DESIRE ME MORE

By Tiffany Clare

Desire Me More
Desire Me Now

DESIRE ME MORE

TIFFANY CLARE

AVONIMPULSE

An Imprint of HarperCollinsPublishers

DESIRE ME MORE

Excerpt from *Desire Me Now* copyright © 2015 by Tiffany Clare.
Excerpt from *Close to Heart* copyright © 2015 by Tina Klinesmith.
Excerpt from *The Maddening Lord Montwood* copyright © 2015 by Vivienne Lorret.
Excerpt from *Chaos* copyright © 2015 by Jamie Shaw.
Excerpt from *The Bride Wore Denim* copyright © 2015 by Lizbeth Selvig.

EPub Edition AUGUST 2015 ISBN: 9780062380463

Print Edition ISBN: 9780062380456

AM 10 9 8 7 6 5 4 3 2 1

For Scott...

CHAPTER ONE

London, 1881

Amelia Somerset stretched out her arms only to find the immoveable force that was Nick lying next to her. Stifling a yawn, she spread her hands over his chest, molding every dip and plane of his body. *What a deliciously wicked way to wake up in the morning.*

Careful not to wake him, Amelia rolled away and grabbed Nick's pocket watch that had been set on her bedside table. Flipping it open, she was pleased to see that it was still early enough that she didn't have to get ready for the day but late enough to rouse Nick from his slumber. A grin tilted up her lips.

She knew that what they did wasn't something polite society would welcome. Women of any standing didn't carry on the way she and Nick were without the sanctity of marriage. She was also sure their intercourse wasn't precisely typical, or at least she never had imagined how many ways she could enjoy her lover. None of that seemed to matter since she was in love with Nick. Without him in her life, she was sure she would have found the past few weeks unbearable.

The man lying next to her had introduced her to an entirely new way of life and love, shown her things she never thought to see. Made her do things that had her blushing just thinking about them now.

Even though he had opened up her mind and her heart to a multitude of feelings she never thought she'd have for another, she was essentially his mistress.

His mistress...and his secretary.

Though she hoped no one yet guessed about the first.

She trailed her hand over his warm body, skimming his right bicep with just the tips of her fingers, making sure to trace every line of muscle as she explored him more thoroughly than she'd ever had the chance to do.

She could do this all day, but they only had an hour before he'd have to sneak back into his room and pretend they hadn't spent the night in delicious sin.

As she grew more daring, her hand lowered to his naval, her fingers circling his toned stomach. Should she caution her actions? Wake him up and get started on the one hundred and one duties that awaited them, or...

Or trail her fingers lower.

Curiosity decided her next course.

With a flick of her hand, she tossed the blanket off his chest and stared in awe at the perfection of his naked body. She loved the fact that he slept *au naturel*, as he was a sight to behold. Her gaze slid lower to see that he was aroused, and the sight had wetness slicking her thighs. She squeezed her legs together, wishing Nick's hand was buried there to ease the need building inside her.

Amelia brushed her fingers against his long, firm manhood. She could make out the dark vein running down the center of his shaft. The skin around the head was pulled back and the plum-colored head of his penis pointed right at her. Almost begging her to take it in her mouth.

His member moved, growing impossibly thicker as semen beaded at the tip. The sight fascinated her. Drew her closer. She had a sudden desire to touch that creamy drop of fluid…feel him like he often felt her. Taste him. She'd had the head of his penis in her mouth before, but she hadn't really known how to pleasure him.

Could she do so now?

Perhaps she could just lick him as he had licked through the folds of her sex. Would that draw more fluid from him?

Glancing up at Nick, she saw his eyes were closed, his breathing even. Turning her focus back to his penis, she lowered her hand enough to touch the wetness that had gathered at the tip. Her breath caught in her throat when his member jerked. She brushed her fingers against it again. Feeling more daring, she curled her hand around the head and squeezed it ever so slightly. Doing this excited her so much, she thought her heart might be pounding loudly enough to awaken him.

Suddenly, Nick wrapped his hand around hers. Her face burned with shame at being caught touching him while he was unaware, but under that shame there was a deep-seated desire, ready to be unleashed.

"You are awake," she said and loosened her hand, though it had nowhere to go with his grip tightening.

"Have been for a while." His voice was low and seductive, and a shiver of understanding shot straight to her core. He wanted to see how far she was willing to go.

Nick guided her hand low enough to cover the root just above his sac. He was so thick, her fingers barely curled around the base of him.

"Pull the skin forward and back." Nick's voice was hoarse.

He showed her how to increase the pressure of her hold. Watching him like this was strangely beautiful, raw, and without pretense. It was about the two of them pleasing each other and seeking their own pleasure, both at the same time. And it was about him giving in to her curiosity.

When she turned her face up to look at him, his eyes were heavy-lidded and lazily focused on her. Her heart skipped a beat and goose bumps rose along her arms. How could he undo her with one look?

He didn't release her from his gaze. He stared at her as though plotting to do very wicked things—and as if he would devour her any second.

She never wanted to get out of bed. She wanted to stay here until neither of them could move or talk and were too sore to even walk.

His breathing grew erratic as her hand stroked his hard length. She liked that he was letting his guard down, letting her see what her touch did to him. She grasped him tighter when his hand encouraged it.

Nick flipped her on her back and hovered over her before she could bring him to completion.

"How do you do this to me?" she asked, breathless.

He did not answer; his gaze locked on hers, his body hard and hot everywhere it pressed into hers. Absently, she stroked his arm, feeling the flex of muscle and the power he held just under the surface. She wanted to scratch her nails along his skin as he entered her but felt suddenly shy.

He leaned in and swept his tongue into her mouth, tasting her deeply. Her body grew heated and needy in a matter of seconds. She wanted him inside her, so in silent plea for more, she spread her legs as wide as her night rail would allow. She tilted her pelvis up, grinding herself against his thigh, trying to find some sort of release.

Nick pushed the material up and out of the way. He had her night rail off before she could offer to help. Her hands molding to the scars that crisscrossed his beautiful back. Every time she touched them she wanted to ask what had happened, who had hurt him, but the words stuck in her throat.

Nick held her hands above her head; then he positioned his body between her legs and worked his rigid penis inside her. Her whole body trembled with relief as he filled her, inch by tortuous inch.

When she tested his hold on her hands, he said, "Move them, and I'll tie you to the bed."

She bit her bottom lip. She almost wanted to dare him. Almost. Instead, she squeezed her thighs around his hips as he pulled out halfway before sliding back into her with a force that shook the bed frame.

Amelia arched her back off the bed, desperate to be closer, to feel him as deep as he could possibly go. Nick stilled once he was fully seated, his hand caressing the side of her face, brushing his fingers through the strands of hair that had come loose from her braid.

Mouth balanced above hers, his tongue swept gently across hers in a seductive dance with which she wanted to keep pace all day. But their morning would eventually end, and she'd make the most of the time they did have. Later, she'd think about the situation in which she kept placing herself and find the courage to ask him what he planned for them in the future.

Nick squeezed one of her nipples between his fingers, the pleasure drawing her attention away from her worries as she focused solely on him.

"I'm apparently not keeping you well enough occupied," he growled.

"It is thoughts of you tangling up my mind."

She kissed his chin and then his neck. Her tongue flicked along his pulse line before she settled against the mattress again.

"Then I will work harder to distract you from coherent thought." He pulled out of her and flipped her onto her knees. "Hold on to the top of the headboard."

Amelia curled her fingers around the cold metal frame. She waited in anticipation for him to slide back inside her. Instead, he kissed her shoulder, lightly at first, then open-mouthed. His teeth bit carefully into her. Amelia's nipples peaked harder and harder with every scrape of his teeth. His hands ran up and down the sides of her ribs, skimming the undersides of her breasts with every pass.

"Nick..." She was panting, breathless from the way he teased her with so simple a touch.

Nick's chest brushed against her back, and the thick hardness of his penis lay demandingly against her backside.

"Hmmm." He moaned, as though she were a tasty treat.

Her head fell back, resting in the crook between his neck and shoulder. "I need you," she said.

"You have me."

"Please."

His hands smoothed over her ribs and waist. "Let me hear the words, Amelia."

"Touch me." She pressed her bottom against him. "I need your touch."

"Tell me where you need me." His hand tickled a seductive path over her hip. It was the barest of caresses as he slid that hand around to her stomach. Too low to touch her aching breasts and tweak with her nipples; too high to spread the juices flowing from her sex. "Or maybe you need me here?" His other hand slid over the front of one thigh and then into the vee of her legs but out of reach of her mound. She squeezed her legs together, wanting to hold him there. Wanting him to touch her more intimately and with more force.

Her breath caught as trembling sensations of arousal snaked through her, warming her and heightening every nerve ending in her body.

"Nick. Please..."

His hand wrenched her legs apart. A cool wash of air brushed over her wet thighs and had her moaning until finally—finally—he touched her clitoris. But the caress was nothing more than a fleeting tease...and not nearly enough. She thought she'd faint if he didn't touch her harder and fill her sheath.

"I want you inside me," she bravely said. "I need you, Nick. Don't deny me this."

"About time you asked," he growled in her ear before sucking her earlobe into his mouth.

Removing his hand from between her legs, he fisted it around his cock and pressed it to her entrance. His groan at the first touch of her wetness fueled her need to have him filling her.

One of his hands gripped the headboard beside her hand as he pressed forward. They both lost themselves in their joining, his chest hair abrading her back with the friction of their bodies as they grew slick with sweat.

His free hand squeezed her breast, and he rolled her nipple between his fingers, heightening her pleasure with the furious propulsion of his body in hers. She bit her bottom lip to keep from screaming out her pleasure, even though the racket they made could surely be heard by anyone on this floor of the house.

Lips hot against her neck, fingers still tweaking her nipples, he overloaded her with sensation, with feeling. Nick surrounded her, filled her, stamped himself on her.

Nick owned her.

Hand lowering, he flicked his finger over her sensitive clitoris, and she could no longer bite back the sounds she'd been holding at bay.

Giving her clit the same treatment he'd given her nipple, he squeezed it between his fingers, letting her grind against his hand as he worked himself inside her.

"Nick," she practically screamed. Her thighs were so slick, so wet, that her juices sluiced a wet path down her legs.

"I could fuck you like this all day," Nick growled in her ear.

She didn't know how to respond, other than to moan his name. Words were beyond her.

"You'd like that, wouldn't you." It wasn't a question. He knew that was exactly what she wanted.

How could one person have so much control over her? How could this man hold the reins of her heart so tightly that she would go anywhere he steered her and do anything he asked?

His words did nothing but inflame her desire further. Her body pushed back against his, needing more yet needing exactly what he was giving her.

"One of these days I'm going to show you what it truly means to be mine."

She shook her head, not able to think his words through. "I don't understand."

"You will...soon."

He grabbed both her hips and pumped into her so hard that the bed frame groaned and creaked with every one of their motions. They would be found out for sure. And while that should concern her, all she did was grasp on tighter, ensuring her hold wouldn't slip and that she stayed exactly where she was so Nick's penis hit her just the right way.

"I want you to come. I know how close you are." He punctuated every word with the movement of their bodies.

He grasped her braid in one hand and yanked it back, exposing her throat to his wicked mouth. "Come for me," he said, licking the sensitive spot between her neck and shoulder.

His legs were between hers, spreading them wide enough that she was sitting atop his lap.

She could feel the slap of his testicles every time she bounced off his lap. And before long, she did scream out. Her orgasm exploded through her. Her sheath gripped his cock so tightly that she felt every ridge of his hardness stroking in and out of her.

With a roar, Nick said, "Fuck."

With a final stroke his seed shot deep inside her, the semen pulsing out of him in a never-ending stream. The slick wetness between them only added to the friction of the short hairs on his sac rubbing and assaulting her clitoris, and she felt herself go off again. Her head fell forward to rest on the frame of the bed as she rotated in tight circles around his shaft, milking every bit of him as her body rode out her climax. Her breasts heaved with the violent breaths she took in and blew out. It was like she'd run a mile, and this was her first chance to pull air into her starved and deprived lungs.

Nick rubbed his hands all over her, as though it would calm her after the race she'd just run with him. Her body collapsed on his, though she couldn't help the slight rotation of her hips from time to time. He wasn't the least bit worn out, and she knew that because he was still hard.

When she finally had her breathing under control, she said, "You're insatiable."

"Only with you. I can never seem to get enough of you, Amelia."

"What if you should grow tired of me?"

"Impossible." He reached for her hands and loosened her grip from the bedpost. All the feeling rushed back into her hands, making them tingle.

Sitting in his lap, she had no desire to move. No desire to start their day. In fact, she would prefer to laze about in bed with Nick all day. That was an impossibility but still a nice dream.

She turned her head to the side to look him in the eyes. "We need to get dressed. If we didn't manage to already wake up the household with our antics, they will be up any minute."

"That makes me think you are trying to get rid of me."

She smiled. She couldn't help it. "I'll see you in the study."

Nick trailed one hand down her sternum and circled her breast. "Mmm, I still haven't had you on my desk."

She swallowed back a groan. Nick was forever trying to commit the wickedest of sins anywhere that wasn't one of their bedrooms, anywhere that they potentially could be caught. She enjoyed the danger of discovery associated with those scenarios, not that she would admit it aloud.

"You have appointments this morning, Nick. You already canceled dinner with Lord Murray last night. I am positive he will send a sour note before the day is through. And at some point you will have to continue working as though nothing has changed." Even though everything had changed since her brother, Jeremy, had tried to remove her from the safety of the house. Since Nick had been forced to take a stand against her brother.

"My priority is and will always be you."

With a heavy sigh, she pulled off his lap. It was pure torture, not being able to sink back down on his hard length. "As I said, we have a busy day."

Nick grabbed her hand before she escaped his reach. He held her at the edge of the bed. "If you want to talk business, then let me say this: I'm concerned your brother will make another appearance while I'm not here. Keeping you in bed seems like the best plan for keeping you safe until he crawls back to Berwick."

"You already have Huxley watching me," she reminded him. Even when she went down for lunch at midday, Huxley was never far behind. Sometimes she resented their close regard, but she understood the necessity.

Her brother had threatened to hurt her and every other servant in the house. He had told her that if she didn't pay him back the money she'd stolen from him, he'd torment the other women who lived here. He also told Amelia that she had to marry a man she despised. A man to whom her brother owed a great deal of money, including the family estate.

With her thoughts maudlin and her good mood taking a turn for the worse, she slipped her hand from Nick's grasp and pulled on her robe as she walked toward the washstand. The rustling of material behind her told her that Nick was donning his clothes too.

When her brother had tried to kidnap her, Nick had been there to stop Jeremy. Amelia would never forget the rage that had filled Nick's eyes as he punched and then threatened her brother if he dared try to get at Amelia again.

The incident had been seen by enough prominent members of society that word had spread of Nick's actions in less than a day. That had been a week ago. And while her brother hadn't come back to the house, she was afraid he would try to get at her again.

When she had run away from her childhood home, she'd promised she would no longer live in fear. But some things were hard to forget, some pasts never forgotten, and her brother hadn't spared her a kind moment in her whole life.

Being with Nick made her feel safe, and she wished she'd never have to leave his arms, but to admit such a thing would make Nick more protective. And really, how could she think that way when her feelings were torn by the fact that she knew so little about him?

She poured water over the linen in the bowl and wrung it out between her shaking hands.

"You're thinking about him again," Nick said, taking the cloth from her.

"It's difficult not to do. I don't know if he has given up his pursuit of me and gone back to Berwick. What if he is waiting for another chance to get me alone?"

Nick's arms wrapped around her as he wiped the cool cloth between her legs, washing away their mingled fluids. Amelia pressed her back against his warm body. She held back a moan, knowing that if she let it slip past her lips, they would end up right back in bed.

"If there's one thing I can promise with certainty, it's that your brother won't come here again."

"I want to believe you. I do. But my doubts have a tendency to consume me at times."

When his finger brushed over her swollen clit, she turned and wrapped her arms around his shoulders.

"I might not leave the house and give my brother a chance to catch me unawares, but he knows Devlin lives here and runs errands for everyone." Devlin was the housekeeper's son, and he'd had a confrontation with Amelia's brother that had resulted in a black eye for the poor boy. Amelia still felt immense guilt over that incident.

"Can you promise me that *everyone* is safe from Jeremy's wrath? I know what my brother is capable of. What lengths he will go to in the name of revenge. There is no decent bone in his body that would make me believe otherwise."

"And you don't know what I'm capable of."

"You're right. You know everything about me, and I know so little about you." She searched his eyes as she admitted this out loud. That very fact had been bothering her for the better part of a week.

Even through his short clipped beard, she could make out the tick high on his cheek. She ran her finger over the harsh line.

"I've promised to protect everyone in this house," he said, "and it's not a promise I make lightly, Amelia. He will never hurt you again."

She wanted to believe him. Trust only in him. And even though she'd confessed her love to him, she had to remind herself that she didn't *really* know much about Nicholas Riley.

She knew where his business interests lay, that he had a sister he doted upon, that his staff was devoted wholly to him. She knew she felt safe and loved when she was in his arms. She knew he'd had a difficult childhood and that he fought hard to reach the position he had in life. Beyond that, she didn't know anything about his past, or why he had the scars on his back. She wanted to know why he sometimes woke up in the grips of a nightmare, yelling incoherently, the words impossible to decipher. He was keeping the deeper parts of himself hidden. The parts that defined him as the man he was.

She trusted that he wouldn't hurt her, but she had more questions than answers where he was concerned.

She pulled Nick's face down to hers and kissed him full on the mouth. She didn't slip her tongue between his lips, even though she wanted to. It was a parting kiss for the morning.

When she let him go, she whispered against his mouth, "I'll meet you in the study once I'm dressed."

Before she could get away, he hugged her hard against his tightly muscled body. She pressed her head to his chest, comforted by the steady beat of his heart.

"I am reluctant to leave you when I know you're mulling over something that has upset you."

"I have so many questions and worries." She bit her lip to keep from saying more.

"About your brother?" He rubbed her back in languorous strokes, drawing a sigh from her.

"My questions are all about you."

"We are taking this one day at a time, Amelia. I have no intentions of letting you go."

But didn't all men grow tired of their mistresses? If that were to come to pass, where would that leave her?

She forced herself to take a step away from him. His gaze was searching.

"We really do have to ready ourselves," she said.

He placed his fingers under her chin and forced her to look at him. "This conversation is far from finished, Amelia."

"I know. And I'm glad for that. We have so much to discuss."

He placed a gentle kiss upon her lips. "You are giving too much thought to what's between us."

"How can you suggest that?"

"Isn't it enough that we are madly, deeply in love with one another?" The seriousness was gone from his tone, and his words held a sternness that took her by surprise.

"Yes and no." Shaking her head, she ushered him toward the door. "You have to leave. I refuse to be caught in a compromising position."

"I'm sure everyone already knows I have thoroughly compromised you."

She laughed as she darted away from his attempt to pull her back into his arms. "You're impossible."

"You like that about me."

"All right, I admit that to be true. Now, will you meet me in the study?"

Nick winked at her as he slipped out the door and closed it softly behind him. Amelia slumped against the wall, thinking about his parting words. Had he really just promised to tell her more about his past? About him? She needed to get dressed immediately so she could ask him all the questions burning in her mind.

CHAPTER TWO

The knocker sounded at the front door as Nick came down the stairs. Huxley emerged from the lower level of the house, but Nick waved him away since he was here anyway. His brows pinched as he opened the door and assessed the uniformed man who stared back at him.

The truncheon at his side and the chinstrap helmet tied just above his cleft chin identified him as a bobby. His coat was slightly rumpled and the buttons drew a crooked line down the center of his chest and tucked under a thick leather belt. The man looked as though he'd been up all night and was coming to the end of his shift.

Nick knew most of the local bobbies, as there was a higher rate of crime near his warehouses on the Thames, but this man was new to him. Nick crossed his arms over his chest. "How can I help you, Constable?"

"Inspector, actually. Inspector Laurie."

"Accept my apologies. What necessity has brought you to my door?" Nick really just wanted to ask what in hell the man was doing here but bit his tongue.

"I'm here about a murder. And you were seen in a precarious situation with this particular man only last week." The inspector produced a notebook from his jacket pocket and thumbed to an empty page. "Do you know the Earl of Berwick?"

Nick nodded. "Only in passing. We were not acquainted." This was perplexing...and disturbing that the inspector was asking Nick about his connection to Jeremy. "The earl is dead?"

"Found him floating in the Thames this morning." He scribbled something down that Nick couldn't make out. "Are you aware that he was residing in London?"

Nick leaned against the doorframe. "What exactly are you asking me, Inspector?"

"You were the last person reportedly seen with Lord Berwick."

Nick narrowed his eyes. "Are you accusing me of something? Because I can assure you I was here all evening. My man of affairs can confirm this if you'd like me to ring for him."

Nick had no intention of bringing Amelia into this. Huxley would vouch for his whereabouts. Though he'd still have to tell her the news about her brother.

How in hell had Jeremy ended up dead? That fool brother of Amelia's might have taken a beating by Nick's hand, but Nick left him breathing—as much as he hadn't wanted to. Did the inspector even have the right man? Something was off here. He needed to investigate this further on his own. Foremost in Nick's thoughts was that it had been a week since he'd seen Amelia's brother, and the inspector said no one had seen him since then. That didn't ring true.

"I'll check with my source again; see if you have been mistaken for someone else. I just needed to ask before I finished my shift."

"If you require some sort of statement from my man of affairs, I can send him over to your headquarters later this morning."

The inspector scratched the side of his jaw where a night's worth of stubble had grown. "No need. My apologies for disturbing you so early."

Nick didn't believe the man, for some reason. He stepped away from the door, ready to say his good-byes, but paused. "Who precisely saw me last night?"

"Unfortunately, I cannot divulge my source while we are actively investigating Lord Berwick's murder."

Nick furrowed his brow. "I see. Good day, Inspector Laurie."

The man assessed him for a moment before he nodded and bounded down the stairs, belying the tiredness that enveloped him.

When Nick closed the front door, a million questions came to mind. He headed to the lower level to find Huxley in the butler's pantry, a small room next to the housekeeper's office. Huxley's room was stacked with rows of wooden crates on every wall, most filled with wine and spirits. There was a desk tucked into one corner where Huxley often came to escape the noise of the house.

Nick closed the door behind him, drawing Huxley's attention away from the inventory ledger he was reviewing. Nick had known Huxley for the better part of a decade, and credited much of his success to their friendship over the years. Nick trusted no one as much as he trusted Huxley.

"Pretty early for visitors. What emergency had them calling so early in the morning?" Huxley asked.

"Lord Berwick was murdered. An inspector came by inquiring about it. He wanted confirmation on my whereabouts last night. Though I don't think it necessary, I said you might go down to his headquarters to say that we remained home last night."

"Berwick found himself some trouble, then."

Huxley didn't question where Nick had been or if he was responsible for any wrongdoing. That kind of trust came from their years of working together. Regardless, Nick had nothing to do with Amelia's brother's murder. But someone would know something, and Nick planned to get to the bottom of it.

"I'll head down to the docks in an hour or so," Huxley said. "I have to do the intake for a shipment transferred from Liverpool at the same time. Don't expect I'll be back before luncheon."

"That is fine. Be sure to talk to the man who watched Lord Berwick last night. He must have witnessed something peculiar."

"Already thinking that. Odd timing, considering you confronted him a week ago."

"I know. I plan to call on Landon this afternoon. If Lord Berwick was murdered, there will be rumors buzzing about Town and I want to know what everyone is saying."

Landon Price, the Earl of Burley, was a friend and business associate of Nick's. He raised sheep in Scotland and had the wool shipped through Nick's company to be sold in London. Landon was also one of the few people Nick trusted implicitly.

"I'll let Liam know we might both be out," Huxley said. "He can watch after the house." Liam, the footman, watched after the house whenever Nick and Huxley both had appointments to attend. "Can't say I'm sorry her brother is dead. Not after the way he treated her, and after the threats he uttered against this house."

"I couldn't agree more with that sentiment," Nick said. "Don't reveal anything about her brother to anyone. Amelia should be the first to know. But I can't tell her anything until I have more information."

Huxley grunted in response.

"I'll let you get on with your day. We can meet tonight before dinner."

"I'll be here," Huxley assured him.

Nick nodded and left the butler's pantry. There was a niggling voice in the back of his mind asking, who was he to keep this news from Amelia?

Nick scrubbed his hand over his face, wishing more than ever that he and Amelia had lazed about in bed all morning. While Amelia didn't profess to love her brother and insisted she never wanted him in her life, Berwick's murder would still wound her deeply. This put him in a moral quandary on keeping this secret from her at all, but his mind was made on the matter.

To Amelia's disappointment, Nick was not in the study when she finally made it downstairs. Perhaps he'd left the house to run errands after all. Although he was a pleasant diversion, she could do without his particular form of distraction for a few hours.

Gathering the letters that had piled up in the front foyer, she resigned herself to responding to Nick's correspondence, and then she would read through the purchase agreements of Lord Murray's lands. They had met with Murray on a few occasions to discuss the sale of his property in Highgate, and it was likely to be transferred to Nick's name over the next few weeks.

The housekeeper entered the study, drawing Amelia's attention away from her scribblings. "Good morning, Mrs. Coleman. How may I assist you?"

"Lord Murray is here with his secretary."

"Mr. Riley isn't here."

"Mr. Riley's occupied in Huxley's office. I told Lord Murray he wasn't available, but he refuses to leave without speaking to Mr. Riley."

Amelia briefly contemplated how best to handle the situation. "I would hate to be the cause of a misunderstanding or for Lord Murray to find someone else to purchase his property. This deal is important to Mr. Riley. Send Lord Murray in here, and let Mr. Riley know I am entertaining Lord Murray until he can join us."

Mrs. Coleman nodded and returned with one very irate-looking Lord Murray. His face was red, and his bushy brows were screwed together tightly in what looked like a permanent scowl. A tall, polished man entered the room with Lord Murray; Amelia assumed this was the secretary. He wore a decent tan coat with waistcoat and dark trousers. His blond hair was neatly parted and pomaded; his green eyes were sharp and focused on her.

Amelia stood to greet them, giving a slight curtsey when she stood before them. "Lord Murray. Shall I have tea brought up while you wait for Mr. Riley? He shouldn't be but a moment."

"That is not necessary," Lord Murray responded. Amelia motioned toward the leather chairs that flanked Nick's desk, but Lord Murray didn't seem inclined to sit.

Since Lord Murray didn't introduce the other man, Amelia took it upon herself to do so. "I'm sorry; we haven't been introduced. I'm Mr. Riley's secretary, Miss Grant."

"Mr. Shauley." His accent was thick, his eyes assessing as he looked her up and down as though she were...lacking. What an odd feeling to have on first meeting someone. "I preside over Lord Murray's business affairs."

Lord Murray didn't exactly have any business other than owning a few lots of land and sitting in the House of Lords.

"It's a pleasure to meet you, Mr. Shauley." She smiled, but he didn't return the gesture; if anything, a frown drew his eyes down and put creases along his forehead.

Mr. Shauley stepped closer to her—too close. Lord Murray was pacing the floor, ignoring them both as he flipped his pocketwatch open, only to snap it shut over and over again.

"What happened to Huxley?" Mr. Shauley inquired.

It was a question she should be used to. And though the question did not precisely bother her, it was the way in which Mr. Shauley said Huxley's name that had her hackles rising.

"Huxley takes care of Mr. Riley's businesses more directly now. I am responsible for the administrative tasks Mr. Riley has, keeping his appointments straight and such."

"I always thought Huxley was a man who could do it all," Mr. Shauley said.

"He most certainly is." She laughed a little, trying to lighten the mood. She didn't like the feeling of being cross-examined by a man she did not know.

"What is it you do, Mr. Shauley? I did not realize Lord Murray was a businessman."

"I manage his estates. And I have done everything in my power to advise against selling Highgate for such a disadvantageous price, but his mind is set."

"Oh?" She was genuinely curious.

"It is worth more. The land alone should be sold at double Riley's offer."

"Then why is Lord Murray selling Highgate?"

As Mr. Shauley took another step toward her, she decided that this particular man was no better than Jeremy, trying to use his presence and taller frame to intimidate her. She held her ground and looked him in the eye. She refused to be cowed by such a man.

Mr. Shauley's nostrils flared for the briefest moment and then he said, "Unfortunately, the house must be sold regardless of whether I agree with the price. Upkeep alone is more than the worth, so it's rotting and in ruins for the most part."

"I hadn't realized." She remembered Nick mentioning that he planned to restore the manor house. But if it was in such a poor state as Mr. Shauley indicated, why go to the trouble?

"Of course not, Miss Grant." He looked at her quizzically. "You're from significantly farther reaches of England. The north, I'd say."

Amelia swallowed back her sudden trepidation. Nick had once said something about her accent not being that of a Londoner, but she didn't think it was so obvious.

Before she could ask more questions of the odd man who was standing far too close, the study door opened, and Amelia couldn't have been happier to see Nick striding in. She looked at him apologetically, though she wasn't sure how she could have righted this situation. Nick's focus lay solely on Mr. Shauley, his gaze filled with something so dark she could only call it hatred.

Did the two men know each other? *Of course they do,* she thought. The negotiations with Lord Murray had been going on since long before she became Nick's secretary.

"Lord Murray." Nick broke the silence that had descended upon the room and turned his attention away from Mr. Shauley. "To what do I owe the pleasure of your company?"

"Cut the small talk, Riley. Did you think I would shrug off your slight?"

Amelia winced at the accusation in Lord Murray's tone. It had been her fault that Nick had canceled his dinner plans with Lord Murray last night.

Nick turned his attention to Amelia. "Miss Grant, would you please send up Huxley? I last saw him in the kitchens."

"Of course." She nodded toward Lord Murray and Shauley before she left, not sure if she was glad for the reprieve of Mr. Shauley's creepy regard or angry with Nick for sending her off as though she played no vital part in the purchase of the property.

Once Amelia left the room, Nick looked toward Lord Murray. "I had a family emergency that needed my attention this week, as the note I sent indicated. Really, Murray, you couldn't wait a few more nights to give me this high-and-mighty speech?"

"We were advised while sitting in the restaurant," Lord Murray responded. "I know what you are about, Riley. You are stringing me along, hoping to get the property for a fraction of its worth." He stood in front of Nick, his face crimson.

"A family emergency," Nick repeated. "It required my *full* attention. Stop acting like a bride jilted at the altar."

Lord Murray sputtered at the insult. "I'll not be treated like a second thought."

"And I will not be hounded in my own house. You forget that I make the rules in this venture of ours." Nick glanced in the direction of Shauley, who had yet to say a word. "I will contact you whenever I damn well please."

Shauley spoke then. "You can play this any way you like, Riley, but by all appearances you haven't come through on your word yet. You have delayed this sale by a month."

"You dare to come into my house and insult me on my word?" Nick sat on the edge of his desk, glaring at Shauley. No one told Nick what he should do, how he should act, or what exactly he was thinking, especially Shauley.

Huxley strolled into the study, and Nick was glad that Amelia was not behind him, though he would have to advise that she stay away from Shauley going forward.

"Good day, Lord Murray," Huxley said, not bothering to greet Shauley.

The tension that had built in the room dispelled with Huxley's arrival.

"It is clear we are of opposing minds," Nick said, "but our meeting has concluded. Miss Grant will advise you tomorrow where and when we will dine to go over any final particulars, Lord Murray. Huxley will show you to the door."

Nick didn't wait for Lord Murray's response as he walked around to the front of the desk and pulled out his chair. Huxley looked on with nothing short of amusement.

"I'll not forget this slight, Riley," Lord Murray said.

"If you want our arrangement to remain mutually beneficial you will guard your temper and leash your pet." Nick looked at Shauley with indifference, though that was the last thing he felt. "I don't need to tell you that my patience is thin when dealing with pompous lords like you. Even thinner for the scum you scraped off the street and dressed up as your man of affairs."

Lord Murray looked as if he was about to have a fit of apoplexy. Instead of another outburst, he turned on his heel and strode out of the study, anger radiating from him like a hive full of disturbed wasps.

Huxley followed Lord Murray out. Shauley, however, placed his hat atop his head and strode toward Nick's desk as though he had all the time in the world before he departed.

"Did I not make myself clear, Shauley?"

"You have certainly turned into a cold bastard over the years."

"If you think that our growing up across a shared laneway gives you any familiarity with me, let me advise you that you are mistaken."

"Now, Nick. You do wound my sensibilities."

Nick snorted, though he wasn't the least bit amused. "Do you have some asinine notion that we will renew our friendship because of my dealings with Lord Murray?"

"It would do you well to remember that I can be the worm in his lordship's ear and persuade him of another course of action."

"Then why let the manor go at all? I know how deeply attached you are to that pile of rubble. *Sentimentality* for your old way of life and all." The depravities of the man standing before him were extreme, and they reminded Nick of a time in his life that he wanted nothing more than to scrub from his brain.

Shauley pinched his lips together, though he didn't take the bait and storm out, as Nick had hoped. "It's no more *sentimentality* for me than it is for you."

It was a place they'd both lost whatever innocence they had as children. While Nick had risen from the ashes of his past, Shauley had smoldered and been molded into a man equally as vile as the vicar who had destroyed their childhood.

"It is mere coincidence that Highgate came up to be purchased at all," Nick explained, though Shauley deserved no reason for Nick's decisions. "I require a manor that has acreage close to the city. Highgate provides that."

Shauley grinned as though he had Nick's purpose figured out. What Shauley didn't realize, however, was Nick's plan to expose the vicar, who still resided in Highgate, as a way to wipe the slate clean from a past that still haunted Nick.

When Shauley didn't seem inclined to leave, Nick pushed out from his desk and stood, ready to throw the man out, if need be. Shauley took the hint but not before parting with, "Did the good old vicar break you after all? I thought you above the old man's machinations."

"Odd how the same cannot be said of you. Broken is the defining character for what you've become." The degeneracies of that vicar had seeped into Shauley long ago.

Shauley laughed shortly before he turned and left Nick's study. Huxley returned a short time later.

"I'd like to say I'm surprised to see them both here, but Shauley has been decidedly quiet since the negotiations were under way for Highgate," Nick mused aloud. Huxley crossed his arms over his chest and waited for Nick to elaborate. "If he comes around the house again, I want to be the first to know."

"Easily done," Huxley said. "Is he a danger to anyone?"

Nick immediately thought of Devlin and Amelia. "Yes. There's no telling who he will try to hurt if he wants to get to me."

"So we bury one problem with Lord Berwick's death, only to have another surface?"

"I'm not convinced the two are singular incidences." Nick pressed his thumbs into his temples. What was he missing that connected the two meetings this morning? "The inspector followed by Shauley's appearance cannot be coincidental, yet why should they be connected at all?"

Nick had never had dealings with Lord Berwick. Did Lord Berwick know Lord Murray? Had Lord Berwick known Shauley? Nick knew that Shauley was Lord Murray's secretary, but Shauley made a point of being scarce for any meetings or dealings directly with Nick. So after two months of avoiding a meeting with Nick, why come around today of all days?

"Where is Amelia?" He hadn't meant to be dismissive when he'd come into the study to find Shauley glaring at her like she was a rabbit set for the dinner plate.

"Said she would break her fast since she wasn't required in the study."

So he'd angered her. *Damn it, this day couldn't possibly get worse.*

Chapter Three

Amelia heard the front door of the house open at nine. She smoothed her fingers over the satin bookmark dividing the pages of the book. She hadn't read more than three words before setting it on the table next to her. She'd waited in the library for Nick's return for nearly two hours now. She headed toward the adjoining study just as a lamp burned to life, chasing away the darkness of the room.

Nick had been gone for the better part of the day. Surprisingly, Huxley hadn't been his usual three feet away from her when Nick wasn't around. Had something happened during the meeting with Murray to take them away from the house? If that were the case, why hadn't Nick told her where he was going?

Had there been a development with her brother? With Huxley's absence, she wondered if Jeremy had gone home.

It wasn't lost on her that she'd had all day to think through her questions, but now that the opportunity presented itself...she didn't know how to ask any of the thoughts that had plagued her throughout day.

Nick was sitting in his chair with his head tilted back and one arm thrown over his eyes.

She broke the silence that had descended upon the room. "Good evening. I wasn't entirely sure we'd see each other tonight."

He removed his hand and looked right at her. The breath froze in her lungs. Just one look from him had the ability to render her speechless.

She looked toward the library, needing to break eye contact with him so she could at least think straight. "I was reading when I heard you come in. I didn't mean to interrupt your solitude."

"Amelia." Her name came out like a question, bidding her to meet his gaze again. Folding her hands in front of her so she wouldn't fidget, she raised her head to look at him. Nick pushed the chair out from his desk and patted one leg. "Will you sit with me for a while?"

Glancing at the door that led to the main corridor of the house, she noted it was slightly ajar. She shook her head. It was one thing for the household to know what they were up to, another thing entirely for the staff to witness their transgressions.

Nick must have noticed where her focus lay. "Close it." He patted his thigh again.

She swallowed and was too tempted not to do his bidding. She locked the door before returning to his side and sat carefully on one of his thighs.

He searched her eyes for a moment and then asked, "How was your day?"

"Fraught with worry."

He merely cocked one eyebrow at her questioningly. "Do elaborate."

She shook her head, not knowing how to voice any of her questions. She stuttered out a few I's and we's but couldn't formulate the words for how she was feeling. "My ability to express myself vanishes whenever we are in the same room."

The side of his mouth kicked up into a half grin. She never saw him smile for anyone but her, and that had her heart pounding to its own tempo in her chest.

"I'll take that as a compliment," he said, smoothing his finger over the creases between her brows. "Tell me what has you worried."

"Us. You. Your expectations of me. You ignoring me after the meeting with Lord Murray and Mr. Shauley this morning, after dismissing me from your company as though my presence was relegated to that of a dimwitted spouse."

Nick sighed heavily. "I regret my reaction to seeing Shauley and you in the same room, but my worry was for your safety. The less he can guess about what is happening between us, the easier it is for me to keep him at arm's length. I should have explained that before I left, but I wasn't thinking clearly."

Mr. Shauley might have seemed creepy, and there was no denying that his presence had made her uncomfortable, but…"Why do you have that opinion of Lord Murray's secretary?"

"I know Shauley more than I care to. We grew up together in St. Giles. Our mothers were in the same…profession. We had a falling out many years ago and have avoided each other since and for good reason. If he can hurt the people I love to get back at me, he will."

Amelia knew she had to pick her questions carefully, for Nick would change the topic and give her nothing of himself if she dug too deep. "Do you care to elaborate on your falling out?"

"He's a dangerous man, Amelia, and you need to avoid him. Trust me in this matter."

None of what he was saying was really an answer, but she would take him at his word. It sounded as though Mr. Shauley knew something more of Nick's past…more than to which she'd been privy. "Did you settle everything with Lord Murray?" she asked.

"He won't be going anywhere anytime soon. He needs my money more than he needs to keep the family lands. He can be as angry as he likes for the delays I've caused. I've been preoccupied by matters far more important to me." Nick ran his thumb over her chin, the move sensual and designed to make her forget the rest of her questions. "He's a concern for another day."

Her eyes slipped shut. Other things had been niggling at the back of her mind all day, but it was hard to recall those questions while he was touching her so innocently…yet so intimately.

She finally remembered. "And us?"

"My expectations?"

She nodded, as she stared at his lips.

"I would never ask for anything more than you are willing to give. You are your own person. What we have isn't shameful, not when we feel the way we do about each other."

"How can you call it anything but? I won't argue that with you, but the rest of the house cannot ever know how we carry on in the evenings."

"Neither of us is naïve enough to believe our time together is a secret to anyone. Least of all those living in this house." Nick placed his fingers under her chin to tilt it up.

He was right. Even though she knew they needed to set clear boundaries that would make everyone believe nothing sinful was happening between them, she found it hard to refuse him anything. What a conundrum she was in—her heart warring with her mind on the right course of action.

"I noticed Huxley's absence today," she said. "Has something happened?"

He curled his hand around hers, his larger size engulfing her, making her feel so small next to him. "I should have told you before I left, but I needed to see the truth for myself. It could have been a hoax, I kept telling myself; it was too easy to happen this way. And it still doesn't feel right."

"It's my brother, isn't it?"

"My sweet Amelia. I have bad news about your brother."

"Did you meet with him today? Is that why Huxley wasn't here?"

He nodded, hesitant.

"Just tell me what has happened."

"If I could shield you from this, I would. But you deserve the truth, as much as it pains me to relay it to you." He paused and entwined their hands. She looked at their fingers, tangled, his tanned skin in juxtaposition to her paleness. "A police inspector was here this morning. Just before Lord Murray's arrival. I'm sorry, Amelia, but…your brother is dead."

She heard a ringing in her ears, and her body suddenly felt numb. Her heart actually skipped a beat with her sudden inhalation. "Huxley said he was staying with a friend this past week. He was—" She swallowed against the nerves making it hard for her talk, and her lip trembled before she could temper the reaction. "I don't understand. How is this possible?"

"I intend to find out what happened." Nick watched her without saying more.

Was he expecting her to cry? There was no press of tears in the back of her eyes. Did that mean something was wrong with her? What kind of person did that make her? She felt nothing except…numb. Everything was numb. She stood from Nick's lap, disentangling their hands as she backed away from him. "This is *impossible*," she whispered.

"I went down to the city morgue myself to confirm what the inspector told me." Nick stood, following her every step.

"How?"

"He was murdered."

Her breath hitched in her lungs. Her hands shook so hard that she had to dig her nails into her palms to steady them. Denials built in her throat, but no sound or words came out.

How was someone supposed to digest the news of a blood relative being murdered?

Should she feel anger? She didn't. Should she feel elated that she didn't have to watch her back constantly? That felt wrong too.

She shook her head. "He's masterminded some sort of trick. He was always good at manipulating everyone around him. This isn't real. It can't be. I know my brother, Nick."

She heard the pleading in her own voice. This was wrong. It was all wrong.

"Amelia." Nick took another step toward her and reached for her arm. He pulled her close, tucking her head against his chest. The steady cadence of his heart in her ear helped even out her breathing, but it did not still the shaking that overtook her whole body.

"I'm sorry to be the bearer of bad news." His arms were strong and steady, and they were the only thing keeping her on her feet.

"This is not possible," she whispered into his shoulder. She felt as though she were in a terrible nightmare, one from which she was unable to wake.

Nick's hand smoothed over her hair, the gesture soothing but far from placating her emotions.

"I didn't believe it either. So I didn't tell you until I'd seen it with my own eyes."

She turned her head up at him. "I need to see him."

Nick looked back at her long and hard. "Foolish girl."

Amelia grasped his jacket at the sleeves. "I won't ever believe it if I don't see him."

"I won't lie to you, Amelia. He is far from resembling the brother you remember."

She appreciated that he didn't deny her this one request. "My brother has tormented me all my life, Nick. It was as though making me miserable was a sick game. I will never believe him gone unless I see him with my own eyes." Her lips trembled, and she took in a shaky breath. "I need closure if I am to move on and put my past behind me, once and for all."

"If that's what you want, I won't stop you. I will never take your choices away from you." He brushed back a stray curl of her hair and tucked it behind her ear. "I'll be right there for you if you need me."

"I wouldn't want anyone but you at my side."

Nick raised her hands to his mouth and pressed kisses to her knuckles.

"You said an inspector told you what had happened?"

He nodded, his gaze never leaving hers.

"Tell me what he said, Nick."

"That I was the last person seen with your brother."

She tried to pull her hands away. Surely he wasn't suspected of killing her brother. "But that was a week ago."

"I know. That's why I left so suddenly this morning. I had to find out who else had been in your brother's company. Huxley went down to see the inspector today and vouched for my whereabouts last night."

"Not…?" Why hadn't he asked her?

Nick rubbed his hands over her arms. "No. I won't ask you to do that."

"What did Huxley think of that?"

"I know he suspects what is happening between us, but he won't ask, and he won't say anything to anyone."

She breathed a small sigh of relief that Huxley would remain circumspect. Though knowing they were not pulling the wool over anyone's eyes should set her straight and make her want to stop their affair…she *couldn't*. Nick was as essential as the air she breathed; without him, she would slowly suffocate.

"We both saw my brother a week ago, as did a number of people outside this house when he accosted me. Surely he's been busy in gambling hells since then. Those places are rife with patrons."

"And prostitutes, criminals, and members of society who don't want to be found out." He kissed her forehead as though to apologize for the reality of that statement. "I know he was never kind to you. I know he made your life a living hell, but I also know how hard it is to lose someone who has been a constant in your life for as long as you can remember."

"I won't mourn him." She squared her shoulders, feeling calmer and more in power of her life now than she'd ever felt before.

"I am not suggesting you do. This once, I'll go along with whatever you tell me. I'm here for you, Amelia. Is that a deal?"

"How are you possible or even real?"

"I'm as real as you are."

"Thank you," she whispered and folded herself in Nick's arms, the place she felt safest.

True to his word, Nick accompanied her to the dead house. Amelia sat in the carriage and waited while Nick went inside to talk to the undertaker. The building looked like any ordinary chapel. Ivy grew along the fascia of the stone building and curled around the lead-paned windows, adding life to a place full of death.

There weren't any places like this in Berwick, so she had nothing to compare to it, but she hadn't expected the exterior to look quite so...pleasant and cheerful. So what had she expected? Some back-alley dungeon filled with rats and filth?

Nick stepped out of the building followed by a slender younger man, clean-shaven, with wheat-blond hair. She looked at him straight on from the carriage, though he was focused on Nick as they conversed.

The undertaker's shirt was rolled up at the sleeves. It had been washed and bleached so many times that it was a soft yellow instead of white. The top of his tan-colored waistcoat was visible under the stained brown leather apron that fell past his knees. The dark stains on the apron spoke to the type of job he performed and grotesquely reminded her of the butcher back home.

Amelia couldn't seem to look away from him. What kind of man would want to take on such a profession?

Banishing her troubling thoughts, she continued to study the bloodstains splashed across his midsection, as if that would prove that she could do this. If she couldn't face what this man did for a living, how would she ever make it past the threshold of the chapel?

As Nick strode toward her, she noted the undertaker's stance: firm, his posture reading irritated by the circumstance.

Well, that made the two of them, didn't it?

Nick held out his hand as he opened the door for her. "Ready then?"

She loved the fact that he didn't question her need to do this, or attempt to change her mind.

She took his hand without hesitation. When she stood before him, he added, "We can leave at any time; just say the words and we'll go. You don't have to prove yourself to anyone, Amelia. I mean that."

"I have to do this."

Threading her arm though Nick's, she walked toward the undertaker with determined steps. She was saved from having to introduce herself, for he turned on his heel and headed back inside. Surely women had visited this place before. Nick had to catch the door so it didn't shut behind the undertaker. The sick scent of death assaulted her senses and had her skin crawling the moment she crossed through the door. She wanted to scratch her arms to rid herself of the feeling, but she soldiered on, refusing to show any weakness.

There would be no peace, no real belief that any of this had happened if she didn't continue on her current path. She had to see her brother one last time.

Amelia stepped into the dark chapel, her steps stalling long enough for her eyes to adjust to the dim lighting. Covering her mouth with her hand, she swallowed back the bile that had climbed up her throat and took in small breaths to acclimate to the strong odor, though she didn't think she'd ever get used to the smell.

Nick leaned in close to her ear. "Just say the words and we can leave."

She shook her head, refusing to give in as she continued deeper into a place fouled right down to the shale foundation with the stench of death. Now that her eyes were adjusted to the dim room, she lowered her hand from her mouth and held her head high as she followed the undertaker.

They walked down a narrow hallway, closer to the stench fouling the air. Nick produced a handkerchief, which she took and pressed over her nose and mouth.

"Watch where you step," the undertaker said as he disappeared into a room just ahead.

Not knowing what to expect, she braved her fears and followed immediately upon his heels, eyes focused on the floor to see her footing. Nick had her elbow and she knew he wouldn't let her walk in the wrong direction.

In a room that's sole purpose appeared to be housing the dead, it was hard not to notice the stone floor covered in filth and other things she never wanted to identify. Lifting her skirts, she took in the rest of her surroundings. Wall sconces kept the room well lit, so she could see altogether too much of what was amassed in the small room.

Half a dozen large slate tables were lined up in two neat rows and spaced evenly in the central part of the room. Half were in use, with unmoving forms atop them but covered with dark sheets of burlap and cloth. Her eyes didn't linger on any one form as she headed toward the table next to which the undertaker hovered.

He gave her a measuring yet solemn look. "You understand he won't be as you remember?" he asked.

In fear that she'd lose the last of her nerves—and her breakfast that now sat heavily in the pit of her stomach—she nodded in answer. Nick was at her back, a solid and reassuring presence. Amelia took a small step back so she was pressed fully along the length of him, taking in the strength he offered by merely being here for her.

Without any further warning, the undertaker pulled back the thin material that covered the lifeless body, revealing her brother's beaten face and bare shoulders.

The undertaker hadn't exaggerated; Jeremy's motionless form didn't resemble the man she'd grown up fearing. The man before her was broken. Lifeless. Not the monster from whom she had constantly cowered. She didn't want to shrink into the background now as she stared at his heavily bruised face. She couldn't seem to take her eyes off him as she studied every cleaned-out cut, every broken part of his body.

When her vision clouded, she turned into Nick's arms, resting her forehead against his chest and closing her eyes to gather any stitch of bravery she had left in her. She needed to collect her own strength, give herself a moment to bring it together in her head and adjust to the reality of her brother's death.

Because this moment was what made it all real.

And the image of her brother would be with her for the rest of her life.

"What happened to him?" she whispered. She didn't need an answer, though, and Nick didn't respond. Her real question was, who could do such a thing to another person, regardless of the circumstances, regardless of the vile man Jeremy was?

Nick's hand pressed against her lower back, holding her close, letting her breathe deeply of his clean scent in a desperate bid to wipe away the foul scent of the room.

Braving her fears, she stepped out of Nick's arms and looked him in the eye. "I would like a minute alone with my brother."

Nick merely nodded and jerked his head toward the exit, indicating to the undertaker that he should give her exactly what she needed. Nick turned at the door. "I'll be one step outside. Call out if you need me, Amelia."

"I will."

She turned away from Nick as tears filled her eyes again and trailed down her cheeks unbidden. She didn't try to stop them or wipe them away. They just were.

She took a step closer to her brother's body. The usual sinister smirk he wore whenever he faced her was absent. Now, he was nothing more than a harmless man, unable to dish out the cruelties he'd delivered over the years. He was a shell. A lifeless shell, and it made her wonder how he had ever wielded any power over her.

Braving herself, she pulled the covering right off him, revealing his full, weak form. The material caught at his booted feet, hanging in a macabre fashion, like he was a fallen flag-bearer who hadn't made it through the battle.

He was unclothed from the waist up, his breeches hanging low on his too-narrow hips. His skin had taken on a yellow-gray waxen tone wherever the miasma of deep red and purple bruises hadn't discolored him. Bruises spidered out over his form, covering his lower ribs and various spots around his slightly distended stomach. His shoulders were red and raw, as though he'd been dragged without a shirt through the streets.

"You've brought this fate upon yourself, brother." She brushed a dirty strand of hair back from his forehead, revealing a deep gash at the edge of his hairline. It had been cleaned out and appeared almost white around the cut, as though it had bled a great deal not so long ago.

Was that the blow that had killed him?

"Who did you cross this time, Jeremy?" No answer came, not that she expected one.

There was only silence.

She was in a room full of the dead; all she could hear was the beat of her own heart and the shallow breaths she took in and out so as not to take in the full odor of the place. She rubbed her hands along her arms, which did nothing to dispel the cold that chilled her to the bone.

"You could have amounted to so much more, but your evil infiltrated you so thoroughly that you're not even a fraction of the man Father was as he lay on his deathbed. Even after all you have done to me, all you've done to others...I pity you. I don't want to, but there you have it. I know that sentiment would anger you, so let me say it again, brother." She leaned in close to his face and whispered, "I pity you in your sad death."

Whoever had done this to her brother had but one intention: to see him gone from this world. There was no one to claim him from this place. Not even she would be stupid enough to tempt fate that way. His past might have caught up with him, but she wanted to remain free of the burdens her brother had placed on her.

Even though he deserved no kind words from her, she rested her hand over his cold chest, and the lack of a heartbeat raised goose bumps through her entire body. "Godspeed, Jeremy. Perhaps forgiveness will find you in your next life."

She reached for the sheet and covered him once again.

There was no love lost between them, and while she was sad, a smidgen of relief filled her at knowing he could never hurt her again. She turned away, her heart heavier than it had been since she'd found out about his death. He had been her last living relative. Her own flesh and blood.

Oddly, his death was at once a yoke about her shoulders and a snapping of the reins that had always kept her in line with her brother's ideals. The freedom that washed through her was sickening, and nothing had ever felt so wrong as this. Maybe that was because her freedom had come at the expense of his life.

True to his word, Nick was waiting just outside the door for her. He wrapped one arm around her shoulders and hugged her tightly to his chest. Her tears had dried, but she felt…empty.

"We have to leave him here, Nick. I can't risk being exposed in my new life by claiming his body for burial."

"I can make any arrangements you want. No one has to know."

She was shaking her head. "I ran away with good reason. And I will not risk being found by anyone. My brother might be the last of my family, but that doesn't make me feel free from his obligations. I still don't know what Lord Ashley has planned, if anything. My brother *should* have a proper burial and mourning period, but I just can't…"

Nick's arm was like a vise around her, holding her tight, making her feel safe. "He deserves less than you think."

"That might be true, but he is still my brother. And he was the last Earl of Berwick. Our family line is no longer extant."

"Then to whom does the estate go?"

"I know of no living relatives who could make a claim for it. Lord Ashley won the cottage in a silly gamble. The rest will revert back to the crown."

"Let's get you home," Nick said against the top of her head, his hand cupping her nape possessively as he turned them toward the exit.

Amelia didn't take a deep breath until they were next to their carriage. The clean air helped clear her senses and shake the icy cloak of death that had wrapped around her while she'd been in that building.

Nick thanked the undertaker and then assisted Amelia inside the carriage.

She took the blue velvet seat opposite him. "Is it wrong that I don't feel any guilt, walking away from my brother's cold, broken corpse?"

"It shows nothing but fortitude."

She looked directly at him as the horses jolted forward. His expression was open, kind. Inviting her to come closer. She switched sides and rested her head against his shoulder. "I feel so odd. Empty of emotion but at the same time, better that I saw him one final time."

Nick kissed the top of her head. "That's normal. Mourn for your brother, Amelia. You needn't think of anything but letting him go."

Amelia slipped her hand over his firm stomach. She was thankful to have him right now. There was no doubt in her mind that she would be lost without him.

"I think the constant threat of my brother precipitated our relationship. And now I wonder if everything between us happened too suddenly."

Nick covered her hand with his, not saying anything to indicate his thoughts on the matter.

"With the danger of my brother eliminated, I'm afraid of what will happen between us," she admitted. She'd been turning that thought over and over since Nick had revealed her brother's fate.

"Nothing will change, so put it out of your mind."

"I can't help that I feel this way. When I ran away from home, I assumed I'd be an aging spinster before any man would catch my attention. We were thrown together by circumstance."

Nick turned up her chin with his fingers so that their gazes were locked. "Do you want to know how I remember the change in our relationship?"

She sucked in her bottom lip and nodded for him to continue.

"I hired you on because I couldn't let you go. That was long before I knew any details about your brother or your past. When we met, I told you that you reminded me of someone."

"I recall but you never said whom."

"Her name was Lillie. She was important to me for the short time she was in my life. And before you believe it to be some grand love affair, you should know she was fifteen when she died. I couldn't have been much older than eleven."

"Why do I remind you of someone so young?"

"Young in age, not in life experience." He rubbed his thumb across her lips.

"Are you saying that you put me on a pedestal before you knew me?" Amelia wasn't sure how she felt about this revelation.

"*After* I met you," he corrected her. "You had the same look in your eyes she often had."

"Which was?"

"Fortitude. You looked ready to take on the world, even though you were at a tether's end with your luck."

Amelia would never forget the day they met, not for as long as she lived. While humiliation should have superseded any other feelings when recalling how she literally fell into his life, had her circumstances not been what they were that fateful day, their paths might never have crossed. She hated to think where that would have left her. Hated to think of a life without Nick in it.

"Do I still remind you of her?"

Nick shook his head. "Life has ways of surprising us. Whether we met because of your brother doesn't change how we feel about each other now. I cannot deny that you make me crazy with need. And while what's between us doesn't scare me, I sometimes worry how far I'll make you go. How far I'll push you before you want to run."

Amelia curled her fingers around his and inched close enough that their mouths were scant inches from touching and their breaths mingled.

"The only thing I fear right now is myself and what I feel for you, Nick."

A dark look came over him, and he was as unreadable as the first time they had met.

CHAPTER FOUR

I f Amelia knew what Nick was thinking, she might change her mind and think carefully about putting that much trust in him. He spanned his hand over her cheek and watched her nibble and suck on her lower lip in tandem. She did that when she was contemplating a problem.

And when she was thinking about kissing him.

But the last thing he should want after their morning was her spread out beneath him, taking her hard and deep as he swallowed her pleasured screams. It didn't matter what time of the day it was, where they were, or how sated they'd been this morning. He wanted her. He always wanted her. Especially when she gave him her complete trust. Even the look in her eyes right now—full of hurt, innocence, wonder—made him want her. He was rock hard inside his trousers, and it took every ounce of control not to press her hand over his erection.

He stared at her mouth, wanting her all the same, no matter how many times he told himself she needed today to mourn her brother's death.

But it was increasingly difficult to feel bad when she had scooted over to his bench to be closer to him. He closed his eyes, trying to banish his thoughts, to clear that look of hope and innocence he saw in her eyes every time she looked at him. But when he closed his eyes, all he could picture was how she'd been spread out naked beneath him.

He was the worst kind of ass.

Still, he couldn't stop himself. He pressed his mouth against hers, wanting nothing more than a small taste of her before they went about the rest of their day. But their mouths didn't linger and stop with a simple kiss. The next he knew, he'd picked her up off the seat, and her soft body was pressed against the length of his as his tongue worked against hers, slicking around her mouth and tasting her deeply. His cock throbbed, needing to be buried deep inside her.

He jerked his head to the side. "Amelia." She was breathing as heavily as he was, telling him that she was just as lost in the moment. "I know I should give you time to grieve. You need time alone."

But hell. He didn't really want that. His need for her was constant, unrelenting.

"I don't need time to myself," she said with a sigh. He swore he could taste her arousal on the air.

Nick took a steadying breath—or at least he tried to; it didn't work. How could he say no to her? He wanted nothing more than to fulfill her request, but he had sent a card to Murray last night, advising him to be at his club for luncheon. They had to finalize their agreement so that Shauley would be forever away from Amelia. And besides, Nick needed Murray's lands *almost* as much as he needed to help Amelia through her grief.

"Help me forget, Nick."

With her breathless sigh, his mind was made. He pulled down the curtains on either side of the carriage windows. Nick slid off the bench so he was on his knees, pushing up her heavy skirts as he settled between her spread thighs.

"Put your feet up on the opposite bench."

She hastened to do his bidding, scooting down so her tailbone rested on the edge of the seat. Nick lifted one of her legs to spread her open. The motion opened up her knickers and brought her sweet cunt closer to his mouth. It was the prettiest sight he'd ever seen, and he wanted to devour her with a fierceness that robbed him momentarily of his breath.

He would help her forget anything she wanted, as long as she let him drink down the juices wetting the hairs of her cunny.

Amelia barely recognized this new brazen side of herself. But she hadn't been like her *old* self since the day she met Nick. The expression in his gaze couldn't be described as anything less than ravenous. She could hardly believe she was doing this—and in a carriage, of all places.

A blush stole over her cheeks when Nick slipped his hand into the slit of her drawers and spread her thighs wider as he breathed a cool stream of air over her mons. A strangled sound escaped her throat as her pelvis tilted toward him. She wanted this. To forget. But more than anything, to feel.

Nick's teeth scraped against her inner thigh, licking away the momentary pain of his nip before he sucked on her sensitive flesh again. But that wasn't where she wanted his mouth.

She wanted to pull his head closer to her sex, but then she'd have to release the layers of her dress that she was holding up. And she wanted to see the look clouding his eyes just as much as she wanted him to kiss her in a more intimate place.

"Nick…please."

"Please what? I can think of a hundred things I want to do in this moment, so be specific in what you want."

She didn't know how to voice her needs. When she didn't respond, he bit her other thigh, and this time she felt a rush of wetness coat her entrance.

She gave a breathless moan and wiggled so far down the seat, she wasn't sure how she didn't fall right into Nick's lap.

"I want your mouth on me," she said, her desperation thick in her request.

He gave her a deep chuckle. "It is on you, love."

"*On* me…"

She demonstrated what she wanted by curling one hand over his shoulder and pulling him deeper into the vee of her legs. While that made him edge a bit closer, it wasn't close enough to get his lips and mouth exactly where she wanted them.

"I want you inside me," she finally said in pure frustration, when all she got was a stream of hot breath along her slick center.

"Is that so? And what will you give me if I fulfill that desire?"

She shook her head. She couldn't think when she just wanted to feel him touching her. "I *need* you inside me."

His fingers thrust inside her before she even finished giving voice to her request. But he wasn't filling her the way she craved most.

She moved against Nick, needing more and less at the same time. Her pelvis undulated as though his hand was another part of his anatomy, and they were in the deepest throes of passion.

Still. Not. Enough.

She needed more. She wanted to be so lost to his touch that she couldn't think.

She loosened her hold on her skirts and squeezed both her thighs around his head. He was forced to pull his fingers from her, his hands slapping against the bench on either side of her hips.

She thought she screamed—mewled, some sound came out of her—loud enough to throw her into a frenzy as he sucked at her with the fervor of a man who'd never feasted at the banquet hall. His tongue wasted no time and slicked through her feminine folds. She felt the scrape of his teeth along the sensitive flesh, but it only had her thrashing harder against him.

When he roughly flicked his tongue against her clitoris, she lost the last of her control, and her body lost its will to hold back the release that had been building from the moment he'd tossed up her skirts. She screamed through her orgasm; Nick's hand covered her mouth to muffle the sounds she made with abandon. The moment stole all sanity from her, and before she could comprehend what was happening and what she was doing, she was straddled over Nick's thighs on the floor of the carriage.

The bench dug into her shoulder painfully, though she didn't mind, as it only heightened her pleasure when she felt so many sensations at once. Nick's hands moved between them, freeing himself from his trousers moments before she sank down on his steel-hard length.

A soft puff of air escaped her the moment she was fully seated atop him. Arms wrapped around his shoulders, she looked him straight in the eye, unable to speak, only able to feel what it was like to be taken by this man.

"Is this what you needed?" he asked, his voice hoarse with mutual desire.

Words were beyond her, so she nodded a second before his mouth stole her next breath in a deep, all-consuming kiss. His tongue was unrelenting as it tangled with hers.

She could taste herself on him, the cream that had spilled into his beard slicked against her tongue, the scent light and—to her surprise—pleasant. And why that fired her desires more she couldn't say. She just knew that the longer he kissed her, the deeper she tasted of him, sucking on his tongue, trying to steal a little of that strong essence of his that she craved, day in and day out.

So lost was she in his kiss, she'd stopped moving over him. His hands were firm as he held on to her thighs, rocking her over his solid manhood.

Her breathing came in pants, her knees grinding into the hard wooden floor where little pebbles cut into her silk stockings. Frantic was the only way to describe the erratic pace of her hips.

Her hands tangling in his hair, she slanted her mouth against his again as he rocked their bodies together in a primitive dance that elicited animalistic sounds from them both. As he promised, there were no thoughts, no niggling doubts. There was only need, reaching that culminating point where they would be lost in each other's arms so that everything else—except for them and this very moment—was drowned out.

With a bruising force, Nick's hands held on to her hips, guiding her every move. And while she was no longer a stranger to his body, she liked it when he took complete control. Craved it, even.

While their bodies grinded together, their tongues swirled and searched. They were breathing each other's air with every pant of pleasure that fell past their lips. The scrape of his beard against her face made her skin prickle with tenderness and her thighs clench around his hips as she remembered its roughness when he had buried his face in that private part of her.

The tingling awareness of her climax started where Nick was working deep inside her, the pounding of his member never ceasing as one of his hands released her hip so his thumb could rub around her clitoris. Her head fell back against the seat, and Nick's mouth sucked and licked at her neck with the same ferocity with which she'd taken his mouth moments ago.

Their coupling had been anything but gentle, so why she thought her climax should be shocked her to the core, when this time it crashed through her so hard she swore her heart actually stopped beating. She stilled altogether, fighting against Nick's movements as she felt liquid heat bubble through her veins a moment before she smashed through the barrier of her orgasm.

Nick shushed her cries with his mouth once again. His hands were around her hips, his body slamming up into her as he rode her through the high that stole any last bit of sense she had. She could do no more than hold on to him. Her arms wrapped tightly around his shoulders, her mouth sucked his tongue and muffled his grunts as he fucked harder and harder into her. The slap of their flesh was louder in her ears than the rut of the carriage along the cobbled road. And the thought that passers-by might hear them and know exactly what they were doing inflamed her need further.

She pulled away from his kiss, taking in a much-needed swallow of air, and she rode him, never wanting her orgasm to end.

"Don't stop. Don't stop. Don't. Stop," she said, panting over and over again, not sure her words even made sense.

Nick leaned her back on the bench, giving his knees leverage as he pounded into her in their awkward position. And it was worth every bit of discomfort as she slowly came down from her state of euphoria. His hand was tangled in her hair, pulling the pins that held her chignon in place. He took her like a man possessed, hell-bent on achieving one thing.

Their coupling was so intense that her core clenched hard around his shaft, milking him, squeezing him, almost as if begging him to join her in the bliss that had washed through her. And that was all it took, for she felt the hot jets of his semen pumping into her, filling her as his movements slowed, and they finally fell back to the floor, temporarily replete.

He nuzzled the side of her face, showering her with light kisses. Amelia closed her eyes and pressed her forehead to his shoulder. Despite being slightly uncomfortable, she didn't want to get up. Getting up would mean facing everything she was avoiding, being responsible, and focusing on the real world.

"I wish we could stay here forever," she said between breaths.

"A sentiment I couldn't agree with more."

His cock twitched inside her. She squirmed in his lap, a smile lifting her lips. "Thank you...for allowing me to forget."

"I can make you forget all night long if you want." Nick placed his hands on her cheeks, moving her head back so she was forced to look at him instead of hiding against his shoulder. "Is that what you really want, though?"

She bit her lip, wondering if it made her a bad person that she never wanted to think about her brother again. She nodded. "It hurts too much right now, when I can barely wrap my mind around everything that's happened in less than a day. Right now, I prefer to forget."

Nick lifted her from his lap, setting her back on the bench. Fixing his trousers and tidying up his rumpled waistcoat and jacket, he sat opposite her. He helped fix her hair and then knocked on the wall of the carriage. Once they slowed to a stop, Nick opened the door to give the driver instructions on where to take them.

When he sat opposite her once again, a wicked gleam sparked in his eyes, the usual calm gray roiling like a storm about to wash over her.

"What are you up to?"

"I have decided to change my plans for the day," Nick said.

"You can't. Murray will be livid. He may not agree to sell you his lands if you keep pushing him off. I know how much you want that house."

"He won't change his mind. I'll worry about him. You"— he grasped her knees and slid her to the edge of the bench so that their noses nearly touched—"need to focus on enjoying the rest of the day. Tomorrow, I won't let you off so easily, but today will be about just us."

She smiled. "I think I can agree to that."

"Perfect, because you're going to love what I have planned next." His words didn't match his tone, not that she brought that to his attention, but he seemed…oddly nervous.

"Where are we?" Amelia stared out the window, studying the busy street. There were layers of filth, garbage, and debris everywhere. The people, for the most part, looked poor and definitely couldn't rub two shillings between the group of them. Women with makeup painting their faces and their skirts hiked up to show their legs whistled and called over the men walking by. An old man sat against a derelict building, tipping a bottle to his lips. Children with dirty faces and tattered clothes ran through the streets, looking to be up to some sort of mischief.

"There's something I want to show you," Nick said. "It will help you focus your attention elsewhere. On better things."

She'd never seen so much poverty, and the sight outside the carriage tugged at her heart. How could she think better things when she saw nothing but broken lives as they drove past? "This place…What is it?"

"St. Giles."

Tearing her gaze away from the window, she gave Nick a questioning look.

"I won't let anything happen to you, Amelia. If there is one thing I can promise, it's that we are as safe here as walking the streets of Mayfair."

She hesitated only a moment before Nick took her hand to help her out of the carriage. He led her down a series of alleys and narrow streets too small for the carriage. After a short time, she was so turned around, she knew she wouldn't be able to find her way back to their carriage, should she attempt to locate it on her own.

There were so many people in one place. No one talked to them as Nick traversed the area as though he was intimately familiar with every nook and cranny. The deeper into the maze of houses they walked, the closer she tucked herself to Nick's side. None of what they saw seemed to shock Nick as they wound their way farther into the slums until they finally came to a less densely populated area.

They paused outside a flagstone wall that had to be four feet high and was topped with a wooden trellis that blocked the view of what lay beyond. Nick reached through a gap in the trellis to unlock a worn and muddy wooden gate from the inside. The noise of children playing met her ears, and she stepped forward, eager now to see what he wanted to show her.

They entered a stone courtyard, where at least a dozen and a half children ran around a lone sapling, chasing a ball. If she had to guess, she'd say they were all between seven and twelve years old, though one girl seemed much older, maybe fifteen or sixteen. She was talking to a young woman who Amelia guessed was in charge of the children.

Nick let go of her hand and shut the gate behind them. The kids kicked the ratty old ball in his direction. Amelia watched in awe and fascination as he joined their game without a moment's hesitation. His demeanor changed, as if a weight was lifted, as he laughed at their teasing taunts and kicked the ball back, only to accept it again from the children.

He didn't try to extricate himself, as many grown men would have. No, he engaged them, dared them to try and take the ball from him as he ran around the small courtyard, dodging this way and that to keep the ball in his possession.

He looked genuinely happy.

Watching him brought to light how little she really knew about him. That she'd given herself to a man of whom she hadn't even skimmed the depths. Not sure what she should do, she leaned against the courtyard wall. She actually was content to wait in the background and watch their game play out.

A woman who'd been standing at the back of the small house approached, holding out her hand. "How do you do? I'm Sera."

"Well." Amelia took Sera's hand, shaking it. "My name is Amelia." She didn't give her last name, as Sera hadn't, though she did add, "I work for Mr. Riley."

The woman had the same uncanny gray eyes as Nick. Was this woman a relative? Their similarities stopped at their identical eyes, though. Her hair was wheat-blonde, not black like Nick's. Her frame slight and fragile-seeming, and her face was perfectly oval.

"And what is your role?" Sera asked, turning to watch the game the children played with Nick.

"I am Mr. Riley's secretary." She didn't know what else to say, so she continued to watch Nick playing with the children.

"I never imagined Huxley would give up the position," Sera finally said.

It shouldn't surprise Amelia that Sera knew Huxley. "Are you Mr. Riley's sister?"

The woman gave Amelia a winning smile, nodding. "Half-brother, at any rate," Sera said. "The odds that we share a father are stacked against us, considering our mother's profession. Considering he's five years old than me, and Mum never had a man around for longer than a few months."

It occurred to Amelia that she hadn't known what Nick's mother's profession was until that moment. The realization was shocking and heartbreaking when she thought of how Nick would have grown up.

"Did my brother mention his reason for stopping by today? He usually comes at the end of the week."

"He didn't say," Amelia lied, not wanting to reveal her own difficulties. She turned back to Sera. "What is this place?"

"A school for the wayward. Nick sets one up in every slum where he amasses properties. It's a way to offer a lower rent to those struggling to work and keep their families going. We grew up in St. Giles, so we have a kinship with the people here."

"How long has the school been here?" Amelia asked.

"Four years now. Not all the kids can stay on for a full and proper education. They're often called away by their parents to work outside of London in the mines when they're of age. A lot of the girls go into the business by the time they hit their fourteenth birthday. Cece"—she nodded in the direction of the young lady wiping down a chalkboard inside the house with a wet rag—"was one of the lucky ones. Her dad works at the docks as a lighterman, and her mother does washing, so Cece's free to pursue her learnings."

"I never would have guessed Nick hid such an amazing thing."

Sera chuckled. "Oh, he's not hiding it. He just lets me manage it as I see fit. It's essentially my school. He supports it through financial means, of course, but I have full say on how this place operates."

How fascinating. "I taught for a short time."

"But now you're a secretary. That's an odd leap in professions, if you don't mind me saying."

"Not at all. I more or less fell into this role. I like the work as much as I liked teaching children."

"Perhaps I'll use you when I'm shorthanded."

It was a genuine offer that brought a smile to Amelia's face. Before she could respond, Nick was jogging toward them, sweat dotting his forehead and temples, which he wiped away with the handkerchief he pulled from the pocket of his waistcoat. She hadn't even seen him strip out of his jacket when she'd been talking with his sister. His shirtsleeves were rolled up and his strong forearms were bare to her hungry gaze. Just seeing him partially unclothed made her cheeks flame. She hoped no one noticed her reaction.

"What brought you by today?" Sera asked her brother as he leaned in and kissed her cheek in greeting.

"I wanted to introduce you to Miss Grant. Huxley," Nick went on, "is required for other duties, and she'll be taking over the day-to-day tasks he once handled. She'll be more than happy to assist with any of the schools, should you require anything."

Amelia didn't fail to notice the odd look his sister gave him, almost like surprise.

"I can offer you some tea, if you plan to stay for a while." Sera posed it as a question.

"We won't keep you long when your class is full," Nick responded. "How is Cece doing?" he asked as they headed through the open doors of the small house. It was set up as a classroom; benches and long tables were lined in three neat rows. There was a small desk at the front of the house, facing those benches. A chalkboard was on an easel, now freshly wiped down.

"Well enough. Her mother wants her to look for employment in one of the houses, but Cece would rather stay here and teach those less fortunate."

"Then draw up an amount for her annual salary, and we'll pay her enough to earn wages for herself and some extra coin so her mother doesn't struggle to make ends meet."

"I thought you'd say as much." Sera elbowed him lightly before she sat on the edge of her desk and faced them both. It was an action Amelia was so used to seeing Nick do that it struck her just how similar their mannerisms were. "You didn't come all this way to ask about Cece, though, did you?"

Nick crossed his arms. "You were always so perceptive."

"More like suspicious," she answered, humor dancing in her eyes. "I've known Huxley since I was a young girl, but you never brought him around while I was teaching."

Amelia watched the exchange and felt their love for each other so viscerally that it made her sad that she and her brother had never had this type of rapport or exchange.

"We might as well get straight to the issue, then, Sera. Miss Grant's role will vary from Huxley's. While she does the usual tasks as my secretary, I also want her to be involved with the rebuild of the old manor." Nick motioned his hand around the quaint little school. "You've outgrown this house faster than we imagined possible. You'll be taking on more children in the coming years, and you won't be able to do everything on your own."

Amelia didn't know what to say or make of that revelation, and she focused her attention on the school children slowly filing into the classroom.

"When the Highgate lands are redeveloped for our purpose, I'll post for teachers if we can't find them from around here," Sera said.

Now it all made sense. The Highgate lands were part of the deal with Lord Murray. His lordship was important because he owned a house close to the city but not so far away that children who attended the school there couldn't easily return to their parents a few days a week. Nick's determination to have that land was now clearer.

"I'll have my hands tied in so many tasks, I'm not sure how I'll keep everything straight," Sera said, looking at Amelia. "But I'm dying to dig in and get to work. Some assistance down the line would be most welcome. You're always thinking three steps ahead, aren't you, Nick?" Sera clapped her hands together and stood. "Now, will you be staying for the lessons? Because I need to get these children in line if we are going to get them back to their parents before supper."

"That's all I needed to tell you. We have to be on our way, as I have a busy night ahead." Nick affectionately embraced his sister and kissed her forehead before returning to Amelia's side. "Send a note or come by the house, should you need anything," he said in parting.

CHAPTER FIVE

Once they were home and settled into the relative privacy of Nick's study, Amelia turned to Nick and said, "I never imagined your intentions with Lord Murray's land would be building a school. I thought you wanted to set up a manor house so you could escape the busy core of the city once in a while." She looked at him sharply. "Does Lord Murray know what you plan?"

Nick pulled her into his arms before she could make it any farther into the adjoining library. His actions were so fast that she collided into his chest, and it left her momentarily breathless. His hands were on her hips, holding her close.

"He won't care what I do with the lands, as long as he has a fat pocket and one less financial burden to keep him up at night."

"How can you be so sure?" She was doing her damnedest to ignore the feeling she got from his closeness. It was so tempting to lose herself in his arms, as she had in the carriage earlier. "Men in his position hate the thought of people talking poorly of them. Like it or not, that's exactly what the residents of Highgate will do when they find out that a school for less-fortunate children will be set up in the manor house. While I think your goals noble and perfectly suited to land not being utilized to its potential, I also know the gentry to be prejudiced against anything that affects their perceived quality of life."

Nick backed her into the library, leading them toward the sofa.

"I could not care less what they think, Amelia. What is right isn't always what people want. And once I own the lands, there's nothing they can do to stop me from accomplishing my goal."

"I don't doubt that for one moment. What you are doing is nothing short of admirable. In fact, I agree wholeheartedly with your plan." She traced her finger over his bearded jawline. "Thank you for today and for giving me something else on which to focus. Most of all, thank you for introducing me to your sister. It means a lot to me."

"You asked to forget about your brother. And I hope you did, for at least a short while. Sera can be a friend, Amelia. Someone you can confide in, if needed. And she is a bit of a mad genius at running the school. Her dream to teach goes back as far as I can remember."

"I'm glad she could make that dream real."

"Our mother always told us to wish for the stars and be content if we only managed to skim the skyline."

"That's beautiful and rather poetic. Your mother sounds like a wonderful woman."

"She was a dreamer. And she allowed herself to be lowered by the men in her life." Nick's mood turned darker with that admission.

She frowned. Had she said something wrong? "No matter your mother's profession, it's obvious how much she loved you."

Nick studied her drawn brows before he said, "Don't you worry about my mother, Amelia. Her greatest accomplishment was ensuring that Sera and I could fend for ourselves. And we eventually did."

"She still sounds like a marvel."

Nick kissed her hard on the mouth. When he pulled away, he said, "I will require your assistance once the acquisition is finalized with Lord Murray. We need to hire architects and builders to make the manor house into a school. It requires extensive work, both inside and out. While all that happens, Sera still needs to run the school. She runs her classes Mondays through Thursdays. You're free to spend time at the school. For friendship, if you desire. Or to assist in teaching, if you miss it."

She recalled her first job as a governess. That calling had been short-lived after her employer had tried to rape her. "While I do love children, I'll leave teaching to those far more capable than I was. What your sister has built in a community that so obviously struggles day to day…it's nothing short of amazing. I respect what she has done and what you help her do."

Nick's hands cupped her face. His mouth was inches from hers. "No less amazing than you."

"Flattery may get you everywhere." She wrapped her arms around his shoulders, her fingers drawing lazy circles over the back of his head, tangling in his slightly longer than fashionable hair. "But in all honesty, today meant more to me than you can possibly imagine."

They broke apart as the echo of footsteps grew louder outside the study. Amelia immediately headed toward her desk, smoothing her hair and then her dress to ensure everything was in place.

"Lord Murray sent a post just now; had it delivered directly to my attention," came Huxley's voice from the study.

Amelia sat in her chair and busied herself with opening the mail, though she kept one ear trained on the study to hear what was discussed.

"When does he want to meet?"

"Says he's found another buyer if you're not interested. He's listed an address where you can find him."

She could hear the rustle of paper. Nick must be reading the missive himself.

"No one else is going to buy that land. This is Shauley's doing."

"It doesn't surprise me," Huxley said. "It was likely to get dirty at some point when he wasn't getting the results he thought he should get."

"Bloody prig." Something thumped down on the desk. "I should let him stew for a while, but the school means too much to my sister, and Landon won't be happy if he finds out I've affected his chances of taking over the town leases."

Amelia listened without saying a word. Now that she better understood why Nick wanted the land, she sympathized with his anger. If there was one thing she'd learned in the weeks living here, it was that Nick hated to be in a position where his hand was forced. Though, she supposed, no one liked to be in a situation where others told one how to act.

She couldn't help but feel as though this was partially her fault. The reason he'd brushed off Lord Murray time and again was because he didn't want to leave her side.

Setting her letter opener down, she made her way into the next room. Huxley stood as she entered.

"I will cancel our dinner reservations at the Langtry with Mr. Hart," Amelia announced.

Nick looked at her as he put on his jacket. "Let Hart know I have business matters that are getting in the way of leisure." Mr. Hart—though she still wasn't sure if Hart was his first name or last, as no one had corrected her as of yet—was a friend of Nick's. She'd only met him on a couple of occasions, but he was a pleasant and kind man.

"Should I be more specific?" she asked.

"That should suffice."

She nodded.

Huxley picked up the crumpled paper from the desk and handed it to Nick. "You'll need this if you're to pay his lordship a visit."

Amelia faced both men, not sure what was going on, but they were looking at each other as if they were both in on a secret, and she wasn't privy to it. "Would you like me to complete anything else while you're out? It's been a bit odd of a day…"

She wasn't quite sure how to occupy her time, and she needed to do something to keep her mind from going to darker, unwanted places. She wasn't comfortable admitting that in front of Huxley, though.

"I should be back in an hour. You can read through the agreement my solicitor drafted for the purchase of the lands.

I expect we will offer less than I was originally willing to part with."

"But..." She was not sure why she should disagree with that stance. It seemed cocky and too sure. What if Lord Murray decided not to sell? That would break his sister's heart. Amelia had to wonder where the school would expand if the Highgate deal fell through.

Nick walked toward her, all dominating, his presence larger than life. She found herself backing up a step, feeling breathless and hot all at once. The second she realized what she'd done, she corrected herself and stepped forward. Nick stopped a foot away from her, respecting her boundaries when Huxley was half listening, half looking like he wanted to find the first excuse he could to escape.

"I think you'll enjoy this process." That could be interpreted so many ways. And his grin said he knew she wasn't thinking about the Highgate deal.

Trying to keep the subject focused, she said, "I've never been much for taking unnecessary risks."

Not when her brother had a knack for losing all their money and their possessions, gambling in games of chance. No, she'd never been one to wager. Money should be saved and used wisely, never spent lavishly or rashly.

"This is a necessary risk, one that will work in our favor." Nick turned and left before she could respond.

She exhaled and stared at Huxley. What should she say to him? Had he noticed Nick's behavior with her? More familiar than an employer should act toward his secretary. These worrying thoughts would be the end of her if she didn't get them under control.

The facts were this: Huxley was intimately aware of the trouble Jeremy had caused. Huxley had been there on the day her brother had tried to drag her off to God-knows-where. He hadn't said anything to her about the incident, so she hadn't brought it up. Did he know her brother was dead? Surely he did, as he hadn't stayed behind yesterday as an additional presence in the house.

"Are you glad you don't have to watch me at all hours of the day when Mr. Riley leaves?"

The scowl lines deepened on Huxley's face. "I didn't so much mind it as you think. My loyalties have always been with Nick, and you're now part of this household, Miss Grant. While that didn't seem to matter where you came from, it means something here."

"Thank you, Huxley." Caught off guard by his honest response, she was suddenly teary-eyed. It was a ridiculous reaction, but she couldn't help it. "I have to get back to my correspondence."

She turned and headed back to the library, not sure what else to say. She busied herself answering letters and invitations, canceling more than she accepted, as that was what her mood called for.

Nick tossed down the letter Lord Murray had the audacity to pen. "You're not in a position to threaten me, Murray."

"How dare you come to my club and speak to me as if you were my better." Lord Murray stood, though his height left something to be desired, as he was a good half foot shorter than Nick.

Nick crossed his arms over his chest and stared down at him. "This afternoon could not be avoided. I have a dozen businesses and more than thirty lots of land to my name in this city. It's guaranteed that I'll miss a few appointments here and there when something comes up that requires my immediate attention."

"I don't give a damn what issues arose today. Our meeting should have taken precedence, had you thought to show me you were serious about purchasing Caldon Manor. I'm more inclined to hold on to it and let it fall to a far worse state of disrepair on principle alone."

Nick curled one hand around the top edge of the wooden chair tucked beneath the table. He could play dirty too, if that was what Lord Murray wanted.

"I do not take lightly to threats, my lord. If your piece-of-shit secretary put you up to this, it's a game you are about to lose. Perhaps you should see where his loyalties lie. I'll agree to two-thirds of the original price being negotiated. *That is* my final offer." Nick turned to leave.

"Wait," Lord Murray said, his voice hushed, defeated.

"Give me one reason," Nick said without turning. They both knew Lord Murray had no choice but to sell one of his properties. The one in Highgate was the better option, as no one could live in the house the way it stood. And until now, the offer on the table had been for a more-than-decent sum, as Nick was anxious to close it for any price, as long as it was his in the end.

Murray was visibly defeated. His shoulders slumped, his usual bearing beaten down. "I need your word the deal will go through before the end of the month."

Nick smiled but hid his reaction before turning to face his foe. Lord Murray was merely a means to an end. "Why should I agree? You think threatening me will make me buy it quicker? I don't know what kind of man you think I am, but you're sorely underqualified in making a deal with me."

"Don't forget that it was you who initially approached me, Riley. Not the other way around."

True, and he regretted his eagerness in the beginning when he'd found out Lord Murray was in financial trouble. It was a mistake he wouldn't repeat. "What you don't understand is that there's no skin off my back if I walk away from the original deal. You, on the other hand…"

The rest didn't need to be said. Perhaps Lord Murray now realized the mistake he'd made in sending that note.

The man visibly paled and sat heavily in his chair. "Heddie wanted the deal done." Heddie was Lord Murray's mistress and a woman of many stage talents. It surprised Nick that the woman hadn't moved on the second she realized his lordship couldn't provide the lavish lifestyle in which she was known to indulge.

As much as Nick wanted to walk away from this deal, he knew he couldn't. But he didn't have to let Lord Murray in on that fact. "Give me one reason not to walk away."

Lord Murray rubbed his hands roughly over his face and then looked Nick straight in the eye. "I know you're after more than the lands. At first, I couldn't figure out why you wanted it or that decrepit house. But I get it now. Your man Huxley's been seen about Highgate. Hard to miss that ugly bastard. He's been watching the locals, questioning the business owners. What I'm interested to know is what you think to find. I have owned that house for thirty years, and there is nothing that goes on at Highgate that I don't know."

Nick knew Lord Murray was pulling at straws. And probably from something Shauley had told him. *When a dog starts sniffing you out, you give it a bone to chew on.* He would not address the reason for Huxley's presence. "I planned on setting up a boarding school for the wayward. But that doesn't need to happen in Highgate."

It was half the truth—and a gamble telling Lord Murray that much.

Lord Murray narrowed his eyes, disbelief and curiosity warring in his expression. "A bloody school?" he sputtered, obviously not expecting that revelation.

Nick turned again, not willing to spend another moment with his lordship, knowing he had to play hard if he was going to succeed in getting what he wanted.

"Where in hell are you going, Riley?"

"To investigate other options."

"So you're no longer interested in Caldon Manor?" Lord Murray followed him out the door, not bothering with his jacket, even though the wind was cutting.

"That is not what I said." Nick gave the older man a bland look. Lord Murray seemed worried he'd lost this deal, but Nick wouldn't give the man any hope. Tomorrow, he planned to see his solicitor about a lower offer for the lands. That should sufficiently anger Shauley, and that thought brought on a smile. Nick would eventually have to deal with Shauley…after the purchase of the lands.

"You can't just leave," Lord Murray called after him.

Nick looked at the man one last time. "Yet that is exactly what I'm doing."

And he left. He needed to stop at Landon's. Landon was Nick's business partner and friend. They were going into this deal together, and they'd have to stand firm on this gamble if they were going to succeed in getting exactly what they wanted in the end. Nicked needed to ensure this deal succeeded. And just maybe Lord Murray would sack Shauley for suggesting they play a harder hand.

Patience, Nick counseled himself. He'd waited nearly twenty years for this opportunity, and he well knew Lord Murray was desperate, for he needed the money and could not afford this deal falling through.

Chapter Six

Amelia woke with a start, not sure what had dragged her from the sweet tangle of limbs that had filled her dreams. Movement beside her had her rolling over to find Nick, who was usually wrapped around her, keeping her warm through the night. The only thing she could make out in the dark of Nick's room was his body twisted in the light blanket that normally was folded at the end of the bed.

Tentatively, she reached out to him. "Nick," she whispered, her voice croaking, still full of sleep. He mumbled something she couldn't make out the words to.

"Nick," she said louder. When he didn't wake, she curled her hand around his bicep, shaking him lightly.

He didn't respond, not that she'd expected it to be so easy to wake him.

She wished she knew why these nightmares gripped him so tightly. This was the third time she'd woken like this in the past week, as though something had triggered the increased frequency. When he was like this, he was unresponsive and sometimes violent, all while he slept. These nightmares frightened her, not for her sake but for his.

Sitting up in the bed, she pressed her hand harder into his chest—he usually woke if she talked for a while. "Nick, you need to wake up. Come back to me. Please…"

She shook him with both hands, feeling desperate to pull him from the nightmare and desperate to protect their privacy. If Huxley heard Nick, as he often did, he'd be in here soon enough. And that was the last thing she wanted.

Leaning over him, she shook him more forcefully. Now that her eyes had adjusted to the darkness, she could see the pained expression that morphed his beautiful face. To see such a strong man made helpless terrified her beyond measure.

She was sprawled over him, doing her damnedest to shake him out of his dream state, but he wasn't responding to her touch or her voice like he usually did. She didn't know what to do. Any minute, Huxley would be here. They'd be found out. And while she knew she couldn't be discovered in here, she would not leave Nick in his current state.

Making a quick decision, she bolted out of Nick's bed and ran to the door to lock it. When she was back on the bed, shaking Nick again, she heard the turn of the latch.

She gazed back at the door. It shook.

Straddling Nick's waist, she squeezed her thighs around his hips. Her voice low and careful as she heard the force of Huxley's shoulder meet the door.

"Please, Nick. Please. You have to get up. I don't know what to do."

When his eyes snapped open, a huge sigh of relief whooshed from her lungs. A second later, their positions were reversed, and his hand was around her throat. Madness lingered in his eyes as he stared back at her without actually seeing her.

"Nick." Her voice was a rasp as his grip tightened. "Nick." She coughed, trying to catch a deep breath as she attempted to yank his hands away from her throat. He eased up, but he didn't let her go, not completely.

A sob escaped her, not so much of fear for herself but of the situation in which they found themselves. Nick would never forgive himself if he hurt her, but she didn't know how to snap him out of what now appeared to be a waking nightmare.

There was a knock at the door, but Nick didn't acknowledge it. She wasn't sure he even heard it. Was he still dreaming? "Please see me," she managed to croak. "Nick. Come back to me."

Huxley's rough voice came through the door. "Nick, answer me if you're awake."

The thud of Huxley's body hitting the door had her heart racing faster and faster as the seconds ticked by. She was running out of time.

Amelia searched Nick's eyes. There was no recognition in the black gaze that stared down at her in the darkness. Tears trailed down the side of her face as she forced herself to remain calm.

Think, Amelia.

While his hand hadn't tightened anymore, it was a little difficult to breath, and she suspected that if she tried to slide out from beneath him, his grip would intensify.

She opened her legs to him, letting him settle in the cradle of her thighs. She tangled her hands in his hair, gripping tightly at the base of his neck.

"Wake up," she demanded. There was no fear left in her voice. *Think, Amelia. Think.*

Straining against his hand, she did the last thing she could think of. She closed her eyes and strained her neck enough that she could kiss him.

The press of their lips was fleeting, as his restraint on her gave her limited mobility. She couldn't move another inch without hurting herself in the process. So she kissed the next best thing she could reach: his lower lip, his chin, the strong cut of his jawline. Between each gentle caress of her lips, she asked Nick to wake up over and over again.

The thickening of his member was almost instantaneous, the heavy weight of it wedged hard between the folds of her sex where their bodies were crushed together. Every muscle in Nick's body grew taut, as though he were preparing for a fight. Amelia continued to kiss him, hoping he awoke before Huxley broke through the door.

The pained look that had taken hold of Nick's expression gradually loosened. Where his eyes had been empty of life, the first flicker of awareness now met her head-on. She breathed a sigh of relief as he released his grip on her throat and tucked his head into her shoulder, as though he needed to catch his breath. Comprehension must have washed through Nick because he cursed a second before he rubbed his lips back and forth over the erratic pulse at her neck.

Her mouth parted on a silent moan, and her knees spread wider, as she tried to wedge the thick hardness of his shaft tighter against her sex. The heavy thud of Huxley ramming into the door brought her back to the reality of their situation.

"I'm fine!" Nick barked, his body stiffening as he held his weight from her. "Go back to bed, Huxley."

There was silence on the other side of the door for long moments before they heard the wood-plank floors creak with Huxley's retreat.

Amelia closed her eyes. "What happened?" she whispered into the dark.

Nick hauled himself off her and went into the plunge bath that was attached to his room. Candlelight flickered, one stub at a time.

She could hear the water running in the sink, but Nick didn't speak to her. She sat at the edge of the bed and waited for him to come back…but he didn't. Was he hiding from her? Did he not want to talk about what had happened? When he didn't return to the bed after five minutes, she reached for her robe on the floor, slipped into the cool silky material, and cinched it at her waist before she followed Nick into the bathing chamber.

Nick's scarred back faced her as she entered the room. His dark head was bowed, and his hands curled over the edge of the white porcelain sink. She approached him slowly, letting him hear every step she took as she walked across the tiled floor.

When she was close enough to touch him, she didn't lay her head against his back and wrap her arms around him, even though that was what she most wanted. She stood tall and firm behind him, knowing she would have to be direct if she wanted answers about what had happened. Answers about how to stop the dreams that tormented him too frequently.

"Nick?"

"Not now, Amelia." His voice was soft, tired.

"Don't shut me out."

"I can't have this conversation right now." His head was shaking back and forth. His body clearly saying no, no, no.

"Can I draw a bath for you?" she offered, refusing to back down.

"Go back to bed. I'll join you soon."

"I'm not leaving you like this, Nick. Help me understand what happened."

He abruptly turned and had her backed up against the cold glass-tiled wall. The look in his eyes was broken. She reached her hand up and pressed her palm to the side of his face, the rough friction of his beard grounding her to the moment. She would not give in so easily to his demands.

"I won't leave because you matter to me. And I cannot help you if I don't understand what happened."

"Stop. Just stop, Amelia. There are things you don't know—can't know. Let it be." His eyes focused on her neck a second before he caressed the back of his hand over her. "I hurt you. I'll never forgive myself for that. I can barely live with myself right now after the way I woke up."

She grasped his hand with her own and lowered it. "What were you dreaming about?"

He yanked himself away from her so fast, she nearly tumbled to the floor.

"You can trust me with your secrets, just as I have trusted you with mine." Her voice was barely above a whisper. If he didn't open himself up to her, how would they ever get beyond this point? "If you shut me out now, I will be forced to believe you do not seek a relationship with me, only someone to warm your bed."

It hurt her to admit that, but if that was the truth, she might as well know sooner rather than later.

"That's not what you are to me." He paced the floor in front of her, looking lost and angry. His hands were buried in his hair and periodically scrubbed over his face, as though he was still trying to shake remnants of the nightmare from his mind.

She walked toward him. How could she give up on him when she could clearly read the torment that hung over him, like a weight that wouldn't let up?

It was obvious that she wasn't going to get the answers she wanted right now. The one thing within her ability to offer was comfort.

Reaching for him, she threaded her fingers through his and led him back into his bedroom. He didn't fight her to leave him be, for which she was thankful, because she wasn't sure what she would have done, had that been the case.

Sitting on the edge of the bed, she tried to pull him down next to her. But he held firm; his expression, hovering on the edge of want and worry, told her he was torn in what to do. She wrapped her arms around his waist and pressed her head against the hard ridges of his stomach. Eventually, he loosened his stance, his hand petting her hair, his penis growing thicker with need between them.

Amelia pressed small kisses against his belly, trailing through the dark hairs that drew a line down to his heavy manhood. He stopped her with his finger under her chin before she could take his member into her mouth.

He shook his head, his expression no longer lost, just…needful. "I don't trust myself right now."

"I know you won't hurt me."

"So sweet and innocent." He brushed the back of his knuckles over her neck and then over her chin. "What I want *is* to hurt you. But not the way I did earlier. In a different way."

Her breath caught in her lungs. His words were a warning that she would be well advised to take to heart, but she wanted to know more.

"Show me what you want, Nick. I trust you."

Instead of answering her, he grasped the braid at the base of her head. "Are you sure you want this?"

She nodded, licking her lips.

"Suck my cock." His voice was gravelly, his need taking over the tormented look that lingered in his eyes.

She would do anything to banish that look completely.

Her fist around the base of his penis, she sucked the head of him into her mouth, her tongue playing with the slit at the top, lapping up the precome before swirling fully around the silky head.

Nick's hand guided her head, making her draw him deeper into her mouth. His hips pumped forward and back, driving him deeper, deeper than she expected she could take him. It was too deep. Her throat closed around him, and she gagged when he pressed too far. Nick eased off, pulling out of her completely, the head of his cock drawing a wet line over her lips, waiting for her to take him again.

"Relax your throat, and you'll be able to take all of me. Go slower this time."

She looked up at his hard expression. Hunger and desire fired his gray eyes, and in place of the haunting dream, something darker was there, darker than she'd ever seen before. She had no words to describe it and recalled his words: *"What I want is to hurt you."* She suspected what he meant, and the thought only made her yearn for more.

With her eyes locked on his, she opened her mouth and let him slide between her lips. She rubbed the flat of her tongue over the thick vein that ran along the bottom of his manhood and took him deeply. Deeper than she had before. And then he started to rock into her mouth like he did her sheath. Spit dribbled out the side of her mouth, but she didn't care. His hand tightened in her hair again, his body strung taut as he held himself back from taking her harder. He was too big for her to take all of him, the head of his cock already touching the back of her throat with each motion of his hips.

Nick stayed in control of the situation, not giving himself over to her fully. He was holding back. And knowing that hurt. His thrusts came faster, shallower, so he wouldn't cause her to gag again. And that control he held over the situation made her angry. Made it difficult for her to lose herself in pleasing him.

Pulling against his hand tangled in her hair, she dislodged his cock from her mouth and looked up at him. His hips were still moving, his need bobbing wetly against her chin.

"You are holding yourself back from me." The hurt was thick in her voice.

"I have to."

"What part of 'I trust you' did you disbelieve?"

With a groan, Nick's hand released her hair, and he hauled her up to her feet.

"You don't know what you're asking."

"I want to be the person you come to when you need to forget what haunts your thoughts. I'm asking you to give me all you have."

He yanked her robe down off her shoulders, trapping her arms at her sides. "The things I want will scare you." When she glared back at him, he pushed her roughly down on the bed, face forward, bottom in the air. His hands were urgent, almost desperate, as he pushed the silky robe off her legs, tearing it in his haste to expose her rear. His hands squeezed each cheek of her buttocks.

"I don't want to scare you," he said.

"And what gave you the impression that I was afraid? I want you to lose yourself in me. Make me lose myself in you," she mumbled against the blanket.

Would he believe her at her word?

He smacked one cheek of her rear hard and then rubbed over the sting. The sound that came out of her was half surprise, half desire.

"Are you sure you're ready for this?"

"Do it, Nick. Take me like you need to." She growled her frustration.

He spread the cheeks of her buttocks. The wetness there was surely visible to the naked eye. The slide of his finger at her entrance brought light to that fact, and he growled something under his breath and then said, "Wet from my rough handling. What will you do when I'm fucking your ass?"

She waited with bated breath for his next move, not able to respond to that question, not sure she was meant to respond or even how she should respond.

It seemed as though he stared and rubbed his finger through her slick folds for ages. She knew deeply that he was fighting with himself over what he should do next. How much of himself he could really give her. Oh, God, she wanted him so badly that she felt a pulse start deep inside her womb.

"I need you, Nick. Please…Give yourself over to me as I have to you."

Hands tight around her hips, he raised her rear higher in the air, placing her knees on the bed. His hard length pressed demandingly against the crease of her bottom. She moved against him, desperate to feel him breach her sheath hard and fast, but he wasn't ready to give her what she wanted. And she suspected he was planning something altogether different.

Releasing her hips, he reached around to her stomach and pulled the tie on the robe loose. She thought he'd pull it right off her, but instead he yanked the material the rest of the way down her arms, until was it was twisted tightly around her wrists, binding them, making sure she couldn't touch him.

His lips pressed against her nape and trailed hotly over her spine. Every touch was like a branding deep in her flesh as he worked his way lower and, skipping the place her hands were tied, over her tailbone.

Going lower yet, the scrape of his beard over her bottom sent a thrill of excitement right to her core and fired her body to an urgent boil. Her hips swayed and her knees spread slightly wider. Why wasn't he filling her? His teeth scraped along the rounded flesh, light at first and then biting her. The sensation only added to her building desire, her need. She needed him more than she ever had before. Her body was so eager to be filled that wetness seeped from her core to trail a path of want down her thighs.

She pulled her arms up, wanting nothing more than to free her hands so that she could pull Nick closer, so he couldn't deny her his body for another second. Nick's hands tightened around the material so she couldn't move from her current position.

"You want me to fill you up, to stuff my cock so deep in you that you feel me in your throat again."

Her nipples pebbled harder, the firm tips scraping along the soft blankets beneath her. The sensation made her pelvis thrust, rubbing them over the blanket, wishing Nick's fingers were plucking and pulling on them instead of her fulfilling her own desires.

When she didn't respond, he pulled away, and cold air washed over her body. She cried out in protest, frustration building in the back of her throat in the form of a growl.

"What do you say to that, Amelia? Do you want me to ride your pretty cunt, fuck you so hard you won't be able to get up from this bed?"

"Yes."

Her eyes slipped closed as he touched her, only this time he ran his finger down between the cheeks of her rear, exploring parts of her that had her heart pounding so hard in her chest that she could hear the thump, thump, thump loud in her ears.

She breathed easy again when his fingers found her slick center, and he slammed two fingers hard and deep. Her sheath tightened around the sweet intrusion. He pulled his fingers out only to repeat the process again and again until the slap of his palm against the skin between her entrance and her anus made wet noises. She was sure his whole hand was soaked with her juices, and she didn't care, didn't think to be embarrassed by her body's reaction. She just needed more.

Nick leaned over her, trapping her hands between their bodies as the heat of him enveloped her from his chest to her back. His mouth was next to her ear, his hard cock heavy between her thighs, but he didn't remove his fingers; if anything, he fucked them into her harder.

"I'm going to own every part of you," he whispered in her ear at the same moment his thumb breached her *other* hole.

Her instinctive reaction was to pull away, but Nick had his arm wrapped around her; she wasn't going anywhere if he didn't want her to.

She made a sound that was half protest and half shock as he worked the tip of his thumb in and out of her, the movement aided by the wetness coating his hand, fingers, and thumb.

"You like that, sweetheart. You want me to fuck this tight hole, don't you?"

She couldn't answer, lost in the euphoric feeling of his surrounding her and being everywhere in her. Desire built inside her like a storm about to rage out of control. She was panting—actually panting, like a cat in heat.

Nick bit at her earlobe, sucking it, his tongue playing with it. His breathing came hard and fast, and his hips were working almost as fast as his hand was stroking deep inside her. He was as affected by their actions as she.

The rigid length of his cock pressed against her thigh. She wanted to squeeze her legs together around that steely length, draw him closer, but she was completely trapped and helpless to his tormenting pleasure.

And she liked that she had no control over what he did. Liked being a slave to his desires, to hers. Powerless to stop him from doing the things that would have her shy away and pull back if she could.

Nick pulled his thumb out of her, and she cried at the loss, her body suddenly feeling too empty.

"Can't be without me, can you."

She shook her head. "I need you back inside me. I—"

He rammed his cock so hard into her sheath that her breath caught on her words, and she moaned instead of begging him to take her. His hips rotated, his rod twisting and gyrating as he took her so hard that her whole body was splayed to him. She felt him on every intimate part of her body, and the sensation was almost too much to process all at once.

"Oh, God. Nick. Nick…"

Her hands curled into fists. She wanted them free so she could give herself enough leverage to push back into him, to urge him to take her harder, even though this was the hardest he'd ever rode her. His hands grasped tightly around her hips, holding her in place as he pumped into her, working her toward that sweet precipice of release.

Amelia strained against her bonds, not sure whether or not she really wanted to be free. And just as quickly as Nick had taken her, he pulled away. She felt empty, needy. How could he stop and leave her wanting?

She looked over her shoulder at him, searching his eyes for the answers she wasn't sure she wanted, when the head of his steely length pressed against the tight puckered hole higher up. The hunger in his eyes nearly undid her. He didn't break his gaze as he pushed forward, breaching the tight hole he'd thumbed earlier.

Her mouth opened on a wordless sound as he stretched her with just the head of his penis, working it in and out of her slowly. Oh, so slowly that she wasn't sure if she was feeling pain or pleasure. It just felt different.

An alien noise rose in the back of her throat. The burn of him working his way in drew her body forward. She hesitated, not sure whether or not she wanted what he was offering. His hand came down hard on one cheek of her buttocks, stilling her.

"Tell me to go slower, if that's what you want, but don't pull away from me, Amelia. I'll own this part of you as much as I own every other part. Is that understood?"

Her face flamed red, knowing she shouldn't want any such thing; she was, after all, her own person. But the truth of the matter was this: she wanted exactly that.

What they were doing felt so far beyond forbidden that she pulled forward another inch and buried her head into the bedding to hide her deep blush. Only the very tip of him remained inside, stretching the tight hole of her bottom. Indecision had her frozen to the spot, unable to move or able to speak.

"Talk to me, Amelia. You said you wanted all of me. Are you still sure you want that?"

She nodded.

"I need to possess every part of you. It's like an obsession, eating me up inside."

"Why?" It was the only word she could form.

"Because I need to own you." His answer came easily, truthfully. But the better question was, did she want that? To be completely controlled by this man?

Yes, she wanted that, but deep down, she felt that was not something she should ever want from anyone. Nick made her feel and think differently. She was losing herself in him, and that scared her more than anything.

"What you're doing feels so…" *Wrong? Strange? Foreign?* "Different."

Nick leaned over her, his beard scraping along her shoulder as he kissed and nibbled her overheated skin. The motion drew him further inside her.

"I can do this all day, my sweet darling." His teeth scraped along her skin, making her shiver.

Reaching around to her front, his fingers slicked through the wet folds of her sex. "Even fucking you this way has cream coating you. I want to lap it all up like a cat, suck it all away 'til I've feasted myself full, but I know you'll only cream more for me if I do that."

She closed her eyes, her breathing shaky as she rolled his words around in her mind. Every dirty word he uttered fired her desire higher. When one of his fingers flicked against her clitoris, there was but one thing on her mind. And that was *more*. She pressed her bottom back into him, needing to pull all of him into her. Needing him completely.

"That's it, Amelia. I'll have you begging for my cock fucking deep inside the tight hole of your rear."

He was relentless with his words, his body. His fingers still rotated around her swollen bud, the sensations blasting through her body and making her pelvis and hips undulate, lodging him deeper until finally it felt like his penis stretched her wide open. There was a slight burn, but it receded the longer he held motionless inside her.

Nick pulled his fingers away seconds before she found her release. She cried out at the loss of his touch, but was filled with an altogether different feeling as he pushed carefully forward, filling her, inch by agonizing inch. Her breath caught, stopped in its tracks, and ended as he slid fully inside. She waited for what felt like forever as his steely length remained still, and her body adjusted to his heavy girth.

"Shh," he whispered next to her ear, sucking her earlobe between his teeth. "The pain will ebb. I promise."

"It doesn't hurt…not really. It's…I can't describe it."

His lips trailed over her shoulder, across her back, and stopped at the little bone at the base of her neck. "Relax."

Lost in the way his lips trailed over her, she was left breathless when he pulled out, only to push back inside her, his pace careful but no less titillating. The slowness was soon a torture in and of itself, and she had to move with him, against him, forward and back. Nick let her move with abandon until her body couldn't keep up with what her heart wanted; her actions grew jerky and erratic. Nick was on his knees behind her, grasping her hips tight, sliding her along his hard length.

Setting a steady pace, he slipped one hand between the folds of her sex again and rubbed her clitoris in hard, even strokes. She unfurled her hands, pressing one palm against his lower abdomen with each plunge forward. His fingers were like magic, building a firestorm in her so high that she was sure she would combust at any moment.

The way he hit her inside only heightened each sensation, drawing her closer to a finale she knew would trump anything she'd ever felt. Her heart skittered and raced; each of his propulsions forward had moans slipping past her lips. His fingers drew on her harder, pulling at the swollen nub between the lips of her sex.

And she begged. "Nick, don't stop. Don't stop. Please. I need to finish. I need you so badly. Please. Please…"

"My minx likes to beg when I'm so close to giving her what she wants."

"I need this."

"And I will give it to you."

He scissored his fingers, sliding them around her clitoris. She cried out his name once more as she flew over the edge and straight into pure ecstasy. She felt impossibly tight, impossibly good. Impossibly free. As her body clenched and released, her cream ran down her thighs with each movement of his hand, each propulsion of his cock in that forbidden place.

Nick shouted, and a second later she felt the pump of his seed deep inside her. He felt so different this way. It was as though she could feel more of him, every twitch, every slide like a thousand hands running over her body in unison. Nick's movements slowed, his body collapsed on top of hers, his hardness diminishing only slightly.

They didn't say anything for some minutes. When their breathing evened out, Amelia spoke first. "The way you make me feel…that scares me about us."

Nick's hand came down to rest near her head. The motion brought him completely out of her bottom, and she exhaled a small sound of relief but felt a twinge of regret at the same time. How could she want *that?*

"Hearing that makes me feel like a monster."

"I don't mean it that way. I just…I don't know who I am without you anymore. Untie me, Nick. Please. I need to touch you."

He sat up on his knees and unwound the material binding her wrists together. Her hands throbbed when they fell forward. Nick flipped her onto her back and rubbed her wrists between his hands.

"Forgive me," he said quietly.

Placing one hand along his jaw, she waited for him to focus on her eyes. "I trust you, Nick. I just need to take this slow. You make me feel things that cause me a great deal of guilt."

"There is nothing wrong with anything we do. Nothing to feel guilty about."

"You'll think me a ninny, but I want to see you and look in your eyes when you want something new. I want to touch you. I feel bereft, having that sense taken away from me."

His thumb lazily circled one of her wrists, drawing the numbness out. "I'll never bind you again."

Amelia buried both her hands in his thick, black hair. "That's not what I want."

"What do you want, then, Amelia? Don't you know I'll give you anything you ask?"

She bit her bottom lip. "I want to do everything with you. But I need to take this one step at a time. We are still learning about each other. The things you want, I would never have dreamed possible. I want to give you complete control, but I also want you to be honest with me. I want you to talk to me and reveal yourself to me, as I've shared myself with you. There's nothing you don't know about me. Nothing."

Nick's thumb brushed back and forth over her lips.

"I won't taint you with my past." One of his hands caressed the side of her face, and he kissed her tenderly on the mouth.

Neither closed their eyes; they watched each other, even as their lips brushed back and forth in a lazy loving.

"Not all of your past is dark…" She was fishing for anything that would chase away the remnants of his dream, of his guilt for taking her in a way that she didn't think many indulged. And to her surprise, she'd do it a hundred times more. For the pleasure and to hand him the reins of control, if that was what he needed to pull back from the darkness.

He pushed off the bed and padded across the floor toward the bathing room, and for the second time that night, she followed him. The water in the tub was running as she entered. Nick retrieved a linen cloth from a cabinet and ran it under the water of the washing stand before wiping himself off. He was still hard, and his member bobbed when he released it and tossed the cloth over the porcelain sink.

The man was insatiable. She blushed and turned away.

"Cat got your tongue now?"

"You are changing the subject."

"It's three in the morning, Amelia. The last thing I want to do is talk about my dreams when you're standing naked, like a feast yet to be tasted. Get in the bath."

She crossed her arms over her middle, the motion plumping up her breasts. "And if I say no?"

"Then I'll happily assist. You're going to be sore. The hot water will help ease any lingering tenseness in your muscles."

She already was feeling a little bruised, not that she'd admit that. "It's going to be difficult to bathe with you here to distract me."

He smiled, and there was nothing innocent about the look her gave her. "I promise only to keep you company."

She gave him a suspicious look and then finally dunked her toes into the hot water. It took her a while to ease in, but when she did, Nick pulled a stool over and washed her hair as she lazed in the water, feeling her muscles loosen the longer she soaked. It didn't escape her that Nick was still closing himself off from her. He couldn't continue doing so. Whatever they had between them wouldn't work if he couldn't he honest with her.

CHAPTER SEVEN

Amelia tapped her fingers along the edge of the velvet bench. Her hired carriage jostled along the uneven road, hitting quite a few bumps that required her to hold on to her seat intermittently.

She couldn't keep her mind from repeatedly wandering back to Nick and the fact that he hadn't roused her this morning so she could sneak back into her room undetected. It did not matter who had guessed they were sleeping in the same bed; what mattered was respecting her wishes that their relationship appear to be no more than professional.

After spending her morning feeling frustrated and ignored by Nick, she knew she needed to get out of the house for a while and focus on anything but matters of the heart. But here she was, thinking about him…again.

Amelia pulled the curtain aside to peek outside. The clouds rolling in promised quite a storm later this afternoon. She hoped to make it to Sera's before the skies opened up.

While Nick had invited Amelia to befriend his sister, she suspected he would not approve of what Amelia had in mind right now. Sera could provide information on Nick's past. Give Amelia the insight into what haunted him so thoroughly that he refused to open up to her. Desperation to understand why he was avoiding her drove her to do this, but it wasn't her sole reason for meeting Sera. She did miss having a friend in whom she could confide. And she had told Sera she wished to discuss the building of the new school.

After only twenty minutes of fretting, the carriage slowed and pulled up in front of a quaint two-story blond-brick townhouse. The front door was painted sage and had an oval section of stained glass in the upper half. Clay flowerpots lined the windows on either side of the door. The pots were empty, though, a testament to the coming winter season.

Amelia stepped out of the carriage, mustering her courage with a deep breath. The street on which Sera lived was quiet. Few people strolled by, but the appearance of those who did seemed to indicate this was a working-class neighborhood.

Before she could change her mind, Amelia tapped the knocker against the wood door. A rotund woman, an apron wrapped around her and a small mobcap covering her hair, opened the door.

"Good day, miss."

"I have an appointment with Miss Riley. She's expecting me at four, but I'm afraid the carriage ride was quicker than anticipated."

"Bella," rang Sera's voice from inside. "Escort Miss Grant into the parlor."

The housekeeper stood to the side so Amelia could enter. Amelia removed her gloves and shawl, which Bella took before leading her into a cozy room just off the front entrance.

Sera stood on seeing Amelia and approached to take her hand in greeting. Sera didn't release Amelia's hand until she had led her over to a seating arrangement of red floral-chintz chairs.

The room was small but perfectly suited for two women catching up on news and gossip. There were four chairs that invited a guest to sink into them, with an ottoman sitting squarely between then. The walls were papered in a gold leaf and ivory-colored design all the way up to the wood-beamed ceiling.

"I apologize for arriving so early, but I had no idea where your address was in relation to Mr. Riley's residence. I thought I would be in the carriage a good deal longer."

"Nonsense. Your timing is impeccable. Bella just brought in the tea service."

Amelia breathed a sigh of relief on the casualness with which Sera handled the change of plans.

Sera placed two teacups on the trolley and filled them. "What do you take, Miss Grant?"

"I drink it black."

Sera handed Amelia the teacup and saucer.

Amelia inhaled the black tea and felt suddenly recharged. "Mr. Riley suggested I help with the school, once the purchase of Caldon Manor is settled. As my note this morning indicated, I am willing to assist in any capacity." Amelia sat in the chair closest to the fireplace, absorbing the warmth, feeling a bit silly for blurting out her plans.

Sera looked at her for a full minute, assessing her in the same uncanny way her brother did. "For some reason, I think you might have come for more than that reason alone."

Amelia tucked a stray curl behind her ear as she met Sera's gaze. "It's been a long time since I could confide in anyone, Miss

Riley." She hadn't really had anyone she could trust, other than Nick and her father, for more years that she cared to admit. "Truthfully, I took a chance coming to London. I do not know anyone here, and have no extended family to speak of. I haven't had tea with another woman since I was a young girl."

"If I might say so, coming to London on your own is an incredibly brave thing to do. I insist on being your first friend and companion."

"Thank you, Miss Riley," Amelia said, ducking her head as the warm infusion of a flush bloomed in her cheeks.

"And I insist that you address me by my Christian name."

A smile lifted Amelia's lips. "And vice versa."

"Absolutely, Amelia."

"If you don't mind my curiosity, I wonder about the origins of your name, as it is uncommon in spelling."

"It's short for Seraphina. My mother called me her little angel for the longest time. I asked her why she would call me that when I caused trouble, and she told me that I was the brightest thing to come into her life and that my name was a sacred order of angels for only the most special people."

"Whenever you and your brother mention your mother, it's with the highest regard and with the most beautiful of stories."

"She was a wonderful woman and an adoring mother. Now, tell me what brought you to my house today."

"In all honesty, I couldn't stop thinking about the school and its importance to the children who will use it. I want to be more involved, but I worry that the difficulties of the deal with Lord Murray will make that impossible. Mr. Riley and Lord Murray seem to see things differently."

"My brother has always made calculated risks during his purchases. I don't think he has ever lost out on a deal about which he was so passionate. And if there is one thing that I can promise, it is that Nick is passionate about this deal."

"He is; I won't argue you that. However, he immensely dislikes Lord Murray."

Sera laughed uproariously. "Amelia, I hope you don't mind my pointing this out, but your experience seems insular, considering the length of time you've been employed by my brother. I should make it clear that he abhors more people than he admires."

Amelia frowned at this revelation. Everyone she'd met, aside from Lord Murray and Shauley, seemed to be a friend of Nick's.

"Now you're thinking of anyone else he hates," Sera suggested. "That's easy—anyone from whom he buys property. As I said, his risks and business interactions are deliberate."

"What is his purpose, then?"

"Retribution. For my mother, for the life we lived when my mother died."

"What does Lord Murray have to do with Mr. Riley's past?"

"Not Lord Murray." Sera took a sip of her tea, watching Amelia curiously. Amelia felt as if she had asked too many questions. "He wants to crush Shauley, and the best way to do that is to make him look bad, to strip away the reputation he has built for himself."

Amelia recalled the tense moment when Nick had sent her away upon discovering Shauley standing in his study. Now it all made sense. "I thought there was unusual tension between Mr. Shauley and Mr. Riley. You know Mr. Shauley, too, don't you?"

"I do. Our mothers were in the same profession. A laneway separated our homes."

"In St. Giles? Nick…" She'd been so caught up in the conversation that she'd forgotten to keep up the front of merely playing the role of secretary. Clearing her throat, she hoped Sera hadn't noted the slip of tongue. "Mr. Riley mentioned growing up in St. Giles."

A smile played on Sera's lips, and Amelia wondered if she was thinking of the familiar way Amelia had addressed Nick. She must mind her tongue.

"If we are to be friends, Amelia, I would at least like the truth from you."

Sera's question caught her off guard, and she sputtered out her tea. "I'm sorry." She set the teacup down, not sure what to say. Not sure what kind of question Sera planned on asking and worrying her charade was up.

"You and my brother? I don't think I would have ever guessed, except he hired you without my having ever heard of you—and your familiarity. You realize what this means, don't you?"

"Please…" Amelia didn't know how to change the direction of their conversation. And she doubted she could lie her way out of this. She'd been foolish to come here at all.

"Oh, you need say no more, Amelia. I will keep your secret."

"Your brother and I haven't exactly come to an understanding, aside from the fact that I am his secretary and he my employer. Please don't make any more of my comments than that. The nature of your brother's ventures means that I work closely with him and sometimes at all hours of the day. I see why you would make an assumption."

"So he hasn't been honest with you."

"I'm not sure what you mean." Amelia put her shoulders back, wishing more than anything she could slink away like a scolded dog. There was no one to blame but herself for allowing her secrets to be so easily read.

"I've scared you. I promised I wouldn't say anything. I won't even bring up the topic with Nick."

"I did wish to discuss the school."

"My brother will get that land from Lord Murray. I know him; I have seen the games of chance he plays, but mark my words—my brother always wins."

"And when he does?"

Sera frowned into her teacup. "I haven't seen the manor house yet. My brother assures me it will have to be practically rebuilt from the bottom up, but he knows a good architect and advised me that I can meet with him just as soon as the deal is firm."

"When do you suppose you will teach from Caldon Manor?"

"It won't be for another two years. But I need to do a lot in the meantime."

"Is it something with which I can help? I genuinely want to be a part of this project."

"I'd be very happy to have you assist me. I know Landon plans to take over the leases, along one of the main strips. I think six or seven properties come with the house; they are only halfway through their lease terms, which I believe is ninety-nine years. Landon is good for finding tenants who want to make something of where they live and work."

"What do Lord Burley's buildings have to do with the manor?"

A wicked grin curved Sera's lips. "An incentive for families with a lot of children to move."

Now Amelia understood. If they couldn't convince parents to let their children attend school outside London center, they needed to entice them to move and build a new life, if they were willing.

Nearly three hours had passed before they realized how much of the afternoon they had used in talking about plans for the school and for their future. Amelia hadn't realized that Sera planned to move into the house that was going to be built for her and situated near Caldon Manor. It was admirable that Nick was giving his sister her lifelong dream.

Amelia learned nothing else about Nick, which was just as well, as she hated to shine another light on just how close she and Nick truly were.

When it came time to part, Sera walked her out to her carriage. Rain had already washed through the city, and everything was damp in the early evening hour. Sera took her hand. "I haven't had this much fun spending time with another in ages. I would love to make this a Friday habit, if we could."

"You honor me. I don't know if I will be able to get away every Friday, but we will make arrangements to see each other soon."

Amelia climbed up into the carriage. Before she could shut the door, Sera stuck her head in. "I see why my brother has taken a liking to you. You are a wonderful person with a big heart. And I have to say that Nick has needed someone like you for far too long."

Sera shut the door before Amelia could respond, and she was left with her thoughts, turning over the revelations during her conversation with Sera.

CHAPTER EIGHT

Nick slipped into Amelia's bedroom well after midnight. The thud of his shoes, no matter how quiet he was trying to be, always woke her. She cracked open her eyes, tiredness still holding her immobile, as Nick pulled his shirt over his head and tossed it on the floor.

The familiar crisscross of scars on his back illuminated by the moon was a constant reminder that he held himself back. She promised herself it wouldn't be long before she ferreted out his secrets. *Tomorrow*, she told herself, and she wouldn't back down until she was satisfied with his answers.

As he came into bed, she rolled over and tucked her back along his chest. His hand wrapped around her stomach and dipped lower.

"Didn't mean to wake you," he whispered in her ear.

"That's all right." She tilted her bottom back, allowing the hard ridge of his penis to lodge between her thighs.

Nick's hand slid lower, grazing the coarse hair covering her mons and sinking his fingers between the folds of her sex.

"You're wet." He kissed her shoulder, lingering there.

She turned her head and pressed a kiss against his mouth. "I think I was dreaming about you."

"Now I wish I'd come to bed earlier." He rolled her onto her back as he came over her, wedging himself between her open legs.

Curling his arm under her thigh, he entered her in one swift motion, eliciting a moan from her. Even though she was trapped beneath his welcome weight, her back arched to position her pelvis in just the right spot that allowed him to sink deeper inside.

He worked into her with long, even strokes. One of her legs curled over his shoulder. His free hand molded to her breast as his fingers played with her nipple, tweaking it, making it longer and firmer.

With his mouth against hers, he caught her moans as they grew in volume. He practically stole the breath from her lungs as their tongues swirled together.

Amelia tangled her hands in his hair, wanting to keep him close. He made a grunting noise with each thrust of their bodies. She cried at the loss of his mouth when he went up on his knees to give himself better leverage. One of his hands wrapped around the frame of her bed; the other grasped tight to her hip as he pounded into her sheath with a vigor that revealed just how desperate he was to claim her.

She gave herself over to him willingly, openly.

"Looking at you like this, I can barely keep control," he said. "Look at the way your breasts bounce, begging me to take hold of them."

He lowered his head and swiftly sucked one nipple into his mouth. She felt dazed when he released her with a pop.

"Pinch your nipples for me."

This was something he hadn't asked her to do before, but she wanted to please him, and she didn't want him to stop the breakneck pace of their pelvises moving together. She rolled her fingers around the firm peak, pulling it enough that the already distended tip grew longer. The sensation was pleasurable, but she needed more.

Nick's hand eventually pushed hers away to cup her and suck the tip of her breast into his mouth. Her whole body convulsed, and her sheath clenched with every pull of his mouth. Her hand curled around his arm, feeling the strength and his muscles flexing with every lunge into her body.

Amelia threw her head back as Nick's mouth trailed higher, biting and licking at the frantic pulse beating at her neck. Her orgasm crept up in her body, slowly at first, her sheath clasping him.

Her body convulsed and trembled. And while her orgasm had started off as a trickle, it now flooded through her at the pace of an exploding geyser. She screamed out his name as sensation upon sensation lashed deliciously against every nerve ending in her body. Her body strained against his, unable to move; the only thing she felt was the pulsating clench of her sheath, trying to milk Nick.

"Fuck, you're so tight right now," Nick muttered against her mouth before pushing his tongue against hers and sealing their mouths in an all-consuming kiss, as he pounded into her until he finally let go. He jerked hard against her, filling her with his seed, as their hearts pounded heavily where their chests were crushed together.

While their breathing evened out, Nick remained buried inside her, still hard, still in need.

My insatiable lover.

He looked down at her, his hand tracing a line along her face. "What I'd give to keep you in bed until we're too wrung out to even walk."

She couldn't help but smile. "While that sounds perfect, we do have appointments we cannot miss tomorrow." She wiggled against him, feeling the flex of his member. "You're always like this, after. Is that normal?"

"Only when I'm with you. I swear, Amelia, I could fuck you all night and still have a raging cockstand at the end of it. I think about throwing you down on my desk all day long. I think about taking you in the library, pressed against the windows. There is no end to my need. It's constant. And when I slide into bed at night and find you naked…" He shuddered, his cock saying what he wasn't as it grew impossibly harder inside her.

"Then don't stop," she said, cradling her legs around his hips.

One of his hands pushed beneath her bottom and titled her pelvis in such a way that he only had to rotate his hips to move inside her.

The way her body responded to him…

Whenever he was inside her, it was hard to care about anything except for this. Amelia grasped his shoulders, keeping herself where she needed to be as he stroked in and out of her body again. Their renewed lovemaking rekindled her desire, igniting a blazing fire of need that struck right through her heart until she was lost in the sensation of their bodies, finding release once again.

"I might just keep you up all night like this," he said.

"I think that plan is the best one I've heard all day." She nibbled on his chin and kissed his throat, allowing the short hair on his beard to abrade her tongue and prick at her skin.

Their lovemaking was slow and indulgent. And as Nick promised, he kept her up all night long.

They didn't talk, other than Nick saying all manner of dirty things that made her blush even to think about them. They just felt, touched, tasted. Tomorrow, Amelia vowed, they would talk. And she wasn't letting him leave her room until they had a few of their issues sorted out—namely, what their future held if he wanted to continue in an illicit matter.

Nick untangled himself from Amelia, hating that he had to leave her at all. But his dreams were escalating, and he couldn't do anything to stop them from stealing his body and mind once he was asleep. Not sleeping seemed like the best solution, though even that was starting to catch up with him.

Every night, he waited until Amelia was asleep before he retreated either to the study or to his room. If she was hurt by his absence, she didn't make it known. In fact, she seemed more and more understanding about his difficulty in talking about his past. She hadn't pushed him for answers, but he knew it was only a matter of time before her questions got the better of her. Before those questions started to affect their…relationship.

He watched Amelia sleep a while longer before pulling on his trousers and slipping his shirt over his head. With one last look at her, he left her room and headed for his. After dressing in something more decent than the rumpled suit from yesterday, he went down to the study.

Huxley was at Nick's desk, writing a note.

"To what do I owe the pleasure of your late-night company?" Nick asked.

"Figured you'd be down," Huxley said morosely. "You've been wandering the house at all hours of the night the whole week."

"It's that obvious." It wasn't a question; he'd just hoped to keep his sleeping difficulties to himself—though it was hard to get anything past Huxley.

"Yes. But I'm sure I'm the only one who's noticed. Keep it up, and the rest of the staff will see something amiss. You look like hell, Nick. Almost as bad as when I pulled you out of the fighting pits you favored."

The last thing Nick wanted to do was take a trip down memory lane.

"Had I not fought for money, I wouldn't be as successful today as I am." Nick plopped himself down in a leather chair and leaned his head back with a yawn. Tiredness and restlessness were a terrible combination. Even if he did try to sleep, his thoughts alone would keep him awake. "I will have it back under control before anyone is the wiser," Nick said, though it felt like an empty promise, even to his own ears. His demons were his own to fight. "What has *you* up so late?"

"Penning a note to my man in Highgate."

Nick sat up. "Didn't take you long to set up someone there."

"Not at all," Huxley gave him a strange look. "I know what's got your thoughts all twisted. And it won't do you no good running from it. Highgate is going to be in your possession soon. You have to decide how you want to handle the business with the vicar."

"This isn't up for debate, Huxley. I will handle him in my own way when the land is transferred to my name." And when he figured out just how he would deal with the vile man.

Huxley and Sera were the only people who knew about Nick's past, but no one really knew the whole of it. Except Shauley.

Huxley bent his head again and started scribbling out more words. "Does she know?"

"I can only assume you mean Amelia."

"Who else? She's been besotted with you from the moment she came here. Didn't think she'd be the type you'd pursue, but she's a good enough lass."

"I didn't come down here to discuss her either."

"Oh, I know. Just thought I'd mention you aren't exactly being circumspect. Neither of you is."

"And what makes you think I would want to be?"

"I don't much care what you do, Nick. We go back too many years to not see a difference in each other. Especially a difference like *her*. But you should tell her your real intentions with the Lord Murray deal. A lass such as she doesn't come by often."

The Lord Murray deal. The vicar. His dealings with Shauley, who had been such a significant part of his past that *that* was the reason sleep eluded him of late. The reason he paced the house with a million thoughts traipsing through his head, unable to shut them out. Thank God the deal was going to be done in the morning.

Nick stood. He couldn't sit here for the rest of the night, discussing the darker days of his life. "I'm going to catch a few hours of sleep before we meet with the solicitors in the morning."

"Probably wise."

"We'll leave at ten."

"Your secretary should attend in my stead."

He was right. But Nick didn't want Amelia anywhere near Shauley, who was sure to be there. He was a slimy bastard. And he suspected the man to be entrenched with Highgate's darker secrets...

Amelia had proven that she could handle herself in any number of situations. She wasn't a delicate flower he needed to shield from the world. And as much as he wanted to do just that, he knew his overprotectiveness might cause her to wither.

"You're right. Amelia will attend with me in the morning." He stood to leave, as he couldn't very well stay in here when he craved solitude. "Good night, Huxley."

Waking up alone again this morning shouldn't have been a surprise to Amelia, but after her resolve to talk to Nick last night, it stung. She'd been patient with him. But that patience was wearing thin. He couldn't continue avoiding her.

She dressed and went down to the kitchens for breakfast. Not everyone had made it down for the day, but Huxley was present, reading the paper as the twins, Jenny and Jessie, set the table.

"Good morning," Amelia said on entering the dining hall.

Huxley looked up and gave her his usual grunt. He was a man of few words unless he wanted to make a point. While he played the role of Nick's man of affairs, anyone could tell they were friends that had a deep appreciation for each other. Amelia guessed that came from knowing someone for so long.

114 TIFFANY CLARE

"Morning," the twins said in unison.

"What's for breakfast today?" she asked of no one in particular. In the first household she'd worked in, she'd never had the camaraderie she had with these people. Misfits, every one of them, including her. Everyone one of them plucked from a bad situation and given a home with a decent job to support themselves.

Mrs. Coleman bustled into the room with a hot dish in her hands. She was like a mother hen to them all. "Kippers, ham, and hash."

"A hearty breakfast," Amelia mused aloud. "How's the weather, then?"

"Getting colder by the day," Mrs. Coleman responded.

Amelia went into the cooking area and said good morning to the cook. "What can I take into the dining hall, Joshua?"

The cook looked at her, his glass eye eerily unmoving. While the sight once had made Amelia uneasy, Joshua was the most jovial and one of the kindest people she'd ever met. "Good morning to you, too, child. Mrs. Coleman's got the breakfast platters taken care of. I'm just finishing up these tomatoes. But if you want to do something, prepare the tea set."

She gave him a smile and did as he asked. She'd never felt kinship with anyone who'd lived in her house when she was growing up, so being at the Riley residence was a relief in so many ways.

Carrying the tea service into the next room, she saw that everyone else was present. Lately, she'd been dining with Mr. Riley in the breakfast room on the second floor, but not these past few days. She missed his company, but was thankful for the friends she had made among the rest of the serving staff.

They remained informal in the dining hall, which helped lend to a welcoming atmosphere. Everyone milled about the table and piled food on their plates before taking a random seat. There was no order to station or position. Everyone was equal here.

Mrs. Coleman prepared Huxley's dish and set it down in front of him. "And what's the gossip today?" Mrs. Coleman asked Huxley.

"This and that. Nothing in particular that might affect this house," he responded.

"Well, that's not what I heard," Jenny said.

"What have you heard, then?" Olive, a young maid of only sixteen, piped in. "The butcher's son came by, he did; gave me a good earful."

"Rumors 'bout Mr. Riley killing a man," Jessie said.

Amelia's fork stopped halfway to her mouth. "Are you sure he meant Mr. Riley?"

"Yes, Miss Grant," said Huxley. "Been expecting it too. Heard it a week ago from my man about the docks and thought that was the end of it. He's got no reason to be killing off people that cross him, whether they're a relation to you or not."

"I never suspected him of being involved with my brother's death, Huxley. Why would Mr. Riley have reason or cause to harm anyone?" Amelia asked. Since the moment she'd arrived, Nick had been nothing but caring and generous, and despite what Sera had told her yesterday, she knew in her heart that Nick wouldn't harm someone to the point of causing death. "Surely none of you believes the rumors."

A chorus of no went around the table, and everyone focused on breakfast again. There were a few tidbits of gossip related to Nick's businesses, but Amelia paid none of it the attention she should. When the meal was finished, she helped clear the plates before she headed upstairs. Huxley wasn't far behind her.

"Is there something I might help you with?" Amelia asked.

"I have errands to run outside the house. Nick wants you present. You'll need to witness, as will Lord Murray's secretary."

"I'll make sure I'm ready before ten." She grabbed up the missives on the foyer table and then turned to call Huxley back. "Where is Mr. Riley this morning?"

"Went to meet Lord Burley at his club."

"Do you know how long it will be before Lord Burley takes over the leases in Highgate?"

Huxley eyed her suspiciously, probably wondering where she'd come by that information. She held her head high and waited for his response. Huxley would have to assume that Nick had told her about that particular arrangement.

"Best you ask Mr. Riley for further clarification. I wouldn't want to give you the wrong information. I've been out of the workings of this deal too long to recall all the details."

While Amelia had a great deal of respect for Huxley, he never let her in on much and often told her to discuss her questions directly with Nick. She supposed that was how he remained loyal to Nick, but it still irritated her to no end when a simple answer or revelation would suffice.

"I will ask him, thank you." Amelia nibbled on her lip as indecision stalled her. "Huxley?"

"Yes, Miss Grant." He folded his arms behind his back as he stood in front of her.

"The rumors about Mr. Riley… Why do you think anyone would believe him possible of killing my brother?"

"Mr. Riley was once a fighter. That was how he made his money, bloodying up other men's faces for high stakes. Anyone with a gambling mind and money in his pocket would remember that."

Her brother had been a gambling man, one without scruples. What would it take for another man to bet against someone being physically harmed? That thought sent revulsion though her whole body and made goose flesh form on her arms.

"Is someone trying to sabotage Mr. Riley's name?" she asked.

"Oh, you're something innocent at times, Miss Grant."

"I could do without the insults, Huxley," she snapped. "I can't learn anything if everyone keeps mum and if you try to coddle me. I'm Mr. Riley's secretary; these things are important to know if I'm to succeed in assisting him."

"They don't care about his name, though they'll enjoy trying to run that into the ground too. They want to frame him for your brother's death. Take him out of the race as a successful landowner and businessman. Let me ask you something, Miss Grant. Being a lady by birth and the daughter of an earl, would your father have considered Nick an equal?"

She mulled over her answer a moment. "My father was a good man, Huxley, and while I want to believe he would accept any man who worked hard as an equal, I can't say for certain if that would have been possible."

"So you see the dilemma with society. Nick is richer than most. He holds more property than they ever will and without the hindrance of being heavily taxed, as the gentry are when someone new successes a title. And while Nick's properties might not be in a desirable location, he holds all the cards on his businesses, and no one can interfere with the empire he's built over the last ten years."

"Except…"

"Men like us don't mingle as equals in any social circle, Miss Grant. We have to conquer and sometimes diminish those around us to get ahead."

"Doesn't every man anger someone on his path to success?"

"Not when you're born into the privilege of money *and* status. Those men are held to a different standard than the rest of the world."

Amelia frowned at this revelation. "I understand what you're saying, but that doesn't explain why anyone would think Mr. Riley capable of killing my brother."

"It's easier to point a finger at him, Miss Grant. That's how it is for men like us. We are a challenge to be crushed, to be diminished, so those with higher social standing can feel vindicated and worthy of their stations in life."

Huxley's words held merit, but that didn't make any of this situation right. Nor did it make it clear why they would want to blame her brother's death on Nick, when Jeremy was a wastrel of the worst sort. The bigger question was, who was trying to destroy Nick's credibility? Who wanted to see him lose everything? Lord Ashley, the man she was supposed to marry to clear her brother's debts? That didn't make sense and seemed unlikely, for she was sure that man was forever out of her life the moment her brother had died. So whom did that leave? How many enemies could Nick possibly have made?

"Thank you for your honesty, Huxley." Before she turned back toward the study, she said, "I plan on answering correspondence before heading out to see the solicitor. Will you be joining us?"

Huxley shook his head. "I'm off to the docks. I got a lead on the buyer who wharfinger's selling Mr. Riley's and Lord Burley's goods to."

A good portion of Nick's goods had gone missing en route to his docking company on the Thames. He brought in wool from Landon's sheep farm in the north of Scotland and consequently, those were the ledgers she had been reviewing for variances, as she had a good head for numbers.

She reached for Huxley's arm and squeezed it gently. "Be careful, Huxley. With everything that's happened over the past month, I want everyone to be vigilant."

"Don't you worry about me, miss. I've been through times more dangerous than this, if you catch what I'm saying." With that, he was off.

Amelia was surprised that Nick hadn't come back to the house before she'd finished her tasks, though he had sent a note advising her that a hired carriage would be waiting for her at half past nine. When she arrived at the solicitor's office—five minutes late, to her everlasting distress; she did hate to be even a minute late—Nick wasn't yet there. Lord Murray, however, was standing outside, his scowl in place.

"Lord Murray." She ducked her head as she approached. "I'm sorry if I kept you waiting. Mr. Riley was held back at his morning appointment. He sent me right away and said he would follow in a short while." She hated to lie, but to date, Lord Murray had been unimpressed with Nick, and she didn't want today to begin inauspiciously.

Mr. Shauley stood next to Lord Murray, watching her to the point that she felt uncomfortable, and she shifted under his scrutiny.

"I don't want to hear your excuses, Miss Grant. It shouldn't surprise me that we are ready to do our sign-offs, and he's nowhere in sight." Lord Murray's response was gruff, and while she was accustomed to his straightforwardness, she still cringed at his harsh words.

"I cannot apologize enough. The streets are overrun with carts and carriages alike. I could have walked here faster, had I the mind for some exercise."

Murray harrumphed but said nothing.

Trying to change the tone to something lighter, she decided to ask about the love of his life, a woman she'd had the pleasure of meeting a few weeks earlier over dinner. "How is Heddie? I did so enjoy our dinner conversation at the Langtry Hotel."

"Good enough. Happier when I unhand this land."

Apparently that left them with nothing else to discuss while they waited on Nick. She was beginning to understand why Nick disliked Lord Murray—he wasn't a great conversationalist, at least not without a never-ending supply of wine.

"Shall we?" Lord Murray said, opening the door to the solicitor's office, allowing her to enter the warmth first. She shivered a little when the heat of the room slapped her in the face but was thankful to get out of the wind. Lord Murray approached the man sitting behind the mahogany desk off to the side of the room.

"Ten o'clock with Mr. Cavendale." His voice boomed around the spacious room.

"Yes, of course, Lord Murray. Mr. Cavendale is just concluding his last appointment. May I offer you refreshment or a hot beverage?"

"We'll wait. Riley's running behind schedule as it is."

Amelia stripped off her gloves and warmed her hands near the burning coals; the red brick of the fireplace covered the whole of one wall. Lord Murray picked up a newspaper and flicked it open as he sat in one of the two dark leather chairs, ignoring both Amelia and Mr. Shauley.

"Mr. Shauley, how was your morning?" Amelia asked, not sure what they should discuss. An instinct told her not to trust this man, so the less personal their topics of conversations, the better—and that might have something to do with Sera's revelation in how far back Nick's acquaintance went with this man.

"How are you keeping as Nick's secretary?" he asked, making her feel more uncomfortable with his familiar use of Nick's name.

"Well." Amelia pulled her hands away from the coals and faced Shauley, determined not to let him frighten her.

"Only 'well'? Surely you can say more about the position than that. I haven't run into any women in this profession, so I am genuinely curious about you."

She couldn't help but feel as though Mr. Shauley was trying to obtain private details of her relationship with Nick. "It's been a great challenge, and Mr. Riley has been a kind employer. I'm still fairly new to the position and learning the role."

"Lady Luck must have been on your side to land such a lofty job after only just arriving in London."

Like the previous comment about her country accent, his familiarity with her sent a shiver of fear across her skin. "I hadn't realized Lord Murray knew of my situation."

Mr. Shauley inched closer, so close that Amelia felt her pulse kick up and goose flesh prickle her skin. "I assure you," he said, "his lordship remains blissfully ignorant."

To say Amelia felt uneasy was an understatement. "You are well informed of my circumstance, Mr. Shauley."

"I make it my business to know every *intimate* detail of anyone with whom Lord Murray has dealings."

While Amelia would have liked to take a step away from Shauley, she refused to be cowed by a man of his ilk. Head high, shoulders back, she faced him unflinchingly.

"I'm curious to know if you'll be staying in London, what with the estate sitting empty and alone in Berwick. All it needs is a male heir, and you are at the prime of your age." His eyes travelled the length of her body, lingering at her breasts and hips.

Amelia swallowed the disgust building low in her belly and forced herself to stand firm even though she wanted to shrink away.

"Did you know my brother?" She wasn't sure how she remained calm, asking that much, but now she understood why this man made her so uncomfortable. Not only did he seem to know an inordinate number of personal details, but she had to wonder how she knew of her brother's death. It wasn't information easily come by.

"Lord Berwick and I had a few dealings."

"Of what nature, Mr. Shauley?" She wished she could have bitten her tongue because she felt like she was borrowing trouble, trying to uncover what this man might know.

"Some mutual endeavors, Miss *Grant*."

If he knew she was using a false name, why not just end her charade? The door to the solicitor's office opened, and Nick made his entrance. A sigh of relief audibly passed Amelia's lips. He looked dashing and in command whenever he entered a room. At least he did to her.

Realizing she'd been staring at him, she made her way to his side. "Mr. Riley." She was a little breathless. Nick's gaze fell on hers and then caught on her lip where she nibbled it. She lowered her gaze. "We are waiting for Mr. Cavendale to conclude his previous appointment."

Nick addressed the men. "Lord Murray. Shauley." Amelia didn't miss the undercurrent of distaste as Nick said the secretary's name. When they finished their affairs here, she planned to ask him why he disliked Shauley as much as he did.

"Riley," Lord Murray said. "Only you would show up late to an important appointment."

"Couldn't be helped. Don't worry; we'll wash our hands of each other soon enough." Strangely, Nick was watching Shauley as he spoke.

They were ushered into the solicitor's office before more sentiments could be exchanged. Amelia also took note that the underlying animosity between Nick and Mr. Shauley didn't end in the waiting room. Their time with the solicitor went by quickly, and before she knew it, they were all standing in the street having concluded their business. Nick was studying her, as though he knew she had a hundred things she wanted to discuss with him, but not while they were in the company of others.

Shauley came within a foot of her as they walked to the edge of the pavement. She bumped into Nick as she tried to put distance between her and Shauley. When she caught Nick's eye, there must have been an expression on her face that indicated her feelings, for Nick said, "Wait here while I talk to Shauley a moment."

She bristled. "I should hear anything you have to say to him." Even though she wanted to be as far from Shauley as possible.

"I promise to tell you every word exchanged between us. For now, stay here by the carriage."

Amelia gave one succinct nod, not happy with being made to stand aside, no matter the situation, no matter the discussion Nick wanted to have with that man.

It took one look on Amelia's face to tell Nick everything he needed to know about what transpired while she'd been stranded with Lord Murray and Shauley.

Fear.

Nick cursed the hired carriage again that had caused his tardiness, when he'd had every intention of arriving prior to Amelia.

"Shauley," he called. As his nemesis turned toward him, Nick took a moment to address Murray. "Your lordship, do you mind if I have a word with Shauley?"

Lord Murray waved him off, indifferent, shouting his directions to the driver as he shut the carriage door.

"I don't have time for you right now," Shauley said. "You've just delayed my next appointment, Riley."

"Our conversation will be quick." Nick hovered so close to Shauley that the man took a step back. "Now that this deal is done with Lord Murray, I don't expect to see you again. And that means you will stay away from anyone who works in my household as well."

"Even your precious Miss Grant…or shall I address her as Lady Amelia Somerset?"

If Nick had hackles, they would have risen just then. And while he raged on the inside, he knew he needed to keep his expression free of reaction so as not to give away his feelings. "Miss Grant, as with anyone living in my house, will be offered the same protection from any potential threats."

"You always did have a sweet spot for the fairer sex."

"And you've always scared them away. I mean it, Shauley; any threat you pose against my household will be acted upon swiftly and without mercy."

Shauley chuckled low. "Should I be worried for my life? I find it odd that people end up floating in the Thames after a confrontation with you."

Nick considered this silently. Inspector Laurie must have used Shauley as a source for information. How else would he know of Lord Berwick and of Miss Grant's true identity? So how did Shauley tie into Lord Berwick's death? Because there was no question in Nick's mind that the two men were somehow tied together.

"Perhaps you should be worried that the last person who got on my bad side ended up dead."

Shauley's eyes lit up. "I have measures in place to deal with the likes of you, Riley. Men of your ilk have fallen down the social rabbit hole with little provocation."

These were all empty threats, meant to incite Nick to act rashly—and he knew it. "You have nothing on me, Shauley."

Nick walked back to Amelia's side and held out his arm for her. He didn't bother turning back to see Shauley's expression at being dismissed so abruptly. After his plans this afternoon concluded, he needed to have a conversation with Huxley. For now, he would reveal a little something about Shauley to Amelia, as she had to understand the danger that man represented.

Chapter Nine

"Tell me what you needed to discuss with Shauley," Amelia said to Nick as soon as they were seated in the carriage.

Nick looked at her a long moment before sighing and placing his top hat on the bench beside him.

"His given name is Michael. We grew up together in St. Giles."

"I know you were once neighbors. I visited your sister a few days ago, and we discussed Shauley to some extent."

A smile tilted up Nick's lips. "I shouldn't have expected anything less. We were once the best of friends. But some men grow stronger from mistreatment, while others change into something twisted and different…I could almost go so far as to call it sinister."

Amelia reached for his hand and clasped it. "We both know the monster my brother was, Nick. I know not all men are cut from the same cloth, no matter their upbringing."

"Michael is a year my junior. His mother was also a prostitute, though she didn't have a place like my mum set up. Michael and I were good friends at one point. We did everything together. My mother saw the attachment we'd formed, so she paid for him to attend school with me."

"What caused you to stop being friends?"

"The school."

"I don't understand."

"There were a handful of teachers there who liked young men." Nick pulled her glove off and massaged the wrist he held captured between his hands. "More specifically, they liked boys."

She still didn't comprehend.

"I wish I could pretend it was nothing but my adolescent imagination, that it was all a dream. I wish I didn't have to reveal any of this to you, but it's important you understand what Shauley is capable of, and why he's capable of it. But I can't lie about this. Not after everything you've been through with your brother. Not when I am starting to think Shauley had a hand in your brother's death…"

"What did he say to you, Nick?"

"Not enough to have a confession but enough to concern me of his involvement."

She'd thought as much—or had been close to that very conclusion. But for the life of her, she couldn't understand why Shauley would cause her brother any harm when she was sure neither knew the other.

"Tell me about the school, Nick."

"As there's no real way to word this delicately, I'm just going to have to spit it out. The teachers liked to rape young boys. The prettier the better. Willing, not willing. They didn't care. They ran a school to fulfill their own base desires." Nick's gaze didn't leave hers as he revealed this.

Amelia's hand flew up to her mouth. There was no covering the shocked sound that escaped her. Tears flooded her eyes. She didn't know what to say and stuttered out a few sounds before saying, "Did they…?"

Oh, God, she couldn't even put words to her questions. They'd hurt Nick; she knew it.

"I was kicked out after four months for stabbing the vicar who…" Even Nick couldn't utter that truth.

She didn't want him to and cleared her throat before redirecting their focus, "And Michael?"

"I visited his mother as she lay on her deathbed. She told me that it was a good thing Michael was able to learn the ins and outs of the business before she was gone."

"She *knew*?" Amelia couldn't temper the shock that flooded that question.

"I always assumed that Michael had told her. He stayed at the school after I left. Received a *scholarship*. We never talked again."

Amelia was sure she'd vomit. She asked Nick to have the carriage pulled over so she could step outside for fresh air. While the day had been cold and she'd found herself chilled to the bone, now she felt only heat and anger boiling in her blood and throughout her body. She took in great gulps of air. Nick stood close by as she paced the laneway they'd pulled into.

Sweat dotted her eyebrow and she swiped it away, agitated by this revelation and situation. As she saw it, there were two problems: the first was what Nick had revealed about his past. And that made her stomach twist again, so she paced faster, trying to ignore her discomfort.

The second: "You think Shauley was responsible for Jeremy's death. Why would he resort to murdering my brother when there are other people more important to you?" Nick's sister, for instance. Or Huxley, or even his old lover, Victoria. "He can't possibly know what we mean to each other."

"Are you so certain, considering the argument I had with your brother? Anyone who heard the threats I uttered toward your brother would know how much you mean to me."

Amelia stopped in front of Nick and studied him. Nick clasped his hands on either of her arms, keeping her from pacing. She'd had a bad feeling about her old employer, who nearly had raped her before she escaped. She'd felt uncomfortable around Shauley too. How poorly she judged men's characters—no, she gave them too much benefit over her doubt. Never again would she give any leeway to what she initially felt.

"Your brother nearly taking you was the end to my good grace, Amelia. I sent someone to watch Jeremy's comings and goings so he wouldn't get a second chance."

"I remember you telling me that." Amelia stepped closer to Nick. Suddenly, she needed to feel his warmth and the comfort of his embrace, and she didn't care that anyone could happen by. He opened his arms to her, inviting her closer.

"The kid I had following your brother came to me today and described a man resembling Shauley as one of your brother's constant companions. He hadn't thought much of it until the kid came by the house and saw Shauley leaving with Lord Murray."

"Why didn't he say something sooner?"

"Didn't think of it when he got caught up in his other tasks. It's not his fault, Amelia. He is but twelve."

Amelia would not fault a child. She pressed her forehead against Nick's chest and inhaled his amber-scented cologne. She could barely comprehend how any of this had happened or why it was happening.

"My brother is a continual nightmare, haunting me from his grave."

"I will ensure Shauley is crushed."

Tilting her head back to look at him, she saw that Nick's expression was resolute and as hard as stone. "I don't doubt you," she said. "But you have to be careful. If he killed my brother, he could harm you too. That's not a risk I'm willing to take, much as you aren't willing to risk my safety."

Nick brushed his thumb across her cheek until his hand stretched behind her nape. "I will always come back to you."

She hoped so, because she couldn't bear the thought of losing Nick.

They embraced a while longer before returning to the carriage. Amelia's thoughts rolled over in her mind. She felt great unease. And distress. How could she not remain in a constant state of uncertainty?

The hired carriage turned toward the shopping strip instead of the townhouse. "Where are we headed?" Amelia asked.

"I made arrangements earlier to spend the afternoon out of the house. I would cancel, except Landon and his wife are meeting us there."

"A day trip sounds like a wonderful plan. It might take our minds off everything else for a short while."

Nick didn't say much else on their ride; he just sat across from her in silent contemplation. Was he concerned he'd revealed too much about his past? She put her own worries from her mind, as she intended to enjoy her afternoon in Nick's company.

Amelia watched the scenery passing through the window as they wound their way through London's hectic midday streets. Finally, the carriage stopped in front of a row of unassuming two-story red brick buildings. There were only a few passers-by in the street; otherwise, it was an unusually quiet spot of London. Inside one of the storefronts, there were people sitting at tables that faced the overlarge windows.

Nick stepped out of the carriage and helped her down.

"It looks absolutely full for being the only shop with visible patrons," she commented.

"It's known for its Turkish coffee. Patrons are willing to go out of their way to come here for that delicacy."

Amelia screwed up her nose. She'd had one taste of coffee and didn't wish to repeat the experience. Nick chuckled at her expression.

"There are other delights aside from the coffee."

She exhaled in a rush. "Well, that's a relief."

"I will get you to like it yet."

"Unlikely. But if you insist on being disappointed by my dislike, by all means"—she motioned her hand in the direction of the entrance—"I will follow your lead."

The atmosphere when they entered was loud and far busier than she could have guessed possible when looking in from the outside. It was also unbearably hot.

Nick led them to a table near the window, tucked in a back corner of the shop. There was a sign that read *reserved*, holding the table empty.

Amelia looked at Nick. "You knew we were coming here all along and didn't think to tell me before you left this morning?"

His only response was a charming grin.

Looking around, she saw men wearing suits, some fine and elegant, some of the lower working class, as well as workmen with shirtsleeves carelessly rolled up their forearms as they sat at tables with their assorted hot beverages and sweets as they boisterously went about their conversation. No one, though, was as finely frocked as Nick. Some of the women wore hats with so many feathers, satin, and lace that they might be about to stroll through Hyde Park to attract a rich suitor. Other women wore the most beautiful walking dresses, the type Amelia expected to see only in the finest of shops around London and far nicer than the drab brown day dress she'd picked to attend the meeting at the solicitor's office.

She felt overwhelmed and less worthy of the man on her arm as she looked from one woman to the next, noticing their focus locked on Nick. The sudden insecurity caught her off guard. She didn't normally think like this, but she felt out of her element.

Nick checked the time on his watch. "We have more time than I thought we would have to ourselves."

"You make that sound as if it's a bad thing."

Nick's hand brushed over her arm as he removed her shawl and folded it over the back of a chair. When he pulled out a seat for her, he stood close enough that she felt the heat of his breath on her cheek, stirring wisps of her hair that curled over her temple. She wanted him to put his arms around her. She craved his touch outside their stolen evenings.

"You're very distracting," he said.

With that comment, he vanquished every one of her insecurities. Nick was so focused on her that he probably hadn't even noticed the other women in the coffee shop. She took her seat without responding, her hands twisting in her lap, her nerves suddenly on edge for an entirely different reason.

She was saved from having to say anything when a robust man approached their table carrying a silver tray with coffee cups and plates. She took the man to be a Turk, since he wore a fez atop his head—something, she was reminded, her brother used to wear in his smoking room. The man's beard rivaled Nick's in length and thickness. The hair on his upper lip was curled and moved as he spoke.

"Mr. Riley. I'll have a coffee service sent over," he said with an accented voice that held a smooth lilt that was almost musical in quality.

"Thank you for saving the table. I know how busy you are at this time of the day."

"It's no trouble for you, Mr. Riley. Now, can I get you something to eat while you wait for your companions?"

"Tea for my lady friend, Adnan. Though I promise to make her try the coffee."

Adnan put his hands together and bowed his head as he left them.

"You must come here often," she observed.

"I do. The patron base is mostly working class. Not too many highbrows come here, which isn't surprising, since it's surrounded by slums."

"I thought women weren't allowed in coffeehouses."

"A fine observation. Adnan is happily ruled by his wife's decisions. She once told me that if they cut off half of London by not allowing women here, they'd never have found success of this magnitude."

"I already adore her and all, without having met her."

Adnan came back carrying a two-tiered copper teapot. It was the oddest thing Amelia had ever seen. Setting it down in front of them, he addressed Nick. "My wife prepared some *lukom* for your lady friend."

A small porcelain dish was placed between them, with small cubes of jelly. She wasn't sure what *lukom* was, but it was dusted with a sugary powder. There were orange and yellow pieces, all similar in size.

"That is very generous, Adnan. She will love them. Thank your wife for her hospitality."

Amelia watched their exchange with interest. Nick seemed so at ease in this place. Normally, he held himself aloof, but just as he'd been in his sister's schoolyard, here he was more relaxed.

"For you, my friend, my wife set aside some *zerde* before it was gone. She garnishes it as we speak."

"Your wife is too kind to lavish me with special treatment."

"We can never be kind enough, Mr. Riley. Now, the tea must sit. I will be back to pour it for your friend." The proprietor turned to Amelia and gave her a smile and wink. "If you like sweets, I will bring you beet sugar too."

She only smiled since she wasn't sure what that was. He was gone again, and Nick was looking at her.

"Beet sugar? Dare I ask?"

"Adnan travels home three times a year and ships back large quantities of traditional items. Mostly teas, spices, and coffee beans. The sugar tastes the same, it's just processed differently."

"What about the squares of jelly?" She pointed at the plate with the dozen small cubes.

"You might know it as Turkish delight." He lifted one of the cubes and held it out to her.

"I do not know what that is. I'm afraid I lived too far north for any cultural variety in cuisine."

"Then you will be pleasantly surprised. Try it."

Amelia's eyes darted around the coffeehouse. "We'll be seen."

"And we won't be judged here. Try it, Amelia, because if you lick your lips one more time, I'm going to want to put my mouth on yours instead of feeding you this tiny morsel of heaven."

She tried to grab it from his hand, but he only tsked and pulled it away before she could snatch it up.

"That's not playing by the rules," he admonished.

"Those are your rules, Nick."

"In case you've forgotten"—he edged closer, his elbows on the table, his knees trapping hers under the small round table—"I like making all the rules."

She felt a blush warm her cheeks. "How could I forget?"

"Now, come here and take it."

She felt absolutely silly and awkward, but she leaned forward anyway because she wanted this flirting to be over. Well, not entirely—she just wished they had a private room at the very least. Nick didn't let it go when her lips touched the jelly; his thumb and finger brushed against her tongue before he slipped them out of her mouth, only to put them in his and suck the sugar clean off his fingers.

Amelia sat back in her chair, feeling suddenly breathless as she bit into the jelly cube. It had a distinct lemon flavor but under that was a flavor noticeably fragrant and floral.

"What's in it?" She picked up one of the orange ones and brought it to her nose. "It smells like roses." She bit into it, tasting a hint of orange zest and that floral scent again.

"Rosewater," Nick said. "Adnan has a lemonade he serves in the summer that has rosewater in it as well."

"Rosewater? Who would think to put that in food?"

"You don't like it?"

She popped another in her mouth, wishing she could steal the plate and eat all the tiny cubes. "I think I'm in love with it."

Nick smiled and leaned forward to brush his thumb over her lip. "You have a little powder here." There was a hunger for more than a mere touch in his eyes.

Her tongue darted out; she made sure there wasn't more sugar on her lips, fearing what she might do if he touched her so provocatively again. Her breath hitched, but before she could contemplate her reaction, Adnan was back, breaking the tension.

He set down a dish in front of Nick of yellow pudding with raisins and chopped nuts sprinkled on it. Holding a towel placed beneath the spout of the small copper pot, he poured Nick's coffee. It was darker than Amelia remembered and foamed at the top. Nick placed a cube of sugar in his cup and thanked Adnan.

The proprietor then placed a strangely shaped glass that looked like the rim had been dipped in gold. Its shape was thin through the middle and rounded on the top and bottom, like a corseted woman. Adnan separated the stacked teapots, pouring out the top one in the glass first. The color was nearly as dark as Nick's coffee.

"We steep the leaves in a small amount of boiled water first. You can dilute to your preference," he said. "We do not serve our tea with milk, like the English prefer, so you must tell me how strong you like it."

"I usually only take lemon and on occasion, sugar."

"Perfect," he lifted the other pot and poured out just as much of the clear boiled water as he had the dark concoction. The colors swirled together until they were a deep red instead of brown.

She inhaled some of the steam that came off the glass. "It smells like black tea."

"It is. Just brewed stronger." Setting the pots together, he bowed again. "I will come again when Lord Burley arrives."

"Thank you, Adnan. And thank your wife for the treats," Nick said.

"It is our pleasure."

Nick motioned toward her glass. "You're meant to drink it while it's hot enough to burn."

Amelia picked it up and tried the tea. It was bitter but still pleasant. She dropped a sugar cube in and stirred it with the small spoon Adnan had left for her.

Clearing her throat, she said, "There are some issues that stand between us that I would like to address."

"Now is not the time, Amelia," Nick said shortly.

"I'm beginning to think there will never be a time for that conversation." She sighed and ate another piece of Turkish delight. If the rest of their party didn't join them soon, she feared she'd eat the whole plate.

Nick took a sip of his coffee. Satisfied, he set it down and scooped up a spoonful of the pudding that sat between them.

"If you won't talk about why you're avoiding me, can you tell me why Lord Burley wasn't part of the deal with Lord Murray, if you are giving him the leases in Highgate?"

"He and Lord Murray go back some years. There was a feud between their fathers. On principle alone, Lord Murray would never have sold the land to Landon."

"But he knows you two are friends, that you do business together."

"Yes, so Shauley was quick to point out on more occasions than I care to recall."

Nick scooped up another spoonful of the pudding and held it out to her. She didn't think twice about taking it. When she realized what she'd done, she looked around her, and while the coffeehouse was brimming and bloated at the seams with business, no one seemed to pay them any mind.

"You shouldn't do that," she whispered.

"Why not?" He pushed his cup across the table. The strong smell of the coffee hit her nose pungently and had her pulling away. "Try it. It's different from the coffee you had at the hotel with me."

"Different how? It smells worse."

Nick laughed but still gave her a firm look. "Someone once told me you should try the things you dislike at least a dozen times before giving up altogether."

"I daresay, they could probably stomach a great deal more than I."

"Perhaps, but you'll never know if you don't sample it."

She nibbled at her lip, looking at the frothy cup of black coffee in front of her. He'd push if she refused. So she picked up the cup and took a small, tentative sip. Her mouth puckered as she swallowed it. "It's very bitter." She set the cup down and pushed it toward him again.

"I see you don't find it nearly as distasteful as you did the last time you tried coffee."

"Oh, I certainly do. I just don't want your friend Adnan to notice my dislike. He's been so generous since we arrived that I would hate to insult him or his wife."

Nick turned the cup where her lips had left a mark and lifted it to his lips. "But now, I can think of what your lips taste like when I'm enjoying my coffee."

His lips touched the cup where hers had just been. She couldn't understand why that felt…erotic, but it made her feel hotter than she currently was and as if Nick was feasting on her mouth instead of sipping his coffee.

"You have to stop doing this to me." Her voice was needy to her own ears. She pinched her lips shut, hating that he could so easily affect her this way.

He leaned forward, elbows on the table again, their faces but a handspan apart. His hand reached under the table and grasped her thigh. Her breath was frozen in her lungs as she stared back at him, feeling a familiar ache at the apex of her thighs.

How could she want him here and now? He'd turned her into a hedonist with only a few words. She was suddenly desperate for his kiss. Thank God the diameter of the table was wide enough that she couldn't accomplish that feat in their current position.

"Tell me something, Amelia. If I manage to get my hand under your skirts and between your legs, just how wet will I find you?"

"You're liable to make me embarrass myself. You need to refrain from such comments," she said, even though that was the last thing she wanted. God help her, she was addicted to this man.

"What if I should slide over to the next seat? My body would cover you enough that no one would guess where my hand is buried."

Amelia swallowed hard, picked up her tea, and took a larger swill than she should have with the temperature still burning. It did bring her back to her senses but did not diminish the ache she had for the things Nick promised.

"When is Lord Burley supposed to arrive?"

Nick's hand flexed over her knee, as though he were fighting whether to lift her skirts or let her be. She was torn on what she wanted too.

"Nick. Didn't think you'd arrive before us," came a masculine voice.

Amelia let out a shaky breath, and as she stood from the table, her chair knocked into the wall behind her. They were squished into a tiny table space, and she couldn't easily maneuver the seating arrangement. Lord Burley and his wife had either interrupted the most erotic tea break she'd ever had or perhaps saved her from committing a sin in public.

"Don't bother yourself, Miss Grant. My wife will sit next to you, if you don't mind."

"Not at all, Lord Burley," she said, ducking her head in greeting.

Lady Burley returned the gesture to those around the table. Amelia had met these friends of Nick's on one occasion, but they'd sat across from each other and hadn't had an opportunity to get to know each other through their last dinner.

"I've heard great things about you, Miss Grant." Lady Burley smoothed her hand over her skirts as she took the seat next to Amelia.

"You flatter me. But I hardly accomplish all that Huxley did, only a fraction of the tasks for which he no longer has time, as he is pulled away from the house constantly for business matters."

"Huxley is a hard man to replace, but from what I hear from my husband, you fill the role well. I'm fascinated by women who take on the workforce like a man would. It's admirable, and had I not married, I'd be tempted to do the very same."

"It was driven from necessity, not a desire to prove women are just as good as any man." Amelia did not explain that she'd gone the usual route and started as a governess, far more typical to women of gentle breeding.

"Let me be the judge. We are apt to spend a great deal of time together over the next few years. I'll be initiating raising funds for the school."

This announcement took Amelia by surprise. "I have spoken at length with Miss Riley and hadn't realized that we would be raising funds for the school."

"I only decided to commit to that recently. Why should all the money come out of my husband's and Mr. Riley's pocketbooks when there are plenty of purses that can be opened in society for such a charitable and community-building endeavor."

"You don't think the residents of Highgate will put up a front against the school?"

"The stores along the main center of the area have been mismanaged for years. Anything to help the local economy will be welcomed with open arms, once my husband turns over the leases on the less-than-desirable tenants."

"You're going to toss everyone out of their homes," Amelia said with alarm.

"Not at all, Miss Grant," interjected Lord Burley. "We are giving them an opportunity to make it a better place to live for everyone. The funds we raise will be used to build residences in the local township for the families of the children accepted into the school. With the integration of more people, more services will be required."

"Was this always your plan?" Amelia asked Nick.

He nodded and sipped his coffee. To think so far in advance of what you could do with a small lot of land with a dilapidated manor house…she admired Nick more and more throughout their conversation.

Adnan served more rounds of tea, coffee, and sweets through the afternoon. And Amelia's imagination was given no opportunity to stray, once she found out that Lady Burley was from Scotland and that they had visited a few of the same places. She also learned they needed to schedule a stay in Highgate this coming week.

Amelia allowed herself to be swept up into the extended friendship she had with Lord and Lady Burley and stuffed away all thoughts of her brother and Shauley for the remainder of the afternoon. Though she knew the escape from reality would be short-lived, she was thankful for a little bit of normalcy. All too soon their meeting came to an end, and they were off in their carriage toward home.

"I'll be dropping you off at the townhouse," Nick advised. "I have to meet Hart at his hotel and then make a few stops to inquire about the inspector who handled your brother's murder."

Just like that, their lovely afternoon was forgotten, and the reality of the past few weeks crashed through her good mood.

"When do you expect to be home?" Really, she wanted to know if she should wait up for Nick.

"Rather late. I'll come to your room when I get in." His focus wasn't on her as he said this; he was looking out the carriage window, staring at the passing scenery.

"Nick?"

When he looked at her, a whoosh of air emitted from her lungs. There was anger mixed with something indefinable as he stared back at her in quiet contemplation.

"What are you going to do to Shauley?"

"Nothing, until I have proof."

"Do you think he'll hurt anyone else?"

"I suspect he knows there is only one way to hurt me, and that's through you."

She did not want to believe that Shauley was capable of anything so sinister. That someone would want to hurt Nick so much that they were willing to commit murder. She wanted to believe that Nick was taking everything out of context, but the truth of the matter was...She trusted Nick's opinion, his belief. And that frightened her.

"Then why hasn't he already tried to hurt me?"

"Because he's playing a game, Amelia."

"Help me understand why."

The carriage slowed, and before he could answer her, he opened the door and helped her down.

"This conversation is far from over," she said, perturbed that he was shutting her out of his thoughts once again.

"I intend to find out a few of the answers myself, Amelia. For now, stay home, and do not leave for any reason."

CHAPTER TEN

Pacing the floor in Hart's office, Nick had one thing on his mind. And that was pummeling Shauley into the same grave that had been dug for Berwick. He felt helpless, and that was not an easy feeling for him.

He hadn't known where to start after leaving Amelia at the townhouse. He just knew he needed to do something, anything, that would have Shauley found out for the monster he truly was.

Hart entered, with a flurry of activity going on behind him in the main staff quarters. He was the same height as Nick, perhaps an inch taller. His frame was thinner but just as strong, and he could fight as lethally as Nick ever had in the ring. Hart looked like the perfect playboy, blond-haired, blue-eyed. Women generally fawned over him. Amelia, Nick remembered, hadn't given Hart a second look.

"I didn't think you'd be this busy," Nick said apologetically.

Hart walked over to the sideboard and poured two glasses of whiskey.

"We have the jewel gallery showing here next month and have to test our security measures after the art fiasco last year. Lewis at the front said it seemed urgent, so I left them to it."

After handing Nick a glass, Hart waved toward the chair arrangement in his office.

"Do you remember Shauley?" Nick asked.

"You mean the pompous bastard always following Lord Murray around like a lapdog?" Hart gave him a wry smile and swirled the contents of his glass around and around.

Nick had known Hart since his fighting days, not as a youth, so his friend would know nothing of Nick's past with Shauley. "The very one."

"Why do I have the feeling you're about to ask for a favor?"

"You have ears in high places."

"And so do you, my friend."

"Not in this case. I need a worm in Lord Murray's ear. Something to cause his trust in Shauley to cease." If it would have helped to go to Lord Murray himself, Nick would have done it, but they didn't see eye-to-eye.

"And what rumor do you want spread?"

So Nick told his friend a secret he'd long kept to himself. One that would not only threaten Shauley's job with Lord Murray but also have him arrested without delay. It was a distraction to keep Shauley off Nick's back as he tried to find evidence to tie the bastard to Berwick's murder.

"You play a hard game, Riley. Does this have anything to do with a certain secretary who's caught your eye?"

Nick downed his whiskey and pointed at Hart. "I'll ask you not to repeat that anywhere."

His friend wore a grin like a Cheshire cat. "Just stating the obvious."

After visiting a few more people who could help root out a few of Shauley's secrets, Nick arrived home after midnight.

He slipped into Amelia's room and climbed into bed behind her. Wrapping his arms around her and holding her close, he fell into the first deep sleep he'd had in weeks. But that sleep was short-lived, and he woke with a start, covered in sweat, sometime around two in the morning.

Sitting on the edge of the bed, he gathered his wits. He shouldn't have come to Amelia when his dreams were always just out of reach from his control. He wondered if they would ever subside. They were always the same. He was back in the school, waking up to the vicar over him.

He wasted no time in dressing, hating to leave Amelia's side at all, but he couldn't sleep now.

The soft click of her door woke her. When she turned over in her bed, it was to see that the covers were mussed where Nick had slept, but he was gone. Had his leaving awakened her? She threw off her blankets with a frustrated huff. This time, she would not be deterred from seeking the path toward which she and Nick had been heading. She was determined to follow him, no matter where he went to escape *them*. Because his sneaking away in the middle of the night needed to stop.

Bleary-eyed and tired, she crawled out of bed and cinched a corset around her waist before pulling on yesterday's dress. They couldn't ignore the problem that made it nearly impossible to move into another phase of their relationship—or whatever it was that they had. She was determined to have an answer to that today too. They'd come leaps and bounds yesterday, but today she would not allow him to close himself off again.

After finding Nick's bedchamber empty, she headed downstairs, only to find him in his study, pacing the floor. His hair was disheveled, his shirt only tucked in at the front. Seeing him thus caused a lot of the frustration building in her to vanish.

She shut the door and flicked over the lock behind her on entering the room. Nick stopped pacing immediately and scrubbed a hand over his face, scratching his beard as his eyes focused on her in the darkness. It broke her heart, seeing him so exhausted from too many sleepless nights.

"I didn't mean to wake you." He sounded genuinely concerned to have disturbed her rest, and that ebbed the rest of the anger that had built while she'd searched the house for him.

"And I didn't intend to let you sneak out of my room yet again."

He rubbed his face again. "I couldn't sleep."

"I could tell. As I have been able to tell every night for weeks, Nick. Please tell me what is going on."

He didn't say anything. Didn't confirm or deny her observation. With a sigh she thought she wasn't meant to hear, he went over to the sideboard and poured two decent-sized glasses of whiskey. He held one out for her to take and motioned toward the library. She didn't normally imbibe in liquor like this but took the glass anyway.

"Sit with me for a while," he said.

He was oddly unsure of himself. Not the Nick she'd grown to know and love since moving into this house. The

Nick who ruled over everything and everyone in his life like each layer was a finely oiled piece of machinery over which he had complete control.

Tumbler in hand, she preceded him into the adjoining room. She didn't sip the liquid fire, afraid it would cloud her thoughts when they needed to have a serious conversation. If she beat around the bush with this, it would give him reason to hide behind the carefully constructed wall he kept erected between her and his emotions.

If she couldn't find a door through that wall, she knew she had to find a way to climb over everything he was avoiding.

Before either of them could sit, she blurted out, "I think you've been avoiding me. Avoiding having another dream while in bed with me. And we need to discuss why." When she looked up, he appeared unperturbed by her questions, so she continued. "Help me understand what it is you're afraid of."

"What confessions do you think to garner from me? I've often been a night wanderer. This is nothing new, and it's unlikely to stop. Telling you what haunts my dreams will not end them."

"Then help me understand why you wander more than you have before. Haven't you noticed the strain it's causing between us? It makes me wonder if you regret what's happened between us. If I'm honest with myself, Nick, I don't think I can go back to being mere acquaintances. But if that's what you want…you have to tell me. My heart's too involved to have you slowly shrink away from me. I don't even know what you want from me. Am I your mistress? Am I your secretary? Do I even mean more to you than that? Because I feel that if I did mean more than that, you would open up to me."

Nick threw his tumbler at the fireplace so fast that a strangled sound caught in her throat at his sudden show of violence. The glass smashed into a thousand shards of glittering crystal that smeared across the brick.

"Nick," she whispered in her shock, fighting tears back.

Nick turned toward her, stalking her with all the grace of a lion eyeing a gazelle. She took a deep, steadying breath and braced herself. The only thing she was certain of was that he wouldn't hurt her.

He pointed at the fireplace. "That is what you do to me inside. That is how I feel. Broken, torn apart, afraid that if I lose you, there will be nothing left of me. I will be destroyed. Do you understand that?" His voice was low and dangerous.

"What do you want from me, Nick? Tell me what I am to you."

"Everything," he said with more force and conviction than she expected.

Amelia vowed to herself that if he wanted to end *them*, then she could handle the news. *Would* handle the news. Maybe. God, let it not be that.

She was sure she could be brave and stand up to Nick, no matter the decision he made. But now that the words she'd been itching to say to him for the past week were out, she wanted to take them all back. To pretend. To continue to love him because she'd been so happy until her brother had ruined it all. But to continue in the way they were, together but apart…it simply wasn't the way she wanted to live.

"Tell me what's wrong, Nick. It's just you and me here. No judgment, no theories. Just us."

"It'll pass. It always does," he said, as if that was the only answer she needed. It wasn't. It was so far from it.

"Stop lying to yourself. Every night that you pull away, I feel a little piece of my heart breaking. Whatever it is, you can trust me. Confide in me. Please. Before it's too late."

His hands braced either of her arms. "That I want you as my own will never change. Is that what you need to hear? That I won't let you go? That you are mine, whether or not you want to be?"

She shook her head and closed her eyes for just a moment—long enough that she could count to five so she didn't lash out at his nonanswer.

Opening her eyes again, she looked straight at him. "You're saying all this because you want to bury a past you think is so much worse than mine. It devastated me to have to tell you what my brother did, Nick. It made me feel half the woman I normally feel when I'm with you. I needed to be honest, and for the sake of our relationship, I let you in. I let you see me at my lowest. I let you see what broke me as a person. Why won't you do the same?"

Nick's forehead pressed against hers. His hands were warm where they covered her arms, looser now than the grip with which he'd originally held her.

"I can't and won't paint a pretty picture of my life growing up, Amelia. So much of it was filled with a darkness so black that it sometimes engulfed and decided my actions. I'm not diminishing what you felt in your situation, but there are some things better left unsaid. Better left in the dark, where they belong."

Tears filled her eyes. She couldn't help her reaction. This wasn't anything more than he'd told her before. None of what he said helped her understand what haunted him. "I can't begin to understand why this makes you the way it does if you won't explain it to me." Her frustrations were mounting, her anger brimming. She wanted to scream. Yell. Anything to make him understand that she could help him through his difficulties.

"I can't," was his answer.

"You won't."

"Trust me for now. Just let me get past this."

"Do you understand the position this puts me in? All I know is that you are pulling away from me. I can't even grasp at a reason. I just…" She dragged herself out of his embrace, not wanting his touch to soothe her. Distract her. "Perhaps we need time away from each other. Maybe I should go to the agency and find another job placement. Because the truth is…I can't live the way we are living. I can't *sin*, night after night, when you're heart isn't in it as much as mine."

Every word tore a new wound in her heart. But this was nothing more than the truth. Time apart might make him realize what he'd given up. Looking at the resolve set in his steely gaze and his unwillingness to talk about the invisible truths standing between them, she didn't think leaving would help them either. But she was out of options. She had no other way to approach this if he wanted to cut her off from his life.

Worse…he said nothing.

Not a damn thing.

His expression was unmoving.

Unable to look at him a moment longer, for she feared she'd completely break down, she turned and ran for the door.

Why hadn't she just stayed in bed? Instead, she'd set herself on an unknown path. One without Nick. Why? She hated this feeling that was ripping her apart from the inside out. It hurt so much and so deeply that she feared the wounds could never be healed.

Biting her bottom lip on a half-escaped sob, she violently wiped her tears away with the back of her hand. Nick caught her as she fumbled with the lock on the study door, spinning her around and wrapping his arms tightly around her, crushing her against his solid body.

She wanted to break down. To just let the tears overtake her. But she held strong.

"I have already told you I can't let you go. Stay, Amelia." His voice was so calm, just above a whisper. "I couldn't bear it if you left me. I can't let you leave. I won't."

Hearing him beg tugged at her heart painfully. Amelia's fists clenched where they were trapped between their bodies. There was only one thing she could do.

She pushed him away, hating that she was seconds away from breaking down. Hating that she knew she had to hold it together when every second in his arms chipped away at her control. "You are breaking my will every day. Making me lose myself in you. Don't ask this of me. Please, Nick. Let me go."

If she stayed, they would only end up back where they were. And she needed more than his physical comfort. He held her tighter against his chest, crushing her between him and the door as if he would *never* let her go.

"I told you I couldn't let you go. Don't try to leave. I warned you that you were mine the night I took your virginity."

Tilting her head back, she stared at him, eyes awash with tears she was helpless to stop from flowing over her cheeks. "Why are you doing this to me?"

The gray of his eyes was stormy, as though waiting to unleash a fury she'd never seen. "Because I can't let you go. Because I love you." His tone brooked no argument, so she said nothing to contradict him, just stared at him for another moment before pushing at his immovable body again. Nick's hand gently cradled her throat, his thumb forcing her head to lean against the door. "I've already told you that I wouldn't let you walk away. You belong to me."

Her lips parted on a half-exasperated groan at his declaration of ownership over her. "How could I belong to you when you close yourself off to me? I will not be controlled by you, no matter what I feel—"

Before she could get out the rest of her sentence, Nick's mouth took hers in an all-consuming kiss, his tongue robbing her of breath as it pushed past the barrier of her lips and tangled with her tongue in wordless need.

Hunger rose in her, but whether it was for physical desire or a need to draw as much of him into her as possible was hard to say. And she hated herself a little for not pushing him away again and again until she won this argument. Not now that she had a small piece of him all to herself. Even if it wouldn't be enough in the end.

Without a doubt in her mind, she'd never crave anything as badly as she craved Nick—his essence, his strength, *him*.

Her hands fisted around his shirtsleeves, holding him close. She didn't want to let go…of him or the moment.

His touch was like a branding iron as he tugged her dress from her shoulders, pulling down the front of the dress. The pull rent the delicate satin material as he pushed down her corset to free one breast. His hand squeezed her, the tips of his short nails digging into her flesh.

Their mouths didn't part once, almost as if Nick wanted to distract her from her original purpose. Keep her thinking of their kiss. The way their tongues slid knowingly against the other. The way he tasted like coffee and danger. Forbidden. Like the apple from the tree, he was a temptation she could not refuse.

His distraction was working.

And his hands were everywhere.

He pushed and pulled at the material of her underclothes, desperate to expose as much of her as he could. He wasn't gentle, and she hated that she loved that so much. That she wanted him to tear every inch of cloth from her body and expose her flesh.

She remained trapped between the solid warmth of Nick's body and the cold hard door at her back as he lifted her. She wrapped her legs around his hips, needing to be closer any way she could. It didn't escape her just how well they fit together. Nick's straining cock wedged powerfully between the folds of her sex, and he stopped kissing her to shove his hand between them, opening his trousers and shucking them impatiently down his hips. Their bodies were so tightly smashed together that his cock landed against her belly first. She moaned; she couldn't help it, and he followed suit when he seated himself deep inside her. Amelia curled her arms around his shoulders and neck to keep from sliding down the door.

This was a bad idea, but she was helpless to stop what was happening. She didn't think she could stop where this was going. She didn't want to. Not really. If this was the end of them, then she would take this memory with her. His complete need to own her body.

He tore his mouth from hers, his body grinding between her legs, building her need, her desire.

"Don't ever run from me." His voice was low, dangerous. And it was full of lust and a demand for complete control that she wanted to obey but knew she wouldn't.

Instead of responding, she pulled herself up higher on his hips, until her mouth was plastered against his again.

He swallowed that sound and ate at her mouth and sucked at her tongue, as if that alone would leave his mark on her. He hitched her hard against the door and fucked her like a man starved for feeling. The quick motions had her shoulders crashing against the wood behind her, causing her to hold on tighter as Nick found an angle that allowed him to drive ever harder and deeper.

He pulled away from their heated kiss and flattened his hands on the door next to her shoulders. Her head leaned back, the position arching her breasts up so Nick could bite and lick at the flesh he'd already exposed. Her hands tangled in his hair, pulling at it, needing to keep him close, needing him tighter inside her.

His cock was unrelenting as it beat into her like a sword, aiming true as it plunged deep. Like it was the only place it wanted to be. Her back was surely bruised; her body ached with a need so profound she could barely skim the surface of understanding just how she could allow this to happen when moments ago they'd been fighting.

Their bodies thrashed, pushed, and pulled. They both needed this.

Nick let her nipple go with a shout, his hands slapped tight around the globes of her buttocks to better grip her so he could pound inside her. She bit her lip and moaned. She'd never felt anything so intoxicating and overwhelming all at once.

"Fuck!" he shouted. "Fuck."

And then he took her harder—hard enough that her head smacked against the back of the door every time his body slapped into hers. He fucked her like a man possessed, bent on one thing: complete abandonment of their emotions.

She made breathless sounds of need as his seed shot inside her. His motions were strong and forceful as he emptied himself. She felt every heavy squirt of his throbbing member and felt her need for completion only grow.

Sated, he rested his forehead against her chest, his hot breath chilling her damp skin and teasing her firm, exposed nipple. She was still primed and ready. And it left her feeling empty.

He pulled out of her without saying a word.

Without looking at her.

Her body felt bruised and sore as her feet touched the floor one at a time. She felt his seed slide down the inside of her thighs and clenched her legs together as she righted her dress, tucking herself back into it and hiding her nakedness.

Nick tucked his penis away, still avoiding her gaze.

"I'm sorry," he said, as though that could explain what had just happened between them.

She hated herself in that moment. Hated that she'd allowed that to happen when it changed nothing between them.

"You have nothing to be sorry about." Only she could claim that.

Nick focused on her, his stormy expression freezing her to the spot, making her second-guess herself. His expression seemed lost, as though he couldn't figure out the next step to take.

Reaching behind her, she clicked over the lock. The sound was audible and undeniable in what it meant.

Was there really anything that could be said between them?

She needed time away from him—to reflect on what had happened and to think about what she'd threatened. She needed to make a decision on whether or not they could work out their differences and move past this hurdle, because she could not continue to be stagnant or carry on how they were. She realized she needed a commitment. But that commitment could only come with his complete honesty.

She turned and did the one thing he'd asked her not to do. She ran from the room—as fast and as far away from him as the house would allow.

"Fuck," Nick mumbled as he smacked the wall with the flat of his hand, hating himself for not holding back. For taking Amelia without a care for her needs. For using her body against her.

She was right; they couldn't carry on how they were. He was keeping his distance from her emotionally. But he wasn't generally someone to confide in another. People either knew about his past, having been there, or they could only guess. But Amelia meant more to him than anyone he'd ever met. He wanted to make her happy. Keep her happy. And what was the harm in telling her the truth? She already knew that he'd been defiled as a youth.

He paused on that thought.

She was innocent in so many ways that it was possible she hadn't fully understood what he'd told her about his time in school with Shauley.

If there was one thing he could give her, it was the truth. Without that, he knew he would lose her. And he couldn't let that happen.

CHAPTER ELEVEN

Was it possible to feel like she'd had too much to drink merely from crying all night long? Her eyes actually hurt and felt overly tired, and her head pounded as she slowly rolled over in her bed. The sun shining through her bedroom window enhanced the pain sitting behind her eyes.

She blinked a few times, trying to clear the haze and fog from view, but that didn't help, and she had to squint at her surroundings for some minutes.

When she could finally focus on her room, she noticed Nick sitting in the chair by her vanity. With elbows perched firmly on his knees, his head was in his hands, eyes toward the ground, so he hadn't yet noticed that she was awake.

She made a study of his rumpled shirt and disheveled appearance, the same way she'd found him last night in the study.

"Nick?" Her voice was soft, worn from crying through the night.

His head lifted. His eyes were red-rimmed and tired as they met hers. Had he been sitting here all night while she slept?

She sat up, pulling the blankets around her in the process. The less he saw, the less vulnerable she felt.

"I couldn't bear the thought of you leaving before I had a chance to explain myself," he said, his voice gravelly.

She waited for him to say more. When he didn't continue, she said, "Then you need to do just that, Nick." She rubbed her eyes, wishing she could go back to sleep. Wishing when she woke up that she could pretend last night hadn't happened.

"I never really explained how my mother supported Sera and me, growing up."

This was a peace offering. She knew it without having to ask.

Nick stood and walked over to the window. He threw the curtains to the side and pressed his hands against the frame as he looked outside. His breath fogged the glass. But she waited for him to continue, knowing she couldn't interrupt him now, or he might never open up to her.

"She was a lovely woman. An Irish immigrant. She came over during the potato famine in '47. The eldest daughter in a family of fourteen." He paused, letting her digest this revelation. "The youngest six didn't survive the famine, and the conditions of those times left my grandparents in poor health, poor enough that seeking work to support their family was impossible. My mother took up that torch, thinking that when she moved to London, as so many of those she knew were doing, she'd be able to send back enough food and money to keep her family going.

"Her first year here, she met more closed doors than anything for decent work. She eventually found herself without a roof over her head as she tried to get into a respectable household. While she waited for the right opportunity to present itself…both her parents died. As did two more siblings. She said the rest had been displaced, and she never knew what became of them."

Nick paused, perhaps lost in his thoughts. Or thinking of how much more to reveal.

When he did nothing but stare outside, she said, "I'm sorry, Nick. No one should be put in such a position when her intentions are noble and her heart is in the right place."

"But it is the reality of this city or any great city. Where there is wealth to be found, there's also poverty that outweighs it in sheer number."

Amelia stood from the bed, holding the blankets around her as she padded over to Nick and pressed her cheek to his back. He was tense and didn't want to be comforted, so she didn't wrap her arms around him even though she almost felt she needed to. "Go on," she encouraged him.

"I remember that my mother was very beautiful. I imagine over time that it grew more and more obvious as to what her options were if she wanted to stay out of the workhouses. She befriended another young woman. Both were smart, both wanted more, but they knew their options were limited. My mother would often joke that her only worth had been her chastity when she'd moved to London. Together, they worked on a plan to sell themselves to the highest bidders. It allowed them to make enough money to open their own place, where they took on patrons regularly."

Amelia swallowed against the lump building in her throat. She could imagine how easily a woman was forced to take on that profession and had been thankful that other options had been open to her. "I'm sorry she was forced to live that kind of life."

"It's the life many women lived when they came over from Ireland."

"Did you know your father?" She wasn't sure what made her ask. Something his sister had said.

"No. I never wanted to. I still don't want to know who he is. Though from my mother's accounts, he wasn't someone I would care to know. I was the product of a rape, an unwilling encounter my mother had with this particular man. Though many didn't paint him to be evil, considering the profession she was in."

Amelia covered her mouth, hoping she didn't give away her shock at that admission. "And your sister?"

"We do not share a father. Sera's father was someone my mother professed to love but who obviously did not return the sentiment, since he didn't stick around when my mother learned she was with child for a second time."

"Why are you telling me this now?"

He turned, pulling her into his arms, resting his chin on top of her head. His arms had found their way under her blanket, and his touch was hot against her back.

"Because I can't lose you, Amelia. When you said you would find other employment last night, something snapped inside me. Something ugly, and I felt like a beast for forcing myself on you when you were vulnerable. Perhaps I'm more like my father than I realize."

"Don't say that." She leaned back to look up at him. "You didn't force yourself. I wanted you just as desperately as you wanted me last night."

"Needed. Not mere want, Amelia. I needed you. Because the thought of losing you…"

His expression was firm and unmoving as he stared back at her. He looked tired. Worn out. She didn't think she was the cause of that, considering he'd been up at all hours of the night this past week.

"Have you slept at all?"

He shook his head. "Not since I was in bed with you last night."

She took his hand and led him toward the bed. Climbing onto the mattress, she carried the blankets with her. Nick paused at the threshold between taking the next step and leaving the room. She tugged him closer; it was a silent plea for him to join her. If he walked out this room right now…she didn't want to contemplate what that would mean. Nick had made one small step in the right direction this morning. Would he take that back from her by closing himself off now?

"We have a few hours before we need to get up. Sleep in here for a spell. I promise not to take advantage of you," she teased slightly. "Besides, my eyes feel like they've got sand in them. I could use more rest."

Nick pulled her hand closer, forcing her to walk over to him on her knees. "Promise me you'll stay, Amelia."

"Only if you promise not to shut me out." She wrapped her arms around his shoulders. Sometimes it seemed like he carried the weight of the world on them, and she didn't want to be a burden. She wanted to stand next to him and take some of that mass. "If you can't trust me, why do you want to be with me?"

"I don't trust anyone as much as I do you. But I've always been a private person."

"Well then, you'll have to consider that I'm in your life, for better or worse, Nick. But I can only remain that way if you share yourself fully with me. A relationship has to work two ways, and holding back your true thoughts and feelings from me makes me believe we want different things and have a different idea of what is between us."

After a light kiss on her lips that held only tenderness and no heat, he climbed onto the bed with her. She lay in the middle; Nick tucked himself tightly along the length of her body. Her head hurt a little less, knowing they had come to an agreement she could live with.

The most delicious feeling bloomed deep in Amelia's belly. She arched her back along Nick's body where it covered her in delightful warmth. Her buttocks tucked tight against the hardness jabbing against her backside. She stretched her arms over her head, wrapping them around his head, and pulled his lips closer to her neck. He scraped his teeth along the column of her throat, sending a shiver of need through her whole body.

"Does this mean we get to start this morning on a different note?" Her voice was barely above a whisper, still filled with tiredness but awakening to other things.

Nick's only response was to suck the skin of her neck into his mouth, making her heart rate pick up in speed with every flick of his tongue. His hand slipped down the front of her naked body, covering her mound. She wasn't sure when he'd taken her clothes off, but she was glad there was no barrier between them.

His fingers split the folds of her sex and slicked the rest of the way to her entrance.

"Already wet for me." He bit at her earlobe as he rolled her onto her back. She tilted her pelvis against his hand, needing him to rub her and fill her. Needing him inside her so badly, she actually ached.

Nick released her mound to push one of her knees out, opening her entrance to him. A cool rush of air hit her slick core, only to inflame her desires further. Where shame once filled her at being exposed this way, need was all she felt.

"I need you inside me," she said, her tone near to begging.

He gave her exactly what she asked, his manhood filling her before she could take her next breath. Her knee was hitched over his arm, her body stretched in a way she'd never been before.

His pace was unhurried, meant to titillate and tease. He was showing her he could be just as gentle as he had been rough. "Tell me you're mine." His demand was hoarse, with a thread of vulnerability.

There was no doubt in her mind that she belonged to this man alone.

"I'm yours, Nick. I'll always be yours." Amelia curled her fingers into the sheets for purchase as he fucked her harder and deeper, rubbing over a sensitive spot that had her toes curling and her hips rotating.

"I want to feel the tight clench of your cunt around my cock, milking me as your cream flows between us. I'm sorry I took that release away from you earlier."

She knew she was on the cusp of giving him just that but couldn't string any words together with their bodies entangled the way they were, with the dirty words he used to describe what he wanted. Even with the way he flicked his finger over her nipple, pulling it taut, and sending stabs of desire right to her womb.

All she could do was moan as their bodies came together, over and over again. His pace was no longer slow and easy. He twisted and rotated his hips and his cock with every plunge into her sheath.

She reached behind her, grabbed on to the metal rods of her headboard, and held on tight. She needed to anchor herself, to hold still for every slap of his body against hers. To keep her grounded in reality before she flew over the edge of release. She wanted this to last forever. To never end, to pretend the world didn't exist beyond this room, this bed.

Nick lowered his hand from her breasts and expertly flicked his thumb over her swollen clitoris. He didn't let up the sweet torture until she was writhing in his arms and desperate to find her own end.

She didn't just reach the threshold to the finale; she smashed right through the wall, her whole body clenching and throbbing simultaneously. She didn't just moan; she cried out so loudly she bit into Nick's shoulder to hush the sounds coming from her.

Nick didn't slow his pace once, and her orgasm continued until she thought she couldn't take it anymore.

"Nick," she said when she released him from her bite. "Nick." Her breathing was erratic, her voice hoarse and dry. She tried to push his hand away from her mound, to ease the pressure at her overly sensitized nub, but he was unrelenting, a man determined to break down every wall keeping her sane right now. Like he could erase what had happened earlier.

She thought she'd break apart if he didn't stop, thought she might never come down from the high of this feeling he filled her with.

Nick jerked in her one final time before stilling. It was as though they were completely in sync, pulsating and rippling together in unison. There were no thoughts, no words; their bodies told the whole story. Amelia could feel each throb of his cock as the seed pumped out of him, filling her, tingling along sensitive nerve endings inside her.

She wasn't sure when his hand had moved from the nub between her feminine folds, but he lazily rolled her nipple between his wet fingers, and the sensations he drew from her skated a thin line between pleasure and pain. His tortuous touch never quite let her desires dissipate, only fueled the fire still burning low in her belly.

"Let's stay in bed the rest of the day," he said.

She wanted nothing more than to say yes. But a voice of reason kicked her thoughts of lazing about aside. "You know very well we can't."

What would the rest of the staff think? What must they think now? Because judging by the light filling her room, it was midday, which meant they'd already overslept.

"Yes, we can." Nick's hand slipped over her hip, gripping her so he could work his still-thick cock in and out of her. His hold was unrelenting, bruising, but she didn't mind it in the least.

Not another word of protest made it past her lips as their motions went from lazy, with obvious intention, to more frantic, with need, in a heartbeat. Nick pulled out of her to reposition them, hoisting her up onto her knees so he could take her from behind.

Amelia steadied herself on her knees and pressed her shoulders to the mattress. She turned her head to the side as she focused on breathing, holding back the moans that wanted to flow freely from her throat. Her fingers curled into the counterpane. She was beginning to think this position let him hide from her.

She tried twisting in his hold, but Nick's hands tightened around her hips, practically lifting her knees from the mattress every time he pumped into her. His pace grew wild, and his motions robbed her of the remainder of her troubles.

Nick surrounded her, and sanity fled as they edged toward a second peak together. Nick leaned over her, covering her back like an animal in rut. His hand slid around her hip and over her stomach, inching those expert fingers of his closer to the folds of her sex. When he reached the bud, he flicked one finger over the sensitive nerve endings of her clitoris. Biting the blanket, Amelia moaned around that material stuffing her mouth.

Nick scissored his fingers around her clitoris, slicking through her folds with every shove of his pelvis against her backside. With a lazy awakening, her orgasm washed through her like waves slapping against the beach, subtler this time but not less powerful. As it ebbed, Nick slammed into her one last time and held deep, rotating and grinding against her core as he came. Every pulse of his cock was swallowed up by the clench and flex of her sheath.

Replete, he slumped over her, pulling them both to their sides, his cock slipping from her and leaving a wet trail along her thigh. His arms wrapped around her waist, one of his hands cupping her breast as he held her close to his chest.

She turned in his arms, putting one arm over his shoulder; the other she curled on the pillow and rested her head in the crook of her elbow.

"I refuse to lie in bed all day," she said to break the silence that descended once their breathing leveled out.

Without missing a beat or giving in to her, he responded, "Then we will stay here all *morning*."

She shook her head. "You know that is impossible… You know *why* we can't."

Mostly, she knew she'd ask him too many questions if she allowed herself to stay in his company for the day. Would he reject that curiosity, or reward it after all they'd been through in these past few days?

"Nick?"

Like a lion well fed, his eyes lazily focused on her. "Amelia."

"I mean it." She pushed playfully at his shoulder. "We don't need to give the members of this household more fodder for their whisperings of what's going on between us."

"I don't give a damn what anyone thinks."

Amelia pushed off the bed and started pulling out fresh clothes for the day. "Well, I do."

And Nick looked for all the world like he didn't give a damn. He lay on her bed, hands tucked behind his head, his nudity on full display. She'd be lying if she said it wasn't tempting to climb over him and straddle his thighs for a third round.

"Come back to bed."

"Absolutely not. They'll think me the whore of Babylon. Oh, hell. I can't believe I didn't think of it sooner. I've shamed myself."

Nick pulled himself up and sat on the edge of her bed, watching her in his contemplative way. He caught her arm and pulled her closer when she walked by him for the tenth time, trying to tie her corset. He turned her around and tightened the strings for her.

"Calm yourself, Amelia. Your first mistake is thinking anyone under this roof would judge what happens in private between us."

"You're a man; you can think that way. They won't care how you behave; you're the master of this house. I have to act above reproach if I want to be valued and respected."

After wrapping the long strings around her front and looping them in a bow at the back, Nick turned her around in the circle of his arms. "I don't agree. You have changed me for the better, Amelia. Everyone here will see that."

She placed her palms against his cheeks. "You haven't changed to me. You've let me into your life. Given me a part of yourself. I don't know any other Nick than the one sitting in front of me."

Her gaze dropped to his lap. He was still semi-erect. She breathed deeply and looked up at Nick's cocky expression before he turned serious again.

"You're the only person I've allowed this close."

"What about Victoria?" Why had she mentioned his ex-lover? She hated herself for having thrown that between them. Nick and Victoria had broken off a while ago, before Amelia had ever come across Nick. "I'm sorry. I don't have the right to ask that."

"That's where you are wrong. You want me to be honest, so I'll be as honest as I can. Victoria is my friend. And she knows nearly as much as you because she grew up in St. Giles, living the life my mother lived. Actually, she was a friend of Sera's growing up."

This revelation surprised Amelia, and she felt a twinge of sympathy toward the woman. "She's made a grand name for herself. Half the women in London would give anything to be in her shoes."

"That wasn't always the case."

Amelia reached around his shoulders, smoothing her fingers along the scars that marred his back. "Tell me how you got these."

He pulled her arms away and gathered her hands in his. "That's a story for another day."

Amelia pinched her lips together. "I'll be patient, but you'll have to tell how it happened. I'd like to wring the neck of whoever caused you so much pain."

"You're my little champion. But it happened a long time ago."

"And the person responsible?" Had he never been caught? Amelia suddenly had a hundred questions she wanted to ask. But they had to take this one step at a time.

"He will have his day of judgment, Amelia. It's not something you can fix. It's something I live with and will deal with in my own time."

"How old you were when it happened?"

"You're inquisitive this morning."

"I usually am when you're not busy avoiding having a real conversation with me."

Nick's mouth tilted up into the smallest of smiles. So small, she thought she was reading it wrong.

"I was eleven," he admitted, breaking her gaze as he did so.

Amelia felt her lips tremble and anchored her teeth into the lower one to still them. How could anyone do that to a child? She bit back a slew of curses building on her tongue. She would not ruin this moment. Nick had given her so much today.

Pulling out of his hold, she changed the topic to something neutral. "So what did we have planned for today?"

"Scheduling our trip to Highgate. As soon as the purchase closes, we'll be headed out there for a week or two; get a feel of the land and the tenants. We should be leaving by week's end."

"We? I hadn't thought Lady Burley was serious that we would all spend time in Highgate."

"I told you I wasn't letting you out of my sight. And we'll be gone at least a week; that's too long a time to be without you."

"And where will we stay?" There was an underlying implausibility about this proposal.

"There's an inn outside of Highgate. A mere horse's ride away. Have you been in the saddle before?"

"I have." Not since she was a child, but she'd cross that bridge when they got to it.

"Landon and his wife will be joining us. My sister will come out a few days later. She hasn't seen the house yet or the state of the land. I want to have a good look around before she arrives. Come up with a preliminary plan for construction."

"Shall I make everyone's arrangements at the inn when I send word of our arrival?"

She hoped Nick intended to reserve two rooms for them. In fact, she'd make those arrangements herself the moment they knew when they were going.

Amelia buckled the bustle around her waist, needing anything to distract her from where her thoughts were going. For anyone to discover what they were up to outside the house...she wasn't sure she was ready for that.

Nick stood behind her, naked and distracting. He lifted the skirts over her head and settled them around her waist to tie them in place. "You can work out those details with Landon's wife." His hands skimmed over her arms, and the warmth of his touch had her sighing and pressing back against him.

"You're wicked."

"Am I?" He kissed her earlobe and then worked his way down her neck. The scratch of his beard was sure to leave a mark, but she didn't care. She tilted her head to the side to give him free access. It was so tempting to fall back into bed with him.

"Very wicked."

"Tell me how to keep you here."

She cleared her throat, coming back to herself. She walked out of his embrace and picked up his pocketwatch from her vanity. "It's half eleven now. We can make luncheon if we hurry."

Turning to face him so she could ward him off, she pulled on the outer shell of her bodice. It buttoned in the front so she wasn't forced to ask for his assistance.

"Break your fast with me in the library," he said.

More time alone wasn't a good idea. They seemed to get into all kinds of naked trouble when there was no one else about.

"I don't think that's wise. Besides, there's plenty to do since we slept the morning away. I'm liable to have a stack of correspondence to go through, and Huxley's probably wondering where you've disappeared."

"He'll think I'm out on errands." He tugged the end of her braid, pulling her closer. "There's no one to interrupt us."

"You think no one will wonder where I'm hiding?" She laughed and drew her braid free from his grasp. Unwinding it, she pulled it back and twisted it into a chignon at her nape and pinned it in place, all the while having to stay out of Nick's reach. He seemed quite determined to get her back in bed.

"You're insatiable." She kissed him on the mouth and headed for the door, practically skipping to stay out of his hold. "I'll see you in the study."

She opened the door enough that she could slip out and so no one would see Nick in her room, standing naked as the day he was born, with his cock deliciously erect and ready for another tumble. Amelia ignored the twinge of regret at leaving him in that state. She also ignored the fact that her lower regions clenched with want. Nick was turning out to be a very bad influence.

CHAPTER TWELVE

Mrs. Coleman smiled at Amelia as she came down the stairs. Before they could offer good mornings, there was a summons at the front door. Amelia hurried into the study and busied herself with going through the correspondence. Perhaps she could make it look as though she'd been at this all morning—though she knew Mrs. Coleman and Huxley would have already been through this room. And she couldn't think up one good excuse for her absence.

Anything was worth a try, she supposed.

Amelia looked up when there was a knock on the study door. Mrs. Coleman came in, her face red and flustered.

"Miss Grant," the housekeeper said stiffly, "there's an inspector here to see you. Shall I show him to the parlor?"

"Yes, please," Amelia said loud enough that the visitor in the hall could hear her response. "Come back in here once that's done, please," she said in a softer tone, giving Mrs. Coleman a curious look. Mrs. Coleman shrugged her shoulders, just as baffled by the man's presence as Amelia.

Why would an inspector want to see her? It was obvious this had to do with her brother. Nick said an inspector had visited him the day before he'd told her of Jeremy's death. Amelia's hands shook, so she clasped them together and took a steadying breath. If this was the same inspector, why had he come back? Had he found news? Did he know who the murderer was?

Mrs. Coleman came back into the study, shutting the door behind her so they weren't heard. "I don't know this one, Amelia."

That comment caught her off guard. "Do you know many?"

"Nick deals with so many down at the docks and throughout St. Giles. Some are better than others. But I don't know this one, and he's specifically asked for you."

Amelia squeezed Mrs. Coleman's arm companionably. "Could you please find Mr. Riley? Let him know there is an inspector here?"

"Of course, Miss Grant."

Amelia released Mrs. Coleman and headed toward the parlor.

If her steps were slower than normal, it was because she had to prepare carefully what she would say. Surely he was here to see her because he knew of her association with Jeremy, knew they were brother and sister.

She shut down those thoughts the moment she stepped over the threshold of the parlor. The inspector was a tall man. His rounded hat sat firmly on his head, with the strap slung across his chin. His long black coat was neatly pressed and buttoned from his Adam's apple down to his knees.

Amelia folded her hands in front of her and dipped her head in greeting. "Good morning, Inspector. How may I assist you?"

"Inspector Laurie," he filled in. "Miss Grant, I presume?"

"I am Miss Grant. Mrs. Coleman said you asked to speak directly with me. With what may I assist you, Inspector Laurie?"

"This is about your brother, Miss *Grant*. Did you know that he was murdered?"

Amelia dug her nails into her palm. So the inspector knew of their relation. "I did. My brother had a lot of enemies, Inspector Laurie. Is this some sort of interrogation on where I was on a particular night in question? Or have you found the responsible party?"

"You're quick. I haven't found anything yet. But I do need to ask about the last time you saw your brother."

"It was more than a month ago. He…he wasn't well." She didn't dare give this man the particulars of that incident. Something about him seemed off. Untrustworthy. And unlike the last few times she'd ignored her discomfort toward certain men, she trusted her instincts on the inspector. The less he knew, the better.

"Why did he seek you out?"

Without missing a beat, she knew the truth would help her here. "He wanted money. I didn't have any to give him."

"Surely a man of Mr. Riley's status could assist."

She bit her tongue on giving him a million reasons why that couldn't be so. It was a crass suggestion, and the inspector knew it.

"It wouldn't have done my brother any good. And as Mr. Riley is my employer, I wasn't in a position to ask such a thing without risking my job. Jeremy had a habit of spending money on the wrong things." Amelia walked around the chairs and invited the inspector to sit. He waved her off, which meant he must not be planning to stay long. Perfect. "What information do you require from me, Inspector Laurie?"

"I'm simply trying to solve a crime that resulted in the Earl of Berwick's death." The inspector gave her pink day dress an up-and-down with his too-assessing eyes. "Considering you are his last relation and his sister, your lack of mourning brings a lot of questions to mind."

"My brother and I had been estranged for some time. We were not close, so while I admit I'm saddened to hear of his death, I have no desire to mourn his passing. If you are investigating me, Inspector, perhaps you should also look into Jeremy's past. You will not find clean ties anywhere. He had a habit of making more enemies than friends."

"I see. I'll keep that in mind. I still need to ask where you were one week after the incident in the street with your brother and Mr. Riley."

"That was a month ago, Inspector. I will have to check my diary."

"By all means." He motioned toward the door. "Why don't you fetch that schedule now."

Amelia tucked her hands behind her back and curled them into fists. This man was infuriating. What was the inspector hoping to find? She didn't have anything to do with her brother's death, and she couldn't even guess who would have killed him. It was exactly as she had said—he had a lot of enemies.

"Of course." Amelia held her head high as she faced the inspector she was fast disliking. "If you'll give me a few minutes, I can verify the schedule."

"If you don't mind, I'll go with you."

How could she say no? Wouldn't that look suspicious? "Yes, if you will follow me."

Amelia led the way to the study. Once there, she pulled out the book from the previous month. "For what day did you require information?"

"The last Thursday in October. If you could copy it out, I would appreciate it."

Amelia flipped through the pages, looking for the date. When she found it, she was almost relieved to see a list of places and appointments Nick had throughout the day, two of which she'd attended.

"This was the day Mr. Riley was finalizing the paperwork with his solicitor on a purchase he was making. Do you require the whole day's events? Or just a particular time?"

The inspector stood over her shoulder, reading off the ledger and taking notes on a small pad of paper he had pulled from his pocket. "I'll take what I need. Were you at this meeting?" He pointed to the line for two in the afternoon that indicated tea at the Langley with Hart and Nick. "I was."

"And after?"

"I was home by dinner, which is served at half six. After that, I spent time going through Mr. Riley's correspondence and preparing replies."

"And when did your day end?"

"I can't say for sure. I usually wait for Mr. Riley to get home, which is around eight or nine, depending on the next day's schedule."

He closed his notebook with a snap and straightened his shoulders. Something about his presence had her taking a step away from him.

"Thank you, Miss Grant...though I have one more question."

"Yes?" she asked, just wanting rid of him.

"Why did you change your name?"

She folded her hands in front of her. That was not an easy answer, and the closest she could come to the truth would be better. "Very few people would have hired Lady Amelia Somerset. I found the change of my name gave me a better opportunity at landing a job once I moved to London. A job that was more challenging than acting as a companion to an aged dowager."

And it gave me a clean slate, she thought, but she didn't say that out loud, knowing it would only bring forth new questions.

"You're a plucky woman, Miss *Grant*." He gave a slight bow. "I'll see myself out and let you know if I require further information."

"Inspector..." When he turned back toward her, she asked, "Have you found any leads or details on what happened to Lord Berwick?"

"I'm working off a tip that named you an accomplice. Just haven't found the kind of clues I like in this instance—or a motive, for that matter."

"Me? I had no reason to want my brother dead."

"And what of Mr. Riley?"

The inspector's reference was obvious. Nick had beaten her brother to a bloody pulp and threatened him in front of every man and woman on the street, shortly before he'd turned up dead. All Nick had been trying to do was protect her. To stop her brother from dragging her away to marry the man he'd sold her to in the name of making good on his debts.

"Mr. Riley didn't personally know my brother. And I can't imagine he'd want such an outcome for anyone."

"Perhaps. That still brings questions forth on his actions toward your brother the week before he was found dead and tossed in the Thames."

The image with which he filled her head had her pressing her lips together. Every bruise and cut on her brother's body was burned into her brain, but to have that small tidbit of information made her sick to her stomach and had bile burning the back of her throat.

"Unfortunately, I don't have those answers. I can only say that a gentleman seeing a woman hauled away against her will is likely to act any way he sees fit." She walked toward the door, hoping to usher him out quickly. She suddenly didn't want to be in his company. She wanted him gone from the house, though she had a feeling she wouldn't be so lucky as to not see him again.

As luck—or bad luck—would have it, Nick walked into the study just as they exited. The smile was suddenly wiped from his face. "Inspector," he said.

"Mr. Riley. A pleasure to see you again." The inspector's voice was anything but friendly, and his tone was cold enough that it stole the warmth from the room as the men eyed each other up and down.

"Mr. Riley." Amelia cut through the tension by walking ahead of both men. "I was just showing Inspector Laurie out."

"Why are you here?" Nick asked, completely ignoring Amelia. In fact, both men were still glaring at each other as if the person who stared longest would be the winner of some manly game.

"I had some questions on Miss *Grant's* whereabouts the night of her brother's murder."

"She's under my employ. You didn't think you should ask my permission to speak with her?"

"I like to get down to the truth of the matter. You're a tricky one, and something's not quite right about this whole scenario. I'll uncover the truth, find out that you killed Berwick, and have you hanged for murder."

"You dare come into my home and threaten me with false accusations? I could have your job for this, Inspector."

"Prove me wrong and it won't be a problem." The inspector gave a smug smile.

"Get out of my house, and don't come back without sending a card."

"My line of work doesn't require me to send word ahead of time. It's hard to catch a criminal in the act if I'm going to advise him of my arrival."

"I'll make sure to spell out my directions to Superintendent Jackson."

"Now who's threatening whom?" the man said before whipping past Amelia in a fury and slamming the door in his wake.

Amelia shrank against the wall, thinking she'd done something wrong. She wasn't sure how to explain what had happened between the two men.

Nick was watching her closely, visibly reining in his frustration at the encounter. "Come into the study."

She felt like a dog with her tail tucked between her legs as she crossed into the next room. Nick left the door open as he entered behind her and walked over to his desk, perching himself on the edge, as he usually did when he was about to interrogate someone.

"What questions did he ask you?"

"He wanted to know my whereabouts on the day Jeremy was murdered."

She looked at the swirling design of the floor rug, so unsure of what had happened and of how she'd handled the situation. There was something she'd missed in dealing with the inspector. Perhaps she should have sent him away without speaking to him.

Nick took a deep breath and rolled his shoulders. "If he comes around again, don't give him an opportunity to ask you any other questions. I will find another way to handle him."

"What do you mean?" She rushed toward him, at odds with whether she wanted to shake him so he explained himself clearly or hold him close and tell him it didn't matter. "Do you plan to handle this the same way you handled my last employer, who thought taking advantage of me was included in my job duties? You can't solve every problem with your fists, Nick. If you're angry with me, that's fine, but don't speak cryptically of your intentions, because it leaves me wondering…"

She didn't believe for one second that Nick had arranged for her brother's murder, but what would happen if the inspector turned up bloody and broken? Nick would find himself in trouble he might not be able to get out of.

"Wonder what? If I killed your brother? Is that what you're asking me?"

"No. Nick…"

"Are you afraid of me?"

She inhaled deeply. Wasn't it only this morning that they'd come to an understanding of where their relationship was headed, that they could work through his secrets one step at a time without her demanding more? Well, this time she *needed* more than his evasive answers.

"I'm not afraid." Her voice was firm. And left no room for interpretation. "Why do you push me away for something that relates to me?"

"Because right now, you are questioning whether or not I had a hand in your brother's death."

Her breath audibly caught. "That's not what I'm suggesting." She shook her head in denial. "Why would you think that?"

"Because you are looking at me with the same trepidation and fear that you gazed at me shortly after you came to live in this house. You were wondering if I had broken your last employer's jaw or if he'd found some other man's fist."

Amelia pressed her fingers against his mouth and tucked her head into his shoulder. "You dealt with Sir Ian the only way he could be dealt with. Any woman who'd just come out of the situation I had would have been wary. And while he deserved what he got, I didn't know you then. But I do now, and I trust you."

"Then why are you questioning me? Don't deny it. I see nothing but accusations in your eyes."

She pulled out of the circle of his arms and gave him a long, measured look. "Do you really think that? That I would think so little of you after everything you have done to help me?"

Nick lifted his hand and rubbed his thumb under her cheek. "It's my nature to assume the worst."

"Don't you know me better than that?"

"I like to think so. But you stand before me with too many questions of doubt." His hand curled around her hip and pulled her pelvis in tight to his.

"Then what do you know of my brother's death?"

"Nothing more than I've told you. I had eyes on your brother after he showed up to the house and tried to take you. Huxley set up a few trusted people to make sure he didn't come back for a second attempt. I thought he would try again; he didn't seem easily persuaded to a different course. Had he not met an unfortunate end, he may have still tried to take you away from me."

"But I'm here now. My brother is dead. And I know I said I didn't want to properly mourn him or do the things I should have for his burial, but it still matters that there's someone out there who killed him in cold blood. What did the boy say when you questioned him about my brother last night?"

"He'd gone on his usual nightly bender. Visited a gambling hell; went to a whorehouse. At the end of the night, he'd had so much to drink he was slurring his words and staggered his way halfway home before passing out. He pissed himself in an alley, woke himself up, and then headed back to the rooms he kept. That's how all his nights were spent. And I've thought it over a hundred times and questioned Brian at least twice that many times to see if there was anything that struck him as odd or different."

"Why didn't you tell the inspector that? Why leave him guessing when you are trying to work out the particulars on your own? What if you both have resources that can help solve the murder?"

Nick rubbed his thumb across her cheek, the motion soothing and speaking to the level of their familiarity with each other. "The inspector can't be trusted, Amelia. Word down at the docks is that he's easily bought."

"How…"

"Superintendent Jackson is a friend. I wasn't lying when I said I would talk to him about the inspector's behavior. The smug blighter is working with someone in the background. Perhaps the killer, or maybe he's working with Shauley. Either way, I promise that I will find out what happened."

"So he's trying to make it look like you did it? He said he more or less suspected me and that the only way to clear me of the crime was to verify my appointments that day."

Nick's hand tightened on her hip. "I'm going to keep Huxley back at the house when I can't be here."

"That's unnecessary, Nick. I doubt he'll come back, and I won't take callers while I'm here. You can't pull Huxley from his duties every time you're worried about me. Had I known…" She shook her head. She would have what?

"I won't argue about this," he said, as if that ended the matter.

"You're the only person arguing."

Nick gave her an exasperated sigh. "You should have stayed in bed with me."

She pushed him away lightly and moved out of his reach. "What would you have done, had my brother come after me again?"

"I would have stopped him."

"How?"

"I would never kill a man in cold blood, Amelia, but had your brother threatened your life, his would have been forfeited."

She flattened her shaking hands against her stomach and felt queasy with that admission. Because she couldn't fault him for the determination and promise in his words. What kind of person did that make her?

She sat on the arm of the leather chair, her head spinning with the events of the day. It seemed as if she had a hundred things to do. One of those things was having a lengthy conversation with Huxley but not while Nick was home. "You have some appointments; it would look odd if you didn't keep them, especially if the inspector is looking for us to slip up in some way. Why don't you visit this friend Jackson and have Huxley keep me company."

"A moment ago, you were eschewing the idea of his being here."

"Now I see the merits."

"What are you up to?" He eyed her suspiciously.

"Nothing. I have a lot to do today, and you've proven to be very distracting."

He didn't look like he believed her, but he didn't say so. "I'm heading down to the kitchens for something to eat. I have a tea scheduled with Victoria midafternoon. Would you like to join us?"

She knew Victoria was on the books, and had Amelia been thinking clearly this morning, she might have asked that they stay in bed all day, just so he wouldn't see his ex-lover.

"I think I might do just that. Tea at her shop sounds like the perfect distraction." Even if she was only present to keep that woman's claws out of Nick. They might be friends, but there was no mistaking the way that woman looked at Nick—she wanted him back in her life. And that was not something Amelia would allow.

Nick came at her, his intention to give her a kiss good-bye clear in his expression.

She shook her head. "You know where that will lead us?" She danced out of his reach.

"And I'll be in a foul mood if I can't taste you once more before I leave."

"Well, they say distance makes the heart grow fonder. Perhaps you should hurry to complete your errands and pick me up before tea with Victoria."

He tried once more to grab her, but she darted backward. "If I come home first, we won't be leaving again."

As tempting as that offer was, Victoria would find another way to see Nick if he didn't show up today. She shook her head and feigned a smile. "I'll meet you there at quarter to two."

He pointed at her. "I'll remember that you owe me a kiss."

"And I won't let you forget."

With a growl of frustration, he turned and strode from the room. Amelia took in a deep breath. She'd give Nick a half an hour to leave; then she'd hunt down Huxley.

Huxley, as it turned out, knew even less than Nick. Or at least he made it seem that way. He was notoriously mum on any sort of gossip about the people living in the house. And while Amelia thought they'd become friends of sorts, she was annoyed for the whole twenty minutes she'd attempted to question him. She finally gave up, knowing it was futile the moment he crossed his arms over his chest and stared back at her with an unamused expression.

"You're only making it more difficult for me to help you," she insisted.

"And why would we be needing your help, Miss Grant? It's man's business you're interfering with. And Mr. Riley isn't likely to be happy you're after so many answers I'm not able to give."

"It was your contact, Brian, watching my brother."

"What are you going on about now?"

"I want to speak with him."

Huxley laughed. It was her turn to cross her arms over her chest, and she glared at him until he looked at her straight on, not a remnant of a smile on his pockmarked face.

"I'm very serious about the matter, Huxley. And if you don't arrange for me to meet this young man, I'll have no choice but to pester you day in and day out. I know and understand my brother better than any of you. If he did the slightest thing that was unlike him, I'll know." She looked at her nails, letting that sink into Huxley's head.

Mrs. Coleman came into the room before Huxley could respond. "Your carriage is here, Miss Grant."

She gazed at the ormolu clock over the fireplace. She'd be early if she left now, which meant she could talk to Victoria prior to Nick's arrival. The timing was perfect.

"Will you at least think about it, Huxley?"

He gave her one succinct nod and held out her pelisse. "I will accompany you to the tea shop. When you're in Miss Victoria's company, I'll be off to take care of a few things."

As they walked out to the carriage, she asked, "Whatever happened to that wharfinger who was stealing wool?"

"That's what I need to take care of when I'm done with you."

"Mr. Riley doesn't want to be present for that?"

"He'll see him lashed, but he doesn't need to be there for the man's arrest."

Huxley opened the carriage door and gave her a hand up. When he rolled the stairs back up, she said, "I thought you were going to see me to the shop?"

"Oh, I will, miss. Just not in there where you can barrage a poor old man with endless questions."

She bit down on her lip to hold back her laugh. "Are you sure? It's awfully cold out."

"Never been surer." He shut the door and climbed up the side of the carriage to sit with the driver.

CHAPTER THIRTEEN

A melia was given a seat at a table by herself in a secondary room, separated from the rest of the patrons at Victoria's Tea Emporium—a room, it seemed, where Victoria conducted meetings that were more private in nature and where men were invited to join her. The young woman who oversaw the teahouse said she'd notify her mistress immediately of Amelia's early arrival. While the woman's demeanor was less than friendly, she'd at least had tea brought to the table while Amelia waited.

The teahouse was like a grand greenhouse without all the plants and flowers on display. The ceilings had to be twenty feet high, the vaulted white beams adding to the delicate way the room was laid out. There were thirty-odd tables, most filled with customers. Everything was white and cream in the decor. The only dash of color was in the orchids placed at the center of each round table and the potted palms at every pillar around the perimeter of the room.

The more lively addition of color was the massive red-and-yellow macaw caged near the entrance of the room that joined the teahouse to the department store. He whistled and purred, saying the odd silly thing that made patrons laugh.

A wall of windows that faced the street allowed patrons to watch the passers-by if they so wished. It was as grand a teahouse as she'd ever seen or been in.

She was saved from wondering if Victoria would delay her appearance until Nick arrived, when the very woman strolled into the room as if the world were at her fingertips and hadn't been really alive until she walked through it. Her dress was the most beautiful color Amelia had ever seen, a light blue that was an icy shade no less beautiful than an aquamarine. Her perfectly styled blonde hair was woven with pearl studs and pins, as though she was Venus fresh from the clamshell. There were so many frills and layers of lace that she looked like a Tissot painting come to life.

Amelia watched as Victoria stopped and talked to a few of the customers, laughing and chatting in a friendly way, before she arrived in the private room. They were closed off from the rest of the teahouse but surrounded in glass and white iron coated in gilt.

Amelia stood, flattening her hands nervously over her pink day dress, one that had been purchased from Victoria's department store and handpicked by this woman she disliked on principle alone. Amelia dipped her head in greeting. "Miss Newgate. A pleasure to see you again."

"Spare me your small talk, Miss Grant. It's unfortunate that we are in the position we are in at all."

"And what position is that?" She hadn't quite expected their meeting to start on a bad note. She'd hoped to at least come to like this woman, since Nick insisted he and she were friends and that status seemed unlikely to change. Not that they would start as friends; she only hoped to work her way up to that point…over a very lengthy time.

"The one where you're making a damnable effort to attract Nick and trap him in some sort of arrangement. I know your type, Miss Grant. You think your virginity is so precious and that offering it up will guarantee you a position as his wife. Nick is not the marrying type, and I dislike anyone taking advantage of the people I care about."

"That couldn't be further from the truth," Amelia said, her cheeks flaming with the assessment of her character, because she had indeed given her virginity to Nick but not to hold that over him and force him to stay with her.

When she didn't seem inclined to respond further, Victoria asked, "Speaking of the man of our lives, where is Nick?"

She wanted to correct her. Nick wasn't Victoria's anything. "He had last-minute errands and said he would meet us here."

"Typical."

"He's been incredibly busy."

Victoria held up her hand to call one of the women on staff over to their private booth. "Aren't we all? I'm not sure if you noticed when you were here last, but there's not a day that I don't have two hundred people through my store and another eighty at the teahouse. I specifically asked that Nick join me for tea to discuss some private business. Your being here changes that."

Amelia chose to ignore that last comment. "Then why did you ask Nick to come at all, if you're too busy to see a friend? You could have made arrangements to visit the house at any time."

"I don't object to spending time with him, Miss Grant. It's only your company I disdain."

"I have given you no reason to dislike me."

What could she say to this woman so she would at least tolerate her presence? While she wished she'd stayed home and badgered Huxley all afternoon, she knew that the woman sitting in front of her would use all of her wiles to tempt Nick. That wasn't to say Amelia didn't trust him, she just couldn't say the same about Victoria. Amelia had never known she could be jealous of anyone.

"Are you sure about that?" Victoria said as another tea serving arrived. Dishes of cake and finger sandwiches were set out between them.

As soon as the server closed the door, Amelia said, "If you're truly a friend of Nick's, you'll let him live his life exactly as he sees fit."

"I intend to, just as soon as I find a way to cut you out of the picture." Victoria's green cat-like eyes flashed in challenge.

Why did this woman care to thwart Amelia's very new and very *secret* relationship with Nick? "I'd advise against it." Amelia stood when she spotted Nick heading in their direction. He couldn't have come sooner and *too soon* at the same time. There were a lot of things she wanted to say to Victoria, and she wasn't sure she'd have another chance beyond today.

"I'm a determined woman, Miss Grant. And I have a tendency to get what I want."

"He broke off with you. Doesn't that tell you everything you need to know?"

"I didn't say I wanted him back in my bed. No, I've found another to fill that role, though he's not nearly as rough as our Nick can get."

Amelia felt her face flame. Not so much with embarrassment as with a rage unlike anything she'd ever felt in her entire life.

"I miss that about him," Victoria continued, as casually as though they were discussing the weather. "But I certainly don't want the likes of you sinking your teeth in and biting off more than you deserve."

"If you were really his friend, you wouldn't be saying any of this to me."

Victoria chuckled and turned just as Nick opened the door. Victoria practically threw herself at him, kissing both his cheeks in greeting as if she were French.

Amelia wanted to haul the woman away by her perfect hair and push her down in the seat farthest from where Nick pulled his chair out. Victoria took his choice as an opportunity to sit next to him. Amelia could do nothing; their relationship had to remain a secret. Though why she bothered when this woman seemed to know exactly what was going on...had Nick told Victoria about them?

"I thought you were coming alone, Nicky. To catch up on old times since we haven't seen each other for an age." Victoria pouted out her bottom lip and gave it a seductive lick before picking up an almond cookie and sucking it like she was sucking...

Amelia dropped her gaze and focused on the tea in front of her. She didn't think Victoria acted like that to draw Nick's attention but more to rile up Amelia. And she would not give Victoria the satisfaction of knowing just how much it affected her.

Taking a breath and raising her gaze only to Nick, Amelia smiled and said, "Victoria was just telling me how much she misses your company, but your schedules rarely allow you to spend time together."

That came out more jealous-sounding than she'd intended. The words couldn't be taken back, and she refused to apologize for her tone.

Nick sat back in his chair, narrowing his eyes in her direction, his question clear. She'd have to tell him that she and Victoria would never be friends, and it was unlikely they'd ever get on amicably. The one burning question she had for him was why he had to remain friends with his old lover at all. She understood that the woman was a friend of his sister's, but that didn't make him obligated to see her again.

"What was your purpose in wanting to see Nick, Miss Newgate?" Amelia asked. "If it was merely to pass an hour, I'd be more than happy to wander around the store and let you have some time alone." Amelia looked right at Nick, hoping he read her discomfort with this situation. That he would declare they needed to leave immediately and say he'd forgotten about a double-booked engagement—anything to get them out of here.

"So that's how it is," Nick said. His steely gaze locked on Victoria. "I thought I was here to discuss Hart's upcoming birthday celebration."

"You can't blame me for wanting to see you again. You haven't visited me in more than a month." The first thread of discomfort filtered into Victoria's thin excuse of an explanation. Amelia would have smiled, were she not seething with resentment.

"Victoria, for the last time, we are friends. Nothing more."

"I'm well aware of that. Don't be a ninny." Victoria leaned forward, showing off her ample décolletage in the square cutout of her dress as she touched his arm. Her hand lingered there.

Amelia pushed out her chair. The sound of the feet skidding across the wood floor broke Victoria and Nick's moment, and she hated that it had taken something external to separate them. She couldn't witness another second of whatever was going on between them. They had unfinished business they needed to sort out, and all she could do was leave them to it.

Nick tried to grab Amelia's hand as she stormed past, but she slipped out the door and through the teahouse. She didn't skulk in the carriage as she wanted to; instead, she made her way into the department store and wandered around to look at all the beautiful wares available for purchase. Not that she would buy anything. She just needed space from that woman.

Victoria and Nick had shared a moment, as if Amelia weren't sitting in the same room with them. That might have been her overactive imagination making her see things that weren't real, but the feeling of jealousy grew in the pit of her stomach and gnawed on her from the inside, making her feel ill.

While her intention in joining Nick for tea was to ensure Victoria didn't try to win Nick back, she knew, after his comment, that she had nothing to worry about. Or at least she hoped she didn't have anything to regret in leaving them alone.

"What in hell was that, Victoria?" Nick pushed out his chair, having every intention of following Amelia. She was hurt. He had seen that in her expression before he'd even sat down.

"Some women are unpredictable when their emotions are overwrought. She'll be well enough in time. I can send someone to follow her if you like."

"You have one minute to give me a good reason to stay."

"I'm trying to protect you." She reached out to touch his arm in that familiar way of hers.

He pulled back, looking at her hand as though it were a stinger. She was not at liberty to touch him. "Don't. You have never had a reason to protect me from anything. What is it *you*, of all people, can guard me from?"

"I see what she's doing to you." Victoria's eyes were clouded with genuine concern. She was one of the best actresses he knew. "I'm worried you'll fall into her carefully devised trap."

Nick wanted to laugh at the assessment. Nick was the one trying to trap Amelia, not the other way around. "And how do you think that's possible? As you said, I haven't seen you in well over a month, Victoria. And I will not allow Miss Grant to be trifled with."

Victoria fell back in her chair, a slight slouch hunching her shoulders forward. "I didn't want to believe it possible when we met at the Langtry for dinner."

"You'll have to be more specific than that."

"You've fallen in love with her. That's the only reason I can think why you've been avoiding me."

"We go back too far for me to lie to you about something like this, Vic. So the truth is, you're right. But if you think for one minute I'll let you interfere, you are sadly mistaken." He stood from the table, done with this conversation. Done with Victoria, if she didn't see the grave mistake she'd made today.

She wrapped her hand around his forearm. "Humor me, Nick. How long have we known each other?"

"A decade, give or take."

"And in that time, I have never known you to fall for any woman. Whoever this Miss Grant is, she's trouble."

Nick gave her a droll look. "You can't be serious."

"I am. I talked to Sera. She said you'd brought your new mistress around to the school."

Nick clenched his teeth so hard that his jaw cracked. "I'll be sure to correct her."

Victoria nibbled on her lip and batted her lashes. She knew better than to try that kind of tactic on him. He crossed his arms over his chest, eager to leave but needing to know what his sister had said so he could correct her assumptions immediately.

"She might not have put it that way exactly."

"Victoria, my patience is running thin…"

"I let her know that I had met your lady friend."

"Let us get one thing straight. Amelia is not a *lady friend*. And you will treat her with the respect she deserves."

"You've lost your head with her." Victoria's voice was slowly rising; her frustration in this argument was not endearing Nick to her cause.

"I know precisely where my head is. The only thing you risk is cutting off our friendship if you insist on treating her poorly."

"We had a conversation, nothing more."

"Don't come around, Victoria. Don't send notes. Don't talk to me until you can apologize to Amelia."

"That's not fair."

"Life generally isn't. Though that's not something I should need to remind you."

He left her standing in the middle of her private room. Eyes were focused on their glass enclosure, and while patrons likely hadn't heard their exchange, they would be well aware that there was a new rift between them. Something for the gossip columns.

Nick stopped at the front counter. "In which direction did the woman wearing the blush-pink dress head?"

"Through the shop, sir."

He headed into the department store, not sure where Amelia would have gone. If she was merely browsing the counters, he'd find her eventually. Surely she wouldn't leave without him. Ladies' Wear was on the third floor, so he'd check there last, as men weren't supposed to be up there. The first floor was antiquities, porcelain, and silver. The second floor was jewelry. He found her walking between two rows of glass cases, with a salesman two steps behind, should she need assistance.

All Nick knew was that he was happy to have found her. Victoria didn't know the danger Amelia was in, so he couldn't blame her completely for the episode that drove Amelia away. But he was happy to see her safe.

Nick nodded the salesman over. He came quickly, Amelia was not even aware she'd been followed around. "I'll signal to you if the lady wants anything."

The man was younger than he originally thought, maybe eighteen. His face still had spots. "Yes, sir," he said enthusiastically.

Nick walked between the rows of glass cases and made his way to Amelia's side. She paused over a series of lockets—gold, silver, a plethora at her fingertips.

"Do you see something you like?"

She jumped, her shoulders hitting his chest as she let out a small squeal of surprise. She pressed her hand to her chest and inhaled deeply. "Nick. You scared the devil out of me."

He caged his arms around her and leaned close enough that he could talk quietly in her ear. Their conversation was for them alone. People could assume what they wanted with his blatant fawning; he didn't care. There was one thing of which Nick was sure: Amelia was his. And everyone in this shop would see and know that. And anything that was his was not to be trifled with.

"Not my intention to scare you."

"What are you doing up here?"

"Apologizing." Nick ran his fingers over the glass display case mere inches from her hand. He wanted to take it up and press a kiss to the inside of her wrist, but the shop was too busy for such an open display of intimacy. "Perhaps a gift is in order."

Amelia ducked her head, shaking it. "No," she said, so quietly he almost didn't catch it.

"Why not?"

"I was only reminiscing." She pointed to a rather plain silver locket in the case with minimal detail stamped in the face. "This one reminded me of one I once had."

"Ah. Did you have something you wanted to put in the locket? I'm happy to make the purchase."

Her white-gloved fingers trailed a seductive path along the edge of the case. "The day we met, mine was stolen, along with my money. I never cared about the money; it wasn't rightfully mine, but the locket was a gift from my parents. I wasn't wearing it because the chain was broken."

"Then let me buy you another. It's the least I can do after Victoria's abhorrent behavior."

She turned her cheek enough to show him her faint smile of appreciation. "It's not the locket that held value but what lay inside. And your friend Victoria is a topic for another time...when there are fewer ears present, I think."

"I can agree to that for now." Nick motioned to the room around them. Jewels, hairpieces, even diadems filled every case. "I want you to pick something else. Anything."

"That's kind of you, but no thank you. I was passing the time in here, waiting for your meeting with Victoria to end. I don't need anything."

"Humor me."

She blushed a pretty shade of pink. "It's too much, Nick. Buying me a present now will prove your friend right."

"I don't care what Victoria thinks."

She pinched her mouth on a smile. "Please, let's go if you're finished."

"I'll cede this once, but only because *I'm* embarrassed by the way Victoria treated you."

Amelia would be lying if she said she wasn't feeling a little defeated by the events of the afternoon. The only thing that made her feel better was that Nick had followed her shortly after she'd departed the teahouse. It might be petty, but it proved that Nick cared more about her than Victoria in that particular instance.

Then there was the guilt she felt. She'd been the cause of their rift. She'd been the one to let Victoria pick a fight with her when Amelia had ample time to fix the direction of their conversation.

Nick had dropped her off at the house and come in long enough to give her a kiss good-bye and apologize once again for his friend's cruel treatment. The second Huxley had arrived, Nick had left for what remained of the afternoon. Amelia wasn't sure where he'd gone, as he had only one appointment in his book, at four, but that was neither here nor there; she had a lot of paperwork she needed to sort through and that would be difficult with Nick hovering over her shoulder.

He came home just as she was closing the study door. Huxley was talking to him, so she remained straight-faced and aloof, as though she hadn't been waiting to see Nick all evening.

They both looked up when the door clicked shut behind her. "Would you like me to open up the study again?" she asked. "I just turned down all the lighting for the night."

"I have some letters to send out before I retire," Nick said.

She ducked her head for the benefit of Huxley, who was still standing there, and backed into the study to turn on the lamps and light the candles.

"It's nearly ten," Nick said as he stepped into the room and shut the door behind him. "I thought you would be in bed by the time I was home."

"I wanted to wait for your return. I had to tell you that I was partially to blame for the disastrous tea with Miss Newgate this afternoon." When he opened his mouth to dispute that, she put up her hand. "Let me finish before you tell me

I had nothing to do with it. I did. The reason I agreed to go with you today was because I hate that you're friends with her, Nick. It eats me up inside, knowing that she had you first, she knew you first. And I was afraid she'd try to tempt you back into her bed."

The last bit she sort of mumbled through because it was difficult to admit that out loud—no matter how many times she'd gone over this speech in her head. "That woman being a part of your life is the only thing that has ever struck a jealous chord in me, Nick. I could have been the better person today and turned the conversation around, but I chose to pick at her comments. *I* was part of the problem and cause in escalating the sour note you came in on. That's not to say I leave her blameless; she has plenty to be blamed for."

Nick cupped her cheek and gave her one of his rare smiles. "I don't expect you to get along with her, Amelia. But Victoria and I go back too far for me to cut her completely out of my life. The one thing that I can promise you, however, is that I'll never find my way back to her bed, nor she mine."

Hearing him say that eased a lot of her troubles.

"And I don't know how we'll work it out going forward, but eventually, I promise to try. Everything is too new between us for you to ask that of me right now. So please give me time to adjust to her. And here…" Amelia held out a linen envelope. "It arrived a few hours ago."

As tempting as it was to burn whatever contents were inside, she knew it was Victoria apologizing for her own bad behavior this afternoon.

He took it and set it on his desk. A small part of her wondered if he wanted to hide whatever contents were contained within the pages of that letter. But the much bigger part of her was saying that he put it down because right now was about them.

"Am I forgiven?" she asked, turning her cheek into his palm and stepping close enough that their bodies brushed ever so lightly from breast and chest and stomach to hip.

Nick's hand wrapped around her waist, and he maneuvered them toward his desk. "I don't know. What do you think would make a good peace offering for all the trouble you've caused today?"

There was a teasing quality to his voice that had her smiling, though she tried to keep her expression serious and play along.

"You didn't lock the door," she pointed out.

"I'm aware. How about we live dangerously tonight?"

She raised one eyebrow at that. "I see. And how does living dangerously look?"

He hitched her up on the edge of his desk and hiked her skirts out of the way so her stockings were visible all the way up to the garter. He bent over her, saying, "Something like this."

Opening the slit in her drawers, his hands slid under her buttocks to tilt her pelvis up so he could lick the seam of her sex. After a swipe that had her cream flowing liberally, he blew a stream of air over her. Amelia fell back on her elbows, spreading her legs wider, wanting to pull his head closer.

Books, paper, and pencils jabbed into her buttocks, as did the bustle fastened around her waist, but she didn't have the wherewithal to concentrate on anything aside from Nick's tongue lashing out and tasting between the folds of her labia, over and over again.

He sucked at her clitoris, flicking his tongue around the swollen nub and making her cry out. Her hands tangled in his hair and pulled him in tight to her body, where he continued the onslaught of pleasure with his tongue. When she started to thrash, her body desperate to be closer to him, to feel him harder against her, he came over her, shoving his trousers down his hips.

His cock sprang out and rubbed along the wet folds of her sex. He rubbed the head of it around her clitoris. "Do you like that?"

She bit her lip to keep her noises to a minimum but nodded heartily. "Kiss me," she cried out. She needed his mouth on her, to smother the sounds she couldn't keep from making when he tortured her with pleasure.

He pushed the head of his rod inside her and nothing more. He wanted her to beg, and she wasn't above doing just that.

"Please," she cried, louder this time, a breathless noise building in her chest as she tilted her hips, trying to lodge him in deeper. "I need you to kiss me."

One of his elbows came down beside her shoulder, his weight finally crushing her just right. "How about here?" he asked, biting her chin and licking a seductive line across her jaw.

She shook her head and placed the arches of her feet on the edge of the desk, forcing him deeper still. The sounds that passed her lips grew in volume. Lost in them, she was less worried about being heard. "Kiss my mouth. Let me taste myself on your tongue."

He gave her exactly that. His tongue was like a weapon all its own as he lashed it against hers, giving her that musky taste. When she sucked on his tongue, he gave her the rest of himself, battering into her sheath with a need so great that the huge mahogany desk groaned beneath them.

His thrusts were shallow, and his hips gyrated and twisted until the folds of her sex were opened up like a flower, the bud abraded by the coarseness of the hair at the base of his manhood.

They kissed so deeply that their teeth hit, and his beard scraped against her face, burning her skin as it rubbed harder and harder over her, his tongue mimicking the motions of his cock.

Impatiently, he ripped at the buttons on her bodice, trying to open the front to get to her breasts. But their bodies moved too frantically together for him to concentrate on doing more than pop a few of them off, making them clink against the floor as they rolled away.

The corner of a book jabbed her in the head, and Amelia pushed it out of the way, making it fall to the floor with a loud thud. Her legs were wrapped around his hips, holding him as close as she could in their clothed state.

Threading her hands through his hair, she held his head, kneading her fingers into his scalp with every sweep of his tongue against hers. She would never get enough of this man. Every forbidden taste didn't sate the craving she had for him; every touch made her burn for more.

That tingling awareness in her nether region started with a pulse in her clitoris and moved through her veins like water through roots, building and building until her whole body let go. When her orgasm hit, a rush of wetness came out of her, soaking them both and making slick, wet noises as Nick tore his mouth from hers and fucked her so hard and furiously that he shouted when he came a moment after her.

His seed added to the slickness between her thighs, making her feel as though she'd...urinated on herself. On him. Oh, good Lord. What had she just done?

She tried to push him away, ashamed and mortified. His lazy, sated gaze was focused on her face; the grin he wore was half cocky, half victorious.

"Nick, please, get off." Her face was flaming and her ears were hot.

"I know you especially enjoyed that, so why are you shy all of a sudden."

"The door is unlocked." It was the only excuse she could come up with fast.

"That didn't bother you a minute ago."

He flexed his hips forward, lodging his penis deeper inside her, despite his hardness having diminished slightly.

She cringed to hear the squish of wetness between them. "We have to clean up."

Nick wrapped his hand around her throat, rubbing his thumb along one side. "You have no reason to be embarrassed, Amelia."

"I...something..." Something had come out of her that shouldn't have. And she couldn't say it, put words to it. It was that devastatingly humiliating. "Fine, I'm embarrassed. Now, will you get off me so that I might clean up?"

He pressed a rather chaste kiss against her mouth and got off her. The grin on his face was starting to irritate her. And it didn't leave his face once as he righted his clothing, though they were rumpled, and it would be obvious they'd been up to something.

"What has you so…jovial," she asked as she took his arm so he could assist her off the desk.

As she stood, she was suddenly aware that her drawers were soaked. Wetness covered her core, her inner thighs, even the bottom of her buttocks and anus. The faster she escaped him, the faster she could clean up.

Nick apparently had other ideas in mind, because he came at her, caught her up in his arms, and headed for the door. She fought to get down. "You can't be serious. Everyone in the household is still awake."

"They won't bother us."

"Nick," she admonished, "you have to put me down."

He was nearing the door. She could fight to get out of his hold, but then they'd likely both end up on the floor.

"I already admitted that I am embarrassed, and your hauling me out of here like some barbarian crusader is not helping matters. I seemed to have had…" An issue? How did one describe a bodily function delicately?

"I'll make you do it again," he said as he hitched her up higher in his arms and pulled down the door handle. "In fact, it's my mission tonight. I will conquer your body so thoroughly that my whole bed will be soaked with your juices."

"What in the world are you talking about?"

He grinned. "Shush now. You don't want to draw anyone's attention to us as I steal you off to my bedroom like a Viking marauder."

She pinched her lips tight. It was no use arguing with him once the door flung open without a care of its hitting the wall it flew against. She inwardly cringed. Thankfully, not one member of the household was to be found.

When they were in Nick's room, he set her down just inside the door. "I'll draw you a bath."

She could do no more than look at him wide-eyed, feeling heat crawl up her whole body.

He leaned in and pressed a kiss to her lips. "You're thinking right now that you pissed while I fucked you."

His words did nothing to calm her, and she felt herself panicking. Her breath pushed in and out of her lungs so rapidly that she suddenly felt…faint. Nick backed her up against the door. "Far from it, love. You gave me a gift instead. A different kind of orgasm. I intend to repeat that performance, or die trying. So a bath is in order, because there will be no sleep until I accomplish my new mission."

Thankfully, there was no repeat of the episode that had happened in the study. But that didn't stop Nick from trying repeatedly to replicate the outcome.

They didn't sleep. Maybe an hour between bouts of lovemaking, but other than that, eight in the morning came too soon for both of them.

Amelia felt better about where she stood with Nick going forward, but everything could still go to hell before they could make something of their newfound appreciation and honesty with each other. And that scared her more than anything.

CHAPTER FOURTEEN

Amelia had opted to go with Nick to gaol. He was to bear witness to the punishment of the wharfinger for stealing from him, something he'd agreed to do instead of a public lashing that would ruin the man's future prospects of finding work, should he be recognized.

She wasn't sure what to expect; she'd never been inside a prison. But she wanted to be there with Nick to gather a better understanding of what he faced when someone tried to profit on the side and steal from him when he was a generous employer. He'd told her she couldn't go a hundred times, but she'd finally worn him down and made him change his mind. She had to take the good with the bad, she'd told him. And she wanted to understand some of the uglier side of his business. See firsthand what he had to deal with.

Huxley hadn't been thrilled about her attending either. He had told her it was no place for a woman, which was typical of Huxley. When she'd pointed out that she had visited the city's dead house to identify her brother's body, they'd lost the argument, and it had been the end of the conversation. Though she couldn't say she was a victor in this.

She did have an ulterior motive for coming. Nick told her his past was too dark to reveal the truth about his scars. What better way to understand what he'd gone through than to watch the details of today unfold. If she could do that without flinching, how could Nick continue to hold himself back from her?

That she thought the prison yard would be a sight better than the dead house was the only shock she got on arriving.

The surgeon of the prison discussed sentencing with Nick and Huxley for the wharfinger's crime. Amelia sat on a bench on the inside of a tall stone wall, looking around her. The place was abysmal and gray, almost as lifeless as the dead house had been.

She couldn't hear what Nick said to the surgeon, but she sat a stone's throw from the man who had stolen a good percentage of the profits for the past four years. It was a place where the public would sit to witness lashings. The man accused of the crime was filthy—though in a cleaner state than the rest of the prison. His shirt was untucked and smeared with dirt, his hands shackled and chained to the wall. He was older, in his midfifties by her estimation. He had a gray beard and balding head. His eyes were dull and empty.

She wondered if this was the sight of a man who had given up. A man who had nothing left to live for. She couldn't help the twinge of sympathy she felt for him.

He called out to her. "Psst."

She focused on his brown eyes, ready to listen—she knew not why—to what he had to say. All she knew about this man was that he had a problem with gin and whores and didn't seem to have any family to support.

"Ne'er be seein' you 'round here 'fore."

Should she answer? She could politely ignore the man, but seeing as he was in line for a lot of painful lashings, she said, "You've committed a grave crime, sir."

"Mebel. Theys calls me. Mebel, miz." He smiled, showing her why his accent was hard to make out…at least half his teeth were missing, the rest rotting in his mouth.

"So why did you do it, Mebel? Hasn't Mr. Riley treated you well and given you a fair wage for the work you do?"

"Don't know no other way. Lost me wife eight years past, me child not long after. Thought it was easier an' all."

"You could have talked to Huxley. He might have helped."

"Didn't want no help. I'd done too many wrongs by then."

"What do you think your punishment will be?"

"Lashings is what I'm set for. They whip thieves here. Make sure they're too broken to be bothered doin' much but get lost in drink to dull the pain afterwards."

"You said you lost your wife?" Amelia felt something crack inside her. She couldn't help it; he was genuine, and there was no lie to his words, though she could be mistaken in her assessment.

"I did. Was in a workhouse. Didn't see her much, as men weren't allowed. Conditions were poor for living, and she got herself sick. Consumption is what the doc told me; daughter followed her to the grave a week later."

And that was when her heart did break for this man she didn't know. Despite the wrongdoings, he was nothing more than a lost soul.

Nick came over before she could say more to the wharfinger. She stood as Nick drew near, placing a hand on his arm. "What will happen to Mebel?"

"I saw you talking to him, Amelia. You can't be so forgiving of his crimes after talking to him for even a few minutes."

"Did you know his wife died?"

"I did. He worked his way up from warehouse laborer to wharfinger. Don't think I haven't given him the opportunity to fix his circumstance. He went behind my back and stole product from my inventory to feed his addictions. I might have looked the other way, had his intentions been noble. But they weren't. He's a criminal and unlikely to change his ways."

Amelia turned away from both men and gulped in a steady breath of air, hoping for fortitude for what she'd agreed to witness. She didn't want to give Nick any reason to regret allowing her to attend.

"I didn't want to bring you here," he reminded her, "but you insisted. You also promised not to interfere."

"I'm not meaning to interfere." His words seemed to give her enough strength to stand taller and face his steady gaze with her own. "What will his punishment be?"

"Forty lashes."

Her breath audibly caught. "He won't survive it. You can't possible agree to that."

"It's the surgeon's suggestion."

"Well, make another. You don't need this man's death on your hands. Surely you have contacts here as you do with the bobbies. Won't someone take another suggestion? Can't you at least spare his life?"

Nick squeezed her arm before leaving her to join the surgeon and Huxley again. They talked for another ten minutes before he was at her side again, taking her arm and letting her lean against him.

"Ten lashings," was all he said to her. "He'll be shipped to Australia next week to live out the remainder of his life."

"I thought they stopped sending convicts over..." But who was she to argue? It was better than the first choice of punishment.

"Only officially."

"Thank you. You have a heart of gold."

"You won't want to thank me after the lashings. I need to stay to witness the punishment. Huxley can take you back to the carriage if you've seen enough."

"No, I will stay."

"The surgeon doesn't want you here, Amelia. Women don't generally witness such things—sometimes the wives of the convicts but no one else."

"Then tell him I'm not just any woman. I won't leave, Nick."

He nodded succinctly in agreement and signaled to the surgeon that he was ready.

She just hoped she hadn't made the wrong choice. Nick had been lashed when he was only eleven, and there were far more than ten scars etched into his back. She wanted to know just how bad it had been for him. And while witnessing someone else's pain seemed intrusive, she felt it was the only way to understand Nick, as he didn't want to talk about what had happened to him.

The lashings were far worse than she could ever have imagined. The blood, the pain, the curdling scream Mebel let out by the time the fourth lash hit his back. Her stomach roiled with each draw of blood. There was so much blood. It ran in a stream and covered the man's trousers and the gray stones beneath him.

At one point—maybe by the sixth lash—she turned around and threw up on the cobblestone. Nick placed his hand at the base of her back and rubbed it in small circles. He didn't say anything, nor did Huxley, though a dark look came to Nick's eyes, and she could tell he wanted her gone from there. She wasn't sure how she watched the rest of it unfold and thought maybe at one point that Nick had put his hand around her waist to keep her upright.

That had happened to Nick. Some man who had wanted to feel superior had done that to Nick when he was only a boy.

As they left gaol, Nick took her hand in his and stopped in front of the carriage. "I'm sorry. I should have insisted you leave or at least have taken you out of there at the first sign of sickness."

She shook her head. "I needed to see what it was like." She closed her eyes, wishing the lash of a whip on skin didn't look so…awful. There really was no other word for it. She would never be able to scrub that image from her mind. And while she might not picture Mebel, she did picture a younger version of Nick, suffering through that same cruelty.

"Perhaps you'll be able to clear your head when we are in Highgate."

They were set to leave in two days. She nodded, though she wasn't sure anything could clear her head of those images. "Will he be all right?"

"He will. A doctor will tend to his wounds before he's shipped off."

"Did you arrange that for my benefit?" She was talking about the doctor, because one hadn't been standing by when they were in there.

"In a sense."

"I would have preferred you'd done it for you."

"I did it for us, Amelia. I did it because I saw your heart breaking the longer you talked with him. I did it because I was stupid enough to agree with your being here today. This isn't a place for women."

"Women are whipped with the same regularity."

"Not women like you." He opened the carriage door. "This isn't up for debate. Just know that Mebel will live out the rest of his days—short or long; it's up to him at this point."

"Thank you." Amelia looked around them. There were too many present for her to kiss him as she wanted to do, so she climbed into the carriage and tried not to picture Nick, bloody and broken, in chains and unable to help himself.

Nick studied her carefully. "Tell me why you wanted to be here."

"To understand." Perhaps she should have lied, but the truth felt right.

"I need you to be more specific."

"You won't talk about it. You won't tell me what would make a grown man lash out at a child."

"You cannot compare the two."

"Yes. I can. Are you going to deny that you didn't go through something similar?"

"No. But I was young, and I was strong. I healed fast enough."

"It doesn't excuse the behavior of an adult taking a lash to you. There is no reason good enough to do that to a child."

Nick pulled her close, tipping her head down so he could kiss the top. "Everything you do makes me love you more."

"And I you. I just hope nothing gets in the way of our happiness."

"I'll keep you safe, Amelia."

But could he? Shauley was still a threat, and the inspector who had practically interrogated her hadn't shown himself in days.

They would be leaving for Highgate soon, and Nick hadn't been able to find Inspector Laurie. When Nick had shown up at the constabulary headquarters, he'd been told that Inspector Laurie hadn't been seen in days. Not since the day he'd last been at Nick's house. Nick chose not to reveal that tidbit.

"Nick," Hart said as he came through the study door.

Nick stood hastily, shutting the door behind his friend. They would have a few minutes alone before Amelia came up from luncheon. And he didn't want her hearing this conversation.

"What has you dithering like an old maid?" Hart asked as he took a seat in one of the leather chairs.

Nick sat across from him. "Word got back to me that Shauley was to be arrested for indecency and sodomy."

"You knew how to play that one." Hart laughed a little, though the sound held no humor. "Bastard was caught with his pants down."

"He's disappeared. Along with the inspector who accused me of murdering Amelia's brother."

"The two are obviously working together."

"I made that conclusion already," Nick snapped. He rubbed at his eyes, hating that he had no control over either man.

Hart's usually carefree expression was wiped from his face as he leaned forward in the chair, elbows on his knees. "Then how can I help you?"

"I'm leaving for Highgate tomorrow. I need the bastards flushed out from whatever hole they're hiding in."

"I'm not sure I can promise that."

"Hart, you run half this town. I don't trust anyone else with this."

"Huxley?"

Nick shook his head. "He's watching my sister's house until she joins us in Highgate at the end of the week."

"I can put extra eyes on her."

Nick nodded, grateful to his friend. Before they could discuss the issues further, the latch turned on the study door, and Amelia entered, hesitating when she realized Nick had company.

"And the most beautiful woman in the world couldn't have arrived at a better time." Hart stood and walked toward Amelia. He took her hand and kissed it with an exaggerated flourish. "You are looking lovely as usual, Miss Grant."

Amelia blushed. "Good afternoon, Hart. Can I have tea brought up?"

"No. I just came from lunch nearby. I had a few minutes, so thought I'd stop in for a quick visit. I have to be heading out or I'll miss my next appointment."

"I'm sorry to have missed your company," Amelia said with a sweet smile that Nick wished was reserved solely for him.

He got up from his chair and walked Hart out.

"I'll write of any developments while you're in Highgate," Hart promised.

"Just keep those extra eyes on Sera."

"It's done. We'll talk when you're back." Hart put his hat on and skipped down the front stairs of Nick's townhouse, whistling a ditty as he went.

Nick rubbed at his eyes again. Something felt wrong about the situation unfolding. That he had no control only angered him more than the thought of Shauley and Laurie wandering freely when both needed to be questioned about their involvement with Lord Berwick. He wished he were so lucky that they'd disappear, now that their plan to frame him for Lord Berwick's murder had failed. This wasn't something he would discuss with Amelia, as he didn't want to unnecessarily worry her. He might not be a praying man, but he'd pray that nothing happened to Amelia by keeping her in the dark on this. He couldn't think of one good reason to enlighten her to the recent developments that would only worry her. And Highgate was a chance to escape the city and enjoy some time alone with each other.

CHAPTER FIFTEEN

Highgate. They'd finally arrived. It was too far into the fall months to call it a nice country visit. Amelia breathed in the clean air. The grass was dull and faded and whipping around fiercely in the bitterly cold wind that seemed to have arrived the moment they'd left the townhouse. The road was long and narrow and the trees sparse, but the farther they rode out of the city, the denser the trees became.

They were just far enough from the city that the stench of coal didn't weigh down the air. It was refreshing to breath in country air again. She hadn't been outside of London since the summer months, and that felt like an age ago. They headed straight to the manor house, since the inn wasn't expecting them for another two hours.

"It's lovely here, Nick. Though I can't say the same for the house." An ominous monstrosity stared back at them as they stood in the front drive. "Are you sure this is suitable for a school?"

Now that she'd seen it, she was skeptical. Nick let out one of his rare laughs. Come to think of it, his laughs were not so rare these days. At least not when he was spending time in her company.

"It'll do. Let me take you through; maybe I can change your mind. It's rather charming on the inside."

Nick took her hand and led her up the graveled path lined with tall grasses and weeds. There was a fountain in the center of the drive, long dried and holding nothing more than dirt.

To say the house was in a state of disrepair was an understatement. The stone was weather-worn and dimpled, and many of the windows were cracked or missing in too many places to begin counting on the first and second levels, though the dormers on the third level appeared to be in decent shape. The sloped roof didn't look to be keeping the rain out, and the building leaned a little to one side and looked as though a strong gale might cause it to tip over.

Thick vines of ivy raced along the wall on the east side, all the way up to the turreted top, where the parapet was collapsed in on one side. The ivy claimed the building in a wildness that matched the unkempt grounds. There was an addition off one side that looked like it might be in a better state of standing than the rest of the house.

The steps flanking the front entrance were pitted and cracked enough that Amelia had to watch her footing so her heels didn't get caught. There was a lock on the outside of the big wooden doors, which looked like they could keep out an army.

Nick pulled a key from his pocket and stuck it in the padlock. "Good thing I brought this along. I don't think we'll want to leave the house open for travelers when we aren't here."

"Is it safe to go inside?" Her question was skeptical. Safe was a relative term, considering the house looked like it might fall at any time.

"Safe enough. Don't worry. I was here a few months back when Lord Murray showed interest in selling. The floors squeak more than they should, the plaster is peeling from the walls, but there were no structural issues."

"That's not reassuring." She looked up at the house. At one time it had been grand and beautiful, and she imagined it had hosted the most beautiful balls and soirées. That time seemed long gone. "I can see why he wanted rid of this property. No one could possibly live here with the state it's in."

"His lordship closed up this house fifteen years ago. I think he ran out of funds to keep it running and to do repairs as they came up. Easier to lock it up and forget about it than pay servants you can't afford to keep on."

The door creaked open, the sound portentous as dead air washed over them. Amelia actually held her breath for the count of five before pulling out a handkerchief to cover her nose. "I'm beginning to think you've paid too much for it. I've seen the drawings and plans, but I just don't see how you'll save this place."

"You need just a little faith. I have one of the best architects lined up to take the job."

They stepped into the foyer, and Amelia tightened her hand around his, telling herself that she didn't do it because she was afraid…well, maybe a smidgen, but that fear stemmed more for their safety than having something jump out at them. Nick let her go to retrieve a lamp hanging on the wall. He pulled out a match from his pocket to light it. He'd come prepared.

The soft glow had shadows dancing on the high vaulted ceiling. Amelia tilted her head back to look at the architecture. It was beautiful. No other word could describe the sight that met her eyes. There was a painting up there, but she couldn't quite make out the finer details. It looked like a frieze of angels dancing through the air. Something black fell from the ceiling and swooped toward her face. She ducked with a scream, her hands covering her head.

"It's just bats," Nick said. "We were liable to find something." He pulled her to his side again, tucking her close as he swatted at another little black beast flying toward them. He swung the lamp around in an arch, and the winged creatures flew out the front door and into the daylight. Amelia's heart raced, and she felt like they were in a gothic novel, about to find danger around every corner.

"I've never been the fainting type, but this changes everything," Amelia admitted, her voice shaky.

Nick chuckled. "Don't faint on me yet. If I drop this lamp, the place is likely to go up like a box of kindling."

She pushed at his shoulder as she stood, keeping her head down just in case. "That's not funny."

"Only the truth. Now, are you ready to explore?"

In a smaller voice, she asked, "How many more bats do you think we're likely to see?"

"This is the tallest point of the house. We'll be safer on the second floor."

With a groan, she walked farther inside and kept her head ducked in case the flying rats took another dive at them. She never quite let go of Nick's sleeve as she headed toward the stairs. It was just one set that swept up and around in a spiral to the second level, which was shut off by a series of doors.

Placing her hand on the intricate wood balustrade, she pulled away before she made it up two steps; it was covered in a heavy layer of dust and grime. She tried to wipe it off her hand but made a mess of her gloves, so she ignored it and took Nick's arm to keep her balance.

"Why would anyone let such a beautiful house lay in waste?"

"Money. It always comes back to money."

"That makes it all the more sad. He should have sold it sooner."

"I think he was hopeful that his financial situation would improve with time. This house has a better purpose than a private home for Lord Murray. One that will be for the betterment of the community."

She laughed at that; she couldn't help herself. "I don't think they'll see it that way, for some reason."

"Probably not, but I have you at my side to help convince any disconcerted resident. Lady Burley is also a marvel. You two will set the town to rights, with my sister advocating for the education of children who need a good place to learn."

"You're so sure of our ability when we haven't met any of the townsfolk."

He pulled her into his arms, one of his hands holding the lamp aloft so they could see each other clearly. "I am. Are you ready to venture upstairs? Shall we see what we will find behind the first door?"

She smiled at him, though she wasn't sure he could see her in the shadows the lamp cast around them, so she squeezed his arm. "Yes, but I think it wise to shine the light ahead of us first…to ensure there aren't any more surprises. I'm trusting you completely with my safely, as I'm not sure about the durability of these floors."

Nick jumped on the spot and laughed when she let out a squeal and held on to him tighter. Creatures stirred in the rafters of the great room, and somewhere deep in the house, something moved about as though it had been awaken from a long slumber.

Amelia was terrified that they would run into some other type of vermin. "You're absolutely diabolical. I'll not step another foot into this house if you do that again."

His expression suddenly turned serious. "You have my word, Miss Grant. I'll be a perfect gentleman." He held out his arm, as though they were set to stroll a garden path.

"Come on," she said pulling him up the stairs after her; really, she was anxious to be away from whatever moved beneath the floors. And she certainly didn't want to be here when night fell. Call her superstitious from her country upbringing, but bats in the house were not something she was willing to face when the sun went down.

She nearly tripped on the last few steps, but Nick caught her around the waist and lifted her the rest of the way up. She took the second door, because it seemed silly to choose the first for some reason.

Throwing it open, they found a grand sitting room. White sheets were draped over a Spartan amount of furniture, all pushed against the walls.

She pulled away from Nick and walked toward the center. The ceiling was painted in gold leaf, and the walls were a faint blue, like a robin's egg that she'd once seen in an encyclopedia. Where paintings once hung on the walls there was a notable difference in the brightness of paint beneath, untouched from sunlight.

"This room is absolutely massive." She spun around, studying it like she was on the dance floor in a grand ballroom. "It will be a great hall for assemblies."

Heavy curtains were drawn against the windows to keep out the exterior temperature and light, making the air stagnant. She pulled one blue velvet curtain back to let in the dreary day so she could get a better view of their surroundings and promptly coughed as dust flew up around her. She waved it away from her nose and turned from the window.

"I probably should leave things as they are." Cracking her eyes open, she saw the way Nick stared at her, and she blushed. That look was a mixture of amusement and ten kinds of naughty, all covered up in a delicious package she wanted to unwrap and indulge in all day long.

She frowned at that thought. That was the last thing that should be on her mind as they toured the dusty old manor and discussed future plans of the property.

"What do you find so amusing?" she asked.

"You." He was walking toward her. There really wasn't anywhere to go, so he backed her up against the wall. The plaster crunched under her as she pressed her shoulders against it.

"Nick." She put her hand out, stopping him from coming even an inch closer. "We can't do this here."

"Why not? There's no one but the two of us. And the sight of you has me starved for a taste."

Amelia's eyes widened. "That doesn't make it right."

His hand was hard and thorough as it rubbed over one of her bound breasts and then the other. "If I take down a few of these buttons"—he traced the ones that marched up the center of her bodice—"and lift up your skirts enough that you can wrap your legs around my waist…there's no one to hear us for miles."

She flattened her hands against his chest. She intended to push him away, but the hard ridges of muscle begged to be traced.

"We can't," she said, but her words belied her actions.

"We can." His hand pressed hers over his pectoral, and she could feel his heart pounding heavily beneath her touch. "Let our first impression of this place be a good one. There are a lot of memories for me here that I prefer to bury."

"What do you mean?"

"Buying this place was only the first step in cleansing my past. And what better way to wipe the slate clean than to bury myself in you until we are so mad with lust that every time we cross the threshold of this house, it's this moment we remember."

It was hard to argue his point. Tracing her hand over his jaw, she bit her tongue in asking what those bad memories were. It wasn't the time or place to ask for that kind of confession when he was giving her so much, just telling her that. She stored the information away for later, when they were at the inn.

"And what of the driver waiting for us outside?" she asked.

"I'll swallow your cries before they reach his ears. Though I don't think he'll hear a sound with the wind stirring the trees outside." It seemed he didn't need to convince her because he was already pressing his groin against hers, mimicking motions they'd make if there weren't clothes hindering them.

Amelia's breath hitched and caught as he proceeded to release the buttons on her bodice. She didn't stop him. And admittedly, she didn't want to.

Nick carefully regarded her expression the whole time. His fingers dipped between her bare skin and the corset so he could pinch and roll her nipples one at a time. Her eyes fell closed, and her mouth parted as a breath hurried out of her in a rush. Her head fell back against the wall. She was sure bits of plaster stuck in her hat, but she was past caring.

The only thing that mattered was standing in front of her, and he was desperate to fill that aching spot between her legs. Who was she to argue with that?

"I crave you constantly," she murmured. She sucked in her bottom lip, biting it. Wishing he was the one nipping her.

"And I you. I get a raging cockstand in the most inconvenient places."

She giggled. And then covered her mouth with her gloved hand. She had never giggled in her whole life.

"That's a sound I want to hear again."

"It's outrageous and something reserved for young women. I hardly fit either of those descriptions."

"It makes my cock twitch."

A wordless sound passed her lips as his head lowered, and he open-mouth kissed the top mounds of her breasts. Her nipples ached for the suction of his mouth, but her breasts were impossible to free in this dress.

"Should we wait to do this on our return to the inn? I'm sure they can prepare our room earlier than we requested."

He hiked up her skirts and stared her right in the eye. "Definitely not. I'll have my fill of you before we leave this room."

A second after that declaration, he dropped to his knees and disappeared beneath her voluminous skirts. His hands were rough as he pushed her knees apart and his mouth found her mons. His tongue sucked on the lips of her sex, making her groan out loud. She had nothing to hold on to with him beneath her skirts, so she pressed her shoulders against the crumbling plaster wall.

He grabbed one of her legs and hitched it over his shoulder, opening the folds of her sex more. She'd forgone drawers at his insistence; now she knew why. One of her hands cupped his head through her skirts. She couldn't get a good hold on him, but it was enough to keep her balanced against the wall as his tongue lashed against her clitoris. His fingers drove deep into her sheath, taking her hard and fast. When she thought she couldn't take anymore, he moved his fingers to her other entrance, drawing her moisture there, and then stuck one finger deep inside.

A scream built in her throat, and the only way she could stop it was to bite down hard on her lip. She drew blood at the same moment her orgasm tore through her body and left her limp in Nick's arms. He was quite literally the only thing holding her up. He kissed her a few times before pulling the skirts over his head and standing before her.

She rubbed her finger along his beard. "Why, Mr. Riley, I do think you've spilled something on yourself."

He pulled out a handkerchief and handed it to her. "Will you do me the honor?"

She took it and cleaned the evidence of her pleasure from his face. When he tucked the linen back into his pocket and grabbed her hand to pull her farther along in the house, she jerked him to a stop. "You didn't find pleasure of your own."

"Oh, I most certainly did."

"Why am I not inclined to believe that?"

He kissed her hard on the mouth and then grabbed her hand. "Come along; let's finish exploring before it's dark."

"Nick..." She couldn't actually say the words for what she wanted to do, so she looked down at his crotch. He was evidently still in a state of arousal. "Let me reciprocate," she said.

"As much as that would please me, I don't want you down on your knees in this place."

She looked at him oddly. What a strange thing to say. "You were on your knees."

"That's different." He dragged her through a door and into a series of other rooms. All were bare, the echo of their voices making this house an eerie place.

They finished the rest of the tour in under an hour. She'd been right in thinking some parts of the house were newer and required less work, but overall the place needed to be redone, top to bottom.

When they were back in the carriage, Amelia didn't let Nick say no to her again. She had him out and in her hand before he could even think to object. Once her mouth was around his cock, his hands assisted in the bob of her head. Because of the proximity of the driver, Nick was forced to remain quiet, not something he was good at. Amelia smiled, making her teeth lightly scrape the underside of him.

He came in her mouth as he reared off the seat, desperate to be in her deeper. When she sat up across from him, she gave him a grin. The look in his eyes was dark and had her shivering. He still craved her. He still wanted her.

"How long before our dinner reservations at the inn?" he asked.

She reached for the watch in his vest pocket, flipped it open, and read the time.

"About three hours."

"Good."

Thank God she'd had enough sense to ask for adjoining rooms. No one would know that she wasn't, in fact, sleeping in her room.

CHAPTER SIXTEEN

Dinner, it turned out, became a private affair that they could have brought up to their room without having to fully dress. Landon had sent a note to say his carriage was stuck in mud and that they wouldn't arrive in Highgate until the evening hours. They didn't expect to see one another until the following day.

Which meant she and Nick had time alone. Away from the worries of the household discovering them and away from the scrutiny of his friends. It also gave her an opportunity to pry into his past.

"When we were at the house, you said you wanted to remember happier things here." She licked the clotted cream from the top of her pastry. "Did you live at Caldon Manor at some point?"

Nick watched her tongue moving over the cream. "I didn't live there."

"Then why does it hold bad memories?"

"I know some of the people who live in this town. And if you don't stop licking at that, I'm going to see what that tastes like on you."

Her eyes widened, and she put the pastry down. She actually wanted him focused on her questions, not on intimacy—that would come later. Preferably when all her questions were answered, but he seemed to be deflecting her before she'd really started.

"You're going to have to be more forthcoming than that, Nick. I don't want to pry, but you leave me with more questions than answers. Sooner or later, you're going to have to tell me what it is your trying so hard to keep a secret."

His hand trailed up her leg. He was trying very hard to distract her. "I'm not trying to keep secrets, Amelia. You know I'm private about my past."

"That's very much the same thing. How can I ever expect to know you fully if you want to hold back the things that make you the person you are?"

"The things in my past might have shaped me along the way, but they did not make me the person sitting before you."

She didn't agree with that but refused to give in to his need to argue.

"Does Victoria know what happened in your past?" she asked, clearly challenging him.

"Victoria has seen and done things that would leave you shocked and with an entirely different view of her."

"I doubt that. I can't picture myself ever liking one of your old lovers."

"When you put it that way…"

Nick dipped his finger into the cream she'd been licking a moment ago. "Now, about that cream."

She scooted away from him and waved her finger back in forth. "Give me one answer first."

He came toward her, a determined glare hooding his eyes. She slid back for every one of his crawls forward, never letting him get as close as he wanted. He stopped and sat on his haunches, the cream still on the tip of his finger.

"One?" he said, the thread of uncertainty in his voice undeniable.

"Just one."

"Then ask me again what you want to know. Just don't ask me about Highgate."

"Why were you whipped as a boy? Was it your mother?"

Nick shook his head. "That was two questions."

"One derives from the other."

"My mother never raised a hand against me. As for the other, that happened at the all-boys school I attended."

The place, he didn't need to remind her, where he'd been sent with Shauley, only to have unspeakable things happen to him. Why hadn't she guessed that was where he'd been whipped?

"I did not please the vicar when given instructions. He thought he could beat the willfulness out of me."

"I'm so sorry." She really hadn't expected that as an answer. Reaching for his hand, she brought it up to her mouth and kissed it.

"It was a long time ago, Amelia. But now you know why I don't like talking about it."

"I almost regret asking."

He'd appeased her curiosity for now. But she wondered how much more she could learn about him before they left Highgate.

"Don't be sorry." He waggled his finger. "Now, again, I must ask about this cream."

She tried to swat his hand away as he came over her, forcing her back onto the mountain of pillows they'd tossed onto the floor for their makeshift indoor picnic.

They were both laughing as Nick smeared the cream down her sternum. Their laughter died when he shoved the chemise from her shoulder and kissed it, following her collarbone across and then working his way over the line of cream. He didn't stop there; he smeared it over her nipples and then sucked her like a babe.

Nick did show her all the places that cream could be put and licked up. They were both a sticky mess by the time dessert was done. The pillows hadn't fared much better. After a shared bath, they eventually found their way to his bed.

Nick sat up with a start. He covered his eyes, feeling a megrim, feeling like he'd sweated through another nightmare. He reached for Amelia, but she wasn't next to him in the bed. Cracking his eyes open, he got a good look around the room.

Amelia wasn't with him at all.

The bedside lamp was turned over and broken, the glass shards littered on the floor. A table was knocked over, and the washbasin had crashed to the floor at some point, as bits of porcelain and water were washed across the floor.

It took a while to realize that the incessant pounding was not his head but someone at the door. Nick stumbled across the room, aware he was naked only when he threw open the door and the wife of the inn's proprietor screamed at his appearance. Her husband tugged her behind his robust form.

Nick's head was spinning, and it took everything in him to stay on his feet. His shoulder crashed into the doorframe as he tried to get a clear view of the man standing in front of him.

"A man came in here, sir. You were making a racket. Had to call the local magistrate when you didn't stop the noise."

"I'm sorry...what racket?" He didn't remember a single event since he and Amelia had crawled into bed, too exhausted to even bother with the blanket. He did remember helping Amelia into her chemise; she'd insisted on wearing it in the event that someone came to the door and she had to run back into her adjoining room.

He recalled that much. After that...

"We've been banging on the door a good twenty minutes. Thought we were going to have to break it down. You've turned over the room, Mr. Riley. You'll have to pay for the damage."

Nick turned back to his chamber, trying to focus on the mess. He spotted his trousers on the floor and stumbled over to the chair to pull them on. Hand against his head, he tried to recall what had happened. His hand came away wet; when he focused on his hand again, it was to see blood smeared across it.

"Shit," he cursed aloud.

He closed his eyes and tried to recall the last thing he remembered. He and Amelia had gone to bed. He hadn't fallen asleep for quite some time, too worried the memories of this town would drag him under, into a nightmare that would wake the whole inn. But he hadn't dreamed.

There was a different kind of fog clouding his head, not from the remnants of a nightmare but from the blow he'd received.

"Twenty minutes, you say?" Nick looked up to the man still standing in his door. The proprietor's wife had left.

"I don't need trouble here," the man said.

Nick rubbed his hand through his hair, feeling a bump at the back of his head. Had he fallen? No…something had hit him.

"My companion?" Nick asked.

At least four other people were in the hall, looking into Nick's room. He glared at them, though he couldn't stare long, as his vision was going in and out.

"Saw her thrown into the back of a carriage. That's why we sent our boy to get the magistrate. Don't think she was awake, as the burly man holding her carried her over his shoulder without much fuss from her. My wife saw him; got a good look at his face, she did."

"Did your wife recognize him?"

"Can't say she did." The proprietor bent down to retrieve Nick's shirt. "I got daughters, sir. You need to be dressed. There's other women staying here too, and I don't need my inn's reputation tarnished more so from tonight's events. You've caused quite the ruckus."

"I'm sorry. I'm having trouble recalling what happened." Nick shook his head as though that would clear his mind, but it didn't.

"Nick!" Landon came charging into the room, his sleeping cap still on and his shirt unbuttoned. He'd dressed in a hurry. He stopped in his tracks and glanced around at the damage to Nick's room. "What in hell happened here?"

"Asked myself the same thing. I think someone took Amelia."

"Miss Grant?" Landon asked. Nick nodded. There would be no delicate way to explain why Amelia had been in his room. He didn't even try or pretend that it was of an innocent nature. It was what it was and if anyone had a problem with that, he didn't mind giving them a goose egg to rival his own.

"Fetch the proprietor's wife, Landon. I need a description of the man who took her."

"You didn't see anything?"

He shook his head. Now that the fog was clearing from his mind, rage started to take its place. Who would dare? He could think of only two people, one of whom knew he'd be in Highgate shortly after the sale.

"Now listen here," the proprietor said. "You can't go running things how you see fit. I have a business to attend here, and you're scaring off my patrons."

"I will pay for everyone's room tonight, as well as a late evening repast, to give them time to settle from the excitement."

The man's mouth snapped shut. "How do I know you're going to be good for that kind of money, sir?"

"If I wasn't, would I have bought the old Caldon Manor in Highgate?"

"You're the man who bought it? The buildings in town too?"

"I did. Now will you let my friend and associate retrieve your wife? I have some questions to ask her."

"I'll get her myself."

Landon came into the room, tucking his shirt into his trousers and properly buttoning it. "Do you know who did this?"

"I suspect, but until it's confirmed, I don't know where to look."

"Why would they take Amelia? Does she have information they need? Is it to do with the purchase of Murray's lands?"

Nick scrubbed his hand over his eyes.

"To get back at me." To make him suffer for ever succeeding. This was all on Shauley.

The proprietor's wife stepped into the room. "Sir, my husband said you needed a description of the man I saw abscond your secretary."

"Yes." Nick stood, perhaps too quickly, because Landon had to catch him around the waist so he didn't totter right over onto the floor.

"There was two, you see…" And Nick did see, as she gave him the description of a man who could only be the inspector.

Even better, he suspected exactly where they'd taken Amelia.

"Landon, procure some horses. I need to see if the magistrate is here yet. We have some business to take care of."

This was something he should have done years ago. As for the inspector, he would enjoy gutting the man if given the opportunity. No one threatened the people under his protection, especially Amelia.

One minute she'd been curled up next to Nick in bed, the next…even her brain couldn't figure out the finer details. She remembered a sack being put over her head and trying to grab onto something with which to hit her kidnapper, but she had only succeeded in knocking over the washstand as she was thrown out of the room she shared with Nick. Then she was dragged over ground with rocks and gravel before she was thrown over someone's brawny shoulders, just before being tossed into a carriage. She'd blacked out after that and had only come to when the inspector slapped her across the face, leaving her cheek stinging even now.

Amelia faced her kidnapper like a crazed woman. Her hair was half tumbled out of its braid and felt like a tangle of knots over her shoulders. Her chemise was torn in too many places to bother taking inventory.

Her arm hurt where the inspector had grabbed hold of her and hadn't bothered to let go until he'd tied a dirty rope around her wrists and arms and hung her on some sort of hook suspended from the low ceiling. The cabin was a single room. It housed a small cooking hearth on one side and a bed on the other. Shelving hung on the wall, with minimal supplies by the door. Other than that, she didn't see anything that would tell her where she was.

"What do you want from me?" she asked, her voice hoarse from having cried for the past half hour, if not longer.

"Can't you figure it out?" he said, leaning back in a wooden chair, studying her like one might a prized mare.

Bile rose in her throat. She knew that look. She had seen it in other men's eyes. The men her brother had allowed to touch her.

"Did you know my brother?"

He tsked at her question.

She was pulling at straws, but how else would she figure out just what kind of trouble she was in, if she couldn't at least figure out what this man's connection was to her life.

"What do you want?" she repeated with more force. She didn't understand what this man had against her. Or what his purpose was. Did he intend to kill her? "Were you responsible for my brother's death? Did you kill him?"

"You've got too many questions. In case you didn't notice, I'm not answering them. Maybe if you ask the right questions, I'll give you a break."

"Where's Nick?" she asked, suddenly realizing he might have been hurt...or worse. Oh, God, if he had met the same fate as her brother, she didn't know how she would survive that news.

"Don't worry about him. You worry about you. Now, what do you think it is I want from you?"

"I don't know," she sobbed. "Please. Let me go. I'll give you whatever I can. Just let me go."

"You disappoint me, Amelia. Here I thought we were old friends."

"Did you kill my brother?" she asked again. She needed the answer. Needed something that might explain why she was here.

"As much as I would have liked to do, I can't take the credit. That was arranged by a mutual friend."

Amelia tugged at the rope burning her wrists, trying to work her hands through the loops, but she only accomplished burning her skin with every twist.

"I wouldn't bother trying to get out of those knots. You'll only hurt yourself more."

She didn't care if she had to break her hand to get free; she would do whatever she needed to find a way out of this situation.

"Who is our mutual friend, *Inspector*?" She was beginning to think he was not an inspector, but an imposter who had come into her and Nick's lives to ferret out information on them.

"You wound me, dearest." He came at her again, his large frame bearing down on her like a bull taking charge. He slapped her across the face, making her ears ring. "You will address me as Inspector Laurie."

"Are you really an inspector?"

"Of course I am. How else could I go about town wearing my uniform?"

"Why do you want to hurt me?" Amelia's lips quivered, but she held back the sobs that wanted to escape.

"Here I thought you were smarter than you let on." He stood so close that she could feel the heat coming off him in sickening waves. And that closeness made her want to vomit all over him. She held back, swallowed against the bile rising in her throat, knowing that if she lost control that would surely drive him over the edge he was walking with sanity.

"Any friend of yours is no friend of mine," Amelia spit out.

He turned her head to the side to examine her face. She noticed she'd left claw marks over the side of his cheek.

"He's not going to like that your face is damaged." The inspector looked down at the rest of her body. She wasn't blind to the fact that she wore only a chemise. Thankfully, he didn't touch her.

"Please, you don't want to hurt me. Let me go. I won't tell anyone I was here."

"You say that as if *here* will be found."

She had to believe that Nick would find her. That was, if he was alive. Tears welled up in her eyes. Now she was sick with worry. Sick at not knowing what had happened and feeling helpless in her current situation. If there was one thing she hated in life, it was being made to feel helpless. She needed to focus on escaping. Focus on how she could help herself, not worry herself sick.

"Where are we?"

The inspector tsked again. "That's a surprise."

"Do you plan on killing me?"

"No, I plan on getting paid for bringing you to the man who wants to get back at Nick."

So the inspector was easily bought. Hadn't Nick told her something to that effect? She stored that information away for later—if he could be bought, who was to say Nick couldn't purchase this man's temporary loyalty for more money?

"Why was my brother killed?"

"A means to an end. It was supposed to look like Riley did it. The situation and timing were perfect. But I misjudged him. Want to know how?"

She nodded, trying to keep him talking as she twisted her hands in the rope.

"Didn't realize Riley was so well connected with the bobbies. Called an investigation into my actions, he did, and my work. Had to run, you know. I need to get back at him for that. I had a good thing set up in London. Was making decent pay as an inspector and even better pay keeping thugs off the streets, and from causing trouble for the businesses."

It seemed she was asking the right questions now, for he was giving her information that might solve the mystery of why she'd been kidnapped.

"How did my brother die?"

"Picked a fight and started a brawl at a whorehouse. I had no hand in killing him. Not directly, anyway. We had men inside that made sure he didn't survive the beating he got."

"What was your purpose in trying to pin my brother's murder on Mr. Riley?"

"Riley had an old debt yet to be paid."

"I'm sure he has the funds to pay any debts outstanding."

His gaze snapped to hers. She stopped moving immediately, not wanting to draw attention to the fact that she was trying to free herself.

"So innocent, yet not. How long have you been Riley's mistress? You played it well, pretending to be his secretary. You almost had me fooled."

It wouldn't do her any good, arguing with him, so she didn't respond to his question and instead asked, "Will you please let me down? I can't feel my hands."

He shook his head. "Wasn't born yesterday, Miss Somerset. I know you'll run. Or at least attempt it, and I don't want to hurt you. Not yet. Not unless you make me."

Amelia looked around the sparse room. "You can tie me to the bedpost. Please, I can't feel my arms." Which was partially true. But more than anything, she needed to put herself in a better position.

"I'm as good as dead if you get away now."

"I promise not to run," she easily lied. Tears flooded her eyes again, making her seem all the more sincere. "Please tell me what will happen to me?"

"Don't much care. My pay on this job is enough to start over in another city."

"Then explain to me why this man wants to get back at Nick."

"Not really any of my business. I just do the job I'm given, take my pay, and move on to the next job. Though if you think about it, it's obvious that getting back at Riley has something to do with this chunk of land."

The inspector had given her two valuable pieces of information.

First, he had confirmed that a *man* wanted to get back at Nick. That could only be Shauley. The second had been the way he'd indicated the cabin as part of the lands. So this must be the groundskeeper's house she'd seen on the property drawings. That put her a mile down the road and in the woods from the house, not that there was anything back at the house that could help her. But it also put her a couple miles from the town and the inn, so she'd have to run east as soon as she found a way out of here.

"This is all Mr. Shauley's doing, isn't it?"

A proud smile lifted the inspector's lips, though it was a bit too frightening to call a smile. "See? I knew you were smart enough to eventually figure it out."

"How can he have the funds to pay you for kidnapping me? Mr. Riley can pay you a decent sum more."

"Don't be so sure."

"Then why didn't he buy the manor house if he didn't want Mr. Riley to have it?"

The inspector shrugged as though that wasn't a matter for him to worry about.

Could that be the only grudge Shauley had against Nick? The manor house seemed so trivial and worthless as a reason to resort to murder and now kidnapping. This obviously had something to do with their childhood. With the school they'd attended.

"What are Shauley's plans for me? Surely he told you something."

"Didn't bother to ask. Don't really care. You're pretty enough and all, but not my type, and certainly not Shauley's type."

The thunder of what sounded like a hundred horses shook the little cabin. The windows rattled and the old wood door shook in its hinges. The inspector stood and pulled out a pistol that had been hanging over the back of the chair. He pointed it at her temple, and Amelia thought for a second he was going to pull the trigger.

"Not a sound," he said. "Or I'll be handing you over with a bullet lodged in your head."

She nodded and sealed her lips, biting back a sob that wanted to escape her. She wasn't sure whether or not he would kill her; and that wasn't a chance she was willing to risk.

The inspector went over to the window and pulled back the dark burlap that covered the glass so he could look outside. He cursed and closed it quickly, obviously needing to seal off the evidence of light from the cabin. He leaned over the rustic table and blew out the lamp, just to be sure there was nothing but darkness in the cramped room.

Amelia felt the cold steel of the pistol head against her arm and bit her lip to keep her trembling still. As she promised, she didn't make a sound. But she did send a prayer up that it was Nick on the other side of that door.

The horses came to a stop, and she could hear their snorts and neighs.

The only sound on the inside of the cabin was her labored breathing. The inspector was like a ghost when he moved away from her. She didn't hear him moving about. There was only the one door, so whoever was on the other side was either going to come in, or the inspector would attempt to go out.

When the door flew open, it was Shauley standing at the threshold.

"What in hell is she doing trussed up there?" Shauley demanded from the inspector.

"Didn't have anywhere else to tie her off."

"She's not a bloody horse, though I'm sure she plays the brood mare well."

Amelia wanted to scream as Shauley charged toward her with his knife out. She closed her eyes when he was a hand-span from her and was surprised to find herself falling to the hard floor. He'd cut the loops that had held her to the hook dangling from the ceiling. She curled her feet under her and pushed herself into a kneeling position. All that mattered now was that she had a better chance of running, and she would find whatever advantage she could.

Shauley turned a chair around and sat astride it. "Give me the pistol," he said to the inspector, who handed it to him without dispute. Shauley pointed the crude piece of metal at her head. "I want nothing more than to shoot you, but I'm afraid you'll make better collateral alive."

"And what do you need collateral for?"

"Safe passage. I know one man who can give that to me."

"Why did you go to the trouble of kidnapping me, then?"

"It's the easiest way to get his cooperation, don't you think?" She wanted to argue, but he was right. "Did you know Nick tried to have me arrested in London?"

"I can't understand why, unless it's for the murder of my brother." She couldn't guard her tongue any longer. If was going to kill her, he'd have done it already. And she believed she was worth more alive than dead to him.

Shauley stood and cuffed her across the face with the back of his hand. Amelia tasted blood in her mouth. "You're very bold for having no say in this matter. I said I needed you alive, but that doesn't mean I can't hand you over bloody and broken."

Amelia pinched her lips closed and turned away from both men. Now it was a matter of waiting for them to strike a deal. She hoped that was soon, because she couldn't stay in this cabin with either of these men for much longer.

The magistrate wanted to call off their search, as the conditions were not ideal for the horses, and traipsing through the woods in full night was likely to cause someone harm. But Nick pushed onward, refusing to give up on Amelia. He'd promised to keep her safe, but tonight he'd failed her.

After checking the manor house, and finding nothing, they had headed back to the village strip and looked in every place near the main road that Shauley and Inspector Laurie could have hidden. They even tried locating the carriage the innkeeper's wife had described. They'd met nothing but dead ends, and there had been no sign of Amelia.

She'd been gone for hours at this point. And he didn't know if he should extend his search beyond Highgate. Landon rode up next to him. His friend had stayed at his side all evening and didn't complain about being out when the first rays of the sun shot through the sky.

"What do you want to do?" Landon asked.

They were walking the horses back toward the inn, though Nick doubted he'd stop searching. He was just trying to work out Shauley's plan. "We didn't leave any stone unturned. I don't know where they could have taken her."

"I was so sure he'd be at the manor house."

"Do you want to head back there? Check it one more time? It's possible he was hiding in plain sight, but we missed him in the dark." Landon motioned toward the lighting sky. "The day ahead is on our side."

Nick rubbed his hand through his hair, wincing when he brushed against the cut at the back. He looked at his friend long and hard. "The manor was the only place that made sense to take her."

"Care to enlighten me as to why?"

"It was a place from my childhood." A place the instructors of the school had brought them to commit their sins when the earl wasn't in residence.

"Shauley and I attended school in Highgate. We used to skip our instructions and hide...I'll be damned. He's at the fucking cabin." Nick mounted his horse and tightened his thighs around the animal, propelling it forward at a quicker pace. He shouted back to his party, "He's at the Caldon Manor cabin."

Why in hell hadn't he thought to look there in the first place? Landon was right; Shauley was hiding in plain sight.

No one questioned him. And though many of the men were tired and their horses were growing weary, they didn't hesitate to follow his lead. Nick rode at a breakneck pace; his only worry was getting to Amelia before anything happened to her.

Amelia's head was throbbing, and her eyes felt like they'd had sand thrown at them. She could barely keep awake, and she felt herself nod off, only to jolt awake the next second. She wasn't sure how long she'd been at the cabin, but she could see the sky lighting up outside through the thin curtain that covered the small window.

The inspector had left a while ago, though she couldn't say precisely how long because she was too focused on trying to keep awake. If she fell asleep, they could move her. And then she'd be at a greater disadvantage, should she have an opportunity to escape. She knocked her head back on the wall, trying to keep it up and keep alert where she was crouched in the corner of the cabin.

Shauley was ignoring her, reading a newspaper at the table situated in the middle of the room. He hadn't said much to her since he'd first arrived, but she held out hope that he didn't intend to hurt her more than he already had.

She wished the inspector were here; he was slightly easier to talk to, and if she didn't start talking, she was apt to fall asleep where she was crouched. Amelia rubbed her eyes with the side of her hands, which were still bound. She wasn't sure she had the strength to stand on her own, but she might have to do so if the gritty feeling in her eyes didn't cease.

"Is the inspector off to make a bargain with Mr. Riley?" Her mouth was dry, and her voice gravelly.

"You're not at liberty to ask anything of me," Shauley said without lifting his head from his paper.

"Why do you hate Nick so much? He told me you were once friends, but friends don't turn on each other."

Shauley spun around on his chair and studied her a moment. "Told you, did he?"

"He did. And about the depravities at the school." She wasn't sure if she'd said too much, but she needed to stay awake and talking was the only thing keeping her mind active. "He won't make a deal with you. Not after the trouble you've caused us."

Shauley stood and came toward her faster than she expected. She tried to shrink away from him, but he didn't hit her. He ripped a strip of her chemise from the hem and held her legs down by kneeling on her when she tried to kick him away.

"I've had about all I can take of you." Shauley held up the strip of her chemise and wrapped it around her mouth before she realized what he was doing. She tried to scream, but it was muffled with the cloth stuffed in her mouth and wrapped around her head where he knotted it.

"Much better," he said and went back to his paper.

Amelia was back to trying to stay awake. Her head bobbed every time she nearly lost her battle with her body.

She swore she heard horses in the distance. She'd heard them last night too, but they hadn't come close to the cabin.

When Shauley stood to peer out the window, she knew her ears weren't fooling her. She pushed her knees under her and pressed her back against the wall to try to stand. If she could make a run for the door and throw it open—she tested her hands, hoping they could grasp the knob and turn it—she might be spotted.

Shauley picked up the pistol from the table and stared in her direction. "Stand, and I won't hesitate to shoot you."

She slid back down the wall, tears tracking down her face. "If you're not in the same spot I left you when I get back, I'll make sure you can't walk. And I promise you, a broken limb or two is going to feel a lot worse than the bump we gave you on your head."

Shauley slipped out the front door, leaving her alone. All Amelia could think was that the threat of a broken leg was better than ending up somewhere unfamiliar. A place that was farther from Nick. She pushed herself up against the wall. Pins and needles ran up and down her numb legs, so she waited a minute as the feeling came back to them. This might be her only opportunity to get free.

Though they tried to be quiet as they approached the cabin, Nick knew it was impossible not to hear the dozen horses that were surrounding and filling the woods. They'd found the carriage used to kidnap Amelia, but no horses, which meant they'd either mounted up and taken Amelia to a new location, or…

He told himself for the millionth time that hurting her would serve no purpose to either man. They'd taken her for ransom; that much was obvious. And that meant they needed to ensure her safety to some degree.

Shauley wasn't a stupid man; he would have had a contingency plan in place, had his plan gone to shit with the murder of Lord Berwick, and it had.

The closer they got to the cabin, the more anxious he grew. He drew the pistol he kept on him when he traveled but had never found reason to use. Today might be an exception.

Nick dismounted a hundred meters or so from the cabin, wanting to blend in with the forest so he could approach undetected. The closer he got, he told himself, the easier it would be to get to Amelia and take her to safety.

Shots rang around the woods, and Nick was forced to take shelter behind a tree. Someone yelled; another of Nick's party shouted, "In the tree line." The report of shots going off sent hundreds of birds to the sky, almost blackening the morning. Nick took the distraction as an opportunity and sprinted toward the cabin entrance, pistol at the ready.

When the door flew open, Amelia let out a muffled scream and fell forward into his arms. "Amelia. Thank God," he found himself uttering as he caught her.

The crack of twigs behind him had him spinning around, taking aim. The inspector held a rifle, and Nick didn't hesitate for a second as he yanked Amelia down to the ground behind him and shot Laurie through the chest. A moment of surprise shaded the inspector's face before he fell to the ground, his chest moving up and down in a whistling breath. Landon broke into the clearing just then with three other men, surrounding the downed inspector. Nick nodded to his friend and turned back to his only concern. Amelia.

He'd found her. She was safe. Her face was bruised and there was blood in her hair, but she was alive. And Nick felt a stab of tears in his eyes.

He dropped his pistol and stripped out of his jacket. He wrapped it around Amelia as he cut through the rope binding her wrists and carefully untied the knot of cloth at the back of her head. She sobbed and buried her head in his chest. He rubbed her back, letting her cry out her relief and fear. Giving him enough time to compose himself before he had to face the rest of the men who had assisted him.

When she stopped shaking, he helped her put her arms through the sleeves in the jacket and buttoned it up in the front.

Once she had calmed, she tried to stand but couldn't seem to get her legs under her. Nick lifted her in his arms and carried her toward his horse. He sat her up in the saddle and pulled himself up behind her, keeping her body cradled tight against his, her legs over to one side so she could wrap her arms tightly around his middle.

Though it wasn't full light, he could still see there were at least eight men milling around, half of them already on their horses. The still form of the inspector lay sprawled out on the ground, a pool of blood growing and spreading from his motionless body. No one said anything, or maybe they did but Nick's only concern now was getting Amelia to safety.

He took the horse at a careful pace so as not to jostle her. She cried into his shirt. Neither said a word as they headed back to the inn. It was enough just to have found each other.

CHAPTER SEVENTEEN

Amelia pushed Nick away. He was inspecting the goose egg in her hairline for the tenth time in the past hour. He hadn't stopped fussing over her since they'd arrived back in his room at the inn.

"Please, I've been poked and prodded with doctor's instruments for the past hour. I just want to sleep."

"The doctor said otherwise," Nick reminded her.

"That doesn't mean I'm not tired. I can at least rest for a while. I just want to forget everything that happened."

Though she doubted she would ever forget the scene that had unfolded as Nick opened the door to the cabin. He'd shot the inspector without hesitation. He'd killed man in front of her without a second thought. She couldn't say if the inspector planned to negotiate something with Nick or pull the trigger on his own gun. Still, it had to have been a hard decision for Nick to make.

"That you were ever put in that position tells me I have let my guard down when it should be highest in this town, of all places." Nick pulled her closer, her body lying half on top of his as she stretched out on the bed beside him.

She played with a button on his shirt. "Did you find Shauley?" she asked. Fear snaked through her body as she asked that. There was no denying that there was something mentally wrong with that man for him to have done all he'd done to her and Nick.

"We didn't. But he'll have everyone in the country looking for him after today. He's a wanted man, and I'm willing to put a price on his head if that keeps him from coming after you again."

When Nick had carried her over to his horse, she had been surprised to see just how many riders had been aiding Nick through the night. Amelia planned to thank every single one of the volunteers who Nick had pulled together as soon as she was rested and able to form coherent sentences. If it hadn't been for them, if it hadn't been for Nick…

It didn't bear thinking.

Nick tilted her chin up, making her look at him. "You're not falling asleep on me, are you?"

"No, thinking."

"Might I ask what about?"

"What did Shauley think to gain in kidnapping me? Why did he kill my brother? Jeremy wasn't anyone I admired or respected, but that his death was avoidable makes me feel as if I was the one who killed him."

"You have nothing to feel guilty about. If you want to blame anyone for what unfolded, blame me."

Amelia sat up so she could better look Nick in the eye. "I could never blame you. You came into my life like a knight on a white steed, and you haven't let me down since."

He swiped his thumb across her cheek, wiping her tears away. But more tears fell, covering her face. "Do you know how perfect you are? How much you mean to me?" he asked.

She shook her head, still not able to talk, not without sobbing.

"Without you in my life, I have nothing to live for."

"Don't say that," she choked out. "You've built an empire. You have helped so many people, and so many others count on you. Don't say that."

He took her hands in his, kissing each finger before kissing the abrasions on her wrists where the rope had burned into her skin.

"What will happen if Shauley is caught?"

Nick let out a long sigh. "He'll be tried, found guilty, and hanged for his crimes."

"I don't know what to say, other than I'm sorry, Nick. I know you haven't been friends with him in a long time, but having once trusted, it must be difficult to believe him capable of what he's done."

"I'm not sorry. Shauley and I haven't been friends for twenty years," he said. "Make no mistake; I would have killed Shauley myself, had I found him before finding you." A dark look clouded his eyes for only a moment before he focused his full attention on her. "I'd rather talk about us," he said, his tone changing.

She looked at him curiously. "Us?" Was there something wrong? "What is it?"

"There are thirty people staying at this inn. It's the only one in a ten-mile radius on the main road."

She tucked her chin closer to her chest, unable to meet his gaze. "They've already labeled me a harlot, haven't they?"

He remained silent.

"It makes our working together impossible, Nick. No one will take me seriously after this. What must your friends think of me?"

"Landon will stand by me, no matter my decisions. He'll stand ready as your friend too."

"How can he? How can Lady Burley? They'll judge me from the events of tonight."

"Marry me. Let us prove the world wrong. Stand at my side as my wife."

She looked up at him, eyes wide, shocked by the proposition and at a complete loss for words or how to respond. "Su-surely you don't mean that."

"I do." He was in earnest. "Let everyone know of our devotion. Let them remove prejudices and labels they've already assigned to our relationship."

She wanted to say yes. She did. But was he only asking out of pity for the situation they now found themselves in? What if the only reason he was offering was in sympathy and regret for their having been found out? Maybe that's what scared her most—that it wasn't a genuine offer but asked out of guilt.

She rubbed her hands over her eyes. This shouldn't be a difficult decision, but it was exactly that. Didn't every young woman want the man she loved to propose marriage?

To make a commitment for the future?

"Are you sure that's what you want?" she asked. Why was she denying him?

A frown creased his brow. "What makes you think I haven't thought this through?"

She opened her mouth to respond but found herself still at a loss for words.

"Would you be offering this, had we not been discovered?"

"It's no lie that I never imagined myself the marrying type."

"And what is the 'marrying type'?" She almost laughed that such a type existed in his mind, but she was too on edge with what he might say, so she bit her lip and waited for his response.

"I've had a difficult life. I've watched the people I love live through some terrible situations. There are things I have done for which polite society would label me a monster."

"If we marry, you have to be open and honest in all things." That was a condition on which she wouldn't budge.

"I'm willing to live with that."

"All things, Nick. I cannot have it any other way. We either have all of each other or nothing."

"I agree to your terms."

"There isn't anything you don't know about me," she countered.

"I know." He chuckled. "But when we leave this room tomorrow, I plan on telling everyone that you are my fiancée."

She felt something grow in her belly and expand outward. Excitement. She suddenly felt alive, and any bit of tiredness left from her ordeal was washed away. She pulled herself up and sat over his thighs, wrapping her arms around his shoulders.

"I will marry you, Nicholas Riley. As long as you don't hide your heart from me."

The last thing she expected was for a smile to light up his whole face. She pressed her hand against his beard and kissed him on the mouth.

When she pulled away, he said, "Amelia, I will give you that and so much more."

Start from the beginning and see where it all started!
Continue reading for an excerpt from

DESIRE ME NOW

<h2 style="text-align:center">An Excerpt from</h2>

<h2 style="text-align:center">DESIRE ME NOW</h2>

She needed to get out of this house—and fast. Sliding out of the bed, trying to make as little noise as possible, she knelt on the cold plank floor and pulled out the sack she'd stowed under the bed. Retrieving what clothes she had, she rolled them up tight and stuffed them into the bag.

At the washbasin, she gathered the last bit of soap she'd taken from her home in Berwick and the silver brush that had been her mother's. She had no other possessions, except a small oil painting of her parents in a broken silver locket, given to her on her tenth birthday and torn from her neck during one of her brother's rages on her eighteenth birthday.

Pulling up a loose floorboard, she retrieved her drawstring reticule with the money she'd stolen from her brother. It wasn't a lot of money, but it had been enough to get her to London and pay for lodgings for a month, if she had needed that long to find a job. The money would be put to good use now.

She packed only what she'd come with, as she didn't want her employer accusing her of thievery. Hopefully, if she left quietly, Sir Ian wouldn't pursue her, as she knew something of the determination of men when they were denied what they wanted.

With her sack tied and slung over one shoulder, and her shawl and mantle over her dress to keep her possessions safe, she tiptoed down the servants' stairs and escaped out the back gate near the stable house. The cool air bit at her cheeks, so she quickened her stride, hoping that would keep her warm.

Once she was on the main streets, Amelia kept her head down so no one would see the tears flooding her eyes. It hit her suddenly that she'd left behind her last hope for a decent job.

Had she known how abhorrent her employer was, she'd have turned down the opportunity to teach his children. Sir Ian hadn't wanted a proper governess for his young boys; he'd wanted a mistress living under his own roof. A woman he could visit in the cover of night, when his ill, bedridden wife was none the wiser.

She covered her mouth with her lace-gloved hand, feeling sick to her stomach. All she could do now was go back to the agency that had placed her and hope to find new employment.

Where would she go if they turned her away?

She picked up her stride, even though she'd developed a stitch in her side that made breathing difficult. She had only been in London for three weeks. Not enough time to make friends or learn her way around. She didn't even know where she could find decent, safe lodgings. She supposed there was enough money to put herself on a train and go back home to her brother.

No. Never that.

She refused to lower herself to that type of desperation. She would find another job. In fact, she would demand a new placement from the agency. She was well educated and the daughter of a once-prominent earl, which made her valuable and an asset for any job requiring someone intelligent and capable.

The only problem was that she'd told no one in London of her true identity.

Someone jostled her shoulder, spinning her from the path she walked.

"Pardon, ma'am," he said, grasping her under the arm to right her footing.

Before she could turn and offer her gratitude, he was just another bobbing hat on the street. Reaching for her reticule to pull out her handkerchief, she came up empty-handed.

"That thief!" she shouted and then slapped her hand over her mouth.

Those around her called up the alarm. She pointed in the direction she was sure the thief had gone, but there wasn't a suspicious soul to be seen.

Amelia started pushing through the crowded street, apologizing along the way when she knocked into a few pedestrians. She grew frantic and inhaled in great gulps, trying to get air into her lungs and to keep at bay the panic that was threatening to rob her of her ability to think rationally.

Eventually, her feet slowed as the cramping in her side worsened. She could barely see beyond the tears falling from her eyes. Her face was damp, and she had nothing to wipe it clean except the sleeve of her day dress. She was unfit to go to the agency, but what other choice did she have?

Despair robbed her of the last of her breath, and she was forced to stop her pursuit.

Bracing one arm against an old stone building, she breathed in and out until she was calm. The last of her tears had dried on her face and made her cheeks stiff.

She should give up, crawl back to her brother, and beg for his eternal forgiveness. There were few viable choices left to her. She couldn't stay out in the streets. Awful things happened to women who had no place to go. Things far worse than what she had escaped, though in a moment of clarity, she might refute that statement.

Walking around to the side of the building where she'd stopped, she threw up the dinner she'd eaten the previous night. Feeling dizzy and unwell, she drew on the last of her courage, straightened her shoulders, and somehow found the strength to continue walking.

She needed to find new employment and accommodations without delay. The agency had been a room full of women; they would understand the situation she'd found herself in. They would help her.

Light-headed, she walked toward Fleet Street, where the agency was tucked neatly behind a printing house. While the day had started rather dreary and dull in so many senses, the odd peek of sunshine cut through the coal-heavy air and pressed against her face. The sun warming her skin gave her a glimmer of optimism.

When the sun disappeared behind the clouds again, she focused on her surroundings and caught sight of a group of urchins, recognizing the tallest of the bunch immediately.

"You little swindler. Give me back what is mine," she cried out loud and clear.

The boy, who had been counting the contents in her reticule, pocketed her money and took off at a full run. His pace was quick and light-footed, and she was sure he took one step to her three, though she still tried to catch up to him.

Shaken, with a cramp in her side and the dizzy feeling growing worse through her body, Amelia refused to give in. When the urchin dodged across a street heavy with traffic, she knew there was no time for hesitation. She needed that money back.

Before she made it halfway across the road, the urchin was lost among the carts. Tears welled in her eyes again, blurring her vision. Someone yelled for her to get off the road; someone else emphasized his point with obscenities she didn't fully comprehend.

Though nearly to the other side, she didn't move quite fast enough for the two-seat open carriage clipping down the street much more swiftly than the other carts.

"Move, you bloody fool," the driver bellowed.

His speeding horses, black as pitch, headed toward her like the devil on her heels. She hiked up her skirts and ran but tripped over the stone curb and tumbled hard to her knees, twisting her foot on the way down. The pain of the impact caused black spots to dot across her vision. As she tried to gain her footing, she collapsed back onto her bruised, pained knees and cried.

A strong arm supported her under her elbow and hauled her to her feet, but it was apparent to them both that she couldn't stand on her own. When the stranger knelt before her, all she saw was his tall beaver hat as he put one arm around her back and shoulders and the other under her legs. That was all the warning he gave before he lifted her into his arms and walked up the lawn as if she weighed nothing.

"Thank you," she said weakly, her heated face pressed into his finely made wool jacket. His cologne was subtle and masculine with undertones of amber and citrus. She inhaled the scent deeper, wanting that comforting smell to wrap around her, wishing it would let her forget just how her day had unfolded.

Instead of releasing her when they were away from the road, he continued walking up the slight incline of the grassy field. A flush washed over her face as she stuttered for words of admonishment that anyone might see this gentleman carrying a poor, injured woman in his arms. She didn't actually want him to put her down, but common decency demanded it of her.

Gazing at the face under his well-made top hat stopped any further protestations. She dropped her gaze and stared at his striped necktie tucked neatly into a charcoal vest.

"You need not carry me. I can find my way," she said, but her request lacked any conviction.

The sun shone through the clouds once more, shining directly in her eyes and allowing her to pull away from the power that radiated from his gaze.

His short, close-clipped beard emphasized the strong line of his jaw. Black hair fanned out a little under his hat, longer than fashionable but suiting to the rough edge this man carried.

She could tell that his mouth, though pinched, was full, the bow on top well defined. The type of lips young ladies tittered and wrote poems about.

"I just witnessed you hike up your skirts well past your shins to run across one of the busiest streets in London." His voice was gruff, with a sensual quality that warmed her right to the very core.

Just as she thought her blush couldn't get worse, she felt her ears burning from the blunt observation of what he'd witnessed.

Amelia cleared her throat, realizing she'd been staring at him too long. "I am sorry you had to witness that."

He settled her down on a slated wood bench under the shade of an ancient burled oak tree. "It's arguable that you did that in a careful manner," he said.

The gentleman removed his leather gloves, set them on the bench beside her, and went down on his knees to stretch out her foot to look at the injury she'd done herself.

She tucked her feet under the bench, away from his searching hands. They were in the open, and anyone could see his familiarity. "I only need to rest a minute. I wish I could repay you for your troubles, but I have nothing of value…"

When he looked at her—really looked at her—she was struck speechless by the sincerity of his regard. His eyes were gray like flint and as hard as steel. *Unusual and beautiful,* she thought. But it wasn't the color that had her at a loss for words. It was the intensity behind his gaze that made her feel that she was the only person in the world he was focused on; almost like nothing but the two of them existed on this tiny patch of grass in the middle of the bustling city.

This perfect man before her, who clearly didn't have to worry about putting a roof over his head or bread on the table, held a maelstrom of emotions in his cool, assessing gaze. She trusted what she saw in his eyes, trusted a man for the first time in she didn't know how long.

She wanted to reach toward his face but grasped the edge of the bench tightly instead.

Just how dire her situation was hit her so hard, she swayed where she sat. Her money was gone, her only picture of her parents taken with it.

And then she cried.

She didn't mean to. She didn't even think she had the energy left for such an outpouring. But she couldn't stop now that the dam had broken on her emotions. Histrionics didn't seem to put her rescuer off, because he only huffed a helpless breath and waited for her to calm herself, which she tried to do in great gulping breaths.

"Let me get you to a doctor." His voice was deep and commanding. He would never have to raise his voice to draw the attention of those around him. It was the kind of voice to which one was naturally drawn, and it stirred something deep inside her.

She shook her head at his offer.

She needed to loosen whatever spell he had over her.

She felt the command of his stare but did not turn her face up to his again.

"Let me see you to a doctor to ensure it is nothing more than a turned ankle," he offered, his voice full of sincerity.

She shook her head again. She tried to explain about the agency, but none of what she said came out coherently, and her tears fell harder.

Before she could attempt saying anything more, her rescuer lifted her in his arms once again and strode toward the street.

Deciding that life had far more to offer than a nine-to-five job, bickering children, and housework of any kind (unless she's on a deadline, when everything is magically spotless), **TIFFANY CLARE** opened up her laptop to write stories she could get lost in. Tiffany writes sexy historical romances set in the Victorian era. She lives in Toronto with her husband, two kids, and two dogs, and you can find out more about her and her books at www.tiffanyclare.com.

Discover great authors, exclusive offers, and more at hc.com.

Give in to your Impulses...
Continue reading for excerpts from
our newest Avon Impulse books.
Available now wherever e-books are sold.

CLOSE TO HEART
By T.J. Kline

THE MADDENING LORD MONTWOOD
THE RAKES OF FALLOW HALL SERIES
By Vivienne Lorret

CHAOS
By Jamie Shaw

THE BRIDE WORE DENIM
A SEVEN BRIDES FOR SEVEN COWBOYS NOVEL
By Lizbeth Selvig

An Excerpt from

CLOSE TO HEART

by T. J. Kline

It only took an instant for actress Alyssa Cole's
world to come crashing down . . . but Heart Fire
Ranch is a place of new beginnings, even for
those who find their way there by accident.

Justin stared at the woman across from him. As familiar as she looked, he couldn't put his finger on where he might have seen her before. Alyssa wasn't from around here, that much was certain. There weren't many women in town who could afford a designer purse, impractical boots, and a luxury vehicle more suited to city jaunts than the winter mountain terrain. But there was something else, some memory niggling at the back of his mind, teasing him, just out of reach.

Her waifish appearance reminded him of a fashion model. She was certainly lovely enough to be one, but the idea didn't suit the woman standing in front of him. Justin assumed models would be accustomed to taking criticism and judgment, and this woman looked as if she'd crumble if he so much as raised his voice.

That was it, he realized. Behind her sadness, he recognized fear. Justin felt the uncontrollable instinct to protect Alyssa swell in his chest. She might not be his responsibility, but he couldn't stop the desire to help her any more than he could have let the dog die. When she glanced up at him again, his mouth opened without acknowledgment from his brain.

"D'you know anything about accounting or running an office? You did pretty well with these guys. You could work here for a while, at least until you get your car fixed or figure something out, since my regular help doesn't seem inclined to answer her phone."

"I guess, but I couldn't let you fire her . . ."

What the hell are you doing? He knew she came from money, since she wore a huge wedding ring. Hell, that ring alone should have been enough reason for him to keep his mouth shut, since she was another man's wife, but his lips continued to move.

Justin laughed out loud, but he wasn't sure whether it was at himself for his stupidity or her comment. "I can't fire her; she's my cousin. But maybe this would be a wake-up call to be more responsible."

Alyssa gave him a slight smile before ducking her head again. He didn't miss the fact that she wasn't able to meet his eyes for more than a few seconds.

"My sister has a ranch with a few guest cabins. I can see if she has one empty. I'm sure she'll let you stay as long as you need to."

Her eyes jumped back up to meet his. He could easily read the gratitude, and a hopeful light flickered to life in her eyes. But there was more—a wariness he couldn't explain and that had no reason to be there.

"Why are you being so nice? You don't know me."

Justin shrugged, as if car crashes and late-night emergency puppy deliveries were commonplace for him. "It's the right thing to do."

The light in her eyes darkened immediately and she frowned, not saying anything more. He reached for the runt, still in front of the oxygen and barely moving. "I don't know

this little guy is going to make it," he warned, slipping the
opper into the puppy's mouth. He wasn't surprised when
puppy didn't even try to suck. It wasn't a good sign.

'We have to help him," she insisted, her voice firm as she
he puppy she was feeding back into the squirming pile of
bodies.

tin looked up at the determination he heard in her
he antithesis of the resignation he'd seen there only
s before. His gaze crashed into hers, and he felt an in-
ob of desire. He cursed the reaction, especially since
ight, he *didn't* know her or her story.

Does this mean you're staying?" The corner of his
ed upward in anticipation of spending some time
nding out how a woman like her ended up in the
owhere like this.

*. You're allowed to help and that's all. That ring on
l that belly say she's committed to someone else.*

*l, that sadness in her eyes and the fact that she's alone
g completely different,* he internally argued with
in wondered what happened to his "no romantic
t" resolution and how quickly this woman was
e him reconsider it. But he couldn't just leave a
stress to figure things out on her own. His father
im better than that.

An Excerpt from

THE MADDENING LORD MONTWOOD
The Rakes of Fallow Hall Series
by Vivienne Lorret

Lucan Montwood is the last man Frances Thorne
should ever trust. A gambler and a rake, he's
known for causing more trouble than he solves.
So when he offers his protection after Frances's
home and job are taken from her, she's more than a
little wary. After all, she knows Lord Montwood's
clever smile can disarm even the most guarded
heart. If she's not mindful, Frances may fall
prey to the most dangerous game of all—love.

An Excerpt from

THE MADDENING LORD MONTWOOD

The Rakes of Fallow Hall Series

by Vivienne Lorret

Lucan Montwood is the last man Frances should ever trust. A gambler and a rake, he's known for causing more trouble than he solves. So when he offers his protection after Frances's home and job are taken from her, she's more than a little wary. After all, she knows better. Lucan Montwood's clever smile can disarm with... most guarded hearts. If she's not mindful, Frances may fall prey to the most dangerous game of all—love.

"**Y**ou've abducted me?" A pulse fluttered at her throat. It came from fear, of course, and alarm. It most certainly did not flutter out of a misguided wanton thrill. At her age, she knew better. Or rather, she *should* know better.

That grin remained unchanged. "Not at all. Rest assured, you are free to leave here at any time—"

"Then I will leave at once."

"As soon as you've heard my warning."

It did not take long for a wave of exasperation to fill her and then exit her lungs on a sigh. "This is in regard to Lord Whitelock again. Will you ever tire of this subject? You have already said that you believe him to be a snake in disguise. I have already said that I don't agree. There is nothing more to say unless you have proof."

"And yet you require no proof to hold ill will against me," he challenged with a lift of his brow. "You have damned me with the same swift judgment that you have elevated Whitelock to sainthood."

What rubbish. "I did not set out to find the good in his lordship. The fact of his goodness came to me naturally, by way of his reputation. Even his servants cannot praise him enough. They are forever grateful for his benevolence. And I can find no fault in a man who would offer a position to a woman who'd been fired by her former employer and whose own father was taken to gaol."

"Perhaps he wants your gratitude," Lucan said, his tone edged with warning as he prowled nearer. "This entire series of events that has put you within his reach reeks of manipulation. You are too sensible to ignore how conveniently these circumstances have turned out in his favor."

"Yet I suppose I'm meant to ignore the *convenience* in which you've abducted me?"

He laughed. The low, alluring sound had no place in the light of day. It belonged to the shadows that lurked in dark alcoves and to the secret desires that a woman of seven and twenty never dare reveal.

"It was damnably hard to get you here," he said with such arrogance that she was assured her desires would remain secret forever. "You have no idea how much liquor Whitelock's driver can hold. It took an age for him to pass out."

Incredulous, she shook her head. "Are you blind to your own manipulations? It has not escaped my notice that you reacted *without* surprise to the news of my recent events. I can only assume that you are also aware of my father's current predicament."

"I have been to Fleet to see him." Lucan's expression lost all humor. "He has asked me to watch over you. So that is what I am doing."

What a bold liar Lucan was—and looking her in the eye all the while, no less. "*If* that is true," she scoffed, "you then interpreted his request as '*Please, sir, abduct my daughter*'? I find it more likely that he would have asked you to pay his debts to gain his freedom."

"He declined my offer."

She let out a laugh. "That is highly suspect. I do not think you are speaking a single word of truth."

"You are putting your faith in the wrong man." Something akin to irritation flashed in his gaze, like a warning shot. He took another step. "Perhaps those spectacles require new lenses. They certainly aren't aiding your sight."

"I wear these spectacles for reading, I'll have you know. Otherwise, my vision is fine," she countered, ignoring the heady static charge in the air between them. "I prefer to wear them instead of risking their misplacement."

"You wear them like a shield of armor."

The man irked her to no end. "Preposterous. I've no need for a shield of any sort. I cannot help it if you are intimidated by my spectacles *and* by my ability to see right through you."

He stepped even closer. An unknown force, hot and barely leashed, crackled in the ever-shrinking space. She watched as he slid the blank parchment toward him before withdrawing the quill from the stand. Ignoring her, he dipped the end into the ink and wrote something on the page.

Undeterred, she continued her harangue. "Though you may doubt it, I can spot those *snakes*—as you like to refer to members of your own sex—quite easily. I can come to an understanding of a man's character within moments of introduction. I am even able to anticipate"—Lucan handed the parchment to her. She accepted it and absently scanned the page—"his actions."

Suddenly, she stopped and read it again. *"As soon as you've finished reading this, I am going to kiss you."*

While she was still blinking at the words, Lucan claimed her mouth.

An Excerpt from

CHAOS

by *Jamie Shaw*

Jamie Shaw's rock stars are back, and a girl from
Shawn's past has just joined the band. But will a
month cooped up on a tour bus rekindle an old
flame . . . or destroy the band as they know it?

"That was a hundred years ago, Kale!" I shout at my closed bedroom door as I wiggle into a pair of skintight jeans. I hop backward, backward, backward—until I'm nearly tripping over the combat boots lying in the middle of my childhood room.

"So why are you going to this audition?"

I barely manage to do a quick twist-and-turn to land on my bed instead of my ass, my furrowed brow directed at the ceiling as I finish yanking my pants up. "Because!"

Unsatisfied, Kale growls at me from the other side of my closed door. "Is it because you still like him?"

"I don't even KNOW him!" I shout at a white swirl on the ceiling, kicking my legs out and fighting against the taut denim as I stride to my closed door. I grab the knob and throw it open. "And he probably doesn't even remember me!"

Kale's scowl is replaced by a big set of widening eyes as he takes in my outfit—tight, black, shredded-to-hell jeans paired with a loose black tank top that doesn't do much to cover the lacy bra I'm wearing. The black fabric matches my wristbands and the parts of my hair that aren't highlighted blue. I turn away from Kale to grab my boots.

"*That* is what you're wearing?"

I snatch up the boots and do a showman's twirl before plopping down on the edge of my bed. "I look hot, don't I?"

Kale's face contorts like the time I convinced him a Sour Patch Kid was just a Swedish Fish coated in sugar. "You're my *sister*."

"But I'm hot," I counter with a confident smirk, and Kale huffs out a breath as I finish tying my boots.

"You're lucky Mason isn't home. He'd never let you leave the house."

Freaking Mason. I roll my eyes.

I've been back home for only a few months—since December, when I decided that getting a bachelor's degree in music theory wasn't worth an extra year of nothing but general education requirements—but I'm already ready to do a kamikaze leap out of the nest again. Having a hyperactive roommate was nothing compared to my overprotective parents and even more overprotective older brothers.

"Well, Mason isn't home. And neither is Mom or Dad. So are you going to tell me how I look or not?" I stand back up and prop my hands on my hips, wishing my brother and I still stood eye to eye.

Sounding thoroughly unhappy about it, Kale says, "You look amazing."

A smile cracks across my face a moment before I grab my guitar case from where it's propped against the wall. As I walk through the house, Kale trails after me.

"What's the point in dressing up for him?" he asks with the echo of our footsteps following us down the hall.

"Who says it's for him?"

"Kit," Kale complains, and I stop walking. At the top of the stairs, I turn and face him.

"Kale, you know this is what I want to do with my life. I've wanted to be in a big-name band since middle school. And Shawn is an amazing guitarist. And so is Joel. And Adam is an amazing singer, and Mike is an amazing drummer . . . This is my chance to be *amazing*. Can't you just be supportive?"

My twin braces his hands on my shoulders, and I have to wonder if it's to comfort me or because he's considering pushing me down the stairs. "You know I support you," he says. "Just . . ." He twists his lip between his teeth, chewing it cherry red before releasing it. "Do you have to be amazing with *him*? He's an asshole."

"Maybe he's a different person now," I reason, but Kale's dark eyes remain skeptical as ever.

"Maybe he's not."

"Even if he isn't, *I'm* a different person now. I'm not the same nerd I was in high school."

I start down the stairs, but Kale stays on my heels, yapping at me like a nippy dog. "You're wearing the same boots."

"These boots are killer," I say—which should be obvious, but apparently needs to be said.

"Just do me a favor?"

At the front door, I turn around and begin backing onto the porch. "What favor?"

"If he hurts you again, use those boots to get revenge where it counts."

An Excerpt from

THE BRIDE WORE DENIM
A Seven Brides for Seven Cowboys Novel
by Lizbeth Selvig

When Harper Lee Crockett returns home
to Paradise Ranch, Wyoming, the last thing
she expects is to fall head-over-heels in lust
for Cole, childhood neighbor and her older
sister's long-time boyfriend. The spirited and
artistic Crockett sister has finally learned to
resist her craziest impulses, but this latest trip
home and Cole's rough and tough appeal might
be too much for her fading self-control.

An Excerpt from

THE BRIDE WORE DENIM

A Seven Brides for Seven Cowboys Novel

by Lizbeth Selvig

When Harper Lee Crockett returns home
to Paradise Ranch, Wyoming, the last thing
she expects is to fall head-over-boots in lust
for Cole, childhood neighbor and her older
sister's long-time boyfriend. The spirited and
artistic Crockett sister has finally learned to
refuse her reckless impulses, but this latest trip
home and Cole's rough and tough appeal might
be too much for her fading self-control.

Thank God for the chickens. *They* knew how to liven up a funeral.

Harper Crockett crouched against the rain-soaked wall of her father's extravagant chicken coop and laughed until she cried. This time, however, the tears weren't for the man who'd built the Henhouse Hilton—as she and her sisters had christened the porch-fronted coop that rivaled most human homes—they were for the eight multi-colored, escaped fowl that careened around the yard like over-caffeinated bees.

The very idea of a chicken stampede on one of Wyoming's largest cattle ranches was enough to ease her sorrow, even today.

She glanced toward the back porch of her parent's huge log home several hundred yards away to make sure she was still alone, and she wiped the tears and the rain from her eyes. "I know you probably aren't liking this, Dad," she said, aiming her words at the sopping chickens. "Chaos instead of order."

Chaos had never been acceptable to Samuel Crockett.

A *bock-bocking* Welsummer rooster, gorgeous with its burnt orange and blue body and iridescent green tail, powered past, close enough for an ambush. Harper sprang from her position and nabbed the affronted bird around its thick, shiny body. "Gotcha," she said as its feathers soaked her sweater. "Back to the pen for you."

The rest of the chickens squawked in alarm at the apprehension and arrest of one of their own. They scattered again scolding and flapping.

Yeah, she thought as she deposited the rooster back in the chicken yard, her father had no choice now but to glower at the bedlam from heaven. He was the one who'd left the darn birds behind.

As the hens fussed, Harper assessed the little flock made up of her father's favorite breeds—all chosen for their easygoing temperaments: friendly, buff-colored cochins; smart, docile, black and white Plymouth rocks; and sweet, shy black Australorps. Oh, what freedom and gang mentality could do—they'd turned into a band of egg-laying gangsters helping each other escape the law.

And despite there being seven chickens still left to corral, Harper reveled in sharing their attempted run for freedom with nobody. She brushed ineffectually at the mud on her soggy blue and brown broom skirt—hippie clothing, in the words of her sisters—and the stains on her favorite, crocheted summer sweater. It would have been much smarter to run back to the house and recruit help. Any number of kids bored with funereal reminiscing would have gladly volunteered. Her sisters—Joely and the triplets, if not Amelia—might have as well. The wrangling would have been done in minutes.

Something about facing this alone, however, fed her need to dredge any good memories she could from the day. She'd chased an awful lot of chickens throughout her youth. The memories served, and she didn't want to share them.

Another lucky grab garnered her a little Australorp who was returned, protesting, to the yard. Glancing around once more to check the empty, rainy yard, Harper squatted back under the eaves of the pretty, yellow chicken mansion and let the half dozen chickens settle. These were not her mother's birds. These were her father's "girls"—creatures who'd sometimes received more warmth than the human females he'd raised.

Good memories tried to flee in the wake of her petty thoughts, and she grabbed them back. Of course her father had loved his daughters. He'd just never been good at showing it. There'd been plenty of good times.

Rain pittered in a slow, steady rhythm over the lawn and against the coop's gingerbread scrollwork. It pattered into the genuine, petunia-filled, window boxes on their actual multipaned windows. Inside, the chickens enjoyed oak-trimmed nesting boxes, two flights of ladders, and chicken-themed artwork. Behind their over-the-top manse stretched half an acre of safely-fenced running yard trimmed with white picket fencing. Why the idiot birds were shunning such luxury to go AWOL out here in the rain was beyond Harper—even if they had found the gate improperly latched.

Wiping rain from her face again, she concentrated like a cat stalking canaries and made three more successful lunges. Chicken wrangling was rarely about mad chasing and much more about patience. She smiled evilly at the remaining three criminals who now eyed her with concern.

"Give yourselves up, you dirty birds," she called. "Your day on the lam is finished."

She swooped toward a fluffy Cochin, a chicken breed

normally known for its lazy friendliness, and the fat creature shocked her by feinting and then dodging. For the first time in this hunt, Harper missed her chicken. A resulting belly-flop onto the grass forced a startled grunt from her throat, and she slid four inches through a puddle. Before she could let loose the mild curse that bubbled up to her tongue, the mortifying sound of clapping echoed through the rain.

"I definitely give that a nine-point-five."

A hot flash of awareness blazed through her stomach, leaving behind unwanted flutters. She closed her eyes, fighting back embarrassment, and she hadn't yet found her voice when a large, sinewy male hand appeared in front of her, accompanied by rich, baritone laughter. She groaned and reached for his fingers.

"Hello, Cole," she said, resignation forcing her vocal chords to work as she let him help her gently but unceremoniously to her feet.

Cole Wainwright stood before her, the knot of his tie pulled three inches down his white shirt front, the two buttons above it spread open. That left the tanned, corded skin of his neck at Harper's eye level, and she swallowed. His brown-black hair was spiked and mussed, as if he'd just awoken, and his eyes sparkled in the rain like blue diamonds. She took a step back.

"Hullo, you," he replied.

CONTACTS 2015

104th EDITION
Published by Spotlight, 7 Leicester Place, London WC2H 7RJ
T 020 7437 7631   **F** 020 7437 5881
E questions@spotlight.com   **W** www.spotlight.com

What is Contacts?

Contacts is the essential handbook for everyone working or wanting to work in the entertainment industry. It has been published by Spotlight since 1947. It contains over 5000 listings for companies, services and individuals across all branches of Television, Stage, Film and Radio. These are updated annually to bring you the most accurate information available.

Also watch out for the 'Information & Advice pages', designed to tell you more about those listed and why you might want to contact them. They include valuable advice from key industry figures - especially helpful if you are just starting out in the industry.

As ever, please send any feedback or suggestions for the next edition to contacts@spotlight.com

How can I / my company appear in the next edition of Contacts?

Contacts is published annually. If you would like to appear in the next edition, either with an advert or a free, text-only listing, please visit: www.contactshandbook.com

How can I change my listing?

If you appear in this edition and wish to inform us of any changes please email: contacts@spotlight.com

How do I buy copies of Contacts?

To purchase copies of Contacts, visit www.contactshandbook.com, email sales@spotlight.com or call 020 7440 5026. It is also available from most good bookshops.

Designed by Consider. www.considercreative.co.uk
Printed and bound in Great Britain by Latimer Trend Company Ltd.

SPOTLIGHT

MANAGING PARTNER

Ben Seale

EDITOR

Kate Poynton

DESIGN & EDITION LAYOUT

Kathy Norrish

ADVERTISING SALES

contacts@spotlight.com

ACCOUNTS

Claire Adams – Chief Financial Officer
Nas Fokeerchand – Head of Accounts
Amelia Barnham

CASTING

Joe Bates – Head of Rooms & Studios
Ilayda Arden Nicholas Peel Liam Simpson

CLIENT RELATIONS

Pippa Harrison – Head of Client Relations
Emma Dyson Holly Janowski

CUSTOMER RELATIONS

Laura Albery – Head of Customer Relations
Sally Barnham
Alice Bruce-Tresnan Joan Queva Elinor Samuels

DATA PROCESSING

Joanna MacLeod – Head of Data Processing
Amanda Lawrence Emma Lear Sharon Mulcahy Caroline Taylor

HEAD OF PRODUCT

Gary Broughton

EDITORIAL

Cindy Dean
Sarah Spahovic (Editor, Case Studies & Information Pages)

HR

Marylin Peach – Head of HR & Facilities
Luke Turvey

IT

Jay Johnston – Chief Technical Officer
Dylan Beattie – Systems Architect
Nathaniel Ghilazghi Pencho Ilchev Tom Parker
James Singleton Adrian Wardle Dan Woodhead

IT SYSTEMS

Rainer Grebin – Operations Manager
Nicola Fahy Terry Fowell Chris Monteiro

MARKETING & SALES

Laura Albery – Head of Marketing & Sales
Lindsay Eyers Rachel Flenley Faye Maitland

PRODUCTION

Neill Kennedy
Hannah Frankel Nick Goldfinch David McCarthy

C →

Contents

Contents

A

Accountants, Insurance & Law   6
(includes Information & Advice pages)

Agents

- Agents & Personal Managers   13
  (includes Information & Advice pages)

- Children & Teenagers   73
  (includes Information & Advice pages)

- Concert & Promoters   90

- Dance   91
  (includes Information & Advice pages)

- Literary   96
  (includes Information & Advice pages)

- Presenters   100
  (includes Information & Advice pages)

- Voice Over   105
  (includes Information & Advice pages)

- Walk-On & Supporting Artists   112
  (includes Information & Advice pages)

Arts Centres   118

C

Casting Directors   122
(includes Information & Advice pages)

Consultants   142

Costumes, Wigs & Make-Up   150

Critics   156

D

Dance Companies   157
(includes Information & Advice pages)

Dance Organisations   163

Dance Training & Professional Classes   166

Drama Schools: Drama UK   170

Drama Training, Schools & Coaches   172
(includes Information & Advice pages)

F

Festivals   205
(includes Information & Advice pages)

Film & Video Facilities   211

Film, Radio, Television & Video Production Companies   213

Film & Television Schools   222
(includes Information & Advice pages)

Film & Television Studios   224

G

Good Digs Guide   225

H

Health & Wellbeing   230
(includes Information & Advice pages)

Contents

N

| Non-Acting Jobs | 237 |

O

| Opera Companies | 240 |
| Organisations | 242 |

P

Photographers: Advertisers Only	249
(includes Information & Advice pages)	
Promotional Services: CVs, Showreels, Websites etc	255
(includes Information & Advice pages)	
Properties & Trades	265
Publications: Print & Online	275
Publicity & Press Representatives	278

R

Radio	
– BBC Radio	280
(includes Information & Advice pages)	
– BBC Local	286
– Independent	288
Rehearsal Rooms & Casting Suites	291
(includes Information & Advice pages)	
Role Play Companies / Theatre Skills in Business	304

S

| Set Construction, Lighting, Sound & Scenery | 306 |

T

Television	
– BBC Television	311
– BBC Regional	315
– Independent	318
Theatre Producers	322
(includes Information & Advice pages)	
Theatre	
– Alternative & Community	336
(includes Information & Advice pages)	
– Children, Young People & TIE	342
– English Speaking in Europe	346
– London	347
– Outer London, Fringe & Venues	349
– Provincial / Touring	355
– Puppet Theatre Companies	360
– Repertory (Regional)	361

U

| Unions, Professional Guilds & Associations | 365 |
| (includes Information & Advice pages) | |

A →

Accountants, Insurance & Law

Agents
- Agents & Personal Managers
- Children & Teenagers
- Concert & Promoters
- Dance
- Literary
- Presenters
- Voice Over
- Walk-On & Supporting Artists

Arts Centres

PMA
For information regarding membership of
the Personal Managers' Association
please contact:

E info@thepma.com
W www.thepma.com

CPMA
For information regarding membership of
the Co-operative Personal Management
Association please contact The Secretary:

E cpmauk@yahoo.co.uk
W www.cpma.coop

Members of the above organisations
are clearly marked as such in the
appropriate listings.

Accountants, Insurance & Law

Why might I need this section?

This section contains listings for a number of companies and services which exist to help performers with the day-to-day administration of their working lives. Performers need to personally manage their business affairs in ways that those in 'normal' jobs do not. For example, unlike most employees, a performer does not have an accounts department to work out their tax and national insurance, or an HR department to take care of contracts or health insurance on their behalf. On top of which, performers can often be away on tour or on set for many months and unable to attend to these matters themselves.

Areas covered in this section include:

Accountants and other financial services

Dedicated companies exist which can help you to manage key financial issues, including national insurance, taxation, benefits, savings and pensions. Specialist mortgage companies also exist for performers and other self-employed workers within the entertainment industry. If you are a member of Equity, the main actors' union in the UK, you can ask them for free financial advice. An Equity pension scheme exists which the BBC, ITV, PACT, TV companies and West End theatre producers will pay into when you have a main part with one of them. Similar schemes also exist for dancers and other performers.

Insurance

Performers may often need specialist insurance for specific jobs, as well as the standard life and health insurance policies held by most people. A number of specialist insurers are listed in this section. Equity also offers a specialist backstage/accident and public liability insurance policy to all of its members.

Legal

There may be times in a performer's career when he/she needs specialist legal advice or representation. This could be because of a performer's high profile, complicated contractual details, or international employment issues. Legal advisers and solicitors are listed in this section. In addition, as part of their membership, Equity performers can also obtain free legal advice regarding professional engagements or personal injury claims.

How should I use these listings?

As when looking to hire any company or individual, contact a number of different companies and carefully compare the services they offer. Ask others in the industry for recommendations. If you are an Equity member, don't forget to check first that the service isn't already available free of charge, as part of your annual membership. For information about joining Equity, visit www.equity.org.uk or see their case study in the 'Unions' section.

Accountants, Insurance & Law

Accountants Breckman & Company have specialised in the arts/ entertainment industry for over 50 years. The firm's offices are located in the heart of London's West End, and more recently Brighton.

I joined the firm in 1991 (and still remember the interview!), I now run the firm with my two partners Kevin Beale and Graham Berry - both of whom have been with the firm in excess of 20 years. Founder Robert Breckman remains as a consultant, therefore we have many years' experience between us. We are a small firm, with a family atmosphere, working closely with our clients.

So you've left drama school and now you're ready to get out there and start working. Obviously, one of the first things you'll do (if you have not done so already) is to get yourself an agent. However, another important thing that you must do is to tell the taxman that you are now freelance. You must submit the relevant form (CWF1) by 5 October after the end of the tax year for which you need a tax return. The tax year runs from 6 April one year to 5 April the next - otherwise he will fine you!

As a freelancer you will be required to pay Class 2 National Insurance contributions and you can pay these either by monthly direct debit or six monthly bills. In addition, you will pay Class 4 National Insurance contributions on your (annual) profits at the current rate of 9%, on profits between £7,755 and £41,450 - on all profits above this a rate of 2% applies. Class 4 contributions are paid with your tax. Performers may have Class 1 contributions deducted at source, and therefore an adjustment can be made to ensure that you do not pay too much.

As of 6 April 2014 performers are no longer treated as employed for National Insurance purposes, and do not have Class 1 contributions deducted at source, therefore need to be prepared for larger tax bills in future.

Let's assume that you start freelancing on 1 August 2014 and therefore your first accounts and tax return go to 5 April 2015. That tax return must be completed and submitted to HMRC by 31 January 2016. The tax due (together with any Class 4 contributions) for that period must also be paid by 31 January 2016. In addition, the taxman will assume that you will earn the same amount in the following tax year to 5 April 2016, and you will be required to pay tax on account (based on the previous year's tax) in January and July. So, each January and July you will make payments on account - if your earnings are similar each year the amounts paid on account will remain similar, although they rarely are in this industry!

We generally recommend to freelance clients that they save at least 30 to 35% of their fees for tax and National Insurance contributions.

In order to complete your freelance accounts and tax return you will need to put together accurate figures for your (freelance) income and expenditure so you must keep adequate records. If you are with an agent they will supply regular statements which will provide you with a record of your income. For business expenses you must keep all receipts and invoices and if there are instances where you do not have a receipt keep a detailed note. A diary can also be a valuable backup for business expense claims.

Expenses claimed must be incurred "wholly and exclusively" for the purpose of your business. Typical examples are agent's commission, motor expenses (business miles only), travel/accommodation/subsistence (you are allowed the cost of an evening meal if an overnight stay is necessary for a business trip, and this extends to breakfast and lunch when overseas on business), use of home as office, equipment, scripts and trade journals, telephone, printing/postage/stationery, subscriptions, advertising/photographs, certain wardrobe, etc.

And finally, please note that if you earn (currently) in excess of £79,000 in any 12 month period you may need to register for VAT. Forms and guidance are available on the HMRC website or via advisers such as ourselves.

Good luck!

To find out more visit www.breckmanandcompany.co.uk

1505 T 020 7112 8750
Book-keeping Packages
20 Bedford Street, London WC2E 9HP
E hello@weare1505.co.uk
W www.weare1505.co.uk

ACCOUNTS ACTION LTD T 020 7437 0301
Arts & Media Accountancy
Suite 210A, Linen Hall
162-168 Regent Street, London W1B 5TB
E nick@accountsaction.net
W www.accountsaction.net

ADDERS T 01604 492534
60 Ashley Lane, Moulton
Northants NN3 7TJ
F 01604 642290
E jim@adders.co.uk
W www.adders.co.uk

ALEXANDER JAMES & CO T 020 8398 4447
Contact: Andrew Nicholson
Admirals Quarters
Portsmouth Road
Thames Ditton, Surrey KT7 0XA
F 020 8398 9989
E actors@alexanderjames.co.uk
W www.alexanderjames.co.uk

ARCHERFIELD PARTNERS LLP T 020 7871 0596
4 Pickering Place, St James's Street
London SW1A 1EA
F 020 7930 4340
E enquiries@archerfieldpartners.com
W www.archerfieldpartners.com

BAMBRIDGE ACCOUNTANTS T 020 3757 9290
1 Mercer Street
London WC2H 9QJ
E info@bambridgeaccountants.co.uk
W www.bambridgeaccountants.co.uk

BLACKMORE, Lawrence T 020 7240 1817
Production Accountant
Suite 5, 26 Charing Cross Road
London WC2H 0DG
E laurieblackmore@aol.com

BLAKE LAPTHORN T 020 7405 2000
Solicitors
Watchmaker Court
33 St John's Lane, London EC1M 4DB
F 020 7814 9421
E info@bllaw.co.uk
W www.bllaw.co.uk

BLINKHORNS T 020 7636 3702
27 Mortimer Street, London W1T 3BL
E info@blinkhorns.co.uk
W www.blinkhorns.co.uk

BOWKER ORFORD T 020 7636 6391
Accountants & Business Advisers
15-19 Cavendish Place, London W1G 0DD
F 020 7580 3909
E mail@bowkerorford.com
W www.bowkerorford.com

BREBNERS T 020 7734 2244
Chartered Accountants
130 Shaftesbury Avenue, London W1D 5AR
F 020 7287 5315
E partners@brebners.com
W www.brebners.com

BRECKMAN & COMPANY T 020 7499 2292
Chartered Certified Accountants. Registered Auditors
49 South Molton Street, London W1K 5LH
E info@breckmanandcompany.co.uk
W www.breckmanandcompany.co.uk

BRECKMAN & COMPANY T 01273 929350
Chartered Certified Accountants. Registered Auditors
95 Ditchling Road, Brighton BN1 4ST
E info@breckmanandcompany.co.uk
W www.breckmanandcompany.co.uk

CARNE, Charlie & CO T 020 8742 2001
Chartered Accountants
49 Windmill Road, London W4 1RN
E info@charliecarne.com

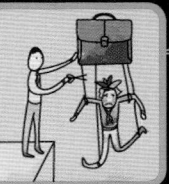

CHARTERED ACCOUNTANTS

Will Advise on Tax, Self Assessment, Accounts, Finance, Limited Companies etc **First meeting Free**

H And S Accountants LTD. 90 Mill Lane, West Hampstead, London NW6 1NL

T: 020 3174 1905 **F:** 020 7788 2984 **E:** hstaxplan@gmail.com

CARR, Mark & CO LTD   **T** 020 7717 8474
Chartered Accountants
90 Long Acre, Covent Garden, London WC2E 9RZ
T 01273 778802
E mark@markcarr.co.uk
W www.markcarr.co.uk

**CBW
(CARTER BACKER
WINTER LLP)**   **T** 020 7309 3800
*Chartered Accountants. Financial Planning. Tax Planning.
Corporate Recovery & Insolvency. Corporate Finance*
66 Prescot Street, London E1 8NN
F 020 7309 3801
E info@cbw.co.uk
W www.cbw.co.uk

**CITY ACCOUNTANTS &
TAX ADVISORS**   **T** 01733 777782
24 Broadway Gardens, Peterborough PE1 4DU
T 07976 244746
E info@cityaccountants.org.uk
W www.cityaccountants.org.uk

CLEARSKY ACCOUNTING   **T** 0808 1471776
Twitter: @ClearSkyEnt
Hampton House, Oldham Road, Manchester M24 1GT
E accountinginfo@clearskybusiness.co.uk
W www.clearskybusiness.co.uk/entertainment

COLLINS & COMPANY   **T** 020 8427 1888
Chartered Accountants
2nd Floor, 116 College Road
Harrow, Middlesex HA1 1BQ
F 020 8863 0068
E hq@collins116.com

COUNT AND SEE LTD   **T** 020 8767 7882
Tax, Accountancy & Book-keeping Services
219 Macmillan Way, London SW17 6AW
E info@countandsee.com
W www.countandsee.com

DUB & CO   **T** 020 7284 8686
7 Torriano Mews, London NW5 2RZ
F 020 7284 8687
E office@dub.co.uk
W www.dub.co.uk

EAM LONDON   **T** 020 3411 1011
Media Accountants
20 Bunhill Row, London EC1Y 8UE
E shayne.savill@eam.co.uk
W www.eam.co.uk

ENCORE INSURE
Online Theatre Insurance
E enquiries@encoreinsure.com
W www.encoreinsure.com

EQUITY INSURANCE SERVICES   **T** 01245 357854
131-133 New London Road
Chelmsford, Essex CM2 0QZ
F 01245 491641
E enquiries@equity-ins-services.com
W www.equity-ins-services.com

**FARROW ACCOUNTING &
TAX LTD**   **T** 020 8876 8020
94-95 South Worple Way
London SW14 8ND
F 020 8876 1116
E info@farrowaccounting.com
W www.farrowaccounting.com

FILM AND BUSINESS LAW LLP   **T** 020 7129 1449
Offices in London, Paris & Los Angeles
17 Cavendish Square
London W1G 0PH
E legal@filmandbusinesslaw.com
W www.filmandbusinesslaw.com

FINDLAY, Richard   **T** 0131 226 3253
Entertainment Lawyer. Business Consultant
1 Darnaway Street
Edinburgh EH3 6DW
T 07850 327725
E mail@richardfindlay.biz

**FISHER PACKMAN
& ASSOCIATES**   **T** 020 8732 5500
Chartered Accountants. In association with Simia Wall
Devonshire House, 582 Honeypot Lane
Stanmore HA7 1JS
F 020 8732 5501
E nik@fisherpackman.com
W www.fisherpackman.com

**FISHER PACKMAN
& ASSOCIATES**   **T** 020 8732 5500
Chartered Accountants. In association with Simia Wall
Sir Robert Peel House
178 Bishopsgate
London EC2M 4NJ
F 020 8732 5501
E nik@fisherpackman.com
W www.fisherpackman.com

FORD, Jonathan & CO LTD   **T** 0151 426 4512
Chartered Accountants
Maxwell House
Liverpool Innovation Park
Liverpool L7 9NJ
E info@jonathanford.co.uk
W www.jonathanford.co.uk

**GALLAGHER
ENTERTAINMENT**   **T** 020 3430 6952
Insurance Brokers
Pinewood Studios, Pinewood Road
Iver, Bucks SL0 0NH
E james_fox@ajg.com
W www.ajg.co.uk

H & S ACCOUNTANTS LTD   **T** 020 3174 1905
Chartered Accountants
90 Mill Lane, West Hampstead
London NW6 1NL
F 020 7788 2984
E hstaxplan@gmail.com
W www.hstaxplan.com

HARDWICKE   **T** 020 7691 0056
Contact: Mark Engelman (Barrister). Media Law
Hardwicke Building
Lincoln's Inn
London WC2A 3SB
T 07720 294667
E mark.engelman@hardwicke.co.uk
W www.hardwicke.co.uk

HARIJYOT LTD   **T** 07958 772581
79 Portland Crescent
Stanmore
Middlesex HA7 1LY
E jignesh@harijyot.co.uk

HILL DICKINSON LLP   **T** 0151 600 8000
1 St Paul's Square
Old Hall Street
Liverpool L3 9SJ
E mediateam@hilldickinson.com
W www.hilldickinson.com

HOOD, Karl LLP   **T** 07916 971998
28A Kings Road, Kingston
Surrey KT2 5HS
E karlhood1@gmail.com

HW LEE ASSOCIATES LLP   **T** 020 7025 4600
New Derwent House
69-73 Theobalds Road
London WC1X 8TA
F 020 7025 4666
E enquiries@hw-lee.com
W www.hw-lee.com

JENKINS, Andrew LTD   **T** 01799 531358
Accountancy Services. Book-keeping. Payroll
The Old House, High Street
Little Chesterford
Saffron Walden
Essex CB10 1TS
T 07977 425518
E andrew@andrewjenkinsltd.com
W www.andrewjenkinsltd.com

**LA PLAYA ARTS
& ENTERTAINMENT**   **T** 01223 200650
Insurance & Financial Services
60 Cannon Street, London EC4N 6NT
T 020 7002 1007
E tracey.mccreath@laplayainsurance.com
W www.laplayainsurance.com

**LACHMAN SMITH
ACCOUNTANTS**   **T** 020 8731 1700
16B North End Road
Golders Green, London NW11 7PH
F 020 8731 1701
E accounts@lachmansmith.co.uk
W www.lachmansmith.co.uk

**LARK INSURANCE
BROKING GROUP**   **T** 020 7543 2800
Ibex House, 42-47 Minories
London EC3N 1DY
F 020 7543 2801
E mailbox@larkinsurance.co.uk
W www.larkinsurance.co.uk

**MARSHAM ACCOUNTANTS &
CONSULTANTS**   **T** 07852 814845
11 Billroth Court, 3 Mornington Close
London NW9 5JQ
E info@marshams.com
W www.marshams.com

MGM ACCOUNTANCY LTD   T 020 7379 9202
3rd Floor, 20 Bedford Street
London WC2E 9HP
E admin@mgmaccountancy.co.uk
W www.mgmaccountancy.co.uk

MGR WESTON KAY LLP   T 020 7625 4545
Chartered Accountants. Business Administration. Touring
55 Loudoun Road, St John's Wood
London NW8 0DL
F 020 7625 5265
E info@mgr.co.uk
W www.mgr.co.uk

MHA MACINTYRE HUDSON   T 020 7429 4100
Media & Entertainment Accountants
New Bridge Street House
30-34 New Bridge Street, London EC4V 6BJ
F 020 7248 8939
E entertainment@mhllp.co.uk
W www.macintyrehudson.co.uk

**MONEYWISE
INVESTMENTS PLC**   T 020 8552 5521
Insurance Brokers
440-442 Romford Road, London E7 8DF
E aadatia@moneywiseplc.co.uk
W www.moneywiseplc.co.uk

NYMAN LIBSON PAUL   T 020 7433 2400
Chartered Accountants
Regina House, 124 Finchley Road
London NW3 5JS
F 020 7433 2401
E entertainment@nlpca.co.uk
W www.nlpca.co.uk

O'DRISCOLL, G. & CO   T 01621 893888
2 Catchpole Lane, Great Totham
Maldon, Essex CM9 8PY
T 07780 662544
E info@godriscoll.co.uk
W www.godriscoll.co.uk

**PERFORMANCE
ACCOUNTANCY**   T 01344 669084
*Chartered Accountants Specialising in Performers
& the Entertainment Industry*
6 Pankhurst Drive, Harmans Water
Bracknell, Berkshire RG12 9PS
F 01344 449727
E louise@performanceaccountancy.co.uk
W www.performanceaccountancy.co.uk

PLANISPHERES   T/F 020 7602 2038
Business & Legal Affairs
Sinclair House, 2 Sinclair Gardens, London W14 0AT
E info@planispheres.com
W www.planispheres.com

RALLI   T 0161 832 6131
Specialising in Personal Injury, IP & Business
Jackson House, Sibson Road, Sale M33 7RR
E enquiries@ralli.co.uk
W www.ralli.co.uk

**REES ASTLEY
INSURANCE BROKERS LTD**   T 01686 626019
Mostyn House, Market Street
Newtown, Powys SY16 2PQ
F 01686 628457
E performingarts@reesastley.co.uk
W www.insurance4performingarts.co.uk

**ROBERTSON TAYLOR W & P
LONGREACH**   T 020 7510 1234
*Contact: Bev Hewes. Specialist Entertainment
Insurance Brokers*
America House
2 America Square
London EC3N 2LU
E enquiries@rtib.co.uk
W www.rtworldwide.com

**SLOANE & CO CHARTERED
CERTIFIED ACCOUNTANTS
& REGISTERED ACCOUNTANTS**   T 020 7221 3292
36-38 Westbourne Grove
Newton Road
London W2 5SH
F 020 7229 4810
E mail@sloane.co.uk
W www.sloane.co.uk

THEATACCOUNTS LLP   T 01905 823177
Twitter: @theataccounts
The Oakley
Kidderminster Road
Droitwich Spa
Worcestershire WR9 9AY
F 01905 799856
E info@theataccounts.co.uk
W www.theataccounts.co.uk

**TOWERGATE
PROFESSIONAL RISKS**   T 0844 3463307
Public Liability Insurance
Kings Court, London Road
Stevenage, Herts SG1 2GA
F 01438 747465
E professionalrisks@towergate.co.uk
W www.performingartsinsurance.co.uk

USMAN ACCOUNTANCY   T 020 3732 4685
26 York Street
London W1U 6PZ
T 07809 448969
E info@usmanaccountancy.co.uk
W www.usmanaccountancy.co.uk

**WISE & CO
CHARTERED ACCOUNTANTS**   T 01252 711244
Contact: Stephen Morgan
Wey Court West, Union Road
Farnham, Surrey GU9 7PT
E smo@wiseandco.co.uk
W www.wiseandco.cc.uk

**WISE & CO
CHARTERED ACCOUNTANTS**   T 01753 656770
Contact: Stephen Morgan
Room 101
Pinewood Studios
Iver Heath, Bucks SL0 0NH
E smo@wiseandco.co.uk
W www.wiseandco.co.uk

WMT LLP   T 01727 838255
Tax Specialists
2nd Floor
45 Grosvenor Road
St Albans, Hertfordshire AL1 3AW
F 01727 861052
E info@wmtllp.com
W www.wmtllp.com

Agents & Personal Managers

Who are agents and personal managers?

There are hundreds of agents and personal managers in the UK, representing thousands of actors and artists. It is their job to promote their clients to casting opportunities and negotiate contracts on their behalf. In return, they take commission ranging from 10-15%. Larger agencies can have hundreds of clients on their books; smaller ones may only have a handful. Agents usually try to represent a good range of artists (age, gender, type) to fill the diverse role types required by casting directors. A personal manager is someone who manages an artist's career on a more one-on-one basis.

What is a co-operative agency?

Co-operative agencies are staffed by actors themselves, who take turns to handle the administrative side of the agency and promote themselves to casting opportunities as a team. If you want more control over your career and can handle the pressures and responsibility that an agent takes away from you, then you might consider joining a co-operative agency. However it is very important that you think carefully about what you are signing up for.

You will be responsible for the careers of others as well as yourself, so you must first of all be able to conduct yourself well when speaking to casting professionals. You will also have to commit some of your time to administrative jobs. You must be prepared to deal with finances and forms – all the boring paperwork you usually hand over to your agent! You must also be aware that the other actors in the agency will want to interview you and, if you are successful, to give you a trial period working with them. The Co-operative Personal Management Association (CPMA) offers advice about joining a co-operative agency on their website www.cpma.coop

Why do I need an agent?

A good agent will have contacts and authority in the entertainment industry that you, as an individual actor, would find more difficult to acquire. Agents, if you want them to, can also deal with matters such as Equity and Spotlight membership renewal. They can offer you advice on which headshots to use, what to include or exclude in your CV as you acquire more skills and experience, what a particular casting director might expect when you are invited to an audition, and so on.

How should I use these listings?

If you are an actor getting started in the industry, or looking to change your agent, the following listings will supply you with up-to-date contact details for many of the UK's leading agencies. Every company listed is done so by written request to us. Members of the Personal Managers' Association (PMA) and the Co-operative Personal Management Association (CMPA) have indicated their membership status under their name.

Some agencies have also chosen to list other information such as relevant contact names, their preferred method of contact from new applicants, whether or not they are happy to receive showreels and/or voicereels with prospective clients' CVs and headshots, the number of performers represented by the agency, the number of agents working for the company, and/or a description of the performance areas they cover. Use this information to narrow down your search for a suitable agent.

How do I choose a new agent?

When writing to agencies, try to research the individual company instead of just sending a 'blanket' letter to every single one. This way you can target your approaches to the most suitable agencies and avoid wasting their time (and yours). As well as using the listing information provided here, look at agency websites and ask around for personal recommendations.

Unfortunately Spotlight is not able to offer personalised advice on choosing an agent, nor is it in a position to handle any financial or contractual queries or complaints, but we have prepared some useful career advice on our website: www.spotlight.com/artists/advice. Click on our Frequently Asked Questions page for general guidance regarding agents, or you may wish to try consulting our list of Independent Advisory Services, for one-to-one tailored advice.

Agents & Personal Managers

You can also contact The Agents' Association www.agents-uk.com or The Personal Managers' Association (PMA) www.thepma.com

If you are a member of Equity then you can contact their legal and welfare department for general information about issues including commissions, fees and contracts. However, Equity is not able to recommend specific agencies or agents.

How do I approach agencies?

Once you have made a list of suitable agencies, consult the listings again. Some agencies have indicated their preferred method of initial contact, whether by post, e-mail or telephone. Do not e-mail them, for example, if they have stated that they wish to receive your headshot, CV and covering letter by post. It is becoming far more common to email agents with applications but if you are doing it by post you should always include a stamped-addressed envelope (SAE) big enough to contain your 10 x 8 photo and with sufficient postage. This will increase your chances of getting a reply. Write your name and telephone number on the back of your headshot in case it gets separated from your CV.

Remember that agents receive hundreds of letters and e-mails each week, so try to keep your communication concise, and be professional at all times. We also recommend that your covering letter has some kind of focus: perhaps you can tell them about your next showcase, or where they can see you currently appearing on stage. This should always be addressed to an individual, not "To whom it may concern" or "Dear Sir or Madam". Some agents have indicated a specific contact to whom you can direct correspondence in their listing, otherwise check the agency's website or give them a call and find out who you should address your letter or e-mail to.

Some agents have indicated that they are happy to receive a showreel and/or voicereel with your CV, but it would be best to exclude these from your correspondence if they are not mentioned. Point out in your covering letter that one is available and the agent can contact you if they want to find out more.

Should I pay an agent to join their books? Or sign a contract?

Equity (the actors' trade union) does not recommend that artists pay an agent to join their client list. Before signing a contract, you should be very clear about the terms and commitments involved. For advice on both of these issues, or if you experience any problems with a current agent, we recommend that you contact Equity www.equity.org.uk. They also produce the booklet *You and your Agent* which is free to all Equity members and available from their website's members' area.

How do I become an agent?

Budding agents will need to get experience of working in an agent's office; usually this is done by working as an assistant. It can be extremely hard work, and you will be expected to give up a lot of your evenings to attend productions. There are two organisations you may find it useful to contact: The Agents' Association www.agents-uk.com and the Personal Managers' Association www.thepma.com

CASE STUDY

Bohemia was opened in 1992 in Los Angeles by Susan Ferris. It was started with 3 actors and a band. Since then The Bohemia Group has grown to 6 offices around the United States (Los Angeles, NYC, New Orleans, Atlanta, Pittsburgh & Dallas) and an office in London. Here she tells us how things work in the USA.

Because our management is very hands on, our lists tend to be smaller and more diverse. We handle actors, writers, directors, musicians, producers and skateboarders (you would be surprised at how much management they need!)

As managers, our job really is not to get you work. That lands squarely on the shoulders of the agents. Although the lines are blurry in the UK they are very clear in the US. Your agent gets you work…. your manager does everything else (sometimes we get you work too!). But we are much more strategists. And generally you should have both. The goal of course is that you have a manager and an agent who work well together so your team is strong and you all share the same vision.

If you already have a visa (or green card), the next big hurdle in the US is going to be the union. If you want to work in the US in television and film, you have to join and it's not cheap. One of the things we have done at Bohemia is become a SAG signatory so that we are able to help facilitate our clients putting together web series that will get them one step closer to the ever elusive SAG card.

Is it key to have a manager in the US? I think it is. Hopefully, a good manager will basically eliminate the first year of growing pains that ALL actors go through. If you are coming to the US with a 0-1 it is best if a manager sponsors it. Over the past year the production companies are getting more and more wary of visas sponsored by lawyers and are insisting a manager or agent be the sponsor or they will not see the actor. Bohemia will only work with actors that we sponsor. It just makes our lives (and yours) easier.

As the world gets smaller and smaller I think it is important that actors keep their options open. Not everyone can work in every country. But that doesn't mean you should not understand how the business works everywhere. We are big advocates of educating folks in the business - not just actors - managers, agents; whatever your chosen profession is in the entertainment

business. No one has to be an expert. But I am constantly fascinated by the amount of information people don't have. And don't necessarily care. Then when things don't happen as fast as they want…. they scratch their heads and don't know why.

I am always amazed when an actor sits in front of me and tells me they don't watch TV! Or they only see art-house films or theatre because they think it makes them smarter or more cultured. If you are an actor and you are not on a job then I expect you to watch everything, at least once…. consider it homework!

What do we expect?

If you are new and building your credits, I expect you to do casting director workshops. Part of a manager's job is to help you be strategic about them - you want casting directors to get to know you while you start building your US credits…. they are a necessary evil.

We expect you to get into class. I am assuming you already know how to act…that is not what being in a class is about. It is about working your muscle. You should always be working the muscle if you are not working on a show. This seems to be a stumbling block for a lot of actors (especially if you have just come out of school) … some of the greatest actors out there are STILL in class. Check the ego at the door…

We expect you to take pictures that look like you. They have to represent what you actually look like and also consider if they represent what the US market wants to see.

We expect you to communicate - a manager should keep your calendar. The assistant at Bohemia has every client's calendar (yes… everyone). If a great opportunity comes up and we call and you are fly fishing in Montana or in Egypt (yes…. both those things REALLY happened) and you didn't think it was important to tell us then it makes us wonder why we are working so hard.

Being a manager is really one of the best jobs in the industry, to have the ability to navigate an actor at any level of their career to the next level (and then the next etc.) is challenging but it's not brain surgery and I can tell you that in our offices not a day goes by that we aren't laughing and loving what we do.

**To find out more visit
www.bohemiaent.com**

Agents & Personal Managers

Matt Chopping joined Waring & McKenna in 2001. He works as an agent alongside Daphne Waring & John Summerfield. They represent actors in all areas of the industry offering high level personal management to nurture the careers of performers both nationally and internationally.

Advice for anyone considering becoming a professional actor:

My advice is, firstly, to fall in love with the craft of acting and be 100% sure it is the career path you wish to follow. Start by studying professional actors: watch them on screen and especially watch them perform their craft on stage. Be inspired by these performers. At the same time, reflect upon how you can bring something new and different to the industry. If you are still at school, get involved in school productions or get some friends together and make a short film. Gaining as much performance experience as possible when you're starting out will reap great rewards in the future. For some, an important step toward becoming a professional actor is to apply for a place at one of the accredited drama schools. Not only does it demonstrate your dedication to pursuing your passion, your acting skills will also be greatly enhanced by the quality training you receive. Towards the end of your training, you will have the opportunity to demonstrate your talents in various drama school productions and showcases. These will be attended by industry professionals such as agents and casting directors.

Pros and cons of the acting industry:

My 13 years' experience in the acting industry has afforded me insight into its pros and cons. There are wonderful moments in my job, such as when a client gets a career-changing job or embarks upon a major theatre role. The acting industry can be dynamic and thrilling, full of wonderful, talented, eccentric and creative individuals. We now work in an international arena which is connected 24/7 and actors with the right management team behind them have the opportunity to audition for work from all over the globe. A client who has the right

ingredients for success combined with a strong management team can achieve the goals they have set themselves. The acting industry also has its cons: it is highly competitive and a high proportion of fees an actor would receive for their work in television, film and theatre in the UK are now relatively low, thus a challenge for actors of all ages to make a decent living. It is an industry which has never been easy to survive, however in my opinion; hard-working, talented, driven actors with the right management can thrive. My advice to anyone who is considering a career in acting is to find a way to fund your early years in the industry, especially if you are based in London. It will also alleviate the pressure on yourself to make a living from acting, and any monies you then earn from acting are a bonus.

What a performer should look for in an agent:

An actor should apply to agents whose clients are working on the same sort of productions that they themselves would like to work on. They should seek to apply to a well-established agent who is well connected with solid relationships in the industry. An agent must also have a strong focus on career management.

What an agent looks for in new clients:

I'm looking to sign talented actors from all walks of life who I feel have a strong chance of a long and rewarding career in the industry. I look for dedicated, driven individuals who I connect with and who I can work closely with on a day-to-day basis to achieve the same goal. When meeting a prospective client, in addition to seeing their work, I focus on how they behave in the meeting. For me, it's an indication of how they will conduct themselves in the professional arena.

How a performer might best approach a new agent:

Most agents advise on how to apply on their website, so list the agencies you wish to apply for then look at their "how to apply to us" page. Send a copy of your photo and CV via the agent's preferred method. Make sure you address the agent correctly by checking on the agency's website. You would be amazed how many applicants get the agent's name wrong, which obviously gives a poor first impression. You can write to "all agents" and your application will be passed around the office. Include a link to your showreel if you have one, and your Spotlight page. Take the time to get a professional photo, it is one of the most important tools you have of not only securing representation, but getting you seen for work throughout your career. Timing is important when you write to an agent. If you are in a production, invite the agent to come and see you. Agents are busy people and need a few weeks' notice, not days. If you have an upcoming television role, mention the air date and time your application accordingly. Remember that your application is a key opportunity to sell yourself. Agencies receive many applications each week so take the time to get it right. Don't blanket agents with the same letter; tailor each application to the particular agent. Take time to look at the work the agent's clients are doing to find a way of writing a letter that is carefully considered rather than rushed without thought. We do read them.

Relationships:

A strong working relationship between agent and actor is extremely important and, for me, is the most rewarding aspect of being an agent. A strong relationship is forged over time. Both actor and agent share the same ambition and work closely, often for many years, to achieve the client's career goals for our mutual benefit. As with any relationship, it thrives on trust, honesty, communication and patience from both parties. Both actor and agent grow and develop in their careers over time and a close professional partnership is crucial for handling the inevitable highs and lows that a career in acting brings. As an agent, my relationships with casting directors and industry professionals have been forged and developed over 13+ years. Many nights have been spent at the theatre together and many phone calls made. These relationships are also built on trust, and our mutual respect for the actors who we look after at Waring & McKenna.

Talent & Hard Work:

If you decide to become professional actor, remember that this will be your chosen career for the next 50-60 years. Take the time in your early career to lay solid foundations for the future. Nurture your relationships over time with casting directors, directors, producers and other actors. It is likely that you will meet them time and time again. Remember that as a professional actor, you are in fact running your own business.

Many successful actors I work with are not only exceptionally talented artists, but work extremely hard at their own self-promotion. They maintain existing contacts and develop new contacts continuously, thus promoting their own business which works in symbiosis with their agent's work. I admire actors who work hard to hone their craft, especially after they have finished training. They continue to take classes to improve existing skills, learn new skills and inevitably increase their employability.

An Agent's Job:

An agent's job is extremely varied. A typical day for me would be submitting clients for roles on Spotlight and calling the casting director, bringing that client to their attention. I will then book clients on work, negotiating their financial deals and contractual obligations to the project. I will arrange to take casting directors to theatre press nights. I will go on a set visit to see a client who is filming. I will speak to my clients. I will visit drama school shows. I will make sure a client gets paid on time. The job of an agent is essentially day-to-day problem solving, drawing on my skills in sales, I.T., negotiation and legal matters. I am very fortunate in that my work also compliments my personal passion for the arts of television, film and theatre. I enjoy looking after my clients day-to-day, which often requires a level of pastoral care and developing a solid working relationship. Ultimately though, the most rewarding aspect of my job is when, after months or years of hard work and development, a client lands a career changing job of major significance. It is a truly wonderful moment for both actor and agent.

To find out more visit www.waringandmckenna.com

1984 PERSONAL MANAGEMENT LTD   **T** 020 7251 8046
CPMA Member. Contact: David Meyer. By Post. Accepts Showreels. 25 Performers
Suite 508, Davina House
137 Goswell Road, London EC1V 7ET
F 020 7250 3031
E info@1984pm.com
W www.1984pm.com

1ST TALENT AGENCY   **T** 0845 6454000
Feature Films. Commercials. Television
1 Beaumont Avenue
West Kensington, London W14 9LP
E 1sttalent@gmail.com
W www.1sttalent.com

21ST CENTURY ACTORS MANAGEMENT LTD   **T** 020 7278 3438
CPMA Member. Contact: By e-mail. Commercials. Film. Stage. Television
206 Panther House, 38 Mount Pleasant
London WC1X 0AN
E 21centuryactors@gmail.com
W www.21stcenturyactors.co.uk

2MA LTD   **T** 023 8074 1354
Sports. Stunts
Spring Vale, Tutland Road
North Baddesley, Hants SO52 9FL
F 023 8074 1355
E mo.matthews@2ma.co.uk
W www.2ma.co.uk

42   **T** 020 7292 0554
8 Flitcroft Street, London WC2H 8DL
E talent@42mp.com

A & B PERSONAL MANAGEMENT LTD   **T** 020 7794 3255
Personal Manager. Contact: By e-mail
PO Box 64671, London NW3 9LH
E b.ellmain@aandb.co.uk

A & J ARTISTS LTD   **T** 020 8342 0542
242A The Ridgeway, Botany Bay
Enfield EN2 8AP
T 020 8367 7139
E jo@ajmanagement.co.uk
W www.ajmanagement.co.uk

A-LIST LOOKALIKES & ENTERTAINMENTS LTD   **T** 0113 253 0563
Top Floor, Crank Mills
New Bank Street, Morley, Leeds LS27 8NT
E info@alistlookalikes.co.uk
W www.alistlookalikes.co.uk

A GENT THE   **T** 07779 595194
16 Globe Row, Dafen
Llanelli, Carmarthenshire SA14 8PA
E mark@theagent.biz
W www.theagent.biz

AARDVARK CASTING LONDON   **T** 020 8667 9812
15 Deans Close, Croydon
London CR0 5PU
T 07587 006176
E london@aardvarkcasting.com
W www.aardvarkcasting.com

ABA MANAGEMENT   **T** 01737 821348
Robert Denholm House, Bletchingley Road
Nutfield, Redhill, Surrey RH1 4HW
E admin@abacusagency.co.uk
W www.abacusaba.com

ABAKPORO, Chris   **T** 07903 192413
Based in London
E chrisabak@hotmail.co.uk

ACA MODELS.COM   **T** 028 9080 9809
381 Beersbridge Road, Belfast BT5 5DT
F 028 9080 9808
E bookings@ACAmodels.com
W www.acamodels.com

ACCESS ARTISTE MANAGEMENT LTD   **T** 020 7866 5444
Contact: Sarah Bryan. By Post/e-mail. Accepts Showreels
71-75 Shelton Street, Covent Garden
London WC2H 9JQ
E mail@access-uk.com
W www.access-uk.com

ACTOR-MUSICIANS @ ACCESS   **T** 020 7866 5444
Personal Manager. Contact: Sarah Bryan. By Post/e-mail. Specialises in Actor-Musicians
c/o Access Artiste Management Ltd
71-75 Shelton Street
Covent Garden, London WC2H 9JQ
E mail@access-uk.com
W www.access-uk.com

ACTORS AGENCY   **T** 0131 228 4040
1 Glen Street, Tollcross, Edinburgh EH3 9JD
E info@stivenchristie.co.uk
W www.stivenchristie.co.uk

ACTORS AGENCY OF SWEDEN THE   **T** 00 46 8 56305400
Contact: Serina Björnbom/Janna Gränesjö
Gamla Brogatan 44, 111 20 Stockholm, Sweden
E janna@actorsagency.se
W www.actorsagency.se

ACTORS ALLIANCE   **T/F** 020 7407 6028
CPMA Member. Contact: By Post. Commercials. Corporate. Film. Stage. Stills. Television
Disney Place House, 14 Marshalsea Road
London SE1 1HL
E actors@actorsalliance.co.uk
W www.actorsalliance.co.uk

ACTORS' CREATIVE TEAM   **T** 020 7278 3388
CPMA Member
Panther House, 38 Mount Pleasant, London WC1X 0AN
F 020 7833 5086
E office@actorscreativeteam.co.uk
W www.actorscreativeteam.co.uk

ACTORS DIRECT LTD   **T** 0161 277 9360
Number 5, 651 Rochdale Road, Manchester M9 5SH
T 07427 616549
E info@actorsdirect.org.uk
W www.actorsdirect.org.uk

ACTORS FILE THE   **T** 020 7582 7923
Personal Manager. Co-operative. CPMA Member. Contact: By Post/e-mail
The White House at Oval House
52-54 Kennington Oval
London SE11 5SW
E theactorsfile@btconnect.com
W www.theactorsfile.co.uk

ACTORS' GROUP THE (TAG)   **T/F** 0161 834 4466
Personal Manager. CPMA Member
Swan Buildings, 20 Swan Street
Manchester M4 5JW
E enquiries@theactorsgroup.co.uk
W www.theactorsgroup.co.uk

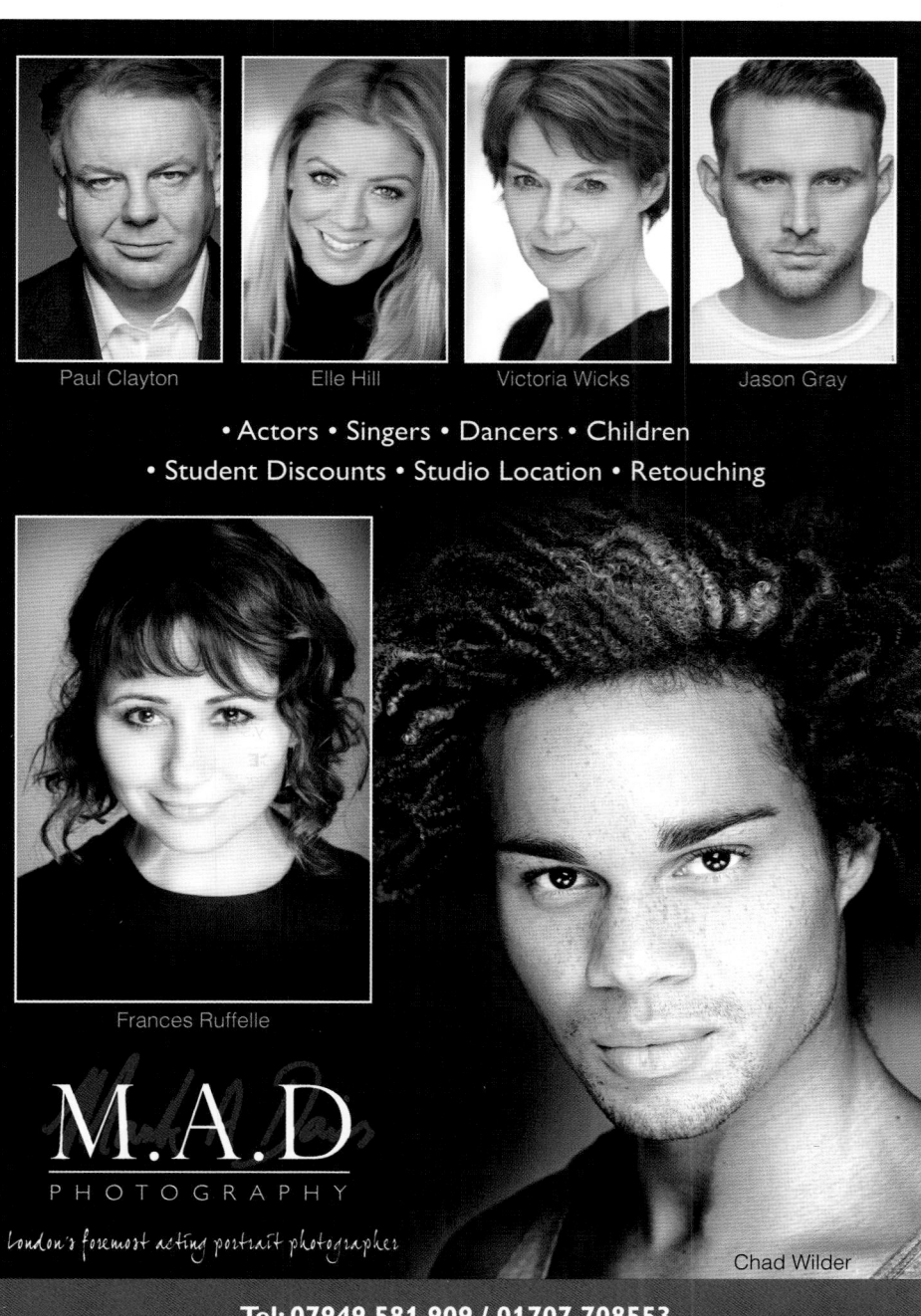

ACTORS IN SCANDINAVIA   T 00 358 4 00540640
Jääkärinkatu 10, 00150, Helsinki, Finland
E laura@actorsinscandinavia.com
W www.actorsinscandinavia.com

ACTORS INTERNATIONAL LTD   T 020 7025 8777
18 Soho Square, London W1D 3QL
F 020 7025 8001
E mail@actorsinternational.co.uk

ACTORS WORLD CASTING   T 07960 332846
13 Briarbank Road, London W13 0HH
T 07870 594388
E katherine@actors-world-production.com
W www.voiceoverworld.eu

ACTORUM LTD   T 020 7636 6978
The Annexe, 25 Eccleston Place, London SW1W 9NF
E info@actorum.com
W www.actorum.com

ADA   T 07951 477015
Contact: Rachael Power. By e-mail. Will Accept
Showreels/Voicereels. 1 Agent represents 25
Performers. Commercials. Film. Stage. Television.
Voice Overs
11 St George's Crescent, Rhyl
Clwyd LL18 3NN
E casting@actorsdirectassociates.net
W www.actorsdirectassociates.net

AESTHETIC CLARITY LTD   T 07812 371225
Contact: By e-mail only. Accepts Showreels
145 Foxhole Road, Paignton
Devon TQ3 3EY
E thenamebehindtheface@yahoo.com
W www.thenamebehindtheface.com

AFA ASSOCIATES   T 020 7682 3677
Unit 101, Business Design Centre
52 Upper Street, London N1 0QH
E afa-associates@hotmail.com

AFA MANAGEMENT   T 07979 737950
Amanda Fairclough Actors Management
14 Cheviot Close, Horwich, Bolton BL6 7DF
T 07929 823110
E info@afamanagement.co.uk
W www.afamanagement.co.uk

AFFINITY MANAGEMENT   T 01342 715275
The Coach House, Down Park
Turners Hill Road, Crawley Down
West Sussex RH10 4HQ
E jstephens@affinitymanagement.co.uk

AGENCY / RED LETTER
FILM AGENCY LTD THE   T 00 353 1 6618535
Contact: Teri Hayden, Karl Hayden
9 Upper Fitzwilliam Street, Dublin 2, Ireland
E admin1@tagency.ie
W www.theagency.ie

AGENCY:105   T 020 7205 2316
Twitter: @agency105
INC Artists Ltd, 90 Long Acre
Covent Garden, London WC2E 9RZ
E chris@international-collective.com
W www.agency105.com

AGENCY OAKROYD   T 01943 600820
Oakroyd, 89 Wheatley Lane
Ben Rhydding, Ilkley, Yorkshire LS29 8PP
T 07840 784337
E paula@agencyoakroyd.com
W www.agencyoakroyd.com

AHA
See HOWARD, Amanda ASSOCIATES LTD

AIM (ASSOCIATED INTERNATIONAL
MANAGEMENT)   T 020 7831 9709
PMA Member
4th Floor, 6-7 Hatton Garden
London EC1N 8AD
E info@aimagents.com
W www.aimagents.com

AIRCRAFT
CIRCUS PERFORMANCE   T 07946 472329
Circus Artists only
7A Melish House, Harrington Way
London SE18 5NR
E lucy@aircraftcircus.com
W www.aircraftcircus.com

ALEXANDER PERSONAL MANAGEMENT LTD
See APM ASSOCIATES

ALL TALENT -
THE SONIA SCOTT AGENCY   T 0141 418 1074
Contact: Sonia Scott Mackay. By Post/e-mail/
Telephone. Accepts Showreels/Voicereels. 2 Agents
represent 40 Performers. Film. Modelling. Television.
Voice Overs. Walk-on & Supporting Artists
The Hub Unit 2.7, 70 Pacific Quay
Glasgow G51 1AE
T 07971 337074
E enquiries@alltalentuk.co.uk
W www.alltalentuk.co.uk

ALLISTON & CO
ARTIST MANAGEMENT   T 020 3390 3456
Suite 2, 3rd Floor, 207 Regent Street
London W1B 3HH
E contact@allistonandco.com
W www.allistonandco.com

ALLSORTS AGENCY   T 020 8472 3924
Waterfront Studios, 1 Dock Road
London E16 1AH
T 07950 490364
E bookings@allsortsagency.com
W www.allsortsagency.com

ALLSORTS DRAMA
FOR CHILDREN   T/F 020 8969 3249
In association with LESLIE, Sasha MANAGEMENT
34 Crediton Road, London NW10 3DU
E sasha@allsortsdrama.com

ALLSTARS ACTORS
MANAGEMENT   T 0161 702 8257
3 Agents. Television. Film. Stage. Corporate. Role Play.
Promotional
23 Falconwood Chase, Worsley
Manchester M28 1FG
T 07584 992429
E michelle@allstarsactors.com
W www.allstarsactors.tv

ALLSTARS CASTING   T 0151 707 2100
66 Hope Street, Liverpool L1 9BZ
T 07739 359737
E sylvie@allstarscasting.co.uk
W www.allstarscasting.co.uk

ALPHA ACTORS   T 020 7241 0077
Co-operative. CPMA Member
Studio B4, 3 Bradbury Street, London N16 8JN
F 020 7241 2410
E alpha@alphaactors.com
W www.alphaactors.com

ALRAUN, Anita
REPRESENTATION   T 01253 343784
PMA Member. Contact: By Post only (SAE)
1A Queensway, Blackpool, Lancashire FY4 2DG
T 07946 630986
E anita@cjagency.demon.co.uk

ALTARAS, Jonathan
ASSOCIATES LTD   T 020 7836 8722
PMA Member
53 Chandos Place, London WC2N 4HS
E info@jaalondon.com

ALW ASSOCIATES   T 020 7388 7018
Contact: Carol Paul
1 Grafton Chambers, Grafton Place
London NW1 1LN
E alw_carolpaul@talktalk.net

AM PERSONAL
MANAGEMENT LTD   T 020 7244 1159
*Contact: Amanda McAllister. Film, Stage & Television
Technical Personnel only*
4 Archel Road, London W14 9QH
E amanda@ampmgt.com
W www.ampmgt.co.uk

AMAZON ARTISTS
MANAGEMENT   T/F 020 8350 4909
27 Inderwick Road, Crouch End, London N8 9LB
T 07957 358767
E amazonartists@gmail.com

AMBER PERSONAL
MANAGEMENT LTD   T 0161 228 0236
No.2 Planetree House, 21-31 Oldham Street
Manchester M1 1JG
E info@amberltd.co.uk
W www.amberltd.co.uk

AMBER PERSONAL
MANAGEMENT LTD   T 020 7734 7887
London
E info@amberltd.co.uk
W www.amberltd.co.uk

AMC MANAGEMENT   T 01438 714652
Contact: Anna McCorquodale, Tricia Howell
31 Parkside, Welwyn
Herts AL6 9DQ
F 01438 718669
E media@amcmanagement.co.uk
W www.amcmanagement.co.uk

  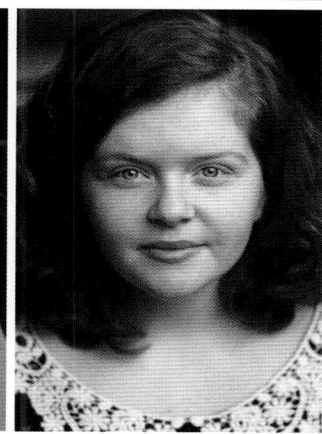

Ryan Molloy   Aisling Jarrett-Gavin   Ami Metcalf

BRANDON BISHOP
t: 020 7275 7468   m: 07931 383 830
www.brandonbishopphotography.com

AMCK MANAGEMENT LTD   T 020 7524 7788
125 Westbourne Studios
242 Acklam Road, Notting Hill
London W10 5JJ
F 020 7524 7789
E info@amck.tv
W www.amck.tv

AMERICAN AGENCY THE   T 020 7485 8883
Contact: By Post/e-mail. 3 Agents represent 81
Performers. Commercials. Corporate. Film. Musical
Theatre. Stage. Television. Voice Overs (American)
14 Bonny Street
London NW1 9PG
E americanagency@btconnect.com
W www.americanagency.tv

AMG ARTISTS   T 07889 241283
Contact: Kyra Morrison. Consulting. Film. Actors.
Directors. Producers. Artists & Writers
E info@amgcom.eu
W www.amgcom.eu

ANA
(ACTORS NETWORK AGENCY)   T 020 7735 0999
Personal Manager. Co-operative. CPMA Member
55 Lambeth Walk
London SE11 6DX
F 020 7735 8177
E info@ana-actors.co.uk
W www.ana-actors.co.uk

ANDREA CASTING   T/F 07092 988083
Actors. Crew. Dancers. Musicians. Presenters.
Voice Overs
Office NA 059A, Centerprise
Dwr-y-Felin Road, Neath SA10 7RF
T 07774 660253
E andreacasting@outlook.com
W www.andreacasting.com

ANDREWS, Amanda AGENCY   T/F 01782 393889
30 Caverswall Road
Blythe Bridge, Stoke-on-Trent
Staffordshire ST11 9BG
T 07711 379770
E amanda@amandaandrewsagency.com
W www.amandaandrewsagency.com

ANGEL, Susan &
FRANCIS, Kevin LTD   T 020 7439 3086
PMA Member
1st Floor, 12 D'Arblay Street
London W1F 8DU
F 020 7437 1712
E agents@angelandfrancis.co.uk
W www.angelandfrancis.co.uk

ANTONY, Christopher
ASSOCIATES   T 020 8994 9952
Studio F5, Grove Park Studios
188-192 Sutton Court Road
London W4 3HR
E info@christopherantony.co.uk
W www.christopherantony.co.uk

APM ASSOCIATES   T 020 8953 7377
PMA Member. Contact: Linda French. By Post/e-mail.
Accepts Showreels/Voicereels. 3 Agents represent
80 Performers
Elstree Studios, Shenley Road
Borehamwood WD6 1JG
F 020 8953 7385
E apm@apmassociates.net
W www.apmassociates.net

ARAENA/COLLECTIVE   T/F 020 8428 0037
10 Bramshaw Gardens, South Oxhey
Herts WD19 6XP
E info@collectivedance.co.uk

A.R.C. ENTERTAINMENTS   T 01740 631292
Contact: By e-mail. 1 Agent represents 800 Active
Performers
10 Church Lane, Redmarshall
Stockton on Tees, Cleveland TS21 1EP
E arcents@btinternet.com
W www.arcents.co.uk

ARCADIA ASSOCIATES   T/F 020 7937 0264
Contact: Hannah Hodgkinson
18B Vicarage Gate, London W8 4AA
E info.arcadia@btopenworld.com

ARENA ENTERTAINMENT
(UK) LTD   T 0113 239 2222
Regent's Court, 39 Harrogate Road, Leeds LS7 3PD
F 0113 239 2016
E info@arenaentertainments.co.uk
W www.arenaentertainments.co.uk

ARENA PERSONAL
MANAGEMENT LTD   T/F 020 7278 1661
Co-operative
Room 11, East Block, Panther House
38 Mount Pleasant, London WC1X 0AN
E arenapmltd@aol.com
W www.arenapmltd.co.uk

A R G
(ARTISTS RIGHTS GROUP LTD)   T 020 7436 6400
PMA Member
4A Exmoor Street, London W10 6BD
F 020 7436 6700
E argall@argtalent.com

ARGYLE ASSOCIATES   T 07905 293319
Personal Manager. Contact: Richard Argyle.
By Post (SAE)
43 Clappers Lane, Fulking, West Sussex BN5 9ND
E argyle.associates@me.com

ARROWSMITH, Martin   T 020 3598 0636
Contact: By Post. Accepts Showreels. 1 Agent. Children.
Commercials. Film. Stage. Television
E office@martinarrowsmith.co.uk
W www.martinarrowsmith.co.uk

ART MIX INTERNATIONAL   T 00 61 0418961104
PO Box 1438 Broadbeach, Gold Coast
Queensland, Australia 4218
E studio@artmixmanagement.com
W www.artmixmanagement.com

ARTEMIS STUDIOS LTD   T 01344 429403
30 Charles Square, Bracknell, Berkshire RG12 1AY
E agency@artemis-studios.co.uk
W www.agency.artemis-studios.co.uk

ARTIST MANAGEMENT UK
LTD   T 0151 523 6222
6 Gondover Avenue, Orrell Park, Liverpool L9 8AZ
T 07948 793552
E chris@artistmanagementuk.com
W www.artistmanagementuk.com

ARTIST PARTNERSHIP THE   T 020 7439 1456
Personal Manager. PMA Member. Contact: By Post only
101 Finsbury Pavement, London EC2A 1RS
F 020 7734 6530
E email@theartistspartnership.co.uk
W www.theartistspartnership.co.uk

SHEILA BURNETT

P H O T O G R A P H Y

Simon Pegg

Imelda Staunton

Patsy Palmer

Ewan McGregor

020 7289 3058 | 07974 731391

www.sheilaburnett-headshots.com

Student Rates

ARUN, Jonathan   **T** 020 7840 0123
Personal Manager. PMA Member. Contact: Jonathan Arun, Amy O'Neill
37 Pearman Street, London SE1 7RB
E info@jonathanarun.com
W www.jonathanarun.com

ASH PRODUCTIONS LIVE LTD   **T** 020 8655 7656
Personal Manager. Contact: Paul Leno (Senior Agent). By Post/e-mail/Telephone. 5 Agents represent 150 Performers. Film. Television. Stage. Musical Theatre. Commercials
3B Nettlefold Place, London SE27 0JW
E office@ashproductionslive.com
W www.ashproductionsliveltd.com

ASQUITH & HORNER   **T** 020 8466 5580
Joined with Elspeth Cochrane Personal Management. Personal Manager. Contact: By Telephone/Post (SAE)/e-mail
The Studio, 14 College Road, Bromley, Kent BR1 3NS
T 07770 482144
E asquith@dircon.co.uk

ASSOCIATED ARTS   **T** 020 8856 4958
Designers. Directors. Movement Directors. Lighting & Sound Designers
8 Shrewsbury Lane, London SE18 3JF
E karen@associated-arts.co.uk
W www.associated-arts.co.uk

ASTON MANAGEMENT   **T** 07742 059762
Aston Farm House, Remenham Lane
Henley on Thames, Oxon RG9 3DE
T 01491 578631
E astonagent@yahoo.co.uk
W www.astonmgt.com

ASTRAL ACTORS MANAGEMENT   **T** 020 8728 2782
22 Parc Starling, Johnstown, Carmarthen SA31 3HX
T 01267 616162
E liz@astralactors.com
W www.astralactors.com

AVALON MANAGEMENT GROUP LTD   **T** 020 7598 8000
4A Exmoor Street, London W10 6BD
F 020 7598 7300
E management@avalonuk.com
W www.avalonuk.com

AVENUE ARTISTES LTD   **T** 023 8076 0930
PO Box 1573, Southampton SO16 3XS
E info@avenueartistes.com
W www.avenueartistes.com

AVIEL TALENT MANAGEMENT INC   **T** 001 514 288 8885
1117 St Catherine Street West, Suite 718
Montreal, Quebec, Canada H3B 1H9
F 001 514 288 0768
E aviel@canadafilm.com

AXIS TALENT   **T** 07854 223376
41 Hastings Avenue, Kent CT9 2SG
E lia@axistalent.co.uk
W www.axistalent.co.uk

AXM (ACTORS EXCHANGE MANAGEMENT)   **T** 020 7837 3304
Co-operative. CPMA Member
Unit J302, J Block, Biscuit Factory
100 Clements Road, Southwark, London SE16 4DG
F 020 7837 7215
E info@axmgt.com
W www.axmgt.com

B A M ASSOCIATES   **T** 01934 852942
Benets, Dolberrow
Churchill, Bristol BS25 5NT
E casting@ebam.tv
W www.ebam.tv

BANANAFISH MANAGEMENT   **T** 0151 708 5509
The Business Hub
40 Devonshire Road
Wirral CH43 1TW
T 07974 206622
E info@bananafish.co.uk
W www.bananafish.co.uk

BARKER, Gavin ASSOCIATES LTD   **T** 020 7499 4777
PMA Member. Contact: Gavin Barker, Michelle Burke
2D Wimpole Street
London W1G 0EB
F 020 7499 3777
E katie@gavinbarkerassociates.co.uk
W www.gavinbarkerassociates.co.uk

BARR, Becca MANAGEMENT   **T** 020 3137 2980
97 Mortimer Street
London W1W 7SU
E info@beccabarrmanagement.co.uk
W www.beccabarrmanagement.co.uk

BEDFORD, Eamonn AGENCY   **T** 020 7395 7528
4th Floor, 80-81 St Martin's Lane
London WC2N 4AA
E info@eamonnbedford.com
W www.eamonnbedford.com

BELFIELD & WARD   **T** 020 3416 5290
PMA Member
26-28 Neal Street, Covent Garden
London WC2H 9QQ
E office@belfieldandward.co.uk
W www.belfieldandward.com

BELFRAGE, Julian ASSOCIATES   **T** 020 7287 8544
PMA Member
3rd Floor, 9 Argyll Street
London W1F 7TG
F 020 7287 8832
E email@julianbelfrage.co.uk

BELL, Olivia MANAGEMENT   **T** 020 7439 3270
PMA Member. Contact: By Post/e-mail. 6 Agents represent 100 Performers. Commercials. Film. Musical Theatre. Stage. Television
193 Wardour Street
London W1F 8ZF
E info@olivia-bell.co.uk
W www.olivia-bell.co.uk

BENJAMIN MANAGEMENT LTD   **T** 020 3714 1111
24-25 Nutford Place, London W1H 5YQ
T 07921 212360
E agent@benjaminmanagement.co.uk

BENNETT DARLING MANAGEMENT   **T** 020 7183 6029
3rd Floor, 207 Regent Street
London W1B 3HH
E info@bdartists.co.uk
W www.bdartists.co.uk

BERLIN ASSOCIATES   **T** 020 7836 1112
PMA Member. Dramatists & Technicians only
7 Tyers Gate, London SE1 3HX
F 020 7632 5296
E agents@berlinassociates.com
W www.berlinassociates.com

"Leading voice on headshot trends" THE STAGE

Peter Ormond

Gillian MacGregor

Bel Powley

Nicôle Lecky

Nicholas Bourne

John Ro'mach

MICHAEL**WHARLEY**
PHOTOGRAPHY

michaelwharley.com
07961 068759

icon actors mangement

tel: 0161 273 3344   **fax:** 0161 273 4567
tanzaro house, ardwick green north, manchester. m12 6fz
info@iconactors.net   www.iconactors.net

icon
actors management

BETTS, Jorg ASSOCIATES   T 020 3405 4546
PMA Member
2 John Street, London WC1N 2ES
E agents@jorgbetts.com

**BIG TIME
ENTERTAINMENT LTD**   T 020 7127 9119
196 High Road, London N22 8HH
F 020 3397 4249
E info@bigtimeentertainment.co.uk
W www.bigtimeentertainment.co.uk

**BILLBOARD PERSONAL
MANAGEMENT**   T 020 7735 9956
Twitter: @billboardpm
45 Lothrop Street, London W10 4JB
T 07791 970773
E billboardpm@btconnect.com
W www.billboardpm.com

BILLY MARSH DRAMA LTD
See MARSH, Billy DRAMA LTD

BIRD AGENCY   T 07889 723995
Personal Performance Manager
The Centre, 27 Station Road
Sidcup, Kent DA15 7EB
T 020 8269 6862
E birdagency@birdcollege.co.uk
W www.birdcollege.co.uk

BLACKBURN MANAGEMENT   T 020 7292 7555
Argyll House, All Saints Passage
London SW18 1EP
E presenters@blackburnmanagement.co.uk
W www.blackburnmanagement.co.uk

**BLAIR, Michelle
MANAGEMENT**   T 020 3664 9897
Personal Manager
The Office, The Elms
Gate Helmsley, Yorkshire YO41 1NE
E info@michelleblairmanagement.co.uk
W www.michelleblairmanagement.co.uk

BLOND, Rebecca ASSOCIATES   T 020 7351 4100
PMA Member
69A Kings Road
London SW3 4NX
F 020 7351 4600
E info@rebeccablond.com
W www.rebeccablond.com

**BLOOMFIELDS WELCH
MANAGEMENT**   T 020 7659 2001
PMA Member
77 Oxford Street, London W1D 2ES
F 020 7659 2101
E info@bloomfieldswelch.com
W www.bloomfieldswelch.com

BLUE STAR ASSOCIATES   T 020 7836 6220
Contact: Barrie Stacey, Keith Hopkins
7-8 Shaldon Mansions, 132 Charing Cross Road
London WC2H 0LA
E bluestar.london.2000@gmail.com

BMA ARTISTS   T 01442 878878
*Personal Manager. Contact: Alex Haddad. By e-mail.
1200 Performers. Children. Commercials. Corporate.
Dancers. Film. Modelling. Presenters. Singers. Television.
Walk-on & Supporting Artists*
346 High Street, Marlow House
Berkhamsted, Hertfordshire HP4 1HT
F 01442 879879
E info@bmaartists.com
W www.bmaartists.com

BODENS AGENCY   T 020 8447 0909
*Personal Manager. Contact: Adam Boden, Sophie
Boden, Katie McCutcheon. By Post/e-mail/Telephone.
3 Agents represent 150 Performers. Children.
Commercials. Film. Television. Walk-on & Supporting
Artists*
99 East Barnet Road, New Barnet, Herts EN4 8RF
T 07545 696888
E info@bodens.co.uk
W www.bodens.co.uk/clients

BODY LONDON   T 020 7371 5858
21 Heathmans Road, London SW6 4TJ
E contact@bodylondon.com
W www.bodylondon.com

BODYWORK AGENCY   T 01223 314461
25-29 Glisson Road, Cambridge CB1 2HA
T 07792 851972
E agency@bodyworkds.co.uk

BOHEMIA GROUP   T 001 323 462 5800
Based in Hollywood with Offices in London and NYC
1680 N. Vine, Suite 412
Los Angeles, California 90028
E management@bohemiaent.com
W www.bohemiaent.com

BOSS CASTING   T 0161 237 0100
Fourways House, 57 Hilton Street, Manchester M1 2EJ
F 0161 236 1237
E cath@bosscasting.co.uk
W www.bosscasting.co.uk

**BOSS CREATIVE
ENTERTAINMENT**   T 020 8299 0478
PMA Member
Office 1, 6 Lordship Lane, London SE22 8HN
E enquiries@bosscreativeentertainment.com
W www.bosscreativeentertainment.com

**BOSS CREATIVE
MANAGEMENT**   T 0161 237 0100
Fourways House, 57 Hilton Street, Manchester M1 2EJ
F 0161 236 1237
E info@bossmodels.co.uk
W www.bossmanagement.co.uk

BOSS LIFESTYLE   T 0161 237 0100
Fourways House
57 Hilton Street, Manchester M1 2EJ
F 0161 236 1237
E info@bossmodels.co.uk
W www.bossmodelmanagement.co.uk

Carole Latimer - Photographer **www.carolelatimer.com**

BOSS MODEL MANAGEMENT **T** 0161 237 0100
Fourways House
57 Hilton Street, Manchester M1 2EJ
F 0161 236 1237
E info@bossmodels.co.uk
W www.bossmodelmanagement.co.uk

**BOX ARTIST MANAGEMENT
LTD - BAM** **T** 020 7713 7313
*Choreographers. Musical Theatre. Commercial Dancers.
Corporate Entertainment*
The Attic, The Old Finsbury Town Hall
Rosebery Avenue, London EC1R 4RP
E hello@boxartistmanagement.com
W www.boxartistmanagement.com

**BOYCE, Sandra
MANAGEMENT** **T** 020 7923 0606
PMA Member
125 Dynevor Road, London N16 0DA
F 020 7241 2313
E info@sandraboyce.com
W www.sandraboyce.com

**BRAIDMAN, Michelle
ASSOCIATES LTD** **T** 020 7237 3523
PMA Member
2 Futura House, 169 Grange Road, London SE1 3BN
F 020 7231 4634
E info@braidman.com
W www.braidman.com

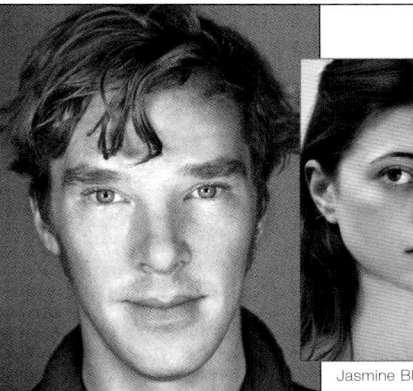
Benedict Cumberbatch

Jasmine Blackborow   Elliot Barnes-Worrell

Natalie Walter

Author of **THE HALF**
Actors Preparing
to go on Stage

30 years' experience
NT, RSC, Royal Court

SIMON ANNAND
PHOTOGRAPHER
www.simonannand.com

Colour and B&W

m: 07884 446776 / £350/310 conc

BRAITHWAITE'S
THEATRICAL AGENCY   T 020 8954 5638
8 Brookshill Avenue, Harrow Weald
Middlesex HA3 6RZ

BREAK A LEG
MANAGEMENT LTD   T/F 020 7250 0662
The City College, University House, Room 33
55 East Road, London N1 6AH
E agency@breakalegman.com
W www.breakalegman.com

BRIDGES:
THE ACTORS' AGENCY   T 0131 554 3073
CPMA Member
Studio S12, Out of the Blue Drill Hall
36 Dalmeny Street, Edinburgh EH6 8RG
E admin@bridgesactorsagency.com
W www.bridgesactorsagency.com

BROAD ACTING
MANAGEMENT LTD   T 0161 834 4716
12 Lever Street, Piccadilly, Manchester M1 1LN
E info@broadactingmanagement.co.uk
W www.broadactingmanagement.co.uk

BROAD ACTING
MANAGEMENT LTD   T 0113 246 9632
67 St Pauls Street, Leeds LS1 2TE
E katy@broadactingmanagement.co.uk
W www.broadactingmanagement.co.uk

BROAD ACTING
MANAGEMENT LTD   T 020 7544 1012
223 Regent Street, London W1B 2QD
E info@broadactingmanagement.co.uk
W www.broadactingmanagement.co.uk

BROADCASTING AGENCY LTD   T 020 3131 0128
Unit 106A Netil House, 1 Westgate Street, London E8 3RL
T 07729 309000
E info@broadcastingagency.co.uk
W www.broadcastingagency.co.uk

BROOD   T 020 3489 4949
PMA Member. Contact: By e-mail. Prospective Client
Applications to broodapplication@aol.com
18 Soho Square, London W1D 3QL
E broodmanagement@aol.com
W www.broodmanagement.com

BROOK, Dolly AGENCY   T 01371 875767
PO Box 5436, Dunmow CM6 1WW
F 01371 875996
E dollybrookcasting@btinternet.com

BROOK, Jeremy LTD   T 020 7434 0398
Contact: Jeremy Brook, James Foster
37 Berwick Street, London W1F 8RS
F 020 7287 8016
E info@jeremybrookltd.co.uk
W www.jeremybrookltd.co.uk

BROOK, Valerie AGENCY   T 0161 486 1631
10 Sandringham Road, Cheadle Hulme
Cheshire SK8 5NH
T 07973 434953
E colinbrook@freenetname.co.uk

BROWN, SIMCOCKS &
ANDREWS   T 020 7953 7484
PMA Member. Contact: Carrie Simcocks, Kelly Andrews
504 The Chandlery, 50 Westminster Bridge Road
London SE1 7QY
F 020 7953 7494
E info@bsaagency.co.uk
W www.brownsimcocksandandrews.co.uk

BRUNO KELLY LTD   T 020 7183 7331
3rd Floor, 207 Regent Street, London W1B 3HH
F 020 7183 7332
E info@brunokelly.com
W www.brunokelly.com

BRUNSKILL MANAGEMENT LTD   T 01768 881430
Personal Manager. PMA Member. Contact: Aude
Powell. By Post only. Accepts Showreels/Voicereels.
Commercials. Corporate. Film. Musical Theatre. Radio.
Stage. Television. Voice Overs
The Courtyard, Edenhall
Penrith, Cumbria CA11 8ST
E accounts@brunskill.com

BSA LTD
See HARRISON, Penny BSA LTD

BSA MANAGEMENT   T 0845 0035301
Personal Manager. Actors & Presenters. Commercials.
Film. Television
Crusader House, 2nd Floor
145-157 St John Street, London EC1V 4PY
E agent@bsamanagement.co.uk
W www.bsamanagement.co.uk

BUCHANAN, Bronia
ASSOCIATES LTD   T 020 7395 1400
PMA Member
2nd Floor, 23 Tavistock Street
London WC2E 7NX
F 020 7379 5560
E info@buchanan-associates.co.uk
W www.buchanan-associates.co.uk

BUCHANAN, Bronia
ASSOCIATES LTD   T 0161 244 5679
PMA Member
2nd Floor, 12 Hilton Street, Manchester M1 1JF
F 0161 228 3930
E manchester@buchanan-associates.co.uk
W www.buchanan-associates.co.uk

BURNETT CROWTHER LTD   T 020 7437 8008
PMA Member. Contact: Barry Burnett, Lizanne Crowther
3 Clifford Street, London W1S 2LF
E associates@bcltd.org
W www.bcltd.org

BURNINGHAM ASSOCIATES   T 07807 176287
Personal Management
4 Victoria Road, Twickenham
Middlesex TW1 3HW
E info@burnassoc.org
W www.burnassoc.org

BUTTERCUP AGENCY   T 0843 2899063
Wyndrums, The Village
Ewhurst, Surrey GU6 7PB
E info@buttercupagency.co.uk
W www.buttercupagency.co.uk

BWH AGENCY LTD THE   T 020 7734 0657
PMA Member
5th Floor, 35 Soho Square
London W1D 3QX
F 020 7734 1278
E info@thebwhagency.co.uk
W www.thebwhagency.co.uk

BYRAM, Paul ASSOCIATES   T 020 3137 3385
PMA Member
Suite B0079, 120 Kingston Road
Wimbledon, London SW19 1LY
E admin@paulbyram.com
W www.paulbyram.com

Ned Wolfgang Kelly

CATHERINE SHAKESPEARE LANE

PORTRAITS

020 7226 7694   www.csl-art.co.uk

BYRON'S MANAGEMENT — T 020 7242 8096
Contact: By Post/e-mail. Accepts Showreels.
Commercials. Film. Musical Theatre. Stage. Television
41 Maiden Lane, London WC2E 7LJ
E office@byronsmanagement.co.uk
W www.byronsmanagement.co.uk

C.A. ARTISTES MANAGEMENT — T 020 8834 1608
26-28 Hammersmith Grove
London W6 7BA
E casting@caartistes.com
W www.caartistes.com

CAMBELL JEFFREY MANAGEMENT — T 01323 730526
Set, Costume & Lighting Designers
7 Homelatch House, St Leonards Road
Eastbourne BN27 3UW
E jeffrey.cambell@btinternet.com

CAPITAL VOICES — T 01372 466228
Contact: Anne Skates. Film. Session Singers. Stage.
Studio. Television
PO Box 364, Esher
Surrey KT10 9XZ
F 01372 466229
E annie@capitalvoices.com
W www.capitalvoices.com

CAREY, Roger ASSOCIATES — T 01932 582890
Personal Manager. PMA Member
Suite 909, The Old House
Shepperton Film Studios
Studios Road, Shepperton
Middlesex TW17 0QD
F 01932 569602
E info@rogercareyassociates.com
W www.rogercareyassociates.com

CAREY DODD ASSOCIATES — T 020 7692 1877
PMA Member
78 York Street, London W1H 1DP
T 020 7504 1087
E agents@careydoddassociates.com
W www.careydoddassociates.com

CARNEY, Jessica ASSOCIATES — T 020 7434 4143
Personal Manager. PMA Member. Prospective Client
Applications to representation@jcarneyassociates.co.uk
with Spotlight Link
4th Floor, 23 Golden Square, London W1F 9JP
E info@jcarneyassociates.co.uk
W www.jessicacarneyassociates.co.uk

CAROUSEL EVENTS — T 0844 2250465
Entertainment for Corporate & Private Events
Incentive House, 23 Castle Street
High Wycombe, Bucks HP13 6RU
F 01494 511501
E info@carouselevents.co.uk
W www.carouselevents.co.uk

CARR, Norrie AGENCY — T 020 7253 1771
Holborn Studios, 49 Eagle Wharf Road
London N1 7ED
F 020 7253 1772
E info@norriecarr.com
W www.norriecarr.com

CASAROTTO MARSH LTD — T 020 7287 4450
Film Technicians
Waverley House, 7-12 Noel Street
London W1F 8GQ
F 020 7287 9128
E info@casarotto.co.uk
W www.casarotto.co.uk

CASCADE ARTISTS LTD — T 020 7437 3175
Contact: By e-mail (No Large File Attachments). Accepts
Links to Showreels & Casting Profiles. 2 Agents represent
25 Performers. Film. Stage. Television. Commercials.
Corporate. Voice Over. TIE. European Connections
Studio Soho, Royalty Mews (entrance by Quo Vadis)
22-25 Dean Street
London W1D 3RA
T 07866 739510
E info@cascadeartists.com
W www.cascadeartists.com

CASTAWAY ACTORS AGENCY — T 00 353 1 6719264
30-31 Wicklow Street, Dublin 2, Ireland
T 00 353 1 6719059
E office@castawayactors.com
W www.castawayactors.com

CASTCALL — T 01582 456213
Casting & Consultancy Service
106 Wilsden Avenue, Luton LU1 5HR
E casting@castcall.co.uk
W www.castcall.co.uk

CAVAT AGENCY — T 020 7018 0536
2nd Floor, 56 Bloomsbury Street
London WC1B 3QT
E enquiries@cavatagency.co.uk
W www.cavatagency.co.uk

C B A INTERNATIONAL — T 00 33 2 32671981
Contact: Cindy Brace
c/o C.M.S. Experts Associés
149 Boulevard Malesherbes
75017 Paris, France
E c_b_a@club-internet.fr
W www.cindy-brace.com

CBL MANAGEMENT — T 01273 321245
PMA Member. Artistes. Creatives
20 Hollingbury Rise, Brighton
East Sussex BN1 7HJ
T 07956 890307
E enquiries@cblmanagement.co.uk
W www.cblmanagement.co.uk

C C A MANAGEMENT — T 020 7630 6303
Personal Manager. PMA Member. Contact: By Post.
Actors. Technicians
Garden Level, 32 Charlwood Street
London SW1V 2DY
E actors@ccamanagement.co.uk
W www.ccamanagementinfo.com

CCM — T 020 7278 0507
CPMA Member
Panther House, 38 Mount Pleasant
London WC1X 0AN
E casting@ccmactors.com
W www.ccmactors.co.uk

CDA — T 020 7937 2749
Personal Manager. PMA Member. Contact: By Post/
e-mail. Accepts Showreels. Film. Stage. Television
167-169 Kensington High Street
London W8 6SH
F 020 7373 1110
E cda@cdalondon.com
W www.cdalondon.com

CELEBRITY GROUP THE — T 0871 2501234
12 Nottingham Place
London W1M 3FA
E info@celebrity.co.uk
W www.celebrity.co.uk

Noel Samuels　　　Lara Honnor　　　Paul Herwig

CENTER STAGE AGENCY　T 00 353 1 4533599
*Personal Manager. Contact: By e-mail. Accepts
Showreels. Commercials. Film. Presenters. Stage.
Television. Voice Overs*
7 Rutledge Terrace
South Circular Road
Dublin 8, Ireland
E geraldinecenterstage@eircom.net
W www.centerstageagency.com

CENTRAL LINE THE　T 0115 941 2937
*Personal Manager. Co-operative. CPMA Member.
Contact: By e-mail/Post*
11 East Circus Street, Nottingham NG1 5AF
E centralline@btconnect.com
W www.thecentralline.co.uk

CHAMBERS MANAGEMENT　T 020 7796 3588
Comedians. Comic Actors
39-41 Parker Street, London WC2B 5PQ
F 020 7831 8598
E info@chambersmgt.com
W www.chambersmgt.com

CHAMPION TALENT　T 020 8761 5395
10 Birkbeck Place, London SE21 8JU
E info@championtalent.co.uk
W www.championtalent.co.uk

CHARKHAM, Esta ASSOCIATES　T 020 8741 2843
16 British Grove, Chiswick, London W4 2NL
F 020 8746 3219
E office@charkham.net
W www.charkham.net

Danny Lee Wynter　　　Sarah MacRae　　　Simon Russell Beale

Arab Actors ~ Voices ~ Presenters

GENUINE ARAB CASTING
TALENT AGENCY
Representing ARAB ACTORS for
Film, Radio, Television & Stage

Recent Clients:
- BBC TV & Radio • Channel 4 • Sky • Paramount
- Left Bank Pictures • Wall to Wall • Closed Circuit (Film)

www.genuinearabcasting.com
Tel: 020 3478 9067 info@genuinearabcasting.com

**CHARLESWORTH, Peter &
ASSOCIATES**   T 020 7792 4600
67 Holland Park Mews, London W11 3SS
F 020 7792 1893
E info@petercharlesworth.co.uk

CHATTO & LINNIT LTD   T 020 7349 7222
Worlds End Studios, 132-134 Lots Road
London SW10 0RJ
E info@chattolinnit.com

CHP ARTIST MANAGEMENT   T 01844 345630
Meadowcroft Barn
Crowbrook Road, Askett
Princes Risborough
Buckinghamshire HP27 9LS
T 07976 560580
E chp.artist.management@gmail.com
W www.chproductions.org.uk

CHRYSTEL ARTS AGENCY   T 01494 773336
6 Eunice Grove, Chesham
Bucks HP5 1RL
T 07799 605489
E chrystelarts@waitrose.com

CIEKABAILEY ASSOCIATES   T 0161 484 5423
7 Ridge Road, Marple
Cheshire SK6 7HL
E enquiries@ciekabailey.com
W www.ciekabailey.com

**CINEL GABRAN
MANAGEMENT**   T 029 2066 6600
*Personal Manager. Contact: By Post. Accepts
Showreels. 40 Performers. Commercials. Corporate.
Film. Musical Theatre. Presenters. Radio. Stage.
Television. Voice Overs*
Ty Cefn, 14-16 Rectory Road
Cardiff CF5 1QL
E mail@cinelgabran.co.uk
W www.cinelgabran.co.uk

**CINEL GABRAN
MANAGEMENT**   T 01947 605376
*Personal Manager. Contact: By Post. Accepts
Showreels. 40 Performers. Commercials. Corporate.
Film. Musical Theatre. Presenters. Radio. Stage.
Television. Voice Overs*
Adventure House, Newholm
Whitby, North Yorkshire YO21 3QL
E mail@cinelgabran.co.uk
W www.cinelgabran.co.uk

**CIRCUIT PERSONAL
MANAGEMENT LTD**   T 01782 285388
*Co-operative. Contact: By Post/e-mail. Accepts
Showreels. Commercials. Corporate. Film. Stage.
Television*
Suite 71 S.E.C., Bedford Street, Shelton
Stoke-on-Trent, Staffs ST1 4PZ
F 01782 206821
E mail@circuitpm.co.uk
W www.circuitpm.co.uk

CITY ACTORS MANAGEMENT   T 020 7793 9888
CPMA Member
Oval House, 52-54 Kennington Oval
London SE11 5SW
E info@cityactors.co.uk
W www.cityactors.co.uk

**CLASS - CARLINE LUNDON
ASSOCIATES**   T 07597 378995
Twitter: @media_legal
25 Falkner Square
Liverpool L8 7NZ
E clundon@googlemail.com
W www.facebook.com/medialegaladvisor

**CLAYMAN, Tony
PROMOTIONS LTD**   T 020 7368 3336
Vicarage House
58-60 Kensington Church Street
London W8 4DB
F 020 7368 3338
E tony@tonyclayman.com
W www.tonyclayman.com

CLAYPOLE MANAGEMENT   T 0845 6501777
PO Box 123, DL3 7WA
E info@claypolemanagement.co.uk
W www.claypolemanagement.co.uk

CLIC AGENCY   T 01248 354420
7 Ffordd Seion, Bangor
Gwynedd LL57 1BS
E clic@btinternet.com
W www.clicagency.co.uk

**COCHRANE, Elspeth PERSONAL
MANAGEMENT**
See ASQUITH & HORNER

**COHEN MAYER, Charlie
ASSOCIATES**   T 07850 077825
Personal Manager & Talent Agency
121 Brecknock Road, Camden
London N19 5AE
E houseofsaintjude@gmail.com

**COLE KITCHENN PERSONAL
MANAGEMENT LTD**   T 020 7427 5681
PMA Member
ROAR House, 46 Charlotte Street
London W1T 2GS
E info@colekitchenn.com
W www.colekitchenn.com

COLLINS, Shane ASSOCIATES   T 020 7253 1010
PMA Member
Suite 112, Davina House
137-149 Goswell Road
London EC1V 7ET
F 0870 4601983
E info@shanecollins.co.uk
W www.shanecollins.co.uk

COMMERCIAL AGENCY THE
See TCA (THE COMMERCIAL AGENCY)

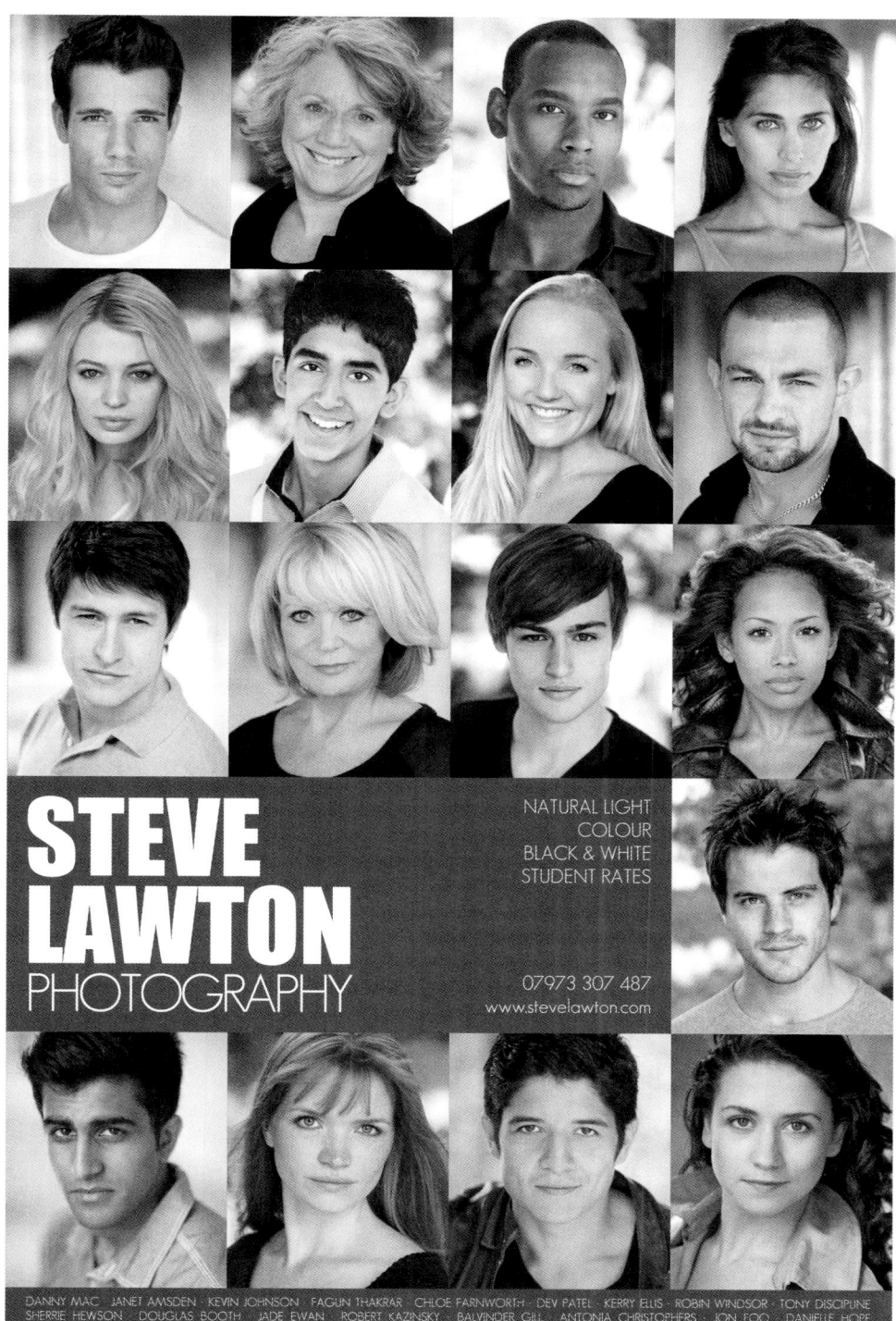

NATURAL LIGHT
COLOUR
BLACK & WHITE
STUDENT RATES

STEVE LAWTON
PHOTOGRAPHY

07973 307 487
www.stevelawton.com

DANNY MAC · JANET AMSDEN · KEVIN JOHNSON · FAGUN THAKRAR · CHLOE FARNWORTH · DEV PATEL · KERRY ELLIS · ROBIN WINDSOR · TONY DISCIPLINE
SHERRIE HEWSON · DOUGLAS BOOTH · JADE EWAN · ROBERT KAZINSKY · BALVINDER GILL · ANTONIA CHRISTOPHERS · JON FOO · DANIELLE HOPE

COMMERCIALS@BBA T 020 7395 1402
Commercials. Corporate
2nd Floor, 23 Tavistock Street
London WC2E 7NX
E commercials@buchanan-associates.co.uk
W www.commercialsatbba.co.uk

CONTI, Italia AGENCY LTD T 020 7608 7500
Contact: By Post/Telephone
Italia Conti House, 23 Goswell Road
London EC1M 7AJ
F 020 7253 1430
E agency@italiaconti.co.uk

**CONWAY VAN GELDER
GRANT LTD** T 020 7287 0077
Personal Manager. PMA Member
3rd Floor, 8-12 Broadwick Street
London W1F 8HW
E info@conwayvg.co.uk

COOKE, Howard ASSOCIATES T 020 7591 0144
*PMA Member. Contact: Howard Cooke. By Post.
2 Agents represent 50 Performers. Commercials. Film.
Stage. Television*
19 Coulson Street
Chelsea, London SW3 3NA
F 020 7591 0155
E mail@hca1.co.uk
W www.hca1.co.uk

**COOPER, Tommy
MAGICAL AGENCY** T 07860 290437
Comedy. Magicians
21 Streatham Court, Ashley Cross
Poole, Dorset BH14 0EX
E info@clivegreenaway.com
W www.tommycooperremembered.co.uk

**COOPER & CHAND TALENT
MANAGEMENT** T 020 3651 9405
69 Teignmouth Road, London NW2 4EA
T 07723 324828
E agents@cooperandchand.com
W www.cooperandchand.com

CORE MGMT T 020 3691 0773
Contact: Sara Sehdev
1st Floor, Artist House, 35 Little Russell Street
London WC1A 2HH
E info@coremgmt.co.uk
W www.coremgmt.co.uk

CORNER, Clive ASSOCIATES T 01305 860267
*Contact: Duncan Stratton. By e-mail. Accepts Showreels
by e-mail only. 2 Agents represent 40 Performers.
Commercials. Film. Musical Theatre. Stage. Television*
'The Belenes', 60 Wakeham
Portland DT5 1HN
E cornerassociates@aol.com

**CORNISH, Caroline
MANAGEMENT LTD** T 020 8743 7337
Technicians only
12 Shinfield Street, London W12 0HN
T 07725 555711
E carolinecornish@me.com
W www.carolinecornish.co.uk

**COULSON, Lou
ASSOCIATES LTD** T 020 7734 9633
PMA Member
1st Floor, 37 Berwick Street
London W1F 8RS
F 020 7439 7569
E info@loucoulson.co.uk

**COULTER MANAGEMENT
AGENCY LTD** T 0141 204 4058
PMA Member. Contact: Anne Coulter, Julie Hamilton
Suite 120 The Pentagon Centre
Washington Street
Glasgow G3 8AZ
E info@coultermanagement.com
W www.coultermanagement.com

CPA MANAGEMENT T 01708 766444
The Studios, 219B North Street
Romford, Essex RM1 4QA
E info@cpamanagement.co.uk
W www.cpastudios.co.uk

CRAWFORDS T 020 8947 9999
PO Box 56662, London W13 3BH
E cr@wfords.com
W www.crawfords.tv

**CREATIVE ARTISTS
MANAGEMENT (CAM)** T 020 7292 0600
PMA Member. Contact: By e-mail only
55-59 Shaftesbury Avenue
London W1D 6LD
E reception@cam.co.uk
W www.cam.co.uk

CREATIVE BLAST AGENCY T 020 8123 6386
13-15 Clarence Road, Grays
Essex RM17 6QA
T 01375 386247
E info@cbagency.co.uk
W www.cbagency.co.uk

CREATIVE DIFFERENCES T 07804 555844
*Contact: Hayley J. Bacon (Agency Director)
Twitter: @CreativeDiffs*
16 Carnforth Gardens, Elm Park
Hornchurch, Essex RM12 5DJ
T 01708 456090
E creativedifferences@outlook.com
W www.creativedifferences.wix.com/agent

**CREATIVE MEDIA
MANAGEMENT** T 020 8584 5363
*PMA Member. No Actors. Film, Television & Stage
Technical Personnel only*
Ealing Studios, Ealing Green
London W5 5EP
F 020 8566 5554
E enquiries@creativemediamanagement.com
W www.creativemediamanagement.com

CRESCENT MANAGEMENT T 020 8987 0191
*Personal Manager. Co-operative. CPMA Member.
Contact: By Post. Accepts Showreels*
Southbank House
Black Prince Road, London SE1 7SJ
E mail@crescentmanagement.co.uk
W www.crescentmanagement.co.uk

**CRUICKSHANK
CAZENOVE LTD** T 020 7735 2933
*PMA Member. Contact: Harriet Cruickshank. By Post.
1 Agent. Choreographers, Designers & Directors only*
97 Old South Lambeth Road
London SW8 1XU
E mail@ccagents.co.uk

CS MANAGEMENT T 01708 708515
35 Chase Cross Road
Romford, Essex RM5 3PJ
T 07818 050424
E linda@csmanagementuk.com
W www.csmanagementuk.com

AM LONDON

Simon Pegg

Julia Sawalha

Kelly-Anne Lyons

Mathew Horne

Amanda Piery

Peter Serafinowicz

Catherine Tate

Gavin Stenhouse

www.am-london.com

C.S.A.   T 020 7420 9351
Contact: By Post/e-mail. Commercials
3rd Floor, Joel House
17-21 Garrick Street, London WC2E 9BL
F 0843 2905796
E csa@shepherdmanagement.co.uk

CURTIS BROWN   T 020 7393 4400
PMA Member
Haymarket House, 28-29 Haymarket, London SW1Y 4SP
E reception@curtisbrown.co.uk
W www.curtisbrown.co.uk

CV ACTOR MANAGEMENT   T 07989 811999
49 Percy Road, Wrexham LL13 7EB
E cvactormanagement@yahoo.co.uk
W www.cvactormanagement.co.uk

DAA MANAGEMENT   T 020 7255 6123
PMA Member. Formerly Debi Allen Associates
Welbeck House, 66-67 Wells Street, London W1T 3PY
F 020 7255 6128
E info@daamanagement.co.uk
W www.daamanagement.co.uk

DALY, David ASSOCIATES   T 020 7384 1036
Contact: David Daly, Louisa Miles
586A King's Road, London SW6 2DX
F 020 7610 9512
E agent@daviddaly.co.uk
W www.daviddaly.co.uk

**DALY, David ASSOCIATES
(MANCHESTER)**   T 01565 631999
Contact: Mary Ramsay
16 King Street, Knutsford, Cheshire WA16 6DL
F 01565 755334
E north@daviddaly.co.uk
W www.daviddaly.co.uk

DALZELL & BERESFORD LTD   T 020 7336 0351
Paddock Suite, The Courtyard
55 Charterhouse Street, London EC1M 6HA
E mail@dbltd.co.uk
W www.dalzellandberesford.com

DANCERS   T 020 7637 1487
Trading as FEATURES AGENCY
1 Charlotte Street, London W1T 1RD
E info@features.co.uk
W www.features.co.uk

DANCERS INC   T 020 7205 2316
Twitter: @dancersincworld
INC Artists Ltd, 90 Long Acre
Covent Garden, London WC2E 9RZ
E miranda@international-collective.com
W www.dancersincworld.com

**DAS IMPERIUM
TALENT AGENCY**   T 00 49 151 19324297
Torstrasse 129, Berlin 10119, Germany
T 00 49 151 61957519
E georg@dasimperium.com
W www.dasimperium.com

**DAVID ARTISTES MANAGEMENT
AGENCY LTD THE**   T 020 8834 1615
26-28 Hammersmith Grove, London W6 7BA
E casting@davidagency.co.uk
W www.davidagency.co.uk

**DAVIS, Chris
MANAGEMENT LTD**   T 020 7240 2116
PMA Member
2nd Floor, 80-81 St Martin's Lane, London WC2N 4AA
E tadams@cdm-ltd.com   W www.cdm-ltd.com

**DAVIS, Chris
MANAGEMENT LTD**   T 01584 819005
PMA Member
Tenbury House, 36 Teme Street
Tenbury Wells, Worcestershire WR15 8AA
F 01584 819076
E tadams@cdm-ltd.com
W www.cdm-ltd.com

**DAVIS, Lena, BISHOP,
John ASSOCIATES**   T 01604 891487
Personal Manager. Contact: By Post. 2 Agents
Cotton's Farmhouse, Whiston Road
Cogenhoe, Northants NN7 1NL
E admin@cottonsfarmhouse.org

**DAVIS GORDON
MANAGEMENT**   T 07989 306252
11 Eastern Avenue, Pinner, London HA5 1NU
E miriam@davisgordon.com
W www.davisgordon.com

**DENMARK STREET
MANAGEMENT**   T 020 7700 5200
*Personal Manager. Co-operative. CPMA Member.
Applications via Website*
Suite 4, Clarendon Buildings
25 Horsell Road, Highbury N5 1XL
E mail@denmarkstreet.net
W www.denmarkstreet.net

DEREK'S HANDS AGENCY   T 020 8834 1609
Hand & Foot Modelling
26-28 Hammersmith Grove, London W6 7BA
E casting@derekshands.com
W www.derekshands.com

**DEVINE ARTIST
MANAGEMENT**   T 020 8865 1955
Contact: By e-mail only
145-157 St John Street, London EC1V 4PW
E mail@devinemanagement.co.uk
W www.devinemanagement.co.uk

**DEVINE ARTIST
MANAGEMENT**   T 0161 726 5726
Tempus Building, 9 Mirabel Street, Manchester M3 1NP
E manchester@devinemanagement.co.uk
W www.devinemanagement.co.uk

de WOLFE, Felix   T 020 7242 5066
PMA Member. Contact: By e-mail
2nd Floor, 20 Old Compton Street
London W1D 4TW
F 020 7242 8119
E info@felixdewolfe.com
W www.felixdewolfe.com

**DHM LTD
(DICK HORSEY MANAGEMENT)**   T 01923 710614
*Personal Manager. Contact: By Post/e-mail/Telephone.
Accepts Showreels/Voicereels. 2 Agents represent
40 Performers. Corporate. Musical Theatre. Stage.
Television*
Suite 1, Cottingham House, Chorleywood Road
Rickmansworth, Herts WD3 4EP
T 07850 112211
E roger@dhmlimited.co.uk
W www.dhmlimited.co.uk

DIAMOND MANAGEMENT   T 020 7631 0400
PMA Member
31 Percy Street, London W1T 2DD
F 020 7631 0500
E agents@diman.co.uk
W www.diamondmanagement.co.uk

Rare Talent Actors Management is a dynamic agency with a fresh approach to acting management.

We supply professional actors to all aspects of the industry including television, film, theatre, corporate and commercials.

tanzaro house, ardwick green north, manchester, m12 6fz
t: 0161 273 4004   **f:** 0161 273 4567
info@raretalentactors.com www.raretalentactors.com

ACTORS MANAGEMENT

DIESTENFELD, Lily   T 07957 968214
Personal Manager. Over 55+ ages. No Unsolicited Post/e-mails/Calls from Actors
E lilyd@talk21.com

**DIRECT PERSONAL
MANAGEMENT**   **T/F** 020 8694 1788
*Co-operative. CPMA Member. Contact: By Post/e-mail.
Commercials. Corporate. Film. Stage. Television.
Voice Overs*
St John's House
16 St John's Vale, London SE8 4EN
E office@directpm.co.uk
W www.directpm.co.uk

**DIRECT PERSONAL
MANAGEMENT**   **T/F** 0113 266 4036
*Co-operative. CPMA Member. Contact: By Post/e-mail.
Film. Stage. Television. Commercials. Corporate.
Voice Overs*
Dukes Studio, Munro House
Duke Street, Leeds LS9 8AG
E office@directpm.co.uk
W www.directpm.co.uk

**DOE, John
MANAGEMENT**   T 020 7871 2969 (London)
T 0161 241 7786 (Manchester)
E casting@johndoemgt.com
W www.johndoemgt.com

DOUBLE ACT   T 020 8381 0151
PO Box 25574
London NW7 3GB
E info@double-act.co.uk
W www.double-act.co.uk

DOUBLEFVOICES   T 01580 830071
Singers
1 Hunters Lodge
Bodiam
East Sussex TN32 5UE
T 07976 927764
E rob@doublefvoices.com

**DOWNES PRESENTERS
AGENCY**   T 07973 601332
E downes@presentersagency.com
W www.presentersagency.com

Rhys Rusbatch

Ingrid Lacey

Tom Dumbleton - Photography
www.tomdumbleton.com
t: 07540251026   e: tom@tomdumbleton.com

DQ MANAGEMENT   T 01273 721221
27 Ravenswood Park, Northwood
Middlesex HA6 3PR
T 07713 984633
E dq.management1@gmail.com
W www.dqmanagement.com

**DRAGON PERSONAL
MANAGEMENT**   T 020 7183 5362
Leighton House, 20 Nantfawr Road
Cyncoed, Cardiff CF23 6JR
T 029 2075 4491
E casting@dragon-pm.com
W www.dragon-pm.com

DS PERSONAL MANAGEMENT   T 020 8743 7777
St Martin's Theatre, West Street
London WC2H 9NZ
E ds@denisesilvey.com
W www.denisesilvey.com

**DYSON, Louise at
VisABLE PEOPLE**   T 01386 555170
Contact: Louise Dyson. Artists with Disabilities
T 07930 345152
E louise@visablepeople.com
W www.visablepeople.com

**EARLE, Kenneth
PERSONAL MANAGEMENT**   T 020 7274 1219
214 Brixton Road, London SW9 6AP
T 01424 434272
E kennethearle@agents-uk.com
W www.kennethearlepersonalmanagement.com

**EARNSHAW, Susi
MANAGEMENT**   T 020 8441 5010
Personal Manager
The Bull Theatre, 68 High Street
Barnet, Herts EN5 5SJ
E casting@susiearnshaw.co.uk
W www.susiearnshawmanagement.com

ECLECTIC ARTISTS   T 001 323 798 5102
1714 North McCadden Place
Suite 2419, Hollywood
Los Angeles, CA 90028, USA
F 001 323 315 4263
E kat@nextstoplax.com

EKA ACTOR MANAGEMENT   T 01925 761210
*Contact: Jodie Keith (Casting Agent). Accepts
Showreels. Commercials. Corporate. Film. Television.
Voice Overs*
The Warehouse Studios, Glaziers Lane
Culcheth, Warrington, Cheshire WA3 4AQ
E jodie@eka-agency.com
W www.eka-agency.com

ELITE TALENT LTD   T 07787 342221
London & Manchester
54 Crosslee Road, Blackley
Manchester M9 6TA
E paul@elitetalent.co.uk
W www.elitetalent.co.uk

ELLICOTT MANAGEMENT   T 01483 428998
*Management Agency for the professional Adult Actors
Formerly with Wings Agency*
4 The Chestnut Suite, Guardian House
Borough Road, Godalming GU7 2AE
T 07745 443448
E admin@ellicottmanagement.com
W www.ellicottmanagement.com

ELLIOTT AGENCY LTD THE   T 01273 454111
17 Osborne Villas, Hove
East Sussex BN3 2RD
E elliottagency@btconnect.com
W www.elliottagency.co.uk

ELLIS, Bill LTD
See A & B PERSONAL MANAGEMENT LTD

ELLITE MANAGEMENT   T 0845 6525361
*Contact: By Post/e-mail. Accepts Showreels. 3 Agents
represent 40 Performers. Dancers*
'The Dancer', 8 Peterson Road, Wakefield WF1 4EB
T 07957 631510
E enquiries@ellitemanagement.co.uk
W www.elliteproductions.co.uk

EMPTAGE HALLETT   T 020 7436 0425
PMA Member
14 Rathbone Place, London W1T 1HT
F 020 7580 2748
E submissions@emptagehallett.co.uk
W www.emptagehallett.co.uk

EMPTAGE HALLETT   T 029 2034 4205
PMA Member
2nd Floor, 3-5 The Balcony
Castle Arcade, Cardiff CF10 1BU
F 029 2034 4206
E cardiff@emptagehallett.co.uk

ENCORE UK CASTING   T 01626 211040
PO Box 251, Newton Abbot
Devon TQ12 1AL
F 01626 202989
E hannah@encorecasting.co.uk
W www.encorecasting.co.uk

**ENGERS, Emma
ASSOCIATES LTD**   T 020 7278 9980
56 Russell Court, Woburn Place, London WC1H 0LW
T 020 7837 1859
E emma@emmaengersassociates.com
W www.emmaengersassociates.com

ENGLISH, Doreen '95   T/F 01243 825968
Contact: By Post/Telephone
48 The Boulevard, Bersted Park
Bognor Regis, West Sussex PO21 5BS

EOC MANAGEMENT   T 0161 724 4880
35 Plymouth Grove, Radcliffe, Manchester M26 3WU
T 07861 778330
E eocmanagement@gmail.com
W www.eoc-management.co.uk

ESSANAY **T** 020 8998 0007
Personal Manager. PMA Member. Contact: By Post
PO Box 56662, London W13 3BH
E info@essanay.co.uk

ETHNICS ARTISTE AGENCY **T** 020 8523 4242
86 Elphinstone Road, Walthamstow
London E17 5EX
F 020 8523 4523
E info@ethnicsaa.co.uk

EUROKIDS CASTING AGENCY **T** 01925 761210
*Contact: Jodie Keith (Casting Agent). Accepts
Showreels. Children & Teenagers. Commercials. Film.
Television. Walk-ons & Supporting Artists*
The Warehouse Studios, Glaziers Lane
Culcheth, Warrington
Cheshire WA3 4AQ
E jodie@eka-agency.com
W www.eka-agency.com

**EVANS, Jacque
MANAGEMENT LTD** **T** 020 8699 1202
Top Floor Suite
14 Holmesley Road
London SE23 1PJ
E jacque@jemltd.demon.co.uk
W www.jacqueevansltd.com

EVANS & REISS **T** 020 8871 0788
104 Fawe Park Road, London SW15 2EA
E janita@evansandreiss.co.uk

EVOLUTION TALENT LTD **T** 020 8733 8206
T 07908 702714
E info@evotalentltd.com
W www.evotalentltd.com

EXCEL AGENCY **T** 01772 755343
1 Sandfield Street, Leyland, Preston PR25 3HJ
T 07570 112022
E XLAgency@yahoo.com
W www.xlagency.com

EXCESS ALL AREAS **T** 020 8761 2384
*Contact: Paul L. Martin (Director). Cabaret, Circus &
Variety Entertainment*
3 Gibbs Square, London SE19 1JN
E info@excessallareas.co.uk
W www.excessallareas.co.uk

**EXPRESSIONS CASTING
AGENCY** **T** 01623 424334
3 Newgate Lane, Mansfield
Nottingham NG18 2LB
E expressions-uk@btconnect.com
W www.expressionsperformingarts.co.uk

EYE CASTING THE **T** 020 7377 7500
1st Floor, 92 Commercial Street
Off Puma Court, London E1 6LZ
E bayo@theeyecasting.com
W www.theeyecasting.com

F4MMODELS **T** 07538 228366
Curve Models. Commercials. Editorials. Music Videos
16 The Vale, London W3 7SB
E hello@face4music.com
W www.f4mmodels.com

FACE MANAGEMENT **T** 0113 245 8667
3 Bowling Green Terrace, Leeds
West Yorkshire LS11 9SP
E info@face-agency.co.uk
W www.face-agency.co.uk

Robert Lister HEADSHOTS www.robertlister.co.uk Bournemouth 07909 824893

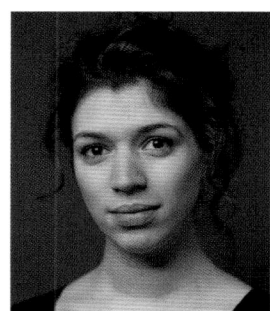

FARINO, Paola T 020 7207 0858
Actors
109 St Georges Road, London SE1 6HY
E info@paolafarino.co.uk
W www.paolafarino.co.uk

FD MANAGEMENT T 07730 800679
18C Marine Square, Brighton BN2 1DN
E vivienwilde@mac.com

**FEA MANAGEMENT
(FERRIS ENTERTAINMENT)** T 07801 493133
London. Belfast. Cardiff. Los Angeles. France. Spain
Number 8, 132 Charing Cross Road
London WC2H 0LA
E info@ferrisentertainment.com
W www.ferrisentertainment.com

FEAST MANAGEMENT LTD T 020 7354 5216
PMA Member
1st Floor, 34 Upper Street, London N1 0PN
F 020 7354 8995
E office@feastmanagement.co.uk

**FEATURED & BACKGROUND
CASTING LTD (FAB)** T 07808 781169
Contact: Suzanne Johns
13A Waldeck House, Waldeck Road
Maidenhead, Berkshire SL6 8BR
E info@fabcastingagency.com
W www.fabcastingagency.com

FEATURES T 020 7637 1487
1 Charlotte Street, London W1T 1RD
E info@features.co.uk
W www.features.co.uk

FFTS MANAGEMENT T 01639 814012
Child & Adult Performers in London & South Wales
Office 4, Sandfields Business Centre
Endeavour Place, Port Talbot, South Wales SA12 7PT
E info@fftsmanagement.com
W www.fftsmanagement.com

FIELD, Alan ASSOCIATES T 020 8441 1137
*Personal Manager. Contact: By e-mail. Celebrities.
Composers. Musical Theatre. Presenters. Singers*
3 The Spinney, Bakers Hill
Hadley Common, Herts EN5 5QJ
T 07836 555300
E alan@alanfield.com

FILM AND BUSINESS LTD T 020 7129 1449
*Personal Manager. Contact: Julia de Cadenet.
Personal Management & Legal Advice. Assistance with
Independent Film Development & Funding Applications.
Offices in London, Paris & California*
17 Cavendish Square, London W1G 0PH
T 07798 695112
E info@filmandbusiness.com
W www.filmandbusinesslaw.com

FILM CAST CORNWALL & SW T 07811 253756
Falmouth, Cornwall
E enquiries@filmcastcornwall.co.uk
W www.filmcastcornwall.co.uk

FILM RIGHTS LTD T 020 7316 1837
Personal Manager. Contact: By Post
Suite 306, Belsize Business Centre
258 Belsize Road, London NW6 4BT
F 020 7624 3629
E information@filmrights.ltd.uk

FINCH & PARTNERS T 020 7851 7140
Top Floor, 35 Heddon Street
London W1B 4BR
F 020 7287 6420
E reception@finchandpartners.com
W www.finchandpartners.com

**FIRST & FOREMOST
ENTERTAINMENT LTD** T 0800 2707567
*Contact: Chris Neilson, Peter Stanford. By Post/
e-mail. Accepts Showreels. 2 Agents represent
175+ Performers. Entertainment Agency & Corporate
Entertainment. Corporate, Musical, Speciality &
Variety Acts*
90 Longridge Avenue, Brighton
East Sussex BN2 8RB
T 07505 565635
E info@firstandforemostentertainment.com
W www.firstandforemostentertainment.com

FIRST CALL MANAGEMENT T 00 353 1 6108842
Beauparc House
Ballydowd, Lucan, Co. Dublin
E fcmeleanor@gmail.com

**FITZGERALD, Sheridan
MANAGEMENT** T 01842 812028
*PMA Member. Contact: Edward Romfourt. By Post only
(SAE). No Phone Calls/e-mails*
16 Pond Lane, Brandon
Suffolk IP27 0LA
W www.sheridanfitzgerald.com

FK ASSOCIATES T 07747 053764
20 Main Road, Tower Park
Poole Lane, Hullbridge
Essex SS5 6PB
E admin@fkassoc.com

FLAIR TALENT T 020 7287 0407
15 Poland Street
London W1F 8QE
E bookings@flairtalent.com
W www.flairtalent.com

FLETCHER ASSOCIATES T 020 8361 8061
*Personal Manager. Contact: Francine Fletcher. Corporate
Speakers. Experts for Radio & Television. Stage*
Studio One, 25 Parkway, London N20 0XN
F 020 8361 8866
W www.fletcherassociates.net

FLETCHER JACOB T 020 3603 7340
Artist Management
162-168 Regent Street, London W1B 5TD
F 020 7038 3707
E info@fletcherjacob.co.uk
W www.fletcherjacob.co.uk

FLICKS FILM & TELEVISION AGENCY   T 00 353 21 4279680
Plunkett Chambers
21-23 Oliver Plunkett Street, Cork 1, Ireland
F 00 353 21 4279690
E info@ddmp.ie
W www.ddmp.ie

FLP MANAGEMENT   T 020 7371 0300
136-144 New Kings Road
Fulham, London SW6 4LZ
F 020 7371 8707
E info@flpmanagement.co.uk
W www.flpmanagement.co.uk

FOCUS TALENT   T 020 3240 1064
*Personal Manager. Representing Actors in Feature Films,
Television, Stage & Commercials. Existing Clients only*
81 Sutherland Avenue, London W9 2HG
T 07532 158818
E info@focustalent.co.uk
W www.focustalent.co.uk

FOGGIE LONDON ASSOCIATES   T 07474 037365
Theatrical Agency
Room 2, 22 Southwark Street
London SE1 1TU
E info@foggielondon.co.uk
W www.foggielondon.co.uk

FOLEY, Kerry MANAGEMENT LTD   T 07747 864001
Communications House
26 York Street, London W1U 6PZ
E contact@kfmltd.com
W www.kerryfoleymanagement.com

FOSTER, Philip COMPANY THE   T 020 3390 2063
16 Carlisle Street
London W1D 3BT
E philip@philipfosterco.com
W www.philipfosterco.com

FOSTER, Sharon MANAGEMENT   T 07919 417812
15A Hollybank Road
Birmingham B13 0RF
E mail@sharonfoster.co.uk
W www.sharonfoster.co.uk

FOX, Clare ASSOCIATES   T/F 020 7328 7494
Set, Lighting & Sound Designers
9 Plympton Road, London NW6 7EH
E clareimfox@gmail.com
W www.clarefox.co.uk

FOX, Julie ASSOCIATES   T/F 01628 777853
*Personal Manager. Contact: Julie Fox. By e-mail only.
Accepts Showreels/Voicereels. 2 Agents represent
50 Performers*
E agent@juliefoxassociates.co.uk
W www.juliefoxassociates.co.uk

FRENCH, Linda
See APM ASSOCIATES

FRESH AGENTS LTD   T 01273 711777
The Dock, Wilbury Villas
Brighton & Hove BN3 6AH
T 0845 4080998
E info@freshagents.co.uk
W www.freshagents.co.uk

PHIL DAVIS   BEVERLEY KLEIN   FREDDIE HIGHMORE

MICHAEL BENNETT PHOTOGRAPHY
020 7100 7584
www.michaelbennett.co.uk

FRESH PARTNERS LTD   **T** 020 7198 8478
1 Hardwick's Square, Wandsworth
London SW18 4AW
E hello@fresh-partners.com
W www.fresh-partners.com

**FRONTLINE ACTORS
AGENCY**   **T** 00 353 1 6359882
30-31 Wicklow Street, Dublin 2, Ireland
E frontlineactors@eircom.net
W www.frontlineactors.com

**FUNKY BEETROOT CELEBRITY
MANAGEMENT LTD**   **T** 07814 010691
Personal Manager. Actors. Television Celebrities
PO Box 307, Herne Bay, Kent CT6 9BQ
E info@funky-beetroot.com
W www.funky-beetroot.com

FUSION MANAGEMENT   **T** 020 7834 6660
201A Victoria Street, London SW1W 5NE
E info@fusionmng.com
W www.fusionmng.com

**GADBURY PERSONAL
MANAGEMENT**   **T** 01942 635556
5 Bolton Road, Atherton, Manchester M46 9JQ
T 07791 737306
E vicky@gadbury-casting.co.uk
W www.gadburycasting.co.uk

**GAELFORCE 10
MANAGEMENT**   **T** 0141 334 6246
14 Bowmont Gardens
Dowanhill, Glasgow G12 9LR
T 07778 296002
E info@gaelforce10.com
W www.gaelforce10.com

GAGAN, Hilary ASSOCIATES   **T** 020 7404 8794
*Personal Manager. PMA Member. Contact: Hilary
Gagan, Shiv Coard*
187 Drury Lane, London WC2B 5QD
F 020 7430 1869
E hilary@hgassoc.co.uk

GALLOWAYS   **T** 020 7636 7770
PMA Member
16 Percy Street, London W1T 1DT
E info@gallowaysagency.com
W www.gallowaysagency.com

GARDNER HERRITY LTD   **T** 020 7388 0088
PMA Member. Contact: Andy Herrity, Nicky James
24 Conway Street, London W1T 6BG
F 020 7388 0688
E info@gardnerherrity.co.uk
W www.gardnerherrity.co.uk

GARRICKS   **T** 020 7738 1600
PMA Member
Angel House, 76 Mallinson Road
London SW11 1BN
E info@garricks.net

GAY, Noel ORGANISATION   **T** 020 7836 3941
PMA Member
19 Denmark Street, London WC2H 8NA
F 020 7287 1816
E info@noelgay.com
W www.noelgay.com

GDA MANAGEMENT   **T** 01322 278879
Contact: By e-mail only. No Post
Suite 793, Kemp House
152 City Road, London EC1V 2NX
T 07974 680439
E info@gdamanagment.co.uk

GENUINE ARAB CASTING   **T** 020 3478 9067
*Contact: By e-mail. Accepts Showreels/Voicereels.
Commercials. Corporate. Film. Television. Voice Overs*
78 York Street, London W1H 1DP
E info@genuinearabcasting.com
W www.genuinearabcasting.com

**GENUINE CASTING TALENT
AGENCY**   **T** 020 3478 9067
*Contact: By e-mail. Accepts Showreels/Voicereels.
Commercials. Corporate. Film. Television. Voice Overs*
78 York Street, London W1H 1DP
E info@genuinecasting.com
W www.genuinecasting.com

**GFM ASSOCIATES
PERSONAL MANAGEMENT**   **T** 020 8878 3105
PMA Member
20 Allenford House, Tunworth Crescent
London SW15 4PG
T 07879 402409
E gillian.gfmassociates@gmail.com
W www.gfmassociates.com

GIELGUD MANAGEMENT   **T** 01444 447020
PMA Member
The Old Cinema, 1st Floor, 59-61 The Broadway
Haywards Heath, West Sussex RH16 3AS
F 01444 447030
E info@gielgudmanagement.co.uk
W www.gielgudmanagement.co.uk

GILBERT & PAYNE   **T** 020 7734 7505
Room 236, 2nd Floor, Linen Hall
162-168 Regent Street, London W1B 5TB
F 020 7494 3787
E ee@gilbertandpayne.com
W www.gilbertandpayne.com

**GILLMAN, Geraldine
ASSOCIATES**   **T** 07799 791586
Harris Primary Academy Crystal Palace, Malcolm Road
Penge, London SE20 8RH
E geraldi.gillma@btconnect.com

**GLADWIN, Elizabeth
ASSOCIATES**   **T** 020 8936 3553
*Personal Manager. Contact: By Post/e-mail. 2 Agents
represent 40 Performers*
2nd Floor, 18-24 Chaseside, London N14 5PA
E info@elizabethgladwinassociates.com
W www.elizabethgladwinassociates.com

GLASS, Eric LTD   **T** 020 7229 9500
25 Ladbroke Crescent, Notting Hill, London W11 1PS
F 020 7229 6220
E eglassltd@aol.com

GLOBAL7   **T/F** 020 7281 7679
Kemp House, 152 City Road, London EC1V 2NX
T 07956 956652
E global7castings@gmail.com
W www.global7casting.com

GLOBAL ARTISTS   **T** 020 7839 4888
*PMA Member. Contact: By e-mail. Accepts
Showreels/Voicereels. 5 Agents*
23 Haymarket, London SW1Y 4DG
F 020 7839 4555
E info@globalartists.co.uk
W www.globalartists.co.uk

**GLOBALWATCH
MANAGEMENT**   **T** 020 3086 9616
1 Berkeley Street, London W1J 8DJ
F 020 3370 7916
E pandrews@globalwatch.com
W www.globalwatch.com

GLYN MANAGEMENT T 01449 737695
The Old School House, Brettenham, Ipswich IP7 7QP
F 01449 736117
E glyn.management@tesco.net

**GMM (GREGG MILLARD
MANAGEMENT)** T 020 3475 3473
2nd Floor, 312 St. Paul's Road, Islington, London N1 2LF
T 07710 562774
E greggmillard.gmm@gmail.com

GOLD AGENCY LTD T/F 01474 561200
Contact: By e-mail. Accepts Showreels. 35 Performers
Britannia House, Lower Road, Ebbsfleet, Kent DA11 9BL
T 07831 764995
E ann@goldagency.co.uk

GOLDMANS MANAGEMENT T 01323 643961
E casting@goldmansmanagement.co.uk
W www.goldmansmanagement.co.uk

GORDON & FRENCH T 020 7734 4818
PMA Member. Contact: By Post
12-13 Poland Street
London W1F 8QB
F 020 7734 4832
E mail@gordonandfrench.co.uk

**GRAHAM, David PERSONAL
MANAGEMENT (DGPM)** T/F 020 7241 6752
The Studio, 107A Middleton Road
London E8 4LN
E info@dgpmtheagency.com

AMERICAN ACTORS UK admin@americanactorsuk.com www.americanactorsuk.com

Need American Actors? American Actors UK is the definitive source of genuine **American** and **Canadian** actors based in the UK. We're not an agency, but a professional network which can connect you to authentic North American performers. To find out more or to join, *get in touch today*.

GRANT, James MEDIA T 020 8742 4950
94 Strand On The Green
Chiswick, London W4 3NN
F 020 8742 4951
E enquiries@jamesgrant.co.uk
W www.jamesgrant.co.uk

GRANTHAM-HAZELDINE LTD T 020 7038 3737
PMA Member
Suite 427, The Linen Hall
162-168 Regent Street
London W1B 5TE
F 020 7038 3739
E agents@granthamhazeldine.com
W www.granthamhazeldine.com

GRAY, Darren MANAGEMENT T 023 9269 9973
Specialising in representing/promoting Australian Artists
2 Marston Lane, Portsmouth
Hampshire PO3 5TW
F 023 9267 7227
E darrengraymanagement@gmail.com
W www.darrengraymanagement.com

GREEN & UNDERWOOD T 020 8998 0007
In association with ESSANAY. Personal Manager.
Contact: By Post
PO Box 56662, London W13 3BH
E ny@greenandunderwood.com

GRESHAM, Carl GROUP T 01274 735880
PO Box 3, Bradford
West Yorkshire BD1 4QN
F 01274 827161
E gresh@carlgresham.co.uk
W www.carlgresham.co.uk

**GRIFFIN, Sandra
MANAGEMENT LTD** T 020 8894 1479
4 First Cross Road, Twickenham TW2 5QA
E office@sandragriffin.com
W www.sandragriffin.com

**GROUNDLINGS
THEATRE COMPANY** T 023 9273 9496
42 Kent Street
Portsmouth, Hampshire PO1 3BS
E richard@groundlings.co.uk
W www.groundlings.co.uk

**GROVES, Rob
PERSONAL MANAGEMENT** T 020 7125 0207
PMA Member. Contact: By e-mail
Hudson House, 8 Tavistock Street
London WC2E 7PP
T 07740 348350
E rob@robgroves.co.uk
W www.robgroves.co.uk

GUBBAY, Louise ASSOCIATES T 01959 573080
69 Paynesfield Road, Tatsfield
Kent TN16 2BG
E louise@louisegubbay.com
W www.louisegubbay.com

**GUBBAY, Louise
ASSOCIATES (LA)** T 01959 573080
10642 Santa Monica Boulevard, Suite 207
Los Angeles, CA 90025, USA
T 001 323 522 5545
E louise@louisegubbay.com
W www.louisegubbay.com

**HALL JAMES
PERSONAL MANAGEMENT** T 020 3036 0558
12 Melcombe Place, London NW1 6JJ
E agents@halljames.co.uk
W www.halljames.co.uk

**HAMBLETON, Patrick
MANAGEMENT** T 020 7226 0947
Top Floor, 136 Englefield Road, London N1 3LQ
T 020 7993 5412
E info@phm.uk.com
W www.phm.uk.com

HAMILTON HODELL LTD T 020 7636 1221
PMA Member
20 Golden Square, London W1F 9JL
E info@hamiltonhodell.co.uk
W www.hamiltonhodell.co.uk

HANCOCK AGENCY THE T 020 3488 0159
E info@thehancockagency.com
W www.thehancockagency.com

HARLEQUIN ARTISTES T 0191 385 8834
Personal Manager
14 Beatrice Terrace, Shiney Row, Durham DH4 4QW
E paul@harlequinartistes.co.uk
W www.harlequinartistes.co.uk

HARRIS AGENCY LTD THE T 01923 211644
71 The Avenue, Watford, Herts WD17 4NU
E theharrisagency@btconnect.com

HARRISON, Penny BSA LTD
Contact: By e-mail
E harrisonbsa@aol.com

HARVEY VOICES T 020 7952 4361
58 Woodlands Road, London N9 8RT
W www.harveyvoices.co.uk

HAT MANAGEMENT T 07891 644767
Contact: Laurence James
67 Granby House, Granby Row
Manchester M1 7AR
E hatactors@hotmail.co.uk
W www.hatactingmanagement.co.uk

**HATTON McEWAN
PENFORD LTD** T 020 7253 4770
Personal Manager. PMA Member. Contact: Stephen Hatton, Aileen McEwan, James Penford. By Post/e-mail
3 Chocolate Studios, 7 Shepherdess Place
London N1 7LJ
E mail@hattonmcewanpenford.com
W www.hattonmcewanpenford.com

HAYES, Cheryl MANAGEMENT　**T** 020 8994 4447
85 Rothschild Road
London W4 5NT
E cheryl@cherylhayes.co.uk
W www.cherylhayes.co.uk

H C A
See COOKE, Howard ASSOCIATES

HEADNOD TALENT AGENCY LTD　**T** 020 3222 0035
RichMix 1st Floor West
35-47 Bethnal Green Road
London E1 6LA
E info@headnodagency.com
W www.headnodagency.com

HENRIETTA RABBIT ENTERTAINERS AGENCY　**T** 0333 000 4567
Contact: Stephanie. By e-mail. 3 Agents represent 21 Performers. Magicians. Clowns. Jugglers. Punch & Judy. Stiltwalkers. Balloonologists. Close-up Magicians. Face Painters. Role Players
The Warren
12 Eden Close
York YO24 2RD
E mrsrabbit1070129@aol.com
W www.henriettarabbit.co.uk

HENRY, Sharon MANAGEMENT　**T** 020 7953 7450
601 The Chandlery
50 Westminster Bridge Road
London SE1 7QY
E info@sharonhenry.co.uk
W www.sharonhenry.co.uk

HICKS, Jeremy ASSOCIATES LTD　**T** 020 7580 5741
Personal Manager. Contact: By Post/e-mail. Accepts Showreels. 2 Agents. Chefs. Comedians. Presenters. Writers
3 Stedham Place, London WC1A 1HU
F 020 7636 3753
E info@jeremyhicks.com
W www.jeremyhicks.com

HIRED HANDS　**T** 020 7267 9212
12 Cressy Road, London NW3 2LY
E info@hiredhandsmodels.com
W www.hiredhandsmodels.com

HOATH, Claire MANAGEMENT　**T** 020 7193 7973
E enquiries@clairehoathmanagement.com
W www.clairehoathmanagement.com

HOBBART & HOBBART　**T** 0047 45465527
Middelthunsgt. 25A
0368 Oslo, Norway
E braathen@hobbart.no
W www.hobbart.co.uk

HOLLAND, Dympna ASSOCIATES　**T** 01753 647551
Casualty Cottage, Kiln Lane, Hedgerley, Bucks SL2 3UT
T 07841 162354
E dympnaster@gmail.com

HOLLOWOOD, Jane ASSOCIATES LTD　**T** 0161 237 9141
Apartment 17, 113 Newton Street, Manchester M1 1AE
T 020 8291 5702
E janehollowood@btconnect.com
W www.janehollowood.co.uk

HOLMES, Kim SHOWBUSINESS ENTERTAINMENT AGENCY LTD   T 0115 930 5088
8 Charles Close, Ilkeston, Derbyshire DE7 5AF
F 0115 944 0390
E kimholmesshowbiz@hotmail.co.uk

HOPE, Sally ASSOCIATES   T 020 7613 5353
PMA Member
108 Leonard Street, London EC2A 4XS
F 020 7613 4848
E casting@sallyhope.biz
W www.sallyhope.biz

HORNCASTLE, Alban MANAGEMENT   T 07557 123022
66 High Street, Sevenoaks, Kent TN13 1JR
E info@albanhorncastlemanagement.co.uk
W www.albanhorncastlemanagement.co.uk

HOWARD, Amanda ASSOCIATES LTD   T 020 7250 1760
PMA Member. Contact: By Post
74 Clerkenwell Road, London EC1M 5QA
E mail@amandahowardassociates.co.uk
W www.amandahowardassociates.co.uk

HOWELL, Philippa
See PHPM (PHILIPPA HOWELL PERSONAL MANAGEMENT)

HOXTON STREET MANAGEMENT   T 020 7503 5131
Hoxton Hall, 130 Hoxton Street
London N1 6SH
E ben@hoxtonstreetmanagement.com
W www.hoxtonstreetmanagement.com

HR CREATIVE ARTISTS   T 020 3286 8830
Contact: By e-mail only
18 Soho Square, London W1D 3QL
E agent@hrca.eu
W www.hrca.eu

HUDSON, Nancy ASSOCIATES LTD   T 020 7499 5548
PMA Member
50 South Molton Street, Mayfair, London W1K 5SB
E agents@nancyhudsonassociates.com
W www.nancyhudsonassociates.com

HUGHES, Steve MANAGEMENT LTD   T 0844 5564670
26 The Tyleshades, Tadburn Gardens
Romsey, Hampshire SO51 5RJ
E management@stevehughesuk.com
W www.stevehughesuk.com

HUNWICK HUGHES LTD   T 0131 229 3094
Personal Manager
Room 8, Argyle House
37 Castle Terrace, Edinburgh EH1 2EL
E maryam@hunwickhughes.com
W www.hunwickhughes.com

I.A.G. (IDENTITY AGENCY GROUP)   T 020 7079 9340
PMA Member
9 Percy Street, London W1T 1DL
E casting@identityagencygroup.com
W www.identityagencygroup.com

ICON ACTORS MANAGEMENT   T 0161 273 3344
Tanzaro House, Ardwick Green North
Manchester M12 6FZ
F 0161 273 4567
E info@iconactors.net
W www.iconactors.net

IMAGE HOSPITALITY   T 01483 243690
3000 Cathedral Hill, Guildford
Surrey GU2 7YB
E jane@i-mage.uk.com
W www.imagehospitality.co.uk

I.M.L.   T/F 020 7587 1080
Personal Manager. CPMA Member. Contact: By Post. Accepts Showreels. 40+ Performers. Commercials. Corporate. Film. Stage. Television
The White House, 52-54 Kennington Oval
London SE11 5SW
E info@iml.org.uk
W www.iml.org.uk

IMPACT INTERNATIONAL MANAGEMENT   T 07941 269849
Personal Manager. Contact: Colin Charles. By e-mail. Accepts Showreels/Voicereels. 1 Agent represents 10 Performers. Cruises. Musical Theatre. Speciality Acts & Events
310 Cascades Tower, 4 Westferry Road
London E14 8JL
E colin.charles310@gmail.com
W www.impact-london.co.uk

IMPERIAL PERSONAL MANAGEMENT LTD   T 0113 244 3222
102 Kirkstall Road
Leeds, West Yorkshire LS3 1JA
T 07890 387758
E katie@ipmcasting.com
W www.ipmcasting.com

IMPERIUM MANAGEMENT   T 020 8819 3155
PMA Member
271 Upper Street, Islington
London N1 2UQ
E info@imperiummgmt.com
W www.imperiummgmt.com

IN GOOD COMPANY   T 00 353 1 2542252 (Ireland)
Also known as IGC Talent. Personal Manager/Talent Agent. Contact: By e-mail. Accepts Showreels/Voicereels. 2 Agents represent 20 Performers. Commercials. Film. Stage. Television
93 St Stephens Green, Dublin 2, Ireland
T 020 7193 4579 (UK)
E info@igctalent.com
W www.igctalent.com

IN HOUSE AGENCY   T 07921 843508
12 Cliffe House, Blackwall Lane, London SE10 0RB
E info@inhouseagency.co.uk
W www.inhouseagency.co.uk

INDEPENDENT TALENT GROUP LTD   T 020 7636 6565
PMA Member. Formerly ICM, London
40 Whitfield Street, London W1T 2RH
F 020 7323 0101
W www.independenttalent.com

INDEPENDENT THEATRE WORKSHOP THE   T 00 353 1 2600831
8 Terminus Mills, Clonskeagh, Dublin 6, Ireland
E itwagency@itwstudios.ie
W www.itwstudios.ie

INFINITY ARTIST MANAGEMENT   T 07740 406224
207 Balgreen Road
Edinburgh EH11 2RZ
E casting@infinityartists.com
W www.infinityartists.com

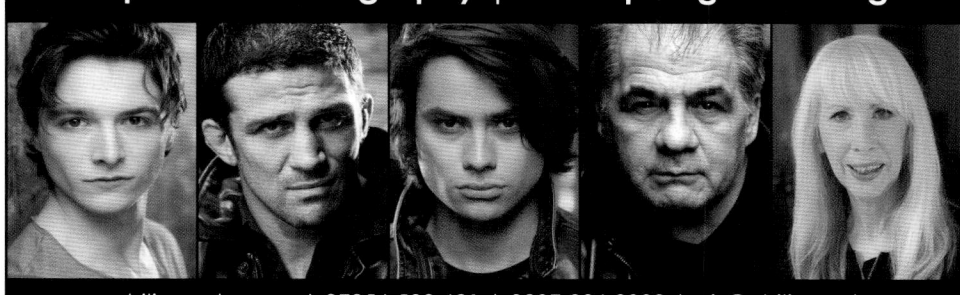

Philip Wade Photography | £175 Spotlight Package

www.philipwade.com | 07956 599 691 | 0207 226 3088 | pix@philipwade.com

INIMITABLE T 07913 597956
1st Floor, 22 West Mall
Clifton, Bristol BS8 4BQ
E bernie@theinimitables.co.uk
W www.theinimitables.co.uk

INSPIRATION MANAGEMENT T 020 7833 2912
Co-operative. CPMA Member. Est 1986
Unit 6, East Block, Panther House
38 Mount Pleasant, London WC1X 0AN
E mail@inspirationmanagement.org.uk
W www.inspirationmanagement.org.uk

INSPIRE ACADEMY T 0115 988 1800
The Attic Studio, 3rd Floor
46-48 Carrington Street
Nottingham NG1 7FG
E admin@inspireacademy.co.uk
W www.inspireacademy.co.uk

INTER-CITY CASTING T/F 01942 321969
*Personal Manager. Contact: By e-mail. Accepts
Showreels. 2 Agents represent 60 Performers*
27 Wigan Lane, Wigan
Greater Manchester WN1 1XR
E intercitycasting@btconnect.com

**INTERNATIONAL ARTISTS
MANAGEMENT** T 020 7435 8065
St Clements House
12 Leyden Street
London E1 7LL
E info@internationalartistsmanagement.co.uk
W www.internationalartistsmanagement.co.uk

**INTERNATIONAL MODEL
MANAGEMENT LTD** T 020 7610 9111
Incorporating Yvonne Paul Management
Elysium Gate, Unit 15
126-128 New Kings Road, London SW6 4LZ
F 020 7736 2221
E info@immmodels.com
W www.immmodels.com

**INTERNATIONAL MODELS &
TALENT AGENCY** T 001 310 760 1082
Contact: Margaret Guiraud
Admin: IMTAgency, PO Box 4475
West Hills, CA 91308, USA
E int.talent@gmail.com

IRISH ACTORS LONDON T 020 7125 0539
Penthouse 11, Bickenhall Mansions
London W1U 6BR
E irishactorslondon@gmail.com
W www.irishactorslondon.co.uk

JAA
See ALTARAS, Jonathan ASSOCIATES LTD

JABBERWOCKY AGENCY T 01580 714306
*Contact: Christina Yates. By e-mail. 4 Agents represent
135 Performers. Children. Teenagers*
Glassenbury Hill Farm
Glassenbury Road
Cranbrook, Kent TN17 2QF
F 01580 714346
E christina@christinayates.com
W www.yt93.co.uk

anna hull photography

t: 07778 399 419
e: info@annahullphotography.com
www.annahullphotography.com

JAFFREY MANAGEMENT LTD   T 01708 732350
Personal Manager. Contact: Kim Barry. By Post/e-mail.
Accepts Showreels/Voicereels (SAE). 80 Performers.
Commercials. Film. Radio. Stage. Television
74 Western Road, Romford, Essex RM1 3LP
T 07790 466206
E mail@jaffreyactors.co.uk
W www.jaffreymanagement.org.uk

JAM2000 AGENCY   T 01895 624755
The Windmill Studio Centre
106-106A Pembroke Road
Ruislip, Middlesex HA4 8NW
E info@jam2000.co.uk
W www.jam2000.co.uk

JAMES, Billie - ORIENTAL CASTING
AGENCY LTD   T 020 8660 0101
Contact: By e-mail/Telephone. Accepts Showreels/
Voicereels. 1 Agent represents 200+ Performers.
Afro/Asian Artists
22 Wontford Road, Purley, Surrey CR8 4BL
E billiejames@btconnect.com

JAMES, Susan
See SJ MANAGEMENT

JB ASSOCIATES   T 0161 237 1808
Personal Manager. Contact: John Basham. By Post/
e-mail. Accepts Showreels/Voicereels. 2 Agents
represent 60 Performers. Commercials. Radio. Stage.
Television
PO Box 173, Manchester M19 0AR
F 0161 249 3666
E info@j-b-a.net
W www.j-b-a.net

JCM MANAGEMENT   T 07866 211647
2 New Street
Bridgtown WS11 0DD
E newtalentjcm@outlook.com

JEFFREY & WHITE
MANAGEMENT LTD   T 01462 429769
Personal Manager. PMA Member
7 Paynes Park, Hitchin
Herts SG5 1EH
E info@jeffreyandwhite.co.uk
W www.jeffreyandwhite.co.uk

JERMIN, Mark MANAGEMENT   T 01792 458855
Contact: By Post/e-mail. Accepts Showreels. 5 Agents
Swansea Metropolitan, University of Wales
Trinity Saint David
Mount Pleasant, Swansea SA1 6ED
E info@markjermin.co.uk
W www.markjermin.co.uk

JERRY MANAGEMENT   T 00 34 69 9281356
Contact: Clara Nieto. Representing Actors & Directors
within the Spanish Market
Calle Martín de los Heros, 19, 4 int izq
Madrid, Spain, 28008
E jerry@jerrymanagement.es
W www.jerrymanagement.com

JEWELL WRIGHT LTD   T 020 7462 0790
Contact: By Post. Accepts Showreels. 2 Agents
represent 90 Performers. Commercials. Creatives. Film.
Musical Theatre. Radio. Stage. Television
17 Percy Street
London W1T 1DU
E agents@jwl-london.com
W www.jwl-london.com

JGPM   T 020 7440 1850
7 Old Park Lane
London W1K 1QR
E victoria@jgpm.co.uk
W www.jgpm.co.uk

J.M. MANAGEMENT   T 020 8908 0502
Personal Representation to a small number of Actors/
Actresses & Magicians in Film Work. No Unsolicited
Showreels/Headshots
20 Pembroke Road, North Wembley
Middlesex HA9 7PD

JOHNSTON & MATHERS
MANAGEMENT   T/F 020 8449 4968
PO Box 3167, Barnet EN5 2WA
E johnstonmathers@aol.com
W www.johnstonandmathers.com

JOYCE, Michael
MANAGEMENT   T 020 3697 1265
Twitter: @michaeljoycetv
6th Floor, International House
223 Regent Street
London W1B 2QP
E michael@michaeljoyce.tv
W www.michaeljoycemanagement.com

JPA MANAGEMENT   T 01494 520978
PMA Member
30 Daws Hill Lane, High Wycombe
Bucks HP11 1PW
F 01494 510479
E jackie.palmer@btinternet.com
W www.jpamanagement.co.uk

K TALENT ARTIST
MANAGEMENT   T 020 7379 1616
Personal Manager. Contact: By Post/e-mail. Accepts
Showreels/Voicereels. 5 Agents represent approx 150
Adult Performers. Children. Commercials. Dancers. Film.
Musical Theatre. Singers. Stage. Television
4th Floor, 43 Aldwych
London WC2B 4DN
E mail@ktalent.co.uk
W www.ktalent.co.uk

KANAL, Roberta AGENCY   T 020 8894 2277
82 Constance Road, Twickenham
Middlesex TW2 7JA
T/F 020 8894 7952
E roberta.kanal@dsl.pipex.com

KDR MANAGEMENT (KDRM)   T 07545 584558
E kdr@kanericca.com
W www.control-london.com

KEDDIE SCOTT ASSOCIATES LTD   T 020 7836 6802
Personal Manager. PMA Member. Contact: By e-mail.
Prospective Client Applications to info@keddiescott.com.
Accepts Showreels. 4 Agents represent 300 Performers.
Commercials. Corporate. Film. Musical Theatre. Radio.
Singers. Stage. Television
Studio 1, 17 Shorts Gardens
Covent Garden, London WC2H 9AT
F 020 7147 1326
E london@keddiescott.com
W www.keddiescott.com

KSA - NORTH   T 07792 022490
PMA Member
c/o Head Office, 17 Shorts Gardens
Covent Garden, London WC2H 9AT
T 07708 202374
E north@keddiescott.com
W www.keddiescott.com

KSA - SCOTLAND   T 07973 235355
Personal Manager. PMA Member. Contact: Paul Harper.
By Post/e-mail. Accepts Showreels/Voicereels. 1 Agent
represents 45 Performers. Film. Musical Theatre. Stage.
Television
c/o Head Office, Studio 1, 17 Shorts Gardens
Covent Garden, London WC2H 9AT
F 020 7147 1326
E scotland@keddiescott.com
W www.keddiescott.com

KELLY, Robert ASSOCIATES (RKA)   T 020 7287 6934
PMA Member
10 Greek Street, London W1D 4DH
E office@rkatalent.com
W www.rktalent.com

KENIS, Steve & CO   T 020 7434 9055
PMA Member
95 Barkston Gardens, London SW5 0EU
F 020 7373 9404
E sk@sknco.com

KEREN ROSE ASSOCIATES   T 07976 435945
Contact: Siobhan Kendall. By Post/e-mail. Commercials.
Film. Stage. Television
Long Lane
Huddersfield HD5 9SG
E agent@kerenrose.co.uk
W www.kerenrose.co.uk

KEW PERSONAL MANAGEMENT   T 07876 457402
PO Box 679
Surrey RH1 6EN
E info@kewpersonalmanagement.com
W www.kewpersonalmanagement.com

KEYLOCK MANAGEMENT   T 01494 563142
Contact: By e-mail. 2 Agents represent 40 Performers.
Commercials. Film. Stage. Television
5 North Dean Cottages
Speen Road
North Dean, Bucks HP14 4NN
T 07712 579502
E agent@keylockmanagement.com
W www.keylockmanagement.com

KHANDO ENTERTAINMENT   T 020 3463 8492
1 Marlborough Court
London W1F 7EE
E info@khandoentertainment.com
W www.khandoentertainment.com

THE INTERNATIONAL HOME OF SHORT, DWARF & TALL ACTORS

REPRESENTING ACTORS FROM 3FT - 5FT AND 6FT 7 - 7FT 7
FOR FILM, TELEVISION AND THEATRE
CONTACT : LISA@OHSOSMALL.COM

WWW.OHSOSMALL.COM

+44 (0) 2920 191622
+44 (0) 7787 788673

KING TALENT INC   **T** 001 604 713 6980
Contact: Lisa King (Personal Manager/Agent), Michael
King (Executive Assistant). Film. Stage. Television
PO Box 1087, Gibsons, B.C.
Vancouver, Canada V0N 1V0
E info@kingtalent.com
W www.kingtalent.com

KMC AGENCIES   **T** 01925 759196
Personal Manager. Actors. Commercials. Corporate.
Dancers. Musical Theatre. Cruise & International Work
Suite 2 Lymm Court, 11 Eagle Brow
Lymm WA13 0LP
F 01925 755821
E casting@kmcagencies.co.uk

KMC AGENCIES   **T** 0845 5193071
Personal Manager. Actors. Commercials. Corporate.
Dancers. Musical Theatre. Cruise & International Work
Garden Studios, 71-75 Shelton Street
Covent Garden, London WC2H 9JQ
E london@kmcagencies.co.uk

KNIGHT, Nic MANAGEMENT   **T** 020 8527 7420
Twitter: @nicknightmgmt
The Black & White Building
74 Rivington Street, London EC2A 3AY
E info@nicknightmanagement.com
W www.nicknightmanagement.com

KNIGHT, Ray CASTING LTD   **T** 020 8327 4244
Contact: Tony Gerrard (Manager)
Elstree Studios, Room 38
John Maxwell Building
Shenley Road, Borehamwood, Herts WD6 1JG
E casting@rayknight.co.uk
W www.rayknight.co.uk

KNIGHT AYTON
MANAGEMENT   **T** 020 7831 4400
Twitter: @KnightAyton
35 Great James Street, London WC1N 3HB
E info@knightayton.co.uk
W www.knightayton.co.uk

KORT, Richard MANAGEMENT   **T** 01636 636686
25 Old Chapel Road, Skellingthorpe
Lincoln LN6 5UB
F 01636 636719
E richardkort@playhouseproductionsltd.co.uk
W www.richardkort.co.uk

KREATE   **T** 020 7401 9007
32 Southwark Bridge Road, London SE1 9EU
E hello@kreate.co.uk
W www.kreate.co.uk

KREATIVE TALENT AGENCY   **T** 020 8133 0687
Professional Adults & Children
Kreative House, 11 Whernside
Ingleby, Cleveland TS17 0QF
T 07772 298789
E sue.francis@kreativetalent.tv
W www.kreativetalent.tv

KREMER ASSOCIATES
See MARSH, Billy DRAMA LTD

KSA - NORTH
See KEDDIE SCOTT ASSOCIATES LTD

KSA - SCOTLAND
See KEDDIE SCOTT ASSOCIATES LTD

L.A. MANAGEMENT   **T** 020 7041 9811
Suite 4, Nixmax House
20 Ullswater Crescent
Ullswater Business Park
Coulsdon
Surrey CR5 2HR
T 07507 276211
E info@lamanagement.biz
W www.lamanagement.biz

LADA MANAGEMENT   **T** 020 3384 5815
Personal Manager. Contact: Richard Boschetto. By
e-mail only. Accepts Showreels/Voicereels. 2 Agents
represent 30 Performers. Film. Musical Theatre. Stage.
Television
23 Austin Friars
London EC2N 2QP
F 020 3384 5816
E info@ladamanagement.com
W www.ladamanagement.com

LADA MANAGEMENT   **T** 01522 837243
Personal Manager. Contact: Richard Boschetto. CVs
& Headshots by e-mail only. Accepts Showreels/
Voicereels. 2 Agents represent 40 Performers. Film.
Musical Theatre. Stage. Television
Sparkhouse Studios
Rope Walk, Lincoln LN6 7DQ
F 01522 837201
E info@ladamanagement.com
W www.ladamanagement.com

LAINE, Betty MANAGEMENT   **T/F** 01372 721815
The Studios
East Street
Epsom, Surrey KT17 1HH
E enquiries@betty-laine-management.co.uk

LAINE MANAGEMENT LTD   **T** 0161 789 7775
Laine House
131 Victoria Road
Hope, Salford M6 8LF
F 0161 787 7572
E sam@lainemanagement.co.uk
W www.lainemanagement.co.uk

LANGFORD ASSOCIATES LTD   **T** 020 7244 7805
Personal Manager. Contact: Barry Langford, Simon
Hayes. By Post/e-mail. Commercials. Film. Stage.
Television
Vicarage House
58-60 Kensington Church Street
London W8 4DB
E barry@langfordassociates.com
W www.langfordassociates.com

LEADING LIGHTS EVENTS   T 07870 696971
Poppy Lodge, London Road
High Wycombe
Bucks HP10 9TJ
E leadinglightsevents@hotmail.co.uk
W www.leading-lights.co.uk

LE BARS, Tessa
MANAGEMENT   T/F 01689 837084
Existing Clients only
54 Birchwood Road, Petts Wood
Kent BR5 1NZ
T 07860 287255
E tessa.lebars@ntlworld.com
W www.galtonandsimpson.com

LEE, Nina MANAGEMENT LTD   T 020 3375 6269
Suite 36, 88-90 Hatton Garden
London EC1N 8PN
E nina@ninaleemanagement.com
W www.ninaleemanagement.com

LEE, Wendy MANAGEMENT   T 020 7703 5187
E wendy-lee@btconnect.com

LEHRER, Jane ASSOCIATES   T 020 7435 9118
Personal Manager. PMA Member. Contact: By Post/
e-mail. 2 Agents
PO Box 66334, London NW6 9QT
F 020 7435 9117
E jane@janelehrer.co.uk
W www.janelehrer.co.uk

LEIGH, Mike ASSOCIATES   T 020 7993 8337
c/o Grand Scheme Media, 27 Maiden Lane
London WC2E 7JS
E info@mikeleighassoc.com
W www.mikeleighassoc.com

LESLIE, Sasha
MANAGEMENT   T/F 020 8969 3249
In association with ALLSORTS DRAMA FOR CHILDREN
34 Crediton Road, London NW10 3DU
E sasha@allsortsdrama.com

LHK MANAGEMENT   T 01744 808907
20 Maltby Close, St Helens WA9 5GJ
E casting@lhkmanagement.co.uk
W www.lhkmanagement.co.uk

LIGHT AGENCY & PRODUCTIONS LTD T 020 8090 0006
Actors. Dancers
27 Mospey Crescent, Epsom, Surrey KT17 4NA
E agency@lightproductions.tv
W www.lightproductions.tv

LIME ACTORS AGENCY & MANAGEMENT LTD T 0161 236 0827
Contact: Georgina Andrew. By Post. Accepts Showreels
Nemesis House, 1 Oxford Court
Bishopsgate, Manchester M2 3WQ
F 0161 228 6727
E georgina@limemanagement.co.uk
W www.limemanagement.tv

LINKSIDE AGENCY T 01233 636188
*Contact: By Post/e-mail. 2 Agents represent 40
Performers. Dancers. Musical Theatre. Singers. Stage.
Television*
57 High Street, Ashford, Kent TN24 8SG
E info@linksideagency.com

LINTON MANAGEMENT T 0161 761 2020
3 The Rock, Bury BL9 0JP
E carol@linton.tv

LINTON MANAGEMENT T 020 7785 7275
27-31 Clerkenwell Close, London EC1R 0AT
E london@linton.tv

LITTLE ALLSTARS CASTING & MODELLING AGENCY T 0161 702 8257
23 Falconwood Chase, Worsley
Manchester M28 1FG
T 07584 992429
E casting@littleallstars.co.uk
W www.littleallstars.co.uk

LIVING THE DREAM TALENT AGENCY T 01727 751613
145-147 St John Street
London EC1V 4PW
T 07845 207501
E agency@livingthedreamcompany.co.uk
W www.livingthedreamcompany.co.uk

LMB MANAGEMENT T 020 7252 4343
In association with The LMB Partnership
Daisy Business Park
19-35 Sylvan Grove
London SE15 1PD
E lisa@lmbmanagement.co.uk
W www.lmbmanagement.co.uk

LONDON THEATRICAL T 020 8748 1478
Contact: Paul Pearson
18 Leamore Street, London W6 0JZ
E agent@londontheatrical.com
W www.londontheatrical.com

LONG, Eva AGENTS T 07736 700849
*Contact: By Post/e-mail. 2 Agents represent 30
Performers. Commercials. Corporate. Film. Musical
Theatre. Radio. Singers. Stage. Television. Voice Overs*
Norwood House, 9 Redwell Road
Wellingborough NN8 5AZ
F 01604 811921
E evalongagents@yahoo.co.uk
W www.evalongagents.co.uk

LONGRUN ARTISTES T 01322 400387
*Contact: Gina Long. By Post. Accepts Showreels/
Voicereels. 3 Agents represent 100 Performers.
Commercials. Corporate. Dancers. Film. Musical
Theatre. Singers. Stage. Television*
32 Ashburnham Road
Belvedere, Kent DA17 6DA
T 07748 723228
E longrunartistes@virginmedia.com
W www.longrunartistes.com

LOOKALIKES T 020 7281 8029
Contact: Susan Scott
106 Tollington Park, London N4 3RB
E susan@lookalikes.info
W www.lookalikes.info

LOOKS AGENCY T 020 8341 4477
*Contact: By Post/e-mail/Telephone. 400 Performers.
Commercials. Corporate. Modelling. Presenters. Walk-on
& Supporting Artists*
PO Box 42783, London N2 0UF
F 020 8442 9190
E lookslondonltd@btconnect.com
W www.lookslondon.com

LOTHERINGTON, Michelle MANAGEMENT LTD T 07785 293806
*Contact: Michelle Lotherington. By e-mail.
Choreographers. Composers. Designers. Directors.
Lighting & Sound Designers. Music Technology. Musical
Directors. Orchestrators*
436 Lordship Lane
London SE22 8NE
E michelle@michellelotherington.com
W www.michellelotherington.com

LOVETT LOGAN ASSOCIATES T 0131 478 7878
Formerly PLA. PMA Member
2 York Place
Edinburgh EH1 3EP
F 0131 478 7070
E edinburgh@lovettlogan.com
W www.lovettlogan.com

Helen McCrory   Dev Patel   Celia Imrie

JP MASCLET photography

headshots@jpmasclet.com   07768 166 727   www.jpmasclet.com

LOVETT LOGAN ASSOCIATES   T 020 7495 6400
Formerly PLA. PMA Member .
40 Margaret Street, London W1G 0JH
F 020 7495 6411
E london@lovettlogan.com
W www.lovettlogan.com

LSW PROMOTIONS   T/F 020 7793 9755
PO Box 31855, London SE17 3XP
E londonswo@hotmail.com

LUXFACTOR GROUP (UK) THE   T 0845 3700589
*Personal Manager. Contact: Michael D. Finch. By
e-mail. 1 Agent represents 20+ Performers. Creatives.
Presenters. Television. Walk-on & Supporting Artists*
Fleet Place, 12 Nelson Drive
Petersfield, Hampshire GU31 4SJ
T 05603 680843
E info@luxfactor.co.uk
W www.luxfactor.co.uk

LYNE, Dennis AGENCY   T 020 7272 5020
PMA Member
503 Holloway Road, London N19 4DD
E info@dennislyne.com
W www.dennislyne.com

M&C SAATCHI MERLIN   T 020 7259 1460
15 Golden Square, London W1F 9EE
E enquiries@mcsaatchimerlin.com
W www.mcsaatchimerlin.com

M&P ARTIST MANAGEMENT   T 020 7734 1051
PMA Member
29 Poland Street, London W1F 8QR
F 020 7287 4481
E info@mandpartistmanagement.com
W www.mandpartistmanagement.com

MA9 MODEL MANAGEMENT   T 020 7096 1191
New Bond House
124 New Bond Street
London W1S 1DX
E info@ma9models.com
W www.ma9models.com

**MACFARLANE CHARD
ASSOCIATES LTD**   T 020 7636 7750
PMA Member
33 Percy Street, London W1T 2DF
F 020 7636 7751
E enquiries@macfarlane-chard.co.uk
W www.macfarlane-chard.co.uk

**MACFARLANE CHARD
ASSOCIATES IRELAND**   T 00 353 1 6638646
7 Adelaide Street, Dun Laoghaire
Co Dublin, Ireland
F 00 353 1 6313649
E derick@macfarlane-chard.ie

**MACFARLANE DOYLE
ASSOCIATES**   T 020 3600 3470
90 Long Acre, Covent Garden, London WC2E 9RZ
E office.mfd@btinternet.com
W www.macfarlanedoyle.com

**MACNAUGHTON LORD
REPRESENTATION**   T 020 7499 1411
*PMA Member. Choreographers. Composers. Designers.
Directors. Lighting Designers. Lyricists. Musical
Directors. Sound Designers. Video Designers. Writers*
44 South Molton Street
London W1K 5RT
E info@mlrep.com
W www.mlrep.com

MAIDA VALE SINGERS **T** 020 7266 1358
Contact: Christopher Dee. Singers for Recordings, Stage,
Film, Radio & Television
7B Lanhill Road, Maida Vale
London W9 2BP
T 07889 153145
E maidavalesingers@cdtenor.freeserve.co.uk
W www.maidavalesingers.co.uk

MAITLAND MANAGEMENT **T** 07508 919946
Personal Manager. Contact: Annie Skates (Director), Lisa
Hull (Partner), James Sharkey (Chairman), David Combes
(Operations Manager)
PO Box 364, Esher KT10 9XS
F 01372 466229
E info@maitlandmanagement.com
W www.maitlandmanagement.com

MAMBAB AGENCY **T** 020 3645 8617
Contact: Nichola D. Hartwell
73 Cornwall Square, Kennington, London SE11 4JP
T 07868 120709
E contacts@mrandmissblackandbeautiful.com
W www.mrandmissblackandbeautiful.com

MANAGEMENT 2000 **T/F** 01352 771231
Contact: Jackey Gerling. By Post. Accepts Showreels.
1 Agent represents 30 Performers. Commercials. Film.
Radio. Stage. Television
11 Well Street, Treuddyn
Flintshire CH7 4NH
E jackey@management-2000.co.uk
W www.management-2000.co.uk

MANS, Johnny PRODUCTIONS **T** 01992 470907
Incorporating Encore Magazine
PO Box 196, Hoddesdon, Herts EN10 7WG
T 07974 755997
E johnnymansagent@aol.com
W www.johnnymansproductions.co.uk

MANTLE MANAGEMENT **T** 01273 454111
17 Osborne Villas, Hove
East Sussex BN3 2RD
E info@mantlemanagement.co.uk
W www.mantlemanagement.co.uk

MARCUS & McCRIMMON
MANAGEMENT **T** 020 7323 0546
Personal Manager. Contact: By Post/e-mail. Accepts
Showreels. 2 Agents represent 100 Performers.
Commercials. Film. Musical Theatre. Stage. Television
Winston House, 3 Bedford Square, London WC1B 3RA
E info@marcusandmccrimmon.com
W www.marcusandmccrimmon.com

MARKHAM AGENCY THE **T** 020 7836 4111
Personal Manager. PMA Member. Contact: John
Markham. By Post/e-mail. Accepts Showreels/Voicereels
405 Strand, London WC2R 0NE
F 020 7836 4222
E info@themarkhamagency.com
W www.themarkhamagency.com

MARKHAM, FROGGATT & IRWIN **T** 020 7636 4412
Personal Manager. PMA Member. Contact: By e-mail
4 Windmill Street, London W1T 2HZ
E admin@markhamfroggattirwin.com
W www.markhamfroggattandirwin.com

MARLOWES AGENCY **T** 07964 589148
HMS President, Victoria Embankment
Blackfriars, London EC4Y 0HJ
T 020 7193 7227
E miles@marlowes.eu
W www.marlowes.eu

MARLOWES AGENCY:
TV, THEATRE & DANCE **T** 020 7193 4484
HMS President, Victoria Embankment
Blackfriars, London EC4Y 0HJ
E mitch@marlowes.eu
W www.marlowesagency.com

MARMALADE MANAGEMENT **T** 01628 483808
Jam Theatre Studios, Archway Court
45A West Street, Marlow, Buckinghamshire SL7 2LS
E info@marmalademanagement.co.uk
W www.marmalademanagement.co.uk

MARSH, Billy
ASSOCIATES LTD **T** 020 7383 9979
PMA Member
4th Floor, 158-160 North Gower Street
London NW1 2ND
F 020 7388 2296
E talent@billymarsh.co.uk
W www.billymarsh.co.uk

MARSH, Billy DRAMA LTD **T** 020 3428 5171
Actors. Actresses
Amadeus House
27B Floral Street, London WC2E 9DP
F 020 3428 5173
E info@billymarshdrama.co.uk

MARSHALL, Ronnie
AGENCY THE **T/F** 020 8368 4958
66 Ollerton Road, London N11 2LA
E theronniemarshallagency@gmail.com
W www.theronniemarshallagency.com

MARSHALL, Scott
PARTNERS LTD **T** 020 7637 4623
PMA Member. Contact: Amanda Evans, Suzy Kenway,
Manon Palmer
2nd Floor, 15 Little Portland Street, London W1W 8BW
F 020 7636 9728
E smpm@scottmarshall.co.uk
W www.scottmarshall.co.uk

MARTIN, Carol
PERSONAL MANAGEMENT **T** 020 8348 0847
19 Highgate West Hill, London N6 6NP
E carolmartin@talktalk.net

MAY, John **T** 020 8962 1606
46 Golborne Road, London W10 5PR
E may505@btinternet.com

MAYER, Cassie LTD **T** 020 7350 0880
PMA Member
5 Old Garden House, The Lanterns
Bridge Lane, London SW11 3AD
E info@cassiemayerltd.co.uk

MBA / MAHONEY BANNON
ASSOCIATES **T** 01273 685970
Part of the John Mahoney Management Group
Concorde House, 18 Margaret Street
Brighton BN2 1TS
E info@mahoney.agency
W www.mahoney.agency

McDONAGH, Melanie MANAGEMENT
(ACADEMY OF PERFORMING ARTS
& CASTING AGENCY) **T** 07909 831409
14 Apple Tree Way
Oswaldtwistle
Accrington, Lancashire BB5 0FB
T 01254 392560
E mcdonaghmgt@aol.com
W www.mcdonaghmanagement.co.uk

McKINNEY MACARTNEY MANAGEMENT LTD   T 020 8995 4747
Technicians
Gable Hse, 18-24 Turnham Green Terrace, London W4 1QP
E mail@mckinneymacartney.com
W www.mckinneymacartney.com

McLEAN, Bill PERSONAL MANAGEMENT LTD   T 020 8789 8191
Personal Manager. Contact: By Post
23B Deodar Road, London SW15 2NP

McLEAN-WILLIAMS LTD   T 020 3567 1090
PMA Member
Chester House (Unit 3:06), Kennington Park
1-3 Brixton Road, London SW9 6DE
E info@mclean-williams.com
W www.mclean-williams.com

McLEAN-WILLIAMS MANCHESTER   T 0161 935 8494
82 King Street, Manchester M2 4WQ
E manchester@mclean-williams.com
W www.mclean-williams.com

McLEOD AGENCY LTD THE   T 01482 565444
1st Floor, 6 The Square
Hessle, East Yorkshire HU13 0AA
E info@mcleodagency.co.uk
W www.mcleodagency.co.uk

McMAHON MANAGEMENT   T 020 8752 0172
28 Cecil Road, London W3 0DB
E info@mcmahonmanagement.co.uk
W www.mcmahonmanagement.co.uk

MEDIA CELEBRITY SERVICES LTD   T 07946 531011
48 Dean Street
London W1B 5BF
T 07809 831340
E info@mcsagency.co.uk
W www.mediacelebrityservices.co.uk

MEDIA LEGAL   T 01732 460592
Existing Clients only
Town House
5 Mill Pond Close
Sevenoaks, Kent TN14 5AW

MF PERSONAL MANAGEMENT   T 01798 344356 (Maggie)
26 Orchard Close, Petworth
West Sussex GU28 0SA
T 07758 052325
E fmmanagement14@gmail.com

MGA MANAGEMENT & CASTING   T 0131 466 9392
207 Balgreen Road
Edinburgh EH11 2RZ
E admin@mgamanagement.com
W www.mgamanagement.com

MIDDLEWEEK NEWTON TALENT MANAGEMENT   T 020 3394 0079
PMA Member
95A Rivington Street
London EC2A 3AY
E agents@mntalent.co.uk
W www.mntalent.co.uk

MILBURN BROWNING ASSOCIATES
T 020 3582 9370
PMA Member
The Old Truman Brewery, 91 Brick Lane
London E1 6QL
F 020 3582 9377
E info@milburnbrowning.com

MIME THE GAP
T 07970 685982
Mime Artistes. Physical Comedy Specialists
17 Cromer Road, Southend on Sea
Essex SS1 2DU
E mimethegap@mac.com
W www.mimethegap.com

MINIMEN THE
T 07875 225168
Contact: Steve Redford. By e-mail. Accepts Showreels/Voicereels. Dwarf & Short Stature Actors & Event Entertainment. 2 Agents represent 32 Performers. Commercials. Corporate. Disabled. Film. Television. Walk-on & Supporting Artists. CGI. Prosthetic. Stunts. Child Stunts. Entertainers
135 Victoria Road, London N9 9BB
E info@theminimen.co.uk
W www.theminimen.co.uk

MISKIN THEATRE AGENCY THE
T 01322 629422
The Miskin Theatre, Oakfield Lane
Dartford, Kent DA1 2JT
T 07709 429354
E miskintheatreagency@yahoo.co.uk

MITCHELL MAAS McLENNAN
T 020 8301 8745
MPA Offices, 29 Thomas Street
Woolwich, London SE18 6HU
T 07540 995802
E agency@mmm2000.co.uk
W www.mmm2000.co.uk

MLR
See MACNAUGHTON LORD REPRESENTATION

MOMENTUM ARTIST MANAGEMENT LLP
T 020 7060 1515
Number 1, 63 Mount Ephraim
Tunbridge Wells, Kent TN4 8BG
E email@momentumtalent.co
W www.momentumtalent.co

MOMENTUM ARTISTS
T 020 3322 6609
Specialising in Musical Theatre & Dance
86-90 Paul Street
London EC2A 4NE
E info@momentumartists.co.uk
W www.momentumartists.co.uk

MONDI ASSOCIATES LTD
T 07817 133349
Personal Manager. PMA Member. Contact: Michelle Sykes. By Post/e-mail. Accepts Showreels/Voicereels. 1 Agent represents 60 Performers. Children. Commercials. Corporate. Dancers. Film. Musical Theatre. Presenters. Radio. Singers. Stage. Television. Voice Overs
Unit 3 O, Cooper House, 2 Michael Road
London SW6 2AD
E info@mondiassociates.com
W www.mondiassociates.com

MONTAGU ASSOCIATES LTD
T 020 7263 3883
Ground Floor, 13 Hanley Road
London N4 3DU
E info@montagus.org

MOORE, Jakki MANAGEMENT
T 01229 776389
Halecote, St Lukes Road
Haverigg, Cumbria LA18 4HB
T 07967 612784
E jakki@jakkimoore.com

MORELLO CHERRY ACTORS AGENCY
T 020 7993 5538
E info@mcaa.co.uk
W www.mcaa.co.uk

MORGAN, Lee MANAGEMENT
T 020 7430 1006
4 Bloomsbury Square, London WC1A 2RP
F 020 7841 1001
E lee@leemorgan.biz
W www.leemorgan.biz

MOUTHPIECE MANAGEMENT
T 01527 850149
18 New Road, Studley
Warwickshire B80 7LY
T 07900 240904
E karin@mouthpiecemanagement.co.uk
W www.mouthpiecemanagement.co.uk

MPC ENTERTAINMENT
T 020 7624 1184
Personal Manager. Contact: Michael P. Cohen (CEO). By e-mail. Accepts Showreels. 4 Agents represent 60 Performers. Corporate. Presenters. Radio. Television
MPC House, 16 Maple Mews
Maida Vale, London NW6 5UZ
F 020 7624 4220
E mpc@mpce.com
W www.mpce.com

M R MANAGEMENT
T 020 7886 0760
PMA Member
19 Bolsover Street, London W1W 5NA
E info@mrmanagement.net
W www.mrmanagement.net

JON HOLLOWAY
H E A D S H O T S
07803 051 083
www.jonhollowayheadshots.co.uk

MRS JORDAN ASSOCIATES   T 020 3151 0710
PMA Member. Contact: By e-mail only. 3 Agents
represent 60 Performers. Commercials. Creatives. Film.
Stage. Television. New Applications:
apps@mrsjordan.co.uk
Communications House, 26 York Street
London W1U 6PZ
T 0161 401 0710
E info@mrsjordan.co.uk
W www.mrsjordan.co.uk

MURPHY, Elaine ASSOCIATES   T 020 8989 4122
Suite 1, 50 High Street
London E11 2RJ
F 020 8989 1400
E elaine@elainemurphy.co.uk

MUSIC INTERNATIONAL   T 020 7359 5183
13 Ardilaun Road, London N5 2QR
F 020 7226 9792
E neil@musicint.co.uk
W www.musicint.co.uk

MV MANAGEMENT   T 020 8889 8231
Co-operative Agency for Graduates of Mountview
Academy of Theatre Arts
Ralph Richardson Memorial Studios
Kingfisher Place
Clarendon Road, London N22 6XF
F 020 8829 1050
E theagency@mountview.org.uk
W www.mvmanagement.org.uk

MVW TALENT AGENCY
IRELAND   T 00 353 87 2480348
Film. Modelling. Musicals. Stage. Television. Voice Overs
23 Burrow Manor, Calverstown, Kilcullen, Kildare, Ireland
F 00 353 45 485464
E mvwtalent@hotmail.com
W www.talentedkidsireland.com

NARROW ROAD
COMPANY THE   T 020 7831 4450
PMA Member
1st Floor, 37 Great Queen Street
London WC2B 5AA
E agents@narrowroad.co.uk

NARROW ROAD
COMPANY THE   T/F 0161 833 1605
PMA Member
2nd Floor, Grampian House, 144 Deansgate
Manchester M3 3EE
E manchester@narrowroad.co.uk

NEALON, Steve ASSOCIATES   T 020 7125 0468
PMA Member
3rd Floor, International House
1-6 Yarmouth Place
Mayfair, London W1J 7BU
T 07949 601935
E admin@stevenealonassociates.co.uk
W www.stevenealonassociates.co.uk

NELSON BROWNE
MANAGEMENT LTD   T 020 7970 6010
PMA Member
40 Bowling Green Lane, London EC1R 0NE
T 07796 891388
E enquiries@nelsonbrowne.com
W www.nelsonbrowne.com

NEVS AGENCY   T 020 7352 4886
Regal House, 198 King's Road
London SW3 5XP
F 020 7352 6068
E getamodel@nevs.co.uk
W www.nevs.co.uk

NEW CASEY AGENCY   T 01923 823182
129 Northwood Way
Northwood HA6 1RF
E newcaseyagency@gmail.com

NEW FACES LTD   T 020 7439 6900
Personal Manager. Contact: Val Horton. By Post/e-mail.
Accepts Showreels. 2 Agents represent 50 Performers.
Stage. Television. Commercials. Film
3rd Floor, The Linen Hall
162-168 Regent Street
London W1B 5TD
F 020 7287 5481
E info@newfacestalent.co.uk
W www.newfacestalent.co.uk

NFD AGENCY   T 01977 681949
The Studio, 21 Low Street
South Milford LS25 5AR
E info@northernfilmanddrama.com
W www.northernfilmanddrama.com

NG PERSONAL MANAGEMENT   T 07810 138535
14 Leafields, Houghton Regis
Dunstable, Bedfordshire LU5 5LX
E info@ngpersonalmanagement.co.uk
W www.ngpersonalmanagement.co.uk

NIC KNIGHT MANAGEMENT
See KNIGHT, Nic MANAGEMENT

NICHOLSON, Jackie ASSOCIATES   T 020 7580 4422
Personal Manager. Contact: Marvin Giles (Agent).
By Post
Suite 44, 2nd Floor, Morley House
320 Regent Street, London W1B 3BD
F 020 7580 4489
E jnalondon@aol.com

N M MANAGEMENT   T 020 8853 4337
16 St Alfege Passage
Greenwich, London SE10 9JS
E nmmanagement@hotmail.com

NMP MANAGEMENT   T 01372 361004
8 Blenheim Court, Brookway
Leatherhead, Surrey KT22 7NA
F 01372 374417
E management@nmp.co.uk
W www.nmpmanagement.co.uk

NOLAN & KAY MANAGEMENT   T 01444 401595
Studio 35 Truggers
Handcross, Haywards Heath
West Sussex RH17 6DQ
T 07966 382766
E info@nolanandkay.co.uk
W www.nolanandkay.co.uk

NORTH OF WATFORD LLP   T 01422 845361
CPMA Member. Twitter: @northofwatford
The Creative Quarter, The Town Hall
St Georges Street, Hebden Bridge
West Yorks HX7 7BY
T 020 3601 3372
E info@northofwatford.com
W www.northofwatford.com

NORTH WEST ACTORS - NIGEL ADAMS   T 0161 761 6437
Personal Manager. Contact: Nigel Adams. By Post.
Accepts Showreels/Voicereels. Commercials. Film.
Radio. Stage. Television
64 Nuttall Street, Bury
Manchester BL9 7EW
E nigel.adams@northwestactors.co.uk
W www.northwestactors.co.uk

NORTHERN LIGHTS MANAGEMENT LTD   T 01422 382203
Dean Clough Mills, West Yorks HX3 5AX
F 01422 330101
E northern.lights@virgin.net

NORTHONE MANAGEMENT   T 020 7359 9666
CPMA Member
The Biscuit Factory, Unit B202.6
Tower Bridge Business Complex
100 Clements Road, London SE16 4DG
E actors@northone.co.uk
W www.northone.co.uk

NS ARTISTES MANAGEMENT   T 07870 969577
113A Enfield Road, Hunt End, Redditch B97 5NE
E nsmanagement@fsmail.net
W www.nsartistes.co.uk

NYLAND MANAGEMENT   T 01663 745629
E susie@nylandmanagement.com
W www.nylandmanagement.com

OBJECTIVE TALENT MANAGEMENT   T/F 020 7202 2300
3rd Floor, Riverside Building, County Hall
Westminster Bridge Road, London SE1 7PB
E corrie@objectivetalentmanagement.com
W www.objectivetalentmanagement.com

OFF THE KERB PRODUCTIONS   T 020 7490 1500
44 Clerkenwell Close, London EC1R 0AZ
F 020 7437 0647
E info@offthekerb.co.uk
W www.offthekerb.co.uk

OH SO SMALL PRODUCTIONS LTD   T 029 2019 1622
Short, Dwarf & Tall Actors Agency. Contact: Lisa
Osmond. By e-mail/Telephone. Extensive Prosthetics.
Creature Work. Full Costume. Motion Capture. CGI.
Stunts. Child Stand-in. Commercials. Corporate. Film.
Stage. Television
6 High Street, Penarth, Cardiff CF64 1EY
T 07787 788673
E lisa@ohsosmall.com
W www.ohsosmall.com

ONE ANOTHER MANAGEMENT LTD   T 020 3627 5255
CPMA Member
84C Gordon Road, London SE15 3RG
T 07410 439517
E info@oneanothermanagement.co.uk

OPERA & CONCERT ARTISTS   T 020 7328 3097
Worldwide Management of Opera Singers
75 Aberdare Gardens, London NW6 3AN
F 020 7372 3537
E enquiries@opera-and-concert-artists.co.uk

ORDINARY PEOPLE   T 020 7267 7007
Actors. Modelling
16 Camden Road, London NW1 9DP
T 07525 932227
E info@ordinarypeople.co.uk
W www.ordinarypeople.co.uk

OREN ACTORS MANAGEMENT   T 0845 4591420
CPMA Member
Chapter Arts Centre, Market Road, Cardiff CF5 1QE
T 029 2023 3321
E info@orenactorsmanagement.co.uk
W www.orenactorsmanagement.co.uk

OTTO PERSONAL MANAGEMENT LTD   T 0114 237 2432
Personal Manager. CPMA Member
Hagglers Corner, 586 Queens Road, Sheffield S2 4DU
T 07587 133212
E admin@ottopm.co.uk
W www.ottopm.co.uk

PADBURY, David ASSOCIATES   T 020 8883 1277
44 Summerlee Avenue, Finchley
London N2 9QP
E info@davidpadburyassociates.com

PALING & JENKINS   T 020 7434 7377
56 Broadwick Street, London W1F 7AJ
T 07500 861535
E enquiries@palingandjenkins.co.uk
W www.palingandjenkins.co.uk

PAN ARTISTS AGENCY LTD   T 07890 715115
Cornerways, 34 Woodhouse Lane
Sale, Cheshire M33 4JX
T 07552 162305
E panartists@btconnect.com
W www.panartists.co.uk

PARADIGM ARTIST MANAGEMENT   T 01554 776836
49 St Josephs Court, Llanelli
Carmarthenshire SA15 1NR
E paradigmartistmgmt@live.co.uk

SJFPHOTO   07581 694934 | photo@sarahjanefield.co.uk | sarahjanefield.co.uk

PARAMOUNT INTERNATIONAL MANAGEMENT   **T** 020 8429 3179
30 Performers. International Comedians
Talbot House, 204-226 Imperial Drive
Harrow, Middlesex HA2 7HH
F 020 8868 6475
E mail@ukcomedy.com
W www.ukcomedy.com

PARKER, Cherry MANAGEMENT (RSM)
See RSM (CHERRY PARKER MANAGEMENT)

PARSONS, Cary MANAGEMENT   **T** 01926 735375
PMA Member. Set, Costume & Lighting Designers & Directors
118 Plymouth Place
Leamington Spa, Warwickshire CV31 1HW
E carylparsons@gmail.com
W www.caryparsons.co.uk

PAYNE MANAGEMENT   **T** 020 7193 1156 (London)
Contact: Natalie Payne
T 0161 408 6715 (Manchester)
E agent@paynemanagement.co.uk
W www.paynemanagement.co.uk

P B J MANAGEMENT LTD   **T** 020 7287 1112
*Personal Manager. PMA Member. Accepts Showreels.
11 Agents represent 115 Performers. Comedians.
Commercials. Corporate. Presenters. Radio. Stage.
Television. Voice Overs. Walk-on & Supporting Artists.
Writers*
22 Rathbone Street, London W1T 1LG
E general@pbjmanagement.co.uk
W www.pbjmanagement.co.uk

PC THEATRICAL, MODEL & CASTING AGENCY   **T** 020 8381 2229
Large Database of Twins
10 Strathmore Gardens
Edgware
Middlesex HA8 5HJ
F 020 8933 3418
E twinagy@aol.com
W www.twinagency.com

PELHAM ASSOCIATES   **T** 01273 323010
Personal Manager. PMA Member. Contact: Peter Cleall
Albert House
82 Queen's Road
Brighton BN1 3XE
E agent@pelhamassociates.co.uk
W www.pelhamassociates.co.uk

PEMBERTON ASSOCIATES LTD   **T** 020 7224 9036
*Contact: Barbara Pemberton. By e-mail. Showreels
on request. 5 Agents represent 130 Performers. Film.
Musical Theatre. Radio. Stage. Television. Voice Overs*
51 Upper Berkeley Street
London W1H 7QW
E general@pembertonassociates.com
W www.pembertonassociates.com

PEOPLEMATTER.TV   **T** 020 7415 7070
40 Bowling Green Lane
Clerkenwell, London EC1R 0NE
F 020 7415 7074
E tony@peoplematter.tv
W www.peoplematter.tv

PEPPERPOT PROMOTIONS T 020 7405 9108
Bands
Suite 20B
20-22 Orde Hall Street
London WC1N 3JW
E chris@pepperpot.co.uk

**PERFORMANCE ACTORS
AGENCY** T 020 7251 5716
Co-operative. CPMA Member
137 Goswell Road, London EC1V 7ET
F 020 7251 3974
E info@performanceactors.co.uk
W www.performanceactors.co.uk

**PERFORMANCE FACTORY
MANAGEMENT THE** T 01792 701570
Kemys Way
Swansea Enterprise Park
Swansea SA1 6JB
W www.theperformancefactorywales.com

**PERFORMING ARTS ARTISTS'
MANAGERS LLP** T 020 7255 1362
*Personal Manager. PMA Member. Contact: By Post/
e-mail. 2 Agents represent 30 Performers. Creative Team
Members only*
6 Windmill Street, London W1T 2JB
E info@performing-arts.co.uk
W www.performing-arts.co.uk

PERRYMENT, Mandy T 020 8941 7907
T 07790 605191
E mail@mandyperryment.com
W www.actorsmanagement.co.uk/
mandyperrymentartists.html

PERSONAL APPEARANCES T/F 020 8343 7748
20 North Mount, 1147-1161 High Road
Whetstone N20 0PH
E patsy@personalappearances.biz
W www.personalappearances.biz

PHILLIPS, Frances T 020 8953 0303
*Personal Manager. PMA Member. Contact: Frances
Zealander. By e-mail. 2 Agents represent 50 Performers*
89 Robeson Way, Borehamwood
Hertfordshire WD6 5RY
T 07957 334328
E frances@francesphillips.co.uk
W www.francesphillips.co.uk

**PHPM (PHILIPPA HOWELL PERSONAL
MANAGEMENT)** T 020 7836 2837
All Correspondence to Sheffield Office
405 The Strand, London WC2R 0NE
T 07790 969024
E philippa@phpm.co.uk
W www.phpm.co.uk

**PHPM (PHILIPPA HOWELL PERSONAL
MANAGEMENT)** T 020 7836 2837
184 Bradway Road
Sheffield S17 4QX
E philippa@phpm.co.uk
W www.phpm.co.uk

PICCADILLY MANAGEMENT T 0161 953 4057
Personal Manager
23 New Mount Street
Manchester M4 4DE
F 0161 953 4001
E info@piccadillymanagement.com
W www.piccadillymanagement.com

PLA
See LOVETT LOGAN ASSOCIATES

**PLATER, Janet
MANAGEMENT LTD** T 0191 221 2490
*Contact: Janet Plater. By e-mail. Commercials. Film.
Radio. Stage. Television*
D Floor, Milburn House
Dean Street, Newcastle upon Tyne NE1 1LF
E info@jpmactors.com
W www.jpmactors.com

PLATINUM ARTISTS T 020 3006 2242
78 York Street, Marylebone, London W1H 1DP
E mail@platinumartists.co.uk
W www.platinumartists.co.uk

PMA MANAGEMENT & AGENCY T 01375 665716
Southend Road, Corringham, Essex SS17 8JT
F 01375 672353
E office@performersmanagement.co.uk
W www.performersmanagement.co.uk

POLLY'S AGENCY T 020 8994 7714
The Bridge, 367 Chiswick High Road, London W4 4AG
E polly@pollysagency.co.uk
W www.pollysagency.co.uk·

**POLLYANNA
MANAGEMENT LTD** T 020 7481 1911
Rayne House, Rayne Street, London E1W 3R0
T 07801 884837
E poliyannamanagement@gmail.com
W www.pollyannatheatre.org

POOLE, Gordon AGENCY LTD T 01275 463222
The Limes, Brockley, Bristol BS48 3BB
F 01275 462252
E agents@gordonpoole.com
W www.gordonpoole.com

POWER PROMOTIONS T/F 0151 230 0070
PO Box 61, Liverpool L13 0EF
E tom2@powerpromotions.co.uk
W www.powerpromotions.com

PREGNANT PAUSE AGENCY T 07970 698868
Pregnant Models, Dancers, Actresses
50 Ditton Hill, Long Ditton KT6 5JD
E sandy@pregnantpause.co.uk
W www.pregnantpause.co.uk

PREMIER ACTING T 0141 255 0255
Contact: Allan Jones
9/2 321 Glasgow Harbour Terrace, Glasgow G11 6BL
T 07885 658316
E info@premieracting.com
W www.premieracting.com

PRENELLE CASTING T 07454 206024
17 Ambleside Terrace, Fulwell, Sunderland SR6 8NP
E barbara@prenellecasting.co.uk
W www.prenellecasting.co.uk

**PRESTON, Morwenna
MANAGEMENT** T/F 020 8835 8147
49 Leithcote Gardens, London SW16 2UX
E info@morwennapreston.com
W www.morwennapreston.com

PRICE GARDNER MANAGEMENT T 020 7610 2111
PMA Member
BM 3162, London WC1N 3XX
F 020 7381 3288
E info@pricegardner.co.uk
W www.pricegardner.co.uk

PRINCIPAL ARTISTES T 020 7637 2120
Personal Manager. Contact: By e-mail
Suite 1, 57 Buckingham Gate
Westminster, London SW1E 6AJ
E enquiries@principalartistes.com

Caroline
Webster
Photography

07867 653019
carolinewebster.co.uk

Dan Whitlam | Lorianne Tika-Lemba | Paul Merton

PROSPECTS ASSOCIATIONS   T 07988 546179
Sessions. Singers
28 Magpie Close, Forest Gate, London E7 9DE
E wasegun@yahoo.co.uk

PV MEDIA LTD   T 01905 616100
County House, St Mary Street, Worcester WR1 1HB
E md@pvmedia.co.uk

QTALENT   T 020 7430 5400
PMA Member
3rd Floor, 161 Drury Lane
Covent Garden, London WC2B 5PN
E reception@qtalent.co.uk
W www.qtalent.co.uk

**RAFFLES, Tim
ENTERTAINMENTS**   T/F 023 8046 5843
*Personal Manager. 2 Agents represent 9 Performers.
Corporate. Cruise Work. Singers. Television*
Victoria House, 29 Swaythling Road
West End, Southampton SO30 3AG
E info@timrafflesentertainments.co.uk
W www.timrafflesentertainments.co.uk

RAGE MODELS   T 020 8749 4760
Ugli Campus, 56 Wood Lane, London W12 7SB
F 020 7402 0507
E ragemodels@ugly.org
W www.ugly.org

**RARE TALENT ACTORS
MANAGEMENT**   T 0161 273 4004
Tanzaro House, Ardwick Green North
Manchester M12 6FZ
F 0161 273 4567
E info@raretalentactors.com
W www.raretalentactors.com

RAY KNIGHT CASTING LTD
See KNIGHT, Ray CASTING LTD

RAZZAMATAZZ MANAGEMENT   T 01342 301617
*Personal Manager. Contact: Jill Shirley. By e-mail/
Telephone. 1 Agent*
204 Holtye Road, East Grinstead
West Sussex RH19 3ES
T 07836 268292
E razzamatazzmanagement@btconnect.com

RbA MANAGEMENT LTD   T 0151 708 7273
*Personal Manager. CPMA Member. Contact: By Post/
e-mail. Accepts Showreels/Voicereels. 20+ Performers*
37-45 Windsor Street, Liverpool L8 1XE
E info@rbamanagement.co.uk
W www.rbamanagement.co.uk

RBM ACTORS   T 020 7976 6021
3rd Floor, 1 Lower Grosvenor Place
London SW1W 0EJ
E info@rbmactors.com
W www.rbmactors.com

RDDC MANAGEMENT AGENCY   T 01706 211161
52 Bridleway, Waterfoot
Rossendale, Lancashire BB4 9DS
T 07811 239780
E info@rddc.co.uk
W www.rddc.co.uk

**RDM CREATIVE TALENT
MANAGEMENT**   T 020 3664 9811
9 Wight Way, Selsey
Chichester, West Sussex PO20 0UD
E mail@rdmfilms.co.uk
W www.rdmfilms.co.uk

**RE-PM (RAIF EYLES PERSONAL
MANAGEMENT)**   T 020 8953 1481
Film. Stage. Television
8 Dacre Gardens, Borehamwood WD6 2JP
T 07794 971733
E info@re-pm.co.uk
W www.re-pm.co.uk

**REACH TO THE SKY
PERSONAL MANAGEMENT**   T 0843 2892503
Actors. Artistes. Entertainers. Musicians
Maxet House, Liverpool Road
Luton, Beds LU1 1RS
E info@reachtothesky.com
W www.reachtothesky.com

steve
ULLATHORNE
PHOTOGRAPHY LONDON

simon callow | miranda hart

colour portfolio online
07961 380 969 **www.SteveUllathorne.com**

REACTORS AGENCY   T 00 353 1 8786833
Contact: By Post/e-mail. Accepts Showreels.
Co-operative of 24 Performers
1 Eden Quay, Dublin 1, Ireland
E info@reactors.ie
W www.reactors.ie

RED 24 MANAGEMENT   T 020 7559 3611
R24, 1st Floor, Kingsway House
103 Kingsway, London WC2B 6QX
E louise@red24management.com
W www.red24management.com

RED CANYON MANAGEMENT   T 07931 381696
T 07939 365578
E info@redcanyon.co.uk
W www.redcanyon.co.uk

RED DOOR MANAGEMENT   T 0161 850 9989
The Greenhouse, Broadway
MediaCityUK, Manchester M50 2EQ
E mail@the-reddoor.co.uk
W www.the-reddoor.co.uk

RED HOT ENTERTAINMENT   T 01279 850618
By e-mail. Accepts Showreels/Voicereels. 4 Agents
represent 45 Performers. Commercials. Disabled. Film.
Musical Theatre. Stage. Television
T 07828 470191
E info@redhotentertainment.biz
W www.redhotentertainment.biz

RED TALENT MANAGEMENT   T 0247 6691900
18 Earlsdon Avenue South, Earlsdon, Coventry CV5 6DT
T 07941 133812
E info@redtalentmanagement.com
W www.redtalentmanagement.com

REDROOFS ASSOCIATES   T 01628 674092
26 Bath Road, Maidenhead, Berkshire SL6 4JT
T 07531 355835 (Holiday Times)
E agency@redroofs.co.uk
W www.redroofsagency.co.uk

REDWOOD TALENT   T 0113 880 0822
15 Queen Square, Leeds LS2 8AJ
T 07712 722282
E info@redwoodtalent.com
W www.redwoodtalent.com

REFLECTIONS TALENT AGENCY   T 07412 833382
International House, 124 Cromwell Road
Kensington SW7 4ET
E info@reflectionstalentagency.co.uk
W www.reflectionstalentagency.co.uk

REGAN MANAGEMENT   T 029 2047 3993
Formerly REGAN RIMMER MANAGEMENT
Contact: Debi MacLean, Leigh-Ann Regan
Unit 2, 11-12 Crichton House
Cardiff Bay, Cardiff CF10 5EE
E debimaclean@reganmanagement.co.uk
W www.reganmanagement.co.uk

REGAN MANAGEMENT   T 020 3735 5429
Formerly REGAN RIMMER MANAGEMENT
Contact: Leigh-Ann Regan, George Smith
Barley Mow Centre, 10 Barley Mow Passage
Chiswick, London W4 4PH
T 07779 321954 (Leigh-Ann)
E leigh-annregan@reganmanagement.co.uk
W www.reganmanagement.co.uk

REGAN MANAGEMENT   T 0161 713 3677
Formerly REGAN RIMMER MANAGEMENT
Contact: Nicola Bolton, Leigh-Ann Regan
MediaCityUK, The Greenhouse
111 Broadway, Salford M50 2EQ
T 07779 321954
E nicolabolton@reganmanagement.co.uk
W www.reganmanagement.co.uk

REGAN RIMMER MANAGEMENT (CARDIFF)
See REGAN MANAGEMENT

REGAN RIMMER MANAGEMENT (LONDON)
See RIMMER, Debbie MANAGEMENT

**REPRESENTATION
UPSON EDWARDS**   T 01782 827222
Voice Coaches only
23 Victoria Park Road, Tunstall
Stoke-on-Trent, Staffs ST6 6DX
F 01782 728004
E sarah.upson@voicecoach.tv
W www.voicecoach.tv

**REYNOLDS, Sandra AGENCY LTD
(COMMERCIALS)**   T 01603 623842
Bacon House, 35 St George's Street
Norwich NR3 1DA
F 01603 219825
E alex@sandrareynolds.co.uk
W www.sandrareynolds.co.uk

**REYNOLDS, Sandra AGENCY LTD
(COMMERCIALS)**   T 020 7387 5858
Amadeus House, 27B Floral Street
London WC2E 9DP
F 020 7387 5848
E jessie@sandrareynolds.co.uk
W www.sandrareynolds.co.uk

RICHARD STONE PARTNERSHIP THE
See STONE, Richard PARTNERSHIP THE

**RICHARDS, Lisa
AGENCY THE**   T 00 353 1 6375000
108 Upper Leeson Street, Dublin 4, Ireland
F 00 353 1 6671256
E info@lisarichards.ie
W www.lisarichards.ie

RICHARDS, Lisa AGENCY THE   T 020 7287 1441
1st Floor, 33 Old Compton Street
London W1D 5JU
E office@lisarichards.co.uk
W www.lisarichards.co.uk

**RICHARDS, Stella
MANAGEMENT**   T 020 7736 7786
Contact: Stella Richards, Julia Lintott.
Existing Clients only
42 Hazlebury Road, London SW6 2ND
E stellagent@aol.com
W www.stellarichards.com

**RIDGEWAY STUDIOS
MANAGEMENT**   T 01992 633775
Office: 106 Hawkshead Road, Potters Bar
Hertfordshire EN6 1NG
E info@ridgewaystudios.co.uk

**RIMMER, Debbie
MANAGEMENT**   T 020 7839 2758
Formerly REGAN RIMMER MANAGEMENT (LONDON)
1st Floor, 23 Haymarket, London SW1Y 4DG
E debbierimmer-office@btconnect.com
W www.debbierimmer.com

**RISQUE MODEL
MANAGEMENT LTD**   T 0870 2283890
Rivington House, 82 Great Eastern Street
London EC2A 3JF
E info@risquemodel.co.uk
W www.risquemodel.co.uk

ROAR GLOBAL   T 020 7462 9060
ROAR House, 46 Charlotte Street, London W1T 2GS
F 020 7462 9061
E info@roarglobal.com
W www.roarglobal.com

Ashley Hodgson

Claire MacKenzie

Jack Bowman

Rory McCallum

Cate Holloway

Vanessa Champion PHOTOGRAPHER
Headshots & Character Shoots • Studio & Location
07747 025361
vanessachampion@live.com
www.vanessachampion.co.uk

RODRIGUEZ, Anxo MANAGEMENT T 00 34 61 9120396
Plaza de la Encarnación, No.3 Bajo Izq.
Madrid, Spain 28013
E anxo@zigguratfilms.com
W www.anxorodriguez.com

ROGUES & VAGABONDS MANAGEMENT LTD T 020 7254 8130
Personal Manager. CPMA Member
The Print House, 18 Ashwin Street
London E8 3DL
F 020 7249 8564
E rogues@vagabondsmanagement.com
W www.vagabondsmanagement.com

ROLE MODELS T 020 7284 4337
12 Cressy Road, London NW3 2LY
E info@rolemodelsagency.com
W www.rolemodelsagency.com

RONAN, Lynda PERSONAL MANAGEMENT T 020 7183 0017
Hunters House, 1 Redcliffe Road
London SW10 9NR
E lynda@lyndaronan.com
W www.lyndaronan.com

ROOM 3 AGENCY T 0845 5678333
The Old Chapel, 14 Fairview Drive
Redland, Bristol BS6 6PH
F 0845 5679333
E kate@room3agency.com
W www.room3agency.com

ROSEBERY MANAGEMENT LTD T 020 7684 0187
CPMA Member. Contact: Lead Agent. Prospective Client Applications should e-mail Spotlight Links only to applications@roseberymanagement.com. Otherwise Applications Accepted with CVs and Headshots by Post. Accepts Showreels.1 Agent represents 35 Performers. Commercials. Film. Musical Theatre. Stage. Television. Voice Overs
87 Leonard Street, London EC2A 4QS
E admin@roseberymanagement.com
W www.roseberymanagement.com

ROSS, Frances MANAGEMENT T 01726 832395
Higher Leyonne, Golant
Fowey, Cornwall PL23 1LA
T 07593 994050
E francesross@btconnect.com
W www.francesrossmanagement.co.uk

ROSS BROWN ASSOCIATES T 07860 558033
Personal Manager
F 020 8398 4111
E sandy@rossbrown.eu

ROSSMORE MANAGEMENT T 020 7258 1953
PMA Member
Broadley House, 48 Broadley Terrace NW1 6LG
E agents@rossmoremanagement.com
W www.rossmoremanagement.com

ROWE ASSOCIATES T/F 01992 640485
33 Percy Street, London W1T 2DF
T 07887 898220
E agents@growe.co.uk
W www.growe.co.uk

ROYCE MANAGEMENT T 020 8650 1096
121 Merlin Grove, Beckenham BR3 3HS
E office@roycemanagement.co.uk
W www.roycemanagement.co.uk

RPM2 T 07795 606087
Studio House, Delamare Road
Cheshunt, Herts EN8 9SH
E rhino-rpm2@hotmail.com
W www.rhino2-rpm.com

RS MANAGEMENT T 020 8257 6477
186 Waltham Way, London E4 8AZ
E info@rsmagency.co.uk
W www.rsmagency.co.uk

RSM (CHERRY PARKER MANAGEMENT) T 01702 522647
15 The Fairway, Leigh, Essex SS9 4QN
T 07976 547066
E info@rsm.uk.net
W www.rsm.uk.net

biutifulpeople.com

photo@danielsutka.com
07737 77 0571

alexruoccophotography
Tel: 07732293231
www.alexruoccophotography.co.uk

RUDEYE DANCE AGENCY   T 020 7014 3023
73 St John Street, London EC1M 4NJ
E dancer110578@hotmail.com
W www.rudeye.com

RUSSELL, Gregory
MANAGEMENT   T 07889 920190
17 Newquay Avenue, Weeping Cross
Stafford ST17 0EB
E info@gregory-russell.co.uk
W www.gregory-russell.co.uk

SAINOU   T 020 7734 6441
PMA Member. Twitter: @Sainou
10-11 Lower John Street, Golden Square
London W1F 9EB
E office@sainou.com
W www.sainou.com

SANDERS, Loesje LTD   T 01394 385260
PMA Member. Contact: Loesje Sanders, Susan Kuhl,
Simon Ash. Choreographers. Designers. Directors.
Lighting Designers
Pound Square, 1 North Hill
Woodbridge, Suffolk IP12 1HH
F 01394 388734
E loesje@loesjesanders.org.uk
W www.loesjesanders.com

SARABAND ASSOCIATES   T 020 8551 9193
Contact: Bryn Newton, Joy Jameson
PO Box 2493, Ilford, Essex IG1 8JW
E brynnewton@btconnect.com

SAROSI, Amanda ASSOCIATES   T 020 7993 6008
1 Holmbury View, London E5 9EG
F 020 7096 2141
E amanda@asassociates.biz

SASHAZE TALENT AGENCY   T 07968 762942
2 Gleannan Close, Omagh, Co. Tyrone BT79 7YA
E info@sashaze.com
W www.sashaze.com

SCA MANAGEMENT   T 01932 503285
Contact: By Post
Suite 17, Wey House
15 Church Street, Weybridge, Surrey KT13 8NA
E agency@sca-management.co.uk
W www.sca-management.co.uk

SCHNABL, Peter   T 01666 502133
The Barn House, Cutwell, Tetbury
Gloucestershire GL8 8EB
F 01666 502998
E peter.schnabl@virgin.net

SCHWARTZ, Marie Claude -
AGENCE CINETEA   T 00 33 1 42781717
9 Rue des Trois Bornes
75011 Paris, France
E cinetea@orange.fr
W www.cinetea.fr

SCOTT MARSHALL PARTNERS LTD
See MARSHALL, Scott PARTNERS LTD

SCOTT, Russell
ENTERTAINMENT LTD   T 0844 5676896
Specialises in Musical Theatre
W www.russellscottentertainment.com

SCOTT, Tim   T 020 8347 8705
PO Box 61776
London SW1V 3UX
E timscott@btinternet.com

SCOTT-PAUL YOUNG
ENTERTAINMENTS LTD   T/F 01753 693250
Artists Representation & Promotions
SPY Record Company
Northern Lights House
110 Blandford Road North
Langley, Nr Windsor
Berks SL3 7TA
E castingdirect@spy-ents.com
W www.spy-artistsworld.com

SCRIMGEOUR, Donald
ARTISTS AGENT   T 020 8444 6248
Choreographers. Principal Dancers. Producers
49 Springcroft Avenue
London N2 9JH
F 020 8883 9751
E vwest@dircon.co.uk
W www.donaldscrimgeour.com

SDM   T 020 7183 8995
120 Ivor Court
Gloucester Place, London NW1 6BS
F 020 7183 9013
E admin@simondrakemanagement.co.uk
W www.simondrakemanagement.co.uk

SEA PERSONAL
MANAGEMENT LTD   T/F 0870 6092629
PMA Member
Moorgate House, 5-8 Dysart Street
London EC2A 2BX
T 07855 460341
E steph@seapmlondon.com
W www.seapmlondon.com

SEA PERSONAL
MANAGEMENT LTD **T/F** 01269 870944
PMA Member
6 Bryn Tirion, Pontyberem
Llanelli, Carmarthenshire SA15 5BX
T 07855 460341
E steph@seapmlondon.com
W www.seapmlondon.com

SECOND SKIN AGENCY LTD **T/F** 01494 730166
26 Wood Pond Close, Seer Green
Beaconsfield, Bucks HP9 2XG
E office@secondskinagency.com
W www.secondskinagency.com

SEDGWICK, Dawn
MANAGEMENT **T** 020 7240 0404
3 Goodwins Court, Covent Garden
London WC2N 4LL
F 020 7240 0415
W www.dawnsedgwickmanagement.com

SELECT MANAGEMENT **T** 07700 059089
PO Box 748, London NW4 1TT
T 07956 131494
E mail@selectmanagement.info
W www.selectmanagement.info

SEVEN AGENCY MANAGEMENT **T** 01785 212266
Staffordshire Office: Suite 3, Tudor House
9 Eastgate Street, Stafford ST16 2NQ
T 07730 130484
E guy@7casting.co.uk
W www.7casting.co.uk

SEVEN CASTING AGENCY **T** 0161 850 1057
Actors. Children. Modelling. Stage. Television
Manchester Office:
82 King Street
Manchester M2 4WQ
T 07730 130484
E guy@7casting.co.uk
W www.7casting.co.uk

SHAPER, Susan
MANAGEMENT **T** 07903 196034
E info@susanshapermanagement.com

SHARKEY & TRIGG LTD **T** 020 7287 1923
PMA Member
44 Lexington Street
London W1F 0LP
E info@sharkeyandtrigg.com
W www.sharkeyandtrigg.com

SHARMAN, Alan AGENCY **T** 0121 212 0090
Office 6, Fournier House
8 Tenby Street, Birmingham B1 3AJ
E info@alansharmanagency.com
W www.alansharmanagency.com

SHELDRAKE, Peter AGENCY **T** 020 8876 9572
Contact: By e-mail. 1 Agent represents 50 Performers.
Commercials. Film. Musical Theatre. Stage. Television
139 Lower Richmond Road
London SW14 7HX
T 07758 063663
E peter.sheldrake3@btinternet.com
W www.petersheldrakeagency.co.uk

SHEPHERD MANAGEMENT　　T 020 7420 9350
PMA Member
3rd Floor, Joel House
17-21 Garrick Street, London WC2E 9BL
F 0843 2905796
E info@shepherdmanagement.co.uk
W www.shepherdmanagement.co.uk

SHEPPERD-FOX　　T 020 7240 2048
PMA Member. Contact: Jane Shepperd, James Davies,
Sophie Renaghan
2nd Floor, 47 Bedford Street, London WC2E 9HA
E info@shepperd-fox.co.uk
W www.shepperd-fox.co.uk

SHOWSTOPPERS!　　T 01376 518486
Events Management & Entertainment
42 Foxglove Close, Witham, Essex CM8 2XW
E mail@showstoppers-group.com
W www.showstoppers-group.com

SHOWTIME CASTINGS　　T 020 7068 6816
112 Milligan Street, Docklands, London E14 8AS
T 07908 008364
E gemma@showtimecastings.com
W www.showtimecastings.com

SILVERLEE MANAGEMENT　　T 07771 194598
Twitter: @SLeemanagement
E info@silverleemanagement.co.uk
W www.silverleemanagement.co.uk

SIMON & HOW ASSOCIATES　　T 020 7739 8865
12-18 Hoxton Street, London N1 6NG
E info@simonhow.com
W www.simonhow.com

SIMPSON FOX
ASSOCIATES LTD　　T 020 7434 9167
PMA Member. Set, Costume & Lighting Designers.
Directors. Choreographers
6 Beauchamp Place, London SW3 1NG
E david.bingham@simpson-fox.com

SINGER, Sandra ASSOCIATES　　T 01702 331616
Personal Manager. Contact: By e-mail. 2 Agents
represent an Adult Section (Boutique Agency).
Specialising in Children & Young Performers up to 23 yrs
for Feature, Film, Television, Commercials, Voice Over,
Musical Theatre. Choreographers
21 Cotswold Road, Westcliff-on-Sea, Essex SS0 8AA
E sandrasingeruk@aol.com
W www.sandrasinger.com

SINGERS INC　　T 020 7205 2316
Twitter: @singers_inc
INC Artists Ltd, 90 Long Acre
Covent Garden, London WC2E 9RZ
E chris@international-collective.com
W www.singersincworld.com

SJ MANAGEMENT　　T 020 7371 0441
8 Bettridge Road, London SW6 3QD
E sj@susanjames.demon.co.uk

SMART MANAGEMENT　　T 020 7837 8822
Contact: Mario Renzullo
PO Box 64377, London EC1P 1ND
E smart.management@virgin.net

SOPHIE'S PEOPLE　　T 020 8812 4999
Contact: Sophie Pyecroft. By Post/e-mail. Accepts
Showreels. 2 Agents represent 400 Performers.
Choreographers. Commercials. Corporate. Dancers.
Film. Television
40 Mexfield Road, London SW15 2RQ
T 0870 7876446
E sophies.people@btinternet.com
W www.sophiespeople.com

S.O.S.　　T 020 7735 5133
Twitter: @SebHolden
85 Bannerman House, Lawn Lane, London SW8 1UA
T 07740 359770
E info@sportsofseb.com
W www.sportsofseb.com

SOUNDCHECK AGENCY THE　　T 020 7437 0290
29 Wardour Street, London W1D 6PS
E casting@soundcheckentertainment.co.uk
W www.soundcheckentertainment.co.uk

SPEAKERS CIRCUIT LTD THE　　T 01892 750131
After Dinner Speakers
The Country Store, The Green
Frant, East Sussex TN3 9DA
T 01892 750921
E speakers-circuit@freenetname.co.uk

SPEAKERS CORNER　　T 020 7607 7070
Award Hosts, Comedians, Facilitators & Keynote
Speakers for Corporate Events & Conferences
Unit 31, Highbury Studios
10 Hornsey Street, London N7 8EL
F 020 7700 8847
E info@speakerscorner.co.uk
W www.speakerscorner.co.uk

SPLITTING IMAGES
LOOKALIKES AGENCY　　T 020 8809 2327
25 Clissold Court, Greenway Close, London N4 2EZ
E info@splitting-images.com
W www.splitting-images.com

SPORTS OF SEB LTD　　T 020 7735 5133
Twitter: @Sebholden
85 Bannerman House, Lawn Lane, London SW8 1UA
T 07740 359770
E info@sportsofseb.com
W www.sportsofseb.com

SPORTS PROMOTIONS (UK)
LTD/SP ACTORS　　T 020 8771 4700
Contact: By e-mail/Telephone. 300+ Performers.
Commercials. Actors. Dancers. Modelling. Presenters.
Sports Models. Stunts
56 Church Road, Crystal Palace, London SE19 2EZ
F 020 8771 4704
E agent@sportspromotions.co.uk
W www.sportspromotions.co.uk

SPYKER, Paul MANAGEMENT　　T 020 7462 0046
PO Box 48848, London WC1B 3WZ
F 020 7462 0047
E belinda@psmlondon.com

SRA PERSONAL
MANAGEMENT　　T 01932 863194
Lockhart Road, Cobham
Surrey KT11 2AX
E agency@susanrobertsacademy.co.uk

SSA MANAGEMENT　　T 07904 817229
E info@ssamanagement.co.uk
W www.ssamanagement.co.uk

S.T. ARTS MANAGEMENT　　T 0845 4082468
Contact: Tarquin Shaw-Young. Actors. Actresses
Suite 2, 1st Floor Offices, Cantilupe Chambers
Cantilupe Road, Ross-on-Wye HR9 7AN
F 0845 4082464
E tarquin@startsmanagement.co.uk
W www.startsmanagement.co.uk

ST JAMES'S MANAGEMENT　　T 01621 772183
Personal Manager. Existing Clients only
7 Smyatts Close, Southminster, Essex CM0 7JT
E jlstjames@btconnect.com

STAGE A MANAGEMENT LTD   T 01798 344356
9 Beech Grove
Midhurst
West Sussex GU29 9JA
T 07837 072775
E stageamanagement@gmail.com
W www.csa-theatreschool.co.uk

**STAGE CENTRE
MANAGEMENT LTD**   T 020 7607 0872
*Co-operative. CPMA Member. Contact: By e-mail/Post.
Commercials. Film. Musical Theatre. Stage. Television*
41 North Road
London N7 9DP
E info@stagecentre.org.uk
W www.stagecentre.org.uk

**STAGEWORKS WORLDWIDE
PRODUCTIONS**   T 01253 342426
*Contact: By e-mail. Cirque Artistes. Corporate. Dancers.
Ice Skaters. Musical Theatre*
525 Ocean Boulevard
Blackpool FY4 1EZ
F 01253 343702
E info@stageworkswwp.com
W www.stageworkswwp.com

**STANTON DAVIDSON
ASSOCIATES**   T 020 7581 3388
*Personal Manager. PMA Member. Contact: Geoff
Stanton, Roger Davidson. By Post only. Accepts
Showreels/Voicereels. Commercials. Corporate. Film.
Musical Theatre. Radio. Stage. Television. Voice Overs*
RADA Studios, 16 Chenies Street, London WC1E 7EX
E contact@stantondavidson.co.uk

STENTORIAN   T 07808 353611
44 Broughton Grove, Skipton BD23 1TL
E stentorian@btinternet.com
W www.stentoriantowncryer.co.uk

STEVENSON, Natasha MANAGEMENT LTD
See STEVENSON WITHERS ASSOCIATES LTD

**STEVENSON WITHERS
ASSOCIATES LTD**   T 020 7720 3355
*Personal Manager. PMA Member. Contact: By e-mail/
Telephone. 2 Agents. Commercials. Corporate. Film.
Radio. Stage. Television*
Studio 7C, Clapham North Arts Centre
Voltaire Road, London SW4 6DH
F 020 7720 5565
E talent@stevensonwithers.com
W www.stevensonwithers.com

STINSON, David AGENCY   T 07500 701521
57 Old Compton Street, London W1D 6HP
E david@davidstinsonagency.com
W www.davidstinsonagency.com

STIRLING MANAGEMENT   T 01204 848333
Contact: Glen Mortimer. By e-mail. Accepts Showreels.
3 Agents represent 100 Performers. Commercials. Film.
Presenters. Stage. Television. Corporate. Photographic
490 Halliwell Road, Bolton
Lancashire BL1 8AN
E admin@stirlingmanagement.co.uk
W www.stirlingmanagement.co.uk

STIVEN CHRISTIE
MANAGEMENT   T 0131 228 4040
Incorporating The Actors Agency of Edinburgh
1 Glen Street, Tollcross
Edinburgh EH3 9JD
E info@stivenchristie.co.uk
W www.stivenchristie.co.uk

STONE, Ian ASSOCIATES   T 020 8667 1627
Suite 262, Maddison House
226 High Street, Croydon CR9 1DF

STONE, Richard
PARTNERSHIP THE   T 020 7497 0849
PMA Member
Suite 3, De Walden Court
85 New Cavendish Street, London W1W 6XD
F 020 7497 0869
E all@thersp.com
W www.thersp.com

STONEHOUSE, Katherine
MANAGEMENT   T 020 8560 7709
Contact: Katherine Stonehouse. By e-mail. 1 Agent
represents 35 Performers. Television. Film. Musical
Theatre. Stage. Commercials
PO Box 64412
London W5 9GU
E katherine@katherinestonehouse.co.uk
W www.katherinestonehouse.co.uk

STOPFORD AGENCY   T 020 8741 6158
Stage
56A Church Road, Barnes, London SW13 0DQ
E info@stopfordagency.com
W www.stopfordagency.com

STRAIGHT LINE
MANAGEMENT   T 020 8393 4220
Division of Straight Line Productions
58 Castle Avenue, Epsom
Surrey KT17 2PH
E hilary@straightlinemanagement.co.uk

SUCCESS   T 020 7734 3356
Room 236, 2nd Floor, Linen Hall
162-168 Regent Street
London W1B 5TB
F 020 7494 3787
E ee@successagency.co.uk
W www.successagency.co.uk

SUMMERS, Mark
MANAGEMENT   T 020 7229 8413
1 Beaumont Avenue, West Kensington
London W14 9LP
E louise@marksummers.com
W www.marksummers.com

SUPERTED.COM   T 07939 664922
2 Chapel Place, Rivington Street
London EC2A 3DQ
E email@superted.com
W www.superted.com

SYMPHONY TALENT
GROUP (STG)   T 020 3488 0159
E us@symphonytalentgroup.com
W www.symphonytalentgroup.com

TAKE2 CASTING AGENCY   T 00 353 87 2563403
28 Beech Park Road, Foxrock
Dublin 18, Ireland
E pamela@take2.ie
W www.take2.ie

TAKE2 MANAGEMENT   T 0161 832 7715
Suite 5, Basil Chambers, 65 High Street
Manchester M4 1FS
F 0161 839 1661
E lois@take2management.co.uk
W www.take2management.co.uk

TAKE2 MANAGEMENT   T 0113 403 2930
34 Park Cross Street, Leeds LS1 2QH
E chris@take2management.co.uk
W www.take2management.co.uk

TALENT4 MEDIA LTD   T 020 7183 4330
Studio LG16
Shepherds Building Central
Charecroft Way, London W14 0EH
F 020 7183 4331
E enquiries@talent4media.com
W www.talent4media.com

TALENT AGENCY LTD THE   T 01483 281500
Contact: Mike Smith
Freshwater House, Outdowns
Effingham, Surrey KT24 5QR
F 01483 281501
E info@thetalentagencyltd.co.uk

TALENT ARTISTS LTD   T 020 7923 1119
Contact: Jane Wynn Owen. No Unsolicited Enquiries
59 Sydner Road, London N16 7UF
E talent.artists@btconnect.com

TALENT NORTH   T 07919 181456
5 Chapel Lane, Garforth LS25 1AG
E sr@talentnorth.co.uk
W www.talentnorth.co.uk

TALENT SCOUT THE   T 01924 464049
19 Edge Road
Dewsbury WF12 0QA
E connect@thetalentscout.org
W www.thetalentscout.org

TALENTED ARTISTS LTD T 020 7520 9412
Suite 17, Adam House
7-10 Adam Street, London WC2N 6AA
E info@talentedartistsltd.com
W www.talentedartistsltd.com

TAVISTOCK WOOD T 020 7494 4767
PMA Member
45 Conduit Street, London W1S 2YN
F 020 7434 2017
E info@tavistockwood.com
W www.tavistockwood.com

TAYLORWOLFE AGENCY T 020 3287 1332
57 Westow Hill, Crystal Palace
London SE19 1TS
E info@taylorwolfeagency.com
W www.taylorwolfeagency.com

**TCA
(THE COMMERCIAL AGENCY)** T 020 7233 8100
12 Evelyn Mansions
Carlisle Place
London SW1P 1NH
E mail@thecommercialagency.co.uk
W www.thecommercialagency.co.uk

**TCG
ARTIST MANAGEMENT LTD** T 020 7240 3600
*Contact: Kristin Tarry (Owner/Director/Agent), Emma
Davidson (Snr Assistant), Cal Griffiths (Snr Assistant). By
Post/e-mail. Accepts Showreels. Film. Television. Stage.
Musical Theatre. Commercials*
14A Goodwin's Court
London WC2N 4LL
E info@tcgam.co.uk
W www.tcgam.co.uk

TEAM PLAYERS T 00 45 20494218
c/o The Danish Filmhouse
Vognmagergade 10, 1st Floor
DK-1120 Copenhagen K, Denmark
T 00 45 20683920
E info@teamplayers.dk
W www.teamplayers.dk

TENNYSON AGENCY THE T 020 8543 5939
10 Cleveland Avenue
Merton Park, London SW20 9EW
E agency@tennysonagency.co.uk

THOMAS, Lisa MANAGEMENT T 0845 9005511
*Contact: Lisa Thomas (Agent). By e-mail. 1 Agent
represents 9+ Performers*
Unit 10, 7 Wenlock Road
London N1 7SL
E lisa@lisathomasmanagement.com
W www.lisathomasmanagement.com

**THOMPSON, David
ASSOCIATES** T 020 8682 3083
7 St Peter's Close
London SW17 7UH
T 07889 191093
E montefioredt@aol.com

THOMSON, Mia ASSOCIATES T 020 7307 5939
PMA Member
3rd Floor, 207 Regent Street
London W1B 3HH
F 020 7580 4729
E assistant@miathomsonassociates.co.uk
W www.miathomsonassociates.co.uk

**THRELFALL, Katie
ASSOCIATES** T 020 8879 0493
PMA Member
13 Tolverne Road, London SW20 8RA
E info@ktthrelfall.co.uk

**THRESH, Melody MANAGEMENT
ASSOCIATES LTD (MTM)** T 0161 457 2110
Imperial Court
2 Exchange Quay
Manchester M5 3EB
E melodythreshmtm@aol.com

**TILDSLEY, Janice
ASSOCIATES** T 020 8521 1888
PMA Member. Contact: Kathryn Kirton
47 Orford Road
London E17 9NJ
E kathryn@janicetildsleyassociates.co.uk
W www.janicetildsleyassociates.co.uk

**TINKER, Victoria
MANAGEMENT** T/F 01403 210653
Non-acting. Technical
Birchenbridge House, Brighton Road
Mannings Heath, Horsham
West Sussex RH13 6HY

**TLA BOUTIQUE
MANAGEMENT** T/F 0113 289 3433
*Formerly LAWRENCE, Tonicha AGENCY. Incorporating
Young Boutique*
T 07766 415996
E tonichalawrence@gmail.com
W www.tlaboutiquemanagement.com

TMG ASSOCIATES   T 020 7437 1383
Formerly Morgan & Goodman
20 Hanover Square
London W1S 1JY
T 07866 589905
E tanya.greep@googlemail.com

TOP TALENT AGENCY LTD   T 01727 855903
Children & Adults. Commercials. Film. Photographic.
Stage. Television
PO Box 860, St Albans
Herts AL1 9BR
F 01727 812666
E admin@toptalentagency.co.uk
W www.toptalentagency.co.uk

TOTAL VANITY   T 07739 381788
15 Walton Way
Aylesbury
Buckinghamshire HP21 7JJ
E richard.williams@totalvanity.com
W www.totalvanity.com

TRENDS ENTERTAINMENT   T 01253 396534
Unit 4, 9 Chorley Road
Blackpool
Lancashire FY3 7XQ
E info@trendsentertainment.com
W www.trendsentertainment.com

TROIKA   T 020 7336 7868
PMA Member
10A Christina Street
London EC2A 4PA
F 020 3544 2919
W www.troikatalent.com

TTA   T 01245 690080
Unit 1, Well Lane Industrial Estate
Well Lane, Danbury
Chelmsford CM3 4AB
E agents@tomorrowstalent.co.uk

TV MANAGEMENTS   T 01425 475544
Brink House, Avon Castle
Ringwood, Hants BH24 2BL
F 01425 480123
E etv@tvmanagements.co.uk

TWINS
See PC THEATRICAL, MODEL & CASTING AGENCY

TWO'S COMPANY   T 020 8299 3714
Existing Clients only. Directors. Stage. Writers
244 Upland Road
London SE22 0DN
E graham@2scompanytheatre.co.uk

UGLY MODELS   T 020 8749 4760
F 020 7402 0507
E info@ugly.org
W www.ugly.org

UK SCREEN ACTING ACADEMY   T 07879 846113
5 Corrie Court, Hamilton
South Lanarkshire ML3 9XE
E stuart@screenactingacademy.co.uk
W www.screenactingacademy.co.uk

UNITED AGENT5S LLP   T 020 3214 0800
Personal Manager. PMA Member
12-26 Lexington Street
London W1F 0LE
E info@unitedagents.co.uk
W www.unitedagents.co.uk

UPBEAT MANAGEMENT   T 020 8668 3332
Theatre Touring & Events. No Actors
10 Lindal Road, London SE4 1EJ
E info@upbeatmanagement.co.uk
W www.upbeat.co.uk

UPSON EDWARDS
See REPRESENTATION UPSON EDWARDS

URBAN COLLECTIVE &
URBAN ASSOCIATES   T 020 7482 3282
The Basement, 17 Burghley Road
London NW5 1UG
E info@urban-collective.co.uk
W www.urban-collective.co.uk

URBAN TALENT   T 0161 228 6866
Nemesis House, 1 Oxford Court
Bishopsgate, Manchester M2 3WQ
E liz@nmsmanagement.co.uk
W www.urbantalent.tv

UTOPIA MODEL
MANAGEMENT   T 07771 884844
7 Ellerbeck, Manchester M28 7XN
F 0871 2180843
E kya@utopiamodels.co.uk

UVA MANAGEMENT LTD   T 0845 0090344
Contact: By e-mail. Commercials. Film. Presenters.
Stage. Television
Pinewood Film Studios, Pinewood Road
Iver Heath, Buckinghamshire SL0 0NH
E berko@uvamanagement.com
W www.uvamanagement.com

VACCA, Roxane
MANAGEMENT   T 020 7383 5971
PMA Member
61 Judd Street, London WC1H 9QT
E info@roxanevacca.co.uk

VALLÉ THEATRICAL
AGENCY THE   T 01992 622861
The Vallé Academy Studios, Wilton House
Delamare Road, Cheshunt, Herts EN8 9SG
F 01992 622868
E agency@valleacademy.co.uk
W www.valleacademy.co.uk

VAM (VAN RENSBURG ARTIST MANAGEMENT)
T 01875 852477
34 Campbell Road, Longniddry
East Lothian EH32 0NP
E michelle@vanartman.co.uk
W www.vanartman.co.uk

VIDAL-HALL, Clare MANAGEMENT
T 020 8741 7647
PMA Member. Choreographers. Composers. Designers.
Directors. Lighting Designers. Musical Supervisors/
Directors. Sound Designers. Video Designers
57 Carthew Road
London W6 0DU
F 020 8741 9459
E info@clarevidalhall.com
W www.clarevidalhall.com

VINE, Michael ASSOCIATES
T 020 8347 2580
Light Entertainment
1 Stormont Road
London N6 4NS
E stephen@michaelvineassociates.com

VISIONARY TALENT
T 020 8133 4622
Suite 36, 88-90 Hatton Garden
Holborn, London EC1N 8PG
E info@visionarytalent.co.uk
W www.visionarytalent.co.uk

VJ MANAGEMENT
T 020 7237 8953
Personal Manager. Contact: Valerie Hodson. By e-mail
with Spotlight number only. 1 Agent represents
44 Clients
15 Jarman House, Hawkstone Road
Surrey Quays, London SE16 2PW
E valerie@vjmgt.co.uk
W www.vjmgt.co.uk

VM TALENT LTD (VIC MURRAY TALENT)
T 020 7112 8938
PMA Member
Unit 40, Battersea Business Centre
99-101 Lavender Hill
London SW11 5QL
E info@vmtalent.com
W www.vmtalent.com

VSA LTD
T 020 7240 2927
PMA Member. Contact: Andy Charles, Tod Weller
186 Shaftesbury Avenue
London WC2H 8JB
F 020 7240 2930
E info@vsaltd.com
W www.vsaltd.com

W ATHLETIC
T 020 8948 2759
34 Hill Street
Richmond-upon-Thames
London TW9 1TW
E london@wathletic.com
W www.wathletic.com

WADE, Suzann
T 020 7486 0746
(Casting/Production only)
Personal Manager. PMA Member. Contact: By Post only
(No Calls). Accepts Showreels via Link on CV. 2 Agents
represent 18 Performers. Film. Musical Theatre. Stage.
Television. Voice Over. Animation/Computer Games.
Radio Drama. Commercials. UK/International Castings
9 Wimpole Mews
London W1G 8PG
E admin@suzannwade.com
W www.suzannwade.com

WARD, Mandy ARTIST MANAGEMENT
T 020 7434 3569
PMA Member
4th Floor, 74 Berwick Street
London W1F 8TE
E info@mwartistmanagement.com
W www.mandywardartistmanagement.com

WARING & McKENNA
T 020 7836 9222
PMA Member
44 Maiden Lane
Covent Garden, London WC2E 7LN
F 020 7836 9186
E dj@waringandmckenna.com
W www.waringandmckenna.com

WELCH, Janet PERSONAL MANAGEMENT
T/F 01761 463238
Contact: By Post
Old Orchard, The Street
Ubley, Bristol BS40 6PJ
E info@janetwelchpm.co.uk

WEST, Ben MANAGEMENT
T 020 7566 4050
Suite 598, Kemp House
152-160 City Road
London EC1V 2NX
F 020 7566 3935
E assistant@benwestmanagement.com
W www.benwestmanagement.com

WEST CENTRAL MANAGEMENT
T/F 020 7833 8134
CPMA Member. Co-operative of 20 Performers. Contact: By Post/e-mail
Room 4, East Block, Panther House
38 Mount Pleasant, London WC1X 0AN
E mail@westcentralmanagement.com
W www.westcentralmanagement.com

WHATEVER ARTISTS MANAGEMENT LTD
T 020 8349 0920
PO Box 72301, London NW7 0HG
E info@wamshow.biz
W www.wamshow.biz

WHITEHALL ARTISTS
T/F 020 8785 3737
6 Embankment, Putney
London SW15 1LB
E whitehallfilms@gmail.com

WILDE MANAGEMENT
T 07759 567639
No 3, 549 Barlow Moor Road
Manchester M21 8AN
E info@wildemanagement.co.uk
W www.wildemanagement.co.uk

WILKINSON, David ASSOCIATES
T 020 7371 5188
Existing Clients only
115 Hazlebury Road, London SW6 2LX
E info@dwassociates.net

WILLIAMS BULLDOG MANAGEMENT LTD
T 020 7585 1518
B404 The Biscuit Factory
Tower Bridges Business Complex
100 Clements Road
London SE16 4DG
E info@williamsbulldog.co.uk
W www.williamsbulldog.co.uk

WILLIAMSON & HOLMES
T 020 7240 0407
Twitter: @WilliamsonHolme
4th Floor, 11 Maiden Lane
London WC2E 7NA
E info@williamsonandholmes.co.uk
W www.williamsonandholmes.co.uk

WILLOW PERSONAL MANAGEMENT
T 01733 240392
Specialist Agency for Short Actors (5 feet & under) & Tall Actors (7 feet & over)
151 Main Street, Yaxley
Peterborough, Cambs PE7 3LD
E office@willowmanagement.co.uk
W www.willowmanagement.co.uk

WILLS, Newton MANAGEMENT
T 07989 398381
Personal Manager. Contact: By Post/e-mail. Accepts Showreels/Voicereels. 3 Agents represent 53 Performers. Actors. Commercials. Dancers. Film. Musical Theatre. Singers. Stage. Television. Voice Overs
12 St Johns Road, Isleworth
Middlesex TW7 6NN
F 00 33 4 68218685
E newton.wills@aol.com
W www.newtonwills.com

WINDMILL ARTISTS MANAGEMENT
T 07900 735566
7 Richmond Close, Princes Gate
Bishops Stortford
Hertfordshire CM23 4PG
T 07512 998007
E info@windmillartistsmanagement.co.uk
W www.windmillartistsmanagement.co.uk

WINSLETT, Dave ASSOCIATES
T 020 8668 0531
4 Zig Zag Road, Kenley
Surrey CR8 5EL
F 020 8668 9216
E info@davewinslett.com
W www.davewinslett.com

WINTERSONS
T 020 7836 7849
PMA Member
59 St Martin's Lane
London WC2N 4JS
E info@nikiwinterson.com
W www.nikiwinterson.com

WIS CELTIC MANAGEMENT
T 07966 302812
Welsh, Irish & Scottish Performers
86 Elphinstone Road, Walthamstow
London E17 5EX
F 020 8523 4523

WISE BUDDAH TALENT
T 020 7307 1600
Contact: Sam Gregory
74 Great Titchfield Street
London W1W 7QP
F 020 7307 1601
E sam.gregory@wisebuddah.com
W www.wisebuddah.com

WMG MANAGEMENT EUROPE LTD
T 020 7009 6000
Sports Management Company
5th Floor, 33 Soho Square
London W1D 3QU
F 020 3230 1053
W www.wmgllc.com

WONDER ARTISTS TALENT AGENT
T 07472 770437
150 Newport Road, Stafford
Staffordshire ST16 2EZ
E wonderartists@blacklightenterprises.co.uk
W www.wonderartists.co.uk

WYMAN, Edward AGENCY
T 029 2075 2351
Contact: Judith Gay. By Post/e-mail. Adults (16+ yrs). Books open for a limited number of new actors. January only. English & Welsh Language. Commercials. Corporate. Television. Voice Overs. Walk-on & Supporting Artists
23 White Acre Close, Thornhill
Cardiff CF14 9DG
E wymancasting@yahoo.co.uk
W www.wymancasting.co.uk

XL MANAGEMENT
T 01926 810449
Edmund House, Rugby Road
Leamington Spa
Warwickshire CV32 6EL
F 01926 811420
E office@xlmanagement.co.uk
W www.xlmanagement.co.uk

YAT MANAGEMENT (YOUNG ACTORS THEATRE MANAGEMENT)
T 020 7278 2101
70-72 Barnsbury Road, London N1 0ES
E agent@yati.org.uk
W www.yati.org.uk

ZWICKLER, Marlene & ASSOCIATES
T/F 0131 343 3030
1 Belgrave Crescent Lane
Edinburgh EH4 3AG
E info@mza-artists.com
W www.mza-artists.com

Children's & Teenagers' Agents

How can my child become an actor?

If your child is interested in becoming an actor, they should try to get as much practical experience as possible. For example, joining the drama club at school, taking theatre studies as an option, reading as many plays as they can and going to the theatre on a regular basis. They could also attend local youth theatres or drama groups. Some theatres offer evening or Saturday classes.

What are the chances of success?

As any agency or school will tell you, the entertainment industry is highly competitive and for every success story there are many children who will never be hired for paid acting work. Child artists and their parents should think very carefully before getting involved in the industry and be prepared for disappointments along the way.

What is the difference between stage schools and agencies?

Stage schools provide specialised training in acting, singing and dancing for under 18s. They offer a variety of full and part-time courses. Please see the 'Drama Training, Schools & Coaches' section for listings. Children's and teenagers' agencies specialise in the representation of child artists, promoting them to casting opportunities and negotiating contracts on their behalf. In return they will take commission, usually ranging from 10-15%. Some larger stage schools also have agencies attached to them. A number of agents are listed in this section.

Why does my child need an agent?

While many parents feel they want to retain control over their child's career, they will not have the contacts and authority a good agent will have in the industry. Casting directors are more likely to look to an agent they know and trust to provide the most suitable children for a job than an independent, unrepresented child. This does not mean to say that a child will never get work without an agent, but it will certainly be more difficult. There are other factors like licensing and chaperoning that agents can organise and give advice on.

How should I use these listings?

This section lists up-to-date contact details for agencies specialising in the representation of children and teenagers. Every company listed is done so by written request to us. Always research agencies carefully before approaching them to make sure they are suitable for your child. Many have websites you can visit, or ask around for personal recommendations. You should make a short-list of the ones you think are most appropriate rather than sending a standard letter to agencies. Please see the main 'Agents & Personal Managers' advice section for further guidance on choosing and approaching agents.

Can Spotlight offer me advice on choosing or changing my child's agent?

Unfortunately Spotlight is not able to advise performers on specific agents, nor is it in a position to handle any financial or contractual queries or complaints. For agent-related queries we suggest you contact The Agents' Association www.agents-uk.com or The Personal Managers' Association (PMA) www.thepma.com, or you could try one of the independent advisers on our website www.spotlight.com/artists/advice

Who can I contact for general advice?

Your local education authority should be able to help with most queries regarding your child's education; working hours, chaperones and general welfare if they are aged 16 or under. You could also try contacting an independent adviser for advice, or for legal guidance please see the 'Accountants, Insurance & Law' section for listings.

Children's & Teenagers' Agents

Can my child join Equity?

Since May 2012, children aged 10 or over can apply for full Equity membership. Please see www.equity.org.uk

Should I pay an agent to represent my child? Or sign a contract?

Equity does not recommend that you pay an agent an upfront fee to place your child on their client list. Before signing a contract, you should be very clear about the terms and commitments involved. For advice on both of these issues, or if you experience any problems with a current agent, we recommend contacting Equity directly.

Why do child actors need licences?

Strict regulations apply to children working in the entertainment industry. These cover areas including the maximum number of performance hours per day/week, rest times, meal times and tutoring requirements. When any child under 16 performs in a professional capacity, the production company must obtain a Child Performance Licence from the child's local education authority.

Who are chaperones?

Child artists must also be accompanied by a chaperone at all times when they are working. Registered chaperones are generally used instead of parents as they have a better understanding of the employment regulations involved, and have professional experience of dealing with production companies.

Listings for a number of child chaperones can be found in the 'Consultants' section, but please ensure that you research any company or individual before proceeding further. Registered chaperones will have been police checked and approved by their local education authority to act in loco parentis. Always contact your local education authority if you have any questions or concerns.

What is Spotlight Children & Young Performers?

Children who are currently represented by an agent or attend a stage school can appear in the Spotlight Children & Young Performers directory. This is a casting resource, used by production teams to source child artists for television, film, stage or commercial work. Each child pays an annual membership fee to have their photo featured in the printed directory along with others represented by the same agency or stage school, as well as receiving their own individual online profile on the Spotlight website, searchable by casting professionals. Please speak to your child's school or agency about joining Spotlight for ongoing promotion to hundreds of casting opportunities.

For further information about the directory visit www.spotlight.com/join

CASE STUDY

Denise Smith started chaperoning approximately 10 years ago and now runs childchaperone.co.uk

I am a married mother of two daughters, now aged 21 and 16 who both attended a theatre school for 12 years. When my youngest daughter was 7 she got her first job in a pantomime and it was a stipulation that I had to get a chaperone licence.

It soon became apparent that a lot of the skills I had acquired as a mother and in previous employments would hold me in good stead for chaperoning. There is often a lot of waiting around required which I had vast experience of waiting outside dance, ballet, gymnastic and swimming lessons. Life skills such as being a good communicator, good time keeping, record keeping and paying attention to detail are all beneficial.

My business has built up over the last 10 years and a high proportion of my work is via recommendations or recurrent bookings, however networking is also a vital work tool for me.

My primary experience is in theatre but I also work in television and film. I have a growing database of chaperones/tutors, therefore I am in a position to undertake multiple posts or enquiries where a larger team is required.

I was appointed head chaperone on the National Theatre's Emil & the Detectives production 2013/2014. This entailed a management/administration role in addition to normal chaperoning as part of a large team. My role as head of department meant I was responsible for overseeing all aspects of the day and liaising with the producer, casting, contracts and stage management. I have worked on many productions at the National Theatre so I was absolutely delighted to have been given this role.

I really love theatre rehearsals, from the start of the read-through to what then transpires onto the stage. It develops from a script into a production through weeks of creative input and is so interesting.

Chaperoning is a huge responsibility, looking after people's children in a place of work. It is the children's safety and wellbeing that is paramount.

There are rules and regulations regarding children's permitted working hours which differ on the child's age, so part of my role is to monitor this and make sure that adequate breaks are given and they are not being overworked. I feel it is also important to maintain a friendly professional relationship with parents in order for them to enjoy the experience too.

In the past two years, I have had multiple trips overseas to Belgium and France on a residential basis in television and opera - being on a residential is 24 hours a day care when children are away from home and family. On one of these trips I decided it would be nice to take 2 teenage boys on a climb of the Belfort Tower in Bruges, all 366 steps up! But also 366 down!! A mammoth task in anyone's book! Phew, I was not as fit as I thought but it seemed like a good idea at the start! Another time whilst in France in a restaurant, a colleague and I had to spring into action to re-plate an entire dinner that a poor young lad had accidentally dropped into his lap, much to his and our bewilderment! So there can be lots of fun and laughter throughout the day, along with the professional side, it can often be light hearted and a fun environment!

The role of a chaperone is quite often under valued but is the most important. It is the law for any production with children to have a licensed chaperone therefore it is not possible without one.

Sometimes it can be challenging with tight schedules etc., so keeping calm and firm in tense situations is advisable.

Advice/tips I would give to parents would be; always be punctual, when a child is late it is unsettling for them. Encourage your children to behave well, be polite and respectful to all people they will meet within their work environment. I think it is also important to find a representative for their child that does not display overt favouritism as I have seen this happen and can be an unpleasant experience.

I think it is wonderful for children to work in the Arts Industry. The skills and experience they can pick up as part of a professional production can benefit them greatly and it can certainly be an education.

**To find out more visit
www.childchaperone.co.uk**

ANNA FIORENTINI — The Agency
THEATRE & FILM SCHOOL

Meet the new crowd

7 to 18 years olds
Drama, Film,
Singing, Dance,
Set & Costume
Design

Clients are exclusive to the Anna Fiorentini School & attend weekly classes

Top Boy
Me & Mrs Jones

Revolting World of
Stanley Brown

Antigone
(National Theatre)

Oliver | West End
The Lion King

My Murder

Song for Marion

T: 020 7682 3677 | E: rhiannon@annafiorentini.com | M: 07904962779
Business Design Centre, Unit 101, Angel, Islington, N1 0QH

www.annafiorentini.com

**1ST TALENT YOUNG
ACTORS AGENCY**   T 0845 6454000
1 Beaumont Avenue, West Kensington, London W14 9LP
E 1sttalent@gmail.com
W www.1sttalent.co.uk

A & J ARTISTS LTD   T 020 8342 0542
Children & Adults
242A The Ridgeway, Botany Bay
Enfield EN2 8AP
T 020 8367 7139
E info@ajmanagement.co.uk
W www.ajmanagement.co.uk

ABACUS AGENCY   T 01737 821348
Robert Denholm House, Bletchingley Road
Nutfield, Redhill, Surrey RH1 4HW
E admin@abacusagency.co.uk
W www.abacusagency.co.uk

ACADEMY ARTS MANAGEMENT   T 01245 422595
6A The Green, Writtle
Chelmsford, Essex CM1 3DU
E info@academyarts.co.uk
W www.academyarts.co.uk

ACT-ON   T 01379 688455
Chapel Cottage, Fen Street
Bressingham, Norfolk IP22 2AQ
E tanya@act-on.org.uk
W www.act-on.org.uk

ACT 2 MANAGEMENT   T 07939 144355
105 Richmond Avenue, Highams Park
London E4 9RR
E management@act2drama.co.uk
W www.act2drama.co.uk

ACT OUT AGENCY   T/F 0161 429 7413
22 Greek Street, Stockport
Cheshire SK3 8AB
E ab22actout@aol.com
W www.abacademytheatreschool.webs.com

AFA MANAGEMENT   T 07979 737950
Amanda Fairclough Actors Management
14 Cheviot Close, Horwich, Bolton BL6 7DF
E toni@afamanagement.co.uk
W www.afamanagement.co.uk

ALL EXPRESSIONS AGENCY   T 020 8892 6185
153 Waverley Avenue, Twickenham TW2 6DJ
E info@allexpressions.co.uk
W www.allexpressions.co.uk

**ALL THE ARTS CHILDREN'S
CASTING AGENCY**   T 020 8850 2384
PO Box 61687, London SE9 9BP
T 07908 618083
E jillian@allthearts.co.uk
W www.allthearts.co.uk

**ALLSORTS CHILDRENS
AGENCY**   T 020 8989 0500
Challenge House, 1st Floor, 57-59 Queens Road
Buckhurst Hill, Essex IG9 5BU
T 07958 511647
E bookings@allsortsagency.com
W www.allsortsagency.com

**ALLSORTS DRAMA
FOR CHILDREN**   T/F 020 8969 3249
In association with LESLIE, Sasha MANAGEMENT
34 Crediton Road, London NW10 3DU
E sasha@allsortsdrama.com

ALLSTARS CASTING   T 0151 707 2100
66 Hope Street, Liverpool L1 9BZ
T/F 07739 359737
E sylvie@allstarscasting.co.uk
W www.allstarscasting.co.uk

ALLSTARZ CASTING AGENCY   T 01268 711180
'Glennines', Ramsden Park Road
Ramsden Bellhouse
Billericay, Essex CM11 1NS
T 07740 922956
E office@allstarzcastingagency.co.uk
W www.allstarzagency.co.uk

ALPHABET KIDZ   T 020 7252 4343
Also known as Alphabet Agency
Daisy Business Park, 19-35 Sylvan Grove
London SE15 1PD
F 020 7252 4341
E contact@alphabetkidz.co.uk
W www.alphabetkidz.co.uk

ANNA'S MANAGEMENT   T 020 8958 7636
Children. Teenagers. Young Adults
25 Tintagel Drive, Stanmore
Middlesex HA7 4SR
E annasmanage@aol.com
W www.annasmanagement.co.uk

ARAENA/COLLECTIVE   T/F 020 8428 0037
10 Bramshaw Gardens, South Oxhey
Herts WD19 6XP
E info@collectivedance.co.uk

ARNOULD KIDZ T 020 8942 1879
1A Brook Gardens, Kingston-upon-Thames
Surrey KT2 7ET
T 07720 427828
E info@arnouldkidz.co.uk
W www.arnouldkidz.co.uk

**ARTEMIS STUDIOS
PERFORMING ARTS SCHOOL** T 01344 429403
30 Charles Square, Bracknell
Berkshire RG12 1AY
E agency@artemis-studios.co.uk
W www.artemis-studios.co.uk

ARTS1 MANAGEMENT T 01908 410700
The Box Studios, Sunrise Parkway
Linford Wood, Milton Keynes MK14 6LS
E info@arts1.co.uk
W www.arts1management.co.uk

**ASHCROFT ACADEMY OF
DRAMATIC ART & AGENCY** T 0844 8005328
Harris Primary Academy Crystal Palace
Malcolm Road, Penge, London SE20 8RH
T 07799 791586
E info@ashcroftacademy.com
W www.ashcroftacademy.com

**AWA - ANDREA WILDER
AGENCY** T 07919 202401
23 Cambrian Drive, Colwyn Bay
Conwy LL28 4SL
F 07092 249314
E andreawilder@fastmail.fm
W www.awagency.co.uk

BACKGROUND WALES T 0845 4082468
Suite 2, 1st Floor Offices, Cantilupe Chambers
Cantilupe Road, Ross-on-Wye HR9 7AN
F 0845 4082464
E tarquin@backgroundwales.co.uk
W www.backgroundwales.co.uk

BANANAFISH MANAGEMENT T 0151 708 5509
The Business Hub, 40 Devonshire Road
Wirral CH43 1TW
T 07974 206622
E info@bananafish.co.uk
W www.bananafish.co.uk

**BIG TALENT SCHOOL &
AGENCY THE** T 029 2046 4506
Contact: Shelley Norton
Unit 2, Crichton House
11-12 Mount Stuart Square, Cardiff CF10 5EE
T 07886 020923
E info@thebigtalent.co.uk
W www.thebigtalent.co.uk

BITESIZE AGENCY T 01978 358320
Unit 6/7 Clwyd Court 2
Rhosddu Industrial Estate
Rhosrobin, Wrexham LL11 4YL
F 01978 756308
E bitesizeagency@btconnect.com
W www.bitesizeagency.co.uk

BIZZYKIDZ T 0845 5200400
Bizzy Studios, 1st Floor Hall
10-12 Pickford Lane
Bexleyheath, Kent DA7 4QW
F 0845 5200401
E bookings@bizzykidzlondon.com
W www.bizzykidz.com

BODENS AGENCY T 020 8447 0909
99 East Barnet Road, New Barnet
Herts EN4 8RF
T 07545 696888
E info@bodens.co.uk
W www.bodens.co.uk/clients

BONNIE & BETTY LTD T 020 8301 8333
9-11 Gunnery Terrace, Royal Arsenal
London SE18 6SW
E agency@bonnieandbetty.com
W www.bonnieandbetty.com

BOSS JUNIORS T 0161 237 0100
Fourways House, 57 Hilton Street
Manchester M1 2EJ
F 0161 236 1237
E info@bossjuniors.co.uk
W www.bossjuniors.co.uk

BOURNE, Michelle
CHILDREN'S MULTICULTURAL
ACADEMY & AGENCY T 07852 932473
E info@michellebourneacademy.co.uk
W www.michellebourneacademy.co.uk

BRADFORD THEATRE ARTS T 07986 713203
Daisy Hill Back Lane, Bradford
West Yorkshire BD9 6DJ
E bradfordtheatrearts@talktalk.net
W www.bradfordtheatrearts.webs.com

BRUCE & BROWN T 020 7624 7333
17 Lonsdale Road, London NW6 6RA
F 020 7625 4047
E info@bruceandbrown.com
W www.bruceandbrown.com

BRUNO KELLY LTD T 020 7183 7331
3rd Floor, 207 Regent Street
London W1B 3HH
F 020 7183 7332
E info@brunokelly.com
W www.brunokelly.com

BUTTERCUP AGENCY T 0843 2899063
Wyndrums, The Village
Ewhurst, Surrey GU6 7PB
E info@buttercupagency.co.uk
W www.buttercupagency.co.uk

BYRON'S MANAGEMENT T 020 7242 8096
Children & Adults
41 Maiden Lane
London WC2E 7LJ
E office@byronsmanagement.co.uk
W www.byronsmanagement.co.uk

CAPITAL ARTS
CHILDREN'S CHOIR T/F 020 8449 2342
Capital Arts Studio, Wyllyotts Theatre
Darkes Lane, Potters Bar
Herts EN6 2HN
T 07855 232414
E capitalarts@btconnect.com
W www.capitalarts.org.uk

CAPITAL ARTS
THEATRICAL AGENCY T/F 020 8449 2342
Capital Arts Studio, Wyllyotts Theatre
Darkes Lane, Potters Bar, Herts EN6 2HN
T 07885 232414
E capitalarts@btconnect.com
W www.capitalarts.org.uk

CARNEY ACADEMY TALENT T 07976 869442
Montgomery Studios, Surrey Street
Sheffield S1
E talent@carneyacademy.co.uk
W www.carneyacademy.co.uk

CARR, Norrie AGENCY T 020 7253 1771
Babies, Children & Adults
Holborn Studios, 49 Eagle Wharf Road
London N1 7ED
F 020 7253 1772
E info@norriecarr.com
W www.norriecarr.com

CAVAT SCHOOL OF
THEATRE ARTS & AGENCY T 020 7018 0536
2nd Floor, 56 Bloomsbury Street
London WC1B 3QT
E enquiries@cavatagency.co.uk
W www.cavatagency.co.uk

CHARKHAM, Esta
ASSOCIATES T 020 8741 2843
16 British Grove, Chiswick
London W4 2NL
F 020 8746 3219
E office@charkham.net
W www.charkham.net

CHEEKY MONKEY MODELS T 020 8960 6277
Unit 211, 5 Buspace Studios
Conlan Street, London W10 5AP
E dione@cheekymonkeymodels.com
W www.cheekymonkeymodels.com

CHILDSPLAY MODELS LLP T 020 8659 9860
114 Avenue Road, Beckenham
Kent BR3 4SA
F 020 8778 2672
E info@childsplaymodels.co.uk
W www.childsplaymodels.co.uk

CHILLI KIDS T 0333 666 2468
1 Badhan Court, Telford TF1 5QX
F 0333 666 2469
E info@chillikids.co.uk
W www.chillikids.co.uk

CHRYSTEL ARTS AGENCY T 01494 773336
6 Eunice Grove, Chesham
Bucks HP5 1RL
T 07799 605489
E chrystelarts@waitrose.com

CIEKABAILEY ASSOCIATES T 0161 484 5423
7 Ridge Road, Marple
Cheshire SK6 7HL
E enquiries@ciekabailey.com
W www.ciekabailey.com

CONTI, Italia AGENCY LTD T 020 7608 7500
Italia Conti House, 23 Goswell Road
London EC1M 7AJ
F 020 7253 1430
E agency@italiaconti.co.uk

CPA AGENCY T 01708 766444
The Studios, 219B North Street
Romford, Essex RM1 4QA
E agency@cpastudios.co.uk
W www.cpastudios.co.uk

CREATIVE KIDZ & ADULTZ T 07908 144802
235 Fox Glove House, Fulham Road
London SW6 5PQ
T 07432 612026
E agency@creativekidzandco.co.uk
W www.creativekidzandco.co.uk

CS MANAGEMENT T 01708 708515
Children & Young Adults
35 Chase Cross Road
Romford, Essex RM5 3PJ
T 07818 050424
E linda@csmanagementuk.com
W www.csmanagementuk.com

CUPCAKE MANAGEMENT T 07583 295898
8 South Drive, Wokingham
Berkshire RG40 2DH
E cupcake_management@yahoo.co.uk

CURTAIN UP T 07974 014490
1 James Close, Holcombe
Radstock, Somerset BA3 5HA
E admin@curtainup.org.uk
W www.curtainup.org.uk

D & B MANAGEMENT T 020 8698 8880
Central Studios, 470 Bromley Road
Bromley, Kent BR1 4PQ
E bonnie@dandbmanagement.com
W www.dandbperformingarts.co.uk

DAISY & DUKES LTD T 01707 377547
30 Great North Road, Stanborough
Herts AL8 7TJ
T 07739 380684
E michelle@daisyanddukes.com
W www.daisyanddukes.com

**⊜d&b
management**

*representing children and young
adults aged 4 - 21 yrs since 1988*

call us
020 8698 8880

email us
bonnie@dandbmanagement.com

visit us
Central Studios, Bromley Road,
Bromley, Kent BR1

Website
www.dandbperformingarts.co.uk

intelligent

directable

natural

character-full

experienced

confident

*We are able to organise workshops and
castings in our studios at short notice.*

DALE HAMMOND ASSOCIATES (DHA)   T 07581 034153
Pixmore Business Centre, Pixmore Avenue
Letchworth, Hertfordshire SG6 1JG
E dalehammondassociates@yahoo.com
W www.dalehammondassociates.com

DD'S CASTING AGENCY   T 020 8502 6866
6 Acle Close, Hainault
Essex IG6 2GQ
T 07957 398501
E ddscasting@ddtst.com
W www.ddtst.com

DEVINE ARTIST MANAGEMENT   T 020 8865 1955
Contact: By e-mail only
145-157 St John Street
London EC1V 4PW
E mail@devinemanagement.co.uk
W www.devinemanagement.co.uk

DEVINE ARTIST MANAGEMENT   T 0161 726 5726
Tempus Building, 9 Mirabel Street
Manchester M3 1NP
E manchester@devinemanagement.co.uk
W www.devinemanagement.co.uk

DODD, Emma SCHOOL OF PERFORMING ARTS THE   T 01473 226422
6-18 yrs
46 Hervey Street, Ipswich
Suffolk IP4 2ET
E emma@emmadodd.com
W www.emmadodd.com

DRAGON DRAMA   T 07590 452436
Improvisational Drama for Children
347 Hanworth Road, Hampton TW12 3EJ
E askus@dragondrama.co.uk
W www.dragondrama.co.uk

DRAMA STUDIO EDINBURGH THE   T 0131 453 3284
19 Belmont Road
Edinburgh EH14 5DZ
E info@thedramastudio.com
W www.thedramastudio.com

EARACHE KIDS (VOICE OVERS)   T 020 7287 2291
177 Wardour Street
London W1F 8WX
F 020 7287 2288
E julie@earachevoices.com
W www.earachevoices.com

EARNSHAW, Susi MANAGEMENT   T 020 8441 5010
The Bull Theatre, 68 High Street
Barnet, Herts EN5 5SJ
E casting@susiearnshaw.co.uk
W www.susiearnshawmanagement.com

ELITE ACADEMY OF PERFORMING ARTS   T 07976 971178
City Studios, 4 Sandford Street
Lichfield, Staffs WS13 6QA
E elitedancing@hotmail.com

ENGLISH, Doreen '95   T 01243 825968
Contact: Gerry Kinner
48 The Boulevard, Bersted Park
Bognor Regis, West Sussex PO21 5BS

ENTER CIC   T/F 01740 655437
2 Chapel Terrace, Ferryhill
Durham DL17 8JL
E info@entercic.org
W www.entercic.org

ESSEX TALENT AGENCY   T/F 01268 812655
33 Basildon Drive, Laindon
Essex SS15 5RN
E info@essextalentagency.co.uk
W www.essextalentagency.co.uk

EUROKIDS CASTING & MODEL AGENCY   T 01925 761083
Contact: Jodie Keith (Casting Agent). Accepts
Showreels. Children & Teenagers. Commercials. Film.
Television. Walk-On. Supporting Artists
The Warehouse Studios, Glaziers Lane
Culcheth, Warrington, Cheshire WA3 4AQ
T 01925 761210
E jodie@eka-agency.com
W www.eka-agency.com

EXPRESSIONS CASTING AGENCY   T 01623 424334
3 Newgate Lane, Mansfield
Nottingham NG18 2LB
E expressions-uk@btconnect.com
W www.expressionsperformingarts.co.uk

FEA MANAGEMENT (FERRIS ENTERTAINMENT)   T 07801 493133
London. Belfast. Cardiff. Los Angeles. France. Spain
Number 8
132 Charing Cross Road
London WC2H 0LA
E info@ferrisentertainment.com
W www.ferrisentertainment.tv

FILM CAST CORNWALL & SW   T 07811 253756
Falmouth, Cornwall
E enquiries@filmcastcornwall.co.uk
W www.filmcastcornwall.co.uk

FIORENTINI, Anna AGENCY   T 020 7682 3677
Islington Business Design Centre, Unit 101
52 Upper Street, London N1 0QH
T 07904 962779
E rhiannon@annafiorentini.com
W www.annafiorentini.com

FOOTSTEPS THEATRE SCHOOL CASTING AGENCY   T 07584 995309
Westfield Lane, Idle
Bradford BD10 8PY
E gwestman500@btinternet.com

FUSION MANAGEMENT   T 020 7834 6660
201A Victoria Street, London SW1W 5NE
E info@fusionmng.com
W www.fusionmng.com

FUSION STARS AGENCY THE   T 07716 371887
Contact: Laura Burrows. Television. Theatre. Modelling.
Film. Voice Overs. 3-17 yrs
Office: 'Red Cottage'
Barleylands Road
Basildon, Essex SS15 4BG
E office@fusionstarsagency.co.uk
W www.fusionstarsagency.co.uk

GALLOWAYS   T 020 7636 7770
16 Percy Street, London W1T 1DT
E info@gallowaysagency.com
W www.gallowaysagency.com

GENESIS THEATRE SCHOOL &
AGENCY T 01536 460928
88 Hempland Close
Great Oakley
Corby, Northants NN18 8LT
T 07745 002821
E info@saracharles.com

GLOBAL7 T/F 020 7281 7679
Kemp House, 152 City Road
London EC1V 2NX
T 07956 956652
E global7castings@gmail.com
W www.global7casting.com

GOBSTOPPERS
MANAGEMENT T 01442 269543
37 St Nicholas Mount
Hemel Hempstead
Herts HP1 2BB
T 07961 372319
E gobstoppersmanagement@hotmail.co.uk

GOLDILOCKS AGENCY T 020 8207 4694
T 07772 479226
E info@goldilocksagency.co.uk
W www.goldilocksagency.co.uk

GOLDMANS MANAGEMENT T 01323 643961
3 Cranborne Avenue
Eastbourne BN20 7TS
E casting@goldmansmanagement.co.uk
W www.goldmansmanagement.co.uk

GROUNDLINGS
MANAGEMENT T 023 9273 9496
Kemp House, 152 City Road
London EC1V 2NX
E richard@groundlings.co.uk
W www.groundlings.co.uk

HAPPY FEET MODELS LTD T 07814 239656
Broadwater House
6 London Road
Tunbridge Wells, Kent TN1 1DQ
T 07912 898692
E info@happyfeetmodels.com
W www.happyfeetmodels.com

HARLEQUIN STUDIOS DANCE &
DRAMA SCHOOL T 01273 581742
122A Phyllis Avenue, Peacehaven
East Sussex BN10 7RQ
E janice@harlequinstudios.co.uk

HARRIS AGENCY LTD T 01923 211644
71 The Avenue, Watford, Herts WD17 4NU
E theharrisagency@btconnect.com

HervL SUPPORTING
ARTISTES LTD T 01322 352766
Children (0-20 yrs). Actors. Extras. Dancers. Models.
Singers
Admiral Park, Victory Way, Crossways Business Park
Dartford, Kent DA2 6QD
E info@hervl.com
W www.hervl.co.uk

HOBSONS KIDS T 020 8995 3628
2 Dukes Gate, Chiswick, London W4 5DX
F 020 8996 5350
E gaynor@hobsons-international.com
W www.hobsons-international.com

HOXTON STREET
MANAGEMENT T 020 7503 5131
Hoxton Hall, 130 Hoxton Street
London N1 6SH
E ben@hoxtonstreetmanagement.com
W www.hoxtonstreetmanagement.com

INDEPENDENT THEATRE
WORKSHOP AGENCY T 00 353 86 8227714
3-19 yrs
8 Terminus Mills, Clonskeagh Road
Ranelagh, Dublin 6
E agency@itwstudios.ie
W www.itwstudios.ie

INSPIRATIONS SCHOOL OF PERFORMING ARTS   T 07946 352305
18 Bryanston Road, Tilbury RM18 8DD
E info@inspirationsspa.co.uk

INSPIRE ACADEMY   T 0115 988 1800
The Attic Studio, 3rd Floor
46-48 Carrington Street, Nottingham NG1 7FG
E admin@inspireacademy.co.uk
W www.inspireacademy.co.uk

INTER-CITY KIDS   T/F 01942 321969
27 Wigan Lane, Wigan
Greater Manchester WN1 1XR
E intercitycasting@btconnect.com

JABBERWOCKY AGENCY   T 01580 714306
Glassenbury Hill Farm, Glassenbury Road
Cranbrook, Kent TN17 2QF
F 01580 714346
E christina@christinayates.com
W www.yt93.co.uk

JCM MANAGEMENT   T 07866 211647
2 New Street, Bridgtown WS11 0DD
E newtalentjcm@outlook.com

JEFFREY & WHITE JUNIORS   T 01462 429769
7 Paynes Park, Hitchin
Hertfordshire SG5 1EH
E info@jeffreyandwhite.co.uk
W www.jeffreyandwhite.co.uk

JERMIN, Mark MANAGEMENT   T 01792 458855
Swansea Metropolitan
University of Wales, Trinity Saint David
Mount Pleasant, Swansea SA1 6ED
E info@markjermin.co.uk
W www.markjermin.co.uk

JIGSAW ARTS MANAGEMENT   T 020 8447 4530
*Representing Children & Young People from Jigsaw
Performing Arts Schools*
64-66 High Street, Barnet
Herts EN5 5SJ
E enquiries@jigsaw-arts.co.uk
W www.jigsaw-arts.co.uk

JM MANAGEMENT   T 07943 347944
Contact: Julia Dickinson, Mark Flitton
44 Redcliffe Street, Swindon
Wiltshire SN2 2BZ
E syactors@gmail.com
W www.swindonyoungactors.com

JOHNSTON & MATHERS MANAGEMENT   T 020 8449 4968
PO Box 3167, Barnet
Herts EN5 2WA
E johnstonmathers@aol.com
W www.johnstonandmathers.com

JPA   T 01494 520978
30 Daws Hill Lane
High Wycombe
Bucks HP11 1PW
E jackie.palmer@btinternet.com
W www.jackiepalmeragency.co.uk

K KIDS   T 020 7379 1616
0-16 yrs. Commercials. Film. Stage
4th Floor, 43 Aldwych
London WC2B 4DN
T 07961 572899
E mail@ktalent.co.uk
W www.ktalent.co.uk

KELLY, Robert ASSOCIATES (RKA)   T 020 7287 6934
10 Greek Street
London W1D 4DH
E youth@rkatalent.com
W www.rkatalent.com

KIDS @ JFA THE   T 01628 771084
E agent@thekidsatjuliefoxassociates.co.uk
W www.thekidsatjuliefoxassociates.co.uk

KIDS LONDON   T 020 7924 9595
67 Dulwich Road, London SE24 0NJ
F 020 7501 8711
E info@kidslondonltd.com
W www.kidslondonltd.com

KIDS MANAGEMENT   T 01444 401595
Studio 35 Truggers, Handcross
Haywards Heath
West Sussex RH17 6DQ
T 07966 382766
E info@kidsmanagement.co.uk
W www.kidsmanagement.co.uk

KIDS PLUS   T 07799 791586
Malcolm House
Harris Primary Academy Crystal Palace
Malcolm Road, Penge
London SE20 8RH
E geraldi.gillma@btconnect.com
W www.kidsplusagency.co.uk

KIDZ 2 DAY   T 01708 747581
74 Western Road
Romford, Essex RM1 3LP
E kim@kidz2day.co.uk
W www.kidz2day.co.uk

KIDZ LTD   T 0871 2180884
7 Ellerbeck Crescent, Worsley
Manchester M28 7XN
F 0871 2180843
E info@kidzltd.com
W www.kidzltd.com

KIDZ ON THE HILL PERFORMING ARTS SCHOOL   T 07881 553480
Classes in Muswell Hill, London
E admin@kidzonthehill.co.uk
W www.kidzonthehill.co.uk

KOOLKIDZ THEATRICAL AGENCY LTD T 07581 232615
Based in West Cornwall
St Johns Hall, Alverton Street
Penzance, Cornwall TR18 2SP
T 07580 596580
E kool-kidz@sky.com
W www.koolkidztheatricalagency.co.uk

KOSKA, Ann AGENCY T 01753 785031
Room 9, Small Process Building
Pinewood Studios
Pinewood Road
Iver Heath, Bucks SL0 0NH
E askpinewood@mac.com
W www.annkoskaagency.com

KRACKERS KIDS THEATRICAL AGENCY T/F 01708 502046
6-7 Electric Parade
Seven Kings Road
Ilford, Essex IG3 8BY
E krackerskids@hotmail.com
W www.krackerskids.co.uk

KREATIVE TALENT AGENCY T 020 8133 0687
Kreative House, 11 Whernside
Ingleby, Cleveland TS17 0QF
T 07772 298789
E sue.francis@kreativetalent.tv
W www.kreativetalent.tv

KYT AGENCY T 01227 730177
Mulberry Croft, Mulberry Hill
Chilham CT4 8AJ
T 07967 580213
E agency@kentyouththeatre.co.uk
W www.kentyouththeatre.co.uk

L.A. MINI MANAGEMENT T 07852 186411
Contact: Amanda Marsh
Nimax House
20 Ullswater Crescent
Coulsdon CR5 2HR
E amanda@lamanagement.biz
W www.lamanagement.biz

LAMONT CASTING AGENCY T 07736 387543
2 Harewood Avenue
Ainsdale
Merseyside PR8 2PH
E diane@lamontcasting.co.uk
W www.lamontcasting.co.uk

LESLIE, Sasha MANAGEMENT T/F 020 8969 3249
In association with ALLSORTS DRAMA FOR CHILDREN
34 Crediton Road, London NW10 3DU
E sasha@allsortsdrama.com

LINTON MANAGEMENT T 0161 761 2020
3 The Rock, Bury BL9 0JP
E carol@linton.tv

LITTLE ADULTS ACADEMY & MODELLING AGENCY LTD T 020 3130 0798
44 Broadway, Stratford, London E15 1XH
E info@littleadults.demon.co.uk
W www.littleadultsagency.co.uk

LITTLE ALLSTARS CASTING &
MODELLING AGENCY   T 0161 702 8257
Representing Babies, Children & Teenagers UK Wide for
Television, Film, Modelling, Stage, Corporate & Role Play
23 Falconwood Chase, Worsley
Manchester M28 1FG
T 07584 992429
E casting@littleallstars.co.uk
W www.littleallstars.co.uk

LIVING THE DREAM
TALENT AGENCY   T 01727 751613
145-147 St John Street, London EC1V 4PW
T 07845 207501
E agency@livingthedreamcompany.co.uk
W www.livingthedreamcompany.co.uk

LUCIA VICTORIA AGENCY
MANAGEMENT LTD   T 01254 207575
Children & Young Performers Casting Agency
22 Highland Drive, Chorley
Lancashire PR7 7AD
E casting@lvagencymanagement.co.uk
W www.lvagencymanagement.co.uk

MAD FISH MANAGEMENT   T 07545 052088
1 Wellington Place, 3-15 Terminus Road
Bexhill On Sea, East Sussex TN39 3LR
T 07957 446612
E madfishmanagement@hotmail.com
W www.madfishmadfish.co.uk

MARMALADE MANAGEMENT   T 01628 483808
Jam Theatre Studios, Archway Court
45A West Street, Marlow
Buckinghamshire SL7 2LS
E info@marmalademanagement.co.uk
W www.marmalademanagement.co.uk

McDONAGH, Melanie MANAGEMENT
(ACADEMY OF PERFORMING
ARTS & CASTING AGENCY)   T 07909 831409
14 Apple Tree Way, Oswaldtwistle
Accrington, Lancashire BB5 0FB
T 01254 392560
E mcdonaghmgt@aol.com
W www.mcdonaghmanagement.co.uk

MGA MANAGEMENT &
CASTING   T 07595 711159
207 Balgreen Road
Edinburgh EH11 2RZ
E admin@mgamanagement.com
W www.mgamanagement.com

MIDDLEWEEK NEWTON
TALENT MANAGEMENT   T 020 3394 0079
95A Rivington Street, London EC2A 3AY
E agents@mntalent.co.uk
W www.mntalent.co.uk

MIM AGENCY   T 0871 2377963
Clayton House, 59 Piccadilly
Manchester M1 2AQ
E info@mimagency.co.uk
W www.mimagency.co.uk

MINI MILLS @ WAM!   T 07900 735566
7 Richmond Close, Princes Gate
Bishops Stortford
Hertfordshire CM23 4PG
T 07512 998007
E info@windmillartistsmanagement.co.uk
W www.windmillartistsmanagement.co.uk

MONDI ASSOCIATES LTD   T 07817 133349
Contact: Michelle Sykes
Unit 3 O, Cooper House
2 Michael Road
London SW6 2AD
E info@mondiassociates.com
W www.mondiassociates.com

NFD AGENCY   T 01977 681949
The Studio, 21 Low Street
South Milford LS25 5AR
E alyson@northernfilmanddrama.com
W www.northernfilmanddrama.com

NG PERSONAL MANAGEMENT   T 07810 138535
14 Leafields
Houghton Regis
Dunstable, Bedfordshire LU5 5LX
E info@ngpersonalmanagement.co.uk
W www.ngpersonalmanagement.co.uk

NOTTINGHAM ACTORS
STUDIO LTD THE   T 0115 860 2179
The Nottingham Actors Studio
Lower Ground Floor
1 Kayes Walk, The Lace Market
Nottingham NG1 1PY
E office@ramayoungactors.co.uk
W www.ramayoungactors.co.uk

O'FARRELL STAGE &
THEATRE SCHOOL   T 020 7474 6466
Babies, Children, Teenagers & Young Adults
36 Shirley Street
Canning Town
London E16 1HU
T 07956 941497
E linda@ofarrells.wanadoo.co.uk

ORA CASTING   T 0151 528 7905
12 Burnham Road, Liverpool
Merseyside L18 6JU
E info@oracasting.com
W www.oracasting.com

ORGANIC KIDZ
TALENT AGENCY   T 020 8449 4968
Boutique Agency. 4-18 yrs
c/o JAM, PO Box 3167
Barnet EN5 2WA
E organickidzagent@aol.com
W www.organickidzagency.co.uk

PACE THEATRE COMPANY   T 0141 8487471
Spires Studios, School Wynd
Paisley, Renfrewshire PA1 2DA
F 0141 8426300
E linsey@pacetheatre.co.uk

PC THEATRICAL, MODEL &
CASTING AGENCY   T 020 8381 2229
10 Strathmore Gardens
Edgware
Middlesex HA8 5HJ
F 020 8933 3418
E twinagy@aol.com
W www.twinagency.com

PD MANAGEMENT   T 020 7794 0905
17 The Heights
Frognal
London NW3 6XS
E pdmanagement1@gmail.com
W www.pdmanagement.org

Mark Jermin
★ ★ ★ Management

www.markjermin.co.uk
Children and young adults from all over the UK

Audition workshops and classes in London, Manchester, Bristol and Wales.
Children with open performance licences, guaranteed to be licensed for any production and at very short notice.
Swansea Metropolitan University of Wales, Trinity Saint David, Mount Pleasant, Swansea SA1 6ED
Phone: 01792 458855   Fax: 01792 458844   Email: info@markjermin.co.uk

PERFORMANCE HOUSE THE   T 07785 614901
Wales-based Agency in conjunction with TPH
Youth Theatre
South Wales, Bridgend CF36
E theperformancehouse@hotmail.co.uk
W www.theperformancehouse.co.uk

PHA YOUTH   T 0161 273 4444
Tanzaro House, Ardwick Green North
Manchester M12 6FZ
F 0161 273 4567
E youth@pha-agency.co.uk
W www.pha-agency.co.uk

PLATFORM TALENT
MANAGEMENT LTD   T 01276 23256
16 Shalbourne Rise, Camberley
Surrey GU15 2EJ
T 07899 080541
E maria@ptmagency.co.uk
W www.ptmagency.co.uk

POLLYANNA
MANAGEMENT LTD   T 020 7481 1911
Raine House, Raine Street
Wapping E1W 3RL
M 07801 884837
E pollyannamanagement@gmail.com
W www.pollyannatheatre.org

PROKIDS MANAGEMENT   T 0151 336 7382
Based in the North West & London
32 Springcroft, Parkgate
Neston, Cheshire CH64 6SE
E mail@prokidsmanagement.co.uk
W www.prokidsmanagement.co.uk

PWASSOCIATES   T 01296 427354
7 Catherine Cottages
Calvert Road
Middle Claydon, Bucks MK18 2HA
E agency@pwacademy.com
W www.pwacademy.com

QUIRKY KIDZ CREATIVE
MANAGEMENT   T 01494 415196
Custodia House
Queensmead Road
Loudwater, High Wycombe
Buckinghamshire HP10 9XA
E hello@quirkykidz.co.uk
W www.quirkykidz.co.uk

RASCALS MODEL AGENCY   T 020 8504 1111
77-79 Station Road, Chingford
London E4 7BU
E kids@rascals.co.uk
W www.rascals.co.uk

RBAPA Agency   T 01189 868985
43 Upper Redlands Road, Reading
Berkshire RG1 5JE
E mail@rbapaagency.com
W www.rbapaagency.co.uk

RDDC MANAGEMENT AGENCY   T 01706 211161
52 Bridleway, Waterfoot
Rossendale, Lancashire BB4 9DS
T 07811 239780
E info@rddc.co.uk
W www.rddc.co.uk

REACT KIDS AGENCY   T 01926 710001
83 Dudley Road, Kenilworth
Warwickshire CV8 1GR
T 07900 921779
E admin@reactkidsagency.co.uk
W www.reactkidsagency.co.uk

REACT MANAGEMENT   T 01254 883692
c/o The Civic Arts Centre, Union Road
Oswaldtwistle, Lancashire BB5 3HZ
E management@reactacademy.co.uk
W www.reactacademy.co.uk

REBEL SCHOOL OF THEATRE
ARTS & CASTING AGENCY LTD   T 01484 603736
Based in Leeds & Huddersfield
PO Box 169, Huddersfield HD8 1BE
T 07808 803637
E sue@rebelschool.co.uk
W www.rebelschool.co.uk

RED 24 MANAGEMENT   T 020 7559 3611
1st Floor, Kingsway House
103 Kingsway, London WC2B 6QX
E louise@red24management.com
W www.red24managment.com

REDROOFS THEATRE
SCHOOL AGENCY   T 01628 674092
26 Bath Road, Maidenhead, Berks SL6 4JT
T 07531 355835 (Holiday Times)
E sam@redroofs.co.uk
W www.redroofs.co.uk

alphabetkidz

TV/Film, Commercial, Photographic, Theatre and Voiceovers
Naturally talented Artists with a multitude of different skills and talents for all your casting needs.
Our philosophy is Fun, Energy, Enthusiasm, Commitment, Equality and Diversity.

t :   020 7252 4343 f: 020 7252 4341
e :   contact@alphabetkidz.co.uk
w: www.alphabetkidz.co.uk

BAFTA AWARD WINNING AGENCY   **alphabetmanagement** | **alphabetagency**

RHODES AGENCY   T 01708 747013
5 Dymoke Road, Hornchurch
Essex RM11 1AA
F 01708 730431
E rhodesarts@hotmail.com

**RIDGEWAY STUDIOS
MANAGEMENT**   T 01992 633775
Office: 106 Hawkshead Road, Potters Bar
Hertfordshire EN6 1NG
E info@ridgewaystudios.co.uk
W www.ridgewaystudios.co.uk

**RISING STARS
PERFORMANCE AGENCY**   T 07709 429354
53 Hurlingham Road, Bexleyheath
Kent DA7 5PE
T 07958 617976
E risingstars_agency@yahoo.co.uk

ROMY LEE MANAGEMENT   T 01704 551877
44 Wayfarers Arcade, Lord Street
Southport, Merseyside PR8 1NT
E info@romyleemanagement.co.uk
W www.romyleemanagement.co.uk

**ROSS, David ACTING
ACADEMY THE**   T 07957 862317
8 Farrier Close, Sale
Cheshire M33 2ZL
E info@davidrossacting.com
W www.davidrossacting.com

ROYCE MANAGEMENT   T 020 8650 1096
121 Merlin Grove, Beckenham
Kent BR3 3HS
E office@roycemanagement.co.uk
W www.roycemanagement.co.uk

RS MANAGEMENT   T 020 8257 6477
186 Waltham Way, London E4 8AZ
E info@rsmagency.co.uk
W www.rsmagency.co.uk

SCALA KIDS CASTING   T 0113 250 6823
42 Rufford Avenue, Yeadon
Leeds LS19 7QR
E office@scalakids.com
W www.scalakids.com

SCALLYWAGS AGENCY LTD   T 020 7739 8820
12-18 Hoxton Street, London N1 6NG
E info@scallywags.co.uk
W www.scallywags.co.uk

SCENE II THEATRICAL AGENCY   T 01371 878020
The Arts Centre, 1 Haslers Lane
Great Dunmow, Essex CM6 1XS
E sceneiiagency@aol.com
W www.sceneii.net

SCHOOL CASTING   T 01325 463383
Liddiard Theatre, Polam Hall, Grange Road
Darlington, Durham DL1 5PA
F 01325 383539
E information@polamhall.com
W www.polamhall.com

SCREAM MANAGEMENT LTD   T 0161 850 1996
The Greenhouse, MediaCityUK
Salford, Manchester M50 2EQ
T 0161 850 1994
E info@screammanagement.com
W www.screammanagement.com

SELECT MANAGEMENT   T 07700 059089
*Actors. Models. Presenters. Dancers. Children.
Teenagers & Adults*
PO Box 748, London NW4 1TT
T 07956 131494
E mail@selectmanagement.info
W www.selectmanagement.info

SEVEN AGENCY   T 01785 212266
Tudor House, 9 Eastgate Street
Stafford ST16 2NQ
E info@7casting.co.uk
W www.7casting.co.uk

SEVEN AGENCY   T 0161 850 1057
82 King Street, Manchester M2 4WQ
E info@7casting.co.uk
W www.7casting.co.uk

SHACK ATTACK   T 07974 235955
1 The Withies, Leatherhead
Surrey KT22 7EY
E lucy@danceshack.co.uk

SHARPE ACADEMY   T 01923 437693
*Based in North West London. Representing Children
3-16 yrs & Adults*
Cardinal Point, Park Road
Rickmansworth, Hertfordshire WD3 1RE
T 07500 569024
E agency@sharpeacademy.co.uk
W www.sharpeacademy.co.uk

SHINE MANAGEMENT   T 07880 721689
Flat 10, Valentine House, Church Road
Guildford, Surrey GU1 4NG
E enquiries@shinemanagement.net
W www.shinemanagement.net

SHOWDOWN THEATRE ARTS   T 01483 893688
*Part-time Theatre School & Agency for Children, Young
Performers & Professional Adults*
16 Garden Close, Shamley Green
Guildford, Surrey GU5 0UW
E info@showdowntheatrearts.co.uk
W www.showdowntheatrearts.co.uk

SINGER, Sandra ASSOCIATES   T 01702 331616
21 Cotswold Road, Westcliff-on-Sea
Essex SS0 8AA
T 07795 144143
E sandrasingeruk@aol.com
W www.sandrasinger.com

SMARTYPANTS AGENCY   T 01277 633772
San-Marie Studios, Southend Road
Billericay CM11 2PZ
T 01277 633712
E office@smartypantsagency.co.uk
W www.smartypantsagency.co.uk

SMITH, Elisabeth LTD   T 0845 8721331
8 Dawes Lane, Sarratt
Rickmansworth, Herts WD3 6BB
E models@elisabethsmith.co.uk
W www.elisabethsmith.co.uk

**SNA / THRESHOLD
THEATRE ARTS**   T 020 7125 0468
3rd Floor, International House
1-6 Yarmouth Place, London W1J 7BU
T 07904 671877
E steve@stevenealonassociates.co.uk

SPEAKE, Barbara AGENCY T 020 8743 6096
East Acton Lane, London W3 7EG
E speakekids2@aol.com
W www.barbaraspeake.com

SRA AGENCY T 01932 863194
Lockhart Road, Cobham
Surrey KT11 2AX
E agency@susanrobertsacademy.co.uk

STAGE A MANAGEMENT LTD T 07837 072775
*Represents Centre Stage Academy & Academy of
Performance Training Students & Selected Adult Artists*
9 Beech Grove, Midhurst
West Sussex GU29 9JA
E stageamanagement@gmail.com
W www.csa-theatreschool.co.uk

STAGE KIDS AGENCY T 01707 328359
Children, Teenagers & Adults
1 Greenfield, Welwyn Garden City
Herts AL8 7HW
E stagekds@aol.com
W www.stagekids.co.uk

**STAGE 84 PERFORMING
ARTS LTD** T 01274 5611984
The Old Fire Station
29A Town Lane, Idle
Bradford, West Yorkshire BD10 8NT
E info@stage84.com

STAGECOACH AGENCY.ie T 0845 4082468
Suite 2, 1st Floor Offices, Cantilupe Chambers
Cantilupe Road, Ross-on-Wye HR9 7AN
F 0845 4082464
E tarquin@stagecoachagency.co.uk
W www.stagecoachagency.ie

**STAGECOACH AGENCY
UK & IRELAND** T 0845 4082468
Suite 2, 1st Floor Offices, Cantilupe Chambers
Cantilupe Road, Ross-on-Wye HR9 7AN
F 0845 4082464
E tarquin@stagecoachagency.co.uk
W www.stagecoachagency.co.uk

**STAGE ONE KIDS THEATRE SCHOOL &
AGENCY** T/F 01992 651222
32 Westbury Lane, Buckhurst Hill
Essex IG9 5PL
E stageone@btinternet.com
W www.stageonekids.co.uk

Elisabeth Smith

Representing children
for over 50 years

• Babies • Children
• Teenagers • Families

T: 0845 872 1331
e: info@elisabethsmith.co.uk
www.elisabethsmith.co.uk

**STAGEWORKS PERFORMING
ARTS SCHOOL** T 07956 176166
The Stablehouse Barn, Remenham Hill
Henley on Thames, Oxon RG9 3HN
E emma_taylor@sky.com
W www.stageworks.org.uk

**STARDOM CASTING AGENCY &
THEATRE SCHOOL** T 07740 091019
15 Gordon Street, Sutton in Craven BD20 7EU
E liz.stardom@btinternet.com
W www.stardom.org.uk

STARMAKER T 0118 988 7959
17 Kendal Avenue, Shinfield
Reading, Berks RG2 9AR
E dave@starmakeruk.org
W www.starmakeruk.org

STARSTRUCK TALENT LTD T 01706 747334
In association with Starstruck Theatre School
1 & 2 St Chads Court, School Lane
Rochdale OL16 1QU
E lisa@starstrucktalent.co.uk
W www.starstrucktalent.co.uk

**STEP ON STAGE
MANAGEMENT** T 07973 900196
5 Poulett Gardens, Twickenham
Middlesex TW1 4QS
E info@steponstagemanagement.co.uk
W www.steponstagemanagement.co.uk

STOMP! MANAGEMENT   T 020 8446 9898
62 Sellwood Drive, Barnet
Herts EN5 2RL
E stompmanagement@aol.com
W www.stompmanagement.com

STUDIO 74 LTD   T 020 8295 4256
The Hall, St Augustines Avenue
Bromley, Kent BR2 8AG
E info@studio74agency.co.uk
W www.studio74dance.co.uk

SUPERARTS AGENCY   T 07721 927714
26/28 Ambergate Street
London SE17 3RX
F 020 7735 4975
E superarts@btinternet.com
W www.superartsagency.com

TAKE2 CASTING AGENCY &
TALENT MANAGEMENT   T 00 353 87 2563403
28 Beech Park Road, Foxrock
Dublin 18, Ireland
E pamela@take2.ie
W www.take2.ie

TAKE2 MANAGEMENT   T 0161 832 7715
Suite 5, Basil Chambers
65 High Street
Manchester M4 1FS
F 0161 839 1661
E lois@take2management.co.uk
W www.take2management.co.uk

TAKE2 MANAGEMENT   T 0113 403 2930
34 Park Cross Street, Leeds LS1 2QH
E chris@take2management.co.uk
W www.take2management.co.uk

TAKE ONE AGENCY   T 07517 313710
Representing Children in Theatre, Television, Film.
Workshops for 5+ yrs
17 Elm Tree Walk, Tring HP23 5EB
E info@takeoneagency.com
W www.takeoneagency.com

TALENTED KIDS PERFORMING ARTS SCHOOL
& AGENCY   T/F 00 353 45 485464
23 Burrow Manor, Calverstown
Kilcullen, Co. Kildare, Ireland
T 00 353 87 2480348
E talentedkids@hotmail.com
W www.talentedkidsireland.com

TANWOOD THEATRICAL
AGENCY   T 07775 991700
Liberatus Studios, Isis Estate
Stratton Road, Swindon SN1 2PG
E tanwood@tiscali.co.uk
W www.tanwood.co.uk

TELEVISION WORKSHOP THE   T 0115 845 0764
Nottingham Group
30 Main Street, Calverton, Notts NG14 6FQ
E ian@thetelevisionworkshop.co.uk

THIS IS YOUTH   T 07956 838843
Children, Teenagers & Young Adults
194B Addington Road, Selsdon
Croydon CR2 8LD
E hello@thisisyouth.com
W www.thisisyouth.com

TICKLEDOM AGENCY   T 020 8341 7044
31 Rectory Gardens
London N8 7PJ
T 07947 139414
E agency@tickledomtheatreschool.com
W www.tickledomtheatreschool.com/agency.html

TIFFIN MANAGEMENT   T 07568 566211
In association with MTPAS
High Street, Stony Stratford
Milton Keynes MK11 7AE
E agency@mtpas.co.uk
W www.tiffin-management.co.uk

TK MANAGEMENT   T 07910 139326
Spires Meade, 4 Bridleways
Wendover, Bucks HP22 6DN
F 01296 623696
E tkpamanagement@aol.com

TOMORROW'S TALENT
AGENCY   T 01245 690080
Contact: By e-mail only
Based in Chelmsford, Essex
E agents@tomorrowstalent.co.uk
W www.tomorrowstalent.co.uk

TOP TALENT AGENCY LTD   T 01727 855903
Representing Child Actors & Models from Babies to
Teenagers
PO Box 860, St Albans
Herts AL1 9BR
F 01727 812666
E admin@toptalentagency.co.uk
W www.toptalentagency.co.uk

TOTS 'N' DARLINGS AGENCY   T 020 7118 2728
Bizzy Studios, 1st Floor Hall
10-12 Pickford Lane
Bexleyheath, Kent DA7 4QW
F 0845 5200401
E agency@totsndarlings.com
W www.totsndarlings.com

TRUE STARS ACADEMY   T 020 7619 9166
6-16 yrs
180 Piccadilly, London W1J 9HF
E queries@truestarsacademy.com
W uk.truestarsacademy.com

TRULY SCRUMPTIOUS LTD   T 020 8888 4204
66 Bidwell Gardens
London N11 2AU
F 020 8888 4584
E bookings@trulyscrumptious.co.uk
W www.trulyscrumptious.co.uk

TUESDAYS CHILD LTD   T/F 01625 501765
Children, Teenagers & Adults
Oakfield House
Springwood Way
Macclesfield SK10 2XA
E admin@tuesdayschildagency.co.uk
W www.tuesdayschildagency.co.uk

TV TALENT   T 07886 825843
36 Armitage Close, Middleton
Manchester, Lancashire M24 4PA
E agency@tvtalentmanagement.co.uk
W www.tvtalentmanagement.co.uk

TWINS
See PC THEATRICAL, MODEL & CASTING AGENCY

London and Hertfordshire based
Representing Children, Teenagers and Professionals in
TV, Film, Photographic and Theatre Work
01727 751613 // AGENCY@LIVINGTHEDREAMCOMPANY.CO.UK
WWW.LIVINGTHEDREAMCOMPANY.CO.UK

URBAN ANGELS T 0845 8387773
PO Box 45453
London SE26 6UZ
F 0845 8387774
E south@urbanangelsagency.com

URBAN ANGELS NORTH T 0845 5191990
Contact: Alysia Lewis
F 0845 8387774
E north@urbanangelsagency.com
W www.urbanangelsagency.com

**VALLÉ THEATRICAL
AGENCY THE** T 01992 622861
The Vallé Academy Studios
Wilton House
Delamare Road
Cheshunt, Herts EN8 9SG
F 01992 622868
E agency@valleacademy.co.uk
W www.valleacademy.co.uk

**VAM (VAN RENSBURG ARTIST
MANAGEMENT)** T 01875 852477
In association with Little Shakespeare Theatre School
34 Campbell Road
Longniddry
East Lothian EH32 0NP
E michelle@vanartman.co.uk
W www.vanartman.co.uk

VISIONS AGENCY T 07857 237806
The Studio
39A Foxbury Road
Bromley, Kent BR1 4DG
E admin@visionsagency.co.uk
W www.visionsagency.co.uk

WE ARE CHARACTERS LTD T 07824 444765
24 Deniston Road
Heaton Moor
Stockport, Cheshire SK4 4RF
E admin@wearecharacters.co.uk
W www.wearecharacters.co.uk

WILLIAMSON & HOLMES T 020 7240 0407
Twitter: @WilliamsonHolme
4th Floor, 11 Maiden Lane
London WC2E 7NA
E carolyn@williamsonandholmes.co.uk
W www.williamsonandholmes.co.uk

WINGS AGENCY T 01483 428998
4 The Chestnut Suite
Guardian House
Borough, Godalming, Surrey GU7 2AE
T 07745 443448
E wingsagency@gmail.com
W www.wingsmanagement.co.uk

WYSE AGENCY T 01223 832288
Hill House, 1 Hill Farm Road
Whittlesford, Cambs CB22 4NB
E frances.wyse@btinternet.com

**YAT MANAGEMENT (YOUNG ACTORS
THEATRE MANAGEMENT)** T 020 7278 2101
70-72 Barnsbury Road, London N1 0ES
E agent@yati.org.uk
W www.yati.org.uk

YOUNG, Sylvia AGENCY T 020 7723 0037
Sylvia Young Theatre School, 1 Nutford Place
London W1H 5YZ
T 07779 145732
E info@sylviayoungagency.com

**YOUNG ACTORS COMPANY
LTD THE** T 07450 033628
3 Marshall Road, Cambridge CB1 7TY
E info@theyoungactorscompany.com
W www.theyoungactorscompany.com

**YOUNGBLOOD THEATRE
COMPANY** T 07870 661243
c/o The BWH Agency Ltd, 35 Soho Square
London W1D 3QX
E ybtc2000@aol.com

**YOUNGSTARS THEATRE
SCHOOL & AGENCY** T 07966 176756
Contact: Coralyn Canfor-Dumas. 4-18 yrs
4 Haydon Dell, Bushey
Herts WD23 1DD
E youngstarsagency@gmail.com
W www.youngstarsagency.co.uk

**ZADEK NOWELL
MANAGEMENT** T 07957 144948
398 Long Lane, London N2 8JX
T 07841 753728
E zadeknowell@gmail.com
W www.zadeknowell.co.uk

REPRESENTING THE BEST JUNIOR TALENT IN THE NORTHWEST, WITH OFFICES IN MANCHESTER & LEEDS

**CASTING DIRECTOR CHRIS MALONEY; FORMERLY OF BEVERLEY KEOGH CASTING, HEADS UP THE TEAM
TO PROVIDE SUPPORT, ADVICE & DIRECTION TO OUR ALREADY TALENTED YOUNG ARTISTS**

TAKE 2 MANAGEMENT

0161 832 7715 0113 403 2930 SUITE 5, BASIL CHAMBERS, 65 HIGH STREET, MANCHESTER M4 1FS
NUMBER 34, PARK CROSS STREET, LEEDS, WEST YORKS LS12 0H
W:WWW.TAKE2MANAGEMENT.CO.UK E:CHRIS@TAKE2MANAGEMENT.CO.UK

ACORN ENTERTAINMENTS LTD T 01285 644622
PO Box 64, Cirencester
Glos GL7 5YD
F 01285 642291
E info@acornents.co.uk
W www.acornents.co.uk

**ARTIST PROMOTION
MANAGEMENT** T 020 7224 1992
113 Great Portland Street, London W1W 6QQ
F 020 7224 0111
E info@harveygoldsmith.com
W www.harveygoldsmith.com

ASKONAS HOLT LTD T 020 7400 1700
Classical Music
Lincoln House, 300 High Holborn
London WC1V 7JH
F 020 7400 1799
E info@askonasholt.co.uk
W www.askonasholt.co.uk

AVALON PROMOTIONS LTD T 020 7598 7333
4A Exmoor Street
London W10 6BD
F 020 7598 7300
E promotions@avalonuk.com
W www.avalonuk.com

**BLOCK, Derek CONCERT
PROMOTIONS** T 020 7724 2101
2D, 4-6 Canfield Place
London NW6 3BT
F 020 7624 1117
E dbcp@derekblock.co.uk

FLYING MUSIC T 020 7221 7799
FM House, 110 Clarendon Road
London W11 2HR
F 020 7221 5016
E info@flyingmusic.co.uk
W www.flyingmusic.com

GUBBAY, Raymond LTD T 020 7025 3750
Dickens House, 15 Tooks Court
London EC4A 1LB
F 020 7025 3751
E info@raymondgubbay.co.uk
W www.raymondgubbay.co.uk

HOBBS, Liz GROUP LTD T 0870 0702702
65 London Road, Newark
Nottinghamshire NG24 1RZ
E info@lizhobbsgroup.com
W www.lizhobbsgroup.com

HOCHHAUSER, Victor T 020 7794 0987
4 Oak Hill Way, London NW3 7LR
F 020 7431 2531
E admin@victorhochhauser.co.uk
W www.victorhochhauser.co.uk

IMG ARTS & ENTERTAINMENT T 020 8233 5300
McCormack House, Burlington Lane
London W4 2TH
F 020 8233 5301
E concerts@imgworld.com
W www.imgworld.com

**McINTYRE, Phil
ENTERTAINMENTS LTD** T 020 7291 9000
3rd Floor, 85 Newman Street
London W1T 3EU
F 020 7291 9001
E info@mcintyre-ents.com
W www.mcintyre-ents.com

RBM COMEDY T 020 7630 7733
3rd Floor, 1 Lower Grosvenor Place
London SW1W 0EJ
E info@rbmcomedy.com
W www.rbmcomedy.com

**ROSENTHAL, Suzanna &
MEADOW, Jeremy** T 020 7436 2244
Something for the Weekend
26 Goodge Street, London W1T 2QG
F 0870 7627882
E admin@sftw.info
W www.sftw.info

**STAGE LEISURE SERVICES &
PROMOTIONS** T 01482 853555
*Specialising in Tribute Shows, Corporate Events, Speakers
& Personal Appearances. Celebrity Occasions & Events*
25 St. Anthonys Close, Kingston-Upon-Hull
East Yorkshire HU6 7FE
E sls.promotions@gmx.co.uk
W www.anightwiththestars.co.uk

Dance Agents

Why do I need a dance agent?

As with any other agent, a dance agent will submit their clients for jobs, negotiate contracts, handle paperwork and offer advice. In return for these services they will charge commission ranging from 10-15%. The agents listed in this section specialise in representing and promoting dancers. They will possess the relevant contacts in the industry that you need to get auditions and jobs.

How should I use these listings?

If you are a dancer getting started in the industry, looking to change your existing agent, or wishing to take on an additional agent that represents you for dance alongside your main acting agent, the following listings will supply you with up-to-date contact details for dance agencies. Every company listed is done so by written request to us. Please see the main 'Agents and Personal Managers' advice section for further guidance on choosing and approaching agents.

Should I pay an agent to join their books? Or sign a contract?

Equity (the actors' trade union) does not recommend that artists pay an agent to join their client list. Before signing a contract, you should be very clear about the terms and commitments involved. For advice on both of these issues, or if you experience any problems with a current agent, we recommend that you contact Equity www.equity.org.uk. They also produce the booklet *You and your Agent* which is free to all Equity members and available from their website's members' area.

Where can I find more information?

Please refer to our dance agent case study in this section and the information and advice pages in the 'Dance Companies' listings for further information about the dance industry.

Dance Agents

Gina Long is the founder/ director of Longrun Artistes Agency, established in 2005.

What does an agent do for their money?

An agent is there to take away the responsibility and time consuming task of finding work for clients. It is this that clients pay you for when they do work, sometimes the daily tasks of an agent are overlooked!

The Longrun office is made up of performers (some from the books), all who are knowledgable both behind the scenes and on stage/television.

Nikki Bond who joined in September 2013 is a hugely experienced dancer, choreographer, casting director and agent who puts on shows all over the world! She is an absolute credit to Longrun for her support and expertise.

Our day is spent searching for work, submitting for jobs, answering calls. Where clients are invited, being sure to take the details down at speed and with accuracy: job name, casting director, venue, time of casting, shoot dates or production dates, money etc. This is then relayed to the client. If successful, contracts have to be read, understood, questioned if necessary, signed and returned, invoices sent and followed up for payment!

Collaboration between agent and client is essential, respect both ways. Whilst our daily work involves the submission part, Longrun has always sent a "Submission Alert" to their clients for them to check the details: am I available as required? do I like the look of this? If not clients are asked to let us know immediately in order to remove them.

Building trusted relationships with casting directors means submitting appropriately and not submitting someone because they have requested it, thinking they are perfect, despite being 10 years too old/young for the job.

We expect you to turn up 5 minutes early and not 10 minutes late to castings/auditions, if there is a script, be "off page" where possible, being familiar with all aspects of any job has to be a bonus.

It is the artist's responsibility to be on top of their game, continuing to learn, taking singing lessons, workshops, and dance classes!! Whichever is appropriate.

Keeping on top of your game is vital; 1 day off, you notice. 2 days off, everybody else notices!!

Those with professional training are of course going to benefit from the endless preparation for a career as a dancer. Dancers are athletes so plenty of rest for the body in between class/rehearsal is imperative as is a good diet. That does not mean diet, you can't! Your body needs fuel to run on just like a car, what goes in is burnt off!

Pilates, yoga and regular massage is always good to enhance strength, peace of mind and physical wellbeing.

Dancers are special, that's what I believe and hopefully you do too!!

It is essential you update your Spotlight profile regularly. If you were going to sell your house you would not leave the beds unmade, not hoover for a fortnight and leave washing up in the sink, would you? So why then would any professional not regularly update their Spotlight profile, change pictures, update showreels on a regular basis etc?

Numbers are huge in this industry. It is up to you to stand out from the crowd, be unique but do not limit yourself with only dance pictures, do not have pictures with short brown hair when now it is blonde and long!!

I started as a Royal Ballet Scholar, here I truly learnt my discipline at a young age, although at times this was hard, it set me on a road of knowledge of how best to sell myself.

I then got a place at Ballet Rambert under the direction of Angela Ellis, Marie Rambert's daughter. I trudged my way around Germany hoping to get a place with a Ballet Company there. I was too small, too skinny, not technical enough, all demoralising stuff but then I returned home auditioned for Scottish

Ballet and got accepted, I stayed for 10 amazing years loving my job and improving my craft. I was then fortunate enough to be in the original cast of *The Snowman* at the Birmingham Rep. We had to sing, I'd never had a singing lesson in my life! I went for several, off the back of that I got the role of "Meg Cover" and Ballet Ensemble in *Phantom of the Opera*. The industry has changed since then however the principles have not.

Only you can practice till perfect, continue classes, improve improve improve in order to stand out for all the right reasons, it is nobody's fault but your own if you are not on top of your game. It is of course a numbers game! But this is where your clients truly matter in order for casting directors to trust your judgement. One person not turning up for an audition or casting can have a negative effect on the people you submit at a later stage, this is totally unforgivable and is not something that an agent can accept unless under exceptional circumstances.

I care about my artists, we all have off-days, we all live life with its trials and tribulations – I do understand, I have been there, feeling inadequate, but we have to toughen up, get on with it and fulfil our dreams, after all there are very few professions that offer a life of doing what you love for a living!

To find out more visit www.longrunartistes.com

AJK DANCE ETC   T 020 7831 9192
8B Lambs Conduit Passage, Holborn
London WC1R 4RH
E info@ajkdance.com
W www.ajkdance.com

A UNITED PRODUCTION   T/F 020 8673 0627
Choreographers, Dancers & Stylists. Twitter: @lyndonlloyd
9 Shandon Road, Clapham, London SW4 9HS
E info@united-productions.co.uk
W www.united-productions.co.uk

BODYWORK AGENCY   T 01223 314461
25-29 Glisson Road, Cambridge CB1 2HA
T 07792 851972
E agency@bodyworkds.co.uk

BOSS DANCE   T 0161 237 0100
Fourways House, 57 Hilton Street, Manchester M1 2EJ
F 0161 236 1237
E info@bossdance.co.uk
W www.bosscasting.co.uk

**BOX ARTIST MANAGEMENT
LTD - BAM**   T 020 7713 7313
*Choreographers. Musical Theatre. Commercial Dancers.
Corporate Entertainment*
The Attic, The Old Finsbury Town Hall
Rosebery Avenue, London EC1R 4RP
E hello@boxartistmanagement.com
W www.boxartistmanagement.com

CREATIVE KIDZ & ADULTZ   T 07908 144802
235 Fox Glove House, Fulham Road, London SW6 5PQ
T 07432 612026
E agency@creativekidzandco.co.uk
W www.creativekidzandco.co.uk

DANCERS   T 020 7637 1487
Trading as FEATURES
1 Charlotte Street, London W1T 1RD
E info@features.co.uk
W www.features.co.uk

DANCERS INC   T 020 7205 2316
Twitter: @dancersincworld
INC Artists Ltd, 90 Long Acre
Covent Garden, London WC2E 9RZ
E miranda@international-collective.com
W www.dancersincworld.com

ELLITE MANAGEMENT   T 0845 6525361
'The Dancer', 8 Peterson Road, Wakefield WF1 4EB
T 07957 631510
E enquiries@ellitemanagement.co.uk
W www.elliteproductions.co.uk

EVENT MODEL MANAGEMENT   T 020 3286 3135
Dancers. Models
Chester House, Fulham Green
81-83 Fulham High Street, London SW6 3JA
T 07581 223738
E info@eventmodel.co.uk
W www.eventmodelmanagement.co.uk

FEATURES   T 020 7637 1487
1 Charlotte Street, London W1T 1RD
E info@features.co.uk
W www.features.co.uk

FUSION MANAGEMENT   T 020 7834 6660
201A Victoria Street, London SW1W 5NE
E info@fusionmng.com
W www.fusionmng.com

**HEADNOD TALENT
AGENCY LTD**   T 020 3222 0035
RichMix 1st Floor West
35-47 Bethnal Green Road, London E1 6LA
E info@headnodagency.com
W www.headnodagency.com

JK DANCE PRODUCTIONS   T 0161 669 4401
T 020 7871 3055
E casting@jkdance.co.uk
W www.jkdance.co.uk

KEW PERSONAL MANAGEMENT   T 07876 457402
PO Box 679, Surrey RH1 9BT
E info@kewpersonalmanagement.com
W www.kewpersonalmanagement.com

KMC AGENCIES   T 0845 5193071
Garden Studios, 71-75 Shelton Street
Covent Garden, London WC2H 9JQ
E london@kmcagencies.co.uk
W www.kmcagencies.co.uk

KMC AGENCIES   T 01925 759196
Suite 2, Lymm Court
11 Eagle Brow, Lymm WA13 0LP
F 01925 755821
E casting@kmcagencies.co.uk
W www.kmcagencies.co.uk

**LIVING THE DREAM TALENT
AGENCY**   T 01727 751613
145-147 St John Street, London EC1V 4PW
T 07845 207501
E agency@livingthedreamcompany.co.uk
W www.livingthedreamcompany.co.uk

LONGRUN ARTISTES   T 01322 400387
Contact: Gina Long
32 Ashburnham Road, Belvedere
Kent DA17 6DA
T 07748 723228
E longrunartistes@virginmedia.com
W www.longrunartistes.com

**MARLOWES AGENCY:
TV, THEATRE & DANCE**   T 020 7193 4484
HMS President, Victoria Embankment
Blackfriars, London EC4Y 0HJ
E mitch@marlowesagency.com
W www.marlowesagency.com

MITCHELL MAAS McLENNAN   T 020 8301 8745
MPA Offices, 29 Thomas Street
Woolwich, London SE18 6HU
T 07540 995802
E agency@mmm2000.co.uk
W www.mmm2000.co.uk

MODELS IN MOTION UK LTD   T 07789 884134
E modelsinmotionlondon@gmail.com
W www.modelsinmotionlondon.com

MOMENTUM ARTISTS   T 020 3322 6609
Specialising in Muscial Theatre & Dance
86-90 Paul Street, London EC2A 4NE
E info@momentumartists.co.uk
W www.momentumartists.co.uk

NEW WAVE AGENCY   T 020 7609 0150
16 Globe Court, 107 Tollington Road
London N7 7JH
E newwaveagency@yahoo.com
W www.newwaveagency.co.uk

**PARADIGM ARTIST
MANAGEMENT LTD**   T 01554 776836
49 St Josephs Court
Llanelli, Carmarthenshire SA15 1NR
E paradigmartistmgnt@live.co.uk
W www.paradigmartistmgnt.com

PRODANCE   T 020 7193 8554
Street Dancers. Choreographers
Wimbledon Studios, 1 Deer Park Road
London SW19 3TL
E info@prodance.co.uk
W www.prodance.co.uk

RAZZAMATAZZ
MANAGEMENT　　　　　**T/F** 01342 301617
204 Holtye Road, East Grinstead RH19 3ES
T 07836 268292
E razzamatazzmanagement@btconnect.com

ROEBUCK, Gavin　　　　**T** 020 7370 7324
51 Earls Court Square, London SW5 9DG
E info@gavinroebuck.com
W www.gavinroebuck.com

RUDEYE DANCE AGENCY　　**T** 020 7014 3023
73 St John Street, London EC1M 4NJ
E dancer110578@hotmail.com
W www.rudeye.com

SCRIMGEOUR, Donald
ARTISTS AGENT　　　　　**T** 020 8444 6248
49 Springcroft Avenue, London N2 9JH
E vwest@dircon.co.uk

SHOW TEAM
PRODUCTIONS THE　　　　**T** 0845 4671010
*Entertainment Production- Event Coordinators, Production
Cast & Musicians. Twitter: @theshowteam*
36 Vine Street, Brighton BN1 4AG
E jo@theshowteam.co.uk
W www.theshowteam.co.uk

SINGER, Sandra ASSOCIATES　**T** 01702 331616
Dancers & Choreographers
21 Cotswold Road, Westcliff-on-Sea, Essex SS0 8AA
E sandrasingeruk@aol.com
W www.sandrasinger.com

S.O.S.　　　　　　　　**T** 020 7735 5133
Twitter: @sebholden
85 Bannerman House, Lawn Lane, London SW8 1UA
T 07740 359770
E info@sportsofseb.com
W www.sportsofseb.com

STUDIO ACCELERATE　　　**T** 020 3130 4040
Accelerate Productions Ltd
374 Ley Street, Ilford IG1 4AE
T 07956 104086
E info@accelerate-productions.co.uk
W www.accelerate-productions.co.uk

SUCCESS　　　　　　　**T** 020 7734 3356
Room 236, 2nd Floor, Linen Hall
162-168 Regent Street, London W1B 5TB
F 020 7494 3787
E ee@successagency.co.uk
W www.successagency.co.uk

SUMMERS, Mark
MANAGEMENT　　　　　**T** 020 7229 8413
1 Beaumont Avenue, West Kensington, London W14 9LP
E louise@marksummers.com
W www.marksummers.com

TASTE OF CAIRO　　　　**T** 07801 413161
Bellydancers. UK & Europe
22 Gilda Crescent Road, Eccles
Manchester M30 9AG
E hello@tasteofcairo.com
W www.tasteofcairo.com

T W MANAGEMENT AGENCY　**T** 01253 292733
66-74 The Promenade, Blackpool
Lancashire FY1 1HB
E marie.cavney@twmanagementagency.co.uk
W www.twmanagementagency.co.uk

W ATHLETIC　　　　　　**T** 020 8948 2759
34 Hill Street, Richmond-upon-Thames
London TW9 1TW
E london@wathletic.com
W www.wathletic.com

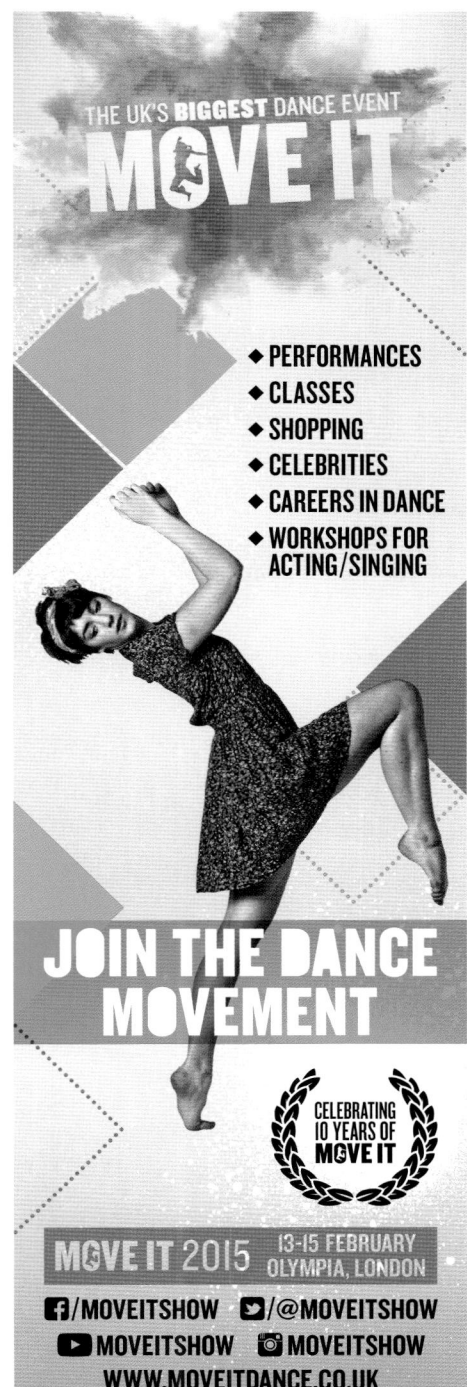

A & B PERSONAL MANAGEMENT LTD   T 020 7794 3255
PO Box 64671, London NW3 9LH
E b.ellmain@aandb.co.uk

AGENCY (LONDON) LTD THE   T 020 7727 1346
PMA Member
24 Pottery Lane, Holland Park, London W11 4LZ
F 020 7727 9037
E info@theagency.co.uk
W www.theagency.co.uk

ASPER, Pauline MANAGEMENT   T/F 01424 870412
PMA Member
Jacobs Cottage, Reservoir Lane
Sedlescombe, East Sussex TN33 0PJ
E pauline.asper@virgin.net

BERLIN ASSOCIATES   T 020 7836 1112
PMA Member
7 Tyers Gate, London SE1 3HX
F 020 7632 5296
E agents@berlinassociates.com
W www.berlinassociates.com

BLAKE FRIEDMANN   T 020 7387 0842
Novels, Non-fiction & TV/Film Scripts
1st Floor, Selous House
5-12 Mandela Street, London NW1 0DU
E info@blakefriedmann.co.uk
W www.blakefriedmann.co.uk

BRITTEN, Nigel MANAGEMENT   T 023 9263 1116
The Studio, Shepherds Cottage
Milberry Lane, Stoughton
West Sussex PO18 9JJ
E office@nbmanagement.com

BRODIE, Alan REPRESENTATION LTD   T 020 7253 6226
Contact: Alan Brodie. PMA Member
Paddock Suite, The Courtyard
55 Charterhouse Street, London EC1M 6HA
F 020 7183 7999
E abr@alanbrodie.com
W www.alanbrodie.com

CANN, Alexandra REPRESENTATION   T 01983 523312
Box 116, 4 Montpelier Street
London SW7 1EE
E alex@alexandracann.co.uk

CASAROTTO RAMSAY & ASSOCIATES LTD   T 020 7287 4450
PMA Member
Waverley House, 7-12 Noel Street
London W1F 8GQ
F 020 7287 9128
E info@casarotto.co.uk
W www.casarotto.co.uk

CLOWES, Jonathan LTD   T 020 7722 7674
PMA/Association of Authors' Agents Member
10 Iron Bridge House, Bridge Approach
London NW1 8BD
F 0871 5283647
E admin@jonathanclowes.co.uk

COCHRANE, Elspeth PERSONAL MANAGEMENT
Existing Clients only. No New Applicants. See ASQUITH & HORNER in Agents & Personal Managers section

COHEN MAYER, Charlie ASSOCIATES   T 07850 077825
Personal Managers. Talent Agency
121 Brecknock Road, Camden
London N19 5AE
E houseofsaintjude@gmail.com

CURTIS BROWN GROUP LTD   T 020 7393 4400
PMA Member
5th Floor, Haymarket House
28-29 Haymarket, London SW1Y 4SP
F 020 7393 4401
E cb@curtisbrown.co.uk
W www.curtisbrown.co.uk

DAISH, Judy ASSOCIATES LTD   T 020 8964 8811
PMA Member
2 St Charles Place, London W10 6EG
F 020 8964 8966
E judy@judydaish.com
W www.judydaish.com

DENCH ARNOLD AGENCY THE   T 020 7437 4551
PMA Member
10 Newburgh Street
London W1F 7RN
F 020 7439 1355
E contact@dencharnold.com
W www.dencharnold.com

de WOLFE, Felix   T 020 7242 5066
PMA Member
2nd Floor, 20 Old Compton Street
London W1D 4TW
F 020 7242 8119
E info@felixdewolfe.com
W www.felixdewolfe.com

FILLINGHAM, Janet ASSOCIATES   T 020 8748 5594
PMA Member
52 Lowther Road, London SW13 9NU
E info@janetfillingham.com
W www.janetfillingham.com

FILM RIGHTS LTD   T 020 7316 1837
Suite 306, Belsize Business Centre
258 Belsize Road, London NW6 4BT
F 020 7624 3629
E information@filmrights.ltd.uk
W www.filmrights.ltd.uk

FITCH, Laurence LTD   T 020 7316 1837
Suite 306, Belsize Business Centre
258 Belsize Road, London NW6 4BT
F 020 7624 3629
E information@laurencefitch.com

FRA   T 020 8255 7755
Formerly FUTERMAN, Rose & ASSOCIATES. PMA Member. TV/Film, Showbiz & Music Business Biographies
91 St Leonards Road
London SW14 7BL
E guy@futermanrose.co.uk
W www.futermanrose.co.uk

FRENCH, Samuel LTD   T 020 7387 9373
PMA Member
52 Fitzroy Street, Fitzrovia, London W1T 5JR
F 020 7387 2161
E theatre@samuelfrench-london.co.uk
W www.samuelfrench-london.co.uk

Literary Agents

Who are literary agents?

Literary agents represent writers and promote their work to publishers, editors and commissioners. Literary agents will also negotiate contracts and sales for their clients and also handle dramatic rights. In return, they take a commission of 10-15%. Some literary agents may represent a specific genre of work whereas others cover a diverse range of writing from books and plays to television, radio and film drama.

Why do I need a literary agent?

A literary agent can help a writer become more marketable and appealing and open up a much wider net of contacts and opportunities. The chances of becoming a published author or successful screenwriter are very small, and only very few experience success. Securing an agent to represent you is a step towards this but in itself is by no means a guarantee of success. For playwrights some theatres welcome submissions directly, however, there are several ways that having an agent can improve your chances; they will work with a writer to get a manuscript or synopsis/pitch in perfect condition, often through extensive editorial work and collaboration. They have years of experience in identifying the right editors, publishers and commissioners who will be interested in a specific work and have invaluable insight into the current market and what type of work is being visioned years in advance. Many 'super' agencies now handle a range of clients from talent through to writers, directors and producers and so have an in-depth knowledge of the market from every perspective. Further down the line, an agent is there to guide their client's career, negotiate contracts, make foreign sales, handle rights and other similar issues.

How do I approach a literary agent?

Consult the listings and make a shortlist of the ones you wish to approach. If they have specified how they want to be contacted, whether by e-mail, post or telephone, make sure you are using this information to your advantage. Most literary agents would prefer post or e-mail rather than a phone call, as it will be your writing that sells you. Do your research and check that the agent handles the kind of writing you do. Some agents only deal with specific genres so make sure you are aware of this before contacting them. Always make sure you are addressing the specific agent and not "sir or madam" or "to whom it may concern". If a contact name is not detailed in the listing, check the website for submission guidelines or try phoning to see who you should send submissions to. Presentation is important; always check spelling and grammar, submissions should be word-processed not handwritten. Your submission should include a short covering letter, a synopsis and a self-addressed envelope with enough postage for the return of your manuscript. Note: legitimate agents do not charge reading or up front fees.

How should I use these listings?

If you are a first-time writer looking to get published or promoted or thinking about changing your agent, the following listings will supply you with up-to-date contact details for many of the UK's leading literary agencies. Every agency listed is done so by written request to us. Members of the Personal Managers' Association (PMA) have indicated their membership status under their name.

Some agencies have also chosen to list other information such as relevant contact names, the fields of work they represent and their preferred method of contact from new applicants. Use this information to narrow down your search and optimise your chances of finding a suitable agent.

GLASS, Eric LTD T 020 7229 9500
25 Ladbroke Crescent, Notting Hill, London W11 1PS
F 020 7229 6220
E eglassltd@aol.com

HANCOCK, Roger LTD T 020 8341 7243
44 South Grove House, South Grove
London N6 6LR
E tim@rogerhancock.com

HIGHAM, David ASSOCIATES LTD T 020 7434 5900
PMA Member
F 020 7437 1072
E dha@davidhigham.co.uk
W www.davidhigham.co.uk

HOSKINS, Valerie ASSOCIATES LTD T 020 7637 4490
PMA Member
20 Charlotte Street, London W1T 2NA
F 020 7637 4493
E vha@vhassociates.co.uk

IMAGINE TALENT T 07876 685515
E christina@imaginetalent.co.uk
W www.imaginetalent.co.uk

INDEPENDENT TALENT GROUP LTD T 020 7636 6565
PMA Member. Formerly ICM, London
40 Whitfield Sreet, London W1T 2RH
F 020 7323 0101
W www.independenttalent.com

JFL AGENCY LTD T 020 3137 8182
PMA Member
48 Charlotte Street, London W1T 2NS
E agents@jflagency.com
W www.jflagency.com

KASS, Michelle ASSOCIATES T 020 7439 1624
PMA Member
85 Charing Cross Road
London WC2H 0AA
F 020 7734 3394
E office@michellekass.co.uk

KENIS, Steve & CO T 020 7434 9055
PMA Member
95 Barkston Gardens, London SW5 0EU
F 020 7373 9404
E sk@sknco.com

MACFARLANE CHARD ASSOCIATES LTD T 020 7636 7750
PMA Member
33 Percy Street, London W1T 2DF
F 020 7636 7751
E enquiries@macfarlane-chard.co.uk
W www.macfarlane-chard.co.uk

MACNAUGHTON LORD REPRESENTATION T 020 7499 1411
PMA Member
44 South Molton Street, London W1K 5RT
E info@mlrep.com
W www.mlrep.com

MANS, Johnny PRODUCTIONS T 01992 470907
Incorporating Encore Magazine
PO Box 196, Hoddesdon
Herts EN10 7WG
E johnnymansagent@aol.com
W www.johnnymansproductions.co.uk

MARJACQ SCRIPTS LTD T 020 7935 9499
Prose. Screenplays. No Stage Plays or Musicals
Submissions: Box 412
19-21 Crawford Street, London W1H 1PJ
F 020 7935 9115
E enquiries@marjacq.com
W www.marjacq.com

MARVIN, Blanche AGENCY T/F 020 7722 2313
Blanche Marvin MBE. Drama Critic for LTR. Critic's Circle Member. No Unsolitcited Materials
21A St Johns Wood High Street
London NW8 7NG
E blanchemarvin17@hotmail.com

M.B.A. LITERARY & SCRIPT AGENTS LTD T 020 7387 2076
PMA Member
62 Grafton Way, London W1T 5DW
E submissions@mbalit.co.uk
W www.mbalit.co.uk

McLEAN, Bill PERSONAL MANAGEMENT LTD T 020 8789 8191
23B Deodar Road
London SW15 2NP

MEMPHIS, THADDAEUS & GOLD TALENT & LITERARY AGENCY T 07850 077825
121 Brecknock Road, Camden
London N19 5AE
E houseofsaintjude@gmail.com

MLR
See MACNAUGHTON LORD REPRESENTATION

MORRIS, William ENDEAVOR ENTERTAINMENT T 020 7534 6800
100 New Oxford Street, London WC1A 1HB
F 020 8929 8400
W www.wma.com

NARROW ROAD COMPANY THE T 020 7831 4450
PMA Member
1st Floor, 37 Great Queen Street
London WC2B 5AA
E richardireson@narrowroad.co.uk

PFD T 020 7344 1000
PMA Member
Drury House
34-43 Russell Street, London WC2B 5HA
E info@pfd.co.uk
W www.peterfraserdunlop.com

ROSICA COLIN LTD T 020 7370 1080
1 Clareville Grove Mews
London SW7 5AN

SAYLE SCREEN LTD T 020 7823 3883
PMA Member. Screenwriters & Directors for Film, Stage & Television
11 Jubilee Place, London SW3 3TD
F 020 7823 3363
E info@saylescreen.com

SEIFERT, Linda MANAGEMENT LTD T 020 3214 8293
PMA Member
48-56 Bayham Place
London NW1 0EU
E contact@lindaseifert.com
W www.lindaseifert.com

SHARLAND ORGANISATION LTD   **T** 01933 626600
The Manor House, Manor Street
Raunds, Northants NN9 6JW
E tso@btconnect.com

SHEIL LAND ASSOCIATES LTD   **T** 020 7405 9351
PMA Member. Literary, Film & Stage
52 Doughty Street, London WC1N 2LS
F 020 7831 2127
E info@sheilland.co.uk

STEEL, Elaine   **T** 01273 739022
PMA Member. Writers' Agent
110 Gloucester Avenue, London NW1 8HX
F 01273 772400
E es@elainesteel.com

STEINBERG, Micheline ASSOCIATES   **T** 020 3214 8292
PMA Member
48-56 Bayham Place
London NW1 0EU
E info@steinplays.com
W www.steinplays.com

STEVENS, Rochelle & CO   **T** 020 7359 3900
PMA Member
2 Terretts Place, Upper Street
London N1 1QZ
F 020 7354 5729
E info@rochellestevens.com
W www.rochellestevens.com

TENNYSON AGENCY THE   **T** 020 8543 5939
10 Cleveland Avenue, Merton Park
London SW20 9EW
E submissions@tenagy.co.uk

TYRRELL, Julia MANAGEMENT   **T** 020 8374 0575
PMA Member
57 Greenham Road, London N10 1LN
F 020 8374 5580
E info@jtmanagement.co.uk
W www.jtmanagement.co.uk

WARE, Cecily LITERARY AGENTS   **T** 020 7359 3787
PMA Member
19C John Spencer Square
London N1 2LZ
F 020 7226 9828
E info@cecilyware.com
W www.cecilyware.com

WEINBERGER, Josef LTD   **T** 020 7580 2827
PMA Member
12-14 Mortimer Street, London W1T 3JJ
F 020 7436 9616
E generalinfo@jwmail.co.uk
W www.josef-weinberger.com

WESSON, Penny   **T** 020 7722 6607
PMA Member
26 King Henry's Road, London NW3 3RP
F 020 7483 2890
E penny@pennywesson.com

WILLIAMSON, Simon AGENCY THE (SWA)   **T** 020 7281 1449
155 Stroud Green Road, London N4 3PZ
E info@swagency.co.uk
W www.swagency.co.uk

Presenters' Agents

How do I become a presenter?

There is no easy answer to this question. Some presenters start out as actors and move into presenting work, others may be 'experts' such as chefs, designers or sports people who are taken on in a presenting capacity. Others may have a background in stand-up comedy. All newsreaders are professional journalists with specialist training and experience. Often presenters work their way up through the production side of broadcasting, starting by working as a runner or researcher and then moving to appear in front of the camera. To get this kind of production work you could contact film and television production companies, many of whom are listed in Contacts. A number of performing arts schools, colleges and academies also offer useful part-time training courses for presenters. See the 'Drama Training, Schools and Coaches' section for college/school listings.

Why do I need a presenting agent?

As with any other agent, a presenting agent will promote their clients to job opportunities, negotiate contracts on their behalf, handle paperwork and offer advice. In return for these services they take commission ranging from 10-15%. The listings in this section will supply you with up-to-date contact details for presenter agencies. They will possess the relevant contacts in the industry that you need to get auditions and jobs.

How should I use these listings?

Before you approach any agency looking for representation, do some research into their current client list and the areas in which they specialise. Many have websites you can visit. Once you have made a short-list of the ones you think are most appropriate, you should send them your CV with a covering letter and a good quality, recent photograph which is a genuine likeness of you. Showreels can also be a good way of showcasing your talents, but only send these if you have checked with the agency first. Enclosing a stamped-addressed envelope with sufficient postage (SAE) will also give you a better chance of a reply. Please see the main 'Agents and Personal Managers' advice section for further guidance on choosing and approaching agents.

Should I pay an agent to join their books? Or sign a contract?

Equity (the actors' trade union) does not recommend that artists pay an agent to join their client list. Before signing any contract, you should be very clear about the terms and commitments involved. For advice on both of these issues, or if you experience any problems with a current agent, we recommend that you contact Equity www.equity.org.uk. They also produce the booklet *You and your Agent* which is free to all Equity members and available from their website's members' area.

CASE STUDY

The Wasserman Media Group is a leading global sports and entertainment agency, specialising in talent management, media rights and consulting. Jonny McWilliams runs the television and broadcasting talent division.

Without wishing to state the obvious, this is an industry based on talent and one's belief in their talent being matched by someone else's – in this case the agent. This can be said of a casting director, commissioner, producer or director, but often it starts with the agent.

The joint decision of the "talent" and the agent to work together, particularly at the beginning of a career, can be the most important career decision they both make. This early endorsement and belief in their talent by their representative can give the performer the confidence they need to go out into an industry and thrive. Similarly, a change in agent at the right time can offer a new perspective to a career and help take it on to the next desired level. We as agents are lucky, we choose to seek out, represent and surround ourselves by people who we believe are talented. In an industry that needs to have a keen eye on the bottom line, with every penny in the budget scrutinised – the business end of "the business" seems ever present; it can be difficult to remember that the business is ultimately all about the talent.

The talent of the actor or presenter sells the project, they are judged the most severely by its merits (or lack thereof) and rightly applauded and lauded for its success. An agent's passionate conviction in their client is a vital part of any performer's progression; the agent's job of identifying and sharing their clients' talent with the industry is key to the whole chain.

As an agency, we specialise in presenter representation, this is a wide and varied form of management, taking in entertainment, features, factual and sports broadcasting; it is also very commercial by nature and means we will spend almost as much time dealing with brands and their PRs as we do with producers and commissioners.

Often we are looking for people who have a unique take and specialise on a subject matter or genre, but universally the most important thing for me is a well thought-out point of difference that we believe can grab the attention of commissioners and producers. The brief in a nutshell is to work with people who you truly believe in regardless of the tribe of television they belong to. Once found and identified, our job is to convince others that we are right!

The comparison of a romantic relationship to that of an agent is reaching for the obvious cliché, but it is a unique and, at its best, a special relationship. The nature of the relationship means that very quickly you know a huge amount about your client. Trusted career advice is sought and dished out, plans are made, diaries are run, deals are struck, contracts are signed, fees invoiced, money paid and careers built – the stakes for all are high.

The idea of talent is a hugely subjective one, but I believe agents choose to work in this industry because they genuinely appreciate the medium (and whisper it quietly, in some cases love it). In a tough and sometimes brutal business it's good to remind ourselves that by keeping positive, playing nice and by really having conviction in your clients (plus a few lunches along the way) it can come good for clients. What is certain is that the union of that special talent and the eager agent looking to build a potential star is as old as the industry itself and luckily still very important to it.

To find out more visit www.wassermantvtalent.com

APM ASSOCIATES   **T** 020 8953 7377
Contact: Linda French
Elstree Studios, Shenley Road
Borehamwood WD6 1JG
F 020 8953 7385
E apm@apmassociates.net
W www.apmassociates.net

**A R G
(ARTISTS RIGHTS
GROUP LTD)**   **T** 020 7436 6400
4A Exmoor Street, London W10 6BD
F 020 7436 6700
E argall@argtalent.com

**ARLINGTON
ENTERPRISES LTD**   **T** 020 7580 0702
1-3 Charlotte Street, London W1T 1RD
F 020 7580 4994
E info@arlington-enterprises.co.uk
W www.arlingtonenterprises.co.uk

BARR, Becca MANAGEMENT   **T** 020 3137 2980
97 Mortimer Street, London W1W 7SU
E info@beccabarrmanagement.co.uk
W www.beccabarrmanagement.co.uk

BLACKBURN MANAGEMENT   **T** 020 7292 7555
Argyll House
All Saints Passage
London SW18 1EP
E presenters@blackburnmanagement.co.uk
W www.blackburnmanagement.co.uk

CAMERON, Sara MANAGEMENT
See TAKE THREE MANAGEMENT

**CHASE PERSONAL
MANAGEMENT**   **T** 07929 447745
T 07775 683955
E sue@chasemanagement.co.uk
W www.chasepersonalmanagement.co.uk

CHP ARTIST MANAGEMENT   **T** 01844 345630
Meadowcroft Barn
Crowbrook Road, Askett
Princes Risborough
Buckinghamshire HP27 9LS
T 07976 560580
E chp.artist.management@gmail.com
W www.chproductions.org.uk

**CINEL GABRAN
MANAGEMENT**   **T** 029 2066 6600
Ty Cefn, 14-16 Rectory Road
Canton, Cardiff CF5 1QL
E info@cinelgabran.co.uk
W www.cinelgabran.co.uk

**CINEL GABRAN
MANAGEMENT**   **T** 01947 605376
Adventure House, Newholm
Whitby, North Yorkshire YO21 3QL
T 07552 168573
E mail@cinelgabran.co.uk
W www.cinelgabran.co.uk

CRAWFORDS   **T** 020 8947 9999
PO Box 56662, London W13 3BH
E cr@wfords.com
W www.crawfords.tv

CURTIS BROWN   **T** 020 7393 4460
Haymarket House, 28-29 Haymarket
London SW1Y 4SP
F 020 7393 4401
E presenters@curtisbrown.co.uk
W www.curtisbrown.co.uk

DAA MANAGEMENT   **T** 020 7255 6123
Formerly Debi Allen Associates
Welbeck House, 66-67 Wells Street, London W1T 3PY
F 020 7255 6128
E info@daamanagement.co.uk
W www.daamanagement.co.uk

**DAVID ANTHONY
PROMOTIONS**   **T** 01925 632496
Twitter: @davewarwick2
PO Box 286, Warrington, Cheshire WA2 8GA
T 07836 752195
E dave@davewarwick.co.uk
W www.davewarwick.co.uk

**DEVINE ARTIST
MANAGEMENT**   **T** 020 8865 1955
Contact by e-mail only
145-157 St John Street, London EC1V 4PW
E mail@devinemanagement.co.uk
W www.devinemanagement.co.uk

**DEVINE ARTIST
MANAGEMENT**   **T** 0161 726 5726
Tempus Building, 9 Mirabel Street
Manchester M3 1NP
E manchester@devinemanagement.co.uk
W www.devinemanagement.co.uk

**DOWNES PRESENTERS
AGENCY**   **T** 07973 601332
E downes@presentersagency.com
W www.presentersagency.com

**EVANS, Jacque
MANAGEMENT LTD**   **T** 020 8699 1202
Top Floor Suite, 14 Holmesley Road
London SE23 1PJ
F 020 8699 5192
E jacque@jemltd.demon.co.uk

EXCELLENT TALENT   **T** 0845 2100111
118-120 Great Titchfield Street
London W1W 6SS
E marie-claire@excellenttalent.com
W www.excellenttalent.com

FLETCHER ASSOCIATES   **T** 020 8361 8061
Broadcasting Experts. Corporate Speakers. Journalists
Studio One, 25 Parkway, London N20 0XN
F 020 8361 8866
W www.fletcherassociates.net

**FORD-CRUSH, June PERSONAL
MANAGEMENT &
REPRESENTATION**   **T** 020 8742 7724
PO Box 57948, London W4 2UJ
T 07711 764160
E june@junefordcrush.com
W www.junefordcrush.com

GAY, Noel ORGANISATION   **T** 020 7836 3941
19 Denmark Street, London WC2H 8NA
F 020 7287 1816
E info@noelgay.com
W www.noelgay.com

GLOBAL7   **T/F** 020 7281 7679
Kemp House, 152 City Road, London EC1V 2NX
T 07956 956652
E global7castings@gmail.com
W www.global7casting.com

GLORIOUS MANAGEMENT   **T** 020 7704 6555
Lower Ground Floor, 79 Noel Road
London N1 8HE
E lisa@glorioustalent.co.uk
W www.gloriousmanagement.com

GRANT, James MEDIA T 020 8742 4950
94 Strand On The Green, Chiswick
London W4 3NN
F 020 8742 4951
E enquiries@jamesgrant.co.uk
W www.jamesgrant.co.uk

**HICKS, Jeremy
ASSOCIATES LTD** T 020 7580 5741
3 Stedham Place, London WC1A 1HU
F 020 7636 3753
E info@jeremyhicks.com
W www.jeremyhicks.com

iCAN TALK LTD T 01858 466749
Palm Tree Mews, 39 Tymecrosse Gardens
Market Harborough, Leicestershire LE16 7US
T 07850 970143
E hello@icantalk.co.uk
W www.icantalk.co.uk

JGPM T 020 7440 1850
4th Floor, 7 Old Park Lane
London W1K 1QR
E victoria@jgpm.co.uk
W www.jgpm.co.uk

**JLA (JEREMY LEE
ASSOCIATES LTD)** T 020 7907 2800
Supplies Celebrities & After Dinner Speakers
80 Great Portland Street
London W1W 7NW
F 020 7907 2801
E talk@jla.co.uk
W www.jla.co.uk

**JOYCE, Michael
MANAGEMENT** T 020 3697 1265
Twitter: @michaeljoycetv
6th Floor, International House
223 Regent Street, London W1B 2QP
T 07903 324405
E michael@michaeljoyce.tv
W www.michaeljoycemanagement.com

KBJ MANAGEMENT LTD T 020 7054 5999
Television Presenters
22 Rathbone Street
London W1T 1LG
E general@kbjmanagement.co.uk
W www.kbjmgt.co.uk

**KNIGHT, Hilary
MANAGEMENT LTD** T 01604 781818
Grange Farm, Church Lane
Old, Northamptonshire NN6 9QZ
E hilary@hkmanagement.co.uk
W www.hkmanagement.co.uk

**KNIGHT AYTON
MANAGEMENT** T 020 7831 4400
35 Great James Street
London WC1N 3HB
E info@knightayton.co.uk
W www.knightayton.co.uk

LEIGH, Mike ASSOCIATES T 020 7993 8337
c/o Grand Scheme Media
27 Maiden Lane
London WC2E 7JS
E info@mikeleighassoc.com
W www.mikeleighassoc.com

**LYTE, Seamus
MANAGEMENT LTD** T 07930 391401
Contact: Seamus Lyte. By e-mail
E seamus@seamuslyte.com
W www.seamuslyte.com

M&C SAATCHI MERLIN T 020 7259 1460
15 Golden Square, London W1F 9EE
E enquiries@mcsaatchimerlin.com
W www.mcsaatchimerlin.com

**MACFARLANE CHARD
ASSOCIATES LTD** T 020 7636 7750
33 Percy Street
London W1T 2DF
F 020 7636 7751
E enquiries@macfarlane-chard.co.uk
W www.macfarlane-chard.co.uk

MARKS PRODUCTIONS LTD T 020 7486 2001
2 Gloucester Gate Mews
London NW1 4AD

**MARSH, Billy
ASSOCIATES LTD** T 020 7383 9979
4th Floor, 158-160 North Gower Street
London NW1 2ND
F 020 7388 2296
E talent@billymarsh.co.uk
W www.billymarsh.co.uk

McKENNA, Deborah LTD T 020 8846 0966
Celebrity Chefs & Lifestyle Presenters only
64-66 Glentham Road, London SW13 9JJ
F 020 8846 0967
E hello@dml-uk.com
W www.dml-uk.com

**MEDIA PEOPLE
(THE CELEBRITY GROUP)** T 0871 2501234
12 Nottingham Place
London W1M 3FA
E info@celebrity.co.uk
W www.celebrity.co.uk

MILES, John ORGANISATION T 01275 854675
Cadbury Camp Lane, Clapton-in-Gordano
Bristol BS20 7SB
F 01275 810186
E john@johnmiles.org.uk
W www.johnmilesorganisation.org.uk

MONDI ASSOCIATES LTD T 07817 133349
Contact: Michelle Sykes
Unit 3 O, Cooper House, 2 Michael Road
London SW6 2AD
E info@mondiassociates.com
W www.mondiassociates.com

MOON, Kate
MANAGEMENT LTD T 01604 686100
Pelham Barn, Draughton, Northampton NN6 9JQ
E kate@katemoonmanagement.com
W www.katemoonmanagement.com

MPC ENTERTAINMENT T 020 7624 1184
Contact: Michael P. Cohen (CEO)
MPC House, 15-16 Maple Mews, London NW6 5UZ
F 020 7624 4220
E info@mpce.com
W www.mpce.com

MTC (UK) LTD T 020 7935 8000
71 Gloucester Place, London W1U 8JW
F 020 7935 8066
E office@mtc-uk.com
W www.mtc-uk.com

NOEL, John MANAGEMENT T 020 7428 8400
Block B, Imperial Works
Perren Street, London NW5 3ED
F 020 7428 8401
E john@johnnoel.com
W www.johnnoel.com

OFF THE KERB
PRODUCTIONS T 020 7490 1500
Comedy Presenters & Comedians
44 Clerkenwell Close, London EC1R 0AZ
F 020 7437 0647
E info@offthekerb.co.uk
W www.offthekerb.co.uk

PANMEDIA UK LTD T 020 8446 9662
18 Montrose Crescent, London N12 0ED
E enquiries@panmediauk.co.uk
W www.panmediauk.com

PEOPLEMATTER.TV T 020 7415 7070
Contact: Tony Fitzpatrick
40 Bowling Green Lane, Clerkenwell, London EC1R 0NE
F 020 7415 7074
E tony@peoplematter.tv
W www.peoplematter.tv

PFD T 020 7344 1000
Presenters. Public Speakers
Drury House, 34-43 Russell Street, London WC2B 5HA
F 020 7836 9539
E info@pfd.co.uk
W www.peterfraserdunlop.com

PV MEDIA LTD T 01905 616100
County House, St Mary Street, Worcester WR1 1HB
E md@pvmedia.co.uk

RARE TALENT ACTORS
MANAGEMENT T 0161 273 4444
Tanzaro House, Ardwick Green North
Manchester M12 6FZ
F 0161 273 4567
E info@raretalentactors.com
W www.raretalentactors.com

RAZZAMATAZZ
MANAGEMENT T/F 01342 301617
204 Holtye Road, East Grinstead
West Sussex RH19 3ES
T 07836 268292
E razzamatazzmanagement@btconnect.com

RED 24 MANAGEMENT T 020 7559 3611
R24 Offices
1st Floor Kingsway House
103 Kingsway, London WC2B 6QX
E info@red24management.com
W www.red24management.com

RED CANYON MANAGEMENT T 07931 381696
T 07939 365578
E info@redcanyon.co.uk
W www.redcanyon.co.uk

RPM2 T 07795 606087
Studio House, Delamare Road
Cheshunt, Hertfordshire EN8 9SH
E rhino-rpm2@hotmail.com
W www.rhino2-rpm.com

SINGER, Sandra ASSOCIATES T 01702 331616
21 Cotswold Road, Westcliff-on-Sea
Essex SS0 8AA
E sandrasingeruk@aol.com
W www.sandrasinger.com

SOMETHIN' ELSE T 020 7250 5500
20-26 Brunswick Place, London N1 6DZ
E info@somethinelse.com
W www.somethinelse.com

TAKE THREE MANAGEMENT T 020 7209 3777
110 Gloucester Avenue, Primrose Hill
London NW1 8HX
F 020 7209 3770
E sara@take3management.com
W www.take3management.co.uk

TALENT4 MEDIA LTD T 020 7183 4330
Studio LG16, Shepherds Building Central
Charecroft Way, London W14 0EH
F 020 7183 4331
E enquiries@talent4media.com
W www.talent4media.com

TRIPLE A MEDIA T/F 020 7637 5839
30 Great Portland Street
London W1W 8QU
E info@tripleamedia.com
W www.tripleamedia.com

TROIKA T 020 7336 7868
10A Christina Street, London EC2A 4PA
F 020 3544 2919
W www.troikatalent.com

WANDER, Jo
MANAGEMENT LTD T 020 7209 3777
110 Gloucester Avenue, Primrose Hill
London NW1 8HX
E jo@jowandermanagement.com
W www.jowandermanagement.com

WISE BUDDAH TALENT T 020 7307 1600
74 Great Titchfield Street, London W1W 7QP
F 020 7307 1601
E talent@wisebuddah.com
W www.wisebuddah.com

ZWICKLER, Marlene & ASSOCIATES
1 Belgrave Crescent Lane, Edinburgh EH4 3AG
E info@mza-artists.com
W www.mza-artists.com

Voice Over Agents

How do I become a voice over artist?

The voice over business has opened up a lot more to newcomers in recent years; you don't have to be a celebrity to be booked for a job. However, it is a competitive industry, and it is important to bear in mind that only a select few are able to earn a living from voice over work. It is more likely that voice over work could become a supplement to your regular income.

In order to get work you must have a great voice and be able to put it to good use. Being able to act does not necessarily mean that you will also be able to do voice overs. Whether your particular voice will get you the job or not will ultimately depend on the client's personal choice, so your technical ability to do voice over work initially comes second in this industry. Once the client has chosen you, however, then you must be able to consistently demonstrate that you can take direction well, you don't need numerous takes to get the job finished, you have a positive attitude and you don't complain if recording goes a little over schedule.

Before you get to this stage, however, you will need a professional-sounding voicereel and, in the majority of cases, an agent.

How do I produce a voicereel?

Please see the 'Promotional Services' section for advice on creating your voicereel.

Why do I need a voice over agent?

As with any other agent, a voice over agent will promote their clients to job opportunities, negotiate contracts on their behalf, handle paperwork and offer advice. In return for these services they take commission ranging from 10-15%. The agents listed in this section specialise in representing and promoting voice over artists, mostly in the commercial and corporate sectors, but also areas such as radio and animation. They will possess the relevant contacts in the industry that you need to get auditions and jobs. In this industry in particular, time is money, and clients are often more likely to trust that an agent can provide someone who can get the job done in the least amount of takes but still sounds good in every project, rather than taking on an unknown newcomer.

How do I find work in radio?

Please see the 'Radio' section of Contacts for further information and advice on this specific area of voice work.

How should I use these listings?

Whether you are completely new to the industry, looking to change your existing agent, or wishing to take on an additional agent to represent you for voice overs alongside your main acting or presenting agent, the listings in this section will supply you with up-to-date contact details for voice over agencies. Every company listed is done so by written request to us. Please see the main 'Agents and Personal Managers' advice section for further guidance on choosing and approaching agents.

Should I pay an agent to join their books? Or sign a contract?

Equity (the actors' trade union) does not recommend that artists pay an agent to join their client list. Before signing a contract, you should be very clear about the terms and commitments involved. For advice on both of these issues, or if you experience any problems with a current agent, we recommend that you contact Equity www.equity.org.uk. They also produce the booklet *You and your Agent* which is free to all Equity members and available from their website's members' area.

Voice Over Agents

CASE STUDY

Rachel Kean has been a voice agent since 2006. She formed Articulate Voices in 2011.

I always have a small moment of dread when I am asked what I do for work because when I divulge that I run a voice over agency called Articulate Voices Ltd, I am very often met with "Oh really? All my friends say I have a good voice and that I should do voice-over work". This is frustrating for two reasons: 1. Because you are suddenly thrown into an awkward situation where you are supposed to tell the person that they do indeed have a lovely voice, even if they sound like Mickey Mouse on helium. And 2. Because it shows a real lack of understanding of the talent and skill involved in voice overs.

The clue is in the name: voice over ARTIST, the voice is used like an instrument and it's no different really from being able to play the oboe say, or the harp. Being a good voice over artist takes time, innate talent and endless self-improvement – it is hard work! Not only that but you have to be able to take those skills and adapt them to any situation the directors choose to throw at you, not to mention you need to be able to interpret the most obscure of directions ("We want you to read these 1000 words in less than 10 seconds but you can't sound rushed. Oh and by the way you're a cartoon cow, so try to sound cow-like").

On top of being a good performer you also have to be a good businessperson. You have to network, self-promote and spend a lot of time trawling through potential new contacts to see whether you can wheedle your way onto a job they're involved in. You have to go on courses, keep adding strings to your bow, work on seemingly endless amounts of low pay productions, or sometimes consider working for free so as to bulk up your CV. You have to be creative in your approach to finding work and constantly find ways to market yourself so that you stand out from the crowd. You will have to do work that is boring, repetitive and on occasion may feel like it goes against your morals. You basically will be the voice over equivalent of a bit of doggy doo on the bottom of a shoe. But then… then comes your first job that excites you, that makes you feel alive and that finally utilises all those millions of accents you've perfected over the years. Then comes the job that actually pays you well and makes you feel valued. Then comes the beginning of regular and more varied work.

And before you know it, you have been working on some big name games, read an audiobook for your favourite author or narrated a documentary on an amazing wildlife series. Then you realise all your hard work has paid off.

All of this can be very daunting for someone just starting out, and it's incredibly difficult to know where to start. But this is where an agent comes in, and that's why picking the right one for you is key. Agents come in many shapes, forms and sizes but the thing they all have in common is that they only exist for the following reasons:

- To give talent a trusted and recognisable platform on which they can shine.
- To promote the talent and ensure all the right industry people hear their voice.
- To ensure the talent gets the best possible monetary deal for their work. This includes advising when to walk away from a job because the rate offered is insulting to the talent and (sometimes) potentially damaging to the industry as a whole.
- To act as a buffer between the production company and the talent and to provide contractual and legal aid if necessary.
- To support the talent and help develop and nurture their career.

In return, agents expect loyalty and (aside from their 15% commission!) hard work. If you've not been put off yet, then it's probably time to get in touch with an agent. Get yourself a professionally made showreel (bedroom recordings on your iPhone simply won't cut the mustard) that really showcases your talent, then contact a select few agents. Make the effort to research the agents; for example make sure there is no one else similar sounding already on their books as they are unlikely to take you on if there is, find out how they prefer to receive submissions, write a personalised cover letter for each submission (don't just cut and paste, it can lead to you addressing the letter to completely the wrong person) and finally, keep it simple – sending sweets, funny pictures or bribes may seem like a good idea but quite frankly it will have been done before and it will probably just get thrown away.

So, good luck out there in voice over land. It is a tough nut to crack but it really is worth the effort, so come on, what are you waiting for?

To find out more visit www.articulatevoices.com

ADVOICE   T 020 7323 2345
40 Whitfield Street, London W1T 2RH
E info@advoice.co.uk
W www.advoice.co.uk

ALPHABET AGENCY   T 020 7252 4343
Also known as Alphabet Kidz Ltd
Daisy Business Park
19-35 Sylvan Grove
London SE15 1PD
E contact@alphabetkidz.co.uk
W www.alphabetkidz.co.uk

**AMERICAN AGENCY
VOICES THE**   T 020 7485 8883
14 Bonny Street, London NW1 9PG
E americanagency@btconnect.com
W www.americanagency.tv

**ANOTHER TONGUE
VOICES LTD**   T 020 7494 0300
The Basement
10-11 D'Arblay Street
London W1F 8DS
F 020 7494 7080
E john@anothertongue.com
W www.anothertongue.com

ASQUITH & HORNER
*Existing Clients only. No New Applicants. See ASQUITH
& HORNER in Agents & Personal Managers*

BABBLE   T 020 7434 0002
30 Great Portland Street
London W1W 8QU
E hello@babblevoices.com
W www.babblevoices.com

**BRAIDMAN, Michelle
ASSOCIATES LTD**   T 020 7237 3523
2 Futura House, 169 Grange Road
London SE1 3BN
F 020 7231 4634
E info@braidman.com

CALYPSO VOICES   T 020 7734 6415
27 Poland Street
London W1F 8QW
F 020 7437 0410
E jane@calypsovoices.com
W www.calypsovoices.com

**CONWAY VAN GELDER
GRANT LTD**   T 020 7287 1070
Twitter: @CvGG_Voices
3rd Floor, 8-12 Broadwick Street
London W1F 8HW
F 020 7287 1940
E kate@conwayvg.co.uk
W www.conwayvangeldergrant.com

CREATIVE KIDZ & ADULTZ   T 07908 144802
235 Fox Glove House
Fulham Road
London SW6 5PQ
T 07432 612026
E agency@creativekidzandco.co.uk
W www.creativekidzandco.co.uk

DAMN GOOD VOICES   T 07702 228185
Chester House, Unit 1:04
1-3 Brixton Road, London SW9 6DE
T 07809 549887
E damngoodvoices@me.com
W www.damngoodvoices.com

EARACHE VOICES   T 020 7287 2291
177 Wardour Street
London W1F 8WX
F 020 7287 2288
E enquiries@earachevoices.com
W www.earachevoices.com

EXCELLENT TALENT   T 0845 2100111
118-120 Great Titchfield Street
London W1W 6SS
F 020 7637 4091
E info@excellenttalent.com
W www.excellenttalent.com

FERRIS ENTERTAINMENT VOICES　T 07801 493133
London. Belfast. Cardiff. Los Angeles. France. Spain
Number 8
132 Charing Cross Road
London WC2H 0LA
E info@ferrisentertainment.com
W www.ferrisentertainment.com

FIRST VOICE AGENCY　T 01494 730166
26 Wood Pond Close, Seer Green
Beaconsfield, Bucks HP9 2XG
E office@firstvoiceagency.com
W www.firstvoiceagency.com

FOREIGN LEGION　T 020 8450 4451
1 Kendal Road, London NW10 1JH
E voices@foreignlegion.co.uk
W www.foreignlegion.co.uk

FOREIGN VERSIONS LTD　T 0333 123 2001
Translation
E info@foreignversions.co.uk
W www.foreignversions.com

GAY, Noel VOICES　T 020 7836 3941
19 Denmark Street
London WC2H 8NA
F 020 7287 1816
E info@noelgay.com
W www.noelgay.com

GLOBAL7　T/F 020 7281 7679
Kemp House, 152 City Road, London EC1V 2NX
T 07956 956652
E global7castings@gmail.com
W www.global7casting.com

foréigñversions

- ~ **Voice Overs**
- ~ **Translations**
- ~ **Script Adaptation**
- ~ **Foreign Copywriting**
- ~ **Studio Production**

Contact:
Margaret Davies, Annie Geary
or Bérangère Capelle on:

Tel: **0333 123 2001**
e-mail: **info@foreignversions.co.uk**

www.foreignversions.com

GREAT BRITISH VOICE COMPANY THE　T 07504 076020
339 Norristhorpe Lane, Liversedge
West Yorkshire WF15 7AZ
E info@gbvcoltd.com
W www.gbvcoltd.com

HAMILTON HODELL LTD　T 020 7636 1221
Contact: Louise Donald
20 Golden Square, London W1F 9JL
E louise@hamiltonhodell.co.uk
W www.hamiltonhodell.co.uk

HARVEY VOICES　T 020 7952 4361
No Unsolicited Correspondence
58 Woodlands Road, London N9 8RT
E info@harveyvoices.co.uk
W www.harveyvoices.co.uk

HOBSONS VOICES　T 020 8995 3628
2 Dukes Gate, Chiswick
London W4 5DX
F 020 8996 5350
E voices@hobsons-international.com
W www.hobsons-international.com

HOPE, Sally ASSOCIATES　T 020 7613 5353
108 Leonard Street
London EC2A 4XS
F 020 7613 4848
E casting@sallyhope.biz
W www.sallyhope.biz

HOWARD, Amanda ASSOCIATES
See JONESES THE

iCAN TALK LTD　T 01858 466749
Palm Tree Mews, 39 Tymecrosse Gardens
Market Harborough, Leicestershire LE16 7US
E hello@icantalk.co.uk
W www.icantalk.co.uk

INTER VOICE OVER　T 020 7262 6937
3rd Floor, 207 Regent Street
London W1B 3HH
E info@intervoiceover.com
W www.intervoiceover.com

J H A VOICE　T 020 7580 5741
3 Stedham Place, London WC1A 1HU
F 020 7636 3753
E info@jeremyhicks.com
W www.jeremyhicks.com

JONESES THE　T 020 7253 8462
74 Clerkenwell Road, London EC1M 5QA
E mail@meetthejoneses.co.uk
W www.meetthejoneses.co.uk

JUST VOICES AGENCY THE　T 020 7881 2567
140 Buckingham Palace Road
London SW1W 9SA
F 020 7881 2569
E info@justvoicesagency.com
W www.justvoicesagency.com

KIDZTALK LTD　T 01737 350808
Young Voices. Children. Teenagers. Twenties
F 01737 352456
E studio@kidztalk.com
W www.kidztalk.com

LEHRER, Jane VOICES　T 020 7435 9118
PO Box 66334, London NW6 9QT
F 020 7435 9117
E voices@janelehrer.co.uk
W www.janelehrer.co.uk/voices.html

theshowreel
London's Spoken-Word Specialists

How would you like to invest your money in a voiceover demo that actually stands you a chance of getting work?

Testimonials

Definitely the best showreels
Leigh Matty - Just Voices Agency

Professional demo reels that the industry expects
Matt Chopping - WAM Voices

Professional, sharp, well presented quality demos
Ben Romer Lee – Vocal Point

The best produced audio reels we receive
Victoria Braverman - Voicebookers.com

Professional and high quality demos
Penny Brown - Voicecall

Unfailingly produce exceptional demos every time
Vicky Crompton - Talking Heads

Great quality reels
Red 24 Management

Professional and unique showreels, 2 very important aspects for a top quality demo
Jennifer & Clair - Shining Management Ltd

Learn the skills needed on our one day voiceover workshop

Learn the "insider" secrets to starting a career in this lucrative industry.

Everyday we get calls and emails from people who want to know how to get started and they come from all walks of life not just from the "acting" side. In fact we've taught news readers, after dinner speakers, sales reps, teachers, actors, DJs, dentists, presenters, vets, lawyers, painters, biochemists and even "Brian" a Concord pilot (seriously) and have come to understand that just because people "tell" you that you've got a good sounding voice doesn't mean you should drop everything and make a demo.

A comprehensive, fun and interactive workshop.

Packed with insider information and loads of "tricks and techniques" on how to succeed in today's industry, this workshop gives you the opportunity to learn the skills and techniques used by working professionals. Small class sizes allow you plenty of time behind the "mic" and the chance to experience what it's really like to be in a commercial recording situation while being directed by one of London's most experienced Voice Producers, JP Orr.

This "heads up" will give you the headstart you need to move your voice career forward.

We know it's not possible to teach you everything there is to know about voiceovers in a single workshop, but we guarantee that having attended this session you will, with our help, be able to make an educated decision about whether voiceovers are for you.

If it is, then we will help you move forward. If it's not, then we will be honest and tell you that you would be wasting your time pursuing this line of work.

We also know that you can't get practical "hands-on" information in any one book, on the internet or at the end of a telephone. We've seen and pretty much heard it all and are willing to share our knowledge with you to help you get started. After all, you only get one chance to "get it right".

It's a serious decision you are about to make. We suggest you at least learn the basics before you spend your hard-earned money on a Voice Showreel you may end up not using.

25 years' working with London's top agents and the best voices in the business.

Our Logo goes on every demo we produce. A badge we've earned by not "just turning out" voice demos that have no chance of getting our clients work. That's why the top London agents choose us to produce their clients' voice demos.

But don't just take our word for it. Call them and ask them. Most will send you to us to "cut" your reel. Why? Because they know we offer a proven process for all our clients. A voiceover plan that works!

- Learn the skills to get started
- Put those skills into practice
- Record your Showreel
- Learn how to market your voice

Information on our One Day Voiceover Workshops, Demo Packages and MORE:

www.theshowreel.com

Please also feel free to call one of our "voice team" if you have any other questions on:

020 7043 8660

The Showreel Limited

LIP SERVICE CASTING LTD   T 020 7734 3393
Contact: By e-mail. Accepts Voicereels. Voice Overs only. Twitter: @lipservicevoice
60-66 Wardour Street
London W1F 0TA
E bookings@lipservice.co.uk
W www.lipservice.co.uk

LONDON VOICE BOUTIQUE THE   T 020 7060 9456
Warwick House, Chapone Place
London W1D 3BF
E info@londonvoiceboutique.com
W www.londonvoiceboutique.com

LOUD & CLEAR VOICES LTD   T 020 8450 7519
27 Mortimer Street
London W1T 3BL
E info@loudandclearvoices.com
W www.loudandclearvoices.com

M2M VOICES   T 020 7631 1721
Specialises in Comedy
21 Foley Street, London W1W 6DR
E info@m2mvoices.com
W www.m2mvoices.com

MARKHAM, FROGGATT & IRWIN   T 020 7636 4412
4 Windmill Street, London W1T 2HZ
E tig@markhamfroggattirwin.com
W www.markhamfroggattandirwin.com

MEMPHIS, THADDAEUS & GOLD TALENT & LITERARY AGENCY   T 07850 077825
121 Brecknock Road, Camden
London N19 5AE
E houseofsaintjude@gmail.com

MONSTER VOICE   T 020 7462 9950
14 Rathbone Place
London W1T 1HT
E mail@monstervoice.co.uk

MONSTER VOICE   T 029 2034 4205
2nd Floor, 3-5 The Balcony
Castle Arcade, Cardiff CF10 1BU
E cardiff@monstervoice.co.uk

MOON, Kate MANAGEMENT LTD   T 01604 686100
Pelham Barn, Draughton
Northampton NN6 9JQ
E kate@katemoonmanagement.co.uk
W www.katemoonmanagement.co.uk

PEMBERTON VOICES   T 020 7224 9036
51 Upper Berkeley Street
London W1H 7QW
E fay@pembertonassociates.com
W www.pembertonvoices.com

QVOICE   T 020 7520 9460
Adam House
7-10 Adam Street
The Strand, London WC2N 6AA
E info@qvoice.co.uk
W www.qvoice.co.uk

RABBIT VOCAL MANAGEMENT LTD   T 020 7287 6466
94 Strand on the Green
London W4 3NN
E info@rabbitvocalmanagement.co.uk
W www.rabbitvocalmanagement.co.uk

RED 24 VOICES   T 020 7559 3611
R24 Office
1st Floor Kingsway House
103 Kingsway, London WC2B 6QX
E miles@red24management.com
W www.red24management.com/voices

RHUBARB VOICES   T 020 8742 8683
1st Floor, 1A Devonshire Road
Chiswick, London W4 2EU
F 020 8742 8693
E enquiries@rhubarbvoices.co.uk
W www.rhubarbvoices.co.uk

RPM2   T 07795 606087
Studio House
Delamare Road
Cheshunt, Hertfordshire EN8 9SH
E rhino-rpm2@hotmail.com
W www.rhino2-rpm.com

SCREAM MANAGEMENT LTD   T 0161 850 1996
The Greenhouse, Broadway
MediaCityUK
Salford M50 2EQ
E info@screammanagement.com
W www.screammanagement.com

SHINING MANAGEMENT LTD   T 020 7734 1981
81 Oxford Street
London W1D 2EU
E info@shiningvoices.com
W www.shiningvoices.com

SUGAR POD VOICES   T 020 8374 4701
Studio 8C, Chocolate Factory 1
5 Clarendon Road
Wood Green, London N22 6XJ
T 07967 673552
E info@sugarpodproductions.com
W www.sugarpodproductions.com

TALKING HEADS   T 020 7292 7575
Argyll House
All Saints Passage
London SW18 1EP
E voices@talkingheadsvoices.com
W www.talkingheadsvoices.com

TERRY, Sue VOICES LTD   T 020 7434 2040
4th Floor, 35 Great Marlborough Street
London W1F 7JF
F 020 7434 2042
E sue@sueterryvoices.com
W www.sueterryvoices.com

TONGUE & GROOVE   T 0161 228 2469
PO Box 173
Manchester M19 0AR
F 0161 249 3666
E info@tongueandgroove.co.uk
W www.tongueandgroove.co.uk

UNITED VOICES   T 020 3214 0937
12-26 Lexington Street
London W1F 0LE
E voices@unitedagents.co.uk
W www.unitedvoices.tv

VOCAL POINT   T 020 7419 0700
131 Great Titchfield Street
London W1W 5BB
E enquiries@vocalpoint.net
W www.vocalpoint.net

VOICE AGENCY THE T 020 7240 2345
Hudson House
8 Tavistock Street
London WC2E 7PP
E info@thevoiceagency.co.uk
W www.thevoiceagency.co.uk

VOICE BANK LTD T 0161 973 8879
PO Box 825, Altrincham
Cheshire WA15 5HH
T 07931 792670
E elinors@voicebankltd.co.uk
W www.voicebankltd.co.uk

VOICE SHOP T 020 8742 7077
1st Floor, Thomas Place
1A Devonshire Road
London W4 2EU
F 020 8742 7011
E info@voice-shop.co.uk
W www.voice-shop.co.uk

VOICE SQUAD T 020 8450 4451
1 Kendal Road
London NW10 1JH
E voices@voicesquad.com
W www.voicesquad.com

**VOICEBANK, THE IRISH
VOICE-OVER AGENCY** T 00 353 1 2350838
35 Thomastown Road
Dun Laoghaire
Co Dublin, Ireland
E voicebank@voicebank.ie
W www.voicebank.ie

VOICECALL T 020 7209 1064
67A Gondar Gardens
London NW6 1EP
T 07920 044615
E voices@voicecall-online.co.uk
W www.voicecall-online.co.uk

**VOICEOVER GALLERY
(LONDON) THE** T 020 7987 0951
12 Cock Lane
London EC1A 9BU
E london@thevoiceovergallery.co.uk
W www.thevoiceovergallery.co.uk

**VOICEOVER GALLERY
(MANCHESTER) THE** T 0161 881 8844
110 Timberwharf
32 Worsley Street
Manchester M15 4LD
E manchester@thevoiceovergallery.co.uk
W www.thevoiceovergallery.co.uk

VOICEOVERS.CO.UK T 020 7099 2264
PO Box 326, Plymouth
Devon PL4 9YQ
E info@voiceovers.co.uk
W www.voiceovers.co.uk

**VOICES AT THE ARTISTS
PARTNERSHIP** T 020 7439 1456
101 Finsbury Pavement
London EC2A 1RS
F 020 7734 6530
E email@theartistspartnership.co.uk
W www.theartistspartnership.co.uk/voices

**VSI - VOICE & SCRIPT
INTERNATIONAL** T 020 7692 7700
Foreign Language Specialists
132 Cleveland Street
London W1T 6AB
F 020 7692 7711
E info@vsi.tv
W www.vsi.tv

WAM VOICES T 020 7836 9222
The Voice Agency of Waring & McKenna
44 Maiden Lane, Covent Garden
London WC2E 7LN
F 020 7836 9186
E info@wamvoices.com
W www.wamvoices.com

WOOTTON, Suzy VOICES T 01604 765872
72 Towcester Road, Far Cotton
Northampton NN4 8LQ
E suzy@suzywoottonvoices.com
W www.suzywoottonvoices.com

WORDS-OUT T 020 7183 0017
Hunters House
1 Redcliffe Road
London SW10 9NR
E karin@words-out.com
W www.words-out.com

YAKETY YAK T 020 7430 2600
Contact: Helen Galway, Jake Lawrence
56 Broadwick Street, London W1F 7AJ
E info@yaketyyak.co.uk
W www.yaketyyak.co.uk

Walk-On & Supporting Artists' Agents

Who are Walk-on & Supporting Artists?

Sometimes known as 'extras', walk-on and supporting artists appear in the background of television and film scenes in order to add a sense of realism, character or atmosphere. They do not have individual speaking roles, unless required to make background/ambient noise.

Working as a walk-on or supporting artist does not require any specific 'look', training or experience as such; however it does involve more effort than people think. Artists are often required to start very early in the morning (6am is not uncommon) and days can be long with lots of waiting around, sometimes in tough conditions on location. It is certainly not glamorous, nor is it a way to become a television or film star!

Artists must be reliable and available at very short notice, which can make it difficult to juggle with other work or family commitments. Requirements vary from production to production and, as with mainstream acting work, there are no guarantees that you will get regular work, let alone be able to earn a living as a walk-on.

How should I use these listings?

If you are serious about working as a walk-on artist, you will need to register with an agency in order to be put forward for jobs. In return for finding you work, you can expect an agency to take between 10-15% in commission. The listings in this section contain contact details of many walk-on and supporting artist agencies. Some will specialise in certain areas, so make sure you research the different companies carefully to see if they are appropriate for you. Many have websites you can visit. It is also worth asking questions about how long an agency has existed, and about their recent production credits.

When approaching an agency for representation, you should send them your CV with a covering letter and a recent photograph which is a genuine, natural likeness of you. Enclosing a stamped-addressed envelope with sufficient postage (SAE) will give you a better chance of a reply.

Should I pay an agent to join their books? Or sign a contract?

Equity (the actors' trade union) does not generally recommend that artists pay an agent to join their client list. Before signing any contract, you should be clear about the terms and commitments involved. Always speak to Equity www.equity.org.uk or BECTU www.bectu.org.uk if you have any concerns or queries. Equity also produces the booklet You and your Agent which is free to all Equity members and available from their website's members' area.

Where can I find more information?

You may find it useful to contact the Film Artists Association, a subdivision of BECTU, who provide union representation for walk-on and supporting artists. For further details visit www.bectu.org.uk/get-involved/background-artistes

BACKGROUND WALES
STAGECOACH AGENCY

The largest provider of children & young performers for film & tv in Wales

'Stella', 'Dr. Who', 'Casualty', 'Wizards Vs Aliens', 'Pobol y Cwm'

For all your casting needs!

Licensed Chaperones - Tutors - Fast Turnaround Children's Licences

Tel: 0845 408 2468 • Email tarquin@backgroundwales.co.uk

www.backgroundwales.co.uk

2020 CASTING LTD T 020 8746 2020
2020 Hopgood Street, London W12 7JU
E info@2020casting.com
W www.2020casting.com

ACADEMY EXTRAS T 01204 417403
Film. Television. Based in the North West
490 Halliwell Road, Bolton, Lancs BL1 8AN
E admin@academyextras.co.uk
W www.academyextras.co.uk

AGENCY OAKROYD T 07840 784337
Oakroyd, 89 Wheatley Lane
Ben Rhydding, Ilkley, Yorkshire LS29 8PP
E paula@agencyoakroyd.com
W www.agencyoakroyd.com

ALLSORTS AGENCY T 020 8472 3924
Waterfront Studios, 1 Dock Road
London E16 1AH
T 07950 490364
E bookings@allsortsagency.com
W www.allsortsagency.com

**ALLSTARS ACTORS
MANAGEMENT** T 0161 702 8257
23 Falconwood Chase, Worsley
Manchester M28 1FG
T 07584 992429
E extras@allstarsactors.tv
W www.allstarsactors.tv

**ARTIST MANAGEMENT
UK LTD** T 0151 523 6222
6 Gondover Avenue, Orrell Park
Liverpool L9 8AZ
E chris@artistmanagementuk.com
W www.artistmanagementuk.com

AVENUE ARTISTES LTD T 023 8076 0930
PO Box 1573, Southampton SO16 3XS
E info@avenueartistes.com
W www.avenueartistes.com

BACKGROUND WALES T 0845 4082468
Suite 2, 1st Floor Offices, Cantilupe Chambers
Cantilupe Road, Ross-on-Wye HR9 7AN
F 0845 4082464
E tarquin@backgroundwales.co.uk
W www.backgroundwales.co.uk

BONNIE & BETTY LTD T 020 8301 8333
9-11 Gunnery Terrace, Royal Arsenal
London SE18 6SW
E agency@bonnieandbetty.com
W www.bonnieandbetty.com

BOSS CASTING T 0161 237 0100
Fourways House, 57 Hilton Street
Manchester M1 2EJ
F 0161 236 1237
E cath@bosscasting.co.uk
W www.bosscasting.co.uk

**BROOK, Dolly
CASTING AGENCY** T 01371 875767
PO Box 5436
Dunmow CM6 1WW
F 01371 875996
E dollybrookcasting@btinternet.com

CASTING CENTRAL LTD T 020 3131 0128
Unit 106A, Netil House
1 Westgate Street
London E8 3RL
E info@castingcentral.co.uk
W www.castingcentral.co.uk

CASTING COLLECTIVE THE T 020 8962 0099
Commercials. Film. Photographic. Television
109-111 Farringdon Road
London EC1R 3BW
E jodie@castingcollective.co.uk
W www.castingcollective.co.uk

CASTING NETWORK LTD THE T 020 8391 2979
4 Vidler Close
Chessington
Surrey KT9 2GL
E info@thecastingnetwork.co.uk
W www.thecastingnetwork.co.uk

Any artist, Any where, Any time

UNI★VERSAL EXTRAS

www.universalextrascasting.co.uk
0845 3700 884

CELEX CASTING LTD   **T** 01332 232445
Adults & Children
PO Box 7317, Derby DE1 0GS
T 07932 066021
E anne@celex.co.uk

CENTRAL CASTING LTD   **T** 020 8327 4244
See also KNIGHT, Ray CASTING LTD
Elstree Studios, Room 38
John Maxwell Building, Shenley Road
Borehamwood, Herts WD6 1JG
E casting@rayknight.co.uk
W www.rayknight.co.uk

COPS ON THE BOX   **T** 07710 065851
Advisers. Walk-ons. Supporting Artists.
Twitter: @copsonthebox1
BM BOX 7301, London WC1N 3XX
E info@cotb.co.uk
W ww.cotb.co.uk

CREATIVE KIDZ & ADULTZ   **T** 07908 144802
235 Fox Glove House, Fulham Road
London SW6 5PQ
T 07432 612026
E agency@creativekidzandco.co.uk
W www.creativekidzandco.co.uk

DARK ARTS   **T** 01782 769213
Alternative Model & Tattooed Character Agency
2 Stamer Street, Stoke-on-Trent
Staffordshire ST4 1DX
T 07514 893326
E info@darkarts.org.uk
W www.darkarts.org.uk

DAVID AGENCY THE   **T** 020 8834 1615
26-28 Hammersmith Grove, London W6 7BA
E casting@davidagency.co.uk
W www.davidagency.co.uk

DK MODEL & CASTING   **T** 0114 257 3480
4 Park Square, Thorncliffe Park
Chapeltown, Sheffield
South Yorkshire S35 2PH
F 0114 257 3482
E mail@dkmodels.net
W www.dkmodels.net

ELLIOTT AGENCY LTD THE   **T** 01273 454111
17 Osborne Villas, Hove
East Sussex BN3 2RD
E elliottagency@btconnect.com
W www.elliottagency.co.uk

ETHNIKA CASTING   **T** 0141 334 6246
14 Bowmont Gardens, Glasgow G12 9LR
T 07778 296002
E ethnikacasting@yahoo.co.uk
W www.ethnikacasting.co.uk

**EUROKIDS & EKA CASTING
AGENCIES**   **T** 01925 761083
Contact: Jodie Keith (Casting Agent).
Accepts Showreels. Children, Teenagers & Adults up
to 85 yrs. Commercials. Film. Television. Walk-on &
Supporting Artists
The Warehouse Studios, Glaziers Lane
Culcheth, Warrington, Cheshire WA3 4AQ
T 01925 761210
E jodie@eka-agency.com
W www.eka-agency.com

EXTRA PEOPLE LTD   **T** 020 3542 3685
London, Birmingham & Manchester
E team@extra-people.com
W www.extra-people.com

FACE MUSIC   **T** 01209 820796
Musicians Representation
Lambourne Farm, TR16 5HA
E facemusic@btinternet.com

FBI AGENCY   **T** 07050 222747
Leeds & Manchester
PO Box 250, Leeds LS1 2AZ
T 07515 567309
E casting@fbi-agency.co.uk
W www.fbi-agency.co.uk

**FEATURED & BACKGROUND
CASTING LTD (FAB)**   **T** 01628 522688
Contact: Suzanne Johns
13A Waldeck House
Waldeck Road, Maidenhead
Berkshire SL6 8BR
T 07808 781169
E suzanne@fabcastingagency.com
W www.fabcastingagency.com

FILM CAST CORNWALL & SW   **T** 07811 253756
Falmouth, Cornwall
E enquiries@filmcastcornwall.co.uk
W www.filmcastcornwall.co.uk

FRESH AGENTS LTD   **T** 01273 711777
Actors. Presenters. Extras. Models. Child Models.
Families. Promotional Event Staff. Work in London and all
over the UK
The Dock, Wilbury Villas
Hove, East Sussex BN3 6AH
T 0845 4080998
E info@freshagents.co.uk
W www.freshagents.co.uk

FUSION MANAGEMENT   **T** 020 7834 6660
201A Victoria Street
London SW1W 5NE
E info@fusionmng.com
W www.fusionmng.com

**GREENLEAF
ENTERTAINMENTS**   **T** 0845 2996614
Hillside Business Centre
Beeston Road
Leeds, West Yorkshire LS11 8ND
E info@greenleafcasting.com
W www.greenleafcasting.com

GUYS & DOLLS CASTING   **T** 020 8906 4144
Trafalgar House, Grenville Place
Mill Hill, London NW7 3SA
E info@guysanddollscasting.com
W www.guysanddollscasting.com

**HERRON, Alana PERSONAL
MANAGEMENT**   **T** 07877 984636
51 Medrox Gardens, Glasgow G67 4AL
E alana@alanaherron.com
W www.alanaherron.com

**HervL SUPPORTING
ARTISTES LTD**   **T** 01322 352766
Admiral Park, Victory Way
Crossways Business Park
Dartford, Kent DA2 6QD
E info@hervl.com
W www.hervl.co.uk

INDUSTRY CASTING   **T** 0161 839 1551
Suite 5, Basil Chambers
65 High Street, Manchester M4 1FS
F 0161 839 1661
E lois@industrycasting.co.uk
W www.industrycasting.co.uk

IPM: IMPERIAL PERSONAL MANAGEMENT LTD   **T** 0113 244 3222
IPM Casting. Contact: Charlotte Blackburn
The Studio, 102 Kirkstall Road
Leeds, West Yorkshire LS3 1JA
E charlotte@ipmcasting.com
W www.ipmcasting.com

JCM MANAGEMENT   **T** 07866 211647
2 New Street, Bridgtown WS11 0DD
E newtalentjcm@outlook.com

JPM EXTRAS   **T** 0191 221 2491
A Division of Janet Plater Management Ltd
D Floor, Milburn House
Dean Street, Newcastle upon Tyne NE1 1LF
E extras@jpmactors.com
W www.jpmactors.com

KNIGHT, Ray CASTING LTD   **T** 020 8327 4244
Elstree Studios, Room 38, John Maxwell Building
Shenley Road, Borehamwood, Herts WD6 1JG
E casting@rayknight.co.uk
W www.rayknight.co.uk

KREATE LIVE MEDIA LTD   **T** 020 7401 9007
32 Southwark Bridge Road
London SE1 9EU
F 020 7401 9008
E hello@kreate.co.uk
W www.kreate.co.uk

LEMON CASTING   **T** 0161 205 2096
The Sharp Project, Thorpe Road
Newton Heath, Manchester M40 5BJ
T 07723 317489
E info@lemoncasting.co.uk

LINTON MANAGEMENT   **T** 0161 761 2020
3 The Rock, Bury BL9 0JP
E mail@linton.tv
W www.lintonmanagement.co.uk

MAD DOG CASTING LTD   **T** 020 7269 7910
The Pavilion Building, Ealing Studios
Ealing Green, London W5 5EP
E info@maddogcasting.com
W www.maddogcasting.com

McDONAGH, Melanie MANAGEMENT (ACADEMY OF PERFORMING ARTS & CASTING AGENCY)   **T** 07909 831409
14 Apple Tree Way, Oswaldtwistle
Accrington, Lancashire BB5 0FB
T 01254 392560
E mcdonaghmgt@aol.com
W www.mcdonaghmanagement.co.uk

MIM AGENCY   **T** 0871 2377963
Clayton House, 59 Piccadilly
Manchester M1 2AQ
E info@mimagency.co.uk
W www.mimagency.co.uk

MINT CASTING AGENCY LTD   **T** 0161 834 7773
Suite 439-440, Royal Exchange
Manchester M2 7EP
E mark@mintcasting.tv
W www.mintcasting.tv

NEMESIS CASTING LTD   **T** 0161 228 6404
Nemesis House, 1 Oxford Court
Bishopsgate, Manchester M2 3WQ
E julie@nmsmanagement.co.uk
W www.nemesiscasting.co.uk

NIDGES CASTING AGENCY
See BOSS CASTING

ONSET EXTRAS   **T** 07795 370678
The Barn
1 Hayley Croft
Duffield, Derbyshire DE56 4HJ
E onsetextras@gmail.com
W www.onsetextras.co.uk

**ORIENTAL CASTING
AGENCY LTD**   **T** 020 8660 0101
Contact: Billie James
22 Wontford Road
Purley, Surrey CR8 4BL
E billiejames@btconnect.com

PAN ARTISTS AGENCY LTD   **T** 07890 715115
Cornerways
34 Woodhouse Lane
Sale, Cheshire M33 4JX
E panartists@btconnect.com
W www.panartists.co.uk

**PC THEATRICAL MODEL &
CASTING AGENCY**   **T** 020 8381 2229
10 Strathmore Gardens
Edgware, Middlesex HA8 5HJ
F 020 8933 3418
E twinagy@aol.com
W www.twinagency.com

PHA CASTING   **T** 0161 273 4444
Tanzaro House
Ardwick Green North
Manchester M12 6FZ
F 0161 273 4567
E info@pha-agency.co.uk
W www.pha-agency.co.uk

PHOENIX CASTING AGENCY   **T** 0117 973 1100
PO Box 387
Bristol BS99 3JZ
F 0117 973 4160
E caron@phoenixagency.biz
W www.phoenixagency.biz

POLEASE   **T** 05600 650524
*Specialist in Police & Military Actors & Supporting
Artistes. Uniform Hire & Props also Available*
1 Noake Road, Hucclecote
Gloucester GL3 3PE
T 07811 504079
E info@polease.co.uk
W www.polease.co.uk

SÉVA
DHALIVAAL
07956 553879

PREMIER ACTING   **T** 0141 255 0255
Contact: Allan Jones
9/2 321 Glasgow Harbour Terrace, Glasgow G11 6BL
T 07885 658316 (Out of Hours)
E info@premieracting.com
W www.premieracting.com

REGENCY AGENCY   **T** 0113 255 8980
25 Carr Road, Calverley
Leeds LS28 5NE

**REYNOLDS, Sandra AGENCY LTD
(COMMERCIALS)**   **T** 020 7387 5858
Commercials
Amadeus House, 27B Floral Street
London WC2E 9DP
F 020 7387 5848
E jessie@sandrareynolds.co.uk
W www.sandrareynolds.co.uk

**REYNOLDS, Sandra AGENCY LTD
(EAST ANGLIA)**   **T** 01603 623842
Commercials
Bacon House, 35 St Georges Street
Norwich NR3 1DA
F 01603 219825
E alex@sandrareynolds.co.uk
W www.sandrareynolds.co.uk

RHODES AGENCY   **T** 01708 747013
5 Dymoke Road, Hornchurch, Essex RM11 1AA
F 01708 730431
E rhodesarts@hotmail.com

**SAINT JUDE - TALENT &
LITERARY AGENCY**   **T** 07850 077825
121 Brecknock Road, Camden
London N19 5AE
E houseofsaintjude@gmail.com

**SAPPHIRES MODEL
MANAGEMENT LTD**   **T** 020 3603 9460
8 Windmill Street, London W1T 2JE
E contact@sapphiresmodel.com
W www.sapphiresmodel.com

SCREAM MANAGEMENT LTD   **T** 0161 850 1996
The Greenhouse, MediaCityUK
Salford, Manchester M50 2EQ
T 0161 850 1995
E extras@screammanagement.com
W www.screammanagement.com

SCREENLITE AGENCY   **T** 01932 561388
Shepperton Studios, Studios Road
Shepperton, Middlesex TW17 0QD
T 01932 592271
E enquiries@screenliteagency.co.uk
W www.screenliteagency.co.uk

SEVEN AGENCY   **T** 0161 850 1057
82 King Street, Manchester M2 4WQ
E info@7casting.co.uk
W www.7casting.co.uk

SHARMAN, Alan AGENCY   **T** 0121 212 0090
Office 6, Fournier House, 8 Tenby Street
Jewellery Quarter, Birmingham B1 3AJ
E info@alansharmanagency.com
W www.alansharmanagency.com

SLICK CASTING LTD   **T/F** 07957 398213
Unit 19, 2nd Floor
5 Blackhorse Lane, London E17 6DS
T 07944 939462
E info@slickcasting.com
W www.slickcasting.com

SOLOMON ARTISTES　　T 020 7748 4409
30 Clarence Street
Southend-on-Sea
Essex SS1 1BD
T 01702 437118
E solomonartistes@hotmail.co.uk
W www.solomon-artistes.co.uk

**SPIRIT MODELS & PROMOTION
AGENCY THE**　　T 0843 6365022
Character & Commercial
91 Stocking Park Road
Lightmoor Village
Telford, Shropshire TF4 3QZ
T 07436 803496
E bookings@spiritmodels.co.uk
W www.spiritmodels.co.uk

**SPORTS PROMOTIONS
(UK) LTD**　　T 020 8771 4700
56 Church Road, Crystal Palace
London SE19 2EZ
F 020 8771 4704
E agent@sportspromotions.co.uk
W www.sportspromotions.co.uk

STAV'S CASTING AGENCY　　T 07539 810640
82 Station Crescent, Tottenham
Haringey, London N15 5BD
E stavros.louca@facebook.com
W www.stavscastingagency.com

**SUMMERS, Mark
MANAGEMENT**　　T 020 7229 8413
1 Beaumont Avenue, West Kensington
London W14 9LP
E louise@marksummers.com
W www.marksummers.com

TUESDAYS CHILD LTD　　T/F 01625 501765
Children & Adults
Oakfield House, Springwood Way
Macclesfield SK10 2XA
E admin@tuesdayschildagency.co.uk
W www.tuesdayschildagency.co.uk

UNI-VERSAL EXTRAS　　T 0845 0090344
Pinewood Studios, Pinewood Road
Iver Heath, Buckinghamshire SL0 0NH
E info@universalextras.co.uk
W www.universalextrascasting.co.uk

ALDERSHOT: West End Centre   **T** 01252 408040
Queens Road, Aldershot
Hants GU11 3JD
BO 01252 330040
E westendcentre@hants.gov.uk
W www.westendcentre.co.uk

BILLERICAY:
Billericay Arts Association   **T** 01277 659286
The Fold, 72 Laindon Road, Billericay
Essex CM12 9LD
E baathefold@yahoo.co.uk
W www.baathefold.org.uk

BINGLEY: Bingley Arts Centre   **T** 01274 519814
Home of Bingley Little Theatre
Main Street, Bingley
West Yorkshire BD16 2LZ
E office@bingleyartscentre.co.uk

BIRMINGHAM:
Custard Factory   **T** 0121 224 7777
Gibb Street, Digbeth
Birmingham B9 4AA
E info@custardfactory.co.uk
W www.custardfactory.co.uk

BOSTON: Blackfriars Theatre &
Arts Centre   **T** 01205 363108
Spain Lane, Boston
Lincolnshire PE21 6HP
F 01205 358855
E director@blackfriarsartscentre.co.uk
W www.blackfriarsartscentre.co.uk

BRACKNELL:
South Hill Park Arts Centre   **T** 01344 484858
Contact: Ron McAllister (Chief Executive)
Ringmead, Bracknell
Berkshire RG12 7PA
BO 01344 484123
E admin@southhillpark.org.uk
W www.southhillpark.org.uk

BRENTFORD: Watermans   **T** 020 8232 1019
40 High Street, Brentford TW8 0DS
BO 020 8232 1010
E info@watermans.org.uk
W www.watermans.org.uk

BRIDGWATER:
Bridgwater Arts Centre   **T** 01278 422700
11-13 Castle Street, Bridgwater
Somerset TA6 3DD
E info@bridgwaterartscentre.co.uk
W www.bridgwaterartscentre.co.uk

BRISTOL: Arnolfini   **T** 0117 917 2300
16 Narrow Quay, Bristol BS1 4QA
F 0117 917 2303
E boxoffice@arnolfini.org.uk

BUILTH WELLS:
Wyeside Arts Centre   **T** 01982 553668
Castle Street, Builth Wells
Powys LD2 3BN
BO 01982 552555
E boxoffice@wyeside.co.uk
W www.wyeside.co.uk

BURY: The Met   **T** 0161 761 7107
Contact: David Agnew (Director)
Market Street, Bury, Lancs BL9 0BW
BO 0161 761 2216
E post@themet.biz
W www.themet.biz

CANNOCK:
Prince of Wales Centre   **T** 01543 466453
Contact: Richard Kay (General Manager)
Church Street, Cannock
Staffs WS11 1DE
BO 01543 578762
E r.k@wllt.org

CARDIFF:
Chapter Arts Centre   **T** 029 2030 4400
Market Road, Canton
Cardiff CF5 1QE
E enquiry@chapter.org
W www.chapter.org

CHIPPING NORTON:
The Theatre   **T** 01608 642349
Contact: John Terry (Director), Ambereene Hitchcox
(Head of Operations), Harriet Mackie (Casting)
2 Spring Street, Chipping Norton
Oxon OX7 5NL
BO 01608 642350
E admin@chippingnortontheatre.com
W www.chippingnortontheatre.com

CHRISTCHURCH:
The Regent Centre   **BO** 01202 499199
Contact: Greg Rawlings (Manager)
51 High Street, Christchurch
Dorset BH23 1AS
E admin@regentcentre.co.uk
W www.regentcentre.co.uk

CIRENCESTER:
New Brewery Arts   **T** 01285 657181
Brewery Court, Cirencester
Glos GL7 1JH
F 01285 644060
E admin@newbreweryarts.org.uk
W www.newbreweryarts.org.uk

COLCHESTER:
Colchester Arts Centre   **T** 01206 500900
Contact: Anthony Roberts (Director)
Church Street, Colchester
Essex CO1 1NF
E info@colchesterartscentre.com
W www.colchesterartscentre.com

COVENTRY:
Warwick Arts Centre   **T** 024 7652 3734
Contact: Alan Rivett (Director)
University of Warwick, Coventry CV4 7AL
BO 024 7652 4524
E arts.centre@warwick.ac.uk
W www.warwickartscentre.co.uk

CUMBERNAULD:
Cumbernauld Theatre   **T** 01236 737235
Kildrum, Cumbernauld G67 2BN
BO 01236 732887
E info@cumbernauldtheatre.co.uk
W www.cumbernauldtheatre.co.uk

DERRY: The Playhouse   **T** 028 7126 8027
5-7 Artillery Street
Derry/Londonderry BT48 6RG
E info@derryplayhouse.co.uk
W www.derryplayhouse.co.uk

EDINBURGH:
Scottish Storytelling Centre   **T** 0131 556 9579
Contact: Reception
43-45 High Street, Edinburgh EH1 1SR
E reception@scottishstorytellingcentre.com
W www.tracscotland.org/scottish-storytelling-centre

Arts Centres

EPSOM: Playhouse   T 01372 742226
Contact: Elaine Teague
Ashley Avenue, Epsom
Surrey KT18 5AL
BO 01372 742555
E eteague@epsom-ewell.gov.uk
W www.epsomplayhouse.co.uk

EXETER: Exeter Phoenix   T 01392 667060
Contact: Patrick Cunningham (Director)
Bradninch Place, Gandy Street
Exeter, Devon EX4 3LS
BO 01392 667080
E admin@exeterphoenix.org.uk
W www.exeterphoenix.org.uk

FAREHAM:
Ashcroft Arts Centre   T 01329 235161
Contact: Annabel Cook (Director/Programmer)
Osborn Road, Fareham
Hants PO16 7DX
BO 01329 223100
E ashcroft@hants.gov.uk
W www.ashcroft.org.uk

FROME: Merlin Theatre   T 01373 461360
Bath Road, Frome
Somerset BA11 2HG
BO 01373 465949
E merlintheatreoffice@gmail.com
W www.merlintheatre.co.uk

GAINSBOROUGH:
Trinity Arts Centre   T 01427 676655
Trinity Street, Gainsborough
Lincolnshire DN21 2AL
E karen.whitfield@west-lindsey.gov.uk
W www.trinityarts.co.uk

GREAT TORRINGTON:
The Plough Arts Centre   T 01805 622552
9-11 Fore Street
Great Torrington
Devon EX38 8HQ
BO 01805 624624
E mail@theploughartscentre.org.uk
W www.theploughartscentre.org.uk

HAVANT: Spring Arts &
Heritage Centre   BO 023 9247 2700
Contact: Sophie Fullerlove (Director)
East Street, Havant
Hants PO9 1BS
E info@thespring.co.uk
W www.thespring.co.uk

HELMSLEY:
Helmsley Arts Centre   T 01439 772112
Contact: Em Whitfield Brooks (Artistic Director)
Meeting House Court
Helmsley
York YO62 5DW
BO 01439 771700
E emhelmsleyarts@yahoo.co.uk
W www.helmsleyarts.co.uk

HEMEL HEMPSTEAD:
Old Town Hall   T 01442 228090
Contact: Sara Railson (Art & Entertainment Manager)
High Street
Hemel Hempstead
Herts HP1 3AE
BO 01442 228091
E othadmin@dacorum.gov.uk
W www.oldtownhall.co.uk

HEXHAM: Queens Hall Arts   BO 01434 652477
Contact: Geof Keys (Artistic Director)
Beaumont Street, Hexham
Northumberland NE46 3LS
E boxoffice@queenshall.co.uk
W www.queenshall.co.uk

HORSHAM: The Capitol   T 01403 756080
North Street, Horsham
West Sussex RH12 1RG
F 01403 756092
W www.thecapitolhorsham.com

HUDDERSFIELD: Kirklees Communities &
Leisure Services   T 01484 221000
4th Floor South, Civic Centre 1
Huddersfield HD1 2YU
E arts.creativity@kirklees.gov.uk
W www.kirklees.gov.uk

INVERNESS: Eden Court   T 01463 239841
Contact: Colin Marr (Director)
Bishop's Road
Inverness IV3 5SA
BO 01463 234234
E admin@eden-court.co.uk
W www.eden-court.co.uk

ISLE OF WIGHT: Quay Arts   T 01983 822490
Sea Street, Newport Harbour
Isle of Wight PO30 5BD
E info@quayarts.org
W www.quayarts.org

JERSEY: Jersey Arts Centre   T 01534 700400
Contact: Daniel Austin (Director)
Phillips Street, St Helier
Jersey JE2 4SW
BO 01534 700444
E enquiries@artscentre.je
W www.artscentre.je

KENDAL: Brewery Arts Centre   BO 01539 725133
Contact: Richard Foster (Chief Executive)
Highgate, Kendal
Cumbria LA9 4HE
E admin@breweryarts.co.uk
W www.breweryarts.co.uk

KING'S LYNN:
King's Lynn Arts Centre   T 01553 779095
29 King Street, King's Lynn
Norfolk PE30 1HA
BO 01553 764864
E info@kingslynnarts.co.uk
W www.kingslynnarts.co.uk

LEICESTER: Phoenix Square   T 0116 242 2803
Midland Street
Leicester LE1 1TG
BO 0116 242 2800
W www.phoenix.org.uk

LICHFIELD: Lichfield Arts   T 01543 262223
Donegal House
Bore Street
Lichfield WS13 6LU
E info@lichfieldarts.org.uk
W www.lichfieldarts.org.uk

LISKEARD: Sterts Theatre   T 01579 362962
Upton Cross, Liskeard
Cornwall PL14 5AZ
T 01579 362382
E office2@stertsarts.org
W www.sterts.co.uk

LONDON: The Albany　T 020 8692 4446
Douglas Way, Deptford
London SE8 4AG
F 020 8469 2253
E reception@thealbany.org.uk
W www.thealbany.org.uk

LONDON: The Amadeus　T 020 7286 1686
50 Shirland Road, Little Venice
London W9 2JA
E info@theamadeus.co.uk
W www.theamadeus.co.uk

LONDON: Artsdepot　BO 020 8369 5454
5 Nether Street, Tally Ho Corner
North Finchley, London N12 0GA
E info@artsdepot.co.uk
W www.artsdepot.co.uk

LONDON:
Battersea Arts Centre　T 020 7223 6557
Lavender Hill, Battersea
London SW11 5TN
BO 020 7223 2223
E boxoffice@bac.org.uk
W www.bac.org.uk

LONDON: Chats Palace　T 020 8533 0227
Contact: Candy Horsbrugh (Centre Director)
42-44 Brooksby's Walk, Hackney
London E9 6DF
E info@chatspalace.com
W www.chatspalace.com

LONDON: The Cockpit　T/BO 020 7258 2925
Gateforth Street
London NW8 8EH
E mail@thecockpit.org.uk
W www.thecockpit.org.uk

LONDON:
The Hangar Arts Trust　T 020 3004 6173
Unit 7A, Mellish House
Harrington Way
London SE18 5NR
E info@hangarartstrust.org
W www.hangarartstrust.org

LONDON:
Hoxton Hall Arts Centre　T 020 7684 0060
Contact: Ben West (Casting Director)
130 Hoxton Street, London N1 6SH
E info@hoxtonhall.co.uk
W www.hoxtonhall.co.uk

LONDON:
Institute of Contemporary Arts　T 020 7930 0493
Contact: Matt Williams (Curator). No in-house
Productions or Castings
The Mall, London SW1Y 5AH
BO 020 7930 3647
W www.ica.org.uk

LONDON:
Islington Arts Factory　T 020 7607 0561
2 Parkhurst Road
London N7 0SF
E info@islingtonartsfactory.org
W www.islingtonartsfactory.org

LONDON: Jacksons Lane　T 020 8340 5226
269A Archway Road
London N6 5AA
BO 020 8341 4421
E admin@jacksonslane.org.uk
W www.jacksonslane.org.uk

LONDON:
Menier Chocolate Factory　T 020 7378 1712
Contact: David Babani (Artistic Director)
53 Southwark Street, London SE1 1RU
BO 020 7378 1713
E office@menierchocolatefactory.com
W www.menierchocolatefactory.com

LONDON: October Gallery　T 020 7242 7367
24 Old Gloucester Street, London WC1N 3AL
F 020 7405 1851
E press@octobergallery.co.uk
W www.octobergallery.co.uk

LONDON: Omnibus Arts Centre　T 020 7498 4699
1 Northside, Clapham Common
London SW4 0QW
E hires@omnibus-clapham.org

LONDON: Ovalhouse　T 020 7582 0080
Contact: Rachel Briscoe & Rebecca Atkinson-Lord
(Directors of Theatre), Deborah Bestwick (Director)
52-54 Kennington Oval, London SE11 5SW
E info@ovalhouse.com
W www.ovalhouse.com

LONDON: Polish Social &
Cultural Association　T 020 8741 1940
238-246 King Street, London W6 0RF

MAIDENHEAD: Norden Farm Centre
for the Arts　T 01628 682555
Contact: Jane Corry (Chief Executive & Artistic Director)
Altwood Road
Maidenhead SL6 4PF
BO 01628 788997
E admin@nordenfarm.org
W www.nordenfarm.org

MAIDSTONE: Hazlitt Theatre　T 01622 753922
Contact: Natalie Price (General Manager)
Earl Street, Maidstone
Kent ME14 1PL
BO 01622 758611
E hazlitt.boxoffice@parkwoodtheatres.co.uk

MANCHESTER: The Lowry　BO 0843 2086000
Contact: Steve Cowton (Senior Theatre Programmer)
Pier 8, Salford Quays M50 3AZ
F 0161 876 2021
E boxofficeadmin@thelowry.com
W www.thelowry.com

MILFORD HAVEN:
Torch Theatre　T 01646 694192
Contact: Peter Doran (Artistic Director)
St Peter's Road, Milford Haven
Pembrokeshire SA73 2BU
BO 01646 695267
E info@torchtheatre.co.uk
W www.torchtheatre.co.uk

NORWICH:
Norwich Arts Centre　T 01603 660387
St Benedicts Street, Norwich
Norfolk NR2 4PG
BO 01603 660352
E pasco@norwichartscentre.co.uk
W www.norwichartscentre.co.uk

NOTTINGHAM:
Lakeside Arts Centre　T 0115 846 7777
University Park
Nottingham NG7 2RD
E lakeside-marketing@nottingham.ac.uk
W www.lakesidearts.org.uk

NUNEATON: Abbey Theatre   T 024 7632 7359
Contact: Tony Deeming (Chairman)
Pool Bank Street
Nuneaton
Warks CV11 5DB
BO 024 7635 4090
E admin@abbeytheatre.co.uk
W www.abbeytheatre.co.uk

**POOLE: Lighthouse Poole Centre
for the Arts**   T 0844 4068666
Kingland Road, Poole
Dorset BH15 1UG
W www.lighthousepoole.co.uk

**RADLETT:
The Radlett Centre**   T 01923 857546
1 Aldenham Avenue, Radlett
Herts WD7 8HL
F 01923 857592
E admin@radlettcentre.com
W www.radlettcentre.co.uk

**ROTHERHAM:
Rotherham Civic Theatre**   T 01709 823621 (T/BO)
Contact: Mark Scott (Theatre Manager)
Catherine Street
Rotherham
South Yorkshire S65 1EB
T 01709 823641 (Admin)
E theatre.tickets@rotherham.gov.uk
W www.rotherhamtheatres.co.uk

**SALISBURY:
Salisbury Arts Centre**   T 01722 343020
Bedwin Street, Salisbury
Wiltshire SP1 3UT
BO 01722 321744
E info@salisburyarts.co.uk
W www.salisburyartscentre.co.uk

**SHREWSBURY: The Gateway
Education & Arts Centre**   T 01743 355159
The Gateway, Chester Street
Shrewsbury
Shropshire SY1 1NB
E gateway.centre@shropshire.gov.uk
W www.shropshire.gov.uk

**STAMFORD:
Stamford Arts Centre**   T 01780 480846
Contact: Graham Burley (General Manager)
27 St Mary's Street, Stamford
Lincolnshire PE9 2DL
BO 01780 763203
E boxoffice@stamfordartscentre.com
W www.stamfordartscentre.com

**STIRLING:
MacRobert Arts Centre**   T 01786 467155
University of Stirling
Stirling FK9 4LA
BO 01786 466666
E info@macrobert.org
W www.macrobert.org

**SWANSEA:
Taliesin Arts Centre**   T 01792 295238
Contact: Sybil Crouch (Head of Cultural Services)
Swansea University
Singleton Park
Swansea SA2 8PZ
BO 01792 602060
E s.e.crouch@swansea.ac.uk
W www.taliesinartscentre.co.uk

**TOTNES:
The Arts at Dartington**   T 01803 847000
Dartington Space
Dartington Hall
Totnes, Devon TQ9 6EN
BO 01803 847070
E arts@dartington.org
W www.dartington.org/arts

**TUNBRIDGE WELLS:
Trinity Theatre**   T 01892 678670
Church Road, Tunbridge Wells
Kent TN1 1JP
BO 01892 678678
E enquiries@trinitytheatre.net

ULEY: Prema   T 01453 860703
Contact: Gordon Scott (Director)
South Street, Uley
Nr Dursley, Glos GL11 5SS
E info@prema.demon.co.uk
W www.prema.org.uk

**VALE OF GLAMORGAN:
St Donats Arts Centre**   T 01446 799309
Contact: Karen Davies (Commercial Director)
St Donats Castle
The Vale of Glamorgan CF61 1WF
BO 01446 799100
E enquiries@stdonats.com

**WAKEFIELD:
Wakefield Arts Centre**   T 01924 789815
Mechanics' Theatre, Wood Street
Wakefield WF1 2EW
E c.lomas@wakefield.ac.uk
W www.facebook.com/mechanicstheatre

**WASHINGTON:
Arts Centre Washington**   T 0191 219 3455
Biddick Lane, Fatfield
Washington
Tyne & Wear NE38 8AB
E acw@sunderland.gov.uk

**WELLINGBOROUGH:
The Castle**   T 01933 229022
*Contact: Darren Walter (Director), Phillip Money (Theatre
Administrator)*
Castle Way, Wellingborough
Northants NN8 1XA
BO 01933 270007
E info@thecastle.org.uk
W www.thecastle.org.uk

WIMBORNE: Layard Theatre   T 01202 847529
*Contact: Chris Thomas (Director of Drama), Christine
Haynes (Administrator)*
Canford School, Canford Magna
Wimborne, Dorset BH21 3AD
BO 01202 847525
E layardtheatre@canford.com

**WINDSOR: The Firestation Centre
for Arts & Culture**   T 01753 866865
The Old Court
St Leonards Road
Windsor, Berks SL4 3BL
E info@firestationartscentre.com
W www.firestationartscentre.com

WREXHAM: Oriel Wrecsam   T 01978 292093
Rhosddu Road
Wrexham LL11 1AU
E oriel.wrecsam@wrexham.gov.uk

C

Casting Directors
Consultants
Costumes, Wigs & Make-Up
Critics

CDG
For information regarding membership of
the Casting Directors' Guild please see:

W www.thecdg.co.uk

Casting Directors

Who are casting directors?

Casting directors are employed by directors/ production companies to source the best available actors for roles across television, film, radio, theatre and commercials. They do the groundwork and present a shortlist of artists to the director, who often makes the final selection. Many casting directors work on a freelance basis, others are employed permanently by larger organisations such as the BBC or the National Theatre. Discovering new and emerging talent also plays an important part in their job.

Why should I approach them?

If you are an actor looking for work, you can promote yourself directly to casting directors by sending them your photo and CV. They keep actors' details on file and may consider you for future productions. Bear in mind that you will not be guaranteed a response as casting directors are physically unable to reply to every one of the vast numbers of letters they receive from actors, but it is worth your while to explore this opportunity to find work.

How should I approach them?

Many of the casting directors in this section have indicated the method in which they prefer actors to contact them for the first time. This tends to be by post but some accept or prefer e-mails. Some are happy to receive telephone calls, but be aware that casting directors are very busy and you should not continually call them with questions or updates once you have sent your CV. If they have not specified whether they prefer postal or e-mail contact, you should send them your CV, a headshot and a covering letter by post only, as this is the traditional method of contacting casting profes sionals. You should always include a stamped-addressed envelope (SAE) big enough to contain your 10 x 8 photo and with sufficient postage. This will increase your chances of getting a reply. Write your name and telephone number on the back of your headshot in case it gets separated from your CV.

Should I send a casting director my showreel and/or voicereel?

Some casting directors have also indicated that they are happy for actors to send showreels and/or voicereels along with their CVs and headshots, but if this is not specified, we would recommend that you leave these out of your correspondence but highlight in your covering letter that they are available or provide links to where they may be able to view online showreels. If a casting director is interested in you, they can contact you later for these items, but they usually prefer not to sift through hundreds of unsolicited showreels until they have first established an interest in an actor.

How do I target my search?

It is not advisable to send a generic CV to every casting director listed in this section. Research the names and companies and then target your letters accordingly. Find out what areas of the industry each one usually casts for (some specify this in their listing) and what productions they have previously cast. Keep an eye on television, film and theatre credits so you become familiar with the casting directors used for different productions. Some of these casting directors have their own websites. If a casting director has 'CDG Member' after their name, it means they are a member of the Casting Directors' Guild, the professional organisation of casting directors working in the UK (see www.thecdg.co.uk for more information and their case study in this section).

How do I write an effective CV and covering letter?

Once you have made a short-list of suitable casting directors you should send them your CV, your headshot, and an individually tailored covering letter. The covering letter should demonstrate that you have researched the casting director and ideally you will have a particular reason for contacting them at this time: perhaps you can tell them about your next showcase, or where they can see you currently appearing. Your CV should be no longer than one page, up-to-date and spell-checked.

Casting Directors

Please see the 'Promotional Services' section of Contacts for further advice on writing CVs and covering letters.

How do I prepare for a casting/audition?

Make sure you are fully prepared with accurate information about the audition time, venue, format and the people you will be meeting. Unless it's a last minute casting, you should always read the script in advance and try to have some opinions on it. If you are asked in advance to prepare a piece, always stick to the brief with something suitable and relevant.

On the day, allow plenty of time to get there so you are not flustered when you arrive. Try to be positive and enjoy yourself. Remember, the casting director doesn't want to spend several days auditioning - they want you to get the job! Never criticise previous productions you have worked on. And at the end of the casting, remember to take your script away unless you are asked to leave it, otherwise it can look as if you're not interested.

Please see 'Rehearsal Rooms and Casting Suites' for more detailed advice on preparing for and attending auditions.

Should I attend a casting in a house or flat?

Professional auditions are rarely held anywhere other than an official casting studio or venue. Be very wary if you are asked to go elsewhere. Trust your instincts. If something doesn't seem right to you, it probably isn't. Always take someone with you if you are in any doubt.

How do I become a casting director?

The best way to gain experience in this field is to work as a casting assistant. Vacancies are sometimes advertised in The Stage www.thestage.co.uk. Alternatively you could try sending your CV to casting directors asking for an internship or work experience. Just as we advise actors, remember to research any casting director you are considering approaching to make sure they actually work in the area you are interested in. Work experience is likely to be unpaid, but the experience and contacts you gain will be invaluable. You may find it helpful to refer to Equity's advice leaflet *Low Pay/No Pay* which is available to all Equity members from their website's members' area.

CASE STUDY

When you read CDG after a casting director's name, you know they are a member of The Casting Directors' Guild and will therefore have a minimum of five years' experience. The current CDG Committee has the following advice for actors.

Casting directors are there to help actors and not to hinder them. We want you to do your best as that reflects back on us, and you should realise that we are only as good as the actors we submit for each role.

Much of our work consists of creating a shortlist of potential actors and reducing it to a suitably sized group to present for audition. We also spend a great deal of time watching you work. Members of the CDG endeavour to cover as many performances as possible on film, television and in the theatre. There is no substitute to seeing you act.

When asked to attend an interview or audition, an actor should feel confident in asking their agent any relevant questions about the role and the project. If this is not forthcoming, arrive early and seek information from the casting director or, better still, contact them the day before. If it is only possible to speak to the casting director on the day, preferably do so before entering the audition room, rather than in front of the director or producer. The casting director will be happy to help.

Sometimes you will only receive pages for a role, but a casting director will always endeavour to give you as much information about a character as is available. When possible, read the entire play/screenplay rather than just the scenes your 'character' appears in, and ideally be able to talk about the script as a whole during the interview. Take your time when reading; preparation is worth a lot but don't be fazed if you get lost over their script. If you feel that a scene is going terribly it's ok to start again.

For most non-theatre jobs these days you will find that your meeting will be recorded. These are then shown to the various producers involved, and this is when the process can slow down. It takes time to build a company and for final casting choices to be made.

Casting is a matter of interpretation. As well as character information derived from the script, the vision of the producer, director, casting director and indeed the actor all come into play.

There are many reasons why one actor will be chosen over another, and even the best audition might not necessarily secure a part. Every aspect of the actor comes into play. Is he/she too young or too mature? Do they work as a family? Could they be mother and son? Does the chemistry work? There is also the frustrating problem of scripts, and parts, being re-written. A character may have an entirely different physical description in a later draft. Sadly we do not have control over this.

When it comes to contacting casting directors, most are happy to receive letters, updated photos and CVs. The best correspondence for casting directors to receive is performance information. Letters should be brief and to the point, with the production name, director, venue and/or television channel clearly stated. If you are enquiring about work be as specific as possible, e.g. "I would like to be seen for the part of … in … because …" or something similar. Dear Sir or Madam letters just don't work.

CVs should be well laid out. List most recent work first and use your spell checker. 6x4 photos are fine to send but include an SAE if you want them returned. Casting directors rarely like unsolicited DVDs and showreels: you must be aware that we do get inundated. Also bear in mind that not receiving a response to your letter does not mean it hasn't been read and filed: it is virtually impossible to reply to the volume of mail received from actors.

In our greener world it's great that Spotlight and other web media now have the facility for us to view CVs, photos and showreels online. Use the technology: it's very easy to keep your CV up-to-date online and you can change your photo, showreel or voicereel at any time of year without having to do a huge mail out to let people know.

Actors are a fundamental tool of this industry: CDG members are aware of this and aim to put actors at their ease. Audition nerves are a given but you should feel secure that the reason you are in the room is because someone wants you to get that role and not because they want to see you fail.

**To find out more visit
www.thecdg.co.uk**

Casting Directors

CASE STUDY

Andy Pryor is a casting director, mainly working in television and occasionally in film. He trained at the Central School of Speech and Drama as a Stage Manager and worked at the Royal Court and Bush Theatre.

As a stage manager, I developed a long standing appreciation and knowledge of actors. Being lucky enough to work in these great new writing theatres, I was incredibly well placed to meet a huge variety of actors and to see at close hand how they worked and responded to new material, to the directors they worked with and to other actors. I then went on to work for Gail Stevens, from whom I learned a huge amount about television and film casting before setting up on my own in the mid 90s.

When I was asked to write for Contacts, I knew that it would be a difficult task to fit a great deal into a relatively short article. Also, each casting director is different, so I can only speak for myself but the tips here, although barely skimming the surface are, I think, helpful and focus on television auditions (although much of this applies to auditions for other media).

We try and get the material for the audition to actors as far ahead as possible. Often, when casting sessions depend on the availability of directors, shooting schedules etc., we are arranging them at quite short notice. We do of course take that into consideration in terms of familiarity with the material. It is however, extremely important that you make yourself as familiar as possible with the scene(s) you have been asked to prepare. Unfortunately, we regularly see actors to whom material has been sent at least two or three days before the audition, then they arrive and say that they haven't had time to learn it, or if a whole script has been sent that they haven't had time to read the whole thing, just their scenes! It can't be stressed enough that preparation makes the crucial difference between a good and a bad audition.

Another extremely important thing to do before an audition is to research. Research the project you are going up for as thoroughly as possible. The internet is a great resource and using sites like IMDb (Internet Movie Database) is extremely worthwhile when seeking information on casting directors, directors, producers etc. Also, if you are going up for an episode of a series that has already been on for at least a season then watch an episode of the show, so that you are familiar with its style and tone. This isn't to say that you need to come in and wax lyrical about the production, or indeed the work of those involved but having this background information is key, not least because it will give you confidence that you know what you are talking about.

It is always good to come in with your own "take" on a character. We are often impressed in the room with an actor's spin on a part (within reason), which may be one that we haven't thought of before. That said, it is also important to be able to take a note and adjust the performance accordingly. Often a director (and the casting director) will want to see that an actor is capable of taking and processing notes so that they know they can successfully communicate with an actor under pressure on set. Even if very often the director might revert to the instinctive performance an actor gave in their first reading, the security a director feels in knowing an actor can respond to them sensitively makes a huge difference.

Every audition will be different and this is the briefest glimpse of things that you will encounter in a television audition. It's always wise to expect the unexpected. For example, some directors are happy for you to read once, that isn't necessarily a reflection on you, it's just the way some directors work. Others will try a scene many times, as that's how they feel they can really get to know how an actor works.

Finally, it's important to remember that good casting directors do what they do because they love actors. They want to help them to be the best they can be. We get you in to the room because we believe in you and want to give you a chance to fulfil your potential, so as daunting as the situation can sometimes be, do remember that. Also, do ask questions if you have them. We are there to help!

Valerie Colgan

- For professional actors who need a voice production "MOT"
- Private individual classes
- Valerie Colgan and a consortium of tutors as appropriate on audition technique

Ex Head of Drama at the City Lit • 5 Drama Schools • The Actors Centre
Tel: 020 7267 2153 The Green, 17 Herbert Street, London NW5 4HA

1066 PRODUCTIONS LTD
34 Pine Hill, Epsom, Surrey KT18 7BG
E admin@1066productions.com
W www.1066productions.com

1505　T 020 7112 8750
20 Bedford Street, London WC2E 9HP
E hello@weare1505.co.uk
W www.weare1505.co.uk

A C A CASTING　T/F 020 7384 2635
Contact: Catherine Arton
London
E catherine@acacasting.com

ACTING-UP.COM CASTING　T 07434 843070
Based in Liverpool & London
PO Box 2732, Liverpool L2 3PF
E casting@acting-up.com
W www.acting-up.com

ADAMSON-PARKER, Jo　T 07787 311270
Contact: By e-mail. Accepts Showreels
E jo@northerndrama.co.uk

AILION, Pippa　T 020 7738 7556
CDG Member
Unit 67B, Eurolink Business Centre
49 Effra Road, London SW2 1BZ
E enquiries@pippaailioncasting.co.uk

ALL DIRECTIONS OF LONDON
Contact: By Post only
7 Rupert Court, Off Wardour Street
London W1D 6EB

ANDERSON, Jane
CDG Member. Contact: By e-mail. Accepts Links to Online Showreels only. Film. Television
E casting@janeandersononline.com
W www.janeandersononline.com

ANDREW, Dorothy CASTING　T 0161 344 2709
CDG Member
E dorothyandrewcasting@gmail.com

ARNELL, Jane
Flat 2, 39 St Peters Square, London W6 9NN
E janearnellcasting@gmail.com

ARNOLD, Jim　T 020 7738 7556
CDG Member. Contact: By e-mail only
c/o Pippa Ailion Casting
E jim@pippaailioncasting.co.uk

ARTHUR, Camilla CASTING　T 07557 220636
Contact: By e-mail. Commercials. Film. Modelling. "Street Casting" & Fashion
12 Westbere Road
London NW2 3SR
E camilla@camillaarthurcasting.com
W www.camillaarthurcasting.com

ASH LIVE CASTING　T 020 8655 7656
3B Nettlefold Place
West Norwood
London SE27 0JW
E casting@ashproductionslive.com
W www.ashproductionsliveltd.com

ASHTON HINKINSON CASTING　T 020 7580 6101
Unit 15, Panther House
38 Mount Pleasant
London WC1X 0AN
E casting@ahcasting.com
W www.ashtonhinkinson.com

BAIG, Shaheen CASTING　T 020 7240 4278
3rd Floor, 20 Denmark Street
London WC2H 8NA
E info@shaheenbaigcasting.com
W www.shaheenbaigcasting.com

BARNES, Derek　T 020 8228 7096
CDG Member
BBC DRAMA SERIES CASTING
BBC Elstree, Room N221
Neptune House, Clarendon Road
Borehamwood, Herts WD6 1JF
F 020 8228 8311

BARNETT, Briony　T 020 7836 3751
CDG Member
11 Goodwins Court, London WC2N 4LL

BEACH CASTING LTD　T 020 7836 6477
Contact: Brendan McNamara
405 Strand, London WC2R 0NE
T 07903 630964
E brendan@beach-casting.com
W www.beach-casting.com

BEASTALL, Lesley CASTING　T 020 7727 6496
Contact: Lesley Beastall
41E Elgin Crescent, London W11 2JD
E casting@lbcasting.co.uk
W www.lesleybeastallcasting.com

BECKLEY, Rowland
BBC DRAMA SERIES CASTING
BBC Elstree, Room N222
Neptune House, Clarendon Road
Borehamwood, Herts WD6 1JF
F 020 8228 7130

BERTRAND, Leila CASTING   **T/F** 020 8964 0683
E leilabcasting@gmail.com
W www.leilabcasting.com

BEVAN, Lucy   **T** 020 8567 6655
CDG Member
Ealing Studios, Ealing Green
London W5 5EP

BEWICK, Maureen   **T** 020 8450 1604
104A Dartmouth Road
London NW2 4HB

BIRD, Sarah   **T** 020 7371 3248
CDG Member
PO Box 32658
London W14 0XA

BLIGH, Nicky
CDG Member
E nicky@nickyblighcasting.com

BRACKE, Siobhan   **T** 020 8891 5686
CDG Member. Contact: By Post
Basement Flat, 22A The Barons
St Margaret's TW1 2AP

BUCKINGHAM, Jo   **T** 07753 605491
CDG Member
E jo@jobuckinghamcasting.co.uk
W www.jobuckinghamcasting.co.uk

CANDID CASTING   **T** 020 7490 8882
2G Woodstock Studios
36 Woodstock Grove
London W12 8LE
E mail@candidcasting.co.uk
W www.candidcasting.co.uk

CANNON, John   **T** 020 8228 7322
CDG Member
BBC DRAMA SERIES CASTING
BBC Elstree, Room N223
Neptune House, Clarendon Road
Borehamwood, Herts WD6 1JF
F 020 8228 8311
E john.cannon@bbc.co.uk

**CANNON DUDLEY &
ASSOCIATES**   **T** 020 7433 3393
*Contact: Carol Dudley (CDG Member). By Post. Film.
Stage. Television*
F 020 7813 2048
E cdacasting@blueyonder.co.uk

CARROLL, Anji   **T** 07957 253769
*CDG Member. Contact: By e-mail. Stage. Film.
Television*
E anji@anjicarroll.tv

CASTING ANGELS THE   **T/F** 020 8313 0443
Based in London & Paris
Suite 4, 14 College Road
Bromley, Kent BR1 3NS

CASTING COMPANY (UK) THE
Contact: Michelle Guish
E casting@michguish.com

CASTING COUCH THE   **T** 07932 785807
Contact: Moira Townsend. No CVs/Photos by Post
213 Trowbridge Road
Bradford on Avon
Wiltshire BA15 1EU
E moira@charactersstageschool.com

CASTING FOX THE   **T** 01628 771084
Contact: By e-mail only
E assistant@thecastingfox.co.uk

CATLIFF, Suzy
CDG Member. Co-author of The Casting Handbook
E soosecat@mac.com
W www.suzycatliff.co.uk

CHAND, Urvashi   **T** 020 8208 3861
CDG Member
Cinecraft, 69 Teignmouth Road
London NW2 4EA
E urvashi@cinecraft.biz

CHARD, Alison   **T** 020 7223 9125
CDG Member
23 Groveside Court
4 Lombard Road
Battersea, London SW11 3RQ
E chardcasting@btinternet.com

CHARKHAM CASTING   **T** 07956 456630
Contact: Beth Charkham
Suite 361, 14 Tottenham Court Road
London W1T 1JY
E charkhamcasting@btconnect.com

CLARK, Andrea   **T** 020 7381 9933
Adults & Children. Commercials. Film. Stage. Television
E andrea@aclarkcasting.com
W www.aclarkcasting.com

CLAYPOLE, Sam CASTING
PO Box 123, Darlington
Durham DL3 7WA
E contact@samclaypolecasting.com
W www.samclaypolecasting.com

CLAYTON, Rosalie   **T** 020 3605 6338
CDG Member
E office@rosalieclayton.com

CLOUTER, Lou CASTING   **T** 07905 146271
79 Empress Avenue
Aldersbrook
London E12 5SA
E lou@loucloutercasting.com
W www.loucloutercasting.com

**COCHRANE, Kharmel
CASTING LTD**   **T** 07885 384196
23 St Michael's Street
London W2 1QU
E kharmel@kharmelcochrane.co.uk
W www.kharmelcochrane.com

COGAN, Ben   **T** 020 8228 7516
BBC DRAMA SERIES CASTING
BBC Elstree, Room N221
Neptune House, Clarendon Road
Borehamwood, Herts WD6 1JF
F 020 8228 8311

COLLYER-BRISTOW, Ellie   **T** 07986 607075
35 Blackheath Park
London SE3 9RW
E elliecollyerbristow@yahoo.co.uk

SHEILA BURNETT
P H O T O G R A P H Y

Damian Lewis

Caroline Quentin

Kitty Lovett

Michael Absalom

020 7289 3058 | 07974 731391
www.sheilaburnett-headshots.com
Student Rates

CORDORAY, Lin
66 Cardross Street
London W6 0DR

COTTON, Irene   T 020 8299 2787
CDG Member
25 Druce Road, Dulwich Village
London SE21 7DW
T 020 8299 1595
E irenecotton@btinternet.com

CRAMPSIE, Julia   T 020 8228 7170
CDG Member. Casting Executive
BBC DRAMA SERIES CASTING
BBC Elstree, Room N224
Neptune House, Clarendon Road
Borehamwood, Herts WD6 1JF
F 020 8228 8311

CRANE, Carole CASTING   T 07976 869442
E crane.shot@virgin.net

**CRAWFORD, Kahleen
CASTING**   T 0141 425 1725
CDG Member
Film City Glasgow, Govan Town Hall
401 Govan Road, Glasgow G51 2QJ
T 07950 414164
E casting@kahleencrawford.com
W www.kahleencrawford.com

**CROCODILE CASTING
COMPANY THE**   T 020 8203 7009
Contact: Claire Toeman, Tracie Saban. By e-mail only
E croccast@aol.com
W www.crocodilecasting.com

CROSS, Louise   T 020 8341 2200
CDG Member
128A North View Road
London N8 7LP
E louisecross@mac.com

CROWE, Sarah CASTING   T 020 7286 5080
75 Amberley Road
London W9 2JL
F 020 7286 5030
E info@sarahcrowecasting.co.uk

CROWLEY, Suzanne
CDG Member. See CROWLEY POOLE CASTING

CROWLEY POOLE CASTING   T 020 7379 5965
*Contact: Suzanne Crowley (CDG Member), Gilly Poole
(CDG Member)*
11 Goodwins Court
London WC2N 4LL
E email@crowleypoole.co.uk

CURTIS, Sophie   T 07786 838588
E casting@sophiecurtis.net

DAVIES, Jane CASTING   T 020 8715 1036
*Contact: Jane Davies (CDG Member), John Connor.
By e-mail only. Film. Television. Comedy*
E info@janedaviescasting.co.uk

DAVIS, Leo (Miss)
See JUST CASTING

DAVY, Gary   T 020 7713 0888
CDG Member. Film. Television
Top Floor, 15 Crinan Street
York Way, Kings Cross, London N1 9SQ
E casting@garydavy.com

DAWES, Gabrielle   T 020 7435 3645
CDG Member
PO Box 52493, London NW3 9DZ
E gdawescasting@tiscali.co.uk

DAWES, Stephanie   T 07802 566642
CDG Member
13 Nevern Square
London SW5 9NW
E stephaniedawes5@gmail.com

DAY, Kate   T/F 01865 858709
Pound Cottage, 27 The Green South
Warborough, Oxon OX10 7DR

DE FREITAS, Paul
CDG Member
E info@pauldefreitas.com

DEITCH, Jane ASSOCIATES   T 07711 856789
14 Nashleigh Hill, Chesham
Bucks HP5 3JF
E casting@janedeitch.co.uk

DICKENS, Laura   T 07958 665468
CDG Member
197 Malpas Road, London SE4 1BH
E dickenscasting@aol.com

DONMAR WAREHOUSE   T 020 7240 4882
Contact: Alastair Coomer (Casting Director)
CDG Member
41 Earlham Street, Covent Garden
London WC2H 9LX
E casting@donmarwarehouse.com
W www.donmarwarehouse.com

DONNELLY, Laura CASTING   T 07917 414014
CV & Showreel on request. Film. Stage. Television
E laura@lauradonnellycasting.com
W www.lauradonnellycasting.com

DOWD, Kate   T 020 7828 8071
3rd Floor, 18 Buckingham Palace Road
London SW1W 0QP

DOWLING, Shakyra CASTING   T 020 7462 0797
Twitter: @shakyradowling
17 Percy Street
London W1T 1DU
T 07958 391198
E me@shakyradowlingcasting.com
W www.shakyradowlingcasting.com

DUDLEY, Carol
CDG Member. See CANNON DUDLEY & ASSOCIATES

DUFF, Julia   T 020 7836 5557
CDG Member
11 Goodwins Court
London WC2N 4LL
E info@juliaduff.co.uk

DUFF, Maureen   T 020 7586 0532
CDG Member
PO Box 47340
London NW3 4TY
E info@maureenduffcasting.com

DUFFY, Jennifer   T 020 7582 1348
CDG Member
9 Bryher Court, Sancroft Street
London SE11 5UQ
E casting@jennyduffy.co.uk

EAST, Irene CASTING   **T** 020 8876 5686
CDG Member. Contact: By Post. Film. Stage
40 Brookwood Avenue
Barnes, London SW13 0LR
E irneast@aol.com

EDWARDS, Daniel CASTING   **T** 020 7835 5616
CDG Member
E daniel@danieledwardscasting.com

EJ CASTING   **T** 07891 632946
E info@ejcastingonline.com
W www.ejcastingonline.com

EMMERSON, Chloe   **T** 020 8748 7595
Contact: By e-mail
E c@chloeemmerson.com

EVANS, Camilla CASTING
CDG Member
E camilla@camillaevans.com
W www.thecdg.co.uk

EVANS, Richard   **T** 020 8994 6304
CDG Member
10 Shirley Road, London W4 1DD
E contact@evanscasting.co.uk
W www.evanscasting.co.uk

EYE CASTING THE   **T** 020 7377 2700
1st Floor, 92 Commercial Street
Off Puma Court, London E1 6LZ
W www.theeyecasting.com

FEARNLEY, Ali CASTING   **T** 020 7613 7320
3rd Floor, 58-60 Rivington Street
London EC2A 3AU
T 07764 945614
E cast@alifearnley.com

FIGGIS, Susie   **T** 020 7482 2200
19 Spencer Rise
London NW5 1AR

FILDES, Bunny CASTING   **T** 020 7935 1254
CDG Member
56 Wigmore Street
London W1

FOX, Celestia   **T** 020 7720 6143
23 Leppoc Road
London SW4 9LS
E celestiafox@me.com

FRANKUM, Marc   **T** 020 8691 2911
CDG Member
PO Box 45293
London SE10 1BF
E marc@marcfrankum.com

FRECK, Rachel   **T/F** 020 8673 2455
CDG Member
E casting@rachelfreck.com

FREE RANGE CASTING   **T** 07854 794007
Contact: Sandy Tedford. Based in London
E sandy@freerangecasting.com
W www.freerangecasting.com

FRISBY, Jane CASTING   **T** 020 8340 7835
Contact: By e-mail. Accepts Showreels Online.
Commercials. Corporates. Feature Films
51 Ridge Road
London N8 9LJ
E janefrisby@hotmail.co.uk

FRUITCAKE   **T** 020 7993 5165
Contact: Thomas Adams, Andrew Mann
Studio 125, 77 Beak Street
London W1F 9DB
T 020 7993 6042
E casting@fruitcakelondon.com
W www.fruitcakelondon.com

FUNNELL, Caroline   **T** 020 7326 4417
CDG Member
25 Rattray Road
London SW2 1AZ

GANE CASTING   **T** 020 8446 2551
Contact: Natasha Gane
52 Woodhouse Road
London N12 0RJ
T 07976 685031
E natasha@ganecasting.com

GIBBONS, Martin CASTING   **T** 07976 912776
15 Lynton Road, Chorlton-cum-Hardy
Manchester M21 9NQ
E info@martingibbons.com
W www.martingibbons.com

GILLHAM, Tracey CASTING   **T** 01932 562112
CDG Member
Suite 929 Old House
Shepperton Studios, Studios Road
Shepperton, Middlesex TW17 0QD
E tracey@traceygillhamcasting.co.uk

GILLON, Tamara CASTING   **T** 020 8766 0099
26 Carson Road
London SE21 8HU
F 020 8265 6330
E tamara@tamaragillon.com
W www.tamaragillon.com

GLOBAL7   **T/F** 020 7281 7679
Kemp House, 152 City Road, London EC1V 2NX
T 07956 956652
E global7castings@gmail.com
W www.global7casting.com

GOLD, Nina   **T** 020 8960 6099
CDG Member
117 Chevening Road
London NW6 6DU
F 020 8968 6777
E info@ninagold.co.uk

GOOCH, Miranda CASTING   **T** 020 8962 9578
Contact: By Post/e-mail. Accepts Showreels/Voicereels.
Film. Stage. Television
102 Leighton Gardens
London NW10 3PR
F 020 8962 9579
E mirandagooch@gmail.com

GREEN, Jill CASTING   **T** 020 7632 4747
CDG Member
Wellington House, 1st Floor
125 Strand, London WC2R 0AP
T 020 7632 4748
E office@jillgreencasting.org

GREENE, Francesca
CASTING   **T** 020 8450 5577
37 Keyes Road, London NW2 3XB
E francescagreene@btinternet.com
W www.francescagreenecasting.com

SPOTLIGHT
The home of casting

Spotlight Database & Website

Browse over 60,000 performers' CVs with photos, showreels, voicereels and contact details

Use Spotlight's award-winning search engine to find exactly the right performer for the part

E-mail casting calls to hundreds of UK agents and performers

Spotlight Rooms and Studios

Hold your auditions in the heart of central London

www.spotlight.com/spaces
020 7440 5030

www.spotlight.com
020 7437 7631
casting@spotlight.com

GROSVENOR, Angela　T 020 8244 5665
CDG Member
66 Woodland Road
London SE19 1PA
E angela.grosvenor@virgin.net

GUISH, Michelle
See CASTING COMPANY (UK) THE

HAMMOND, Louis　T 020 7610 1579
E louis@louishammond.co.uk

**HAMMOND COX
CASTING**　T 020 7734 3335 (Office)
Contact: Michael Cox, Thom Hammond
2nd Floor
22 Noel Street
Soho, London W1F 8GS
T 07834 362691 (Michael)
E office@hammondcoxcasting.com
W www.hammondcoxcasting.com

HAMPSON, Janet CASTING　T 07931 513223
Based in Manchester. CDG Member
E janet@janethampson.co.uk
W www.janethampson.co.uk

HANCOCK, Gemma
CDG Member. Contact: By e-mail
E gemma@hancockstevenson.com

HARKIN, Julie CASTING　T 020 7278 0735
CDG Member
3rd Floor, 15 Crinan Street
London N1 9SQ
E info@julieharkincasting.com

HAWES, Jo　T 01628 773048
CDG Member. Children's Casting & Administration
21 Westfield Road, Maidenhead
Berkshire SL6 5AU
T 07824 337222
E joanne.hawes2013@gmail.com
W www.johawes.com

HAWSER, Gillian CASTING　T 020 7731 5988
CDG/CSA Member. Contact: Gillian Hawser
24 Cloncurry Street
London SW6 6DS
F 020 7731 0738
E gillianhawser@btinternet.com

HB CASTING　T 020 7871 2969
London
T 07957 114175
E hannah@hbcasting.com
W www.hbcasting.com

HB CASTING　T 0161 241 7786
Manchester
T 07957 114175
E hannah@hbcasting.com
W www.hbcasting.com

HILL, Serena　T 00 61 2 92501727
Sydney Theatre Company
Pier 4, Hickson Road
Walsh Bay, NSW 2000, Australia
E shill@sydneytheatre.com.au

HINTON, Maddy CASTING　T 020 8940 5535
270C Kew Road, TW9 3EE
E casting@maddyhinton.com
W www.maddyhinton.com

HOLM, Lissy
See JUST CASTING

HOOTKINS, Polly　T 020 7692 1184
CDG Member. Contact: By e-mail
T 07545 784294
E phootkins@clara.net

HORAN, Julia　T 020 7267 5261
CDG Member
26 Falkland Road, London NW5 2PX
E horancasting@aol.com

HOWE, Gary CASTING　T 029 2045 3883
34 Orbit Street, Roath
Cardiff, South Wales CF24 0JX
E garyhowecasting@talktalk.net

HUBBARD CASTING　T 020 7631 4944
*Contact: Dan Hubbard (CDG Member), Amy Hubbard
(CDG Member), Ros Hubbard (CDG Member)
John Hubbard (CDG Member). No Showreels*
14 Rathbone Place
London W1T 1HT
F 020 7636 7117

HUGHES, Sarah　T 020 8291 0304
CDG Member
E sarahhughescasting@gmail.com
W www.sarahhughescasting.co.uk

HUGHES, Sylvia　T 07770 520007
Casting Suite, The Deanwater
Wilmslow Road, Woodford
Cheshire SK7 1RJ
T 07826 946999
E sylviahughes007@gmail.com

IN HOUSE CASTING　T 07921 843508
12 Cliffe House, Blackwall Lane
London SE10 0RB
E mark@inhousecasting.com
W www.inhousecasting.com

JAFFA, Janis CASTING　T 020 8740 1629
CDG Member
2 Landor Walk
London W12 9AP
E janis@janisjaffacasting.co.uk

JAFFREY, Jennifer　T 07973 617168
Contact: By Post
136 Hicks Avenue, Greenford
Middlesex UB6 8HB
E jennifer.jaffrey@gmail.com

JAY, Jina CASTING　T 020 8607 8887
CDG Member
Office 2, Sound Centre
Twickenham Film Studios
The Barons, St Margarets
Twickenham, Middlesex TW1 2AW

JENKINS, Lucy
CDG Member. See JENKINS McSHANE CASTING

JENKINS, Victor
CDG Member. See VHJ CASTING

JENKINS McSHANE CASTING　T 020 8943 5328
Contact: Lucy Jenkins (CDG Member)
74 High Street, Hampton Wick
Kingston upon Thames KT1 4DQ
E lucy@jenkinsmcshanecasting.com

JENKINS McSHANE CASTING   T 020 8693 7411
Contact: Sooki McShane (CDG Member)
86A Underhill Road
London SE22 0QU
E sooki@jenkinsmcshanecasting.com

JENNER, Rebecca   T 07903 347958
Studio 3
549 Barlow Moor Road
Manchester M21 8AN
E casting@rebeccajenner.com
W www.rebeccajenner.com

JEWELL, Jimmy   T 020 7462 0790
17 Percy Street
London W1T 1DU
E jimmy@ladidagroup.com
W www.ladidagroup.com

JN PRODUCTION & CASTING   T 020 7324 2630
Contact: Paul Hunt, Tina Newland
27 Cowper Street
London EC2A 4AP
E paul@jncasting.com

JOHN, Priscilla   T 020 8741 4212
CDG Member
PO Box 22477
London W6 0GT
F 020 8741 4005

JOHNSON, Alex CASTING   T 020 7229 8779
Contact: By e-mail. Accepts Showreels. Children.
Commercials. Film. Modelling. Stage. Television
1 Clarendon Cross
London W11 4AP
E alex@alexjohnsoncasting.com

JOHNSON, Marilyn   T 020 7497 5552
CDG Member
1st Floor
11 Goodwins Court
London WC2N 4LL
E casting@marilynjohnsoncasting.com

JONES, Sue
CDG Member
E info@suejones.net

JUST CASTING   T 020 7229 3471
Contact: Leo Davis, Lissy Holm
20th Century Theatre
291 Westbourne Grove
London W11 2QA
F 020 7792 2143

KATE & LOU CASTING   T 020 7323 1952
Twitter: @kateandloucast
The Basement, Museum House
25 Museum Street
London WC1A 1JT
T 07885 763429
E cast@kateandloucasting.com
W www.kateandloucasting.com

KENNEDY, Anna
CASTING LTD   T 020 8677 6710
8 Rydal Road
London SW16 1QN
T 07973 119269
E anna@kennedycasting.com

KEOGH, Beverley
CASTING LTD　　　**T** 0161 273 4400
Contact: Beverley Keogh. CDG Member
29 Ardwick Green North
Ardwick Green
Manchester M12 6DL
F 0161 273 4401
E drama@beverleykeogh.tv

KESTER, Gaby
E casting@gabykester.com

KHANDO CASTING　　　**T** 020 3463 8492
1 Marlborough Court
London W1F 7EE
E casting@khandoentertainment.com
W www.khandoentertainment.com

KING, Belinda CASTING　　　**T** 020 7470 8747
Contact: By Post/e-mail/Telephone. Accepts Showreels.
Dancers. Musical Theatre. Stage. Cruise Ships
Suite S201, Garden Studios
71-75 Shelton Street
Covent Garden, London WC2H 9JQ
E casting@belindaking.com

KING, Cassandra CASTING　　　**T** 020 8977 2345
73 Victor Road, Teddington TW11 8SP
T 07813 320673
E cassyking@yahoo.co.uk

KINNEAR, Kirsty　　　**T** 020 8354 7388
E kinnearcast@virginmedia.com

KLIMEK, Nana CASTING　　　**T** 020 3222 0035
RichMix 1st Floor West
35-47 Bethnal Green Road
London E1 6LA
E casting@nanaklimek.com
W www.nanaklimek.com

KNIGHT-SMITH, Jerry　　　**T** 0161 615 6761
CDG Member
c/o Royal Exchange Theatre Company
St Ann's Square
Manchester M2 7DH

KOREL, Suzy　　　**T** 07973 506793
CDG Member
E suzy@korel.org

KRUGER, Beatrice　　　**T** 00 39 06 92956808
FBI CASTING S.r.l.
17 via della Scala
00153 Roma, Italy
F 00 39 06 23328203
E beatrice.kruger@fbicasting.it
W www.fbicasting.com

KYLE, Greg　　　**T** 020 8876 6763
71B North Worple Way, Mortlake
London SW14 8PR
T 07967 744056
E kylecasting@btinternet.com

LARCA LTD　　　**T** 07779 321954
Welsh Language/English. Commercials. Film. Stage.
Television
Unit 2, Crichton House
11-12 Mount Stuart Square
Cardiff CF10 5EE
E leigh-annregan@btconnect.com
W www.larca.co.uk

LEVENE, Jon　　　**T** 020 7792 8501
T 07977 570899
E jonlevene@mac.com
W www.jonlevenecasting.co.uk

LINDSAY-STEWART, Karen　　　**T** 020 7439 0544
CDG Member
E asst@klscasting.co.uk

LOVE CASTING　　　**T** 07722 668815
Contact: Chris Maloney. Nationwide Casting Service
E lovecasting@email.com

LUNN, Maggie　　　**T** 020 7226 8334
CDG Member
T 07973 785645
E maggie@maggielunn.co.uk

MAD DOG CASTING LTD　　　**T** 020 7269 7910
Contact: By Post/e-mail. Accepts Showreels/Voicereels.
Real People. Street Casting
The Pavilion Building, Ealing Studios
Ealing Green, London W5 5EP
E enquiry@maddogcasting.com
W www.maddogcasting.com

MAGSON, Kay　　　**T** 0113 236 0251
CDG Member. Contact: By e-mail. Stage
PO Box 175, Pudsey
Leeds LS28 7WY
E kay.magson@btinternet.com

MARCH, Heather CASTING　　　**T** 020 3056 8862
Contact: By e-mail. Commercials. Idents. Photographic
32 Threadneedle Street
London EC2R 8AY
E hello@heathermarchcasting.com
W www.heathermarchcasting.com

McDAID-WREN, Ri　　　**T** 07814 803808
Contact: By e-mail
Based in London
E ri@ri-mcd.com

McLEOD, Carolyn CASTING　　　**T** 07946 476425
Contact: By e-mail only. Commercials. Film. Television
1st Floor, 193 Wardour Street
London W1F 8ZF
E info@cmcasting.co.uk
W www.cmcasting.co.uk

McLEOD, Thea　　　**T** 07941 541314
E mcleodcasting@hotmail.com

McMURRICH, Chrissie　　　**T** 020 8568 0137
Contact: By Post. Accepts Showreels
16 Spring Vale Avenue, Brentford
Middlesex TW8 9QH

McSHANE, Sooki
CDG Member. See JENKINS McSHANE CASTING

McWILLIAMS, Debbie　　　**T** 020 7564 8860
CDG Member
T 07785 575805
E debbie@castingconsultancy.com

MEULENBERG, Thea　　　**T** 00 31 20 6265846
Keizersgracht 116
1015 CW Amsterdam
The Netherlands
E info@theameulenberg.com
W www.theameulenberg.com

MILLER, Hannah
CDG Member. See ROYAL SHAKESPEARE COMPANY

MOISELLE, Frank   T 00 353 1 2802857
7 Corrig Avenue
Dun Laoghaire
Co. Dublin, Ireland
F 00 353 1 2803277

MOISELLE, Nuala   T 00 353 1 2802857
7 Corrig Avenue
Dun Laoghaire
Co. Dublin, Ireland
F 00 353 1 2803277

MOORE, Stephen   T 020 8228 7109
CDG Member
E stephen@stephenmoorecasting.co.uk

MORGAN, Andy
CASTING LTD   T 020 8674 5375
Contact: Andy Morgan. CDG Member
E andy@andymorgan.org

MORLEY, Adam   T 07855 133836
The Lodge, Wentworth Hall
The Ridgeway
Mill Hill, London NW7 1RJ
E adam.e.morley@gmail.com

MORRISON, Melika   T/F 020 7381 1571
Contact: By Post. Accepts Showreels. Film. Radio.
Television
12A Rosebank
Holyport Road
London SW6 6LG

MOUNTJOY, Lee
CASTING   T 0161 850 1656 (Manchester)
T 020 7112 8353 (London)
E info@leemountjoy.com
W www.leemountjoy.com

MURDER MY DARLINGS   T 020 7386 0560
Contact: Sue Pocklington
Based in London
E office@murdermydarlings.com

MURPHY, Sabrina CASTING   T 07956 450755
E casting@sabrinamurphy.co.uk
W www.murphycharpentier.co.uk

NATIONAL THEATRE
CASTING DEPARTMENT   T 020 7452 3336
Contact: Wendy Spon, Head of Casting (CDG Member),
Charlotte Bevan, Casting Associate (CDG Member),
Juliet Horsley, Casting Associate (CDG Member),
Charlotte Sutton, Casting Assistant. By Post
Upper Ground, South Bank
London SE1 9PX
F 020 7452 3340
W www.nationaltheatre.org.uk

NEEDLEMAN, Sue   T 020 8959 1550
CDG Member
19 Stanhope Gardens, London NW7 2JD

NORCLIFFE, Belinda   T 020 8992 1333
Contact: Belinda Norcliffe, Matt Selby
23 Brougham Road
London W3 6JD
T 020 8992 8643
E belinda@bncasting.co.uk

NORTH, Sophie　　T 020 3372 4878
Bridges House, Branbridges Road
Kent TN12 5HD
T 07956 516606
E sophie@sophienorthcasting.com

O'BRIEN, Debbie　　T 01462 742919
72 High Street, Ashwell
Nr Baldock, Herts SG7 5NS
F 01462 743110
E info@debbieobrien.net

O'CONNOR, Orla　　T 0131 553 0559
CDG Member
The Out of the Blue Drill Hall
36 Dalmeny Street
Edinburgh EH6 8RG
E info@orlaoconnorcasting.co.uk
W www.orlaoconnorcasting.co.uk

O'DONNELL, Rory　　T 07940 073165
E rory@raindance.co.uk

PALMER, Helena
CDG Member. See ROYAL SHAKESPEARE COMPANY

PARRISS, Susie CASTING　　T 020 8543 3326
CDG Member
PO Box 40, Morden SM4 4WJ

**PEREIRA HIND, Simone
CASTING**　　T 07973 818885
CDG Member. Formerly 'Simone Ireland'
Argyle House, 37 Castle Terrace
Edinburgh EH3 9SJ
E simonepereirahind@gmail.com
W www.simonepereirahind.com

PETTS, Tree CASTING　　T 020 8458 8898
125 Hendon Way
London NW2 2NA
T 07966 283252
E casting@treepetts.co.uk
W www.treepettscasting.com

PLANTIN, Kate　　T 01932 782350
CDG Member
4 Riverside, Lower Hampton Road
Sunbury on Thames TW16 5PW
E kate@kateplantin.com
W www.kateplantin.com

POOLE, Gilly
CDG Member. See CROWLEY POOLE CASTING

PROCTOR, Carl　　T 020 7681 0034
CDG Member
15B Bury Place
London WC1A 2JB
T 07956 283340
E carlproctorcasting@gmail.com
W www.carlproctor.com

PRYOR, Andy　　T 020 7492 1726
CDG Member
31-35 Kirby Street
London EC1N 8TE

PURO CASTING　　T 020 7193 8799
F 07006 056678
E office@purocasting.com
W www.purocasting.com

RADCLIFFE, Gennie　　T 0161 952 0580
CDG Member
ITV PLC
Trafford Wharf Road
Trafford, Manchester M17 1FZ

**RANCH CASTING
COMPANY THE**　　T 020 8374 6072
*Contact: By e-mail/Telephone. Commercials. Corporate.
Idents. Photographic Campaigns. Pop Promos*
F 020 8442 9190
E info@theranchcasting.co.uk
W www.theranchcasting.co.uk

REICH, Liora　　T 020 8444 1686
25 Manor Park Road
London N2 0SN
E casting@liorareich.fsnet.co.uk

RENNIE, Nadine　　T 020 7478 0104
CDG Member
Soho Theatre
21 Dean Street
London W1D 3NE
E nadine@sohotheatre.com

REVOLVER CASTING LTD　　T 07958 922829
70 Sylvia Court
Cavendish Street
London N1 7PG
E waynesearcher@mac.com
W www.revolvercasting.com

REYNOLDS, Gillian CASTING　　T 028 9091 8218
Scottish Provident Building
7 Donegall Square West
Belfast
County Antrim BT1 6JH
E gillreynoldscasting@gmail.com
W www.gillianreynoldscasting.com

REYNOLDS, Gillian CASTING　　T 0872 619718
25 Saint Kevin's Parade
Portobello, Dublin 8
E gillreynoldscasting@gmail.com
W www.gillianreynoldscasting.com

REYNOLDS, Simone　　T 020 8672 5443
CDG Member
60 Hebdon Road
London SW17 7NN
E simone-r@dircon.co.uk

RHODES JAMES, Kate　　T 020 8943 3265
CDG Member
KRJ Casting Ltd
E office@krjcasting.com

RICHTER, Ilisa　　T 020 3131 0128
Unit 106A Netil House
1 Westgate Street
London E8 3RL
E ilisarichter@live.co.uk

RIPLEY, Jane　　T 020 8340 5123
E jane@janeripleycasting.co.uk

ROBERTS, Barbara　　T 07811 568925
CDG Member. Children
E barbara@robertscasting.com

ROBERTSON, Sasha CASTING T 020 8993 8118
Contact: Sasha Robertson (CDG Member)
5 Cumberland Road
London W3 6EX
E casting@sasharobertson.com
W www.sasharobertsoncasting.com

RONANE, Jessica CASTING T 020 8607 0836
CDG Member
12 Richmond Lodge
Twickenham Studios
The Barons, Twickenham TW1 2AW
E jessica@jessicaronane.com

ROSE, Dionne T 020 3664 9811
9 Wight Way, Selsey
Chichester
West Sussex PO20 0UD
T 07810 824567
E casting@rdmfilms.co.uk
W www.rdmfilms.co.uk

ROWAN, Amy CASTING T 00 353 1 2140514
PO Box 10247, Blackrock
Co. Dublin, Ireland

ROWE, Annie CASTING T 020 8354 2699
98 St Albans Avenue
London W4 5JR
W www.annierowe-casting.com

**ROYAL SHAKESPEARE
COMPANY** T 020 7845 0530
*Contact: Hannah Miller, Head of Casting (CDG Member),
Helena Palmer (CDG Member), Annelie Powell,
Matthew Dewsbury*
Casting Department
1 Earlham Street
London WC2H 9LL
E suggestions@rsc.org.uk
W www.rsc.org.uk

**RUBIN, Shaila EUROPEAN
CASTING SERVICE** T 00 39 06 72901906
Cinecitta Studios Via Tuscolana 1055
00173 Roma
Teatro 6/7 Stanza 8, Italy
E sernass@gmail.com

RUTHERFORD, Neil T 07960 891911
Neil Rutherford Casting
7 Falkland Avenue
London N3 1QR
E neil@neilrutherford.com
W www.neilrutherford.com

SCHILLER, Ginny T 020 8806 5383
CDG Member
9 Clapton Terrace
London E5 9BW
E ginny.schiller@virgin.net

SCHOFIELD, Gilly
CDG Member
E gillyschofield1@btinternet.com

SCOTT, Laura T 020 7978 6336
CDG Member
56 Rowena Crescent
London SW11 2PT
E laurascottcasting@mac.com

SEARCHERS THE T 07958 922829
70 Sylvia Court
Cavendish Street
London N1 7PG
F 020 7684 5763
E waynesearcher@mac.com

SEECOOMAR, Nadira T 020 8892 8478
E nadira.seecoomar@gmail.com

SELECT CASTING LTD T 07700 059089
PO Box 748
London NW4 1TT
T 07956 131494
E info@selectcasting.co.uk
W www.selectcasting.co.uk

SHAW, David
CDG Member. See KEOGH, Beverley CASTING LTD

SHAW, Phil T 020 8715 8943
Contact: By Post. Commercials. Film. Stage. Television
Suite 476
2 Old Brompton Road
South Kensington
London SW7 3DQ
E shawcastlond@aol.com

SHEPHERD, Debbie CASTING T 020 7240 0400
Suite 16, 63 St Martin's Lane
London WC2N 4JS
E debbie@debbieshepherd.com

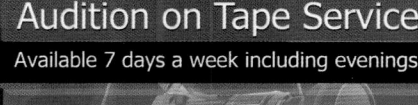

SID PRODUCTIONS LTD **T** 01932 863194
Susan Head (Director)
T 07766 761267
E casting@sidproductions.co.uk
W www.sidproductions.co.uk

SIMPSON, Georgia **T** 028 9147 0800
CDG Member
E georgia@georgiasimpsoncasting.com
W www.georgiasimpsoncasting.com

SINGER, Sandra ASSOCIATES **T** 01702 331616
Contact: By e-mail
21 Cotswold Road
Westcliff-on-Sea
Essex SS0 8AA
E sandrasingeruk@aol.com
W www.sandrasinger.com

**SMITH, Michelle
CASTING LTD** **T** 0161 439 6825
*Contact: Michelle Smith (CDG Member). Television. Film.
Animation. Commercials. Corporate*
220 Church Lane
Stockport SK7 1PQ
E enquiries@michellesmithcasting.co.uk

SMITH, Suzanne **T** 020 7278 0045
CDG Member
99 Leighton Road
Kentish Town
London NW5 2RB
E zan@dircon.co.uk

SNAPE, Janine CASTING
CDG Member
c/o Melbourne Theatre Company
Australia
E j.snape@mtc.com.au

SOLOMON, Alison **T** 0121 245 2023
Centenary Square, Broad Street
Birmingham B1 2EP

SPORTSCASTINGS.COM **T** 07973 863263
Contact: Penny Burrows
3 Thornlaw Road
London SE27 0SH
E info@sportsmodels.com
W www.sportsmodels.com

STAFFORD, Aaron **T** 020 8372 0611
Freelance. Commercials. Film. Television
14 Park Avenue, Enfield
Middlesex EN1 2HP
E aaron.stafford@blueyonder.co.uk

STAFFORD, Emma CASTING **T** 0161 833 4263
T 020 3137 7351
E info@emmastafford.tv
W www.emmastafford.tv

STAFFORD, Helen **T** 020 8360 6329
14 Park Avenue, Enfield
Greater London EN1 2HP
E helen.stafford@blueyonder.co.uk

STARK CASTING **T** 020 8800 0060
T 07956 150689
E anna@starkcasting.com
W www.starkcasting.com

STERNE, Robert **T** 020 8960 6099
CDG Member
Nina Gold Casting
117 Chevening Road
London NW6 6DU
T 07793 405150
E robert@ninagold.co.uk

STEVENS, Gail CASTING **T** 020 7253 6532
CDG Member
Greenhill House
90-93 Cowcross Street
London EC1M 6BF
E office@gailstevenscasting.com

**STEVENS MILLEFIORINI,
Danny** **T** 00 39 389 4352200
Via Sillaro 14, Cerveteri
Rome 00052, Italy
T 00 39 348 268015
E dannystevens62@gmail.com

STEVENSON, Sam
CDG Member
E sam@hancockstevenson.com

STOLL, Liz **T** 020 8228 8285
BBC DRAMA SERIES CASTING
BBC Elstree, Room N223
Neptune House, Clarendon Road
Borehamwood, Herts WD6 1JF

STYRING, Faye **T** 020 7157 3000
ITV, The Television Centre
Leeds LS3 1JS
E faye.styring@itv.com

SUMMERS, Mark CASTING **T** 020 7229 8413
Twitter: @marksummerscast
1 Beaumont Avenue
West Kensington
London W14 9LP
E mark@marksummers.com
W www.marksummers.com

SYSON GRAINGER CASTING **T** 020 7287 5327
*Contact: Lucinda Syson (CDG/CSA Member),
Elaine Grainger (CDG Member)*
Rooms 7-8, 2nd Floor
83-84 Berwick Street
London W1F 8TS
F 020 7287 3629
E office@sysongraingercasting.com

TABAK, Amanda
CDG Member. See CANDID CASTING

**THOMAS, Hazel
PRODUCTIONS** **T** 07948 211083
Flat 6, Highwood Manor
21 Constitution Hill
Ipswich, Suffolk IP1 3RG
E htproductions@live.co.uk
W www.hazel-thomas.wix.com/htproductions

TOPPING, Nicci **T** 07802 684256
Panther House, Studio 4, East Block
38 Mount Pleasant
London WC1X 0AN
E general@toppscasting.co.uk
W www.toppscasting.co.uk

Van Dyck Photography www.vandyckphotography.com 07947 378178

15% Discount if you mention Spotlight · Notting Hill, London W11

TOPPING, Nicci T 0161 818 6568
10 Haddon Road, Chorlton, Manchester M21 7QU
E general@toppscasting.co.uk
W www.toppscasting.co.uk

TOPPING, Nicci T 07802 684256
The Media Centre, 7 Northumberland Street
West Yorkshire HD1 1RL
T 01484 511988
E general@toppscasting.co.uk
W www.toppscasting.co.uk

TREVELLICK, Jill T 020 8340 2734
CDG Member
92 Priory Road, London N8 7EY
E jill@jilltrevellick.com

TREVIS, Sarah T 020 8354 2398
CDG Member
E info@sarahtrevis.com

VALENTINE HENDRY, Kelly
CDG Member. See VHJ CASTING

VAUGHAN, Sally T 020 7735 6539
CDG Member
2 Kennington Park Place, London SE11 4AS
E svaughan12@btinternet.com

VHJ CASTING T 020 7255 6146
Contact: Kelly Valentine Hendry (CDG Member),
Victor Jenkins (CDG Member)
Welbeck House, 66-67 Wells Street
London W1T 3PY
E assistant@vhjcasting.com
W www.vhjcasting.com

VOSSER, Anne CASTING T 01252 404716
156 Lower Farnham Road, Aldershot
Hampshire GU12 4EL
T 07968 868712
E anne@vosser-casting.co.uk
W www.vosser-casting.co.uk

WEIR, Fiona T 020 7727 5600
CDG Member
2nd Floor, 138 Portobello Road, London W11 2DZ

WEST, June
CDG Member
E info@junewestcasting.com
W www.junewestcasting.com

WESTERN, Matt T 07740 702077
Newhouse Farm
Broughton Gifford SN12 8NX
T 020 3603 1130
E matt@mattwestern.co.uk
W www.mattwestern.co.uk

WHALE, Toby T 020 8993 2821
CDG Member
80 Shakespeare Road
London W3 6SN
F 020 8993 8096
E toby@whalecasting.com
W www.whalecasting.com

WICKSTEED, Rose T 020 7249 8386
CSA Member
Based in London
T 07854 831636
E casting@rosewicksteed.com
W www.rosewicksteed.com

WILDMANHALL CASTING T 020 7373 2036
Contact: Vicky Wildman, Buffy Hall
1 Child's Place, London SW5 9RX
E wildmanhall@mac.com

WILLIS, Catherine T 020 7255 6131
CDG Member. Contact: By e-mail
Wellbeck House
66-67 Wells Street
London W1T 3PY
E catherine@cwcasting.co.uk

WRIGHT, Rebecca CASTING T 020 3371 1531
CDG Member
E office@rebeccawrightcasting.com
W www.rebeccawrightcasting.com

YOUNGSTAR CASTING T 023 8047 7717
Children & Teenagers only
5 Union Castle House, Canute Road
Southampton SO14 3FJ
E info@youngstar.tv
W www.youngstar.tv

ZIMMERMANN, Jeremy CASTING T 020 7478 5161
3rd Floor, 50 Bedford Street
London WC2E 9HA
E info@zimmermanncasting.com

A1 ANIMALS   T/F 0844 3351733
Farm, Domestic & Exotic Animals
70 Frobisher Road, Bilton
Rugby, Warwickshire CV22 7HU
T 07860 416545
E a1animals@btinternet.com
W www.a1animals.co.uk

A-Z ANIMALS LTD   T 01372 377111
The Bell House, Bell Lane, Fetcham, Surrey KT22 9ND
T 07836 721288
E info@a-zanimals.co.uk
W www.a-zanimals.co.uk

ACADEMY OF PERFORMANCE
COMBAT THE   T 07963 206803
197 Church Road, Northolt UB5 5BE
E info@theapc.org.uk
W www.theapc.org.uk

ACTING AUDITION SUCCESS   T 020 8731 6686
Audition Coaching for Drama UK Schools. Camera
Technique. Career Advice
53 West Heath Court, London NW11 7RG
E philiproschactor@gmail.com
W www.actingauditionsuccess.co.uk

ACTORS' ADVISORY SERVICE   T 020 8287 2839
Provides Advice to Actors, Agents, Photographers etc
29 Talbot Road, Twickenham
Middlesex TW2 6SJ

ACTOR'S ONE-STOP SHOP THE   T 020 8279 8073
Showreels Edited & Filmed
2B Dale View Crescent, Chingford
London E4 6PQ
T 07894 152651
E info@actorsonestopshop.com
W www.actorsonestopshop.com

AGENTFILE   T 07050 683662
Software for Agents
E admin@agentfile.com
W www.agentfile.com

AKA   T 020 7836 4747
Advertising. Design. Digital. Marketing. Promotions. Sales
& Ticketing
1st Floor, 115-117 Shaftesbury Avenue
Cambridge Circus, London WC2H 8AF
F 020 7836 8787
E aka@akauk.com
W www.akauk.com

ALTERNATIVE ANIMALS   T 07956 564715
Contact: Trevor Smith. Animatronics. Taxidermy
56 Lance Way, High Wycombe, Bucks HP13 7BU
F 07770 666088
E animalswork1@yahoo.co.uk
W www.animalswork.co.uk

ANIMAL ACTING   T 01253 853953
Animals. Horse-drawn Vehicles. Props. Stunts
33 Broadhurst Road, Thornton-Cleveleys
Lancashire FY5 3HR
T 07831 800567
E information@animalacting.com
W www.animalacting.com

ANIMAL ACTORS   T 07710 348777
Animals. Birds. Reptiles
95 Ditchling Road, Brighton
Sussex BN1 4ST

ANIMAL AMBASSADORS   T 01993 778847
Contact: Kay Weston. Animal Consultant &
Trainer/ Animal Agent
The Glades, 119 Brize Norton Road
Minster Lovell, Oxon OX29 0SH
T 07831 558594
E kay@animalambassadors.co.uk
W www.animalambassadors.co.uk

ANIMALS GALORE LTD   T 01342 842400
208 Smallfield Road, Horley
Surrey RH6 9LS
E info@animals-galore.co.uk
W www.animals-galore.co.uk

ARTS VA THE   T 01789 552559
Contact: Bronwyn Robertson (Experienced PA).
Admin Support
T 07815 192135
E bronwyn@theartsva.com
W www.theartsva.com

ASSOCIATED STUDIOS THE   T 020 7385 2038
The Hub @ St Alban's Fulham, 2 Margravine Road
London W6 8HJ
E info@associatedstudios.co.uk
W www.associatedstudios.co.uk

AUDIO DESCRIPTION
For Blind & Visually Impaired Audiences. West End &
on Tour
E info@theatredescription.com

AUTOMOBILE ASSOCIATION
(THE AA)   T 01256 492640
Fanum House, Basing View
Basingstoke RG21 4EA
E lindsey.szegota@theaa.com

BAILEY, Bernice   T 01306 741310
Tutor & Chaperone
Spur Lacey, Camilla Drive
Westhumble, Surrey RH5 6BU
E bpbailey_uk@yahoo.co.uk

BAM! BAIRD ARTISTS MANAGEMENT
CONSULTING   T/F 001 705 424 6507
Specialising in US & Canadian Visas, Work Permits,
Withholding, Taxes etc
7132 County Road #21, PO Box 597
Alliston, Ontario, Canada L9R 1V7
E robert@bairdartists.com
W www.bairdartists.com

BARTERCARD   T 0800 8406333
Churchill House, 1 London Road
Slough, Berkshire SL3 7FJ
E info@uk.bartercard.com
W www.bartercard.co.uk

BIG PICTURE   T 020 7371 4455
Contact: Jayne Thorburn (Field Marketing)
13 Netherwood Road
London W14 0BL
E humanresources@ebigpicture.co.uk
W www.ebigpicture.co.uk

BLACK, Liam A.   T 01383 610711
Magic & Illusion Consultant. Custom & Off-the-shelf
Illusions, Magic & Special Effects Props
12 Downfield, Cowdenbeath
Fife KY4 9JE
E kandlblack@btinternet.com

THE KNIGHTS OF MIDDLE ENGLAND

The Knights of Middle England are a professional Jousting Stunt Team providing a range of services for the Theatre, Film & TV industry and are the UK's leading Jousting School.

We offer: • Trained Horses & Riders for the TV & Film Industry • Medieval Knights Sword Fighting
• 5 Day Intensive Horse Riding Course for Actors
• Learn Stunt Riding, Jousting & Horseback Archery with our Tailor Made Courses or Experience Days

Based in the heart of the Midlands in Warwick, Warwickshire. Direct Trains – Euston to Coventry – 1hr only / London Marylebone to Warwick – 1hr 15 mins – pick up available
e: info@knightsofmiddleengland.co.uk   t: 00 44 (0)1926 400401   www.knightsofmiddleengland.com

---

BOARDMAN, Emma T 07976 294604
Creative Event Producer. Private Party Planner. Media Spokesperson for the UK Events Industry
Weybridge, Surrey KT13
E hq@thelovelypartycompany.com
W www.thelovelypartycompany.com

BRITISH ASSOCIATION OF DRAMATHERAPISTS T/F 01242 235515
Waverley, Battledown Approach
Cheltenham, Glos GL52 6RE
E info@badth.org.uk
W www.badth.org.uk

BYFORD, Simon PRODUCTION MANAGEMENT SERVICES T 01273 623972
Production & Event Management
22 Freshfield Place, Brighton
East Sussex BN2 0BN
T 07885 474455
E simon@simonbyfordpms.com
W www.simonbyfordpms.com

BYRNE, John T 07720 847831
One-to-one Advice from The Stage's Career Adviser
E johnbyrnecontact@gmail.com
W www.performingcareers.com

CAP PRODUCTION SOLUTIONS LTD T 07973 432576
Technical Production Services
116 Wigmore Road, Carshalton, Surrey SM5 1RQ
E leigh@leighporter.com

CASTLE MAGICAL SERVICES T/F 01904 709500
Contact: Michael Shepherd. Magical Effect Consultants
Broompark, 131 Tadcaster Road
Dringhouses, York YO24 1QJ
E admin@castlemagicalservices.co.uk

CAULKETT, Robin Dip SM MIIRSM T 07970 442003
Abseiling. Rope Work
3 Churchill Way, Mitchell Dean, Glos GL17 0AZ
E robincaulkett@talktalk.net

CELEBRITIES WORLDWIDE LTD T 020 7637 4178
Celebrity Contacts & Booking
E claire@celebritiesworldwide.com
W www.celebritiesworldwide.com

CELEBRITY REPTILES T/F 020 8659 0877
11 Tramway Close, London SE20 7DF
E info@celebrityreptiles.co.uk
W www.celebrityreptiles.co.uk

CHAPERONE T/F 020 8650 8997
For Children in Performing Arts
31 Whitecroft Way, Beckenham, Kent BR3 3AQ
T 07930 353381
E elaineboyle@msn.com

CHAPERONEAGENCY T 07960 075928
E chaperoneagency@hotmail.co.uk
W www.chaperoneagency.com

CHAPERONES & TUTORS LTD T 0845 4670067
Covering the whole of the UK to Film, Television & Stage. Offices based in the Midlands & London
T 07535 337423
E arlene@chaperonesandtutors.co.uk
W www.chaperonesandtutors.co.uk

CHARCOALBLUE LLP T 020 7928 0000
17 Short Street, Bankside
London SE1 8LJ
E studio@charcoalblue.com
W www.charcoalblue.com

CHEESEMAN, Virginia T 01628 522632
Entomological Supplier
21 Willow Close, Flackwell Heath
High Wycombe, Bucks HP10 9LH
T 07971 838724
E virginia@virginiacheeseman.co.uk
W www.virginiacheeseman.co.uk

CHEKHOV, Michael CENTRE UK T 020 8696 7372
Information Centre for the Work of Michael Chekhov in the UK including Biographies, Academic Contacts, International Links, Training Links & other Information
E info@michaelchekhov.org.uk
W www.michaelchekhov.org.uk

CHILDCHAPERONE.CO.UK T 07956 427442
Contact: Denise Smith. Licensed Chaperone. Stage, Television & Film Industry
E denisesmith916@btinternet.com
W www.childchaperone.co.uk

CLASS - CARLINE LUNDON ASSOCIATES T 07597 378995
25 Falkner Square, Liverpool L8 7NZ
E clundon@googlemail.com

COBO MEDIA T 020 8291 7079
Performing Arts, Entertainment & Leisure Marketing
43A Garthorne Road
London SE23 1EP
F 020 8291 4969
E admin@cobomedia.com
W www.cobomedia.com

COLCLOUGH, John T 020 8873 1763
Practical Independent Guidance for Actors & Actresses
E info@johncolclough.com
W www.johncolclough.com

COMBAT INTERNATIONAL T 01259 731010
27 High Street, Kincardine
Alloa FK10 4RJ
E info@clanranald.org
W www.clanranald.org

COPS ON THE BOX T 020 8650 9828
Twitter: @copsonthebox1
BM BOX 7301, London WC1N 3XX
T 07710 065851
E info@cotb.co.uk
W www.cotb.co.uk

COTSWOLD FARM PARK T 01451 850307
Rare Breed Farm Animals
Guiting Power, Cheltenham
Gloucestershire GL54 5UG
F 01451 850423
E info@cotswoldfarmpark.co.uk

**CREATIVE MAGIC DIRECTOR
(TONY MIDDLETON)** T 01727 838656
67 De Tany Court, St Albans
Herts AL1 1TX
T 07738 971077
E anthonyjjmiddleton@gmail.com
W www.middletonenterprisesuk.com

CREATURE FEATURE T/F 01387 860648
Animal Agent
Gubhill Farm, Ae, Dumfries
Scotland DG1 1RL
T 07770 774866
E david@creaturefeature.co.uk
W www.creaturefeature.co.uk

CROFTS, Andrew T/F 01403 864518
Book Writing Services
Westlands Grange, West Grinstead
Horsham, West Sussex RH13 8LZ
E croftsa@aol.com
W www.andrewcrofts.com

DALLA VECCHIA, Sara T 07877 404743
Italian Teacher
13 Fauconberg Road
London W4 3JZ
E saraitaliantuition@gmail.com
W www.italiantuition.com

DHALIVAAL, Séva T 07956 553879

DOLBADARN FILM HORSES T/F 01286 870277
Dolbadarn Hotel, High Street, Llanberis
Gwynedd, North Wales LL55 4SU
T 07710 461341
E info@filmhorses.co.uk
W www.filmhorses.co.uk

DR VOICE T 07850 697807
3 Mills Studios, London E3 3DU
E drvoice@drvoice.tv
W www.drvoice.tv

**DUDLEY, Yvonne
LRPS ARAD FISTD** T 020 8989 1528
Stories for Films & Television
55 Cambridge Park, Wanstead
London E11 2PR
T 07870 372637

**EARLE, Kenneth
PERSONAL MANAGEMENT** T 020 7274 1219
214 Brixton Road
London SW9 6AP
F 020 7274 9529
E kennethearle@agents-uk.com
W www.kennethearlepersonalmanagement.com

ENGLISH TUTOR THE T 0118 958 9330
EFL/TEFL English Tutor
2 Baron Court, Western Elms Avenue
Reading, Berks RG30 2BP
E theenglishtutorno1@gmail.com

ES GLOBAL LTD T 020 7055 7200
3 Vyner Street, London E2 9DG
E info@esglobalsolutions.com
W www.esglobalsolutions.com

FACADE T 020 8291 7079
Creation & Production of Musicals
43A Garthorne Road, London SE23 1EP
F 020 8291 4969
E facade@cobomedia.com

**FERRIS ENTERTAINMENT
MUSIC** T 07801 493133
*Music for Film & Television. London. Cardiff. Belfast.
Los Angeles. France. Spain*
Number 8, 132 Charing Cross Road
London WC2H 0LA
E info@ferrisentertainment.com
W www.ferrisentertainment.com

**FIGHT CHOREOGRAPHER & ACTION
DIRECTOR** T 07739 184418
*Contact: Nic Main (Professional Actor, Film Fighting
Choreographer)*
Based in the South East
E nicmain1@hotmail.com
W www.nicmain.com

FILM & TV HORSES T/F 01753 864464
Crown Farm, Eton Wick Road
Eton, Windsor SL4 6PG
T 07831 629662
E filmhorses@yahoo.co.uk
W www.filmhorses.com

**FLAMES MARTIAL ARTS
ACADEMY** T 07950 396389
Contact: Adam Richards
Unit 2, 128 Milton Road Business Park, Gravesend
Kent DA12 2PG
E stunts@adamrichardsstunts.co.uk
W www.adamrichardsfightdirector.com

GET STUFFED T 020 7226 1364
Taxidermy
105 Essex Road, London N1 2SL
T 07831 260062
E taxidermy@thegetstuffed.co.uk
W www.thegetstuffed.co.uk

**GHOSTWRITER/AUTHOR/
SCRIPTWRITER** T 01227 721071
Contact: John Parker
Dove Cottage, The Street, Ickham CT3 1QP
T 07702 999920
E ghostwriterforyourbook@ymail.com
W www.ghostwriteruk.info

**GILMOUR Rev/Prof/Dr Glenn Msc.D IMM
SHsc.D Dip.Coun. BCMA.Reg** T 0114 321 6500
*Fully Qualified/International Medium & Clairvoyant.
Healer/Counsellor. Holistic Therapist. Consultant
Paranormal/Metaphysics/Occult for Radio & Television*
45 Studfield Road, Sheffield S6 4ST
E drglenngilmour@yahoo.com
W www.drglenngilmour.com

**GLOBAL ACCESS WORLD-WIDE
ENTERTAINMENT VISAS**   T 001 323 936 7100
5670 Wilshire Boulevard, Suite 1970
Los Angeles 90036, USA
F 001 323 936 7197
E info@globalaxs.net
W www.globalaxs.net

GOLDIELLE PROMOTIONS   T 07977 936826
Event Management & Entertainment
68 Lynton Drive, Hillside
Southport, Merseyside PR8 4QQ
T 01704 566604
E goldielle@yahoo.co.uk
W www.goldiellepromotions.com

GRADY, Chris ORGANISATION   T 07713 643971
Gothic House, High Road
Great Finborough, Suffolk IP14 3AQ
E chris@chrisgrady.org
W www.chrisgrady.org

GRAY, Robin COMMENTARIES   T 01420 23347
*Equestrian Equipment. Horse Race Commentaries.
Voice Overs*
Comptons, Isington, Alton, Hants GU34 4PL
T 07831 828424
E comptons1@hotmail.co.uk

HANDS UP PUPPETS   T 07909 824630
Contact: Marcus Clarke
7 Cavendish Vale, Nottingham NG5 4DS
E enquiries@handsuppuppets.com
W www.handsuppuppets.com

HARLEY PRODUCTIONS   T 020 7486 2986
78 York Street, London W1H 1DP
F 020 8202 8863
E harleyprods@aol.com

HAYES, Susan   T 07721 927714
*Choreographer. Body Worker & Psychotherapist.
Director of Superarts Agency & Irene Hayes School of
Performing Arts*
46 Warrington Crescent, London W9 1EP
E susan22@btconnect.com

**HERITAGE RAILWAY
ASSOCIATION**   T 01993 883384
10 Hurdeswell, Long Hanborough
Witney, Oxfordshire OX29 8DH
E john.crane@hra.gb.com
W www.heritagerailways.com

HILTON HORSES   T 07958 292222
Contact: Samantha Jones
478 London Road, Ashford, Middlesex TW15 3AD
E samantha@hilton-horses.com
W www.hilton-horses.com

IMAGE DIGGERS   T 020 8455 4564
Slide/Stills/Audio/Video Library. Theme Research
618B Finchley Road, London NW11 7RR
E lambhorn@gmail.com

iTREND RESEARCH LTD   T 01799 531358
*Contact: Andrew Jenkins. Audience Research. Audience
Surveys. Focus Groups*
The Old House, High Street
Little Chesterford, Saffron Walden, Essex CB10 1TS
T 07977 425518
E andrew@itrendresearch.com
W www.itrendresearch.com

JOE PUBLIC   T 020 7831 7077
The Dutch House
307-308 High Holborn
London WC1V 7LL
E mail@joepublicmarketing.com
W www.joepublicmarketing.com

JOHNSON, Gareth LTD   T 01239 891368
1st Floor, 19 Garrick Street
London WC2E 9AX
T 07770 225227
E gjltd@mac.com
W www.garethjohnsonltd.com

JOHNSON, Gareth LTD   T 01239 891368
Plas Hafren, Eglwyswrw
Crymych
Pembrokeshire SA41 3UL
T 07770 225227
E gjltd@mac.com
W www.garethjohnsonltd.com

**JORDAN, Richard
PRODUCTIONS LTD**   T 020 7243 9001
*Festivals. General Management. Production
Consultancy. UK & International Productions*
Mews Studios, 16 Vernon Yard
London W11 2DX
F 020 7313 9667
E info@richardjordanproductions.com

KEAN LANYON LTD   T 020 7697 8453
*Contact: Sharon Kean, Iain Lanyon. PR & Web/
Graphic Consultants*
United House, North Road
Islington, London N7 9DP
T 07973 843133
E sharon@keanlanyon.com
W www.keanlanyon.com

KELLER, Don   T 020 8800 4882
Marketing Consultancy. Project Management
65 Glenwood Road, Harringay
London N15 3JS
E info@donkeller.co.uk

KIEVE, Paul   T 07939 252526
Magical Effects for Film & Stage
2 St Philip's Road
London E8 3BP
E mail@stageillusion.com
W www.stageillusion.com

KNIGHTS OF ARKLEY THE   T/F 01269 861001
Glyn Sylen Farm, Five Roads
Llanelli SA15 5BJ
E penny@knightsofarkley.fsnet.co.uk
W www.knightsofarkley.com

**KNIGHTS OF MIDDLE
ENGLAND THE**   T 01926 400401
Horses & Riders for Film, Opera & Television
Warwick International School of Riding, Guys Cliffe
Coventry Road
Warwick CV34 5YD
E info@knightsofmiddleengland.co.uk
W www.knightsofmiddleengland.com

LAMBOLLE, Robert   T 020 8455 4564
Script Evaluation & Editing
618B Finchley Road
London NW11 7RR
E lambhorn@gmail.com

LAWINSPORT.COM   T 020 3286 8003
*Contact: Sean Cottrell (CEO). International Sports Law
Publication Providing High Quality Daily Sports Law &
Business Information, Topical Articles of Legal Opinion,
Blogs & Videos by those working in the field. Information
about Sports Law Firms, Books, Conferences & Courses*
E sean.cottrell@lawinsport.com
W www.lawinsport.com

LAWSON LEAN, David   T 01932 230273
Chaperone Service for Children in Entertainment
72 Shaw Drive
Walton-on-Thames
Surrey KT12 2LS
E dlawsonlean@aol.com
W www.davidlawsonlean.com

LEEP MARKETING & PR   T 07973 558895
Marketing. Press. Publicity
5 Hurdwick Place
London NW1 2JE
E philip@leep.biz

**LEO MEDIA & ENTERTAINMENT
GROUP THE**   T 00 37 7 93258797
*In Association with Argentum of Monaco. Executive
Production. Film, Television & Literary Consultancy.
Legal Work*
PO Box 68006
London NW4 9FW
E info@leomediagroup.com
W www.argentum.mc

LES AMIS D'ONNO   T 01835 869757
*Performing Horses, Stunt Riders & Performing Dogs for
Film & Television*
Lanton Hill Farm
Jedburgh TD8 6SY
E lesamisdonno@btinternet.com
W www.lesamisdonno.com

**LOCATION TUTORS
NATIONWIDE**   T 020 7978 8898
*Fully Qualified & Experienced Teachers Working with
Children on Film Sets & Covering all Key Stages of
National Curriculum*
16 Poplar Walk, Herne Hill
London SE24 0BU
T 07806 887471
E locationtutorsnationwide@gmail.com
W www.locationtutors.co.uk

LONDON COMPUTER DOCTOR   T 020 7652 4296
Computer Support
66 Heath Road, Clapham
London SW8 3BD
E joe@londoncomputerdoctor.com
W www.londoncomputerdoctor.com

**LONDON LITERARY PUB CRAWL
COMPANY THE**   T 020 8090 5082
*Promotes the Art & Literature of London through
Tours & Infodramas*
2nd Floor, 12 Fouberts Place
Carnaby Street, London W1F 7PA
T 07435 362424
E tours@mavericktheatre.co.uk
W www.londonliterarypubcrawl.com

**LOVE, Billie
HISTORICAL PHOTOGRAPHS**   T 01983 812572
*Picture Research. Formerly 'Amanda' Theatrical
Portraiture*
3 Winton Street, Ryde
Isle of Wight PO33 2BX
E billielove@tiscali.co.uk

LUXFACTOR GROUP (UK) THE   T 0845 3700589
Twitter: @luxfactor
Fleet Place, 12 Nelson Drive
Petersfield, Hampshire GU31 4SJ
F 0845 3700588
E info@luxfactor.co.uk
W www.luxfactor.co.uk

MAGICIANS.CO.UK   T 0845 0062442
Entertainers. Magic Consultants
Burnhill House, 50 Burnhill Road
Beckenham BR3 3LA
F 0845 0062443
E mail@magicians.co.uk

MAGICIANS IN LONDON   T 07973 512845
*Contact: Mike Alan. Magician and Magical Adviser for
the BBC*
The House of Magic
45 Bedford Street
London WC2E 9HA
E mikealan25@yahoo.com
W www.magiciansinlondon.co.uk

MAIN, Nic   T 07739 184418
*Experienced Stage, Television & Film Action/Fight
Director/Actor*
62 Kingsway, Blackwater
Camberley, Surrey GU17 0JB
E nicmain1@hotmail.com
W www.nicmain.com

**MALAGUEIRA, Fatima THEATRICAL AGENT
CONSULTANT**   T 07775 708460
For Actors, Agents & PR Companies
89 Harbord Street, London SW6 6PL
E fatima.malagueira@gmail.com
W www.roomtobreathe.uk.com

MATTLX GROUP   T 0845 6808692
*Lighting. Design. Production Engineering. Safety.
Training. IOSH-approved Training Provider*
Unit 3, Vinehall Business Centre
Vinehall Road, Robertsbridge
East Sussex TN32 5JW
E intray@mattlx.com
W www.mattlx.com

MAYS, Lorraine T 01494 771029
Face Painting & Entertainment Trainer
Park View, Stanley Avenue
Chesham, Bucks HP5 2JF
T 07778 106552
E lorrainebmays@aol.com

McKENNA, Deborah LTD T 020 8846 0966
Celebrity Chefs & Lifestyle Presenters only
64-66 Glentham Road, London SW13 9JJ
F 020 8846 0967
E hello@dml-uk.com
W www.dml-uk.com

MEDIA LEGAL T 01732 460592
Jurisconsults
Town House, 5 Mill Pond Close
Sevenoaks, Kent TN14 5AW

**MEYER, Robert -
CHAPERONE** T/F 020 8933 0076
*Licensed Chaperone for Children in the Entertainment
Industry*
1 Edward Court, London Road
Harrow, Middlesex HA1 3NW
T 07989 702950
E robmeyer4@aol.com

MILDENBERG, Vanessa T 07796 264828
Movement Director. Choreographer. Director
Flat 6, Cameford Court
New Park Road, London SW2 4LH
E vanessamildenberg@me.com
W www.vanessamildenberg.com

**MILITARY ADVISORY & INSTRUCTION
SPECIALISTS** T 01904 491198
*Contact: Johnny Lee Harris. Advice on Weapons, Drill,
Period to Present. Ex-Army Instructor. Health & Safety.
IOSH. Military Bugler & Drummer. Actor. PSV Licence.
Own Scarlets (Scarlet Uniform), Bugle & Drum. Chieftain
Tank Driver & Gunner. Horse Rider*
38 Knapton Close, Strensall
York YO32 5ZF
T 07855 648886
E johnmusic1@hotmail.com

MILLENNIUM BUGS T 07770 666088
Live Insects
28 Greaves Road, High Wycombe
Bucks HP13 7JU
T 07956 566252
E animalswork1@yahoo.co.uk
W www.animalworld.org.uk

MINIMAL RISK T 01432 379950
Security Consultancy
Rural Enterprise Centre, Hereford HR2 6FE
E enquiries@minimalrisk.co.uk
W www.minimalrisk.co.uk

MINISTRY OF FUN THE T 020 7708 6116
Entertainment. Promotions. PR Marketing Campaigns
Unit A&B, 22 Amelia Street
London SE17 3BZ
E james@ministryoffun.net
W www.ministryoffun.net

**MORGAN, Jane
ASSOCIATES (JMA)** T 020 7263 9867
Marketing. Media
8 Heathville Road, London N19 3AJ
E jma@janemorganassociates.com

MORTON, Matt T 01430 860185
Shire Horse & Equipment
Hasholme Carr Farm
Holme on Spalding Moor
York YO43 4BD
T 07768 346905

MUSIC SOLUTIONS LTD T 020 7866 8160
Garden Studios, 71-75 Shelton Street
London WC2H 9JQ
E mail@musicsolutionsltd.com

**NORDIC NOMAD TRAINING /
BUSINESS ADVICE** T 07980 619165
*Workshops, Courses, Books & One-to-One Advice
Sessions on 'Making a Living' & 'Running a Successful
Arts Business' for Actors, Dancers & Performers*
E tanja@nordicnomad.com
W www.nordicnomad.com

OATWAY, Christopher T 07873 485265
Social Media, Editing Scripts. Twitter: @djchrisoatway
495 Altrincham Road, Baguley Hall
Manchester M23 1AR
E christopherjoatway@gmail.com

**ORANGE TREE STUDIO LTD & RICHARD
PARDY MUSIC SERVICES** T 07768 146200
*Saxophone, Woodwinds, Brass Section & Bands for
Hire (Live or in Studio). Original Music/Composition &
Production*
31A New Road, Croxley Green
Herts WD3 3EJ
E richard@orangetreestudio.com
W www.redhornz.co.uk

**PA & ADMIN SUPPORT
SERVICES** T 07939 954575
*Louise Carmichael. Professional PA. Admin Services
including CV Formatting*
3 Clough Mill, Walsden
West Yorkshire, England OL14 7QX
E louisecarmichaelpa@gmail.com

PENROSE, Scott T 07767 336882
Magic & Illusion Effects for Film, Stage & Television
17 Berkeley Drive, Billericay
Essex CM12 0YP
E mail@stagemagician.com
W www.stagemagician.com

**POLICING EXPERIENCE
UNLEASHED** T 020 7205 2999
Suite 36, 88-90 Hatton Garden
London EC1N 8PG
E enquiries@policingexperienceunleashed.com
W www.policingexperienceunleashed.com

PSYCHOLOGY GROUP THE T 0870 6092445
*Assessments. Counselling. Expert Opinion. Presentation.
Psychotherapy*
F 0845 2805243
E info@psychologygroup.co.uk
W www.psychologygroup.co.uk

PUKKA PRESENTING T 020 8455 1385
*Training in Television Presenting & Presentation
Techniques*
Appletree Cottage, 51 Erskine Hill
London NW11 6EY
E kathryn@pukkapresenting.co.uk
W www.pukkapresenting.co.uk

PUPPET CENTRE   **T** 020 7228 5335
Development & Advocacy Agency for Puppetry & Related Animated Theatre
BAC, Lavender Hill
London SW11 5TN
E pct@puppetcentre.org.uk
W www.puppetcentre.org.uk

RAINBOW BIGBOTTOM   **T** 01494 771029
Children's Warm-up Artist for Stage & Television. Agent: Mark Starr, Keyhold Management
Park View, Stanley Avenue
Chesham, Bucks HP5 2JF
W www.mrpanda.co.uk

RB HEALTH & SAFETY SOLUTIONS LTD   **T** 0845 2571489
Specialists in Theatre & Production Health & Safety Audits, Consultancy, Risk Assessments & Training
Blacklands Business Centre, 15 Fearon Road
Hastings, East Sussex TN40 1DA
E richard@rbhealthandsafety.co.uk
W www.rbhealthandsafety.co.uk

REACH TO THE SKY   **T** 0843 2892503
Contact: Dr J. Success Life Coach
Brook Street, Mayfair, London W1K 4HR
T 07961 911027
E drj@reachtothesky.com
W www.reachtothesky.com

RED HOT ID - THE BRANDING SERVICE FOR ACTORS   **T** 01279 850618
F 01279 850625
E id@redhotentertainment.biz
W www.redhotentertainment.biz

RICHARDS, Adam   **T** 07950 396389
Fight Director
Unit 2, 128 Milton Road Business Park
Gravesend, Kent DA12 2PG
E stunts@adamrichardsstunts.co.uk
W www.adamrichardsfightdirector.com

RIPLEY-DUGGAN PARTNERSHIP THE   **T** 020 7436 1392
Tour Booking
26 Goodge Street, London W1T 2QG
E info@ripleyduggan.com

ROCKWOOD ANIMALS ON FILM   **T** 029 2088 5420
Lewis Terrace, Llanbradach, Caerphilly CF83 3JZ
T 07973 930983
E martin@rockwoodanimals.com
W www.rockwoodanimals.com

ROSCH, Philip   **T** 020 8731 6686
Audition Coaching for Drama UK Schools. Camera Technique. Career Advice
53 West Heath Court, London NW11 7RG
E philiproschactor@gmail.com
W www.actingauditionsuccess.co.uk

SCHOOL OF NATIONAL EQUITATION LTD   **T** 01509 852366
Contact: Sam Humphrey
Bunny Hill Top, Costock
Loughborough, Leicestershire LE12 6XN
T 07977 930083
E sam@bunnyhill.co.uk
W www.bunnyhill.co.uk

SHADEÈ, Magus Lynius: RITUAL FORMAN, INVOCATIONS   **T** 07740 043156
Direct Voice Communication. Materialisations. Psychic. Occult Investigator. Consultant
Suite 213, 91 Western Road
Brighton BN1 2NW
E maguslyniusshadee@hotmail.com
W www.occultcentre.com

SINCLAIR, Andy   **T** 07831 196675
Mime
E andynebular@hotmail.com
W www.andyjsinclair.co.uk

SOUTHAM FERRARI, Maggie   **T** 01798 344356
26 Orchard Close
Petworth
West Sussex GU28 0SA
T 07758 052325
E margaret.ferrari@btinternet.com

SPORTS PROMOTIONS (UK) LTD   **T** 020 8771 4700
Production Advisers. Safety. Sport. Stunts
56 Church Road
Crystal Palace
London SE19 2EZ
F 020 8771 4704
E cameron@sportspromotions.co.uk
W www.sportspromotions.co.uk

STAGE CRICKET CLUB   **T** 020 7402 7543
Cricketers & Cricket Grounds
39-41 Hanover Steps
St George's Fields
Albion Street, London W2 2YG
F 020 7262 5736
E brianjfilm@aol.com
W www.stagecc.co.uk

STAGECOACH AGENCY CHAPERONES   **T** 0845 4082468
Suite 2, 1st Floor Offices
Cantilupe Chambers
Cantilupe Road
Ross-on-Wye HR9 7AN
F 0845 4082464
E tarquin@stagecoachagency.co.uk
W www.stagecoachagency.co.uk

STREET DEFENCE   **T** 07919 350290
Commando Krav Maga Instructor, Screen Combatant & Celebrity Personal Trainer
6 Clive Close, Potters Bar
Hertfordshire EN6 2AE
E streetdefence@hotmail.co.uk
W www.streetdefenceuk.com

STUNT ACTION SPECIALISTS (S.A.S.)   **T** 01273 230214
Corporate & Television Stunt Work
110 Trafalgar Road
Portslade
East Sussex BN41 1GS
E mail@stuntactionspecialists.co.uk
W www.stuntactionspecialists.co.uk

STUNT DOGS & ANIMALS   **T/F** 01869 338546
3 The Chestnuts, Clifton
Deddington
Oxon OX15 0PE
E gill@stuntdogs.net

STYLES, John -
MAGICAL MART **T/F** 020 8300 3579
Magic, Ventriloquism & Punch & Judy Consultant
42 Christchurch Road, Sidcup
Kent DA15 7HQ
W www.johnstylesentertainer.co.uk

SYNCREDIBLE MEDIA **T** 020 7117 6776
Licensing & Media Marketing Communications
26-28 Hammersmith Grove, Hammersmith
London W6 7BA
E contact@syncredible.com
W www.syncredible.com

TALENT SCOUT THE **T** 01924 464049
Referral Service. Agents & Managers
19 Edge Road, Thornhill
Dewsbury, West Yorkshire WF12 0QA
E connect@thetalentscout.org

THEATRE PROJECTS
CONSULTANTS **T** 020 7482 4224
4 Apollo Studios
Charlton Kings Road
London NW5 2SW
F 020 7284 0636
E uk@theatreprojects.com
W www.theatreprojects.com

THERAPEDIA LONDON
BRIGHTON **T** 07941 300871
93 Gloucester Place, London W1U 6JQ
E info@gregmadison.net
W www.gregmadison.net

TODD, Carole **T** 07775 566275
Director. Choreographer. Show Doctor. Consultancy for
Acts Development & Audition Advice
E ctdirector@gmail.com

TOP NOTCH NANNIES **T** 020 7824 8209
142 Buckingham Palace Road
London SW1W 9TR
T 020 7881 0893
E jean@topnotchnannies.com
W www.topnotchnannies.com

TUTORS ON LOCATION **T** 0800 0488864
Holly House, Village Road
Christleton, Chester, Cheshire CH3 7AS
E enquiries@tutorsonlocation.co.uk
W www.tutorsonlocation.co.uk

TWINS FX THE **T** 0845 0523683
Special Effects for Film, Stage & Television Productions
T 07971 589186
E info@thetwinsfx.com
W www.thetwinsfx.com

UNITED KINGDOM
COPYRIGHT BUREAU **T** 01273 277333
Script Services
110 Trafalgar Road, Portslade
East Sussex BN41 1GS
E info@copyrightbureau.co.uk
W www.copyrightbureau.co.uk

VERNON, Doremy **T/F** 020 8767 6944
Archivist. Author 'Tiller Girls'. Dance Routines
Tiller Girl Style
16 Ouseley Road, London SW12 8EF
E mrs.worthington@hotmail.co.uk

VOCALEYES **T** 020 7375 1043
Audio Description "Describing The Arts"
1st Floor, 54 Commercial Street
London E1 6LT
E enquiries@vocaleyes.co.uk
W www.vocaleyes.co.uk

WELBOURNE, Jacqueline **T** 07977 247287
Choreographer. Circus Trainer. Consultant
43 Kingsway Avenue, Kingswood
Bristol BS15 8AN
E jackie.welbourne@gmail.com

WHITE DOVES
COMPANY LTD THE **T** 020 8508 1414
Provision of up to 300 Doves for Release
Suite 210 Sterling House, Langston Road
Loughton, Essex IG10 3TS
F 020 8502 2461
E thewhitedovecompany@yahoo.co.uk
W www.thewhitedovecompany.co.uk

WHITE, Leonard **T** 01273 514473
Stage & Television Credits
Highlands, 40 Hill Crest Road
Newhaven, Brighton
East Sussex BN9 9EG
E leoguy.white@virgin.net

WILD FANGS **T** 07969 434050
Animals for all Media Work, Specialising in Reptiles &
Snakes
78 Beversbrook Road, London N19 4QH
E wildfangs@outlook.com
W www.wildfangsuk.wordpress.com

WINDOW, S. PHOTOS **T** 07455 011639
Archival Documentation of Performance, Practice,
Design & Architecture
269 Southborough Lane, Bromley
Kent BR2 8AT
E info@swindowphotos.com
W www.swindowphotos.com

WISE MONKEY FINANCIAL
COACHING **T** 01273 691223
Contact: Simonne Gnessen
14 Eastern Terrace Mews
Brighton BN2 1EP
E simonne@financial-coaching.co.uk
W www.financial-coaching.co.uk

WOLF SPECIALISTS THE **T** 0118 971 3330
The UK Wolf Conservation Trust
UK Wolf Centre
Butlers Farm, Beenham
Berks RG7 5NT
E ukwct@ukwolf.org
W www.ukwolf.org

YOUNGBLOOD **T** 020 7193 3207
Fight Co-ordinators & Directors
E info@youngblood.co.uk
W www.youngblood.co.uk

YOUR GOLF DAY **T** 0845 1309517
Event Management & Promotions. Specialising in
Golf Days
Roche Hill, Bury Road
Rochdale OL11 5EU
E jennifer@yourgolfday.co.uk
W www.yourgolfday.co.uk

ACADEMY COSTUMES LTD T 020 7620 0771
50 Rushworth Street
London SE1 0RB
E info@academycostumes.com
W www.academycostumes.com

ADMIRAL COSTUMES T 01908 372504
Contact: Ruth Hewitt
86 Westbrook End
Newton Longville
Milton Keynes, Bucks MK17 0BX
E info@admiralcostumes.co.uk
W www.admiralcostumes.co.uk

ALL-SEWN-UP T/F 01422 843407
Mechanics Institute, 7 Church Street
Heptonstall, West Yorks HX7 7NS
E nwheeler_allsewnup@hotmail.com
W www.allsewnup.org.uk

ANELLO & DAVIDE T 020 7938 2255
Handmade Shoes
15 St Albans Grove, London W8 5BP
E enquiries@handmadeshoes.co.uk
W www.handmadeshoes.co.uk

ANGELS T 020 7836 5678
Fancy Dress. Revue
119 Shaftesbury Avenue
London WC2H 8AE
F 020 7240 9527
E fun@fancydress.com
W www.fancydress.com

ANGELS THE COSTUMIERS T 020 8202 2244
1 Garrick Road, London NW9 6AA
F 020 8202 1820
E angels@angels.uk.com
W www.angels.uk.com

ANGELS WIGS T 020 8202 2244
Facial Hair Suppliers. Wig Hire/Makers
1 Garrick Road, London NW9 6AA
F 020 8202 1820
E wigs@angels.uk.com
W www.angels.uk.com

ANTOINETTE COSTUME HIRE T 020 3490 8060
Events. Film. Stage
Rear of 184-190 Farnaby Road
Bromley, Kent BR2 0BB
E antoinettehire@aol.com
W www.costumehirelondon.com

ARMS & ARCHERY T 01920 460335
*Armour. Banners. Chainmail. Medieval Tents. Warrior
Costumes. Weaponry*
Thrift Lane, Off London Road
Ware, Herts SG12 9QS
E armsandarchery@btconnect.com

ATTLE COSTUMIERS LTD T 07707 143273
*Contact: Jamie Attle. Designs, Makes & Hires Costumes
to Professional & Amateur Theatre Companies, Film
Students & School Productions. Stock of Pantomime
Costumes to Hire. Based in Wimbledon*
E info@attlecostumiers.com
W www.attlecostumiers.com

BAHADLY, R. T 01625 615878
*Hair & Make-up Artist. Hair Extensions. Bald Caps.
Ageing & Casualty. Available for Test Shots*
47 Ploughmans Way
Macclesfield
Cheshire SK10 2UN
T 07973 553073
E rosienico@hotmail.co.uk

**BALLETPRO LTD, THE GRISHKO
DISTRIBUTORS** T 01223 861425
Importer & Distributor of Dance Shoes & Dancewear
The Old Sunday School, Chapel Street
Waterbeach, Cambridge CB25 9HR
F 01223 280388
E info@grishko.co.uk
W www.grishko.co.uk

**BELLIN, Sophie
COSTUME MAKING** T 07726 181148
Specialist in Dance & Physical Disciplines
E sophie.bellinhansen@hotmail.com
W www.sophiebellin.eu

BERTRAND, Henry T 020 7424 7000
London Stockhouse for Silk
52 Holmes Road, London NW5 3AB
F 020 7424 7001
E sales@henrybertrand.co.uk
W www.henrybertrand.co.uk

BIRMINGHAM COSTUME HIRE T 0121 622 3158
Suites 209-210, Jubilee Centre
130 Pershore Street, Birmingham B5 6ND
F 0121 622 2758
E info@birminghamcostumehire.co.uk
W www.facebook.com/BirminghamCostume

BLAIR, Julia T 07917 877742
Make-up Artist. Film. Photographic. Stage. Television
6A Boston Parade, London W7 2DG
E julia0blair@gmail.com
W www.juliablair.co.uk

BRADLEY-HILL, Justine T 07962 177733
Bespoke Milliner
The Studio, 29 Green Lane
Addingham, Ilkley, West Yorkshire LS29 0JH
E info@justinebradley-hill.co.uk
W www.justinebradley-hill.co.uk

BRIGGS, Ron DESIGN T 020 8444 8801
*Theatrical Tailors. Costume Design & Making. Bespoke
Embroidery. Rhinestone Application*
1 Bedford Mews, London N2 9DF
E costumes@ronbriggs.com
W www.ronbriggs.com

BRODY, Shirley
Freelance Hair & Make-up Artist & Hair Decorations
Based in London
E s.brody@blueyonder.co.uk
W www.lalatiara.com

BURGESS, Romy T 07731 633865
Hair & Theatrical Make-up Artist
Flat 3, 77 Montpelier Road
Brighton, East Sussex BN1 3BD
E romy_932@hotmail.com

BURLINGTONS BOUTIQUE T 0844 8008884
Hairdressers
14 John Princes Street, London W1G 0JS
E reception@burlingtonsboutique.com
W www.burlingtonsboutique.com

CALICO FABRICS T 020 8541 5274
*Suppliers of Unbleached Calico Fabrics for Stage,
Costumes, Backdrops plus Cotton, Silks, Linens, Jersey,
Tweeds, Velvets including Liberty Prints & James Hare
Silks. Visit Shop or Website*
3 Ram Passage, High Street
Kingston-upon-Thames, Surrey KT1 1HH
F 020 8546 7755
E amir@calicofabrics.co.uk
W www.calicofabrics.co.uk

CAPEZIO LONDON T 020 7379 6042
Dance Products
33 Endell Street, London WC2H 9BA
E capeziolondon@capezio.com
W www.capezio.com

CHRISANNE LTD T 020 8640 5921
Specialist Fabrics & Accessories for Dance & Stage
110-112 Morden Road, Mitcham
Surrey CR4 4XB
F 020 8640 2106
E sales@chrisanne.com
W www.chrisanne.com

CLANRANALD COSTUME T 01259 731010
27 High Street, Kincardine
Alloa FK10 4RJ
E info@clanranald.org
W www.clanranald.org

CLASSIQUE DANCE SHOP T 023 9223 3334
3-5 Stakes Hill Road, Waterlooville
Hampshire PO7 7JB
E audreyhersey@gmail.com
W www.classiquedance.co.uk

COLTMAN, Mike
See COSTUME CONSTRUCTION LTD

COOK, Sheila TEXTILES T 020 7603 3003
Vintage Textiles, Costumes & Accessories for Sale/Hire
26 Addison Place, London W11 4RJ
E sheilacook@sheilacook.co.uk
W www.sheilacook.co.uk

COSPROP LTD T 020 7561 7300
Accessories. Costumes
469-475 Holloway Road
London N7 6LE
F 020 7561 7310
E enquiries@cosprop.com
W www.cosprop.com

COSTUME BOUTIQUE T 020 7193 6877
Costume Hire for Events & Parties
38 Great Western Studios, 65 Alfred Road
London W2 5EU
T 07973 794450
E costumeboutique@me.com
W www.costumeboutique.co.uk

COSTUME CONSTRUCTION LTD T/F 01242 581847
Costumes. Masks. Props. Puppets
Unit 1 Crooks Industrial Estate, Croft Street
Cheltenham GL53 0ED
E mike@costumeconstruction.co.uk
W www.costumeconstruction.co.uk

COSTUME CREATIONS T 01902 738282
10 Olinthus Avenue
Wolverhampton WV11 3DE
E yourcostume@googlemail.com
W www.costumecreations.co.uk

COSTUME SOLUTIONS T 020 7603 9035
Costume Stylist
43 Rowan Road, London W6 7DT
E sequinedslippers@hotmail.com

COSTUME STORE LTD THE T 01273 479727
Costume Accessories
3 Upper Stalls, Iford
Lewes, East Sussex BN7 3EJ
F 01273 477191
E enquiries@thecostumestore.co.uk
W www.thecostumestore.co.uk

COSTUME STUDIO LTD T 020 7275 9614
Costumes. Wigs
Montgomery House, 159-161 Balls Pond Road
London N1 4BG
T/F 020 7923 9065
E costume.studio@btconnect.com
W www.costumestudio.co.uk

**COUTURE BEADING &
EMBELLISHMENT** T 020 8925 2714
108 Hiltongrove Business Centre
Hatherley Mews
Walthamstow, London E17 4QP
T 07866 939401
E enquiries@couturebeading.com
W www.couturebeading.com

**CRAZY CLOTHES
CONNECTION** T 020 7221 3989
*Vintage Clothing, Shoes & Accessories. Male & Female.
1920s-1980s. Sale or Hire. Open Fridays/Saturdays
11.30-6.30 only*
134 Lancaster Road, Ladbroke Grove
London W11 1QU
W www.crazy-clothes.co.uk

DANCIA INTERNATIONAL T 020 7831 9483
The Dancer's Shop
168 Drury Lane, London WC2B 5QA
E london@dancia.co.uk
W www.dancia.co.uk/london

**DAVIES, Bryan Philip
COSTUMES** T 01273 481004
Lavish Pantomime. Musical Shows. Opera
68 Court Road, Lewes, East Sussex BN7 2SA
T 07931 249097
E bryan@bpdcostumes.co.uk
W www.bpdcostumes.co.uk

DELAMAR ACADEMY T/F 020 8579 9511
Make-up Training
Ealing Studios, Building D, 2nd Floor
Ealing Green, London W5 5EP
E info@delamaracademy.co.uk
W www.delamaracademy.co.uk

DESIGN AND ALTER T 020 7498 4360
Restyling
220A Queenstown Road
Battersea, London SW8 4LP
T 020 3011 1788
E info@designeralterations.com
W www.designeralterations.com

DR. BOO T 020 8693 4823
*Independent Cosmetic Make-up Studio/
Treatment Rooms*
22 North Cross Road, East Dulwich
London SE22 9EU
E boogirls@hotmail.co.uk
W www.drboo.co.uk

EASTON, Derek T/F 01273 588262
Wigs For Film, Stage & Television
1 Dorothy Avenue, Peacehaven, East Sussex BN10 8LP
T 07768 166733
E wigs@derekeastonwigs.co.uk
W www.derekeastonwigs.co.uk

EDA ROSE MILLINERY T 01491 837174
Ladies' Hats. Design & Manufacture
Lalique, Mongewell
Wallingford, Oxon OX10 8BP
F 01491 835909
E edarose.lawson@btconnect.com

**EIA MILLINERY DESIGN /
EIAHATART** T 001 773 206 9330
By Appointment
1620 West Nelson Street, Chicago
Illinois 60657-3027, USA
E info@eiahatart.com

**EVOLUTION SETS &
COSTUMES LTD** T 01304 615333
Set & Costume Hire
Langdon Abbey, West Langdon
Dover, Kent CT15 5HJ
F 01304 615353
E dorcas@evolution-productions.co.uk

FOTONICA T 07840 550097
233 Russell Court, Woburn Place
London WC1H 0ND
E sheree.tams@gmail.com
W www.shereetams.com

FOX, Charles H. LTD T 020 7240 3111
The Professional Make-up Centre
22 Tavistock Street
London WC2E 7PY
F 020 7379 3410
E makeup@charlesfox.co.uk
W www.charlesfox.co.uk

FOXTROT PRODUCTIONS LTD T 020 8964 3555
Armoury Services. Costume & Prop Hire. Firearms
3B Brassie Avenue
East Acton
London W3 7DE
E info@foxtrot-productions.co.uk
W www.foxtrot-productions.co.uk

FREED OF LONDON T 020 7240 0432
Dance Shoes. Dancewear
94 St Martin's Lane
London WC2N 4AT
F 020 7240 3061
E shop@freed.co.uk
W www.freedoflondon.com

FUNN LTD T 0870 8743866
*Silk, Cotton & Wool Stockings. Opaque Opera Tights.
40's Rayon Stockings (over the Knee, Stay-ups)*
PO Box 102, Steyning
West Sussex BN44 3EB
F 0870 8794450
E funnsales@lycos.com

GAMBA THEATRICAL
See THEATRE SHOES LTD

**GAV NICOLA
THEATRICAL SHOES** T 07961 974278
T 00 34 673803783
E gavnicola@yahoo.com
W www.theatricalshoes.com

GILLHAM, Felicite T 01761 437142
Wig Makers for Film, Opera & Stage
Gallis Ash, Kilmersdon
Near Bath, Somerset BA3 5SZ
T 07802 955908
E felicite@gillywigs.com

**GREASEPAINT SCHOOL OF
MAKE-UP & HAIR** T 020 8840 6000
143 Northfield Avenue
Ealing
London W13 9QT
E info@greasepaint.co.uk
W www.greasepaint.co.uk

GROUNDLINGS COSTUME HIRE T 023 9273 9496
Over 11,000 Period & Modern Costumes
42 Kent Street, Portsmouth
Hampshire PO1 3BS
E wardrobe@groundlings.co.uk
W www.groundlings.co.uk

GROVE, Sue DESIGNS T 023 8078 6849
Costume Designers & Makers. Historical Specialist
12 Ampthill Road, Shirley
Southampton, Hants SO15 8LP
E sue.grove1@tiscali.co.uk

HAIRAISERS T 020 8965 2500
Hair Extensions. Wigs
9-11 Sunbeam Road, Park Royal
London NW10 6JP
F 020 8963 1600
E info@hairaisers.com
W www.hairaisersshop.com

HAND & LOCK T 020 7580 7488
Bespoke Embroidery for Costumes, Fashion & Interiors
86 Margaret Street
London W1W 8TE
F 020 7580 7499
E enquiries@handembroidery.com
W www.handembroidery.com

HANSEN, Kasper THEATRE DESIGNER T 07847 316196
Design Set & Costume for Theatre, Dance, Ballet & Opera
29C Grosvenor Park, London SE5 0NH
E contact@kasper-hansen.com
W www.kasper-hansen.com

HARVEYS OF HOVE T 01273 430323
Military Specialists. Theatrical Costumes
110 Trafalgar Road, Portslade
Sussex BN41 1GS
E harveys.costume@ntlworld.com
W www.harveysofhove.co.uk

HENRY, Lewis LTD T 020 7636 6683
Dress Makers
111-113 Great Portland Street
London W1W 6QQ
E info@lewishenrydesigns.com

HIREARCHY T 01202 394465
Classic & Contemporary Costume
45-47 Palmerston Road, Boscombe
Bournemouth, Dorset BH1 4HW
E hirearchy1@gmail.com
W www.hirearchy.co.uk

HISTORY IN THE MAKING T 023 9225 3175
Historically Correct Costumes & Armour for Film, Television & Theatre
4A Aysgarth Road, Waterlooville
Hampshire PO7 7UG
E info@history-making.com
W www.history-making.com

HODIN, Annabel T 020 7431 8761
Costume Designer & Stylist. Personal Shopper
12 Eton Avenue, London NW3 3EH
T 07836 754079
E annabelhodin@aol.com

HOPKINS, Trisha T 01704 873055
6 Willow Grove, Formby L37 3NX
T 07957 368598
E trisha_hopkins@hotmail.co.uk

JULIETTE DESIGNS T 020 7263 7878
Diamante Jewellery Manufacturers
90 Yerbury Road, London N19 4RS
F 020 7281 7326
E juliettedesigns@hotmail.com
W www.stagejewellery.com

KATIE'S WIGS T 07900 250853
Wig Supplier & Maker
4 Round Hill Road, Leeds LS28 8BJ
E katie.hunt@katieswigs.com

KIDD, Ella J. T 01603 304445
Bespoke Millinery, Wigs & Head-dresses for Film, Stage & Television
W www.ellajkidd.co.uk

LARGER THAN LIFE STAGEWEAR T 020 8466 9010
Theatrical Costumes for Hire
Unit E36 Big Yellow Store, 12 Farwig Lane
Bromley, Kent BR1 3RB
T 07802 717714
E info@largerthanlifestagewear.co.uk
W www.largerthanlifestagewear.co.uk

LG CREATIVE T 07590 237289
Contact: Lauren Gregory. Make-up Artist. SFX. Prosthetics
15C Healey Street, London NW1 8SR
E lauren@lg-creative.com
W www.lg-creative.com

LOCK, Josie T 07722 358425
Make-up Artist
66 Castle Road, St Albans
Hertfordshire AL1 5DG
E hello@josielock.co.uk
W www.josielockmakeup.co.uk

MADDERMARKET THEATRE COSTUME HIRE T 01603 626292
Costume & Wig Hire. Period Clothing
St John's Alley, Norwich NR2 1DR
F 01603 661357
E office@maddermarket.org
W www.maddermarket.co.uk

MAKE-UP ARTIST & HAIR STYLIST T 07973 216468
Freelancer
16 Tempest Avenue, Potters Bar
Hertfordshire EN6 5JX
E magui@magui.co.uk
W www.mm-mua.co.uk

MAKE-UP LONDON ACADEMY T 020 7272 9848
12 Brecknock Road, London N7 0DD
E info@makeuplondonacademy.co.uk
W www.makeuplondonacademy.com

MASCOTS UK & HIRE LTD T 01525 405889
*Professional Character Mascot Costumes available to
Hire & Buy*
3-5 Kings Arms Yard, Church Street
Ampthill, Beds MK45 2PJ
E sales@mascotuk.com
W www.mascotsuk.com

MASTER CLEANERS THE T 020 7431 3725
*Dry Cleaning of Theatrical Costumes & Antique
Garments*
189 Haverstock Hill, London NW3 4QG
E info@themastercleaners.com
W www.themastercleaners.com

McCORMACK, Mitsuki
*Media Make-up Artist. Make-up, Hair Styling,
SFX & Airbrush*
Based in London
W www.mitsukimccormack.webs.com

McGAHERN, Becky T 07771 800172
Hair & Make-up Artist
26A Wadley Road, London E11 1JF
E becky@beckymcgahern.com
W www.beckymcgahern.com

MEANANDGREEN.COM T 0845 8991133
87 Darlington Street
Wolverhampton WV1 4EX
E custserv@meanandgreen.com
W www.meanandgreen.com

**MEDIA INTERNATIONAL
FOUNDATION** T 07765 927008
*Film/Wardrobe Asssistant. Designs, Alters & Makes any
Costumes*
227 Earls Court Road, London SW5 9BL
E mediacorp1@yahoo.com

MORRIS, Heather T 020 8771 7170
Hair Replacement. Wigs
Fortyseven, 47A Westow Street
Crystal Palace, London SE19 3RW
W www.fortysevenhair.co.uk

NATIONAL THEATRE T 020 7820 1358 (Props)
Costume, Furniture & Props Hire
Chichester House
Kennington Park Estate
1-3 Brixton Road, London SW9 6DE
T 020 7452 3970 (Costume)
E costume_hire@nationaltheatre.org.uk

ONE REPRESENTS LTD T 020 7467 1400
3rd Floor, 66-68 Margaret Street
London W1W 8SR
F 020 7467 1401
E info@onerepresents.com
W www.onerepresents.com

ORIGINAL KNITWEAR T 01726 844807
Contact: Gina Pinnick. Includes Stretch Fake Fur
Avalon, Tregoney Hill
Mevagissey, Cornwall PL26 6RG
T 07957 376855
E okgina@btinternet.com
W www.originalknitwear.co.uk

PACE, Terri MAKE-UP DESIGN T 07939 698999
E info@terripace.com
W www.terripace.com

PAINTED LADY THE T 07895 820041
Make-up Consultant & Trainer
581 London Road, Stoke on Trent
Staffordshire ST4 5AZ
E ashaleeblueeyes@hotmail.co.uk

PATEY (LONDON) LTD T 020 8291 4820
The Hat Workshop
Connaught Business Park
Malham Road, London SE23 1AH
F 020 8291 6275
E trevor@pateyhats.com
W www.pateyhats.com

PHA CREATIVES T 0161 273 4444
Hair & Make-up Artists
Tanzaro House, Ardwick Green North
Manchester M12 6FZ
E info@pha-agency.co.uk
W www.pha-agency.co.uk

PINK POINTES DANCEWEAR T/F 01708 438584
1A Suttons Lane, Hornchurch
Essex RM12 6RD
E pink.pointes@btconnect.com

PORSELLI T 0845 0170817
4 Frensham Road
Sweet Briar Industrial Estate
Norwich NR3 2BT
F 01603 406676
E porselliuk@aol.com
W www.dancewear.co.uk

RAINBOW PRODUCTIONS LTD T 020 8254 5300
Manufacture & Handling of Costume Characters
Unit 3, Green Lea Park
Prince George's Road
London SW19 2JD
F 020 8254 5306
E info@rainbowproductions.co.uk
W www.rainbowproductions.co.uk

REPLICA WAREHOUSE T/F 01477 534075
Costumiers. Props
200 Main Road, Goostrey
Cheshire CW4 8PD
E lesleyedwards@replicawarehouse.co.uk
W www.replicawarehouse.co.uk

ROBBINS, Sheila T 01865 735524
Wig Hire
Broombarn, 7 Ivy Cottages
Hinksey Hill, Oxford OX1 5BQ

**ROYAL EXCHANGE
THEATRE COSTUME HIRE** T/F 0161 819 6660
Period Costumes & Accessories
47-53 Swan Street
Manchester M4 5JY
E costume.hire@royalexchange.co.uk
W www.royalexchange.co.uk

**ROYER, Hugo
INTERNATIONAL LTD** T 01252 878811
Hair & Wig Materials
10 Lakeside Business Park, Swan Lane
Sandhurst, Berkshire GU47 9DN
F 01252 878852
E enquiries@royer.co.uk
W www.hugoroyer.com

RSC COSTUME HIRE T 01789 205920
28 Timothy's Bridge Road, Stratford Enterprise Park
Stratford-upon-Avon
Warwickshire CV37 9UY
E costume.hire@rsc.org.uk

RUMBLE, Jane   T 020 8904 6462
Masks, Millinery & Helmets Made to Order
121 Elmstead Avenue, Wembley
Middlesex HA9 8NT

SAGUARO, Jen   T 07773 385703
Costume, Drape & Fabric Commissions
35 Southey Street
Bristol BS2 9RE
E jrsaguaro@googlemail.com

SEXTON, Sallyann   T 01923 211644
Hair & Make-up Stylist
c/o The Harris Agency Ltd
71 The Avenue
Watford, Herts WD17 4NU
T 07973 802842
E theharrisagency@btconnect.com

SINGER, Sandra ASSOCIATES   T 01702 331616
*Fashion Stylists for Stage & Television. Costume/
Designer*
21 Cotswold Road, Westcliff-on-Sea
Essex SS0 8AA
E sandrasingeruk@aol.com
W www.sandrasinger.com

SLEIMAN, Hilary   T 020 8555 6176
Specialist & Period Knitwear
72 Godwin Road, London E7 0LG
T 07940 555663
E hilarysleiman1@gmail.com

SOFT PROPS   T 020 7587 1116
Costume & Model Makers
92 Fentiman Road, London SW8 1LA
F 020 7207 0062
E jackie@softprops.co.uk

**STAGEWORKS WORLDWIDE
PRODUCTIONS**   T 01253 342426
Largest Costume Wardrobe in the North
525 Ocean Boulevard
Blackpool FY4 1EZ
F 01253 342702
E simone.bolajuzon@stageworkswwp.com
W www.stageworkswwp.com

STEVENS, Anita   T 07713 132456
*Freelance Make-up Artist and Hair Stylist for Fashion,
Television and Film*
21 Ryculff Square, Blackheath
London SE3 0SN
E anita@anitastevens.com
W www.anitastevens.com

STRIBLING, Joan   T 07791 758480
*Film. Television. Stage (ex BBC). Hair, Make-up &
Prosthetics Designer. BAFTA Craft, RTS & Design & Arts
Director's Awards. BAFTA & WFTV Member. Wales Film
Screen Commission (Crew)*
Based in London / West Country
E joanstribling@hotmail.com
W www.joanstribling.co.uk

SWINFIELD, Rosemarie   T 07976 965520
Rosie's Make-up Box. Make-up Design & Training
E rosiesmake-up@uw.club.net
W www.rosemarieswinfield.com

TALK TO THE HAND PUPPETS   T 020 7627 1052
Custom Puppets for Film, Stage & Television
Studio 27B, Spaces Business Centre
15-17 Ingate Place, London SW8 3NS
T 07855 421454
E iestynmevans@hotmail.com
W www.talktothehandpuppets.com

THEATRE SHOES LTD   T 020 8529 9195
Trading as GAMBA Theatrical
Unit 1A, Lee Valley Trading Estate
Rivermead Road, London N18 3QW
F 020 8529 7995
E info@theatreshoes.com

**THEATRICAL
SHOEMAKERS LTD**   T 020 8884 4484
Footwear
Unit 1A, Lee Valley Trading Estate
Rivermead Road, London N18 3QW
E info@theatreshoes.com
W www.shoemaking.co.uk

TRENDS ENTERTAINMENTS   T 01253 396534
Theatrical Costume Hire, Design & Making
Unit 4, 9 Chorley Road
Lancashire FY3 7XQ
T 07506 171054
E info@trendsentertainment.com
W www.trendsentertainment.com

TRYFONOS, Mary MASKS   T 020 7502 7883
Designer & Maker of Masks & Costume Properties
59 Shaftesbury Road, London N19 4QW
T 07764 587433
E marytryfonos@aol.com

TUTU-TOPIA
Pembrokeshire, Wales SA73
E sales@tutu-topia.co.uk
W www.tutu-topia.co.uk

**WEST YORKSHIRE
FABRICS LTD**   T/F 0113 225 6550
*Barathea. Crepe. Linen. Stretch Fabrics. Suiting.
Venetian. Cut Lengths*
Unit 5 Milestone Court, Stanningley
Leeds LS28 6HE
E neil@wyfabrics.com

**WEST YORKSHIRE
PLAYHOUSE**   T 0113 213 7242
Costume Hire
6 St Peter's Building, St Peter's Square
Leeds, West Yorkshire LS2 8AH
E sally.stone@wyp.org.uk
W www.wyp.org.uk/about-us/what-we-do/costume-hire

WIG ROOM THE   T 01256 415737
22 Coronation Road, Basingstoke
Hants RG21 4HA
E darren@wigroom.co.uk

WIG SPECIALITIES LTD   T 020 7724 0020
Handmade Wigs, Facial Hair & Wig Hire
77 Ashmill Street, London NW1 6RA
F 020 7724 0069
E wigspecialities@btconnect.com
W www.wigspecialities.co.uk

WIGS BY TRACEY BRIDGE   T 01453 765329
21A Dudbridge Meadow, Dudbridge
Stroud, Gloucestershire GL5 3NH
T 07505 529039
E wigsbytraceybridge@yahoo.com
W www.wigsbytraceybridge.com

**WIGS, MAKE-UP &
COSTUME SPECIALIST**   T 07516 323000
12 Waterford Lane, Witney, Oxfordshire OX28 1GB
E rachellisajones@hotmail.co.uk

WILLIAMS, Emma   T 07710 130345
Costume Designer & Stylist. Film, Stage & Television
E ewuk@mac.com

DAILY EXPRESS T 020 8612 7773
Contact: Caroline Jowett, Arts Editor (Stage, Film, Dance, Opera, Books)
Northern Shell Building
10 Lower Thames Street
London EC3R 6EN
E arts.editor@express.co.uk

DAILY MAIL T 020 7938 6000
Contact: Quentin Letts (Stage), Chris Tookey (Film), Baz Bamigboye (Chief Showbiz Writer), Adrian Thrills (Music)
Northcliffe House
2 Derry Street
Kensington
London W8 5TT

DAILY STAR T 020 8612 7000
Contact: Alan Frank (Film & Video), Nigel Pauley (Showbiz Report)
Northern Shell Building
10 Lower Thames Street
London EC3R 6EN

DAILY TELEGRAPH T 020 7931 2000
Contact: Ross Jones (Film), Serena Davies (TV & Radio), Sarah Compton (Arts & Dance), Paul Gent (Classical Music, Theatre & Opera), Bernadette McNulty (Music), Sameer Rahim (Books), Mark Monahan (Comedy), Tom Hoggins (Video Games)
111 Buckingham Palace Road
London SW1W 0DT

FINANCIAL TIMES T 020 7873 3000
Contact: Nigel Andrews (Film), Martin Hoyle (Television)
1 Southwark Bridge
London SE1 9HL

GUARDIAN T 020 3353 2000
Contact: Michael Billington (Stage), Sam Wollaston (Television)
King's Place, 90 York Way
London N1 9GU
E michael.billington@guardian.co.uk

INDEPENDENT T 020 7005 2000
Contact: Gerard Gilbert (Television)
2 Derry Street
London W8 5HF

LONDON EVENING STANDARD T 020 3367 7000
Contact: Henry Hitchings, Fiona Mountford (Stage), David Sexton, Charlotte O'Sullivan (Film), Barry Millington (Classical Music & Opera)
Northcliffe House
2 Derry Street
Kensington, London W8 5TT
W www.thisislondon.co.uk

MAIL ON SUNDAY T 020 7938 6000
Contact: Georgina Brown (Stage), Jason Solomons (Cinema & DVDs), Matthew Bond (Film)
Review Section
Northcliffe House
2 Derry Street
London W8 5TT

MIRROR T 020 7510 3000
Contact: David Edwards (Film), James Simon (Television Previews)
Mirror Group Newspapers Ltd
1 Canada Square, Canary Wharf
London E14 5AP

MORNING STAR T 020 8510 0815
Contact: Cliff Cocker (Arts Editor)
William Rust House
52 Beachy Road
London E3 2NS

OBSERVER T 020 3353 2000
Contact: Sarah Donaldson (Arts Editor)
King's Place, 90 York Way
London N1 9GU

PEOPLE T 020 7293 3000
Contact: Chris Hunneysett (Film), Adam Postans (Television & Radio), Nada Farhoud (Features), Katie Hind (Show Business)
1 Canada Square, Canary Wharf
London E14 5AP

SUN T 020 7782 4000
Contact: Ally Ross (Features Writer)
3 Thomas More Square
London E98 1XY

SUNDAY EXPRESS T 020 8612 7000
Contact: Michael Arditti (Stage), Henry Fitzherbert (Film), David Stephenson (Television), Clare Heal (Radio), Clair Woodward (Arts Editor), Clare Colvin (Opera), Jeffery Taylor (Dance)
Northern Shell Building
10 Lower Thames Street
London EC3R 6EN

SUNDAY MIRROR T 020 7510 3000
Contact: Kevin O'Sullivan (Stage & Television), Mark Adams (Film)
Mirror Group
1 Canada Square
Canary Wharf
London E14 5AP

SUNDAY TELEGRAPH T 020 7931 2000
Contact: Tim Walker (Stage), Jenny McCartney (Film), John Allison (Classical Music & Opera)
111 Buckingham Palace Road
London SW1W 0DT

SUNDAY TIMES T 020 7782 5000
Contact: Christopher Hart (Stage), A. A. Gill (Television), Paul Donovan (Radio)
3 Thomas More Square
London E98 1XY

TIMES T 020 7782 5000
Contact: Kate Muir (Film), James Jackson (Television), Ed Potton (Music)
3 Thomas More Square
London E98 1XY

D

Dance Companies
Dance Organisations
Dance Training & Professional Classes
Drama Schools: Drama UK
Drama Training, Schools & Coaches

DRAMA UK
For information about Drama UK
please see:
W www.dramauk.co.uk

CDET
For information
regarding membership
of the Council for Dance
Education and Training
please see:
W www.cdet.org.uk

Dance Companies

How do I become a professional dancer?

Full-time vocational training can start from as young as ten years old. A good starting point for researching the different schools and courses available is CDET (Council for Dance Education & Training) www.cdet.org.uk. There are 24 dance colleges offering professional training accredited by CDET, and nearly three hundred university courses which include some form of dance training. It is estimated that over one thousand dancers graduate from vocational training schools or university courses every year, so it is a highly competitive career. Therefore anyone wanting to be a professional dancer must obtain as many years of training and experience as possible, plus go to see plenty of performances spanning different types and genres of dance. If you require further information on vocational dance schools, applying to accredited dance courses, auditions and funding, contact CDET's information line 'Answers for Dancers' on 020 7240 5703.

What are dance companies?

There are more than two hundred dance companies in the UK, spanning a variety of dance styles including ballet, contemporary, hip hop and African. A dance company will either be resident in a venue, be a touring company, or a combination of both. Many have websites which you can visit for full information. Most dance companies employ ensemble dancers on short to medium contracts, who may then work on a number of different productions for the same company over a number of months. In addition, the company will also employ principal/leading dancers on a role-by-role basis.

What are dance organisations?

There are numerous organisations which exist to support professional dancers; covering important areas including health and safety, career development, networking and legal and financial aspects. Other organisations (e.g. regional/ national dance agencies) exist to promote dance within the wider community.

I have already trained to be a dancer. Why do I need further training?

Dance training should not cease as soon as you get your first job or complete a course. Throughout your career you should continuously strive to maintain your fitness levels, enhance and develop your existing skills and keep learning new ones in order to retain a competitive edge. You must also be prepared to continuously learn new dance styles and routines for specific roles. Ongoing training and classes can help you stay fit and active, and if you go through a period of unemployment you can keep your mind and body occupied, ready to take on your next job.

How should I use these listings?

The following listings will supply you with up-to-date contact details for a wide range of dance companies and organisations, followed by listings for dance training and professional classes. Members of CDET have indicated their membership status under their name. Always research schools and classes thoroughly, obtaining copies of prospectuses where available. Most vocational schools offer two and three year full-time training programmes, many also offer excellent degree programmes. Foundation courses offer a sound introduction to the profession, but they can never replace a full-time vocational course. Many schools, organisations and studios also offer part-time/evening classes which offer a general understanding of dance and complementary technique or the opportunity to refresh specific dance skills; they will not, however, enable a student to become a professional dancer.

How else can I find work as a dancer?

Dance also plays a role in commercial theatre, musicals, opera, film, television, live music and video, corporate events and many other industries. Dancers may also want to be represented by an agent. Agents have many more contacts within the industry than an individual dancer can have and can offer advice and negotiate contracts on your behalf as well as submit you for jobs. A number of specialist dance agencies are listed in the 'Agents: Dance' section.

What other careers are available in dance?

Opportunities also exist to work as a teacher, choreographer, technician or manager. For information about teaching, contact CDET. Dance UK (www.danceuk.org) is a good source for information for anyone considering working in a supporting role within the industry.

What should I do to avoid injury?

An injury is more likely to occur if you are inflexible and unprepared for sudden physical exertion. The last thing you want to do is to pick up an injury, however minor, and be prevented from working, so continuous training during both employment and unemployment will help you to minimise the risk of an injury during a performance or rehearsal. If you do sustain an injury you will want to make sure it does not get any worse by getting treatment with a specialist. The British Association for Performing Arts Medicine (BAPAM) provides specialist health support for performers, free health assessment clinics and a directory of performing arts health practitioners and specialists. Visit www.bapam.org.uk for more information.

I'm not a professional dancer but I enjoy dancing. Why should I use these listings?

People don't just dance to perform, teach or advise within the industry. Dance can be pursued for fun, recreation, social reasons and for health. Training and professional advice should still be pursued to ensure that you do not injure yourself while dancing and prevent yourself from working. You can also use the 'Dance Training & Professional Classes' listings to find suitable dance lessons in your area, which you could attend to make friends, keep fit and stay occupied.

Where can I find more information?

For further advice about the dance industry, you could try contacting CDET (www.cdet.org.uk) for training information, Dance UK (www.danceuk.org) regarding the importance and needs of dance and dancers, or BAPAM (www.bapam.org.uk) for health issues. You may want to get involved with MOVE IT! – the UK's biggest dance exhibition which takes place every year in the spring. For more information visit www.moveitdance.co.uk. If you are looking for a dance agent to promote you to job opportunities, please see the 'Agents: Dance' section of Contacts.

Dance Companies

Love, Learn, Teach Dance

As a registered educational charity, The Imperial Society of Teachers of Dancing (ISTD) is one of the world's leading dance examination boards. The ISTD's mission is to educate the public in the art of dancing in all its forms, to promote and provide knowledge of dance, to provide up-to-date techniques for members and to maintain and improve teaching standards.

As a professional dancer, you may decide to make a transition in your career and become a teacher. If you're keen to share your passion for dance with others, then this is often the natural next step. Everyone remembers their favourite teacher and this seems particularly true in the world of dance.

Dance teachers need to have good technical skills plus the ability to communicate and motivate. Increasingly today you also need to have good business skills and a thorough knowledge of health and safety. Getting the right training can help you sharpen your skills these areas.

The training you get is crucial to providing the right opportunities and opening doors for you to work in a wide variety of settings. If you are interested in a career as a dance teacher, the ISTD is a source of research, training and information.

THE ISTD AT A GLANCE

- The ISTD's mission is to "educate the public in the art of dancing in all its forms"
- Over 100 years of expertise and 250,000 dance examinations taken every year
- 12 specialist faculties including the latest styles and techniques to train dancers for the profession
- ISTD syllabus grades, vocational levels, medal tests and class exams held in dance schools and professional institutions located through out the world
- Training courses and opportunities for further learning are available to support members at every stage of their teaching career
- Teaching qualifications in all theatre dance and dancesport genres
- A wide range of accredited and ISTD specific teaching qualifications - globally recognised and industry leading - from Level 3 to MA level

We periodically make syllabus revisions to ensure our teaching frameworks reflect the demands required of dancers in today's world. This is about providing teachers with the best possible skills and tools to train young dancers ready for the profession. We offer the training activities you need to learn revisions to our syllabi, and we also host courses where we can engage with members and create networking opportunities for them. The ISTD publishes numerous syllabus guides and DANCE, a quarterly magazine to keep members informed of syllabus updates.

In addition to syllabus training, the ISTD offers courses for members and non-members to support their continuing professional development (CPD) including the opportunity to study many essential elements of our Level 6 Diploma in Dance Pedagogy (DDP) in the form of short weekend sessions. These hugely popular courses offer teachers a flexible and affordable way to enhance their skills, and provide a route for the very busiest teachers to continue their professional development journey.

To find out more visit www.istd.org

AKADEMI SOUTH ASIAN DANCE UK   T 020 7691 3210
Hampstead Town Hall
213 Haverstock Hill
London NW3 4QP
E info@akademi.co.uk
W www.akademi.co.uk

ANJALI DANCE COMPANY   T 01295 251909
The Mill Arts Centre
Spiceball Park
Banbury, Oxfordshire OX16 5QE
E info@anjali.co.uk
W www.anjali.co.uk

BALLET CYMRU   T 01633 892927
E dariusjames@welshballet.co.uk
W www.welshballet.co.uk

BALLETBOYZ   T 020 8549 8814
52A Canbury Park Road
Kingston-Upon-Thames
Surrey KT2 6JX
E info@balletboyz.com
W www.balletboyz.com

BALLROOM, LONDON THEATRE OF   T 020 8722 8798
Contact: Paul Harris® (Artistic Director)
24 Montana Gardens
Sutton, Surrey SM1 4FP
E office@londontheatreofballroom.com
W www.londontheatreofballroom.com

BIRMINGHAM ROYAL BALLET   T 0121 245 3500
Thorp Street
Birmingham B5 4AU
F 0121 245 3570
E brbinfo@brb.org.uk
W www.brb.org.uk

BOY BLUE ENTERTAINMENT   T 020 7256 6849
Barbican Centre
c/o Stage Door
Silk Street, London EC2Y 8DS
E info@boyblueent.com
W www.boyblueent.com

CANDOCO DANCE COMPANY   T 020 7704 6845
2T Leroy House
436 Essex Road
London N1 3QP
F 020 7704 1645
E info@candoco.co.uk
W www.candoco.co.uk

COMPANY OF CRANKS   T 07963 617981
1st Floor
62 Northfield House
London SE15 6TN
E mimetic16@yahoo.com
W www.mimeworks.com

CREATIVE KIDZ STAGE SCHOOL & PERFORMANCE TEAM   T 07908 144802
Samuel Lewis Trust Community Centre
Vanston Place
Fulham
London SW6 1AS
T 07432 612026
E info@creativekidzandco.co.uk
W www.creativekidzandco.co.uk

DAVIES, Siobhan DANCE   T 020 7091 9650
Investigative Contemporary Arts Organisation, Applying Choreography across a Wide Range of Creative Disciplines
Siobhan Davies Studios
85 St George's Road
London SE1 6ER
F 020 7091 9669
E info@siobhandavies.com
W www.siobhandavies.com

DV8 PHYSICAL THEATRE   T 020 7655 0977
Artsadmin
Toynbee Studios
28 Commercial Street
London E1 6AB
F 020 7247 5103
E dv8@artsadmin.co.uk
W www.dv8.co.uk

ENGLISH NATIONAL BALLET LTD   T 020 7581 1245
Markova House
39 Jay Mews
London SW7 2ES
F 020 7225 0827
E info@ballet.org.uk
W www.ballet.org.uk

ENGLISH YOUTH BALLET   T 01689 856747
Appledowne
The Hillside
Orpington
Kent BR6 7SD
T 07732 383600
E misslewis@englishyouthballet.co.uk
W www.englishyouthballet.co.uk

GREEN CANDLE DANCE COMPANY   T 020 7739 7722
Oxford House
Derbyshire Street
Bethnal Green
London E2 6HG
E info@greencandledance.com
W www.greencandledance.com

IJAD DANCE COMPANY   T 07930 378639
33 Allison Road
London NW10 2DD
E hello@ijaddancecompany.com
W www.ijaddancecompany.com

JEYASINGH, Shobana DANCE COMPANY   T 020 7697 4444
Omnibus Office 113
39-41 North Road
London N7 9DP
E admin@shobanajeyasingh.co.uk
W www.shobanajeyasingh.co.uk

KHAN, Akram COMPANY   T 020 7354 4333
Unit 232A, 35A Britannia Row
London N1 8QH
F 020 7354 5554
E office@akramkhancompany.net
W www.akramkhancompany.net

KOSH THE   T/F 020 7263 7419
Physical Theatre
59 Stapleton Hall Road
London N4 3QF
E info@thekosh.com

LUDUS DANCE   T 01524 35936
Assembly Rooms, King Street
Lancaster LA1 1RE
F 01524 847744
E info@ludusdance.org
W www.ludusdance.org

NEW ADVENTURES   T 020 7713 6766
Sadler's Wells
Rosebery Avenue
London EC1R 4TN
E info@new-adventures.net
W www.new-adventures.net

NORTHERN BALLET   T 0113 220 8000
2 St Cecilia Street
Quarry Hill
Leeds LS2 7PA
F 0113 220 8001
E info@northernballet.com
W www.northernballet.com

PAVILION DANCE SOUTH WEST   T 01202 203630
Westover Road
Bournemouth BH1 2BU
E info@pdsw.org.uk
W www.pdsw.org.uk

PHOENIX DANCE THEATRE   T 0113 236 8130
2 St Cecilia Street
Quarry Hill
Leeds LS2 7PA
E info@phoenixdancetheatre.co.uk
W www.phoenixdancetheatre.co.uk

PLACE THE   T 020 7121 1000
17 Duke's Road, London WC1H 9PY
F 020 7121 1142
E info@theplace.org.uk
W www.theplace.org.uk

PMB PRESENTATIONS LTD   T 020 7368 3337
Vicarage House
58-60 Kensington Church Street
London W8 4DB
E info@pmbpresentations.co.uk
W www.pmbpresentations.co.uk

RAMBERT   T 020 8630 0600
99 Upper Ground, London SE1 9PP
F 020 8747 8323
E info@rambert.org.uk
W www.rambert.org.uk

RETINA DANCE COMPANY   T 0115 947 6202
*UK-based Contemporary Dance Company Touring
Nationally & Internationally*
College Street Centre
College Street
Nottingham NG1 5AQ
E admin@retinadanceuk.com
W www.retinadanceuk.com

ROTIE, Marie-Gabrielle PRODUCTIONS
1 Christchurch Square
London E9 7HU
E rotieproductions@googlemail.com
W www.rotieproductions.com

ROYAL BALLET THE   T 020 7240 1200
Royal Opera House, Covent Garden
London WC2E 9DD
F 020 7212 9121
E balletcompany@roh.org.uk
W www.roh.org.uk

SCOTTISH BALLET   T 0141 331 2931
Tramway, 25 Albert Drive
Glasgow G41 2PE
W www.scottishballet.co.uk

SCOTTISH DANCE THEATRE   T 01382 342600
Dundee Repertory Theatre, Tay Square
Dundee DD1 1PB
F 01382 228609
E sdt@scottishdancetheatre.com
W www.scottishdancetheatre.com

SPLITZ THEATRE ARTZ   T 01223 880389
5 Cow Lane, Fulbourn
Cambridge CB21 5HB
E clare@splitz-ta.net
W www.splitz-ta.co.uk

SPRINGS DANCE COMPANY   T 01634 817523
65 John Kennedy Court
Newington Green Road
London N1 4RT
T 07775 628442
E info@springsdancecompany.org.uk
W www.springsdancecompany.org.uk

TWITCH EVENT CHOREOGRAPHY
E info@twitch.uk.com
W www.twitch.uk.com

UNION DANCE   T 020 7836 7837
Top Floor, 6 Charing Cross Road
London WC2H 0HG
F 020 7836 7847
E info@uniondance.co.uk
W www.uniondance.co.uk

ZIKZIRA PHYSICAL THEATRE   T 020 7460 1371
46 Highlever Road, London W10 6PT
E zz@zikzira.com
W www.zikzira.com

ACCELERATE PRODUCTIONS LTD   T 020 3130 4040
Studio Accelerate, 374 Ley Street
Ilford IG1 4AE
E info@accelerate-productions.co.uk
W www.accelerate-productions.co.uk

AKADEMI SOUTH ASIAN DANCE UK   T 020 7691 3210
Hampstead Town Hall
213 Haverstock Hill
London NW3 4QP
E info@akademi.co.uk
W www.akademi.co.uk

ALLIED DANCING ASSOCIATION   T 0151 724 1829
137 Greenhill Road, Mossley Hill
Liverpool L18 7HQ
E carolparryada@yahoo.co.uk

ASSOCIATION OF DANCE OF THE AFRICAN DIASPORA   T 020 7841 7357
The Old Finsbury Town Hall
Rosebery Avenue, London EC1R 4QT
F 020 7833 2363
E info@adad.org.uk
W www.adad.org.uk

AWARENESS THROUGH DANCE   T 0844 2412987
International Volunteer Experiences for Performing Artists
18 Gainsford Street
London SE1 2NE
E info@awarenessthroughdance.org
W www.awarenessthroughdance.org

BENESH INSTITUTE THE   T 020 7326 8035
36 Battersea Square
London SW11 3RA
T 020 7326 8031
E beneshinstitute@rad.org.uk
W www.benesh.org

BRITISH ARTS THE   T 01708 756263
12 Deveron Way, Rise Park
Romford RM1 4UL
E sally.chennelle1@ntlworld.com
W www.britisharts.org

BRITISH ASSOCIATION OF TEACHERS OF DANCING   T 0141 427 3699
Pavilion, 8 Upper Level
Watermark Business Park
315 Govan Road
Glasgow G51 2SE
E enquiries@batd.co.uk
W www.batd.co.uk

BRITISH BALLET ORGANIZATION   T 020 8748 1241
Dance Examining Society. Teacher Training
E info@bbo.org.uk
W www.bbo.org.uk

BRITISH THEATRE DANCE ASSOCIATION   T 0845 1662179
Garden Street
Leicester LE1 3UA
F 0116 251 4781
E info@btda.org.uk
W www.btda.org.uk

CHISENHALE DANCE SPACE   T 020 8981 6617
64-84 Chisenhale Road, Bow
London E3 5QZ
E mail@chisenhaledancespace.co.uk
W www.chisenhaledancespace.co.uk

COUNCIL FOR DANCE EDUCATION & TRAINING (CDET)   T 020 7240 5703
Old Brewer's Yard
17-19 Neal Street
Covent Garden, London WC2H 9UY
F 020 7240 2547
E info@cdet.org.uk
W www.cdet.org.uk

DANCE4   T 0115 941 0773
Twitter: @dance_4
College Street Centre, College Street
Nottingham NG1 5AQ
E info@dance4.co.uk
W www.dance4.co.uk

DANCE BASE NATIONAL CENTRE FOR DANCE   T 0131 225 5525
Twitter: @DanceBase
14-16 Grassmarket
Edinburgh EH1 2JU
E dance@dancebase.co.uk
W www.dancebase.co.uk

DANCE HOUSE   T 0141 552 2442
The Briggait, 141 Bridgegate
Glasgow G1 5HZ
E info@dancehouse.org
W www.dancehouse.org

DANCE IN DEVON   T 01803 868116
Dartington Space
Dartington Hall
Totnes, Devon TQ9 6EN
E administrator@danceindevon.org.uk
W www.danceindevon.org.uk

DANCE MANCHESTER   T 0161 232 7179
Z-arts, Stretford Road
Hulme, Manchester M15 5ZA
E info@dancemanchester.org.uk
W www.dancemanchester.org

DANCE UK   T 020 7713 0730
Including the Healthier Dancer Programme & The National Institute of Dance Medicine & Science
Unit A402A, The Biscuit Factory
Drummond Road, London SE16 4DG
F 020 7833 2363
E info@danceuk.org
W www.danceuk.org

DANCE UMBRELLA   T 020 7407 1200
1 Brewery Square
London SE1 2LF
F 020 7378 8405
E mail@danceumbrella.co.uk
W www.danceumbrella.co.uk

DANCEEAST   T 01473 295230
Jerwood DanceHouse
Foundry Lane
Ipswich IP4 1DW
E info@danceeast.co.uk
W www.danceeast.co.uk

DANCERS' CAREER DEVELOPMENT   T 020 7831 1449
Twitter: @dcd_dancers
Plouviez House, 19-20 Hatton Place
London EC1N 8RU
E admin@thedcd.org.uk
W www.thedcd.org.uk

DANCEXCHANGE   T 0121 689 3170
National Dance Agency
Birmingham Hippodrome
Thorp Street
Birmingham B5 4TB
E info@dancexchange.org.uk
W www.dancexchange.org.uk

DAVIES, Siobhan DANCE   T 020 7091 9650
Studio & Events Hires. Professional Development for Dance Artists
Siobhan Davies Studios, 85 St George's Road
London SE1 6ER
F 020 7091 9669
E info@siobhandavies.com
W www.siobhandavies.com

EAST LONDON DANCE   T 020 8279 1050
Stratford Circus, Theatre Square
London E15 1BX
E office@eastlondondance.org
W www.eastlondondance.org

EVERYBODY DANCE   T 07870 429528
Contact: Rachel Freeman. Aerial & Community Dance for Disabled & Non-disabled Artists of All Ages
Longlands Barn, Whitbourne
Worcester
Worcestershire WR6 5SG
E rfeverybodydance@gmail.com

FOUNDATION FOR COMMUNITY DANCE   T 0116 253 3453
LCB Depot
31 Rutland Street
Leicester LE1 1RE
F 0116 261 6801
E info@communitydance.org.uk
W www.communitydance.org.uk

GREENWICH DANCE   T 020 8293 9741
The Borough Hall, Royal Hill
London SE10 8RE
E info@greenwichdance.org.uk
W www.greenwichdance.org.uk

IDTA (INTERNATIONAL DANCE TEACHERS' ASSOCIATION)   T 01273 685652
International House
76 Bennett Road
Brighton, East Sussex BN2 5JL
F 01273 674388
E info@idta.co.uk
W www.idta.co.uk

IMPERIAL SOCIETY OF TEACHERS OF DANCING   T 020 7377 1577
Examination Board & Educational Charity offering Dance Teacher Qualifications
22-26 Paul Street, London EC2A 4QE
F 020 7655 8869
E marketing@istd.org
W www.istd.org

LANGUAGE OF DANCE CENTRE   T 020 7749 1131
Oxford House, Derbyshire Street
London E2 6HG
E info@lodc.org
W www.lodc.org

**LONDON CONTEMPORARY
DANCE SCHOOL**   T 020 7121 1111
The Place, 17 Duke's Road
London WC1H 9PY
F 020 7121 1142
E lcds@theplace.org.uk
W www.lcds.ac.uk

LUDUS DANCE   T 01524 35936
The Assembly Rooms, King Street, Lancaster LA1 1RE
F 01524 847744
E info@ludusdance.org
W www.ludusdance.org

MDI   T 0151 708 8810
National Dance Agency
24 Hope Street, Liverpool L1 9BX
E info@mdi.org.uk
W www.mdi.org.uk

**NATIONAL RESOURCE
CENTRE FOR DANCE**   T 01483 689316
University of Surrey, Guildford GU2 7XH
F 01483 689500
E nrcd@surrey.ac.uk
W www.surrey.ac.uk/nrcd

**PAVILION DANCE
SOUTH WEST**   T 01202 203630
Pavilion Theatre, Westover Road
Bournemouth BH1 2BU
E info@pdsw.org.uk
W www.pdsw.org.uk

PLACE THE   T 020 7121 1000
17 Duke's Road, London WC1H 9PY
F 020 7121 1142
E info@theplace.org.uk
W www.theplace.org.uk

**PROFESSIONAL TEACHERS
OF DANCING**   T 01935 848547
Contact: Jo Pillinger
The Studios, Morcombelake
Dorset DT6 6DY
E ptdenquiries@msn.com
W www.professionalteachersofdancing.co.uk

SOUTH EAST DANCE   T 01273 696844
*National Development Organisation for Dance in South
East England*
28 Kensington Street
Brighton BN1 4AJ
F 01273 697212
E sed@southeastdance.org.uk
W www.southeastdance.org.uk

SWINDON DANCE   T 01793 601700
National Dance Agency
Town Hall Studios
Regent Circus
Swindon SN1 1QF
E info@swindondance.org.uk
W www.swindondance.org.uk

YORKSHIRE DANCE   T 0113 243 9867
Dance Development Agency
3 St Peters Buildings
St Peters Square
Leeds LS9 8AH
F 0113 259 5700
E admin@yorkshiredance.com
W www.yorkshiredance.com

ACADEMY FOR THEATRE ARTS THE T 01782 660818
1 Vale View, Porthill, Newcastle under Lyme
Staffordshire ST5 0AF
E no1theacademy@aol.com
W www.jillclewes.co.uk

AIRCRAFT CIRCUS LTD T 020 8317 8401
Unit 7A, Mellish House
Harrington Way, London SE18 5NR
E info@aircraftcircus.com
W www.aircraftcircus.com

ARTS EDUCATIONAL SCHOOLS LONDON T 020 8987 6666
CDET Member
Cone Ripman House, 14 Bath Road
Chiswick, London W4 1LY
E receptionist@artsed.co.uk
W www.artsed.co.uk

ATENEO DELLA DANZA T 00 39 0577 222774
Professional Training Centre
Via dei Pispini 39/45, Siena 53100
Tuscany, Italy
E info@ateneodelladanza.it
W www.ateneodelladanza.it

AVIV DANCE STUDIOS T/F 01923 250000
Watford Boys Grammar School
Rickmansworth Road
Watford WD18 7JF
E info@avivdance.com
W www.avivdance.com

BALLROOM, LONDON THEATRE OF T 020 8722 8798
Artistic Director: Paul Harris® (Mentor "Faking It")
24 Montana Gardens, Sutton
Surrey SM1 4FP
E office@londontheatreofballroom.com
W www.londontheatreofballroom.com

BHAVAN CENTRE T 020 7381 3086
Training in Indian Classical Music, Dance, Languages & Yoga
4A Castletown Road, London W14 9HE
E info@bhavan.net
W www.bhavan.net

BIRD COLLEGE DANCE MUSIC & THEATRE PERFORMANCE T 020 8300 6004
CDET Member. Professional Training in Dance & Musical Theatre. HE & FE Programmes
The Centre, 27 Station Road
Sidcup, Kent DA15 7EB
F 020 8308 1370
E performance@birdcollege.co.uk
W www.birdcollege.co.uk

BODENS PERFORMING ARTS T 020 8447 0909
Contact: Adam Boden. Acting Workshops. Audition Technique. Dancing. Improvisation. Singing. Part-time. Performing Arts Classes
Bodens Performing Arts, 99 East Barnet Road
New Barnet, Herts EN4 8RF
E info@bodens.co.uk
W www.bodens.co.uk

CAMBRIDGE PERFORMING ARTS AT BODYWORK COMPANY DANCE STUDIOS T 01223 314461
CDET Member
Bodywork Company Dance Studios
25-29 Glisson Road, Cambridge CB1 2HA
E admin@bodyworkds.co.uk
W www.bodywork-dance.co.uk

CANDOCO DANCE COMPANY T 020 7704 6845
2T Leroy House, 436 Essex Road
London N1 3QP
E info@candoco.co.uk
W www.candoco.co.uk

CENTRAL SCHOOL OF BALLET T 020 7837 6332
Full Time Vocational Training. Open Classes Beginner/Professional Level
10 Herbal Hill, Clerkenwell Road, London EC1R 5EG
F 020 7833 5571
E info@csbschool.co.uk
W www.centralschoolofballet.co.uk

CENTRE PERFORMING ARTS COLLEGE THE T 01634 848009
CDET Member
681 Maidstone Road, Rochester
Kent ME1 3QJ
E dance@thecentrepac.com
W www.thecentrepac.com

CLASSIQUE SCHOOL OF DANCE T 02392 233334
Ballet. Contemporary. Jazz. Modern. Tap. Stage (2 yrs-Adult). Drama. Singing
3-5 Stakes Hill Road, Waterlooville
Hampshire PO7 7JB
E classique_enquiries@yahoo.co.uk
W www.classiquedance.co.uk

COLLECTIVE DANCE & DRAMA T/F 020 8428 0037
The Studio, Rectory Lane
Rickmansworth, Herts WD3 1FD
E info@collectivedance.co.uk
W www.collectivedance.co.uk

CONTI, Italia ACADEMY OF THEATRE ARTS T 020 7608 0044
CDET Member. Drama UK Member. Courses: Performing Arts Diploma, 3 yr. Performing Arts with Teacher Training, 3 yr. Intensive Performing Arts, Acting, 1 yr. Foundation Performing Arts, 1 yr. BA (Hons) Acting, 3 yr. Foundation Acting, 1 yr. Singing, 1 yr. Theatre Arts School (academic yrs 7-11)
Italia Conti House, 23 Goswell Road, London EC1M 7AJ
E admin@italiaconti.co.uk
W www.italiaconti.com

COUNCIL FOR DANCE EDUCATION & TRAINING (CDET) T 020 7240 5703
Old Brewer's Yard, 17-19 Neal Street
Covent Garden, London WC2H 9UY
F 020 7240 2547
E info@cdet.org.uk
W www.cdet.org.uk

CPA STUDIOS T 01708 766007
CDET Member
The Studios, 219B North Street
Romford, Essex RM1 4QA
E collegeadmin@cpastudios.co.uk
W www.cpastudios.co.uk

D&B SCHOOL OF PERFORMING ARTS & D&B THEATRE SCHOOL T 020 8698 8880
Central Studios, 470 Bromley Road
Bromley, Kent BR1 4PQ
E info@dandbperformingarts.co.uk
W www.dandbperformingarts.co.uk

DANCE BASE NATIONAL CENTRE FOR DANCE T 0131 225 5525
14-16 Grassmarket, Edinburgh EH1 2JU
E dance@dancebase.co.uk
W www.dancebase.co.uk

Paul Harris®
Choreographer
2014·2015

Choreography and Coaching in Period and Contemporary Social Dance

TV: **The Great Fire** | **Call The Midwife**
Film: **Far From The Madding Crowd (starring Carey Mulligan)**

www.paulharris.uk.com | office @ paulharris.uk.com | *Swing Waltz Pavane Salsa Tango Quadrille Charleston Schottische*

DANCE HOUSE   T 0141 552 2442
The Briggait, 141 Bridgegate, Glasgow G1 5HZ
E info@dancehouse.org
W www.dancehouse.org

DANCE LONDON   T 0844 2412987
18 Gainsford Street, London SE1 2NE
E info@dance-london.com
W www.dance-london.com

DANCE RESEARCH COMMITTEE -
IMPERIAL SOCIETY OF TEACHERS
OF DANCING   T 01233 712469
Training in Historical Dance
c/o Ludwell House, Charing, Kent TN27 0LS
F 01233 712768
E n.gainesarmitage@tiscali.co.uk
W www.istd.org

DANCE STUDIO
LEEDS LTD THE   T 0113 242 1550
Mill 6, 1st Floor, Mabgate Mills
Leeds, West Yorkshire LS9 7DZ
E katie@thedancestudioleeds.com
W www.thedancestudioleeds.com

DANCE STUDIO THE   T 020 8360 5700
Evening & Weekend Classes (3-18 yrs)
843-845 Green Lanes, Winchmore Hill
London, N21 2RX
E thedancestudio@btconnect.com
W www.thedancestudio.co.uk

DANCEWORKS   T 020 7629 6183
Also Fitness, Yoga & Martial Arts Classes
16 Balderton Street, London W1K 6TN
E info@danceworks.net
W www.danceworks.net

DAPA   T 01254 699221
Dance. Drama. Music. Singing. All Ages & Abilities
The Wharf Studios, Eanam Wharf
Blackburn, Lancashire BB1 5BY
E info@dapacentre.co.uk
W www.dapa.info

DAVIES, Siobhan STUDIOS   T 020 7091 9650
Daily Professional Classes. Open Dance & Body
Conditioning Classes for Wider Community
85 St George's Road, London SE1 6ER
F 020 7091 9669
E info@siobhandavies.com
W www.siobhandavies.com

DIRECTIONS THEATRE ARTS
CHESTERFIELD LTD   T/F 01246 854455
1A-2A Sheffield Road, Chesterfield
Derbyshire S41 7LL
E julie.cox5@btconnect.com
W www.directionstheatrearts.org

D M ACADEMY   T 01274 585317
The Studios, Briggate
Shipley, Bradford, West Yorks BD17 7BT
E info@dmacademy.co.uk
W www.dmacademy.co.uk

DUFFILL, Drusilla
THEATRE SCHOOL   T 01444 232672
Suite F, KBF House, 55 Victoria Road
Burgess Hill, West Sussex RH15 9LH
E drusilladschool@btclick.com
W www.drusilladuffilltheatreschool.co.uk

EAST LONDON DANCE   T 020 8279 1050
Stratford Circus, Theatre Square
London E15 1BX
E office@eastlondondance.org
W www.eastlondondance.org

ELMHURST SCHOOL
FOR DANCE   T 0121 472 6655
CDET Member
249 Bristol Road, Edgbaston
Birmingham B5 7UH
F 0121 472 6654
E enquiries@elmhurstdance.co.uk
W www.elmhurstdance.co.uk

ENGLISH NATIONAL
BALLET SCHOOL   T 020 7376 7076
CDET Member
Carlyle Building, Hortensia Road
London SW10 0QS
F 020 7376 3404
E info@enbschool.org.uk
W www.enbschool.org.uk

EXPRESSIONS ACADEMY OF
PERFORMING ARTS   T 01623 424334
CDET Member
3 Newgate Lane, Mansfield
Nottingham NG18 2LB
E expressions-uk@btconnect.com
W www.expressionsperformingarts.co.uk

GEORGIE SCHOOL OF
THEATRE ARTS   T/F 01484 606994
101 Lane Head Road, Shepley
Huddersfield, West Yorkshire HD8 8DB

GREASEPAINT ANONYMOUS   T 020 8360 9785
Flat 13, Oak Lodge, 50 Eversley Park Road
London N21 1JL
T 07930 421216
E info@greasepaintanonymous.co.uk
W www.greasepaintanonymous.co.uk

HAMMOND SCHOOL THE   T 01244 305350
CDET Member
Hoole Bank, Mannings Lane
Chester CH2 4ES
F 01244 305351
E info@thehammondschool.co.uk
W www.thehammondschool.co.uk

HARRIS, Paul   T 07958 784462
Contact: Paul Harris®. Choreography. Movement for
Actors. Tuition in Period & Contemporary Social Dance
24 Montana Gardens, Sutton, Surrey SM1 4FP
E office@paulharris.uk.com
W www.paulharris.uk.com

ISLINGTON ARTS FACTORY　T 020 7607 0561
2 Parkhurst Road, London N7 0SF
E info@islingtonartsfactory.org
W www.islingtonartsfactory.org

KS DANCE LTD　T 01925 837693
CDET Member
9A Centre 21, Bridge Lane
Woolston, Warrington, Cheshire WA1 4AW
E admin@ksd-online.co.uk
W www.ksd-online.co.uk

LAINE THEATRE ARTS　T 01372 724648
CDET Member
The Studios, East Street, Epsom, Surrey KT17 1HH
F 01372 723775
E webmaster@laine-theatre-arts.co.uk
W www.laine-theatre-arts.co.uk

**LIVERPOOL INSTITUTE
FOR PERFORMING ARTS**　T 0151 330 3000
CDET Member
Mount Street, Liverpool L1 9HF
E admissions@lipa.ac.uk
W www.lipa.ac.uk

LIVERPOOL THEATRE SCHOOL　T 0151 728 7800
CDET Member. Musical Theatre & Professional Classes
19 Aigburth Road, Liverpool, Merseyside L17 4JR
T 07515 282877
E info@liverpooltheatreschool.co.uk
W www.liverpooltheatreschool.co.uk

**LONDON CONTEMPORARY
DANCE SCHOOL**　T 020 7121 1111
*Full-time Vocational Training at Degree &
Postgraduate Level*
The Place, 17 Duke's Road, London WC1H 9PY
F 020 7121 1145
E lcds@theplace.org.uk
W www.lcds.ac.uk

LONDON DANCE PROGRAMME　T 0844 2412987
77 Blackfriars Road, Number 2, London SE1 8HA
E info@londondanceprogramme.com
W www.londondanceprogramme.com

**LONDON SCHOOL
OF CAPOEIRA**　T 020 7281 2020
Unit 1-2 Leeds Place, Tollington Park
London N4 3RF
E info@londonschoolofcapoeira.com
W www.londonschoolofcapoeira.com

LONDON STUDIO CENTRE　T 020 7837 7741
CDET Member
artsdepot, 5 Nether Street, Tally Ho Corner
North Finchley, London N12 0GA
F 020 7837 3248
E info@londonstudiocentre.org
W www.londonstudiocentre.org

**MANN, Stella COLLEGE OF
PERFORMING ARTS LTD**　T 01234 213331
*CDET Member. Professional Training Course for
Performers & Teachers*
10 Linden Road, Bedford
Bedfordshire MK40 2DA
F 01234 217284
E stellamanncollege@hotmail.com
W www.stellamanncollege.co.uk

**MGA ACADEMY OF
PERFORMING ARTS THE**　T 0131 466 9392
207 Balgreen Road, Edinburgh EH11 2RZ
E info@themgaacademy.com
W www.themgaacademy.com

MIALKOWSKI, Andrzej　T 01604 239755
*Choreographer. Teacher. IDTA Member. Ballroom.
Latin American. Street. Zumba. Ballet*
Step By Step Dance School
24 Henry Street, Northampton
Northamptonshire NN1 4JE
T 07849 331430
E info@danceschool-stepbystep.com
W www.danceschool-stepbystep.com

**MIDLANDS ACADEMY OF
DANCE & DRAMA**　T/F 0115 911 0401
CDET Member
Century House, Building B
428 Carlton Hill, Nottingham NG4 1QA
E admin@maddcollege.supanet.com
W www.maddcollege.co.uk

**MILLENNIUM PERFORMING
ARTS LTD**　T 020 8301 8744
CDET Member
29 Thomas Street, Woolwich, London SE18 6HU
E info@md2000.co.uk
W www.md2000.co.uk

**NEW LONDON PERFORMING
ARTS CENTRE**　T 020 8444 4544
*Performing Arts Classes (3-19 yrs). Teacher Training.
DDI & DDE Training. All Dance Styles. GCSE Course.
A-Levels. RAD & ISTD Exams*
76 St James Lane, Muswell Hill, London N10 3RD
E info@nlpac.co.uk
W www.nlpac.co.uk

**NORTHERN ACADEMY OF
PERFORMING ARTS**　T 01482 310690
Anlaby Road, Hull HU1 2PD
F 01482 212280
E napa@northernacademy.org.uk
W www.northernacademy.org.uk

NORTHERN BALLET SCHOOL　T 0161 237 1406
CDET Member
The Dancehouse, 10 Oxford Road, Manchester M1 5QA
F 0161 237 1408
E enquiries@northernballetschool.co.uk
W www.northernballetschool.co.uk

**NORTHERN SCHOOL OF CONTEMPORARY
DANCE THE**　T 0113 219 3000
98 Chapeltown Road, Leeds LS7 4BH
E info@nscd.ac.uk
W www.nscd.ac.uk

PERFORMERS COLLEGE　T 01375 672053
CDET Member
Southend Road, Corringham, Essex SS17 8JT
F 01375 672353
E lesley@performerscollege.co.uk
W www.performerscollege.co.uk

PINEAPPLE DANCE STUDIOS　T 020 7836 4004
7 Langley Street, London WC2H 9PA
F 020 7836 0803
W www.pineapple.uk.com

PLACE THE　T 020 7121 1000
17 Duke's Road, London WC1H 9PY
F 020 7121 1142
E info@theplace.org.uk　　W www.theplace.org.uk

**PROFESSIONAL TEACHERS
OF DANCING**　T 01935 848547
Contact: Jo Pillinger
The Studios, Morcombelake, Dorset DT6 6DY
E ptdenquiries@msn.com
W www.professionalteachersofdancing.co.uk

RAMBERT SCHOOL OF BALLET &
CONTEMPORARY DANCE   **T** 020 8892 9960
Clifton Lodge, St Margaret's Drive
Twickenham, Middlesex TW1 1QN
F 020 8892 8090
E info@rambertschool.org.uk
W www.rambertschool.org.uk

RETINA DANCE COMPANY   **T** 0115 947 6202
Weekly Classes. Training. Workshops. Residencies
College Street Centre
College Street
Nottingham NG1 5AQ
E retinadance@uk.com
W www.retinadance.uk.com

RIDGEWAY STUDIOS PERFORMING
ARTS CENTRE   **T** 01992 633775
Cheshunt & Cuffley Studios
Office: 106 Hawkshead Road, Potters Bar
Hertfordshire EN6 1NG
E info@ridgewaystudios.co.uk
W www.ridgewaystudios.co.uk

RIVERSIDE REFLECTIONS
BATON TWIRLING TEAM   **T/F** 01322 410003
34 Knowle Avenue
Bexleyheath, Kent DA7 5LX
T 07958 617976
E clare@riversidereflections.co.uk
W www.riversidereflections.co.uk

ROEBUCK, Gavin   **T** 020 7370 7324
Classical Ballet
51 Earls Court Square, London SW5 9DG
E info@gavinroebuck.com

ROJO Y NEGRO   **T** 020 8520 2726
Argentine Tango School of Dance
Latvian Club, 1st Floor
72 Queensborough Terrace, London W2 3SH
T 07748 648322
E info@rojoynegroclub.com
W www.rojoynegroclub.com

ROJO Y NEGRO TANGO   **T** 020 8520 2726
Argentine Tango Academy
Union Tavern - Upstairs
52 Lloyd Baker Street
Farringdon, Kings Cross
London WC1X 9AA
T 07748 648322
E info@rojoynegroclub.com
W www.rojoynegroclub.com

ROYAL ACADEMY OF DANCE   **T** 020 7326 8000
36 Battersea Square, London SW11 3RA
F 020 7924 3129
E info@rad.org.uk
W www.rad.org.uk

SAFREY ACADEMY OF
PERFORMING ARTS   **T** 07986 966533
Classes at: South London Liberal Synagogue, 1 Prentis
Road, Streatham, London SW16 1ZW
Correspondence only:
10 St Julians Close, London SW16 2RY
F 020 8488 9121
E info@safreyarts.co.uk
W www.safreyarts.co.uk

SLP COLLEGE   **T** 0113 286 8136
CDET Member
Chapel Lane, Leeds LS25 1AG
E info@slpcollege.co.uk
W www.slpcollege.co.uk

STARMAKERZ
THEATRE SCHOOL   **T** 07771 595171
Oxted School, Bluehouse Lane
Oxted, Surrey RH8 0AB
E vicky@starmakerz.co.uk
W www.starmakerz.co.uk

TIFFANY THEATRE COLLEGE   **T** 01702 710069
969-973 London Road
Leigh on Sea
Essex SS9 3LB
E info@tiffanytheatrecollege.com
W www.tiffanytheatrecollege.com

TRING PARK SCHOOL FOR
THE PERFORMING ARTS   **T** 01442 824255
CDET Member
Tring Park, Tring
Hertfordshire HP23 5LX
E info@tringpark.com
W www.tringpark.com

TRINITY LABAN CONSERVATOIRE
OF MUSIC & DANCE   **T** 020 8305 9400
Creekside, London SE8 3DZ
F 020 8691 8400
E info@trinitylaban.ac.uk
W www.trinitylaban.ac.uk

URDANG ACADEMY   **T** 020 7713 7710
CDET Member
The Old Finsbury Town Hall
Rosebery Avenue
London EC1R 4RP
F 020 7278 6727
E info@theurdangacademy.com
W www.theurdang.com

VALLÉ ACADEMY OF
PERFORMING ARTS   **T** 01992 622862
The Vallé Academy Studios
Wilton House, Delamare Road
Cheshunt, Herts EN8 9SG
F 01992 622868
E enquiries@valleacademy.co.uk
W www.valleacademy.co.uk

WAINWRIGHT, Benjamin   **T** 07950 811327
Choreography. Teaching
11 Laburnum Avenue
Sunnyside
Rotherham, South Yorkshire S66 3PR
E b-wainwright@live.co.uk

WIVELL, Betty ACADEMY OF
PERFORMING ARTS THE   **T** 020 8764 5500
Ballet. Jazz. Modern. Tap. Drama. Singing
52 Norbury Court Road
Norbury, London SW16 4HT
E ereeves@bettywivell.com
W www.bettywivell.com

YOUNG ACTORS THEATRE   **T** 020 7278 2101
70-72 Barnsbury Road
Islington, London N1 0ES
E yolande@yati.org.uk
W www.yati.org.uk

YOUNG, Sylvia
THEATRE SCHOOL   **T** 020 7258 2330
1 Nutford Place
London W1H 5YZ
F 020 7724 8371
E syoung@syts.co.uk
W www.syts.co.uk

ALRA (ACADEMY OF LIVE & RECORDED ARTS)   T 020 8870 6475
Studio 24-25
The Royal Victoria Patriotic Building
John Archer Way
London SW18 3SX
E info@alra.co.uk
W www.alra.co.uk

ARTS EDUCATIONAL SCHOOLS LONDON   T 020 8987 6666
14 Bath Road
London W4 1LY
F 020 8987 6699
E receptionist@artsed.co.uk
W www.artsed.co.uk

BIRMINGHAM SCHOOL OF ACTING   T 0121 331 7220
Millennium Point
Curzon Street
Birmingham B4 7XG
F 0121 331 7221
E info@bsa.bcu.ac.uk
W www.bcu.ac.uk/bsa

BRISTOL OLD VIC THEATRE SCHOOL   T 0117 973 3535
1-2 Downside Road
Clifton
Bristol BS8 2XF
F 0117 980 9258
E enquiries@oldvic.ac.uk
W www.oldvic.ac.uk

CONTI, Italia ACADEMY   T 020 7733 3210
Avondale, 72 Landor Road
London SW9 9PH
E acting@italiaconti.co.uk
W www.italiaconti-acting.co.uk

DRAMA CENTRE LONDON   T 020 7514 7936
Central Saint Martins College of Arts & Design
Granary Building
1 Granary Square
London N1C 4AA
E drama@arts.ac.uk
W www.arts.ac.uk/csm/drama-centre-london

DRAMA STUDIO LONDON   T 020 8579 3897
Grange Court
1 Grange Road
London W5 5QN
F 020 8566 2035
E admin@dramastudiolondon.co.uk
W www.dramastudiolondon.co.uk

EAST 15 ACTING SCHOOL   T 020 8508 5983
Hatfields
Rectory Lane
Loughton IG10 3RY
E east15@essex.ac.uk
W www.east15.ac.uk

GSA, GUILDFORD SCHOOL OF ACTING   T 01483 684040
University of Surrey
Stag Hill Campus
Guildford
Surrey GU2 7XH
E gsaenquiries@gsa.surrey.ac.uk
W www.gsauk.org

GUILDHALL SCHOOL OF MUSIC & DRAMA   T 020 7628 2571
Silk Street, Barbican
London EC2Y 8DT
E info@gsmd.ac.uk
W www.gsmd.ac.uk

LAMDA   T 020 8834 0500
155 Talgarth Road
London W14 9DA
F 020 8834 0501
E enquiries@lamda.org.uk
W www.lamda.org.uk

LIVERPOOL INSTITUTE FOR PERFORMING ARTS THE   T 0151 330 3000
Mount Street
Liverpool L1 9HF
F 0151 330 3131
E reception@lipa.ac.uk
W www.lipa.ac.uk

MANCHESTER SCHOOL OF THEATRE AT MANCHESTER METROPOLITAN UNIVERSITY   T 0161 247 1305
The Mabel Tylecote Building
Cavendish Street
Manchester M15 6BG
E theatre@mmu.ac.uk
W www.theatre.mmu.ac.uk

MOUNTVIEW ACADEMY OF THEATRE ARTS   T 020 8881 2201
Ralph Richardson Memorial Studios
1 Kingfisher Place
Clarendon Road
London N22 6XF
F 020 8829 0034
E enquiries@mountview.org.uk
W www.mountview.org.uk

OXFORD SCHOOL OF DRAMA THE   T 01993 812883
Sansomes Farm Studios
Woodstock
Oxford OX20 1ER
F 01993 811220
E info@oxforddrama.ac.uk
W www.oxforddrama.ac.uk

ROSE BRUFORD COLLEGE   T 020 8308 2600
Lamorbey Park
Burnt Oak Lane
Sidcup, Kent DA15 9DF
F 020 8308 0542
E enquiries@bruford.ac.uk
W www.bruford.ac.uk

ROYAL ACADEMY OF DRAMATIC ART   T 020 7636 7076
62-64 Gower Street
London WC1E 6ED
F 020 7323 3865
E enquiries@rada.ac.uk
W www.rada.ac.uk

ROYAL CENTRAL SCHOOL OF SPEECH & DRAMA THE   T 020 7722 8183
Eton Avenue, Swiss Cottage
London NW3 3HY
E enquiries@cssd.ac.uk
W www.cssd.ac.uk

Photo: Anna Karenina/BSA Birmingham School of Acting

Drama UK quality assures the top drama training in the UK and provides help and advice to drama students of all ages through its website.

dramauk.co.uk

Download the latest Guide to Professional Training and access:

- **Course listings**
- **Regularly updated info & advice**
- **Articles from industry experts**

Drama UK was formed in 2012 following the merger of CDS and NCDT.

Drama Training

Why do I need drama training?

The entertainment industry is an extremely competitive one, with thousands of performers competing for a small number of jobs. In such a crowded market, professional training will increase an actor's chances of success, and professionally trained artists are also more likely to get representation. Drama training can begin at any age and should continue throughout an actor's career.

I have already trained to be an actor. Why do I need further training?

Drama training should not cease as soon as you graduate or get your first job. Throughout your career you should strive to enhance your existing skills and keep up-to-date with the techniques new actors are being taught, even straight after drama school, in order to retain a competitive edge. You must also be prepared to learn new skills for specific roles if required. Ongoing drama training and classes can help you stay fit and active, and if you go through a period of unemployment you can keep your mind and body occupied, ready to take on your next job.

What kind of training is available?

For the under 18s, stage schools provide specialist training in acting, singing and dancing. They offer a variety of full and part-time courses. After 18, students can attend drama school. The standard route is to take a three-year, full-time course, in the same way you would take a university degree. Some schools also offer one or two-year courses.

What is Drama UK?

Drama UK comprises Britain's leading drama schools. It exists in order to strengthen the voice of the member schools, to set and maintain the highest standards of training within the vocational drama sector, and to make it easier for prospective students to understand the range of courses on offer and the application process. The member schools listed in the section 'Drama Schools: Drama UK' offer courses in Acting, Musical Theatre, Directing and Technical Theatre training. For more information you can visit their website www.dramauk.co.uk

How should I use these listings?

The following listings provide up-to-date contact details for a wide range of performance courses, classes and coaches. Every company listed is done so by written request to us. Some companies have provided contact names, areas of specialisation and a selection of courses on offer.

I want to apply to join a full-time drama course. Where do I start?

Your first step should be to research as many different courses as possible. Have a look on each school's website and request a prospectus. Ask around to find out where other people have trained or are training now and who they recommend. You would be advised to begin your search by considering Drama UK courses. Please refer to the *Drama UK Guide to Professional Training in Drama & Technical Theatre* for a description of each school, its policy and the courses it offers together with information about funding, available from www.dramauk.co.uk

What types of courses are available?

Drama training courses generally involve three-year degree or diploma courses, or one-year postgraduate courses if you have already attended university or can demonstrate a certain amount of previous experience. Alternatively, short-term or part-time foundation courses are available, which can serve as an introduction to acting but are not a substitute for a full-time drama course.

When should I apply?

Deadlines for applications to drama courses vary between schools so make sure you check each school's individual deadlines. Most courses start in September. If the school you are considering requires you to apply via UCAS, you must submit your application between mid-September 2014 and 15th January 2015 to guarantee that your application will be considered for a course beginning in 2015. You can apply after that until 30th June, but the school is then under no obligation to consider your application.

See www.ucas.ac.uk/students/applying/whentoapply or contact the individual school for more details.

What funding is available to me?

Drama courses are unavoidably expensive. Most students have to fund their own course fees and other expenses, whether from savings, part-time work or a student loan. However, if you are from a low-income household you may qualify for a maintenance grant from the government to cover some of the costs. Some Drama UK accredited courses offer a limited number of students Dance and Drama Awards (DaDA) scholarships, introduced to increase access to dance, drama and stage management training for talented students. These scholarships include help with both course fees and living expenses. Find out what each school offers in terms of potential financial support before applying.

Another possibility is to raise funds from a charity, trust or foundation. As with applying to agents and casting professionals for representation and work, do your research first and target your letters to explain how your needs meet each organisation's objectives, rather than sending a generalised letter to everyone. You are much more likely to be considered if you demonstrate that you know the background of the organisation and what they can offer performers.

How can my child become an actor?

If your child is interested in becoming an actor, they should try to get as much practical experience as possible. They could also join a stage school or sign with an agent. Contact details for stage schools can be found among the listings in this section. Please also see the 'Agents: Children & Teenagers' section for more information.

What about other forms of training?

Building on your initial acting course is essential for both new and more experienced actors. There are so many new skills you can learn – you could take stage fighting classes, hire a vocal coach, attend singing and dance lessons and many more. These will enhance your CV and will give you a competitive edge. It is also extremely useful to take occasional 'refresher' courses on audition skills, different acting techniques and so on in various forms such as one-to-one lessons, one-off workshops or evening classes, to make sure you are not rusty when your next audition comes along.

Where can I find more information?

The Actors Centre runs over 1700 classes and workshops a year to encourage performers to develop their talent throughout their career in a supportive environment. They also run introductory classes for people who are interested in becoming actors but currently have no training or experience. Visit their website www.actorscentre.co.uk for more information.

The Actors' Guild (TAG) offers on-going professional development for actors in the UK, through actor-led workshops and services. See www.actorsguild.co.uk for more information.

You may also want to refer to the 'Dance Training & Professional Classes' section for listings which will help you to add additional skills to your CV as well as keep fit. If you are interested in a career behind rather than in front of the camera or stage, please see the *Drama UK Guide to Careers Backstage*, available from www.dramauk.co.uk

Drama Training

CASE STUDY

Benjamin Warren is one of the founding members of The Actors' Guild - the largest membership organisation offering on-going training to professional actors in the UK. Actor built and actor led TAG is an independent not-for-profit organisation that offers industry leading workshops, professional development, bursaries and support. They bring together key industry professionals, strict joining criteria and a low membership fee to create a centre for professionals.

Those who went to drama school can often find the transition from full-time training to life as a jobbing actor quite traumatic. In a similar vein those who have found other routes into the profession may feel disconnected and outside of the loop.

Of course, those who have been out of work for a prolonged period sometimes even struggle to see themselves as actors - even if the passion is still very much alive deep inside. Whatever stage you are at, the profession can be challenging - there is no escaping that - but perhaps with a shift in perception, a refocusing in attitude, it is possible not only to see yourself as a professional actor but also to engage with, create even, a meaningful, fulfilling career – and carve a unique position for yourself within the profession.

We often see at The Actors' Guild the benefits of belonging to a community within our profession. Our industry can sometimes be quite disparate and the journey nomadic. But coming together is not just about support. I believe a successful career starts by engaging with your peers. So often projects are born out of collaboration. One person meets another and through their contacts a project is launched. The point is, on-going professional development is so much more than taking the odd workshop – although pick the right one, led by the right person, and it's a great place to start!

Actors get used to comparing their own career trajectory against others whilst being surrounded by people talking of casting 'types'. Perhaps though you are far more interesting than that – perhaps you have far more to give. Whilst there may always be some crossovers with others, the spectrum of your casting bracket is, of course, totally unique to you - but it is a wise actor who also understands how the profession 'sees' them at any particular stage in their career and then know how to use that information to create positive results.

It's about combining your artistic goals with a good business acumen.

At TAG we have one rule that is central to our programme – those who work, teach. We combine the need to develop artistically with the opportunity of working with the very people who are currently shaping our industry. It's also about finding the right environment for you – and surrounding yourself with the right kind of people. When looking at a workshop always do your research, are you looking for an acting tutor or a working director? Is the workshop leader creating the kind of work that you would like to do? Look people up on the web, if their CV interests you and the price is clearly reasonable then that's a good start – but ask questions too. How many others will be in the workshop, and really importantly - will they be a similar standard to you?

Being out of work should be as far from resting as you can get. Of course holding down a job that supports you in these times can be extremely testing – but there is nothing more attractive at an audition than an actor who is engaged with their profession – someone who is interested and interesting. Whether that manifests itself in keeping your skills sharp (something that no longer needs to cost the earth) or meeting and creating with friends, peers and colleagues.

Remember your job is not to be good, or even excellent. If the casting director has done their job well, everyone who gets to audition stage should offer that – you have to raise the bar, to offer that little bit more. Auditions are often last minute and we don't always have enough time to perfect a particular skill before we are called in. Those at the top of their game are constantly sharpening their skills, and when you go up for that gig you may well be up against these people in the audition room. But it doesn't have to cost the earth. TAG membership is designed to save you far more than it costs (a max of £24 a year, but often less) and there are many very reasonably priced workshops out there – with Spotlight's support some of our workshops are even free of charge! But value does not come from the workshop alone - it's also the contacts you make, the actors you meet and the networks that come from such opportunities. It's about finding affordable and meaningful on-going training relevant to our times with a supportive network of artists, and, crucially, where the actor is not on the outside of their profession but, from the outset, firmly at the very centre of it.

To find out more visit www.actorsguild.co.uk

Members of Drama UK offer their students the highest quality training in the industry. Graduates from these schools are in a strong position to advise anyone thinking of following in their path. We asked two recent graduates to share their thoughts on the benefits of drama training.

Sam Valentine

Photo: AM London

Sam graduated from RADA with a BA in Acting. He was the winner of the Spotlight Prize at the Showcase in 2014.

As far as I can remember, (and according to my mum, pretty much since I could breathe) I've been a performer. I have vague recollections of my finger-puppet shows and evenings fuelled by the magic garments of the dressing-up chest.

When I was seven, I joined Kick Off Youth Theatre in Bristol. It ran every Wednesday night in a church hall, opposite my primary school. We would create wonderful, surreal characters, without much judgement or care for 'getting it right'. We just wanted to make each other laugh.

As one of my A Level projects, I was given the challenge of playing in Pinter's *(One For The Road)* which was completely out of my league, yet I found a sudden intense well of determination; in an attempt to understand, inhabit and then share the vivid world that Pinter had created. I love the collaboration of acting; the melting pot of ideas; people sparking off each other; I haven't encountered anything quite like it.

I then applied to LAMDA, RADA and Guildhall. I made it to the fourth round at RADA, but fell at the last hurdle. Before applying again the following year, I helped set up a theatre company and we put on a devised version of the Greek myth, Pandora's Box. Then in 2011, I got into RADA. What a feeling it is to hear that news!

My time at RADA has been the biggest challenge of my life and the most invaluable. My advice to anyone applying to drama school would be: breathe deeply, be determined, and be open. I think you probably already know if acting is what you need to do with your life, the question is: are you mad enough to have a go? If so…commit with everything.

Joseph Prowen

Photo: Simon Annand

Joseph trained at the London Academy of Music and Dramatic Art (LAMDA) on the three year BA Hons Acting Course. He won the Highly Commended Actor award at the 2014 Spotlight Showcase.

I was taken to the theatre a lot as a child. I loved it. By the age of about ten I had grasped the concept that you could act for a living and so I thought: fantastic, I want to do that. As I got older I realised it isn't always that easy and a lot of hard work and often disappointment has to go in before you achieve success. However this didn't deter me as it was the only thing I wanted to do, and I was lucky enough to be accepted into LAMDA when I was 18.

Everybody's journey is different though. I applied for six drama schools and got into one. Some of my friends got into a few. Some took five or six years of auditioning before being accepted. But we all felt as though we had got into the right place at the right time.

I knew funding was going to be an issue; however I was very fortunate to get a scholarship. Anyone who is considering drama school but concerned about not being able to cover the costs should look into scholarships, grants and bursaries. You'd be surprised how many people are willing to help out aspiring actors! Don't be afraid to ask your drama school for advice as well.

The highlight of my training was probably the diversity of experiences! Performing in plays, musicals, short films, radio plays, working with amazing tutors, actors, directors…it's also possibly the only time in your life when you get to be creative every day! That's a fantastic opportunity.

The most important piece of advice I could give to a drama student is look after yourself and one another. Three years is a long time to spend every day with the same group of 30 or so people but it flies by. Make the most of it. And just remember that you're all in the same boat. Some people do really well very soon, others take more time. Don't over analyse it. Keep looking forward.

VOICE POWER WORKS
Irene Bradshaw - *Training tomorrow's actors today*

| voice coaching | audition preparation | public speaking | presentations

t: 020 7794 5721   www.voice-power-works.co.uk   e: irene@irenebradshaw.fsnet.co.uk

---

A B ACADEMY
THEATRE SCHOOL   T/F 0161 429 7413
Act Out Ltd, 22 Greek Street
Stockport, Cheshire SK3 8AB
E ab22actout@aol.com

ABBI ACTING MA BA Hons
*Accredited Drama School Tutor & Actress. 1-2-1 Sessions
in Auditioning, Speech & Voice, Corporate Presentation,
Public Speaking, Shakespeare & Text, Relaxation*
Based in London NW10
E stephanie.schonfield@googlemail.com

ABOMELI TUTORING
*Contact: Charles Abomeli BA LLAM. Development
Coach. Stage & Screen Acting Technique*
E charlesabm@aol.co.uk
W www.charlesabomeli.com

ACADEMY ARTS THEATRE
SCHOOL & AGENCY   T 01245 422595
6A The Green, Writtle
Chelmsford, Essex CM1 3DU
E info@academyarts.co.uk
W www.academyarts.co.uk

ACADEMY OF
CREATIVE TRAINING   T 01273 818266
*Contact: Janette Eddisford. Actor Training in Brighton,
Hove & Eastbourne*
8-10 Rock Place, Brighton
East Sussex BN2 1PF
T 07740 468338
E info@actbrighton.org
W www.actbrighton.org

ACADEMY OF PERFORMANCE
COMBAT THE   T 07963 206803
197 Church Road, Northolt
Middlesex UB5 5BE
E info@theapc.org.uk
W www.theapc.org.uk

ACADEMY OF PERFORMANCE TRAINING
(APT THE DRAMA SCHOOL)
*Courses: Professional Acting Diploma, 2 yrs. Television &
Film Acting, 1yr. Drama School Preparation, 1 yr.*
Guildford, Surrey
W www.aptraining.co.uk

ACCENT @ THE RICHER VOICE   T 07967 352551
Contact: Richard Ryder. Accent Specialist
9 Kamen House, 17-21 Magdalen Street
London Bridge, London SE1 2RH
E richard@therichervoice.com
W www.therichervoice.com

ACCENT KIT THE   T 07967 352551
Free iPhone App
9 Kamen House, 17-21 Magdalen Street
London SE1 2RH
E theaccentkit@gmail.com
W www.theaccentkit.com

ACKERLEY STUDIOS OF SPEECH, DRAMA &
PUBLIC SPEAKING   T 0151 724 3449
Est. 1919. Contact: Margaret Parsons
16 Fawley Road, Allerton
Liverpool L18 9TF
E johnmutch@talktalk.net

ACT 2 CAM   T 0191 270 4255
Sudio B3, Linskill Centre
Linskill Terrace, North Shields
Tyne & Wear NE30 2AY
E info@act2cam.com
W www.act2cam.com

ACT 2 DRAMA SCHOOL   T 07939 144355
Performing Arts School (5-18 yrs)
105 Richmond Avenue
Highams Park
London E4 9RR
E management@act2drama.co.uk
W www.act2drama.co.uk

ACT & VOICE   T 07850 910237 (Dee)
*Contact: Dee Mardi, Andrew Alton-Read. Drama
& Performance Classes (5-16 yrs). Drama School
Preparation, Coaching in Acting & Singing for
Children & Adults*
Based in Chelmsford, Essex
T 07854 536817 (Andrew)
E enquiries@actandvoice.co.uk
W www.actandvoice.co.uk

ACT NOW! PERFORMING ARTS
ACADEMY   T 07920 855410
Performing Arts Training (4-21 yrs). Part-time
Trestle Arts Base, Russett Drive
St Albans, Hertfordshire AL4 0JQ
E actnowperformingarts@mac.com
W www.actnowperformingartsschool.co.uk

ACT ONE DRAMA STUDIO   T 07904 339024
PO Box 4776, Sheffield S11 0EX
E info@actonedramastudio.co.uk
W www.actonedramastudio.co.uk

ACT UP   T 020 7924 7701
*Acting Classes for Everyone. Acting Workshops. Audition
Technique. Pre-Drama School (18+ yrs). Public Speaking.
Vocal Coaching. Casting & Production*
Unit 88, Battersea Business Centre
99-109 Lavender Hill
London SW11 5QL
E info@act-up.co.uk
W www.act-up.co.uk

ACTING AUDITION SUCCESS   T 020 8731 6686
*Contact: Philip Rosch. Audition Coaching for Drama UK
Schools. Audition Technique. Drama School Preparation.
Improvisation. Private Acting Classes*
53 West Heath Court
London NW11 7RG
E philiproschactor@gmail.com
W www.actingauditionsuccess.co.uk

ACTION LAB   **T** 020 8810 0412
Contact: Miranda French, Peter Irving. Part-time Acting Courses & Private Coaching. Based in London & West Dorset
34 Northcote Avenue, London W5 3UT
T 07979 623987
E miranda@mirandafrench.com

ACTORS CENTRE THE   **T** 020 7632 8001
Career and Casting Advice. Voice. Accent/Dialect Coaching. Acting for Camera. Audition Technique. Television Presenting. Voice Overs. Showreels. Shakespeare. The Meisner Technique. Performance Workshops
1A Tower Street, London WC2H 9NP
E reception@actorscentre.co.uk
W www.actorscentre.co.uk

ACTORS COMPANY LA THE
Based in Hollywood & London
916A North Formosa Avenue, West Hollywood
Los Angeles, CA 90004, USA
E info@theactorscompanyla.co.uk
W www.theactorscompanyla.co.uk

ACTORS PLATFORM LTD
Contact: Melissa Osborne. Courses: Weekly Casting Director Workshops, Quarterly Agent Workshops, Quarterly Industry Showcases
Based in Central London
E melissa@actorsplatform.com
W www.actorsplatform.com

ACTORS STUDIO   **T** 01753 650951
Acting Workshops. Audition Technique. Improvisation. Screen Acting Technique. Private Acting Classes. Stage School for Children
Main Admin, Pinewood Studios
Pinewood Road, Iver Heath
Bucks SL0 0NH
E info@actorsstudio.co.uk
W www.actorsstudio.co.uk

ACTORS' SURGERY THE   **T** 07956 344255
Contact: Katie Morgan (BA Hons, PG Dip, PGCE). Acting Classes for Adults in London taught by Professional Actress/Coach. Group & one-to-one Coaching Available. Audition Preparation. Drama School Entry. Improvisation. Meisner Technique. Working the Text. Confidence Building. General Skills. Coaching/Consulting for Plays, Television, Films
E theactorssurgery@gmail.com
W www.theactorssurgery.com

ACTOR'S TEMPLE THE   **T** 020 3004 4537
13-14 Warren Street
London W1T 5LG
E info@actorstemple.com
W www.actorstemple.com

ACTORS' THEATRE SCHOOL   **T** 020 8450 0371
Foundation Course
32 Exeter Road, London NW2 4SB
E info@theactorstheatreschool.co.uk
W www.theactorstheatreschool.co.uk

ACTORS TRAINING STUDIO   **T** 07710 172477
Part-time, Evening & Weekend Acting Workshops & Short Courses in London
c/o The Red Hedgehog
255-257 Archway
Highgate, London N6 5BS
E workshops@actorstrainingstudio.co.uk
W www.actorstrainingstudio.co.uk

ACTS   **T** 020 8360 0352
Ayres-Clark Theatre School
c/o 12 Gatward Close
Winchmore Hill
London N21 1AS
E actsn21@talktalk.net

ALEXANDER, Helen   **T** 020 8543 4085
Audition Technique. Drama School Entry
14 Chestnut Road
Raynes Park
London SW20 8EB
E helen-alexander@virginmedia.com

ALL EXPRESSIONS THEATRE SCHOOL   **T** 020 8892 6185
153 Waverley Avenue
Twickenham
Middlesex TW2 6DJ
E info@allexpressions.co.uk
W www.allexpressions.co.uk

ALLSORTS - DRAMA   **T/F** 020 8969 3249
Part-time Courses & Drama Training (3-18 yrs). Based in Kensington, Notting Hill, Hampstead, Fulham & Putney
34 Crediton Road
London NW10 3DU
E info@allsortsdrama.com
W www.allsortsdrama.com

ALLSTARS ACTORS MANAGEMENT DRAMA SCHOOL FOR ADULTS   **T** 0161 702 8257
Based in Manchester
T 07584 992429
E michelle@allstarsactors.tv
W www.allstarsactors.tv

ALRA (ACADEMY OF LIVE & RECORDED ARTS)
See DRAMA SCHOOLS: DRAMA UK

AMERICAN DIALECT
COACHING & RP　　　　T 07956 602508
Contact: Anne Wittman. Private Coaching in American Dialects & RP. All USA Dialects Covered. Accent Correction for Foreign Speakers. Acting Coaching & Audition Preparation
Based in London N8
E wittmananne@yahoo.com
W www.spokenstates.com

AMERICAN MUSICAL THEATRE
ACADEMY OF LONDON　　　T 020 7253 3118
Europa House, 13-17 Ironmonger Row
London EC1V 3QG
E info@americanacademy.co.uk
W www.americanacademy.co.uk

AMERICAN VOICES　　　　T 07875 148755
Contact: Lynn Bains. Acting Teacher & Director. American Accent/Dialect Coach
20 Craighall Crescent, Edinburgh EH6 4RZ
E mail@lynnbains.com

AND ALL THAT JAZZ　　　　T 020 8993 2111
Contact: Eileen Hughes. Accompanist. Vocal Coaching
163 Gunnersbury Lane, Acton Town, London W3 8LJ

ARABESQUE SCHOOL OF
PERFORMING ARTS　　　T/F 01243 531144
Quarry Lane, Chichester PO19 8NY
E arabesqueschool@aol.com
W www.arabesqueschool.com

ARDEN SCHOOL OF
THEATRE THE　　　　　T 0161 920 4890
BA (Hons) Acting for Live & Recorded Media. BA (Hons) Musical Theatre. HNC Acting for Camera. FdA Theatre & Performance. FdA Dance & Performance
The Manchester College, Nicholls Campus
Ardwick, Manchester M12 6BA
E enquiries@themanchestercollege.ac.uk
W www.themanchestercollege.ac.uk

ARTEMIS SCHOOL OF
THE LIVING WORD　　　T/F 01342 321330
Peredur Centre of The Arts, West Hoathly Road
East Grinstead, West Sussex RH19 4NF
E office@artemisspeechanddrama.org.uk
W www.artemisspeechanddrama.org.uk

ARTEMIS STUDIOS　　　　T 01344 429403
30 Charles Square, Bracknell, Berkshire RG12 1AY
E info@artemis-studios.co.uk
W www.artemis-studios.co.uk

ARTS1 SCHOOL OF
PERFORMANCE　　　　　T 01908 604756
Classes in Acting, Singing & Dance. RAD, ISTD, LAMDA. CDET Recognised School
The Box Studios, Sunrise Parkway
Linford Wood, Milton Keynes MK14 6LS
E info@arts1.co.uk
W www.arts1.co.uk

ARTS EDUCATIONAL SCHOOLS LONDON
See DRAMA SCHOOLS: DRAMA UK

ARTS UNIVERSITY
BOURNEMOUTH THE　　　T 01202 533011
7 Fern Barrow, Wallisdown, Poole, Dorset BH12 5HH
E hello@aub.ac.uk
W www.aub.ac.uk

ASHCROFT ACADEMY
OF DRAMATIC ART THE　　T/F 0844 8005328
Dance ISTD. Drama LAMDA. Singing (4-18 yrs)
Harris Primary Academy Crystal Palace, Malcolm Road
Penge, London SE20 8RH
T 07799 791586
E info@ashcroftacademy.com
W www.ashcroftacademy.com

ASHFORD, Clare BSc PGCE LLAM ALAM
(Recital) ALAM (Acting)　　T 020 8660 9609
20 The Chase, Coulsdon
Surrey CR5 2EG
E clareashford@rocketmail.com

ASSOCIATED STUDIOS THE　　T 020 7385 2038
Contact: Hannah Taylor, Yvonne I'Anson. Professional Development & Training
The Hub @ St Alban's Fulham
2 Margravine Road, London W6 8HJ
E info@associatedstudios.co.uk
W www.associatedstudios.co.uk

AUDITION COACH　　　　　T 0161 969 1444
Contact: Martin Harris. Acting Workshops. Audition Techniques. Group Evening Classes. Private Acting Classes
32 Baxter Road, Sale, Manchester M33 3AL
T 07788 723570
E martin@auditioncoach.co.uk
W www.auditioncoach.co.uk

AUDITION DOCTOR　　　　T 020 7357 8237
1 Gloucester Court, Swan Street
London SE1 1DQ
T 07764 193806
E tilly@auditiondoctor.co.uk
W www.auditiondoctor.co.uk

AUDITIONS: THE COMPLETE GUIDE
E info@auditionsthecompleteguide.com
W www.auditionsthecompleteguide.com

AVERY-CLARK, Kenneth　　　T 020 7253 3118
Musical Theatre. Voice Coach
Europa House, 13-17 Ironmonger Row
London EC1V 3QG
T 07734 509810
E ken@americanacademy.co.uk

BATE, Richard MA (Theatre) LGSM (TD) PGCE
(FE) Equity　　　　　　T 07720 865774
Audition Technique. Vocal & Acting Training. Drama School Entry
45A Derngate, Derngate Mews
Northampton, Northamptonshire NN1 1UE
E rich.bate@yahoo.co.uk

BATES, Esme　　　　　　T 0118 958 9330
BA Hons Royal Central School of Speech & Drama. Actress. Youth Theatre Director. LAMDA Tutor
2 Baron Court, Western Elms Avenue
Reading, Berks RG30 2BP
T 07941 700941
E batesesme@gmail.com
W www.esmebates.weebly.com

BATTERSEA ARTS
CENTRE (BAC)　　　　　T 020 7326 8210
Young People's Theatre Workshops & Performance Projects (12-25 yrs)
Lavender Hill, London SW11 5TN
F 020 7978 5207
E homegrown@bac.org.uk
W www.bac.org.uk

BENCH, Paul MEd LGSM ALAM FRSA LJBA (Hons) PGCE ACP (Lings) (Hons) MASC (Ph) MIFA (Reg)　　**T/F** 01743 233164
Audition Technique. Corporate Vocal Presentation. LAMDA Exams, Grades to Diploma Level. Private Acting Classes. Public Speaking. Stress Management. Vocal Coaching
1 Whitehall Terrace
Shrewsbury, Shropshire SY2 5AA
E pfbench@aol.com
W www.paulbench.co.uk

BEST SCHOOL OF ACTING　　**T** 0845 9011908
PO Box 749, St Albans
Herts AL1 4YW
E info@bestschoolofacting.com
W www.bestschoolofacting.com

BEST THEATRE ARTS　　**T** 01727 759634
PO Box 749
St Albans AL1 4YW
E bestarts@aol.com
W www.besttheatrearts.com

BIG ACT THE　　**T** 0870 8810367
14-16 Wilson Place
Bristol BS2 9HJ
E info@thebigact.com
W www.thebigact.com

BIG LITTLE THEATRE SCHOOL　　**T** 01202 434499
Acting Examination & Audition Prep (LAMDA). All Grades up to Grade 8 Gold. Early Years Drama & Dance. Performance in Education Workshops. Professional Development Programme. RAD Ballet, Tap & Modern, Performance Dance & Tap. Singing Technique Classes & Private Lessons. Musical Theatre Classes. Summer Schools. Themed Holiday Workshops. Youth Theatre Companies. Senior Musical Projects
Garnet House, 2A Harvey Road
Bournemouth
Dorset BH5 2AD
E info@biglittle.biz
W www.biglittle.biz

BIG TALENT SCHOOL & AGENCY THE　　**T** 029 2046 4506
Contact: Shelley Barrett-Norton
Unit 2, Crichton House
11-12 Mount Stuart Square
Cardiff CF10 5EE
T 07886 020923
E info@thebigtalent.co.uk
W www.thebigtalent.co.uk

BIG VOICE - LITTLE VOICE　　**T** 01706 812420
Contact: Russell Richardson LLAM DipDram. Audition Techniques. Drama School Preparation. LAMDA Speech Exams. Private Acting Classes. Public Speaking. Vocal Coaching
The Mill House, 3 Clough Mill
Walsden, West Yorkshire OL14 7QX
T 07939 215458
E russellrichardson5864@gmail.com

BIRD COLLEGE　　**T** 020 8300 6004
Professional Dance & Musical Theatre College
The Centre
27 Station Road
Sidcup, Kent DA15 7EB
F 020 8308 1370
E performance@birdcollege.co.uk
W www.birdcollege.co.uk

BIRMINGHAM SCHOOL OF ACTING
See DRAMA SCHOOLS: DRAMA UK

**BIRMINGHAM THEATRE
SCHOOL THE** T 0121 440 1665
The Old Fire Station
285-287 Moseley Road
Highgate, Birmingham B12 0DX
E info@birminghamtheatreschool.co.uk
W www.birminghamtheatreschool.com

**BLACKSTONE, Sarah
VOICE COACHING** T 07804 048541
Voice, Accent & Singing Coach
E info@sbvoiceworks.com
W www.sbvoiceworks.com

**BODENS COLLEGE OF
PERFORMING ARTS** T 020 8447 0909
*Contact: Adam Boden. Full time college (16-19 yrs).
Level 3 BTEC & Trinity Diploma*
99 East Barnet Road, New Barnet
Herts EN4 8RF
E adam@bodens.co.uk
W www.performingartscollege.co.uk

BODENS PERFORMING ARTS T 020 8447 0909
*Contact: Adam Boden. Acting Workshops. Audition
Technique. Dancing. Improvisation. Part-time Performing
Arts Classes. Singing*
Bodens Performing Arts
99 East Barnet Road
New Barnet, Herts EN4 8RF
E info@bodens.co.uk
W www.bodens.co.uk

BOWES, Sara T 07830 375389
Child Acting Coach for Film & Commercials
25 Holmes Avenue, Hove BN3 7LA
E saracrowe77@gmail.com

BOYD, Beth T 020 8398 6768
Private Acting Coach
10 Prospect Road, Long Ditton
Surbiton, Surrey KT6 5PY

BRADSHAW, Irene T 020 7794 5721
Private Coach. Voice & Audition Preparation
Flat F, Welbeck Mansions
Inglewood Road
West Hampstead, London NW6 1QX
T 07949 552915
E irene@irenebradshaw.fsnet.co.uk
W www.voice-power-works.co.uk

**BRAITHWAITE'S
ACROBATIC SCHOOL** T 020 8954 5638
8 Brookshill Avenue, Harrow Weald
Middlesex HA3 6RZ

BRANSTON, Dale T 020 8696 9958
Singing Teacher. Audition Preparation. Repertoire
Ground Floor Flat, 16 Fernwood Avenue
Streatham, London SW16 1RD
T 07767 261713
E branpickle@yahoo.co.uk

**BREAK A LEG
MANAGEMENT LTD** T/F 020 7250 0662
The City College
University House, Room 33
55 East Road, London N1 6AH
E agency@breakalegman.com
W www.breakalegman.com

**BRIDGE THEATRE
TRAINING COMPANY THE** T 020 7424 0860
*Contact: Mark Akrill. Drama School (over 18 yrs).
Acting. Dance. Film, Television & Radio Technique.
Improvisation. Movement. Professional Studies.
Singing. Stage Combat. Voice. Courses: Professional
Acting Course, 2 yr, full-time, Diploma. Postgraduate
Professional Acting Course (over 21 yrs), 1 yr,
full-time, Diploma*
90 Kingsway, Tally Ho Corner
North Finchley, London N12 0EX
E admin@thebridge-ttc.org
W www.thebridge-ttc.org

BRIGHTER VOICE T 07976 329611
*Voice Coaching. Accent Softening. Voice Over
Technique*
The Light Centre, 114 London Wall, London EC2M 5QA
E info@brightervoice.com
W www.brightervoice.com

BRISTOL OLD VIC THEATRE SCHOOL
See DRAMA SCHOOLS: DRAMA UK

**BRIT SCHOOL FOR PERFORMING ARTS &
TECHNOLOGY THE** T 020 8665 5242
60 The Crescent, Croydon CR0 2HN
F 020 8665 8676
E admin@brit.croydon.sch.uk
W www.brit.croydon.sch.uk

**BRITISH ACTION
ACADEMY LTD** T 0844 4146007
Screen Action Training
Shieling House, 30 Invincible Road
Farnborough, Hampshire GU14 7QU
E info@britishactionacademy.com
W www.britishactionacademy.com

**BRITISH AMERICAN
DRAMA ACADEMY** T 020 7487 0730
14 Gloucester Gate, Regent's Park, London NW1 4HG
F 020 7487 0731
E info@badaonline.com
W www.badaonline.com

BROWN, Michael BA MFA
*International Workshops: Physical Performance Skills,
Clown, Commedia, Mask Performance, Storytelling.
Acting Technique. Audition Technique/Preparation.
Private Acting Coach. Teacher at LAMDA & LISPA.
Workshops in UK & USA*
E brown.michaelanthony@gmail.com

CAMERON BROWN, Jo PGDVS
*Dialect. Dialogue. Voice Coaching for Film, Stage,
Television & Auditions*
E jocameronbrown@hotmail.com
W www.jocameronbrown.com

CAMPBELL, Jon T 07854 697971
36 Fentiman Road, London SW8 1LF
E jon@joncampbellacting.co.uk
W www.joncampbellacting.co.uk

**CAMPBELL, Ross
ARCM Dip RCM (Perf)** T 01252 510228
*Professor, Royal Academy of Music. Head of Singing
& Music, GSA, 2004-2011. Director & Head of Musical
Theatre, Musical Theatre Ireland. Private Teaching
Studios in London & Surrey*
17 Oldwood Chase, Farnborough, Hants GU14 0QS
T 07956 465165
E rosscampbell@ntlworld.com
W www.rosscampbell.biz

CANNON, Dee T 07586 313390
Freelance Acting Coach in Film, Television & Theatre.
Author of "In-Depth Acting"
Flat 9, 2A Regina Road
London N4 3QH
E dee@deecannon.com
W www.deecannon.com

CAPITAL ARTS
THEATRE SCHOOL T/F 020 8449 2342
Capital Arts Studio, Wyllyotts Theatre
Darkes Lane, Potters Bar, Herts EN6 2HN
T 07885 232414
E capitalarts@btconnect.com
W www.capitalarts.org.uk

CAPO FERRO
FIGHT ENSEMBLE T 07791 875902
Contact: Paul Casson-Yardley. Acting Workshops.
Drama School (over 18 yrs). Improvisation. Private Acting
Classes. Stage School for Children. Courses: Basic
Introduction to Stage Fighting, Fight Choreography,
Stage Combat Past & Present, Stage Combat with
Weapons & Props. All Abilities. All Courses Day/Half Day
168 Richmond Road, Sheffield
Yorkshire S13 8TG
E capo.ferro.ensemble@gmail.com

CELEBRATION THEATRE COMPANY
FOR THE YOUNG T 020 8994 8886
Contact: Neville Wortman. Drama School (over 18 yrs).
Drama School Preparation & 13-15 yrs LAMDA Bronze,
Silver & Gold Medals. Private Acting Classes. Summer
School. Vocal Coaching. Courses: Audition & Interview
Techniques, 'Shakespeare Today', Speaking in Public,
'The Confident Voice', 10 week Saturday Classes
School of Economic Science Building
Studio 11-13, Mandeville Place
London W1U 3AJ
T 07976 805976
E neville@speakwell.co.uk
W www.speakwell.co.uk

CENTRAL LONDON
DRAMA COACHING T 07950 720868
Audition Technique. Text Analysis. Vocal Presentation
Skills. Trinity Examinations. CRB Checked
Based in WC1
E euniceroberts1@gmail.com

CENTRE FOR SOLO
PERFORMANCE T 07952 960424
Conway Hall, 25 Red Lion Square
London WC1R 4RL
E luke@centreforsoloperformance.com
W www.centreforsoloperformance.com

CENTRE STAGE ACADEMY
THEATRE SCHOOL T 07773 416593
Weekend Theatre School in Midhurst & Chichester
(5-20 yrs)
9 Beech Grove, Midhurst & Haslemere
West Sussex GU29 9JA
E brett.east@hotmail.com
W www.csatheatreschool.co.uk

CENTRE STAGE SCHOOL
OF PERFORMING ARTS T 020 8886 4264
Students (4-18 yrs). Based in North London
The Croft, 7 Cannon Road
Southgate, London N14 7HE
F 020 8886 7555
E carole@centrestageuk.com
W www.centrestageuk.com

CENTRE STAGE
THEATRE ACADEMY **T** 01689 330557
Performing Arts Training for Children. Four Branches
across South London/Kent
91 Eldred Drive, Orpington, Kent BR5 4PE
E info@centrestagetheatreacademy.com
W www.centrestagetheatreacademy.com

CENTRESTAGE SCHOOL
OF PERFORMING ARTS **T** 020 7328 0788
Drama School Auditions. Private Coaching for
Professionals
Centrestage House, 117 Canfield Gardens
London NW6 3DY
E vickiwoolf@centrestageschool.co.uk
W www.centrestageschool.co.uk

CHARD, Verona
LRAM Dip RAM **T** 020 8992 1571
Private Pupils Welcome. British & International Vocal
Academy Founder. Visiting Singing Tutor at Royal Central
School of Speech & Drama. Vocal Expert X Factor,
Poland, 2012. Coach of Award-winning Jazz Singers &
West End Leads. Vocal Producer for Record Labels
Ealing House, 33 Hanger Lane
London W5 3HJ
E verona@veronachard.com

CHARRINGTON, Tim **T** 020 7987 3028
Dialect/Accent Coaching
54 Topmast Point, Strafford Street, London E14 8SN
T 07967 418236
E tim.charrington@gmail.com
W www.timcharrington.co.uk

CHASE, Stephan
PRODUCTIONS LTD **T** 020 8878 9112
Private Coach for Acting, Auditions, Public Speaking &
Script Work. Originator of Managing Authentic Presence
The Studio, 22 York Avenue, London SW14 7LG
E stephan@stephanchase.com
W www.stephanchase.com

CHEKHOV, Michael
STUDIO LONDON **T** 020 8696 7372
Contact: Graham Dixon. Monthly Acting Workshops.
Private Acting Classes. Summer School. Vocal Coaching
48 Vectis Road, London SW17 9RG
E info@michaelchekhovstudio.org.uk
W www.michaelchekhovstudio.org.uk

CHERRY PIE PERFORMANCE **T** 07939 422081
Workshops for Actors, Performers, Presenters &
Professionals
20 Coronation Court, Croston
Lancs PR26 9HF
E enquiries@cherrypieperformance.co.uk
W www.cherrypieperformance.co.uk

CHRISKA STAGE SCHOOL **T** 01928 739166
37-39 Whitby Road, Ellesmere Port
Cheshire L64 8AA
E chrisbooth41@hotmail.com
W www.chriska.co.uk

CHRYSTEL ARTS
THEATRE SCHOOL **T** 01494 785589
Part-time Classes for Children, Teenagers & Young
Adults in Dance, Drama & Musical Theatre. ISTD &
LAMDA Examinations
Edgware Parish Hall, Rectory Lane
Edgware, Middlesex HA8 7LG
T 020 8952 6010
E chrystelarts@waitrose.com

CHURCHER, Mel MA **T** 07778 773019
Acting & Vocal Coach
E melchurcher@hotmail.com
W www.melchurcher.com

CHURCHER, Teresa
(Life Coach MASC) **T** 07807 103295
Screen Acting & Career Coaching
E info@theactingangel.co.uk
W www.theactingangel.co.uk

CIRCOMEDIA **T/F** 0117 947 7288
Centre for Contemporary Circus & Physical Performance
Britannia Road, Kingswood, Bristol BS15 8DB
E info@circomedia.com
W www.circomedia.com

CITY LIT **T** 020 7492 2542
Accredited & Non-Accredited part-time & full-time Day
& Evening Courses. Acting Workshops. Shakespeare,
Stanislavski, Meisner Audition Techniques. Screen &
Radio Acting/Presenting. Camera Training. Dancing.
Dialect/Accent Coaching. Directing. Elocution Coaching.
Improvisation. Presenting. Professional Preparation.
Agent & Casting Directors Masterclasses. Public
Speaking. Clowning. Stand-up Comedy. Singing. Story
Telling. Stage & Fighting for Film. CL Rep Company
1-10 Keeley Street
Covent Garden, London WC2B 4BA
E drama@citylit.ac.uk
W www.citylit.ac.uk/dramaschool

CLANRANALD TRUST: COMBAT
INTERNATIONAL **T** 01259 731010
27 High Street, Kincardine, Alloa FK10 4RJ
E info@clanranald.org
W www.clanranald.org

CLEMENTS, Anne
MA LGSM FRSA **T** 020 7435 1211
Audition Technique. Role Exploration. Dialect/Accent/
Voice Coaching. Drama School Advice & Preparation.
Close to Hampstead Tube NW3
E woodlandcreature10@hotmail.com

COLDIRON, M. J. **T** 07941 920498
Audition Preparation & Presentation Skills. Private
Coaching
54 Millfields Road, London E5 0SB
E jiggs@blueyonder.co.uk

COLGAN, Valerie **T** 020 7267 2153
Audition Technique. Voice Production
The Green, 17 Herbert Street, London NW5 4HA

COMBAT ACTOR SCHOOL **T** 07950 024561
6A Rushock Trading Estate, Droitwich Road
Droitwich, Worcestershire WR9 0NR
E info@combatactorschool.co.uk
W www.combatactorschool.co.uk

COMBER, Sharrone BA
(Hons) MAVS (CSSD) PGCE **T** 07752 029422
Audition & Monologue Speech Technique for Drama &
Performing Arts School Entry. Vocal Coach Specialist.
Dialect & Accent Coaching. Elocution. Presentation
Skills. Private Acting Classes. Public Speaking
E sharronecomber@hotmail.com

COMPLETE WORKS THE **T** 020 7377 0280
The Old Truman Brewery, 91 Brick Lane, London E1 6QL
F 020 7247 7405
E info@tcw.org.uk
W www.tcw.org.uk

CONTI, Italia ACADEMY
See DRAMA SCHOOLS: DRAMA UK

CONTI, Italia ACADEMY
OF THEATRE ARTS   T 020 7608 0044
Courses: Performing Arts Diploma, 3 yr. Professional Dance Diploma, 3 yr. Performing Arts with Teacher Training, 3 yr. Intensive Performing Arts, 1 yr. Foundation Performing Arts, 1 yr. BA (Hons) Acting, 3 yr. Foundation Acting, 1 yr. Singing, 1 yr. Theatre Arts School (Academic yrs 7-11)
Italia Conti House, 23 Goswell Road
London EC1M 7AJ
F 020 7253 1430
E admin@italiaconti.co.uk
W www.italiaconti.com

CORNER, Clive AGSM LRAM   T 01305 860267
Qualified Teacher. Audition Training. Private Coaching
'The Belenes', 60 Wakeham
Portland DT5 1HN
E cornerassociates@aol.com

COURT THEATRE
TRAINING COMPANY   T/F 020 7739 6868
The Courtyard Theatre, Bowling Green Walk
40 Pitfield Street, London N1 6EU
E info@courttheatretraining.org.uk
W www.courttheatretraining.org.uk

COX, Gregory BA Joint Hons   T 07931 370135
Bristol Old Vic Graduate with 35 Years' Experience. Audition Coaching. Drama Coaching. Sight Reading Skills. Voice Work
Based in South West London
E gregoryedcox@hotmail.com

COX, Jerry MA PGCE BA (Hons)   T 07957 654027
Acting Coach. Audition Technique. Preparation/Entry for Drama School. Private Acting Classes
4 Stevenson Close, London EN5 1DR
E jerrymarwood@hotmail.com

CPA STUDIOS   T 01708 766007
3 yr Professional Musical Theatre Diploma Course
The Studios, 219B North Street
Romford, Essex RM1 4QA
F 01708 766077
E collegeadmin@cpastudios.co.uk
W www.cpastudios.co.uk

CREATIVE
PERFORMANCE LTD   T 020 8908 0502
Mobile Workshop in Circus Skills & Drama TIE. Events Management for Libraries, Schools, Youth Clubs & Play Schemes
20 Pembroke Road, North Wembley
Middlesex HA9 7PD
E creative.performance@yahoo.co.uk

CROSKIN, Phil   T 07837 712323
RADA Trained. Auditions, Presentation Skills & Public Profiles
E philcroskin@fastmail.fm

CROWE, Ben   T 07952 784911
Accent, Acting & Audition Tuition
25 Holmes Avenue, Hove BN3 7LA
E bencrowe@hotmail.co.uk

CYGNET THEATRE   T 01392 277189
Friars Gate, Exeter, Devon EX2 4AZ
E info@cygnettheatre.co.uk
W www.cygnettheatre.co.uk

D&B SCHOOL OF PERFORMING ARTS & D&B
THEATRE SCHOOL   T 020 8698 8880
Central Studios, 470 Bromley Road, Bromley BR1 4PQ
E info@dandbperformingarts.co.uk
W www.dandbperformingarts.co.uk

DAVIDSON, Clare   T 020 8348 0132
30 Highgate West Hill, London N6 6NP
E davidson_clare@hotmail.com
W www.claredavidson.co.uk

DEBUT SCHOOL OF
PERFORMING ARTS   T 01274 618288
12 Tenterfields House, Meadow Road
Apperley Bridge, Bradford BD10 0LQ
E jacqui.debut@btinternet.com
W www.debuttheatreschool.co.uk

DE COURCY, Bridget   T 020 8883 8397
Singing Teacher
19 Muswell Road, London N10
E singinglessons@bridgetdecourcy.co.uk

De FLOREZ, Jane LGSM PG Dip   T 020 7602 0741
Singing. Acting for Singers. Audition Technique. Drama School Audition Preparation. Language Tutoring. Music Theory for Singers. Public Speaking. Speech & Drama Tuition. Singing. Vocal Coaching. Courses: Musical Theatre, 1 yr, part-time. Classical/Opera Singing, 2 yrs, part-time. General Singing & Music Theory, 1 yr, part-time. Choir Preparation, 6 months, part-time
Kensington, London W14 9AS
E janedeflorez@gmail.com
W www.singingteacherlondon.com

DIGNAN, Tess MA   T 07528 576915
Audition, Text & Voice Coach
004 Oregon Building, Deals Gateway
Lewisham SE13 7RR
E tess.dignan@gmail.com

DIRECTIONS THEATRE ARTS
(CHESTERFIELD) LTD   T/F 01246 854455
Musical Theatre School
Studios: 1A-2A Sheffield Road, Chesterfield
Derby S41 7LL
T 07973 768144
E julie.cox5@btconnect.com
W www.directionstheatrearts.org

DOGGETT, Antonia   T 07814 155090
Courses: Cold Reading, 3 weeks, part-time. Shakespeare, 6 weeks, part-time. Advanced LAMDA Grades/Drama School Audition Preparation, 6 weeks, part-time. Acting Techniques, 6 weeks, part-time. Acting Workshops. Audition Technique, Drama Scool Preparation. Private Acting Classes, Public Speaking, Vocal Coaching. Accent Softening
Conway Hall, 25 Red Lion Square, London WC1R 4RL
E antoniadoggettcontact@gmail.com
W www.antoniadoggett.co.uk

DORSET SCHOOL OF
ACTING THE   T 01202 922675
Courses: Foundation in Acting & Musical Theatre, 1yr, full-time. Trinity ATCL Level 4 Qualification. Adult Acting Courses. Youth Theatre Programmes, part-time. Acting Classes. Musical Theatre Classes. Audition Technique. Dancing. Drama School Preparation. Improvisation. Singing. Summer Schools. Vocal Coaching
c/o Lighthouse, 21 Kingland Road
Poole, Dorset BH15 1UG
E admin@dorsetschoolofacting.co.uk
W www.dorsetschoolofacting.co.uk

**DRAMA ASSOCIATION
OF WALES**   T 029 2045 2200
Workshops for Amateur Actors & Directors
Unit 2, The Malting, East Tyndall Street
Cardiff Bay, Cardiff CF24 5EA
E office@dramawales.org.uk

DRAMA CENTRE LONDON
See DRAMA SCHOOLS: DRAMA UK

DRAMA FOR KIDS   T 07973 513619
22 Aughantarragh Road, Armagh
County Armagh BT60 4QG
E narelleallen@yahoo.co.uk
W www.dramaforkids.org.uk

**DRAMA STUDIO
EDINBURGH THE**   T 0131 453 3284
Children's Weekly Drama Workshops
19 Belmont Road, Edinburgh EH14 5DZ
E info@thedramastudio.com
W www.thedramastudio.com

DRAMA STUDIO LONDON
See DRAMA SCHOOLS: DRAMA UK

DULIEU, John   T 020 8696 9958
Acting Coach. Audition & Role Preparation
16 Fernwood Avenue
Streatham
London SW16 1RD
T 07803 289599
E john_dulieu@yahoo.com

DUNMORE, Simon
Acting & Audition Tuition
E simon.dunmore@btinternet.com

DURRENT, Peter   T 01787 248263
Audition & Rehearsal Pianist. Vocal Coach
40 Water Street
Lavenham
Sudbury, Suffolk CO10 9RN
E tunefuldurrent@gmail.com

DYSON, Kate LRAM   T 01273 607490
Audition Technique Coaching. Drama
39 Arundel Street
Kemptown BN2 5TH
T 07812 949875
E kate.dyson@talktalk.net

John Colclough Advisory
Practical independent guidance for actors and actresses

www.johncolclough.com | t: 020 8873 1763 | e: info@johncolclough.com

---

EARNSHAW, Susi
THEATRE SCHOOL　　　　**T** 020 8441 5010
Full-time Stage School (11-18 yrs). GCSEs & Vocational
Qualifications. Saturday Theatre School (5-16 yrs). After
School & Holiday Courses
The Bull Theatre, 68 High Street
Barnet, Herts EN5 5SJ
E info@sets.org.uk
W www.susiearnshaw.co.uk

EAST 15 ACTING SCHOOL
See DRAMA SCHOOLS: DRAMA UK

EASTON, Lydia　　　　**T** 07977 511621
Singing Teacher
72 Palmerston Road, London N22 8RF
E lydzeaston@yahoo.com

ÉCOLE INTERNATIONALE DE THÉÂTRE
JACQUES LECOQ　　　　**T** 00 33 1 47704478
Acting Workshops. Drama School (over 21 yrs). Mime.
Movement & Creative Theatre. Play Writing
57 rue du Faubourg Saint-Denis
75010 Paris, France
F 00 33 1 45234014
E contact@ecole-jacqueslecoq.com
W www.ecole-jacqueslecoq.com

EDINBURGH LIGHTING &
SOUND SCHOOL (ELSS)　　　　**T** 07590 015957
c/o Black Light, West Shore Trading Estate
West Shore Road, Edinburgh EH5 1QF
E contact@edinburghlightingandsoundschool.co.uk
W www.edinburghlightingandsoundschool.co.uk

EDUCATION IN STAGE & THEATRE ARTS
(E.S.T.A.)　　　　**T** 020 8741 2843
16 British Grove, Chiswick
London W4 2NL
F 020 8746 3219
E esta@charkham.net
W www.estatheatreschool.com

EEDLE, Ben　　　　**T** 07587 526286
273 Camberwell New Road
London SE5 0TF
E ben@theenglishbears.com
W www.theenglishbears.com

EXPRESSIONS ACADEMY OF
PERFORMING ARTS　　　　**T** 01623 424334
3 Newgate Lane, Mansfield
Nottingham NG18 2LB
E expressions-uk@btconnect.com
W www.expressionsperformingarts.co.uk

FAIRBROTHER, Victoria
MA CSSD LAMDA Dip　　　　**T** 07877 228990
Audition Technique. Improvisation. Private Acting
Classes. Public Speaking. Vocal Coaching
15A Devonport Road, Shepherd's Bush
London W12 8NZ
E victoriafairbrother1@hotmail.com

FAIRCLOUGH, Amanda
STAGE & FILM SCHOOL　　　　**T** 07929 823110
Children 5-18 yrs
Horwich Resource Centre, Beaumont Road
Horwich, Bolton, Lancashire BL6 7BG
E info@stageandfilmschool.co.uk
W www.stageandfilmschool.co.uk

FAITH, Gordon
BA IPA Dip.REM.Sp LRAM　　　　**T** 020 7328 0446
Speech & Voice
1 Wavel Mews, Priory Road
West Hampstead, London NW6 3AB
E gordon.faith@tiscali.co.uk
W www.gordonfaith.co.uk

FERRIS, Anna Theresa　　　　**T** 01258 881098
MA Voice Studies, Royal Central School of Speech &
Drama. Voice & Text Coach working in Dorset, Somerset
& Wiltshire
E annabellaferris@gmail.com

FERRIS ENTERTAINMENT
PERFORMING ARTS　　　　**T** 07801 493133
London. Belfast. Cardiff. Los Angeles. France. Spain
Number 8, 132 Charing Cross Road
London WC2H 0LA
E info@ferrisentertainment.com
W www.ferrisentertainment.com

FINBURGH, Nina　　　　**T** 020 7435 9484
Cold & Prepared Readings Specialist. Masterclasses &
Individuals. (Equity Members only)
1 Buckingham Mansions
West End Lane
London NW6 1LR
E ninafinburgh@aol.com

FOOTSTEPS THEATRE SCHOOL
& AGENCY　　　　**T/F** 07554 761307
Dance, Drama & Singing Training
Westfield Lane, Bradford
West Yorkshire BD10 8PY
E gwestman500@btinternet.com

FORD, Carole Ann ADVS　　　　**T** 020 8815 1832
Acting Coach. Communication Skills
Based in N10
E emko2000@aol.com

FOURTH MONKEY　　　　**T** 020 8150 0076
Actor Training Programmes, 1 & 2 yr, full-time &
part-time. Repertory & Ensemble Focused Training
49 South Molton Street
London W1K 5LH
E office@fourthmonkey.co.uk
W www.fourthmonkey.co.uk

FRANKLIN, Michael
Meisner Technique
Correspondence: c/o Spotlight, 7 Leicester Place
London WC2H 7RJ
E info@acteach.info

FRANKLYN, Susan   T 01306 884913
Audition Speeches. Confidence. Interview Technique.
Presentation. Sight Reading
T 07780 742891
E susan.franklyn1@btinternet.com

FURNESS, Simon   T 07702 619665
Actor Training. Audition Preparation & Technique
c/o The Actors' Temple
13-14 Warren Street
London W1T 5LG
E simon@actorstemple.com

**GFCA (GILES FOREMAN CENTRE
FOR ACTING)**   T 020 7437 3175
Formerly Caravanserai Productions & Acting Studio.
4 Term Postgraduate Equivalent Level Intensive Acting
& Acting/Directing/Writing Diploma & 1 yr Foundation
ATCL Diploma. Part-time Courses: 12 week Acting, All
Levels inc Professionals, 10 week Movement, Voice,
Improvisation, Meisner, On-Camera. Malmgren/
Laban Analysis. Short Courses: International Acting
Masterclasses & Workshops, Summer School, Audition
Technique. Private Acting Coaching.
Twitter: @gilesForeman1
Studio Soho, Royalty Mews (entrance by Quo Vadis)
22-25 Dean Street
London W1D 3RA
E info@gilesforeman.com
W www.gilesforeman.com

**GMA TELEVISION
PRESENTER TRAINING**   T 01628 673078
Presenting for Television, Radio, Live Events. Autocue.
Improvisation. Scriptwriting. Talkback. Vocal Coaching
86 Beverley Gardens, Maidenhead
Berks SL6 6SW
T 07769 598625
E geoff@gma-training.co.uk
W www.gma-training.co.uk

GRAYSON, John   T 07702 188031
Audition Coaching. Vocal Technique. Improvisation
Skills. Also Coaching for Public Speaking. Experienced
Classical & Musical Theatre Performer. Singing Lessons.
Vocal Coaching
2 Jubilee Road, St Johns
Worcester WR2 4LY
E jgbizzybee@btinternet.com

GREASEPAINT ANONYMOUS   T 020 8360 9785
Youth Theatre & Training Company. Part-time Theatre
Workshops run weekly through School Term Time.
Holiday Courses at Easter & Summer. Acting Workshops.
Dancing. Singing (4-30 yrs)
Flat 13 Oak Lodge
50 Eversley Park Road
London N21 1JL
T 07930 421216
E info@greasepaintanonymous.co.uk

GROUNDLINGS THEATRE   T 023 9273 9496
Drama School Training for Young People & Adults
42 Kent Street, Portsmouth
Hampshire PO1 3BT
E richard@groundlings.co.uk
W www.groundlings.co.uk

GROUT, Philip   T 020 8881 1800
Theatre Director. Drama Coaching. Tuition for Students
& Professionals
81 Clarence Road, London N22 8PG
E philipgrout@hotmail.com

GRYFF, Stefan T 020 7723 8181
Screen Acting Coach

GSA, GUILDFORD SCHOOL OF ACTING
See DRAMA SCHOOLS: DRAMA UK

GUILDHALL SCHOOL OF MUSIC & DRAMA
See DRAMA SCHOOLS: DRAMA UK

HABER, Margie STUDIO T 001 310 854 0462
On-camera Audition Technique Training in Los Angeles
971 N. La Cienega Boulevard, #207
Los Angeles, CA 90069
F 001 310 854 0870
E info@margiehaber.com
W www.margiehaber.com

HANCOCK, Allison LLAM T/F 020 8891 1073
Acting. Audition Coach. Dramatic Art. Elocution. Speech Correction. Voice
38 Eve Road, Isleworth
Middlesex TW7 7HS
E allisonhancock@blueyonder.co.uk

HARLEQUIN STUDIOS
PERFORMING ARTS SCHOOL T 01273 581742
Drama & Dance Training
122A Phyllis Avenue
Peacehaven
East Sussex BN10 7RQ

HARRIS, Sharon NCSD LRAM LAM STSD IPA
Dip DA (London Univ) T 01923 211644
Speech & Drama Specialist Teacher. Private Acting Coach for Screen & Stage. Training for RADA, LAMDA & ESB Exams. Audition Technique. Drama School & National Youth Theatre Audition Preparation
71 The Avenue, Watford
Herts WD17 4NU
T 07956 388716
E theharrisagency@btconnect.com

HARRISON RUTHERFORD, Lucie MA Voice
Studies, BA (Hons) Drama T 07773 798440
Voice Tutor & Acting Coach
Based in Richmond upon Thames
E info@lucieharrison.co.uk
W www.lucieharrison.co.uk

HASS, Leontine
Vocal Coach
E leontine@associatedstudios.co.uk
W www.leontinehass.com

HESTER, John LLCM (TD) T 020 8224 9580
Member of The Society of Teachers of Speech & Drama. Acting Courses for all Ages. Acting Workshops. Audition Technique. Dialect/Accent Coaching. Drama School Auditions (over 18 yrs). Elocution Coaching. Private Acting Classes. Public Speaking. Stage School for Children. Vocal Coaching
105 Stoneleigh Park Road
Epsom
Surrey KT19 0RF
E hjohnhester@aol.com

HETHERINGTON, Caro T 07723 620728
Voice & Dialect Coach
7 Dodcott Barns
Burleydam
Whitchurch, Cheshire SY13 4BQ
E carolinehetherington@gmail.com
W www.carohetherington.co.uk

HIGGS, Jessica T 020 7701 8477
Voice
34 Mary Datchelor House
2D Camberwell Grove, London SE5 8FB
T 07940 193631
E juhiggs@aol.com

HOFFMANN-GILL, Daniel T 07946 433903
Acting & Audition Tuition
E danielhg@gmail.com

HOOKER, Jennifer Jane T 07725 977146
Private Acting Coach. Based in North West London. Nearest tube Marylebone
E jj@jjhooker.com
W www.jjhooker.com

HOOPLA IMPRO T 07976 975348
Improvised Comedy Courses & Classes. All Levels of Experience. Various Venues around London
E hooplaimpro@gmail.com
W www.hooplaimpro.com

HOPE STREET LTD T 0151 708 8007
Professional Development Opportunities for Emerging & Established Artists
13A Hope Street, Liverpool L1 9BQ
E peter@hope-street.org
W www.hope-street.org

HOPKINS, Abigail T 07847 420882
Audition & Acting Coach
E creativeacting@hotmail.co.uk

HOPNER, Ernest LLAM T 0151 625 5641
Elocution. Public Speaking. Vocal Coaching
70 Banks Road
West Kirby CH48 0RD

HOUSEMAN, Barbara T 07767 843737
Ex-RSC Voice Dept. Author 'Finding Your Voice' & 'Tackling Text'. Voice. Text. Acting. Confidence
E barbarahouseman@hotmail.com
W www.barbarahouseman.com

HOWARD, Ashley BA MA T 07821 213752
Voice Coach
5 St John's Street, Aylesbury
Bucks HP20 1BS
E ashleynormanhoward@me.com
W www.ashleyhoward.me

HUDSON, Mark T 0161 238 8900
Film & Television Acting & Dialect Coach
14-32 Hewitt Street
Manchester M15 4GB
E actorclass@aol.com

HUGHES, Dewi T 07836 545717
Voice. Text. Accents. Auditions
Flat 1, 4 Fielding Road, London W14 0LL
E dewi.hughes@gmail.com

HUGHES-D'AETH, Charlie T 07811 010963
RSC Text & Voice Coach. Acting & Audition Technique. Presentation Skills. Public Speaking. Vocal Coaching
E chdaeth@aol.com

IDENTITY DRAMA SCHOOL T 020 7702 7008
160-170 Cannon Street Road
London E1 2LH
E studentadmin@identitydramaschool.com
W www.identitydramaschool.com

RICK LIPTON | DIALECT COACH

American accents coaching from an American based in London
Film, TV and Theatre with 18+ years experience • **100s of shows and 1000s of actors coached**
07961 445247   rl@ricklipton.com   ricklipton.com

IMPULSE COMPANY THE   **T/F** 07525 264173
Meisner-Based Core Training
E info@impulsecompany.co.uk
W www.impulsecompany.co.uk

INDEPENDENT THEATRE WORKSHOP THE   **T** 00 353 1 2600831
8 Terminus Mills, Clonskeagh, Dublin 6, Ireland
E agency@itwstudios.ie
W www.itwstudios.ie

INTERACT   **T** 07961 982198
Contact: Lauren Bigby (LGSM). Acting Workshops.
Audition Technique. Elocution Coaching. Private Acting
Classes. Public Speaking
18 Knightbridge Walk, Billericay
Essex CM12 0HP
E renbigby@hotmail.com

INTERNATIONAL PERFORMING ARTS & THEATRE LTD   **T** 020 3714 3393
Accredited Awarding Body. Programmes in Dance,
Singing, Acting & Musical Theatre
E info@i-path.biz
W www.i-path.biz

INTERNATIONAL SCHOOL OF SCREEN ACTING   **T** 020 8709 8719
Courses: 1 yr Advanced, full-time. 2 yr, full-time. Drama
School (over 18 yrs)
3 Mills Studios, The Old Lab
Three Mill Lane, London E3 3DU
E office@screenacting.co.uk
W www.screenacting.co.uk

J VOX VOCAL ACADEMY   **T** 07546 100745
Contact: Jay Henry. The Voice, BBC Vocal Coach. Vocal
Training & Audition Preparation for Television & Reality
Shows. Microphone Technique
Dunbar, Latimer Road
Barnet EN5 5NF
T 07854 596916
E info@jvox.co.uk
W www.jvoxacademy.com

JACK, Andrew   **T** 07836 615839
Dialect Coach
Vrouwe Johanna, 24 The Moorings
Willows Riverside
Windsor, Berks SL4 5TG
W www.andrewjack.com

JACK, Paula T 01753 646677
Dialect Coach. Language Specialist
E dialect.guru@mac.com
W www.paulajack.com

JAM ACADEMY THE T 01628 483808
Jam Theatre Company, 45A West Street
Marlow, Bucks SL7 3NH
E info@thejamacademy.co.uk
W www.thejamacademy.co.uk

JAMES, Linda
RAM Dip Ed IPD LRAM T 020 8568 2390
Dialect & Speech Coach
25 Clifden Road, Brentford
Middlesex TW8 0PB

JAQUARELLO, Roland BA T 020 8567 5988
Audition Technique. Drama School Entrance.
Radio Coaching
11 Chesnut Grove, London W5 4JT
T 07808 742307
E rolandjaquarello@gmail.com
W www.rolandjaquarello.com

JARVIS, Nathan T 07970 963282
Singing Teacher. Audition Preparation & Technique
44E Croydon Road, Penge, London SE20 7AE
E nathanjarvis81@hotmail.com
W www.nathancjarvis.co.uk

JG DANCE LTD T 01491 572000
Melody House, 198 Grey's Road
Henley-on-Thames, Oxon RG9 1QU
E info@jgdance.co.uk
W www.jgdance.co.uk

JIGSAW PERFORMING
ARTS SCHOOLS T 020 8447 4530
64-66 High Street, Barnet, Herts EN5 5SJ
F 020 8447 4531
E enquiries@jigsaw-arts.co.uk
W www.jigsaw-arts.co.uk

JINGLES, Jo T 01494 778989
1 Boismore Road, Chesham, Bucks HP5 1SH
E headoffice@jojingles.co.uk
W www.jojingles.com

JOHNSON, David DRAMA T 07969 183481
PO Box 618, Oldham
Greater Manchester OL1 9GU
E johnsondrama@googlemail.com
W www.davidjohnsondrama.co.uk

JUDE'S DRAMA ACADEMY
& MANAGEMENT T 0161 624 5378
Manor House, Oldham Road
Springhead, Oldham OL4 4QJ
E judesdrama@yahoo.co.uk
W www.judesdrama.co.uk

K-BIS THEATRE SCHOOL T 01273 566739
Clermont Hall, Cumberland Road
Brighton, East Sussex BN1 6SL
E k-bis@live.co.uk
W www.kbistheatreschool.co.uk

KADHIM, Najwa T 07977 603483
Arabic Language & Dialect Specialist. Arabic Native
Speaker
7 Cotman Close, Westleigh Avenue
London SW15 6RG
E najwakadhim@gmail.com

KENT YOUTH THEATRE STAGE
& SCREEN ACADEMY T 01227 730177
Contact: Richard Andrews. Weekly Classes plus Stage
& Screen Productions. From 3 yrs upwards. KYT Agency
for Professional Work
Office: Mulberry Croft, Mulberry Hill, Chilham CT4 8AJ
T 07967 580213
E richard@kentyouththeatre.co.uk
W www.kentyouththeatre.co.uk

KERR, Louise T 020 8509 2767
Voice Coach
20A Rectory Road, London E17 3BQ
T 07780 708102
E louise@resonancevoice.com
W www.resonancevoice.com

KIDZ ON THE HILL T 07881 553480
Weekly Classes in Street Dance, Acting, Singing &
Ballet. Free Trials
Pages Lane, Muswell Hill
London, Haringey N10 1PP
E admin@kidzonthehill.co.uk
W www.kidzonthehill.co.uk

KINGSTON JUNIOR
DRAMA COMPANY T 01932 230273
Youth Theatre (10-14 yrs)
72 Shaw Drive, Walton-on-Thames, Surrey KT12 2LS
E kingstonjdc@aol.com
W www.davidlawsonlean.com

KIRKLEES COLLEGE T 01484 437047
Courses in Acting, Dance & Musical Theatre (BTEC)
Highfields Annexe, New North Road
Huddersfield HD1 5NN
E info@kirkleescollege.ac.uk

KNYVETTE, Sally T 020 7385 2216
Drama Tuition. Specialising in Drama School Entrance.
Particular Focus on Shakespeare. Audition Speech
Preparation for Theatre, Film & Television (includes filmed
playback). References available. West Brompton nearest
Tube. 74 & 430 Buses to the Door
239 Lillie Road, Fulham, London SW6 7LN
T 07958 972425
E salkny@gmail.com
W www.sallyknyvette.co.uk

KOGAN ACADEMY
OF DRAMATIC ARTS T 020 7272 0027
9-15 Elthorne Road, London N19 4AJ
F 020 7272 0026
E info@scienceofacting.com
W www.scienceofacting.com

KRIMPAS, Titania T 07957 303958
One-to-one Tuition, all Levels. Tailored to Suit
Experienced Actors & Beginners
36 Deronda Road, London SE24 9BG
E titaniakrimpas@gmail.com

KSA PERFORMING ARTS T 020 8090 5801
Beckenham Halls, 4 Bromley Road
Beckenham BR3 5JE
E info@ksapa.co.uk
W www.ksapa.co.uk

LAINE THEATRE ARTS T 01372 724648
The Studios, East Street
Epsom, Surrey KT17 1HH
F 01372 723775
E info@laine-theatre-arts.co.uk
W www.laine-theatre-arts.co.uk

city lit

exceptional, affordable, vocational training

Approximately 500 part-time courses for adults available ranging from beginners to professionals.

Call the Drama, dance and speech department on **020 7492 2542** or e-mail: **drama@citylit.ac.uk**

Request a course guide at: **www.citylit.ac.uk**

- Professional Acting Diploma (2 year)
- Foundation and Access Acting courses
- Acting and Dance classes
- Agent and Casting Directors Master-classes
- Method and Meisner classes
- TV Presenting, Radio, Voice-over and Screen Acting
- Story-telling, Stand-up Comedy, Performing Magic
- Weekend workshops
- Technical Theatre Skills (Foundation and Rep Company Crew)
- Stage fighting - Beginners and Advanced classes
- Musical Theatre etc.

drama | uk recognised

LAMDA
See DRAMA SCHOOLS: DRAMA UK

LAMONT DRAMA SCHOOL & CASTING AGENCY   T 07736 387543
Contact: Diane Lamont. Acting Skills. Audition Technique. Coaching. Part-time Lessons
2 Harewood Avenue, Ainsdale
Merseyside PR8 2PH
E diane@lamontcasting.co.uk
W www.lamontcasting.co.uk

LAURIE, Rona   T 020 7262 4909
Audition Coach. Public Speaking. Voice & Speech Technique
Flat 1, 21 New Quebec Street
London W1H 7SA

LEAN, David Lawson BA Hons PGCE   T 01932 230273
Acting Tuition for Children. LAMDA Exams. Licensed Chaperone
72 Shaw Drive, Walton-on-Thames
Surrey KT12 2LS
E dlawsonlean@aol.com
W www.davidlawsonlean.com

LEE, Steven   T 07771 665582
Performance Pianist & Piano Teacher
80 Kimberley Road, Southbourne
Bournemouth, Dorset BH6 5BY
E stevenleepianist@yahoo.com

LEE THEATRE SCHOOL THE   T 01268 793090
Office: 48 Brook Road
Benfleet, Essex SS7 5JF
E lynn.theatre@gmail.com
W www.poultonlee.com

LESLIE, Maeve   T 020 7834 4912
Classical & Musicals. Presentations. Singing. Voice Production
60 Warwick Square
London SW1V 2AL

LEVENTON, Patricia BA Hons   T 020 7624 5661
Audition & Dialect Coach. RP, Irish, American etc. Sight Reading. Drama School Entry
113 Broadhurst Gardens
West Hampstead
London NW6 3BJ
T 07703 341062
E patricia@lites2000.com

LHK YOUTH THEATRE COMPANY   T 01744 808907
6-18 yrs
20 Maltby Close
St Helens WA9 5GJ
E info@lhkproductions.co.uk
W www.lhkyouththeatre.co.uk

LIPTON, Rick   T 07961 445247
Dialect/Accent Coaching
14 Lock Road
Richmond
Surrey TW10 7LH
E info@ricklipton.com
W www.ricklipton.com

LIR, NATIONAL ACADEMY OF DRAMATIC ART THE   T 00 353 1 896 2559
Trinity Technology and Enterprise Campus
Pearse Street, Dublin 2
E info@thelir.ie
W www.thelir.ie

LITTLE ACTORS THEATRE CLUB LIVERPOOL   T 0151 336 4302
Community Stage School for Children. Dance. Drama. Singing
c/o 9 Carlton Close
Parkgate, Neston
Cheshire CH64 6TD
E mail@littleactorstheatre.com
W www.littleactorstheatre.com

LITTLE ACTORS THEATRE
CLUB NESTON T 0151 336 4302
Dance, Drama & Singing Training (2-11 yrs)
9 Carlton Close, Parkgate
Neston, Cheshire CH64 6TD
E mail@littleactorstheatre.com
W www.littleactorstheatre.com

LITTLE ALLSTARS CASTING
DRAMA SCHOOL T 0161 702 8257
Children & Young Performers
T 07584 992429
E michelleactress@me.com
W www.littleallstars.co.uk

LITTLE SHAKESPEARE
THEATRE SCHOOL T 07724 937331
*Classes, Workshops, Shakespearean Performances &
Training for Young Actors led by Professional Actors*
34 Campbell Road, Longniddry
East Lothian EH32 0NP
E michelle@littleshakespearetheatreschool.co.uk
W www.littleshakespearetheatreschool.co.uk

LIVERPOOL INSTITUTE FOR PERFORMING
ARTS THE
See DRAMA SCHOOLS: DRAMA UK

LLOYD, Gabrielle T 020 8946 4042
*Audition Technique. Drama School Entrance. LAMDA
Exams. Private Acting Classes. Public Speaking.
Vocal Coaching*
Based in South West London
E gubilloyd@hotmail.com

LOCATION TUTORS
NATIONWIDE T 020 7978 8898
*Fully Qualified & Experienced Teachers Working with
Children on Film Sets & Covering all Key Stages of
National Curriculum*
16 Poplar Walk, Herne Hill, London SE24 0BU
T 07806 887471 (Text Messages)
E locationtutorsnationwide@gmail.com
W www.locationtutors.co.uk

LONDON ACTORS WORKSHOP T 07748 846294
Workshop Studio based in Endell Street, Covent Garden
Enquiries: 29B Battersea Rise, London SW11 1HG
E info@londonactorsworkshop.co.uk
W www.londonactorsworkshop.co.uk

LONDON INTERNATIONAL SCHOOL OF
PERFORMING ARTS T 020 8215 3390
Bridge House, 3 Mills Studios
Three Mill Lane, London E3 3DU
F 020 8215 3392
E welcome@lispa.co.uk
W www.lispa.co.uk

LONDON LANGUAGE
TRAINING T 07941 468639
*English Language Coaching for Overseas Actors Looking
to Improve Fluency, Pronunciation & Intonation. All
Courses Taught by English Language Teacher, Trainer &
Author Luke Vyner*
E luke@londonlanguagetraining.co.uk
W www.londonlanguagetraining.co.uk

LONDON REPERTORY
COMPANY ACADEMY T/F 020 7258 1944
PO Box 59385, London NW8 1HL
E academy@londonrepertorycompany.com
W www.londonrepertorycompany.com

LONDON SCHOOL OF
DRAMATIC ART T 020 7581 6100
*Foundation & Advanced Diplomas in Acting (full &
part-time). Drama School (over 18 yrs). Short Summer
Courses*
4 Bute Street, South Kensington
London SW7 3EX
E enquiries@lsda-acting.com
W www.lsda-acting.com

LONDON SCHOOL OF
MUSICAL THEATRE T 020 7407 4455
83 Borough Road, London SE1 1DN
E info@lsmt.co.uk

LONDON SCHOOL OF PERFORMING
ARTS PRACTICES T 07852 348144
*Western Tradition of Dramatic Practices. Ancient
Performance Techniques*
9 Hurley Court, 215 Mitcham Road
London SW17 9DE
E info@lspap.com
W www.lspap.com

LONDON STUDIO CENTRE T 020 7837 7741
*Courses in Theatre Dance, 3 yrs, full-time, BA. Saturday
Classes & Summer Courses*
artsdepot, 5 Nether Street
Tally Ho Corner
North Finchley, London N12 0GA
F 020 7837 3248
E info@londonstudiocentre.org
W www.londonstudiocentre.org

LONG OVERDUE THEATRE
SCHOOL THE T 0845 8382994
16 Butterfield Drive, Amesbury
Wiltshire SP4 7SJ
E stefpearmain@hotmail.com
W www.tlots.co.uk

LONGMORE, Wyllie T 0161 264 0089
Acting Techniques. Voice & Speech. Presentation Skills.
Based in Manchester
E info@wyllielongmore.co.uk
W www.wyllielongmore.co.uk

MACKINNON, Alison T 07973 562132
Accent. Audition Preparation. Presentation. Voice
Based in London SE6
E alimac810@gmail.com

MAD RED THEATRE SCHOOL AT THE
MADDERMARKET THEATRE,
NORWICH T 01603 628600
*Contact: Jen Dewsbury. Courses: Youth Theatre, 1
term, part-time. Adult Evening Classes, 1 term, part-time.
Open Stagers (55 yrs), 1 term, part-time. Youth Summer
School, 1 week Intensive, full-time. Acting Workshops.
Drama School (over 18 yrs). Drama School Preparation.
Private Acting Classes. Stage School for Children*
Maddermarket Theatre, St John's Alley
Norwich NR2 1DR
F 01603 661357
E jenny.dewsbury@maddermarket.org
W www.mad-red.co.uk

MANCHESTER SCHOOL
OF ACTING T/F 0161 238 8900
14-32 Hewitt Street, Manchester M15 4GB
E info@manchesterschoolofacting.co.uk
W www.manchesterschoolofacting.co.uk

MANCHESTER SCHOOL OF THEATRE AT MANCHESTER METROPOLITAN UNIVERSITY
See DRAMA SCHOOLS: DRAMA UK

MARLOW, Chris T 07792 309992
Voice & Speech Teacher
RDDC, 52 Bridleway
Waterfoot, Rossendale
Lancashire BB4 9DS
E rddc@btinternet.com
W www.rddc.co.uk

MARLOW, Jean LGSM T 020 8450 0371
32 Exeter Road
London NW2 4SB

MARPLE DRAMA T 07874 216681
Drama Workshops & Acting Classes for Children & Adults
7 Ridge Road, Marple
Cheshire SK6 7HL
E enquiries@marpledrama.com
W www.marpledrama.com

MARTIN, Liza GRSM GRSM (Recital) ARMCM (Singing & Piano) T 020 8348 0346
Piano Accompanist. Singing Tuition

MARTIN, Mandi SINGING TECHNIQUE T 020 8950 7525
Previously at London Studio Centre, Bodywork & Millennium Performing Arts. Currently Available for Private Lessons
T 07811 758656
E mandi.martin@sky.com

MARTONE, Sergio T 07742 148418
Acting
14 Netherhall Gardens, Hampstead
London NW3 5TQ
E sergiomartone@mac.com

MASTERS PERFORMING ARTS COLLEGE LTD T 01268 777351
Performing Arts Course
Arterial Road, Rayleigh
Essex SS6 7UQ
E info@mastersperformingarts.co.uk

McDAID, Marj T 07815 993203
1 Chesholm Road
Stoke Newington
London N16 0DP
E marjmcdaid@hotmail.com
W www.voicings.co.uk

McDONAGH, Melanie MANAGEMENT (ACADEMY OF PERFORMING ARTS & CASTING AGENCY) T 07909 831409
14 Apple Tree Way, Oswaldtwistle
Accrington, Lancashire BB5 0FB
T 01254 392560
E mcdonaghmgt@aol.com
W www.mcdonaghmanagement.co.uk

McKEAND, Ian T 07768 960530
Audition Technique. Drama School Entry
Based in Lincoln
E ian.mckeand@ntlworld.com
W http://homepage.ntlworld.com/ian.mckeand1

McKELLAN, Martin T 07973 437237
Acting Workshops. Dialect/Accent Coaching. Private Acting Classes. Vocal Coaching
Covent Garden, London WC2H 9PA
E dialectandvoice@yahoo.co.uk

MELAINEY, John
THE CASTING COACH T 07952 232255
Casting Technique. Sight Reading. Coaching. Audition Coaching. Audition on Camera Service
49 Herbert Road, Wimbledon
London SW19 3SQ
E john@johnmelainey.com
W www.121auditioncoach.com

MELBOURNE ACTING STUDIO:
LONDON T 07752 948351
Contact: Bruce Alexander
University House, 55 East Road
London N1 6AH
E info@melbourneactingstudio.com
W www.melbourneactingstudio.co.uk

MELLECK, Lydia T 020 7794 8845
Pianist & Coach for Auditions & Repertoire, RADA, Mountview. Accompanist. Singing for Beginners. Vocal Coaching. Workshops on Sondheim
10 Burgess Park Mansions, London NW6 1DP
E lyd.muse@yahoo.co.uk

MGA ACADEMY OF
PERFORMING ARTS THE T 0131 466 9392
207 Balgreen Road, Edinburgh EH11 2RZ
E info@themgaacademy.com
W www.themgaacademy.com

MICHAELJOHN'S
ACTING ACADEMY T 020 3463 8492
In association with Khando Entertainment. Contact: Ajay Nayyar
E info@khandoentertainment.com

MICHEL, Hilary ARCM T 020 8343 7243
Singing Teacher & Vocal Coach. Audition Songs. Accompanist. Piano, Recorder & Theory Teacher
21 Southway, Totteridge
London N20 8EB
T 07775 780182
E hilarymich@optimamail.co.uk

MILLER, Robin T 07957 627677
Audition Coaching. Dialect/Accent Coaching
Based in St Margarets/Twickenham
E robinjenni@hotmail.com

MORE DRAMATIC THEATRE
COMPANY T 07869 130735
Acting, Dancing & Musical Theatre Classes
37 Carthall Road, Coleraine BT51 3LP
E info@moredrama.co.uk
W www.moredrama.co.uk

MORLEY COLLEGE T 020 7450 1889
Acting, Writing & Public Speaking Courses for all levels. Accredited Courses for Vocational Study. Courses: Acting. Audition Workshops. Directing. Drama Theory. Improvisation. Mime. Physical Theatre. Presentation Skills. Public Speaking. Scriptwriting. Shakespeare. Stand-up
61 Westminster Bridge Road, London SE1 7HT
E drama@morleycollege.ac.uk
W www.morleycollege.ac.uk

MORRISON, Elspeth T 07790 919870
Accent & Dialect Coach
E elsp.morrison@talk21.com

MORRISON, J Stuart MA Voice Studies
(RCSSD) FVCM (TD)
(Hons) FIfL FRSA T 020 3651 2100
Voice, Speech & Acting Coach
24 Deans Walk, Coulsdon
Surrey CR5 1HR
T 07825 618596
E stuartvoicecoach@yahoo.co.uk
W www.voiceandspeechtrainer.com

MOTHERWELL COLLEGE/NEW COLLEGE,
LANCASHIRE MOTHERWELL
CAMPUS T 01698 232323
Courses: Acting. Musical Theatre. HNC/D, BA Hons
1 Enterprise Way
Motherwell ML1 2TX
E information@newcollegelancashiremotherwellcampus.co.uk
W www.motherwell.co.uk

MOUNTVIEW ACADEMY OF THEATRE ARTS
See DRAMA SCHOOLS: DRAMA UK

MTA THE T 020 8882 8181
T 07904 987493
E info@themta.co.uk
W www.themta.co.uk

MURRAY, Barbara LGSM LALAM T 01923 823182
129 Northwood Way, Northwood
Middlesex HA6 1RF
E barbarahalliwell@gmail.com

MUSICAL KIDZ COMPANY THE T 07989 353673
Spires Meade, 4 Bridleways
Wendover, Bucks HP22 6DN
F 01296 623696
E themusicalkidz@aol.com
W www.themusicalkidz.co.uk

MUSICAL THEATRE AUDITIONS
Information, Tips & Resources for Musical Theatre Auditions
Based in London
E hello@musicaltheatreauditions.info
W www.musicaltheatreauditions.info

NATHENSON, Zoë T 07956 833850
Audition Technique. Film Acting. Sight Reading. Group Classes
E zoe.act@btinternet.com
W www.zoenathenson.com

NEIL, Andrew T 07979 843984
Audition Technique. Private Acting Classes. Public Speaking
2 Howley Place, London W2 1XA
E andrewneil@talktalk.net

NEO - NUNCHAKU EXERCISE
ORGANISATION T 020 8337 6181
Fight Scene Staging, Planning & Training. Training in the use of Nunchaku vs Nunchaku & Other Weapons. Venue based in Kingston, London
Mail to: 202 Bridgewood Road
Worcester Park
Sutton, Surrey KT4 8XU
E neo@neo-nunchaku.co.uk
W www.neo-nunchaku.co.uk

NEW LONDON PERFORMING ARTS CENTRE   T 020 8444 4544
Courses in Performing Arts (3-19 yrs). Dance. Drama. Singing. Instruments. GCSE/A-Level Courses, LAMDA, ISTD & RAD. Holiday Workshops. Specialist Professional Preparation Classes
76 St James Lane, Muswell Hill
London N10 3RD
E info@nlpac.co.uk
W www.nlpac.co.uk

NEWNHAM, Caryll   T 01255 670973
Singing Teacher
69 Old Road, Frinton
Essex CO13 9BX
T 07976 635745
E caryllnewnham@gmail.com

NOBLE, Penny PSYCHOTHERAPY   T 07506 579895
Character-Centred Counselling & Training. Character Development. Performance Support. Safe Emotion Memory Work. Script Work. Self-esteem & Confidence
8 Shaftesbury Gardens, Victoria Road
North Acton, London NW10 6LJ
E pennynobletherapy@googlemail.com
W www.pennynoblepsychotherapy.com

NORTHERN: DRAMA ACTING SCHOOL   T 07787 311270
Led by Jo Adamson-Parker
c/o The Carriageworks Theatre
Leeds LS1
E ndas@northerndrama.co.uk

NORTHERN ACADEMY OF PERFORMING ARTS   T 01482 310690
Anlaby Road, Hull HU1 2PD
F 01482 212280
E napa@northernacademy.org.uk
W www.northernacademy.org.uk

NORTHERN FILM & DRAMA   T 01977 681949
Acting Workshops. Television Audition Technique. Drama School. On Location Filming. Film & Television Training. Improvisation. Private Acting Classes. Stage School for Children
The Studio, 21 Low Street
South Milford, Leeds LS25 5AR
E info@northernfilmanddrama.com
W www.northernfilmanddrama.com

NPAS @ THE STUDIOS   T/F 00 353 1 8944660
NPAS The Factory, 35A Darrow Street
Dublin 4, Ireland
E info@npas.ie
W www.npas.ie

O.J. SONUS   T 020 8963 0702
Voice Over Workshops. Voicereel Production with Professional Coaching Available
14-15 Main Drive
East Lane Business Park
Wembley HA9 7NA
T 07929 859401
E info@ojsonus.com
W www.ojsonus.com

OLLERENSHAW, Maggie BA (Hons) Dip Ed   T 020 7286 1126
Acting Workshops. Audition Technique. Career Guidance. Private Acting. Television & Theatre Coaching
151D Shirland Road, London W9 2EP
T 07860 492699
E maggieoll@aol.com

OLSON, Lise   T 0121 331 7220
Acting through Song. American Accents. Vocal Coaching. Working with Text
c/o Birmingham School of Acting
Millennium Point
Curzon Street, Birmingham B4 7XG
E lise.olson@bcu.ac.uk

OMOBONI, Lino　　　　**T/F** 020 8741 2038
Private Acting Classes
182 Riverside Gardens, London W6 9LQ
T 07525 187468
E bluewand@btinternet.com

OPEN VOICE　　　　**T** 07704 704930
Contact: Catherine Owen. Auditions. Consultancy.
Personal Presentations
9 Bellsmains
Gorebridge, Near Edinburgh EH23 4QD
E catherineowenopenvoice@gmail.com

ORAM, Daron　　　　**T** 07905 332497
Voice, Text & Accent Coach. Teaches on the Actor
Training & Voice Teacher Training Courses at the Royal
Central School of Speech & Drama. Also Coached for
the RSC, West End & National Tours. A Designated
Linklater Voice Teacher
E darono@yahoo.com

OSBORNE HUGHES, John　　　　**T** 020 8653 7735
Spiritual Psychology of Acting
Miracle Tree Productions Training Department
51 Church Road, London SE19 2TE
T 07801 950916
E info@miracletreeproductions.com
W www.spiritualpsychologyofacting.com

OSCARS THEATRE ACADEMY　　　　**T** 01484 545519
Contact: Paula Danholm
Oscars Management, Spring Bank House
1 Spring Bank, New North Road
Huddersfield, West Yorkshire HD1 5NR
E management@oscarsacademy.co.uk

OXFORD SCHOOL OF DRAMA THE
See DRAMA SCHOOLS: DRAMA UK

PALMER, Jackie
STAGE SCHOOL　　　　**T** 01494 510597
30 Daws Hill Lane, High Wycombe
Bucks HP11 1PW
F 01494 510479
E info@jackiepalmerstageschool.co.uk
W www.jackiepalmerstageschool.co.uk

PARKES, Frances MA AGSM　　　　**T/F** 020 8542 2777
Contact: Frances Parkes, Sarah Upson. Dialect/Accent
Coaching & Script Coach. Interview Skills for Castings.
Presenting. Private Acting Classes. Public Speaking.
Speak English Clearly Programme for Actors with English
as a Second Language
Suite 5, 3rd Floor, 1 Harley Street
London W1G 9QD
T 01782 827222 (Upson Edwards)
E frances@maxyourvoice.com
W www.maxyourvoice.com

PERFORMANCE
BUSINESS THE　　　　**T** 01932 888885
78 Oatlands Drive, Weybridge
Surrey KT13 9HT
E michael@theperformance.biz
W www.theperformance.biz

PERFORMANCE
FACTORY STAGE SCHOOL THE　　　　**T** 01792 701570
c/o 26 Pine Crescent, Morriston
Swansea SA6 6AR
E info@tpfwales.com
W www.tpfwales.com

PERFORMANCE FREQUENCY　　　　**T** 07876 298613
Vocal Training
9 Tennyson Road
Stoke, Coventry
West Midlands CV2 5HX
E info@performancefrequency.com
W www.performancefrequency.com

PERFORMANCE PREPARATION
ACADEMY (PPA)　　　　**T** 01483 459080
Unit 5, Riverside Business Centre
Walnut Tree Close
Guildford, Surrey GU1 4UG
E enquiries@ppaacademy.co.uk
W www.ppacademy.co.uk

PERFORMERS COLLEGE　　　　**T** 01375 672053
Contact: Brian Rogers, Susan Stephens
Southend Road, Corringham
Essex SS17 8JT
F 01375 672353
E lesley@performerscollege.co.uk
W www.performerscollege.co.uk

PERFORMERS
THEATRE SCHOOL　　　　**T** 0151 708 4000
Classes in Drama, Dance & Singing. Stage School for
Children. Holiday & Summer Schools
8 Vernon Street
Liverpool L2 2AY
E info@performerstheatre.co.uk
W www.performerstheatre.co.uk

PERFORMERZONE
(BRIGHTON & LONDON)　　　　**T** 07973 518643
Contact: William Pool (ARCM). Singing. Tuition.
Workshops
33A Osmond Road, Hove
East Sussex BN3 1TD
E pool.william@gmail.com
W www.performerzone.co.uk

PG ACTING COACH　　　　**T** 07786 512841
One-to-one Tuition & Meisner Training in Small Groups
with Qualified Acting Coach based in Altrincham, South
Manchester & Leek, North Staffordshire. Courses
arranged elsewhere on request
E coaching@pruegillett.com
W www.pruegillett.com/coaching

POLLYANNA TRAINING
THEATRE　　　　**T** 020 7481 1911
Raine House, Raine Street
London E1W 3RL
T 07801 884837
E pollyannamanagement@gmail.com
W www.pollyannatheatre.org

POLYDOROU, Anna MA　　　　**T** 07833 545292
Vocal Coaching. MA Voice Studies, Royal Central School
of Speech & Drama
147C Fernhead Road
Maida Hill
Queens Park W9 3ED
E annahebe@yahoo.co.uk

POOR SCHOOL　　　　**T** 020 7837 6030
242 Pentonville Road
London N1 9JY
E acting@thepoorschool.com
W www.thepoorschool.com

COURT Theatre Training Company

BA (Hons) Acting
Intensive 2 Year Course

Train for a life in the theatre by working in the theatre...

P.G. Dipl.
• Technical Theatre
• Acting
• Directing

1 Year Courses

Court Theatre Training Company, The Courtyard Theatre, Bowling Green Walk, 40 Pitfield St, London N1 6EU
t/f: 020 7739 6868   e: info@courttheatretraining.org.uk   www.courttheatretraining.org.uk

POPPIES YOUTH THEATRE & AGENCY   T 07795 370678
Stockbrook House
8 King Street
Duffield, Derbyshire DE56 4EU
E poppies09@live.co.uk
W www.poppies-yta.co.uk

PRICE, Janis R.   T 07977 630829
Voice Coach
E janis@janisprice.fsnet.co.uk

QUEEN MARGARET UNIVERSITY, EDINBURGH   T 0131 474 0000
Queen Margaret University Drive
Musselburgh, East Lothian EH21 6UU
F 0131 474 0001
E admissions@qmu.ac.uk
W www.qmu.ac.uk

QUESTORS THEATRE EALING THE   T 020 8567 0011
12 Mattock Lane
London W5 5BQ
E academy@questors.org.uk
W www.questors.org.uk

RAPIERSHARP (STAGE & SCREEN COMBAT)   T 07710 763735
Performance Combat & Fight Directing Services for Stage, Film & Television. Specialised Weapons & Unarmed Combat Training leading to British Academy of Dramatic Combat (BADC) qualifications. Training & Workshops for all Levels. Consultancy & Weapon Hire
E rapiersharp@hotmail.com
W www.rapiersharp.com

RAZZAMATAZ THEATRE SCHOOLS   T 01228 550129
2nd Floor, Atlas Works, Nelson Street
Denton Holme, Carlisle CA2 5NB
E franchise@razzamataz.co.uk
W www.razzamataz.co.uk

RC-ANNIE LTD   T 020 8123 5936
Fight Directing Services. Stage & Screen Combat Training. Theatrical Blood Supplies
34 Pullman Place
London SE9 6EG
E info@rc-annie.com
W www.rc-annie.com

REACT ACADEMY OF THEATRE ARTS   T 01254 883692
Specialist Training in Drama, Musical Theatre, Dance & Music Production
c/o The Civic Arts Centre, Union Road
Oswaldtwistle, Lancashire BB5 3HZ
E info@reactacademy.co.uk
W www.reactacademy.co.uk

REALLY YOUTHFUL THEATRE COMPANY THE   T/F 01926 494533
Audition Technique. LAMDA/Trinity Guildhall. Arts Award. Private Acting Classes (Children & Adults). Stage School for Children. Summer School
17 West End Court, Crompton Street
Warwick, Warwickshire CV34 6NA
T 07909 083939
E info@rytc.co.uk
W www.rytc.co.uk

REBEL SCHOOL OF THEATRE ARTS & CASTING AGENCY LTD   T 01484 603736
Based in Leeds & Huddersfield
PO Box 169, Huddersfield HD8 1BE
T 07808 803637
E sue@rebelschool.co.uk
W www.rebelschool.co.uk

REDROOFS THEATRE SCHOOL   T 01628 674092
26 Bath Road, Maidenhead, Berkshire SL6 4JT
T 07531 355835
E sam@redroofs.co.uk
W www.redroofs.co.uk

REP COLLEGE THE   T 0118 942 1144
17 St Mary's Avenue, Purley on Thames, Berks RG8 8BJ
E tudor@repcollege.co.uk
W www.repcollege.co.uk

RICHMOND DRAMA SCHOOL   T 020 8891 5907 ext 4018
Contact: Dr Fern-Chantele Carter (Director of Courses). Acting Workshops. Audition Technique. Drama School (over 18 yrs). Drama School Preparation. Public Speaking. Courses: 1 yr Foundation. Access to HE Drama, BTEC Ext Cert L2 Performing Arts (Acting), Richmond Drama School Advanced Certificate, all 1 yr, part-time
Richmond Adult & Community College, Parkshot
Richmond, Surrey TW9 2RE
E fern-chantelecarter@racc.ac.uk

**RIDGEWAY STUDIOS PERFORMING
ARTS COLLEGE**   T 01992 633775
Office: 106 Hawkshead Road
Potters Bar
Hertfordshire EN6 1NG
E info@ridgewaystudios.co.uk
W www.ridgewaystudios.co.uk

RISING STARS DRAMA SCHOOL   T 0845 2570127
*Contact: Jessica Andrews. Acting Workshops.
Audition Technique. Filming Techniques. Films Made.
Improvisation. LAMDA Examinations*
10 Orchard Way, Measham
Derbyshire DE12 7JZ
E info@risingstarsdramaschool.co.uk
W www.risingstarsdramaschool.co.uk

ROSCH, Philip   T 020 8731 6686
*Contact: Philip Rosch. Audition Coaching for Drama UK
Schools. Audition Technique. Drama School Preparation.
Improvisation. Private Acting Classes*
53 West Heath Court
London NW11 7RG
E philiproschactor@gmail.com
W www.actingauditionsuccess.co.uk

ROSE BRUFORD COLLEGE
See DRAMA SCHOOLS: DRAMA UK

**ROSS, David ACTING
ACADEMY THE**   T 07957 862317
*Contact: David Ross. Acting Workshops. Audition
Technique. Dialect/Accent Coaching. Drama School
Preparation. Improvisation. Stage School for Children.
Vocal Coaching*
8 Farrier Close, Sale
Cheshire M33 2ZL
E info@davidrossacting.com
W www.davidrossacting.com

**ROSSENDALE DANCE &
DRAMA CENTRE**   T 01706 211161
*Contact: Chris Marlow. LAMDA LCM TCL Grade &
Diploma Courses & Exams. Acting Workshops. Audition
Technique. Dancing. Dialect/Accent Coaching. Drama
School (over 18 yrs). Elocution. Improvisation. Private
Acting Classes. Public Speaking. Stage School for
Children. Vocal Coaching*
52 Bridleway, Waterfoot
Rossendale, Lancs BB4 9DS
E rddc@btinternet.com

ROYAL ACADEMY OF DRAMATIC ART
See DRAMA SCHOOLS: DRAMA UK

ROYAL ACADEMY OF MUSIC   T 020 7873 7483
Musical Theatre Department
Marylebone Road
London NW1 5HT
E mth@ram.ac.uk
W www.ram.ac.uk/mth

**ROYAL CENTRAL SCHOOL OF SPEECH &
DRAMA THE**
See DRAMA SCHOOLS: DRAMA UK

**ROYAL CONSERVATOIRE
OF SCOTLAND**   T 0141 332 4101
100 Renfrew Street
Glasgow G2 3DB
E registry@rcs.ac.uk
W www.rcs.ac.uk

**ROYAL WELSH COLLEGE
OF MUSIC & DRAMA**   T 029 2039 1361
Drama Department, Castle Grounds
Cathays Park, Cardiff CF10 3ER
F 029 2039 1301
E admissions@rwcmd.ac.uk
W www.rwcmd.ac.uk

RUMBELOW, Sam   T 020 7622 9742
*Acting & Method Acting Coach. Classes held at
Brick Lane E1*
84 Union Road, London SW4 6JU
E main@methodacting.co.uk
W www.methodacting.co.uk

SALES, Stephanie   T 020 8995 9127
61 Brookfield Road, Chiswick
London W4 1DF
E steph@stephaniesales.co.uk
W www.stephaniesales.co.uk/dramacoaching

SAMPSON PILATES   T 01328 712116
*Pilates Teacher Training (Active IQ Level 3 - Cert).
Physical Coaching. Specialing in Physical Rehabilitation*
7A Park Road, Holkham
Wells-next-the-Sea, Norfolk NR23 1RG
E info@sampsonpilates.com
W www.sampsonpilates.com

SAMUELS, Marianne   T 07974 203001
Voice, Accents, Text & Public Speaking
Based in Nottingham
E marianne@voice-ms.com
W www.voice-ms.com

**SCALA SCHOOL OF
PERFORMING ARTS**   T 0113 250 6823
*Children & Young Performers. Drama Workshops.
Training for Musical Theatre, Dance, Voice Training &
Group Singing. Stage School & Casting Agency for
Children*
Office: 42 Rufford Avenue, Yeadon
Leeds LS19 7QR
E office@scalakids.com
W www.scalakids.com

SCHER, Anna THEATRE   T 020 8527 7420
St Silas Church, Pentonville
Penton Street, London N1 9UL
E enquiries@nicknightmanagement.com
W www.annaschertheatre.com

SELF TAPING: THE ACTOR'S GUIDE
Illustrated ebook. Advice & Resources for Self Taping
E info@selftaping.com
W www.selftaping.com

**SEMARK, Rebecca
LLAM, LaLAM**   T 07956 850330
*Elocution. Voice & Vocal Coaching. Audition Technique.
Drama School Preparation. LAMDA Exams. Private
Acting Classes & Public Speaking for Children & Adults.
Stage School Entry for Children including Singing*
Based in Epping, Essex
E rebecca@semark.biz
W www.semark.biz

SHAPES IN MOTION   T 07802 709933
*Contact: Sarah Perry. Movement & Acting Coaching.
Workshops. Laban. Yoga*
Based in London
E sarah@shapesinmotion.com
W www.shapesinmotion.com

UNDERGRADUATE & POSTGRADUATE DEGREES

ROYAL CENTRAL
SCHOOL OF SPEECH & DRAMA
UNIVERSITY OF LONDON

W www.cssd.ac.uk/spotlight @CSSDLondon CSSDLondon

SHAW, Phil　　T 020 8715 8943
Actors' Consultancy Service. Acting Workshops. Audition Technique. Drama School Preparation. Private Acting Classes. Vocal Coaching
Suite 476, 2 Old Brompton Road
South Kensington
London SW7 3DQ
E shawcastlond@aol.com

SHENEL, Helena　　T 020 7724 8793
Singing Teacher
205 John Aird Court
London W2 1UX

**SHINE TIME MUSICAL THEATRE
& ACTING**　　T 07880 721689
Contact: Laura Green. Audition Technique. Dancing. Drama School Preparation. Improvisation. LAMDA Acting Solo Examinations. Musical Theatre & Acting Holiday Workshops. Private Acting Classes. Singing. Stage School for Children. Vocal Coaching
Flat 10, Valentine House
Church Road
Guildford
Surrey GU1 4NG
E shinetime@hotmail.co.uk
W www.shinetimeworkshops.com

SHOWSONG ACCOMPANIST　　T 020 8993 2111
163 Gunnersbury Lane
London W3 8LJ

SIMMONS, Ros MA　　T 020 8347 8089
Accents/Dialects. Voice. Auditions. Presentations
The Real Speaking Company
120 Hillfield Avenue
Crouch End
London N8 7DN
T 07957 320572
E info@realspeaking.co.uk
W www.realspeaking.co.uk

SINGER, Sandra ASSOCIATES　　T 01702 331616
LAMDA & ISTD Exams. Acting Workshops. Audition Technique. Dancing. Dialect/Accent Coaching. Part-time Drama School (over 18 yrs). Improvisation. Private Acting Classes. Singing. Stage School for Children. Vocal Coaching
21 Cotswold Road
Westcliff-on-Sea
Essex SS0 8AA
E sandrasingeruk@aol.com
W www.sandrasinger.com

SINGER STAGE SCHOOL　　T 01702 331616
Part-time Vocational Stage School & Summer School. 6-21 yrs. Acting Workshops. Audition Technique. Dancing. Dialect/Accent Coaching for Entry to Drama School (over 18 yrs). Improvisation. ISTD. Private Acting Classes. LAMDA. Singing. Stage School for Children. Member of National Youth Theatre
Office: 21 Cotswold Road
Westcliff-on-Sea
Essex SS0 8AA
E sandrasingeruk@aol.com
W www.sandrasinger.com

SLP COLLEGE　　T 0113 286 8136
5 Chapel Lane
Garforth
Leeds
West Yorkshire LS25 1AG
F 0113 287 4487
E info@slpcollege.co.uk
W www.slpcollege.co.uk

SO-MEDIA　　T 020 8789 7495
Professional Screen Acting Courses. 16+ yrs
7 Knight House
22 Scott Avenue
Putney SW15 3PB
E info@so-media.co.uk
W www.so-media.co.uk

SHAPES IN MOTION

Movement & Acting Coaching
Movement Directing
Motion Capture
Yoga & Laban Tuition

Sarah Perry
+44/0 7802 709 933
sarah@shapesinmotion.com
www.shapesinmotion.com

SOCIETY OF TEACHERS OF SPEECH & DRAMA THE   **T** 01623 627636
Registered Office: 73 Berry Hill Road
Mansfield, Notts NG18 4RU
E ann.k.jones@btinternet.com
W www.stsd.org.uk

SONNETS THEATRE ARTS SCHOOL   **T** 0845 0038910
Thorneycombe, Vernham Dean
Andover, Hampshire SP11 0JY
E sonnetsagency@hotmail.co.uk
W www.sonnets-tas.co.uk

SPEAK EASILY   **T** 020 3174 1316
Voice, Speech & Accent Specialists
E morwenna.rowe@speak-easily.com
W www.speak-easily.com

SPEAKE, Barbara STAGE SCHOOL & AGENCY   **T** 020 8743 1306
Full-time Drama School. Coaches. Part-time School.
Theatrical Agency. Casting Studio
East Acton Lane
London W3 7EG
F 020 8743 2746
E speakekids3@aol.com
W www.barbaraspeake.com

SPEED, Anne-Marie Hon ARAM MA (Voice Studies) CSSD ADVS BA   **T** 07957 272554
Vanguard Estill Practitioner. Accents. Auditions.
Coaching. Vocal Technique for Speaking & Singing
E info@thevoiceexplained.com
W www.thevoiceexplained.com

SPIRITUAL PSYCHOLOGY OF ACTING THE   **T** 020 8653 7735
51 Church Road, London SE19 2TE
E info@spiritualpsychologyofacting.com
W www.spiritualpsychologyofacting.com

SPLITZ THEATRE ARTZ   **T** 01223 880389
5 Cow Lane, Fulbourn
Cambridge CB21 5HB
E clare@splitz-ta.net
W www.splitz-ta.net

SPONTANEITY SHOP THE   **T** 020 7788 4080
85-87 Bayham Street
London NW1 0AG
E info@the-spontaneity-shop.com
W www.the-spontaneity-shop.com

SPYMONKEY   **T** 01273 670282
Unit 7B Level 3N, New England House
New England Street
Brighton, East Sussex BN1 4GH
E education@spymonkey.co.uk
W www.spymonkey.co.uk

STAGE2 YOUTH THEATRE   **T** 07961 018841
Saturdays. Twitter: @Stage2YT
Millennium Point, Curzon Street
Birmingham B4 7XG
E info@stage2.org
W www.stage2.org

STAGE2 YOUTH THEATRE   **T** 07961 018841
Administration: 12 Valentine Road, Kings Heath
Birmingham, West Midlands B14 7AN
E info@stage2.org
W www.stage2.org

STAGE 84 PERFORMING ARTS LTD   **T** 01274 611984
Evening & Weekend Classes & Summer Schools
The Old Fire Station, 29A Town Lane, Idle
Bradford, West Yorkshire BD10 8NT
E info@stage84.com

STAGECOACH THEATRE ARTS   **T** 01932 254333
The Courthouse, Elm Grove
Walton-on-Thames, Surrey KT12 1LZ
F 01932 222894
E mail@stagecoach.co.uk
W www.stagecoach.co.uk

STAGEFIGHT & ECSPC   **T** 07813 308672
138 Wilden Lane, Stourport-on-Severn
Worcestershire DY13 9LP
E info@stagefight.co.uk
W www.stagefight.co.uk

STARLIGHT STAGE SCHOOL   **T** 07581 368677
Holly Road, Thornton Cleveleys
Lancashire FY5 4HH
E charlotte_starlight@hotmail.com
W www.starlight-stageschool.co.uk

STEP ON STAGE ACADEMY OF PERFORMING ARTS   **T** 07973 900196
Contact: Emma-Louise Tinniswood. Stage School
for Children. Acting Workshops & Audition Coaching.
Musical Theatre Courses & Workshops. Acting for Stage
& Screen. Dancing. Singing. Summer School. School
Workshops & Teacher INSET. Courses: GCSE Drama,
1 yr, part-time. LAMDA, 1 term-1 yr, part-time. Acting.
Musical Theatre. Audition Technique. Film Acting. Stage
Make-up. Stage Combat
5 Poulett Gardens, Twickenham
Middlesex TW1 4QS
E info@steponstageacademy.co.uk
W www.steponstageacademy.co.uk

STEPHENSON, Sarah GMusRNCM PGDip RNCM   **T** 020 8425 1225
Vocal Coach. Piano Accompanist. Audition Preparation
8A Edgington Road, Streatham, London SW16 5BS
T 07581 716233
E s.stephenson@ntlworld.com

STINSON, David THEATRE SCHOOL   **T** 07500 701521
Professional Training in Ballet, Jazz, Tap, Street, Acting
& Singing
I-PATH Head Office, 57 Old Compton Street
London W1D 6HP
E info@i-path.biz
W www.davidstinsontheatreschool.com

STINSON STAGE ACADEMY   **T** 020 3714 3393
Located at Arts Ed. Every Sunday. Ballet, Musical
Theatre & Street
1 Brandreth Drive, Giltbrook, Nottingham NG16 2UN
E london@i-path.biz
W www.stinsonstageacademy.com

STIRLING ACADEMY   **T** 01204 848333
Contact: Glen Mortimer. Acting Workshops. Audition
Techniques. Audition Training for Camera. Drama
School. Improvisation. Private Acting Classes. Showreels
490 Halliwell Road, Bolton, Lancashire BL1 8AN
F 0844 4128689
E admin@stirlingacademy.co.uk
W www.stirlingacademy.co.uk

STOCKTON RIVERSIDE COLLEGE T 01642 865400
Further Education & Training
Harvard Avenue, Thornaby
Stockton TS17 6FB
W www.stockton.ac.uk

STOMP! THE SCHOOL OF PERFORMING ARTS T 020 8446 9898
Stage School for Children. Street Dance. Acting & Singing Classes (5-19 yrs). Weekends. Mill Hill Area
62 Sellwood Drive, Barnet
Herts EN5 2RL
E stompschoolnw7@aol.com
W www.stompschool.com

STREET DEFENCE T 07919 350290
Commando Krav Maga Instructor. Screen Combatant
6 Clive Close, Potters Bar
Hertfordshire EN6 2AE
E streetdefence@hotmail.co.uk
W www.streetdefenceuk.com

STREETON, Jane T 07968 788857
Singing Teacher, RADA. Author of 'Singing on Stage: An Actor's Guide'
24 Richmond Road, Leytonstone
London E11 4BA
E janestreetonsop@aol.com
W www.singingonstage.co.uk

STUDIOS THE T 01628 777853
Office: 47 Furze Platt Road
Maidenhead SL6 7NF
E julie.fox@virgin.net

SUPERSTARS IN THE MAKING T 07531 814820
St John's Hall, Beryl Road
Barry CF62 8DN
E director@superstarsinthemaking.com
W www.superstarsinthemaking.com

TALENTED KIDS PERFORMING ARTS SCHOOL & MVW TALENT AGENCY T/F 00 353 45 485464
Contact: Maureen V. Ward. Agency. Acting Workshops. Audition Technique. Dance. Drama School (over 18 yrs). Elocution. Improvisation. Modelling. Musical Theatre. Singing. Stage School for Children. Vocal Coaching
23 Burrow Manor, Calverstown
Kilcullen, Co. Kildare, Ireland
T 00 353 87 2480348
E talentedkids@hotmail.com
W www.talentedkidsireland.com

THAT'S A WRAP ACTING SCHOOL FOR CHILDREN & TEENAGERS T 01753 650951
Acting Workshops. Audition Technique. Improvisation
Actors Studio, Admin Building, Pinewood Studios
Pinewood Road, Iver Heath, Bucks SL0 0NH
E info@actorsstudio.co.uk
W www.actorsstudio.co.uk

THEATRETRAIN T 01327 300498
Performing Arts for 6-18 yrs. Annual Large Scale Productions. Open to All. No Experience Required
Orchard Studio, PO Box 42
Hitchin, Herts SG4 8FS
E admin@theatretrain.co.uk
W www.theatretrain.co.uk

THREE4ALL THEATRE COMPANY T 01227 276217
57 Millstrood Road, Whitstable, Kent CT5 1QF
E alison@three4all.org
W www.three4all.org/dramatraining.php

TIP TOE STAGE SCHOOL T 07940 521864
Dance, Drama, Singing & Performing Arts part-time Training
For correspondence only: 65 North Road
South Ockendon, Essex RM15 6QH
E julie@tiptoestageschool.co.uk
W www.tiptoestageschool.co.uk

TO BE OR NOT TO BE   **T** 07958 996227
Contact: Anthony Barnett. LAMDA Exams. Showreels.
Theatre/Audition Pieces. Television/Film Acting
Technique
40 Gayton Road, King's Lynn, Norfolk PE30 4EL
E tony@tobeornottobe.org.uk
W www.showreels.org.uk

TODD, Paul   **T** 020 7229 9776
Singing. Audition Technique. Acting. Percussion.
Improvisation. Vocal Coaching. Any age, any level
3 Rosehart Mews, London W11 3JN
T 07813 985092
E paultodd@talk21.com

TOMORROW'S TALENT   **T** 01245 690080
Theatre School & Agency for Young Performers. Acting.
Singing. Dance. Musical Theatre. Audition Preparation.
Drama School Coaching
Based in Chelmsford, Essex
E mail@tomorrowstalent.co.uk
W www.tomorrowstalent.co.uk

TOP HAT STAGE &
SCREEN SCHOOL   **T/F** 01727 812666
Contact: Warren Bacci. Acting Workshops. Dancing.
Singing. Stage School for Children. Courses: School
Term Weekends, part-time. Easter & Summer Holidays,
part-time. Youth Theatre, Weeknights, part-time.
Schools in Potters Bar, Welwyn, Stevenage, St Albans,
Harpenden & Surrey
PO Box 860, St Albans
Herts AL1 9BR
E admin@tophatstageschool.co.uk
W www.tophatstageschool.co.uk

TRING PARK SCHOOL
FOR THE PERFORMING ARTS   **T** 01442 824255
Contact: Adelia Wood-Smith. Courses: Dance, 3 yrs,
full-time. Qualification: Diploma in Dance. Drama, 2 yrs,
full-time. Musical Theatre, 2 yrs, full-time. Commercial
Music, 2 yrs, full-time. Audition Technique, Drama
School Preparation. Improvisation. Singing. Summer
School. Vocal Coaching
Tring Park, Tring, Hertfordshire HP23 5LX
E info@tringpark.com
W www.tringpark.com

TROLLOPE, Ann   **T** 07943 816276
Voice/Acting Coach
Solihull, West Midlands
E ann-t@uwclub.net

TROTTER, William
BA MA PGDVS   **T/F** 020 8459 7594
25 Thanet Lodge, Mapesbury Road
London NW2 4JA
T 07946 586719
E william.trotter@ukspeech.co.uk
W www.ukspeech.co.uk

TUCKER, John   **T** 07903 269409
Voice Coach
503 Mountjoy House, Barbican, London EC2Y 8BP
E mail@john-tucker.com
W www.john-tucker.com

TWICKENHAM
THEATRE WORKSHOP   **T** 020 8898 5882
Katie Abbott LTCL
29 Campbell Road, Twickenham, Middlesex TW2 5BY
E frabbt@aol.com

UK DRAMA EDUCATION   **T** 0118 958 9330
LAMDA Examinations
2 Baron Court, Western Elms Avenue
Reading, Berks RG30 2BP
E ukdramaeducation@live.co.uk

URQUHART, Moray   **T** 020 7731 3419
Private Coaching for Auditions, Schools, Showbiz etc
61 Parkview Court, London SW6 3LL
E nmuphelps@yahoo.co.uk

VALLÉ ACADEMY OF
PERFORMING ARTS   **T** 01992 622862
The Vallé Academy Studios
Wilton House, Delamare Road, Cheshunt, Herts EN8 9SG
F 01992 622868
E enquiries@valleacademy.co.uk
W www.valleacademy.co.uk

VERNON ACTING METHOD   **T** 0161 773 7670
Screen Acting
20 Ruskin Road, Manchester M25 9GL
E info@vernonactingmethod.co.uk
W www.vernonactingmethod.co.uk

VERRALL, Charles   **T** 020 7833 1971
19 Matilda Street, London N1 0LA
E info@charlesverrall.com
W www.learntoact.co.uk

VIVIAN, Michael   **T** 020 8876 2073
Acting Workshops. Audition Technique. Improvisation.
Private Acting Classes. Public Speaking
15 Meredyth Road, Barnes, London SW13 0DS
T 07958 903911
E vivcalling@aol.com

VOCAL CONFIDENCE
Contact: Alix Longman. Voice & Acting Technique.
All Vocal Problems Attended. Audition Preparation
Presentation. Accent & Dialect Coaching
E alix@vocalconfidence.com
W www.vocalconfidence.com

VOICE & DIALECT COACH   **T** 07723 620728
Contact: Caroline Hetherington
7 Dodcott Barns, Burleydam, Whitchurch SY13 4BQ
E voice@carohetherington.co.uk
W www.carohetherington.co.uk

VOICE MASTER
INTERNATIONAL   **T** 020 8455 1666
Creators of the Hudson Voice Technique: Unique
Technique for Voiceovers, Actors & Autocue
88 Erskine Hill, London NW11 6HR
T 07921 210400
E info@voicemaster-international.com
W www.voicemaster.co.uk

VOICEATWORK   **T** 07973 871479
Voice Coach
5 Anhalt Road, London SW11 4NZ
E kateterris@voiceatwork.co.uk
W www.voiceatwork.co.uk

VOICES & PERFORMANCE   **T** 07712 624083
Contact: Julia Gaunt ALCM TD-Musical Theatre. Audition
Technique. Corporate Training. Community Workshops.
Courses: Singing for Musical Theatre, 1-2 days. Voice
Care, 1 day
E joolsmusicbiz@aol.com
W www.joolsmusicbiz.com

actor training for an EVOLVING industry

Fourth Monkey
Theatre Company

VOICES LONDON   **T** 07774 445637
Contact: Ann Leberman. Estill Certified Master Teacher.
Technical Singing Coach
E ann@voicesvocal.co.uk
W www.voicesvocal.co.uk

VOXTRAINING LTD   **T** 020 7434 4404
Demo CDs. Voice Over Training
20 Old Compton Street, London W1D 4TW
E info@voxtraining.com
W www.voxtraining.com

WALLACE, Elaine BA   **T** 07856 098334
Voice
249 Goldhurst Terrace, London NW6 3EP
E im@voicebiz.biz

WALSH, Anne   **T** 07932 440043
Accents. Dialect. Speech. RP. Accent-softening
The Pronunciation Rooms, The Garden Studios
71-75 Shelton Street, London WC2H 9JQ
E anne@confidentlyspeaking.co.uk
W www.confidentlyspeaking.co.uk

WALSH, Genevieve   **T** 020 7627 0024
Acting Tuition. Audition Coaching
37 Kelvedon House, Guildford Road
Stockwell, London SW8 2DN
T 07801 948864

WALTZER, Jack   **T** 07949 136862 (London)
Professional Acting Workshops
5 Minetta Street Apt 2B, New York, NY 10012, USA
T 001 212 840 1234
E jackwaltzer@hotmail.com
W www.jackwaltzer.com

WEAKLIAM, Brendan PGDipMusPerf
BMusPerf Dip ABRSM   **T** 07724 558955
Singing Teacher. Voice Coach
23 Alders Close, Wanstead, London E11 3RZ
E brendanweakliam@gmail.com

WEBB, Bruce   **T** 01508 518703
Audition Technique. Singing
Abbots Manor, Kirby Cane, Bungay, Suffolk NR35 2HP

WELBOURNE, Jacqueline   **T** 07977 247287
Choreographer. Circus Trainer. Consultant
43 Kingsway Avenue
Kingswood, Bristol BS15 8AN
E jackie.welbourne@gmail.com

WERKKIT   **T** 07830 120536
2/21 Culmington Road, Ealing, London W13 9NJ
E info@werkkit.com
W www.werkkit.com

WESTMINSTER KINGSWAY
COLLEGE   **T** 0870 0609800
Performing Arts, Musical Theatre & Music
King's Cross Centre, 211 Gray's Inn Road
London WC1X 8RA
E courseinfo@westking.ac.uk
W www.westking.ac.uk

WHITE, Susan BA TEFL LGSM MA Voice
Studies Distinction   **T** 020 7244 0402
Coach of Professional Spoken Voice & Personal
Presence. Resonance Specialist via one-to-one for
Actors, Days for Individuals & Summer Pause 'Presence'
Masterclass - Central London
E susan@per-sona.com
W www.per-sona.com

WILDCATS THEATRE SCHOOL
& POST-16 ACADEMY   **T** 07725 915333
Contact: Emma Hancock. Courses: Performing Arts -
Musical Theatre, 2 yrs, full-time. Qualification:
BTEC Level 3. Performing Arts (Performance), 2 yrs,
full-time. Qualification: HND. Stage School for Children.
Summer School
Castle House, St Peter's Hill, Stamford PE9 2PE
E admin@wildcats-uk.com
W www.wildcatstheatreschool.co.uk

HOLLY WILSON LLAM.

Actor Teacher-London Drama Schools
Voice / Speech & Drama / Audition coaching / Private tuition

T: 020 8878 0015   e: hbwilson@fastmail.co.uk

SCREEN ACTING STEFAN GRYFF (DGGB) (LLB)

"I believe that for film and TV an actor's quality is more important than their level of talent."

I will provide:
- Special training for beginners and artists unused to camera acting
- Preparation of showreels for Casting Directors and Agents
- Classes for experienced actors currently employed in TV or film

Marble Arch Studio
T: 020 7723 8181

WILDER, Andrea   T 07919 202401
23 Cambrian Drive, Colwyn Bay
Conwy LL28 4SL
F 07092 249314
E andreawilder@fastmail.fm
W www.awagency.co.uk

WILSON, Holly   T 020 8878 0015
3 Worple Street, Mortlake, London SW14 8HE
E hbwilson@fastmail.co.uk

WIMBUSH, Martin Dip GSMD   T 020 8877 0086
Audition Technique. Drama School Entry. Elocution.
Public Speaking. Vocal Coaching
Flat 4, 289 Trinity Road
Wandsworth Common
London SW18 3SN
T 07930 677623
E martinwimbush@btinternet.com
W www.martinwimbush.com

WINDLEY, Joe   T 07867 780856
Accent, Speech, Voice, Text & Presentation Skills for
Film, Stage & Television
91 Lyric Road, Barnes
London SW13 9QA
E joe.windley@gmail.com

WINDSOR, Judith Ph. D   T 01782 827222
American Accents/Dialects
Woodbine, Victoria Road
Deal, Kent CT14 7AS
E sarah.upson@voicecoach.tv

WOOD, Tessa Teach Cert
AGSM CSSD PGDVS   T 020 8896 2659
Voice Coach
43 Woodhurst Road
London W3 6SS
T 07957 207808
E tessaroswood@aol.com

WOODHOUSE, Alan
AGSM ADVS   T 07748 904227
Acting Coach. Acting Workshops. Audition Technique.
Drama School Preparation. Elocution. Private Acting
Classes. Public Speaking. Vocal Coaching
33 Burton Road
Kingston upon Thames
Surrey KT2 5TG
E alanwoodhouse50@hotmail.com
W www.woodhouse-voice.co.uk

WORTMAN, Neville   T 07976 805976
Speech Coach. Voice Training
School of Economic Science Building
11 Mandeville Place
London W1U 3AJ
E neville@speakwell.co.uk
W www.speakwell.co.uk

WYNN, Madeleine   T 01394 450265
Audition Technique. Acting & Directing Coach. Drama
School Entry. LAMDA Exams. Acting Classes. Public
Speaking. LAMDA Teacher Training
40 Barrie House
Hawksley Court
Albion Road, London N16 0TX
E madeleinewynn@toucansurf.com
W www.plainspeaking.co.uk

YOUNG, Sylvia
THEATRE SCHOOL   T 020 7258 2330
Full-time Academic/Vocational School. Part-time Acting
Workshops. Audition Technique. Dancing. Improvisation.
Singing. Vocal Coaching
1 Nutford Place
London W1H 5YZ
F 020 7724 8371
E syoung@syts.co.uk
W www.syts.co.uk

YOUNG ACTORS THEATRE   T 020 7278 2101
70-72 Barnsbury Road
London N1 0ES
E info@yati.org.uk
W www.yati.org.uk

YOUNGSTARS THEATRE SCHOOL
& AGENCY   T 020 8950 5782
Contact: Coralyn Canfor-Dumas. Part-time Children's
Theatre School (4-18 yrs). Commercials. Dance. Drama.
Film. Singing. Stage. Television. Voice Overs
4 Haydon Dell, Bushey
Herts WD23 1DD
T 07966 176756
E youngstarsagency@gmail.com
W www.youngstarsagency.co.uk

YOUNGSTAR TELEVISION & FILM ACTING
SCHOOLS   T 023 8047 7717
Part-time Schools across the UK (8-20 yrs).
Twitter: @ystvproductions
Head Office
20 Hilldene Way
Westend, Southampton SO30 3DW
E info@youngstar.tv
W www.youngstar.tv

YOURVOICECOACH   T 01273 204779
Contact: Dee Forrest (Associate Voice Tutor, School
of Acting/Surrey University). Accents/Dialects, Vocal
Technique, Vocal Power, Articulation (Elocution). Text
Delivery. Sightreading. Confidence Building/NLP. Public
Speaking. Vocal Coaching. London & Brighton Studios.
Skype Coaching Available
20 Landseer Road
Hove BN3 7AF
T 07957 211065
E yourvoicecoach@hotmail.co.uk
W www.yourvoicecoach.co.uk

F →

Festivals

Film & Video Facilities

Film, Radio, Television & Video
Production Companies

Film & Television Schools

Film & Television Studios

Festivals

What do I need to know about the listed festivals?

The festivals listed in this section are all dedicated to creative and performing arts. Festivals are an opportunity for like-minded people to gather together to appreciate and learn from both well-established and new and up-and-coming acts and performers.

Why should I get involved?

Being a spectator at a festival is a chance to see others in action and to see a variety of shows that are not necessarily mainstream. This is an opportunity to see talent in its rawest form, which is exactly why casting directors often attend drama festivals: they may spot someone who is just what they are looking for, who would otherwise have gone unnoticed in a pile of CVs.

Taking part in festivals will be something else to add to your CV and will help develop your skills. This not only means performance skills but social skills as well: you will meet hundreds of new faces with the same passion for their work as you, so this is a great opportunity to make friends and useful contacts in the industry.

What do I need to bear in mind?

Before committing to performing at a festival, there are a number of issues to take into consideration. You will usually be unpaid and you will have to set aside enough money to fund the time spent rehearsing for and performing at the festival, not to mention travel, accommodation and food expenses. Not only that, you must also consider that you will be putting yourself out of the running for any paid work offered to you during this time. Make sure you let your agent know the dates you will be unavailable for work. You may find it helpful to refer to Equity's *Low Pay/No Pay* advice leaflet which is available to all Equity members from their website's members' area.

You may be required to not just perform but help out with any odd jobs involved with your show, such as setting up the stage and handing out flyers. If you are considering taking your own show to a festival, you will have to think well in advance about entrance fees, choosing and hiring a suitable venue, publicising your show,

casting if necessary, finding technicians, buying or hiring props, costumes, sets and so on. You must weigh up the financial outlays and potential headaches with the learning and networking opportunities that come with being involved in festivals.

How can I get involved?

If you are a performer at a festival, casting professionals could be there looking for you! Let them know that you will be performing and where and when. Send them a covering letter giving details and enclose your CV and headshot if you have not already done so in previous correspondence. You could do the same with agents if you are currently searching for new representation.

Spotlight members performing at the Edinburgh Festival Fringe can access a number of free services including a Spotlight VIP area, a series of career advice seminars, one-to-one advice sessions with a Spotlight expert and free Wi-Fi. For full information or to book tickets for seminars please visit www.edfringe.com from June onwards and enter 'Spotlight' in the show/performer field.

Most festivals have websites which you can browse for further information on what to expect and how to get involved. Even if you simply go as a spectator to a festival, you will learn a lot and will have the opportunity to network. If you are performing in or organising a show, make sure you know exactly what you are letting yourself in for and make the most of your time there!

CASE STUDY

Annelie Powell is the assistant casting director at the RSC and also works on freelance projects. Her first Edinburgh Fringe was in 2002.

I've attended in several capacities, having had the very senior jobs of chief flyer-er, junior company manager, general tea person, and since 2007 as a casting director. I regularly go and try to work out how to see seventy hundred and eleven shows in 3 days. I always return home exhausted, happy and with a bit of a hangover. Just how the Fringe should be.

The Fringe can be a wonderful place. It can be the place where your play sells out, gets 5 stars reviews and does two consecutive tours. It can be the place to develop your craft, find a capability for drinking whisky, the best belly laughs of your lifetime, new best friends and true love.

*It can also be a place where you play to two people per show if you are lucky, and return broken hearted with an alcohol intolerance, exhaustion, and viral videos of the time you thought you could outwit the comics at 2am at Spank! (Trust me, you can't)

So how can you try to be the former, and not the latter?

Go first as a visitor. Festivals are wonderful places to discover actors, writers, directors, companies, stand-ups, spoken word, physical theatre and much more - it's a melting pot of creativity. Also many projects have found that a festival can be just the start of something, they provide a wonderful opportunity to immerse yourself in your chosen field. Seek out companies you like. Write to them and see if they'll be taking work the following year. The more you know, the more you know.

If you are auditioning for something and it's very low pay, ask if they will be flexible with rehearsals and see if you can get a job around the show while you are up there, so you can afford to eat at the very least. I once took a job helping a cabaret singer change backstage and had to help her aim a cup for her to pee in as there were no toilet facilities and her quick change was incredibly quick. It wasn't the highlight of my month there, but it made being able to feed myself less of a financial burden.

If you are a young company taking your own project, trial it out somewhere first, and take on feedback. Don't rush the process. The Fringe will be there for many years to come, and your show will be better for not rushing. Many a successful show has been trialled out the year before in London for a few nights, before raising money (Kickstarter, fundraisers, sponsored activities, trusts) and taking it the following year. It's a marathon, not a race, and you shouldn't take anything that you are not completely proud of. It represents you.

Eat healthy. Have nights in. Be prepared to network. Be match fit. Write to casting directors and directors so it's not just your parents who see your work. Be positive and proactive while you are there. Sleep properly. Dive in. Climb a few peaks. See something you know nothing about. Enjoy it.

*This all happened to a friend. A friend. Honest.

Festivals

Katherine Thorogood

Photo: Peter Marsh

Katherine has just finished studying BA English & Theatre at the University of Warwick and will be graduating with a First Class Degree.

Involvement with drama and performance has for me been the hallmark of my time at Warwick, whether it's drama, opera, or musical theatre, there is a vast amount of output from the student body from which I have learned and benefitted. It was through my involvement with an exciting piece of new writing (Lulu Raczka's *Nothing*) being produced by Barrel Organ Theatre that I came into contact with NSDF and along with the rest of the company (comprising a group of Warwick students) made it to Scarborough for the 2014 festival.

I wouldn't presume to advise anyone on how best to do what they want to do, but I would say that one of the most important things I've discovered during my study and experience to date would be that challenging yourself is not to be under-estimated. Doing stuff outside your comfort zone, trying projects and opportunities which aren't necessarily very 'you' is far more valuable than sitting pretty in a box in which you feel secure. The style and concept of *Nothing* was a completely new animal to me and it remains the most rewarding project of which I have ever been a part. I have just finished playing in Shakespeare Shorts with Action To The Word at the Camden People's Theatre, and after shooting a short film over summer and then the Edinburgh Fringe run of *Nothing*, I hope to be exploring potential avenues of further training.

My future ambitions with regard to theatre include expanding my writing practice, and widening my experience as a stage actor – I absolutely hope to continue working with Barrel Organ, which is made up of the most amazing group of actors and creatives.

Angus Imrie

Angus attends the University of Warwick, studying BA English and Theatre (graduating in 2015).

I have been to NSDF for the past two years and only now, a few months on from this year's festival, realise what a brilliant opportunity it is. The festival exhibits selected student theatre in an environment which can be as punishing as it is rewarding, but what you learn from the criticism is absolutely invaluable. Those who run NSDF are some of the most talented and innovative theatre-makers in the country (many of whom encouragingly went to the festival when they were students) and they are truly interested in the kind of work being produced. Their advice and friendship endures way beyond the week in Scarborough. It's not a showcase festival – it's a forum for investigating how theatre can move forward.

This year, the selected show I performed in was *Road* by Jim Cartwright. The play is a depiction of life in a Lancashire town in the early 1980s, under the Thatcher government – I played a few different characters including Brink and Skinlad. My friend (who played Scullery) and I auditioned on the last day of the festival and were cast in Slunglow's adaptation of Moby Dick, The White Whale to be performed in Leeds in September (Slunglow is a theatre company run by festival selector, Alan Lane and workshop leader, Lucy Hind). Other friends from NSDF have similarly got professional work as a result of their success at the festival.

Spotlight's immensely generous awards are a real boost – I think all actors need is a bit of a confidence lift (and a year of not having to pay for membership doesn't half help either…). To any students wanting to apply for NSDF, don't hesitate – do work you believe in, defend it tooth and nail, make pals and listen. There are some brilliant people you're going want to work with.

ALDEBURGH FESTIVAL OF MUSIC & THE ARTS
T 01728 687100
12-28 June 2015
Aldeburgh Music
Snape Maltings Concert Hall
Snape, Suffolk IP17 1SP
BO 01728 687110
E enquiries@aldeburgh.co.uk
W www.aldeburgh.co.uk

BATH CHILDREN'S LITERATURE FESTIVAL
T 01225 462231
26 September-5 October 2015
Bath Festivals
Abbey Chambers
Kingston Buildings, Bath BA1 1NT
BO 01225 463362
E info@bathfestivals.org.uk
W www.bathfestivals.org.uk

BATH INTERNATIONAL MUSIC FESTIVAL
T 01225 462231
May 2015
Bath Festivals, Abbey Chambers
Kingston Buildings, Bath BA1 1NT
BO 01225 463362
E info@bathfestivals.org.uk
W www.bathfestivals.org.uk

BATH LITERATURE FESTIVAL
T 01225 462231
27 February-8 March 2015
Bath Festivals, Abbey Chambers
Kingston Buildings, Bath BA1 1NT
BO 01225 463362
E info@bathfestivals.org.uk
W www.bathfestivals.org.uk

BRIGHTON DOME & BRIGHTON FESTIVAL
T 01273 700747
2-24 May 2015
12A Pavilion Buildings
Castle Square
Brighton BN1 1EE
BO 01273 709709
E info@brightonfestival.org
W www.brightonfestival.org

BRIGHTON FRINGE
T 01273 764900
1-31 May 2015
5 Palace Place, Brighton BN1 1EF
E participantservices@brightonfringe.org
W www.brightonfringe.org

BUXTON FESTIVAL
T 01298 70395
10-25 July 2015
3 The Square, Buxton
Derbyshire SK17 6AZ
BO 0845 1272190
E info@buxtonfestival.co.uk
W www.buxtonfestival.co.uk

DANCE UMBRELLA
T 020 7407 1200
15-31 October 2015
1 Brewery Square
London SE1 2LF
E mail@danceumbrella.co.uk
W www.danceumbrella.co.uk

DUBLIN THEATRE FESTIVAL
T 00 353 1 6778439
24 September-11 October 2015
44 East Essex Street
Temple Bar
Dublin 2, Ireland
F 00 353 1 6797709
E marketing@dublintheatrefestival.com
W www.dublintheatrefestival.com

EDINBURGH FESTIVAL FRINGE
T 0131 226 0026
7-31 August 2015
Edinburgh Festival Fringe Society Ltd
180 High Street
Edinburgh EH1 1QS
BO 0131 226 0000
E admin@edfringe.com
W www.edfringe.com

EDINBURGH INTERNATIONAL FESTIVAL
BO 0131 473 2000
7-31 August 2015
The Hub, Castlehill
Edinburgh EH1 2NE
E boxoffice@eif.co.uk
W www.eif.co.uk

HARROGATE INTERNATIONAL FESTIVAL
T 01423 562303
1-26 July 2015
32 Cheltenham Parade
Harrogate
North Yorkshire HG1 1DB
F 01423 521264
E info@harrogate-festival.org.uk
W www.harrogateinternationalfestival.com

HENLEY FRINGE & FILM (TRUST) THE
T 07742 059762
20-28 July 2015
Aston Farm House
Remenham Lane
Henley on Thames, Oxon RG9 3DE
E info@henleyfringe.org
W www.henleyfringe.org

INTERNATIONAL PLAYWRITING FESTIVAL
T 020 7580 1000
June 2015. Annual Competition with Selected Plays Showcased in Festival Weekend
87 Great Titchfield Street, London W1W 6RL
E intplayfest@outlook.com
W www.internationalplaywritingfestival.com

KING'S LYNN FESTIVAL
T 01553 767557
12-25 July 2015
Suite 2, 3rd Floor
Bishops Lynn House
18 Tuesday Market Place
King's Lynn, Norfolk PE30 1JW
BO 01553 764864 (open from mid April)
E info@kingslynnfestival.org.uk
W www.kingslynnfestival.org.uk

LIFT
T 020 7968 6800
Bi-Annual Festival. June 2016
3rd Floor, Institute of Contemporary Arts
12 Carlton House Terrace
London SW1Y 5AH
E kate@liftfestival.com
W www.liftfestival.com

LONDON SKETCH COMEDY FESTIVAL
T 07782 244248
May 2015
149-157 St John Street, London EC1V 4PW
E admin@londonsketchfest.com
W www.londonsketchfest.com

LUDLOW ARTS FESTIVAL LTD
T 01584 819005
13 June-5 July 2015
Tenbury House, 36 Teme Street
Tenbury Wells, Worcs WR15 8AA
E admin@ludlowartsfestival.co.uk
W www.ludlowartsfestival.co.uk

MOVE IT 2015
T 020 7288 6734
13-15 February 2015
Olympia, Hammersmith Road
London W14 8UX
E info@moveitdance.co.uk
W www.moveitdance.co.uk

NATIONAL STUDENT DRAMA FESTIVAL (NSDF)
T 020 7036 9027
28 March-3 April 2015
Registered Office: 49 South Molton Street
London W1K 5LH
E info@nsdf.org.uk
W www.nsdf.org.uk

PERFORM 2015
T 020 7288 6625
13-15 February 2015
Olympia, Hammersmith Road, London W14 8UX
E info@performshow.co.uk
W www.performshow.co.uk

ULSTER BANK BELFAST FESTIVAL AT QUEEN'S
T 028 9097 1034
12 October-1 November 2015
Lanyon North, Belfast BT7 1NN
BO 028 9097 1197
E belfastfestival@qub.ac.uk
W www.belfastfestival.com

WEST END LIVE
T 020 7641 3297
June 2015
E westendlive@westminster.gov.uk
W www.westendlive.co.uk

ACTOR'S ONE-STOP SHOP THE
T 020 8279 8073
Showreels- Edited & Filmed
2B Daleview Crescent
London E4 6PQ
T 07894 152651
E info@actorsonestopshop.com
W www.actorsonestopshop.com

ALBANY THE
T 020 8692 4446
Douglas Way
London SE8 4AG
F 020 8469 2253
E hires@thealbany.org.uk
W www.thealbany.org.uk

ARRI MEDIA
T 01895 457100
3 Highbridge
Oxford Road
Uxbridge
Middlesex UB8 1LX
F 01895 457101
E info@arrimedia.com
W www.arrimedia.com

CENTRELINE VIDEO LTD
T 0118 941 0033
138 Westwood Road
Tilehurst
Reading RG31 6LL
W www.centrelinevideo.co.uk

CHANNEL 2020 LTD
T 0844 8402020
Phoenix Square
4 Midland Street
Leicester LE1 1TG
E info@channel2020.co.uk
W www.channel2020.co.uk

CHANNEL 2020 LTD
T 0844 8402020
3rd Floor
28 Marshalsea Road
London SE1 1HF
E info@channel2020.co.uk
W www.channel2020.co.uk

CLICKS MEDIA STUDIOS LTD
T 01634 723838
Contact: Peter Snell
40 Holborn Viaduct
London EC1N 2PB
E info@clicksmediastudios.com
W www.clicksmediastudios.com

CRYSTAL MEDIA
T 0131 240 0988
28 Castle Street
Edinburgh EH2 3HT
F 0131 240 0989
E hello@crystal-media.co.uk
W www.crystal-media.co.uk

DELUXE 142
T 020 7878 0000
Post-production Facilities
Film House
142 Wardour Street
London W1F 8DD
W www.deluxe142.co.uk

EXECUTIVE AUDIO VISUAL
T 020 7723 4488
DVD Editing & Duplication Service. Photography Services
E chris.jarvis60@gmail.com

GREENPARK PRODUCTIONS LTD
T 01566 782107
Film & Video Archives
Illand, Launceston
Cornwall PL15 7LS
E info@greenparkimages.co.uk
W www.greenparkimages.co.uk

HARLEQUIN PRODUCTIONS
T 020 8653 2333
15-17 Church Road
London SE19 2TF
E neill@harlequinproductions.co.uk
W www.harlequinproductions.co.uk

HARVEY HOUSE FILMS LTD
T 07968 830536
Animation. Full Pre/Post-production. Graphics. Showreels
The Mission Hall
Cunnington Street, London W4 5ER
E chris@harveyhousefilms.co.uk
W www.harveyhousefilms.co.uk

HIREACAMERA.COM
T 01435 873028
Equipment Hire. Video & Photography. Accessories. Lenses
Unit 5, Wellbrook Farm
Berkeley Road, Mayfield
East Sussex TN20 6EH
F 01435 874841
E info@hireacamera.com
W www.hireacamera.com

HUNKY DORY PRODUCTIONS LTD
T 020 8440 0820
Crew. Facilities. Also Editing: Non-linear
57 Alan Drive, Barnet
Herts EN5 2PW
T 07973 655510
E adrian@hunkydory.tv
W www.hunkydory.tv

MPC (THE MOVING PICTURE COMPANY)
T 020 7434 3100
Post-production
127 Wardour Street, London W1F 0NL
F 020 7287 5187
E mailbox@moving-picture.com
W www.moving-picture.com

ONSIGHT LTD
T 020 7637 0888
Film Equipment Rental
Shepperton Studios
Middlesex TW17 0QD
F 01932 592246
E hello@onsight.co.uk
W www.onsight.co.uk

PANAVISION UK
T 020 8839 7333
The Metropolitan Centre
Bristol Road, Greenford
Middlesex UB6 8GD
F 020 8839 7300
W www.panavision.co.uk

PLACE THE
T 020 7121 1000
17 Duke's Road, London WC1H 9PY
F 020 7121 1142
E info@theplace.org.uk
W www.theplace.org.uk

SPOTLIGHT
SHOWREELS

Having the perfect showreel on your Spotlight profile is a crucial part of getting yourself noticed by casting professionals.

Working with our experienced editors in our Spotlight-based edit suites, we can create a high resolution, professionally produced showreel to your specification.

Your session includes:

- **Up to three hours of sit-in editing time**
- **Upload to your Spotlight profile**
- **5 x labelled DVD copies**
- **High-resolution mpeg4 video file (for upload to Vimeo, YouTube etc.)**

www.spotlight.com/artists/showreelediting

PRO-LINK RADIO SYSTEMS LTD   **T** 01527 577788
Walkie Talkie & Communications Hire & Sales
84 Wynall Lane, Stourbridge
West Midlands DY9 9AQ
F 01527 577757
E admin@prolink-radio.com
W www.prolink-radio.com

RICH TV LTD   **T** 0161 635 6207
Houldsworth Mill, Studio 1.6
Meadow Mill
Water Street SK1 2BU
E sales@richtv.co.uk
W www.richtv.co.uk

SALON LTD   **T** 020 8963 0530
Editing Equipment Hire. Post-production
D12 Genesis Business Park
Whitby Avenue
London NW10 7SE
E hire@salonrentals.com
W www.salonrentals.com

SOUNDHOUSE LTD THE   **T** 0161 832 7299
MediaCityUK, Blue
Manchester M50 2HQ
E mike@thesoundhouse.com
W www.thesoundhouse.tv

TEN80MEDIA   **T** 07814 406251
Studio: 517 Foleshill Road
Coventry
West Midlands CV6 5AU
E info@ten80media.com
W www.ten80media.com

VIDEO INN PRODUCTION   **T** 01604 864868
AV Equipment Hire. Conferences & Events
Glebe Farm, Wooton Road
Quinton, Northampton NN7 2EE
E enquiries@videoinn.co.uk
W www.videoinn.co.uk

VSI - VOICE & SCRIPT INTERNATIONAL   **T** 020 7692 7700
Dubbing. DVD Encoding & Authoring Facilities. Editing. Subtitling. Voice Overs
132 Cleveland Street
London W1T 6AB
F 020 7692 7711
E info@vsi.tv
W www.vsi.tv

W6 STUDIO   **T** 020 7385 2272
Editing Facilities. Music Videos. Photography. Showreels. Video Production
359 Lillie Road, Fulham
London SW6 7PA
T 07836 357629
E kazkam@hotmail.co.uk
W www.w6studio.co.uk

WARNER BROTHERS DE LANE LEA   **T** 020 7432 3800
Film & TV Sound Dubbing & Editing Suite
75 Dean Street, London W1D 3PU
F 020 7494 3755
E solutions@delanelea.com
W www.delanelea.com

1066 PRODUCTIONS LTD
34 Pine Hill, Epsom, Surrey KT18 7BG
E admin@1066productions.com
W www.1066productions.com

2PRODUCTION   T 020 8440 4848
Professional Management. Voice Over Direction & CDs
E info@2production.com
W www.2production.com

30 BIRD PRODUCTIONS   T 07970 960995
Cambridge Junction, Clifton Way
Cambridge CB1 7GX
E info@30bird.org
W www.30bird.org

ACADEMY   T 020 7395 4155
16 West Central Street, London WC1A 1JJ
F 020 7240 0355
E post@academyfilms.com
W www.academyfilms.com

ADASTRA DEVELOPMENT   T 01487 823608
Contact: Martin Franks. TV & Media Production
The Lilacs, West End
Woodhurst, Huntingdon, Cambridge PE28 3BH
E mfranks@adastradevelopment.com
W www.adastradevelopment.com

AGILE FILMS   T 020 7000 2882
Unit 1, 68-72 Redchurch Street
London E2 7DP
E info@agilefilms.com
W www.agilefilms.com

ALGORITHM-GROUP   T 07549 892062
Film, Television & Animation. Manchester & Los Angeles
13 The Highgrove, Bolton
Lancashire BL1 5PX
E andy@algorithm-group.com
W www.algorithm-group.com

AN ACQUIRED TASTE TV CORP   T 020 8686 1188
51 Croham Road, South Croydon CR2 7HD
F 020 8686 5928
E cbennetttv@aol.com

ASF PRODUCTIONS LTD   T 07770 277637
*Contact: Alan Spencer, Malcolm Bubb. Commercials.
Corporate Videos. Documentaries. Feature Films. Films*
38 Clunbury Court, Manor Street
Berkhamsted, Herts HP4 2FF
E info@asfproductions.co.uk

**ASHFORD ENTERTAINMENT
CORPORATION LTD THE**   T 020 8660 9609
*Contact: Frazer Ashford. By e-mail. Documentaries.
Drama. Feature Films. Films. Television*
20 The Chase, Coulsdon, Surrey CR5 2EG
E info@ashford-entertainment.co.uk
W www.ashford-entertainment.co.uk

ASSOCIATED PRESS   T 020 7482 7400
The Interchange, Oval Road
Camden Lock, London NW1 7DZ
F 020 7413 8312

AVALON TELEVISION LTD   T 020 7598 8000
4A Exmoor Street, London W10 6BD
F 020 7598 7281
W www.avalonuk.com

BAILEY, Catherine LTD   T 020 7483 3330
110 Gloucester Avenue, Primrose Hill
London NW1 8JA
W www.cbltd.net

BBC WORLDWIDE LTD   T 020 8433 2000
Media Centre, Media Village
201 Wood Lane W12 7TQ
W www.bbcworldwide.com

BROADSIDE FILMS   T 07581 670525
Independent Film Company run by Young People
13 Pleasant View, Llanelli SA15 4LF
E broadsidefilms@hotmail.com

BRUNSWICK FILMS LTD   T 020 8960 0066
Formula One Motor Racing Archive
26 Macroom Road, Maida Vale, London W9 3HY
F 020 8960 4997
E info@brunswickfilms.com
W www.brunswickfilms.com

BRYANT WHITTLE LTD   T 020 8311 8752
49 Federation Road, Abbey Wood
London SE2 0JT
E amanda@bryantwhittle.com
W www.bryantwhittle.com

CARDINAL BROADCAST   T 01753 639210
Room 114, N&P Building, Pinewood Studios
Iver Heath, Bucks SL0 0NH
W www.mentalhealthtv.co.uk

**CENTRE SCREEN
PRODUCTIONS**   T 0161 832 7151
Eastgate, Castle Street
Castlefield, Manchester M3 4LZ
F 0161 832 8934
E info@centrescreen.co.uk
W www.centrescreen.co.uk

CHANNEL 2020 LTD   T 0844 8402020
Phoenix Square, 4 Midland Street
Leicester LE1 1TG
E info@channel2020.co.uk
W www.channel2020.co.uk

CHANNEL X LTD   T 0845 9002940
4 Candover Street, London W1W 7DJ
E info@channelx.co.uk
W www.channelx.co.uk

CLEVER BOY MEDIA LTD   T 01753 650951
Pinewood Studios, Pinewood Road
Iver Heath, Bucks SL0 0NH
E tim@cleverboymedia.com
W www.cleverboymedia.com

COLLINGWOOD & CO   T 020 8993 3666
10-14 Crown Street, Acton, London W3 8SB
F 020 8993 9595
E info@collingwoodandco.co.uk
W www.collingwoodandco.co.uk

COMMUNICATOR LTD   T 01763 852635
76 Station Road, Steeple Morden
Royston, Herts SG8 0NS
E info@communicator.ltd.uk

COMPLETE WORKS THE   T 020 7377 0280
The Old Truman Brewery, 91 Brick Lane
London E1 6QL
F 020 7247 7405
E info@tcw.org.uk
W www.tcw.org.uk

COMTEC LTD   T 0844 8805238
Unit 19, Tait Road, Croydon, Surrey CR0 2DP
F 0844 8805239
E info@comtecav.co.uk
W www.comtecav.co.uk

COURTYARD PRODUCTIONS T 01732 700324
Film & Television Post Production
Little Postlings Farmhouse, Four Elms
Kent TN8 6NA
E courtyard@mac.com

CPL PRODUCTIONS LTD T 020 7240 8101
38 Long Acre, London WC2E 9JT
F 020 7836 9633
E info@cplproductions.co.uk
W www.cplproductions.co.uk

CREATIVE PARTNERSHIP THE T 020 7439 7762
115-117 Shaftesbury Avenue, London WC2H 8AF
F 020 7437 1467
W www.thecreativepartnership.co.uk

CROFT TELEVISION T 01628 668735
Contact: Nick Devonshire. By e-mail. Commercials.
Corporate Videos. Live Events
Croft House, Progress Business Centre, Whittle Parkway
Slough, Berkshire SL1 6DQ
F 01628 668791
E nick@croft-tv.com
W www.croft-tv.com

CUPSOGUE PICTURES T 020 3411 2058
81 Brook Street, Raunds NN9 6LL
E enquiries@cupsoguepictures.com
W www.cupsoguepictures.com

DANCETIME LTD T/F 020 8742 0507
1 The Orchard, Chiswick, London W4 1JZ
E berry@tabletopproductions.com
W www.tabletopproductions.com

DARLOW SMITHSON
PRODUCTIONS LTD T 020 7482 7027
1st Floor, Shepherds Building Central, Charecroft Way
Shepherd's Bush, London W14 0EE
E mail@dsp.tv
W www.dsp.tv

DELUXE 142 T 020 7878 0000
Film House, 142 Wardour Street
London W1F 8DD
W www.deluxe142.co.uk

DISNEY, Walt COMPANY THE T 020 8222 1000
3 Queen Caroline Street, Hammersmith
London W6 9PE
F 020 8222 2795
W www.disney.co.uk

DISTANT OBJECT
PRODUCTIONS LTD T 01635 281760
Video Production. Corporate. Documentary. Internet
Broadcasting
11 Lime Tree Mews, 2 Lime Walk
Headington, Oxford OX3 7DZ
E production@distantobject.com
W www.distantobject.com

DLT ENTERTAINMENT UK LTD T 020 7631 1184
10 Bedford Square, London WC1B 3RA
F 020 7636 4571
W www.dltentertainment.com

DOLPHIN CASTING T 020 3697 7121
14-16 Dowgate Hill, London EC4R 2SU
E dolphincasting522@gmail.com

DRAMATIS PERSONAE LTD T 020 7834 9300
Contact: Nathan Silver, Nicolas Kent
19 Regency Street, London SW1P 4BY
E ns@nathansilver.com

DREADNOUGHT
PRODUCTIONS LTD T 01708 222938
10 Dee Close, Upminster
Essex RM14 1QD
E terence@terencemustoo.com
W www.terencemustoo.com

DREAMING WILL
INITIATIVE THE T/F 020 7793 9755
PO Box 38155, London SE17 3XP
E londonswo@hotmail.com
W www.lswproductions.co.uk

DREAMWORKS ANIMATION
6 Agar Street, London WC2N 4HN
W www.dreamworksanimation.com

ECOSSE FILMS LTD T 020 7371 0290
Brigade House, 8 Parsons Green
London SW6 4TN
F 020 7736 3436
E info@ecossefilms.com
W www.ecossefilms.com

EDGE PICTURE
COMPANY LTD THE T 020 7836 6262
20-22 Shelton Street, London WC2H 9JJ
F 020 7836 6949
E ask.us@edgepicture.com
W www.edgepicture.com

EFFINGEE PRODUCTIONS LTD T 07946 586939
Contact: Lesley Kiernan. By e-mail. Television
E info@effingee.com
W www.effingee.com

ENDEMOL UK PLC T 0870 3331700
Including Endemol UK Productions, Initial, Remarkable
& Zeppotron
Shepherds Building Central, Charecroft Way
Shepherd's Bush, London W14 0EE
F 0870 3331800
E info@endemoluk.com
W www.endemoluk.com

ENGINE CREATIVE T 01604 453177
The Church Rooms, Agnes Road
Northampton, Northants NN2 6EU
E wecancreate@enginecreative.co.uk
W www.enginecreative.co.uk

ENLIGHTENMENT
INTERACTIVE T 01695 727555
East End House, 24 Ennerdale
Skelmersdale WN8 6AJ
W www.trainingmultimedia.co.uk

EON PRODUCTIONS LTD T 020 7493 7953
Eon House, 138 Piccadilly, London W1J 7NR
F 020 7408 1236

EXTRA DIGIT LTD
1 Nutford Place, London W1H 5YZ
W www.extradigit.com

EYE FILM & TELEVISION T 0845 6211133
Epic Studios, 112-114 Magdalen Street
Norwich NR3 1JD
E production@eyefilmandtv.co.uk
W www.eyefilmandtv.co.uk

FARNHAM FILM COMPANY THE T 01252 710313
34 Burnt Hill Road, Lower Bourne, Farnham GU10 3LZ
F 01252 725855
E info@farnfilm.com
W www.farnfilm.com

FEELGOOD FICTION LTD T 020 8746 2535
49 Goldhawk Road
London W12 8QP
E feelgood@feelgoodfiction.co.uk
W www.feelgoodfiction.co.uk

FENIXX PRODUCTIONS T 07837 338990
*Music Video Specialists. Commercial Production
Company & Creative Team*
E us.fenixx@gmail.com
W www.fenixx.tv

**FERRIS ENTERTAINMENT
FILMS** T 07801 493133
London. Belfast. Cardiff. Los Angeles. France. Spain
Number 8, 132 Charing Cross Road
London WC2H 0LA
E info@ferrisentertainment.com
W www.ferrisentertainment.tv

**FESTIVAL FILM &
TELEVISION LTD** T 020 8297 9999
Festival House, Tranquil Passage
London SE3 0BJ
F 020 8297 1155
E info@festivalfilm.com
W www.festivalfilm.com

FIFTY ONE PRODUCTIONS T 01639 648672
Office NA 059A, Centerprise
Dwr-y-Felin Road, Neath SA10 7RF
F 07092 987858
E info@fiftyoneproductions.co

FILMS OF RECORD LTD T 020 7428 3100
6 Anglers Lane, Kentish Town
London NW5 3DG
F 020 7284 0626
W www.filmsofrecord.com

**FOCUS PRODUCTIONS
PUBLICATIONS** T 01789 298948
58 Shelley Road
Stratford-upon-Avon
Warwickshire CV37 7JS
F 01789 294845
E maddern@focuspublishers.co.uk
W www.focusproductions.co.uk

**FREMANTLEMEDIA /
FREMANTLEMEDIA UK** T 020 7691 6000
1 Stephen Street, London W1T 1AL
W www.fremantlemedia.com

GALA PRODUCTIONS LTD T 020 8741 4200
25 Stamford Brook Road, London W6 0XJ
E info@galaproductions.co.uk
W www.galaproductions.co.uk

GALLEON FILMS LTD T 020 8310 7276
Head Office: 50 Openshaw Road
London SE2 0TE
E alice@galleontheatre.co.uk
W www.galleontheatre.co.uk

GAY, Noel TELEVISION LTD T 07738 124362
PO Box 4613, Ascot
Berks SL5 5BU
E charles.armitage@virgin.net

GHA GROUP T 020 7439 8705
33 Newman Street, London W1T 1PY
F 020 7636 4448
E info@ghagroup.co.uk
W www.ghagroup.co.uk

GOLDHAWK ESSENTIAL T 020 7439 7113
Radio Productions
20 Great Chapel Street, London W1F 8FW
E lucinda@essentialmusic.co.uk

**GRANT NAYLOR
PRODUCTIONS LTD** T 01932 592175
David Lean Building
Shepperton Studios
Studios Road, Shepperton
Middlesex TW17 0QD
E enquiries@grantnaylor.co.uk

GREAT GUNS LTD T 020 7692 4444
43-45 Camden Road, London NW1 9LR
F 020 7692 4422
E reception@greatguns.com
W www.gglondon.tv

GUERILLA FILMS LTD T 020 8758 1716
35 Thornbury Road, Isleworth
Middlesex TW7 4LQ
E david@guerilla-films.com
W www.guerilla-films.com

**HAMMERWOOD
FILM PRODUCERS** T 01273 277333
110 Trafalgar Road, Portslade, Sussex BN41 1GS
E filmangels@freenetname.co.uk
W www.filmangel.co.uk

HANDS UP PRODUCTIONS LTD T 07909 824630
7 Cavendish Vale, Sherwood
Nottingham NG5 4DS
E marcus@handsuppuppets.com
W www.handsuppuppets.com

**HARRISON, Stephen FILM &
PRODUCTION SERVICES** T 07970 723097
42 Pembroke, Bracknell
Berkshire RG12 7RD
E spharrison@me.com
W www.stephenharrison.me.uk

HARTSWOOD FILMS T 020 3668 3060
3A Paradise Road, Richmond
Surrey TW9 1RX
F 020 3668 3050
W www.hartswoodfilms.co.uk

HEAD, Sally PRODUCTIONS T 020 8994 8650
60 Strand on the Green, London W4 3PE
E sally.head@sallyheadproductions.com

HEADSTRONG PICTURES T 020 7239 1010
85 Gray's Inn Road, London WC1X 8TX
F 020 7239 1011
E mail@walltowall.co.uk
W www.shedproductions.com

HEAVY ENTERTAINMENT LTD T 020 7494 1000
111 Wardour Street, London W1F 0UH
F 020 7494 1100
E info@heavy-entertainment.com
W www.heavy-entertainment.com

**HERMES ENTERTAINMENT
INC LTD (HE)** T 07875 628299
*Contact: Modeste Jean-Marc (Producer/Distributor).
Production & Distribution. Specialising in Motion Picture
Industry based in Paris/London/Hollywood*
72/6 Grove Lane, Camberwell Green
London SE5 8TW
F 020 7703 7927
E modeste500@gmail.com

HIT ENTERTAINMENT LTD **T** 020 7554 2500
5th Floor, Maple House
149 Tottenham Court Road, London W1T 7NF
F 020 7388 9321
E creative@hitentertainment.com
W www.hitentertainment.com

HOLMES ASSOCIATES &
OPEN ROAD FILMS **T** 020 7813 4333
The Studio, 37 Redington Road
London NW3 7QY
E holmesassociates@blueyonder.co.uk

HOWARD, Danny **T** 01625 875170
Director. Television, Video & Online Web Production
AmbitActivate Ltd, 52 Shrigley Road
Poynton, Cheshire SK12 1TF
E danny@ambitactivate.co.uk
W www.ambitactivate.co.uk

HUNGRY MAN LTD **T** 020 7239 4550
1-2 Herbal Hill, London EC1R 5EF
F 020 7239 4589
E ukreception@hungryman.com
W www.hungryman.com

HUNKY DORY
PRODUCTIONS LTD **T** 020 8440 0820
57 Alan Drive, Barnet
Herts EN5 2PW
T 07973 655510
E adrian@hunkydory.tv
W www.hunkydory.tv

HURRICANE FILMS LTD **T** 0151 707 9700
13 Hope Street, Liverpool L1 9BQ
E info@hurricanefilms.co.uk
W www.hurricanefilms.net

ICE PRODUCTIONS LTD **T** 0121 288 4864
The Mail Box, Lonsdale House
52 Blucher Street, Birmingham B1 1QU
E admin@ice-productions.com
W www.ice-productions.com

ICON FILMS LTD **T** 0117 910 2030
3rd Floor College House, 32-36 College Green
Bristol BS1 5SP
F 0117 910 2031
W www.iconfilms.co.uk

IMAGE PRODUCTIONS **T** 07729 304795
Makes Films with Children for Children
PO Box 133, Bourne
Lincolnshire PE10 1DE
E info@imageproductions.co.uk
W www.imageproductions.co.uk

INGLENOOK
PRODUCTIONS LTD **T** 07814 077708
Victoria Warehouse
Trafford Wharf Road
Manchester M17 1AB
E hello@inglenookproductions.com
W www.inglenookproductions.com

IRREGULAR FEATURES LTD **T** 07771 665382
11 Keslake Road, London NW6 6DJ
E mforstater@msn.com

J. I. PRODUCTIONS **T** 07732 476409
90 Hainault Avenue, Giffard Park
Milton Keynes, Bucks MK14 5PE
E jasonimpey@live.com
W www.jiproductions.co.uk

JACKSON, Brian FILMS LTD **T** 020 7402 7543
39-41 Hanover Steps, St George's Fields
Albion Street, London W2 2YG
F 020 7262 5736
W www.brianjacksonfilms.com

JMP-MEDIA **T** 07947 241821
Corporate Videos. Television
18 Westmead, Princes Risborough
Buckinghamshire HP27 9HR
E carolyn@jmp-media.tv
W www.jmp-media.tv

JMS GROUP LTD THE **T** 01603 811855
Park Farm Studios, Hethersett
Norwich, Norfolk NR9 3DL
F 01603 812255
E info@jms-group.com
W www.jms-group.com

JUNCTION 15 PRODUCTIONS **T** 01782 562531
EMMY Award Winners. Corporate. Television
Unit 10, Rosevale Road
Parkhouse Estate
Newcastle under Lyme ST5 7EF
E info@junction15.com
W www.junction15.com

KHANDO ENTERTAINMENT **T** 020 3463 8492
Contact: By e-mail (for Script Submissions)
1 Marlborough Court, London W1F 7EE
E production@khandoentertainment.com

KNOWLES, Dave FILMS **T** 023 8084 2190
Contact: Jenny Knowles. Corporate, Training & Project
Documentary Video Productions
34 Ashleigh Close, Hythe SO45 3QP
E mail@dkfilms.co.uk
W www.dkfilms.co.uk

LANDSEER
PRODUCTIONS LTD **T** 020 7794 2523
27 Arkwright Road, London NW3 6BJ
E kchoward1@mac.com
W www.landseerfilms.com

LIGHT AGENCY &
PRODUCTIONS LTD **T** 020 8090 0006
Contact: Lucy Misch. By Post/e-mail/Telephone.
Commercials. Corporate Videos. Documentaries.
Music Videos. Television. Showreel Editing. Software
Development
27 Mospey Crescent, Epsom, Surrey KT17 4NA
E production@lightproductions.tv
W www.lightproductions.tv

LIME PICTURES **T** 0151 722 9122
Campus Manor, Childwall
Abbey Road, Liverpool L16 0JP
F 0151 722 6839

MALLINSON TELEVISION
PRODUCTIONS **T** 0141 332 0589
Commercials
29 Lynedoch Street, Glasgow G3 6EF
F 0141 332 6190
E reception@mtp.co.uk

MANS, Johnny PRODUCTIONS **T** 01992 470907
Incorporating Encore Magazine
PO Box 196, Hoddesdon
Herts EN10 7WG
T 07974 755997
E johnnymansagent@aol.com
W www.johnnymansproductions.co.uk

MANSFIELD, Mike PRODUCTIONS   T 020 8947 6884
4 Ellerton Road, London SW20 0EP
E mikemantv@aol.com

MARTIN, William PRODUCTIONS   T 01865 390258
The Studio, Tubney Warren Barns
Tubney, Oxfordshire OX13 5QJ
F 01865 390148
E info@wmpcreative.com
W www.wmpcreative.com

MAVERICK MOTION LTD   T 020 7460 1371
46 Highlever Road, London W10 6PT
E mm@maverickmotion.com
W www.maverickmotion.com

MAVERICK TELEVISION   T 0121 771 1812
Progress Works, Heath Mill Lane
Birmingham B9 4AL
F 0121 771 1550
E mail@mavericktv.co.uk
W www.mavericktv.co.uk

MBP TV   T 01403 741620
Saucelands Barn, Coolham
Horsham, West Sussex RH13 8QG
F 01403 741647
E info@mbptv.com
W www.mbptv.com

McINTYRE, Phil TELEVISION LTD   T 020 7291 9000
3rd Floor, 85 Newman Street, London W1T 3EU
F 020 7291 9001
E info@mcintyre-ents.com
W www.mcintyre-ents.com

MEMPHIS & GOLD FILMS   T 07850 077825
121 Brecknock Road, Camden
London N19 5AE
E houseofsaintjude@gmail.com

MENTORN MEDIA   T 020 7258 6800
77 Fulham Palace Road, London W6 8JA
F 020 7258 6888
E reception@mentorn.tv

MET FILM PRODUCTION   T 020 8280 9127
Ealing Studios, Ealing Green
London W5 5EP
F 020 8280 9111
E assistant@metfilm.co.uk
W www.metfilm.co.uk

MINAMONFILM   T 020 8674 3957
Contact: Min Clifford. By e-mail/Telephone. Corporate Videos. Documentaries. Drama. Films. Online Promotions
117 Downton Avenue, London SW2 3TX
E studio@minamonfilm.co.uk
W www.minamonfilm.co.uk

MISTRAL FILMS LTD   T 020 7284 2300
31 Oval Road, London NW1 7EA
F 020 7284 0547
E info@mistralfilm.co.uk

MUMMU LTD   T 020 7012 1673
Independent Studio Creating Animated, Filmed & Illustrated Content
Unit 1.1, 128 Hoxton Street, London N1 6SH
E info@mummu.co.uk
W www.mummu.co.uk

MURPHY, Patricia FILMS LTD   T 020 7267 0007
Office 133, 33 Parkway
Camden, London NW1 7PN
E office@patriciamurphy.co.uk

MY SPIRIT PRODUCTIONS LTD   T 01634 323376
Paranormal & Psychic Radio & Television Production
Maidstone TV Studios, Vinters Park
Maidstone ME14 5NZ
E info@myspiritradio.com
W www.myspiritradio.com

NANAK FILM PVT LTD   T 00 91 22 23511363
Producers & Distributors of Films, Tele-films, Television, Serials, Documentaries & Music Videos
132, 1st Floor, Arun Chambers
Next to Tardeo A.C. Market
Tardeo Road, Bombay 400 034, India
F 00 91 22 23510328
E info@devnani23.com
W www.devnani23.com

NEAL STREET PRODUCTIONS LTD   T 020 7240 8890
1st Floor, 26-28 Neal Street
London WC2H 9QQ
F 020 7240 7099
E post@nealstreetproductions.com
W www.nealstreetproductions.com

NEW MOON TELEVISION   T 020 7479 7010
63 Poland Street, London W1F 7NY
F 020 7479 7011
E production@new-moon.co.uk
W www.new-moon.co.uk

NEW PLANET FILMS LTD   T 020 8426 1090
PO Box 640, Pinner HA5 9JB
E info@newplanetfilms.com
W www.newplanetfilms.com

NEXUS PRODUCTIONS LTD   T 020 7749 7500
Animation, Mixed Media, Live Action & Interactive Production for Commercials, Broadcast, Pop Promos & Title Sequences
113-114 Shoreditch High Street
London E1 6JN
F 020 7749 7501
E info@nexusproductions.com
W www.nexusproductions.com

NFD PRODUCTIONS LTD   T/F 01977 681949
Contact: By Post/e-mail/Telephone. Children's Entertainment. Commercials. Corporate Videos. Drama. Films. Television. Short Films. Showreels. Twitter: @platform2c
The Studio, 21 Low Street
South Milford, Leeds
Yorkshire LS25 5AR
T 07966 473455
E contact@nfdproductions.com
W www.nfdproductions.com

NOMADIC FILMS   T 020 7221 7775
Features. Documentaries. Music Videos. Commercials. Corporate Promos
15 Poland Street
London W1F 8QE
E info@nomadicfilms.com
W www.nomadicfilms.com

OMNI PRODUCTIONS LTD   T 0117 954 7170
14-16 Wilson Place, Bristol BS2 9HJ
E info@omniproductions.com
W www.omniproductions.co.uk

ON SCREEN PRODUCTIONS LTD   T 01291 636300
Ashbourne House, 33 Bridge Street
Chepstow, Monmouthshire NP16 5GA
F 01291 636301
E action@onscreenproductions.com
W www.onscreenproductions.com

OPEN SHUTTER PRODUCTIONS LTD   T 01753 841309
Contact: John Bruce. Documentaries. Drama. Films. Television
100 Kings Road, Windsor
Berkshire SL4 2AP
T 07753 618875
E openshutterproductions@googlemail.com

OVC MEDIA LTD   T 020 7402 9111
Contact: Eliot M. Cohen. By e-mail. Animation. Documentaries. Drama. Feature Films. Films. Television
88 Berkeley Court, Baker Street
London NW1 5ND
F 020 7723 3064
E eliot@ovcmedia.com
W www.ovcmedia.com

P4FILMS   T 01242 542760
Film & Video for Television, Commercials & Corporate
Cheltenham Film Studios, Hatherley Lane
Cheltenham, Gloucestershire GL51 6PN
E info@p4films.com
W www.p4films.com

PARK VILLAGE LTD   T 020 7387 8077
1 Park Village East, London NW1 7PX
E info@parkvillage.co.uk

PASSION PICTURES LTD   T 020 7323 9933
Animation. Documentary. Television
1st Floor-4th Floor, 33-34 Rathbone Place
London W1T 1JN
F 020 7323 9030
E info@passion-pictures.com

PATHE PICTURES LTD   T 020 7323 5151
4th Floor, 6 Ramillies Street
London W1F 7TY
F 020 7631 3568
W www.pathe.co.uk

PICTURE PALACE FILMS LTD   T 020 7586 8763
13 Egbert Street, London NW1 8LJ
F 020 7586 9048
E info@picturepalace.com
W www.picturepalace.com

PIER PRODUCTIONS LTD   T 01273 691401
8 St Georges Place, Brighton BN1 4GB
E info@pierproductionsltd.co.uk

PINBALL LONDON   T 0845 2733893
20 Attneave Street, London WC1X 0DX
E info@pinballonline.co.uk
W www.pinballonline.co.uk

PINEWOOD PICTURES   T 020 7637 2612
3rd Floor, 12 Great Portland Street
London W1W 8QN
F 020 7636 5481

PLASTER CAST PRODUCTIONS   T 07737 946492
34 Advent House, 3 Every Street
Manchester M4 7ED
E john@plastercastproductions.co.uk
W www.plastercastproductions.co.uk

PODCAST COMPANY THE   T 0844 5041226
101 Wardour Street, London W1F 0UG
E info@thepodcastcompany.co.uk
W www.thepodcastcompany.co.uk

PODCAST COMPANY THE   T 0844 5041226
3 The Avenue, London N3 2LB
E info@thepodcastcompany.co.uk
W www.thepodcastcompany.co.uk

POSITIVE IMAGE LTD   T 01753 842248
25 Victoria Street, Windsor
Berkshire SL4 1HE
E theoffice@positiveimage.co.uk

POTBOILER PRODUCTIONS LTD   T 020 7734 7372
9 Greek Street, London W1D 4DQ
F 020 7287 5228
E info@potboiler.co.uk
W www.potboiler.co.uk

POZZITIVE TELEVISION LTD   T 020 7255 1112
1st Floor, 25 Newman Street
London W1T 1PN
E pozzitive@pozzitive.co.uk
W www.pozzitive.co.uk

PRETTY CLEVER PICTURES   T 01730 817899
Hurst Cottage, Old Buddington Lane
Hollist Lane, Eastbourne
Midhurst, West Sussex GU29 0QN
T 07836 616981
E pcpics@globalnet.co.uk

PRODUCERS THE   T 020 7636 4226
111 Priory Road, London NW6 3NN
E info@theproducersfilms.co.uk
W www.theproducersfilms.co.uk

QUADRILLION   T 01628 487522
17 Balvernie Grove, London SW18 5RR
E enqs@quadrillion.tv
W www.quadrillion.tv

RAW TALENT COMPANY THE   T 0131 510 0133
Contact: Helen Raw. Film Production & Actor Training Workshops
E helen@therawtalentcompany.co.uk
W www.therawtalentcompany.co.uk

RDM FILMS   T 020 3664 9811
9 Wight Way, Selsey
Chichester, West Sussex PO20 0UD
T 07810 824567
E mail@rdmfilms.co.uk
W www.rdmfilms.co.uk

READ, Rodney   T 020 8891 2875
45 Richmond Road, Twickenham
Middlesex TW1 3AW
T 07956 321550
E rodney_read@hotmail.co.uk
W www.rodney-read.com

RECORDED PICTURE COMPANY LTD   T 020 7636 2251
24 Hanway Street, London W1T 1UH
F 020 7636 2261
E rpc@recordedpicture.com

RED KITE ANIMATION   T 0131 554 0060
89 Giles Street, Edinburgh EH6 6BZ
E info@redkite-animation.com
W www.redkite-animation.com

RED ROSE CHAIN T 01473 603388
Gippeswyk Hall, Gippeswyk Avenue
Ipswich, Suffolk IP2 9AF
E info@redrosechain.com
W www.redrosechain.com

REDRUSH TALENT T 02891 878146
22 Burnsall Street, London SW3 3ST
T 07803 594961
E janice@redrushtalent.com
W www.redrushtalent.com

REDWEATHER PRODUCTIONS T 0117 916 6456
Brunswick Court, Brunswick Square
Bristol BS2 8PE
E production@redweather.co.uk
W www.redweather.co.uk

RENIERMEDIA T 01462 892669
Television & Film Production & Consulting
11 The Twitchell, Baldock SG7 6DN
E renierv@aol.com
W www.reniermedia.com

REPLAY FILM & NEW MEDIA T 020 7637 0473
*Contact: Danny Scollard. Animation. Corporate Videos.
Documentaries. Drama. E-Learning. Live Events. Script
Writing. Web Design*
Museum House, 25 Museum Street
London WC1A 1JT
E sales@replayfilms.co.uk
W www.replayfilms.co.uk

REUTERS LTD T 020 7250 1122
The Thompson Reuters Building, South Collonade
Canary Wharf, London E14 5EP

RIVERSIDE TV STUDIOS T 020 8237 1123
Riverside Studios, Crisp Road
London W6 9RL
F 020 8237 1121
E info@riversidetv.co.uk
W www.riversidetv.co.uk

ROEBUCK PRODUCTIONS T 01937 835900
Commer House, Station Road
Tadcaster, North Yorkshire LS24 9JF
F 01937 835901
E john@roebuckproductions.com
W www.roebuckproductions.com

RSA FILMS T 020 7437 7426
42-44 Beak Street, London W1F 9RH
F 020 7734 4978
W www.rsafilms.com

SANDS FILMS STUDIOS T 020 7231 2209
82 St Marychurch Street, London SE16 4HZ
F 020 7231 2119
E info@sandsfilms.co.uk
W www.sandsfilms.co.uk

SCALA PRODUCTIONS LTD T 020 7916 4771
249 Gray's Inn Road, London WC1X 8QZ
E scalaprods@aol.com

SCREEN FIRST LTD T 01248 716973
Cil-y-Coed, Llansadwrn
Menai Bridge, Anglesey LL59 5SE
E paul.madden@virgin.net

SEPTEMBER FILMS LTD T 020 8563 9393
Glen House, 22 Glenthorne Road
Hammersmith, London W6 0NG
F 020 8741 7214
E info@septemberfilms.com

SEVENTH ART PRODUCTIONS T 01273 777678
63 Ship Street, Brighton BN1 1AE
F 01273 323777
E info@seventh-art.com
W www.seventh-art.com

SHELL FILM & VIDEO UNIT T 020 7934 3318
Shell Centre, York Road
London SE1 7NA
E jane.poynor@shell.com

SIGHTLINE T 01483 813311
*Video & Interactive Media. Full Creative & Technical
Production Resources for Producing Videos (Promotion,
Training, Employee Communications), E-Learning,
Interactive Presentations, Apps for Mobile Devices
Based in Guildford*
F 01483 813317
E keith@sightline.co.uk
W www.sightline.co.uk

SILK SOUND T 020 7434 3461
Commercials. Corporate Videos. Documentaries
13 Berwick Street, London W1F 0PW
F 020 7494 1748
E bookings@silk.co.uk
W www.silk.co.uk

SINDIBAD FILMS LTD T 020 7259 2707
Tower House, 226 Cromwell Road
London SW5 0SW
E info@sindibad.co.uk
W www.sindibad.co.uk

SITCOM SOLDIERS LTD T 07712 669097
Windy Yetts, Windy Harbour Lane
Bromley Cross, Bolton BL7 9AP
E info@sitcomsoldiers.com
W www.sitcomsoldiers.com

SNEEZING TREE FILMS T 020 7436 8036
1st Floor, 37 Great Portland Street, London W1W 8QH
E firstname@sneezingtree.com
W www.sneezingtree.com

**SNOWBALL
PRODUCTIONS LTD** T 07412 833383
International House, 221 Bow Road
Bow, London E3 2SJ
E info@snowballproductions.co.uk
W www.snowballproductions.co.uk

**SOLOMON THEATRE
COMPANY LTD** T 01725 518760
Penny Black, High Street, Damerham
Nr Fordingbridge, Hampshire SP6 3EU
E office@solomontheatre.co.uk
W www.solomontheatre.co.uk

SONY PICTURES T 020 7533 1000
25 Golden Square, London W1F 9LU
F 020 7533 1015

SPACE CITY PRODUCTIONS T 020 7371 4000
77-79 Blythe Road, London W14 0HP
F 020 7371 4001
E info@spacecity.co.uk
W www.spacecity.co.uk

**SPEAKEASY
PRODUCTIONS LTD** T 01738 828524
Wildwood House, Stanley, Perth PH1 4NH
F 01738 828419
E info@speak.co.uk
W www.speak.co.uk

SPECIFIC FILMS LTD   **T** 020 7580 7476
33 Percy Street, London W1T 2DF
F 020 7636 6886
E info@specificfilms.com

SPIRAL PRODUCTIONS LTD   **T** 020 7428 9948
Unit 17-18, The Dove Centre
109 Bartholomew Road
London NW5 2BJ
F 020 7485 1845
E info@spiral.co.uk
W www.spiral.co.uk

**STAFFORD, Jonathan
PRODUCTIONS**   **T** 01932 562611
Shepperton Studios, Studios Road
Shepperton, Middlesex TW17 0QD
E jon@staffordproductions.com

STANDFAST FILMS   **T** 020 8466 5580
The Studio, 14 College Road
Bromley, Kent BR1 3NS

STANTON MEDIA   **T** 01296 489539
6 Kendal Close, Aylesbury
Bucks HP21 7HR
E info@stantonmedia.com
W www.stantonmedia.com

**STONE PRODUCTIONS
CREATIVE LTD**   **T** 01255 822172
Lakeside Studio, 62 Mill Street
St Osyth, Essex CO16 8EW
F 01255 822160
E kevin@stone-productions.co.uk
W www.stone-productions.co.uk

STUDIO AKA   **T** 020 7434 3581
Animation
30 Berwick Street, London W1F 8RH
F 020 7437 2309
E nikki@studioaka.co.uk
W www.studioaka.co.uk

TABARD PRODUCTIONS LTD   **T/F** 020 7497 0830
*Contact: John Herbert. By e-mail. Corporate Videos.
Documentaries*
4 Bloomsbury Place
London WC1A 2QA
E johnherbert@tabard.co.uk
W www.tabardproductions.com

TABLE TOP PRODUCTIONS   **T** 020 8994 1269
*Contact: Alvin Rakoff. By e-mail. Feature Films.
Television. Theatre*
1 The Orchard, Bedford Park
Chiswick, London W4 1JZ
T/F 020 8742 0507
E alvin@alvinrakoff.com

TAKE 3 PRODUCTIONS LTD   **T** 020 7288 1818
79 Essex Road, London N1 2SF
E mail@take3.co.uk
W www.take3.co.uk

TAKE FIVE PRODUCTIONS   **T** 020 7287 2120
37 Beak Street, London W1F 9RZ
F 020 7287 3035
E info@takefivestudio.com
W www.takefivestudio.com

TALKBACKTHAMES   **T** 020 7861 8000
20-21 Newman Street, London W1T 1PG
F 020 7861 8001
W www.fremantlemediauk.com

TALKING PICTURES   **T** 01753 650000
Pinewood Studios, Pinewood Road
Iver Heath, Bucks SL0 0NH
F 01865 890504
E info@talkingpictures.co.uk
W www.talkingpictures.co.uk

TANDEM CREATIVE   **T** 01442 261576
Corporate Videos, Time Lapse & Documentaries
Charleston House, 13 High Street
Hemel Hempstead, Herts HP1 3AA
E info@tandem.tv
W www.tandem.tv

THEATRE WORKSHOP   **T** 0131 555 3854
Film. Theatre
Out of the Blue Drill Hall, 36 Dalmeny Street
Edinburgh EH6 8RG
W www.theatre-workshop.com

THEOTHER COMPANY LTD   **T** 020 8858 6999
*Contact: Sarah Boote. By e-mail. Drama.
Documentaries. Music Videos. Corporate Videos*
30 Glenluce Road, Blackheath
London SE3 7SB
E contact@theothercompany.co.uk
W www.theothercompany.co.uk

THIN MAN FILMS   **T** 020 7734 7372
9 Greek Street, London W1D 4DQ
F 020 7287 5228
E info@thinman.co.uk

**TIGER ASPECT
PRODUCTIONS**   **T** 020 7434 6700
Shepherds Building Central, Charecroft Way
London W14 0EE
F 020 8222 4700
E general@tigeraspect.co.uk
W www.tigeraspect.co.uk

TOP BANANA   **T** 01562 700404
The Studio, Broome
Stourbridge, West Midlands DY9 0HA
F 01562 700930
E enquiries@top-b.com
W www.top-b.com

TOPICAL TELEVISION LTD   **T** 023 8071 2233
61 Devonshire Road, Southampton SO15 2GR
F 023 8033 9835
E post@topical.co.uk

TRAFALGAR 1 LTD   **T** 020 7722 7789
*Contact: Hasan Shah. By Post/e-mail. Documentaries.
Feature Films. Films. Music Videos. Television*
153 Burnham Towers, Fellows Road, London NW3 3JN
F 020 7483 0662
E t1ltd@blueyonder.co.uk

TUALEN PICTURES   **T** 020 7193 7995
95 Old Woolwich Road, Greenwich, London SE10 9PP
E production@tualen.co.uk
W www.tualen.co.uk

**TV PRODUCTION
PARTNERSHIP LTD**   **T** 01264 861440
4 Fullerton Manor, Fullerton, Hants SP11 7LA
E dbj@tvpp.tv
W www.tvpp.tv

TV STUDIO THE   **T** 020 8677 7143
85 Lewin Road, London SW16 6JX
E info@thetvstudio.co.uk
W www.thetvstudio.co.uk

TWOFOUR   **T** 01752 727400
Corporate Videos. Documentaries. Live Events.
Television
Twofour Studios, Estover
Plymouth PL6 7RG
F 01752 727450
E enquiries@twofour.co.uk
W www.twofour.co.uk

TYBURN ENTERTAINMENT LTD   **T** 01494 670335
2 Chapel Court
London SE1 1HH
F 01753 691785
E tyburngeneral@btconnect.com

**TYBURN FILM
PRODUCTIONS LTD**   **T** 01494 670335
2 Chapel Court, London SE1 1HH
F 01753 691785
E tyburngeneral@btconnect.com

VECTOR PRODUCTIONS   **T** 0844 8019770
Corporate Videos, Television & Film Production
Moulton Park Industrial Estate
Northampton NN3 6AQ
E production@vectortv.co.uk
W www.vectortv.co.uk

VERA PRODUCTIONS LTD   **T** 020 7292 1480
165 Wardour Street, London W1F 8WW
F 020 7292 1481
E info@vera.co.uk

VIDEO ENTERPRISES   **T** 01494 534144
Contact: Maurice Fleisher. Corporate Videos.
Documentaries. Live Events. Television
12 Barbers Wood Road
High Wycombe
Bucks HP12 4EP
T 07831 875216
E videoenterprises@ntlworld.com
W www.videoenterprises.co.uk

VIDEOTEL PRODUCTIONS   **T** 020 7299 1800
Corporate Videos
84 Newman Street, London W1T 3EU
F 020 7299 1818

**VSI - VOICE & SCRIPT
INTERNATIONAL**   **T** 020 7692 7700
132 Cleveland Street
London W1T 6AB
E info@vsi.tv
W www.vsi.tv

W3KTS LTD   **T** 01904 647822
10 Portland Street, York YO31 7EH
T 0845 8727949
E info@w3kts.com

W6 STUDIO   **T** 020 7385 2272
Editing Facilities. Music Video. Photography.
Video Production
359 Lillie Road, Fulham
London SW6 7PA
T 07836 357629
E kazkam@hotmail.co.uk
W www.w6studio.co.uk

WALKING FORWARD MEDIA   **T** 01480 496309
29 Hampton Close, Fenstanton
Cambridgeshire, PE28 9HB
E info@walkingforward.co.uk
W www.walkingforward.co.uk

WALKOVERS VIDEO LTD   **T** 01249 750428
Facilities. Production
Kington Langley, Chippenham
North Wiltshire SN15 5NU
T 07831 828022
E walkoversvideo@btinternet.com

WALSH BROS LTD   **T/F** 020 8858 6870
Contact: By e-mail. Animation. Documentaries. Drama.
Feature Films. Films. Television
29 Trafalgar Grove, Greenwich
London SE10 9TB
E info@walshbros.co.uk
W www.walshbros.co.uk

**WARNER BROS
PRODUCTIONS LTD**   **T** 020 3427 7777
Warner Suite (Bldg. 242)
Warner Bros Studios Leavesden
Warner Drive, Leavesden, Herts WD25 7LP

**WARNER SISTERS
PRODUCTIONS LTD**   **T** 020 8567 6655
Ealing Studios, Ealing Green
London W5 5EP
E ws@warnercini.com

WEST DIGITAL   **T** 020 8743 5100
Broadcast Post-production
59 Goldhawk Road, London W12 8EG
F 020 8743 2345
E jackie@westdigital.co.uk

WHITEHALL FILMS   **T** 020 8785 3737
6 Embankment, Putney
London SW15 1LB
F 020 8788 2340
E whitehallfilms@gmail.com

WORKING TITLE FILMS LTD   **T** 020 7307 3000
26 Aybrook Street, London W1U 4AN
F 020 7307 3002
W www.workingtitlefilms.com

WORLD PRODUCTIONS LTD   **T** 020 3002 3113
101 Finsbury Pavement
London EC2A 1RS
E enquiries@world-productions.com
W www.world-productions.com

WORLD WIDE PICTURES   **T** 020 7613 6580
103 The Timber Yard, Drysdale Street
London N1 6ND
E info@worldwidepictures.tv
W www.worldwidepictures.tv

WORLD'S END TELEVISION   **T** 020 7240 3439
10 Denmark Street, London WC2H 8LS
E info@worldsendproductions.com
W www.worldsendproductions.com

WORTHWHILE MOVIE LTD   **T** 001 416 469 0459
Providing the Services of Bruce Pittman as Film Director
191 Logan Avenue, Toronto
Ontario, Canada M4M 2NT
E bruce.pittman@sympatico.ca

YA I NO PRODUCTIONS   **T/F** 01482 650483
Lowfield House, Lowfield Road
Anlaby, East Riding of Yorkshire HU10 7BA
E info@yainoproductions.com
W www.yainoproductions.com

ZEPHYR FILMS LTD   **T** 020 7794 0011
E info@zephyrfilms.co.uk

Film & Television Schools

What are film and television schools?

The schools listed in this section offer various courses to those who wish to become part of the behind-camera world of the entertainment industry. These courses include filmmaking, producing, screenwriting and animation, to name a few. Students taking these courses usually have to produce a number of short films in order to graduate. The following advice has been divided into two sections: for potential students and for actors.

Advice for filmmakers/writers:

Why should I take a course?

The schools listed here offer courses which enable a budding filmmaker or scriptwriter to develop their skills with practical training. These courses are designed to prepare you for a career in a competitive industry. They also provide you with an opportunity to begin networking and making contacts with industry professionals.

How should I use these listings?

Research a number of schools carefully before applying to any courses. Have a look at the websites of the schools listed first to get an idea of the types of courses on offer, what is expected from students, and the individual values of each school. Request a prospectus from the school if they do not have full details online. Word of mouth recommendations are invaluable if you know anyone who has attended or taught at a school. You need to decide what type of course suits you – don't just sign up for the first one you read about. See what is available and give yourself time to think about the various options.

Advice for actors:

Why should I get involved?

Student films can offer new performers the chance to develop skills and experience in front of a camera; learning scripts, working with other actors and working with crew members. Making new contacts and learning how to get on with those you are working with, whether in front of or behind camera, is a vital part of getting along in the acting community.

In addition, you are likely to receive a certain amount of exposure from the film. The student filmmaker may show it to teachers, other students, other actors, and most importantly directors when applying for jobs, and you would

normally be given your own copy of the film which you can show to agents or casting directors if requested, or use a clip of it in your showreel.

For more experienced actors, working on a student film can offer the opportunity to hone existing skills and keep involved within the industry. It can also be useful to observe new actors and keep up-to-date with new training ideas and techniques.

How do I get involved?

It may be helpful to see if the schools' websites have any advice for actors interested in being considered for parts in student films and suggesting how they should make contact. If there is no advice of this kind, it would be worth either phoning or e-mailing to ask if the school or its students would consider actors previously unknown to them. If this is the case, ask who CVs and headshots should be sent to, and whether they would like to see a showreel or voicereel (for animation courses).

If you are asked to play a role in a student film, make sure you are not going to a student's home and that someone knows where you are going and when. Equity also recommends that actors request a contract when working on any film; you could receive payment retrospectively if the film becomes a success. You may find it helpful to refer to Equity's *Low Pay/No Pay* advice leaflet which is available to all Equity members from their website's members' area, and to check if your employer has signed the Equity Film School Agreement, which will ensure you will receive the minimum wage.

Should I use a clip of a student film on my showreel?

Casting directors would generally prefer to see some form of showreel than none at all. If you do not have anything else you can show that has been professionally broadcast, or do not have the money to get a showreel made from scratch, then a student film is an acceptable alternative. See the 'Promotional Services' section for more information on showreels.

Where can I find more information?

Students and actors may want to visit Shooting People's website www.shootingpeople.org for further advice and daily e-mail bulletins of student/ short film and TV castings. Filmmakers can upload their films to the site for others to view.

BRIGHTON FILM SCHOOL T 01273 602070
*Head of School: Gary Barber. HNC & HND in
Filmmaking. Diploma in Cinematography & Directing.
Short Courses in Filmmaking & Screenwriting*
The Brighton Forum
95 Ditchling Road
Brighton BN1 4ST
E info@brightonfilmschool.co.uk
W www.brightonfilmschool.co.uk

LEEDS BECKETT UNIVERSITY T 0113 812 8053
*Courses: Filmmaking, MA & BA (Hons). Animation,
BA (Hons)*
Northern Film School
Leeds Beckett University
Electric Press, 1 Millennium Square
Leeds LS2 3AD
F 0113 812 8080
E aetenquiries@leedsmet.ac.uk
W www.leedsbeckett.ac.uk

**LONDON COLLEGE OF
COMMUNICATION** T 020 7514 6569
Film & Video Course
Elephant & Castle, London SE1 6SB
F 020 7514 6843
E info@lcc.arts.ac.uk
W www.arts.ac.uk/lcc

LONDON FILM ACADEMY T 020 7386 7711
The Old Church
52A Walham Grove
London SW6 1QR
E info@londonfilmacademy.com
W www.londonfilmacademy.com

LONDON FILM SCHOOL THE T 020 7836 9642
*Courses: Filmmaking, 2 yr, MA. Screenwriting, 1 yr, MA.
International Film Business, 1 yr, MA (in association with
University of Exeter). PhD Film by Practice. Specialised
Professional Short Courses & Workshops*
24 Shelton Street
London WC2H 9UB
F 020 7497 3718
E info@lfs.org.uk
W www.lfs.org.uk

**LONDON SCHOOL OF FILM,
MEDIA & PERFORMANCE** T 020 7487 7505
Regent's College
Inner Circle
Regent's Park, London NW1 4NS
F 020 7487 7425
E lsfmp@regents.ac.uk
W www.regents.ac.uk/lsfmp

MIDDLESEX UNIVERSITY T 020 8411 5555
Television Production Course
School of Arts & Education
Hendon Campus, The Burroughs
Hendon, London NW4 4BT
W www.mdx.ac.uk

**NATIONAL FILM &
TELEVISION SCHOOL** T 01494 671234
*MA & Diploma Courses in the Key Filmmaking
Disciplines. Short Courses for Freelancers*
Beaconsfield Studios, Station Road
Beaconsfield, Bucks HP9 1LG
F 01494 674042
E info@nfts.co.uk
W www.nfts.co.uk

**NATIONAL YOUTH
FILM ACADEMY** T 0845 3096239
For Young Actors & Film-makers aged 16-25
Gateshead International Business Centre
Mulgrave Terrace, Gateshead, Newcastle NE8 1AN
E info@nyfa.org.uk
W www.nyfa.org.uk

NORTHERN FILM SCHOOL T 0113 812 8000
Leeds Beckett University
Electric Press, 1 Millennium Square, Leeds LS2 3AD
E aetenquiries@leedsmet.ac.uk
W www.leedsbeckett.co.uk

**RAINDANCE FILM
PARTNERSHIP LLP** T 020 7930 3412
Short Courses. 1 yr Postgraduate Degrees
10 Craven Street, London WC2N 5PE
E info@raindance.co.uk
W www.raindance.org

**UNIVERSITY FOR THE
CREATIVE ARTS** T 01252 892883
*Pre-degree, Undergraduate & Postgraduate Degrees in
Creative Arts Courses*
Falkner Road
Farnham, Surrey GU9 7DS
E enquiries@ucreative.ac.uk
W www.ucreative.ac.uk

**UNIVERSITY OF WESTMINSTER SCHOOL OF
MEDIA ARTS & DESIGN** T 020 7911 5000
*Undergraduate Courses: Film & Television Production.
Contemporary Media Practice. Postgraduate Courses:
Theory, Culture & Industry*
Admissions & Enquiries:
Watford Road, Northwick Park
Harrow, Middlesex HA1 3TP
W www.westminster.ac.uk/film

3 MILLS STUDIOS
T 020 7363 3336
Three Mill Lane, London E3 3DU
F 0871 5944028
E info@3mills.com
W www.3mills.com

ANIMAL PROMOTIONS LTD
T 07778 156513
White Rocks Farm, Underriver
Sevenoaks, Kent TN15 0SL
F 01732 763767
E happyhoundschool@yahoo.co.uk
W www.whiterocksfarm.co.uk

ARDMORE STUDIOS LTD
T 00 353 1 2862971
Herbert Road, Bray
Co. Wicklow, Ireland
E film@ardmore.ie
W www.ardmore.ie

BACKSTAGE CENTRE THE
T 020 3668 5753
25m x 35m Sound Stage, 100 Tonne Rigging, 1000kVA
High House Production Park
Vellacott Close
Purfleet, Essex RM19 1RJ
E info@thebackstagecentre.com
W www.thebackstagecentre.com

CLAPHAM ROAD STUDIOS
T 020 7582 9664
Animation. Live Action
161 Clapham Road, London SW9 0PU
W www.claphamroadstudios.co.uk

COLD CITY STUDIOS LTD
T 020 8811 2861
Photo & Film Location
Unit B2, 2A Askew Crescent
Shepherd's Bush
London W12 9DP
E info@coldcitystudios.co.uk
W www.coldcitystudios.co.uk

EALING STUDIOS
T 020 8567 6655
Ealing Green, London W5 5EP
F 020 8758 8658
E firstname.lastname@ealingstudios.com
W www.ealingstudios.com

ELSTREE STUDIOS
T 020 8953 1600
Shenley Road, Borehamwood
Hertfordshire WD6 1JG
F 020 8905 1135
E info@elstreestudios.co.uk
W www.elstreestudios.co.uk

LONDON STUDIOS THE
T 020 7157 5555
London Television Centre
Upper Ground
London SE1 9LT
F 020 7157 5757
E sales@londonstudios.co.uk
W www.londonstudios.co.uk

PINEWOOD STUDIOS
T 01753 651700
Pinewood Road, Iver Heath
Buckinghamshire SL0 0NH
W www.pinewoodgroup.com

REUTERS TELEVISION
T 020 7250 1122
The Reuters Thompson Building
South Colonnade
Canary Wharf
London E14 5EP

RIVERSIDE STUDIOS
T 020 8237 1000
Crisp Road, London W6 9RL
F 020 8237 1001
E reception@riversidestudios.co.uk
W www.riversidestudios.co.uk

SANDS FILMS STUDIOS
T 020 7231 2209
82 St Marychurch Street
London SE16 4HZ
F 020 7231 2119
E info@sandsfilms.co.uk
W www.sandsfilms.co.uk

SHEPPERTON STUDIOS
T 01932 562611
Studios Road, Shepperton
Middlesex TW17 0QD
W www.pinewoodgroup.com

SILVER ROAD STUDIOS
T 020 8746 2000
Green Screen Studios. Filming & Photographic Studios.
Conference/Function Room. Cinema/Screening Room.
Casting Room. Make-up Rooms. Voice Overs. Editing.
In-house Equipment Hire. Maintenance. Free Parking
2 Silver Road, White City
London W12 7SG
E info@silverroadstudios.co.uk
W www.silverroadstudios.co.uk

TWICKENHAM STUDIOS LTD
T 020 8607 8888
The Barons, Twickenham TW1 2AW
F 020 8607 8889
E enquiries@twickenhamstudios.com
W www.twickenhamstudios.com

G

Good Digs Guide
Compiled by Janice Cramer
and David Banks

This is a list of digs recommended by those who have used them.

To keep the list accurate please send recommendations for inclusion to:

Good Digs Guide
Spotlight, 7 Leicester Place
London WC2H 7RJ

E contacts@spotlight.com

If you are a digs owner wishing to be listed, your application must include 2 recommendations from performers who have stayed in your accommodation.

Good Digs Guide

ABERDEEN: Milne, Mrs A. T 01224 638951
5 Sunnyside Walk, Aberdeen AB24 3NZ

ABERYSTWYTH:
Vegetarian Penrhiw T 07837 712323
Farmhouse near Aberystwyth providing Accommodation
& Vegetarian Breakfasts
Penrhiw, Llanafan, Aberystwyth, Dyfed SY23 4BA
E penrhiw@fastmail.fm
W www.vegetarianpenrhiw.com

AYR: Dunn, Sheila T 01292 284531
The Dunn-Thing Guest House
13 Park Circus, Ayr KA7 2DJ

BATH: Tapley, Jane T 01225 446561
Camden Lodgings, 3 Upper Camden Place
Bath BA1 5HX
E peter@tapley.ws

BIRMINGHAM: Hurst, Mr P. T 0121 449 8220
41 King Edward Road, Moseley
Birmingham B13 8HR
E phurst1com@aol.com

BIRMINGHAM:
Mountain, Marlene P. T 0121 454 5900
268 Monument Road, Edgbaston
Birmingham B16 8XF

BIRMINGHAM: Wilson, Mrs T 0121 440 5182
17 Yew Tree Road, Edgbaston
Birmingham B15 2LX
E yolandewilson17@gmail.com

BLACKPOOL: Lees, Jean T 01253 621059
Ascot Flats, 6 Hull Road
Central Blackpool FY1 4QB

BLACKPOOL:
Somerset Apartments T/F 01253 346743
22 Barton Avenue, Blackpool FY1 6AP
E somersetapartments@tiscali.co.uk
W www.blackpool-somerset-apartments.co.uk

BLACKPOOL:
Waller, Veronica & Bob T 01253 627003
The Brooklyn Hotel, 7 Wilton Parade, Blackpool FY1 2HE
E brooklyn@live.co.uk
W www.brooklynblackpool.co.uk

BOLTON: Duckworth, Paul T 07762 545129
19 Burnham Avenue, Bolton BL1 6BD
E pauljohnathan@msn.com

BOURNEMOUTH: Sitton, Martin T 01202 293318
Flat 2, 9 St Winifreds Road
Meyrick Park, Bournemouth BH2 6NX
E martinbmouth@hotmail.co.uk

BRADFORD: Smith, Theresa T 01274 778568
8 Moorhead Terrace, Shipley
Bradford BD18 4LA
E theresaannesmith@hotmail.com

BRIGHTON: Benedict, Peter T 07752 810122
19 Madeira Place, Brighton BN2 1TN
E peter@peterbenedict.co.uk
W www.madeiraplace.co.uk

BRIGHTON: Chance, Michael &
Drinkel, Keith T 01273 779585
6 Railway Street, Brighton BN1 3PF
T 07876 223359
E mchance@lineone.net

BRIGHTON: Dyson, Kate T 01273 607490
39 Arundel Street
Kemptown BN2 5TH
T 07812 949875
E kate.dyson@talktalk.net

BRISTOL: Ham, Phil & Jacqui T 0117 902 5213
Double room. Walking distance from town
78 Stackpool Road, Bristol BS3 1NN
T 07956 962422
E jacqui@tiptopmusic.com

BURY ST EDMUNDS:
Bird, Mrs S. T 01284 754492
30 Crown Street, Bury St Edmunds
Suffolk IP33 1QU
E josandsue@homebird2.plus.com

BURY ST EDMUNDS:
Harrington-Spier, Sue T 01284 768986
39 Well Street, Bury St Edmunds
Suffolk IP33 1EQ
E sue.harringtonspier@gmail.com

BUXTON: Kitchen, Mrs G. T 01298 26555
Silverlands Holiday Apartments
c/o 156 Brown Edge Road
Buxton, Derbyshire SK17 7AA
T 01298 79381
E swiftcaterequip2@aol.com

CAMBRIDGE: Dunn, Anne T 01954 210291
The Dovecot, 1 St Catherine's Hall
Coton, Cambridge CB23 7GU
T 07774 131797
E dunn@annecollet.fsnet.co.uk

CANTERBURY: Ellen, Nikki T 01227 720464
Crockshard Farmhouse, Wingham
Canterbury CT3 1NY
E crockshard_bnb@yahoo.com
W www.crockshard.com

CANTERBURY: Waugh, Gilda T 07730 040602
Two Bedrooms. 15 min walk from Central Canterbury.
Park & Ride 5 mins walk
185 Wincheap, Canterbury CT1 1TG

CARDIFF: Blade, Mrs Anne T 029 2022 5860
25 Romilly Road, Canton
Cardiff CF5 1FH

CARDIFF: Julia's Homely Digs T 07989 203011
4 Inglefield Avenue, Heath
Cardiff, South Glamorgan CF14 3PZ
E jbrams69@hotmail.com

CARDIFF: Kelly, Sheila T 029 2039 5078
166 Llandaff Road, Canton
Cardiff CF11 9PX
T 07875 134381
E mgsmkelly1@gmail.com

CARDIFF: Kennedy, Rosie T 07746 946118
Duffryn Mawr Farm House, Pendoylan
Vale of Glamorgan
E rosie@duffrynmawrcottages.com
W www.duffrynmawrcottages.co.uk

CARDIFF: Lewis, Nigel T 029 2049 4008
66 Donald Street, Roath
Cardiff CF24 4TR
T 07813 069822
E nigel.lewis66@btinternet.com

CARDIFF:
Ty Rosa Boutique B&B   T 029 2022 1964
118 Clive Street, Cardiff CF11 7JE
F 029 2002 7930
E info@tyrosa.com
W www.tyrosa.com/theatre-digs

CHESTERFIELD: Cook, Chris   T 01246 202631
27 Tennyson Avenue, Chesterfield, Derbyshire S40 4SN
T 07969 989558
E chris_cook@talk21.com

CHESTERFIELD:
Foston, Mr & Mrs   T 01246 235412
Anis Louise Guest House, 34 Clarence Road
Chesterfield S40 1LN
E anislouise@gmail.com
W www.anislouiseguesthouse.co.uk

COVENTRY:
Snelson, Paddy & Bob   T 01926 852850
Banner Hill Farmhouse, Rouncil Lane
Kenilworth CV8 1NN

DARLINGTON: Bird, Mrs   T 01748 822771
Gilling Old Mill, Gilling West
Richmond, N Yorks DL10 5JD
E admin@yorkshiredales-cottages.com

DARLINGTON: George Hotel   T 01325 374576
Piercebridge, Darlington DL2 3SW
E george@bulldogmail.co.uk
W www.george-ontees.co.uk

DERBY: Boddy, Susan   T 01332 701384
St Wilfrids, Church Lane
Barrow-upon-Trent, Derbyshire DE73 7HB

DERBY: Coxon, Mary   T 01332 347460
Short Term Accommodation. Theatricals only
1 Overdale Road, Derby DE23 6AU
T 07850 082943
E marycoxon@hotmail.co.uk

EASTBOURNE: Allen, Peter   T 07712 439289
16 Enys Road, Eastbourne BN21 2DN

EDINBURGH: ACS Properties   T 01620 826880
Contact: Ashley Smith, Carole Smith. Short Term Letting in Edinburgh
Office: 7 St Lawrence, Haddington
East Lothian EH41 3RL
T 07875 667752
E ashley@acs-properties.com
W www.acs-properties.com

EDINBURGH: Glen Miller, Edna   T 0131 556 4131
£90 per person, per week
25 Bellevue Road, Edinburgh EH7 4DL

EDINBURGH: Tyrrell, Helen   T 0131 229 7219
Two single rooms in flat overlooking city-centre park.
10 mins walk from several Edinburgh theatres. Wi-fi, full
access to kitchen & sitting room. Charges: £100 per
week (including breakfast, reductions for students),
£18 per day
9 Lonsdale Terrace, Edinburgh EH3 9HN
T 07929 960510
E hkmtyrrell@gmail.com

GLASGOW: Baird, David W.   T 0141 423 1340
6 Beaton Road, Maxwell Park, Glasgow G41 4LA
T 07842 195597
E b050557@yahoo.com

GLASGOW:
Leslie-Carter, Simon   T 01475 732204
52 Charlotte Street, Glasgow G1 5DW
T 07814 891351
E slc@52charlottestreet.co.uk
W www.52charlottestreet.co.uk

INVERNESS: Blair, Mrs   T 01463 232878
McDonald House Hotel, 1 Ardross Terrace
Inverness IV3 5NQ
E f.blair@homecall.co.uk

IPSWICH: Ball, Bunty   T 01473 256653
56 Henley Road, Ipswich IP1 3SA
E bunty.ball.t21@btinternet.com

IPSWICH: Bennett, Liz   T 01473 623343
Gayfers, Playford
Ipswich IP6 9DR
E lizzieb@clara.co.uk

LEEDS: Cannon, Rosie   T 0113 262 3550
14 Toronto Place, Chapel Allerton
Leeds LS7 4LJ
T 07969 832955
E cannon.rosey42@googlemail.com

LINCOLN: Carnell, Andrew   T 01522 569892
Tennyson Court Cottages, 3 Tennyson Street
Lincoln LN1 1LZ
E andrew@tennyson-court.co.uk
W www.tennyson-court.co.uk

LINCOLN: Sharpe, Mavis S.   T 01522 534477
Bight House, 17 East Bight
Lincoln LN2 1QH

LIVERPOOL: Maloney, Anne   T 0151 734 4839
16 Sandown Lane, Wavertree
Liverpool L15 8HY
T 07977 595040

LLANDUDNO:
Blanchard, Mr D. & Mrs A.   T 01492 877822
Oasis Hotel, 4 Neville Crescent
Central Promenade, Llandudno LL30 1AT
E oasishotel4@btconnect.com

LONDON: Allen, Mrs I.   T 020 7723 3979
Flat 2, 9 Dorset Square
London NW1 6QB
E neddyallen@mypostoffice.co.uk

LONDON: Cavanah, Anne Marie   T 07939 220299
Upper Flat, 66 Elsinore Road
Forest Hill, London SE23 2SL
E anmariecavanah@aol.com

LONDON: Home Rentals B&B   T 020 8840 1071
Agency
7 Park Place, Ealing
London W5 5NQ
E home_rentals@btinternet.com

LONDON: Horn, Cryn   T 020 8470 4868
27 Donald Road, Upton Park
London E13 0QF
T 07958 107620
E crynhorn@easynet.co.uk

LONDON: Kempton, Victoria   T 020 8888 5595
66 Morley Avenue, London N22 6NG
T 07946 344697
E vjkempton@onetel.com

LONDON: Mesure, Nicholas   T 020 8853 4337
16 St Alfege Passage, Greenwich
London SE10 9JS
T 07941 043841
E info@st-alfeges.co.uk

LONDON: Montagu, Beverley   T 020 7263 3883
13 Hanley Road, London N4 3DU
E beverley@montagus.org

LONDON: Rothner, Stephanie   T 020 8446 1604
44 Grove Road, North Finchley
London N12 9DY
T 07956 406446

LONDON: Shaw, Lindy   T 020 8567 0877
11 Baronsmede, London W5 4LS
E lindy.shaw@talktalk.net

LONDON: Walsh, Genevieve   T 020 7627 0024
37 Kelvedon House, Guildford Road
Stockwell, London SW8 2DN
T 07801 948864

LONDON: Warren, Mrs Sally   T 020 8994 0560
28 Prebend Gardens, Chiswick
London W4 1TW

LONDON: Wilson, Sylvia   T 07758 265351
1 Marlborough Mansions, 39 Bromells Road
Clapham SW4 0BA
E sylvia.wilson155@gmail.com

LONDON: Wood, Hilary   T 020 8331 6639
59 Prince John Road, Eltham
London SE9 6QB
F 07092 315384
E rainbowtheatrelondoneast@yahoo.co.uk

MALVERN: McLeod, Mr & Mrs   T 01684 574994
Sidney House, 40 Worcester Road
Malvern WR14 4AA
E info@sidneyhouse.co.uk
W www.sidneyhouse.co.uk

MANCHESTER:
Dyson, Mrs Edwina   T 0161 434 5410
33 Danesmoor Road, West Didsbury
Manchester M20 3JT
T 07947 197755
E edwinadyson@hotmail.com

MANCHESTER: Heaton, Miriam   T 0161 773 4490
58 Tamworth Avenue, Whitefield
Manchester M45 6UA

MANCHESTER: Higgins, Mark   T 07454 202880
New build less than 1 mile from Lowry or Opera House.
Pictures available on request. Parking Available
72 Camp Street, Manchester M7 1LG
T 0161 879 4712
E icenlemon30@hotmail.com

MANCHESTER:
Jones, Miss P. M.   T 0161 766 9243
'Forget-me-not Cottages', 12 Livsey Street
Whitefield, Manchester M45 6AE
E patricia@whitefieldcottages.co.uk

MANCHESTER: Prichard, Fiona   T 0161 434 4877
45 Bamford Road, Didsbury
Manchester M20 2QP
T 07771 965651
E fionaprichard@hotmail.com

MANCHESTER: Twist, Susan   T 0161 225 1591
45 Osborne Road
Levenshulme
Manchester M19 2DU
E sue.twist@o2.co.uk

MANSFIELD: Ward, Judith   T 01623 431359
4 Bedrooms. 5 minutes from Palace Mansfield Theatre
16 Watson Avenue, Mansfield
Nottinghamshire NG18 2BS
T 07926 601034
E judithaward@hotmail.com

MILFORD HAVEN:
Henricksen, Bruce & Diana   T 01646 695983
Belhaven House Hotel near Torch Theatre
29 Hamilton Terrace
Milford Haven SA73 3JJ
T 07436 582854
E brucehenricksen@mac.com
W www.westwaleshotel.com

NEWCASTLE UPON TYNE:
Rosebery Hotel   T 0191 281 3363
Contact: The Manager
2 Rosebery Crescent, Jesmond
Newcastle upon Tyne NE2 1ET
W www.roseberyhotel.co.uk

NEWCASTLE UPON TYNE:
Theatre Digs Newcastle   T 0191 226 1345
73 Moorside North
Newcastle upon Tyne NE4 9DU
E pclarerowntree@yahoo.co.uk
W www.theatredigsnewcastle.co.uk

NEWPORT: Price, Mrs Dinah   T 01633 420216
Great House, Isca Road
Old Village, Caerleon, Gwent NP18 1QG
E dinahprice123@btinternet.com
W www.greathousebb.co.uk

NORWICH:
Busch, Julia Cornaby   T 01603 612833
8 Chester Street, Norwich NR2 2AY
T 07920 133250
E juliacbusch@aol.com

NOTTINGHAM: Davis, Mrs B.   T 0115 947 4179
3 Tattershall Drive, The Park
Nottingham NG7 1BX

NOTTINGHAM: Offord, Mrs   T 0115 947 6924
5 Tattershall Drive, The Park
Nottingham NG7 1BX

NOTTINGHAM: Santos, Mrs S.   T 0115 966 3018
Eastwood Farm
Hagg Lane, Epperstone
Nottingham NG14 6AX
E info@eastwoodfarm.co.uk

NOTTINGHAM: Seymour Road
Studios Bed & Breakfast   T 07946 208211
42 Seymour Road
West Bridgford
Nottingham NG2 5EF
E fran@seymourroadstudios.co.uk
W www.seymourroadstudios.co.uk

NOTTINGHAM: Walker, Christine   T 0115 947 2485
18A Cavendish Crescent North, The Park
Nottingham NG7 1BA
E walker.ce@virgin.net

OXFORD: Petty, Susan   **T** 01993 703035
Self-catering Cottages. Sleeps 4-10. 12 miles from Oxford
Witney, Oxfordshire
E ianpetty@btinternet.com

PETERBOROUGH: Smith, J.   **T** 01733 211847
Fen-Acre
20 Barber Drove North
Crowland, Peterborough PE6 0BE
T 07759 661896
E julie@fen-acreholidaylet.com
W www.fen-acreholidaylet.com

PLYMOUTH: Ball, Fleur   **T** 01752 670967
3 Hoe Gardens
Plymouth PL1 2JD
E fleurball@blueyonder.co.uk

PLYMOUTH: Carson, Mr & Mrs   **T** 01752 872124
Beech Cottages
Parsonage Road
Newton Ferrers, Nr Plymouth PL8 1AX
T 07791 108146
E beechcottages@aol.com

PLYMOUTH:
Humphreys, John & Sandra   **T** 01752 220176
Lyttleton House, 4 Crescent Avenue
Plymouth PL1 3AN

PLYMOUTH: Mead, Teresa   **T** 01752 664046
Ashgrove House, 218 Citadel Road
The Hoe, Plymouth PL1 3BB
E ashgroveho@aol.com

PLYMOUTH:
Spencer, Hugh & Eloise   **T** 01752 664066
10 Grand Parade, Plymouth PL1 3DF
T 07966 412839
E hugh.spencer@hotmail.com

POOLE: Saunders, Mrs   **T** 01202 741637
1 Harbour Shallows
15 Whitecliff Road
Poole BH14 8DU
E saunders.221@btinternet.com

PORTSMOUTH: Dave &
Gerald's Theatrical Digs   **T** 023 9275 3359
10 mins from King's Theatre & 20 mins from New Theatre Royal
26 Wimborne Road, Southsea
Portsmouth, Hants PO4 8DE
E d.yetman@btinternet.com

SALISBURY: Brumfitt, Ms S.   **T** 01722 334877
26 Victoria Road, Salisbury
Wilts SP1 3NG
E slbrumfitt@gmail.com

SCARBOROUGH:
Holly Croft B&B   **T** 01723 375376
28 Station Road, Scalby
Scarborough, North Yorkshire YO13 0QA
E christine.goodall@tesco.net
W www.holly-croft.co.uk

SHEFFIELD: Slack, Penny   **T** 0114 234 0382
Rivelin Glen Quarry
Rivelin Valley Road
Sheffield S6 5SE
E pennyslack@aol.com
W www.quarryhouse.org.uk

SHOREHAM: Cleveland, Carol   **T** 01273 567954
Near Brighton
1 Oxen Court, Oxen Avenue
Shoreham-by-Sea BN43 5AS
T 07973 363939
E info@carolcleveland.com

SOUTHSEA & PORTSMOUTH:
Tyrell, Wendy   **T** 023 9282 1453
Douglas Cottage, 27 Somerset Road
Southsea PO5 2NL

STOKE-ON-TRENT:
Hindmoor, Mrs   **T** 01782 264244
Self-catering & B&B
Verdon Guest House
44 Charles Street
Hanley, Stoke-on-Trent ST1 3JY
E debbietams@ymail.com
W www.verdonguesthouse.co.uk

STOKE-ON-TRENT:
Meredith, Mr K.   **T** 01782 502160
2 Bank End Farm Cottage
Hammond Avenue
Brown Edge, Stoke-on-Trent, Staffs ST6 8QU
E kenmeredith@btinternet.com

STRATFORD-UPON-AVON:
Caterham House   **T** 01789 267309
58-59 Rother Street
Stratford-upon-Avon CV37 6LT
E caterhamhousehotel@btconnect.com

TAUNTON: Parker, Sue   **T** 01278 458580
Admirals Rest, 5 Taunton Road
Bridgwater TA6 3LW
E info@admiralsrest.co.uk

TAUNTON: Read, Mary   **T** 01823 334148
Pyreland Farm, Cheddon Road
Taunton, Somerset TA2 7QX

WINCHESTER:
South Winchester Lodges   **T** 01962 820490
The Green, South Winchester Golf Club
Winchester, Hampshire SO22 5SW

WOLVERHAMPTON:
Riggs, Peter A.   **T** 01902 846081
'Bethesda', 56 Chapel Lane
Codsall, Nr Wolverhampton WV8 2EJ
T 07930 967809

WOLVERHAMPTON: York Hotel   **T** 01902 758211
138 Tettenhall Road, Wolverhampton
West Midlands WV6 0BQ
E frontdesk@theyorkhotel.com
W www.theyorkhotel.com

WORTHING: Symonds, Mrs Val   **T** 01903 201557
23 Shakespeare Road
Worthing BN11 4AR
T 07951 183252

YORK: Blacklock, Tom   **T** 01904 620487
155 Lowther Street
York YO31 7LZ
E thomas.blacklock@btinternet.com

YORK: Harrand, Greg   **T** 01904 637404
Hedley House Hotel & Apts
3 Bootham Terrace, York YO30 7DH
E greg@hedleyhouse.com

Health & Wellbeing

Please note: Readers should take care to research any company or individual before agreeing to treatment or services listed in this section.

Health & Wellbeing

How should I use these listings?

You will find a variety of companies in this section which could help you enhance your health and wellbeing physically and mentally. They include personal fitness and lifestyle coaches, counsellors, exercise classes and beauty consultants amongst others. You should research any company or service you are considering using. Many of these listings have websites which you can browse. Even if you feel you have your career and lifestyle under control, you may still find the following advice helpful:

Your body is part of your business

Your mental and physical health is vital to your career as a performer. Just from a business perspective, your body is part of your promotional package and it needs to be maintained. Try to keep fit and eat healthily to enhance both your outward appearance and your inner confidence. This is particularly important if you are not working currently. You need to ensure that if you are suddenly called for an audition you look suitable for and feel positive about the part you are auditioning for.

Injury

Keeping fit also helps you to minimise the risk of an injury during a performance. The last thing you want to do is to be prevented from working. An injury is more likely to occur if you are inflexible and unprepared for sudden physical exertion. If you do pick up an injury or an illness you will want to make sure it does not get any worse by getting treatment with a specialist.

Mental health

Mental health is just as important as bodily health. Just as you would for any physical injury or illness, if you suffer from a psychological problem such as stage fright, an addiction or depression, you should make sure that you address your concerns and deal with the issues involved. You may need to see a counsellor or a life coach for guidance and support.

Unemployment

If you are unemployed, it can be difficult to retain a positive mindset. The best thing you can do is to keep yourself occupied. You could join a dance or drama class, which would help to maintain your fitness levels as well as developing contacts and keeping involved within the industry. Improve your CV by learning to speak a new language or play a musical instrument. Think about taking on temporary or part-time work outside of acting to earn money until the next job comes along (see the 'Non-Acting Jobs' section), or you could put yourself forward for acting work in a student film (see 'Film & Television Schools' for more information).

Where can I find more information?

For more information on health and wellbeing you may wish to contact the British Association for Performing Arts Medicine (BAPAM) www.bapam.org.uk. Please refer to the 'Drama Training, Schools & Coaches' and 'Dance Training & Professional Classes' sections if you are interested in taking drama or dance courses or lessons to improve your fitness, keep your auditioning skills sharp between jobs and/or stay occupied and motivated.

Working as a performer can be a stressful and sometimes isolating career. Spotlight members should keep an eye on the Spotlight website www.spotlight.com for useful career advice and news on forthcoming events and initiatives designed to support them and their wellbeing.

And remember, if you feel that things are getting to you, or you are worried about a colleague or friend, The Samaritans offer a confidential service, 24 hours a day, 365 days a week. Call 08457 90 90 90 or visit www.samaritans.org.uk

Health & Wellbeing

arts&minds

Looking after the industry

Spotlight is proud to be a founding partner of the Arts & Minds campaign, recognising that life can be the hardest act of all.

Arts & Minds is a joint initiative between Spotlight, Equity and The Stage, working together to end mental health discrimination within the industry and to support performers in need. It aims to:

- Raise awareness of mental health issues within the acting profession
- Support those currently in crisis, by signposting to specialists
- Promote good mental health within the acting profession

In 2013 there were a number of notable suicides amongst actors working in our industry. These tragic events caused much comment in the press, on social media channels and from individuals who had concerns about the issue of stress and mental wellbeing in the creative industries.

Spotlight, Equity and The Stage came together to discuss their responsibility as key industry organisations to raise awareness about the particular pressures of our sector and about available support networks. The result is the Arts & Minds initiative with a range of activities underway.

We are working with mental health practitioners and organisations such as BAPAM to ensure all the necessary resources are available and relevant to our industry.

As part of the 2014 Edinburgh Fringe, Spotlight, Equity and the Fringe Society ran a Sanctuary on three separate days during the festival. This was designed to provide a calm, quiet place within Fringe Central where participants could get away from things. The Sanctuary also included access to specialist support for one-to-one conversations and a neck and shoulder massage therapist.

Arts & Minds posters have been distributed in theatres, these provide sources of immediate help like The Samaritans, SANE and Mind.

www.artsminds.co.uk is an online resource, set up to raise awareness of mental health issues, support those currently in crisis, and promote good mental health within the acting profession.

As part of our commitment to the Arts & Minds campaign, Spotlight will be signing the Time to Change Pledge. This is an aspirational statement with meaning, indicating to employees, clients and the public that an organisation wants to take action to tackle the stigma and discrimination around mental health.

Signing the pledge highlights the key issues that have motivated us to come together for this campaign. It is also important to include actions that tackle stigma in the work environment so that our message runs throughout, both internally and externally.

We hope and believe the Arts & Minds initiative will prompt real change and progress in the entertainment industry.

**To find out more visit
www.artsminds.co.uk**

1ST SUCCESS   T 01628 780470
Empowerment, Confidence & Stress Therapies.
Challenge Blocks, Anxieties, Stresses & Fears
The Amber Zone, 13 St Mark's Crescent
Maidenhead, Berks SL6 5DA
E joanna@1stsuccess.com
W www.1stsuccess.com

ALEXANDER ALLIANCE   T 01727 843633
Alexander Technique. Audition & Voice Coaching
3 Hazelwood Drive, St Albans, Herts
E bev.keech@ntlworld.com
W www.alextech.co.uk

ALEXANDER TECHNIQUE   T 020 7731 1061
Contact: Jackie Coote MSTAT
27 Britannia Road, London SW6 2HJ
E jackiecoote@alexandertec.co.uk
W www.alexandertec.co.uk

ALKALI   T 020 8788 8588
Cosmetic Dentistry. Straightening. Whitening
226A Upper Richmond Road
Putney, London SW15 6TG
E hello@alkaliaesthetics.co.uk
W www.alkaliaesthetics.co.uk

AURA DENTAL SPA   T 020 7722 0040
Cosmetic Dentistry. Invisible Braces & Teeth Whitening,
50% Discount
5 Queens Terrace, London NW8 6DX
E info@auradentalspa.com
W www.auradentalspa.com

BEYONDYOGA   T 07837 355362
Holistic Bespoke Yoga in the Familial Lineage of
Krishnamacharya
Apartment 307, 3 Eastfields Avenue, London SW18 1GN
E tissie@beyondyoga.co.uk
W www.beyondyoga.co.uk

BLOOMSBURY ALEXANDER
CENTRE THE   T 020 7404 5348
Alexander Technique
Bristol House, 80A Southampton Row
London WC1B 4BB
T 07884 015954
E enquiries@alexcentre.com
W www.alexcentre.com

BODY CLINIC THE   T 0800 5424809
Skincare Specialists
33 Percy Street, London W1T 1DF
E info@thebodyclinic.co.uk
W www.thebodyclinic.co.uk

BODY CLINIC THE   T 0800 5424809
Skincare Specialists
85 Main Road, RM2 5EL
E info@thebodyclinic.co.uk
W www.thebodyclinic.co.uk

BODYWISE YOGA &
NATURAL HEALTH   T 020 3116 2098
21 Old Ford Road, London E2 9PL
E info@bodywisehealth.org
W www.bodywisehealth.org

BOXMOOR HOUSE
DENTAL PRACTICE   T 01442 253253
451 London Road, Hemel Hempstead HP3 9BE
F 01442 244454
E reception@boxmoordental.com

BREATHE FITNESS
PERSONAL TRAINING   T 07840 180094
Twitter: @BreatheFitPT
29 Rope Street, London SE16 7TE
E anthony@breathefitness.uk.com
W www.breathefitness.uk.com

BURGESS, Chris   T 07985 011694
Counsellor. Psychotherapist
New Road Consultancy Practice
28 New Road, Brighton BN1 1NG
E chrisburgess@netcom.co.uk

BURT, Andrew   T 020 8992 5992
Counselling
74 Mill Hill Road, London W3 8JJ
E burt.counsel@tiscali.co.uk
W www.andrewburtcounselling.co.uk

COACHING FOR LEADERS LTD   T 0845 1701300
Executive Coaching. Management & Team Development
& Training
90 Long Acre, Covent Garden
London WC2E 9RZ
E coaching@coachingforleaders.co.uk
W www.coachingforleaders.co.uk

COGNITIVE BEHAVIOURAL THERAPY (CBT)
Based in West & North London
E info@therapycbt.co.uk
W www.therapycbt.co.uk

COLLEGE PRACTICE THE   T 020 7267 6445
Massage. Osteopathy. Pilates. Podiatry. Sports Therapy
60 Highgate Road, London NW5 1PA
E thecollegepracticeuk@gmail.com
W www.thecollegepractice.com

**CONSTRUCTIVE
TEACHING CENTRE LTD**   **T** 020 7727 7222
Alexander Technique Teacher Training
13 The Boulevard, Imperial Wharf
Fulham, London SW6 2UB
E constructiveteachingcentre@gmail.com
W www.constructiveteachingcentre.com

CORTEEN, Paola MSTAT   **T** 020 8882 7898
Alexander Technique
10A Eversley Park Road, London N21 1JU
E pmcorteen@yahoo.co.uk

COURTENAY, Julian   **T** 07973 139376
NLP Hypnotherapy
42 Langdon Park Road, London N6 5QG
E julian@mentalfitness.uk.com

**CRAIGENTINNY
DENTAL CARE**   **T** 0131 669 2114
57 Duddingston Crescent, Milton Road
Edinburgh EH15 3AY
E office@craigentinny.co.uk
W www.craigentinny.co.uk

CROWE, Sara   **T** 07830 375389
Holistic Massage. Pregnancy Treatment. Reflexology
Holmes Avenue
Hove BN3 7LB
E saracrowe77@gmail.com

DAVIES, Siobhan STUDIOS   **T** 020 7091 9650
Complementary Therapies
Treatment Room, 85 St George's Road
London SE1 6ER
F 020 7091 9669
E info@siobhandavies.com
W www.siobhandavies.com

DIAMOND WHITE SMILE   **T** 07540 242098
2 Essella Road, Ashford, Kent TN24 8AN
E diamondwhitesmile@yahoo.com
W www.diamondwhitesmile.com

E(IN)MOTION   **T** 07766 062910
*Contact: Tiziana Silvestre. Physical Theatre, Movement
Coaching & Fitness for Performers & Productions on
Stage & Set. Based in London*
E3 4JJ
E tiziana.silvestre.Einm@gmail.com

**EDGE OF THE WORLD
HYPNOTHERAPY & NLP**   **T** 01206 391050
*Contact: Graham Howes. ASHPH GHR Registered.
GHSC Regulated. Gastric Band/Weight Loss
Hypnotherapy. Specialist Help for Performers: Anxiety,
Audition/Stage Fright, Problems with Line Learning,
Stress. Quit Smoking*
Based in Central London, Essex/Suffolk
T 07875 720623
E info@edgehypno.com
W www.edgehypno.com

**EDWARDS, Simon MCAHyp DABCH MHS MHA
MAPHP SQHP**   **T** 020 7467 8498
*Hypnotherapy for Professionals in Film, Stage &
Television*
10 Harley Street, London W1G 9PF
T 07889 333680
E simonedwardsharleystreet@gmail.com
W www.simonedwards.com

ELITE SPORTS SKILLS
*Personal Training. Sports Coaching. Level 4 in
Fitness & Coaching*
E esskills@hotmail.com
W www.elitesportsskills.com

ENLIGHTENEDSELFINTEREST.COM
56 Bloomsbury Street, London WC1B 3QT
T 07910 157064
E maggie@enlightenedselfinterest.com

EVOLVE WELLNESS CENTRE   **T** 020 7581 4090
10 Kendrick Mews, South Kensington
London SW7 3HG
E info@evolvewellnesscentre.com
W www.evolvewellnesscentre.com

**EXPERIENTIAL FOCUSING
THERAPY SESSIONS**   **T** 07941 300871
Contact: Dr Greg Madison
93-95 Gloucester Place
London W1
E info@gregmadison.net
W www.gregmadison.net

**EXPERIENTIAL FOCUSING
THERAPY SESSIONS**   **T** 07941 300871
Contact: Dr Greg Madison
40 Wilbury Road, Brighton BN1
E info@gregmadison.net
W www.gregmadison.net

**EXPLORING U COUNSELLING,
CENTRE FOR WELLBEING**   **T** 01787 829141
Practices in Colchester, Sudbury & Saffron Walden
54 Station Road, Sudbury
Suffolk CO10 2SP
T 07841 979450
E euc@exploringucounselling.co.uk
W www.exploringucounselling.co.uk

EXPOLRING U COUNSELLING   **T** 01787 829141
Dealing with Stress, Addictions & Lack of Confidence
The Old Press Rooms, 54 Station Road
Sudbury, Suffolk CO10 2SP
E info@exploringucounselling.co.uk
W www.exploringucounselling.co.uk

FABULOUS IMPACT   **T** 07958 984195
*Confidence & Positive Focus Coaching for Performers.
NLP*
E nicci@nicciroscoe.com
W www.nicciroscoe.com

**FAITH, Gordon
BA MCHC (UK) Dip.REM.Sp**   **T** 020 7328 0446
*Focusing. Hypnotherapy. Obstacles to Performing.
Positive Affirmation*
1 Wavel Mews, Priory Road
West Hampstead, London NW6 3AB
E gordon.faith@tiscali.co.uk
W www.hypnotherapy.gordonfaith.co.uk

FIT 4 THE PART   **T** 020 8311 9676
*Contact: Jon Trevor (Celebrity Trainer). Health & Fitness.
Stage & Screen. Production Services. TV Experts*
Based in North London
E info@fit4thepart.com
W www.fit4thepart.com

FITNESS COACH THE   **T** 020 7300 1414
Contact: Jamie Baird
Agua at The Sanderson
50 Berners Street
London W1T 3NG
T 07970 782476
E jamie@thefitnesscoach.com

**FOOTPRINT COACHING &
PERSONAL TRAINING**   **T** 07984 251903
Based in London & Kent
E georgina@georginaburnett.com
W www.footprintcoaching.org.uk

 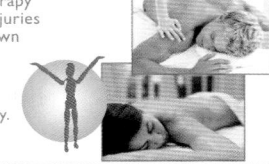

THE **CollegePractice**
Osteopathic Clinic
60 Highgate Road London NW5 1PA

- The College Practice's osteopathy, physiotherapy and Pilates treatments will help to prevent injuries and everyday aches and pains slowing you down
- Our practitioners offer effective treatments
- We also offer massage and chiropody

Call **020 7267 6445** to book a consultation today.
Or visit **www.thecollegepractice.com**
to learn more about our services.

HAMMOND, John B. Ed (Hons) ICHFST T/F 01277 632830
Fitness Consultancy. Sports & Relaxation Massage
4 Glencree, Billericay, Essex CM11 1EB
T 07703 185198
E johnhammond69@googlemail.com

HARLEY HEARING CENTRE T 020 7935 5486
Hearing Protection. Invisible Hearing Aids. Tinnitus Maskers
109 Harley Street, London W1G 6AN
E info@hearing-aid-devices.co.uk

HARLEY STREET VOICE CENTRE THE T 020 7224 2350
The Harley Street ENT Clinic, 109 Harley Street
London W1G 6AN
F 020 7935 7701
E info@harleystreetent.com
W www.harleystreetent.com

HAYWARD, Sarah T 07834 608833
Reflexology, Reiki, Meditation & other Therapies
27C Lyford Road, London SW18 3LU
E eyelovelight2012@gmail.com
W www.eyelovelight.co.uk

HEAL:TH WORKS T 07837 355362
Pilates, Acupuncture, Yoga, Massage & More
Apartment 307, 3 Eastfields Avenue
London SW18 1GN
E tissie@beyondyoga.co.uk

HORN, Cryn T 020 8470 4868
Gentle Yoga with a Therapeutic Focus
27 Donald Road
Plaistow, London E13 0QF
E crynhorn@easynet.co.uk

HYL ENERGISER T 07768 321092
10 Little Newport Street
London WC2H 7JJ
E info@hylenergiser.com
W www.hylenergiser.com

JOSHI CLINIC THE T 020 7487 5456
Holistic Healthcare
57 Wimpole Street, London W1G 8YW
E reception@joshiclinic.co.uk
W www.joshiclinic.co.uk

LIFE PRACTICE UK LTD T/F 01462 431112
Specialists in Coaching, Mentoring, NLP & Hypnotherapy
Suite 1, 107 Bancroft
Hitchin, Herts SG5 1NB
E info@lifepractice.co.uk
W www.lifepractice.co.uk

MAGIC KEY PARTNERSHIP THE T 0844 3320234
Contact: Lyn Burgess. Media Life Coach
151A Moffat Road
Thornton Heath, Surrey CR7 8PZ
E lyn@magickey.co.uk
W www.magickey.co.uk

MATRIX ENERGY FIELD THERAPY T 01304 379466
Accredited Healer
Deal Castle House, 31 Victoria Road
Deal, Kent CT14 7AS
T 07762 821828
E donnie@lovingorganization.org

McCALLION, Anna T 020 7602 5599
Alexander Technique. Voice
Flat 2, 11 Sinclair Gardens, London W14 0AU
E hildegarde007@yahoo.com

MIESSENCE T 07962 454206
Organic Natural Skincare. Wholefood Superfood Nutritionals
4 Little Dimocks, London SW12 9JH
E oxana.nico@gmail.com
W www.naturalhealthbeauty.miessence.com

NOBLE, Penny PSYCHOTHERAPY T 07506 579895
8 Shaftesbury Gardens, Victoria Road
North Acton, London NW10 6LJ
E pennynobletherapy@googlemail.com
W www.pennynoblepsychotherapy.com

NORTON, Michael R. T 020 7486 9229
Implant/Reconstructive Dentistry
104 Harley Street, London W1G 7JD
F 020 7486 9119
E linda@nortonimplants.com
W www.nortonimplants.com

NUTRITIONAL THERAPY FOR PERFORMERS T 07962 978763
Contact: Vanessa May BSc CNHC NTC & BANT Reg
18 Oaklands Road, Ealing, London W7 2DR
E vanessa@wellbeingandnutrition.co.uk
W www.wellbeingandnutrition.co.uk

ODYSSEY FITNESS T 07527 571443
Berwick-upon-Tweed, TD15 1PX
E lyons.a.michelle@gmail.com

OGUNLARU, Rasheed T 020 7207 1082
Life & Business Coach
The Coaching Studio, 223A Mayall Road
London SE24 0PS
E rasheed@rasaru.com
W www.rasaru.com

OWOADE, Simon T 07877 520266
Author. Motivational Speaker
Based in West London
E beinspiredtosucceed@hotmail.com
W www.simonowoade.co.uk

PEAK PERFORMANCE TRAINING T 01628 633509
Contact: Tina Reibl. Hypnotherapy. NLP. Success Strategies
42 The Broadway, Maidenhead, Berkshire SL6 1LU
E tina.reibl@gmail.com
W www.maidenhead-hypnotherapy.co.uk

POLAND, Ken
DENTAL STUDIOS   T 020 7935 6919
Film & Stage Dentistry
1 Devonshire Place, London W1G 6HH
F 020 7486 3952
E robpoland@btconnect.com

PSYCHOTHERAPY &
MEDICAL HYPNOSIS   T 07956 217266
Contact: Karen Mann DCH DHP. Including Performance
Improvement, Guilt & Anger Issues. Telephone
Appointments Available. Also in Hampstead
10 Harley Street, London W1G 9PF
E emailkarenmann@googlemail.com
W www.karenmann.co.uk

REACH TO THE SKY   T 0843 2892503
Contact: Dr J. Success Life Coach
Brook Street, Mayfair, London W1K 4HR
T 07961 911027
E drj@reachtothesky.com
W www.reachtothesky.com

ROGERS, Helen
HYPNOTHERAPY   T 07915 093588
Lower Ground Floor, 5 College Fields, Bristol BS8 3HP
E helen@helenrogers.co.uk
W www.helenrogers.co.uk

SERENDIPITY   T 07809 458270
Remedial Sports Massage Therapist
Based in North West
E mail@serendipity-spa.co.uk
W www.serendipity-spa.co.uk

SEYRI, Kayvan
MSc CSCS*D CES   T 07881 554636
Athletic Performance Specialist. Master Personal Trainer
E info@ultimatefitpro.com
W www.ultimatefitpro.com

SHAPES IN MOTION   T 07802 709933
Contact: Sarah Perry. Movement Coaching. Yin, Viniyoga
& Children's Yoga
Based in London
E yoga@shapeinmotion.com
W www.shapeinmotion.com

SHENAS, Dr DENTAL CLINIC   T 020 7589 2319
51 Cadogan Gardens, Sloane Square
Chelsea, London SW3 2TH
E info@shenasdental.co.uk
W www.shenasdental.co.uk

SHIATSU HEALTH CENTRE   T 01908 679834
E japaneseyoga@btinternet.com
W www.shiatsuhealth.com

SMILE NW DENTAL PRACTICE   T 020 8458 2333
Contact: Dr Veronica Morris. Cosmetic & General Dentist
17 Hallswelle Parade, Finchley Road
Temple Fortune, London NW11 0DL
F 020 8458 5681
E enquiries@smile-nw.co.uk
W www.smile-nw.co.uk

SMILE SOLUTIONS   T 020 7449 1760
Dental Practice
24 Englands Lane, London NW3 4TG
F 020 7449 1769
E enquiries@smile-solutions.info
W www.smile-solutions.info

STAT (THE SOCIETY OF TEACHERS OF THE
ALEXANDER TECHNIQUE)   T 020 7482 5135
1st Floor Linton House, 39-51 Highgate Road
London NW5 1RT
F 020 7482 5435
E enquiries@stat.org.uk   W www.stat.org.uk

STEP 'N' FLEX- ZUMBA
CLASSES   T 07801 741892
Zumba® Fitness Classes across South West London.
Oval, Vauxhall & Kennington
E sarahfrench123@hotmail.com
W www.sarahfrench.zumba.com

STRANGE, Victoria   T 07854 052602
4 Richmond Road, Westoning
Bedfordshire MK45 5JZ
E veceighty@hotmail.com

STREET DEFENCE   T 07919 350290
Commando Krav Maga Instructor, Screen Combatant &
Celebrity Personal Trainer
6 Clive Close, Potters Bar
Hertfordshire EN6 2AE
E streetdefence@hotmail.co.uk
W www.streetdefenceuk.com

TEAM DAN ROBERTS   T 020 7989 0338
Personal Training. Nutrition, Yoga & Martial Arts.
Specialising in Training Athletes, Models & Actors.
Regularly Consults on Hollywood Films. Based in
Kensington, London
E info@danrobertstraining.com
W www.danrobertstraining.com

TOPOLSKI, Suzy   T 07702 476843
Life & Performance Coaching
69 Randolph Avenue, Little Venice, London W9 1DW
E suzytopolski@aol.com

VIE MEDIC SERVICES LTD   T 07581 144538
Contact: Paul Holmes. Professional First Aid & Medical
Services. Quality First Aid Courses
West House, West Street
Wath-upon-Dearne, South Yorkshire S63 7QX
E enquiries@viemedic.co.uk
W www.viemedic.co.uk

VITAL TOUCH (UK) LTD THE   T 07976 263691
50 Greenham Road, Muswell Hill, London N10 1LP
E suzi@thevitaltouch.com
W www.thevitaltouch.com

WALK-IN BACKRUB   T/F 020 7436 9875
On-site Massage Company
14 Neals Yard, London WC2H 9DP
E info@walkinbackrub.co.uk
W www.walkinbackrub.co.uk

WALSH, Gavin
PERSONAL TRAINING   T 07782 248687
22 Stirling Court, Tavistock Street
London WC2E 7NU
E gavin@gavinwalsh.co.uk
W www.gavinwalsh.co.uk

WELLBEING   T 07957 333921
Contact: Leigh Jones. Personal Training. Tai Chi. Yoga
22 Galloway Close
Broxbourne, Herts EN10 6BU
E williamleighjones@hotmail.com

WOODFORD HOUSE
DENTAL PRACTICE   T 020 8504 2704
162 High Road, Woodford Green, Essex IG8 9EF
E info@improveyoursmile.co.uk
W www.improveyoursmile.co.uk

WORSLEY, Victoria   T 07711 088765
Feldenkrais Practitioner. Addresses Habits of Moving &
Breathing which Limit Range of Movement, Cause Pain
or Affect the Voice
32 Clovelly Road, London N8 7RH
E v.worsley@virgin.net
W www.feldenkraisworks.co.uk

N →

Non-Acting Jobs

**42ND STREET
RECRUITMENT**　　　　T 020 7734 4422
Linen Hall
162-168 Regent Street
London W1B 5TD
E info@42ndstreetrecruitment.com
W www.42ndstreetrecruitment.com

ALLSTARS STAFF LTD　　T 0161 702 8258
2 Buttermere Road
Partington, Manchester
Greater Manchester M31 4WE
T 07584 992429
W www.allstarsactors.com

ARTISAN PEOPLE　　　　T 020 7813 2121
*Temporary Non-acting Positions available in Museums &
Retail Promotions in London*
Tudor House, 35 Gresse Street
London W1T 1QY
F 020 7813 1414
E simon@artisanpeople.com

**AT YOUR SERVICE EVENT
STAFFING LTD**　　　　　T 020 7610 8610
Temporary Event Staff
Unit 6, The Talina Centre, Bagley's Lane
Fulham, London SW6 2BW
F 020 7610 8616
E joanna@ays.co.uk
W www.ays.co.uk/apply

ATTITUDE EVENTS　　　T 020 7953 7935
Event Consultation & Staffing
412 Coppergate House
16 Brune Street, London E1 7NJ
E nikki@attitude-events.com
W www.attitude-events.com

BREEZE PEOPLE　　　　T 023 8001 5000
Promotional Staffing Agency
Wessex House, Upper Market Street
Eastleigh, Hampshire SO50 9FD
E peepz@breezepeople.co.uk
W www.breezepeople.co.uk/staff

**BRISTOW, Lucy
APPOINTMENTS**　　　　T 0117 925 5988
Recruitment for Office Staff
12 Orchard Street
Bristol BS1 5EH
E enquire@lucybristow.com
W www.lucybristow.com

CATERINGTEMPS.COM LTD　T 020 7713 8772
*Suppliers of Temporary Staff to the Catering &
Hospitality Industry*
108-110 Judd Street, London WC1H 9PX
F 020 7713 6297
E enquiries@cateringtemps.com
W www.cateringtemps.com

**CENTRAL EMPLOYMENT
AGENCY**　　　　　　　T 0191 232 4816
34-36 St Mary's Place
Newcastle upon Tyne NE1 7PQ
F 0191 261 2203
E enquiries@centralemployment.co.uk
W www.centralemployment.co.uk

COVENT GARDEN BUREAU　T 020 7734 3374
Recruitment Consultants
5-6 Argyll Street
London W1F 7TE
E cv@coventgardenbureau.co.uk
W www.coventgardenbureau.co.uk

**FISHER, Judy
ASSOCIATES**　　　　　T 020 7437 2277
Media & Arts Recruitment Specialists
7 Swallow Street
London W1B 4DE
E cv@judyfisher.co.uk
W www.judyfisher.co.uk

**FOUR SEASONS
RECRUITMENT**　　　　　T 020 8237 8900
Recruitment Company. Beauty. Fashion. Retail
The Triangle
5-17 Hammersmith Grove
London W6 0LG
F 020 8237 8999
E info@fsrl.co.uk
W www.fsrl.co.uk

HANDLE RECRUITMENT　　T 020 7569 9999
*Recruitment for Arts, Media, Entertainment &
Inspirational Brands*
7 Portman Mews South
London W1H 6AY
E david.bishop@handle.co.uk
W www.handle.co.uk

JAM STAFFING LTD　　　T 020 7237 2228
*Events Company. Part-time Flexible Bar & Waiting Work
at London Events*
Unit 104
The Light Box
111 Power Road
London W4 5PY
E jeremy@jamstaffing.com
W www.jamstaffing.com

JFL SEARCH & SELECTION　T 020 7009 3500
Recruitment Consultants
27 Beak Street
London W1F 9RU
F 020 7734 6501
E info@jflrecruit.com
W www.jflrecruit.com

LEISUREJOBS　　　　　T 020 7622 8500
*Temporary, Promotional & Permanent Positions within
Leisure*
Cloisters House
8 Battersea Park Road
London SW8 4BG
E info@leisurejobs.com
W www.leisurejobs.com

**LUMLEYS HOSPITALITY &
CATERING**　　　　　　T 020 7630 0545
Private & Corporate Hospitality, Catering & Events
Grosvenor Gardens House
35-37 Grosvenor Gardens
London SW1W 0BS
E admin@greycoatlumleys.co.uk
W www.greycoatlumleys.co.uk

MORTIMER, Angela T 020 7287 7788
Recruitment Specialists for Perm & Temp PAs & Support
Staff in the UK & Europe
37-38 Golden Square
London W1F 9LA
E info@angelamortimer.com
W www.angelamortimer.com

NETWORK THE T 020 8742 4336
Field Marketing & Promotions
Merlin House
20 Belmont Terrace
Chiswick, London W4 5UG
F 020 8742 4051
E recruitment@thenetwork-uk.com
W www.thenetwork-uk.com

OFF TO WORK T 020 7381 8222
Non-acting Employment. Promotional Work at Events
across the UK
3rd Floor
79 Knightsbridge
London SW1X 7RB
E abbie.paulman@offtowork.co.uk
W www.offtowork.co.uk

RSVP T 020 7536 3548
Telemarketing/Agency
Northern & Shell Tower
4 Selsdon Way
London E14 9GL
E jobs@rsvp.co.uk
W www.rsvp.co.uk/careers

SENSE STAFFING T 020 7034 2000
Promotional Staffing for Experiential Marketing
1st Floor
100 Oxford Street
London W1D 1LN
E staff@senselondon.com
W www.senselondon.com

SMITH, Amanda
RECRUITMENT LTD T 020 7681 6180
Recruitment of Temporary, Permanent & Contract Office
Support Staff
88 Kingsway
Holborn
London WC2B 6AA
E info@as-recruitment.co.uk

STUCKFORSTAFF.CO.UK T 0844 5869595
Promotions, Field Marketing & Brand Experience
116 Zellig
Custard Factory
Gibb Street, Birmingham B9 4AA
E info@stuckforstaff.com
W www.stuckforstaff.co.uk

TRIBE MARKETING LTD T 020 7702 3600
Experiential Marketing & Promotional Staffing Agency
The Wool House
74 Back Church Lane
Whitechapel
London E1 1LX
E talent@tribemarketing.co.uk
W www.tribemarketing.co.uk

Opera Companies
Organisations

CANTAMUSICA T 020 8449 2342
Young Professionals' Chorus for Opera, Recordings & Concerts
Capital Arts Studio
Wyllyotts Theatre, Darkes Lane
Potters Bar, Hertfordshire EN6 2HN
T 07885 232414
E capitalarts@btconnect.com
W www.capitalarts.org.uk

CO-OPERA CO T 020 8699 8650
Touring Productions. Education. Training. Workshops
5 Metro Business Centre
Kangley Bridge Road
London SE26 5BW
E admin@co-opera-co.org
W www.co-opera-co.org

ENGLISH NATIONAL OPERA T 020 7836 0111
London Coliseum
St Martin's Lane
London WC2N 4ES
F 020 7845 9277
W www.eno.org

ENGLISH TOURING OPERA T 020 7833 2555
3rd Floor
63 Charterhouse Street
London EC1M 6HJ
E admin@englishtouringopera.org.uk
W www.englishtouringopera.org.uk

GARSINGTON OPERA T 01865 368201
The Old Garage, The Green
Great Milton, Oxford OX44 7NP
F 01865 961545
W www.garsingtonopera.org

GLYNDEBOURNE T 01273 812321
Lewes, East Sussex BN8 5UU
E info@glyndebourne.com
W www.glyndebourne.com

GRANGE PARK OPERA T 01962 737360
24-26 Broad Street, Alresford
Hampshire SO24 9AQ
E info@grangeparkopera.co.uk
W www.grangeparkopera.co.uk

GUBBAY, Raymond LTD T 020 7025 3750
Dickens House
15 Tooks Court
London EC4A 1LB
F 020 7025 3751
E info@raymondgubbay.co.uk
W www.raymondgubbay.co.uk

KENTISH OPERA T 01732 700993
Contact: Sally Langford
Lakefields Farmhouse
Ide Hill Road
Bough Beech, Kent TN8 7PW
E sl.sweald@fsmail.net
W www.kentishopera.com

**LONDON CHILDREN'S
OPERA COMPANY** T/F 020 8449 2342
Rehearsals at Dragon Hall, Covent Garden. Students aged 8-18
T 07885 232414
E capitalarts@btconnect.com
W www.capitalarts.org.uk

MUSIC THEATRE LONDON T 07831 243942
c/o Capriol Films, The Coach House
35 High Street, Holt, Norfolk NR25 6BN
T 01263 712600
E tony.britten@capriolfilms.co.uk
W www.capriolfilms.co.uk

OPERA CAPITAL ARTS T 020 8449 2342
Rehearsals held at Dragon Hall, Covent Garden WC2B 5LT
Capital Arts Studio
Wyllyotts Theatre, Darkes Lane
Potters Bar, Hertfordshire EN6 2HN
T 07885 232414
E capitalarts@btconnect.com
W www.capitalarts.org.uk

OPERA DELLA LUNA T 01869 325131
7 Cotmore House, Fringford
Bicester, Oxfordshire OX27 8RQ
E enquiries@operadellaluna.org
W www.operadellaluna.org

OPERA NORTH T 0113 243 9999
Grand Theatre, 46 New Briggate
Leeds LS1 6NU
F 0113 244 0418
E info@operanorth.co.uk
W www.operanorth.co.uk

OPERAUK LTD T 020 7628 0025
Charity
177 Andrewes House, Barbican
London EC2Y 8BA
E rboss4@aol.com
W www.operauk.co.uk

**PEGASUS OPERA
COMPANY LTD** T/F 020 7501 9501
The Brix, St Matthew's
Brixton Hill, London SW2 1JF
E admin@pegopera.org
W www.pegasus-opera.net

PIMLICO OPERA T 01962 737360
24 Broad Street, Alresford
Hampshire SO24 9AQ
E pimlico@grangeparkopera.co.uk
W www.grangeparkopera.co.uk

PMB PRESENTATIONS LTD T 020 7368 3337
Vicarage House, 58-60 Kensington Church Street
London W8 4DB
E info@pmbpresentations.co.uk
W www.pmbpresentations.co.uk

ROYAL OPERA THE T 020 7240 1200
Royal Opera House, Bow Street
Covent Garden, London WC2E 9DD
W www.roh.org.uk

SCOTTISH OPERA T 0141 248 4567
39 Elmbank Crescent, Glasgow G2 4PT
E information@scottishopera.org.uk
W www.scottishopera.org.uk

WELSH NATIONAL OPERA T 029 2063 5000
Wales Millennium Centre, Bute Place
Cardiff CF10 5AL
F 029 2063 5099
E marketing@wno.org.uk
W www.wno.org.uk

ABTT (ASSOCIATION OF BRITISH THEATRE TECHNICIANS) T 020 7242 9200
4th Floor, 55 Farringdon Road, London EC1M 3JB
F 020 7242 9303
E office@abtt.org.uk
W www.abtt.org.uk

ACADEMY OF PERFORMANCE COMBAT THE
Teaching Body of Stage Combat
197 Church Road, Northolt, Middlesex UB5 5BE
E info@theapc.org.uk
W www.theapc.org.uk

ACTORS' BENEVOLENT FUND T 020 7836 6378
6 Adam Street, London WC2N 6AD
F 020 7836 8978
E office@abf.org.uk
W www.actorsbenevolentfund.co.uk

ACTORS CENTRE (LONDON) THE T 020 7632 8001
Charity. Over 1700 Workshops & Courses per year for Professional Actors. Advice & Information. Introductory Courses
1A Tower Street, London WC2H 9NP
E reception@actorscentre.co.uk
W www.actorscentre.co.uk

ACTORS' CHILDREN'S TRUST T 020 7636 7868
Provides Grants & Support for Actors' Children
58 Bloomsbury Street, London WC1B 3QT
E robert@tactactors.org
w www.tactactors.org

ACTORS' GUILD OF GREAT BRITAIN (TAG) T 020 7112 8458
Non-profit. Workshops. Networking. Bursaries. Support
TAG Hub at Spotlight, 2nd Floor
7 Leicester Place, London WC2H 7RJ
E mail@actorsguild.co.uk
W www.actorsguild.co.uk

ADVERTISING ASSOCIATION T 020 7340 1100
7th Floor North, Artillery House
11-19 Artillery Row, London SW1P 1RT
F 020 7222 1504
E aa@adassoc.org.uk
W www.adassoc.org.uk

AGENTS' ASSOCIATION (GREAT BRITAIN) T 020 7834 0515
54 Keyes House
Dolphin House, London SW1V 3NA
E association@agents-uk.com
W www.agents-uk.com

ARTS & BUSINESS T 020 7566 8650
137 Shepherdess Walk, London N1 7RQ
E info@bitc.org.uk
W www.bitc.org.uk

ARTS CENTRE GROUP T 0845 4581881
c/o Paintings in Hospitals, 51 Southwark Street
London SE1 1RU
T 020 7407 1881
E info@artscentregroup.org.uk
W www.artscentregroup.org.uk

ARTS COUNCIL ENGLAND T 0845 3006200
T 020 7973 6564 (Textphone)
W www.artscouncil.org.uk

ARTS COUNCIL OF NORTHERN IRELAND T 028 9038 5200
MacNeice House, 77 Malone Road, Belfast BT9 6AQ
F 028 9066 1715
E info@artscouncil-ni.org
W www.artscouncil-ni.org

ARTS COUNCIL OF WALES T 0845 8734900
Bute Place, Cardiff CF10 5AL
F 029 2044 1400
E information@artswales.org.uk
W www.artscouncilofwales.org.uk

ARTS COUNCIL OF WALES T 0845 8734900
The Mount, 18 Queen Street
Carmarthen SA31 1JT
F 01267 233084
E information@artscouncilofwales.org.uk
W www.artscouncilofwales.org.uk

ARTS COUNCIL OF WALES T 01492 533440
36 Prince's Drive, Colwyn Bay, Conwy LL29 8LA
F 01492 533677
E information@artscouncilofwales.org.uk
W www.artscouncilofwales.org.uk

ASSOCIATED STUDIOS THE T 020 7385 2038
The Hub @ St Alban's Fulham, 2 Margravine Road
London W6 8HJ
E info@associatedstudios.co.uk
W www.associatedstudios.co.uk

ASSOCIATION OF LIGHTING DESIGNERS T 07817 060189
PO Box 955, Southsea PO1 9NF
E office@ald.org.uk
W www.ald.org.uk

ASSOCIATION OF MODEL AGENTS T 020 7422 0699
11-29 Fashion Street, London E1 6PX
E amainfo@btinternet.com
W www.associationofmodelagents.org

BASCA - BRITISH ACADEMY OF SONGWRITERS, COMPOSERS & AUTHORS T 020 7636 2929
2nd Floor, British Music House
26 Berners Street, London W1T 3LR
F 020 7636 2212
E info@basca.org.uk
W www.basca.org.uk

BFI SOUTH BANK T 020 7928 3232
Belvedere Road, South Bank
London SE1 8XT
W www.bfi.org.uk

BRITISH ACADEMY OF FILM & TELEVISION ARTS (BAFTA) T 020 7734 0022
195 Piccadilly, London W1J 9LN
E info@bafta.org
W www.bafta.org

BRITISH ACADEMY OF FILM & TELEVISION ARTS LOS ANGELES T 001 323 658 6590
8469 Melrose Avenue, West Hollywood
CA 90069, USA
E office@baftala.org
W www.bafta.org/losangeles

BRITISH ACADEMY OF STAGE & SCREEN COMBAT T 07898 670186
Suite 280, 10 Great Russell Street
London WC1B 3BQ
E info@bassc.org
W www.bassc.org

BRITISH ASSOCIATION FOR PERFORMING ARTS MEDICINE (BAPAM) T 020 7404 5888
Charity
4th Floor, Totara Park House
34-36 Gray's Inn Road, London WC1X 8HR
E clinic@bapam.org.uk
W www.bapam.org.uk

sport
music
dance
drama
childcare
uniform
trips
equipment
clothing
university

help for actors' children

Are you:
- a professional actor?
- parent of a child under 21?
- worried about money?

TACT helps children who are ill or have special needs, families in financial crisis, or where a parent is unwell or cannot work.

Confidential and friendly.

TACT
The Actors' Children's Trust
020 7636 7868
www.tactactors.org
registered charity 206809

BRITISH ASSOCIATION OF DRAMATHERAPISTS THE T 01242 235515
Waverley, Battledown Approach
Cheltenham, Glos GL52 6RE
E enquiries@badth.org.uk
W www.badth.org.uk

BRITISH BOARD OF FILM CLASSIFICATION T 020 7440 1570
3 Soho Square, London W1D 3HD
F 020 7287 0141
E feedback@bbfc.co.uk
W www.bbfc.co.uk

BRITISH COUNCIL T 0161 957 7755
Arts Group
10 Spring Gardens, London SW1A 2BN
E arts@britishcouncil.org
W www.britishcouncil.org/arts

BRITISH EQUITY COLLECTING SOCIETY T 020 7670 0360
1st Floor, Guild House
Upper St Martin's Lane, London WC2H 9EG
E becs@equity.org.uk
W www.equitycollecting.org.uk

BRITISH FILM INSTITUTE T 020 7255 1444
21 Stephen Street, London W1T 1LN
F 020 7436 0165
W www.bfi.org.uk

BRITISH LIBRARY SOUND ARCHIVE T 020 7412 7831
96 Euston Road, London NW1 2DB
F 020 7412 7691
E sound-archive@bl.uk
W www.bl.uk/soundarchive

BRITISH MUSIC HALL SOCIETY T 01727 768878
Contact: Daphne Masterton (Secretary). Charity
45 Mayflower Road, Park Street
St Albans, Herts AL2 2QN
E geoff.bowden1@btinternet.com
W www.britishmusichallsociety.com

CATHOLIC ASSOCIATION OF PERFORMING ARTS T 020 7240 1221
Contact: Ms Molly Steele (Hon Secretary). By Post (SAE)
1 Maiden Lane
London WC2E 7NB
E secretary@caapa.org.uk
W www.caapa.org.uk

CEG PRODUCTIONS T 01379 888179
Provision of Technical Support for all Theatre Events
Unit 23 Court Industrial Estate, Vinces Road
Diss, Norfolk IP22 4BF
E info@cegproductions.co.uk
W www.cegproductions.co.uk

CELEBRITY BULLETIN THE T 020 8672 3191
Tower Point, 44 North Road
Brighton, East Sussex BN1 1YR
E enquiries@celebrity-bulletin.co.uk

CIDA CO T 0113 373 1754
The Creative & Innovation Company
Munro House, Duke Street, Leeds LS9 8AG
E info@cida.org
W www.cidaco.org

CINEMA & TELEVISION BENEVOLENT FUND (CTBF) T 020 7437 6567
22 Golden Square, London W1F 9AD
F 020 7437 7186
E charity@ctbf.co.uk
W www.ctbf.co.uk

CINEMA EXHIBITORS' ASSOCIATION T 020 7734 9551
3 Soho Square, London W1D 3HD
F 020 7734 6147
E info@cinemauk.org.uk
W www.cinemauk.org.uk

CLUB FOR ACTS & ACTORS T 020 7836 3172
Incorporating Concert Artistes Association
20 Bedford Street
London WC2E 9HP
E office@thecaa.org
W www.thecaa.co.uk

COMPANY OF CRANKS T 07963 617981
1st Floor, 62 Northfield House
Frensham Street, London SE15 6TN
E mimetic16@yahoo.com
W www.mimeworks.com

COUNCIL FOR DANCE EDUCATION & TRAINING (CDET) T 020 7240 5703
Old Brewer's Yard, 17-19 Neal Street
London WC2H 9UY
F 020 7240 2547
E info@cdet.org.uk
W www.cdet.org.uk

CREATIVE SCOTLAND T 0141 302 1700
249 West George Street
Glasgow G2 4QE
F 0141 302 1711
E enquiries@creativescotland.com
W www.creativescotland.com

CRITICS' CIRCLE THE T 020 7732 9636
Contact: William Russell
50 Finland Road, Brockley
London SE4 2JH
E williamfinland@gmail.com
W www.criticscircle.org.uk

DANCE HOUSE T 0141 552 2442
The Briggait, 141 Bridgegate
Glasgow G1 5HZ
E info@dancehouse.org
W www.dancehouse.org

DANCE UK T 020 7713 0730
Including the Healthier Dancer Programme, the National Institute for Dance Medicine & Science & 'The UK Choreographers' Directory'. Professional Body & Charity, providing Advice, Information & Support
Unit A402A, The Biscuit Factory
Drummond Road
London SE16 4DG
F 020 7833 2363
E info@danceuk.org
W www.danceuk.org

DENVILLE HALL T 01923 825843
Provides Residential, Nursing & Dementia Care to Actors & other Theatrical Professions
62 Ducks Hill Road, Northwood
Middlesex HA6 2SB
E office@denvillehall.org.uk
W www.denvillehall.org.uk

DIRECTORS UK T 020 7240 0009
8-10 Dryden Street, London WC2E 9NA
E info@directors.uk.com
W www.directors.uk.com

DON'T PLAY ME PAY ME CAMPAIGN
Campaigning for a Greater Representation of Disabled Talent in the Entertainment Industry
E peoplenotpunchlines@gmail.com
W www.dontplaymepayme.com

**D'OYLY CARTE
OPERA COMPANY**　T 0844 6060007
Unit 302 Northlock
Westminster Business Square
London SE11 5JH
F 020 7820 0240
E ian@doylycarte.org.uk
W www.doylycarte.org.uk

**DRAMA ASSOCIATION
OF WALES**　T 029 2045 2200
Specialist Drama Lending Library
Unit 2, The Maltings
East Tyndall Street
Cardiff Bay
Cardiff CF24 5EA
E chair@dramawales.org.uk
W www.dramawales.org.uk

DRAMA UK　T 020 3393 6141
*Drama UK Champions Quality Drama Training &
Provides a Link between the Theatre, Media & Broadcast
Industries & Drama Training Providers in the UK. Offering
Help & Advice to Drama Students of all Ages. Awarding
a Quality Kite Mark to the very Best Drama Training
Available. Created in 2012 following the Merger of the
Conference of Drama Schools (CDS) and the National
Council for Drama Training (NCDT). Charity. Professional
Body. Provides Advice. Provides Information. Social
Membership*
Woburn House
20 Tavistock Square
London WC1H 9HB
E info@dramauk.co.uk
W www.dramauk.co.uk

DRAMATURGS' NETWORK
*Supports Theatre Makers, Dramaturgs, Literary
Managers & Educational Professionals Involved in
Dramaturgical Practice. Twitter: @dramaturgs_net*
Flat 1, Westmorland House
Fieldway Crescent
London N5 1QE
E info@dramaturgy.co.uk
W www.dramaturgy.co.uk

**ENGLISH FOLK DANCE &
SONG SOCIETY**　T 020 7485 2206
Cecil Sharp House, 2 Regent's Park Road
London NW1 7AY
F 020 7284 0534
E info@efdss.org
W www.efdss.org

EQUITY CHARITABLE TRUST　T 020 7831 1926
Plouviez House, 19-20 Hatton Place
London EC1N 8RU
E info@equitycharitabletrust.org.uk

FILM LONDON　T 020 7613 7676
Suite 6.10, The Tea Building
56 Shoreditch High Street, London E1 6JJ
F 020 7613 7677
E info@filmlondon.org.uk
W www.filmlondon.org.uk

GLASGOW FILM OFFICE　T 0141 287 0424
Free Advice & Liaison Support for all Productions
231 George Street, Glasgow G1 1RX
F 0141 287 0311
E info@glasgowfilm.com

Patron: H.R.H. The Prince of Wales

Registered Charity No. 206524

Help us to help actors unable to work because of illness or frail old age by including the Fund in your will or sending a donation today.

If you know someone who needs our help please contact me in confidence:
Willie Bicket   020 7836 6378
6 Adam Street London WC2N 6AD
Fax: 020 7836 8978 Email: office@abf.org.uk
www.actorsbenevolentfund.co.uk

GRAND ORDER OF WATER RATS   T 020 7278 3248
328 Gray's Inn Road
London WC1X 8BZ
E info@gowr.net
W www.gowr.net

GROUP LINE   T 020 7420 9700
Group Bookings for London Theatre
37 Long Acre
Covent Garden
London WC2E 9JT
E tix@groupline.com
W www.groupline.com

HAMMER FILMS PRESERVATION SOCIETY
Fan Club
E maylott@btinternet.com

IDEASTAP
A Charity that Supports Creative People through Opportunities, Funding, Arts Jobs & Career Development. Twitter: @IdeasTap
Woolyard, 54 Bermondsey Street
London SE1 3UD
E info@ideastap.com
W www.ideastap.com

INDEPENDENT THEATRE COUNCIL (ITC)   T 020 7403 1727
Professional Body offering Advice, Information, Support & Political Representation
The Albany, Douglas Way
London SE8 4AG
E admin@itc-arts.org
W www.itc-arts.org

INGMAR SAUER NETWORKS   T 00 31 6 16242010
Mathenesserdijk 288b
3026 GP Rotterdam
The Netherlands
E info@ingmarsauernetworks.com
W www.ingmarsauernetworks.com

INTERNATIONAL CENTRE FOR VOICE
The Royal Central School of Speech & Drama
Eton Avenue
London NW3 3HY
E icv@cssd.ac.uk
W www.icvoice.co.uk

IRVING SOCIETY THE
Contact: Megan Hunter
E theirvingsociety@gmail.com
W www.theirvingsociety.org.uk

LONDON SCHOOL OF CAPOEIRA   T 020 7281 2020
Units 1 & 2 Leeds Place, Tollington Park
London N4 3RF
E info@londonschoolofcapoeira.com
W www.londonschoolofcapoeira.com

LONDON SHAKESPEARE WORKOUT   T/F 020 7793 9755
PO Box 31855, London SE17 3XP
E londonswo@hotmail.com
W www.lswproductions.co.uk

MAKE A DIFFERENCE TRUST THE   T 07956 019853
Provides Practical Support to Members of the Entertainment Industry Experiencing Hardship due to Ill Health as well as Specific HIV & AIDS Support, Education & Care in the UK & Southern Africa. UK Charity Registration No. 1124014
c/o Theatre Delicatessen, 1st Floor, 119 Farringdon Road
London EC1R 3DA
E office@madtrust.org.uk
W www.madtrust.org.uk

NATIONAL ASSOCIATION OF YOUTH THEATRES (NAYT)   T 07804 254651
Contact: Henry Raby. Founded in 1982, NAYT works with over 1,000 Groups & Individuals to Support the Development of Youth Theatre Activity through Information & Support Services, Advocacy, Training, Participation & Partnerships
c/o Riding Lights Theatre, Friargate Theatre
Lower Friargate, York YO1 9SL
E info@nayt.org.uk
W www.nayt.org.uk

NATIONAL RESOURCE CENTRE FOR DANCE   T 01483 689316
University of Surrey, Guildford, Surrey GU2 7XH
F 01483 689500
E nrcd@surrey.ac.uk
W www.surrey.ac.uk/nrcd

NODA (NATIONAL OPERATIC & DRAMATIC ASSOCIATION)   T 01733 374790
Charity. Providing Advice, Information & Support. Largest Umbrella Body for Amateur Theatre in the UK offering Advice & Assistance on all Aspects of Amateur Theatre plus Workshops, Summer School and Social Events
15 The Metro Centre, Woodston
Peterborough PE2 7UH
F 01733 237286
E info@noda.org.uk
W www.noda.org.uk

THE RALPH AND MERIEL RICHARDSON FOUNDATION

Please support us as we provide grants to relieve the need, hardship, or distress of British actors and actresses, their spouses and children.

Please consider including the Foundation in your Will, or sending a donation to the address below, as any amount will be warmly welcomed.

Please help to spread awareness of this very special charity and encourage anyone who needs assistance to be in contact with us.

Please contact: Manager **E:** manager@sirralphrichardson.org.uk **W:** sirralphrichardson.org.uk **T:** 07733 688120
Address for correspondence: c/o 179 Great Portland Street, London W1W 5LS
Charity No: 1074030

OFCOM   T 0300 1234000
Ofcom Media Office, Riverside House
2A Southwark Bridge Road
London SE1 9HA
E ofcomnews@ofcom.org.uk
W www.ofcom.org.uk

PACT   T 020 7380 8230
Trade Association for Independent Television, Feature Film & New Media Production Companies
3rd Floor, Fitzrovia House
153-157 Cleveland Street, London W1T 6QW
E info@pact.co.uk
W www.pact.co.uk

PRS FOR MUSIC   T 020 7580 5544
29-33 Berners Street, London W1T 3AB
F 020 7306 4455
W www.prsformusic.com

**RICHARDSON, Ralph & Meriel
FOUNDATION**   T 020 7546 8889
Charity. Contact: Brian Eagles
c/o HowardKennedyFsi
179 Great Portland Street
London W1W 5LS
E manager@sirralphrichardson.org.uk
W www.sirralphrichardson.org.uk

ROYAL TELEVISION SOCIETY   T 020 7822 2810
Kildare House, 3 Dorset Rise, London EC4Y 8EN
F 020 7822 2811
E info@rts.org.uk
W www.rts.org.uk

ROYAL THEATRICAL FUND   T 020 7836 3322
Provides Financial Assistance for Members of the Entertainment Profession of all Ages & their Dependants plus Help for those who have Experienced Illness, Accident, Bereavement or other Personal Misfortune, including Grants, Advice & Friendship
11 Garrick Street, London WC2E 9AR
E admin@trtf.com

SAMPAD SOUTH ASIAN ARTS   T 0121 446 3260
Promotes the Appreciation & Practice of South Asian Arts
c/o Mac Birmingham
Cannon Hill Park, Birmingham B12 9QH
E info@sampad.org.uk
W www.sampad.org.uk

SOCIETY OF AUTHORS   T 020 7373 6642
Trade Union for Professional Writers. Providing Advice, Funding, Information & Support
84 Drayton Gardens, London SW10 9SB
E info@societyofauthors.org
W www.societyofauthors.org

**SOCIETY OF BRITISH
THEATRE DESIGNERS**   T 029 2039 1346
Professional Body. Charity. Providing Advice & Information
Theatre Design Department
Royal Welsh College of Music & Drama
Castle Grounds, Cathays Park
Cardiff CF10 3ER
E admin@theatredesign.org.uk
W www.theatredesign.org.uk

SOCIETY OF LONDON THEATRE THE (SOLT)   T 020 7557 6700
32 Rose Street, London WC2E 9ET
F 020 7557 6799
E enquiries@soltukt.co.uk

SOCIETY OF TEACHERS OF SPEECH & DRAMA THE   T 01623 627636
Registered Office: 73 Berry Hill Road, Mansfield
Nottinghamshire NG18 4RU
E ann.k.jones@btinternet.com
W www.stsd.org.uk

SOCIETY OF THEATRE CONSULTANTS   T 020 8455 4640
Contact: Michael Holden (Chairman)
27 Old Gloucester Street, London WC1N 3AX
E info@theatreconsultants.org.uk
W www.theatreconsultants.org.uk

STAGE CRICKET CLUB   T 020 7402 7543
39-41 Hanover Steps, St George's Fields
Albion Street, London W2 2YG
F 020 7262 5736
E brianjfilm@aol.com
W www.stagecc.org

STAGE GOLFING SOCIETY   T 020 8940 8861
Sudbrook Park, Sudbrook Lane
Richmond, Surrey TW10 7AS
E sgs@richmondgolfclub.co.uk

STAGE MANAGEMENT ASSOCIATION   T 020 7403 7999
*Supporting Excellence in Performance. Advice,
Information & Support; Representation & Advocacy for
& about Stage Management. Offers Help Finding Work,
Information, Training & Networking Opportunities for
SMA Members*
89 Borough High Street, London SE1 1NL
E admin@stagemanagementassociation.co.uk
W www.stagemanagementassociation.co.uk

STAGE ONE   T 020 7557 6737
Operating Name of The Theatre Investment Fund Ltd
32 Rose Street, London WC2E 9ET
F 020 7557 6799
E enquiries@stageone.uk.com
W www.stageone.uk.com

TECHNICAL THEATRE AWARDS   T 020 7112 8907
*Awards to Highlight Outstanding Achievement in the
Technical Theatre Industry*
39 Equinox House, Barking, Essex IG11 8RN
E general@technicaltheatreawards.com
W www.technicaltheatreawards.com

THEATRE CHAPLAINCY UK   T 020 7240 0344
St Paul's Church, Bedford Street, London WC2E 9ED
E actorschurchunion@gmail.com

THEATRES TRUST THE   T 020 7836 8591
*Contact: Kate Carmichael (Resources Adviser). National
Advisory Public Body for Theatres, Protecting Theatres
for Everyone. Statutory Consultee, Charity. Provides
Advice, Support & Information, Resources & Small
Capital Grants. Twitter: @TheatresTrust*
22 Charing Cross Road, London WC2H 0QL
F 020 7836 3302
E info@theatrestrust.org.uk
W www.theatrestrust.org.uk

THEATRICAL GUILD THE   T 020 7240 6062
The Charity for Backstage & Front of House
11 Garrick Street, London WC2E 9AR
E admin@ttg.org.uk
W www.ttg.org.uk

TYA - UK CENTRE OF ASSITEJ   T 0121 245 2092
*International Association of Theatre for Children & Young
People. Network for Makers & Promoters of Professional
Theatre for Young Audiences*
c/o Birmingham Repertory Theatre
Centenary Square
Broad Street, Birmingham B1 2EP
E secretary@tya.uk.org
W www.tya-uk.org

UK CHOREOGRAPHERS' DIRECTORY THE
See DANCE UK

UK THEATRE   T 020 7557 6700
32 Rose Street, London WC2E 9ET
F 020 7557 6799
E enquiries@soltukt.co.uk
W www.uktheatre.org

UK THEATRE CLUBS   T 020 8459 3972
54 Swallow Drive
London NW10 8TG
E uktheatreclubs@aol.com

UNITED KINGDOM COPYRIGHT BUREAU   T 01273 277333
110 Trafalgar Road, Portslade
East Sussex BN41 1GS
E info@copyrightbureau.co.uk
W www.copyrightbureau.co.uk

UNIVERSITY OF BRISTOL THEATRE COLLECTION   T 0117 331 5086
*Incorporating the Mander & Mitcheson Theatre
Collection*
Cantocks Close, Bristol BS8 1UP
E theatre-collection@bristol.ac.uk

VARIETY & LIGHT ENTERTAINMENT COUNCIL (VLEC)   T 020 7834 0515
54 Keyes House, Dolphin Square
London SW1V 3NA
E association@agents-uk.com
W www.vlec.org.uk

VARIETY, THE CHILDREN'S CHARITY   T 020 7428 8100
Variety Club House, 93 Bayham Street
London NW1 0AG
F 020 7428 8111
E info@variety.org.uk
W www.variety.org.uk

WILLIAMS, Tim AWARDS   T 020 7793 9755
*In Memory of LSW's Late Musical Director. Seeking
to Support Excellence in the Composition of
Theatrical Song*
PO Box 31855, London SE17 3XP
E londonswo@hotmail.com
W www.lswproductions.co.uk

WOMEN IN FILM & TELEVISION (UK)   T 020 7287 1400
*WFTV is the Premier Membership Organisation for
Women working in Creative Media in the UK and part
of an International Network of over 10,000 Women
Worldwide. Provides Advice, Information, Social
Membership & Support*
E info@wftv.org.uk
W www.wftv.org.uk

YOUTH MUSIC THEATRE UK (YMT)   T 020 8563 7725
Galena House, 8-30 Galena Road
London W6 0LT
E mail@ymtuk.org
W www.youthmusictheatreuk.org

P

Photographers: Advertisers Only
Promotional Services:
CVs, Showreels, Websites etc
Properties & Trades
Publications: Print & Online
Publicity & Press Representatives

Each photographer listed in this section
has taken an advertisement in this edition.
See the Advertisers' Index to view each
advertisement.

Photographers

How do I find a photographer?

Having a good quality, up-to-date promotional headshot is crucial for every performer. Make sure you choose your photographer very carefully: do some research and try to look at different examples. Photographers' adverts run throughout this edition, featuring many sample shots, although to get a real feel for their work you should also try to see their portfolio or website since this will give a more accurate impression of the quality of their photography.

If you live in or around London, please feel free to visit the Spotlight offices and look through current editions of our directories to find a style you like. We also have nearly sixty photographers' portfolios available for you to browse, many of them from photographers listed in this edition. Our offices are open Monday - Friday, 10.00am - 5.30pm at 7 Leicester Place, London WC2H 7RJ (nearest tube is Leicester Square).

What should I expect from the photo shoot?

When it comes to your photo shoot, bear in mind that a casting director, agent or production company will want to see a photo of the 'real' you. Keep your appearance as neutral as possible so that they can imagine you in many different roles, rather than type-casting yourself from the outset and limiting your opportunities.

Your eyes are your most important feature, so make sure they are visible: face the camera straight-on and try not to smile too much because it makes them harder to see. Wear something simple and avoid jewellery, hats, scarves, glasses or props, since these will all add character. Do not wear clothes that detract from your face such as polo necks, big collars, busy patterns or logos. Always keep your hands out of the shot.

Also consider the background: some photographers like to do outdoor shots. A contrast between background and hair colour works well, whereas dark backgrounds work less well with dark hair, and the same goes for light hair on light backgrounds.

Which photograph should I choose?

When you get your contact sheet or digital proofs back from the photographer, make sure you choose a photo that looks like you - not how you would like to look. If you are unsure, ask friends or your agent for an honest opinion. Remember, you will be asked to attend meetings and auditions on the basis of your photograph, so if you turn up looking completely different you will be wasting everyone's time.

Due to copyright legislation, you must always credit the photographer when using the photo.

How should I submit my photo to Spotlight and to casting professionals?

All photographs submitted to Spotlight must be of the highest possible quality, otherwise casting professionals will not see you in the best possible light. When sending a digital image by e-mail or disk, we have certain technical specifications which can be found on our website. We would recommend that you follow similar guidelines when sending your headshot directly to casting professionals.

What are Spotlight portfolio photographs?

Every Spotlight performer can also add extra photographs to their online profile, in addition to their principal photograph. These are called portfolio photos, and they give you the opportunity to show yourself in a range of different shots and/or roles. Members can upload up to 15 digital photos to their online profile free of charge.

Although you are allowed a maximum of 15 photos on your profile, it doesn't necessarily mean that this is advisable. 2-3 well chosen photos can make for a stronger profile than 15 poor quality ones, so be selective.

To find out more visit www.spotlightcom/artists/ multimedia/photoguidelines

CASE STUDY

Pete Bartlett has been shooting actor headshots for 8 years, having previously worked in the film industry. He is based in Notting Hill.

To be taken seriously at all an actor has to have a good, professionally taken headshot. Its main purpose is to get you to an audition. In order to do that it needs to look like an honest representation of you, a casting director will not be interested if they cannot be sure that you will turn up at an audition looking exactly like your picture, but you on a really, really good day.

When looking for a photographer make sure their pictures look real. At the same time they need to really sing off the page. Once you've shortlisted the ones whose pictures you like, I would be looking for the seasoned pros amongst them by seeing whose portfolio contains a lot of actors with the top London agents, ie. who are actually getting work!

I would also then consider price and be prepared to pay the top end of whatever your budget is. Like most things in life you tend to get what you pay for. I'd then look for the details, such as length of session and amount of shots etc. However, I wouldn't be swayed much on promises of extras, since 50 stunning shots will be worth far more than 500 mediocre ones.

Lastly, of the few remaining I'd go with my gut. Whose website gives me the feeling I'd like to work with them?

To prepare for the session think through all the expressions and looks you'd like to achieve; what does it look like to smoulder, what does playful look like, etc. Practice in the mirror, become familiar with how your face looks at different angles.

Keep the clothes simple. Plain block colours are best and V necklines draw the eye to the face nicely.

Get help in choosing the pictures after the session. You want to pick the ones that represent you best as an actor, not necessarily where you think you look best. You want a range to put up on your Spotlight profile, 4 to 5 from a session should suffice.

Lastly I'd urge you to try to enjoy the day of your headshots. Treat yourself that day, coffees, taxis etc. Your sense of fun, relaxation and feeling special will show up in the pictures!

Having previously worked in the film industry, I've now been shooting actor headshots for the last 8 years. I am lucky enough to include many of London's top agents as my clients. What I love most about the job, clichéd though it may be, is that I love meeting people. I am genuinely interested in each and every client I have and I'm pretty sure that that factor translates into successful pictures more than any other.

To find out more visit www.petebartlett.com

Photographers

Michael Wharley studied acting and worked as a successful stage actor for 6 years before re-training as a photographer in 2010. He shoots film, theatre and comedy advertising imagery as well as working with actors on their headshots. He runs 'Take Control of Your Headshots' seminars for drama schools and at industry events.

Taking Control of Your Headshots

Whether you're prepping for a session, adding new photos, or want to get more out of your existing portfolio, you have to take control of your headshots.

Used properly, the headshot portfolios on your Spotlight profile, personal websites or other casting services offer an amazing opportunity to subtly present your range to casting professionals and employers alike.

So, while having headshots taken can be expensive, not to mention a fear-inducing prospect, remember you are in control of a large part of the success of your next session.

Before and during the session:

- Choosing a photographer: it's a buyer's market, so use the hardcopy photographers' portfolios at Spotlight, web tools like Headshot Hunter and friend's recommendations to make a shortlist, and then compare details like prices, session length and photos included. Don't forget to trust your gut feeling, though; it's a very personal choice.

- Based on current UK trends, a session can cost anything from £50 to over £500. You can get good shots at knock-down prices, but to ensure industry-standard photos and a decent length of time with a good photographer, expect to spend a minimum of £150-250.

- Headshots are all about the eyes: look for detail and light in the eyes as a basic guide to whether a photographer takes good portraits.

- Session Time: The shortest session can seem attractive, but it can often take a while to relax and get good photos, especially in your first shoot.

- Brief your photographer before you shoot – whether it's about the sorts of role you get, or the type of shot you want – and your photos will be better tailored to the jobs you need them to do.

- Take an array of tops with contrasting necklines, textures and colours to help create range. A colour that chimes with your eye colour will help them pop, but keep things neutral and not too fashiony.

- Posing for headshots is about subtlety: feel don't show thoughts, breathe deeply, and take every chance to keep your face and body relaxed while shooting.

- Few people like being photographed, but bring energy and detail to the shoot, and make sure you review photos throughout to tweak hair, clothing and makeup, and to help calibrate your 'performance' for the stills camera.

After: managing your headshot portfolio

- Choosing photos: get feedback from as many people as possible: your peers, tutors and friendly industry contacts – to ensure you choose shots that fit your casting types/career ambitions, instead of the ones that make you look best.

- 3-6 photos shows range, but is manageable to view. You might include a good quality performance shot, to give a sense of your body shape and you 'in-action'.

- Have colour shots in your portfolio. Black and white still has its place, but the industry increasingly expects colour. It offers a better preview of your eye colour, hair colour, and skin tone, which might get you work.

- Curate your portfolio: take a step back and try to see it as others do. Ask yourself, 'What is each photo selling me on?' e.g. is it a subtle difference of status, a different part of your playing range, or a tonal change, perhaps bright and commercial, versus edgy and moody?

- And keep it fresh: review regularly to make sure each shot earns its place on merit. Most actors renew their photos every 18 months-2 years.

- But don't throw out your old shots too quickly. You might achieve a nice balance out of one session, or blend together shots from different photographers to create a dynamic mix.

- If you are getting new shots, think first. Use what the old photos have taught you, and reflect on the sorts of auditions they got you and the feedback you've been given, to make your next session even more successful.

- Headshots are part of your branding as an artist and a business: use them consistently across social media, personal websites and in print to reinforce that brand.

- Create a balanced promotional tool-kit: headshots are still central to the casting process, but remember that video and audio are increasingly important as well, so blend your promotional tools to create a vibrant presence on Spotlight.

To find out more visit www.michaelwharley.com, @MichaelWharley on Twitter, blog: wharleywords.co.uk & Facebook: facebook.com/ michaelwharleyphotography

AM LONDON
W www.am-london.com

ANKER, Matt   T 07835 241835
W www.mattanker.com

ANNAND, Simon   T 07884 446776
W www.simonannand.com

BARTLETT, Pete   T 07971 653994
E info@petebartlett.com
W www.petebartlett.com

BENNETT, Michael   T 020 7100 7584
W www.michaelbennett.co.uk

BISHOP, Brandon   T 020 7275 7468
T 07931 383830
W www.brandonbishopphotography.com

BOLTON, Peter   T 07768 818378
W www.peterboltonphotoart.com

BREWER, Nev   T 07967 993458
E nevbrewer@gmail.com
W www.nevbrewerphotography.co.uk

BURNETT, Sheila   T 020 7289 3058
T 07974 731391
W www.sheilaburnett-headshots.com

CARTER Charlie   T 07989 389493
E charlie@charliecarter.com
W www.charliecarter.com

CASTING IMAGE   T 07905 311408
W www.castingimage.com

CHAMPION, Vanessa   T 07747 025361
E vanessachampion@live.com
W www.vanessachampion.co.uk

DUMBLETON, Tom   T 07540 251026
E tom@tomdumbleton.com
W www.tomdumbleton.com

HOLLOWAY, Jon   T 07803 051083
W www.jonhollowayheadshots.co.uk

HULL, Anna   T 07778 399419
E info@annahullphotography.com
W www.annahullphotography.com

LADENBURG, Jack   T 07932 053743
E info@jackladenburg.co.uk
W www.jackladenburg.co.uk

LATIMER, Carole
W www.carolelatimer.com

LAWTON, Steve   T 07973 307487
W www.stevelawton.com

LISTER, Robert   T 07909 824893
W www.robertlister.co.uk

M.A.D. PHOTOGRAPHY   T 07949 581909
T 01707 708553
E info@mad-photography.co.uk
W www.mad-photography.co.uk

MARKS, Patrick
T 020 7183 7798
E info@thefactorycoventgarden.co.uk
W www.patrickmarks.com

MASCLET, JP   T 07768 166727
E headshots@jpmasclet.com
W www.jpmasclet.com

MISTY MORNING MEDIA   T 07544 010622
W www.mmmist.co.uk

MITCHELL, Jason   T 07794 378575
E info@jasonstuartmitchell.co.uk
W www.jasonstuartmitchell.co.uk

MOSTOFI, Kamal
W www.head-shot.photography

OLD, Dominic
E contactme@dominicold.com
W www.dominicold.com

PROCTOR, Carl   T 07956 283340
E carlproctorphotos@gmail.com
W www.carlproctorphotography.com

READING, John   T 07970 840922
E johnreading@mac.com
W www.johnreading.co.uk

REDDINGTON, Kirstin   T 07904 927020
E info@krheadshots.com
W www.krheadshots.com

RUOCCO, Alex   T 07732 293231
W www.alexruoccophotography.co.uk

SAYER, Howard   T 020 8123 0251
E howard@howardsayer.com
W www.howardsayer.co.uk

SCOTT, Karen   T 07958 975950
E info@karenscottphotography.com
W www.karenscottphotography.com

SHAKESPEARE LANE, Catherine   T 020 7226 7694
W www.csl-art.co.uk

SJFPHOTO   T 07581 694934
E photo@sarahjanefield.co.uk
W www.sarahjanefield.co.uk

SUTKA, Daniel   T 07737 770571
E photo@danielsutka.com
W www.biutifulpeople.com

ULLATHORNE, Steve   T 07961 380969
W www.steveullathorne.com

VALENTINE, Vanessa   T 07904 059541
W www.vanessavalentinephotography.com

VAN DYCK PHOTOGRAPHY   T 07947 378178
W www.vandyckphotography.com

WADE, Philip   T 07956 599691
T 020 7226 3088
E pix@philipwade.com
W www.philipwade.com

WEBSTER, Caroline   T 07867 653019
W www.carolinewebster.co.uk

WHARLEY, Michael   T 07961 068759
W www.michaelwharley.com

WORKMAN, Robert   T 020 7385 5442
W www.robertworkman.demon.co.uk

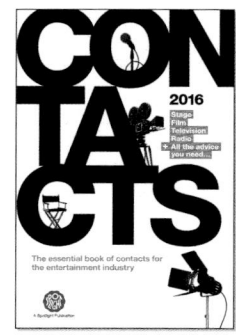

Promotional Services

What are promotional services?

This section contains listings for companies who provide practical services to help performers promote themselves. You might need to improve or create your CV; record a showreel or voicereel; design your own website; duplicate CDs; or print photographic repros, CVs or Z-cards: all essential ways to create a good impression with those that count in the industry.

Why do I need to promote myself?

Performers need to invest in marketing and promotion as much as any other self-employed business-person. Even if you have trained at a leading drama school, have a well-known agent, or have just finished work on a popular television series, you should never sit back and wait for the phone to ring or for the next job opportunity just to knock on your door. In such a competitive industry, successful performers are usually the ones who market themselves pro-actively and treat their careers as a 'business'.

Having up-to-date and well-produced promotional material makes a performer look professional and serious about their career: and hence a desirable person for a director or agent to work with.

Why is my CV important?

Poor presentation, punctuation and grammar create a bad first impression and you risk your CV being dismissed before it is even read. Make sure that you continually update your CV – you don't want it to look as if you haven't been working recently when you have, and you don't want to miss out on an audition because you haven't included skills you have put time and effort into achieving. Your CV should be kept to a maximum of one page and printed on good-quality paper.

Why do I need a covering letter?

Always include a covering letter to introduce your CV and persuade casting professionals that it is worth reading. Remember that they receive hundreds each week. Keep your communication concise and be professional at all times. We also recommend that your letter has some kind of focus: perhaps you can tell them about your next showcase, or where they can see you currently appearing on stage. Ideally this should be addressed to an individual, not "Dear Sir or Madam".

Why is my headshot important?

Your CV should feature, or be accompanied by, a recent headshot which is an accurate current likeness. See the 'Photographers' section for more information about promotional photography. You may need to print copies of your headshot through a repro company, some of whom are listed in this section.

Why do I need a voicereel?

If you are interested in voice over and/or radio work, you will need a professional-sounding voicereel to show agents, casting directors and potential employers what your voice is capable of. For commercial and corporate voice over work this should be no more than two minutes long with a number of short clips demonstrating your range, but showcase the strengths of your natural voice as much as possible. It should contain a mixture of commercials and narrations.

A radio voicereel should be around eight minutes long, with four clips no longer than two minutes each, and read in your natural voice. To achieve a good balance of material, one clip should be 'classical', one 'contemporary', one 'comic' and one a poem. This is designed to give an overview of your suitability to various areas of radio work.

Record your voicereel in a professional studio to ensure a high-quality result, otherwise you are unlikely to be considered in this competitive industry. For further information please see the 'Agents: Voice Over' and 'Radio' sections.

Why do I need a showreel?

Some casting directors will only consider a performer for an audition if they have first seen them demonstrating their skills in a showreel. A CV and headshot give some indication of your potential, but can only provide a basic summary.

What should I do if I don't currently have anything on film?

Showreels are expensive to produce if you don't currently have any broadcasted material to use, but it is advisable to get one professionally recorded and edited if at all possible. Showreels help you to promote yourself, but a casting

Promotional Services

director may be put off by a poor quality one. You might want to consider a Spotlight Monologue as a temporary alternative to a full showreel.

How long should my showreel be?

We would recommend no more than three or four minutes. Casting professionals receive thousands of CVs and showreels and do not have time to watch every actor for ten minutes each. This is why we suggest you do not send your showreel out with your CV, but instead mention in your covering letter that one is available.

What should I use in my showreel?

Rather than one long excerpt, it is more beneficial to demonstrate your versatility with a number of different clips. Focus on your strongest characters to enable the casting director to picture you in the roles you play best.

The first 30 seconds are the most important in your showreel, and may be the only part a busy casting director or agent has time to look at. You may wish to start with a headshot of yourself so that they know who to watch out for in the following scenes. Avoid noisy musical/uptempo soundtracks where possible and cut straight to the action.

The focus should be on you, not on the other actors, so close-up shots ought to be included. You should be speaking most if not all of the time. A visual contrast is good, whether this means filming in a different location or setting, or changing your outfit. You should avoid well-known scripts in order to prevent drawing comparisons between yourself and previous successful interpretations.

How should I use the listing in this section?

If you are looking for a company to help you with any of these promotional items, browse through this section carefully and get quotes from a number of places to compare. If you are a Spotlight member, some companies offer a discount on their services. Always ask to see samples of a company's work and ask friends in the industry for their own recommendations.

CASE STUDY

At Spotlight, we do everything we can to help you promote yourself. We offer free video and voice uploads and you can edit your showreel or film your Spotlight Monologue in our offices.

Get your showreel just right with our editing service

The process of making a showreel can be a minefield. It needs to be the best showcase of your acting ability, and a slick production that will catch a casting director's eye. But how do you go about getting your showreel just right?

Our showreel editors will collaborate with you and help you to create a showreel that casting directors will take notice of. Here are some of their top tips for the perfect showreel:

- First and foremost, keep it simple. All casting directors want to see is your acting ability. There's no need for montages, text flying across the screen or unnecessary background music.

- The scenes don't need to make sense within the context of the piece it is extracted from. A casting director knows they're viewing something out of context. You want it to make as much sense as possible, but trying to using longer footage for the sake of putting it in context can be wasting the little time you have to show yourself off.

- The first scene should be one where the you are talking; ideally in your native accent - it gives the casting director an immediate and honest impression of you.

- The ideal length of the showreel is about three minutes. Five minutes is getting a little too long. If you have lots of good quality footage then you may want it to be longer but never feel like you have to fill the time out. Always remember, quality over quantity!

Working with a professional editor in our Spotlight-based edit suite, we can create a high resolution DVD showreel. You can book on the phone or using our online booking system. We'll then give you a call a few days before the edit and discuss requirements. Use the advice of your agent, teacher/coach, even an honest friend to choose the scenes you want to take with you.

The session includes:

- Up to three hours of sit-in editing time
- Upload to your Spotlight profile
- 5x labelled DVD copies
- High-resolution .mpeg4 video file (for upload to Vimeo, YouTube etc)

The cost is £195 (incl. VAT). Follow-up or additional editing time is charged at £75 per hour (incl. VAT).

Armed with the perfect showreel, it's never been easier to get noticed

Spotlight members can add up to five minutes of video and audio. For performers with large amounts of media, there is also an option to upgrade your account. Your material will play in high-quality video and audio players which are optimised for mobile devices.

How else can you promote yourself on Spotlight?

A Spotlight Monologue is an opportunity for you to have a scene of your choice recorded and uploaded to your Spotlight profile. They are filmed in our studio where you'll have half an hour with an experienced camera operator to record one monologue and choose your preferred take. Your Spotlight Monologue will appear on your Spotlight profile for casting directors to watch. You can also take a copy away on DVD if you wish.

Make sure you are fully prepared before you come to our studios. Decide beforehand what you want to achieve from your Monologue and choose a suitable piece. Make sure you are comfortable with it and know it well. If you have an agent, it's a good idea to discuss the

monologue with them and get their opinion on the choice of material. We recommend that it is no longer than three minutes in length.

If you have been out of the industry for a while and only have old footage, a Spotlight Monologue is a good alternative to a showreel. It means you have something recent on your profile, gives the casting director a good idea of how you look and act now so it can be more useful than making a showreel full of dated footage.

It costs £50 (inc VAT) to record your Spotlight Monologue and add this to your web profile. DVD copies cost £12 each. We record Spotlight Monologues every Monday to Friday and have four appointments daily: 10.00, 10.30, 16.00 or 16.30.

> **To find out more, book a showreel editing or Spotlight Monologue session, visit www.spotlight.com, email studios@spotlight.com or call 020 7437 7631**

10X8PRINTS.COM T 07773 108108
32 High Street, Laurencekirk
Aberdeenshire AB30 1AB
E snappingsam@mac.com
W www.10x8prints.com

2PRODUCTION T 020 8440 4848
Professional Management Voice Over Direction & CDs
E info@2production.com
W www.2production.com

4VOICES MEDIA T 07860 466302
Voicereels. Auditions. Workshops. Advice
8 Gower Close, London SW4 9LX
E info@4voicesmedia.com
W www.4voicesmedia.com

A1 VOX LTD T 020 7434 4404
*Audio Clips. Demo CDs. ISDN Links. Spoken Word
Audio. Soundpicture Work & Foley*
20 Old Compton Street, London W1D 4TW
E info@a1vox.com
W www.a1vox.com

ABBEY ROAD STUDIOS T 020 7266 7000
3 Abbey Road, St John's Wood
London NW8 9AY
F 020 7266 7250
E bookings@abbeyroad.com
W www.abbeyroad.com

ABSOLUTE WORKS LTD T 01525 385400
Danson House, Manor Farm Lane
Ledburn, Bucks LU7 0UG
T 07778 934307
E nigelmpark@gmail.com
W www.absoluteworks.com

ACTOR SHOWREELS T 07853 637965
Showreel Service
97B Central Hill, London SE19 1BY
E post@actorshowreels.co.uk
W www.actorshowreels.co.uk

ACTORS CENTRE T 020 7240 3940
1A Tower Street, London WC2H 9NP
E film@actorscentre.co.uk
W www.actorscentre.co.uk

ACTOR'S ONE-STOP SHOP THE T 07894 152651
Showreels, CVs & Websites for Performing Artists
2B Dale View Crescent, London E4 6PQ
E info@actorsone-stopshop.com
W www.actorsone-stopshop.com

ACTORSHOP.CO.UK T 07970 381944
Showreels. Voicereels. Websites
E info@actorshop.co.uk
W www.actorshop.co.uk

**AIR-EDEL RECORDING
STUDIOS LTD** T 020 7486 6466
18 Rodmarton Street, London W1U 8BJ
F 020 7224 0344
E tom.bullen@air-edel.co.uk
W www.air-edelstudios.co.uk

AN ACTOR'S LIFE FOR ME T 07855 342161
722B High Road, North Finchley
London N12 9QD
E anactorslifeforme@hotmail.com
W www.anactorslifeforme.com

**ANGEL RECORDING
STUDIOS LTD** T 020 7354 2525
311 Upper Street, London N1 2TU
F 020 7226 9624
E bookings@angelstudio.co.uk

**ANT FARM STUDIOS
VOICE OVERS** T 07905 691353
Southend Farm, Southend Lane
Waltham Abbey EN9 3SE
E antfarmstudio@yahoo.co.uk
W www.antfarmstudios.co.uk

APPLE VIDEO FACILITIES T 01204 847974
The Studio, 821 Chorley Old Road
Bolton, Lancs BL1 5SL
F 01204 495020
E info@applevideo.co.uk
W www.applevideo.co.uk

ARTS HOSTING T 0121 433 4511
46 Glenmore Drive, Birmingham
West Midlands B38 8YR
E hosting@artshosting.co.uk
W www.artshosting.co.uk

BESPOKE REELS T 020 7580 3773
Contact: Charlie Lort-Phillips. Twitter: @charlielortp
3rd Floor, 83 Charlotte Street
London W1T 4PR
T 07538 259748
E charlie@bespokereels.com
W www.bespokereels.com

BLUE CHECKBOX LTD T 0843 2894414
Website Design
13 Portman House, 136 High Road
London N22 6DF
E contact@bluecheckbox.com
W www.bluecheckbox.com

CASTING COACH THE T 07952 232255
*Records & Uploads Password Protected Self-tape
Castings*
49 Herbert Road, Wimbledon
London SW19 3SQ
E john@johnmelainey.com
W www.auditiononcamera.co.uk

CHANNEL 2020 LTD T 0844 8402020
Phoenix Square, 4 Midland Street
Leicester LE1 1TG
E info@channel2020.co.uk
W www.channel2020.co.uk

CHANNEL 2020 LTD T 0844 8402020
3rd Floor, 28 Marshalsea Road, London SE1 1HF
E info@channel2020.co.uk
W www.channel2020.co.uk

CHASE, Stephan PRODUCTIONS LTD T 020 8878 9112
Producer of Voice Overs & Showreels
The Studio, 22 York Avenue, London SW14 7LG
E stephan@stephanchase.com
W www.stephanchase.com

CONSIDER CREATIVE T 020 3397 3816
Integrated Creative Approach. Print. Digital. Advertising & Branding
1st Floor, The Italian Building
41 Dockhead, London SE1 2BS
E ben@considercreative.co.uk
W www.considercreative.co.uk

CONSIDER THIS UK LTD T 01895 619900
Design. Marketing. Print. Web
Brook House, 54A Cowley Mill Road
Uxbridge, Middlesex UB8 2QE
F 01895 251048
E develop@considerthisuk.com
W www.considerthisuk.com

COURTWOOD PHOTOGRAPHIC LTD T 01736 741222
Photographic Reproduction
Profile Prints, Freepost TO55
Penzance, Cornwall TR20 8DU
E images@courtwood.co.uk
W www.courtwood.co.uk

CRE8 LIFESTYLE CENTRE T 020 8533 1691
80 Eastway, Hackney Wick, London E9 5JH
E shellyann@cre8lifestyle.org.uk
W www.cre8lifestyle.org.uk

CreateAV (UK) LTD T 01992 789759
Unit 14, Studio House, Delamare Road
Cheshunt EN8 9SH
F 01992 625180
E connect@createav.com
W www.createav.com

CRICKCRACK PRODUCTIONS T 01268 416195
Contact: Charlie Wilson. Professionally Equipped Recording Facility for Voice Overs
23 Kings Road, Laindon
Basildon, Essex SS15 4AB
E charlie@crickcrack.com
W www.crickcrackproductions.com

CROWE, Ben T 07952 784911
Voice Clip Recording
25 Holmes Avenue, Hove BN3 7LB
E bencrowe@hotmail.co.uk

CRYING OUT LOUD PRODUCTIONS T 07809 549887 (Simon)
Contact: Simon Cryer, Marina Caldarone. Voice Over Demo Specialists. Voice Training & Studio Hire
1:04 Chester House, 1-3 Brixton Road
London SW9 6DE
T 07946 533108 (Marina)
E simon@cryingoutloud.co.uk
W www.cryingoutloud.co.uk

CRYSTAL MEDIA T 0131 240 0988
28 Castle Street, Edinburgh EH2 3HT
F 0131 240 0989
E hello@crystal-media.co.uk
W www.crystal-media.co.uk

CUTGLASS PRODUCTIONS T 01929 400758
Contact: Phill Corran. Voice Showreel Production
Tides, Britwell Drive
West Lulworth, Dorset BH20 5RS
T 07966 280033
E phil@cutglassproductions.com
W www.cutglassproductions.com

DELUXE 142 T 020 7878 0000
Film House, 142 Wardour Street, London W1F 8DD
W www.deluxe142.co.uk

DENBRY REPROS LTD T 01442 242411
Photographic Reproduction
57 High Street, Hemel Hempstead
Herts HP1 3AF
E info@denbryrepros.com
W www.denbryrepros.com

DV2BROADCAST   T 0161 736 5300
3 Carolina Way, Salford M50 2ZY
E info@dv2broadcast.co.uk
W www.dv2broadcast.co.uk

ELMS STUDIOS   T 020 3556 1515
Contact: Phil Lawrence. Composing/Scoring for Film &
Television
10 Empress Avenue
London E12 5ES
T 07956 275554
E info@elmsstudios.com
W www.elmsstudios.co.uk

ESQUIRE SHOWREELS   T 07540 566569
19 Hillside Close, Knaphill
Woking, Surrey GU21 2HR
E simsjamie@icloud.com
W www.jamie-sims.com

ESSENTIAL MUSIC   T 020 7439 7113
20 Great Chapel Street
London W1F 8FW
E david@essentialmusic.co.uk

EXECUTIVE AUDIO VISUAL   T/F 020 7723 4488
DVD Duplication Service. Showreels for Actors &
Presenters
E chris.jarvis60@gmail.com

FLIXELS LTD   T 020 7193 8171
1 Bermondsey Square
London SE1 3UN
E info@flixels.co.uk
W www.flixels.co.uk

GENESIS TEE SHIRTS
& HOODIES   T 01654 710137
18 Pendre Enterprise Park, Tywyn
Gwynedd LL36 9LW
F 01654 712461
E info@genesis-uk.com
W www.genesis-uk.com

GENESIS UK LTD   T 01654 710137
Unit 18, Pendre Enterprise Park
Tywyn, Gwynedd LL36 9LW
E info@genesis-uk.com
W www.genesis-uk.com

GINGER SHOWREELS   T 020 8442 4017
Flat 7, 117 Cazenove Road
London N16 6AX
E info@gingershowreels.com
W www.gingershowreels.com

GYROSCOPE STUDIOS   T 00 46 86 459223
Contact: Frank Sanderson
Hökmossevägen 34
SE12642 Hägersten, Sweden
E frank@gyroscope-studios.com
W www.gyroscope-studios.com

HARVEY HOUSE FILMS LTD   T 07968 830536
Animation. Showreels. Video Production
The Mission Hall
Cummington Street
London W4 5ER
E chris@harveyhousefilms.co.uk
W www.harveyhousefilms.co.uk

HEAVY ENTERTAINMENT LTD   T 020 7494 1000
111 Wardour Street, London W1F 0UH
F 020 7494 1100
E info@heavy-entertainment.com
W www.heavy-entertainment.com

HOTQS CREATIVE   T 07903 017819
Animation. Graphics. Showreels. Websites
E info@hotqs.uk
W www.hotqs.uk

HOTREELS   T 020 7952 4362
Voice & Showreels
E info@hotreels.co.uk
W www.hotreels.co.uk

IMAGE PHOTOGRAPHIC   T 020 7602 1190
Online Only
E digital@imagephotographic.com
W www.imagephotographic.com

JEN X FILMS   T 020 8743 7635
Showreels
56 Wood Lane, Ugli Campus
London W12 7SB
E info@jenxfilms.com
W www.jenxfilms.com

JMS GROUP LTD THE   T 01603 811855
Park Farm Studios, Norwich Road
Hethersett, Norfolk NR9 3DL
F 01603 812255
E info@jms-group.com
W www.jms-group.com

KEAN LANYON LTD   T 020 7697 8453
Design of Websites, Print & Front of House, from Touring to West End
United House, North Road
Islington, London N7 9DP
E iain@keanlanyon.com
W www.keanlanyon.com

McANDREW, Shane   T 07941 640124
Professional Video Editing Services
2 Croft Cottage, Thrigby Road
Great Yarmouth, Norfolk NR29 3DP
E shane.j.mcandrew@gmail.com
W www.shanemcandrew.co.uk

MIGHTY REELS
11 Romola Road, London SE24 9BA
E info@mightyreels.com
W www.mightyreels.com

MINAMONFILM   T 020 8674 3957
Specialist in Showreels
117 Downton Avenue, London SW2 3TX
E studio@minamonfilm.co.uk
W www.minamonfilm.co.uk

**MOF STUDIOS
(MINISTRY OF FUN)**   T 020 7708 6116
22 Amelia Street, London SE17 3BZ
E studio@ministryoffun.net
W www.mofstudios.net

MOO.COM   T 020 7392 2780
Online Printers. Business Cards
32-38 Scrutton Street, London EC2A 4RQ
W www.moo.com

**MOTIVATION SOUND
STUDIOS**   T 020 7328 8305
35A Broadhurst Gardens, London NW6 3QT
F 020 7624 4879
E info@motivationsound.co.uk
W www.motivationsound.co.uk

MUSIC IN MOTION LTD   T 07813 070961
London
E neil@neilmyers.com
W www.neilmyers.com

O.J. SONUS   T 020 8963 0702
Recording Studio. Voice Over Recording. Voicereel Production. Voice Over Workshops. Professional Coaching Available
14-15 Main Drive
East Lane Business Park
Wembley HA9 7NA
T 07929 859401
E info@ojsonus.com
W www.ojsonus.com

OLD, Dominic   T 07970 101135
Web Designer
TB-111, Telegraph Buildings
2nd Floor Studios & Arts
Studio TW27, Harrington Way
London SE18 5NR
E contactme@dominicold.com
W www.dominicold.com

OLYMPIC RECORDS STUDIO   T 07956 951090
58 Selhurst New Road, South Norwood
London SE25 5PU
E olympicrecords@tiscali.co.uk
W www.olympicrecordsuk.com

Shoe String Filming
London Based
SHOWREELS
www.shoestringfilming.com
Make An Impact With A Bespoke Showreel & Your Own Unique Scripts Tailored To Your Needs
Phone Alexandre : 07955736926 showreels@shoestringfilming.com

PINPOINT   T 020 8963 0702
Specialised Voice Over Studio. Voice Over Recording.
Voicereel Production. Voice Over Workshops.
Professional Coaching Available
14-15 Main Drive
East Lane Business Park, Wembley HA9 7NA
T 07929 859401
E info@voice-overstudio.co.uk
W www.voice-overstudio.co.uk

PRESENTER STUDIO THE   T 020 8677 7143
85 Lewin Road, London SW16 6JX
E info@presenterstudio.com
W www.presenterstudio.com

PROFILE PRINTS   T 01736 741222
Photographic Reproduction
Unit 2, Plot 1A, Rospeath Industrial Estate
Crowlas, Cornwall TR20 8DU
E sales@courtwood.co.uk
W www.courtwood.co.uk

PURE LEMON   T 05602 625262
6 Millan Court, Lumphanan, Aberdeenshire AB31 4QF
E music@lemondesign.net
W www.lemondesign.net

RARELY PURE, NEVER SIMPLE   T 07809 142048
Showreels
145-147 St John's Street, Clerkenwell
London EC1V 4PW
E info@rarelypureneversimple.com
W www.rarelypureneversimple.com

RE:AL   T 01622 200123
Print. Creative. Marketing. Digital
Unit 2, Tovil Green Business Park
Maidstone, Kent ME15 6TA
E info@realprintandmedia.com
W www.realprintandmedia.com

RED FACILITIES   T 0131 555 2288
61 Timber Bush, Leith, Edinburgh EH6 6QH
F 0131 555 0088
E doit@redfacilities.com
W www.redfacilities.com

**REEL DEAL SHOWREEL
CO THE**   T 020 8647 1235
6 Charlotte Road, Wallington, Surrey SM6 9AX
E info@thereel-deal.co.uk
W www.thereel-deal.co.uk

REEL GEEKS.COM THE   T 07951 757024
Showreel Editing for Actors
Based in West Kensington, London
E thereelgeeks@hotmail.com
W www.thereelgeeks.com

REPLAY FILM & NEW MEDIA   T 020 7637 0473
Showreels & Performance Recording
Museum House, 25 Museum Street
London WC1A 1JT
E sales@replayfilms.co.uk
W www.replayfilms.co.uk

**ROUND ISLAND SHOWREELS
& VOICEREELS**   T 07939 540458
Contact: Ben Warren, Guy Michaels
T 07973 445328
E mail@roundisland.net
W www.roundisland.net

SEARCH THE ARTS   T 01895 619900
Online Search Directory for Contacts & Events within
the Arts
Brook House, 54A Cowley Mill Road
Uxbridge UB8 2QE
F 01895 251048
E develop@considerthisuk.com
W www.considerthisuk.com

SETTLE THE SCORE   T 07853 643346
E toby@settlethescore.co.uk
W www.settlethescore.co.uk

SHOE STRING FILMING   T 07955 736926
Specialises in Shooting & Editing Showreels
E showreels@shoestringfilming.com
W www.shoestringfilming.com

SHOTS & REELS   T 07825 639006
Showreels
Based in Dalston, London E8 2LH
E sam@shotsandreels.com
W www.shotsandreels.com

SHOWCASE SITES   T 020 3490 2202
Unit 13, Kelday Building, 2 Spencer Way
London E1 2PW
E showcase@showcasesites.co.uk
W www.showcasesites.co.uk

SHOWREEL LTD THE   T 020 7043 8660 (Bookings)
Voice Over Demo Services. Training & Workshops
Soho Recording Studios
The Heals Building, 22-24 Torrington Place
London WC1E 7HJ
E info@theshowreel.com
W www.theshowreel.com

SHOWREELS 4 U   T 01923 352385
Actors Showreels Filmed & Edited in HD. Voicereels.
Based near Elstree
15 Pippin Close, Shenley
Radlett, Herts WD7 9EU
E showreels4u@hotmail.com
W www.showreels4u.blogspot.com

SHOWREELZ   T 020 8994 7927
28 Eastbury Grove, Chiswick
London W4 2JZ
T 07885 253477
E brad@showreelz.com
W www.showreelz.com

**SILVER~TONGUED
PRODUCTIONS**   T 020 8309 0659
Specialising in the Recording & Production of Voicereels
E contactus@silver-tongued.co.uk
W www.silver-tongued.co.uk

SILVERTIP FILMS LTD T 01483 407533
*Actor Showreel Production. Edits Existing Material.
Shoots New Material*
8 Quadrum Park
Old Portsmouth Road
Guildford, Surrey GU3 1LU
E info@silvertipfilms.co.uk
W www.silvertipfilms.co.uk

SKATTA LTD T 07472 321113
Skatta Studios, BBC Lighthouse
London W12 7TQ
E info@skatta.tv
W www.skatta.tv

SLICK SHOWREELS T 020 7099 8269
Imperial House
15-19 Kingsway WC2B 6UN
T 07543 016194
E info@slickshowreels.co.uk
W www.slickshowreels.co.uk

SMALL SCREEN SHOWREELS T 020 8816 8896
Showreel Editing for Actors
London
E info@smallscreenshowreels.co.uk
W www.smallscreenshowreels.co.uk

SOHO SHOWREELS T 0844 5040731
101 Wardour Street, London W1F 0UG
E info@sohoshowreels.co.uk
W www.sohoshowreels.co.uk

SONICPOND STUDIO T 020 7690 8561
Specialising in Voicereels. MT Demos. Showreels
70 Mildmay Grove South, Islington
London N1 4PJ
E info@sonicpond.co.uk
W www.sonicpond.co.uk

SOUND T 0117 924 5853
Pembroke House
7 Brunswick Square
Bristol BS2 8PE
E kenwheeler@mac.com
W www.soundat7.com

SOUND COMPANY LTD T 020 7580 5880
23 Gosfield Street
London W1W 6HG
F 020 7580 6454
E bookings@sound.co.uk
W www.sound.co.uk

SOUND HOUSE LTD THE T 0161 832 7299
MediaCityUK, Blue
Salford, Manchester M50 2HQ
F 0161 832 7266
E mail@thesoundhouse.tv
W www.thesoundhouse.tv

SOUND MARKETING T 01225 701600
Strattons House, Strattons Walk
Melksham, Wiltshire SN12 6JL
F 01225 701601
E nicki@soundm.com
W www.soundm.com

**STAGES CAPTURE
THE MOMENT** T 020 7193 8519
Showreels
30 Byewaters, Croxley Green
Watford, Herts WD18 8WJ
T 07786 813812
E info@stagescapturethemoment.com
W www.stagescapturethemoment.com

**STIRLING SHOWREEL
SERVICE** T 01204 848333
490 Halliwell Road, Bolton
Lancashire BL1 8AN
E admin@stirlingmanagement.co.uk
W www.stirlingmanagement.co.uk

**STRAY DOG CAFE
PRODUCTIONS LTD** T 07455 011639
*Digital Producing: Audio, Video, Photography, Websites
& Social Media*
269 Southborough Lane, Bromley
Kent BR2 8AT
E corinne@straydogcafeproductions.com
W www.straydogcafeproductions.com

STUDIO 359 T 07791 516859
*Websites & Showreels for Actors, Presenters &
Performers*
219 New Park Road, London SW2 4HN
E hello@studio359.co.uk
W www.studio359.co.uk

**SUGAR LENS
PRODUCTIONS LTD** T 07952 907168
Showreels
10 Foreland Close, Christchurch
Dorset BH23 2TQ
E info@sugarlensproductions.com
W www.sugarlensproductions.com

SUGAR POD PRODUCTIONS　T 020 8374 4701
Voice Showreels & Production Studio
Studio 8C, Chocolate Factory 1
5 Clarendon Road
Wood Green, London N22 6XJ
T 07967 673552
E info@sugarpodproductions.com
W www.sugarpodproductions.com

SUPER SHOWREELS　T 07877 023154
141 Riverbank Tower
Bridgewater Street
Manchester M3 7JY
E supershowreelsuk@gmail.com
W www.supershowreels.co.uk

SYNCREDIBLE AGENCY　T 020 7117 6776
26-28 Hammersmith Grove
London W6 7BA
E contact@syncredible.com
W www.syncredible.com

TAKE FIVE CASTING STUDIO　T 020 7287 2120
Showreels
37 Beak Street, London W1F 9RZ
F 020 7287 3035
E info@takefivestudio.com
W www.takefivestudio.com

**TOUCHWOOD AUDIO
PRODUCTIONS**　T 0113 278 7180
6 Hyde Park Terrace, Leeds
West Yorkshire LS6 1BJ
T 07745 377772
E bruce@touchwoodaudio.com
W www.touchwoodaudio.com

**TV PRESENTER TRAINING -
ASPIRE**　T 0800 0305471
3 Mills Studios, Three Mill Lane
London E3 3DU
E info@aspirepresenting.com
W www.aspirepresenting.com

TWITCH FILMS　T 020 7266 0946
Showreels
22 Grove End Gardens, 18 Abbey Road
London NW8 9LL
E post@twitchfilms.co.uk
W www.twitchfilms.co.uk

**UNIVERSAL SOUND
(JUST PLAY LTD)**　T 01494 723400
Old Farm Lane, London Road East
Amersham, Buckinghamshire HP7 9DH
E foley@universalsound.co.uk
W www.universalsound.co.uk

VISUALEYES　T 020 7323 7430
Photographic Reproduction
95 Mortimer Street, London W1W 7ST
F 020 7323 7438
E imaging@visualeyes.co.uk
W www.visualeyes.co.uk

**VOICE MASTER
INTERNATIONAL**　T 020 8455 1666
*Creators of the Hudson Voice Technique. Unique
Technique for Voice Overs*
88 Erskine Hill
London NW11 6HR
T 07921 210400
E info@voicemaster.co.uk
W www.voicemaster.co.uk

VOICEREELS.CO.UK　T 07989 602880
Based in London SW16
E rob@voicereels.co.uk
W www.voicereels.co.uk

**VSI - VOICE & SCRIPT
INTERNATIONAL**　T 020 7692 7700
*Foreign Language Specialists. Casting. Dubbing. Editing.
Recording Studios. Subtitling. Translation*
132 Cleveland Street
London W1T 6AB
F 020 7692 7711
E info@vsi.tv
W www.vsi.tv

**WARNER BROS
DE LANE LEA SOUND**　T 020 7432 3800
Post-production. Re-recording Studios
75 Dean Street, London W1D 3PU
F 020 7494 3755
E solutions@delanelea.com
W www.delanelea.com

WE THEATRE　T 020 3327 3877
*Flyer, Poster, Programme & Website Design for
Fringe Theatre*
239 Lewisham Way
London SE4 1XF
E info@wetheatre.co.uk
W www.wetheatre.co.uk

WEBVID.CO.UK　T 020 8133 1728
*Contact: Neil Bentley (Heart, Capital, Galaxy), James,
Vince. Web & Video Production Company. Bespoke
Website Design & Video Filming/Editing*
Based in South London
E hello@webvid.co.uk
W www.webvid.co.uk

WORLDWIDE PICTURES LTD　T 020 7613 6580
103 The Timber Yard
Drivedale Street
London N1 6ND
E info@worldwidepictures.tv
W www.worldwidepictures.tv

WORTH VALLEY WEB　T 07944 023597
Showreel Editing, VHS to DVD Conversion & Websites
103/105 Lidget
Oakworth, Keighley
West Yorkshire BD22 7HN
E info@worthvalleyweb.co.uk
W www.worthvalleyweb.co.uk

BAPTY & CO

WWW.BAPTY.CO.UK

Supplying props to the entertainment industry
Bapty & Co.
Witley Gardens, Norwood Green, Middx UB2 4ES
+44 (0)20 8574 7700   +44 (0)20 8571 5700

---

10 OUT OF 10 PRODUCTIONS LTD T 020 8659 2558
Lighting & Sound. Design. Hire. Installation. Sales
5 Metro Business Centre, Kangley Bridge Road
London SE26 5BW
E sales@10outof10.co.uk
W www.10outof10.co.uk

147RESEARCH T 01665 714777
Sources Anything Needed for Period or Modern Productions
Manderville, Amble Morpeth NE65 0SB
T 07778 002147
E jenniferdalton@147research.com
W www.147research.com

3D CREATIONS LTD T 01493 652055
Production Design. Prop Makers. Scenery Contractors. Scenic Artists
Berth 33, Malthouse Lane
Gorleston, Norfolk NR31 0GW
F 01493 443124
E info@3dcreations.co.uk
W www.3dcreations.co.uk

ACROBAT PRODUCTIONS T 01442 843377
Advisers. Artistes
4 Bridgewater Court, Little Gaddesden
Berkhamsted, Herts HP4 1PX
T 07771 907030
E roger@acrobatproductions.com
W www.acrobatproductions.com

ACTION 99 CARS LTD T 01923 266373
Westwick Road Farm, Westwick Row
Hemel Hempstead HP2 4UB
E david@nineninecars.com
W www.nineninecars.com

ADAMS ENGRAVING T 01483 725792
Unit G1A, The Mayford Centre, Mayford Green
Woking GU22 0PP
E adamsengraving@pncl.co.uk
W www.adamsengraving.co.uk

AF WILTSHIRE (DUNSFOLD) LTD T 01483 200516
Agricultural Vehicle Engineers, Repairs etc
The Agricultural Centre, Alfold Road
Dunsfold, Surrey GU8 4NP
F 01483 200491
E team@afwiltshire.co.uk

AIRBOURNE SYSTEMS INTERNATIONAL T 01245 268772
All Skydiving Requirements Arranged. Parachute Hire (Period & Modern)
8 Burns Crescent, Chelmsford, Essex CM2 0TS

ALCHEMICAL LABORATORIES ETC T 01636 707836
Medieval Science & Technology Recreated for Museums & Films
2 Stapleford Lane, Coddington
Newark, Nottinghamshire NG24 2QZ
E alchemyjack@gmail.com
W www.jackgreene.co.uk

ALCOHOL-FREE SHOP THE T 0800 2448024
Alcohol-free Drinks for Television & Film Sets
Units 1 & 2 Manchester Industrial Park
Newton Heath, Manchester M40 5AX
E info@alcoholfree.co.uk
W www.alcoholfree.co.uk

ALL STARS AMERICAN LIMOS T 07747 130685
30 Henley Meadows, Tenterden TN30 6EN
E limohire@live.co.uk
W www.limo-hire-sussex-kent.co.uk

ANELLO & DAVIDE T 020 7938 2255
Handmade Shoes
15 St Albans Grove, London W8 5BP
E enquiries@handmadeshoes.co.uk
W www.handmadeshoes.co.uk

ANNUAL CLOWNS DIRECTORY.COM T 01268 745791
Contact: Salvo The Clown
13 Second Avenue, Kingsleigh Park
Thundersley, Essex SS7 3QD
E salvo@annualclownsdirectory.com
W www.annualclownsdirectory.com

AQUATECH SURVEY LTD T 01452 740559
Camera Boats
2 Cobbies Rock, Epney, Gloucestershire GL2 7LN
F 01452 741958
E office@aquatech-uk.com
W www.aquatech-uk.com

ARMS & ARCHERY T 01920 460335
Armour. Chainmail. Longbows. Tents. Weaponry. X-bows
Thrift Lane, Off London Road, Ware, Herts SG12 9QS
E armsandarchery@btconnect.com

ART *
Art Consultant. Supplier of Paintings & Sculpture
E h@art8star.co.uk
W www.art8star.co.uk

ART DIRECTORS & TRIP PHOTO LIBRARY T 020 8642 3593
Digital Scans & Colour Slides (All Subjects)
57 Burdon Lane, Cheam, Surrey SM2 7BY
F 020 8395 7230
E images@artdirectors.co.uk
W www.artdirectors.co.uk

A. S. DESIGNS T 01279 722416
Theatrical Designer. Costumes, Heads, Masks, Puppets, Sets etc

ASH, Riky T 01476 407383
Equity Registered Stuntman/Stunt Co-ordinator
T 07850 471227
E stuntmanriky@fallingforyou.tv
W www.fallingforyou.tv

AWESOME UPHOLSTERY & CUSTOM INTERIORS T 01480 461195
Member of The Guild of Master Craftsmen
Unit 7, Monsal Works, Somersham Road, St Ives
Cambridgeshire PE27 3LY
E info@awesome.eu.com
W www.awesome.eu.com

BAPTY (2000) LTD T 020 8574 7700
Dressing, Props, Weapons etc
1A Witley Gardens, Norwood Green
Southall, Middlesex UB2 4ES
F 020 8571 5700
E team@bapty.co.uk
W www.bapty.co.uk

BEAT ABOUT THE BUSH LTD T 020 8960 2087
Musical Instrument Hire
Unit 23, Enterprise Way, Triangle Business Centre
Salter Street (Off Hythe Road), London NW10 6UG
F 020 8969 2281
E info@beataboutthebush.com
W www.beataboutthebush.com

BIANCHI AVIATION FILM SERVICES T 01494 449810
Historic & Other Aircraft
Wycombe Air Park, Booker Marlow
Buckinghamshire SL7 3DP
F 01494 461236
E info@bianchiaviation.com
W www.bianchiaviation.com

BIG BREAK CARDS T 01386 438952
*Theatrical Greetings Cards for First Nights, featuring
Hamlet the Pig, drawn by Harry Venning, as seen in The
Stage. Made by Actors for Actors*
E info@bigbreakcards.co.uk
W www.bigbreakcards.co.uk

BLUE MILL LTD T 0116 248 8130
Dyers. Finishers
84 Halstead Street, Leicester LE5 3RD
F 0116 253 7633
E info@bluemill.co.uk
W www.bluemill.co.uk

BLUEBELL RAILWAY PLC T 01825 720800
*Period Stations. Pullman Coaches. Steam Locomotives.
Extensive Film Experience*
Sheffield Park Station, East Sussex TN22 3QL
F 01825 720804
E info@bluebell-railway.co.uk
W www.bluebell-railway.com

BOLDGATE COMMERCIAL SERVICES LTD T 01895 236666
Unit 12, Brook Business Centre, Cowley Mill Road
Uxbridge, Middlesex UB8 2FX
F 01895 237962
E info@boldgate.co.uk
W www.boldgate.co.uk

BOSCO LIGHTING T 020 8769 3470
Design/Technical Consultancy
47 Woodbourne Avenue, London SW16 1UX
E boscolx@lineone.net

BOUNCY CASTLES BY P. A. LEISURE T 01282 453939
Specialists in Amusements & Fairground Equipment
Delph House, Park Bridge Road
Towneley Park, Burnley
Lancs BB10 4SD
T 07968 399053
E info@paleisure.co.uk
W www.paleisure.co.uk

BRISTOL (UK) LTD T 01923 779333
Scenic Paint & StageFloor Duo Suppliers. VFX Solutions
Unit 1, Sutherland Court
Tolpits Lane, Watford WD18 9SP
F 01923 779666
E tech.sales@bristolpaint.com
W www.bristolpaint.com

BRODIE & MIDDLETON LTD T 020 7836 3289
Theatrical Suppliers. Glitter, Paints, Powders etc
68 Drury Lane, London WC2B 5SP
F 020 7497 0554
E info@brodies.net
W www.brodies.net

BURTON EXECUTIVE CARS LTD T 07792 013117
Unit 3 Farmers Court, 16-17 High Street, Tutbury
Burton on Trent, Staffordshire DE13 9LP
E enquiries@burtonexecutivecars.co.uk
W www.burtonexecutivecars.co.uk

CANDLE MAKERS SUPPLIES T 020 7602 1812
Rear of 102-104 Shepherds Bush Road
(Entrance in Batoum Gardens)
London W6 7PD
E candles@candlemakers.co.uk
W www.candlemakers.co.uk

CARLINE PRIVATE HIRE T 01293 430430
12A Bridge Industrial Estate, Balcombe Road
Horley, West Sussex RH6 9HU
F 01293 430432
E carlinehire@yahoo.co.uk
W www.albioncarsgatwick.co.uk

CHRISANNE LTD T 020 8640 5921
Specialist Fabrics & Accessories for Theatre & Dance
Chrisanne House, 110-112 Morden Road
Mitcham, Surrey CR4 4XB
F 020 8640 2106
E sales@chrisanne.com
W www.chrisanne.com

CIRCUS PROMOTIONS T 01892 537964
Circus Hire. Entertainers. Big Tops etc
Hey Presto House, 36 St Lukes Road
Tunbridge Wells, Kent TN4 9JH
T 07973 512845
E mike@heypresto.orangehome.co.uk
W www.heyprestoentertainments.co.uk

CLASSIC CAR AGENCY THE T 07788 977655
Advertising. Film. Promotional. Publicity
The G&A Building, Sendall's Yard
Crawley Road, Horsham
West Sussex RH12 4HG
E theclassiccaragency@btopenworld.com
W www.theclassiccaragency.com

CLASSIC CAR HIRE T 020 8939 3987
Over 30 Classic & Vintage Vehicles
Unit 2 Hampton Court Estate, Summer Road
Thames Ditton KT7 0RG
E info@classic-hire.com
W www.classic-hire.com

CLASSIC OMNIBUS T 01303 248999
Vintage Open-Top Buses & Coaches
44 Welson Road, Folkestone
Kent CT20 2NP
W www.opentopbus.co.uk

COBO MEDIA T 020 8291 7079
Performing Arts, Entertainment & Leisure Marketing
43A Garthorne Road, London SE23 1EP
F 020 8291 4969
E admin@cobomedia.com
W www.cobomedia.com

COMPTON, Mike & Rosi T 020 8680 4364
Costumes. Models. Props
11 Woodstock Road, Croydon
Surrey CR0 1JS
T 07900 258646
E mikeandrosicompton@btopenworld.com

CONCEPT ENGINEERING LTD T 01628 825555
Smoke, Fog, Snow etc
7 Woodlands Business Park
Woodlands Park Avenue
Maidenhead, Berkshire SL6 3UA
F 01628 826261
E info@conceptsmoke.com
W www.conceptsmoke.com

COOK, Sheila TEXTILES T 020 7603 3003
Textiles, Costumes & Accessories for Hire/Sale
26 Addison Place, London W11 4RJ
E sheilacook@sheilacook.co.uk
W www.sheilacook.co.uk

COPS ON THE BOX T 020 8650 9828
Twitter: @copsonthebox1
BM BOX 7301, London WC1N 3XX
T 07710 065851
E info@cotb.co.uk
W www.cotb.co.uk

**COSTUMES &
SHOWS UNLIMITED** T 01253 827092
Costume Rental & Design. Ice Rink Rental. Show Production
Crammond, Hillylaid Road
Thornton-Cleveleys, Lancs FY5 4EG
T 07881 970398
E iceshowpro@aol.com

CRESTA BLINDS LTD T 01902 765408
Supplier of Vertical Blinds
PO Box 6976, Wolverhampton WV1 9YP
E info@blindsbycresta.co.uk
W www.crestablindsltd.co.uk

CROFTS, Andrew T/F 01403 864518
Book Writing Services
Westlands Grange, West Grinstead
Horsham, West Sussex RH13 8LZ
E croftsa@aol.com
W www.andrewcrofts.com

**CUE ACTION POOL
PROMOTIONS** T 07881 828077
Advice for UK & US Pool, Snooker, Trick Shots
4 Hillview Close, Rowhedge
Colchester, Essex CO5 7HT
E sales@cueaction.com
W www.stevedaking.com

DESIGN PROJECTS T 01883 730262
Perrysfield Farm
Broadham Green
Old Oxted, Surrey RH8 9PG
T 07712 490004
W www.designprojects.co.uk

**DEVEREUX
DEVELOPMENTS LTD** T 01642 560854
Haulage. Removals. Trucking
Daimler Drive
Cowpen Industrial Estate
Billingham, Cleveland TS23 4JD
F 01642 566664
E mikebell@britdev.com

**DORANS PROPMAKERS /
SET BUILDERS** T/F 01335 300064
53 Derby Road, Ashbourne, Derbyshire DE6 1BH
E info@doransprops.com
W www.doransprops.com

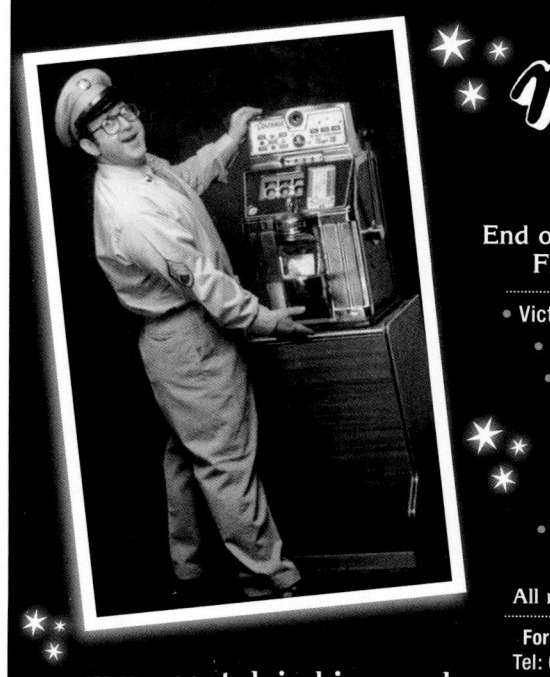

DRAMA T'S　　　　**T** 07587 094808
Branded Merchandise for Stage Professionals
(T-shirts/Hoodies etc)
Based in London
E info@dramats.com
W www.dramats.com

DURRENT, Peter　　　**T** 01787 248263
Audition & Rehearsal Pianist. Cocktail Pianist. Composer.
Vocalist
40 Water Street, Lavenham
Sudbury, Suffolk CO10 9RN
E tunefuldurrent@gmail.com

EAT TO THE BEAT　　　**T** 01494 790700
Production & Location Caterers
Global Infusion Court, Nashleigh Hill
Chesham, Bucks HP5 3HE
F 01494 790701
E hello@eattothebeat.com
W www.globalinfusiongroup.com

ELECTRO SIGNS LTD　　**T** 020 8521 8066
97 Vallentin Road, London E17 3JJ
F 020 8520 8127
E info@electrosigns.co.uk

ESCORT GUNLEATHER　　**T** 01268 792769
Custom Leathercraft
602 High Road, Benfleet, Essex SS7 5RW
E info@escortgunleather.com
W www.escortgunleather.com

EYE 4 DESIGN
UPHOLSTERY LTD　　　**T** 01775 680109
Reupholstery, Bespoke Upholstery, Antique Restoration,
Television, Theatre & Set Work
154 Station Road, Surfleet
Spalding, Lincolnshire PE11 4DG
E enquiries@eye4designupholstery.co.uk
W www.eye4designupholstery.co.uk

FACADE　　　　　**T** 020 8291 7079
Musical Production Services
43A Garthorne Road, London SE23 1EP
F 020 8291 4969
E facade@cobomedia.com

FELLOWES, Mark
TRANSPORT SERVICES　　**T** 020 7386 7005
Transport. Storage
59 Sherbrooke Road, London SW6 7QL
T 07850 332818
W www.fellowesproductions.com

FILM MEDICAL SERVICES　**T** 020 8961 3222
Units 5 & 7, Commercial Way
Park Royal, London NW10 7XF
F 020 8961 7427
E info@filmmedical.co.uk
W www.filmmedical.co.uk

FINAL CREATION　　　**T** 01530 249100
Unit 19, The Loft Studio, Hill Lane Industrial Estate
Markfield, Leicestershire LE67 9PN
F 01530 249400
E gemma@finalcreation.co.uk
W www.finalcreation.co.uk

FIREBRAND　　　**T/F** 01546 870310
Real Flame Torches. Hire & Sales
Leac Na Ban, Tayvallich
By Lochgilphead, Argyll PA31 8PF
W www.studiobarnargyll.co.uk

FIRST NIGHT DESIGN　　**T** 07773 770781
Original & Vintage Art
E info@firstnightdesign.co.uk
W www.firstnightdesign.co.uk

FLAME RETARDING　　　**T** 01621 818477
Grove Farm, Grove Farm Road
Tolleshunt Major, Maldon, Essex CM9 8LR
F 07092 036931
E email@flameretarding.co.uk
W www.flameretarding.co.uk

FLAMENCO PRODUCTIONS　**T** 01905 424083
Entertainers
Sevilla 4 Cormorant Rise
Lower Wick, Worcester WR2 4BA
E delphineflamenco@tiscali.co.uk

FLINTS　　　　　**T** 020 7703 9786
Queen's Row, London SE17 2PX
F 020 7708 4189
E sales@flints.co.uk　　**W** www.flints.co.uk

FLYING BY FOY　　　**T** 020 8236 0234
Flying Effects for Stage, Television, Corporate Events etc
Unit 4, Borehamwood Enterprise Centre
Theobald Street, Borehamwood, Herts WD6 4RQ
F 020 8236 0235
E enquiries@flyingbyfoy.co.uk
W www.flyingbyfoy.co.uk

FROST, John NEWSPAPERS
Historical Newspaper Archives
E andrew@johnfrostnewspapers.com
W www.johnfrostnewspapers.com

GARRATT, Jonathan FRSA　**T** 01725 517700
Suppliers of Traditional & Unusual Garden Pots &
Installations. Glazed Tableware
Hare Lane Farmhouse, Cranborne, Dorset BH21 5QT
E jonathan.garratt@talk21.com
W www.jonathangarratt.com

GAV NICOLA
THEATRICAL SHOES　　**T** 07961 974278
T 00 34 673803783
E gavnicola@yahoo.com
W www.theatricalshoes.com

GET STUFFED　　　**T** 020 7226 1364
Taxidermy
105 Essex Road, London N1 2SL
T 07831 260062
E taxidermy@thegetstuffed.co.uk
W www.thegetstuffed.co.uk

GHOSTWRITER / AUTHOR /
SCRIPTWRITER　　　**T** 01227 721071
Contact: John Parker
Dove Cottage, The Street, Ickham CT3 1QP
T 07702 999920
E ghostwriterforyourbook@ymail.com
W www.ghostwriteruk.info

GIG...FYI　　　　**T** 01494 790700
Corporate Hospitality Caterers
Global Infusion Court, Nashleigh Hill
Chesham, Bucks HP5 3HE
F 01494 790701
E hello@gigfyi.com
W www.gigfyi.com

GORGEOUS GOURMETS LTD　**T** 020 8944 7771
Furniture & Catering Equipment Hire
Gresham Way, Wimbledon SW19 8ED
E hire@gorgeoushire.co.uk
W www.gorgeoushire.co.uk

GOULD, Gillian ANTIQUES　**T** 020 8455 1747
Scientific & Marine Antiques & Collectables
38 Denman Drive South, London NW11 6RH
T 07831 150060
E gillgould@dealwith.com
W www.gilliangouldantiques.co.uk

GREENPROPS Foliage * Flowers * Fruit & Veg
Importers, Stockists & Makers

The Artificial STAGE SUPPLIERS, serving The West End, The UK and Europe
T: 01398 361531   trevor@greenprops.org   www.greenprops.org

‖‖‖

GRADAV HIRE & SALES LTD T 020 8803 7400
Lighting & Sound Hire/Sales
Units C6 & C9 Hastingwood Trading Estate
Harbet Road, Edmonton
London N18 3HU
F 020 8803 5060
E office@gradav.co.uk

GRAND HIRE T 020 7281 9555
Short & Long Term Piano Hire
465 Hornsey Road, London N19 4DR
F 020 7263 0154
E piano@grandhire.co.uk
W www.grandhire.co.uk

GRAY, Robin COMMENTARIES T 01420 23347
Voice Overs. Hunting Attire. Racing Colours. Saddles
Comptons, Isington
Alton, Hampshire GU34 4PL
T 07831 828424
E comptons1@hotmail.co.uk

GREENPROPS T 01398 361531
Prop Suppliers. Replica Flowers, Fruit, Raffia Grass,
Foliage, Trees etc
E trevor@greenprops.org
W www.greenprops.org

GREENSOURCE
SOLUTIONS LTD T 0845 3100200
Providers of Mobile Phone Props. Supplies & Recycles
Printer Consumables
14 Kingsland Trading Estate
St Phillips Road
Bristol BS2 0JZ
F 0117 304 2391
E props@greensource.co.uk
W www.greensource.co.uk

HANDS UP PUPPETS T 07909 824630
7 Cavendish Vale, Nottingham
Nottinghamshire NG5 4DS
E marcus@handsuppuppets.com
W www.handsuppuppets.com

HARLEQUIN FLOORS
(BRITISH HARLEQUIN PLC) T 01892 514888
Floors for Dance, Display, Entertainment & the
Performing Arts
Festival House, Chapman Way
Tunbridge Wells, Kent TN2 3EF
T 0800 289932
E enquiries@harlequinfloors.com
W www.harlequinfloors.com

HERON & DRIVER T 020 7394 8688
Scenic Furniture & Prop Makers
Unit 7, Dockley Road Industrial Estate
Rotherhithe, London SE16 3SF
E mail@herondriver.co.uk
W www.herondriver.co.uk

HI-FLI T 0161 278 9352
Flying Effects
18 Greencourt Drive
Manchester M38 0BZ
E mikefrost@hi-fli.co.uk

HISTORICAL INTERPRETER &
ROLE PLAYING T 020 8866 2997
Contact: Donald Clarke
80 Warden Avenue, Rayners Lane
Harrow, Middlesex HA2 9LW
T 07811 606285
E info@historicalinterpretations.co.uk
W www.historicalinterpretations.co.uk

HISTORY IN THE MAKING LTD T 023 9225 3175
Weapon & Costume Hire
4A Aysgarth Road, Waterlooville
Hampshire PO7 7UG
E info@history-making.com
W www.history-making.com

HOME JAMES
CHAUFFEUR SERVICE T 0121 356 5088
Moor Lane, Witton
Birmingham B6 7HH
E enquiries@homejamescars.com
W www.homejamescars.com

HOMESITE ESTATE AGENTS T 020 7243 3535
16 Lambton Place, London W11 2SH
F 020 7243 5794
E info@homesite.co.uk
W www.homesite.co.uk

HOWARD, Rex DRAPES T 020 8955 6940
Trading Division of Hawthorns
Unit F, Western Trading Estate
London NW10 7LU
E hire@hawthorns.uk.com

IMPACT T 020 8579 9922
Private & Contract Hire of Coaches
1 Leighton Road, Ealing
London W13 9EL
F 020 8840 4880
E info@impactgroup.co.uk
W www.impactgroup.co.uk

IMPACT MARKETING T 020 7729 5978
Print Distribution & Display
Tuscany Wharf, 4B Orsman Road
London N1 5QJ
F 020 7729 5994
E contactus@impactideas.co.uk
W www.impactideas.co.uk

IMPACT PERCUSSION T 020 8299 6700
Percussion Instruments for Sale
Unit 7, Goose Green Trading Estate
47 East Dulwich Road
London SE22 9BN
F 020 8299 6704
E sales@impactpercussion.com

JAPAN PROMOTIONS T/F 020 7278 4099
Japanese Costumes & Props
200 Russell Court
3 Woburn Place
London WC1H 0ND
E info@japan-promotions.co.uk
W www.japan-promotions.co.uk

JULIETTE DESIGNS T 020 7263 7878
Diamante Jewellery Manufacturer: Necklaces,
Crowns etc
90 Yerbury Road, London N19 4RS
F 020 7281 7326
E juliettedesigns@hotmail.com
W www.stagejewellery.com

KEIGHLEY & WORTH VALLEY
LIGHT RAILWAY LTD T 01535 645214
Crew. Props. Carriages, Engines & Stations
The Railway Station, Haworth
Keighley, West Yorkshire BD22 8NJ
F 01535 647317
E admin@kwvr.co.uk
W www.kwvr.co.uk

KENSINGTON EYE CENTRE T 020 7937 8282
Opticians. Special Eye Effects
37 Kensington Church Street, London W8 4LL
E kensingtoneyecentre@gmail.com
W www.kensingtoneyecentre.com

KIRBY'S AFX LTD T/F 020 8723 8552
8 Greenford Avenue, Hanwell, London W7 3QP
T 07958 285608
E mail@afxuk.com
W www.afxuk.com

KNEBWORTH HOUSE,
GARDENS & PARK T 01438 812661
Knebworth, Herts SG3 6PY
E info@knebworthhouse.com
W www.knebworthhouse.com

LAREDO, Alex T 01306 889423
Expert with Ropes, Bullwhips, Shooting & Riding
29 Lincoln Road, Dorking
Surrey RH4 1TE
T 07745 798118

LAREDO WILD WEST TOWN T 01580 891790
Wild West Entertainment
1 Bower Walk, Staplehurst
Tonbridge, Kent TN12 0LU
T 07947 652771
E colin.winter123@btinternet.com
W www.laredo.org.uk

LEES-NEWSOME LTD T 0845 0708005
Manufacturers of Flame Retardant Fabrics
Ashley Works, Unit 2, Rule Business Park
Grimshaw Lane, Middleton, Manchester M24 2AE
F 0845 0708006
E info@leesnewsome.co.uk
W www.leesnewsome.co.uk

LEIGHTON HALL T 01524 734474
Historic House
Carnforth, Lancashire LA5 9ST
F 01524 720357
E info@leightonhall.co.uk
W www.leightonhall.co.uk

LEVRANT, Stephen - HERITAGE
ARCHITECTURE LTD T 020 8748 5501
Architects. Historic Building Consultants
62 British Grove, Chiswick, London W4 2NL
F 020 8748 4992
E info@heritagearchitecture.co.uk

LIGHT ARMOURIES T 07761 219755
Hand-made Latex & Foam Weapons, Shields, Props &
Armour
Unit 16, Chase Farm, Vicarage Lane West
North Weald, Essex CM16 6AL
E mikel42@hotmail.co.uk
W www.lightarmoury.co.uk

LIMELIGHT ENTERTAINMENT T 020 8853 9570
Theatre Merchandise
Unit 13, The io Centre
The Royal Arsenal, Seymour Street, London SE18 6SX
F 020 8853 9579
E enquiries@thelimelightgroup.co.uk

LONDON MUSEUM OF WATER &
STEAM THE T 020 8568 4757
Green Dragon Lane, Brentford
Middlesex TW8 0EN
F 020 8569 9978
E museum@waterandsteam.org.uk
W www.waterandsteam.org.uk

LONDON QUALITY
DRY CLEANERS LTD T 020 7935 7316
Dry Cleaners. Dyers. Launderers. Costumes &
Stage Curtains
222 Baker Street, London NW1 5RT

LONO DRINKS T 0800 8250035
Units 1 & 2, Manchester Industrial Estate, Holt Street
Newton Heath, Manchester M40 5AX
E info@lono.co.uk
W www.lono.co.uk

LOS KAOS T 01291 680074
Animatronics. Puppetry. Street Theatre
Quay House, Quayside
Brockweir, Gloucestershire NP16 7NQ
E kaos@loskaos.co.uk
W www.loskaos.co.uk

LUCKINGS T 020 8332 2000
Stage Hands. Storage. Transporters
Boston House, 69-75 Boston Manor Road
Brentford, Middlesex TW8 9JJ
F 020 8332 3000
E info@luckings.co.uk
W www.luckings.co.uk

LUCKINGS SCREEN SERVICES T 020 8332 2000
Artists' Trailers/Splits/2-3 Ways
Boston House, 69-75 Boston Manor Road
Brentford, Middlesex TW8 9JJ
F 020 8332 3000
E info@luckings.co.uk
W www.luckings.co.uk

LYON EQUIPMENT T 01539 626250
Petzl & Beal Rope Access Equipment (PPE) for Industrial
& Theatrical Work
Junction 38, M6, Tebay, Cumbria CA10 3SS
F 01539 624857
E work.rescue@lyon.co.uk
W www.lyon.co.uk

M A C T 0161 969 8311
Sound Hire
1-2 Attenburys Park, Park Road
Altrincham, Cheshire WA14 5QE
F 0161 962 9423
E hire@macsound.co.uk
W www.macsound.co.uk

MACKIE, Sally LOCATIONS T 01451 830294
Location Finding & Management
Cownham Farm, Broadwell
Moreton-in-Marsh, Gloucestershire GL56 0TT
E sally@mackie.biz
W www.sallymackie-locations.com

MAGICAL MART T/F 020 8300 3579
Magic. Punch & Judy. Ventriloquists' Dolls. Hire &
Advising. Callers by Appointment
42 Christchurch Road, Sidcup, Kent DA15 7HQ
W www.johnstylesentertainer.co.uk

MAINSTREAM LEISURE GROUP   T 020 3044 2923
Riverboat/Canal Boat Hire
Trident Court, 1 Oakcroft Road
Chessington, Surrey KT9 1BD
F 020 3044 2926
E info@mainstreamleisure.co.uk
W www.mainstreamleisure.co.uk

MARCUS HALL PROPS   T 020 7252 6291
Contact: Chris Marcus, Jonathan Hall
Unit 2BC Vanguard Court, 36-38 Peckham Road
London SE5 8QT
E chris@marcushallprops.com
W www.marcushallprops.com

MARKSON PIANOS   T 020 7935 8682
8 Chester Court, Albany Street
London NW1 4BU
F 020 7224 0957
E info@marksonpianos.com
W www.marksonpianos.com

MATTLX GROUP   T 0845 6808692
Lighting. Design. Production Engineering. Safety. Training
Unit 3, Vinehall Business Centre
Vinehall Road, Robertsbridge
East Sussex TN32 5JW
E intray@mattlx.com
W www.mattlx.com

McDONAGH, Melanie MANAGMENT   T 07908 225278
*TV Horse-drawn Cinderella Carriage. As seen in
'Marriage and Mayhem', 'Britain's Got Talent', 'Don't Tell
the Bride', 'Sweet Sixteen (UK)', 'This Morning' & 'Four
Weddings'. Used at Charity Events including Unicef
Cinderella Ball*
T 07909 831409
E info@famouscinderellacarriage.co.uk
W www.mcdonaghmanagement.co.uk

McNEILL, Brian   T 01706 812291
Vintage Truck & Coaches
Hawk Mount, Kebs Road
Todmorden, Lancashire OL14 8SB
E autotrans@uk2.net
W www.rollingpast.com

MICHELLE, Sabah   T 001 954 566 6219 (Office)
*UK Stylist/Designer/Coordinator. Based in Ft.
Lauderdale, Florida. Specialising in Fashion & Wardrobe*
2841 N. Ocean Boulevard Apt 501, Fort Lauderdale
Florida 33308, USA
T 001 954 383 2179 (Mobile)
E sabah561@aol.com

MIDNIGHT ELECTRONICS   T 0191 224 0088
Sound Hire
Off Quay Building, Foundry Lane
Newcastle upon Tyne NE6 1LH
E info@midnightelectronics.co.uk
W www.midnightelectronics.co.uk

MILITARY, MODELS & MINIATURES   T 020 7700 7036
Model Figures
38A Horsell Road, London N5 1XP
F 020 7700 4624
E pevans113@btinternet.com

MODDED MOTORS AGENCY   T 07989 128131
Suppliers of Modified Cars
38 Williamson Way, Rickmansworth
Hertfordshire WD3 8GL
E contact@moddedmotorsagency.com
W www.moddedmotorsagency.com

MODELBOX   T 01837 810923
Computer Aided Design. Design Services
41C Market Street, Hatherleigh, Devon EX20 3JP
E info@modelbox.co.uk
W www.modelboxplans.com

MOORFIELDS PHOTOGRAPHIC LTD   T 0151 236 1611
2 Old Hall Street, Liverpool L3 9RQ
E info@moorfieldsphoto.com
W www.moorfieldsphoto.com

MORGAN, Dennis   T 07915 662767
Cinematographer
Cornwall
E info@dennismorgan.co.uk

MORTON, G. & L.   T 01430 860185
Farming. Horses
Hashome Carr, Holme-on-Spalding Moor
Yorkshire YO43 4BD
E janet_morton@hotmail.com

MOTORHOUSE HIRE LTD   T 020 7495 1618
Contact: Michael Geary. Action Vehicles
Oatleys Hall, Turweston
Northants NN13 5JX
F 01280 704944
E michael@motorhouseltd.co.uk

NEWMAN HIRE COMPANY   T 020 8743 0741
Lighting Hire
16 The Vale, Acton, London W3 7SB
E info@newmanhire.co.uk

NORTHERN LIGHT   T 0131 622 9100
Assembly Street, Leith
Edinburgh EH6 7RG
E enquiries@northernlight.co.uk
W www.northernlight.co.uk

NOSTALGIA AMUSEMENTS   T 020 8398 2141
Contact: Brian Davey
22 Greenwood Close, Thames Ditton, Surrey KT7 0BG
T 07973 506869
E bdavey@globalnet.co.uk
w www.nostalgia-hire.co.uk

NOTTINGHAM JOUSTING ASSOCIATION SCHOOL OF NATIONAL EQUITATION LTD   T 01509 852366
*Jousting & Medieval Tournaments. Horses & Riders for
Films & Television*
Bunny Hill Top, Costock
Loughborough, Leicestershire LE12 6XN
E info@bunnyhill.co.uk
W www.bunnyhill.co.uk

OCEAN LEISURE   **T** 020 7930 5050
Scuba Diving. Watersports Retail. Underwater & Extreme Camera Specialists
11-14 Northumberland Avenue, London WC2N 5AQ
F 020 7930 3032
E info@oceanleisure.co.uk
W www.oceanleisure.co.uk

OFFSTAGE BOOKS   **T** 020 8444 4717
BlackGull Bookshop, 121 High Road
London N2 8AG
E offstagebooks@gmail.com

PAPERFLOW PLC   **T** 020 8331 2000
Office Equipment. Stationery
Unit 6, Meridian Trading Estate
20 Bugsbys Way, Charlton, London SE7 7SJ
F 020 8331 2001
E sales@paperflowgroup.com

PAPERPROPMAKER   **T** 07545 281486
Paper Props Created for Stage, Film & Television. Letters, Notebooks, Paper Ephemera etc. Handwritten or Printed. Any Style or Period Reproduced
Based in London
E sianwillis@live.co.uk

PATCHETTS EQUESTRIAN CENTRE   **T** 01923 852255
Location
Hillfield Lane, Aldenham
Watford, Herts WD25 8PE
F 01923 859289
E info@patchetts.co.uk
W www.patchetts.co.uk

PATERSON, Helen   **T** 020 7730 6428
Typing Services
40 Whitelands House, London SW3 4QY
E pater@waitrose.com

PERIOD PETROL PUMP COLLECTION   **T** 01379 643978
c/o Diss Ironworks, 7 St Nicholas Street
Diss, Norfolk IP22 4LB
E info@dissironworks.co.uk
W www.periodpetrolpumps.co.uk

PHOSPHENE   **T** 01449 770011
Lighting & Sound. Design. Hire. Sales
Milton Road South, Stowmarket
Suffolk IP14 1EZ
E phosphene@btconnect.com
W www.phosphene.co.uk

PIANO PEOPLE THE   **T** 020 7281 3280
Piano Hire & Transport
74 Playford Road, London N4 3PH
E info@pianopeople.co.uk
W www.pianopeople.co.uk

PINK POINTES DANCEWEAR   **T/F** 01708 438584
1A Suttons Lane, Hornchurch
Essex RM12 6RD
E pink.pointes@btconnect.com

PLUNGE PRODUCTIONS   **T** 01273 421819
Creative Services. Graphic Design. Props
Unit 3, Bestwood Works
Drove Road, Brighton BN41 2PA
E info@plungeproductions.com
W www.plungeproductions.com

PLUSFILM LTD   **T** 01489 895559
Action Vehicle Hire & SFX Vehicles Designed & Built
T 07885 619783
E stephen.lamonby@gmail.com
W www.plusfilm.com

POLAND, Anna: SCULPTOR & MODELMAKER   **T** 023 8040 5166
Sculpture, Models, Puppets, Masks etc
Salterns, Old Bursledon
Southampton, Hampshire SO31 8DH
E polandanna@hotmail.com

POLLEX PROPS / FIREBRAND   **T/F** 01546 870310
Prop Makers
Leac Na Ban, Tayvallich
Lochgilphead, Argyll PA31 8PF
E firebrand.props@btinternet.com

PREMIER CHAUFFEUR SERVICES   **T** 01925 299112
164 Haydock Street, Newton-le-Willows
Merseyside WA12 9DH
T 07890 661050
E mike.vizard@hotmail.co.uk

PRINTMEDIA GROUP
E info@printmediagroup.eu
W www.printmediagroup.eu

PROBLOOD   **T/F** 01728 723865
11 Mount Pleasant, Framlingham, Suffolk IP13 9HQ

PROFESSOR PATTEN'S PUNCH & JUDY   **T** 01707 873262
Hire & Performances. Advice on Traditional Show
14 The Crest, Goffs Oak
Hertfordshire EN7 5NP
E dennis@dennispatten.co.uk
W www.dennispatten.co.uk

PROP FARM LTD   **T** 01909 723100
Contact: Pat Ward
Grange Farm, Elmton
Nr Creswell, North Derbyshire S80 4LX
F 01909 721465
E pat@propfarm.co.uk

PROP STUDIOS LTD   **T** 01444 250088
Unit 3 Old Kiln Works
Ditchling Common Industrial Estate
Hassocks BN6 8SG
F 01444 250089
E info@propstudios.co.uk
W www.propstudios.co.uk

PUNCH & JUDY PUPPETS & BOOTHS   **T/F** 020 8300 3579
Hire & Advisory Service. Callers by Appointment
42 Christchurch Road, Sidcup
Kent DA15 7HQ
W www.johnstylesentertainer.co.uk

RAINBOW PRODUCTIONS LTD   **T** 020 8254 5300
Creation & Appearances of Costume Characters. Stage Shows
Unit 3, Greenlea Park
Prince George's Road, London SW19 2JD
F 020 8254 5306
E info@rainbowproductions.co.uk
W www.rainbowproductions.co.uk

RE:AL   **T** 01622 200123
Print. Creative. Marketing. Digital
Unit 2, Tovil Green Business Park
Maidstone, Kent ME15 6TA
E info@realprintandmedia.com
W www.realprintandmedia.com

RENT-A-CLOWN   **T/F** 020 7608 0312
Contact: Mattie Faint
37 Sekforde Street, Clerkenwell, London EC1R 0HA
E mattiefaint@gmail.com

REPLAY FILM & NEW MEDIA   T 020 7637 0473
Showreels. Television Facilities Hire
Museum House
25 Museum Street, London WC1A 1JT
E sales@replayfilms.co.uk
W www.replayfilms.co.uk

ROBERTS, Chris INTERIORS   T 07956 512074
*Specialist Painters & Decorators. Classic & Modern
Decorating*
117 Colebrook Lane
Loughton IG10 2HP
E procopi@hotmail.com

ROOTSTEIN, Adel LTD   T 020 7381 1447
Mannequin Manufacturer
9 Beaumont Avenue, London W14 9LP
F 020 7386 9594
W www.rootstein.com

RORKIES BUS   T 07846 022119
*London Routemaster Bus Available for Film Work,
Advertising & Private Hire*
Flat 4, 26 Devonshire Gardens
Margate, Kent CT9 3AE
E rorke.steve@yahoo.co.uk
W www.rorkiesbus.co.uk

**ROYAL HORTICULTURAL
HALLS THE**   T 0845 3704606
*Film Location: Art Deco & Edwardian Buildings.
Conferences. Events. Exhibitions. Fashion Shows*
80 Vincent Square, London SW1P 2PE
E horthalls@rhs.org.uk
W www.rhhonline.co.uk

RUDKIN DESIGN   T 01327 301770
*Design Consultants. Advertising, Brochures,
Corporate etc*
10 Cottesbrooke Park
Heartlands Business Park
Daventry, Northamptonshire NN11 8YL
E arudkin@rudkindesign.co.uk
W www.rudkindesign.co.uk

RUMBLE, Jane   T 020 8904 6462
Props to Order. No Hire
121 Elmstead Avenue, Wembley
Middlesex HA9 8NT

SALVO THE CLOWN   T 01268 745791
13 Second Avenue, Kingsleigh Park
Thundersley, Essex SS7 3QD
E salvo@annualclownsdirectory.com
W www.annualclownsdirectory.com

SAPEX SCRIPTS   T 020 8236 1600
The Maxwell Building
Elstree Film Studios, Shenley Road
Borehamwood, Herts WD6 1JG
F 020 8324 2771
E scripts@sapex.co.uk
W www.sapex.co.uk

**SCHULTZ & WIREMU FABRIC
EFFECTS LTD**   T/F 020 8469 0151
Distressing. Dyeing. Printing
Unit 6, Titan Business Estate, Finch Street
London SE8 5QA
E swfabricfx@london.com
W www.schultz-wiremufabricfx.co.uk

SCRIPTRIGHT   T 020 8749 9179
*Contact: S.C. Hill. Script & Manuscript Typing Services.
Script Reading & Assessment Services*
St Saviour's Vicarage Cottage, Cobbold Road
London W12 9LN
E samc.hill@virgin.net

SCRIPTS BY ARGYLE   T 07905 293319
*Play, Film & Book Typing/Editing in Professional Layout.
London Collection of Manuscript on Request*
43 Clappers Lane
Fulking, West Sussex BN5 9ND
E argyle.associates@me.com

**SHIRLEY LEAF &
PETAL COMPANY**   T/F 01424 427793
Flower Makers Museum & Manufacturers
58A High Street, Old Town
Hastings, East Sussex TN34 3EN

SIDE EFFECTS   T 020 7587 1116
FX. Models. Props
92 Fentiman Road
London SW8 1LA
F 020 7207 0062
E sfx@lineone.net

SNOW BUSINESS   T/F 01453 840077
Snow & Winter Effects on any Scale
The Snow Mill, Bridge Road
Ebley, Stroud, Gloucestershire GL5 4TR
E snow@snowbusiness.com
W www.snowbusiness.com

SOFT PROPS   T 020 7587 1116
Modelmakers
92 Fentiman Road, London SW8 1LA
F 020 7207 0062
E jackie@softprops.co.uk

**STANSTED AIRPORT TAXIS &
CHAUFFEURS**   T 0845 6436705
55 Croasdaile Road
Stansted Airport
Essex CM24 8DW
E enquiries@stanstedtaxiservice.co.uk
W www.stanstedtaxiservice.co.uk

**STEELDECK RENTALS /
SALES LTD**   T 020 7833 2031
Modular Staging. Stage Equipment Hire
Unit 58
T Marchant Trading Estate
42-72 Verney Road
London SE16 3DH
F 020 7232 1780
E rentals@steeldeck.co.uk
W www.steeldeck.co.uk

STEVENSON, Scott   T 07739 378579
Prop Maker
60 Ripley Road, Sawmills
Belper, Derbyshire DE56 2JQ
E scott.stevenson317@gmail.com

**STOKE BRUERNE BOAT
COMPANY LTD**   T 07966 503609
Passenger Boat Operator
Wharf Cottage, Stoke Bruerne
Northants NN12 7SE
W www.stokebruerneboats.co.uk

SUPERHIRE PROPS LTD   T 0871 2310900
Prop Hire Specialist. Victorian to Present Day
55 Chase Road
London NW10 6LU
F 020 8965 8107
E dawn@superhire.com
W www.superhire.com

SUPERSCRIPTS   T 01256 769376
1 Bluehaven Walk, Hook
Hampshire RG27 9SX
T 07793 160138
E super_scripts@sky.com

TAYLOR, Charlotte   T 020 8876 9085
Stylist/Set Decorator
18 Eleanor Grove, Barnes
London SW13 0JN
T 07836 708904
E charlottetaylor.info@gmail.com

**THAMES LUXURY
CHARTERS LTD**   T 020 7357 7751
Eagle Wharf, 53 Lafone Street
London SE1 2LX
F 020 7378 1359
E sales@thamesluxurycharters.co.uk
W www.thamesluxurycharters.co.uk

THEATRESEARCH LTD   T 01423 780497
Theatre Consultants
Dacre Hall, Dacre
North Yorkshire HG3 4ET
F 01423 781957
E office@theatresearch.co.uk
W www.theatresearch.co.uk

**THEATRICAL
SHOEMAKERS LTD**   T 020 8884 4484
Footwear
Unit 1A, Lee Valley Trading Estate
Rivermead Road, London N18 3QW
E info@theatreshoes.com
W www.shoemaking.co.uk

THEME TRADERS LTD   T 020 8452 8518
Props. Prop Hire. Party Planners. Productions
The Stadium, Oaklands Road
London NW2 6DL
F 020 8450 7322
E mailroom@themetraders.com
W www.themetraders.com

TOP SHOW   T/F 01904 750022
Props. Scenery. Conference Specialists
North Lane, Huntington
Yorks YO32 9SU

TRANSCRIPTS   T 07973 200197
*Conferences. Interviews. Post-production Scripts.
Proofreading. Videos. Working Formats: Digital,
CD/DVD, Tapes*
E lucy@transcripts.demon.co.uk

TRYFONOS, Mary MASKS   T 020 7502 7883
Mask, Headdress & Puppet Specialist
59 Shaftesbury Road
London N19 4QW
T 07764 587433
E marytryfonos@aol.com

TURN ON LIGHTING   T/F 020 7359 7616
Antique Lighting c1850-1950
11 Camden Passage, London N1 8EA
E info@turnonlighting.co.uk
W www.turnonlighting.co.uk

**UK SAME DAY
DELIVERY SERVICE**   T 07785 717179
Contact: Philip Collings
18 Billingshurst Road, Broadbridge Heath
Horsham, West Sussex RH12 3LW
F 01403 266059
E philcollings60@hotmail.com

UPSTAGE   T 020 7403 6510
Live Communications Agency
Studio A, 7 Maidstone Buildings Mews
72-76 Borough High Street, London SE1 1GD
F 020 7403 6511
E loretta@upstagecommunications.com
W www.upstagecommunications.com

**VENTRILOQUIST
DOLLS HOME**   T/F 020 8300 3579
Hire & Helpful Hints. Callers by Appointment
42 Christchurch Road, Sidcup
Kent DA15 7HQ
W www.johnstylesentertainer.co.uk

VENTRILOQUIST DUMMY HIRE   T 01707 873262
Contact: Dennis Patten. Hire & Advice
14 The Crest, Goffs Oak
Herts EN7 5NP
E dennis@dennispatten.co.uk
W www.dennispatten.co.uk

VINMAG ARCHIVE LTD   T 020 8533 7588
84-90 Digby Road
London E9 6HX
E pictures@vinmagarchive.com
W www.vintagemagazinecompany.co.uk

VINTAGE CARRIAGES TRUST   T 01535 680425
*Owners of the Museum of Rail Travel at Ingrow
Railway Centre*
Keighley, West Yorkshire BD21 5AX
F 01535 610796
E admin@vintagecarriagestrust.org
W www.vintagecarriagestrust.org

VOCALEYES   T 020 7375 1043
Audio Description "Describing the Arts"
1st Floor, 54 Commercial Street
London E1 6LT
F 020 7247 5622
E enquiries@vocaleyes.co.uk
W www.vocaleyes.co.uk

WALKING YOUR DOG   T 01322 634807
Dog Walking & Pet Services for South East London
T 07867 502333
E info@walkingyourdog.net
W www.walkingyourdog.net

**WEBBER, Peter
RITZ STUDIOS**   T 020 8870 1335
Music Equipment Hire. Rehearsal Studios
Courtyard Studios, The Bridge
Esmond Street, London SW15 2LP
E ben@peterwebberhire.com
W www.ritzstudios.com

**WESTED LEATHERS
COMPANY**   T 01322 660654
Suede & Leather Suppliers/Manufacturers
Little Wested House, Wested Lane
Swanley, Kent BR8 8EF
F 01322 667039
E wested@wested.com

WESTWARD, Lynn BLINDS   T 020 8742 8333
Window Blind Specialist
458 Chiswick High Road
London W4 5TT
F 020 8742 8444
E info@lynnwestward.com
W www.lynnwestward.com

WHITE ROOM STUDIO   T 020 8674 8151
Unit 03, 45 Morrish Road
London SW2 4EE
E info@whiteroomstudio.co.uk
W www.whiteroomstudio.co.uk

WORBEY, Darryl STUDIOS   T 020 7639 8090
Specialist Puppet Design & Construction
Ground Floor, 33 York Grove
London SE15 2NY
T 07815 671564
E info@darrylworbeystudios.com

ACTIONS: THE ACTORS'
THESAURUS　　　　　T 020 8749 4953
By Marina Caldarone & Maggie Lloyd-Williams
Nick Hern Books, The Glasshouse
49A Goldhawk Road, London W12 8QP
F 020 8735 0250
E info@nickhernbooks.co.uk
W www.nickhernbooks.co.uk

ACTORS & PERFORMERS
YEARBOOK　　　　　T 020 7631 5600
Methuen Drama, Bloomsbury Publishing Plc
50 Bedford Square, London WC1B 3DP
F 020 7631 5800
E actorsyb@bloomsbury.com
W www.actorsandperformers.com

AMATEUR STAGE MAGAZINE　T 020 7096 1603
3rd Floor, 207 Regent Street, London W1B 3HH
F 020 7681 3867
E editor@amateurstagemagazine.co.uk
W www.amateurstagemagazine.co.uk

ANNUAIRE DU
CINEMA BELLEFAYE　　　T 00 33 1 42335252
French Actors' Directory, Production, Technicians & all
Technical Industries & Suppliers
30 rue Saint Marc
75002 Paris, France
F 00 33 1 42963303
E contact@bellefaye.com
W www.bellefaye.com

ARTISTES & AGENTS　　　T 020 7224 9666
Richmond House Publishing Co Ltd
Suite D2, 4-6 Canfield Place
London NW6 3BT
E sales@rhpco.co.uk
W www.rhpco.co.uk

AUDITIONS: THE COMPLETE GUIDE
E info@auditionsthecompleteguide.com
W www.auditionsthecompleteguide.com

AUDITIONS UNDRESSED　　T 020 7839 4888
By Dan Bowling
c/o Global Artists, 23 Haymarket
London SW1Y 4DG
E michaelgarrett@globalartists.co.uk

AURORA METRO PRESS
(1989)　　　　　　　T 020 3261 0000
Biography, Drama, Fiction, Humour, Reference &
International Literature in English Translation
67 Grove Avenue, Twickenham TW1 4HX
E info@aurorametro.com
W www.aurorametro.com

BEAT MAGAZINE　　　　T 01753 866865
Arts & Culture Magazine
c/o Firestation Centre for Arts & Culture
The Old Court, St Leonards Road
Windsor, Berks SL4 3BL
E editor@beatmagazine.co.uk
W www.beatmagazine.co.uk

BRITISH PERFORMING
ARTS YEARBOOK　　　　T 020 7333 1723
Rhinegold Publishing, Rhinegold House
20 Rugby Street, London WC1N 3QZ
E bpay@rhinegold.co.uk
W www.rhinegold.co.uk

BRITISH THEATRE.COM　　T 020 7096 1603
3rd Floor, 207 Regent Street
London W1B 3HH
F 020 7681 3867
E sales@3foldmedia.co.uk
W www.britishtheatre.com

BRITISH THEATRE DIRECTORY　T 020 7224 9666
Richmond House Publishing Co Ltd, Suite D2
4-6 Canfield Place
London NW6 3BT
E sales@rhpco.co.uk
W www.rhpco.co.uk

BROADCAST　　　　　T 020 3033 2872
MBI, 101 Finsbury Pavement
London EC2A 1RS
T 01604 828706 (Subscriptions)
E help@subscribe.broadcastnow.co.uk
W www.broadcastnow.co.uk

BROADWAY BABY　　　　T 020 3327 3872
Reviewer at Edinburgh & Brighton Fringe & also in
London. Print & Online Reviews
239 Lewisham Way, London SE4 1XF
E pressreleases@broadwaybaby.com
W www.broadwaybaby.com

CASTCALL　　　　　　T 01582 456213
Casting Information Services. Incorporating Castfax
106 Wilsden Avenue, Luton LU1 5HR
E admin@castcall.co.uk
W www.castcall.co.uk

CASTNET LTD　　　　　T 020 8420 4209
Jobs Information, Casting & Personal Websites for UK
Actors & Casting
20 Sparrows Herne
Bushey, Herts WD23 1FU
E admin@castnet.co.uk
W www.castnet.co.uk

CASTWEB　　　　　　T 020 7720 9002
7 St Luke's Avenue, London SW4 7LG
E info@castweb.co.uk
W www.castweb.co.uk

CELEBRITY BULLETIN THE　T 020 8672 3191
FENS Information
Tower Point
44 North Road, Brighton BN1 1YR
E enquiries@celebrity-bulletin.co.uk

CONFERENCE & INCENTIVE
TRAVEL MAGAZINE　　　T 020 8267 4285
Teddington Studios, Broom Road
Teddington, Middlesex TW11 9BE
E cit@haymarket.com
W www.citmagazine.com

CREATIVE REVIEW
HANDBOOK　　　　　T 020 7970 6455
Centaur Media Plc
79 Wells Street, London W1T 3QN
W www.chb.com

DRAMACLASSES.BIZ　　　T 01923 721109
Directory of Drama & Performing Arts Schools
44 Nightingale Road
Rickmansworth
Hertfordshire WD3 7DB
E lynn@dramaclasses.biz
W www.dramaclasses.biz

EQUITY MAGAZINE　　　T 020 7670 0211
Guild House, Upper St Martin's Lane
London WC2H 9EG
F 020 7379 7001
E ppemberton@equity.org.uk
W www.equity.org.uk

FORESIGHT-NEWS　　　T 020 7970 4293
The Profile Group, Centaur Media Plc
Wells Point, London W1T 3QN
F 020 7970 4293
E info@foresightnews.co.uk
W www.foresightnews.co.uk

FOURTHWALL MAGAZINE   T 020 3371 0995
Incorporating The Drama Student Magazine
3rd Floor, 207 Regent Street
London W1B 3HH
E editor@fourthwallmagazine.co.uk
W www.fourthwallmagazine.co.uk

HERN, Nick BOOKS   T 020 8749 4953
Theatre Publishers. Performing Rights Agents
The Glasshouse, 49A Goldhawk Road
London W12 8QP
F 020 8735 0250
E info@nickhernbooks.co.uk
W www.nickhernbooks.co.uk

JASPER PUBLISHING   T 01604 590315
155 Harlestone Road, Northampton NN5 7AQ
F 01604 591077
E sales@jasperpublishing.com
W www.jasperpublishing.com

**KAY'S UK & EUROPEAN
PRODUCTION MANUALS**   T 020 8960 6900
Pinewood Studios, Pinewood Road
Iver Heath, Bucks SL0 0NH
E info@kays.co.uk
W www.kays.co.uk

KFTV   T 020 7549 2596
Formerly KEMPS
Wilmington Publishing & Information Ltd
6-14 Underwood Street
London N1 7JQ
E skeegan@wilmington.co.uk
W www.kftv.com

KNOWLEDGE THE
6-14 Underwood Street, London N1 7JQ
E knowledge@wilmington.co.uk
W www.theknowledgeonline.com

METHUEN DRAMA   T 020 7631 5600
Bloomsbury Publishing
50 Bedford Square, London WC1B 3DP
F 020 7631 5800
E methuendrama@bloomsbury.com/drama
W www.bloomsbury.com/drama

MOVIE MEMORIES MAGAZINE
*3 Issues per yr. Devoted to Films & Stars of the 40s,
50s & 60s*
10 Russet Close, Scunthorpe
N Lincs DN15 8YJ
E crob.mvm@ntlworld.com

OBERON BOOKS LTD   T 020 7607 3637
521 Caledonian Road, London N7 9RH
F 020 7607 3629
E info@oberonbooks.com
W www.oberonbooks.com

**OFFICIAL LONDON SEATING
PLAN GUIDE THE**   T 020 7224 9666
Richmond House Publishing Co Ltd
Suite D2, 4-6 Canfield Place
London NW6 3BT
E sales@rhpco.co.uk
W www.rhpco.co.uk

OFFICIALTHEATRE.COM   T 020 7183 7183
35 Kingsland Road, Shoreditch
London E2 8AA
E rebecca@officialtheatre.com

PA ENTERTAINMENT   T 0870 1203200
292 Vauxhall Bridge Road, Victoria
London SW1V 1AE
F 0870 1203201
E jane.kew@pressassociation.com
W www.pressassociation.com

PACKED TO THE RAFTERS   T 020 7096 1603
Silvermoon Publications, 3rd Foor
207 Regent Street
London W1B 3HH
F 020 7681 3867
E doug@silvermoonpublishing.co.uk
W www.packedrafterspr.co.uk

PINTER & MARTIN LTD   T 020 7737 6868
6 Effra Parade, Brixton
London SW2 1PS
E info@pinterandmartin.com
W www.pinterandmartin.com

PLAYERS DIRECTORY   T 001 310 247 3058
*Casting Directory Published in January & July. Hard
Copy & eBook. Contains Actor Photos, Representation,
Resume & Demo Reels. Published since 1937*
2210 W. Olive Avenue, Suite 320
Burbank, California 91506, USA
E info@playersdirectory.com
W www.playersdirectory.com

PLAYS INTERNATIONAL   T 020 7720 1950
33A Lurline Gardens
London SW11 4DD
E info@playsinternational.org
W www.playsinternational.org.uk

PRESENTERS CLUB THE   T 07782 224207
Presenter Promotions
123 Corporation Road
Gillingham, Kent ME7 1RG
E info@presenterpromotions.com
W www.presenterpromotions.com

PRODUCTION INTELLIGENCE   T 020 7549 2503
Hosted on The Knowledge. Contact: Matthew Wright
6-14 Underwood Street
London N1 7JQ
E mwright@wilmington.co.uk
W www.theknowledgeonline.com/production-
intelligence

RADIO TIMES   T 020 7150 5000
Formerly Published by BBC Magazines
Immediate Media
Vineyard House, 44 Brook Green
Hammersmith, London W6 7BT
E enquiries@immediate.co.uk
W www.radiotimes.com

**RICHMOND HOUSE
PUBLISHING COMPANY LTD**   T 020 7224 9666
Suite D2, 4-6 Canfield Place
London NW6 3BT
E sales@rhpco.co.uk
W www.rhpco.co.uk

ROUTLEDGE PUBLISHING   T 020 7017 6000
2 Park Square, Milton Park
Abington, Oxon OX14 4RN
F 020 7017 6699
E book.orders@tandf.co.uk
W www.routledge.com

SCREEN INTERNATIONAL   T 020 3638 5000
MBI, 101 Finsbury Pavement, London EC2A 1RS
E mai.le@mb-insight.com
W www.screendaily.com

SELF TAPING: THE ACTOR'S GUIDE
Illustrated ebook. Advice & Resources for Self Taping
E info@selftaping.com
W www.selftaping.com

SHOWBIZ FRIENDS
*Social Networking Website for Professional Showbiz
People*
W www.showbizfriends.com

SHOWCASE   T 01892 530460
Annual Handbook for the Worldwide Music Production Industry
The Warehouse, 1 Draper Street
Southborough, Tunbridge Wells
Kent TN4 0PG
E james@showcase-music.com
W www.showcase-music.com

SHOWCAST   T 00 61 2 46552820
PO Box 7035, Mount Annan
NSW 2567 Australia
E danelle@showcast.com.au
W www.showcast.com.au

SHOWDIGS.CO.UK
E amy.vs@showdigs.co.uk
W www.showdigs.co.uk

SIGHT & SOUND   T 020 7255 1444
British Film Institute
21 Stephen Street
London W1T 1LN
E s&s@bfi.org.uk
W www.bfi.org.uk/sightandsound

**SO YOU WANT TO BE
AN ACTOR?**   T 020 8749 4953
By Timothy West & Prunella Scales
Nick Hern Books, The Glasshouse
49A Goldhawk Road, London W12 8QP
F 020 8735 0250
E info@nickhernbooks.co.uk
W www.nickhernbooks.co.uk

**SO YOU WANT TO BE
A THEATRE DIRECTOR?**   T 020 8749 4953
By Stephen Unwin
Nick Hern Books, The Glasshouse
49A Goldhawk Road, London W12 8QP
F 020 8735 0250
E info@nickhernbooks.co.uk
W www.nickhernbooks.co.uk

**SO YOU WANT TO BE A
THEATRE PRODUCER?**   T 020 8749 4953
By James Seabright
Nick Hern Books, The Glasshouse
49A Goldhawk Road, London W12 8QP
F 020 8735 0250
E info@nickhernbooks.co.uk
W www.nickhernbooks.co.uk

**SO YOU WANT TO BE A
TV PRESENTER?**   T 020 8749 4953
By Kathryn Wolfe
Nick Hern Books, The Glasshouse
49A Goldhawk Road, London W12 8QP
F 020 8735 0250
E info@nickhernbooks.co.uk
W www.nickhernbooks.co.uk

**SO YOU WANT TO BE
IN MUSICALS?**   T 020 8749 4953
By Ruthie Henshall with Daniel Bowling
Nick Hern Books, The Glasshouse
49A Goldhawk Road, London W12 8QP
F 020 8735 0250
E info@nickhernbooks.co.uk
W www.nickhernbooks.co.uk

**SO YOU WANT TO DO
A SOLO SHOW?**   T 020 8749 4953
By Gareth Armstrong
Nick Hern Books, The Glasshouse
49A Goldhawk Road, London W12 8QP
F 020 8735 0250
E info@nickhernbooks.co.uk
W www.nickhernbooks.co.uk

**SO YOU WANT TO
WORK IN THEATRE?**   T 020 8749 4953
By Susan Elkin
Nick Hern Books, The Glasshouse
49A Goldhawk Road, London W12 8QP
F 020 8735 0250
E info@nickhernbooks.co.uk
W www.nickhernbooks.co.uk

**SOCIETY OF LONDON
THEATRE THE (SOLT)**   T 020 7557 6700
Latest News & London Theatre Listings
32 Rose Street, London WC2E 9ET
E enquiries@soltukt.co.uk
W www.officiallondontheatre.co.uk

SPOTLIGHT   T 020 7437 7631
Twitter: @SpotlightUK
7 Leicester Place, London WC2H 7RJ
E questions@spotlight.com
W www.spotlight.com

STAGE MEDIA COMPANY LTD   T 020 7939 8483
47 Bermondsey Street, London SE1 3XT
F 020 7939 8478
E editor@thestage.co.uk
W www.thestage.co.uk

SUPERNOVA BOOKS   T 020 3261 0000
Contact: Rebecca Gillieron (Publisher/Editor). Publishing Books on Film, Art & Music
67 Grove Avenue, Twickenham TW1 4HX
E rebecca@aurorametro.com
W www.supernovabooks.co.uk

TEACHING DRAMA MAGAZINE   T 07785 613149
Rhinegold House, 20 Rugby Street
London WC1N 3QZ
E teaching.drama@rhinegold.co.uk
W www.teaching-drama.co.uk

TELEVISUAL MEDIA UK LTD   T 020 3008 5750
48 Charlotte Street, London W1T 2NS
F 020 3008 5784
E advertising@televisual.com
W www.televisual.com

TIME OUT GROUP LTD   T 020 7813 3000
Universal House
251 Tottenham Court Road
London W1T 7AB
F 020 7813 6001
W www.timeout.com

TV TIMES   T 020 3148 5615
IPC Media, Blue Fin Building
110 Southwark Street, London SE1 0SU
F 020 3148 8115

WHATSONSTAGE LTD   T 020 7317 9100
5th Floor, 81 Oxford Street
London W1D 2EU
E feedback@whatsonstage.com
W www.whatsonstage.com

WHITE BOOK THE   T 020 8971 8282
Mash Media Group Ltd, 4th Floor, Sterling House
6-10 St Georges Road
London SW19 4DP
E spascal@mashmedia.net
W www.whitebook.co.uk

YAMAHA MUSIC LONDON   T 020 7432 4400
Sheet Music. Musical Instruments. Guitars. Keyboards. Pianos
152-160 Wardour Street
London W1F 8YA
F 020 7432 4410
E enquiries@yamahamusiclondon.com
W www.yamahamusiclondon.com

ANTONY BARLOW ASSOCIATES   T 020 8401 1108
*Publicity & Promotion for Musicians (Concerts & CDs),
Dance & Theatre Companies*
Flat 4, 15 Brambledown Road
Wallington, Surrey SM6 0TH
T 07711 929170
E artspublicity@hotmail.com

ARTHUR LEONE PR   T 020 7836 7660
Suite 5, 17 Shorts Gardens, London WC2H 9AT
E anna@arthurleone.com
W www.arthurleone.com

AVALON PROMOTIONS   T 020 7598 8000
Arts. Marketing. PR
4A Exmoor Street, London W10 6BD
F 020 7598 7223
E sophias@avalonuk.com
W www.avalonuk.com

CHESTON, Judith PUBLICITY   T 01608 661198
30 Telegraph Street, Shipston-on-Stour
Warwickshire CV36 4DA
F 01608 663772
E jacheston@tiscali.co.uk

CLARKE, Duncan PR   T 01904 345247
Twitter: @duncancpr
24 Severus Street, York, North Yorkshire YO24 4NL
E duncanclarkepr@live.co.uk
W www.duncanclarkepr.wordpress.com

CLOUT COMMUNICATIONS LTD   T 020 8362 0803
15 Carlton Road, London N11 3EX
E enquiries@cloutcom.co.uk
W www.cloutcom.co.uk

ELSON, Howard PROMOTIONS   T 01494 784760
*Management. Marketing. PR. Theatre Tour Publicity &
Promotion*
16 Penn Avenue, Chesham
Buckinghamshire HP5 2HS
T 07768 196310
E howardelson@btinternet.com

EMPICA LTD   T 01275 394400
1 Lyons Court, Long Ashton Business Park
Yanley Lane, Bristol BS41 9LB
F 01275 393933
E info@empica.com
W www.empica.com

**FIVEASH, Nick PR &
MANAGEMENT**   T 07971 240987
1st Floor, 4 Baxendale Street, London E2 7BY
E nickfiveash@me.com

FLICKS MORRIS PR   T 07917 875625
Specialist Comedy & Theatre Publicist
11 Harrington Court, Barnet, Herts EN5 1PZ
E flicks@flicksmorrispr.com
W www.flicksmorrispr.com

GADABOUTS LTD   T 020 8445 5450
Theatre Marketing & Promotions
54 Friary Road, London N12 9PB
F 0870 7059140
E info@gadabouts.co.uk
W www.gadabouts.co.uk

GAYNOR, Avril ASSOCIATES   T 07958 623013
126 Brudenell Road, London SW17 8DE
E gaynorama@aol.com

**GOODMAN, Deborah
PUBLICITY (DGPR)**   T 020 8959 9980
25 Glenmere Avenue, London NW7 2LT
F 020 8959 7875
E publicity@dgpr.cc.uk
W www.dgpr.co.uk

GRIFFIN, Alison ASSOCIATES   T 07768 964935
4th Floor, St Martin's House
St Martin's Lane, London WC2N 4JS
E alison@alisongriffin.co.uk

GUNG HO   T 0121 604 6366
Contact: Paul Phedon
Unit 9, 133-137 Newhall Street
Birmingham B3 1SF
E paul@gunghoco.com
W www.gungohoco.com

**HYMAN, Sue
ASSOCIATES LTD**   T 020 7379 8420
St Martin's House, 59 St Martin's Lane
London WC2N 4JS
T 07976 514449
E sue.hyman@btinternet.com
W www.suehyman.com

IMPACT AGENCY THE   T 020 7580 1770
1 Bedford Avenue, London WC1B 3AU
F 020 7580 7200
E mail@impactagency.co.uk
W www.theimpactagency.com

JM PR   T 020 8621 8920
Contact: Jerome Morrow
1A Exeter Road, London NW2 4SJ
E mail@jm-pr.co.uk

KEAN LANYON LTD   T 020 7697 8453
Contact: Sharon Kean
United House, North Road, Islington, London N7 9DP
T 07973 843133
E sharon@keanlanyon.com
W www.keanlanyon.com

KELLER, Don   T 020 8800 4882
Arts Marketing
65 Glenwood Road, Harringay, London N15 3JS
E info@donkeller.co.uk

LEEP MARKETING & PR   T 07973 558895
Marketing. Press. Publicity
5 Hurdwick Place, London NW1 2JE
E philip@leep.biz

LONDON FLAIR PR   T 020 3371 7945
*Entertainment Specialists for Actors & Celebrities. Film.
Television*
6th Floor, International House
223 Regents Street, London W1B 2QD
E cls@londonflairpr.com
W www.londonflairpm.com

MATTHEWS, Liz PR   T 020 7253 1639
The Smokehouse, Smokehouse Yard
44-46 St John Street, London EC1M 4DF
E liz@lizmatthewspr.com
W www.lizmatthewspr.com

MAYER, Anne PR   T 020 3659 8482
82 Mortimer Road, London N1 4LH
T 07764 192842
E annemayer@btopenworld.com

**McAULEY ARTS MARKETING LTD /
MAKESTHREE**   T 020 7021 0927
25 Short Street, London SE1 8LJ
E sam@makesthree.org
W www.makesthree.org

MITCHELL, Jackie   T 01372 465041
JM Communications
4 Sims Cottages, The Green, Claygate
Surrey KT10 0JH
F 01372 471073
E jackie@jackiem.com
W www.jackiem.com

MOBIUS   T 020 3195 6269
2nd Floor, 34-35 Great Sutton Street
Clerkenwell, London EC1V 0DX
E info@mobiusindustries.com
W www.mobiusindustries.com

**MORGAN, Jane
ASSOCIATES (JMA)**   T 020 7263 9867
Marketing. Media
8 Heathville Road, London N19 3AJ
E jma@janemorganassociates.com

NELKIN, Chloe CONSULTING   T 07711 033205
Boutique PR agency for Theatre, Art & Opera
Laurel Farmhouse
Totteridge Green
London N20 8PH
E info@chloenelkinconsulting.com
W www.chloenelkinconsulting.com

**NELSON BOSTOCK
GROUP LTD**   T 020 7229 4400
Compass House, 22 Redan Place
London W2 4SA
F 020 7727 2025
E info@nelsonbostock.com
W www.nelsonbostock.com

OATWAY, Christopher   T 07873 485265
495 Altrincham Road
Baguley Hall
Manchester M23 1AR
E christopherjoatway@gmail.com

PR PEOPLE THE   T 0161 976 2729
1 St James Drive, Sale
Cheshire M33 7QX
E graham@pr-people.uk.com
W www.pr-people.uk.com

PREMIER   T 020 7292 8330
91 Berwick Street, London W1F 0NE
F 020 7734 2024
W www.premiercomms.com

**PRESS COMPLAINTS
COMMISSION**   T 020 7831 0022
Halton House, 20-23 Holborn
London EC1N 2JD
E complaints@pcc.org.uk
W www.pcc.org.uk

**PUBLIC EYE
COMMUNICATIONS LTD**   T 020 7351 1555
Suite 313, Plaza
535 Kings Road, London SW10 0SZ
F 020 7351 1010
E assistant@publiceye.co.uk

**PURPLE REIGN
PUBLIC RELATIONS**   T 07809 110982
8 Belmont Hill, Lewisham
London SE13 5BD
E monique@purplereignpr.co.uk
W www.purplereignpr.co.uk

**RICHMOND TOWERS
COMMUNICATIONS LTD**   T 020 7388 7421
The Tapestry, 51-52 Frith Street
Soho, London W1D 4SH
F 020 7388 7761
W www.rt-com.com

RKM COMMUNICATIONS LTD   T 020 3130 7090
Based in London & Los Angeles
14-15 Manette Street
London W1D 4AP
E info@rkmcom.com
W www.rkmcom.com

**SHIPPEN, Martin
MARKETING & MEDIA**   T 020 8968 1943
88 Purves Road
London NW10 5TB
T 07956 879165
E m.shippen@virgin.net

SILVEY, Denise   T 020 8743 7777
St Martin's Theatre, West Street
London WC2N 9NH
T 07711 245848
E ds@denisesilvey.com
W www.denisesilvey.com

SKPR THEATRE PUBLICITY   T 07966 578607
*Theatre & Dance PR Agency. London, Edinburgh &
National Touring*
1 Heath Hall Lodge, French Hill
Thursley, Godalming
Surrey GU8 6NQ
E sheridan@sheridanskitchen.com

SNELL, Helen LTD   T 020 7240 5537
4th Floor, 80-81 St Martin's Lane
London WC2N 4AA
F 020 7240 2947
E info@helensnell.com

**SOCIETY OF LONDON
THEATRE (SOLT)**   T 020 7557 6727
*Contact: Anthony McNeill (Press & Communications
Manager)*
32 Rose Street, London WC2E 9ET
E anthony@soltukt.co.uk

STAFFORD, Abi   T 07954 371083
Freelance Journalist & Photographer
289 Birmingham Road
Birmingham
West Midlands B72 1ED
E abistafford@hotmail.com

TARGET LIVE LTD   T 020 3372 0950
Design. Marketing. Media. Press
45-51 Whitfield Street
London W1T 4HD
E info@target-live.co.uk
W www.target-live.co.uk

**TAYLOR HERRING
PUBLIC RELATIONS**   T 020 8206 5151
11 Westway Centre, 69 St Marks Road
London W10 6JG
F 020 8206 5155
E james.herring@taylorherring.com
W www.taylorherring.com

TRE-VETT, Eddie   T 01425 475544
Brink House, Avon Castle
Ringwood, Hampshire BH24 2BL

TREVIS, Maria MARKETING   T 07814 304443
Associate of the Chartered Institute of Marketing
28 Ardler Road, Caversham
Reading, Berkshire RG4 5AE
E mtrevis@hotmail.com

**WILLIAMS, Tei PRESS &
ARTS MARKETING**   T 01869 337940
Post Office Cottage, Clifton
Oxon OX15 0PD
T 07957 664116
E artsmarketing@btconnect.com

**WINGHAM, Maureen
PRESS & PUBLIC RELATIONS**   T 01449 771200
69 Bury Street, Stowmarket
Suffolk IP14 1HD
E maureen.wingham@mwmedia.uk.com

R →

Radio
- BBC Radio
- BBC Local
- Independent

Rehearsal Rooms & Casting Suites

Role Play Companies / Theatre Skills in Business

Radio

Why should I work in radio?

To make a smooth transition from stage or camera to radio acting, everything that would otherwise be conveyed through body language and facial expressions must all be focused into the tone and pitch of the actor's voice.

If you have only ever considered visual acting work before, pursuing radio work would certainly enable you to expand your horizons and add additional skills to your CV. It is an opportunity to work in a different way and meet new requirements. Rehearsal and recording time is reduced in radio, which may allow you to pursue visual and radio acting alongside each other. Time constraints can be a pressure, and you have to get used to working without props (just sound effects), but this 'back to basics' existence is appealing to a lot of actors.

How can I become a radio presenter?

Presenting work in any medium comes under a different category as this is not classed as acting. It is a skill in its own right. Please refer to the 'Agents: Presenters' section for more information.

Do I need a voicereel?

This has to be your first and most important step into getting work as a radio actor. Your CV is not enough to get you a job without a professional-sounding voicereel. Voice over work in commercial and corporate sectors requires a different type of reel. Please see the 'Promotional Services' section for more detailed voicereel advice in either area.

Do I need an agent?

It is not strictly necessary to have an agent for radio work. The BBC is by far the main producer of radio drama and welcomes applications directly from actors, but some independent radio stations prefer using agents to put actors forward. It might be worth doing some research on your local radio stations and finding out their preferred method of contact and making a decision from there. If you are looking for a new agent and are interested in radio work as well as straight acting work, find out whether they deal with this area of the industry before signing up. If you only want to pursue radio and/or voice over work, or are looking for a specialist agent in addition to your main agent, please see the 'Agents: Voice Over' section for further advice and listings.

How do I find work in radio?

You can send your CV and voicereel directly out to producers of radio drama, but make sure you target your search. Listen to radio plays and make a note of any producers whose work you particularly liked. This may also help you to identify what types of dramas you feel your voice would be most suited to.

Once you have done your research and made a shortlist, send your voicereel with a personalised letter. Mention the plays you liked and explain that you feel he or she will be able to use your voice in productions like these. This method is likely to be much more effective than sending out a generic covering letter en masse, and will make you stand out.

You don't need to send a headshot with your CV, but you could incorporate your photo in the body of your CV. It would be a good idea to have your name and contact details professionally printed onto your voicereel CD in case it becomes separated from your CV – see 'Promotional Services' for listings of companies that can do this for you.

Radio

Carys Eleri was one of two winners of the 2013 Norman Beaton Fellowship which earned her a five month contract at the BBC Radio Drama Rep. She has been working as an actress in Wales since 2004 and lives and works bilingually (in Welsh and English).

Why should I work in radio?

This is a completely different medium to work in as an actor. Theatre, television or film have their obvious differences - one's performances become more subtle and contained. In radio, your whole performance is given through the voice, therefore your entire range of characterisation tools such as facial expressions, physicality, hair and costume are all transferred into your reasoning, pitch, vocal tones and accents. You will find yourself exploring microphone technique as opposed to a camera. Creating a character entirely out of your own vocal abilities is very exciting and rewarding. The turn around is far quicker than other mediums too - so you are constantly kept on your toes and it is possible to pursue other work alongside it. As a workplace, I found that radio is possibly the most humbling of places for all actors. There is a sense of 'we're all in this together' - no separate dressing rooms, no special treatments. Each actor is there for their love and respect of this cherished craft.

Do I need a voicereel?

A voicereel is important for those who submit applications directly to the radio drama department. Winners of the Carleton Hobbs Bursary and the Norman Beaton Fellowship will be given the opportunity to record these at the BBC before embarking on their full time contracts. Your voicereel is distributed amongst producers along with a note of your range of accents. If these accents come up, they will reference your voicereel before hiring you. Ensure your voicereel shows enough range, and make a point of recording your natural accent also. I have a strong Welsh accent, that wasn't used very frequently but really gave me lots of unique opportunities.

Do I need an agent?

An agent isn't completely necessary. Some actors on the BBC radio drama rep didn't have an agent. I do have an agent, but because of the nature of the Norman Beaton Fellowship and Carleton Hobbs Bursary - you would apply for either scheme yourself via the BBC Soundstart website (Norman Beaton) or through your drama college (Carleton Hobbs). Nowadays, actors tend to have separate voice agents too as not all companies deal with radio and voice over work as well as the other mediums. Smaller, independent companies might prefer to turn to agencies to put actors forward. As the main producer of radio drama - the BBC does welcome individual applications from actors. Again - a voicereel is a must-have in this situation.

How do I find work in radio?

Send your voicereels and CVs directly to radio drama producers. Listen out for their names during the credits at the end of broadcasts, or search for them on iplayer. Do remember that there are many radio drama departments producing radio plays across the UK within the BBC - so do not be disheartened if you don't live in London and would like to work in radio. Many plays are produced in Cardiff, Birmingham, Salford and Edinburgh. Do your research - personalise your cover letters. Producers like to know that you are on board with and understand their way of making things. Sending a headshot isn't necessary - but make sure a photo of yourself is sent within the body of your CV along with your contact details.

I found work within radio drama in a different way. As I had mentioned earlier, I was lucky enough to have won the Norman Beaton Fellowship in 2013. This competition was open to professional actors who had not attended an accredited drama school and had found other paths and ways into the industry. You can apply for this via the BBC's Soundstart website. You will be auditioned by your regional BBC radio drama department in the initial rounds. This is a great way to get to know your most local radio drama department, as you will spend a lot of time getting to know the producers at this stage. So even if you don't progress through to the very end of the 'competition' - a contact has been made, and you may have something completely different to offer as an actor for their future productions. For instance - BBC Cardiff had hired me for a production a month before I had entered the final round of the NBF. You can enter this competition as many times as you like if you aren't a previous winner.

Alternatively - if you are currently studying at an accredited drama school - I'm sure you will come across the Carleton Hobbs Bursary. There are 4 winners every year, and this is such an amazing kick start for the careers of young actors straight out of drama schools.

CASE STUDY

John Norton is an actor, DJ, composer, and artistic director of Give It A Name Theatre. He was one of the two winners of the Norman Beaton Fellowship in 2013. He gained a BA in Drama from Manchester University in 1993, became a professional DJ and then returned to acting in 1999. Since his time on the RDC he has regularly worked as a freelancer for BBC Radio in Cardiff, where he lives.

The Norman Beaton Fellowship

Ok, so you've been invited to audition for the Norman Beaton Fellowship. You ought to be pleased already: someone somewhere thinks you are worth a punt. Now get to work, it is a tough competition and you have got to want it. Listen to radio drama, read scripts, choose your pieces, think about the medium, get a friend or colleague to listen and challenge and direct you. Borrow a microphone, record your scenes, listen back, be critical and start again. Remember to show your range, and that radio can be very intimate. And don't be put off in the first round when you look up from your script to see the entire panel with their heads buried in their hands – they are not in despair, they are listening.

Being on the rep

One of the great benefits of The Carleton Hobbs/ Norman Beaton Fellowship awards is that all you really need is raw talent and the desire to do the job, because when you arrive you get a whole week of on-the-job training by some of the world's top professionals. This covers the all the basics of microphones, how to approach the script and character, creating movement in the sound space, and acting with your backgrounds (stormy seas, arctic wind, city traffic). At the end of the week, you feel fully equipped, if still a little nervous.

What can I say about the rep?

Well, it's brilliant. The RDC is one of the few real repertory jobs left in the UK. It's an actor's dream to turn up for work on Monday and find a whole load of new scripts waiting for you. For once, you don't have to think about where to find your next job – it's in a tray with your name on near the green room. And you are a company member, with a really happy medium between the camaraderie of being in a permanent company, and meeting new people every week.

Most dramas (in my experience) are performed by a combination of the RDC and a few guest artists. You will often end up mopping up several smaller roles, skilled as you now are in adaptability, whilst the guest artists will play leads. These guest artists are often actors of international renown, but Radio Drama is delightfully egalitarian: one Green Room, one Studio, two (ish) microphones, several cups of tea. And as the resident, you sometimes get to be host, show them around, or demonstrate the sublime technique of radio horse-riding. Otherwise you get to learn as much as you can from them, or just have a good laugh jumping out of an imaginary plane together.

Radio Drama at the BBC is a quick turnaround, with single plays usually taking between 2 to 3 days to record, which means you can be dealing with 2 or 3 dramas per week, as well as fitting in the odd reading, or news item.

In fact, although the job primarily involves working in Radio Drama, the RDC is used as a resource by many other departments, which means you can get asked to do a whole range of exciting voice work. You can get booked by news to voice over a journalist's anonymous source, or by readings to read an extract of a novel that won a prize, or by documentaries...you get the idea. One morning I was deeply touched to be asked by World Service to read some song lyrics for an obituary piece about Lou Reed.

Yes the job is diverse – and sometimes really stretching. In my 5 months I learned fragments of 3 entirely new languages, as well as a host of accents I had never dreamed of. But thankfully there's something called the pronunciation department. And I got to know the British Library Sound Archive pretty well too.

I can't finish without a short homage to wild tracks. These are the bespoke audio recordings for many a radio drama, which are made by the company, in the studio, and then masterfully mixed with sound effects by the curiously named Studio Managers (that's old BBC speak for phenomenally skilled sound artist). This is some of the oddest and simply playful professional work you will ever do. My first proper day on the job was recording a series of wild tracks for some WW1 dramas and for a visit to Hades. Some orchestrated battlefield charges past the mic, a few dying groans, some 1914 style group singing around the piano, followed by lost souls suffering, orgasmic nymphs...

A final thought:

We are visual creatures in a highly visual culture: there is something amazing and liberating about channelling all of your performance into sound. Stravinsky, writing about music, claimed that "the more constraints one imposes, the more one frees oneself" and I'm inclined to agree.

You will have a ball. You will work with some truly brilliant actors, producers, writers, and studio managers. You will be stretched, and you will emerge a smarter, quicker, lither, leaner, better actor.

BBC RADIO

**BBC Broadcasting House
Portland Place, London W1A 1AA
T 020 7580 4468 (Main Switchboard)**

Many BBC Departments are now based at MediaCityUK, Salford Quays, Salford. They include BBC Children's, BBC Radio 5 live, parts of Future Media & Technology, BBC Learning, BBC Sport and BBC Breakfast. For further information about BBC North please contact the BBC's main London switchboard.

If you are interested in working for the BBC in a production role, you can submit your CV to the BBC Production Talent website at www.bbcproductiontalent.co.uk

• DRAMA

**Head of Audio
  Drama UK** Alison Hindell (BBC Wales)

Drama & Books Production – London

Editor, Drama	Toby Swift
Editor, Books	Di Speirs
Radio Drama Company/ Production Executive	Rebecca Wilmshurst

Drama Producers – London

Sally Avens	Marion Nancarrow
Marc Beeby	Tracey Neale
Nandita Ghose	Jonquil Panting
David Hunter	Mary Peate
Peter Kavanagh	Saha Yevtushenko
Abigail le Fleming	

Books Producers - London

Elizabeth Allard	Duncan Minshull
Emma Harding	Justine Willett
Gemma Jenkins	

Drama Production – Birmingham

Editor, The Archers	Sean O'Connnor
Producers, The Archers	
Julie Beckett	Rosemary Watts
Kim Greengrass	
Editor, Home Front	Jessica Dromgoole
Producer, Home Front	Lucy Collingwood
Production Executive	Rebecca Wilmhurst

Drama Producers – Manchester

Editor	Sue Roberts
Development	
Gary Brown	Nadia Molinari
Pauline Harris	Charlotte Riches
Production Executive	Amanda Queiroz

Producers - BBC Bristol

Tim Dee	Mark Smalley

Christine Hall	Mary Ward Lowery
Production Executive	Amanda Queiroz

Drama Producers – BBC Wales

Helen Perry	James Robinson

Drama Producers – BBC Scotland

Editor	Bruce Young
Development	
Kirsteen Cameron	Allegra McIlroy
David Ian Neville	Gaynor Macfarlane

Drama Production – BBC Northern Ireland

All enquiries to Gemma McMullan, Executive Producer
Writersroom
Creative Director Kate Rowland

• RADIO COMEDY/RADIO PRODUCTION

Head of Radio Comedy	Jane Berthoud
Executive Producers	
Julia McKenzie	Alison Vernon-Smith
Producers	
Adnan Ahmed	Victoria Lloyd
Colin Anderson	Sam Michell
Amab Chanda	Ed Morrish
Carl Cooper	Charlie Perkins
Lyndsay Fenner	Alexandra Smith
Tilusha Ghelani	Katie Tyrrell
Claire Jones	
Production Manager	Hayley Nathan

• NEWS AND CURRENT AFFAIRS

Director, News & Current Affairs	James Harding
Deputy Director, News & Current Affairs	Fran Unsworth
Head of Programmes	Ceri Thomas
Head of BBC Newsroom	Mary Hockaday
Managing Editor	Keith Blackmore
Editor News	Gavin Allen
Head of Newsgathering	Jonathan Munro
Controller of BBC News Channel (inc. News at One)	Sam Taylor
Editor Six & Ten O'clock	Paul Royall
Chief Technology Officer	Peter Coles
Head of Political Programmes, Analysis & Research	Sue Inglish
Head of TV Current Affairs & Deputy to the Head of News Programmes	Jim Gray
Head of Commissioning, Knowledge (& Commisioner for Current Affairs Independent Productions)	Clive Edwards
Editor, Newsnight	Ian Katz
Editor, Breakfast	Adam Bullimore

Editor, Panorama	Tom Giles
Editor, BBC News Online	Steve Herrmann
Controller of BBC Parliament	Peter Knowles
Head of BBC Weather	Liz Howell

Radio Programmes

Executive Editor, Radio Current Affairs	Nicola Meyrick
Editor, Today	Jamie Angus
Editor, PM/Broadcasting House	Joanna Carr
Editor, The World Tonight	Alistair Burnett
Editor, The World this Weekend/ The World at One	Nick Sutton
Editor, Newsbeat Radio 1	Louisa Compton
Editor, Today in Parliament	Peter Knowles
Editor, Westminster Hour	Terry Dignan

• RADIO SPORT

Head of BBC Sports News & BBC Radio Sport	Richard Burgess
Controller, Radio 5 live	Jonathan Wall

• CONTROLLERS

Director of Audio & Music	Helen Boaden

RADIO 1

Controller	Ben Cooper

RADIO 2

Controller	Bob Shennan

RADIO 3

Controller	Roger Wright

RADIO 4 & RADIO 4 EXTRA

Controller	Gwyneth Williams

RADIO 5 LIVE

Controller	Jonathan Wall

• BBC NEW WRITING

**BBC Writersroom, BBC Grafton House
379-381 Euston Road, London NW1 3AU
T 020 8743 8000 (Main Switchboard)
E writersroom@bbc.co.uk
W www.bbc.co.uk/writersroom**

Creative Director	Kate Rowland
Development Producers	
Abigail Gonda	Henry Swindell

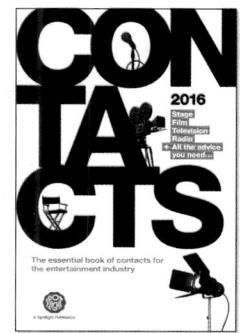

BBC RADIO BRISTOL   T 0117 974 1111
Contact: Tim Pemberton (Managing Editor)
Bristol Broadcasting House
Whiteladies Road, Bristol BS8 2LR
E radio.bristol@bbc.co.uk
W www.bbc.co.uk/bristol

**BBC RADIO
CAMBRIDGESHIRE**   T 01223 259696
Contact: Dave Harvey (Managing Editor)
Cambridge Business Park, Cowley Road
Cambridge CB4 0WZ
E cambs@bbc.co.uk
W www.bbc.co.uk/cambridgeshire

BBC RADIO CORNWALL   T 01872 275421
Contact: Pauline Causey (Managing Editor)
Phoenix Wharf, Truro, Cornwall TR1 1UA
F 01872 240679
W www.bbc.co.uk/cornwall

**BBC COVENTRY &
WARWICKSHIRE**   T 024 7653 9222
Contact: Rupert Upshon (News Desk Editor)
Priory Place, Coventry CV1 5SQ
F 024 7655 2000
E coventry.warwickshire@bbc.co.uk
W www.bbc.co.uk/coventry

BBC RADIO CUMBRIA   T 01228 592444
Contact: Mark Elliot (Managing Editor)
Annetwell Street, Carlisle, Cumbria CA3 8BB
F 01228 511195
E radio.cumbria@bbc.co.uk
W www.bbc.co.uk/radiocumbria

BBC RADIO DERBY   T 01332 361111
Contact: Simon Cornes (Editor)
56 St Helen's Street, Derby DE1 3HY
E radio.derby@bbc.co.uk
W www.bbc.co.uk/derby

BBC RADIO DEVON   T 01752 260323
Contact: Mark Grinnell (Managing Editor)
PO Box 1034, Plymouth PL3 5BD
F 01752 234595
E radio.devon@bbc.co.uk
W www.bbc.co.uk/devon

BBC ESSEX   T 01245 616000
Contact: Gerald Main (Managing Editor)
PO Box 765, Chelmsford, Essex CM2 9AB
F 01245 616025
E essex@bbc.co.uk
W www.bbc.co.uk/essex

**BBC RADIO
GLOUCESTERSHIRE**   T 01452 308585
Contact: Mark Hurrell (Managing Editor)
London Road, Gloucester GL1 1SW
E radio.gloucestershire@bbc.co.uk
W www.bbc.co.uk/gloucestershire

BBC GUERNSEY   T 01481 200600
*Contact: Sarah Solstley (Managing Editor), Kay Langlois
(Assistant Editor), David Earl, Jim Cathcart, Ben Chapple
(Senior Broadcast Journalists)*
Broadcasting House, Bulwer Avenue
St Sampsons, Guernsey GY2 4LA
F 01481 200361
E bbcguernsey@bbc.co.uk
W www.bbc.co.uk/guernsey

**BBC HEREFORD &
WORCESTER**   T 01905 748485
Contact: Jeremy Pollock (Managing Editor)
Hylton Road, Worcester WR2 5WW
W www.bbc.co.uk/herefordandworcester

BBC RADIO HUMBERSIDE   T 01482 323232
Contact: Simon Pattern (Managing Editor)
Queens Court
Queens Gardens
Hull HU1 3RH
F 01482 226409
E radio.humberside@bbc.co.uk
W www.bbc.co.uk/humberside

BBC RADIO JERSEY   T 01534 870000
*Contact: Jon Gripton (Editor), Matthew Price
(Assistant Editor)*
18 & 21 Parade Road, St Helier
Jersey JE2 3PL
F 01534 732569
E radiojersey@bbc.co.uk
W www.bbc.co.uk/jersey

BBC RADIO KENT   T 01892 670000
Contact: Gordon Davidson (Managing Editor)
The Great Hall, Mount Pleasant Road
Tunbridge Wells, Kent TN1 1QQ
E radio.kent@bbc.co.uk
W www.bbc.co.uk/kent

BBC RADIO LANCASHIRE   T 01254 262411
Contact: John Clayton (Editor)
20-26 Darwen Street
Blackburn
Lancashire BB2 2EA
E radio.lancashire@bbc.co.uk
W www.bbc.co.uk/lancashire

BBC RADIO LEEDS   T 0113 224 7303
Contact: Rozina Breen (Managing Editor)
BBC Yorkshire
2 St Peter's Square
Leeds LS9 8AH
F 0113 224 7316
E radioleeds@bbc.co.uk
W www.bbc.co.uk/leeds

BBC RADIO LEICESTER   T 0116 251 6688
Contact: Jane Hill (Managing Editor)
9 St Nicholas Place
Leicester LE1 5LB
F 0116 251 1463
E radio.leicesternews@bbc.co.uk
W www.bbc.co.uk/radioleicester

BBC RADIO LINCOLNSHIRE   T 01522 511411
Contact: Charlie Partridge (Managing Editor)
Newport, Lincoln LN1 3XY
F 01522 511058
W www.bbc.co.uk/lincolnshire

**BBC LONDON
94.9 FM**   T 020 7224 2000 (Live Studio)
Contact: David Robey (Managing Editor)
Egton House, Portland Place
London W1A 1AA
T 020 8743 8000 (Switchboard)
E yourlondon@bbc.co.uk
W www.bbc.co.uk/london

BBC RADIO MANCHESTER   T 0161 335 6000
Contact: John Ryan (Managing Editor)
MediaCityUK
Salford M50 2EQ
W www.bbc.co.uk/manchester

BBC RADIO MERSEYSIDE   T 0151 708 5500
Contact: Sue Owen (Managing Editor)
PO Box 95.8
Liverpool L69 1ZJ
E radio.merseyside@bbc.co.uk
W www.bbc.co.uk/liverpool

BBC NEWCASTLE   T 0191 232 4141
Contact: Andrew Robson (Managing Editor)
Broadcasting Centre
Barrack Road
Newcastle upon Tyne NE99 1RN
F 0191 221 0796
E bbcnewcastle.news@bbc.co.uk
W www.bbc.co.uk/tyne

BBC RADIO NORFOLK   T 01603 617411
Contact: David Clayton (Managing Editor)
The Forum, Millennium Plain
Norwich NR2 1BH
E norfolk@bbc.co.uk
W www.bbc.co.uk/norfolk

BBC NORTHAMPTON   T 01604 239100
Contact: Jess Rudkin (Manager)
Broadcasting House
Abington Street
Northampton NN1 2BH
F 01604 230709
E northampton@bbc.co.uk
W www.bbc.co.uk/northampton

BBC RADIO NOTTINGHAM   T 0115 955 0500
Contact: Mike Bettison (Editor)
London Road
Nottingham NG2 4UU
F 0115 902 1984
E radio.nottingham@bbc.co.uk
W www.bbc.co.uk/nottingham

BBC RADIO SHEFFIELD   T 0114 267 5440
Contact: Martyn Weston (Managing Editor)
54 Shoreham Street
Sheffield S1 4RS
E radio.sheffield@bbc.co.uk
W www.bbc.co.uk/sheffield

BBC RADIO SHROPSHIRE   T 01743 248484
Contact: Tim Beech (Editor), Tim Page (Senior Broadcast Journalist, News)
2-4 Boscobel Drive, Shrewsbury
Shropshire SY1 3TT
F 01743 271702
E radio.shropshire@bbc.co.uk
W www.bbc.co.uk/shropshire

BBC RADIO SOLENT   T 023 8063 1311
Contact: Chris Carney (Managing Editor)
Broadcasting House
10 Havelock Road
Southampton SO14 7PW
F 023 8033 9648
E radio.solent@bbc.co.uk
W www.bbc.co.uk/solent

BBC RADIO STOKE   T 01782 208080
Contact: Gary Andrews (Managing Editor)
Cheapside, Hanley
Stoke-on-Trent
Staffordshire ST1 1JJ
F 01782 289115
E radio.stoke@bbc.co.uk
W www.bbc.co.uk/radiostoke

BBC RADIO SUFFOLK   T 01473 250000
Contact: Peter Cook (Editor)
Broadcasting House
St Matthews Street
Ipswich IP1 3EP
F 01473 210887
E radiosuffolk@bbc.co.uk
W www.bbc.co.uk/suffolk

BBC SURREY   T 01273 320400
Contact: Sara David (Managing Editor)
Broadcasting Centre
Guildford
Surrey GU2 7AP
F 01483 304952
E sussex@bbc.co.uk
W www.bbc.co.uk/sussex

BBC SUSSEX   T 01273 320400
Contact: Sara David (Managing Editor)
40-42 Queen's Road
Brighton BN1 3YB
F 01483 304952
E sussex@bbc.co.uk
W www.bbc.co.uk/sussex

BBC TEES   T 01642 225211
Contact: Dan Thorpe (Acting Managing Editor)
Broadcasting House, Newport Road
Middlesbrough TS1 5DG
F 01642 211356
E tees.studios@bbc.co.uk
W www.bbc.co.uk/tees

BBC THREE COUNTIES RADIO   T 01582 637400
Contact: Laura Moss (Managing Editor)
1 Hastings Street
Luton LU1 5XL
F 01582 401467
E 3cr@bbc.co.uk
W www.bbc.co.uk/threecounties

BBC WEST MIDLANDS   T 0121 567 6767
The Mailbox
Birmingham B1 1RF
E midlandstoday@bbc.co.uk
W www.bbc.co.uk/westmidlands

BBC WILTSHIRE   T 01793 513626
Contact: Tony Worgan (Managing Editor)
Broadcasting House
56-58 Prospect Place
Swindon SN1 3RW
E wiltshire@bbc.co.uk
W www.bbc.co.uk/wiltshire

BBC RADIO YORK   T 01904 641351
Contact: Managing Editor
20 Bootham Row, York YO30 7BR
E radio.york@bbc.co.uk
W www.bbc.co.uk/york

ABERDEEN: Northsound Radio T 01224 337000
Abbotswell Road, West Tullos
Aberdeen AB12 3AJ
F 01224 400003
W www.northsound1.com

AYR: West Sound Radio T 01292 283662
Incorporating West Sound 1035 AM & West 96.7 FM
Radio House, 54A Holmston Road
Ayr KA7 3BE
E carolyn.mcallister@westsound.co.uk
W www.westsound.co.uk

**BELFAST: City Beat 96.7 FM &
102.5 FM** T 028 9023 4967
2nd Floor, Arena Building
85 Ormeau Road, Belfast BT7 1SH
F 028 9089 0101
E info@citybeat.co.uk
W www.citybeat.co.uk

BELFAST: Cool FM T 028 9181 7181
Kiltonga Industrial Estate, Newtownards
Co Down BT23 4ES
E info@coolfm.co.uk
W www.coolfm.co.uk

BELFAST: Downtown Radio T 028 9181 5555
Kiltonga Industrial Estate, Newtownards
Co Down BT23 4ES
E info@downtown.co.uk
W www.downtown.co.uk

**BERKSHIRE &
NORTH HAMPSHIRE: Heart** T 0118 945 4400
PO Box 2020, Reading
Berkshire RG31 7FG
E thamesvalley.news@heart.co.uk
W www.heart.co.uk

BIRMINGHAM: Free Radio 96.4 T 0121 566 5200
9 Brindleyplace, 4 Oozells Square, Birmingham B1 2DJ
F 0121 566 5239
W www.freeradio.co.uk

BORDERS THE: Radio Borders T 01896 759444
Tweedside Park, Galashiels TD1 3TD
F 0845 3457080
E info@radioborders.com
W www.radioborders.com

**BRADFORD:
Sunrise Radio Yorkshire** T 01274 735043
55 Leeds Road, Bradford BD1 5AF
F 01274 728534
E info@sunriseradio.fm
W www.sunriseradio.fm

**BRADFORD, HUDDERSFIELD, HALIFAX,
KEIGHLEY & DEWSBURY:
Pulse & Pulse 2** T 01274 203040
Forster Square, Bradford BD1 5NE
E general@pulse.co.uk
W www.pulse2.net

**CAMBRIDGESHIRE &
PETERBOROUGH: Heart** T 01733 281370
Enterprise House, Division Park
Histon, Cambridgeshire CB24 9ZR
T 01733 460460
E cambridgeshire.news@heart.co.uk
W www.heart.co.uk

CARDIFF & NEWPORT: Capital FM & Gold FM
W www.capitalfm.com

**CHESTER, NORTH WALES &
WIRRAL: Heart** T 01978 752202
Contact: Paul Holmes (Programme Controller)
The Studios, Mold Road
Wrexham LL11 4AF
E northwestwales.news@heart.co.uk
W www.heart.co.uk

DUMFRIES: West Sound FM T 01387 250999
Unit 40, The Loreburn Centre
High Street, Dumfries DG1 2BD
F 01387 265629
W www.westsoundradio.com

**DUNDEE & PERTH:
Radio Tay AM** T 01382 200800
6 North Isla Street, Dundee DD3 7JQ
E tayam@radiotay.co.uk
W www.radiotay.co.uk

**EAST MIDLANDS:
Capital East Midlands** T 0115 873 1500
Incorporating Ram FM, Leicester Sound & Trent FM
Chapel Quarter, Maid Marian Way
Nottingham NG1 6HQ
W www.capitalfm.com

EDINBURGH: Radio Forth T 0131 556 9255
Forth House, Forth Street
Edinburgh EH1 3LE
E info@radioforth.com
W www.radioforth.com

EXETER & TORBAY: Heart T 01392 354200
Hawthorn House, Exeter Business Park
Exeter EX1 3QS
F 01392 354209
W www.heart.co.uk

FALKIRK: Central FM T 01324 611164
The Studio, 9 Munroe Road
Springkerse Industrial Estate
Sterling FK7 7UU
F 01324 611168
W www.centralfm.co.uk

GLASGOW: Radio Clyde Ltd T 0141 565 2200
3 South Avenue, Clydebank Business Park
Glasgow G81 2RX
W www.clyde1.com

GLASGOW: Radio Clyde 2 T 0141 565 2200
3 South Avenue, Clydebank Business Park
Glasgow G81 2RX
W www.clyde2.com

**GLOUCESTER &
CHELTENHAM: Heart 102.4** T 01452 572400
The Eastgate Shopping Centre
Gloucester GL1 1SS
F 01452 572409
W www.heart.co.uk/gloucestershire

GUILDFORD: 96.4 Eagle Radio T 01483 300964
Eagle Radio Ltd, Dolphin House, 3 North Street
Guildford, Surrey GU1 4AA
F 01483 454443
E onair@964eagle.co.uk
W www.964eagle.co.uk

HEREFORD & WORCESTER:
Free Radio   **T** 01905 545500
1st Floor, Kirkham House
John Comyn Drive, Worcester WR3 7NS
W www.freeradio.co.uk

HOME COUNTIES: Heart   **T** 01604 795600
Bedford, Beds, Bucks, Herts, Milton Keynes &
Northamptonshire
4th Floor, CBX11, 382-428 Midsummer Boulevard
Milton Keynes MK9 2EA
E fourcounties.news@heart.co.uk
W www.heart.co.uk

INVERNESS: Moray Firth Radio   **T** 01463 224433
PO Box 271, Scorguie Place
Inverness IV3 8UJ
E mfr@mfr.co.uk
W www.mfr.co.uk

ISLE OF WIGHT:
Isle of Wight Radio   **T** 01983 822557
Dodnor Park, Newport, Isle of Wight PO30 5XE
F 01983 822109
E studio@iwradio.co.uk
W www.iwradio.co.uk

KENT: Heart   **T** 01227 772004
Radio House, John Wilson Business Park
Whitstable, Kent CT5 3QX
E news.kent@heart.co.uk
W www.heart.co.uk/kent

LIVERPOOL: Radio City   **T** 0151 472 6800
St John's Beacon, 1 Houghton Street
Liverpool L1 1RL
W www.radiocity.co.uk

LONDON: Absolute Radio   **T** 020 7434 1215
1 Golden Square, London W1F 9DJ
W www.absoluteradio.co.uk

LONDON: Captial Extra   **T** 020 7766 6810
Global Radio
30 Leicester Square, London WC2H 7LA
F 020 7766 6100
W www.thisisglobal.com

LONDON: Classic FM   **T** 020 7343 9000
Global Radio
30 Leicester Square, London WC2H 7LA
F 020 7344 2789
W www.thisisglobal.com

LONDON: Gold   **T** 020 7054 8000
Global Radio
30 Leicester Square, London WC2H 7LA
W www.thisisglobal.com

LONDON:
Independent Radio News   **T** 020 7182 8591
Mappin House, 4 Winsley Street
London W1W 8HF
E irn@bskyb.com
W www.irn.co.uk

LONDON:
London Greek Radio   **T** 020 8349 6950
437 High Road, Finchley
London N12 0AP
E info@lgr.co.uk
W www.lgr.co.uk

LONDON: Magic 105.4 FM   **T** 020 7182 8233
Mappin House, 4 Winsley Street
London W1W 8HF
W www.magic.co.uk

LONDON: Smooth Radio   **T** 0161 886 8800
26-27 Castlereagh Street
London W1H 5DL
E info@smoothradio.co.uk
W www.smoothradio.co.uk

MANCHESTER:
Key 103 FM & Magic 1152   **T** 0161 288 5000
Piccadilly Radio Ltd, Castle Quay
Castle Field, Manchester M15 4PR
F 0161 288 5151
W www.key103.co.uk

MANCHESTER:
Wythenshawe FM   **T** 0161 499 7982
Forum Learning Room G24
Forum Centre, Forum Square
Wythenshawe, Manchester M22 5RX
E jk@wfmradio.org
W www.wfmradio.org

NORFOLK & SUFFOLK:
Heart FM   **T** 01603 630621
St Georges Plain, 47-49 Colegate
Norwich NR3 1DB
W www.heart.co.uk

NORTHAMPTONSHIRE: Connect FM 97.2,
106.8 FM, 107.4 FM & DAB   **T** 01536 513664
55 Headlands, Kettering
Northampton NN15 7EU
W www.connectfm.com

OXFORD & BANBURY: Heart   **T** 01865 871000
The Chase, Calcot
Reading RG31 7RB
W www.heart.co.uk

PLYMOUTH & DEVON:
Heart South West   **T** 01752 275600
Hawthorn House
Exeter Business Park EX1 3QS
W www.heart.co.uk

PORTSMOUTH & SOUTHAMPTON:
Capital South Coast   **T** 01489 589911
Global Radio
Radio House, Whittle Avenue
Segensworth West
Fareham, Hampshire PO15 5SX
W www.capitalfm.com

PORTSMOUTH &
SOUTHAMPTON: Heart   **T** 01489 589911
Global Radio
Radio House, Whittle Avenue
Segensworth West, Fareham
Hampshire PO15 5SX
W www.heart.co.uk

SOUTH MANCHESTER & CHESHIRE:
Imagine 104.9 FM   **T** 0161 476 7340
Waterloo Place, Watson Square
Stockport, Cheshire SK1 3AZ
E studio@imaginefm.net
W www.imaginefm.net

STOKE-ON-TRENT & STAFFORD: Signal Radio   T 01782 441300
Stoke Road, Stoke-on-Trent
Staffordshire ST4 2SR
E info@signalradio.com
W www.signal1.co.uk

SUSSEX: Heart   T 01273 430111
Radio House, Franklin Road
Portslade
East Sussex BN41 1AS
F 01273 316909
W www.heart.co.uk

SWANSEA: The Wave 96.4 FM   T 01792 511964
Victoria Road, Gowerton
Swansea SA4 3AB
W www.thewave.co.uk

TEESSIDE: Magic 1170   T 01642 888222
55 Degrees North, Pilgrim Street
Newcastle NE1 6BF
W www.magic1170.co.uk

TEESSIDE: TFM Radio   T 01642 888222
55 Degrees North, Pilgrim Street
Newcastle NE1 6BF
W www.tfmradio.com

TYNE & WEAR, NORTHUMBERLAND & DURHAM: Magic 1152   T 0191 230 6100
55 Degrees North, Pilgrim Street
Newcastle upon Tyne NE1 6BF
W www.magic1152.co.uk

TYNE & WEAR, NORTHUMBERLAND & DURHAM: Metro Radio   T 0191 230 6100
55 Degrees North, Pilgrim Street
Newcastle upon Tyne NE1 6BF
W www.metroradio.co.uk

WEST COUNTRY: Heart   T 0117 984 3200
1 Passage Street, Bristol BS2 0JF
F 0117 984 3229
W www.heart.co.uk

WOLVERHAMPTON & BLACK COUNTRY / SHREWSBURY & TELFORD: Free Radio   T 01902 461200
267 Tettenhall Road, Wolverhampton WV6 0DE
W www.freeradio.co.uk

YORKSHIRE: Hallam FM & Magic AM   T 0114 209 1000
Radio House, 900 Herries Road
Hillsborough, Sheffield S6 1RH
W www.hallamfm.co.uk

YORKSHIRE: Seaside Radio   T 07583 100370
Community Radio for Southern Holderness
Shores Centre, 29-31 Seaside Road
Withernsea, East Yorkshire HU19 2DL
E justin@seasideradio.co.uk
W www.seasideradio.co.uk

YORKSHIRE & LINCOLNSHIRE: Viking 96.9 FM & Magic 1161 AM   T 01482 325141
Commercial Road, Hull HU1 2SG
W www.vikingfm.co.uk

Rehearsal Rooms & Casting Suites

How should I prepare for an audition?

When you are called to a casting you should make sure you are fully prepared with accurate information about the audition time, venue and format. Research the casting director too: look on his or her website and pay attention to media news. What productions have they worked on previously? What do they seem to look for and expect from the actors they cast?

For most auditions you will be given a script to learn, but you could be provided with a brief in advance and asked to find something suitable yourself. It would be advisable to have about five or six pieces ready to choose from that demonstrate your range before you are even called to a casting. You should select two relevant but contrasting pieces of about two to three minutes each for your audition, with the others as backups. If you can, read the whole play in addition to your speech.

It is generally best not to use 'popular' or very well-known pieces and instead to use original modern speeches, as this prevents the likelihood of the casting director comparing you, perhaps unfavourably, with anyone else. Having said this, however, you should still rehearse at least one Shakespeare piece. To find suitable speeches you should read widely for inspiration, or you could search online. If you are still struggling, think about who your favourite playwrights are and find out if they have written anything that is not too well-known.

What should I expect when I arrive at the audition?

Arrive early for your audition, but be prepared to wait! Time slots are allocated but auditions can overrun for various reasons. Be presentable and think about how your character might choose to dress, but overall you will feel more comfortable and confident if you don't differ too much from what you would normally wear. Don't come in costume unless specifically asked.

When you enter the audition room, you may have just the casting director in the room, or you could be confronted with a panel including the director and/or producer, and an editor and cameraman if you are being filmed. Don't let this disconcert you. Nerves are to be expected, but try to be positive and enjoy yourself. Remember, the casting director doesn't want to spend several days auditioning – they want you to get the job!

Take a few moments to work out where you should stand and where everything is. Don't ask too many questions as this can be irritating but you could ask whether to address your monologue to the casting director/camera, or whether to speak into the 'middle distance'. Make sure that your face, and in particular your eyes, can be seen as much as possible.

Once you have performed your monologue, pause and wait for the casting director to speak to you. Don't ask if they want to see a second speech. If they want another one, and if there's time, they will ask you. You may be asked your opinion on the speech so be prepared with possible answers. Never criticise previous productions you have worked on. At the end of the casting, remember to take your script away unless you are asked to leave it, otherwise it can look as if you're not interested.

Auditions are never a waste of time, even if you don't get the part. You may have performed well but you might not have been quite right for that particular role. Every audition is great practice and experience, and the casting director may very well keep you in mind for future productions.

Should I attend a casting in a house or flat?

Professional auditions are rarely held anywhere other than an official casting studio or venue. Be very wary if you are asked to go elsewhere. Trust your instincts. If something doesn't seem right to you, it probably isn't. Always take someone with you if you are in any doubt.

BRIXTON COMMUNITY BASE
* FORMERLY BRIXTON ST VINCENT'S COMMUNITY CENTRE *

◄ REHEARSAL STUDIO 16 x 7.5 metres ►

SECOND SPACE AVAILABLE

Piano / keyboards / showers / facility for aerial work / WiFi

Full Disabled Access

TEL - 020 7326 4417 / 07958 448690

Brixton Tube – Victoria line   **www.bsvcc.org**   Talma Road SW2 1AS

---

3 MILLS STUDIOS   T 020 7363 3336
Three Mill Lane, London E3 3DU
F 0871 5944028
E info@3mills.com
W www.3mills.com

ABACUS ARTS   T 020 7277 2880
2A Browning Street, Southwark, London SE17 1LN
E info@abacus-arts.org.uk
W www.abacus-arts.org.uk

ACTING SUITE LTD   T 020 7462 0792
*Fully Equipped Film, Television, Commercial & Theatrical
Casting & Rehearsal Studios*
17 Percy Street, London W1T 1DU
E jimmy@actingsuite.com
W www.actingsuite.com

**ACTORS CENTRE
(LONDON) THE**   T 020 7632 8012
Auditioning. Casting. Rehearsals. Room Hire
1A Tower Street, London WC2H 9NP
T 020 7240 3940
E operations@actorscentre.co.uk
W www.actorscentre.co.uk

ACTOR'S TEMPLE THE   T 020 3004 4537
Basement, 13-14 Warren Street, London W1T 5LG
E info@actorstemple.com
W www.actorstemple.com

ALBANY THE   T 020 8692 0231
Douglas Way, Deptford, London SE8 4AG
F 020 8469 2253
E hires@thealbany.org.uk
W www.thealbany.org.uk

ALFORD HOUSE   T 020 7735 1519
Aveline Street, London SE11 5DQ
E tim@alfordhouse.org.uk
W www.alfordhouse.org.uk

**ALRA (ACADEMY OF LIVE &
RECORDED ARTS)**   T 020 8870 6475
The Royal Victoria Patriotic Building
John Archer Way, London SW18 3SX
E info@alra.co.uk
W www.alra.co.uk

**AMERICAN CHURCH IN
LONDON THE**   T 020 7580 2791
Contact: Monty Strikes
Whitefield Memorial Church
79A Tottenham Court Road, London W1T 4TD
F 020 7580 5013
E latchcourt@amchurch.co.uk
W www.latchcourt.com

ARCH 468 THEATRE STUDIO   T 07973 302908
Arch 468, 209A Coldharbour Lane, London SW9 8RU
E rebecca@arch468.com
W www.arch468.com

ARTEMIS STUDIOS LTD   T 01344 429403
30 Charles Square
Bracknell, Berkshire RG12 1AY
E niki@artemis-studios.co.uk
W www.artemis-studios.co.uk

ARTSADMIN   T 020 7247 5102
Toynbee Studios
28 Commercial Street, London E1 6AB
F 020 7247 5103
E admin@artsadmin.co.uk
W www.artsadmin.co.uk

AVIV DANCE STUDIOS   T/F 01923 250000
Watford Boys Grammar School
Rickmansworth Road, Watford WD18 7JF
E info@avivdance.com
W www.avivdance.com

**BATTERSEA ARTS
CENTRE (BAC)**   T 020 7326 8211
Lavender Hill, London SW11 5TN
F 020 7978 5207
E venues@bac.org.uk
W www.bac.org.uk/hires

BIG ACT THE   T 0870 8810367
14-16 Wilson Place, Bristol BS2 9HJ
E info@thebigact.com
W www.thebigact.com

**BREAK A LEG
MANAGEMENT LTD**   T/F 020 7250 0662
The City College, University House, Room 33
55 East Road, London N1 6AH
E agency@breakalegman.com
W www.breakalegman.com

**BRIDGE THEATRE TRAINING
COMPANY THE**   T 020 7424 0860
Various Large Studios & Meeting Rooms
90 Kingsway, Tally Ho Corner
North Finchley, London N12 0EX
E admin@thebridge-ttc.org
W www.thebridge-ttc.org

BRIXTON COMMUNITY BASE   T 020 7326 4417
Formerly Brixton St Vincent's Community Centre
Talma Road, London SW2 1AS
T 07958 448690
E info@brixtoncommunitybase.org
W www.bsvcc.org

**CALDER THEATRE
BOOKSHOP LTD THE**   T 020 7620 2900
*Central London Rehearsal Space, Fringe Venue &
Theatre Bookshop*
51 The Cut, London SE1 8LF
E info@calderbookshop.com
W www.calderbookshop.com

CASTING CABIN LTD THE   T 020 7812 1399
Panther House, Unit 4, East Block
38 Mount Pleasant
Holborn, London WC1X 0AN
T 07767 445640
E thecastingcabin@gmail.com
W www.thecastingcabin.com

CASTING SUITE   T 020 7427 5681
ROAR House, 46 Charlotte Street, London W1T 2GS
E info@castingsuite.net

CECIL SHARP HOUSE   T 020 7241 8954
2 Regent's Park Road, London NW1 7AY
F 020 7284 0534
E hire@efdss.org
W www.cecilsharphouse.org

**CENTRAL LONDON
GOLF CENTRE**   T 020 8871 2468
Burntwood Lane, London SW17 0AT
F 020 8874 7447
E info@clgc.co.uk   W www.clgc.co.uk

CENTRAL STUDIOS T 020 8698 8880
470 Bromley Road, Bromley, Kent BR1 4PQ
E info@dandbperformingarts.co.uk
W www.dandbperformingarts.co.uk

CHARING CROSS THEATRE T 020 7930 5868
Formerly New Players Theatre
The Arches, Off Villiers Street, London WC2N 6NL
E info@charingcrosstheatre.co.uk
W www.charingcrosstheatre.co.uk

CHATS PALACE T 020 8533 0227
42-44 Brooksby's Walk, Hackney, London E9 6DF
E info@chatspalace.com
W www.chatspalace.co.uk

CHELSEA THEATRE T 020 7349 7811
Contact: Francis Alexander
World's End Place, King's Road, London SW10 0DR
T 020 7352 1967
E admin@chelseatheatre.org.uk
W www.chelseatheatre.org.uk

CLEAN BREAK T 020 7482 8600
2 Patshull Road, London NW5 2LB
F 020 7482 8611
E general@cleanbreak.org.uk
W www.cleanbreak.org.uk

CLUB FOR ACTS & ACTORS T 020 7836 3172
Incorporating Concert Artistes Association
20 Bedford Street, London WC2E 9HP
E office@thecaa.org
W www.thecaa.co.uk

COLOMBO CENTRE THE T 020 7261 1658
Audition & Rehearsal Space
34-68 Colombo Street, London SE1 8DP
E colombodm@jubileehalltrust.org
W www.colombo-centre.org

COPTIC STREET STUDIO LTD T 020 7636 2030
9 Coptic Street, London WC1A 1NH
E studio@copticstreet.com

**COVENT GARDEN
DRAGON HALL TRUST** T 020 7404 7274
17 Stukeley Street, London WC2B 5LT
E bookings@dragonhall.org.uk
W www.dragonhall.org.uk

CUSTARD FACTORY T 0121 224 7777
Gibb Street, Digbeth, Birmingham B9 4AA
E info@custardfactory.co.uk
W www.custardfactory.co.uk

DANCE ATTIC STUDIOS T 020 7610 2055
368 North End Road, Fulham, London SW6 1LY
E danceattic@hotmail.com

DANCE COMPANY STUDIOS T 020 8402 2424
76 High Street, Beckenham BR3 1ED
E hire@dancecompanystudios.co.uk
W www.dancecompanystudios.co.uk

**DANCE STUDIO
LEEDS LTD THE** T 0113 242 1550
Mill 6, 1st Floor, Mabgate Mills
Leeds, West Yorkshire LS9 7DZ
E katie@thedancestudioleeds.com
W www.thedancestudioleeds.com

DANCEWORKS T 020 7318 4100
16 Balderton Street, London W1K 6TN
E info@danceworks.net
W www.danceworks.net

DAVIES, Siobhan STUDIOS T 020 7091 9650
Rehearsal Studios, Meeting Rooms & Events Hires
85 St George's Road, London SE1 6ER
F 020 7091 9669
E info@siobhandavies.com
W www.siobhandavies.com

DIE-CAST STUDIOS T 020 7494 4630
39A Berwick Street, Soho, London W1F 8RU
E studio@diecaststudios.co.uk
W www.diecaststudios.co.uk

DIORAMA ARTS STUDIOS T 020 7383 0727
201 Drummond Street, Regents Place
London NW1 3FE
E info@diorama-arts.org.uk
W www.diorama-arts.org.uk

EALING STUDIOS T 020 8567 6655
Ealing Green, London W5 5EP
F 020 8758 8658
E bookings@ealingstudios.com
W www.ealingstudios.com

**ELMS LESTERS
PAINTING ROOMS** T 020 7836 6747
1-3-5 Flitcroft Street, London WC2H 8DH
F 020 7379 0789
E info@elmslesters.co.uk
W www.elmslesters.co.uk

**ENGLISH FOLK DANCE &
SONG SOCIETY** T 020 7485 2206
Cecil Sharp House, 2 Regent's Park Road
London NW1 7AY
F 020 7284 0534
E hire@efdss.org   W www.efdss.org

ENGLISH NATIONAL OPERA T 020 7624 7711
Lilian Baylis House, 165 Broadhurst Gardens
London NW6 3AX
F 020 7625 3398
E receptionlbh@eno.org   W www.eno.org

ENGLISH TOURING THEATRE T 020 7450 1990
25 Short Street, Waterloo, London SE1 8LJ
E admin@ett.org.uk
W www.ett.org.uk

ETCETERA THEATRE T 020 7482 4857
(Above the Oxford Arms)
265 Camden High Street, London NW1 7BU
E admin@etceteratheatre.com
W www.etceteratheatre.com

**EUROKIDS & EKA CASTING
STUDIOS** T 01925 761083
Contact: Jodie Keith (Casting Agent)
The Warehouse Studios, Glaziers Lane
Culcheth, Warrington, Cheshire WA3 4AQ
T 01925 761210
E jodie@eka-agency.com
W www.eka-agency.com

EXCHANGE THE   T 01258 475137
Old Market Hill, Sturminster Newton DT10 1FH
E info@stur-exchange.co.uk
W www.stur-exchange.co.uk

EXPRESSIONS STUDIOS   T 020 7813 1580
Linton House, 39-51 Highgate Road, London NW5 1RT
E info@expressionsstudios.org.uk
W www.expressionsstudios.org.uk

FACTORY FITNESS &
DANCE CENTRE THE   T 020 7272 1122
407 Hornsey Road, London N19 4DX
E info@factorylondon.com   W www.factorylondon.com

FSU LONDON STUDY CENTRE   T 020 7813 3223
99 Great Russell Street, London WC1B 3LH
F 020 7813 3270

GRAEAE THEATRE COMPANY   T 020 7613 6900
Bradbury Studios, 138 Kingsland Road
London E2 8DY
E info@graeae.org   W www.graeae.org

GROUNDLINGS THEATRE   T 023 9273 9496
42 Kent Street, Portsmouth, Hampshire PO1 3BS
E richard@groundlings.co.uk
W www.groundlings.co.uk

HAMPSTEAD THEATRE   T 020 7449 4200
Eton Avenue, Swiss Cottage, London NW3 3EU
F 020 7449 4201
E info@hampsteadtheatre.com
W www.hampsteadtheatre.com

HANGAR ARTS TRUST   T 020 3004 6173
Unit 7A, Mellish House
Harrington Way, London SE18 5NR
E info@hangarartstrust.org
W www.hangarartstrust.org

HEYTHROP COLLEGE   T 020 7795 6600
University of London, 23 Kensington Square
London W8 5HN
E conferences@heythrop.ac.uk
W www.heythrop.ac.uk

HOLLY LODGE COMMUNITY
CENTRE   T 020 8342 9524
Hall for Hire for Weekdays, Evenings & Weekends
30 Makepeace Avenue, London N6 6HL
E hollylodgelondon@hotmail.com   W www.hlcchl.org

HOLY INNOCENTS CHURCH   T 020 8748 2286
Paddenswick Road, London W6 0UB
E bookings@hisj.co.uk   W www.hisj.co.uk

HOLY TRINITY W6　**T** 020 7603 3832
Holy Trinity Parish Centre, 41 Brook Green
London W6 7BL
E brookgreen@rcdow.org.uk　**W** www.trinityfocus.org

HOPE STREET LTD　**T** 0151 708 8007
13A Hope Street, Liverpool L1 9BQ
E sarah@hope-street.org　**W** www.hope-street.org

HOXTON HALL THEATRE &
YOUTH ARTS CENTRE　**T** 020 7684 0060
130 Hoxton Street, London N1 6SH
E info@hoxtonhall.co.uk　**W** www.hoxtonhall.co.uk

IMT GALLERY　**T** 020 8980 5475
Unit 2, 210 Cambridge Heath Road
London E2 9NQ
E mail@imagemusictext.com
W www.imagemusictext.com

INVISIBLE DOT THE　**T** 020 7424 8918
2 Northdown Street, London N1 9BG
E hire@theinvisibledot.com
W www.theinvisibledot.com

ISLINGTON ARTS FACTORY　**T** 020 7607 0561
2 Parkhurst Road, London N7 0SF
E info@islingtonartsfactory.org
W www.islingtonartsfactory.org

ISTD DANCE STUDIOS　**T** 020 7655 8801
346 Old Street, London EC1V 9NQ
E reception.istd2@istd.org　**W** www.istd.org

JACKSONS LANE　**T** 020 8340 5226
Various Spaces including Rehearsal Rooms &
Theatre Hire
269A Archway Road, London N6 5AA
E admin@jacksonslane.org.uk
W www.jacksonslane.org.uk

JAM THEATRE STUDIOS　**T** 01628 483808
Air-conditioned Studios
Archway Court, 45A West Street
Marlow, Buckinghamshire SL7 2LS
E office@jamtheatre.co.uk　**W** www.jamtheatre.co.uk

JERWOOD SPACE　**T** 020 7654 0171
171 Union Street, London SE1 0LN
F 020 7654 0172
E space@jerwoodspace.co.uk
W www.jerwoodspace.co.uk

LARCA STUDIOS　**T** 07779 321954
Studio Space with Adjustable Lighting. 7M x 4M
Unit 2, Crichton House, 11-12 Mount Stuart Square
Cardiff, South Glamorgan CF10 5EE
E lizlarca@gmail.com　**W** www.larca.co.uk

LIVE THEATRE　**T** 0191 261 2694
Broad Chare, Quayside, Newcastle upon Tyne NE1 3DQ
E info@live.org.uk　**W** www.live.org.uk

LONDON BUBBLE THEATRE
COMPANY LTD　**T** 020 7237 4434
5 Elephant Lane, London SE16 4JD
E admin@londonbubble.org.uk
W www.londonbubble.org.uk

LONDON SCHOOL
OF CAPOEIRA　**T** 020 7281 2020
Units 1 & 2 Leeds Place, Tollington Park
London N4 3RF
E studiohire@londonschoolofcapoeira.com
W www.londonschoolofcapoeira.com

LONDON THEATRE THE　**T** 020 8694 1888
Lower Space, 443 New Cross Road
New Cross, London SE14 6TA
E thelondontheatre@live.co.uk
W www.thelondontheatre.com

LONDON WELSH CENTRE　**T** 020 7837 3722
157-163 Gray's Inn Road, London WC1X 8UE
E administrator@lwcentre.demon.co.uk
W www.londonwelsh.org

LS-LIVE　**T** 01977 659888
Arena-sized Studio
Unit 53, Langthwaite Business Park
Lidgate Crescent, South Kirkby, Wakefield
West Yorkshire WF9 3NR
E sales@ls-live.com　**W** www.ls-live.com

LYRIC HAMMERSMITH　**T** 020 8741 6850
King Street, London W6 0QL
E enquiries@lyric.co.uk　**W** www.lyric.co.uk

MA WORKS LTD　**T** 07828 105125
Ground Floor, 6 Bakers Yard
London EC1R 3DD
E emily@modeladvice.info　**W** www.maworks.co.uk

MACKINTOSH, Cameron
REHEARSAL STUDIO　**T** 020 7372 6611
The Tricycle, 269 Kilburn High Road, London NW6 7JR
F 020 7328 0795
E admin@tricycle.co.uk　**W** www.tricycle.co.uk

MAKEBELIEVE ARTS　**T** 020 8691 3803
3 Spaces Available for Hire
The Deptford Mission, 1 Creek Road, London SE8 3BT
E info@makebelievearts.co.uk
W www.makebelievearts.co.uk

MENIER CHOCOLATE
FACTORY　**T** 020 7378 1712
53 Southwark Street, London SE1 1RU
F 020 7234 0447
E office@menierchocolatefactory.com
W www.menierchocolatefactory.com

MOBERLY SPORTS &
EDUCATION CENTRE   T 020 7641 4807
101 Kilburn Lane, Kensal Rise, London W10 4AH
E moberly@enquiries@gll.org

MOVING EAST STUDIO   T 020 7503 3101
Harlequin Sprung Floor. Quadrophonic Sound System
St Matthias Church Hall, Wordsworth Road
London N16 8DD
E admin@movingeast.co.uk
W www.movingeast.co.uk

NATIONAL YOUTH THEATRE
OF GREAT BRITAIN   T 020 3696 7066
111 Buckingham Palace Road, London SW1W 0DT
E info@nyt.org.uk   W www.nyt.org.uk

NEALS YARD
MEETING ROOMS   T/F 020 7436 9875
14 Neals Yard
Covent Garden
London WC2H 9DP
E info@walkinbackrub.co.uk
W www.meetingrooms.org.uk

NLPAC
PERFORMING ARTS   T 020 8444 4544
Casting & Production Office Facilities. Performing
Arts School
76 St James Lane
Muswell Hill, London N10 3RD
E info@nlpac.co.uk   W www.nlpac.co.uk

SOUTH LONDON DANCE STUDIOS

- 3 large dance studios for hire
- Sprung floors, mirrors, barres & piano
- Spacious changing & waiting facilities
- Suitable for auditions, castings & rehearsals

130 Herne Hill, London SE24 9QL, *10 mins from Victoria by train* 020 7978 8624

info@southlondondancestudios.co.uk   www.southlondondancestudios.co.uk

OBSERVATORY STUDIOS THE   T 020 7437 2823
45-46 Poland Street, London W1F 7NA
F 020 7437 2830
E info@theobservatorystudios.com
W www.theobservatorystudios.com

OCTOBER GALLERY   T 020 7831 1618
24 Old Gloucester Street, London WC1N 3AL
F 020 7405 1851
E events@octobergallery.co.uk
W www.octobergallery.co.uk

OLD VIC THEATRE THE   T 020 7928 2651
The Cut, London SE1 8NB
E hires@oldvictheatre.com
W www.oldvictheatre.com

OMNIBUS ARTS CENTRE   T 020 7498 4699
1 North Side Clapham Common, London SW4 0QW
E hires@omnibus-clapham.org

ONLY CONNECT UK   T 0845 3707990
32 Cubitt Street, London WC1X 0LR
T 020 7278 8939
E info@oclondon.org
W www.oclondon.org

DRAGON HALL
COVENT GARDEN
TRUST

Photo: David Andrew

17 Stukeley Street, Covent Garden
London, WC2B 5LT

020 7404 7274
bookings@dragonhall.org.uk
www.dragonhall.org.uk

OPEN DOOR COMMUNITY CENTRE   T/F 020 8871 8172
Beaumont Road, Wimbledon, London SW19 6TF
E dconstantinou@wandsworth.gov.uk
W www.wandsworth.gov.uk

OUT OF JOINT   T 020 7609 0207
7 Thane Works, Thane Villas, London N7 7NU
F 020 7609 0203
E ojo@outofjoint.co.uk
W www.outofjoint.co.uk

OVALHOUSE   T 020 7582 0080
52-54 Kennington Oval, London SE11 5SW
E hire@ovalhouse.com
W www.ovalhouse.com/hire

PAINES PLOUGH REHEARSAL & AUDITION SPACE   T 020 7240 4533
4th Floor, 43 Aldwych, London WC2B 4DN
F 020 7240 4534
E office@painesplough.com
W www.painesplough.com

PARK THEATRE   T 020 7167 6628
Morris Space available for Rehearsals
Clifton Terrace, Finsbury Park, London N4 3JP
E hire@parktheatre.co.uk
W www.parktheatre.co.uk

PEREGRINES PIANOS   T 020 7242 9865
Auditioning. Casting. Filming. Piano Hire
137A Gray's Inn Road, London WC1X 8TU
E info@peregrines-pianos.com
W www.peregrines-pianos.com

PHA CASTING SUITE   T 0161 273 4444
Tanzaro House, Ardwick Green North
Manchester M12 6FZ
F 0161 273 4567
E casting@pha-agency.co.uk
W www.pha-agency.co.uk/castingstudio

PINEAPPLE DANCE STUDIOS   T 020 7836 4004
7 Langley Street, Covent Garden, London WC2H 9JA
F 020 7836 0803
W www.pineapple.uk.com

PLACE THE   T 020 7121 1000
17 Duke's Road, London WC1H 9PY
F 020 7121 1142
E info@theplace.org.uk
W www.theplace.org.uk

PLAYGROUND STUDIO THE   T/F 020 8960 0110
Unit 8, Latimer Road, London W10 6RQ
E info@the-playground.co.uk
W www.the-playground.co.uk

POOR SCHOOL THE   T 020 7837 6030
242 Pentonville Road, London N1 9JY
E roomhire@thepoorschool.com
W www.thepoorschool.com

PRETZEL FILMS   T 020 7580 9595
2 Bermondsey Exchange, 179-181 Bermondsey Street
London SE1 3UW
E info@pretzelfilms.com   W www.pretzelfilms.com

PRICE STUDIOS T 020 7228 6862
110 York Road, London SW11 3RD
E info@pricestudios.co.uk
W www.pricestudios.co.uk

QUESTORS THEATRE
EALING THE T 020 8567 0011
12 Mattock Lane, London W5 5BQ
F 020 8567 2275
E enquiries@questors.org.uk
W www.questors.org.uk

RAG FACTORY THE T 020 7183 3048
16-18 Heneage Street, London E1 5LJ
E hello@ragfactory.org.uk
W www.ragfactory.org.uk

RAINDANCE FILM
CENTRE REHEARSAL ROOMS T 020 7930 3412
10 Craven Street, London WC2N 5PE
E roombookings@raindance.co.uk
W www.raindance.org

RAMBERT T 020 8630 0600
99 Upper Ground, London SE1 9PP
F 020 8747 8323
E info@rambert.org.uk
W www.rambert.org.uk

REALLY USEFUL
THEATRES GROUP LTD T 020 7379 4981
Contact: Jessica Nowell
Theatre Royal Drury Lane, Catherine Street
London WC2B 5JF
E jessica.nowell@reallyuseful.co.uk
W www.reallyusefultheatres.co.uk

RED HEDGEHOG THE T 07817 109093
2 Spaces available for ad hoc Rehearsal Hire
255-257 Archway Road, Highgate, London N6 5BS
E clare.f@theredhedgehog.co.uk
W www.redhedgehog.co.uk

RIDGEWAY STUDIOS T 01992 633775
Office: 106 Hawkshead Road, Potters Bar
Herts EN6 1NG
E info@ridgewaystudios.co.uk

RITZ STUDIOS T 020 8870 1335
*Provides Rehearsals/Backline & Sound Hire for
Musicians*
The Courtyard, Esmond Street, Putney SW15 2LP
E lee@ritzstudios.com
W www.ritzstudios.com

ROCHELLE SCHOOL T 020 7033 3539
Gallery. Conferences. Events. Venue Hire
Arnold Circus, London E2 7ES
E info@rochelleschool.org
W www.rochelleschool.org

ROOFTOP STUDIO THEATRE T 01785 761233
Rooftop Studio, High Street Arcade
Stone, Staffordshire ST15 8AU
F 01785 818176
E elaine@pssa.co.uk
W www.rooftopstudio.co.uk

ROOMS ABOVE THE T 020 3503 0038
Westheath Yard, (Beside Davids Deli)
174 Mill Lane, West Hampstead, London NW6 1TB
E info@theroomsabove.org.uk
W www.theroomsabove.org.uk

ROSE STUDIO & GALLERY T 020 8546 6983
Rose Theatre, Kingston, 24-26 High Street
Kingston upon Thames, Surrey KT1 1HL
F 020 8546 8783
E hiresandevents@rosetheatrekingston.org
W www.rosetheatrekingston.org

Raindance Film Centre Rehearsal Rooms
10 Craven Street, Charing Cross, WC2N 5PE

Room 1 6.1m x 7.3m **Room 2** 6.2m x 9.1m
Central Location | Free WiFi | Tea and Coffee Facilities | Piano
Perfect for castings, rehearsals and workshops.

T 020 7930 3412 **W** www.raindance.org/room-hire **E** roombookings@raindance.co.uk

ROYAL ACADEMY OF DANCE **T** 020 7326 8000
36 Battersea Square, London SW11 3RA
F 020 7924 3129
E info@rad.org.uk
W www.rad.org.uk

**ROYAL ACADEMY OF
DRAMATIC ART** **T** 020 7908 4822
Including The RADA Studios
62-64 Gower Street, London WC1E 6ED
F 020 7307 5062
E venues@radaenterprises.org
W www.rada.ac.uk/venues

**ROYAL SHAKESPEARE
COMPANY** **T** 020 7819 8700
35 Clapham High Street, London SW4 7TW
F 020 7819 8708
W www.rsc.org.uk

RUDEYE STUDIOS **T** 020 7014 3023
73 St John Street, Farringdon, London EC1M 4NJ
E info@rudeye.com
W www.rudeye.com

SADLER'S WELLS STUDIOS **T** 020 7863 8065
Rosebery Avenue, London EC1R 4TN
E events@sadlerswells.com
W www.sadlerswells.com/venue-hire/studios

SANDS FILM STUDIOS **T** 020 7231 2209
82 St Marychurch Street, London SE16 4HZ
F 020 7231 2119
E ostockman@sandsfilms.co.uk
W www.sandsfilms.co.uk

SOHO GYMS **T** 020 7482 4524
Camden Town Gym, 193-199 Camden High Street
London NW1 7BT
F 020 7267 0500 **W** www.sohogyms.com

SOHO GYMS **T** 020 7720 0321
Clapham Common Gym, 95-97 Clapham High Street
London SW4 7TB
F 020 7720 6510
E clapham@sohogyms.com **W** www.sohogyms.com

SOHO GYMS **T** 020 7242 1290
Covent Garden Gym, 12 Macklin Street
London WC2B 5NF
F 020 7242 0899
W www.sohogyms.com

SOHO GYMS **T** 020 7370 1402
Earl's Court Gym, 254 Earl's Court Road
London SW5 9AD
F 020 7244 6893
W www.sohogyms.com

SOHO GYMS **T** 020 7261 9798
Waterloo Gym, 11-15 Brad Street, London SE1 8TG
F 020 7928 8623
W www.sohogyms.com

SOHO THEATRE **T** 020 7287 5060
21 Dean Street, London W1D 3NE
F 020 7287 5061
E hires@sohotheatre.com
W www.sohotheatre.com

**SOUTH LONDON
DANCE STUDIOS** **T** 020 7978 8624
130 Herne Hill, London SE24 9QL
E info@southlondondancestudios.co.uk
W www.southlondondancestudios.co.uk

SPACE @ CLARENCE MEWS **T** 020 8986 5260
40 Clarence Mews, London E5 8HL
T 07871 190500
E 40cmews@gmail.com
W www.clarencemews.wordpress.com

SPACE ARTS CENTRE THE **T** 020 7515 7799
269 Westferry Road, London E14 3RS
E info@space.org.uk
W www.space.org.uk

SPACE CITY STUDIOS **T** 020 7371 4000
79 Blythe Road, London W14 0HP
F 020 7371 4001
E info@spacecity.co.uk
W www.spacecitystudios.co.uk

SPOTLIGHT ROOMS **T** 020 7440 5030
Casting Studios. Room Hire. Twitter: @SpotlightUK
7 Leicester Place, London WC2H 7RJ
E rooms@spotlight.com
W www.spotlight.com/rooms

SPOTLIGHT STUDIOS **T** 020 7440 5030
Casting Studios. Room Hire. Twitter: @SpotlightUK
7 Leicester Place, London WC2H 7RJ
E studios@spotlight.com
W www.spotlight.com/spaces

ST AGNES CHURCH **T** 020 7582 0032
St Agnes Place, Kennington Park, London SE11 4BB
E keith.potter@talk21.com

ST ANDREW'S CHURCH **T** 020 7633 9819
*Casting Suites. Meetings. Rehearsal Room. Workshops
& Classes*
Short Street, Southbank, London SE1 8LJ
E bookings@stjohnswaterloo.org
W www.stjohnswaterloo.org

HANGAR ARTS TRUST
- Creation, Rehearsal and Studio Spaces
- Large green screen for CGI Effects
- Fully Riggable for flying and Effects
- Sprung Dance Floors
- Free Parking • Nr Greenwich and The O2 Centre
Studio 1 - 10m High, 15m x 18m
Studio 2 - 10m High, 10m x 10m

Contact us: 020 8317 8401 020 3004 6173
www.hangarartstrust.org info@hangarartstrust.org
Hangar Arts Trust, Unit 7A, Mellish House
Harrington Way, London SE18 5NR

SPOTLIGHT
The home of casting

Spotlight Rooms and Studios
Hold your auditions in the heart of central London

Spotlight Database & Website
Browse over 60,000 performers' CVs with photos, showreels, voicereels and contact details

Use Spotlight's award-winning search engine to find exactly the right performer for the part

E-mail casting calls to hundreds of UK agents and performers

www.spotlight.com/spaces
020 7440 5030

www.spotlight.com
020 7437 7631
casting@spotlight.com

ST GEORGE'S CHURCH BLOOMSBURY T 020 7242 1979
Vestry Hall, 6 Little Russell Street, London WC1A 2HR
E hiring@stgb.org.uk
W www.stgeorgesbloomsbury.org.uk

ST JAMES'S CHURCH, PICCADILLY T 020 7292 4861
197 Piccadilly, London W1J 9LL
E roomhire@sjp.org.uk
W www.sjp.org.uk

ST MARTIN-IN-THE-FIELDS T 020 7766 1130
Trafalgar Square, London WC2N 4JJ
E music@smitf.org
W www.smitf.org

ST MARY ABBOTS CENTRE T 020 7937 8885
Vicarage Gate, Kensington, London W8 4HN
E adam.norton@stmaryabbotschurch.org
W www.smacentre.co.uk

ST MARY MAGDALENE ACADEMY T 020 7697 0123
475 Liverpool Road, Islington, London N7 8PG
E alistair.moulton@smmacademy.org
W www.smmacademy.org/facilities_hire/page/contact_us

STUDIO THE T 01746 787153
Burwarton, Nr Bridgnorth, Shropshire WV16 6QJ
E meghawkins@btinternet.com
W www.meghawkins.com

STUDIO SOHO T 020 7437 3175
*Also Premises of The Giles Foreman Centre for Acting.
2 Large Air-conditioned Modern Customised Spaces.
Wi-Fi. Reception. Kitchen. Changing Room. Showers.
Step-free Access via Stair-lift. HD Video Recording/
Projection Available*
Studio Soho, Royalty Mews (entrance by Quo Vadis)
22-25 Dean Street, London W1D 3RA
E info@gilesforeman.com
W www.gilesforeman.com

SUMMERS, Mark CASTING STUDIOS T 020 7229 8413
1 Beaumont Avenue, West Kensington
London W14 9LP
E louise@marksummers.com
W www.marksummers.com

SUMMIT STUDIOS T 020 8840 2200
2-4 Spring Bridge Mews, Ealing, London W5 2AB
F 020 8840 2446
E info@summitstudios.co.uk
W www.summitstudios.co.uk

TAKE FIVE CASTING STUDIO T 020 7287 2120
Casting Suite
37 Beak Street, London W1F 9RZ
F 020 7287 3035
E info@takefivestudio.com
W www.takefivestudio.com

THEATRE ALIBI T/F 01392 217315
Emmanuel Hall, Emmanuel Road, Exeter EX4 1EJ
E info@theatrealibi.co.uk
W www.theatrealibi.co.uk/hire.php

THEATRES TRUST THE T 020 7836 8591
1st Floor Resource Centre with 2 Rooms for Day-time, Evening & Weekend Hire
22 Charing Cross Road
London WC2H 0QL
E info@theatrestrust.org.uk
W www.theatrestrust.org.uk

THEATRO TECHNIS T 020 7387 6617
26 Crowndale Road
London NW1 1TT
E info@theatrotechnis.com
W www.theatrotechnis.com

TOOTING & MITCHAM COMMUNITY SPORTS CLUB T 020 8685 6193
Imperial Fields, Bishopsford Road
Morden, Surrey SM4 6BF
F 020 8685 6190
E info@tmunited.org
W www.tmunited.org

TREADWELL'S T 020 7419 8507
33 Store Street, Bloomsbury
London WC1E 7BS
E info@treadwells-london.com
W www.treadwells-london.com/london-shop/room-hire/

TRESTLE ARTS BASE T 01727 850950
Home of Trestle Theatre Company
Russet Drive, St Albans
Herts AL4 0JQ
E admin@trestle.org.uk
W www.trestle.org.uk

TRICYCLE THE T 020 7372 6611
269 Kilburn High Road
London NW6 7JR
F 020 7328 0795
E trish@tricycle.co.uk
W www.tricycle.co.uk

TT DANCE STUDIO T 07904 771980
Parkwood Health & Fitness Centre
Darkes Lane, Potters Bar
Herts EN6 1AA
T 07930 400647
E info@talenttimetheatre.com
W www.talenttimetheatre.com

UNICORN THEATRE T 020 7645 0500
147 Tooley Street
London SE1 2HZ
E stagedoor@unicorntheatre.com
W www.unicorntheatre.com

UNION SOHO THE T 020 7734 4113
50 Greek Street
London W1D 4EQ
E info@unionclub.co.uk
W www.unionclub.co.uk

UNIT TWENTY THREE T 01379 882200
Unit 23, Vince's Road
Court Industrial Estate, Diss, Norfolk IP22 4BF
E info@unittwentythree.co.uk
W www.unit23.co

Rehearsal Spaces for hire

Two new, purpose built studios for hire just 15 minutes by tube from the West End. Suitable for dance, musicals, large scale rehearsals, meetings or intimate one on one work.

For full details visit our website:
www.losttheatre.co.uk
or call us on 020 7622 9208

Tube: Stockwell (Victoria & Northern Lines)
Vauxhall (Northern & Overground lines)

**UPSTAIRS AT THE
ARTS THEATRE**   T 020 7836 8463
6-7 Great Newport Street, London WC2H 7JB
E upstairs@artstheatrewestend.co.uk
W www.artstheatrewestend.co.uk

URDANG ACADEMY THE   T 020 7713 7710
The Old Finsbury Town Hall
Rosebery Avenue, London EC1R 4RP
F 020 7278 6727
E studiohire@theurdangacademy.com
W www.theurdangacademy.com

WATERMANS   T 020 8232 1019
40 High Street, Brentford TW8 0DS
E info@watermans.org.uk   W www.watermans.org.uk

**Y TOURING THEATRE
COMPANY**   T 020 7520 3090
One KX, 120 Cromer Street, London WC1H 8BS
E d.jackson@ytouring.org.uk
W www.theatreofdebate.com

**YOUNG, Sylvia
THEATRE SCHOOL**   T 020 7258 2336
1 Nutford Place, London W1H 5YZ
T 020 7258 2339
E syoung@syts.co.uk
W www.syts.co.uk

YOUNG ACTORS THEATRE   T 020 7278 2101
70-72 Barnsbury Road, London N1 0ES
E info@yati.org.uk   W www.yati.org.uk

St James's Church, Piccadilly
Versatile Space for Hire in the West End

Conference Room
Perfect for large scale meetings, presentations, press launches, workshops and rehearsals.
10m x 7.5m

Meeting Room
Ideal for meetings, presentations, workshops, press launches, rehearsals and castings.
7.5m x 5m

Central location, competitive rates, free Wi-Fi, access to kitchen facilities

St James's Church, 197 Piccadilly, London W1J 9LL
020 7292 4861 • roomhire@sjp.org.uk

Is your CV up-to-date?

Top tips for promoting yourself!

- **Keep your credits up-to-date**

  An absolute must – always take responsibility for updating your own profile, as and when you gain credits and new skills.

- **Review your skills**

  Add new skills as they are learnt; remove old skills that you can no longer complete. The more skilled you are, the more you maximise your marketability.

- **Make sure your professional training appears**

  Also, remember to update this section as you undertake further training across your career.

- **Update your photograph**

  Ensure that you are representing yourself as you would now appear at an audition.

- **Add multimedia**

  Make sure casting professionals see and hear just how good you are with video and audio clips.

ACT UP T 020 7924 7701
Unit 88
99-109 Lavender Hill
London SW11 5QL
E info@act-up.co.uk
W www.act-up.co.uk

ACTIVATION T 020 8783 9494
Riverside House
Feltham Avenue
Hampton Court
Surrey KT8 9BJ
F 020 8783 9345
E info@activation.co.uk
W www.activation.co.uk

APROPOS PRODUCTIONS LTD T 020 7739 2857
53 Greek Street
London W1D 3DR
E info@aproposltd.com
W www.aproposltd.com/talent

BROWNE, Michael ASSOCIATES LTD T/F 01462 812483
The Cloisters
168C Station Road
Lower Stondon
Bedfordshire SG16 6JQ
E enquiries@mba-roleplay.co.uk
W www.mba-roleplay.co.uk

CRAGRATS T 0844 8111184
Lawster House
140 South Street
Dorking
Surrey RH4 2EU
E enquiries@cragrats.com
W www.cragrats.com

DRAMANON LTD T 01753 647795
Langtons House
Templewood Lane
Farnham Common
Buckinghamshire SL2 3HD
F 01753 647783
E info@dramanon.co.uk
W www.dramanon.co.uk

FRANK PARTNERS LLP T 0117 908 5384
14 Brynland Avenue
Bristol BS7 9DT
E neil@frankpartners.co.uk
W www.frankpartners.co.uk

GLOBAL7 T/F 020 7281 7679
Kemp House
152 City Road, London EC1V 2NZ
T 07956 956652
E global7castings@gmail.com
W www.global7casting.com

INTERACT T 020 7793 7744
138 Southwark Bridge Road
London SE1 0DG
E cv@interact.eu.com
W www.interact.eu.com

NORTH OF WATFORD LLP T 01422 845361
The Creative Quarter
The Town Hall
Hebden Bridge
Yorkshire HX7 7BY
E info@northofwatford.com
W www.northofwatford.com

NV MANAGEMENT LTD
Central Office
Minerva Mill Innovation Centre
Station Road
Alcester
Warwickshire B49 5ET
E hello@nvmanagement.co.uk
W www.nvmanagement.co.uk

**PERFORMANCE
BUSINESS THE** T 01932 888885
The Coach House
78 Oatlands Drive
Weybridge, Surrey KT13 9HT
E lucy@theperformance.biz
W www.theperformance.biz

RADA IN BUSINESS T 020 7908 4810
The Royal Academy of Dramatic Art
18-22 Chenies Street
London WC1E 7PA
F 020 7908 4811
E customerservice@radaenterprises.org
W www.radaenterprises.org

ROLEPLAY UK T 0333 121 3003
5 St Peters Street
Stamford
Lincolnshire PE9 2PQ
E bookings@roleplayuk.com
W www.roleplayuk.com

**STEPS DRAMA LEARNING
DEVELOPMENT** T 020 7403 9000
Suite 10, Baden Place
Crosby Row
London SE1 1YW
F 020 7403 0909
E mail@stepsdrama.com
W www.stepsdrama.com

THEATRE& LTD T 01484 664078
25 Queens Square Business Park
Huddersfield Road
Honley
West Yorkshire HD9 6QZ
F 01484 660079
E cmitchell@theatreand.com
W www.theatreand.com

WIZARD THEATRE T 0800 5832373
Blenheim Villa
Burr Street
Harwell
Oxfordshire OX11 0DT
E admin@wizardtheatre.co.uk
W www.wizardtheatre.co.uk

S →

3D SET COMPANY LTD   **T** 0161 273 8831
Construction. Exhibition Stands. Scenery Design. Sets
Unit 8 Temperance Street
Manchester M12 6HR
F 0161 273 6786
E twalsh@3dsetco.com
W www.3dsetco.com

ALBEMARLE SCENIC STUDIOS   **T** 0845 6447021
Suppliers of Scenery & Costumes Construction/Hire
Admin: PO Box 240, Rotherfield TN6 9BN
E albemarle.productions@virgin.net
W www.albemarleproductions.com

ALPHA CREW   **T** 020 3691 9683
Stage & Technical Crew for London & Midlands
88-90 Hatton Garden, Holborn
London EC1N 8PG
E info@alphacrew.co.uk
W www.alphacrew.co.uk

AVW CONTROLS LTD   **T** 01379 898340
Stage Automation Specialists
Unit 12 Willow Farm Business Centre
Allwood Green, Rickinghall, Diss, Norfolk IP22 1LT
F 01379 898386
E sales@avw.co.uk
W www.avw.co.uk

BONDINI LTD   **T** 01763 852691
*Cabaret, Magic & Illusion. Scenery Construction. Venue
Decor. AV Equipment*
Low Farm, Brook Road
Bassingbourn, Royston
Herts SG8 5NT
F 01763 853946
E hello@bondini.co.uk
W www.bondini.co.uk

BRISTOL (UK) LTD   **T** 01923 779333
Scenic Paint
Unit 1, Southerland Court
Tolpits Lane, Watford WD18 9SP
F 01923 779666
E tech.sales@bristolpaint.com
W www.bristolpaint.com

CAP PRODUCTION SOLUTIONS   **T** 07973 432576
116 Wigmore Road, Carshalton, Surrey SM5 1RQ
E leigh@leighporter.com

CAROUSEL LIGHTS LTD   **T** 07944 654349
86-90 Paul Street, London EC2A 4NE
E hello@carousellights.com
W www.carousellights.com

**CARTEY & CO LTD MANUFACTURERS
AGENT- UK & ITALY**   **T** 07878 977970
*Film, Television & Theatre Lighting, Screen & Scenic
Solutions*
Suite 80, 26 The Hornet
Chichester, West Sussex PO19 7BB
E clivecartey@gmail.com
W www.cartey.co.uk

CCT LIGHTING UK LTD   **T** 0115 985 8919
Lighting. Dimmers. Sound & Stage Machinery
Unit 3, Ellesmere Business Park
Haydn Road, Sherwood, Nottingham NG5 1DX
F 0115 985 7091
E office@cctlighting.co.uk
W www.cctlighting.com

CLOCKWORK SCENERY   **T** 01483 427531
*Hand-crafted Scenery for Theatres, Cruise Ships,
Exhibitions, Television & Film*
Secretts Farm, Chapel Lane
Milford, Surrey GU8 5HU
E enquiries@clockworkscenery.com
W www.clockworkscenery.com

COD STEAKS LTD   **T** 0117 980 3910
*Costume. Design. Exhibitions. Model Making.
Set Construction. Exhibition Designers*
2 Cole Road, Bristol BS2 0UG
E mail@codsteaks.com
W www.codsteaks.com

DAP STUDIO   **T** 07973 406830
55 Longdown Lane North
Epsom, Surrey KT17 3JB
E james@dapstudio.co.uk
W www.dapstudio.co.uk

DMN DESIGN BUILD   **T** 0844 8711801
Unit 1, Calder Trading Estate
Lower Quarry Road
Bradley, Huddersfield HD5 0RR
E enquiries@dmndesignbuild.co.uk
W www.dmndesignbuild.com

EVANS, Peter STUDIOS LTD   **T** 01582 725730
Scenic Embellishment. Vacuum Forming
12-14 Tavistock Street, Dunstable
Bedfordshire LU6 1NE
F 01582 481329
E sales@peterevansstudios.co.uk
W www.peterevansstudios.co.uk

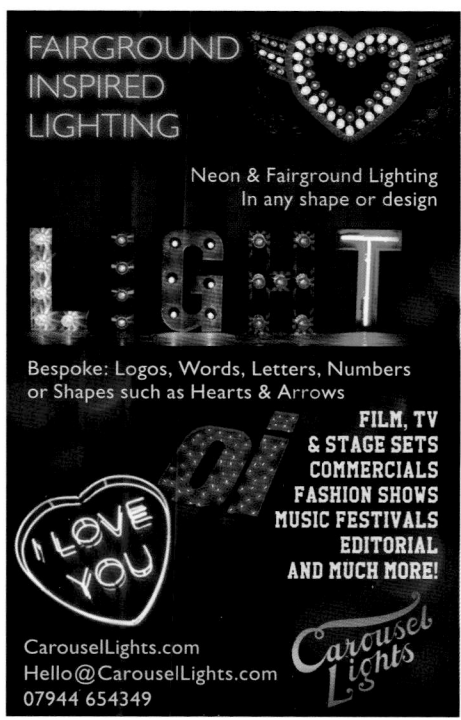

FULL EFFECT THE T 020 3553 5747
Event Designers & Producers
Millennium Studios
Bedford Technology Park
Thurleigh
Bedfordshire MK44 2YP
E mark.harrison@tfe.co.uk
W www.thefulleffect.co.uk

FUTURIST SOUND & LIGHT LTD T 0113 279 0033
Unit 1, White Swan Yard
Boroughgate, Otley LS21 1AE
F 0113 242 0022
E info@futurist.co.uk
W www.futurist.co.uk

GILL, Perry T 07815 048164
Installation. Production Management. Set Construction
E perry_gill100@hotmail.com

HALL STAGE LTD T 01582 439440
Unit 4, Cosgrove Way
Luton, Beds LU1 1XL
F 01582 720904
E sales@hallstage.com
W www.hallstage.com

HALO LIGHTING T 0844 8440484
98-124 Brewery Road
London N7 9PG
E info@halo.co.uk
W www.halo.co.uk

HAND & LOCK T 020 7580 7488
Embroidery for Costumes & Interiors
86 Margaret Street
London W1W 8TE
F 020 7580 7499
E enquiries@handembroidery.com
W www.handembroidery.com

HARLEQUIN FLOORS T 01892 514888
Festival House
Chapman Way
Tunbridge Wells
Kent TN2 3EF
F 01892 514222
E enquiries@harlequinfloors.com
W www.harlequinfloors.com

HENSHALL, John T 01793 790333
Director of Lighting & Photography
6 Divinity Close, Wanborough
Swindon SN4 0EH
E john@epi-centre.com

HERON & DRIVER T 020 7394 8688
Scenic Furniture & Structural Prop Makers
Unit 7, Dockley Road
Industrial Estate
Rotherhithe
London SE16 3SF
E mail@herondriver.co.uk
W www.herondriver.co.uk

IOGIG LTD T 020 7112 8907
Production Services including Set Construction, Lighting & Sound Hire, Stage & Production Management, Marketing & Online Design
39 Equinox House, Barking, Essex IG11 8RN
E info@iogig.com
W www.iogig.com

LIGHT WORKS LTD T 020 7249 3627
2A Greenwood Road, London E8 1AB
F 020 7254 0306

LS-LIVE T 01977 659888
Arena-sized Studio. Set Design & Construction. Equipment Rental
Unit 53, Langthwaite Business Park
Lidgate Crescent
South Kirkby, Wakefield
West Yorkshire WF9 3NR
E sales@ls-live.com
W www.ls-live.com

MALTBURY STAGING T 0333 800 8881
Portable Staging Sales & Consultancy
87 Church Road, Hove BN3 2BB
F 0333 800 8882
E info@maltbury.com
W www.maltbury.com

MATTLX GROUP T 0845 6808693
Lighting. Design. Production Engineering. Safety. Training
Unit 3, Vinehall Business Centre
Vinehall Road, Robertsbridge
East Sussex TN32 5JW
E intray@mattlx.com
W www.mattlx.com

MODELBOX T 01837 810923
Computer Aided Design. Design Services
41C Market Street
Hatherleigh, Devon EX20 3JP
E info@modelbox.co.uk
W www.modelboxplans.com

MODERNEON LONDON LTD T 020 8650 9690
LED Lighting. Signage
Cromwell House, 7 Brabourne Rise
Park Langley, Beckenham, Kent BR3 6SQ
F 020 8658 2770
E info@moderneon.co.uk
W www.moderneon.co.uk

MOUNSEY, Matthew T 07941 355450
Scenic Artist
E mmounsey@yahoo.com

NEED, Paul J.   T 020 8659 2558
Lighting Designer
5 Metro Business Centre
Kangley Bridge Road, London SE26 5BW
F 020 8778 9217
E paul@10outof10.co.uk
W www.pauljneed.co.uk

NORTHERN LIGHT   T 0131 622 9100
Communications, Lighting, Sound & Stage Equipment
Assembly Street, Leith
Edinburgh EH6 7RG
F 0131 622 9101
E info@northernlight.co.uk
W www.northerlight.co.uk

ORBITAL SOUND LTD   T 020 7501 6868
Sound Hire & Design
57 Acre Lane
Brixton, London SW2 5TN
F 020 7501 6869
E hire@orbitalsound.co.uk
W www.orbitalsound.co.uk

PANALUX   T 020 8233 7000
12 Waxlow Road, London NW10 7NU
F 020 8233 7001
E info@panalux.biz
W www.panalux.biz

PMB THEATRE &
EXHIBITION SERVICES LTD   T 01763 852691
Low Farm, Brook Road
Bassingbourn, Royston, Herts SG8 5NT
F 01763 853946
E info@creatingtheimpossible.co.uk
W www.creatingtheimpossible.co.uk

PRODUCTION STORE   T 0845 6808692
Lighting. Production Engineering. Special Projects
Unit 3, Vinehall Business Centre
Vinehall Road, Robertsbridge
East Sussex TN32 5JW
E sales@mattlx.com
W www.mattlx.com

REVOLVING STAGE
COMPANY LTD THE   T 024 7668 7055
Unit F5, Little Heath Industrial Estate
Old Church Road, Coventry
Warwickshire CV6 7ND
E enquiries@therevolvingstagecompany.co.uk
W www.therevolvingstagecompany.co.uk

RK RESOURCE   T 01233 750180
2 Wyvern Way
Henwood, Ashford
Kent TN24 8DW
F 01233 750133
E rkresource2007@aol.co.uk
W www.rk-resourcekent.com

S + H TECHNICAL
SUPPORT LTD   T 01271 866832
Starcloths. Drapes
Starcloth Way, Mullacott Industrial Estate
Ilfracombe, Devon EX34 8PL
F 01271 865423
E shtsg@aol.com
W www.starcloth.co.uk

STAGEWORKS®
WORLDWIDE PRODUCTIONS

Technical

Stageworks

Sets, scenery & props
Aerial flying systems
Specialist rigging
Lighting, sound
and staging
Ice floors

Whatever you need in technical management, from the creation of special lighting effects and sound design, to providing experienced technical support teams, Stageworks can deliver a turnkey solution.

00 44 **(0) 1253 342426**
00 44 **(0) 1253 336341**
info@stageworkswwp.com
stageworkswwp.com

S2 EVENTS   T 020 7928 5474
*Design, Equipment Hire, Production, Scenery/Set
Construction & Technical Services for Creative
Live Events*
3-5 Valentine Place
London SE1 8QH
F 020 7928 6082
E info@s2events.co.uk
W www.s2events.co.uk

SCENA PRODUCTIONS LLP   T 020 7703 4444
Set Construction
240 Camberwell Road
London SE5 0DP
F 020 7703 7012
E info@scenapro.com
W www.scenapro.com

SCENIC WORKSHOPS LTD   T 0151 933 6677
Baltic Road, Bootle
Liverpool L20 1AW
E info@scenicworkshops.co.uk
W www.scenicworkshops.co.uk

**SCOTT FLEARY
PRODUCTIONS LTD**   T 0870 4441787
Unit 1-4, Vale Industrial Park
170 Rowan Road
London SW16 5BN
F 0870 4448322
E info@scottfleary.com

SET CREATIONS   T 020 7274 2044
Unit 7, Dominion Business Park
Goodwin Road, Edmonton
London N9 0BG
F 020 7738 3099
E info@setcreations.com
W www.setcreations.com

SET CREATIONS LTD   T 020 7274 2044
Unit 14, Studio House
Delamare Road
Cheshunt EN8 9SH
F 01992 625180
E nash@setcreations.com
W www.setcreations.com

SMITH, Paul Don   T 07949 710306
Graffiti Mural Artist. Graphics. Scenery
11A Cadogan Road
Surbiton
Surrey KT6 4DQ
E firedon_1@hotmail.com
W www.pauldonsmith.com

SPICKNELL, Jackie   T 07752 831095
Freelance Scenic Painter
55 Tavistock Street, Luton
Bedfordshire LU1 3UT
E jackie_jackiecool@hotmail.com
W www.jacquelinespicknell.webeden.co.uk

SPLINTER   T 0161 633 6787
Supplier of Touring Theatre Scenery
The Gasworks
Higginshaw Lane
Oldham, Greater Manchester OL1 3LB
F 0161 633 6851
E splintermail@aol.com
W www.splinterscenery.co.uk

**STAGE MANAGEMENT
COMPANY**   T 01274 669259
Audio. Lighting. Production
Unit 12 Commerce Court, Challenge Way
Bradford BD4 8NW
E info@stagemanagementcompany.com
W www.stagemanagementcompany.com

STAGE SYSTEMS   T 01509 611021
*Designers & Suppliers of Modular Staging, Tiering &
Auditorium Seating*
Stage House, Prince William Road
Loughborough LE11 5GU
F 01509 233146
E info@stagesystems.co.uk
W www.stagesystems.co.uk

**STAGECRAFT
PRODUCTION SERVICES**   T 01722 326055
*Hire & Sales of Audio Visual, Lighting, Sound & Staging
for Conferences & Live Events*
F 01202 599900
E hire@cpsgroup.co.uk
W www.cpsgroup.co.uk

**STAGEWORKS WORLDWIDE
PRODUCTIONS**   T 01253 342426
Lighting. Props. Scenery. Sound
525 Ocean Boulevard
Blackpool FY4 1EZ
F 01253 342702
E info@stageworkswwp.com
W www.stageworkswwp.com

STEWART, Helen   T 07887 682186
Theatre Designer
29C Hornsey Rise Gardens
London N19 3PP
E helen@helenstewart.co.uk
W www.helenstewart.co.uk

STORM LIGHTING LTD   T 01483 757211
Warwick House
Monument Way West
Woking, Surrey GU21 5EN
F 01483 757710
E hire@stormlighting.co.uk
W www.stormlighting.co.uk

TOP SHOW   T 01904 750022
Props. Scenery. Conference Specialists
North Lane, Huntington
York YO32 9SU

WELLINGTON SCENIC   T/F 01522 794260
*Full Scenery Design & Build Services, also with
Pantomime Sets for Hire*
Units 1 & 2 Karglen Ind Est
Potterhanworth Road
Branston, Lincoln
Lincolnshire LN4 1HY
T 01636 636625
E info@wellingtonscenic.com
W www.wellingtonscenic.com

WEST, John   T 07753 637451
Art Director. Draughtsman
103 Abbotswood Close
Winyates Green
Redditch, Worcestershire B98 0QF
E johnwest@blueyonder.co.uk
W www.johnwestportfolio.com

T

Television
- BBC Television
- BBC Regional
- Independent

Theatre Producers

Theatre
- Alternative & Community
- Children, Young People & TIE
- English Speaking in Europe
- London
- Outer London,
  Fringe & Venues
- Provincial / Touring
- Puppet Theatre
  Companies
- Repertory (Regional)

BBC TELEVISION

• RIGHTS, LEGAL & BUSINESS AFFAIRS

**BBC Broadcasting House
Zone B, 6th Floor, Portland Place
London W1A 1AA**

Controller of Rights, Legal & Business Affairs	Roger Leatham
Head of Legal	Kathryn Richardson
Head of Contributor Rights	Rob Kirkham
Head of Programme Rights	Jo Korn

• RADIO & MUSIC

**BBC Brock House
4th Floor, 19 Langham Street
London W1W 6BP**

Head of Commercial & Business Development, Rights & Business Affairs	Isabel Begg
Head of Legal & Business Affairs	Emma Trevelyan

Business Affairs Managers

Simon Brown	Lesley Eaton
Sarah Daly	Daniel Miller

• COMEDY & ENTERTAINMENT

**BBC Broadcasting House
Zone A, 7th Floor, Portland Place
London W1A 1AA**

Controller of Business	Tamara Howe
Head of Legal & Business Affairs	Mike Griffiths

Business Affairs Managers

Natalie Alvarado	Susan Dean
Tessa Beckett	Vanessa Wilson
Murray Carrad	

• KNOWLEDGE & DAYTIME (inc. Bristol)

**BBC Broadcasting House
Zone D, 6th Floor, Portland Place
London W1A 1AA**

Controller of Business	Lisa Opie
Head of Legal & Business Affairs	Jennifer Barrett

Business Affairs Managers

Jane Armstrong	James Dundas
Jane Bentham	Phil Gibbs
Angelique Brook	Clive Illenden
Dawn Cleaver	Fiona MacDonald
Andrew Downey	

• DRAMA, FILMS & ACQUISITIONS

**BBC Broadcasting House, Zone A, 7th Floor
Portland Place, London W1A 1AA**

Controller of Business	Nick Betts
Head of Legal & Business Affairs	Zoe Brown

Business Affairs Managers

Kate Boyle	Dan Leon
Helen Giles	Natasha Ross
David Hudson	Livy Sandler
Nadia Lachman	Emmanuel Whinnery

• RLBA, BBC North - Salford (inc. Birmingham)

**BBC MediaCityUK
Quay House
Salford M50 2QH**

Head of Business Affairs & Partnerships	Jessica Yelas

Business Affairs Managers

Simon Ashwood	Penny Woodhams
Mark Bennett	Jessica Yales

• RLBA, BBC Cymru Wales

**Broadcasting House
E2106 Llantristant Road
Llandaff
Cardiff CF5 2YQ**

Head of Rights, Legal & Business Affairs	Donna Spencer

Business Affairs Managers

Ifer Arch	Clare Jenrick
Debbie Cross	Ifty Khan

• RLBA, BBC Scotland & Northern Ireland

**Zone 1.04, 40 Pacific Quay
Glasgow G51 1DA**

**Broadcasting House
2nd Floor Ormeau Avenue
Belfast BT2 8HQ**

Head of Rights & Business Affairs	Alison Denvir

Business Affairs Managers

Suzanne Elrick	Kathleen Magee (NI)
Jane Gilmartin	Claire O'Neill
Kay MacPherson	Annie Paterson

• DRAMA

**BBC Drama Production
4th Floor, BBC Grafton House
379-381 Euston Road
London NW1 3AU
T 020 8743 8000 (Main Switchboard)**

Head of Production	Susy Liddell
Head of Production, Series & Serials	Gordon Ronald
Head of Production UK, Continuing Drama	Nikki Saunders
Creative Director, Drama Production	Katie McAleese

Executive Producers - Drama Production

Sarah Brown	Lisa Osbourne
Phillippa Giles	Anne Pivcevic
Sue Hogg	Jess Pope
Oliver Kent	Hilary Salmon
Elizabeth Kilgarriff	Caroline Skinner
Lorraine Newman	Will Trotter

Executive Producer, EastEnders — Dominic Treadwell-Collins

• COMMISSIONING

Director, BBC Television	Danny Cohen
Controller, Factual Commissioning	Emma Swain
Controller, Drama Commissioning	Ben Stephenson
Head of Independent Drama	Polly Hill
Head of Drama Production UK	Kate Harwood
Commissioning Editor, Drama	Lucy Richer
Acting Controller, BBC Two & BBC Four	Adam Barker

• FACTUAL PRODUCTION

Pacific Quay, Glasgow G51 1DA
T 0141 422 6000

Controller Factual & Daytime
Production — Natalie Humphreys

History & Business – London
Broadcasting House
Portland Place, London W1A 1AA

Head — Dominic Crossley-Holland
History Executives
Chris Granlund — Eamon Hardy

Science – London & Glasgow
Broadcasting House
7th Zone, Zone C
Portland Place
London W1A 1AA

Head — Andrew Cohen (London)

Pacific Quay, Glasgow G51 1DA
T 0141 422 6000

Executives:

Will Aslett (Glasgow)	Jonathan Renouf (London)
Tina Fletcher (London)	Jacqui Smith (Glasgow)
Mark Hedgecoe (Glasgow)	Helen Thomas (London)
Nigel Paterson (London & Glasgow)	

Editor, Horizon — Steve Crabtree (London)

Arts – Glasgow, London & Bristol
Pacific Quay, Glasgow G51 1DA

Broadcasting House
7th Zone, Zone C
Portland Place, London W1A 1AA

Broadcasting House
Whiteladies Road
Bristol BS8 2LR

Head — Jonty Claypole, (based in Glasgow)
Executives

Richard Bright (Glasgow)	Janet Lee (London)
Basil Comely (London)	Franny Moyle (Glasgow))
Tanya Hudson (Glasgow)	John Mullen (London)
Pauline Law (Glasgow)	Mike Poole (Bristol)

Daytime - Cardiff, Bristol, Belfast
Broadcasting House
Llantrisant Road, Llandaff CF5 2YQ

Broadcasting House
Whiteladies Road, Bristol BS8 2LR

Broadcasting House
Ormeau Avenue
Belfast BT2 8HQ

Head — Jeff Anderson (Cardiff)
Executives
Paul Connelly (Belfast) — Karen Plumb (Bristol)
Roger Farrant (Bristol)

Documentaries – London, Bristol & Glasgow
Broadcasting House
7th Zone, Zone C
Portland Place, London W1A 1AA

Broadcasting House
Whiteladies Road
Bristol BS8 2LR

Pacific Quay
Glasgow G51 1DA

Head — Aysha Rafaele
Executives

Simon Ford (London)	Fergus O'Brien (London)
Sacha Mirzoeff (Bristol)	Clare Sillery (London)

Natural History Unit – Bristol
Broadcasting House
Whiteladies Road
Bristol BS8 2LR

Head — Wendy Darke
Executives

Vanessa Berlowitz	Bill Lyons
Julian Hector	Tim Martin
James Honeyborne	Tim Scoones
Jonny Keeling	Jo Skinner

Features – Bristol, Cardiff, Belfast, London
Broadcasting House
Whiteladies Road
Bristol BS8 2LR

Broadcasting House
7th Zone, Zone C
Portland Place, London W1A 1AA

Broadcasting House
Ormeau Avenue, Belfast BT2 8HQ

Broadcasting House
Llantristant Road
Llandaff, Cardiff CF5 2YQ

Executives
Robi Dutta (Bristol)   Joe Mather (Cardiff)
Bill Lyons (Bristol)

Religion & Ethics - Salford
Dock House, BBC MediaCityUK
Salford M50 2LH
T 0161 836 0020

Head   Aaqil Ahmed

Executives
Christine Morgan   David Taviner
Juliian Mercer

Consumer & Live
Broadcasting House, 7th Zone
Zone C, Portland Place, London W1A 1AA

Creative Director, Factual Production   Lisa Auden
Editor, Watchdog   Alan Holland

Is your CV up-to-date?

Top tips for promoting yourself!

- **Keep your credits up-to-date**
  An absolute must – always take responsibility for updating your own profile, as and when you gain credits and new skills.

- **Review your skills**
  Add new skills as they are learnt; remove old skills that you can no longer complete. The more skilled you are, the more you maximise your marketability.

- **Make sure your professional training appears**
  Also, remember to update this section as you undertake further training across your career.

- **Update your photograph**
  Ensure that you are representing yourself as you would now appear at an audition.

- **Add multimedia**
  Make sure casting professionals see and hear just how good you are with video and audio clips.

The One Show
Media Centre at
New Broadcasting House
London W1A 1AA

Editor   Sandy Smith
Executives
Michael Armit   Gareth Collet

• CHILDREN

Director   Joe Godwin
Controller, CBBC   Cheryl Taylor
Controller, CBeebies   Kay Benbow
CBBC Head of Production   Helen Bullough
Head of Children's Programmes,
  Scotland   Sara Harkins
Head of CBeebies Production, Animations
  & Aquisitions   Alison Stewart

• CLASSICAL MUSIC & TV PERFORMANCE BBC MUSIC TELEVISION

Head of Commissioning, Music & Events TV (All
  Production In-House & Indie)   Jan Younghusband
Commissioning Editor
  (All Production)   Greg Sanderson
Business Affairs (Music)   Jason Emerton
Head of Music Television
  (BBC In-House London)   Mark Cooper
Head of Music Television
  (BBC In-House Wales)   Paul Bullock
Head of Events (BBC London)   Phil Dolling
Assistant to Jan Younghusband   Sarah Hayes

•SPORT

Director of Sport   Barbara Slater
Head of TV Sport   Philip Bernie
Head of Interactive & Formula 1 Ben Gallop
Head of Sports News &
  BBC Radio Sport   Richard Burgess
Head of Production   Paula Stringer
HR Partner   Andrea Wilkinson
Head of Communications,
  Sport & 5 Live   Vicky Owens
Finance Partner   Daniel Chaffer

• NEW WRITING

BBC Writersroom
BBC Grafton House
379-381 Euston Road
London NW1 3AU
T 020 8743 8000 (Main Switchboard)
E writersroom@bbc.co.uk
W www.bbc.co.uk/writersroom

Creative Director   Kate Rowland
Development Producers
Abigail Gonda   Henry Swindell

BBC BIRMINGHAM

The Mailbox
Birmingham B1 1AY
F 0121 567 6875   **T 0121 567 6767**

English Regions

Controller, English Regions	David Holdsworth
Head of New Media Services, English Regions	Laura Ellis
Chief Operating Officer, English Regions	Ian Hughes
Head of Communications, BBC South	Tamsin Morgan
Adviser - Accountability BBC Trust	Lydia Thomas
Head of Regional & Local Programmes, West Midlands	David Jennings
Head of Business Development	Tommy Nagra

Drama

BBC Birmingham TV Drama Village
Archibald House
1059 Bristol Road
Selly Oak
Birmingham B29 6LT   **T 0121 567 7417**

Executive Producer	Will Trotter

BBC BRISTOL

PAN-UK Production Hub

Acting Head of Features	Jeff Anderson
Head of Daytime, UK	Jeff Anderson
Managing Editor, Returning Series & Features	Robi Dutta
Executive Producers Features	
Bill Lyons	Simon Shaw
Editor, Features	Liz Rumbold
Executive Producer, Daytime	Karen Plumb
Executive Producer, Arts	Mike Poole
Executive Producer, Documentaries	Sacha Mirzoeff
Head of Natural History Unit	Wendy Darke
Creative Director, Natural History	Mike Gunton
Executive Producers, Natural History	
Vanessa Berlowitz	Jonny Keeling
Julian Hector	Tim Martin
James Honeyborne	Tim Scoones
Editor Springwatch/ Autumn Watch	Rosemary Edwards
Head of Production Talent, Natural History, Features, Documentaries & Daytime	Christopher Hutchins

BBC LONDON

2nd Floor
Egton Wing Broadcasting House
10-22 Portland Place
London W1A 1AA   **T 020 8743 8000**

BBC London News

TV: The Politics Show
Radio: BBC London Radio 94.9FM
Online: BBC London online

Head of BBC London	Michael MacFarlane
TV Editor	Antony Dore
Editor, Inside Out	Dippy Chaudhary
Managing Editor, BBC Radio London 94.9FM	David Robey
Political Editor	Tim Donovan
Editor, BBC London Online	Claire Timms

BBC NORTH WEST

New Broadcasting House
Oxford Road
Manchester M60 1SJ

W www.bbc.co.uk/manchester
W www.bbc.co.uk/liverpool
W www.bbc.co.uk/lancashire   **T 0161 200 2020**

Religion & Ethics

Head of Religion & Ethics & Commissioning Editor for Religion TV	Aaqil Ahmed
Executive Editor & Head of Radio, Religion & Ethics	Christine Morgan
Head of Television Religion	Julian Mercer

Regional & Local Programmes

Head of Regional & Local Programmes, North West	Aziz Rashid
Head of Regional & Local Programmes, North East & Cumbria	Phil Roberts

BBC SOUTH

Havelock Road
Southampton SO14 7PU   **T 023 8022 6201**

Head of Regional & Local Programmes	Jason Horton
TV News Editor	Lee Desty
Managing Editor, BBC Radio Oxford & BBC Radio Berkshire	Marianne Bell
Managing Editor, BBC Solent	Sarah Miller
Deputy Editor, BBC Radio Berkshire	Duncan McLarty

BBC SOUTH EAST

The Great Hall Arcade
Mount Pleasant Road
Tunbridge Wells
Kent TN1 1QQ   **T 01892 670000**

Head of Regional & Local Programmes,
  BBC South East   Michael Macfarlane
Managing Editor,
  BBC Radio Kent   Gordon Davidson
Managing Editor, BBC Radio Surrey &
  BBC Radio Sussex   Sara David
Editor, BBC South East Today   Quentin Smith
Editor, Inside Out   Linda Bell
Assistant Editor, Politics Show Dan Fineman

BBC SOUTH WEST

Seymour Road
Mannamead
Plymouth PL3 5BD   **T 01752 229201**

Head of BBC South West   Leo Devine
Acting Editor, TV Current Affairs Sam Smith
Output Editor   Simon Read

BBC WEST

Broadcasting House
Whiteladies Road
Bristol BS8 2LR   **T 0117 973 2211**

For the latest local news and information about your area, visit our websites:

Bristol: www.bbc.co.uk/bristol
Gloucestershire: www.bbc.co.uk/gloucestershire
Somerset: www.bbc.co.uk/somerset
Wiltshire/
Swindon: www.bbc.co.uk/wiltshire
Points West: www.bbc.co.uk/pointswest

Head of Regional & Local Programmes,
  including BBC West, BBC Radio Bristol,
  BBC Somerset, BBC Gloucestershire,
  BBC Wiltshire   Lucio Mesquita
Editor, TV News   Neil Bennett

BBC SCOTLAND

40 Pacific Quay
Glasgow G51 1DA
W www.bbc.co.uk/scotland   **T 0141 422 6000**

Scottish Executive Board

Director, Scotland   Ken MacQuarrie
Head of Programmes &
  Services   Donalda MacKinnon
Head of Public Policy   Ian Small
Chief Operating Officer   Alan Dickson
Head of Commonwealth Games,
  BBC   Bruce Malcolm
Head of Talent &
  Editorial Operations   Donald-Iain Brown
Head of HR & Development   Wendy Aslett
Head of Service, BBC Alba   Margaret Mary Murray
Head of Marketing &
  Communications   Mairead Ferguson
Controller Factual Network Productions,
  Pan UK   Natalie Humphreys
Head of Strategy   Catherine Smith
Head of News & Current Affairs John Boothman
Commissioning Editor, Television &
  Head of Sport   Ewan Angus
Head of Radio, Scotland   Jeff Zycinski

Genre Heads

Service Editor, BBC Alba   Marion MacKinnon
Head of Factual   Andrea Miller
Head of Drama, Television   Christopher Aird
Head of Drama, Radio   Bruce Young
Creative Director, Documentaries
  & Acting Head of New Media,
  Learning & Outreach   Neil McDonald
Creative Director, Children's Scotland Sara Harkins
Head of Entertainment & Events Eileen Herlihy
Head of New Media, Learning &
  Outreach   Matthew Lee
Director, BBC Scottish Symphony
  Orchestra   Gavin Reid

Commissioning

Executive Editor, Entertainment
  Commissioning   Alan Tyler
Commissioning Executive, BBC Daytime,
  Scotland & Northern Ireland   Jo Street

BBC Scotland provides television and radio programmes for Scotland and the UK networks as well as online and interactive content. Based in Glasgow's digital headquarters, there are also centres throughout Scotland which includes City Halls, the home of the BBC Scottish Symphony Orchestra.

Aberdeen

Broadcasting House
Beechgrove Terrace
Aberdeen AB15 5ZT   **T 01224 625233**

Dumbarton

Dumbarton Studios, Studio Way
Dumbarton G82 2QW   **T 01389 736666**

Dumfries
Elmbank, Lover's Walk
Dumfries DG1 11NZ T 01387 268008

Dundee
Nethergate Centre
4th Floor, 66 Nethergate
Dundee DD1 4ER T 01382 202481

Edinburgh
The Tun, 4 Jackson's Entry
111 Holyrood Road
Edinburgh EH8 8PJ T 0131 557 5888

Glasgow
Glasgow City Halls
(BBC Scottish Symphony Orchestra)
87 Albion Street
Glasgow G1 1NQ T 0141 552 0909

Inverness
7 Culduthel Road
Inverness IV2 4AD T 01463 720720

Orkney
Castle Street, Kirkwall
Orkney KW15 1DF T 01856 873939

Portree
Clydesdale Bank Buildings
Somerled Square
Isle of Skye IV51 9EH T 01478 612005

Selkirk
Unit 1, Ettrick Riverside
Dunsdale Road
Selkirk TD7 5EB T 01750 724567

Shetland
Pitt Lane, Lerwick
Shetland ZE1 0DW T 01595 694747

Stornoway
Radio nan Gaidheal
Rosebank
52 Church Street
Isle of Lewis HS1 2LS T 01851 705000

BBC CYMRU/WALES
Broadcasting House
Llandaff
Cardiff CF5 2YQ T 029 2032 2000

Director Rhodri Talfan-Davies
Head of Programmes &
  Services (Welsh) Sian Gwynedd
Head of Programmes &
  Services (English) Adrian Davies
Head of Marketing, Communications &
  Audiences Richard Thomas
Head of News & Current Affairs Mark O'Callaghan
Lead HR Business Partner for Wales Wendy Rees
Chief Operating Officer Gareth Powell
Head of Drama Faith Penhale
Head of Sport Geoff Williams
Head of Factual & Music Judith Winnan
Editor, Radio Wales Steve Austins
Editor, Radio Cymru Betsan Powys
Editor, Interactive Learning Iain Tweedale

BBC NORTHERN IRELAND
Belfast
BBC Broadcasting House
Ormeau Avenue
Belfast BT2 8HQ T 028 9033 8000
W www.bbc.co.uk/ni

Director, BBC Northern Ireland Peter Johnston
Head of BBC NI Productions Steve Carson
Head of Drama Stephen Wright
Head of News Kathleen Carragher
Chief Operating Officer Mark Taylor
Head of Corporate & Community Affairs Mark Adair
Head of Marketing, Communications &
  Audiences Kathy Martin
Head of TV Current Affairs Jeremy Adams
Editor, Sport Shane Glynn
Head of Local TV Commissioning Susan Lovell
Head of Radio Ulster Fergus Keeling
Editor, Radio Foyle Larry Deeny

BBC Radio Ulster
BBC Broadcasting House
Ormeau Avenue
Belfast BT2 8HQ T 028 9033 8000
W www.bbc.co.uk/radioulster

BBC Radio Foyle
8 Northland Road
Londonderry BT48 7JD T 028 7126 2244

CHANNEL 4 TELEVISION CORPORATION
London Office

124 Horseferry Road
London SW1P 2TX
Textphone 020 7396 8691   **T 020 7396 4444**

Non-Executive Directors
Monica Burch	Stewart Purvis
Lord Terry Burns (Chairman)	MT Rainy
Alicja Lesniak	Richard Rivers
Paul Potts	Josie Rourke
Mark Price	

Executives / Board Members
Chief Executive	David Abraham
Chief Creative	Officer Jay Hunt
Sales Director	Jonathan Allan
Director of Audience Technologies & Insight	Gill Whitehead
Director of Marketing & Communications	Dan Brooke
Director of Human Resources	Diane Herbert
Controller of Film & Drama	Tessa Ross, CBE
Group Finance Director	Glyn Isherwood
Director of Stage & Technology	Keith Underwood
Director of Commercial Affairs	Martin Baker

Heads of Departments
Director of Planning	Paula Carter
Director of Commercial Affairs	Martin Baker
Channel Manager	Richard Brent
Director, Commercial & Business Development	Sarah Rose
Head of Business Assurance	Rob Mattey
Head of Corporate Relations	Sophie Jones
Director, Creative Diversity	Stuart Cosgrove
Head of Distribution & Broadcast Technology	David Dorans
Head of Comedy	Phil Clarke
Head of Entertainment	Justin Gorman
Head of Corporate Services	Julie Kortens
Head of Factual Entertainment	Liam Humphreys
Controller, Film & Drama	Tessa Ross, CBE
Director, Finance	Glyn Isherwood
Controller, Legal & Compliance	Prash Naik
Head of News & Current Affairs	Dorothy Byrne
Head of Online	Richard Davidson-Houston
Head of Airtime & Ad Operations	Tanya O'Sullivan
Head of Specialist Factual	Ralph Lee
Chief Information Officer	Kevin Gallagher
Chief Technology Officer	TBC
Head of Agency Sales	Damon Lafford

Controller, Press & Publicity	Jane Fletcher
Head of Production, 4Creative	Mary Seiler
Head of Music	Mark Adams
Head of Film4	Julia Wrigley
Head of Business Affairs, Film4 & Scripted	Geraldine Atlee
Head of Production, Film4	Tracey Josephs
Head of Rights	Jeremy Kimberlin

CHANNEL 5 BROADCASTING LTD

10 Lower Thames Street
London EC3R 6EN
W www.channel5.com   **T 020 8612 7000**

Chairman	Richard Desmond
Chief Operating Officer	Paul Dunthorne
Director of Programmes	Ben Frow
PA to Chief Operating Officer & Director of Programmes	Anna Humphries
Head of Scheduling	Craig Morris
Commissioning Editor, Entertainment, Daytime & Soaps	Greg Barnett
Head of Children's	Jessica Symons
Aquisitions & Channel Manager	Sebastian Cardwell
Head of Acquisitions	Kate Keenan
Creative Director	Rich Thrift
Head of Campaign & Pictures	Nicola Moran
Commercial Sales Director	Nick Bampton
Director of Legal & Commercial Affairs	Marcus Lee
Group Finance Director	Rob Sanderson
General Counsel	Marcus Lee
Head of Channel Management: Channel 5, 5*, 5USA, Channel 5 + 24	Craig Morris

INDEPENDENT TELEVISION NEWS

200 Gray's Inn Road
London WC1X 8XZ   **T 020 7833 3000**

Chief Executive	John Hardie
Editor, ITV News	Geoff Hill
Editor, Channel 4 News	Ben De Pear

ITV PLC
Registered Office

The London Television Centre
Upper Ground, London SE1 9LT
F 020 7849 9344
W www.itv.com   **T 020 7157 3000**

Board of Directors & Management Team

Chairman	Archie Norman
Chief Executive	Adam Crozier
Senior Independent Director	Andy Haste
Group Finance Director	Ian Griffiths
Group Communications & Corporate Affairs Director	Mary Fagan
Director of Television	Peter Fincham
Group Legal Director	Andrew Garard
Managing Director of Commercial & Online	Fru Hazlitt
Managing Director	Kevin Lygo
Director of Strategy & Technology	Simon Pitts

Non-Executive Directors

Sir Peter Bazalgette	Baroness Lucy Nelville-Rolfe
Roger Faxon	John Ormerod

Casting Directors at ITV Studios

Manchester

Casting Director	Gennie Radcliffe
Assistant Casting Director	Katy Belshaw

Leeds

Casting Director	Faye Styring
Casting Assistant	Amy Hill

If you would like one of the casting teams to cover your performance in a stage production, please e-mail casting@itv.com including your name, the theatre and the dates.

ITV ANGLIA
Head Office

**Anglia House
Norwich NR1 3JG
Twitter: @ITVAnglia
E anglianews@itv.com
W www.itv.com/anglia   T 0844 8816900**

East of England: Weekday & Weekend

Regional News Centres
Cambridge

**Link House, Station Road
Great Shelford
Cambridge CB22 5LT   T 0844 8816985 (News)**

Northampton

**Portfolio Innovation Centre
University of Northampton
St George's Avenue
Northampton NN2 6JD   T 0844 8816974**

ITV BREAKFAST

**London Television Centre
Upper Ground, London SE1 9TT
F 020 7827 7001
W www.itv.com/daybreak   T 020 7827 7000**

Good Morning Britain

Editor	Neil Thompson
Deputy Editor Programme	Annemarie Leahy
Deputy Editor News	Simon Cole
Head of Features	Corinne Bishop
Heads of Planning	
Terry O'Sullivan	Caroline Sigley
Head of Entertainment	Amy Vosburgh
Day Editors	
Nick Caldon	Vivek Sharma
Night Editors	
Owen Masters	Daniel Robinson
Chief Sub Editor	Mark Kiff
Head of Graphics	Fiona Skinner
Production Executive	Helen Killeen

Lorraine

Editor	Sue Walton
Series Editor	Pauline Haase
Acting Head of Features	Helen Addis

ITV CHANNEL TELEVISION LTD
Registered Office

**The Television Centre
La Pouquelaye, St Helier
Jersey JE1 3ZD, Channel Islands
F 01534 816817
W www.channelonline.tv   T 01534 816816**

Channel Islands: Weekday and Weekend

Managing Director/Head of News Programmes	Karen Rankine
Programme Editor	India Camm
Director of Resources & Transmission/Ops Manager	Kevin Banner

ITV MERIDIAN

ITV Meridian is part of ITV Plc

**Fusion 3, 1200 Parkway
Whiteley, Hants PO15 7AD
F 0844 8812074   T 0844 8812000**

Meridian Board

Regional Sales Manager	Matt Corse

Executives

Finance Manager	Malcolm Beasley
Head of News	Robin Britton

ITV TYNE TEES & ITV BORDER

Television House
The Watermark
Gateshead NE11 9SZ   **T 0844 8815000**

Teesside News Gathering
6 Belasis Court
Billingham
Cleveland TS23 4AZ
E tttvnews@itv.com   **T 0844 8815000**

North East and North Yorkshire: Weekday and Weekend

Border TV Regional Offices

ITV Border, 1 Clifford Court
Cooper Way, Parkhouse
Carlisle CA3 0JG   **T 0844 8815885**

Managing Editor   Catherine Houlihan

ITV Border, Room P2.08
The Scottish Parliament
Holyrood
Edinburgh EH99 1SP

ITV Border
7 Bakehouse Close
Edinburgh EH8 8DD

ITV Border
Ettrick Riverside
Dunsdale Road, Selkirk
Selkirkshire TD7 5EB

Executive Chair ITV   Adam Crozier
Head of News   Michaela Byrne
Managing Director, SignPost   Malcolm Wright

ITV CYMRU WALES

3 Assembly Square
Brittania Quay, Cardiff Bay CF10 4PL
E wales@itv.com
W www.itv.com/wales   **T 0844 8810375**

Wales: All week

Head of News & Programmes   Phil Henfrey

ITV WEST & ITV WESTCOUNTRY

470 Bath Road
Bristol BS4 3HG   **T 0844 8812345**

Head of News   Sarah Norman

ITV YORKSHIRE

The Television Centre
Leeds LS3 1JS
F 0113 244 5107
W www.itv.com   **T 0113 222 7000**

London Office

London Television Centre
Upperground, London SE1 9LT   **T 020 7157 3000**

Executives

Head of News   Margaret Emsley
Creative Director ITV Studios   John Whiston

S4C

Parc Tŷ Glas
Llanishen, Cardiff CF14 5DU
F 029 2075 4444
E s4c@s4c.co.uk
W www.s4c.co.uk   **T 029 2074 7444**

The Welsh Fourth Channel Authority

Chair   Huw Jones

Authority Members

Dr Carol Bell   Aled Eirug
Elan Closs Stephens   Rheon Tomos
John Davies   Marian Wyn Jones

Senior Staff

Chief Executive   Ian Jones
Content Director   Dafydd Rhys
Director of Communications,
  Marketing & Partnerships   Garffild Lloyd Lewis
Director of Finance   Kathryn Morris
Director of Corporate & Commercial   Elin Morris

SKY SATELLITE TELEVISION BRITISH SKY BROADCASTING LTD (BSkyB)

Grant Way, Isleworth
Middlesex TW7 5QD
W www.sky.com/corporate   **T 020 7705 3000**

Chief Executive   Jeremy Darroch
Chief Financial Officer & MD,
  Commercial Businesses   Andrew Griffith
Managing Director,
  Sales & Marketing   Stephen Van Rooyen
Managing Director, Content   Sophie Turner Laing
Director for People   Deborah Baker
Group Director of
  Corporate Affairs   Graham McWilliam
General Counsel   James Conyers
Managing Director, Sky Sports   Barney Francis
Managing Director, Product Design &
  Development   Alun Webber
Chief Technology Officer   Didier Lebrat
Managing Director, Customer Group   Chris Stylianou
Group Director of Strategy &
  Business Development   Mia Fyfield

STV

Glasgow Office

Pacific Quay
Glasgow G51 1PQ
W www.stv.tv
T 0141 300 3000

Aberdeen Office

Television Centre
Craigshaw Business Park
West Tullos
Aberdeen AB12 3QH
W www.stv.tv
T 01224 848848

London Office

2nd Floor, Bewlay House
2 Swallow Place
London W1B 2AE
W www.stv.tv
T 020 7494 5747

Director of Channels	Bobby Hain
Head of News & Current Affairs	Gordon MacMillan
Chief Executive	Rob Woodward
Director of Content	Alan Clements
Deputy Director of Content	Liam Hamilton
Head of Entertainment	Gary Chippington
Head of Drama	Margaret Enefer

UTV MEDIA PLC

Head Office
Ormeau Road, Belfast BT7 1EB
E info@u.tv
W www.utvmedia.com
T 028 9032 8122

Based in the UK & Ireland, UTV Media plc incorporates Broadcasting & Digital Media Assets across its Radio & Television Divisions

Directors

Chairman	Richard Huntingford
Group Chief Executive	John McCann
Board Members	
Andy Anson	Stephen Kirkpatrick
Helen Kirkpatrick	Coline McConville

Officers

Group Commercial Director	Nigel Robbins
Group HR Director	Mairead Regan
Group Finance Director	Norman McKeown
Managing Director, UTV Television	Michael Wilson
News Editor	Chris Hagan
Head of Communications	Orla McKibbin
Managing Director, GB Radio	Scott Taunton

Theatre Producers

What is a theatre producer?

A theatre producer is someone who oversees and organises a theatre show. They will find, or arrange for other professionals to find, a suitable script, design, director and cast for each production, while also managing all finances and marketing.

How should I use these listings?

Theatre producers tend to use casting directors to put forward suitable actors for the parts in forthcoming productions, but you could also try approaching them yourself.

Rather than sending your CV and headshot to every producer listed, it would be best to do some research first in order to target your search. You need to decide what type of work you want to do first, as there is no need to waste your time and the producer's time sending your CV to unsuitable companies. Then find out what each company has produced in the past, what they are currently working on and if possible what they are considering producing in the future, and only send your CV to those most relevant to the roles you want to play.

Don't forget to include a covering letter which states why you are contacting this producer in particular: this could be because you feel you are perfect for a particular role in their next production, for example. Personalising and targeting your correspondence in this way gives you the best chance of your CV being considered in a favourable light.

How should I approach theatre producers?

You should contact theatre producers by post or e-mail only. We would advise against calling them, especially when approaching them for the first time. Address your correspondence to an individual within the company, as this demonstrates that you have done your research. If you are unsure as to the best method of applying to theatre producers, as with other casting professionals it is safest to post your CV and headshot in the traditional way rather than e-mailing it.

Remember to put your name and telephone number on the back of the photo in case it gets separated from your CV. It would be a good idea to include a SAE big enough to contain your photo if you send hard copy and with sufficient postage to increase your chances of getting a reply. Do not enclose your showreel but you

can mention that you have one available in your covering letter, and if the producer is interested in viewing it they will contact you.

When should I approach theatre producers?

Listen to industry news and have a look at theatre producers' websites for forthcoming production details. The casting process usually takes place around three months prior to rehearsals, so bear this in mind when you are writing your covering letter.

How do I become a theatre producer?

The best way to learn about producing is to work in producing. Internships are a good way to get to grips with the industry; research the theatre producers listed over the following pages by checking their websites' jobs sections for vacancies. Remember to make sure they actually work in the area you are interested in before making contact. You should also try to build up a good general knowledge of the industry by going to see as many theatrical productions as you can and keeping track of which producers work on which types of shows.

CASE STUDY

Metal Rabbit was set up in 2012 (www.metalrabbit.org.uk) by producer George Warren. Martha Rose Wilson joined the company as producer in 2014. Metal Rabbit's mission is to create visceral, high quality and stimulating theatre in London and beyond. They have a particular interest in new and undiscovered work.

The role of the producers at Metal Rabbit is fairly standard within the industry. Our chief foci are discovering, creating and bringing together projects that we are passionate about. That includes putting together production teams, financing and marketing projects and generally providing the impetus to get a show off the ground. Most recently Metal Rabbit produced *Johnny Got His Gun* and it is perhaps useful to take this show as an example of how we work.

An interesting note to make about *Johnny Got His Gun* was the way in which the project came about. Having cast uber talented actor Jack Holden on Ernest Hemmingway's *Fiesta: The Sun Also Rises* at Trafalgar Studios, (a co-production between Metal Rabbit and Oiffy), we were keen to work with him again. We spent quite a lot of time looking for a script together that would provide Jack with a great part to showcase his talents as well as give Metal Rabbit the opportunity to produce a quality piece of theatre. After looking for a while we found *Johnny Got His Gun* and decided it was the right project. Jack was then involved in the process of finding a director and had a general view over the entire production process.

The way in which the project came about is not what we would call typical – just as often we start with wanting to tackle a particular subject matter or script as wanting to collaborate with a specific actor - but it is a demonstration that there can be more to the relationship between actor and producer than simply a one way street, with the actor the supplicant and the producer with all the power. Theatre is the ultimate collaborative medium, and often the best parts for an actor grow out a continuing dialogue, not simply coming onto a project that is already set up. It is all very well to dream of being cast in the next West End hit, but often doing a smaller show with the producer who knows your abilities and wants to base a piece of work around them is the better showcase for the future.

That is not to say that actors should take any work that is offered to them, but it often worth considering whether working with people you admire or would like a continuing relationship with could be worth taking smaller or less well paid roles. It is also a demonstration that having established a working relationship with a producer it is always worth keeping tabs on what they are doing; even if they do not have work for you themselves they can be your biggest champions. The fringe producers and directors of today are quite possibly the West End impresarios and artistic directors of tomorrow, and as in all industries they take their colleagues with them. The process is as much about an actor talent spotting a director or producer they believe has talent as the other way around.

London is a superb place to live and work in terms of theatre – there are brilliant shows and opportunities galore – but it is also, notoriously, a saturated market. It's an obvious point but an important one – anything you can do to make your show stand out is a massive bonus. Increasingly touring our productions has become a vital component of our business model as a

way to insure ourselves against a difficult London run. It is also something that we immensely enjoy and consider to be a duty of those companies that are able; theatre has a tendency to be London-centric and we have often found captive audiences in the farthest flung reaches of the UK.

Luckily for us *Johnny Got His Gun* is an eminently 'tourable' piece (being a one-man show and having no discernible set helps hugely!) When we are considering actors, their willingness to tour is always a factor. It is expensive to recast and re-rehearse for a tour, and we would always prefer to cast actors who are willing to go on the road. The realities of touring a show are that it is often tiring and relentless work, and an actor has to really believe in the benefits of the work to sustain the level of their performance. The stress of touring also means that there is no room for divas. Believe us when we say that there have been plenty of times when two actors are similar in ability but one is simply more hassle and does not get the job. A balance has to be found between knowing what is needed to produce the optimum performance and a recognition of the realities of theatre. Getting yourself a bit more knowledge of what is involved in other roles in theatre is an invaluable asset in knowing when to dig your heels in over an issue and when to let it go for the good of the production.

When it comes to contacting a producer our first tip would be do your research. We recently had an email congratulating us on a Metal Rabbit show someone had seen and loved, which hadn't yet opened! This is not a great start but sending project ideas, CVs or scripts that you think may be of interest, can be. We receive a lot of potential projects but we always endeavour to read it all – sooner or later – and, again, anything that makes your work stand out will make us more likely to sit up and pay attention. Do invite producers to read-throughs and workshops and do introduce yourselves to us at any upcoming Metal Rabbit shows – you never know where your next great project is going to come from so be open, enthusiastic and ambitious.

Most of all, our advice is to be polite and persistent. We producers are humans too, often overworked and under-organised, so if we do not get back all of the time it is as likely to be because we are trying to stop our set falling down as that we are not interested. It can be frustrating when you are not getting replies, but a positive attitude is vital. And do chase us up every now and again, we do not always have parts available at the time but we plan to do many more shows in the coming years!

10TH PLANET PRODUCTIONS
T/F 020 8442 2659
75 Woodland Gardens, London N10 3UD
E admin@10thplanetproductions.com
W www.10thplanetproductions.com

1505
T 020 7112 8750
3rd Floor, 20 Bedford Street
London WC2E 9HP
E hello@weare1505.co.uk
W www.weare1505.co.uk

30 BIRD PRODUCTIONS
T 01223 403362
Twitter: @30Bird
Cambridge Junction, Clifton Way
Cambridge CB1 7GX
E info@30bird.org
W www.30bird.org

ACORN ENTERTAINMENTS LTD
T 01285 644622
PO Box 64, Cirencester, Glos GL7 5YD
F 01285 642291
E info@acornents.co.uk
W www.acornents.co.uk

ACT PRODUCTIONS LTD
T 020 7484 5292
Golden Cross House, 8 Duncannon Street
London WC2N 4JF
E info@actproductions.co.uk
W www.actproductions.co.uk

ACTORS PLATFORM LTD
Showcases for Professional Actors
Based in Central London
E melissa@actorsplatform.com
W www.actorsplatform.com

ACTOR'S TEMPLE THE
T 020 3004 4537
Basement, 13-14 Warren Street
London W1T 5LG
E info@actorstemple.com
W www.actorstemple.com

ACTORS TOURING COMPANY
T 020 7930 6014
Contact: Nick Williams (Executive Director)
Institute of Contemporary Arts (ICA)
12 Carlton House Terrace
London SW1Y 5AH
E atc@atctheatre.com
W www.atctheatre.com

AGENCY:105
T 020 7205 2316
Twitter: @agency105
INC Artists Ltd, 90 Long Acre
Covent Garden
London WC2E 9RZ
E chris@international-collective.com
W www.agency105.com

AJTC THEATRE COMPANY
T/F 01483 232795
28 Rydes Hill Crescent, Guildford
Surrey GU2 9UH
W www.ajtctheatre.co.uk

AMBASSADOR THEATRE GROUP
T 020 7534 6100
39-41 Charing Cross Road
London WC2H 0AR
F 020 7534 6109
E ccrreception@theambassadors.com
W www.atgtickets.com

ANTIC DISPOSITION
T 020 7284 0760
4A Oval Road, London NW1 7EB
E info@anticdisposition.co.uk
W www.anticdisposition.co.uk

AOD (ACTORS OF DIONYSUS)
T/F 01273 673691
Twitter: @aodtheatre
25 St Lukes Road, Brighton BN2 9ZD
E info@actorsofdionysus.com
W www.actorsofdionysus.com

APROPOS PRODUCTIONS LTD
T 020 7739 2857
53 Greek Street, London W1D 3DR
E info@aproposltd.com
W www.aproposltd.com

ARCADE PRODUCTIONS LTD
Contact: Henry Filloux-Bennett, Stephen Makin,
Nick Rogers, Kellie Spooner (Producers)
418 St John Street, Angel
London EC1V 4NJ
E info@arcadeproductions.co.uk
W www.arcadeproductions.co.uk

ARDEN ENTERTAINMENT
T 020 7395 5433
Ambassadors Theatre, West Street
London WC2H 9ND
E douglas@arden-entertainment.co.uk
W www.arden-entertainment.co.uk

ARIA ENTERTAINMENT
T 07947 074887
7 Northiam, Cromer Street
London WC1H 8LB
E info@aria-entertainment.com
W www.aria-entertainment.com

ASH PRODUCTIONS LIVE LTD
T 020 8655 7656
UK & International Theatre Producers
3B Nettlefold Place, West Norwood
London SE27 0JW
E antony@ashproductionslive.com
W www.ashproductionsliveltd.com

ASHTON GROUP THEATRE THE
T 01229 430636
The Cooks, 104 Abbey Road
Barrow-in-Furness, Cumbria LA14 5QR
E theashtongroup@btconnect.com
W www.ashtongroup.co.uk

ATTIC THEATRE COMPANY (LONDON) LTD
T 020 8640 6800
Mitcham Library, 157 London Road
Mitcham CR4 2YR
E info@attictheatrecompany.com
W www.attictheatrecompany.com

AVVA LAFF! PRODUCTIONS
T 07798 692373
Family Entertainment Shows. Comedy.
Children's Theatre
10B Harcourt Road, Windsor
Berkshire SL4 5NB
E jane@avvalaff.co.uk
W www.avvalaff.co.uk

BEE & BUSTLE ENTERPRISES
T 020 8450 0371
32 Exeter Road, London NW2 4SB
F 020 8450 1057
E info@beeandbustle.co.uk
W www.beeandbustle.co.uk

BIRMINGHAM STAGE COMPANY THE
T 020 7437 3391
Contact: Neal Foster (Actor/Manager), Philip Compton
(Executive Producer), Peter Holand (General Manager)
Suite 228, The Linen Hall
162 Regent Street, London W1B 5TB
F 020 7437 3395
E info@birminghamstage.com
W www.birminghamstage.com

BIRMINGHAM STAGE COMPANY THE   T 0121 605 5116
Contact: Neal Foster (Actor/Manager)
The Old Rep Theatre, Station Street
Birmingham B5 4DY
BO 0800 3587070
E info@birminghamstage.com
W www.birminghamstage.com

BLUE BOX ENTERTAINMENT LTD   T 020 7395 7520
Top Floor, 80-81 St Martin's Lane, London WC2N 4AA
F 020 3292 1699
E info@newbluebox.com
W www.newbluebox.com

BLUE STAR PRODUCTIONS   T 020 7836 6220
Contact: Barrie Stacey, Keith Hopkins
7-8 Shaldon Mansions, 132 Charing Cross Road
London WC2H 0LA
E bluestar.london.2000@gmail.com

BORDER CROSSINGS   T 020 8829 8928
13 Bankside, Enfield EN2 8BN
F 020 8366 5239
E info@bordercrossings.org.uk
W www.bordercrossings.org.uk

BOTELLO, Catalina   T 07939 060434
48 New Cavendish Street, London W1G 8TG
E contact@outoftheboxproductions.org
W www.outoftheboxproductions.org

BRITISH THEATRE SEASON IN MONACO   T 020 8455 3278
1 Hogarth Hill, London NW11 6AY
E mail@montecarlotheatre.co.uk
W www.montecarlotheatre.com

BROOKE, Nick LTD   T 020 7240 3901
3rd Floor, 62 Shaftesbury Avenue, London W1D 6LT
F 020 7494 4905
E nick@nickbrooke.com
W www.nickbrooke.com

BRUNJES, Emma PRODUCTIONS LTD   T 020 7820 9332
37 Peninsula Heights, 93 Albert Embankment
London SE1 7TY
E info@emmabrunjesproductions.com
W www.emmabrunjesproductions.com

BUDDY WORLDWIDE LTD   T 020 7240 9941
PO Box 293, Letchworth Garden City
Herts SG6 9EU
F 01462 684851
E info@buddyshow.com
W www.buddythemusical.com

BUSH THEATRE   T 020 8743 3584
7 Uxbridge Road, Shepherd's Bush
London W12 8LJ
E info@bushtheatre.co.uk
W www.bushtheatre.co.uk

CAP PRODUCTION SOLUTIONS LTD   T 07973 432576
116 Wigmore Road, Carshalton, Surrey SM5 1RQ
F 07970 763480
E leigh@leighporter.com

CENTRELINE PRODUCTIONS & THE TOURING CONSORTIUM THEATRE COMPANY   T 07710 522438
41 Beresford Road, London N8 0AL
E jenny@centrelinenet.com
W www.touringconsortium.com

CHAIN REACTION   T/F 020 8981 9572
Millers, Three Mills Lane
London E3 3DU
E admin@chainreactiontheatre.co.uk
W www.chainreactiontheatre.co.uk

CHANNEL THEATRE PRODUCTIONS LTD   T 01963 362937
5 Gold Street, Stalbridge
Dorset DT10 2LX
E info@channel-theatre.co.uk
W www.scenethreecreative.co.uk

CHAPMAN, Duggie ASSOCIATES   T/F 01253 403177
Concerts. Musicals. Pantomime
Clifton House, 106 Clifton Drive
Blackpool FY4 1RR
E info@duggiechapmanassociates.com
W www.duggiechapman.com

CHEEK BY JOWL   T 020 7382 2391
Contact: Beth Byrne
Stage Door, Barbican Centre
Silk Street, London EC2Y 8DS
E info@cheekbyjowl.com
W www.cheekbyjowl.com

CHICHESTER FESTIVAL THEATRE   T 01243 784437
Oaklands Park, Chichester
West Sussex PO19 6AP
F 01243 787288
E admin@cft.org.uk
W www.cft.org.uk

CHICKENSHED   T 020 8351 6161
290 Chase Side, Southgate, London N14 4PE
E info@chickenshed.org.uk
W www.chickenshed.org.uk

CHOL THEATRE   T 01484 536008
Contact: Susan Burns (Director). Twitter: @choltheatre
48A Byram Arcade, Westgate
Huddersfield HD1 1ND
E info@choltheatre.co.uk
W www.choltheatre.co.uk

CHURCHILL THEATRE BROMLEY LTD   T 020 8464 7131
Producing Theatre
The Churchill, High Street, Bromley, Kent BR1 1HA
F 020 8290 6968
W www.atgtickets.com/churchill

CLEAN BREAK   T 020 7482 8600
Theatre Education. New Writing
2 Patshull Road, London NW5 2LB
F 020 7482 8611
E general@cleanbreak.org.uk
W www.cleanbreak.org.uk

CODRON, Michael PLAYS LTD   T 020 7240 8291
Aldwych Theatre Offices, London WC2B 4DF
F 020 7240 8467

COLE KITCHENN   T 020 7427 5681
ROAR House, 46 Charlotte Street
London W1T 2GS
E info@colekitchenn.com

COMPLICITE   T 020 7485 7700
Twitter: @Complicite
14 Anglers Lane, London NW5 3DG
E email@complicite.org
W www.complicite.org

CONCORDANCE　T 020 7244 7439
Contact: Neil McPherson
Finborough Theatre, 118 Finborough Road
London SW10 9ED
E admin@concordance.org.uk
W www.concordance.org.uk

CONTEMPORARY STAGE COMPANY
9 Finchley Way, London N3 1AG
E contemp.stage@hotmail.co.uk

**CONWAY, Clive CELEBRITY
PRODUCTIONS LTD**　T 01865 514830
32 Grove Street, Oxford OX2 7JT
F 01865 514409
E admin@celebrityproductions.org
W www.celebrityproductions.info

CREATIVE BLAST COMPANY　T 01375 386247
13-15 Clarence Road, Grays, Essex RM17 6QA
E info@creativeblastcompany.com
W www.creativeblastcompany.com

**CREATIVE MANAGEMENT &
PRODUCTIONS (CMP) LTD**　T 020 7240 3033
1st Floor, 26-28 Neal Street, London WC2H 9QQ
F 020 7240 3037
E mail@cmplimited.com
W www.cmplimited.com

DEAD EARNEST THEATRE　T 07855 866292
Sheffield Design Studio, 40 Ball Street
Sheffield S3 8DB
E info@deadearnest.co.uk
W www.deadearnest.co.uk

DEAN, Lee　T 020 7497 5111
PO Box 10703, London WC2H 9ED
E admin@leedean.co.uk

DEBUT PRODUCTIONS　T 07505 677994
Actor Showcases in London's West End & Manchester
65 Norton Way North, Letchworth
Herts SG6 1BH
E submissions@debutproductions.co.uk
W www.debutproductions.co.uk

**DISNEY THEATRICAL
PRODUCTIONS (UK)**　T 020 7845 0900
Lyceum Theatre, 21 Wellington Street
London WC2E 7RQ

DK PRODUKTIONS LTD　T 01628 605981
Specialising in Children's Shows & Pantomimes
42 Coalmans Way, Slough SL1 7NX
E info@dk-pro.co.uk
W www.dk-pro.co.uk

DONEGAN, David LTD　T 07957 358909
PO Box LB689, London W1A 9LB
E daviddonegan@hotmail.co.uk

DRAMATIS PERSONAE LTD　T 020 7834 9300
Contact: Nathan Silver
19 Regency Street, London SW1P 4BY
E ns@nathansilver.com

**EASTERN ANGLES
THEATRE COMPANY**　T 01473 218202
The Sir John Mills Theatre
Gatacre Road, Ipswich, Suffolk IP1 2LQ
E admin@easternangles.co.uk
W www.easternangles.co.uk

ELDARIN YEONG STUDIO　T 020 3714 9580
40 Gracechurch Street, London EC3V 0BT
E info@eldarin-yeong-studio.co.uk
W www.eldarin-yeong-studio.co.uk

ELLIOTT, Paul LTD　T 020 3435 6439
18 Exeter Street, London WC2E 7DU
E paul@paulelliott.ltd.uk

ENGLISH NATIONAL OPERA　T 020 7836 0111
London Coliseum, St Martin's Lane, London WC2N 4ES
F 020 7845 9277
W www.eno.org

**ENGLISH STAGE
COMPANY LTD**　T 020 7565 5050
Royal Court Theatre, Sloane Square
London SW1W 8AS
F 020 7565 5001
E info@royalcourttheatre.com
W www.royalcourttheatre.com

**ENGLISH TOURING
THEATRE (ETT)**　T 020 7450 1990
25 Short Street, London SE1 8LJ
F 020 7633 0188
E admin@ett.org.uk
W www.ett.org.uk

**ENTERTAINMENT
BUSINESS LTD THE**　T 020 3714 1114
25 Nutford Place, London W1H 5YQ
F 020 7691 7218
E joanne.benjamin@entbiz.co.uk
W www.entbiz.co.uk

EUROPEAN THEATRE COMPANY THE
15 Beverley Avenue, London SW20 0RL
E admin@europeantheatre.co.uk
W www.europeantheatre.co.uk

EXCESS ALL AREAS LTD　T 020 8761 2384
3 Gibbs Square, London SE19 1JN
E paul@excessallareas.co.uk
W www.excessallareas.co.uk

FACADE　T 020 8291 7079
Musicals
43A Garthorne Road, London SE23 1EP
F 020 8291 4969
E facade@cobomedia.com

FAIRBANK PRODUCTIONS
E info@fairbankproductions.co.uk
W www.fairbankproductions.co.uk

FEATHER PRODUCTIONS LTD
E anna@featherproductions.com
W www.featherproductions.com

**FIELD, Anthony
ASSOCIATES LTD**　T 020 7240 5453
Top Floor, 80-81 St Martin's Lane, London WC2N 4AA
F 020 7240 2947
E info@anthonyfieldassociates.com
W www.anthonyfieldassociates.com

FIERY ANGEL PARTNERS LLP　T 020 7734 9600
2nd Floor National House, 60-66 Wardour Street
London W1F 0TA
E mail@fiery-angel.com
W www.fiery-angel.com

**FORBIDDEN THEATRE
COMPANY**　T 07852 942588
56 Handsworth Road, London N17 6DE
E info@forbidden.org.uk
W www.forbidden.org.uk

FORD, Vanessa PRODUCTIONS　T 01483 278203
Upper House Farm, Upper House Lane
Shamley Green, Surrey GU5 0SX
E vanessa.ford8@gmail.com

FOX, Robert LTD T 020 7584 6855
6 Beauchamp Place, London SW3 1NG
F 020 7225 1638
E info@robertfoxltd.com
W www.robertfoxltd.com

FRANK, Lina B. / AUSFORM
Circus & Theatre. Twitter: @ausform
Room 206, The Exchange, Corn Street
Bristol BS1 1JQ
E info@ausform.co.uk
W www.ausform.co.uk

FRESH GLORY PRODUCTIONS T 020 7240 1941
59 St Martin's Lane
London WC2N 4JS
E fg@freshglory.com
W www.freshglory.com

**FRIEDMAN, Sonia
PRODUCTIONS** T 020 7845 8750
Duke of York's Theatre, 104 St Martin's Lane
London WC2N 4BG
F 020 7845 8759
E office@soniafriedman.com
W www.soniafriedman.com

**GALLEON THEATRE
COMPANY LTD** T 020 8310 7276
Contact: Alice De Sousa
Head Office, Greenwich Playhouse
50 Openshaw Road, London SE2 0TE
E boxoffice@galleontheatre.co.uk
W www.galleontheatre.co.uk

GBM PRODUCTIONS LTD T 01837 871522
Bidlake Toft, Roadford Lake
Germansweek, Devon EX21 5BD
E gbm@bidlaketoft.com
W www.musicaltheatrecreations.com

**GIANT CHERRY
PRODUCTIONS LTD** T 07814 171929
*Specialising in LGBT Productions for Theatre,
Film & Television*
26 Cranbourne Road, London E15 2DB
E info@giantcherryproductions.com
W www.giantcherryproductions.com

GIANT STEPS LTD T 020 8567 5988
11 Chesnut Grove, London W5 4JT
T 07808 742307
E giantstepstheatre@googlemail.com
W www.giantsteps.info

GOUCHER, Mark LTD T 020 7438 9570
1st Floor, 19 Garrick Street
London WC2E 9AX
E michael@markgoucher.com

GRADELINNIT COMPANY THE T 020 7349 7222
Worlds End Studios, 132-134 Lots Road
London SW10 0RJ
E info@gradelinnit.com

GRAEAE THEATRE COMPANY T 020 7613 6900
Bradbury Studios, 138 Kingsland Road
London E2 8DY
E info@graeae.org
W www.graeae.org

**GRAHAM, David
ENTERTAINMENT LTD** T 020 7175 7170
3rd Floor, 14 Hanover Street
London W1S 1YH
E info@davidgraham.co.uk
W www.davidgrahamentertainment.com

**GRANDAGE, Michael
COMPANY** T 020 3582 7210
4th Floor, Gielgud Theatre
Shaftesbury Avenue, London W1D 6AR
E info@michaelgrandagecompany.com

HALL & CHILDS LTD T 07778 984365
Producers/General Managers
3 Thrifts Hall Farm Mews, Abridge Road
Theydon Bois, Essex CM16 7NL
E tc@hallandchilds.com
W www.hallandchilds.com

**HAMPSTEAD THEATRE
PRODUCTIONS LTD** T 020 7449 4200
Eton Avenue, Swiss Cottage, London NW3 3EU
F 020 7449 4201
E info@hampsteadtheatre.com
W www.hampsteadtheatre.com

HAPPYSTORM THEATRE
Contact: By e-mail
11 Old Mill Close, Pendlebury
Greater Manchester M27 4DW
E info@happystormtheatre.co.uk
W www.happystormtheatre.co.uk

**HARLEY PRODUCTIONS
CONSULTANTS** T 020 7486 2986
78 York Street, London W1H 1DP
F 020 8202 8863
E harleyprods@aol.com

HARRISON, Garth T 01508 530849
Michaelmas Barn, Long Stratton
Norfolk NR15 2PY
E garthsfp@hotmail.co.uk

**HAYDEN SCOTT
PRODUCTIONS** T 07879 897900
Contact: Daniel Sparrow, Mike Walsh
44B Floral Street, London WC2E 9DA
E info@danielsparrowproductions.com
W www.danielsparrowproductions.com

HAYMARKET THE T 01256 819797
c/o The Anvil Trust, Wote Street
Basingstoke, Hampshire RG21 7NW
F 01256 331733
E christine.bradwell@anvilarts.org.uk
W www.anvilarts.org.uk

HEADLONG THEATRE LTD T 020 7478 0270
3rd Floor, 34-35 Berwick Street, London W1F 8RP
F 020 7438 1749
E info@headlong.co.uk
W www.headlong.co.uk

**HENDERSON, Glynis
PRODUCTIONS LTD** T 020 7580 9644
16-17 Little Portland Street, London W1W 8BP
F 020 7183 3298
E info@ghmp.co.uk
W www.ghmp.co.uk

**HENDRY, Jamie
PRODUCTIONS LTD** T/F 020 7183 5630
13 Regent Street, 6th Floor, London SW1Y 4LR
E office@jamiehendryproductions.com
W www.jamiehendryproductions.com

**HENNEGAN, Nicholas
ASSOCIATES** T 020 8090 5082
2nd Floor, 12 Fouberts Place
Carnaby Street, London W1F 7PA
E info@nicholashennegan.com
W www.nicholashennegan.com

HESTER, John PRODUCTIONS   T/F 020 8224 9580
Intimate Mysteries Theatre Company
105 Stoneleigh Park Road, Epsom
Surrey KT19 0RF
E hjohnhester@aol.com

HISS & BOO COMPANY LTD THE   T 01444 881707
Contact: Ian Liston. By Post (SAE). No Unsolicited Scripts
Nyes Hill, Wineham Lane
Bolney, West Sussex RH17 5SD
E email@hissboo.co.uk
W www.hissboo.co.uk

HISTORIA THEATRE COMPANY   T 020 7837 8008
8 Cloudesley Square
London N1 0HT
T 07811 892079
E kateprice@lineone.net
W www.historiatheatre.com

HOLLOW CROWN PRODUCTIONS   T 07930 530948
2 Old Hall Farm
Halesworth Road
Reydon, Suffolk IP18 6SG
E enquiries@hollowcrown.co.uk
W www.hollowcrown.co.uk

HOLMAN, Paul ASSOCIATES LTD   T 020 8845 9408
Morritt House, 58 Station Approach
South Ruislip, Middlesex HA4 6SA
E enquiries@paulholmanassociates.co.uk
W www.paulholmanassociates.co.uk

HOLT, Thelma LTD   T 020 7812 7455
Noel Coward Theatre
85 St Martin's Lane
London WC2N 4AU
F 020 7812 7550
E thelma@dircon.co.uk
W www.thelmaholt.co.uk

HUGHES, Steve MANAGEMENT LTD   T 0844 5564670
26 The Tyleshades, Tadburn Gardens
Romsey, Hampshire SO51 5RJ
E productions@stevehughesuk.com
W www.stevehughesuk.com

HULL TRUCK THEATRE   T 01482 224800
50 Ferensway, Hull HU2 8LB
F 01482 581182
E admin@hulltruck.co.uk
W www.hulltruck.co.uk

HUNTLEY, Peter PRODUCTIONS
E info@peterhuntley.net
W www.peterhuntley.net

I&I PRODUCTIONS LTD   T 07825 261687
27 Heol Y Dryw, Rhoose Point
Barry CF62 3LR
E iandiproductionsltd@gmail.com
W www.iandiproductionsltd.co.uk

IAN, David PRODUCTIONS   T 020 7427 8380
5th Floor, 53 Parker Street
London WC2B 5PT
F 020 7427 8381
E hello@davidianproductions.com
W www.davidianproductions.com

IBSEN STAGE COMPANY   T 020 7607 6992
97 Richmond Avenue, London N1 0LT
T 07958 566274
E ask@ibsenstage.com
W www.ibsenstage.com

ICARUS THEATRE COLLECTIVE   T 020 7998 1562
4 Ivor Court, Gloucester Place
London NW1 6BJ
E info@icarustheatre.co.uk
W www.icarustheatre.co.uk

IMAGE MUSICAL THEATRE   T 020 8743 9380
197 Church Road, Northolt
Middlesex UB5 5BE
F 020 8181 6279
E admin@imagemusicaltheatre.co.uk
W www.imagemusicaltheatre.co.uk

INCISOR   T 07979 498450
41 Edith Avenue, Peacehaven
East Sussex BN10 8JB
E sarahmann7@hotmail.co.uk
W www.theatre-company-incisor.com

INGRAM, Colin LTD   T 020 7038 3906
Suite 526, Linen Hall
162-168 Regent Street
London W1B 5TE
F 020 7038 3907
E info@coliningramltd.com
W www.coliningramltd.com

INSIDE INTELLIGENCE   T/F 020 8986 8013
Theatre, including West End. New Writing. Contemporary Opera. Music Theatre
13 Athlone Close, London E5 8HD
E admin@inside-intelligence.org.uk
W www.inside-intelligence.org.uk

INSTANT WIT   T 0117 974 5734
Comedy Improvisation Theatre Show. Corporate/ Conference Entertainment Show. Drama Based Training
6 Worrall Place, Worrall Road
Clifton, Bristol BS8 2WP
T 07711 644094
E info@instantwit.co.uk
W www.instantwit.co.uk

JAM THEATRE COMPANY   T 01628 483808
Jam Theatre Studios, Archway Court
45A West Street, Marlow
Buckinghamshire SL7 2LS
E office@jamtheatre.co.uk
W www.jamtheatre.co.uk

JERSEY BOYS UK LTD   T 020 3427 3720
Hudson House, 8 Tavistock Street
London WC2E 7PP
E jerseyboyslondon@dodger.com
W www.jerseyboyslondon.com

JOHNSON, David   T 020 7284 3733
85B Torriano Avenue, London NW5 2RX
E david@johnsontemple.co.uk

JOHNSON, Gareth LTD   T 01239 891368
1st Floor, 19 Garrick Street, London WC2E 9AX
T 07770 225227
E gjltd@mac.com
W www.garethjohnsonltd.com

JORDAN, Andy PRODUCTIONS LTD   T 07775 615205
130 Newland Street West, Lincoln LN1 1PH
E andyjandyjordan@aol.com

JORDAN, Richard PRODUCTIONS LTD — T 020 7243 9001
Mews Studios, 16 Vernon Yard
London W11 2DX
F 020 7313 9667
E info@richardjordanproductions.com

JORDAN PRODUCTIONS LTD — T 01323 417745
The Coach House, 5B Commercial Road
Eastbourne, East Sussex BN21 3XE
E info@jordanproductionsltd.co.uk

KEAN PRODUCTIONS — T 020 3151 2710
Communications House, 26 York Street
London W1U 6PZ
E info@keanprods.com
W www.keanprods.com

KELLY, Robert C. — T 0141 533 5856
PO Box 5597, Glasgow G77 9DH
E office@robertckelly.co.uk
W www.robertckelly.co.uk

KENWRIGHT, Bill LTD — T 020 7446 6200
BKL House, 1 Venice Walk, London W2 1RR
F 020 7446 6222
E info@kenwright.com
W www.kenwright.com

KING, Belinda CREATIVE PRODUCTIONS — T 01604 720041
BK Studios, 157 Clarence Avenue
Kingsthorpe, Northampton NN2 6NY
F 01604 721448
E office@belindaking.com
W www.belindaking.com

KING'S HEAD THEATRE — T 020 7226 8561
Contact: Adam Spreadbury-Maher (Artistic Director)
115 Upper Street, Islington
London N1 1QN
BO 020 7478 0160
E info@kingsheadtheatre.com
W www.kingsheadtheatre.com

LATCHMERE THEATRE — T 020 7978 2620
Contact: Chris Fisher
Unit 5A, Spaces Business Centre
Ingate Place, London SW8 3NS
E latchmere@fishers.org.uk

LEIGH-PEMBERTON, David — T 020 7112 8445
43-44 Berners Street
London W1T 3ND
E david@leigh-pemberton.co.uk
W www.davidleigh-pemberton.co.uk

LHK PRODUCTIONS LTD — T 01744 808907
20 Maltby Close, St Helens WA9 5GJ
E info@lhkproductions.co.uk
W www.lhkproductions.co.uk

LHP LTD — T 07973 938634
9 Coombe Court, Hayne Road
Beckenham, Kent BR3 4XD
E lhpltd@msn.com

LIMELIGHT PRODUCTIONS — T 020 8853 9570
Unit 13, The io Centre, The Royal Arsenal
Seymour Street, London SE18 6SX
F 020 8853 9579
E enquiries@thelimelightgroup.co.uk

LINNIT PRODUCTIONS LTD — T 020 7349 7222
Worlds End Studios
132-134 Lots Road
London SW10 0RJ

Richard Jordan Productions Ltd

- **Producing**
- **General Management**
  UK and International Productions
  and International Festivals
- **Consultancy**

Richard Jordan Productions Ltd
Mews Studios, 16 Vernon Yard, London W11 2DX
T: 020 7243 9001   F: 020 7313 9667
e-mail: info@richardjordanproductions.com

LIVE THEATRE — T 0191 261 2694
Broad Chare, Quayside
Newcastle upon Tyne NE1 3DQ
E info@live.org.uk
W www.live.org.uk

LONDON BUBBLE THEATRE COMPANY LTD — T 020 7237 4434
5 Elephant Lane, London SE16 4JD
E admin@londonbubble.org.uk
W www.londonbubble.org.uk

LONDON CLASSIC THEATRE — T 020 8395 2095
The Production Office, 63 Shirley Avenue
Sutton, Surrey SM1 3QT
E admin@londonclassictheatre.co.uk
W www.londonclassictheatre.co.uk

LONDON MANAGEMENT (UK) LTD — T 01202 522711
The Old Dairy, Throop Road
Bournemouth BH8 0DL
F 01202 522311
E nicky@london-management.co.uk
W www.london-management.co.uk

LONDON MANAGEMENT (UK) LTD — T 01202 522711
4th Floor, EON House
138 Piccadilly, London W1J 7NR
F 01202 522311
W www.london-management.co.uk

LONDON PRODUCTIONS LTD — T 020 7497 5111
PO Box 10703, London WC2H 9ED
E admin@leedean.co.uk

LONDON REPERTORY COMPANY — T/F 020 7258 1944
PO Box 59385, London NW8 1HL
E info@londonrepertorycompany.com
W www.londonrepertorycompany.com

LOVE & PRODUCE — T 07455 011639
Performance Art & Devised Theatre
269 Southborough Lane, Bromley
Kent BR2 8AT
E info@loveandproduce.com
W www.loveandproduce.com

MACKINTOSH, Cameron LTD — T 020 7637 8866
Contact: Melanie Watts (Casting Assistant)
1 Bedford Square, London WC1B 3RB
F 020 7436 2683
E melanie@camack.co.uk

MACNAGHTEN PRODUCTIONS   T 01223 577974
19 Grange Court, Grange Road
Cambridge CB3 9BD

**MALCOLM, Christopher
PRODUCTIONS LTD**   T 07850 555042
26 Rokeby Road, London SE4 1DE
E cm@christophermalcolm.co.uk
W www.christophermalcolm.co.uk

MANS, Johnny PRODUCTIONS   T 01992 470907
Incorporating Encore Magazine
PO Box 196, Hoddesdon, Herts EN10 7WG
T 07974 755997
E johnnymansagent@aol.com
W www.johnnymansproductions.co.uk

**MASTERSON, Guy
PRODUCTIONS**   T/F 01707 330360
The Hawthorne Theatre, Campus West
Welwyn Garden City, Herts AL8 6BX
E admin@theatretoursinternational.com
W www.theatretoursinternational.com

MAYK   T 07707 363572
c/o Bristol Old Vic, King Street
Bristol BS1 4ED
E matthewandkate@mayk.org.uk
W www.mayk.org.uk

**McCABE, Michael
PRODUCTIONS LTD**   T 020 7831 7077
The Dutch House, 307-308 High Holborn
London WC1V 7LL
E mailbox@michaelmccabe.net
W www.michaelmccabe.net

McKITTERICK, Tom LTD   T/F 001 212 431 7697
113 Greene Street, New York 10012, USA
E tommckitterick@aol.com

McLAUGHLIN, Dermot   T 07957 491036
Freelance Producer
Brighton/London
E dermotmclaughlin@me.com
W www.dermotmclaughlin.com

MENZIES, Lee LTD   T 020 7240 4070
19 Garrick Street, London WC2E 9AX
F 020 7681 3670
E leemenzies@leemenzies.co.uk
W www.leemenzies.co.uk

METAL RABBIT LTD   T 07813 640858
London Based Commercial Theatre Producers
360A Clapham Road, London SW9 9AR
E gjwarren@metalrabbit.org.uk
W www.metalrabbit.org.uk

**MIDDLE GROUND
THEATRE CO LTD**   T 01684 577231
3 Gordon Terrace, Malvern Wells
Malvern, Worcestershire WR14 4ER
F 01684 574472
E middleground@middlegroundtheatre.co.uk
W www.middlegroundtheatre.co.uk

MJE PRODUCTIONS LTD   T 01858 461177
Contact: Carole Winter, Michael Edwards
7 Sutton Lodge, Sutton Lane
Dingley, Market Harborough LE16 8HL
E info@mjeproductions.com
W www.mjeproductions.com

MOKITAGRIT   T 07980 564849
75D Humber Road, London SE3 7LR
E mail@mokitagrit.com
W www.mokitagrit.com

MOVING THEATRE   T 01323 815726
16 Laughton Lodge, Nr Lewes
East Sussex BN8 6BY
F 01323 815736
E info@movingtheatre.com
W www.movingtheatre.com

MUSIC THEATRE LONDON   T 07831 243942
c/o Capriol Films, The Coach House
35 High Street, Holt
Norfolk NR25 6BN
T 01263 712600
E tony.britten@capriolfilms.co.uk
W www.capriolfilms.co.uk

NADINE'S WINDOW
Theatre Company
E nadineswindow@yahoo.co.uk
W www.nadineswindow.com

NATIONAL ANGELS   T 020 7349 7060
Worlds End Studios
132-134 Lots Road
London SW10 0RJ
E admin@nationalangels.com

NATIONAL THEATRE   T 020 7452 3333
Upper Ground, South Bank
London SE1 9PX
F 020 7452 3344
W www.nationaltheatre.org.uk

**NEAL STREET
PRODUCTIONS LTD**   T 020 7240 8890
1st Floor, 26-28 Neal Street
London WC2H 9QQ
F 020 7240 7099
E post@nealstreetproductions.com

NEW PERSPECTIVES   T 0115 927 2334
Park Lane Business Centre, Park Lane
Nottingham NG6 0DW
E info@newperspectives.co.uk
W www.newperspectives.co.uk

NEWPALM PRODUCTIONS   T 020 8349 0802
26 Cavendish Avenue, London N3 3QN
F 020 8346 8257
E newpalm@btopenworld.com
W www.newpalm.co.uk

**NICHOLAS, Paul & IAN,
David ASSOCIATES LTD**   T 020 7427 8380
5th Floor, 53 Parker Street, London WC2B 5PT
F 020 7427 8381
E hello@davidianproductions.com
W www.davidianproductions.com

NITRO
E info@nitro.co.uk
W www.nitro.co.uk

NORDIC NOMAD PRODUCTIONS   T 07980 619165
*Contact: Tanja Raaste (Creative Producer). Specialising
in New Writing, Site Specific & Interactive Work, Tango
& Dance Events & Festivals. Training & Workshops:
Business Skills for Performers, Writing Workshops,
One-to-one Business Advice Sessions. Nordic Nomad
Blog: Articles on Arts & Business, Good Food & Travel*
E info@nordicnomad.com
W www.nordicnomad.com

**NORTHERN BROADSIDES
THEATRE COMPANY**   T 01422 369704
Dean Clough, Halifax HX3 5AX
E sue@northern-broadsides.co.uk
W www.northern-broadsides.co.uk

NORTHERN STAGE (THEATRICAL PRODUCTIONS) LTD **T** 0191 242 7200
Barras Bridge, Newcastle upon Tyne NE1 7RH
F 0191 242 7257
E info@northernstage.co.uk
W www.northernstage.co.uk

NORTHUMBERLAND THEATRE COMPANY (NTC) **T** 01665 602586
The Playhouse, Bondgate Without
Alnwick, Northumberland NE66 1PQ
F 01665 605837
E admin@northumberlandtheatre.co.uk
W www.northumberlandtheatre.co.uk

OLD VIC PRODUCTIONS PLC **T** 020 7928 2651
The Old Vic Theatre, The Cut
Waterloo, London SE1 8NB
F 020 7981 0991
E becky.barber@oldvictheatre.com

ONE NIGHT BOOKING COMPANY THE **T** 020 8455 3278
1 Hogarth Hill, London NW11 6AY
E mail@onenightbooking.com
W www.onenightbooking.com

OUT OF JOINT **T** 020 7609 0207
7 Thane Works, Thane Villas, London N7 7NU
F 020 7609 0203
E ojo@outofjoint.co.uk
W www.outofjoint.co.uk

OVATION **T** 020 8340 4256
Upstairs at The Gatehouse, Highgate Village
London N6 4BD
E events@ovationproductions.com
W www.ovationtheatres.com

PAINES PLOUGH **T** 020 7240 4533
4th Floor, 43 Aldwych, London WC2B 4DN
F 020 7240 4534
E office@painesplough.com
W www.painesplough.com

PAPATANGO THEATRE COMPANY **T** 07834 958804
37A Harold Road, London SE19 3PL
E info@papatango.co.uk
W www.papatango.co.uk

PAPER MOON THEATRE COMPANY **T** 020 7060 0550
Contact: Jan Hunt (Producer/Director). Specialising in Traditional Victorian Music Hall
6 Thames Meadow, West Molesey
Surrey KT8 1TQ
E jan@papermoontheatre.co.uk

PASSWORD PRODUCTIONS LTD **T** 020 7284 3733
Contact: John Mackay
85B Torriano Avenue, London NW5 2RX
E johnmackay2001@aol.com

PENDLE PRODUCTIONS LTD **T** 01253 839375
Bridge Farm, 249 Hawes Side Lane
Blackpool FY4 4AA
F 01253 792930
E admin@pendleproductions.co.uk
W www.pendleproductions.co.uk

PENTABUS THEATRE **T** 01584 856564
Bromfield, Ludlow
Shropshire SY8 2JU
E info@pentabus.co.uk
W www.pentabus.co.uk

PEOPLE SHOW **T** 020 7729 1841
Brady Arts Centre
192-196 Hanbury Street, London E1 5HU
E people@peopleshow.co.uk
W www.peopleshow.co.uk

PERFECT PITCH MUSICALS LTD **T** 020 7930 1087
5A Irving Street, London WC2H 7AT
E andy@perfectpitchmusicals.com
W www.perfectpitchmusicals.com

PERFORMANCE BUSINESS THE **T** 01932 888885
78 Oatlands Drive, Weybridge, Surrey KT13 9HT
E info@theperformance.biz
W www.theperformance.biz

PILOT THEATRE **T** 01904 635755
Performance Work across Platforms & National Touring
York Theatre Royal, St Leonard's Place, York YO1 7HD
E info@pilot-theatre.com
W www.pilot-theatre.com

PLANTAGENET PRODUCTIONS **T** 01635 253322
Drawing Room Recitals
Westridge Open Centre, Star Lane
Highclere, Nr Newbury RG20 9PJ

PLAYFUL PRODUCTIONS **T** 020 7811 4600
4th Floor, 41-44 Great Queen Street, London WC2B 5AD
F 020 7811 4622
E aboutus@playfuluk.com
W www.playfuluk.com

POLKA THEATRE **T** 020 8545 8323
240 The Broadway, Wimbledon SW19 1SB
F 020 8545 8365
E stephen@polkatheatre.com
W www.polkatheatre.com

POPULAR PRODUCTIONS LTD **T** 020 8292 5305
448 Muswell Hill Broadway, Muswell Hill
London N10 1BS
E info@popularproductions.com
W www.popularproductions.com

PORTER, Richard LTD **T** 07884 183404
214 Grange Road, London SE1 3AA
E office@richardporterltd.com
W www.richardporterltd.com

POSTER, Kim **T** 020 7240 3098
Stanhope Productions Ltd
4th Floor, 80-81 St Martin's Lane
London WC2N 4AA
F 020 7504 8656
E admin@stanhopeprod.com

PROMENADE PRODUCTIONS **T** 020 7240 3407
20 Thayer Street, London W1U 2DD
E hharrison@promenadeproductions.com
W www.promenadeproductions.com

PUGH, David & ROGERS, Dafydd **T** 020 7292 0390
David Pugh Ltd, Wyndhams Theatre
Charing Cross Road, London WC2H 0DA
F 020 7292 0399
E dpl@davidpughltd.com

PURSUED BY A BEAR PRODUCTIONS **T** 01252 745445
Farnham Maltings, Bridge Square
Farnham GU9 7QR
E pursuedbyabear@yahoo.co.uk
W www.pursuedbyabear.co.uk

PW PRODUCTIONS LTD T 020 7395 7580
2nd Floor, 80-81 St Martin's Lane, London WC2N 4AA
F 020 7240 2947
E info@pwprods.co.uk
W www.pwprods.co.uk

QDOS ENTERTAINMENT T 01723 500038
Qdos House, Queen Margaret's Road
Scarborough, North Yorkshire YO11 2YH
F 01723 361958
E info@qdosentertainment.co.uk
W www.qdosentertainment.co.uk

QUAIFE, James PRODUCTIONS
Contact: James Quaife
E office@jamesquaifeproductions.com
W www.jamesquaifeproductions.com

QUANTUM THEATRE T 020 8317 9000
The Old Button Factory
1-11 Bannockburn Road
Plumstead, London SE18 1ET
E office@quantumtheatre.co.uk
W www.quantumtheatre.co.uk

RAGS & FEATHERS
THEATRE COMPANY T 020 8224 2203
80 Summer Road, Thames Ditton
Surrey KT7 0QP
T 07958 724374
E jilldowning.tls@gmail.com

RAIN OR SHINE THEATRE
COMPANY T 0330 660 0541
Twitter: @rainorshineUK
25 Paddock Gardens, Longlevens
Gloucester GL2 0ED
E theatre@rainorshine.co.uk
W www.rainorshine.co.uk

REAL CIRCUMSTANCE THEATRE COMPANY
22 Erle Harvard Road, West Bergholt
Colchester CO6 3BW
E info@realcircumstance.com
W www.realcircumstance.com

REALLY USEFUL
GROUP LTD THE T 020 7240 0880
Theatre Licensing & Production
17 Slingsby Place, London WC2E 9AB
F 020 7240 1204

RED ROOM THE T 020 7470 8790
The Garden Studio, 71-75 Shelton Street
London WC2H 9JQ
E admin@theredroom.org.uk
W www.theredroom.org.uk

RED ROSE CHAIN T 01473 603388
Gippeswyk Hall, Gippeswyk Avenue
Ipswich, Suffolk IP2 9AF
E info@redrosechain.com
W www.redrosechain.com

RED SHIFT
THEATRE COMPANY T/F 020 8540 1271
PO Box 60151, London SW19 2TB
E redshift100@gmail.com
W www.redshifttheatreco.co.uk

REDROOFS THEATRE
COMPANY T 01628 674092
Contact: By Post
Novello Theatre, High Street
Sunninghill, Ascot SL5 9NE
E info@redroofs.co.uk
W www.redroofs.co.uk/novellotheatre

REDUCED CIRCUMSTANCES T 07585 155534
Contact: Emma Keele
E info@reducedcircumstances.co.uk
W www.reducedcircumstances.co.uk

REGENT'S PARK
THEATRE LTD T 0844 3753460
Open Air Theatre
Stage Door Gate, Inner Circle
Regent's Park, London NW1 4NU
W www.openairtheatre.com

REVEAL THEATRE
COMPANY LTD T 07525 480164
72 Barnfield Road, Stoke on Trent ST6 3DH
E enquiries@revealtheatre.co.uk
W www.revealtheatre.co.uk

RGC PRODUCTIONS T 07740 286727
260 Kings Road, Kingston, Surrey KT2 5HX
E info@rgcproductions.com
W www.rgcproductions.com

RHO DELTA LTD T 020 7436 1392
Contact: Greg Ripley-Duggan
26 Goodge Street, London W1T 2QG
E info@ripleyduggan.com

ROCKET THEATRE T 0161 969 1444
32 Baxter Road, Sale, Manchester M33 3AL
T 07788 723570
E martin@rockettheatre.co.uk
W www.rockettheatre.co.uk

ROLLING JUNK
PRODUCTIONS LTD T 020 7240 4004
8 Sheridan Buildings, Martlett Court, London WC2B 5SD
E info@rollingjunkproductions.co.uk
W www.rollingjunkproductions.co.uk

ROSE THEATRE, KINGSTON T 020 8546 6983
Contact: Jerry Gunn (Executive Producer), Naomi Webb
(Assistant Producer)
24-26 High Street, Kingston Upon Thames
Surrey KT1 1HL
F 020 8546 8783
E admin@rosetheatrekingston.org
W www.rosetheatrekingston.org

ROSENTHAL, Suzanna &
MEADOW, Jeremy T 020 7436 2244
26 Goodge Street, London W1T 2QG
F 0870 7627882
E info@meadowrosenthal.com

ROYAL COURT THEATRE
PRODUCTIONS LTD T 020 7565 5050
Sloane Square, London SW1W 8AS
F 020 7565 5001
E info@royalcourttheatre.com
W www.royalcourttheatre.com

ROYAL EXCHANGE THEATRE T 0161 833 9333
St Ann's Square, Manchester M2 7DH
W www.royalexchange.co.uk

ROYAL SHAKESPEARE
COMPANY T 020 7845 0500
1 Earlham Street, London WC2H 9LL
F 020 7845 0505
W www.rsc.org.uk

ROYAL SHAKESPEARE
COMPANY T 01789 296655
Royal Shakespeare Theatre, Waterside
Stratford-upon-Avon CV37 6BB
F 01789 403710
W www.rsc.org.uk

RUBINSTEIN, Mark LTD T 020 7021 0787
25 Short Street, London SE1 8LJ
F 0870 7059731
E info@mrluk.com

SCAMP THEATRE LTD T 01462 734843
44 Church Lane, Arlesey
Beds SG15 6UX
E admin@scamptheatre.com
W www.scamptheatre.com

SCENE THREE CREATIVE T 01963 362937
Creative Services. Project Management. Theatre
Production. Writing
5 Gold Street, Stalbridge
Dorset DT10 2LX
E info@scenethreecreative.co.uk
W www.scenethreecreative.co.uk

SEABRIGHT
PRODUCTIONS LTD T 020 7439 1173
Palace Theatre, Shaftesbury Avenue
London W1D 5AY
F 020 7183 6023
E office@seabrightproductions.com
W www.seabrightproductions.com

SELL A DOOR THEATRE
COMPANY LTD T 020 3355 8567
Athelney House, 161-165 Greenwich High Road
London SE10 8JA
E info@selladoor.com
W www.selladoor.com

SHAKESPEARE'S MEN T 01708 222938
10 Dee Close, Upminster
Essex RM14 1QD
E terence@terencemustoo.com
W www.terencemustoo.com

SHARED EXPERIENCE T 01865 305321
c/o Oxford Playhouse, Beaumont Street
Oxford OX1 2LW
E admin@sharedexperience.org.uk
W www.sharedexperience.org.uk

SHOW OF STRENGTH T 0117 902 0235
74 Chessel Street, Bedminster
Bristol BS3 3DN
E info@showofstrength.org.uk
W www.showofstrength.org.uk

SHOWCASE ENTERTAINMENTS
INTERNATIONAL LTD T 01325 316224
Contact: Geoffrey J.L. Hindmarch (Executive Producer),
Paul Morgan (Creative Director). Theatre. Cruises.
Hotels. Corporate
2 Lumley Close, Newton Aycliffe
Co Durham DL5 5PA
E gjl@showcaseproductions.co.uk
W www.showcaseproductions.co.uk

SILVEY, Denise T 020 8743 7777
St Martin's Theatre, West Street, London WC2N 9NH
E ds@denisesilvey.com
W www.denisesilvey.com

SIMPLY THEATRE T 00 41 22 8600518
Avenue de Choiseul 23A, 1290 Versoix
Switzerland
E info@simplytheatre.com
W www.simplytheatre.com

SINDEN, Marc PRODUCTIONS T 020 8455 3278
1 Hogarth Hill, London NW11 6AY
E mail@sindenproductions.com
W www.sindenproductions.com

SIXTEENFEET PRODUCTIONS T 020 7326 4417
25 Rattray Road, London SW2 1AZ
T 07958 448690
E info@sixteenfeet.co.uk
W www.sixteenfeet.co.uk

SOHO THEATRE COMPANY T 020 7287 5060
21 Dean Street, London W1D 3NE
F 020 7287 5061
W www.sohotheatre.com

SPARROW, Daniel & WALSH, Mike
PRODUCTIONS T 020 7252 5757
1/2, 44B Floral Street, Covent Garden
London WC2E 9DA
T 07879 897900
E info@danielsparrowproductions.com
W www.danielsparrowproductions.com

SPHINX THEATRE COMPANY T 07768 332564
Oval House, 52-54 Kennington Oval
London SE11 5SY
E info@sphinxtheatre.co.uk
W www.sphinxtheatre.co.uk

SPLATS ENTERTAINMENT T 07944 283659
Contact: Mike Redwood
5 Denmark Street, London WC2H 8LP
E mike@splatsentertainment.com
W www.splatsentertainment.com

SPLITMOON THEATRE T 020 7252 8126
PO Box 58891, London SE15 9DE
E info@splitmoontheatre.org
W www.splitmoontheatre.org

SQUAREDEAL
PRODUCTIONS LTD T/F 020 7249 5966
Contact: Jenny Topper
24 De Beauvoir Square, London N1 4LE
T 07785 394241
E jenny@jennytopper.com

STAGE ENTERTAINMENT
UK LTD T 020 7632 4700
Wellington House, 125 Strand, London WC2R 0AP
E info@seuk.uk.com
W www.stage-entertainment.co.uk

STANHOPE
PRODUCTIONS LTD T 020 7240 3098
4th Floor, 80-81 St Martin's Lane, London WC2N 4AA
F 020 7504 8656
E admin@stanhopeprod.com

STELLAR QUINES
THEATRE COMPANY T 0131 229 3851
30B Grindlay Street, Edinburgh EH3 9AX
E admin@stellarquines.co.uk
W www.stellarquines.com

STEPHENSON, Ian
PRODUCTIONS LTD T 07960 999374
E soholondon@aol.com

STRAIGHT LINE
PRODUCTIONS T 020 8393 4220
58 Castle Avenue, Epsom
Surrey KT17 2PH
E hilary@straightlinemanagement.co.uk

TALAWA THEATRE COMPANY T 020 7251 6644
Ground Floor, 53-55 East Road
London N1 6AH
F 020 7251 5969
E hq@talawa.com
W www.talawa.com

TAMASHA THEATRE COMPANY　T 020 7749 0090
RichMix, 35-47 Bethnal Green Road
London E1 6LA
F 020 7729 8906
E info@tamasha.org.uk
W www.tamasha.org.uk

TBA MUSIC　T 0845 1203722
1 St Gabriels Road, London NW2 4DS
F 0700 607 0808
E peter@tbagroup.co.uk

TEG PRODUCTIONS LTD
See ROSENTHAL, Suzanna & MEADOW, Jeremy

THAT'S ENTERTAINMENT PRODUCTIONS　T 07803 050714
PO Box 223, Bexhill-on-Sea
East Sussex TN40 9DP
E chris@thatsentertainmentproductions.co.uk
W www.thatsentertainmentproductions.co.uk

THEATRE ABSOLUTE　T 07799 292957
Shop Front Theatre, 38 City Arcade
Coventry CV1 3HW
E info@theatreabsolute.co.uk
W www.theatreabsolute.co.uk

THEATRE ALIVE!
13 St Barnabas Road, London E17 8JZ
E andrew@andrewvisnevski.com
W www.theatrealive.org.uk

THEATRE NA N'OG　T 01639 641771
Unit 3, Millands Road Industrial Estate
Neath SA11 1NJ
F 01639 647941
E drama@theatr-nanog.co.uk
W www.theatr-nanog.co.uk

THEATRE OF COMEDY COMPANY LTD　T 020 7379 3345
Shaftesbury Theatre
210 Shaftesbury Avenue
London WC2H 8DP
F 020 7836 8181
E info@shaftesburytheatre.com

THEATRE ROYAL HAYMARKET PRODUCTIONS　T 020 7930 8890
Theatre Royal Haymarket
18 Suffolk Street, London SW1Y 4HT
E nigel@trh.co.uk

THEATRE ROYAL STRATFORD EAST　T 020 8534 0310
Gerry Raffles Square, Stratford
London E15 1BN
F 020 8534 8381
E theatreroyal@stratfordeast.com
W www.stratfordeast.com

THEATRE SANS FRONTIERES　T 01434 603114
Queen's Hall, Beaumont Street
Hexham NE46 3LS
F 01434 607206
E info@tsf.org.uk
W www.tsf.org.uk

THEATRE TOURS INTERNATIONAL　T/F 01707 330360
Contact: Guy Masterson
The Hawthorne Theatre, The Campus West
Welwyn Garden City, Herts AL8 6BX
E admin@theatretoursinternational.com
W www.theatretoursinternational.com

THEATRE WORKOUT LTD　T 020 8144 2290
13A Stratheden Road, Blackheath
London SE3 7TH
E enquiries@theatreworkout.com
W www.theatreworkout.com

THOMAS, Hazel PRODUCTIONS　T 07948 211083
Flat 6, Highwood Manor
21 Constitution Hill
Ipswich, Suffolk IP1 3RG
E htproductions@live.co.uk
W www.hazel-thomas.wix.com/htproductions

TIATA FAHODZI　T 020 3435 6508
Waterloo House, 207 Waterloo Road
London SE1 8XD
E info@tiatafahodzi.com
W www.tiatafahodzi.com

TOPPER, Jenny　T 07785 394241
SquaredDeal Productions Ltd
24 De Beauvoir Square
London N1 4LE
E jenny@jennytopper.com

TOWER THEATRE COMPANY　T/F 020 7353 5700
Full-time, Non-professional
St Bride Foundation, Bride Lane
London EC4Y 8EQ
E info@towertheatre.freeserve.co.uk
W www.towertheatre.org.uk

TOWNSEND PRODUCTIONS　T 07949 635910
5 Moorhills Road, Wing
Bucks LU7 0NG
E townsendproductions@hotmail.co.uk
W www.townsendproductions.org.uk

TREAGUS, Andrew ASSOCIATES LTD
32-33 St James's Place
London SW1A 1NR
E admin@at-assoc.co.uk

TRENDS ENTERTAINMENT　T 01253 396534
Unit 4, 9 Chorley Road, Blackpool
Lancashire FY3 7XQ
T 07506 171054
E info@trendsentertainment.com
W www.trendsentertainment.com

TRESTLE THEATRE COMPANY　T 01727 850950
Visual/Physical Theatre. Music. Choreography.
New Writing
Trestle Arts Base, Russet Drive
Herts, St Albans AL4 0JQ
F 01727 855558
E admin@trestle.org.uk
W www.trestle.org.uk

TRICYCLE THEATRE COMPANY　T 020 7372 6611
269 Kilburn High Road
London NW6 7JR
F 020 7328 0795
E admin@tricycle.co.uk
W www.tricycle.co.uk

TRIUMPH ENTERTAINMENT LTD　T 020 3435 6439
18 Exeter Street, London WC2E 7DU
E paul@paulelliott.ltd.uk

TRIUMPH PROSCENIUM PRODUCTIONS LTD　T 01243 527186
The Cottage, West Lavant
Chichester, West Sussex PO18 9AH

TURTLE KEY ARTS   T 020 8964 5060
Ladbroke Hall
79 Barlby Road
London W10 6AZ
F 020 8964 4080
E admin@turtlekeyarts.org.uk
W www.turtlekeyarts.org.uk

TWO'S COMPANY   T 020 8299 3714
244 Upland Road
London SE22 0DN
E graham@2scompanytheatre.co.uk

UK ARTS INTERNATIONAL
Theatre Royal Margate
Addington Street
Margate CT9 1PW
E janryan@ukarts.com
W www.ukarts.com

UK PRODUCTIONS LTD   T 01483 423600
Churchmill House, Ockford Road
Godalming, Surrey GU7 1QY
F 01483 418486
E mail@ukproductions.co.uk
W www.ukproductions.co.uk

UNRESTRICTED VIEW   T 020 7704 2001
Above Hen & Chickens Theatre Bar
109 St Paul's Road
London N1 2NA
E henandchickens@aol.com
W www.henandchickens.com

**UPSTART CROWS
THEATRE COMPANY**   T 020 8543 4085
14 Chesnut Road, Raynes Park
London SW20 8EB
E upstartcrows@virginmedia.com

**VANDER ELST, Anthony
PRODUCTIONS**   T 020 8466 5580
The Studio, 14 College Road
Bromley, Kent BR1 3NS

**VOLCANO THEATRE
COMPANY LTD**   T 01792 464790
229 High Street
Swansea SA1 1NY
E mail@volcanotheatre.co.uk
W www.volcanotheatre.co.uk

WALKING FORWARD   T 01480 496309
29 Hampton Close, Fenstanton
Cambridgeshire PE28 9HB
E info@walkingforward.co.uk
W www.walkingforward.co.uk

WALLACE, Kevin LTD   T 020 7812 7238
Amadeus House, 27B Floral Street
London WC2E 9DP
E info@kevinwallace.co.uk

WAREHOUSE PHOENIX LTD   T 020 7580 1000
*Ex-Warehouse Theatre Croydon. Producers of
International Playwriting Festival*
87 Great Titchfield Street
London W1W 6RL
E warehousephoenix@outlook.com
W www.warehousephoenix.co.uk

WAX, Kenny LTD   T 020 7437 1736
3rd Floor
62 Shaftesbury Avenue
London W1D 6LT
W www.kennywax.com

**WELDON, Duncan C.
PRODUCTIONS LTD**   T 01243 527186
The Cottage, West Lavant
Chichester, West Sussex PO18 9AH

**WESTENDFRONT
PRODUCTIONS LTD**   T 020 8150 7294
19A Goodge Street
London W1Y 2PH
E info@westendfrontproductions.co.uk
W www.westendfrontproductions.co.uk

WHITALL, Keith   T 01323 844882
25 Solway, Hailsham
East Sussex BN27 3HB

WHITEHALL, Michael   T/F 020 8785 3737
6 Embankment, Putney
London SW15 1LB
E whitehallfilms@gmail.com

WILDER, David PRODUCTIONS   T 07710 907221
1 Elmlea Drive, Olney
Bucks MK46 5HU
E info@davidwilderproductions.co.uk
W www.davidwilderproductions.co.uk

**WILLS, Newton
MANAGEMENT**   T 07989 398381
12 St Johns Road, Isleworth
Middlesex TW7 6NN
F 00 33 4 68218685
E newton.wills@aol.com
W www.newtonwills.com

**WILSON, Jamie
PRODUCTIONS LTD**   T 020 7240 0748
18 Exeter Street
London WC2E 7DU
E info@jamiewilsonproductions.com
W www.jamiewilsonproductions.com

WIZARD THEATRE   T 0800 5832373
Blenheim Villa, Burr Street
Harwell, Oxfordshire OX11 0DT
E admin@wizardtheatre.co.uk
W www.wizardtheatre.co.uk

**WORD & MUSIC
COMPANY THE**   T 020 7385 2038
The Hub @ St Alban's Fulham
2 Margravine Road
London W6 8HJ
E info@associatedstudios.co.uk
W www.associatedstudios.co.uk

**WORTMAN UK / POLESTAR
PICTURES UK / US**   T 020 8994 8886
Film & Television Productions
48 Chiswick Staithe, London W4 3TP
T 07976 805976
E neville@speakwell.co.uk
W www.speakwell.co.uk

YELLOW EARTH THEATRE   T 020 8694 6631
The Albany, Douglas Way
London SE8 4AG
E admin@yellowearth.org
W www.yellowearth.org

YOUNG VIC THEATRE   T 020 7922 2800
66 The Cut, London SE1 8LZ
F 020 7922 2801
E info@youngvic.org
W www.youngvic.org

Theatre

There are hundreds of theatres and theatre companies in the UK, varying dramatically in size and type. The theatre sections are organised under headings which best indicate a theatre's principal area of work. A summary of each of these is below.

Alternative & Community

Many of these companies tour to arts centres, small and middle-scale theatres, and non-theatrical venues which do not have a resident company, or they may be commissioned to develop site-specific projects. The term 'alternative' is sometimes used to describe work that is more experimental in style and execution.

Children, Young People & TIE

The primary focus of these theatre companies is to reach younger audiences. They often tour to smaller theatres, schools and non-theatrical venues. Interactive teaching – through audience participation and workshops – is often a feature of their work.

English Speaking Theatre Companies in Europe

These work principally outside of the UK. Some are based in one venue whilst others are touring companies. Their work varies enormously and includes theatre for young people, large-scale musicals, revivals of classics and dinner theatre. Actors are employed either for an individual production or a 'season' of several plays.

London Theatres

Larger theatres situated in the West End and Central London. A few are producing houses, but most are leased to theatre producers who take responsibility for putting together a company for a run of a single show. In such cases it is they and not the venue who cast productions (often with the help of casting directors). Alternatively, a production will open outside London and tour to provincial theatres, then subsequently, if successful, transfer to a London venue.

Outer London, Fringe & Venues

Small and middle-scale theatres in Outer London and around the country. Some are producing houses, others are only available for hire. Many of the London venues have provided useful directions on how they may be reached by public transport.

Provincial / Touring

Theatre producers and other companies sell their ready-made productions to the provincial/touring theatres, a list of larger venues outside London. A run in each theatre varies between a night and several weeks, but a week per venue for tours of plays is usual. Even if a venue is not usually a producing house, most provincial theatres and arts centres put on a family show at Christmas.

Puppet Theatre Companies

Some puppet theatres are one-performer companies who literally create their own work from scratch. The content and style of productions varies enormously. For example, not all are aimed at children, and some are more interactive than others. Although we list a few theatres with puppet companies in permanent residence, this kind of work often involves touring. As with all small and middle scale touring, performers who are willing, and have the skills, to involve themselves with all aspects of company life are always more valuable.

Repertory (Regional) Theatres

Theatres situated outside London which employ a resident company of actors (i.e. the 'repertory company') on a play-by-play basis or for a season of several plays. In addition to the main auditorium (usually the largest acting space) these theatres may have a smaller studio theatre attached, which will be home to an additional company whose focus is education or the production of new plays (see 'Theatre: Children, Young People & TIE'). In recent years the length of repertory seasons has become shorter; this means that a number of productions are no longer in-house. It is common for gaps in the performance calendar to be filled by tours mounted by theatre producers, other repertory theatres and non-venue based production companies.

1623 THEATRE COMPANY   T 01332 285434
QUAD, Market Place
Cathedral Quarter
Derby DE1 3AS
E messages@1623theatre.co.uk
W www.1623theatre.co.uk

ABERYSTWYTH ARTS CENTRE   T 01970 621512
Penglais, Aberystwyth
Ceredigion SY23 3DE
F 01970 622883
E ggo@aber.ac.uk
W www.aber.ac.uk/artscentre

ADMIRATION THEATRE   T 07010 041579
Twitter: @theatre.com
E email@admirationtheatre.com
W www.admirationtheatre.com

**AGE EXCHANGE
THEATRE TRUST**   T 020 8318 9105
Contact: Suzanne Lockett (Director of Operations)
Number 11, Blackheath Village
London SE3 9LA
E administrator@age-exchange.org.uk
W www.age-exchange.org.uk

ALTERNATIVE ARTS   T 020 7375 0441
Top Studio, Montefiore Centre
Hanbury Street, London E1 5HZ
E info@alternativearts.co.uk
W www.alternativearts.co.uk

ANGLES THEATRE THE   BO 01945 474447
Alexandra Road, Wisbech
Cambridgeshire PE13 1HQ
E office@anglestheatre.co.uk

APELT, Steve PRODUCTIONS   T 01278 458253
20 Sandpiper Road
Blakespool Park
Bridgwater, Somerset TA6 5QU
E steve.apelt@virgin.net
W www.steveapelt.co.uk

ARUNDEL JAILHOUSE   T/F 01903 889821
Arundel Town Hall, Arundel
West Sussex BN18 9AP
E info@arundeljailhouse.co.uk
W www.arundeljailhouse.co.uk

**ASHTON GROUP
THEATRE THE**   T 01229 430636
The Cooks, 104 Abbey Road
Barrow-in-Furness
Cumbria LA14 5QR
E theashtongroup@btconnect.com
W www.ashtongroup.co.uk

ATTIC THEATRE COMPANY   T 020 8640 6800
Mitcham Library
157 London Road
Mitcham CR4 2YR
E info@attictheatrecompany.com
W www.attictheatrecompany.com

BANNER THEATRE   T 0845 4581909
23 Endwood Court Road
Birmingham B20 2RX
E info@bannertheatre.co.uk

BECK THEATRE   T 020 8561 7506
Grange Road, Hayes
Middlesex UB3 2UE
BO 020 8561 8371
E enquiries@becktheatre.org.uk
W www.becktheatre.org.uk

**BLUEYED THEATRE
PRODUCTIONS**   T 07799 137487
59B Crystal Palace Park Road
London SE26 6UT
E info@blueyedtheatreproductions.co.uk
W www.blueyedtheatreproductions.co.uk

**BLUNDERBUS THEATRE
COMPANY LTD**   T 01636 678900
The Old Painters Store, Cliff Nook Lane
Newark, Nottinghamshire NG24 1LY
E admin@blunderbus.co.uk
W www.blunderbus.co.uk

**CAPITAL ARTS
YOUTH THEATRE**   T/F 020 8449 2342
Capital Arts Studio
Wyllyotts Theatre, Darkes Lane
Potters Bar, Herts EN6 2HN
T 07885 232414
E capitalarts@btconnect.com
W www.capitalarts.org.uk

CARIB THEATRE COMPANY   T/F 020 8903 4592
73 Lancelot Road, Wembley
Middlesex HA0 2AN
E antoncarib@yahoo.co.uk

**CENTRE FOR
PERFORMANCE RESEARCH**   T 01970 622133
The Foundry, Parry Williams
Penglais Campus SY23 3AJ
F 01970 622132
E info@thecpr.org.uk
W www.thecpr.org.uk

CHAIN REACTION   T/F 020 8981 9527
Millers, Three Mills Lane
London E3 3DY
E admin@chainreactiontheatre.co.uk
W www.chainreactiontheatre.co.uk

CHATS PALACE   T 020 8533 0227
42-44 Brooksby's Walk, Hackney
London E9 6DF
E info@chatspalace.com
W www.chatspalace.co.uk

CHEESE & CRACKERS LTD   T 07982 429350
*Comedy & Theatre Entertainment Company based in the
North East*
33 Cambourne Close, Hemlington
Teesside TS8 9QD
E cheesecrackersltd@gmail.com
W www.cheeseandcrackersltd.wix.com/
cheeseandcrackers

CHICKENSHED   T 020 8216 2733
290 Chase Side, Southgate
London N14 4PE
BO 020 8292 9222
E susanj@chickenshed.org.uk
W www.chickenshed.org.uk

CHOL THEATRE   T 01484 536008
Contact: Susan Burns (Director)
Lawrence Batley Theatre
8 Queen Street
Huddersfield, West Yorkshire HD1 2SP
F 01484 425336
E info@choltheatre.co.uk
W www.choltheatre.co.uk

CITIZENS LEARNING   T 0141 429 5561
Citizens' Theatre, 119 Gorbals Street
Glasgow G5 9DS
F 0141 429 7374
E info@citz.co.uk
W www.citz.co.uk

**CLOSE FOR COMFORT
THEATRE COMPANY**   T 07710 258290
34 Boleyn Walk, Leatherhead
Surrey KT22 7HU
T 01372 378613
E close4comf@aol.com
W www.closeforcomforttheatre.co.uk

COMPLETE WORKS THE   T 020 7377 0280
The Old Truman Brewery
91 Brick Lane
London E1 6QL
F 020 7247 7405
E info@tcw.org.uk
W www.tcw.org.uk

**CORNELIUS & JONES
ORIGINAL PRODUCTIONS**   T/F 01908 612593
49 Carters Close, Sherington
Newport Pagnell
Buckinghamshire MK16 9NW
E admin@corneliusjones.com
W www.corneliusjones.com

CURZON KNUTSFORD   T 01565 633005
Primarily Cinema with Hire Spaces
Toft Road, Knutsford
Cheshire WA16 0PE
E manager.knutsford@curzon.com
W www.curzoncinemas.com

CUT-CLOTH THEATRE   T 07950 542346
41 Beresford Road, Highbury
London N5 2HR

EALDFAEDER   T 01787 238257
Anglo Saxon Living History & Re-enactment
12 Carleton Close, Great Yeldham
Essex CO9 4QJ
E pete@gippeswic.demon.co.uk
W www.ealdfaeder.org

ELECTRIC CABARET   T 07714 089763
*Specialising in Physical Theatre, Mime, Street Theatre,
Clowns & Workshops*
50 Oakthorpe Road, Oxford OX2 7BE
E richard@electriccabaret.co.uk
W www.electricccabaret.co.uk

EUROPEAN THEATRE COMPANY THE
15 Beverley Avenue
London SW20 0RL
E admin@europeantheatre.co.uk
W www.europeantheatre.co.uk

**FEMME FATALE
THEATRE COMPANY**   T 07779 611414
30 Creighton Avenue, Muswell Hill
London N10 1NU
E dianelefley@yahoo.com
W www.femmefataletheatrecompany.com

**FOREST FORGE
THEATRE COMPANY**   T 01425 470188
The Theatre Centre
Endeavour Park, Crow Arch Lane
Ringwood, Hampshire BH24 1SF
E info@forestforge.co.uk
W www.forestforge.co.uk

FOUND THEATRE   T 01629 813083
The Byways, Church Street
Monyash, Derbyshire DE45 1JH
E found_theatre@yahoo.co.uk
W www.foundtheatre.org.uk

**FRANTIC THEATRE
COMPANY**   T/F 0870 1657350
32 Woodlane, Falmouth TR11 4RF
E bookings@frantictheatre.com
W www.frantictheatre.com

**GALLEON THEATRE
COMPANY LTD**   T 020 8310 7276
Head Office, Greenwich Playhouse
50 Openshaw Road
London SE2 0TE
E boxoffice@galleontheatre.co.uk
W www.galleontheatre.co.uk

GRANGE THEATRE   T 0161 785 4239
Rochdale Road, Oldham
Greater Manchester OL9 6EA
E grangetheatre@oldham.ac.uk
W www.oldham.ac.uk/grangetheatre

GREASEPAINT ANONYMOUS   T 020 8360 9785
Youth Theatre Company
13 Oak Lodge, 50 Eversley Park Road
London N21 1JL
T 07930 421216
E info@greasepaintanonymous.co.uk

HALL FOR CORNWALL   T 01872 321971
Contact: Isobel King (Education Manager)
Back Quay, Truro
Cornwall TR1 2LL
E isobelk@hallforcornwall.org.uk
W www.hallforcornwall.co.uk

**HEBE THEATRE
COMPANY THE**   T 07818 459561
Presents The Ruba'iya't of Omar Khayya'm
7 Harvest House, Cobbold Road
Felixstowe, Suffolk IP11 7SP
E c.mugleston672@btinternet.com
W www.thehebetheatrecompany.onesuffolk.net

HIJINX THEATRE   T 029 2030 0331
*Touring Theatre Company. Producers of Inclusive
Theatre*
Wales Millennium Centre, Bute Place
Cardiff CF10 5AL
E info@hijinx.org.uk
W www.hijinx.org.uk

HISTORIA THEATRE COMPANY T 020 7837 8008
8 Cloudesley Square
London N1 0HT
T 07811 892079
E kateprice@lineone.net
W www.historiatheatre.com

ICON THEATRE T 01634 813179
The Brook Theatre
Old Town Hall
Chatham, Kent ME4 4SE
E nancy@icontheatre.org.uk
W www.icontheatre.org.uk

IMAGE MUSICAL THEATRE T 020 8743 9380
197 Church Road, Northolt
Middlesex UB5 5BE
F 020 8181 6279
E admin@imagemusicaltheatre.co.uk
W www.imagemusicaltheatre.co.uk

IMMEDIATE THEATRE T 020 7923 8180
Unit 18, Springfield House
5 Tyson Street, London E8 2LY
E info@immediate-theatre.com
W www.immediate-theatre.com

INOCENTE ART & FILM LTD T 07973 518132
Film. Multimedia. Music Videos. Two Rock 'n' Roll Musicals
Flat 2, 76 Highdown Road
Hove BN3 6EB
E tarascas@btopenworld.com
W www.tanglehead.co.uk

ISOSCELES T 020 8946 3905
7 Amity Grove, Raynes Park
London SW20 0LQ
E patanddave@isosceles.biz
W www.isosceles.biz

KING'S HEAD THEATRE BO 020 7478 0160
Contact: Adam Spreadbury-Maher (Artistic Director)
115 Upper Street, Islington
London N1 1QN
T 020 7226 8561
E info@kingsheadtheatre.com
W www.kingsheadtheatre.com

KNEEHIGH T 01872 267910
Twitter: @wearekneehigh
15 Walsingham Place, Truro
Cornwall TR1 2RP
E office@kneehigh.co.uk
W www.kneehigh.co.uk

KOMEDIA T 01273 647101
44-47 Gardner Street
Brighton BN1 1UN
E info@komedia.co.uk
W www.komedia.co.uk

KORU THEATRE T 020 8579 1029
11 Clovelly Road
London W5 5HF
E info@korutheatre.com
W www.korutheatre.com

LIVE THEATRE T 0191 261 2694
New Writing
Broad Chare, Quayside
Newcastle upon Tyne NE1 3DQ
F 0191 232 2224
E info@live.org.uk
W www.live.org.uk

LONDON ACTORS THEATRE COMPANY T 020 7978 2620
Unit 5A, Imex Business Centre
Ingate Place, London SW8 3NS
E latchmere@fishers.org.uk

LONDON BUBBLE THEATRE COMPANY LTD T 020 7237 4434
5 Elephant Lane
London SE16 4JD
E admin@londonbubble.org.uk
W www.londonbubble.org.uk

LONG OVERDUE THEATRE COMPANY THE T 0845 8382994
16 Butterfield Drive, Amesbury
Wiltshire SP4 7SJ
E stefpearmain@hotmail.com
W www.tlots.co.uk

LSW JUNIOR INTER-ACT T/F 020 7793 9755
PO Box 31855
London SE17 3XP
E londonswo@hotmail.com
W www.londonshakespeare.org.uk

LSW PRISON PROJECT T/F 020 7793 9755
PO Box 31855, London SE17 3XP
E londonswo@hotmail.com
W www.lswproductions.co.uk

LSW SENIOR RE-ACTION T/F 020 7793 9755
PO Box 31855, London SE17 3XP
E londonswo@hotmail.com
W www.lswproductions.co.uk

LYRICS & LAUGHTER PRODUCTIONS T 01425 612830
Music Hall. Comedy. Revues. Themed Shows.
Locally Based
35 Barton Court Avenue
Barton on Sea, Hants BH25 7EP
E lyricsandlaughter@outlook.com
W www.lyricsandlaughter.info

M6 THEATRE COMPANY T 01706 355898
Studio Theatre, Hamer CP School
Albert Royds Street
Rochdale OL16 2SU
F 01706 712601
E admin@m6theatre.co.uk
W www.m6theatre.co.uk

MADDERMARKET THEATRE T 01603 626560
Resident Community Theatre Company. Small-scale Producing & Receiving House
St John's Alley
Norwich NR2 1DR
E office@maddermarket.org
W www.maddermarket.co.uk

MAGIC HAT PRODUCTIONS **T** 07769 560991
Based in London
E general@magichat-productions.com
W www.magichat-productions.com

MANCHESTER ACTORS COMPANY **T** 0161 227 8702
c/o 31 Leslie Street
Manchester M14 7NE
E steve.boyes1411@gmail.com
W www.manactco.org.uk

MAVERICK THEATRE COMPANY LTD **T** 020 8090 5082
2nd Floor, 12 Fouberts Place
Carnaby Street, London W1F 7PA
T 07531 138248
E info@mavericktheatre.co.uk
W www.mavericktheatre.co.uk

MIKRON THEATRE COMPANY LTD **T** 01484 843701
Marsden Mechanics, Peel Street
Marsden, Huddersfield HD7 6BW
E admin@mikron.org.uk
W www.mikron.org.uk

NATURAL THEATRE COMPANY **T** 01225 469131
Street Theatre. Touring. Corporate
Widcombe Institute, Widcombe Hill
Bath BA2 6AA
E info@naturaltheatre.co.uk
W www.naturaltheatre.co.uk

NEW PERSPECTIVES **T** 0115 927 2334
Park Lane Business Centre, Park Lane
Basford, Nottingham NG6 0DW
E info@newperspectives.co.uk
W www.newperspectives.co.uk

NEWFOUND THEATRE COMPANY
Contact: By e-mail
E newfoundtheatre@gmail.com
W www.newfoundtheatre.com

NORTH COUNTRY THEATRE **T** 01748 825288
3 Rosemary Lane, Richmond
North Yorkshire DL10 4DP
E office@northcountrytheatre.com
W www.northcountrytheatre.com

NORTHERN STAGE (THEATRICAL PRODUCTIONS) LTD **T** 0191 242 7200
Barras Bridge
Newcastle upon Tyne NE1 7RH
F 0191 242 7257
E info@northernstage.co.uk
W www.northernstage.co.uk

NORTHUMBERLAND THEATRE COMPANY (NTC) **T** 01665 602586
Touring Regionally & Nationally
The Playhouse, Bondgate Without
Alnwick, Northumberland NE66 1PQ
F 01665 605837
E admin@northumberlandtheatre.co.uk
W www.northumberlandtheatre.co.uk

OPEN STAGE PRODUCTIONS **T/F** 0121 777 9086
49 Springfield Road, Moseley
Birmingham B13 9NN
E info@openstage.co.uk
W www.openstage.co.uk

PASCAL THEATRE COMPANY **T** 020 7383 0920
35 Flaxman Court, Flaxman Terrace
Bloomsbury, London WC1H 9AR
E pascaltheatrecompany@gmail.com
W www.pascal-theatre.com

PEOPLE'S THEATRE COMPANY THE
69 Manor Way, Guildford
Surrey GU2 7RR
E ptc@ptc.org.uk
W www.ptc.org.uk

PHANTOM CAPTAIN THE **T** 020 8455 4564
618B Finchley Road, London NW11 7RR
E lambhorn@gmail.com

PLAYTIME THEATRE COMPANY **T** 01227 266272
18 Bennells Avenue, Whitstable
Kent CT5 2HP
F 01227 266648
E playtime@dircon.co.uk
W www.playtimetheatre.co.uk

POWERHOUSE THEATRE COMPANY **T** 01483 232690
Contact: Geoff Lawson (Artistic Director)
58 Oak Hill, Wood Street
Guildford GU3 3ER
T 07949 821567
E powerhousetheatre@hotmail.co.uk
W www.powerhousetheatre.co.uk

PROTEUS THEATRE COMPANY **T** 01256 354541
Multimedia & Cross-artform Work
Proteus Creations Space
Council Road, Basingstoke
Hampshire RG21 3DH
E info@proteustheatre.com
W www.proteustheatre.com

PURSUED BY A BEAR PRODUCTIONS **T** 01252 745445
Farnham Maltings, Bridge Square
Farnham GU9 7QR
E pursuedbyabear@yahoo.co.uk
W www.pursuedbyabear.co.uk

Q20 THEATRE LTD **T** 01274 221360
Dockfield Road, Shipley
West Yorkshire BD17 7AD
E info@q20theatre.co.uk

RIDING LIGHTS THEATRE COMPANY **T** 01904 655317
Friargate Theatre, Lower Friargate
York YO1 9SL
F 01904 651532
E info@rltc.org
W www.ridinglights.org

SALTMINE THEATRE COMPANY (SALTMINE TRUST) T 01384 454807
61 The Broadway, Dudley DY1 3EB
E creative@saltmine.org
W www.saltminetrust.org.uk

SPANNER IN THE WORKS T 020 7193 7995
95 Old Woolwich Road, Greenwich
London SE10 9PP
T 07850 313986
E info@spannerintheworks.org.uk
W www.spannerintheworks.org.uk

SPARE TYRE T/F 020 7061 6454
Contact: Arti Prashar (Artistic Director). Theatre Without Prejudice. For Performers who are Female, Older or have Learning Disabilities
Unit 3.22, Canterbury Court
Kennington Park, 1-3 Brixton Road
London SW9 6DE
E info@sparetyre.org
W www.sparetyre.org

SPECTACLE THEATRE T 01443 430700
Coleg Morgannwg Rhondda, Llwynypia
Tonypandy CF40 2TQ
F 01443 439640
E info@spectacletheatre.co.uk
W www.spectacletheatre.co.uk

SPONTANEITY SHOP THE T 020 7788 4080
85-87 Bayham Street, London NW1 0AG
E info@the-spontaneity-shop.com
W www.the-spontaneity-shop.com

TAKING FLIGHT THEATRE COMPANY T 029 2023 0020
Chapter Arts Centre, Market Road
Canton, Cardiff CF5 1QE
E takingflighttheatre@yahoo.co.uk
W www.takingflighttheatre.co.uk

TARA ARTS GROUP LTD T 020 8333 4457
Tara Theatre, 356 Garratt Lane
London SW18 4ES
F 020 8870 9540
E tara@tara-arts.com
W www.tara-arts.com

THEATRE& LTD T 01484 664078
25 Queens Square Business Park
Huddersfield Road
Honley, West Yorkshire HD9 6QZ
F 01484 660079
E cmitchell@theatreand.com
W www.theatreand.com

THEATRE & FILM WORKSHOP T 0131 555 3854
Out of the Blue Drill Hall
36 Dalmeny Street
Edinburgh EH6 8RG
W www.theatre-workshop.com

THEATRE PECKHAM T 020 7708 5401
Havil Street, London SE5 7SD
E admin@theatrepeckham.co.uk
W www.theatrepeckham.co.uk

TOBACCO FACTORY THEATRES T 0117 902 0345
1st Floor, Raleigh Road, Southville
Bristol BS3 1TF
E theatre@tobaccofactorytheatres.com
W www.tobaccofactorytheatres.com

TROY THEATRE COMPANY T 07710 431741
New Plays Considered for Festivals & Fringe Venues
184 Wandle Road, Morden
Surrey SM4 6AB
E jane.sheraton@gmail.com

UPTKREEK THEATRE T 07935 822939
82 St Stephens Road, Saltash
Cornwall PL12 6DA
E uptkreek@live.co.uk

WAREHOUSE PHOENIX LTD T 020 7580 1000
Ex-Warehouse Theatre Croydon
87 Great Titchfield Street
London W1W 6RL
E warehousephoenix@outlook.com
W www.warehousephoenix.co.uk

WOMEN & THEATRE BIRMINGHAM LTD T 0121 449 7117
Twitter: @womenandtheatre
The Old Lodge, Uffculme
50 Queensbridge Road, Moseley
Birmingham B13 8QY
E info@womenandtheatre.co.uk
W www.womenandtheatre.co.uk

Y TOURING THEATRE COMPANY T 020 7520 3090
One KX, 120 Cromer Street
London WC1H 8BS
E d.jackson@ytouring.org.uk
W www.theatreofdebate.com

YELLOW EARTH THEATRE T 020 8694 6631
The Albany, Douglas Way
London SE8 4AG
E admin@yellowearth.org
W www.yellowearth.org

YELLOWCHAIR PERFORMANCE EXPERIENCE THE
First Breaks on the London Fringe for New Talent
89 Birchanger Lane
Bishop Stortford CM23 5QF
E contacttype@gmail.com
W www.wix.com/yellowchair/type

YORICK INTERNATIONALIST THEATRE ENSEMBLE T/F 020 7836 7637
Yorick Theatre & Film
4 Duval Court, 36 Bedfordbury
Covent Garden, London WC2N 4DQ
E yorickx@hotmail.com

YOUNG VIC THEATRE T 020 7922 2800
66 The Cut, London SE1 8LZ
BO 020 7922 2922
E info@youngvic.org
W www.youngvic.org

A THOUSAND CRANES T 07801 269772
48 Brunswick Crescent, London N11 1EB
E kumiko@athousandcranes.org.uk
W www.athousandcranes.org.uk

ACTION STATION UK LTD THE T 0870 7702705
4-6 Canfield Place, London NW6 3BT
E info@theactionstation.co.uk
W www.theactionstation.co.uk

ACTION TRANSPORT THEATRE T 0151 357 2120
*New Writing. Professional Production for, by & with
Young People*
Whitby Hall, Stanney Lane
Ellesmere Port, Cheshire CH65 9AE
E info@actiontransporttheatre.org
W www.actiontransporttheatre.org

ACTIONWORK WORLDWIDE LTD T 01934 815163
Theatre & Film Productions with Young People
PO Box 433, Weston-super-Mare
Somerset BS24 0WY
E admin@actionwork.com
W www.actionwork.com

**AESOP'S TOURING
THEATRE COMPANY** T/F 01483 724633
Professional TIE Theatre Company Touring Nationally
The Arches, 38 The Riding
Woking, Surrey GU21 5TA
T 07836 731872
E info@aesopstheatre.co.uk
W www.aesopstheatre.co.uk

**AKADEMI SOUTH
ASIAN DANCE UK** T 020 7691 3210
Hampstead Town Hall, 213 Haverstock Hill
London NW3 4QP
E info@akademi.co.uk
W www.akademi.co.uk

APELT, Steve PRODUCTIONS T 01278 458253
20 Sandpiper Road, Blakespool Park
Bridgwater, Somerset TA6 5QU
E steve.apelt@virgin.net
W www.steveapelt.co.uk

**ARTY-FACT THEATRE
COMPANY LTD** T 07020 962096
18 Weston Lane, Crewe, Cheshire CW2 5AN
F 07020 982098
E artyfact@talktalk.net
W www.arty-fact.co.uk

ASHCROFT YOUTH THEATRE T 0844 8005328
Ashcroft Academy of Dramatic Art, Harris Primary
Academy Crystal Palace
Malcolm Road, Penge, London SE20 8RH
T 07799 791586
E info@ashcroftacademy.com
W www.ashcroftacademy.com

**BARKING DOG
THEATRE COMPANY** T 020 7117 6321
Building 3, Chiswick Park
566 Chiswick High Road, London W4 5YA
T 07803 773160
E mike@barkingdog.co.uk
W www.barkingdog.co.uk

BECK THEATRE T 020 8561 7506
Grange Road, Hayes, Middlesex UB3 2UE
BO 020 8561 8371
E enquiries@becktheatre.org.uk
W www.becktheatre.org.uk

BIG ACT THE T 0870 8810367
14-16 Wilson Place, Bristol BS2 9HJ
E info@thebigact.com
W www.thebigact.com

BIG WOODEN HORSE T 020 8567 8431
Twitter: @bigwoodenhorse1
30 Northfield Road, West Ealing, London W13 9SY
E info@bigwoodenhorse.com
W www.bigwoodenhorse.com

**BIRMINGHAM STAGE
COMPANY THE** T 020 7437 3391
*Contact: Neal Foster (Actor/Manager), Philip Compton
(Executive Producer)*
Suite 228, The Linen Hall, 162 Regent Street
London W1B 5TB
F 020 7437 3395
E info@birminghamstage.com
W www.birminghamstage.com

BITESIZE THEATRE COMPANY T 01978 358320
8 Green Meadows, New Broughton
Wrexham LL11 6SG
F 01978 756308
E admin@bitesizetheatre.co.uk
W www.bitesizetheatre.co.uk

**BLUNDERBUS THEATRE
COMPANY LTD** T 01636 678900
The Old Painter's Store, Cliff Nook Lane
Newark, Notts NG24 1LY
E hello@blunderbus.co.uk
W www.blunderbus.co.uk

**BOOSTER CUSHION
THEATRE LTD** T 01727 873874
75 How Wood, Park Street
St Albans, Herts AL2 2RW
F 01727 872597
E admin@booster-cushion.co.uk
W www.boostercushiontheatreforchildren.com

BRIDGE HOUSE THEATRE T 01926 776437
Professional & School Productions. Visiting Companies
Warwick School Site, Myton Road
Warwick CV34 6PP
E boxoffice@warwick.org
W www.bridgehousetheatre.co.uk

**CAMBRIDGE TOURING
THEATRE** T/F 01223 246533
29 Worts Causeway, Cambridge CB1 8RJ
E info@cambridgetouringtheatre.co.uk
W www.cambridgetouringtheatre.co.uk

CHAIN REACTION T/F 020 8981 9527
Millers, Three Mills Lane, London E3 3DU
E admin@chainreactiontheatre.co.uk
W www.chainreactiontheatre.co.uk

CHICKENSHED T 020 8351 6161
290 Chase Side, Southgate
London N14 4PE
BO 020 8292 9222
E susanj@chickenshed.org.uk
W www.chickenshed.org.uk

**CLWYD THEATR CYMRU
THEATRE FOR YOUNG PEOPLE** T 01352 701575
Contact: Nerys Edwards (Administrator)
Raikes Lane, Mold, Flintshire CH7 1YA
F 01352 701558
E ctctyp@clwyd-theatr-cymru.co.uk
W www.ctctyp.co.uk

COMPLETE WORKS THE   T 020 7377 0280
Contact: Phil Evans (Artistic Director)
The Old Truman Brewery
91 Brick Lane
London E1 6QL
F 020 7247 7405
E info@tcw.org.uk
W www.tcw.org.uk

CRAGRATS   T 0844 8111184
Lawster House, 140 South Street
Dorking, Surrey RH4 2EU
E enquiries@cragrats.com
W www.cragrats.com

DAYLIGHT THEATRE   T 01453 763808
66 Middle Street, Stroud
Gloucestershire GL5 1EA

DONNA MARIA COMPANY   T 020 8670 7814
16 Bell Meadow, Dulwich
London SE19 1HP
E info@donnamariasworld.co.uk
W www.donna-marias-world.co.uk

DRAGON DRAMA   T 07590 452436
Theatre Company. Parties. Tuition. Workshops
347 Hanworth Road
Hampton TW12 3EJ
E askus@dragondrama.co.uk
W www.dragondrama.co.uk

**EUROPA CLOWNS
THEATRE SHOW**   T 01892 537964
36 St Lukes Road
Tunbridge Wells, Kent TN4 9JH
T 07973 512845
E mike@heypresto.orangehome.co.uk
W www.clownseuropa.co.uk

EUROPEAN THEATRE COMPANY THE
Contact: By Post/e-mail
15 Beverley Avenue
London SW20 0RL
E admin@europeantheatre.co.uk
W www.europeantheatre.co.uk

**FUTURES THEATRE
COMPANY**   T 020 7928 2832
St John's Crypt, 73 Waterloo Road
London SE1 8UD
F 020 7928 6724
E info@futurestheatrecompany.co.uk
W www.futurestheatrecompany.co.uk

GAZEBO THEATRE COMPANY   T 01902 497222
The Town Hall, Church Street
Bilston, West Midlands WV14 0AP
F 01902 497244
E admin@gazebotie.org
W www.gazebotie.org

**GREENWICH & LEWISHAM YOUNG
PEOPLE'S THEATRE (GLYPT)**   T 020 8854 1316
The Tramshed
51-53 Woolwich New Road
London SE18 6ES
E info@glypt.co.uk
W www.glypt.co.uk

GROUP 64 YOUTH THEATRE   T 020 8788 6935
Putney Arts Theatre, Ravenna Road
London SW15 6AW
E group.64@virgin.net
W www.g64.org.uk

**HALF MOON YOUNG
PEOPLE'S THEATRE**   T 020 7265 8138
43 White Horse Road
London E1 0ND
F 020 7709 8914
E admin@halfmoon.org.uk
W www.halfmoon.org.uk

HOXTON HALL   T 020 7684 0060
130 Hoxton Street
London N1 6SH
E info@hoxtonhall.co.uk
W www.hoxtonhall.co.uk

IMAGE MUSICAL THEATRE   T 020 8743 9380
197 Church Road, Northolt
Middlesex UB5 5BE
F 020 8181 6279
E admin@imagemusicaltheatre.co.uk
W www.imagemusicaltheatre.co.uk

INDIGO MOON THEATRE   T 07855 328552
35 Waltham Court, Beverley
East Yorkshire HU17 9JF
E info@indigomoontheatre.com
W www.indigomoontheatre.com

INTERACT YOUTH THEATRE   T 0151 336 4302
New Writing for Young People
9 Carlton Close, Parkgate
Neston, Cheshire CH64 6TD
E interactyouththeatre@gmail.com
W www.littleactorstheatre.com

INTERPLAY THEATRE   T 0113 263 8556
Armley Ridge Road, Leeds LS12 3LE
E info@interplayleeds.co.uk
W www.interplayleeds.co.uk

**KINETIC THEATRE
COMPANY LTD**   T 020 8286 2613
Suite H, The Jubilee Centre
Lombard Road, Wimbledon
London SW19 3TZ
F 020 8286 2645
E sarah@kinetictheatre.co.uk
W www.kinetictheatre.co.uk

KOMEDIA   T 01273 647101
44-47 Gardner Street
Brighton BN1 1UN
E info@komedia.co.uk
W www.komedia.co.uk

**LEAVENERS THE
(QUAKER COMMUNITY ARTS)**   T 0121 414 0099
1 The Lodge, 1046 Bristol Road
Birmingham B29 6LJ
E timi@leaveners.org
W www.leaveners.org

**LITTLE ACTORS
THEATRE COMPANY**   T 0151 336 4302
9 Carlton Close Road, Parkgate
Cheshire CH64 6TD
E mail@littleactorstheatre.com
W www.littleactorstheatre.com

M6 THEATRE COMPANY   T 01706 355898
Studio Theatre, Hamer CP School
Albert Royds Street
Rochdale OL16 2SU
F 01706 712601
E admin@m6theatre.co.uk
W www.m6theatre.co.uk

MAGIC CARPET THEATRE T 01482 709939
18 Church Street, Sutton-on-Hull HU7 4TS
E jon@magiccarpettheatre.com
W www.magiccarpettheatre.com

**NATIONAL ASSOCIATION OF YOUTH
THEATRES (NAYT)** T 07804 254651
*Works with Youth Theatres & other Organisations in
Regional Venues to Host Festivals & Events*
c/o Riding Lights Theatre Company, Friargate Theatre
Lower Friargate, York YO1 9SL
E info@nayt.org.uk
W www.nayt.org.uk

**NATIONAL STUDENT
DRAMA FESTIVAL** T 020 7036 9027
Woolyard, 54 Bermondsey Street, London SE1 3UD
E info@nsdf.org.uk
W www.nsdf.org.uk

**NATIONAL YOUTH MUSIC
THEATRE** T 020 7802 0386
Adrian House, 27 Vincent Square, London SW1P 2NN
F 020 7821 0458
E enquiries@nymt.org.uk
W www.nymt.org.uk

**NATIONAL YOUTH THEATRE
OF GREAT BRITAIN** T 020 3696 7066
111 Buckingham Palace Road, London SW1W 0DT
F 020 7036 9031
E info@nyt.org.uk
W www.nyt.org.uk

**NOTTINGHAM PLAYHOUSE
ROUNDABOUT** T 0115 947 4361
Nottingham Playhouse, Wellington Circus
Nottingham NG1 5AF
F 0115 947 5759
E roundabout@nottinghamplayhouse.co.uk

OILY CART T 020 8672 6329
*Creates Work for the under 6 yrs & for Young People
3-19 yrs with Profound & Multiple Learning Disabilities
(PMLD) or ASD*
Smallwood School Annexe, Smallwood Road
London SW17 0TW
E oilies@oilycart.org.uk
W www.oilycart.org.uk

ONATTI PRODUCTIONS LTD T 01594 562033
Contact: Andrew Bardwell (Artistic Director)
The Old Chapel, Yorkley, Gloucestershire GL15 4SB
F 0870 1643629
E info@onatti.co.uk
W www.onatti.co.uk

OUTLOUD PRODUCTIONS LTD T 07946 357521
TIE Company. Drama Workshops
21-23 Glendale Gardens, Leigh on Sea, Essex SS9 2PA
E info@outloudproductions.co.uk
W www.outloudproductions.co.uk

**PANDEMONIUM TOURING
PARTNERSHIP** T 029 2047 2060
228 Railway Street, Cardiff CF24 2NJ
T 07885 280635
E paul@pandemoniumtheatre.com

**PIED PIPER THEATRE
COMPANY** T/F 01428 684022
1 Lilian Place, Coxcombe Lane
Chiddingfold, Surrey GU8 4QA
E twpiedpiper@aol.com
W www.piedpipertheatre.co.uk

PLAY HOUSE THE T 0121 265 4425
c/o Birmingham Repertory Theatre, Centenary Square
Broad Street, Birmingham B1 2EP
F 0121 233 0652
E info@theplayhouse.org.uk
W www.theplayhouse.org.uk

**PLAYTIME THEATRE
COMPANY** T 01227 266272
*TIE Company Touring Drama & Workshops Nationally &
Internationally*
18 Bennells Avenue, Whitstable
Kent CT5 2HP
T 01227 266648
E playtime@dircon.co.uk
W www.playtimetheatre.co.uk

POLKA THEATRE T 020 8545 8323
240 The Broadway, Wimbledon SW19 1SB
F 020 8545 8365
E stephen@polkatheatre.com
W www.polkatheatre.com

Q20 THEATRE LTD T 01274 221360
Creative Arts Hub, Dockfield Road
Shipley, West Yorkshire BD17 7AD
F 0871 9942226
E info@q20theatre.co.uk

QUANTUM THEATRE T 020 8317 9000
*Contact: Michael Whitmore, Jessica Selous
(Artistic Directors)*
The Old Button Factory, 1-11 Bannockburn Road
Plumstead, London SE18 1ET
E office@quantumtheatre.co.uk
W www.quantumtheatre.co.uk

RAINBOW BIGBOTTOM T 01494 771029
84 Broadway, Chesham
Bucks HP5 1EG
T 07778 106552
E lorrainebmays@aol.com
W www.mrpanda.co.uk

**RAINBOW THEATRE
LONDON EAST** T 020 8331 6639
59 Prince John Road, Eltham
London SE9 6QB
F 07092 315384
E rainbowtheatrelondoneast@yahoo.co.uk
W www.rainbow-theatre.com

ROYAL & DERNGATE T 01604 626222
19-21 Guildhall Road
Northampton NN1 1DP
E arts@royalandderngate.co.uk
W www.royalandderngate.co.uk

SCOTTISH YOUTH THEATRE T 0141 552 3988
The Old Sheriff Court, 105 Brunswick Street
Glasgow G1 1TF
E info@scottishyouththeatre.org
W www.scottishyouththeatre.org

**SHAKESPEARE 4 KIDZ
THEATRE COMPANY THE** T 01342 894548
Oxted Production Office, PO Box 287
Oxted, Surrey RH8 8BX
E office@shakespeare4kidz.com
W www.shakespeare4kidz.com

SHAKESPEAREWORKS T/F 01865 241281
22 Chilswell Road, Oxford OX1 4PJ
E info@shakespeareworks.co.uk
W www.shakespeareworks.co.uk

SHEFFIELD THEATRES TRUST T 0114 249 5999
Contact: Dan Bates (Chief Executive)
55 Norfolk Street, Sheffield S1 1DA
F 0114 249 6003
E info@sheffieldtheatres.co.uk
W www.sheffieldtheatres.co.uk/
creativedevelopmentprogramme

**SHOOTING STAR
ENTERTAINMENTS** T 07708 390137
63 Charlton Street, Maidstone
Kent ME16 8LB
E enquiries@shootingstarents.co.uk
W www.shootingstarents.co.uk

**SOLOMON THEATRE
COMPANY** T 01725 518760
Penny Black, High Street
Damerham, Fordingbridge
Hants SP6 3EU
E office@solomontheatre.co.uk
W www.solomontheatre.co.uk

**SOUTH WEST YOUTH
THEATRE** T 07778 579005
*New Writing for Young People. Based in London SW18.
Ages 10+*
c/o 9 Carlton Close, Parkgate
Neston, Cheshire CH64 6TD
E swyt@littleactorstheatre.com
W www.littleactorstheatre.com

SPECTACLE THEATRE T 01443 430700
Coleg Morgannwg, Rhondda, Llwynypia
Tonypandy CF40 2TQ
F 01443 439640
E info@spectacletheatre.co.uk
W www.spectacletheatre.co.uk

**STORYTELLERS THEATRE
COMPANY THE** T 01253 839375
Bridge Farm, 249 Hawes Side Lane
Blackpool FY4 4AA
F 01253 792930
E admin@pendleproductions.co.uk
W www.pendleproductions.co.uk

**TALEGATE THEATRE
PRODUCTIONS** T 01777 708333
5 Station Road, Retford
Nottinghamshire DN22 7DE
E info@talegatetheatre.co.uk
W www.talegatetheatre.co.uk

TALL STORIES T 020 8348 0080
Jacksons Lane, 269A Archway Road
London N6 5AA
E info@tallstories.org.uk
W www.tallstories.org.uk

THEATR IOLO LTD T 029 2061 3782
Market Chapter Arts Centre
Market Road
Canton, Cardiff CF5 1QE
E admin@theatriolo.com
W www.theatriolo.com

THEATRE& LTD T 01484 664078
25 Queens Square Business Park
Huddersfield Road
Honley, West Yorkshire HD9 6QZ
F 01484 660079
E cmitchell@theatreand.com
W www.theatreand.com

THEATRE ALIBI T/F 01392 217315
Adults & Young People
Emmanuel Hall, Emmanuel Road
Exeter EX4 1EJ
E info@theatrealibi.co.uk
W www.theatrealibi.co.uk

THEATRE CENTRE T 020 7729 3066
National Touring. New Writing for Young Audiences
Shoreditch Town Hall, 380 Old Street
London EC1V 9LT
F 020 7739 9741
E admin@theatre-centre.co.uk
W www.theatre-centre.co.uk

**THEATRE COMPANY
BLAH BLAH BLAH** T 0113 380 5646
Roundhay Road Resource Centre
233-237 Roundhay Road, Leeds LS8 4HS
E cas@blahs.co.uk
W www.blahs.co.uk

THEATRE HULLABALOO T 01325 352004
The Meeting Rooms, 5 Skinner Gate
Darlington, County Durham DL3 7NB
E info@theatrehullabaloo.org.uk
W www.theatrehullabaloo.org.uk

THEATRE WORKOUT LTD T 020 8144 2290
13A Stratheden Road, Blackheath
London SE3 7TH
E education@theatreworkout.com
W www.education.theatreworkout.com

TRICYCLE THEATRE T/F 020 7372 6611
*Contact: Mark Londesborough (Creative Learning
Director)*
269 Kilburn High Road, London NW6 7JR
E education@tricycle.co.uk
W www.tricycle.co.uk

UNICORN THEATRE T 020 7645 0500
147 Tooley Street, London SE1 2HZ
F 020 7645 0550
E office@unicorntheatre.com
W www.unicorntheatre.com

WIZARD THEATRE T 0800 5832373
*Contact: Leon Hamilton (Artistic Director), Emmy
Bradbury (Company Manager), Oliver Gray (Associate
Producer)*
Blenheim Villa, Burr Street
Harwell, Oxon OX11 0DT
E admin@wizardtheatre.co.uk
W www.wizardtheatre.co.uk

YOUNG ACTORS THEATRE T 020 7278 2101
70-72 Barnsbury Road, Islington, London N1 0ES
E andrew@yati.org.uk
W www.yati.org.uk

**YOUNG SHAKESPEARE
COMPANY** T 020 8368 4828
*Contact: Christopher Geelan, Sarah Gordon (Artistic
Directors)*
213 Fox Lane, Southgate
London N13 4BB
E youngshakespeare@mac.com
W www.youngshakespeare.org.uk

ZEST THEATRE T 01522 569590
The Terrace, Grantham Street
Lincoln, Lincolnshire LN2 1BD
E hello@zesttheatre.com
W www.zesttheatre.com

AUSTRIA, VIENNA: Vienna's
English Theatre **T/F** 01304 813330
UK Representative: VM Theatre Productions Ltd
16 The Street, Ash, Canterbury, Kent CT3 2HJ
E vanessa@vmtheatre.demon.co.uk
W www.englishtheatre.at

DENMARK, COPENHAGEN:
The London Toast Theatre **T** 00 45 33228686
Contact: Vivienne McKee (Artistic Director), Soren Hall
(Administrator)
Kochsvej 18, DK-1812 Frb. C, Denmark
E mail@londontoast.dk
W www.londontoast.dk

FRANCE, LYON: Theatre from Oxford (Touring
Europe & Beyond)
Contact: Robert Southam
B.P. 10, F-42750 St-Denis-de-Cabanne, France
E fm.oxford@gmail.com

GERMANY, FRANKFURT AM MAIN: The English
Theatre Frankfurt **T** 00 49 69 24231615
Contact: Daniel Nicolai (Artistic & Managing Director)
Gallusanlage 7, 60329, Frankfurt am Main, Germany
F 00 49 69 24231614
E mail@english-theatre.de
W www.english-theatre.de

GERMANY, HAMBURG: The English Theatre of
Hamburg **T** 00 49 40 2277925
Contact: Robert Rumpf, Clifford Dean
Lerchenfeld 14, 22081 Hamburg
Germany
BO 00 49 40 2277089
W www.englishtheatre.de

GERMANY, TOURING GERMANY:
White Horse Theatre **T** 00 49 29 21339339
Contact: Peter Griffith, Michael Dray
Boerdenstrasse 17, 59494 Soest, Germany
F 00 49 29 21339336
E theatre@white-horse-theatre.eu
W www.whitehorse.de

ICELAND, REYKJAVIK: Light Nights - The
Summer Theatre **T** 00 354 5519181
Contact: Kristine G. Magnus (Artistic Director)
The Travelling Theatre
Baldursgata 37
IS-101 Reykjavik, Iceland
E info@lightnights.com
W www.lightnights.com

ITALY, SANREMO: Theatrino & Melting Pot
Theatre - ACLE **T** 00 39 0184 506070
Via Roma 54
18038 Sanremo (IM), Italy
F 00 39 0184 509996
E info@acle.org
W www.acle.org

SWEDEN, GOTHENBURG: Gothenburg English
Studio Theatre (GEST) **T** 00 46 3142 5065
Chapmanstorg 10 BV
Gothenburg
Sweden 41454
E info@gest.se
W www.gest.se

SWITZERLAND, GENEVA:
Simply Theatre **T** 00 41 22 8600518
Avenue de Choiseul 23A
1290 Versoix
Switzerland
F 00 41 22 8600519
E info@simplytheatre.com
W www.simplytheatre.com

UNITED KINGDOM, YORKLEY:
Onatti Productions Ltd **T** 01594 562033
Contact: Andrew Bardwell
The Old Chapel
Yorkley
Gloucestershire GL15 4SB
F 0870 1643629
E info@onatti.co.uk
W www.onatti.co.uk

ADELPHI T 020 7836 1166
409-412 Strand, London WC2R 0NS
BO 0844 4124651

ALDWYCH T 020 7836 5537
Aldwych, London WC2B 4DF
W www.aldwychtheatre.com

ALMEIDA T 020 7288 4900
Almeida Street, London N1 1TA
BO 020 7359 4404
E info@almeida.co.uk

AMBASSADORS T 020 7828 0600
West Street, London WC2H 9ND
BO 0844 8112334
E enquiries@theambassadorstheatre.co.uk
W www.theambassadorstheatre.co.uk

APOLLO T 020 7494 5834
Shaftesbury Avenue, London W1D 7EZ
BO 0844 4124658
E enquiries@nimaxtheatres.com
W www.nimaxtheatres.com

APOLLO VICTORIA T 020 7834 6318
17 Wilton Road, London SW1V 1LG
W www.apollovictorialondon.org.uk

ARTS T 020 7836 8463 (T/BO)
6-7 Great Newport Street, London WC2H 7JB
E productions@artstheatrewestend.co.uk
W www.artstheatrewestend.co.uk

BARBICAN T 020 7638 4141
Barbican Centre, Stage Door
Silk Street, London EC2Y 8DS
BO 020 7638 8891
E theatre@barbican.org.uk
W www.barbican.org.uk

BLOOMSBURY T 020 7679 2777
15 Gordon Street, London WC1H 0AH
BO 020 7388 8822
E admin@thebloomsbury.com
W www.thebloomsbury.com

BUSH T 020 8743 3584
7 Uxbridge Road, London W12 8LJ
BO 020 8743 5050
E info@bushtheatre.co.uk
W www.bushtheatre.co.uk

CAMBRIDGE T 020 7850 8710
Earlham Street, Seven Dials
Covent Garden, London WC2H 9HU
BO 020 7850 8715
W www.reallyuseful.com

CHARING CROSS T 020 7930 5868
Formerly New Players Theatre
The Arches, Off Villiers Street, London WC2N 6NL
E info@charingcrosstheatre.co.uk
W www.charingcrosstheatre.co.uk

**COLISEUM
(ENGLISH NATIONAL OPERA)** T 020 7836 0111
St Martin's Lane, London WC2N 4ES
BO 020 7845 9300
W www.eno.org

CRITERION T 020 7839 8811
2 Jermyn Street, Piccadilly, London SW1Y 4XA
BO 0844 8471778
E admin@criterion-theatre.co.uk
W www.criterion-theatre.co.uk

DOMINION T 020 7927 0900
268-269 Tottenham Court Road, London W1T 7AQ
BO 0844 8471775
W www.dominiontheatre.com

DONMAR WAREHOUSE T 020 7240 4882
41 Earlham Street, London WC2H 9LX
BO 0844 8717624
E office@donmarwarehouse.com
W www.donmarwarehouse.com

DRURY LANE T 020 7850 8790
Theatre Royal, Catherine Street, London WC2B 5JF
BO 0844 8588877
W www.rutheatres.com

DUCHESS T 020 7632 9600
Catherine Street, London WC2B 5LA
BO 0844 4124659
E general@nimaxtheatres.com

DUKE OF YORK'S T 020 7565 6500
St Martin's Lane, London WC2N 4BG
BO 0844 8717623

EVENTIM APOLLO T 020 8563 3800
Queen Caroline Street, London W6 9QH
BO 0844 2491000
E info@eventimapollo.com
W www.eventimapollo.com

FORTUNE T 020 7010 7900
Russell Street, Covent Garden, London WC2B 5HH
BO 0844 8717627

GARRICK T 020 7520 5692
2 Charing Cross Road, London WC2H 0HH
BO 020 7520 5693
E enquiries@nimaxtheatres.com

GIELGUD T 020 7292 1320
Shaftesbury Avenue, London W1D 6AR
BO 0844 4825130

HACKNEY EMPIRE T 020 8510 4500
291 Mare Street, London E8 1EJ
BO 020 8985 2424
E info@hackneyempire.co.uk
W www.hackneyempire.co.uk

HAMPSTEAD T 020 7449 4200
Eton Avenue, Swiss Cottage, London NW3 3EU
BO 020 7722 9301
E info@hampsteadtheatre.com
W www.hampsteadtheatre.com

HAROLD PINTER T 020 7321 5300 (SD)
Formerly Comedy Theatre
Panton Street, London SW1Y 4DN
BO 0844 8717622
E rachaellund@theambassadors.com
W www.atgtickets.com

HER MAJESTY'S T 020 7850 8750 (SD)
Haymarket, London SW1Y 4QL

LONDON PALLADIUM T 020 7850 8770
Argyll Street, London W1F 7TF
BO 0844 4122957

LYCEUM T 020 7420 8100
21 Wellington Street, London WC2E 7RQ
BO 0844 8713000

LYRIC T 020 7494 5840
29 Shaftesbury Avenue, London W1D 7ES
BO 0844 4124661
E general@nimaxtheatres.com

LYRIC HAMMERSMITH T 020 8741 6850
Lyric Square, King Street, London W6 0QL
E enquiries@lyric.co.uk W www.lyric.co.uk

NATIONAL T 020 7452 3333
South Bank, Upper Ground, London SE1 9PX
BO 020 7452 3000
W www.nationaltheatre.org.uk

NEW LONDON T 020 7242 9802
Drury Lane, London WC2B 5PW
BO 0844 4124654
E cuqui.rivera@reallyuseful.co.uk

NOEL COWARD T 020 7759 8010
Formerly Albery Theatre
St Martin's Lane, London WC2N 4AU
BO 0844 4825140

NOVELLO T 020 7759 9611
Formerly Strand
5 Aldwych, London WC2B 4LD
BO 0844 4825115

OLD VIC T 020 7928 2651
The Cut, London SE1 8NB
BO 0844 8717628
E ovtcadmin@oldvictheatre.com
W www.oldvictheatre.com

PALACE T 020 7434 0088
Shaftesbury Avenue, London W1D 5AY
BO 0844 4829676
W www.nimaxtheatres.com

PEACOCK T 020 7863 8268
For Administration see SADLER'S WELLS
Portugal Street, Kingsway, London WC2A 2HT
BO 0844 4124322
E info@sadlerswells.com
W www.sadlerswells.com

PHOENIX T 020 7438 9600
110 Charing Cross Road, London WC2H 0JP
BO 0844 8717629
E jaimebrent@theambassadors.com

PICCADILLY T 020 7478 8800
Denman Street, London W1D 7DY
BO 020 7478 8805
E piccadillymanager@theambassadors.com

PLAYHOUSE T 020 7839 4292
Northumberland Avenue
London WC2N 5DE
BO 0844 8717631

PRINCE EDWARD T 020 7440 3021
28 Old Compton Street, London W1D 4HS
BO 0844 4825151
W www.delfont-mackintosh.co.uk

PRINCE OF WALES T 020 7766 2100
Coventry Street, London W1D 6AS
BO 0844 4825110
E powmanagers@delmack.co.uk
W www.delfontmackintosh.co.uk

QUEEN'S T 020 7292 1350
Contact: Nicolas Shaw (Manager)
51 Shaftesbury Avenue, London W1D 6BA
BO 0844 4825160

REGENT'S PARK OPEN AIR T 0844 3753460
Inner Circle, Regent's Park, London NW1 4NU
BO 0844 8264242
W www.openairtheatre.com

RIVERSIDE STUDIOS T 020 8237 1000
Crisp Road, Hammersmith
London W6 9RL
BO 020 8237 1111
E info@riversidestudios.co.uk
W www.riversidestudios.co.uk

ROYAL COURT T 020 7565 5050
Sloane Square, London SW1W 8AS
BO 020 7565 5000
E info@royalcourttheatre.com
W www.royalcourttheatre.com

ROYAL OPERA HOUSE T 020 7240 1200
Bow Street, Covent Garden
London WC2E 9DD
BO 020 7304 4000

SADLER'S WELLS T 020 7863 8034
Rosebery Avenue, London EC1R 4TN
BO 0844 4124300
E info@sadlerswells.com
W www.sadlerswells.com

SAVOY T 020 7845 6050
Savoy Court, Strand
London WC2R 0ET
BO 0844 8717687
E savoytheatremanagement@theambassadors.com
W www.atgtickets.com

SHAFTESBURY T 020 7379 3345
Theatre of Comedy Company
210 Shaftesbury Avenue, London WC2H 8DP
BO 020 7379 5399
E info@shaftesburytheatre.com
W www.shaftesburytheatre.com

SHAKESPEARE'S GLOBE T 020 7902 1400
21 New Globe Walk
Bankside, London SE1 9DT
BO 020 7401 9919
E info@shakespearesglobe.com
W www.shakespearesglobe.com

SHAW T 020 7666 9037
100-110 Euston Road, London NW1 2AJ
BO 0844 2485075
E info@shaw-theatre.com
W www.shaw-theatre.com

SOHO T 020 7287 5060
21 Dean Street, London W1D 3NE
BO 020 7478 0100
E box1@sohotheatre.com
W www.sohotheatre.com

ST MARTIN'S T 020 7828 0600
West Street, London WC2H 9NZ
BO 0844 4991515
E enquiries@stmartinstheatre.co.uk
W www.the-mousetrap.co.uk

THEATRE ROYAL T 020 7930 8890
Haymarket, London SW1Y 4HT
BO 020 7930 8800

TRICYCLE T 020 7372 6611
269 Kilburn High Road
London NW6 7JR
BO 020 7328 1000
E info@tricycle.co.uk
W www.tricycle.co.uk

VAUDEVILLE T 020 7632 9538
404 Strand, London WC2R 0NH
BO 020 7836 3191

VICTORIA PALACE T 020 7828 0600
Victoria Street, London SW1E 5EA
BO 0844 2485000
E enquiries@victoriapalace.co.uk
W www.victoriapalace.co.uk

WYNDHAM'S T 020 7759 8077
Charing Cross Road, London WC2H 0DA
BO 0870 9500925

YOUNG VIC T 020 7922 2800
66 The Cut, London SE1 8LZ
BO 020 7922 2922
E info@youngvic.org
W www.youngvic.org

ALBANY THE BO 020 8692 4446
Douglas Way, Deptford
London SE8 4AG
E reception@thealbany.org.uk
W www.thealbany.org.uk

APROPOS PRODUCTIONS LTD T 020 7739 2857
53 Greek Street, London W1D 3DR
E info@aproposltd.com
W www.aproposltd.com

ARCH 468 THEATRE STUDIO T 07973 302908
Arch 468, 209A Coldharbour Lane
London SW9 8RU
E rebecca@arch468.com
W www.arch468.com

ARCOLA THEATRE T 020 7503 1645
*Contact: Mehmet Ergen (Artistic Director), Leyla Nazli
(Executive Producer). Route: Victoria Line to Highbury
& Islington, then Main Line to Dalston Kingsland then 5
min walk. Buses: 38 or 242 from West End, 149 from
London Bridge*
24 Ashwin Street, Dalston, London E8 3DL
BO 020 7503 1646
E info@arcolatheatre.com
W www.arcolatheatre.com

ARTSDEPOT T 020 8369 5454
5 Nether Street, Tally Ho Corner
North Finchley, London N12 0GA
E info@artsdepot.co.uk
W www.artsdepot.co.uk

BARONS COURT THEATRE T 020 8932 4747
*'The Curtain's Up'. Route: Piccadilly or District Lines to
West Kensington or Barons Court*
28A Comeragh Road, West Kensington
London W14 9HR
E londontheatre@gmail.com
W www.offwestend.com

BATES, Tristan THEATRE T 020 7632 8010
Contact: Ben Monks, Will Young (Creative Producers)
The Actors Centre, 1A Tower Street
London WC2H 9NP
BO 020 7240 6283
E tbt@actorscentre.co.uk
W www.tristanbatestheatre.co.uk

**BATTERSEA ARTS
CENTRE (BAC)** BO 020 7223 2223
*Route: Victoria or Waterloo (Main Line) to Clapham
Junction then 5 min walk or Northern Line to Clapham
Common then 20 min walk*
Lavender Hill, London SW11 5TN
E boxoffice@bac.org.uk
W www.bac.org.uk

BECK THEATRE T 020 8561 7506
*Route: Metropolitan Line to Uxbridge then buses 427 or
607 or Paddington Main Line to Hayes Harlington then
buses 90, H98 or 195 (10 min)*
Grange Road, Hayes
Middlesex UB3 2UE
BO 020 8561 8371
E enquiries@becktheatre.org.uk
W www.becktheatre.org.uk

BEDLAM THEATRE BO 0131 225 9893
11B Bristo Place, Edinburgh EH1 1EZ
E bedlam@bedlamtheatre.co.uk
W www.bedlamtheatre.co.uk

BIKE SHED THEATRE THE T 01392 434169
162-163 Fore Street, Exeter EX4 3AT
E info@bikeshedtheatre.co.uk
W www.bikeshedtheatre.co.uk

BLACKHEATH HALLS T 020 8318 9758
23 Lee Road, Blackheath, London SE3 9RQ
BO 020 8463 0100
E k.murray@trinitylaban.ac.uk
W www.blackheathhalls.com

BLOOMSBURY THEATRE T 020 7679 2777
Route: Tube to Euston, Euston Square or Warren Street
15 Gordon Street, Bloomsbury, London WC1H 0AH
BO 020 7388 8822
E admin@thebloomsbury.com
W www.thebloomsbury.com

BRENTWOOD THEATRE T 01277 230833
*Contact: David Zelly (Production Manager). Route:
Liverpool Street Main Line to Shenfield, then 15 min walk*
15 Shenfield Road, Brentwood
Essex CM15 8AG
BO 01277 200305
E david@brentwood-theatre.org
W www.brentwood-theatre.org

BRIDEWELL THEATRE THE T 020 7353 3331
*Route: Circle Line to Blackfriars. City Thameslink Capital
Connect. 15 different bus routes*
St Bride Foundation, Bride Lane
Fleet Street, London EC4Y 8EQ
E info@sbf.org.uk
W www.sbf.org.uk

**BROADWAY STUDIO
THEATRE THE** T 020 8690 1000
*Contact: Martin Costello (General Manager). Route:
Charing Cross to Catford Bridge*
Catford, London SE6 4RU
BO 020 8690 0002
E martin@broadwaytheatre.org.uk
W www.broadwaytheatre.org.uk

BROADWAY THEATRE THE T 020 8507 5610
The Broadway, Barking IG11 7LS
BO 020 8507 5607
E admin@thebroadwaybarking.com
W www.thebroadwaybarking.com

**CALDER THEATRE
BOOKSHOP LTD** T 020 7620 2900
*40 Seat Theatre Venue. Wide Selection of Plays on Sale
in Bookshop. Rehearsal Space for Hire*
51 The Cut, London SE1 8LF
E info@calderbookshop.com

CAMDEN PEOPLE'S THEATRE T 020 7419 4841
*Route: Victoria or Northern Line to Euston or Warren
Street, Hammersmith & City Line, Metropolitan or Circle
Line to Euston Square (2 min walk either way)*
58-60 Hampstead Road, London NW1 2PY
E admin@cptheatre.co.uk
W www.cptheatre.co.uk

CANAL CAFE THEATRE THE T 020 7289 6056
Contact: Emma Taylor (Artistic Director)
The Bridge House, Delamere Terrace
Little Venice, London W2 6ND
BO 020 7289 6054
E mail@canalcafetheatre.com
W www.canalcafetheatre.com

CHARING CROSS THEATRE T 020 7930 5868
Formerly New Players Theatre
The Arches, Villiers Street, London WC2N 6NL
E info@charingcrosstheatre.co.uk
W www.charingcrosstheatre.co.uk

CHATS PALACE T 020 8533 0227
42-44 Brooksby's Walk, Hackney, London E9 6DF
E info@chatspalace.com
W www.chatspalace.co.uk

CHELSEA THEATRE   **T** 020 7352 1967
Route: District or Circle Line to Sloane Square then short bus ride 11 or 22 down King's Road
World's End Place, King's Road
London SW10 0DR
E admin@chelseatheatre.org.uk
W www.chelseatheatre.org.uk

CHICKENSHED   **T** 020 8351 6161
Contact: Mary Ward MBE (Artistic Director). Route: Piccadilly Line to Oakwood, turn left outside tube & walk 8 min down Bramley Road or take 307 bus. Buses 298, 299, 699 or N19. Car Parking Available & Easy Access Parking by Reservation
290 Chase Side, Southgate, London N14 4PE
BO 020 8292 9222
E susanj@chickenshed.org.uk
W www.chickenshed.org.uk

CHRIST'S HOSPITAL THEATRE   **T** 01403 247435
Contact: Melanie Bloor-Black (Director)
Horsham, West Sussex RH13 0JD
BO 01403 247434
E mbb@christs-hospital.org.uk

CHURCHILL THE   **T** 020 8290 8255
Contact: Chris Glover (General Manager)
High Street, Bromley, Kent BR1 1HA
BO 0844 8717620
W www.atgtickets.com/bromley

CLUB FOR ACTS & ACTORS THE   **T** 020 7836 3172
Contact: Malcolm Knight (Concert Artistes Association). Route: Piccadilly or Northern Line to Leicester Square then few mins walk
20 Bedford Street, London WC2E 9HP
E office@thecaa.org
W www.thecaa.co.uk

COCKPIT THE   **T** 020 7258 2925 (12-6 Mon-Sat)
Gateforth Street, Marylebone
London NW8 8EH
E mail@thecockpit.org.uk
W www.thecockpit.org.uk

COLOUR HOUSE THEATRE THE   **T** 020 8542 5511
Merton Abbey Mills, Watermill Way
London SW19 2RD
E info@colourhousetheatre.co.uk
W www.colourhousetheatre.co.uk

CONSTRUCTIVE INTERFERENCE   **T** 07972 162392
40 Stockwell Street, Greenwich, London SE10 8EY
E creative@constructiveinterference.co.uk
W www.constructiveinterference.co.uk

CORBETT THEATRE   **T** 020 8508 5983
Route: Central Line (Epping Branch) to Debden then 6 min walk
East 15 Acting School, Hatfields
Rectory Lane, Loughton IG10 3RY
E east15@essex.ac.uk
W www.east15.ac.uk

COURTYARD THEATRE THE   **T** 020 7729 2202
Contact: June Abbott, Tim Gill (Joint Artistic Directors)
Bowling Green Walk, 40 Pitfield Street
London N1 6EU
BO 0844 4771000
E info@thecourtyard.org.uk
W www.thecourtyard.org.uk

CUSTARD FACTORY   **T** 0121 224 7777
Gibb Street, Digbeth, Birmingham B9 4AA
E info@custardfactory.co.uk
W www.custardfactory.co.uk

DRILL HALL THE
See RADA: THE STUDIO THEATRE

EDINBURGH FESTIVAL FRINGE SOCIETY   **T** 0131 226 0026
180 High Street, Edinburgh EH1 1QS
E admin@edfringe.com
W www.edfringe.com

EMBASSY THEATRE & STUDIOS   **T** 020 7722 8183
Route: Jubilee Line to Swiss Cottage then 1 min walk
The Royal Central School of Speech & Drama
64 Eton Avenue
Swiss Cottage, London NW3 3HY
E enquiries@cssd.ac.uk
W www.cssd.ac.uk

EPSOM PLAYHOUSE THE   **T** 01372 742226
Contact: Elaine Teague (Assistant Manager). Main Auditorium Seats 450. Myers Studio Seats 80
Ashley Avenue, Epsom, Surrey KT18 5AL
BO 01372 742555
E eteague@epsom-ewell.gov.uk
W www.epsomplayhouse.co.uk

ETCETERA THEATRE   **T** 020 7482 4857
Hire Venue. In-house Productions.
Twitter: @EtceteraTheatre
265 Camden High Street, London NW1 7BU
E admin@etceteratheatre.com
W www.etceteratheatre.com

FAIRFIELD HALLS   **T** 020 8681 0821
Route: Victoria & London Bridge Main Line to East Croydon then 5 min walk
Ashcroft Theatre & Concert Hall, Park Lane
Croydon CR9 1DG
BO 020 8688 9291
E info@fairfield.co.uk
W www.fairfield.co.uk

FINBOROUGH THEATRE   **T** 020 7244 7439
Contact: Neil McPherson (Artistic Director). Route: District or Piccadilly Line to Earls Court then 5 min walk. Buses 74, 328, C1, C3 then 3 min walk
118 Finborough Road, London SW10 9ED
BO 0844 8471652
E admin@finboroughtheatre.co.uk
W www.finboroughtheatre.co.uk

GATE THEATRE   **T** 020 7229 5387
Route: Central, Circle or District Line to Notting Hill Gate (exit 3) then 1 min walk. Buses 23, 27, 28, 31, 52, 70, 94, 148, 328, 390, 452
11 Pembridge Road, Above Prince Albert Pub
Notting Hill, London W11 3HQ
BO 020 7229 0706
E boxoffice@gatetheatre.co.uk
W www.gatetheatre.co.uk

GREENWICH PLAYHOUSE   **T** 020 8310 7276
Contact: Alice De Sousa
Head Office, 50 Openshaw Road, London SE2 0TE
E boxoffice@galleontheatre.co.uk
W www.galleontheatre.co.uk

GREENWICH THEATRE   **T** 020 8858 4447
Contact: James Haddrell (Executive Director). Route: Jubilee Line (change Canary Wharf) then DLR to Greenwich Cutty Sark, 3 min walk or Charing Cross Main Line to Greenwich, 5 min walk
Crooms Hill, Greenwich
London SE10 8ES
BO 020 8858 7755
E info@greenwichtheatre.org.uk
W www.greenwichtheatre.org.uk

GROUNDLINGS THEATRE T 023 9273 9496
42 Kent Street, Portsmouth
Hampshire PO1 3BT
E richard@groundlings.co.uk
W www.groundlings.co.uk

**GUILDHALL SCHOOL OF
MUSIC & DRAMA** T 020 7628 2571
*Route: Hammersmith & City, Circle or Metropolitan Line
to Barbican or Moorgate (also served by Northern Line)
then 5 min walk*
Silk Street, Barbican, London EC2Y 8DT
E info@gsmd.ac.uk
W www.gsmd.ac.uk

HACKNEY EMPIRE THEATRE T 020 8510 4500
Route: North London Line to Hackney Central
291 Mare Street, Hackney, London E8 1EJ
BO 020 8985 2424
E info@hackneyempire.co.uk
W www.hackneyempire.co.uk

HEN & CHICKENS THEATRE T 020 7704 2001
*Route: Victoria Line or Main Line to Highbury & Islington,
directly opposite station*
Unrestricted View, Above Hen & Chickens Theatre Bar
109 St Paul's Road, Islington, London N1 2NA
E henandchickens@aol.com
W www.henandchickens.com

ICA THEATRE T 020 7930 0493
*No CVs. Venue only. Route: Nearest stations Piccadilly &
Charing Cross*
The Mall, London SW1Y 5AH
BO 020 7930 3647
W www.ica.org.uk

IVY ARTS CENTRE BO 01483 686876
University of Surrey, Stag Hill, Guildford GU2 7XH
E boxoffice@surrey.ac.uk
W www.gsauk.org

JACK STUDIO THEATRE THE T 020 8291 6354
410 Brockley Road, London SE4 2DH
E admin@brockleyjack.co.uk
W www.brockleyjack.co.uk

JACKSONS LANE T 020 8340 5226
269A Archway Road, London N6 5AA
E admin@jacksonslane.org.uk
W www.jacksonslane.org.uk

**JERMYN STREET
THEATRE** T 020 7434 1443 (Admin)
*Contact: Anthony Biggs (Artistic Director), Penny Horner
(General Manager)*
16B Jermyn Street, London SW1Y 6ST
BO 020 7287 2875
E info@jermynstreettheatre.co.uk
W www.jermynstreettheatre.co.uk

KING'S HEAD THEATRE T 020 7226 8561
*Contact: Adam Spreadbury-Maher (Artistic Director).
Route: Northern Line to Angel then 5 min walk. Approx
halfway between Angel and Highbury & Islington tube
stations*
115 Upper Street, Islington, London N1 1QN
BO 020 7478 0160
E info@kingsheadtheatre.com
W www.kingsheadtheatre.com

**KING'S LYNN CORN
EXCHANGE** T 01553 765565
Tuesday Market Place, King's Lynn
Norfolk PE30 1JW
BO 01553 764864
E entertainment_admin@west-norfolk.gov.uk
W www.kingslynncornexchange.co.uk

KOMEDIA T 01273 647101
Contact: Marina Kobler (Programmer)
44-47 Gardner Street
Brighton BN1 1UN
BO 01273 647100
E info@komedia.co.uk
W www.komedia.co.uk

LANDMARK ARTS CENTRE T 020 8977 7558
Ferry Road, Teddington
Middlesex TW11 9NN
E info@landmarkartscentre.org
W www.landmarkartscentre.org

LANDOR THEATRE THE T 020 7737 7276
*Contact: Robert McWhir (Artistic Director). Route:
Northern Line to Clapham North then 2 min walk*
70 Landor Road
London SW9 9PH
E info@landortheatre.co.uk
W www.landortheatre.co.uk

**LEICESTER SQUARE
THEATRE** T 020 7534 1740
6 Leicester Place, London WC2H 7BX
BO 0844 8733433
E info@leicestersquaretheatre.com
W www.leicestersquaretheatre.com

**LEIGHTON BUZZARD
THEATRE** T 0300 3008130
Lake Street, Leighton Buzzard
Bedfordshire LU7 1RX
BO 0300 3008125
E lbtboxoffice@centralbedfordshire.gov.uk
W www.leightonbuzzardtheatre.co.uk

LIBRARY THEATRE THE T 0114 273 4102
*260 Seat Civic Theatre for Hire. Traditional 1930s Art
Deco Style*
Central Library, Tudor Square
Sheffield, South Yorkshire S1 1XZ
E philip.repper@sheffield.gov.uk
W www.sheffield.gov.uk/libraries/librarytheatre

LILIAN BAYLIS STUDIOS T 020 7863 8065
Rosebery Avenue, London EC1R 4TN
BO 0844 4124300
E events@sadlerswells.com
W www.sadlerswells.com

LIVE THEATRE T 0191 261 2694
Broad Chare, Quayside
Newcastle upon Tyne NE1 3DQ
BO 0191 232 1232
E info@live.org.uk
W www.live.org.uk

LONDON THEATRE THE T 020 8694 1888
Lower Space, 443 New Cross Road
New Cross, London SE14 6TA
E thelondontheatre@live.co.uk
W www.thelondontheatre.com

LOST THEATRE T 020 7622 9208
208 Wandsworth Road
London SW8 2JU
E info@losttheatre.co.uk
W www.losttheatre.co.uk

MADDERMARKET THEATRE T 01603 626560
*Contact: Peter Beck, Stash Kirkbride (Joint Creative
Directors)*
St John's Alley, Norwich NR2 1DR
BO 01603 620917
E office@maddermarket.org
W www.maddermarket.co.uk

MENIER CHOCOLATE FACTORY   T 020 7378 1712
53 Southwark Street, London SE1 1RU
BO 020 7378 1713
E office@meniferchocolatefactory.com
W www.meniferchocolatefactory.com

NEW DIORAMA THEATRE THE   T 020 7916 5467
*Hire Venue. Route: Circle & District Line to Great
Portland Street then 5 min walk or Victoria & Northern
Lines to Warren Street then 5 min walk*
15-16 Triton Street, Regents Place
London NW1 3BF
BO 020 7383 9034
E hello@newdiorama.com
W www.newdiorama.com

NEW WIMBLEDON THEATRE & STUDIO   T 020 8545 7900
*Route: Main Line or District Line to Wimbledon, then 3
min walk. Buses 57, 93, 155*
The Broadway, Wimbledon, London SW19 1QG
BO 0844 8717646
W www.atgtickets.com/venue/new-wimbledon-theatre

NORTHBROOK THEATRE THE   BO 01903 273333
Contact: Theatre Co-ordinator
Northbrook College, Littlehampton Road
Worthing, West Sussex BN12 6NU
E box.office@nbcol.ac.uk
W www.northbrooktheatre.co.uk

NORWICH PUPPET THEATRE   T 01603 615564
St James, Whitefriars, Norwich NR3 1TN
BO 01603 629921
E info@puppettheatre.co.uk
W www.puppettheatre.co.uk

NOVELLO THEATRE THE   T 01344 620881
*Redroofs Theatre Company. Route: Waterloo Main Line
to Ascot then 1 mile from station*
2 High Street, Sunninghill
Nr Ascot, Berkshire SL5 9NE

OLD RED LION THEATRE   T 020 7833 3053
*Contact: Stewart Pringle (Artistic Director). Route:
Northern Line to Angel, then 1 min walk*
418 St John Street, Islington
London EC1V 4NJ
BO 0844 4124307
E info@oldredliontheatre.co.uk

ORANGE TREE   T 020 8940 0141 (Admin)
*Contact: Paul Miller (Artistic Director). Route: District
Line, Waterloo Main Line or Overground, then virtually
opposite station*
1 Clarence Street, Richmond TW9 2SA
BO 020 8940 3633
E admin@orangetreetheatre.co.uk

ORCHARD, DARTFORD THE   T 01322 220099
*Contact: Chris Glover (Theatre Director)
Route: Charing Cross Main Line to Dartford*
Home Gardens, Dartford
Kent DA1 1ED
BO 01322 220000
E info@orchardtheatre.co.uk
W www.orchardtheatre.co.uk

OVALHOUSE   T 020 7582 0080
*Route: Northern Line to Oval then 1 min walk, or Victoria
Line & Main Line to Vauxhall then 10 min walk*
52-54 Kennington Oval, London SE11 5SW
BO 020 7582 7680
E info@ovalhouse.com
W www.ovalhouse.com

OVATION THEATRES LTD   T 020 8340 4256
*Route: Northern Line to Highgate then 10 min walk.
Buses 143, 210, 214, 271*
Upstairs at the Gatehouse
Corner of Hampstead Lane/North Road
Highgate, London N6 4BD
BO 020 8340 3488
E events@ovationproductions.com
W www.upstairsatthegatehouse.com

PARK THEATRE   T 020 7870 6876
*Route: 1 min walk from Finsbury Park via tube (Victoria/
Piccadilly Lines), Main Line or bus*
Clifton Terrace, Finsbury Park
London N4 3JP
E info@parktheatre.co.uk
W www.parktheatre.co.uk

PAVILION THEATRE   T 00 353 1 2312929
Marine Road, Dun Laoghaire
County Dublin, Ireland
E info@paviliontheatre.ie
W www.paviliontheatre.ie

PENTAMETERS   T 020 7435 3648
*Route: Northern Line to Hampstead then 1 min walk.
Buses 46, 268*
(Theatre Entrance in Oriel Place)
28 Heath Street
London NW3 6TE
W www.pentameters.co.uk

PLACE THE   T 020 7121 1101
*Main London Venue for Contemporary Dance.
Route: Northern or Victoria Lines to Euston; Circle,
Hammersmith & City, Metropolitan, Northern, Piccadilly
or Victoria Lines to King's Cross St Pancras; Circle,
Hammersmith & City or Metropolitan Lines to Euston
Square; Piccadilly Line to Russell Square. All easy
walking distance*
17 Duke's Road
London WC1H 9PY
BO 020 7121 1100
E theatre@theplace.org.uk
W www.theplace.org.uk

PLATFORM THEATRE
Central Saint Martins College of Arts & Design, University
of the Arts London
Handyside Street, King's Cross
London N1C 4AA
E platformboxoffice@arts.ac.uk
W www.csm.arts.ac.uk/platform-theatre

PLEASANCE ISLINGTON   T 020 7619 6868
*Contact: Anthony Alderson. 180-280 Seat Mainhouse
plus 60 Seat Studio. 2 Rehearsal Rooms & Production
Offices. Route: Piccadilly Line to Caledonian Road, turn
left, walk 50 yds, turn left into North Road, 3 min walk.
Buses 17, 91, 259, 393, N91*
Carpenters Mews, North Road
(Off Caledonian Road), London N7 9EF
BO 020 7609 1800
E info@pleasance.co.uk
W www.pleasance.co.uk

POLKA THEATRE   T 020 8545 8323
*Route: Waterloo Main Line or District Line to Wimbledon
then 10 min walk. Northern Line to South Wimbledon
then 10 min walk. Tram to Wimbledon, Buses 57, 93,
219, 493*
240 The Broadway
Wimbledon SW19 1SB
BO 020 8543 4888
E stephen@polkatheatre.com
W www.polkatheatre.com

PRINCESS THEATRE HUNSTANTON T 01485 532252 (T/BO)
13 The Green, Hunstanton
Norfolk PE36 5AH
E boxoffice@princesshunstanton.co.uk
W www.princesshunstanton.co.uk

PRINT ROOM THE T 020 7221 6036
34 Hereford Road, Notting Hill
London W2 5AJ
E hello@the-print-room.org

PUTNEY ARTS THEATRE T 020 8788 6943
Ravenna Road
Putney SW15 6AW
E info@putneyartstheatre.org.uk
W www.putneyartstheatre.org.uk

QUEEN'S THEATRE T 01708 462362
Contact: Bob Carlton (Artistic Director). Route: District Line to Hornchurch. Main Line Train to Romford or Gidea Park. 15 miles drive from West End via A13, A1306 then A125, or A12 then A127
Billet Lane, Hornchurch
Essex RM11 1QT
BO 01708 443333
E info@queens-theatre.co.uk
W www.queens-theatre.co.uk

QUESTORS THEATRE EALING THE T 020 8567 0011
Route: Central or District Line to Ealing Broadway then 5 min walk. Buses 65, 83, 207, 427, 607, E2, E7, E8, E11
12 Mattock Lane, London W5 5BQ
BO 020 8567 5184
E jane@questors.org.uk
W www.questors.org.uk

RADA: THE CLUB THEATRE T 020 7307 5060 (T/BO)
Formerly The Drill Hall
16 Chenies Street
London WC1E 7EX
T 020 7307 5075 (Theatre Hire)
E venues@radaenterprises.org
W www.rada.ac.uk/venues

RADA: GBS THEATRE (GEORGE BERNARD SHAW) T 020 7908 4800 (T/BO)
Malet Street
London WC1E 6ED
T 020 7307 5075 (Theatre Hire)
E venues@radaenterprises.org
W www.rada.ac.uk/venues

RADA: GIELGUD, John THEATRE T 020 7908 4800 (T/BO)
Malet Street, London WC1E 6ED
T 020 7908 4822 (Theatre Hire)
E venues@radaenterprises.org
W www.rada.ac.uk/venues

RADA: JERWOOD VANBRUGH THEATRE T 020 7908 4800 (T/BO)
Malet Street, London WC1E 6ED
T 020 7908 4822 (Theatre Hire)
E venues@radaenterprises.org
W www.rada.ac.uk/venues

RADA: THE STUDIO THEATRE T 020 7307 5060 (T/BO)
Formerly The Drill Hall
16 Chenies Street
London WC1E 7EX
T 020 7908 4822 (Theatre Hire)
E venues@radaenterprises.org
W www.rada.ac.uk/venues

RED HEDGEHOG THE T 07817 109093
255-257 Archway Road, Highgate
London N6 5BS
BO 020 8348 5050
E theatre@theredhedgehog.co.uk
W www.theredhedgehog.co.uk

RED LADDER THEATRE COMPANY LTD T 0113 245 5311
3 St Peter's Buildings, York Street
Leeds LS9 8AJ
E rod@redladder.co.uk
W www.redladder.co.uk

RICHMOND THEATRE T 020 8332 4500
Contact: Kate Wrightson (General Manager). Route: 20 min from Waterloo (South West Trains) or District Line to Richmond then 2 min walk
The Green, Richmond, Surrey TW9 1QJ
BO 0844 8717651
E richmondstagedoor@theambassadors.com
W www.atgtickets.com/richmond

RIVERSIDE STUDIOS T 020 8237 1000
Route: District, Piccadilly or Hammersmith & City Line to Hammersmith then 5 min walk. Buses 9, 10, 27, 33, 72, 190, 209, 211, 266, 267, 283, 295, 391, 419
Crisp Road, London W6 9RL
BO 020 8237 1111
E info@riversidestudios.co.uk
W www.riversidestudios.co.uk

ROSE THEATRE, KINGSTON T 020 8546 6983
Contact: Jerry Gunn (Executive Producer), Naomi Webb (Assistant Producer)
24-26 High Street, Kingston upon Thames
Surrey KT1 1HL
E admin@rosetheatrekingston.org
W www.rosetheatrekingston.org

ROSEMARY BRANCH THEATRE T 020 7704 6665
Route: Tube to Bank, Moorgate or Old Street (exit 5), then 21, 76 or 141 bus to Baring Street, or 271 bus from Highbury & Islington
2 Shepperton Road, London N1 3DT
E rosemarybranchtheatre@googlemail.com
W www.rosemarybranch.co.uk

SAGE GATESHEAD T 0191 443 4661
St Mary's Square, Gateshead Quays
Gateshead NE8 2JR
F 0191 443 4551
E ticketoffice.mail@sagegateshead.com
W www.sagegateshead.com

SCOTTISH STORYTELLING CENTRE T 0131 556 9579
Netherbow Theatre
43-45 High Street, Edinburgh EH1 1SR
E reception@scottishstorytellingcentre.com
W www.tracscotland.org/scottish-storytelling-centre

SHAW THEATRE @ PULLMAN LONDON ST PANCRAS T 020 7666 9037
100-110 Euston Road, London NW1 2AJ
BO 0844 2485075
E info@shaw-theatre.com

SOUTH HILL PARK ARTS CENTRE T 01344 484858
Route: Waterloo Main Line to Bracknell then 10 min bus ride or taxi rank at station
Bracknell, Berkshire RG12 7PA
BO 01344 484123
E enquiries@southhillpark.org.uk
W www.southhillpark.org.uk

SOUTH LONDON THEATRE   **T** 020 8670 3474
*Route: Victoria or London Bridge Main Line to West
Norwood then 2 min walk or Victoria Line to Brixton then
buses 2, 68, 196, 322*
Bell Theatre & Prompt Corner
2A Norwood High Street
London SE27 9NS
E southlondontheatre@yahoo.co.uk
W www.southlondontheatre.co.uk

SOUTHWARK PLAYHOUSE   **T** 020 7407 0234
*Contact: Chris Smyrnios (Chief Executive). Route: Trains
to Borough or Elephant & Castle, Jubilee/Northern Line
to London Bridge. Buses 47, 381, RV1, N47, N381. River
service to London Bridge City*
77-85 Newington Causeway, London SE1 6BD
E admin@southwarkplayhouse.co.uk
W www.southwarkplayhouse.co.uk

SPACE ARTS CENTRE THE   **T** 020 7515 7799
269 Westferry Road, London E14 3RS
E info@space.org.uk
W www.space.org.uk

ST JOHN'S CHURCH   **T** 020 7633 9819
*Hosts Classical Concerts, Conferences, Large Meetings
& Lectures*
Waterloo Road, Southbank
London SE1 8TY
E bookings@stjohnswaterloo.org
W www.stjohnswaterloo.org

TABARD THEATRE   **T** 020 8995 6035
*Contact: Collin Hilton, Fred Perry (Artistic Directors),
Simon Reilly (Theatre Manager)*
2 Bath Road, London W4 1LW
E info@tabardtheatre.co.uk
W www.tabardtheatre.co.uk

THEATRE503   **T** 020 7978 7040
*Route: Main Line Train to Clapham Junction from Victoria
or Waterloo then 10 min walk, or buses 44, 49, 319,
344, 345, or tube to South Kensington then buses 49 or
345 or tube to Sloane Square then bus 319*
The Latchmere Pub, 503 Battersea Park Road
London SW11 3BW
E info@theatre503.com
W www.theatre503.com

THEATRE ALIBI   **T/F** 01392 217315
Emmanuel Hall, Emmanuel Road
Exeter EX4 1EJ
E info@theatrealibi.co.uk
W www.theatrealibi.co.uk

**THEATRE ROYAL
STRATFORD EAST**   **T** 020 8534 7374
*Contact: Kerry Michael (Artistic Director). Route: Central
or Jubilee Lines, DLR, Overground or National Express
trains to Stratford then 2 min walk*
Gerry Raffles Square, London E15 1BN
BO 020 8534 0310
E theatreroyal@stratfordeast.com
W www.stratfordeast.com

THEATRO TECHNIS   **T** 020 7387 6617
*Contact: George Eugeniou (Artistic Director). Route:
Northern Line to Mornington Crescent then 3 min walk*
26 Crowndale Road, London NW1 1TT
E info@theatrotechnis.com
W www.theatrotechnis.com

**TOBACCO FACTORY
THEATRES**   **T** 0117 902 0345
Raleigh Road, Southville
Bristol BS3 1TF
E theatre@tobaccofactorytheatres.com
W www.tobaccofactorytheatres.com

TRICYCLE THEATRE   **T** 020 7372 6611
*Contact: Indhu Rubasingham (Artistic Director), Kate
Devey (Executive Director), Bridget Kalloushi (Executive
Producer). Route: Jubilee Line to Kilburn then 5 min walk
or buses 16, 32, 189, pass the door, 31, 98, 206, 316,
332 pass nearby*
269 Kilburn High Road, London NW6 7JR
BO 020 7328 1000
E admin@tricycle.co.uk
W www.tricycle.co.uk

TRON THEATRE   **T** 0141 552 3748
63 Trongate, Glasgow G1 5HB
BO 0141 552 4267
E boxoffice@tron.co.uk
W www.tron.co.uk

UNION THEATRE THE   **T** 020 7261 9876
*Contact: Sasha Regan (Artistic Director), Ben De
Wynter (Associate Director), Michael Strassen (Resident
Director), Iain Dennis (Technical Director). Route: Jubilee
Line to Southwark then 2 min walk*
204 Union Street, Southwark
London SE1 0LX
E sashareganunion@gmail.com
W www.uniontheatre.biz

WATERLOO EAST THEATRE   **T** 020 7928 0060
Brad Street, London SE1 8TN
E info@waterlooeast.co.uk
W www.waterlooeast.co.uk

WATERLOO EAST THEATRE   **T** 020 7928 0060
Admin: 3 Wootton Street, London SE1 8TG
E info@waterlooeast.co.uk
W www.waterlooeast.co.uk

WATERMANS   **T** 020 8232 1019
40 High Street, Brentford TW8 0DS
BO 020 8232 1010
E info@watermans.org.uk
W www.watermans.org.uk

WESTRIDGE (OPEN CENTRE)   **T** 01635 253322
Drawing Room Recitals
Star Lane, Highclere
Nr Newbury, Berkshire RG20 9PJ

WHITE BEAR THEATRE   **T** 020 7793 9193
*Favours New Writing. Route: Northern Line to
Kennington (2 min walk)*
138 Kennington Park Road, London SE11 4DJ
E info@whitebeartheatre.co.uk
W www.whitebeartheatre.co.uk

WILTON'S MUSIC HALL   **T** 020 7702 2789
*Route: Under 10 min walk from Aldgate East (exit for
Leman Street) & Tower Hill Tube. DLR: Shadwell or
Tower Gateway. Car: Follow the yellow AA signs to
Wilton's Music Hall from the Highway, Aldgate or
Tower Hill*
Graces Alley, Off Ensign Street
London E1 8JB
E info@wiltons.org.uk
W www.wiltons.org.uk

WYCOMBE SWAN   **T** 01494 514444
St Mary Street, High Wycombe
Buckinghamshire HP11 2XE
BO 01494 512000
E enquiries@wycombeswan.co.uk
W www.wycombeswan.co.uk

WYVERN THEATRE   **T** 01793 535534
Theatre Square, Swindon, Wiltshire SN1 1QN
BO 01793 524481
E info@wyverntheatre.org.uk
W www.wyverntheatre.org.uk

ABERDEEN:
His Majesty's Theatre   T 0845 2708200
Rosemount Viaduct
Aberdeen AB25 1GL
BO 01224 641122
E hmtinfo@aberdeenperformingarts.com
W www.aberdeenperformingarts.com

ABERYSTWYTH:
Aberystwyth Arts Centre   T 01970 622882
Penglais, Aberystwyth
Ceredigion SY23 3DE
BO 01970 623232
E ggo@aber.ac.uk
W www.aber.ac.uk/artscentre

BACUP: Royal Court Theatre   BO 01706 874080
Rochdale Road
Bacup OL13 9NR
E managingdirectorscp@brct.co
W www.brct.co

BASINGSTOKE:
The Haymarket Theatre   T 01256 819797
Wote Street, Basingstoke RG21 7NW
BO 01256 844244
E box.office@anvilarts.org.uk
W www.anvilarts.org.uk

BATH: Theatre Royal   T 01225 448815
Sawclose, Bath BA1 1ET
BO 01225 448844
E forename.surname@theatreroyal.org.uk
W www.theatreroyal.org.uk

BELFAST: Grand Opera House   T 028 9024 0411
Great Victoria Street
Belfast BT2 7HR
BO 028 9024 1919
E info@goh.co.uk
W www.goh.co.uk

BILLINGHAM: Forum Theatre   T 01642 551389
Town Centre
Billingham TS23 2LJ
E forumtheatre@btconnect.com
W www.forumtheatrebillingham.co.uk

BIRMINGHAM: Hippodrome   BO 0844 3385000
Hurst Street, Southside
Birmingham B5 4TB
E info@birminghamhippodrome.com
W www.birminghamhippodrome.com

BIRMINGHAM:
New Alexandra Theatre   T 0121 230 9070
Station Street
Birmingham B5 4DS
BO 0844 8713011
W www.atgtickets.com/birmingham

BLACKPOOL: Grand Theatre   T 01253 290111
33 Church Street
Blackpool FY1 1HT
BO 01253 290190
E geninfo@blackpoolgrand.co.uk
W www.blackpoolgrand.co.uk

BLACKPOOL: Opera House   T 01253 625252
Church Street
Blackpool FY1 1HW
BO 0844 8561111
W www.wintergardensblackpool.co.uk

BOURNEMOUTH:
Pavilion Theatre   T 01202 456400
Westover Road
Bournemouth BH1 2BU
BO 0844 5763000
E paul.griffiths@bhlive.co.uk
W www.bic.co.uk

BRADFORD: Alhambra Theatre   T 01274 432375
Morley Street
Bradford BD7 1AJ
BO 01274 432000
E administration@ces.bradford.gov.uk
W www.bradford-theatres.co.uk

BRADFORD:
Theatre in the Mill   BO 01274 233200
University of Bradford
Shearbridge Road
Bradford BD7 1DP
E theatre@bradford.ac.uk
W www.bradford.ac.uk/theatre

BRIGHTON: Brighton Dome &
Brighton Festival   T 01273 700747
The Dome, Corn Exchange & Pavilion Theatres
12A Pavilion Buildings
Castle Square, Brighton BN1 1EE
BO 01273 709709
E info@brightondome.org
W www.brightondome.org

BRIGHTON: Spymonkey   T 01273 670282
Unit 7B, Level 3N
New England House
New England Street
Brighton BN1 4GH
E info@spymonkey.co.uk
W www.spymonkey.co.uk

BRIGHTON:
Theatre Royal Brighton   T 01273 764400
New Road, Brighton BN1 1SD
BO 0844 8717650
W www.atgtickets.com/brighton

BRISTOL: Bristol Hippodrome   T 0117 302 3310
St Augustines Parade
Bristol BS1 4UZ
BO 0844 8713012
W www.atgtickets.com/bristol

BROXBOURNE:
Broxbourne Civic Hall   BO 01992 441946
High Street, Hoddesdon, Herts EN11 8BE
E civic.leisure@broxbourne.gov.uk
W www.broxbourne.gov.uk/whatson

BURY ST EDMUNDS:
Theatre Royal   T 01284 829944
Westgate Street
Bury St Edmunds IP33 1QR
BO 01284 769505
E admin@theatreroyal.org
W www.theatreroyal.org

BUXTON: Buxton Opera House &
Pavilion Arts Centre   T 01298 72050
Water Street
Buxton SK17 6XN
BO 0845 1272190
E admin@boh.org.uk
W www.buxtonoperahouse.org.uk

CAMBERLEY:
The Camberley Theatre   BO 01276 707600
Knoll Road, Camberley
Surrey GU15 3SY
E camberley.theatre@surreyheath.gov.uk
W www.camberleytheatre.biz

CAMBRIDGE: Cambridge Arts
Theatre Trust Ltd   T 01223 578904
6 St Edward's Passage
Cambridge CB2 3PJ
BO 01223 503333
E info@cambridgeartstheatre.com
W www.cambridgeartstheatre.com

CAMBRIDGE: Mumford Theatre   T 01223 417748
Anglia Ruskin University
East Road, Cambridge CB1 1PT
BO 0845 1962320
E mumford@anglia.ac.uk

CANTERBURY: Gulbenkian   BO 01227 769075
Theatre & Cinema
University of Kent, Canterbury CT2 7NB
E boxoffice@kent.ac.uk
W www.thegulbenkian.co.uk

CANTERBURY:
The Marlowe Theatre   BO 01227 787787
The Friars, Canterbury
Kent CT1 2AS
E marlowetheatre@marlowetheatre.com
W www.marlowetheatre.com

CARDIFF: New Theatre   T 029 2087 8787
Park Place, Cardiff CF10 3LN
BO 029 2087 8889
E ntmailings@cardiff.gov.uk
W www.newtheatrecardiff.co.uk

CARDIFF:
Wales Millennium Centre   T 029 2063 6400
Bute Place, Cardiff CF10 5AL
BO 029 2063 6464
E stagedoor@wmc.org.uk
W www.wmc.org.uk

CHELTENHAM:
Everyman Theatre   T 01242 512515
Regent Street
Cheltenham GL50 1HQ
BO 01242 572573
E admin@everymantheatre.org.uk
W www.everymantheatre.org.uk

CHICHESTER:
Festival Theatre   T 01243 784437
Oaklands Park, Chichester PO19 6AP
BO 01243 781312
E admin@cft.org.uk
W www.cft.org.uk

CRAWLEY: The Hawth   T 01293 552941
Hawth Avenue, Crawley
West Sussex RH10 6YZ
BO 01293 553636
E hawthadmin@parkwoodtheatres.co.uk
W www.hawth.co.uk

CREWE: Lyceum Theatre   BO 01270 638242
Heath Street, Crewe CW1 2DA
E admin@crewelyceum.co.uk
W www.crewelyceum.co.uk

DARLINGTON: Civic Theatre   T 01325 387775
Parkgate, Darlington DL1 1RR
BO 01325 486555
E info@darlingtonarts.gov.uk
W www.darlingtonarts.co.uk

DUBLIN: Gaiety Theatre   T 00 353 1 6795622
South King Street
Dublin 2, Ireland
BO 0818 719388
E info@gaietytheatre.com
W www.gaietytheatre.com

DUBLIN: Gate Theatre   T 00 353 1 8744368
1 Cavendish Row, Dublin 1, Ireland
BO 00 353 1 8744045
E info@gate-theatre.ie
W www.gatetheatre.ie

DUBLIN:
The Olympia Theatre   T 00 353 1 6725883
72 Dame Street, Dublin 2, Ireland
BO 00 353 1 6793323
E info@olympia.ie
W www.olympia.ie

EASTBOURNE:
Congress Theatre   T 01323 415500
Admin Office: Winter Garden
Compton Street, Eastbourne BN21 4BP
BO 01323 412000
E theatres@eastbourne.gov.uk
W www.eastbournetheatres.co.uk

EASTBOURNE:
Devonshire Park Theatre   T 01323 415500
Admin Office: Winter Garden
Compton Street, Eastbourne BN21 4BP
BO 01323 412000
E theatres@eastbourne.gov.uk
W www.eastbournetheatres.co.uk

EDINBURGH: King's Theatre   T 0131 662 1112
2 Leven Street
Edinburgh EH3 9LQ
BO 0131 529 6000
E empire@edtheatres.com
W www.edtheatres.com

EDINBURGH:
Playhouse Theatre   T 0131 524 3333
18-22 Greenside Place, Edinburgh EH1 3AA
BO 0844 8713014
E edinburghadministrator@theambassadors.com
W www.atgtickets.com/edinburgh

GLASGOW: King's Theatre   T 0141 240 1300
297 Bath Street, Glasgow G2 4JN
BO 0844 8717648
E glasgowstagedoor@theambassadors.com
W www.atgtickets.com

GLASGOW: Theatre Royal   T 0141 332 3321
282 Hope Street, Glasgow G2 3QA
BO 0844 8717647
W www.atgtickets.com/glasgow

GRAYS THURROCK:
Thameside Theatre   T 01375 413981
Orsett Road, Grays Thurrock RM17 5DX
BO 0845 3005264
E thameside.theatre@thurrock.gov.uk
W www.thurrock.gov.uk/theatre

HARLOW: Harlow Playhouse   T 01279 446760
Playhouse Square
Harlow CM20 1LS
BO 01279 431945
E playhouse@harlow.gov.uk
W www.playhouseharlow.com

HARROGATE:
Harrogate International Centre   T 01423 500500
Kings Road
Harrogate HG1 5LA
E sales@harrogateinternationalcentre.co.uk
W www.hicyorkshire.co.uk

HASTINGS:
White Rock Theatre   T 01424 462283
White Rock
Hastings TN34 1JX
BO 01424 462288
E enquiries@whiterocktheatre.org.uk
W www.whiterocktheatre.org.uk

HATFIELD:
The Hawthorne Theatre   T 01707 330360
Campus West
Welwyn Garden City
Herts AL8 6BX
E guymasterson@hawthornetheatre.co.uk
W www.hawthornetheatre.co.uk

HAYES: Beck Theatre   T 020 8561 7506
Grange Road, Hayes
Middlesex UB3 2UE
BO 020 8561 8371
E enquiries@becktheatre.org.uk
W www.becktheatre.org.uk

HIGH WYCOMBE:
Wycombe Swan   T 01494 514444
St Mary Street
High Wycombe HP11 2XE
BO 01494 512000
E enquiries@wycombeswan.co.uk
W www.wycombeswan.co.uk

HUDDERSFIELD:
Lawrence Batley Theatre   T 01484 425282
Queen's Square, Queen Street
Huddersfield HD1 2SP
BO 01484 430528
E theatre@thelbt.org
W www.thelbt.org

HULL: Hull New Theatre   T 01482 613818
Kingston Square
Hull HU1 3HF
BO 01482 300300
E theatre.management@hullcc.gov.uk
W www.hullcc.gov.uk

HULL: Hull Truck Theatre   T 01482 224800
50 Ferensway
Hull HU2 8LB
BO 01482 323638
E admin@hulltruck.co.uk
W www.hulltruck.co.uk

ILFORD:
Kenneth More Theatre   T 020 8553 4464
Oakfield Road, Ilford IG1 1BT
BO 020 8553 4466
E admin@kmtheatre.co.uk
W www.kmtheatre.co.uk

IPSWICH:
Sir John Mills Theatre   T 01473 218202
Eastern Angles Theatre Company
Gatacre Road, Ipswich IP1 2LQ
BO 01473 211498
E admin@easternangles.co.uk
W www.easternangles.co.uk

JERSEY: Jersey Opera House   T 01534 511100
Gloucester Street
St Helier, Jersey JE2 3QR
BO 01534 511115
E admin@jerseyoperahouse.co.uk
W www.jerseyoperahouse.co.uk

KINGSTON: Rose Theatre   T 020 8546 6983
24-26 High Street
Kingston Upon Thames
Surrey KT1 1HL
F 020 8546 8783
E admin@rosetheatrekingston.org
W www.rosetheatrekingston.org

KIRKCALDY:
Adam Smith Theatre   T 01592 583301
Bennochy Road
Kirkcaldy KY1 1ET
BO 01592 583302
E boxoffice.adamsmith@onfife.com
W www.onfife.com

LEATHERHEAD:
The Leatherhead Theatre   T 01372 365130
7 Church Street
Leatherhead, Surrey KT22 8DN
BO 01372 365141
E info@the-theatre.org
W www.theleatherheadtheatre.org

LEEDS:
City Varieties Music Hall   T 0113 391 7777
Swan Street, Leeds LS1 6LW
BO 0113 243 0808
E info@cityvarieties.co.uk
W www.cityvarieties.co.uk

LEEDS:
Grand Theatre & Opera House   T 0113 245 6014
46 New Briggate
Leeds LS1 6NZ
BO 0844 8482705
E boxoffice@leedsgrandtheatre.com
W www.leedsgrandtheatre.com

LICHFIELD:
The Lichfield Garrick   T 01543 412110
Castle Dyke
Lichfield WS13 6HR
BO 01543 412121
E garrick@lichfieldgarrick.com
W www.lichfieldgarrick.com

LINCOLN: LADA Productions   T 01522 837242
Sparkhouse Studios, Ropewalk
Lincoln, Lincs LN6 7DQ
F 01522 837201
E productions@lada.org.uk
W www.lada.org.uk

LINCOLN: Theatre Royal   T 01522 519999
Clasketgate, Lincoln LN2 1JJ
E boxoffice@lincolntheatreroyal.com
W www.lincolntheatreroyal.com

LIVERPOOL: Empire Theatre   T 0151 702 7320
Lime Street, Liverpool L1 1JE
BO 0844 8713017
W www.atgtickets.com/liverpool

LLANDUDNO: Venue Cymru   T 01492 879771
Promenade, Llandudno, Conwy
North Wales LL30 1BB
BO 01492 872000
E info@venuecymru.co.uk
W www.venuecymru.co.uk

MALVERN: Malvern Theatres   T 01684 569256
Festival & Forum Theatres
Grange Road, Malvern WR14 3HB
BO 01684 892277
E post@malvern-theatres.co.uk
W www.malvern-theatres.co.uk

MANCHESTER:
O2 Apollo Manchester   T 0161 273 6921
Stockport Road, Ardwick Green
Manchester M12 6AP
BO 0844 4777677
E o2apollomanchester@livenation.co.uk
W www.o2apollomanchester.co.uk

MANCHESTER: Opera House   T 0161 828 1700
Quay Street, Manchester M3 3HP
BO 0844 8713018
W www.atgtickets.com/manchester

MANCHESTER: Palace Theatre   T 0161 245 6600
Oxford Street, Manchester M1 6FT
BO 0844 8713019
E manchesterstagedoor@theambassadors.com
W www.palaceandoperahouse.org.uk

MARGATE:
Theatre Royal Margate   T 01843 296111
Addington Street
Margate, Kent CT9 1PW
BO 01843 292795
E admin@theatreroyalmargate.com
W www.theatreroyalmargate.com

MILTON KEYNES:
Milton Keynes Theatre   T 01908 547500
500 Marlborough Gate
Central Milton Keynes MK9 3NZ
BO 0844 8717652
W www.atgtickets.com/miltonkeynes

NEWARK: Palace Theatre   T 01636 655750
Appletongate, Newark NG24 1JY
BO 01636 655755
E carys.coultonjones@nsdc.info
W www.palacenewark.com

NEWCASTLE UPON TYNE: Northern Stage
(Theatrical Productions) Ltd   T 0191 242 7200
Barras Bridge
Newcastle upon Tyne NE1 7RH
BO 0191 230 5151
E info@northernstage.co.uk
W www.northernstage.co.uk

NEWCASTLE UPON TYNE:
Theatre Royal   T 0191 244 2500
100 Grey Street
Newcastle upon Tyne NE1 6BR
BO 0844 8112121
W www.theatreroyal.co.uk

NORTHAMPTON:
Royal & Derngate Theatres   T 01604 626222
19-21 Guildhall Road, Northampton NN1 1DP
BO 01604 624811
E ashley.bishop@namtrust.co.uk
W www.royalandderngate.co.uk

NORWICH:
Norwich Theatre Royal   T 01603 598500
Theatre Street, Norwich NR2 1RL
BO 01603 630000
W www.theatreroyalnorwich.co.uk

NOTTINGHAM: Royal Centre   T 0115 989 5500
Theatre Royal & Royal Concert Hall
Theatre Square, Nottingham NG1 5ND
BO 0115 989 5555
E enquiry@trch.co.uk
W www.trch.co.uk

OXFORD: New Theatre   T 01865 320760
George Street, Oxford OX1 2AG
BO 0844 8713020
E oxfordstagedoor@theambassadors.com

OXFORD: Oxford Playhouse   T 01865 305300
11-12 Beaumont Street
Oxford OX1 2LW
BO 01865 305305
E admin@oxfordplayhouse.com
W www.oxfordplayhouse.com

POOLE: Lighthouse, Poole's
Centre for the Arts   BO 0844 4068666
Kingland Road, Poole BH15 1UG
W www.lighthousepoole.co.uk

READING: The Hexagon   T 0118 937 2123
Queen's Walk, Reading RG1 7UA
BO 0118 960 6060
E boxoffice@readingarts.com
W www.readingarts.com

RICHMOND, N YORKS:
Georgian Theatre Royal   T 01748 823710
Victoria Road, Richmond
North Yorkshire DL10 4DW
BO 01748 825252
E admin@georgiantheatreroyal.co.uk
W www.georgiantheatreroyal.co.uk

RICHMOND, SURREY:
Richmond Theatre   T 020 8332 4500
The Green, Richmond
Surrey TW9 1QJ
BO 0844 8717651
E richmondstagedoor@theambassadors.com
W www.atgtickets.com/richmond

ROCHDALE:
Gracie Fields Theatre   T 01706 716689
Hudsons Walk
Rochdale, Lancashire OL11 5EF
E enquiries@graciefieldstheatre.com
W www.graciefieldstheatre.com

SHEFFIELD:
Sheffield Theatres Trust   T 0114 249 5999
Crucible, Lyceum & Crucible Studio
55 Norfolk Street, Sheffield S1 1DA
BO 0114 249 6000
E info@sheffieldtheatres.co.uk
W www.sheffieldtheatres.co.uk

SHERINGHAM: Little Theatre   T 01263 822117
2 Station Road
Sheringham, Norfolk NR26 8RE
BO 01263 822347
E boxoffice@sheringhamlittletheatre.com
W www.sheringhamlittletheatre.com

SOMERSET:
Warehouse Theatre   T 01460 57857
Brewery Lane
Ilminster, Somerset TA19 9AD
E annabowerman4@aol.com
W www.thewarehousetheatre.org.uk

SOUTHAMPTON:
The Mayflower Theatre   T 023 8071 1800
Empire Lane, Southampton SO15 1AP
BO 023 8071 1811
E info@mayflower.org.uk
W www.mayflower.org.uk

SOUTHEND:
Southend Theatres   T 01702 390657
Cliffs Pavilion, Palace Theatre & Dixon Studio
Southend on Sea, Station Road
Westcliff-on-Sea, Essex SS0 7RA
BO 01702 351135
E info@southendtheatres.org.uk
W www.southendtheatres.org.uk

ST ALBANS: Abbey Theatre   T 01727 847472
Holywell Hill, St Albans AL1 2DL
BO 01727 857861
E manager@abbeytheatre.org.uk
W www.abbeytheatre.org.uk

ST ALBANS: Alban Arena   T 01727 861078
Civic Centre, St Albans AL1 3LD
BO 01727 844488
E alban.arena@leisureconnection.co.uk
W www.alban-arena.co.uk

ST HELENS: Theatre Royal   T 01744 756333
Corporation Street
St Helens WA10 1LQ
BO 01744 756000
E info@sthelenstheatreroyal.co.uk
W www.sthelenstheatreroyal.com

STAFFORD:
Stafford Gatehouse Theatre   T 01785 253595
Eastgate Street, Stafford ST16 2LT
BO 01785 254653
E gatehouse@staffordbc.gov.uk
W www.staffordgatehousetheatre.co.uk

STEVENAGE:
Gordon Craig Theatre   T 01438 363200 (T/BO)
Stevenage Arts & Leisure Centre
Lytton Way
Stevenage SG1 1LZ
E gordoncraig@stevenage-leisure.co.uk
W www.gordon-craig.co.uk

SUNDERLAND:
Sunderland Empire   T 0191 566 1040 (Admin)
High Street West
Sunderland SR1 3EX
BO 0844 8713022
E sunderlandboxoffice@theambassadors.com
W www.atgtickets.com/sunderland

SWANAGE: Mowlem Theatre   BO 01929 422239
Shore Road, Swanage BH19 1DD
E mowlem.theatre@gmail.com

TAMWORTH: Assembly Rooms   T 01827 709619
Corporation Street
Tamworth B79 7DN
BO 01827 709618
E tarenquiries@tamworth.gov.uk
W www.tamworthassemblyrooms.gov.uk

TEWKESBURY:
The Roses Theatre   T 01684 853061 (Admin)
Sun Street, Tewkesbury GL20 5NX
BO 01684 295074
E assistant@rosestheatre.org
W www.rosestheatre.org

TORQUAY:
Babbacombe Theatre   BO 01803 328385
Babbacombe Downs
Torquay TQ1 3LU
E info@babbacombe-theatre.com
W www.babbacombe-theatre.com

TORQUAY: Princess Theatre   T 01803 206360
Torbay Road, Torquay TQ2 5EZ
BO 0844 8713023
E wendybennett@theambassadors.com
W www.atgtickets.com/torquay

TRURO: Hall For Cornwall   T 01872 321969
Back Quay, Truro
Cornwall TR1 2LL
BO 01872 262466
E mwhite@hallforcornwall.org.uk
W www.hallforcornwall.co.uk

WAKEFIELD: Theatre Royal   T 01924 215531
Drury Lane, Wakefield
West Yorkshire WF1 2TE
F 01924 215525
E murray.edwards@theatreroyalwakefield.co.uk
W www.theatreroyalwakefield.co.uk

WINCHESTER: Theatre Royal   T 01962 844600
21-23 Jewry Street
Winchester SO23 8SB
BO 01962 840440
E kate.raines@theatreroyalwinchester.co.uk
W www.theatreroyalwinchester.co.uk

WORCESTER: Swan Theatre   T 01905 726969
The Moors, Worcester WR1 3ED
BO 01905 611427
E info@worcesterlive.co.uk
W www.worcesterlive.co.uk

WORTHING: Connaught Theatre, Pavilion
Theatre & The Assembly Hall   T 01903 231799
Union Place, Worthing BN11 1LG
BO 01903 206206
E theatres@adur-worthing.gov.uk
W www.worthingtheatres.co.uk

YEOVIL: Octagon Theatre   T 01935 845900
Hendford, Yeovil BA20 1UX
BO 01935 422884
E octagontheatre@southsomerset.gov.uk
W www.octagon-theatre.co.uk

YORK: Grand Opera House   T 01904 678700
Cumberland Street
York YO1 9SW
BO 0844 8713024
E yorkboxoffice@theambassadors.com
W www.atgtickets.com/york

AUTHENTIC PUNCH & JUDY T/F 020 8300 3579
Contact: John Styles. Booths. Presentations. Puppets
42 Christchurch Road, Sidcup
Kent DA15 7HQ
W www.johnstylesentertainer.co.uk

COMPLETE WORKS THE T 020 7377 0280
Contact: Phil Evans (Artistic Director)
The Old Truman Brewery, 91 Brick Lane
London E1 6QL
F 020 7247 7405
E info@tcw.org.uk
W www.tcw.org.uk

**CORNELIUS & JONES
ORIGINAL PRODUCTIONS** T/F 01908 612593
49 Carters Close, Sherington
Newport Pagnell
Buckinghamshire MK16 9NW
E admin@corneliusjones.com
W www.corneliusjones.com

**DNA PUPPETRY &
VISUAL THEATRE CO** T 0161 408 1720
Hope Villa, 18 Woodland Avenue
Thornton Cleveleys, Lancashire FY5 4HB
E dna@dynamicnewanimation.co.uk
W www.dynamicnewanimation.co.uk

INDIGO MOON THEATRE T 07855 328552
35 Waltham Court, Beverley
East Yorkshire HU17 9JF
E info@indigomoontheatre.com
W www.indigomoontheatre.com

JACOLLY PUPPET THEATRE T 01822 852346
Redbar, Kirkella Road, Yelverton
West Devon PL20 6BB
E theatre@jacolly-puppets.co.uk
W www.jacolly-puppets.co.uk

LITTLE ANGEL THEATRE T 020 7226 1787
14 Dagmar Passage, Off Cross Street, London N1 2DN
E info@littleangeltheatre.com
W www.littleangeltheatre.com

**MAJOR MUSTARD'S
TRAVELLING SHOW** T 0121 426 4329
1 Carless Avenue, Harborne, Birmingham B17 9EG
E mm@majormustard.com

NORWICH PUPPET THEATRE T 01603 615564
St James, Whitefriars, Norwich NR3 1TN
F 01603 617578
E info@puppettheatre.co.uk
W www.puppettheatre.co.uk

**PROFESSOR PATTEN'S
PUNCH & JUDY** T 01707 873262
Magic. Puppetry
14 The Crest, Goffs Oak, Herts EN7 5NP
E dennis@dennispatten.co.uk
W www.dennispatten.co.uk

PUPPET THEATRE WALES T 01446 790634
22 Starling Road, St Athan
Vale of Glamorgan CF62 4NJ
E info@puppettheatrewales.co.uk
W www.puppettheatrewales.co.uk

**SLAPSTICK & TICKLE PUPPET
COMPANY** T 07970 141005
14 Brackerns Way, Lymington SO41 3TL
E slapstickandtickle@gmail.com

TOPPER, Chris PUPPETS T 0151 424 8692
Puppets & Costume Characters Created & Performed
75 Barrows Green Lane, Widnes
Cheshire WA8 3JH
E christopper@ntlworld.com
W www.christopperpuppets.co.uk

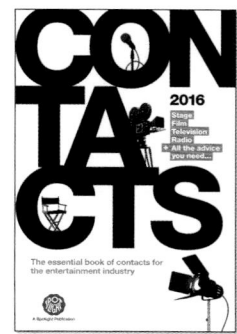

ALDEBURGH:
Summer Theatre   **BO** 01728 454022
July-August
The Jubilee Hall, Crabbe Street
Aldeburgh IP15 5BN
W www.southwoldtheatre.org

BELFAST: Lyric Theatre   **T** 028 9038 5685
Contact: Cat Rice (Admin Assistant), Jimmy Fay
(Executive Producer), Morag Keating (Admin Manager),
Ciaran McAuley (Chief Executive)
55 Ridgeway Street
Belfast BT9 5FB
E info@lyrictheatre.co.uk
W www.lyrictheatre.co.uk

BIRMINGHAM:
Birmingham Repertory Theatre   **T** 0121 245 2000
Contact: Roxana Silbert (Artistic Director), Stuart Rogers
(Executive Director)
Centenary Square
Broad Street
Birmingham B1 2EP
BO 0121 236 4455
E info@birmingham-rep.co.uk

BIRMINGHAM:
Blue Orange Theatre   **T** 0121 212 2643
118 Great Hampton Street
Jewellery Quarter
Birmingham, West Midlands B18 6AD
E info@blueorangetheatre.co.uk
W www.blueorangetheatre.co.uk

BOLTON: Octagon Theatre   **T** 01204 529407
Contact: David Thacker (Artistic Director), Roddy Gauld
(Chief Executive), Vicky Entwistle (Theatre Administrator),
Olly Seviour (Head of Production)
Howell Croft South
Bolton BL1 1SB
BO 01204 520661
E info@octagonbolton.co.uk
W www.octagonbolton.co.uk

BRISTOL:
Theatre Royal & Studio   **T** 0117 949 3993
Contact: Tom Morris (Artistic Director), Emma Stenning
(Executive Director)
Bristol Old Vic, King Street
Bristol BS1 4ED
BO 0117 987 7877
E admin@bristololdvic.org.uk
W www.bristololdvic.org.uk

CARDIFF: Sherman Cymru   **T** 029 2064 6901
Contact: Rachel O'Riordan (Artistic Director), Margaret
Jones (General Manager)
Senghennydd Road
Cardiff CF24 4YE
E artistic@shermancymru.co.uk

CHICHESTER:
Chichester Festival Theatre   **T** 01243 784437
Contact: Jonathan Church (Artistic Director), Alan Finch
(Executive Director), Janet Bakose (Theatre Manager)
Oaklands Park
Chichester
West Sussex PO19 6AP
BO 01243 781312
E admin@cft.org.uk
W www.cft.org.uk

CHICHESTER: Minerva Theatre
at Chichester Festival Theatre   **T** 01243 784437
Contact: Jonathan Church (Artistic Director), Alan Finch
(Executive Director), Janet Bakose (Theatre Manager)
Oaklands Park, Chichester
West Sussex PO19 6AP
BO 01243 781312
E admin@cft.org.uk
W www.cft.org.uk

COLCHESTER: Mercury Theatre   **T** 01206 577006
Contact: Daniel Buckroyd (Artistic Director), Steve Mannix
(Executive Director)
Balkerne Gate, Colchester
Essex CO1 1PT
BO 01206 573948
E info@mercurytheatre.co.uk
W www.mercurytheatre.co.uk

COVENTRY: Belgrade Main Stage
& B2 Auditorium   **T** 024 7625 6431
Contact: Hamish Glen (Artistic Director/CEO), Joanna
Reid (Executive Director), Nicola Young (Director of
Communications)
Belgrade Square, Coventry
West Midlands CV1 1GS
BO 024 7655 3055
E admin@belgrade.co.uk
W www.belgrade.co.uk

DERBY: Derby LIVE   **BO** 01332 255800
Market Place
Derby DE1 3AH
E derbylive@derby.gov.uk
W www.derbylive.co.uk

DERBY: Derby Theatre   **T** 01332 593939 (BO)
Twitter: @derbytheatre
15 Theatre Walk
St Peters Quarter
Derby DE1 2NF
T 01332 593900 (SD)
E tickets@derbytheatre.co.uk
W www.derbytheatre.co.uk

DUBLIN: Abbey Theatre Amharclann na
Mainistreach   **T** 00 353 1 8872200
Contact: Fiach MacConghail (Director)
26 Lower Abbey Street
Dublin 1, Ireland
BO 00 353 1 8787222
E info@abbeytheatre.ie
W www.abbeytheatre.ie

DUNDEE:
Dundee Repertory Theatre   **T** 01382 227684
Contact: Ian Alexander (General Manager)
Tay Square, Dundee DD1 1PB
BO 01382 223530
E info@dundeereptheatre.co.uk
W www.dundeerep.co.uk

EDINBURGH: Royal Lyceum
Theatre Company   **T** 0131 248 4800
Contact: Mark Thomson (Artistic Director)
30B Grindlay Street
Edinburgh EH3 9AX
BO 0131 248 4848
E info@lyceum.org.uk
W www.lyceum.org.uk

EDINBURGH:
Traverse Theatre　　T 0131 228 3223 (Admin)
Contact: Orla O'Loughlin (Artistic Director), Linda Crooks
(Executive Producer). New Writing. Own Productions.
Touring & Visiting Companies
10 Cambridge Street
Edinburgh EH1 2ED
BO 0131 228 1404
E admin@traverse.co.uk
W www.traverse.co.uk

EXETER:
Exeter Northcott Theatre　　T 01392 223999
Contact: Kate Tyrrell (Executive Director). Mid-Scale
Receiving Theatre
Stocker Road, Exeter
Devon EX4 4QB
BO 01392 493493
E info@exeternorthcott.co.uk
W www.exeternorthcott.co.uk

FRINTON:
Frinton Summer Theatre　　T 07905 589792
July-September
The McGrigor Hall, Fourth Avenue
Frinton-on-Sea, Essex CO13 9EB
E mtproductions@btconnect.com
W www.frintonsummertheatre.co.uk

GLASGOW: Citizens Theatre　　T 0141 429 5561
Contact: Dominic Hill (Artistic Director), Judith Kilvington
(Executive Director), Graham Sutherland (Head of
Production)
Gorbals, Glasgow G5 9DS
BO 0141 429 0022
E info@citz.co.uk
W www.citz.co.uk

GUILDFORD:
Yvonne Arnaud Theatre　　T 01483 440077
Contact: James Barber (Director)
Millbrook, Guildford
Surrey GU1 3UX
BO 01483 440000
E yat@yvonne-arnaud.co.uk
W www.yvonne-arnaud.co.uk

HARROGATE:
Harrogate Theatre　　T 01423 502710
Contact: David Bown (Chief Executive). Mainly
Co-productions. Touring & Visiting Companies
Oxford Street
Harrogate HG1 1QF
BO 01423 502116
E info@harrogatetheatre.co.uk
W www.harrogatetheatre.co.uk

HULL: Hull Truck Theatre　　T 01482 224800
Contact: Mark Babych (Artistic Director), Janthi
Mills-Ward (Executive Director)
50 Ferensway, Hull HU2 8LB
E admin@hulltruck.co.uk
W www.hulltruck.co.uk

IPSWICH:
The New Wolsey Theatre　　T 01473 295900
Contact: Peter Rowe (Artistic Director), Sarah Holmes
(Chief Executive)
Civic Drive, Ipswich IP1 2AS
E info@wolseytheatre.co.uk
W www.wolseytheatre.co.uk

KESWICK: Theatre by the Lake　　T 01768 772282
Contact: Ian Forrest (Artistic Director), Patric Gilchrist
(Executive Director)
Lakeside, Keswick
Cumbria CA12 5DJ
BO 01768 774411
E enquiries@theatrebythelake.com
W www.theatrebythelake.com

LANCASTER: The Dukes　　T 01524 598505
Contact: Joe Sumsion (Director)
Moor Lane, Lancaster
Lancashire LA1 1QE
BO 01524 598500
E info@dukes-lancaster.org
W www.dukes-lancaster.org

LEEDS:
West Yorkshire Playhouse　　T 0113 213 7800
Contact: James Brining (Artistic Director/Chief
Executive), Sheena Wrigley (Joint Chief Executive),
Henrietta Duckworth (Producer)
Playhouse Square, Quarry Hill
Leeds LS2 7UP
W www.wyp.org.uk

LEICESTER: Curve　　T 0116 242 3560
Contact: Verity Bartesch (Assistant Producer), Paul
Kerryson (Artistic Director), Fiona Allan (Chief Executive),
Chris Stafford (Executive Producer)
Rutland Street
Leicester LE1 1SB
E c.stafford@curvetheatre.co.uk
W www.curveonline.co.uk

LIVERPOOL: Everyman &
Playhouse Theatres　　T 0151 708 3700
Contact: Gemma Bodinetz (Artistic Director), Deborah
Aydon (Executive Director)
Everyman: 9-11 Hope Street
Liverpool L1 9BH

Playhouse: Williamson Square
Liverpool L1 1EL
BO 0151 709 4776
E enquiries@everymanplayhouse.com
W www.everymanplayhouse.com

MANCHESTER: Contact　　T 0161 274 0600
Oxford Road
Manchester M15 6JA
E info@contactmcr.com
W www.contactmcr.com

MANCHESTER: Home　　T 0161 228 7621
Contact: Dave Moutrey (Chief Executive),
Walter Meierjohann (Artistic Director)
Cornerhouse & HOME, GMAC Ltd
70 Oxford Street
Manchester M1 5NH
E admin@homemcr.org
W www.homemcr.org

MANCHESTER:
Royal Exchange Theatre　　T 0161 833 9333
Contact: Gregory Hersov, Sarah Frankcom (Artistic
Directors), Richard Morgan (Producer/Studio),
Jerry Knight-Smith (Casting Director)
St Ann's Square
Manchester M2 7DH
BO 0161 833 9833
W www.royalexchange.co.uk

MILFORD HAVEN:
Torch Theatre   T 01646 694192
Contact: Peter Doran (Artistic Director)
St Peter's Road
Milford Haven
Pembrokeshire SA73 2BU
BO 01646 695267
E info@torchtheatre.co.uk
W www.torchtheatre.co.uk

MOLD: Clwyd Theatr Cymru   T 01352 756331
Repertoire. 4 Weekly. Also Touring
Mold, Flintshire
North Wales CH7 1YA
BO 0845 3303565
E admin@clwyd-theatr-cymru.co.uk
W www.clwyd-theatr-cymru.co.uk

MUSSELBURGH: The Brunton   T 0131 665 9900
*Contact: Lesley Smith (General Manager). Annual
Programme of Theatre, Dance, Music, Comedy &
Children's Work. Also available for Private &
Corporate Hire*
Ladywell Way
Musselburgh EH21 6AA
BO 0131 665 2240
E mhegarty@eastlothian.gov.uk
W www.thebrunton.co.uk

NEWBURY: Watermill Theatre   T 01635 45834
*Contact: Hedda Beeby (Artistic & Executive Director),
Clare Lindsay (General Manager). 4-8 Weekly.
February-January*
Bagnor, Newbury
Berkshire RG20 8AE
BO 01635 46044
E admin@watermill.org.uk
W www.watermill.org.uk

NEWCASTLE-UNDER-LYME:
New Vic Theatre   T 01782 717954
*Contact: Theresa Heskins (Artistic Director),
Fiona Wallace (Executive Director)*
Etruria Road
Newcastle-under-Lyme
Staffordshire ST5 0JG
BO 01782 717962
E administration@newvictheatre.org.uk
W www.newvictheatre.org.uk

NEWCASTLE UPON TYNE:
Northern Stage
(Theatrical Productions) Ltd   T 0191 242 7210
Contact: Susan Cotter (Chief Executive)
Barras Bridge
Newcastle upon Tyne NE1 7RH
BO 0191 230 5151
E info@northernstage.co.uk
W www.northernstage.co.uk

NORTHAMPTON:
Royal & Derngate   T 01604 626222
*Contact: Martin Sutherland (Chief Executive), James
Dacre (Artistic Director), Dani Parr (Associate Director),
John Manning (Producer)*
19-21 Guildhall Road
Northampton NN1 1DP
BO 01604 624811
E arts@royalandderngate.co.uk
W www.royalandderngate.co.uk

NOTTINGHAM:
Nottingham Playhouse   T 0115 947 4361
*Contact: Stephanie Sirr (Chief Executive), Giles Croft
(Artistic Director)*
Nottingham Playhouse Trust Ltd
Wellington Circus
Nottingham NG1 5AF
BO 0115 941 9419
E enquiry@nottinghamplayhouse.co.uk
W www.nottinghamplayhouse.co.uk

OLDHAM: Coliseum Theatre   T 0161 624 1731
Contact: Kevin Shaw (Chief Executive). 3-4 Weekly
Fairbottom Street, Oldham
Lancashire OL1 3SW
BO 0161 624 2829
E mail@coliseum.org.uk
W www.coliseum.org.uk

PERTH: Perth Theatre   T 01738 472700
*Contact: Kenny Miller (Creative Director) Graeme Wallace
(Head of Planning & Resources), Colin McMahon
(Chief Executive)*
Horsecross Arts, 185 High Street
Perth PH1 5UW
BO 01738 621031
E info@horsecross.co.uk
W www.horsecross.co.uk

PETERBOROUGH: Key Theatre   T 01733 207237
Touring & Occasional Seasonal
Embankment Road, Peterborough
Cambridgeshire PE1 1EF
BO 01733 207239
E key.theatre@vivacity-peterborough.com

PITLOCHRY:
Pitlochry Festival Theatre   T 01796 484600
Contact: John Durnin (Chief Executive/Artistic Director)
Pitlochry, Perthshire PH16 5DR
BO 01796 484626
E admin@pitlochryfestivaltheatre.com
W www.pitlochryfestivaltheatre.com

PLYMOUTH: Theatre Royal &
Drum Theatre   T 01752 668282
*Contact: Simon Stokes (Artistic Director), Adrian Vinken
(Chief Executive)*
Royal Parade, Plymouth
Devon PL1 2TR
BO 01752 267222
E info@theatreroyal.com
W www.theatreroyal.com

READING: The Mill at
Sonning Theatre   T 0118 969 6039
Contact: Sally Hughes (Artistic Director). 8 Weekly
Sonning Eye, Reading RG4 6TY
BO 0118 969 8000
W www.millatsonning.com

SALISBURY: Playhouse &
Salberg Studio   T 01722 320117
*Contact: Gareth Machin (Artistic Director), Sebastian
Warrack (Executive Director). 3-4 Weekly*
Malthouse Lane, Salisbury
Wiltshire SP2 7RA
BO 01722 320333
E info@salisburyplayhouse.com
W www.salisburyplayhouse.com

SCARBOROUGH:
Stephen Joseph Theatre T 01723 370540
*Contact: Chris Monks (Artistic Director), Stephen Wood
(Executive Director). Repertoire/Repertory*
Westborough, Scarborough
North Yorkshire YO11 1JW
BO 01723 370541
E enquiries@sjt.uk.com
W www.sjt.uk.com

SHEFFIELD: Crucible, Studio &
Lyceum Theatres T 0114 249 5999
Contact: Dan Bates (Chief Executive)
55 Norfolk Street, Sheffield S1 1DA
BO 0114 249 6000
E info@sheffieldtheatres.co.uk
W www.sheffieldtheatres.co.uk

SHERINGHAM:
Sheringham Little Theatre T 01263 822117
Contact: Debbie Thompson (Theatre Director)
2 Station Road, Sheringham
Norfolk NR26 8RE
E debbie@sheringhamlittletheatre.com
W www.sheringhamlittletheatre.com

Is your CV up-to-date?

Top tips for promoting yourself!

- **Keep your credits up-to-date**

  An absolute must – always take responsibility for updating your own profile, as and when you gain credits and new skills.

- **Review your skills**

  Add new skills as they are learnt; remove old skills that you can no longer complete. The more skilled you are, the more you maximise your marketability.

- **Make sure your professional training appears**

  Also, remember to update this section as you undertake further training across your career.

- **Update your photograph**

  Ensure that you are representing yourself as you would now appear at an audition.

- **Add multimedia**

  Make sure casting professionals see and hear just how good you are with video and audio clips.

SIDMOUTH:
Manor Pavilion Theatre T 01395 576798
Weekly. June-September
Manor Road, Sidmouth
Devon EX10 8RP
BO 01395 514413
W www.manorpavillion.com

SOUTHAMPTON:
Nuffield Theatre T 023 8031 5500
*Contact: Sam Hodges (Creative & Executive Director).
September-July. Tours*
University Road
Southampton SO17 1TR
BO 023 8067 1771
E info@nuffieldtheatre.co.uk
W www.nuffieldtheatre.co.uk

SOUTHWOLD & ALDEBURGH:
Summer Theatre T 01502 724462
*Contact: Suffolk Summer Theatres Ltd (Producer).
July-September*
4 Foster Close, Southwold
Suffolk IP18 6LE
E enquiries@southwoldtheatre.org
W www.southwoldtheatre.org

STRATFORD-UPON-AVON: Royal Shakespeare
Company T 0844 8001110 (T/BO)
Waterside, Stratford-upon-Avon
Warwickshire CV37 6BB
E info@rsc.org.uk
W www.rsc.org.uk

WATFORD:
Watford Palace Theatre T 01923 235455
*Contact: Brigid Larmour (Artistic Director/Chief
Executive), Mathew Russell (Executive Director)*
20 Clarendon Road, Watford
Hertfordshire WD17 1JZ
BO 01923 225671
E enquiries@watfordpalacetheatre.co.uk
W www.watfordpalacetheatre.co.uk

WINDSOR: Theatre Royal T 01753 863444
Contact: Simon Pearce (Director)
32 Thames Street, Windsor
Berkshire SL4 1PS
BO 01753 853888
E info@theatreroyalwindsor.co.uk
W www.theatreroyalwindsor.co.uk

WOKING: New Victoria Theatre,
The Ambassadors T 01483 545999
Peacocks Centre
Woking GU21 6GQ
BO 0844 8717645
E wokingboxoffice@theambassadors.com
W www.atgtickets.com/woking

YORK: Theatre Royal T 01904 658162
*Contact: Damian Cruden (Artistic Director), Liz Wilson
(Chief Executive)*
St Leonard's Place
York YO1 7HD
BO 01904 623568
E admin@yorktheatreroyal.co.uk
W www.yorktheatreroyal.co.uk

U →

Unions, Professional Guilds & Associations

Unions

What are performers' unions?

The unions listed in this section exist to protect and improve the rights, interests and working conditions of performers. They offer very important services to their members, such as advice on pay and conditions, help with contracts and negotiations, legal support and welfare advice. To join a performers' union there is usually a one-off joining fee and then an annual subscription fee calculated in relation to an individual's total yearly earnings.

Equity is the main actors' union in the UK. See www.equity.org.uk and their case study in this section for more details.

Do similar organisations exist for other sectors of the entertainment industry?

In addition to representation by trade unions, some skills also have professional bodies, guilds and associations which complement the work of trade unions. These include directors, producers, stage managers, designers and casting directors. These can also be found in the following listings.

What is the FIA?

The FIA (International Federation of Actors) www.fia-actors.com is an organisation which represents performers' trade unions, guilds and associations from all around the world. It tackles the same issues as individual actors' unions, but on an international rather than local level.

I'm a professionally trained actor from overseas and I want to work in the UK. How do I get started?

If you are a national of a country in the European Economic Area (EEA) or Switzerland (excluding Bulgaria and Romania) you do not need to apply for permission from the Home Office in order to work as an actor in the UK. You will be able to look for and accept offers of work without needing a visa. Visit www.ukba.homeoffice.gov.uk/eucitizens/rightsandresponsibilites for details of your rights to enter, live in and work in the UK.

If you are from a country outside the EEA you will need to apply for a visa before you can work as an actor in the UK. You might want to visit www.bia.homeoffice.gov.uk/visas-immigration/working for full information.

You may also wish to join the UK's actors' union, Equity. For more information please visit their website www.equity.org.uk. If you can prove that you have relevant professional acting training and/or experience, you can also apply to join Spotlight to promote yourself to casting opportunities.

I am a UK resident and I want to work as an actor elsewhere in Europe. Where do I start?

A good starting point would be to contact the actors' union in the country in which you are hoping to work for information on their employment legislation. Contact details for performers' unions in Europe can be found in the following listings or obtained from the FIA www.fia-actors.com, who in most cases will be able to advise on what criteria you need to fulfil to be eligible for work.

As a UK national, you have the right to work in any country which is a member of the EEA without a work permit. You will be given the same employment rights as nationals of the country you are working in, but these rights will change according to the country you choose to work in and may not be the same as the UK.

For more general advice, the Foreign and Commonwealth Office (FCO) offers advice on living overseas and provides information on contacting the UK embassy in and relevant entry requirements for the country of your choice. Please see www.fco.gov.uk/en/travel-and-living-abroad for details. You could also visit Directgov's website www.direct.gov.uk/en/BritonsLivingAbroad for further useful guidance for British citizens living abroad.

You should also go further and start researching agents, casting directors, production companies and so on which are based in the country you wish to live and work in. Begin your search online and then decide whether to approach a person or company for further information once you have found out more about them. Learning the culture and becoming as fluent as possible in the language of your chosen country would be advisable, as this opens up a far wider range of job opportunities.

What are English Speaking Theatres?

English Speaking Theatres can provide British actors with an opportunity to work abroad in theatre. These companies vary greatly in terms of the plays they put on and the audiences they attract: they may aim to teach English to schoolchildren; help audiences develop an appreciation of English plays; or may exist simply because there is a demand for English speaking entertainment. Some are based in one venue while others tour round the country. Actors may be employed for an individual production or, especially if touring, for a series of plays. Performers interested in the possibility of working for this type of theatre company should refer to the 'Theatre: English Speaking in Europe' section for listings.

I am a UK resident and I want to work as an actor in the USA. Where do I start?

To work in America you will need a Green Card – a visa which entitles the holder to live and work there permanently as an immigrant – but you will not qualify for one unless you are sponsored by a prospective employer in the US or a relative who is a US citizen. Visit the US Embassy's website http://london.usembassy.gov/visas.html or alternatively visit the US Department of State's Bureau of Consular Affairs' website http://travel.state.gov/visa for information about the criteria you must meet and the fees you will have to pay.

Don't expect to be granted immediate entry to the USA. There is a limit to the number of people who can apply for immigrant status every year, so you could be on the waiting list for several years depending on the category of your application. You could enter the Green Card Lottery at www.greencard.co.uk for a chance to fast-track the processing of your application, although your visa will still have to be approved.

Finding employment from outside the USA will be difficult. You might want to try signing with an American talent agent to submit you for work, although there is huge competition for agents. Try the Association of Talent Agents (ATA) www.agentassociation.com for US agent details. The most effective way to gain an American agent's interest would be to get a personal referral from an industry contact, such as a casting director or acting coach. You should also promote yourself as you would with Spotlight by signing up with casting services such as www.breakdownservices.com

Acting employment in America is divided into union work and non-union work. The major actors' unions are AEA www.actorsequity.org and SAG-AFTRA www.sagaftra.org. As with any other union they protect and enhance the rights of their members and offer various services and benefits. You will only become eligible for membership once you have provided proof of a contract for a job which comes under a particular union's jurisdiction. Non-members can work on union jobs if a producer is willing to employ them. You can join more than one union, but once you have joined at least one you will be unable to accept any non-union work.

You may have to begin your career in America with non-union work, as experience or union membership in the UK does not make you eligible to join a union in the US. Work ungoverned by the unions could include student and independent films, small stage productions, commercials, voice overs, extra work, and so on. You are unlikely to be paid well as non-union contracts are not governed by the minimum wages set by the unions, but you will be able to build on your CV and begin making yourself known in the US acting industry.

Unions

Phil Pemberton is the Campaigns & Publications Officer at Equity, the trade union for the UK entertainment industry. He works to provide a voice of authority for performers and the industry in general.

There are lots of good reasons to join a performers' union. The issues that impact most upon you as a performer will depend on your personal circumstances and your career, amongst other things, but the one thing that performers can be sure of is that Equity is the union that best represents your interests. So, why should you join Equity? Here are ten good reasons to get you thinking…

1. Pay: Equity contracts set the minimum rates for employment throughout the entertainment industry and the provisions in our contracts protect members from exploitation and deliver minimum standards. The stronger we become, the more we push for improved deals. When members come together we can make real progress.

2. Decent Treatment At Work: On everything from holiday entitlement to meal breaks and from health and safety protection to maximum working time, Equity has negotiated agreements across the industry to protect you from exploitation by unscrupulous employers and to increase awareness of best practice.

3. Equal Treatment: Regardless of your gender, your race or your sexuality, Equity works for equal opportunities across the entertainment industry and to end discrimination. Recent campaigns for greater opportunities for older women and for a media that is more representative of all sectors of the community have been high profile and continue to attract considerable support.

4. Protection: If your employers, managers or agents are treating you unfairly, Equity will be by your side to ensure that your rights are protected. Equity has a team of specialist organisers working full-time to represent your needs and we have strong legal support for when you need it.

5. Public Liability: For many performers, Equity's public liability insurance (which provides coverage of up to £10 million) is an essential protection for their working lives and provides unbeatable value. If someone gets hurt during your act or if something gets damaged, then the knowledge that full insurance comes with your membership can help take the drama out of a crisis.

6. Compensation: If you are injured or get ill because of your working conditions our legal services can ensure you get proper compensation. We have specialist legal support and a 24 hour helpline if you need to make a personal injury claim.

7. Belonging: By becoming an Equity member you make a statement about your commitment to your vocation and your place within our industry. For almost 80 years Equity membership has been a symbol of unity in an industry where work is often transitory and geographically diverse. Your Equity card is a symbol of your professionalism.

8. Contribute: If you are serious about making a contribution to improving conditions for yourself and those you work with, the best way to help is to get involved in your union. In Equity our democratic structures mean your voice can be heard and that you can genuinely make a difference to your own working life and that of your fellow performers.

9. Influence: Equity is a major voice in the entertainment industry, contributing to public debate at local, regional, national and international levels. Our influence comes from the strength of our membership. Although we are not affiliated to any political party, we work with other entertainment unions to influence politicians and to protect your interests and the interests of the arts and media in general.

10. Pride: By being part of Equity you can be proud of your contribution to making your industry a safer and more rewarding place for everyone who works. Your membership makes our union stronger; your involvement gives your union greater influence. Working together we can make Equity a union we can all be proud of.

To find out more visit www.equity.org.uk

UNITED KINGDOM: AMERICAN ACTORS UK
Contact: By e-mail only
E admin@americanactorsuk.com
W www.americanactorsuk.com

UNITED KINGDOM: BECTU - Broadcasting, Entertainment, Cinematograph & Theatre Union   **T** 020 7346 0900
373-377 Clapham Road, London SW9 9BT
F 020 7346 0901
E info@bectu.org.uk
W www.bectu.org.uk

UNITED KINGDOM: CDG - Casting Directors' Guild
Contact: Sophie Hallett
PO Box 64973, London SW20 2AW
E info@thecdg.co.uk
W www.thecdg.co.uk

UNITED KINGDOM: CPMA - Co-operative Personal Management Association
Contact: The Secretary
E cpmauk@yahoo.co.uk
W www.cpma.coop

UNITED KINGDOM: DGGB - Directors Guild of Great Britain   **T** 020 8871 1660
Studio 24, RVP Building
John Archer Way, London SW18 3SX
E info@dggb.org
W www.dggb.org

UNITED KINGDOM: EQUITY inc Variety Artistes' Federation   **T** 020 7379 6000
Guild House, Upper St Martin's Lane, London WC2H 9EG
E info@equity.org.uk
W www.equity.org.uk

UNITED KINGDOM: EQUITY inc Variety Artistes' Federation (Midlands)   **T/F** 024 7655 3612
Office 1, Steeple House, Percy Street, Coventry CV1 3BY
E tjohnson@midlands-equity.org.uk
W www.equity.org.uk

UNITED KINGDOM: EQUITY inc Variety Artistes' Federation (North West & Isle of Man)   **T** 0161 244 5995
Express Networks, 1 George Leigh Street
Manchester M4 5DL
F 0161 244 5971
E northwestengland@equity.org.uk
W www.equity.org.uk

UNITED KINGDOM: EQUITY inc Variety Artistes' Federation (Scotland & Northern Ireland)   **T** 0141 248 2472
114 Union Street, Glasgow G1 3QQ
F 0141 248 2473
E scotland@equity.org.uk
W www.equity.org.uk

UNITED KINGDOM: EQUITY inc Variety Artistes' Federation (Wales & South West)   **T** 029 2039 7971
1 Cathedral Road, Cardiff CF11 9SD
E southwestengland@equity.org.uk
W www.equity.org.uk

UNITED KINGDOM: FAA - Film Artistes' Association   **T** 020 7346 0900
Amalgamated with BECTU
373-377 Clapham Road, London SW9 9BT
F 020 7346 0925
W www.bectu.org.uk

UNITED KINGDOM:
Musicians' Union   T 020 7582 5566
60-62 Clapham Road, London SW9 0JJ
E info@themu.org
W www.themusiciansunion.org

UNITED KINGDOM: PMA - Personal Managers'
Association Ltd   T 0845 6027191
E info@thepma.com
W www.thepma.com

UNITED KINGDOM: Writers' Guild
of Great Britain   T 020 7833 0777
1st Floor, 134 Tooley Street, London SE1 2TU
E admin@writersguild.org.uk
W www.writersguild.org.uk

BELGIUM: ACV/TRANSCOM -
Cultuur   T 00 32 47 0130600
Galerij Agora, Grasmarkt 105, 1000 Brussels
E info@acvcultuur.be
W www.acvcultuur.be

BELGIUM: Centrale Générale
des Services Publics   T 00 32 2 2261375
Rue de Congrès 17-19, 1000 Brussels
F 00 32 2 2261362
W www.acod.be

BELGIUM: FIA - International
Federation of Actors   T 00 32 2 2345653
40 Rue Joseph II, Box 4, 1000 Brussels
F 00 32 2 2350870
E office@fia-actors.com
W www.fia-actors.com

DENMARK: DAF -
Dansk Artist Forbud   T 00 45 33326677
Dronningensgade 68, 4.sal, 1420 Copenhagen K
F 00 45 33337330
E artisten@artisten.dk
W www.artisten.dk

DENMARK:
Dansk Skuespillerforbund   T 00 45 33242200
Sankt Knuds Vej 26, 1903 Frederiksberg C
E dsf@skuespillerforbundet.dk
W www.skuespillerforbundet.dk

FINLAND: SNL -
Suomen Näyttelijäliitto   T 00 358 9 25112135
Meritullinkatu 33, 00170 Helsinki
F 00 358 9 25112139
E toimisto@nayttelijaliitto.fi
W www.nayttelijaliitto.fi

FRANCE: SFA-Syndicat Français
des Artistes-Interprètes   T 00 33 1 53250909
1 rue Janssen, 75019 Paris
F 00 33 1 53250901
E info@sfa-cgt.fr
W www.sfa-cgt.fr

GERMANY: GDBA - Genossenschaft Deutscher
Bühnenangehöriger   T 00 49 40 43282440
Postfach 57 04 29, 22773 Hamburg, Germany
E gdba@buehnengenossenschaft.de
W www.buehnengenossenschaft.de

GREECE: HAU -
Hellenic Actors' Union   T 00 30 210 3833742
33 Kaniggos Street, 106 82 Athens
F 00 30 210 3808651
E support@sei.gr
W www.sei.gr

IRELAND: IEG -
Irish Equity Group   T 00 353 1 8586403
SIPTU
Liberty Hall, Dublin 1
E equity@siptu.ie
W www.irishequity.ie

ITALY: Sindicato Lavorati
Commucazione   T 00 39 06 42048204
Piazza Sallustio 24, 00187 Rome
F 00 39 06 4824325
E segreteria.nazionale@slc.cgil.it
W www.slc-cgil.it

LUXEMBOURG: OGB - L Onofhänege
Gewerkschaftbond Lëtztbuerg   T 00 352 496005
19 Rue d'Epernay, B.P. 2031
1020 Luxembourg, Luxembourg
F 00 352 486949
E leon.jenal@ogb-l.lu
W www.ogb-l.lu

NORWAY: NSF - Norsk Skuespillerforbund /
NORWEIGAN ACTORS'
EQUITY ASSOCIATION   T 00 47 21027190
Welhavens Gate 1, 0166 Oslo
F 00 47 21027191
E nsf@skuespillerforbund.no
W www.skuespillerforbund.no

PORTUGAL: STE - Sindicato dos Trabalhadores
de Espectáculos   T 00 351 21 8852728
Rua da Fé 23, 2º Piso
1150-149 Lisbon, Portugal
F 00 351 21 8853787
E stespectaculos@hotmail.com
W www.stespectaculos.com

SPAIN: CC.OO. - Comisiones Obreras -
Comunicación, Artes,
Cultura y Deporte   T 00 34 91 5409295
Plaza Cristino Martos 4
6A Planta, 28015 Madrid
E internacional@fsc.ccoo.es
W www.fsc.ccoo.es/medios

SPAIN: FAEE - Federación de Artistas del
Estado Español   T 00 34 91 5222804
C/ Montera 34, 1ro Piso, 28013 Madrid
F 00 34 91 5226055
E federaciondeartistas@faee.es
W www.faee.es

SWEDEN: TF -
Teaterförbundet   T 00 46 8 4411300
Kaplansbacken 2A
Box 12 710, 112 94 Stockholm
F 00 46 8 6539507
E info@teaterforbundet.se
W www.teaterforbundet.se

UNITED STATES OF AMERICA:
SAG-AFTRA   T 001 323 954 1600
5757 Wilshire Boulevard, 7th Floor
Los Angeles, CA 90036 - 3600
F 001 323 549 6792
E sagaftrainfo@sagaftra.org
W www.sagaftra.org/home

UNITED STATES OF AMERICA:
SAG-AFTRA   T 001 212 944 1030
1900 Broadway, 5th Floor
New York, NY 10023
E newyork@sagaftra.org
W www.sagaftra.org

Index To Advertisers

Alphabetical Listing Of Advertisers

Index To Advertisers Contacts 2015

ACCOUNTANTS, INSURANCE & LAW

Breckman & Company	11
H and S Accountants Ltd	10
Harijyot Ltd	9
MGM Accountancy Ltd	9

AGENTS

All The Arts Casting Agency	81
Alphabet Kidz	85
Background Wales	113
Bodens	78
Boss Casting	117
Boss Juniors	83
D & B Management	79
Damn Good Voices	111
Anna Fiorentini Theatre & Film School	76
Genuine Arab Casting	32
iCan Talk	111
Icon Actors Management	26
Industry Casting	115
Mark Jermin Management	85
Living The Dream Talent Agency	89
Mint Casting Agency Ltd	117
Oh So Small	50
Personal Appearances	21
Quirky Kidz Creative Management	77
Rare Talent Actors Management	37
Rebel School of Theatre Arts Ltd & Casting Agency	82
Alan Sharman Agency	71
Elisabeth Smith	87
S.T. Arts Management	47
The Stagecoach Agency UK & Ireland	81
Stageworks Worldwide Productions	49
Take2 Management	40, 89
Top Talent Agency	83
Tuesdays Child	78
Uni-versal Extras	113
Willow Management	69

CONSULTANTS

Animal Ambassadors	145
John Colclough	68, 186
Foreign Versions	108
The Knights of Middle England	143
Reduced Circumstances	65
RSVP	239
Stagecoach Chaperones	87

COSTUMIERS/WARDROBE SERVICES

Ron Briggs Design	153
Genesis UK	258
Stageworks Worldwide Productions	151

ENTERTAINERS/ACTORS/CHOREOGRAPHERS

Séva Dhalival	116
Paul Harris	167

FESTIVALS

NSDF	209
Move It	95
Perform	210

HEALTH & WELLBEING

The College Practice	235

ORGANISATIONS

The AA	Inside Front Cover
The Actors' Benevolent Fund	246
The Actors Centre	247
The Actors' Children's Trust	243
The Agents' Association	67
American Actors UK	44
British Association for Performing Arts Medicine (BAPAM)	233
The Casting Directors' Guild	137
Council for Dance Education & Training	163
Dance UK	161

The Directors Guild of Great Britain
& Directors Guild Trust | 245
Drama UK | 171
Equity | 369
The Ralph & Meriel Richardson
Foundation | 247

PHOTOGRAPHERS

AM London | 35
Matt Anker | 55
Simon Annand | 27
Pete Bartlett | 31
Michael Bennett | 41
Brandon Bishop | 21
Peter Bolton | 70
Nev Brewer | 51
Sheila Burnett | 23, 129
Charlie Carter | 31
Castingimage | 67
Vanessa Champion | 63
Tom Dumbleton | 38
Jon Holloway | 57
Anna Hull | 48
Jack Ladenburg | 131
Carole Latimer | 27
Steve Lawton | 33
Robert Lister | 39
M.A.D. Photography | 19
Patrick Marks | Inside Back Cover
JP Masclet | 53
Misty Morning Media | 139
Jason Mitchell | 51
Kamal Mostofi | 71
Dominic Old | 69
Carl Proctor | 43
John Reading | 59
Kirstin Reddington | 55
Alex Ruocco | 64
SJF Photo | 59
Howard Sayer | 56
Karen Scott | 45
Catherine Shakespeare Lane | 29

Daniel Sutka | 63
Steve Ullathorne | 61
Vanessa Valentine | 65
Van Dyck Photography | 141
Philip Wade | 47
Caroline Webster | 61
Michael Wharley | 25
Robert Workman | 37

PROPERTIES & TRADES

Bapty & Co | 265
Greenprops | 269
Kirby's AFX Ltd | 271
Nostalgia Amusements | 267

PUBLICATIONS & PUBLISHERS

Castnet | 52
The Stage | 135

REHEARSAL/AUDITION ROOMS/ CASTING SUITES

Alford House | 293
Brixton Community Base | 292
Covent Garden Dragon Hall Trust | 298
Diorama Arts Studios | 297
Hangar Arts Trust | 300
Invisible Dot | 293
ISTD2 Dance Studios | 294
Jerwood Space | 297
Lost Theatre | 303
PHA Casting Studio | 295
The Questors Theatre | 293
Raindance Film Centre | 300
Sadler's Wells Events | 295
South London Dance Studios | 298
Spotlight Rooms & Studios | 133, 301
St James's Church | 303
St Mary Abbots Centre | 302
Take Five Studio | 296
The Urdang Academy | 299

ROLE PLAY COMPANIES

Interact 305

SET CONSTRUCTION

3D Creations 308
Carousel Lights Ltd 307
Stageworks Worldwide Productions ... 309

SHOWREELS, VOICE TAPES, CVS, PRODUCTION & WEB DESIGN

Bespoke Reels 261
Blue Checkbox 263
Crying Out Loud Productions 111
Cutglass Productions 107
Re:al 260
Replay 259
Shoe String Filming 262
The Showreel Ltd 109
Silver-Tongued Productions 261
Sonicpond Studio 107
Stages Capture the Moment 263
Take Five Studio 259

REPRO COMPANIES & PHOTOGRAPHIC RETOUCHING

10x8 Prints 264
Visualeyes 43

THEATRE PRODUCERS

Richard Jordan Productions 329

TRAINING (Private Coaches)

John Melainey 139
Mel Churcher 185
Valerie Colgan 127
Gordon Faith 201
Dee Forrest 197
Stefan Gryff 204
Paul Harris 167

Rick Lipton 189
Zoë Nathenson 191
Philip Rosch 181
Holly Wilson 203

TRAINING (Schools, Companies & Workshops)

The Actors Centre 183
Associated Studios 189
Bristol Old Vic Theatre School 179
City Lit 187, 191
Court Theatre Training Company 197
Cygnet Training Theatre 193
Drama Studio London 185
Giles Foreman Centre for Acting 195
Fourth Monkey Theatre Company 203
GSA, Guildford School of Acting 195
International School of Screen Acting ... 201
Leeds Beckett Film,
Music & Performing Arts Short Courses ... 223
Royal Central School of
   Speech & Drama 199
Shapes in Motion 199
SLP College 177
Voice Power Works 176

A

The AA	Inside Front Cover
The Actors' Benevolent Fund	246
The Actors Centre	183, 247
The Actors' Children's Trust	243
The Agents' Association	67
Alford House	293
All The Arts Casting Agency	81
Alphabet Kidz	85
AM London	35
American Actors UK	44
Animal Ambassadors	145
Matt Anker	55
Simon Annand	27
Associated Studios	189

B

Background Wales	113
Bapty & Co	265
Pete Bartlett	31
Michael Bennett	41
Bespoke Reels	261
Blue Checkbox	263
Brandon Bishop	21
Bodens	78
Peter Bolton	70
Boss Casting	117
Boss Juniors	83
Breckman & Company	11
Nev Brewer	51
Ron Briggs Design	153
Bristol Old Vic Theatre School	179
British Association for Performing Arts Medicine (BAPAM)	233
Brixton Community Base	292
Sheila Burnett	23, 129

C

Carousel Lights Ltd	307
Charlie Carter	31
The Casting Directors' Guild	137
Castingimage	67
Castnet	52
Vanessa Champion	63
Mel Churcher	185
City Lit	187, 191
John Colclough	68, 186
Valerie Colgan	127
The College Practice	235
Council for Dance Education & Training	163
Court Theatre Training Company	197
Covent Garden Dragon Hall Trust	298
Crying Out Loud Productions	111
Cutglass Productions	107
Cygnet Training Theatre	193

D

D & B Management	79
Damn Good Voices	111
Dance UK	161
Séva Dhalival	116
Diorama Arts Studios	297
The Directors Guild of Great Britain & Directors Guild Trust	245
Drama Studio London	185
Drama UK	171
Tom Dumbleton	38

E

Equity	369

F

Gordon Faith	201
Anna Fiorentini Theatre & Film School	76
Foreign Versions	108
Giles Foreman Centre for Acting	195
Dee Forrest	197
Fourth Monkey Theatre Company	203

G

Genesis UK	258
Genuine Arab Casting	32
Greenprops	269
Stefan Gryff	204
GSA, Guildford School of Acting	195

H

H and S Accountants Ltd	10
Hangar Arts Trust	300
Paul Harris	167
Harijyot Ltd	9
Jon Holloway	57
Anna Hull	48

I

iCan Talk	111
Icon Actors Management	26
Industry Casting	115
Interact	305
International School of Screen Acting	201
Invisible Dot	293
ISTD2 Dance Studios	294

J

Mark Jermin Management	85
Jerwood Space	297
Richard Jordan Productions	329

K

Kirby's AFX Ltd	271
The Knights of Middle England	143

L

Jack Ladenburg	131
Carole Latimer	27
Steve Lawton	33
Leeds Beckett Film, Music & Performing Arts Short Courses	223
Rick Lipton	189
Robert Lister	39
Living The Dream Talent Agency	89
Lost Theatre	303

M

M.A.D. Photography	19
Patrick Marks	Inside Back Cover
JP Masclet	53
John Melainey	139
MGM Accountancy Ltd	9
Mint Casting Agency Ltd	117
Misty Morning Media	139
Jason Mitchell	51
Kamal Mostofi	71
Move It	95

N

Zoë Nathenson	191
NSDF	209
Nostalgia Amusements	267

O

Oh So Small	50
Dominic Old	69

P

Perform	210
Personal Appearances	21
PHA Casting Studio	295
Carl Proctor	43

Q

The Questors Theatre	293
Quirky Kidz Creative Management	77

R

Raindance Film Centre	300
Rare Talent Actors Management	37
John Reading	59
Re:al	260
Rebel School of Theatre Arts Ltd & Casting Agency	82
Replay	259
Kirstin Reddington	55
Reduced Circumstances	65
The Ralph & Meriel Richardson Foundation	247
Philip Rosch	181
Royal Central School of Speech & Drama	199
RSVP	239
Alex Ruocco	64

S

Sadler's Wells Events	295
Howard Sayer	56
Karen Scott	45
Catherine Shakespeare Lane	29
Shapes in Motion	199
Alan Sharman Agency	71
SJF Photo	59
Shoe String Filming	262
The Showreel Ltd	109
Silver-Tongued Productions	261

SLP College	177
Elisabeth Smith	87
South London Dance Studios	298
Sonicpond Studio	107
Spotlight Rooms & Studios	133, 301
S.T. Arts Management	47
St James's Church	303
St Mary Abbots Centre	302
The Stage	135
Stages Capture the Moment	263
The Stagecoach Agency UK & Ireland	81
Stagecoach Chaperones	87
Stageworks Worldwide Productions	49, 151, 309
Daniel Sutka	63

T

3D Creations	308
10x8 Prints	264
Take2 Management	40, 89
Take Five Studio	259, 296
Top Talent Agency	83
Tuesdays Child	78

U

Steve Ullathorne	61
Uni-versal Extras	113
The Urdang Academy	299

V

Vanessa Valentine	65
Van Dyck Photography	141
Visualeyes	43
Voice Power Works	176

W

Philip Wade	47
Caroline Webster	61
Michael Wharley	25
Willow Management	69
Holly Wilson	203
Robert Workman	37

N

Notes

Notes

Notes